D1810868

The Christmas Books, Ghost Stories & Other Tales

CHARLES DICKENS

WORDSWORTH LIBRARY COLLECTION

For my husband
ANTHONY JOHN RANSON
with love from your wife, the publisher.
Eternally grateful for your unconditional love,
not just for me but for our children,
Simon, Andrew and Nichola Trayler

Readers who are interested in other titles from
Wordsworth Editions are invited to visit our website at
www.wordsworth-editions.com

For our latest list and a full mail-order service, contact
Bibliophile Books, 5 Datapoint, South Crescent, London E16 4TL
TEL: +44 (0)20 7474 2474 FAX: +44 (0)20 7474 8589
ORDERS: orders@bibliophilebooks.com
WEBSITE: www.bibliophilebooks.com

This edition, part of the Wordsworth Library Collection,
first published in 2010 by Wordsworth Editions Limited
8B East Street, Ware, Hertfordshire SG12 9HJ

ISBN 978 1 84022 654 6

Text © Wordsworth Editions Limited 2010

Wordsworth® is a registered trademark of
Wordsworth Editions Limited,
the company founded by Michael Trayler in 1987

Cover design Robert Mathias
Cover illustration: Fireside Scene at Christmas
by Lavinia Hamer (contemporary artist)
Private collection / Bridgeman Art Library, London

Typeset in Great Britain by Antony Gray
Printed and bound by Clays Ltd, St Ives plc

CONTENTS

A CHRISTMAS CAROL

Being a Ghost Story of Christmas

LIST OF CHARACTERS IN
THE CHRISTMAS CAROL

Bob Cratchit, clerk to Ebenezer Scrooge

Peter Cratchit, a son of the preceding

Tim Cratchit ('Tiny Tim'), a cripple, youngest son of Bob
Cratchit

Mr Fezziwig, a kind-hearted, jovial old merchant

Fred, Scrooge's nephew

Ghost of Christmas Past, a phantom showing things past

Ghost of Christmas Present, a spirit of a kind, generous
and hearty nature

Ghost of Christmas Yet to Come, an apparition showing
the shadows of things which yet may happen

Ghost of Jacob Marley, a spectre of Scrooge's former
partner in business

Joe, a marine-store dealer and receiver of stolen goods

Ebenezer Scrooge, a grasping, covetous old man, the
surviving partner of the firm of Scrooge & Marley

Mr Topper, a bachelor

Dick Wilkins, a fellow apprentice of Scrooge's

Belle, a comely matron, an old sweetheart of Scrooge's

Caroline, wife of one of Scrooge's debtors

Mrs Cratchit, wife of Bob Cratchit

Belinda and Martha Cratchit, daughters of the
preceding

Mrs Dilber, a laundress

Fan, the sister of Scrooge

Mrs Fezziwig, the worthy partner of Mr Fezziwig

Marley's Ghost

Marley was dead, to begin with. There is no doubt whatever about that. The register of his burial was signed by the clergyman, the clerk, the undertaker and the chief mourner. Scrooge signed it. And Scrooge's name was good upon 'Change for anything he chose to put his hand to. Old Marley was as dead as a doornail.

Mind! I don't mean to say that I know of my own knowledge, what there is particularly dead about a doornail. I might have been inclined, myself, to regard a coffin-nail as the deadest piece of ironmongery in the trade. But the wisdom of our ancestors is in the simile; and my unhallowed hands shall not disturb it, or the country's done for. You will, therefore, permit me to repeat, emphatically, that Marley was as dead as a doornail.

Scrooge knew he was dead? Of course he did. How could it be otherwise? Scrooge and he were partners for I don't know how many years. Scrooge was his sole executor, his sole administrator, his sole assign, his sole residuary legatee, his sole friend, and sole mourner. And even Scrooge was not so dreadfully cut up by the sad event but that he was an excellent man of business on the very day of the funeral, and solemnised it with an undoubted bargain.

The mention of Marley's funeral brings me back to the point I started from. There is no doubt that Marley was dead. This must be distinctly understood, or nothing wonderful can come of the story I am going to relate. If we were not perfectly convinced that Hamlet's father died before the play began, there would be nothing more remarkable in his taking a stroll at night, in an easterly wind, upon his own ramparts, than there would be in a breezy spot – say St Paul's Churchyard, for instance – literally to astonish his son's weak mind.

Scrooge never painted out Old Marley's name. There it stood, years afterwards, above the warehouse door: Scrooge and Marley. The firm was known as Scrooge and Marley. Sometimes people new to the business called Scrooge Scrooge, and sometimes Marley, but he answered to both names. It was all the same to him.

Oh! but he was a tight-fisted hand at the grindstone, Scrooge! a squeezing, wrenching, grasping, scraping, clutching, covetous old sinner! Hard and sharp as flint, from which no steel had ever struck out generous fire; secret, and self-contained, and solitary as an oyster. The cold within him froze his old features, nipped his pointed nose, shrivelled his cheek, stiffened his gait; made his eyes red, his thin lips blue; and spoke out shrewdly in his grating voice. A frosty rime was on his head, and on his eyebrows, and his wiry chin. He carried his own low temperature always about with him; he iced his office in the dog-days, and didn't thaw it one degree at Christmas.

External heat and cold had little influence on Scrooge. No warmth could warm, no wintry weather chill him. No wind that blew was bitterer than he, no falling snow was more intent upon its purpose, no pelting rain less open to entreaty. Foul weather didn't know where to have him. The heaviest rain, and snow, and hail, and sleet could boast of the advantage over him in only one respect. They often 'came down' handsomely, and Scrooge never did.

Nobody ever stopped him in the street to say, with gladsome looks, 'My dear Scrooge, how are you? When will you come to see me?' No beggars implored him to bestow a trifle, no children asked him what it was o'clock, no man or woman ever once in all his life enquired the way to such and such a place, of Scrooge. Even the blind men's dogs appeared to know him; and, when they saw him coming on, would tug their owners into doorways and up courts; and then would wag their tails as though they said, 'No eye at all is better than an evil eye, dark master!'

But what did Scrooge care? It was the very thing he liked. To edge his way along the crowded paths of life, warning all human sympathy to keep its distance, was what the knowing ones call 'nuts' to Scrooge.

Once upon a time – of all the good days in the year, on Christmas Eve – old Scrooge sat busy in his counting-house. It was cold, bleak, biting weather; foggy withal; and he could hear the people in the court outside go wheezing up and down, beating their hands upon their breasts, and stamping their feet upon the pavement stones to warm them. The City clocks had only just gone three, but it was quite dark already – it had not been light all day – and candles were flaring in the windows of the neighbouring offices, like ruddy smears upon the palpable brown air. The fog came pouring in at every chink and keyhole, and was so dense without, that, although the court was of the narrowest, the houses opposite were mere phantoms. To see the dingy cloud come drooping down, obscuring everything, one might have thought that nature lived hard by, and was brewing on a large scale.

The door of Scrooge's counting-house was open, that he might keep his eye upon his clerk, who in a dismal little cell beyond, a sort of tank, was copying letters. Scrooge had a very small fire, but the clerk's fire was so very much smaller that it looked like one coal. But he couldn't replenish it, for Scrooge kept the coal-box in his own room; and so surely as the clerk came in with the shovel, the master predicted that it would be necessary for them to part. Wherefore the clerk put on his white comforter, and tried to warm himself at the candle; in which effort, not being a man of strong imagination, he failed.

'A merry Christmas, uncle! God save you!' cried a cheerful voice. It was the voice of Scrooge's nephew, who came upon him so quickly that this was the first intimation he had of his approach.

'Bah!' said Scrooge. 'Humbug!'

He had so heated himself with rapid walking in the fog and frost, this nephew of Scrooge's, that he was all in a glow; his face was ruddy and handsome; his eyes sparkled, and his breath smoked again.

'Christmas a humbug, uncle!' said Scrooge's nephew. 'You don't mean that, I am sure?'

'I do,' said Scrooge. 'Merry Christmas! What right have you to be merry? What reason have you to be merry? You're poor enough.'

'Come, then,' returned the nephew gaily. 'What right have you to be dismal? What reason have you to be morose? You're rich enough.'

Scrooge, having no better answer ready on the spur of the moment, said, 'Bah!' again; and followed it up with 'Humbug!'

'Don't be cross, uncle!' said the nephew.

'What else can I be,' returned the uncle, 'when I live in such a world of fools as this? Merry Christmas! Out upon merry Christmas! What's Christmastime to you but a time for paying bills without money; a time for finding yourself a year older, and not an hour richer; a time for balancing your books, and having every item in 'em through a round dozen of months presented dead against you? If I could work my will,' said Scrooge indignantly, 'every idiot who goes about with "Merry

Christmas" on his lips should be boiled with his own pudding, and buried with a stake of holly through his heart. He should!'

'Uncle!' pleaded the nephew.

'Nephew!' returned the uncle sternly, 'keep Christmas in your own way, and let me keep it in mine.'

'Keep it!' repeated Scrooge's nephew. 'But you don't keep it.'

'Let me leave it alone, then,' said Scrooge. 'Much good may it do you! Much good it has ever done you!'

'There are many things from which I might have derived good, by which I have not profited, I dare say,' returned the nephew; 'Christmas among the rest. But I am sure I have always thought of Christmastime, when it has come round – apart from the veneration due to its sacred name and origin, if anything belonging to it can be apart from that – as a good time; a kind, forgiving, charitable, pleasant time; the only time I know of, in the long calendar of the year, when men and women seem by one consent to open their shut-up hearts freely, and to think of people below them as if they really were fellow-passengers to the grave, and not another race of creatures bound on other journeys. And therefore, uncle, though it has never put a scrap of gold or silver in my pocket, I believe that it *has* done me good and *will* do me good; and I say, God bless it!'

The clerk in the tank involuntarily applauded. Becoming immediately sensible of the impropriety, he poked the fire, and extinguished the last frail spark for ever.

'Let me hear another sound from *you*,' said Scrooge, 'and you'll keep your Christmas by losing your situation! You're quite a powerful speaker, sir,' he added, turning to his nephew. 'I wonder you don't go into Parliament.'

'Don't be angry, uncle. Come! Dine with us tomorrow.'

Scrooge said that he would see him in h— Yes, indeed he did. He went the whole length of the expression, and said that he would see him in that extremity first.

'But why?' cried Scrooge's nephew. 'Why?'

'Why did you get married?' said Scrooge.

'Because I fell in love.'

'Because you fell in love!' growled Scrooge, as if that were the only one thing in the world more ridiculous than a merry Christmas. 'Good-afternoon!'

'Nay, uncle, but you never came to see me before that happened. Why give it as a reason for not coming now?'

'Good-afternoon,' said Scrooge.

'I want nothing from you; I ask nothing of you; why cannot we be friends?'

'Good-afternoon!' said Scrooge.

'I am sorry, with all my heart, to find you so resolute. We have never had any quarrel to which I have been a party. But I have made the trial in homage to Christmas, and I'll keep my Christmas humour to the last. So A Merry Christmas, uncle!'

'Good-afternoon,' said Scrooge.

'And a Happy New Year!'

'Good-afternoon!' said Scrooge.

His nephew left the room without an angry word, notwithstanding. He stopped at the outer door to bestow the greetings of the season on the clerk, who, cold as he was, was warmer than Scrooge; for he returned them cordially.

'There's another fellow,' muttered Scrooge, who overheard him: 'my clerk, with fifteen shillings a week, and a wife and family, talking about a merry Christmas. I'll retire to Bedlam.'

This lunatic, in letting Scrooge's nephew out, had let two other people in. They were portly gentlemen, pleasant to behold, and now stood, with their hats off, in Scrooge's office. They had books and papers in their hands, and bowed to him.

'Scrooge and Marley's, I believe,' said one of the gentlemen, referring to his list. 'Have I the pleasure of addressing Mr Scrooge, or Mr Marley?'

'Mr Marley has been dead these seven years,' Scrooge replied. 'He died seven years ago, this very night.'

'We have no doubt his liberality is well represented by his surviving partner,' said the gentleman, presenting his credentials.

It certainly was; for they had been two kindred spirits. At the ominous word 'liberality' Scrooge frowned, and shook his head, and handed the credentials back.

'At this festive season of the year, Mr Scrooge,' said the gentleman, taking up a pen, 'it is more than usually desirable that we should make some slight provision for the poor and destitute, who suffer greatly at the present time. Many thousands are in want of common necessaries; hundreds of thousands are in want of common comforts, sir.'

'Are there no prisons?' asked Scrooge.

'Plenty of prisons,' said the gentleman, laying down the pen again.

'And the Union workhouses?' demanded Scrooge. 'Are they still in operation?'

'They are. Still,' returned the gentleman, 'I wish I could say they were not.'

'The Treadmill and the Poor Law are in full vigour, then?' said Scrooge.

'Both very busy, sir.'

'Oh! I was afraid, from what you said at first, that something had occurred to stop them in their useful course,' said Scrooge. 'I am very glad to hear it.'

'Under the impression that they scarcely furnish Christian cheer of mind or body to the multitude,' returned the gentleman, 'a few of us are endeavouring to raise a fund to buy the Poor some meat and drink, and means of warmth. We choose this time, because it is a time, of all others, when Want is keenly felt, and Abundance rejoices. What shall I put you down for?'

'Nothing!' Scrooge replied.

'You wish to be anonymous?'

'I wish to be left alone,' said Scrooge. 'Since you ask me what I wish, gentlemen, that is my answer. I don't make merry myself at Christmas, and I can't afford to make idle people merry. I help to support the establishments I have mentioned – they cost enough: and those who are badly off must go there.'

'Many can't go there; and many would rather die.'

'If they would rather die,' said Scrooge, 'they had better do it, and decrease the surplus population. Besides – excuse me – I don't know that.'

'But you might know it,' observed the gentleman.

'It's not my business,' Scrooge returned. 'It's enough for a man to understand his own business, and not to interfere with other people's. Mine occupies me constantly. Good-afternoon, gentlemen!'

Seeing clearly that it would be useless to pursue their point, the gentlemen withdrew. Scrooge resumed his labours with an improved opinion of himself, and in a more facetious temper than was usual with him.

Meanwhile the fog and darkness thickened so, that people ran about with flaring links, proffering their services to go before horses in carriages, and conduct them on their way. The ancient tower of a church, whose gruff old bell was always peeping slily down at Scrooge out of a Gothic window in the wall, became invisible, and struck the hours and quarters in the clouds, with tremulous vibrations afterwards, as if its teeth were chattering in its frozen head up there. The cold became intense. In the main street, at the corner of the court, some labourers were repairing the gas-pipes, and had lighted a great fire in a brazier, round which a party of ragged men and boys were gathered: warming their hands and winking their eyes before the blaze in rapture. The water-plug being left in solitude, its over-flowings suddenly congealed, and turned to misanthropic ice. The brightness of the shops, where holly sprigs and berries crackled in the lamp heat of the windows, made pale faces ruddy as they passed. Poulterers' and grocers' trades became a splendid joke: a glorious pageant, with which it was next to impossible to believe that such dull principles as bargain and sale had anything to do. The Lord Mayor, in the stronghold of the mighty Mansion House, gave orders to his fifty cooks and butlers to keep Christmas as a Lord Mayor's household should; and even the little tailor, whom he had fined five shillings on the previous   Monday for being drunk and bloodthirsty in the streets, stirred up tomorrow's pudding in his garret, while his lean wife and the baby sallied out to buy the beef.

Foggier yet, and colder! Piercing, searching, biting cold. If the good St Dunstan had but nipped the Evil Spirit's nose with a touch of such weather as that, instead of using his familiar weapons, then indeed he would have roared to lusty purpose. The owner of one scant young nose, gnawed and mumbled by the hungry cold as bones are gnawed by dogs, stooped down at Scrooge's keyhole to regale him with a Christmas carol; but, at the first sound of

> 'God bless you, merry gentleman,
> May nothing you dismay!'

Scrooge seized the ruler with such energy of action that the singer fled in terror, leaving the keyhole to the fog, and even more congenial frost.

At length the hour of shutting up the counting-house arrived. With an ill-will Scrooge dismounted from his stool, and tacitly admitted the fact to the expectant clerk in the tank, who instantly snuffed his candle out, and put on his hat.

'You'll want all day tomorrow, I suppose?' said Scrooge.

'If quite convenient, sir.'

'It's not convenient,' said Scrooge, 'and it's not fair. If I was to stop half a crown for it, you'd think yourself ill used, I'll be bound?'

The clerk smiled faintly.

'And yet,' said Scrooge, 'you don't think *me* ill used when I pay a day's wages for no work.'

The clerk observed that it was only once a year.

'A poor excuse for picking a man's pocket every twenty-fifth of December!' said Scrooge, buttoning his greatcoat to the chin. 'But I suppose you must have the whole day. Be here all the earlier next morning.'

The clerk promised that he would; and Scrooge walked out with a growl. The office was closed in a twinkling, and the clerk, with the long ends of his white comforter dangling below his waist (for he boasted no greatcoat), went down a slide on Cornhill, at the end of a lane of boys, twenty times, in honour of its being Christmas Eve, and then ran home to Camden Town as hard as he could pelt, to play at blindman's-buff.

Scrooge took his melancholy dinner in his usual melancholy tavern; and having read all the newspapers, and beguiled the rest of the evening with his banker's book, went home to bed. He lived in chambers which had once belonged to his deceased partner. They were a gloomy suite of rooms, in a lowering pile of building up a yard, where it had so little business to be, that one could scarcely help fancying it must have run there when it was a young house, playing at hide-and-seek with other houses, and have forgotten the way out again. It was old enough now, and dreary enough; for nobody lived in it but Scrooge, the other rooms being all let out as offices. The yard was so dark that even Scrooge, who knew its every stone, was fain to grope with his hands. The fog and frost so hung about the black old gateway of the house, that it seemed as if the Genius of the Weather sat in mournful meditation on the threshold.

Now, it is a fact that there was nothing at all particular about the knocker on the door, except that it was very large. It is also a fact that Scrooge had seen it, night and morning, during his whole residence in that place; also that Scrooge had as little of what is called fancy about him as any man in the City of London, even including – which is a bold word – the corporation, aldermen, and livery. Let it also be borne in mind that Scrooge had not bestowed one thought on Marley since his last mention of his seven-years'-dead partner that afternoon. And then let any man explain to me, if he can, how it happened that Scrooge, having his key in the lock of the door, saw in the knocker, without its undergoing any intermediate process of change – not a knocker, but Marley's face.

Marley's face. It was not in impenetrable shadow, as the other objects in the yard were, but had a dismal light about it, like a bad lobster in a dark cellar. It was not angry or ferocious, but looked at Scrooge as Marley used to look; with ghostly spectacles turned up on its ghostly forehead. The hair was curiously stirred, as if by breath or hot air; and, though the eyes were wide open, they were perfectly motionless. That, and its livid colour, made it horrible; but its horror seemed to be in spite of the face, and beyond its control, rather than a part of its own expression.

As Scrooge looked fixedly at this phenomenon, it was a knocker again.

To say that he was not startled, or that his blood was not conscious of a terrible sensation to which it had been a stranger from infancy, would be untrue. But he put his hand upon the key he had relinquished, turned it sturdily, walked in, and lighted his candle.

He *did* pause, with a moment's irresolution, before he shut the door; and he *did* look cautiously behind it first, as if he half expected to be terrified with the sight of Marley's pigtail sticking out into the hall. But there was nothing on the back of the door, except the screws and nuts that held the knocker on, so he said, 'Pooh, pooh!' and closed it with a bang.

The sound resounded through the house like thunder. Every room above, and every cask in the wine-merchant's cellars below, appeared to have a separate peal of echoes of its own. Scrooge was not a man to be frightened by echoes. He fastened the door, and walked across the hall, and up the stairs: slowly, too: trimming his candle as he went.

You may talk vaguely about driving a coach and six up a good old flight of stairs, or through a bad young Act of Parliament; but I mean to say you might have got a hearse up that staircase, and taken it broadwise, with the splinter-bar towards the wall, and the door towards the balustrades: and done it easy. There was plenty of width for that, and room to spare; which is perhaps the reason why Scrooge thought he saw a locomotive hearse going on before him in the gloom. Half a dozen gas-lamps out of the street wouldn't have lighted the entry too well, so you may suppose that it was pretty dark with Scrooge's dip.

Up Scrooge went, not caring a button for that. Darkness is cheap, and

Scrooge liked it. But, before he shut his heavy door, he walked through his rooms to see that all was right. He had just enough recollection of the face to desire to do that.

Sitting-room, bedroom, lumber-room. All as they should be. Nobody under the table, nobody under the sofa; a small fire in the grate; spoon and basin ready; and the little saucepan of gruel (Scrooge had a cold in his head) upon the hob. Nobody under the bed; nobody in the closet; nobody in his dressing-gown, which was hanging up in a suspicious attitude against the wall. Lumber-room as usual. Old fireguard, old shoes, two fish baskets, washing-stand on three legs, and a poker.

Quite satisfied, he closed his door, and locked himself in; double locked himself in, which was not his custom. Thus secured against surprise, he took off his cravat; put on his dressing-gown and slippers, and his nightcap; and sat down before the fire to take his gruel.

It was a very low fire indeed; nothing on such a bitter night. He was obliged to sit close to it, and brood over it, before he could extract the least sensation of warmth from such a handful of fuel. The fireplace was an old one, built by some Dutch merchant long ago, and paved all round with quaint Dutch tiles, designed to illustrate the Scriptures. There were Cains and Abels, Pharaoh's daughters, Queens of Sheba, Angelic messengers descending through the air on clouds like feather-beds, Abrahams, Belshazzars, Apostles putting off to sea in butter-boats, hundreds of figures to attract his thoughts; and yet that face of Marley, seven years dead, came like the ancient Prophet's rod, and swallowed up the whole. If each smooth tile had been a blank at first, with power to shape some picture on its surface from the disjointed fragments of his thoughts, there would have been a copy of old Marley's head on every one.

'Humbug!' said Scrooge; and walked across the room.

After several turns he sat down again. As he threw his head back in the chair, his glance happened to rest upon a bell, a disused bell, that hung in the room, and communicated, for some purpose now forgotten, with a chamber in the highest storey of the building. It was with great astonishment, and with a strange, inexplicable dread, that, as he looked, he saw this bell begin to swing. It swung so softly in the outset that it scarcely made a sound; but soon it rang out loudly, and so did every bell in the house.

This might have lasted half a minute, or a minute, but it seemed an hour. The bells ceased, as they had begun, together. They were succeeded by a clanking noise deep down below as if some person were dragging a heavy chain over the casks in the wine-merchant's cellar. Scrooge then remembered to have heard that ghosts in haunted houses were described as dragging chains.

The cellar door flew open with a booming sound, and then he heard the noise much louder on the floors below; then coming up the stairs; then coming straight towards his door.

'It's humbug still!' said Scrooge. 'I won't believe it.'

His colour changed, though, when, without a pause, it came on through the heavy door and passed into the room before his eyes. Upon its coming in, the dying flame leaped up, as though it cried, 'I know him! Marley's Ghost!' and fell again.

The same face: the very same. Marley in his pigtail, usual waistcoat, tights, and boots; the tassels on the latter bristling, like his pigtail, and his coat-skirts, and the hair upon his head. The chain he drew was clasped about his middle. It was long, and wound about him like a tail; and it was made (for Scrooge observed it closely) of cash-boxes, keys, padlocks, ledgers, deeds, and heavy purses wrought in steel. His body was transparent: so that Scrooge, observing him, and looking through his waistcoat, could see the two buttons on his coat behind.

Scrooge had often heard it said that Marley had no bowels, but he had never believed it until now.

No, nor did he believe it even now. Though he looked the phantom through and through, and saw it standing before him; though he felt the chilling influence of its death-cold eyes, and marked the very texture of the folded kerchief bound about its head and chin, which wrapper he had not observed before, he was still incredulous, and fought against his senses.

'How now!' said Scrooge, caustic and cold as ever. 'What do you want with me?'

'Much!' Marley's voice; no doubt about it.

'Who are you?'

'Ask me who I *was*.'

'Who *were* you, then?' said Scrooge, raising his voice. 'You're particular, for a shade.' He was going to say '*to* a shade', but substituted this, as more appropriate.

'In life I was your partner, Jacob Marley.'

'Can you – can you sit down?' asked Scrooge, looking doubtfully at him.

'I can.'

'Do it, then.'

Scrooge asked the question, because he didn't know whether a ghost so transparent might find himself in a condition to take a chair; and felt that in the event of its being impossible, it might involve the necessity of an embarrassing explanation. But the ghost sat down on the opposite side of the fireplace, as if he were quite used to it.

'You don't believe in me,' observed the ghost.

'I don't,' said Scrooge.

'What evidence would you have of my reality beyond that of your own senses?'

'I don't know,' said Scrooge.

'Why do you doubt your senses?'

'Because,' said Scrooge, 'a little thing affects them. A slight disorder of the stomach makes them cheats. You may be an undigested bit of beef, a blot of mustard, a crumb of cheese, a fragment of an underdone potato. There's more of gravy than of grave about you, whatever you are!'

Scrooge was not much in the habit of cracking jokes, nor did he feel in his heart by any means waggish then. The truth is, that he tried to be smart, as a means of distracting his own attention, and keeping down his terror; for the spectre's voice disturbed the very marrow in his bones.

To sit staring at those fixed, glazed eyes in silence, for a moment, would play, Scrooge felt, the very deuce with him. There was something very awful, too, in the spectre's being provided with an infernal atmosphere of his own. Scrooge could not feel it himself, but this was clearly the case; for though the ghost sat perfectly motionless, its hair, and skirts, and tassels were still agitated as by the hot vapour from an oven.

'You see this toothpick?' said Scrooge, returning quickly to the charge, for the reason just assigned; and wishing, though it were only for a second, to divert the vision's stony gaze from himself.

'I do,' replied the ghost.

'You are not looking at it,' said Scrooge.

'But I see it,' said the ghost, 'notwithstanding.'

'Well!' returned Scrooge, 'I have but to swallow this, and be for the rest of my days persecuted by a legion of goblins, all of my own creation. Humbug, I tell you: humbug!'

At this the spirit raised a frightful cry, and shook its chain with such a dismal and appalling noise, that Scrooge held on tight to his chair, to save

Marley's Ghost

himself from falling in a swoon. But how much greater was his horror when the phantom, taking off the bandage round his head, as if it were too warm to wear indoors, its lower jaw dropped down upon its breast!

Scrooge fell upon his knees, and clasped his hands before his face.

'Mercy!' he said. 'Dreadful apparition, why do you trouble me?'

'Man of the worldly mind!' replied the ghost, 'do you believe in me or not?'

'I do,' said Scrooge; 'I must. But why do spirits walk the earth, and why do they come to me?'

'It is required of every man,' the ghost returned, 'that the spirit within him should walk abroad among his fellow-men, and travel far and wide; and, if that spirit goes not forth in life, it is condemned to do so after death. It is doomed to wander through the world – oh, woe is me! and witness what it cannot share, but might have shared on earth, and turned to happiness!'

Again the spectre raised a cry, and shook its chain and wrung its shadowy hands.

'You are fettered,' said Scrooge, trembling. 'Tell me why?'

'I wear the chain I forged in life,' replied the ghost. 'I made it link by link, and yard by yard; I girded it on of my own free will, and of my own free will I wore it. Is its pattern strange to *you*?'

Scrooge trembled more and more.

'Or would you know,' pursued the ghost, 'the weight and length of the strong coil you bear yourself? It was full as heavy and as long as this seven Christmas Eves ago. You have laboured on it since. It is a ponderous chain!'

Scrooge glanced about him on the floor, in the expectation of finding himself surrounded by some fifty or sixty fathoms of iron cable; but he could see nothing.

'Jacob!' he said imploringly. 'Old Jacob Marley, tell me more! Speak comfort to me, Jacob!'

'I have none to give,' the ghost replied. 'It comes from other regions, Ebenezer Scrooge, and is conveyed by other ministers, to other kinds of men. Nor can I tell you what I would. A very little more is all permitted to me. I cannot rest, I cannot stay, I cannot linger anywhere. My spirit never walked beyond our counting-house – mark me – in life my spirit never roved beyond the narrow limits of our money-changing hole; and weary journeys lie before me!'

It was a habit with Scrooge, whenever he became thoughtful, to put his hands in his breeches pockets. Pondering on what the ghost had said, he did so now, but without lifting up his eyes, or getting off his knees.

'You must have been very slow about it, Jacob,' Scrooge observed in a businesslike manner, though with humility and deference.

'Slow!' the ghost repeated.

'Seven years dead,' mused Scrooge. 'And travelling all the time?'

'The whole time,' said the ghost. 'No rest, no peace. Incessant torture of remorse.'

'You travel fast?' said Scrooge.

'On the wings of the wind,' replied the ghost.

'You might have got over a great quantity of ground in seven years,' said Scrooge.

The ghost, on hearing this, set up another cry, and clanked its chain so hideously in the dead silence of the night, that the Ward would have been justified in indicting it for a nuisance.

'Oh! captive, bound, and double-ironed,' cried the phantom, 'not to know that ages of incessant labour, by immortal creatures, for this earth must pass into eternity before the good of which it is susceptible is all developed! Not to know that any Christian spirit working kindly in its little sphere, whatever it may be, will find its mortal life too short for its vast means of usefulness! Not to know that no space of regret can make amends for one life's opportunities misused! Yet such was I! Oh, such was I!'

'But you were always a good man of business, Jacob,' faltered Scrooge, who now began to apply this to himself.

'Business!' cried the ghost, wringing its hands again. 'Mankind was my business. The common welfare was my business; charity, mercy, forbearance, and benevolence were, all, my business. The dealings of my trade were but a drop of water in the comprehensive ocean of my business!'

It held up its chain at arm's-length, as if that were the cause of all its unavailing grief, and flung it heavily upon the ground again.

'At this time of the rolling year,' the spectre said, 'I suffer most. Why did I walk through crowds of fellow-beings with my eyes turned down, and never raise them to that blessed Star which led the Wise Men to a poor abode? Were there no poor homes to which its light would have conducted *me*?'

Scrooge was very much dismayed to hear the spectre going on at this rate, and began to quake exceedingly.

'Hear me!' cried the ghost. 'My time is nearly gone.'

'I will,' said Scrooge. 'But don't be hard upon me! Don't be flowery, Jacob! Pray!'

'How it is that I appear before you in a shape that you can see, I may not tell. I have sat invisible beside you many and many a day.'

It was not an agreeable idea. Scrooge shivered, and wiped the perspiration from his brow.

'That is no light part of my penance,' pursued the ghost. 'I am her tonight to warn you that you have yet a chance and hope of escaping my fate. A chance and hope of my procuring, Ebenezer.'

'You were always a good friend to me,' said Scrooge. 'Thankee!'

'You will be haunted,' resumed the ghost, 'by Three Spirits.'

Scrooge's countenance fell almost as low as the ghost's had done.

'Is that the chance and hope you mentioned, Jacob?' he demanded in a faltering voice.

'It is.'

'I – I think I'd rather not,' said Scrooge.

'Without their visits,' said the ghost, 'you cannot hope to shun the path I tread. Expect the first tomorrow when the bell tolls One.'

'Couldn't I take 'em all at once, and have it over, Jacob?' hinted Scrooge.

'Expect the second on the next night at the same hour. The third, upon the next night when the last stroke of Twelve has ceased to vibrate. Look to see me no more; and look that, for your own sake, you remember what has passed between us!'

When it had said these words, the spectre took its wrapper from the table, and bound it round its head as before. Scrooge knew this by the smart sound its teeth made when the jaws were brought together by the bandage. He ventured to raise his eyes again, and found his supernatural visitor confronting him in an erect attitude, with its chain wound over and about its arm.

The apparition walked backward from him; and, at every step it took, the window raised itself a little, so that, when the spectre reached it, it was wide open. It beckoned Scrooge to approach, which he did. When they were within two paces of each other, Marley's Ghost held up its hand, warning him to come no nearer. Scrooge stopped.

Not so much in obedience as in surprise and fear; for, on the raising of the hand, he became sensible of confused noises in the air; incoherent sounds of lamentation and regret; wailings inexpressibly sorrowful and self-accusatory. The spectre, after listening for a moment, joined in the mournful dirge; and floated out upon the bleak, dark night.

Scrooge followed to the window: desperate in his curiosity. He looked out.

The air was filled with phantoms

The air was filled with phantoms, wandering hither and thither in restless haste, and moaning as they went. Every one of them wore chains like Marley's Ghost; some few (they might be guilty governments) were linked together; none were free. Many had been personally known to Scrooge in their lives. He had been quite familiar with one old ghost in a white waistcoat, with a monstrous iron safe attached to its ankle, who cried piteously at being unable to assist a wretched woman with an infant, whom it saw below upon a doorstep. The misery with them all was clearly, that they sought to interfere, for good, in human matters, and had lost the power for ever.

Whether these creatures faded into mist, or mist enshrouded them, he could not tell. But they and their spirit voices faded together; and the night became as it had been when he walked home.

Scrooge closed the window, and examined the door by which the ghost had entered. It was double locked, as he had locked it with his own hands, and the bolts were undisturbed. He tried to say 'Humbug!' but stopped at the first syllable. And being, from the emotions he had undergone, or the fatigues of the day, or his glimpse of the Invisible World, or the dull conversation of the ghost, or the lateness of the hour, much in need of repose, went straight to bed without undressing and fell asleep upon the instant.

The First of the Three Spirits

When Scrooge awoke it was so dark that, looking out of bed, he could scarcely distinguish the transparent window from the opaque walls of his chamber. He was endeavouring to pierce the darkness with his ferret eyes, when the chimes of a neighbouring church struck the four quarters. So he listened for the hour.

To his great astonishment, the heavy bell went on from six to seven, and from seven to eight, and regularly up to twelve; then stopped. Twelve! It was past two when he went to bed. The clock was wrong. An icicle must have got into the works. Twelve!

He touched the spring of his repeater, to correct this most preposterous clock. Its rapid little pulse beat twelve, and stopped.

'Why, it isn't possible,' said Scrooge, 'that I can have slept through a whole day and far into another night. It isn't possible that anything has happened to the sun, and this is twelve at noon!'

The idea being an alarming one, he scrambled out of bed, and groped his way to the window. He was obliged to rub the frost off with the sleeve of his dressing-gown before he could see anything; and could see very little then. All he could make out was, that it was still very foggy and extremely cold, and that there was no noise of people running to and fro, and making a great stir, as there unquestionably would have been if night had beaten off bright day, and taken possession of the world. This was a great relief, because 'Three days after sight of this First of Exchange pay to Mr Ebenezer Scrooge or his order,' and so forth, would have become a mere United States security if there were no days to count by.

Scrooge went to bed again, and thought, and thought, and thought it over and over, and could make nothing of it. The more he thought, the more perplexed he was; and, the more he endeavoured not to think, the more he thought.

Marley's Ghost bothered him exceedingly. Every time he resolved within himself, after mature enquiry, that it was all a dream, his mind flew back again, like a strong spring released, to its first position, and presented the same problem to be worked all through, 'Was it a dream or not?'

Scrooge lay in this state until the chime had gone three-quarters more, when he remembered, on a sudden, that the ghost had warned him of a visitation when the bell tolled one. He resolved to lie awake until the hour was passed; and, considering that he could no more go to sleep than go to heaven, this was, perhaps, the wisest resolution in his power.

The quarter was so long, that he was more than once convinced he must have sunk into a doze unconsciously, and missed the clock. At length it broke upon his listening ear.

'Ding, dong!'

'A quarter past,' said Scrooge, counting.

'Ding, dong!'

'Half past,' said Scrooge.

'Ding, dong!'

'A quarter to it,' said Scrooge.

'Ding, dong!'

'The hour itself,' said Scrooge triumphantly, 'and nothing else!'

He spoke before the hour bell sounded, which it now did with a deep, dull, hollow, melancholy One. Light flashed up in the room upon the instant, and the curtains of his bed were drawn.

The curtains of his bed were drawn aside, I tell you, by a hand. Not the curtains at his feet, nor the curtains at his back, but those to which his face was addressed. The curtains of his bed were drawn aside; and Scrooge, starting up into a half-recumbent attitude, found himself face to face with the unearthly visitor who drew them: as close to it as I am now to you, and I am standing in the spirit at your elbow.

It was a strange figure – like a child; yet not so like a child as like an old man, viewed through some supernatural medium, which gave him the appearance of having receded from the view, and being diminished to a child's proportions. Its hair, which hung about its neck and down its back, was white, as if with age; and yet the face had not a wrinkle in it, and the tenderest bloom was on the skin. The arms were very long and muscular; the hands the same, as if its hold were of uncommon strength. Its legs and feet, most delicately formed, were, like those upper members, bare. It wore a tunic of the purest white; and round its waist was bound a lustrous belt, the sheen of which was beautiful. It held a branch of fresh green holly in its hand; and, in singular contradiction of that wintry emblem, had its dress trimmed with summer flowers. But the strangest thing about it was, that from the crown of its head there sprang a bright clear jet of light, by which all this was visible; and which was doubtless the occasion of its using, in its duller moments, a great extinguisher for a cap, which it now held under its arm.

Even this, though, when Scrooge looked at it with increasing steadiness, was *not* its strangest quality. For, as its belt sparkled and glittered, now in one part and now in another, and what was light one instant at another time was dark, so the figure itself fluctuated in its distinctness; being now a thing with one arm, now with one leg, now with twenty legs, now a pair of legs without a head, now a head without a body: of which dissolving parts no outline would be visible in the dense gloom wherein they melted away. And, in the very wonder of this, it would be itself again; distinct and clear as ever.

'Are you the Spirit, sir, whose coming was foretold to me?' asked Scrooge.

'I am!'

The voice was soft and gentle. Singularly low, as if, instead of being so close behind him, it were at a distance.

'Who and what are you?' Scrooge demanded.

'I am the Ghost of Christmas Past.'

'Long past?' enquired Scrooge, observant of its dwarfish stature.

'No. Your past.'

Perhaps Scrooge could not have told anybody why, if anybody could have asked him; but he had a special desire to see the Spirit in his cap, and begged him to be covered.

'What!' exclaimed the ghost, 'would you so soon put out, with worldly hands, the light I give? Is it not enough that you are one of those whose passions made this cap, and force me through whole trains of years to wear it low upon my brow?'

Scrooge reverently disclaimed all intention to offend or any knowledge of having wilfully 'bonneted' the Spirit at any period of his life. He then made bold to enquire what business brought him there.

'Your welfare!' said the ghost.

Scrooge expressed himself much obliged, but could not help thinking that a night of unbroken rest would have been more conducive to that end. The Spirit must have heard him thinking, for it said immediately –

'Your reclamation, then. Take heed!'

It put out its strong hand as it spoke, and clasped him gently by the arm.

'Rise! and walk with me!'

It would have been in vain for Scrooge to plead that the weather and the hour were not adapted to pedestrian purposes; that bed was warm, and the thermometer a long way below freezing; that he was clad but lightly in his slippers, dressing-gown, and nightcap; and that he had a cold upon him at that time. The grasp, though gentle as a woman's hand, was not to be resisted. He rose; but, finding that the Spirit made towards the window, clasped its robe in supplication.

'I am a mortal,' Scrooge remonstrated, 'and liable to fall.'

'Bear but a touch of my hand *there*,' said the Spirit, laying it upon his heart, 'and you shall be upheld in more than this!'

As the words were spoken, they passed through the wall, and stood upon an open country road, with fields on either hand. The city had entirely vanished. Not a vestige of it was to be seen. The darkness and the mist had vanished with it, for it was a clear, cold, winter day, with snow upon the ground.

'Good Heaven!' said Scrooge, clasping his hands together, as he looked about him. 'I was bred in this place. I was a boy here!'

The Spirit gazed upon him mildly. Its gentle touch, though it had been light and instantaneous, appeared still present to the old man's sense of feeling. He was conscious of a thousand odours floating in the air, each one connected with a thousand thoughts, and hopes, and joys, and cares long, long forgotten!

'Your lip is trembling,' said the ghost. 'And what is that upon your cheek?'

Scrooge muttered, with an unusual catching in his voice, that it was a pimple; and begged the ghost to lead him where he would.

'You recollect the way?' enquired the Spirit.

'Remember it!' cried Scrooge with fervour; 'I could walk it blindfold.'

'Strange to have forgotten it for so many years!' observed the ghost. 'Let us go on.'

They walked along the road, Scrooge recognising every gate, and post, and tree, until a little market-town appeared in the distance, with its bridge, its church, and winding river. Some shaggy ponies now were seen trotting towards them with boys upon their backs, who called to other boys in country gigs and carts, driven by farmers. All these boys were in great spirits, and shouted to each other, until the broad fields were so full of merry music, that the crisp air laughed to hear it.

'These are but shadows of the things that have been,' said the ghost. 'They have no consciousness of us.'

The jocund travellers came on; and as they came, Scrooge knew and named them everyone. Why was he rejoiced beyond all bounds to see them? Why did his cold eye glisten, and his heart leap up as they went past? Why was he filled with gladness when he heard them give each other Merry Christmas, as they parted at crossroads and byways for their several homes? What was merry Christmas to Scrooge? Out upon merry Christmas! What good had it ever done to him?

'The school is not quite deserted,' said the ghost. 'A solitary child, neglected by his friends, is left there still.'

Scrooge said he knew it. And he sobbed.

They left the highroad by a well-remembered lane and soon approached a mansion of dull red brick, with a little weathercock surmounted cupola on the roof, and a bell hanging in it. It was a large house, but one of broken fortunes; for the spacious offices were little used, their walls were damp and mossy, their windows broken, and their gates decayed. Fowls clucked and strutted in the stables; and the coach-houses and sheds were overrun with grass. Nor was it more retentive of its ancient state within; for, entering the dreary hall, and glancing through the open doors of many rooms, they found them poorly furnished, cold, and vast. There was an earthy savour in the air, a chilly bareness in the place, which associated itself somehow with too much getting up by candlelight and not too much to eat.

They went, the ghost and Scrooge, across the hall, to a door at the back of the house. It opened before them, and disclosed a long, bare, melancholy room, made barer still by lines of plain deal forms and desks. At one of these a lonely boy was reading near a feeble fire; and Scrooge sat down upon a form, and wept to see his poor forgotten self as he had used to be.

Not a latent echo in the house, not a squeak and scuffle from the mice behind the panelling, not a drip from the half-thawed waterspout in the dull yard behind, not a sigh among the leafless boughs of one despondent poplar, not the idle swinging of an empty storehouse door, no, not a clicking in the fire, but fell upon the heart of Scrooge with softening influence, and gave a freer passage to his tears.

The Spirit touched him on the arm, and pointed to his younger self, intent upon his reading. Suddenly a man in foreign garments, wonderfully real and distinct to look at, stood outside the window, with an axe stuck in his belt, and leading by the bridle an ass laden with wood.

'Why, it's Ali Baba!' Scrooge exclaimed in ecstasy. 'It's dear old honest Ali Baba! Yes, yes, I know. One Christmastime, when yonder solitary child was left here all alone, he *did* come, for the first time, just like that. Poor boy! And Valentine,' said Scrooge, 'and his wild brother, Orson; there they go! And what's his name, who was put down in his drawers, asleep, at the gate of Damascus; don't you see him? And the Sultan's Groom turned upside down by the Genii; there he is upon his head! Serve him right! I'm glad of it. What business had *he* to be married to the Princess?'

To hear Scrooge expending all the earnestness of his nature on such subjects, in a most extraordinary voice between laughing and crying; and to see his heightened and excited face; would have been a surprise to his business friends in the City, indeed.

'There's the Parrot!' cried Scrooge. 'Green body and yellow tail, with a thing like a lettuce growing out of the top of his head; there he is! Poor Robin Crusoe he called him, when he came home again after sailing round the island. "Poor Robin Crusoe, where have you been, Robin Crusoe?" The man thought he was dreaming, but he wasn't. It was the Parrot, you know. There goes Friday, running for his life to the little creek! Halloa! Hoop! Halloo!'

Then, with a rapidity of transition very foreign to his usual character, he said, in pity for his former self, 'Poor boy!' and cried again.

'I wish,' Scrooge muttered, putting his hand in his pocket, and looking about him, after drying his eyes with his cuff; 'but it's too late now.'

'What is the matter?' asked the Spirit.

'Nothing,' said Scrooge. 'Nothing. There was a boy singing a Christmas carol at my door last night. I should like to have given him something: that's all.'

The ghost smiled thoughtfully, and waved its hand, saying as it did so, 'Let us see another Christmas!'

Scrooge's former self grew larger at the words, and the room became a little darker and more dirty. The panels shrunk, the windows cracked; fragments of plaster fell out of the ceiling, and the naked laths were shown instead; but how all this was brought about Scrooge knew no more than you do. He only knew that it was quite correct; that everything had happened so; that there he was, alone again, when all the other boys had gone home for the jolly holidays.

He was not reading now, but walking up and down despairingly. Scrooge looked at the ghost, and, with a mournful shaking of his head, glanced anxiously towards the door.

It opened; and a little girl, much younger than the boy, came darting in, and, putting her arms about his neck, and often kissing him, addressed him as her 'dear, dear brother.'

'I have come to bring you home, dear brother!' said the child, clapping her tiny hands, and bending down to laugh. 'To bring you home, home, home!'

'Home, little Fan?' returned the boy.

'Yes!' said the child, brimful of glee. 'Home for good and all. Home for ever and ever. Father is so much kinder than he used to be, that home's like heaven! He spoke so gently to me one dear night when I was going to bed, that I was not afraid to ask him once more if you might come home; and he said Yes, you should; and sent me in a coach to bring you. And you're to be a man!' said the child, opening her eyes; 'and are never to come back here; but first we're to be together all the Christmas long, and have the merriest time in all the world.'

'You are quite a woman, little Fan!' exclaimed the boy.

She clapped her hands and laughed, and tried to touch his head; but, being too little laughed again, and stood on tiptoe to embrace him. Then she began to drag him, in her childish eagerness, towards the door; and he, nothing loath to go, accompanied her.

A terrible voice in the hall cried, 'Bring down Master Scrooge's box, there!' and in the hall appeared the schoolmaster himself, who glared on Master Scrooge with a ferocious condescension, and threw him into a dreadful state of mind by shaking hands with him. He then conveyed him and his sister into the veriest old well of a shivering best parlour that ever was seen, where the maps upon the wall, and the celestial and terrestrial globes in the windows, were waxy with cold. Here he produced a decanter of curiously light wine, and a block of curiously heavy cake, and administered instalments of those dainties to the young people; at the same time sending out a meagre servant to offer a glass of 'something' to the postboy, who answered that he thanked the gentleman, but, if it was the same tap as he had tasted before, he had rather not. Master

Scrooge's trunk being by this time tied on to the top of the chaise, the children bade the schoolmaster goodbye right willingly; and, getting into it, drove gaily down the garden sweep; the quick wheels dashing the hoarfrost and snow from off the dark leaves of the evergreens like spray.

'Always a delicate creature, whom a breath might have withered,' said the ghost. 'But she had a large heart!'

'So she had,' cried Scrooge. 'You're right. I will not gainsay it, Spirit. God forbid!'

'She died a woman,' said the ghost, 'and had, as I think, children.'

'One child,' Scrooge returned.

'True,' said the ghost. 'Your nephew!'

Scrooge seemed uneasy in his mind, and answered briefly, 'Yes.'

Although they had but that moment left the school behind them, they were now in the busy thoroughfares of a city, where shadowy passengers passed and repassed; where shadowy carts and coaches battled for the way, and all the strife and tumult of a real city were. It was made plain enough, by the dressing of the shops, that here, too, it was Christmastime again; but it was evening, and the streets were lighted up.

The ghost stopped at a certain warehouse door, and asked Scrooge if he knew it.

'Know it!' said Scrooge. 'Was I apprenticed here?'

They went in. At sight of an old gentleman in a Welsh wig, sitting behind such a high desk, that if he had been two inches taller, he must have knocked his head against the ceiling, Scrooge cried in great excitement –

'Why, it's old Fezziwig! Bless his heart, it's Fezziwig alive again!'

Old Fezziwig laid down his pen, and looked up at the clock, which pointed to the hour of seven. He rubbed his hands; adjusted his capacious waistcoat; laughed all over himself, from his shoes to his organ of bene-volence; and called out, in a comfortable, oily, rich, fat, jovial voice –

'Yo ho, there! Ebenezer! Dick!'

Scrooge's former self, now grown a young man, came briskly in, accompanied by his fellow-'prentice.

'Dick Wilkins, to be sure!' said Scrooge to the ghost. 'Bless me, yes. There he is. He was very much attached to me, was Dick. Poor Dick! Dear, dear!'

'Yo ho, my boys!' said Fezziwig. 'No more work tonight. Christmas Eve, Dick. Christmas, Ebenezer! Let's have the shutters up,' cried old

Mr Fezziwig's ball

Fezziwig, with a sharp clap of his hands, 'before a man can say Jack Robinson!'

You wouldn't believe how those two fellows went at it! They charged into the street with the shutters – one, two, three – had 'em up in their places – four, five, six – barred 'em and pinned 'em – seven, eight, nine – and came back before you could have got to twelve, panting like racehorses.

'Hilli-ho!' cried old Fezziwig, skipping down from the high desk with wonderful agility. 'Clear away, my lads, and let's have lots of room here! Hilli-ho, Dick! Chirrup, Ebenezer!'

Clear away! There was nothing they wouldn't have cleared away, or couldn't have cleared away, with old Fezziwig looking on. It was done in a minute. Every movable was packed off, as if it were dismissed from public life for evermore; the floor was swept and watered, the lamps were trimmed, fuel was heaped upon the fire; and the warehouse was as snug, and warm, and dry, and bright a ballroom as you would desire to see upon a winter's night.

In came a fiddler with a music-book, and went up to the lofty desk, and made an orchestra of it, and tuned like fifty stomachaches. In came Mrs Fezziwig, one vast substantial smile. In came the three Miss Fezziwigs, beaming and lovable. In came the six young followers whose hearts they broke. In came all the young men and women employed in the business. In came the housemaid, with her cousin the baker. In came the cook with her brother's particular friend the milkman. In came the boy from over the way, who was suspected of not having board enough from his master; trying to hide himself behind the girl from next door but one, who was proved to have had her ears pulled by her mistress. In they all came, one after another; some shyly, some boldly, some gracefully, some awkwardly, some pushing, some pulling; in they all came, anyhow and every how. Away they all went, twenty couple at once; hands half round and back again the other way; down the middle and up again; round and round in various stages of affectionate grouping; old top couple always turning up in the wrong place; new top couple starting off again as soon as they got there; all top couples at last, and not a bottom one to help them! When this result was brought about, old Fezziwig, clapping his hands to stop the dance, cried out, 'Well done!' and the fiddler plunged his hot face into a pot of porter, especially provided for that purpose. But, scorning rest upon his reappearance, he instantly began again, though there were no dancers yet, as if the other fiddler had been carried home, exhausted, on a shutter, and he were a bran-new man resolved to beat him out of sight, or perish.

There were more dances, and there were forfeits, and more dances, and there was cake, and there was negus, and there was a great piece of Cold Roast, and there was a great piece of Cold Boiled, and there were mincepies, and plenty of beer. But the great effect of the evening came after the Roast and Boiled, when the fiddler (an artful dog, mind! The sort of man who knew his business better than you or I could have told it him!) struck up 'Sir Roger de Coverley'. Then old Fezziwig stood out to dance with Mrs Fezziwig. Top couple, too; with a good stiff piece of work cut out for them; three or four and twenty pair of partners; people who were not to be trifled with; people who would dance, and had no notion of walking.

But if they had been twice as many – ah! four times – old Fezziwig would have been a match for them, and so would Mrs Fezziwig. As to *her*, she was worthy to be his partner in every sense of the term. If that's not high praise, tell me higher, and I'll use it. A positive light appeared to issue from Fezziwig's calves. They shone in every part of the dance like moons. You couldn't have predicted, at any given time, what would become of them next. And when old Fezziwig and Mrs Fezziwig had gone all through the dance; advance and retire, both hands to your partner, bow and curtsy, corkscrew, thread-the-needle, and back again to your place: Fezziwig 'cut' – cut so deftly, that he appeared to wink with his legs, and came upon his feet again without a stagger.

When the clock struck eleven, this domestic ball broke up. Mr and Mrs Fezziwig took their stations, one on either side the door, and, shaking hands with every person individually as he or she went out, wished him or her a Merry Christmas. When everybody had retired but the two 'prentices, they did the same to them; and thus the cheerful voices died away, and the lads were left to their beds; which were under a counter in the back-shop.

During the whole of this time Scrooge had acted like a man out of his wits. His heart and soul were in the scene, and with his former self. He corroborated everything, remembered everything, enjoyed everything, and underwent the strangest agitation. It was not until now, when the bright faces of his former self and Dick were turned from them, that he remembered the ghost, and became conscious that it was looking full upon him, while the light upon its head burnt very clear.

'A small matter,' said the ghost, 'to make these silly folks so full of gratitude.'

'Small!' echoed Scrooge.

The Spirit signed to him to listen to the two apprentices, who were pouring out their hearts in praise of Fezziwig; and when he had done so, said, 'Why! Is it not? He has spent but a few pounds of your mortal money: three or four, perhaps. Is that so much that he deserves this praise?'

'It isn't that,' said Scrooge, heated by the remark, and speaking unconsciously like his former, not his latter self. 'It isn't that, Spirit. He has the power to render us happy or unhappy; to make our service light or burdensome; a pleasure or a toil. Say that his power lies in words and looks; in things so slight and insignificant that it is impossible to add and count 'em up: what then? The happiness he gives is quite as great as if it cost a fortune.'

He felt the Spirit's glance, and stopped.

'What is the matter?' asked the ghost.

'Nothing particular,' said Scrooge.

'Something, I think?' the ghost insisted.

'No,' said Scrooge, 'no. I should like to be able to say a word or two to my clerk just now. That's all.'

His former self turned down the lamps as he gave utterance to the wish; and Scrooge and the ghost again stood side by side in the open air.

'My time grows short,' observed the Spirit. 'Quick!'

This was not addressed to Scrooge, or to anyone whom he could see, but it produced an immediate effect. For again Scrooge saw himself. He was older now; a man in the prime of life. His face had not the harsh and rigid lines of later years; but it had begun to wear the signs of care and avarice. There was an eager, greedy, restless motion in the eye, which showed the passion that had taken root, and where the shadow of the growing tree would fall.

He was not alone, but sat by the side of a fair young girl in a mourning dress: in whose eyes there were tears, which sparkled in the light that shone out of the ghost of Christmas Past.

'It matters little,' she said softly. 'To you, very little. Another idol has displaced me; and, if it can cheer and comfort you in time to come as I would have tried to do, I have no just cause to grieve.'

'What Idol has displaced you?' he rejoined.

'A golden one.'

'This is the evenhanded dealing of the world!' he said. 'There is nothing on which it is so hard as poverty; and there is nothing it professes to condemn with such severity as the pursuit of wealth!'

'You fear the world too much,' she answered gently. 'All your other hopes have merged into the hope of being beyond the chance of its sordid reproach. I have seen your nobler aspirations fall off one by one, until the master passion, Gain, engrosses you. Have I not?'

'What then?' he retorted. 'Even if I have grown so much wiser, what then? I am not changed towards you.'

She shook her head.

'Am I?'

'Our contract is an old one. It was made when we were both poor, and content to be so, until, in good season, we could improve our worldly fortune by our patient industry. You *are* changed. When it was made you were another man.'

'I was a boy,' he said impatiently.

'Your own feeling tells you that you were not what you are,' she returned. 'I am. That which promised happiness when we were one in heart is fraught with misery now that we are two. How often and how keenly I have thought of this I will not say. It is enough that I *have* thought of it, and can release you.'

'Have I ever sought release?'

'In words. No. Never.'

'In what, then?'

'In a changed nature; in an altered spirit; in another atmosphere of life; another Hope as its great end. In everything that made my love of any worth or value in your sight. If this had never been between us,' said the girl, looking mildly, but with steadiness, upon him; 'tell me, would you seek me out and try to win me now? Ah, no!'

He seemed to yield to the justice of this supposition in spite of himself. But he said, with a struggle, 'You think not.'

'I would gladly think otherwise if I could,' she answered. 'Heaven knows! When *I* have learned a Truth like this, I know how strong and irresistible it must be. But if you were free today, tomorrow, yesterday, can even I believe that you would choose a dowerless girl – you who, in your very confidence with her, weigh everything by Gain: or, choosing her, if for a moment you were false enough to your one guiding principle to do so, do I not know that your repentance and regret would surely follow? I do; and I release you. With a full heart, for the love of him you once were.'

He was about to speak; but, with her head turned from him, she resumed, 'You may – the memory of what is past half makes me hope you will – have pain in this. A very, very brief time, and you will dismiss the recollection of it gladly, as an unprofitable dream, from which it happened well that you awoke. May you be happy in the life you have chosen!'

She left him, and they parted.

'Spirit!' said Scrooge, 'show me no more! Conduct me home. Why do you delight to torture me?'

'One shadow more!' exclaimed the ghost.

'No more!' cried Scrooge. 'No more! I don't wish to see it. Show me no more!'

But the relentless ghost pinioned him in both his arms, and forced him to observe what happened next.

They were in another scene and place; a room, not very large or handsome, but full of comfort. Near to the winter fire sat a beautiful young girl, so like that last that Scrooge believed it was the same, until he saw *her*, now a comely matron, sitting opposite her daughter. The noise in this room was perfectly tumultuous, for there were more children there than Scrooge in his agitated state of mind could count; and, unlike the celebrated herd in the poem, they were not forty children conducting themselves like one, but every child was conducting itself like forty. The consequences were uproarious beyond belief; but no one seemed to care; on the contrary, the mother and daughter laughed heartily, and enjoyed it very much; and the latter, soon beginning to mingle in the sports, got pillaged by the young brigands most ruthlessly. What would I not have given to be one of them! Though I never could have been so rude, no, no! I wouldn't for the wealth of all the world have crushed that braided hair, and torn it down; and for the precious little shoe, I wouldn't have plucked it off, God bless my soul! to save my life. As to measuring her waist in sport, as they did, bold young brood, I couldn't have done it; I should have expected my arm to have grown round it for a punishment, and never come straight again. And yet I should have dearly liked, I own, to have touched her lips; to have questioned her, that she might have opened them; to have looked upon the lashes of her downcast eyes, and never raised a blush; to have let loose waves of hair, an inch of which would be a keepsake beyond price: in short, I should have liked, I do confess, to have had the lightest licence of a child, and yet to have been man enough to know its value.

But now a knocking at the door was heard, and such a rush immediately ensued that she, with laughing face and plundered dress, was borne towards it the centre of a flushed and boisterous group, just in time to greet the father, who came home attended by a man laden with Christmas toys and presents. Then the shouting and the struggling, and the onslaught that was made on the defenceless porter! The scaling him, with chairs for ladders, to dive into his pockets, despoil him of brown-paper parcels, hold on tight by his cravat, hug him round his neck, pummel his back, and kick his legs in irrepressible affection! The shouts of wonder and delight with which the development of every package was received! The terrible announcement that the baby had been taken in the act of putting a doll's frying pan into his mouth, and was more than suspected of having swallowed a fictitious turkey, glued on a wooden platter! The immense relief of finding this a false alarm! The joy, and gratitude, and ecstasy! They are all indescribable alike. It is enough that, by degrees, the children and their emotions got out of the parlour, and, by one stair at a time, up to the top of the house, where they went to bed, and so subsided.

And now Scrooge looked on more attentively than ever, when the master of the house, having his daughter leaning fondly on him, sat down with her and her mother at his own fireside; and when he thought that such another creature, quite as graceful and as full of promise, might have called him father, and been a springtime in the haggard winter of his life, his sight grew very dim indeed.

'Belle,' said the husband, turning to his wife with a smile, 'I saw an old friend of yours this afternoon.'

'Who was it?'

'Guess!'

'How can I? Tut, don't I know?' she added in the same breath, laughing as he laughed. 'Mr Scrooge.'

'Mr Scrooge it was. I passed his office window; and as it was not shut up, and he had a candle inside, I could scarcely help seeing him. His partner lies upon the point of death, I hear; and there he sat alone. Quite alone in the world, I do believe.'

'Spirit!' said Scrooge in a broken voice, 'remove me from this place.'

'I told you these were shadows of the things that have been,' said the ghost. 'That they are what they are do not blame me!'

'Remove me!' Scrooge exclaimed, 'I cannot bear it!'

He turned upon the ghost, and seeing that it looked upon him with a face in which in some strange way there were fragments of all the faces it had shown him, wrestled with it.

'Leave me! Take me back. Haunt me no longer!'

In the struggle, if that can be called a struggle in which the ghost with no visible resistance on its own part was undisturbed by any effort of its adversary, Scrooge observed that its light was burning high and bright; and dimly connecting that with its influence over him, he seized the extinguisher-cap, and by a sudden action pressed it down upon its head.

The Spirit dropped beneath it, so that the extinguisher covered its whole form; but though Scrooge pressed it down with all his force, he could not hide the light, which streamed from under it, in an unbroken flood upon the ground.

He was conscious of being exhausted, and overcome by an irresistible drowsiness; and, further, of being in his own bedroom. He gave the cap a parting squeeze, in which his hand relaxed; and had barely time to reel to bed, before he sank into a heavy sleep.

Though Scrooge pressed it down with all his force, he could not hide the light

The Second of the Three Spirits

Awaking in the middle of a prodigiously tough snore, and sitting up in bed to get his thoughts together, Scrooge had no occasion to be told that the bell was again upon the stroke of One. He felt that he was restored to consciousness in the right nick of time, for the especial purpose of holding a conference with the second messenger despatched to him through Jacob Marley's intervention. But finding that he turned uncomfortably cold when he began to wonder which of his curtains this new spectre would draw back, he put them every one aside with his own hands, and, lying down again, established a sharp lookout all round the bed. For he wished to challenge the Spirit on the moment of its appearance, and did not wish to be taken by surprise and made nervous.

Gentlemen of the free-and-easy sort, who plume themselves on being acquainted with a move or two, and being usually equal to the time of day, express the wide range of their capacity for adventure by observing that they are good for anything from pitch-and-toss to manslaughter; between which opposite extremes, no doubt, there lies a tolerably wide and comprehensive range of subjects. Without venturing for Scrooge quite as hardily as this, I don't mind calling on you to believe that he was ready for a good broad field of strange appearances, and that nothing between a baby and a rhinoceros would have astonished him very much.

Now, being prepared for almost anything, he was not by any means prepared for nothing; and consequently, when the bell struck One, and no shape appeared, he was taken with a violent fit of trembling. Five minutes, ten minutes, a quarter of an hour went by, yet nothing came. All this time he lay upon his bed, the very core and centre of a blaze of ruddy light, which streamed upon it when the clock proclaimed the hour; and which, being only light, was more alarming than a dozen ghosts, as he was powerless to make out what it meant, or would be at; and was sometimes apprehensive that he might be at that very moment an interesting case of spontaneous combustion, without having the consolation of knowing it. At last, however, he began to think – as you or I would have thought at first; for it is always the person not in the predicament who knows what ought to have been done in it, and would unquestionably have done it too – at last, I say, he began to think that the source and secret of this ghostly light might be in the adjoining room, from whence, on further tracing it, it seemed to shine. This idea taking full possession of his mind, he got up softly, and shuffled in his slippers to the door.

The moment Scrooge's hand was on the lock a strange voice called him by his name, and bade him enter. He obeyed.

It was his own room. There was no doubt about that. But it had undergone a surprising transformation. The walls and ceiling were so hung with living green, that it looked a perfect grove; from every part of which bright gleaming berries glistened. The crisp leaves of holly, mistletoe, and ivy reflected back the light, as if so many little mirrors had been scattered there; and such a mighty blaze went roaring up the chimney as that dull petrification of a hearth had never known in Scrooge's time, or Marley's, or for many and many a winter season gone. Heaped up on the floor, to form a kind of throne, were turkeys, geese, game, poultry, brawn, great joints of meat, sucking-pigs, long wreaths of sausages, mincepies, plum-puddings, barrels of oysters, red-hot chestnuts, cherry-cheeked apples, juicy oranges, luscious pears, immense twelfth-cakes, and seething bowls of punch, that made the chamber dim with their delicious steam. In easy state upon this couch there sat a jolly Giant, glorious to see; who bore a glowing torch, in shape not unlike Plenty's horn, and held it up, high up, to shed its light on Scrooge as he came peeping round the door.

'Come in!' exclaimed the ghost. 'Come in! and know me better, man!'

Scrooge entered timidly, and hung his head before this Spirit. He was not the dogged Scrooge he had been; and though the Spirit's eyes were clear and kind, he did not like to meet them.

'I am the Ghost of Christmas Present,' said the Spirit. 'Look upon me!'

Scrooge reverently did so. It was clothed in one simple deep green robe, or mantle, bordered with white fur. This garment hung so loosely on the figure, that its capacious breast was bare, as if disdaining to be warded or concealed by any artifice. Its feet, observable beneath the ample

Scrooge's third visitor, the Ghost of Christmas Present

folds of the garment, were also bare; and on its head it wore no other covering than a holly wreath, set here and there with shining icicles. Its dark-brown curls were long and free; free as its genial face, its sparkling eye, its open hand, its cheery voice, its unconstrained demeanour, and its joyful air. Girded round its middle was an antique scabbard; but no sword was in it, and the ancient sheath was eaten up with rust.

'You have never seen the like of me before!' exclaimed the Spirit.

'Never,' Scrooge made answer to it.

'Have never walked forth with the younger members of my family; meaning (for I am very young) my elder brothers born in these later years?' pursued the phantom.

'I don't think I have,' said Scrooge. 'I am afraid I have not. Have you had many brothers, Spirit?'

'More than eighteen hundred,' said the ghost.

'A tremendous family to provide for,' muttered Scrooge.

The Ghost of Christmas Present rose.

'Spirit,' said Scrooge submissively, 'conduct me where you will. I went forth last night on compulsion, and I learned a lesson which is working now. Tonight if you have aught to teach me, let me profit by it.'

'Touch my robe!'

Scrooge did as he was told, and held it fast.

Holly, mistletoe, red berries, ivy, turkeys, geese, game, poultry, brawn, meat, pigs, sausages, oysters, pies, puddings, fruit, and punch, all vanished instantly. So did the room, the fire, the ruddy glow, the hour of night, and they stood in the city streets on Christmas morning, where (for the weather was severe) the people made a rough, but brisk and not unpleasant kind of music, in scraping the snow from the pavement in front of their dwellings, and from the tops of their houses, whence it was mad delight to the boys to see it come plumping down into the road below, and splitting into artificial little snowstorms.

The house-fronts looked black enough, and the windows blacker, contrasting with the smooth white sheet of snow upon the roofs, and with the dirtier snow upon the ground; which last deposit had been ploughed up in deep furrows by the heavy wheels of carts and wagons: furrows that crossed and recrossed each other hundreds of times where the great streets branched off; and made intricate channels, hard to trace in the thick yellow mud and icy water. The sky was gloomy, and the shortest streets were choked up with a dingy mist, half thawed, half frozen, whose heavier particles descended in a shower of sooty atoms, as if all the chimneys in Great Britain had, by one consent, caught fire, and were blazing away to their dear hearts' content. There was nothing very cheerful in the climate or the town, and yet was there an air of cheerfulness abroad that the clearest summer air and brightest summer sun might have endeavoured to diffuse in vain.

For the people who were shovelling away on the house-tops were jovial and full of glee; calling out to one another from the parapets, and now and then exchanging a facetious snowball – better-natured missile far than many a wordy jest – laughing heartily if it went right, and not less heartily if it went wrong. The poulterers' shops were still half open, and the fruiterers' were radiant in their glory. There were great, round, potbellied baskets of chestnuts, shaped like the waistcoats of jolly old gentlemen, lolling at the doors, and tumbling out into the street in their apoplectic opulence. There were ruddy, brown-faced, broad-girthed Spanish onions, shining in the fatness of their growth like Spanish friars, and winking from their shelves in wanton slyness at the girls as they went by, and glanced demurely at the hung-up mistletoe. There were pears and apples clustered high in blooming pyramids; there were bunches of grapes, made, in the shopkeepers' benevolence, to dangle from conspicuous hooks that people's mouths might water gratis as they passed; there were piles of filberts, mossy and brown, recalling, in their fragrance, ancient walks among the woods, and pleasant shufflings ankle deep through withered leaves; there were Norfolk Biffins, squab and swarthy, setting off the yellow of the oranges and lemons, and, in the great compactness of their juicy persons, urgently entreating and beseeching to be carried home in paper bags and eaten after dinner. The very gold and silver fish, set forth among these choice fruits in a bowl, though members of a dull and stagnant-blooded race, appeared to know that there was something going on; and, to a fish, went gasping round and round their little world in slow and passionless excitement.

The Grocers'! oh, the Grocers'! nearly closed, with perhaps two shutters down, or one; but through those gaps such glimpses! It was not alone that the scales descending on the counter made a merry sound, or that the twine and roller parted company so briskly, or that the canisters were rattled up and down like juggling tricks, or even that the blended scents of tea and coffee were so grateful to the nose, or even that the raisins were so plentiful and rare, the almonds so extremely white, the sticks of cinnamon so long and straight, the other spices so delicious, the candied fruits so caked and spotted with molten sugar as to make the coldest lookers-on feel faint, and subsequently bilious. Nor was it that the figs were moist and pulpy, or that the French plums blushed in modest tartness from their highly-decorated boxes, or that everything was good to eat and in its Christmas dress; but the customers were all so hurried and so eager in the hopeful promise of the day, that they tumbled up against each other at the door, crashing their wicker baskets wildly, and left their purchases upon the counter, and came running back to fetch them, and committed hundreds of the like mistakes, in the best humour possible; while the grocer and his people were so frank and fresh, that the polished hearts with which they fastened their aprons behind might have been their own, worn outside for general inspection, and for Christmas daws to peck at if they chose.

But soon the steeples called good people all to church and chapel, and away they came, flocking through the streets in their best clothes and with their gayest faces. And at the same time there emerged, from scores of by-streets, lanes, and nameless turnings, innumerable people, carrying their dinners to the bakers' shops. The sight of these poor revellers appeared to interest the Spirit very much, for he stood with Scrooge beside him in a baker's doorway, and, taking off the covers as their bearers passed, sprinkled incense on their dinners from his torch. And it was a very uncommon kind of torch, for once or twice, when there were angry words between some dinner-carriers who had jostled each other, he shed a few drops of water on them from it, and their good-humour was restored directly. For they said, it was a shame to quarrel upon Christmas Day. And so it was! God love it, so it was!

In time the bells ceased, and the bakers were shut up; and yet there was a genial shadowing forth of all these dinners, and the progress of their cooking, in the thawed blotch of wet above each baker's oven, where the pavement smoked as if its stones were cooking too.

'Is there a peculiar flavour in what you sprinkle from your torch?' asked Scrooge.

'There is. My own.'

'Would it apply to any kind of dinner on this day?' asked Scrooge.

'To any kindly given. To a poor one most.'

'Why to a poor one most?' asked Scrooge.

'Because it needs it most.'

'Spirit!' said Scrooge, after a moment's thought, 'I wonder you, of all the beings in the many worlds about us, should desire to cramp these people's opportunities of innocent enjoyment.'

'I!' cried the Spirit.

'You would deprive them of their means of dining every seventh day, often the only day on which they can be said to dine at all,' said Scrooge; 'wouldn't you?'

'I!' cried the Spirit.

'You seek to close these places on the Seventh Day,' said Scrooge. 'And it comes to the same thing.'

'I seek!' exclaimed the Spirit.

'Forgive me if I am wrong. It has been done in your name, or at least in that of your family,' said Scrooge.

'There are some upon this earth of yours,' returned the Spirit, 'who lay claim to know us, and who do their deeds of passion, pride, ill-will, hatred, envy, bigotry, and selfishness in our name, who are as strange to us, and all our kith and kin, as if they had never lived. Remember that, and charge their doings on themselves, not us.'

Scrooge promised that he would; and they went on, invisible, as they had been before, into the suburbs of the town. It was a remarkable quality of the ghost (which Scrooge had observed at the baker's), that notwithstanding his gigantic size, he could accommodate himself to any place with ease; and that he stood beneath a low roof quite as gracefully and like a supernatural creature as it was possible he could have done in any lofty hall.

And perhaps it was the pleasure the good Spirit had in showing off this power of his, or else it was his own kind, generous, hearty nature, and his sympathy with all poor men, that led him straight to Scrooge's clerk's; for there he went, and took Scrooge with him, holding to his robe; and on the threshold of the door the Spirit smiled, and stopped to bless Bob Cratchit's dwelling with the sprinklings of his torch. Think of that! Bob had but fifteen 'Bob' a week himself; he pocketed on Saturdays but fifteen copies of his Christian name; and yet the Ghost of Christmas Present blessed his four-roomed house!

Then up rose Mrs Cratchit, Cratchit's wife, dressed out but poorly in a twice-turned gown, but brave in ribbons, which are cheap, and make a goodly show for sixpence; and she laid the cloth, assisted by Belinda Cratchit, second of her daughters, also brave in ribbons; while Master

Peter Cratchit plunged a fork into the saucepan of potatoes, and getting the corners of his monstrous shirt-collar (Bob's private property, conferred upon his son and heir in honour of the day), into his mouth, rejoiced to find himself so gallantly attired, and yearned to show his linen in the fashionable Parks. And now two smaller Cratchits, boy and girl, came tearing in, screaming that outside the baker's they had smelt the goose, and known it for their own; and basking in luxurious thoughts of sage and onion, these young Cratchits danced about the table, and exalted Master Peter Cratchit to the skies, while he (not proud, although his collars nearly choked him) blew the fire, until the slow potatoes, bubbling up, knocked loudly at the saucepan-lid to be let out and peeled.

'What has ever got your precious father, then?' said Mrs Cratchit. 'And your brother, Tiny Tim? And Martha warn't as late last Christmas Day by half an hour!'

'Here's Martha, mother!' said a girl, appearing as she spoke.

'Here's Martha, mother!' cried the two young Cratchits. 'Hurrah! There's *such* a goose, Martha!'

'Why, bless your heart alive, my dear, how late you are!' said Mrs Cratchit, kissing her a dozen times, and taking off her shawl and bonnet for her with officious zeal.

'We'd a deal of work to finish up last night,' replied the girl, 'and had to clear away this morning, mother!'

'Well! never mind so long as you are come,' said Mrs Cratchit. 'Sit ye down before the fire, my dear, and have a warm, Lord bless ye!'

'No, no! There's father coming,' cried the two young Cratchits, who were everywhere at once. 'Hide, Martha, hide!'

So Martha hid herself, and in came little Bob, the father, with at least three feet of comforter, exclusive of the fringe, hanging down before him, and his threadbare clothes darned up and brushed to look seasonable, and Tiny Tim upon his shoulder. Alas for Tiny Tim, he bore a little crutch, and had his limbs supported by an iron frame!

'Why, where's our Martha?' cried Bob Cratchit, looking round.

'Not coming,' said Mrs Cratchit.

'Not coming!' said Bob, with a sudden declension in his high spirits; for he had been Tim's blood-horse all the way from church, and had come home rampant. 'Not coming upon Christmas Day!'

Martha didn't like to see him disappointed, if it were only in joke; so she came out prematurely from behind the closet door, and ran into his arms, while the two young Cratchits hustled Tiny Tim, and bore him off into the wash-house, that he might hear the pudding singing in the copper.

'And how did little Tim behave?' asked Mrs Cratchit when she had rallied Bob on his credulity, and Bob had hugged his daughter to his heart's content.

'As good as gold,' said Bob, 'and better. Somehow, he gets thoughtful, sitting by himself so much, and thinks the strangest things you ever heard. He told me, coming home, that he hoped the people saw him in the church, because he was a cripple, and it might be pleasant to them to remember upon Christmas Day who made lame beggars walk and blind men see.'

Bob's voice was tremulous when he told them this, and trembled more when he said that Tiny Tim was growing strong and hearty.

His active little crutch was heard upon the floor, and back came Tiny Tim before another word was spoken, escorted by his brother and sister to his stool beside the fire; and while Bob, turning up his cuffs – as if, poor fellow, they were capable of being made more shabby – compounded some hot mixture in a jug with gin and lemons, and stirred it round and round, and put it on the hob to simmer, Master Peter and the two ubiquitous young Cratchits went to fetch the goose, with which they soon returned in high procession.

Such a bustle ensued that you might have thought a goose the rarest of all birds; a feathered phenomenon, to which a black swan was a matter of course – and, in truth, it was something very like it in that house. Mrs Cratchit made the gravy (ready beforehand in a little saucepan) hissing hot; Master Peter mashed the potatoes with incredible vigour; Miss Belinda sweetened up the apple sauce; Martha dusted the hot plates; Bob took Tiny Tim beside him in a tiny corner at the table; the two young Cratchits set chairs for everybody, not forgetting themselves, and, mounting guard upon their posts, crammed spoons into their mouths, lest they should shriek for goose before their turn came to be helped. At last the dishes were set on, and grace was said. It was succeeded by a breathless pause, as Mrs Cratchit, looking slowly all along the carving-knife, prepared to plunge it in the breast; but when she did, and when the long-expected gush of stuffing issued forth, one murmur of delight arose all round the board, and even Tiny Tim, excited by the two young Cratchits, beat on the table with the handle of his knife and feebly cried Hurrah!

There never was such a goose. Bob said he didn't believe there ever was such a goose cooked. Its tenderness and flavour, size and cheapness, were the themes of universal admiration. Eked out by apple sauce and mashed potatoes, it was a sufficient dinner for the whole family; indeed, as Mrs Cratchit said with great delight (surveying one small atom of a bone upon the dish), they hadn't ate it all at last! Yet everyone had had enough, and the youngest Cratchits, in particular, were steeped in sage and onion to the eyebrows! But now, the plates being changed by Miss Belinda, Mrs Cratchit left the room alone – too nervous to bear witnesses – to take the pudding up, and bring it in.

Suppose it should not be done enough! Suppose it should break in turning out! Suppose somebody should have got over the wall of the backyard and stolen it, while they were merry with the goose – a supposition at which the two young Cratchits became livid! All sorts of horrors were supposed.

Hallo! A great deal of steam! The pudding was out of the copper. A smell like a washing-day! That was the cloth. A smell like an eating-house and a pastrycook's next door to each other, with a laundress's next door to that! That was the pudding! In half a minute Mrs Cratchit entered – flushed, but smiling proudly – with the pudding, like a speckled cannonball, so hard and firm, blazing in half of half a quartern of ignited brandy, and bedight with Christmas holly stuck into the top.

Oh, a wonderful pudding! Bob Cratchit said, and calmly too, that he regarded it as the greatest success achieved by Mrs Cratchit since their marriage. Mrs Cratchit said that, now the weight was off her mind, she would confess she had her doubts about the quantity of flour. Everybody had something to say about it, but nobody said or thought it was at all a small pudding for a large family. It would have been flat heresy to do so. Any Cratchit would have blushed to hint at such a thing.

At last the dinner was all done, the cloth was cleared, the hearth swept, and the fire made up. The compound in the jug being tasted, and considered perfect, apples and oranges were put upon the table, and a shovel full of chestnuts on the fire. Then all the Cratchit family drew round the hearth in what Bob Cratchit called a circle, meaning half a one; and at Bob Cratchit's elbow stood the family display of glass. Two tumblers and a custard cup without a handle.

These held the hot stuff from the jug, however, as well as golden goblets would have done; and Bob served it out with beaming looks, while the chestnuts on the fire sputtered and cracked noisily. Then Bob proposed: 'A merry Christmas to us all, my dears. God bless us!'

Which all the family re-echoed.

'God bless us, every one!' said Tiny Tim, the last of all.

He sat very close to his father's side, upon his little stool. Bob held his withered little hand to his, as if he loved the child, and wished to keep him by his side, and dreaded that he might be taken from him.

'Spirit,' said Scrooge, with an interest he had never felt before, 'tell me if Tiny Tim will live.'

'I see a vacant seat,' replied the ghost, 'in the poor chimney corner, and a crutch without an owner, carefully preserved. If these shadows remain unaltered by the Future, the child will die.'

'No, no,' said Scrooge. 'Oh no, kind Spirit! say he will be spared.'

'If these shadows remain unaltered by the Future none other of my race,' returned the ghost, 'will find him here. What then? If he be like to die, he had better do it, and decrease the surplus population.'

Scrooge hung his head to hear his own words quoted by the Spirit, and was overcome with penitence and grief.

'Man,' said the ghost, 'if man you be in heart, not adamant, forbear that wicked cant until you have discovered what the surplus is, and where it is. Will you decide what men shall live, what men shall die? It may be that, in the sight of Heaven, you are more worthless and less fit to live than millions like this poor man's child. O God! to hear the insect on the leaf pronouncing on the too much life among his hungry brothers in the dust!'

Scrooge bent before the ghost's rebuke, and, trembling, cast his eyes upon the ground. But he raised them speedily on hearing his own name.

'Mr Scrooge!' said Bob. 'I'll give you Mr Scrooge, the Founder of the Feast!'

'The Founder of the Feast, indeed!' cried Mrs Cratchit, reddening. 'I wish I had him here. I'd give him a piece of my mind to feast upon, and I hope he'd have a good appetite for it.'

'My dear,' said Bob, 'the children! Christmas Day.'

'It should be Christmas Day, I am sure,' said she, 'on which one drinks the health of such an odious, stingy, hard, unfeeling man as Mr Scrooge. You know he is, Robert! Nobody knows it better than you do, poor fellow!'

'My dear!' was Bob's mild answer. 'Christmas Day.'

'I'll drink his health for your sake and the Day's,' said Mrs Cratchit, 'not for his. Long life to him! A merry Christmas and a happy New Year! He'll be very merry and very happy, I have no doubt!'

The children drank the toast after her. It was the first of their proceedings which had no heartiness in it. Tiny Tim drank it last of all, but he didn't care twopence for it. Scrooge was the Ogre of the family. The mention of his name cast a dark shadow on the party, which was not dispelled for full five minutes.

After it had passed away they were ten times merrier than before, from the mere relief of Scrooge the Baleful being done with. Bob Cratchit told them how he had a situation in his eye for Master Peter, which would bring in, if obtained, full five-and-sixpence weekly. The two young Cratchits laughed tremendously at the idea of Peter's being a man of business; and Peter himself looked thoughtfully at the fire from between his collars, as if he were deliberating what particular investments he should favour when he came into the receipt of that bewildering income. Martha, who was a poor apprentice at a milliner's, then told them what kind of work she had to do, and how many hours she worked at a stretch and how she meant to lie abed tomorrow morning for a good long rest; tomorrow being a holiday she passed at home. Also how she had seen a countess and a lord some days before, and how the lord 'was much about as tall as Peter'; at which Peter pulled up his collar so high that you couldn't have seen his head if you had been there. All this time the chestnuts and the jug went round and round; and by and by they had a song, about a lost child travelling in the snow, from Tiny Tim, who had a plaintive little voice, and sang it very well indeed.

There was nothing of high mark in this. They were not a handsome family; they were not well dressed; their shoes were far from being waterproof; their clothes were scanty; and Peter might have known, and very likely did, the inside of a pawnbroker's. But they were happy, grateful, pleased with one another, and contented with the time; and when they faded, and looked happier yet in the bright sprinklings of the Spirit's torch at parting, Scrooge had his eye upon them, and especially on Tiny Tim, until the last.

By this time it was getting dark, and snowing pretty heavily; and as Scrooge and the Spirit went along the streets, the brightness of the roaring fires in kitchens, parlours, and all sorts of rooms was wonderful Here, the flickering of the blaze showed preparations for a cosy dinner, with hot plates baking through and through before the fire, and deep red curtains, ready to be drawn to shut out cold and darkness. There, all the children of the house were running out into the snow to meet their married sisters, brothers, cousins, uncles, aunts, and be the first to greet them. Here, again, were shadows on the window-blinds of guests assembling; and there a group of handsome girls, all hooded and fur-booted, and all chattering at once, tripped lightly off to some near neighbour's house; where, woe upon the single man who saw them enter – artful witches, well they knew it – in a glow!

But, if you had judged from the numbers of people on their way to friendly gatherings, you might have thought that no one was at home to give them welcome when they got there, instead of every house expecting company, and piling up its fires half-chimney high. Blessings on it, how the ghost exulted! How it bared its breadth of breast, and opened its capacious palm, and floated on, outpouring with a generous hand its bright and harmless mirth on everything within its reach! The very lamplighter, who ran on before, dotting the dusky street with specks of light, and who was dressed to spend the evening somewhere, laughed out loudly as the Spirit passed, though little kenned the lamplighter that he had any company but Christmas.

And now, without a word of warning from the ghost, they stood upon a bleak and desert moor, where monstrous masses of rude stone were cast about, as though it were the burial-place of giants; and water spread itself wheresoever it listed; or would have done so, but for the frost that held it prisoner; and nothing grew but moss and furze, and coarse, rank grass. Down in the west the setting sun had left a streak of fiery red, which glared upon the desolation for an instant, like a sullen eye, and frowning lower, lower, lower yet, was lost in the thick gloom of darkest night.

'What place is this?' asked Scrooge.

'A place where miners live, who labour in the bowels of the earth,' returned the Spirit. 'But they know me. See!'

A light shone from the window of a hut, and swiftly they advanced towards it. Passing through the wall of mud and stone, they found a cheerful company assembled round a glowing fire. An old, old man and woman, with their children and their children's children, and another generation beyond that, all decked out gaily in their holiday attire. The old man, in a voice that seldom rose above the howling of the wind upon the barren waste, was singing them a Christmas song; it had been a very old song when he was a boy; and from time to time they all joined in the chorus. So surely as they raised their voices, the old man got quite blithe and loud; and so surely as they stopped, his vigour sank again.

The Spirit did not tarry here, but bade Scrooge hold his robe, and, passing on above the moor, sped whither? Not to sea? To sea. To Scrooge's horror, looking back, he saw the last of the land, a frightful range of rocks, behind them; and his ears were deafened by the thundering of water, as it rolled and roared, and raged among the dreadful caverns it had worn, and fiercely tried to undermine the earth.

Built upon a dismal reef of sunken rocks, some league or so from shore, on which the waters chafed and dashed, the wild year through, there stood a solitary lighthouse. Great heaps of seaweed clung to its base, and storm-birds – born of the wind, one might suppose, as seaweed of the water – rose and fell about it, like the waves they skimmed.

But, even here, two men who watched the light had made a fire, that through the loophole in the thick stone wall shed out a ray of brightness on the awful sea. Joining their horny hands over the rough table at which they sat, they wished each other Merry Christmas in their can of grog; and one of them – the elder too, with his face all damaged and scarred with hard weather, as the figurehead of an old ship might be – struck up a sturdy song that was like a gale in itself.

Again the ghost sped on, above the black and heaving sea – on, on – until being far away, as he told Scrooge, from any shore, they lighted on a ship. They stood beside the helmsman at the wheel, the lookout in the bow, the officers who had the watch; dark, ghostly figures in their several stations; but every man among them hummed a Christmas tune, or had a Christmas thought, or spoke below his breath to his companion of some bygone Christmas Day, with homeward hopes belonging to it. And every man on board, waking or sleeping, good or bad, had had a kinder word for one another on that day than on any day in the year; and had shared to some extent in its festivities; and had remembered those he cared for at a distance, and had known that they delighted to remember him.

It was a great surprise to Scrooge, while listening to the moaning of the wind, and thinking what a solemn thing it was to move on through the lonely darkness over an unknown abyss, whose depths were secrets as profound as death: it was a great surprise to Scrooge, while thus engaged, to hear a hearty laugh. It was a much greater surprise to Scrooge to recognise it as his own nephew's and to find himself in a bright, dry, gleaming room, with the Spirit standing smiling by his side, and looking at that same nephew with approving affability!

'Ha, ha!' laughed Scrooge's nephew. 'Ha, ha, ha!'

If you should happen, by any unlikely chance, to know a man more blessed in a laugh than Scrooge's nephew, all I can say is, I should like to know him too. Introduce him to me, and I'll cultivate his acquaintance.

It is a fair, even-handed, noble adjustment of things, that while there is infection in disease and sorrow, there is nothing in the world so irresistibly contagious as laughter and good-humour. When Scrooge's nephew laughed in this way – holding his sides, rolling his head, and twisting his face into the most extravagant contortions – Scrooge's niece, by marriage, laughed as heartily as he. And their assembled friends, being not a bit behindhand, roared out lustily.

'Ha, ha! Ha, ha, ha, ha!'

'He said that Christmas was a humbug, as I live!' cried Scrooge's nephew. 'He believed it, too!'

'More shame for him, Fred!' said Scrooge's niece indignantly. 'Bless those women! they never do anything by halves. They are always in earnest.'

She was very pretty; exceedingly pretty. With a dimpled, surprised-looking, capital face; a ripe little mouth, that seemed made to be kissed – as no doubt it was; all kinds of good little dots about her chin, that melted into one another when she laughed; and the sunniest pair of eyes you ever saw in any little creature's head. Altogether she was what you would have called provoking, you know; but satisfactory, too. Oh, perfectly satisfactory!

'He's a comical old fellow,' said Scrooge's nephew, 'that's the truth; and not so pleasant as he might be. However, his offences carry their own punishment, and I have nothing to say against him.'

'I'm sure he is very rich, Fred,' hinted Scrooge's niece. 'At least, you always tell *me* so.'

'What of that, my dear?' said Scrooge's nephew. 'His wealth is of no use to him. He don't do any good with it. He don't make himself comfortable with it. He hasn't the satisfaction of thinking – ha, ha, ha! – that he is ever going to benefit Us with it.'

'I have no patience with him,' observed Scrooge's niece. Scrooge's niece's sisters, and all the other ladies, expressed the same opinion.

'Oh, I have!' said Scrooge's nephew. 'I am sorry for him; I couldn't be angry with him if I tried. Who suffers by his ill whims? Himself always. Here he takes it into his head to dislike us, and he won't come and dine with us. What's the consequence? He don't lose much of a dinner.'

'Indeed, I think he loses a very good dinner,' interrupted Scrooge's niece. Everybody else said the same, and they must be allowed to have been competent judges, because they had just had dinner; and with the dessert upon the table, were clustered round the fire, by lamplight.

'Well! I am very glad to hear it,' said Scrooge's nephew, 'because I haven't any great faith in these young housekeepers. What do *you* say, Topper?'

Topper had clearly got his eye upon one of Scrooge's niece's sisters, for he answered that a bachelor was a wretched outcast, who had no right to express an opinion on the subject. Whereat Scrooge's niece's sister – the plump one with the lace tucker: not the one with the roses – blushed.

'Do go on, Fred,' said Scrooge's niece, clapping her hands. 'He never finishes what he begins to say! He is such a ridiculous fellow!'

Scrooge's nephew revelled in another laugh, and as it was impossible to keep the infection off, though the plump sister tried hard to do it with aromatic vinegar, his example was unanimously followed.

'I was only going to say,' said Scrooge's nephew, 'that the consequence of his taking a dislike to us, and not making merry with us, is, as I think, that he loses some pleasant moments, which could do him no harm. I am sure he loses pleasanter companions than he can find in his own thoughts, either in his mouldy old office or his dusty chambers. I mean to give him the same chance every year, whether he likes it or not, for I pity him. He may rail at Christmas till he dies, but he can't help thinking better of it – I defy him – if he finds me going there, in good temper, year after year, and saying, "Uncle Scrooge, how are you?" If it only put him in the vein to leave his poor clerk fifty pounds, *that's* something; and I think I shook him yesterday.'

It was their turn to laugh now, at the notion of his shaking Scrooge. But being thoroughly good-natured, and not much caring what they laughed at, so that they laughed at any rate, he encouraged them in their merriment, and passed the bottle, joyously.

After tea they had some music. For they were a musical family, and knew what they were about when they sung a Glee or Catch, I can assure you: especially Topper, who could growl away in the bass like a good one, and never swell the large veins in his forehead, or get red in the face over it. Scrooge's niece played well upon the harp; and played, among other tunes, a simple little air (a mere nothing: you might learn to whistle it in two minutes) which had been familiar to the child who fetched Scrooge from the boarding-school, as he had been reminded by the Ghost of Christmas Past. When this strain of music sounded, all the things that ghost had shown him came upon his mind; he softened more and more; and thought that if he could have listened to it often, years ago, he might have cultivated the kindnesses of life for his own happiness with his own hands, without resorting to the sexton's spade that buried Jacob Marley.

But they didn't devote the whole evening to music. After a while they played at forfeits; for it is good to be children sometimes, and never better than at Christmas, when its mighty Founder was a child himself. Stop! There was first a game at blindman's-buff. Of course there was. And I no more believe Topper was really blind than I believe he had eyes in his boots. My opinion is, that it was a done thing between him and Scrooge's nephew; and that the Ghost of Christmas Present knew it. The way he went after that plump sister in the lace tucker was an outrage on the credulity of human nature. Knocking down the fire-irons, tumbling over the chairs, bumping up against the piano, smothering himself amongst the curtains, wherever she went, there went he! He always knew where the plump sister was. He wouldn't catch anybody else. If you had fallen up against him (as some of them did) on purpose, he would have made a feint of endeavouring to seize you, which would have been an affront to your understanding, and would instantly have sidled off in the direction of the plump sister. She often cried out that it wasn't fair; and it really was not. But when, at last, he caught her; when, in spite of all her silken rustlings, and her rapid flutterings past him, he got her into a corner whence there was no escape; then his conduct was the most execrable. For his pretending not to know her; his pretending that it was necessary to touch her headdress, and further to assure himself of her identity by pressing a certain ring upon her finger, and a certain chain about her neck; was vile, monstrous! No doubt she told him her opinion of it when, another blind man being in office, they were so very confidential together behind the curtains.

Scrooge's niece was not one of the blind man's-buff party, but was made comfortable with a large chair and a footstool, in a snug corner where the ghost and Scrooge were close behind her. But she joined in the forfeits, and loved her love to admiration with all the letters of the alphabet. Likewise at the game of How, When, and Where, she was very great, and, to the secret joy of Scrooge's nephew, beat her sisters hollow; though they were sharp girls too, as Topper could have told you. There might have been twenty people there, young and old, but they all played, and so did Scrooge; for wholly forgetting, in the interest he had in what was going on, that his voice made no sound in their ears, he sometimes came out with his guess quite loud, and very often guessed right, too; for the sharpest needle, best Whitechapel, warranted not to cut in the eye, was not sharper than Scrooge, blunt as he took it in his head to be.

The ghost was greatly pleased to find him in this mood, and looked upon him with such favour that he begged like a boy to be allowed to stay until the guests departed. But this the Spirit said could not be done.

'Here is a new game,' said Scrooge. 'One half-hour, Spirit, only one!'

It was a game called Yes and No, where Scrooge's nephew had to think of something, and the rest must find out what, he only answering to their questions yes or no, as the case was. The brisk fire of questioning to which he was exposed elicited from him that he was thinking of an animal, a live animal, rather a disagreeable animal, a savage animal, an animal that growled and grunted sometimes, and talked sometimes and lived in London, and walked about the streets, and wasn't made a show of, and wasn't led by anybody, and didn't live in a menagerie, and was never killed in a market, and was not a horse, or an ass, or a cow, or a bull, or a tiger, or a dog, or a pig, or a cat, or a bear. At every fresh question that was put to him, this nephew burst into a fresh roar of laughter; and was so inexpressibly tickled, that he was obliged to get up off the sofa and stamp.

At last the plump sister, falling into a similar state, cried out, 'I have found it out! I know what it is, Fred! I know what it is!'

'What is it?' cried Fred.

'It's your Uncle Scro–o–o–o–oge.'

Which it certainly was. Admiration was the universal sentiment, though some objected that the reply to 'Is it a bear?' ought to have been 'Yes'; inasmuch as an answer in the negative was sufficient to have diverted their thoughts from Mr Scrooge, supposing they had ever had any tendency that way.

'He has given us plenty of merriment, I am sure,' said Fred, 'and it would be ungrateful not to drink his health. Here is a glass of mulled wine ready to our hand at the moment; and I say, "Uncle Scrooge!" '

'Well! Uncle Scrooge!' they cried.

'A merry Christmas and a happy New Year to the old man, whatever he is!' said Scrooge's nephew. 'He wouldn't take it from me, but may he have it, nevertheless. Uncle Scrooge!'

Uncle Scrooge had imperceptibly become so gay and light of heart, that he would have pledged the unconscious company in return, and thanked them in an inaudible speech, if the ghost had given him time. But the whole scene passed off in the breath of the last word spoken by his nephew; and he and the Spirit were again upon their travels.

Much they saw, and far they went, and many homes they visited, but always with a happy end. The Spirit stood beside sick-beds, and they were cheerful; on foreign lands, and they were close at home; by struggling men, and they were patient in their greater hope; by poverty, and it was rich. In almshouse, hospital, and gaol, in misery's every refuge, where vain man in his little brief authority had not made fast the door, and barred the Spirit out, he left his blessing and taught Scrooge his precepts.

It was a long night, if it were only a night; but Scrooge had his doubts of this, because the Christmas holidays appeared to be condensed into the space of time they passed together. It was strange, too, that, while Scrooge remained unaltered in his outward form, the ghost grew older, clearly older. Scrooge had observed this change, but never spoke of it until they left a children's Twelfth-Night party, when, looking at the Spirit as they stood together in an open place, he noticed that its hair was grey.

'Are spirits' lives so short?' asked Scrooge.

'My life upon this globe is very brief,' replied the ghost. 'It ends tonight.'

'Tonight!' cried Scrooge.

'Tonight at midnight. Hark! The time is drawing near.'

The chimes were ringing the three-quarters past eleven at that moment.

'Forgive me if I am not justified in what I ask,' said Scrooge, looking intently at the Spirit's robe, 'but I see something strange, and not belonging to yourself, protruding from your skirts. Is it a foot or a claw?'

'It might be a claw, for the flesh there is upon it,' was the Spirit's sorrowful reply. 'Look here!'

From the foldings of its robe it brought two children, wretched, abject, frightful, hideous, miserable. They knelt down at its feet, and clung upon the outside of its garment.

'O Man! look here! Look, look down here!' exclaimed the ghost.

They were a boy and girl. Yellow, meagre, ragged, scowling, wolfish, but prostrate, too, in their humility. Where graceful youth should have filled their features out, and touched them with its freshest tints, a stale and shrivelled hand, like that of age, had pinched and twisted them, and pulled them into shreds. Where angels might have sat enthroned, devils lurked, and glared out menacing. No change, no degradation, no perversion of humanity in any grade, through all the mysteries of wonderful creation, has monsters half so horrible and dread.

This boy is Ignorance. This girl is Want.

Scrooge started back, appalled. Having them shown to him in this way, he tried to say they were fine children, but the words choked themselves, rather than be parties to a lie of such enormous magnitude.

'Spirit! are they yours?' Scrooge could say no more.

'They are Man's,' said the Spirit, looking down upon them. 'And they cling to me, appealing from their fathers. This boy is Ignorance. This girl is Want. Beware of them both, and all of their degree, but most of all beware this boy, for on his brow I see that written which is Doom, unless the writing be erased. Deny it!' cried the Spirit, stretching out his hand towards the city. 'Slander those who tell it ye! Admit it for your factious purposes, and make it worse! And bide the end!'

'Have they no refuge or resource?' cried Scrooge.

'Are there no prisons?' said the Spirit, turning on him for the last time with his own words. 'Are there no workhouses?'

The bell struck Twelve.

Scrooge looked about him for the ghost, and saw it not. As the last stroke ceased to vibrate, he remembered the prediction of old Jacob Marley, and, lifting up his eyes, beheld a solemn phantom, draped and hooded, coming like a mist along the ground towards him.

The Last of the Spirits

The phantom slowly, gravely, silently approached. When it came near him, Scrooge bent down upon his knee; for in the very air through which this Spirit moved it seemed to scatter gloom and mystery.

It was shrouded in a deep black garment, which concealed its head, its face, its form, and left nothing of it visible, save one outstretched hand. But for this, it would have been difficult to detach its figure from the night, and separate it from the darkness by which it was surrounded.

He felt that it was tall and stately when it came beside him, and that its mysterious presence filled him with a solemn dread. He knew no more, for the Spirit neither spoke nor moved.

'I am in the presence of the Ghost of Christmas Yet to Come?' said Scrooge.

The Spirit answered not, but pointed onward with its hand.

'You are about to show me shadows of the things that have not happened, but will happen in the time before us,' Scrooge pursued. 'Is that so, Spirit?'

The upper portion of the garment was contracted for an instant in its folds, as if the Spirit had inclined its head. That was the only answer he received.

Although well used to ghostly company by this time, Scrooge feared the silent shape so much that his legs trembled beneath him, and he found that he could hardly stand when he prepared to follow it. The Spirit paused a moment, as observing his condition, and giving him time to recover.

But Scrooge was all the worse for this. It thrilled him with a vague, uncertain horror to know that, behind the dusky shroud, there were ghostly eyes intently fixed upon him, while he, though he stretched his own to the utmost, could see nothing but a spectral hand and one great heap of black.

'Ghost of the Future!' he exclaimed, 'I fear you more than any spectre

I have seen. But as I know your purpose is to do me good, and as I hope to live to be another man from what I was, I am prepared to bear your company, and do it with a thankful heart. Will you not speak to me?'

It gave him no reply. The hand was pointed straight before them.

'Lead on!' said Scrooge. 'Lead on! The night is waning fast, and it is precious time to me, I know. Lead on, Spirit!'

The phantom moved away as it had come towards him. Scrooge followed in the shadow of its dress, which bore him up, he thought, and carried him along.

They scarcely seemed to enter the City; for the City rather seemed to spring up about them, and encompass them of its own act. But there they were in the heart of it; on 'Change, amongst the merchants, who hurried up and down, and chinked the money in their pockets, and conversed in groups, and looked at their watches, and trifled thoughtfully with their great gold seals, and so forth, as Scrooge had seen them often.

The Spirit stopped beside one little knot of business men. Observing that the hand was pointed to them, Scrooge advanced to listen to their talk.

'No,' said a great fat man with a monstrous chin, 'I don't know much about it either way. I only know he's dead.'

'When did he die?' enquired another.

'Last night, I believe.'

'Why, what was the matter with him?' asked a third, taking a vast quantity of snuff out of a very large snuffbox. 'I thought he'd never die.'

'God knows,' said the first, with a yawn.

'What has he done with his money?' asked a red-faced gentleman with a pendulous excrescence on the end of his nose, that shook like the gills of a turkey-cock.

'I haven't heard,' said the man with the large chin, yawning again. 'Left it to his company, perhaps. He hasn't left it to *me*. That's all I know.'

This pleasantry was received with a general laugh.

'It's likely to be a very cheap funeral,' said the same speaker; 'for, upon my life, I don't know of anybody to go to it. Suppose we make up a party, and volunteer?'

'I don't mind going if a lunch is provided,' observed the gentleman with the excrescence on his nose. 'But I must be fed if I make one.'

Another laugh.

'Well, I am the most disinterested among you, after all,' said the first speaker, 'for I never wear black gloves, and I never eat lunch. But I'll offer to go if anybody else will. When I come to think of it, I'm not at all sure that I wasn't his most particular friend; for we used to stop and speak whenever we met. Bye-bye!'

Speakers and listeners strolled away, and mixed with other groups. Scrooge knew the men, and looked towards the Spirit for an explanation.

The phantom glided on into a street. Its finger pointed to two persons meeting. Scrooge listened again, thinking that the explanation might lie here.

He knew these men, also, perfectly. They were men of business: very wealthy, and of great importance. He had made a point always of standing well in their esteem in a business point of view, that is; strictly in a business point of view.

'How are you?' said one.

'How are you?' returned the other.

'Well!' said the first, 'old Scratch has got his own at last, hey?'

'So I am told,' returned the second. 'Cold, isn't it?'

'Seasonable for Christmastime. You are not a skater, I suppose?'

'No, no. Something else to think of. Good-morning!'

Not another word. That was their meeting, their conversation, and their parting.

Scrooge was at first inclined to be surprised that the Spirit should attach importance to conversations apparently so trivial; but feeling assured that they must have some hidden purpose, he set himself to consider what it was likely to be. They could scarcely be supposed to have any bearing on the death of Jacob, his old partner, for that was Past, and this ghost's province was the Future. Nor could he think of anyone immediately connected with himself to whom he could apply them. But nothing doubting that, to whomsoever they applied, they had some latent moral for his own improvement, he resolved to treasure up every word he heard, and everything he saw; and especially to observe the shadow of himself when it appeared. For he had an expectation that the conduct of his future self would give him the clue he missed, and would render the solution of these riddles easy.

He looked about in that very place for his own image, but another man stood in his accustomed corner; and though the clock pointed to his usual time of day for being there, he saw no likeness of himself among the multitudes that poured in through the Porch. It gave him little surprise, however; for he had been revolving in his mind a change of life, and thought and hoped he saw his newborn resolutions carried out in this.

Quiet and dark, beside him stood the phantom, with its outstretched hand. When he roused himself from his thoughtful quest, he fancied, from the turn of the hand, and its situation in reference to himself, that the Unseen Eyes were looking at him keenly. It made him shudder, and feel very cold.

They left the busy scene, and went into an obscure part of the town, where Scrooge had never penetrated before, although he recognised its situation and its bad repute. The ways were foul and narrow; the shops and houses wretched; the people half naked, drunken, slipshod, ugly. Alleys and archways, like so many cesspools, disgorged their offences of smell and dirt, and life upon the straggling streets; and the whole quarter reeked with crime, with filth, and misery.

Far in this den of infamous resort, there was a low-browed, beetling shop, below a penthouse roof, where iron, old rags, bottles, bones, and greasy offal were bought. Upon the floor within were piled up heaps of rusty keys, nails, chains, hinges, files, scales, weights, and refuse iron of all kinds. Secrets that few would like to scrutinise were bred and hidden in mountains of unseemly rags, masses of corrupted fat, and sepulchres of bones. Sitting in among the wares he dealt in, by a charcoal stove made of old bricks, was a grey-haired rascal, nearly seventy years of age, who had screened himself from the cold air without by a frouzy curtaining of miscellaneous tatters hung upon a line, and smoked his pipe in all the luxury of calm retirement.

Scrooge and the phantom came into the presence of this man, just as a woman with a heavy bundle slunk into the shop But she had scarcely entered, when another woman, similarly laden, came in too; and she was closely followed by a man in faded black, who was no less startled by the sight of them than they had been upon the recognition of each other. After a short period of blank astonishment, in which the old man with the pipe had joined them, they all three burst into a laugh.

'Let the charwoman alone to be the first!' cried she who had entered first. 'Let the laundress alone to be the second; and let the undertaker's man alone to be the third. Look here, old Joe, here's a chance! If we haven't all three met here without meaning it!'

'You couldn't have met in a better place,' said old Joe, removing his pipe from his mouth. 'Come into the parlour. You were made free of it long ago, you know; and the other two an't strangers. Stop till I shut the door of the shop. Ah! how it skreeks! There an't such a rusty bit of metal in the place as its own hinges, I believe; and I'm sure there's no such old bones here as mine. Ha! ha! We're all suitable to our calling, we're well matched. Come into the parlour. Come into the parlour.'

The parlour was the space behind the screen of rags. The old man raked the fire together with an old stair-rod, and having trimmed his smoky lamp (for it was night) with the stem of his pipe, put it into his mouth again.

While he did this, the woman who had already spoken threw her bundle on the floor, and sat down in a flaunting manner on a stool, crossing her elbows on her knees, and looking with a bold defiance at the other two.

'What odds, then? What odds, Mrs Dilber?' said the woman. 'Every person has a right to take care of themselves. *He* always did!'

'That's true, indeed!' said the laundress. 'No man more so.'

'Why, then, don't stand staring as if you was afraid, woman! Who's the wiser? We're not going to pick holes in each other's coats, I suppose?'

'No, indeed!' said Mrs Dilber and the man together. 'We should hope not.'

'Very well then!' cried the woman. 'That's enough. Who's the worse for the loss of a few things like these? Not a dead man, I suppose?'

'No, indeed,' said Mrs Dilber, laughing.

'If he wanted to keep 'em after he was dead, a wicked old screw,' pursued the woman, 'why wasn't he natural in his lifetime? If he had been, he'd have had somebody to look after him when he was struck with Death, instead of lying gasping out his last there, alone by himself.'

'It's the truest word that ever was spoke,' said Mrs Dilber. 'It's a judgement on him.'

'I wish it was a little heavier judgement,' replied the woman: 'and it should have been, you may depend upon it, if I could have laid my hands on anything else. Open that bundle, old Joe, and let me know the value of it. Speak out plain. I'm not afraid to be the first, nor afraid for them to see it. We knew pretty well that we were helping ourselves before we met here, I believe. It's no sin. Open the bundle, Joe.'

But the gallantry of her friends would not allow of this; and the man in faded black, mounting the breach first, produced *his* plunder. It was not extensive. A seal or two, a pencil-case, a pair of sleeve-buttons, and a brooch of no great value, were all. They were severally examined and appraised by old Joe, who chalked the sums he was disposed to give for each upon the wall, and added them up into a total when he found that there was nothing more to come.

'That's your account,' said Joe, 'and I wouldn't give another sixpence, if I was to be boiled for not doing it. Who's next?'

Mrs Dilber was next. Sheets and towels, a little wearing apparel, two old fashioned silver teaspoons, a pair of sugar-tongs, and a few boots. Her account was stated on the wall in the same manner.

'I always give too much to ladies. It's a weakness of mine, and that's the way I ruin myself,' said old Joe. 'That's your account. If you asked me for another penny, and made it an open question, I'd repent of being so liberal, and knock off half a crown.'

'And now undo *my* bundle, Joe,' said the first woman.

Joe went down on his knees for the greater convenience of opening it, and, having unfastened a great many knots, dragged out a large heavy roll of some dark stuff.

'What do you call this?' said Joe. 'Bed-curtains?'

'Ah!' returned the woman, laughing and leaning forward on her crossed arms. 'Bed-curtains!'

'You don't mean to say you took 'em down, rings and all, with him lying there?' said Joe.

'Yes, I do,' replied the woman. 'Why not?'

'You were born to make your fortune,' said Joe, 'and you'll certainly do it.'

'I certainly shan't hold my hand, when I can get anything in it by reaching it out, for the sake of such a man as he was, I promise you, Joe,' returned the woman coolly. 'Don't drop that oil upon the blankets, now.'

'His blankets?' asked Joe.

'Whose else's do you think?' replied the woman. 'He isn't likely to take cold without 'em, I dare say.'

'I hope he didn't die of anything catching? Eh?' said old Joe, stopping in his work, and looking up.

'Don't you be afraid of that,' returned the woman. 'I an't so fond of his company that I'd loiter about him for such things, if he did. Ah! you may look through that shirt till your eyes ache, but you won't find a hole in it, nor a threadbare place. It's the best he had, and a fine one too. They'd have wasted it, if it hadn't been for me.'

'What do you call wasting of it?' asked old Joe.

'Putting it on him to be buried in, to be sure,' replied the woman, with a laugh. 'Somebody was fool enough to do it, but I took it off again. If calico an't good enough for such a purpose, it isn't good enough for anything. It's quite as becoming to the body. He can't look uglier than he did in that one.'

Scrooge listened to this dialogue in horror. As they sat grouped about their spoil, in the scanty light afforded by the old man's lamp, he viewed them with a detestation and disgust which could hardly have been greater, though they had been obscene demons marketing the corpse itself.

'Ha, ha!' laughed the same woman when old Joe producing a flannel bag with money in it, told out their several gains upon the ground. 'This is the end of it, you see! He frightened everyone away from him when he was alive, to profit us when he was dead! Ha, ha, ha!'

'Spirit!' said Scrooge, shuddering from head to foot. 'I see, I see. The case of this unhappy man might be my own. My life tends that way now. Merciful heaven, what is this?'

He recoiled in terror, for the scene had changed, and now he almost touched a bed – a bare, uncurtained bed – on which, beneath a ragged sheet, there lay a something covered up, which, though it was dumb, announced itself in awful language.

The room was very dark, too dark to be observed with any accuracy, though Scrooge glanced round it in obedience to a secret impulse, anxious to know what kind of room it was. A pale light, rising in the outer air, fell straight upon the bed; and on it, plundered and bereft, unwatched, unwept, uncared for, was the body of this man.

Scrooge glanced towards the phantom. Its steady hand was pointed to the head. The cover was so carelessly adjusted that the slightest raising of it, the motion of a finger upon Scrooge's part, would have disclosed the face. He thought of it, felt how easy it would be to do, and longed to do it; but he had no more power to withdraw the veil than to dismiss the spectre at his side

Oh, cold, cold, rigid, dreadful Death, set up thine altar here, and dress it with such terrors as thou hast at thy command; for this is thy dominion! But of the loved, revered, and honoured head thou canst not turn one hair to thy dread purposes, or make one feature odious. It is not that the hand is heavy, and will fall down when released; it is not that the heart and pulse are still; but that the hand was open, generous, and true; the heart brave, warm, and tender, and the pulse a man's. Strike, Shadow, strike! And see his good deeds springing from the wound, to sow the world with life immortal!

No voice pronounced these words in Scrooge's ears, and yet he heard them when he looked upon the bed. He thought, if this man could be raised up now, what would be his foremost thoughts? Avarice, hard dealing, griping cares? They have brought him to a rich end, truly!

He lay in the dark, empty house, with not a man, a woman, or a child to say he was kind to me in this or that, and for the memory of one kind word I will be kind to him. A cat was tearing at the door, and there was a sound of gnawing rats beneath the hearthstone. What *they* wanted in the room of death, and why they were so restless and disturbed, Scrooge did not dare to think.

'Spirit!' he said, 'this is a fearful place. In leaving it, I shall not leave its lesson, trust me. Let us go!'

Still the ghost pointed with an unmoved finger to the head.

'I understand you,' Scrooge returned, 'and I would do it if I could. But I have not the power, Spirit. I have not the power.'

Again it seemed to look upon him.

'If there is any person in the town who feels emotion caused by this man's death,' said Scrooge, quite agonised, 'show that person to me, Spirit, I beseech you!'

The phantom spread its dark robe before him for a moment, like a wing; and, withdrawing it, revealed a room by daylight, where a mother and her children were.

She was expecting someone, and with anxious eagerness; for she walked up and down the room, started at every sound, looked out from the window, glanced at the clock, tried, but in vain, to work with her needle, and could hardly bear the voices of her children in their play.

At length the long-expected knock was heard. She hurried to the door, and met her husband; a man whose face was careworn and depressed, though he was young. There was a remarkable expression in it now, a kind of serious delight of which he felt ashamed; and which he struggled to repress.

He sat down to the dinner that had been hoarding for him by the fire, and when she asked him faintly what news (which was not until after a long silence), he appeared embarrassed how to answer.

'Is it good,' she said, 'or bad?' to help him.

'Bad,' he answered

'We are quite ruined?'

'No. There is hope yet, Caroline.'

'If *he* relents,' she, said, amazed, 'there is! Nothing is past hope, if such a miracle has happened.'

'He is past relenting,' said her husband. 'He is dead.'

She was a mild and patient creature, if her face spoke truth; but she was thankful in her soul to hear it, and she said so with clasped hands. She prayed forgiveness the next moment, and was sorry; but the first was the emotion of her heart.

'What the half-drunken woman, whom I told you of last night, said to me when I tried to see him and obtain a week's delay – and what I thought was a mere excuse to avoid me – turns out to have been quite true. He was not only very ill, but dying, then.'

'To whom will our debt be transferred?'

'I don't know. But, before that time, we shall be ready with the money; and even though we were not, it would be bad fortune indeed to find so merciless a creditor in his successor. We may sleep tonight with light hearts, Caroline!'

Yes. Soften it as they would, their hearts were lighter. The children's faces, hushed and clustered round to hear what they so little understood, were brighter; and it was a happier house for this man's death! The only emotion that the ghost could show him, caused by the event, was one of pleasure.

'Let me see some tenderness connected with a death,' said Scrooge; 'or that dark chamber, Spirit, which we left just now, will be for ever present to me.'

The ghost conducted him through several streets familiar to his feet; and as they went along, Scrooge looked here and there to find himself, but nowhere was he to be seen. They entered poor Bob Cratchit's house; the dwelling he had visited before; and found the mother and the children seated round the fire.

Quiet. Very quiet. The noisy little Cratchits were as still as statues in one corner, and sat looking up at Peter, who had a book before him. The mother and her daughters were engaged in sewing. But surely they were very quiet!

' "And he took a child, and set him in the midst of them." '

Where had Scrooge heard those words? He had not dreamed them.

The boy must have read them out as he and the Spirit crossed the threshold. Why did he not go on?

The mother laid her work upon the table, and put her hand up to her face.

'The colour hurts my eyes,' she said.

The colour? Ah, poor Tiny Tim!

'They're better now again,' said Cratchit's wife. 'It makes them weak by candlelight; and I wouldn't show weak eyes to your father when he comes home for the world. It must be near his time.'

'Past it rather,' Peter answered, shutting up his book. 'But I think he has walked a little slower than he used, these few last evenings, mother.'

They were very quiet again. At last she said, and in a steady, cheerful voice, that only faltered once:

'I have known him walk with – I have known him walk with Tiny Tim upon his shoulder very fast indeed.'

'And so have I,' cried Peter. 'Often.'

'And so have I,' exclaimed another. So had all.

'But he was very light to carry,' she resumed, intent upon her work, 'and his father loved him so, that it was no trouble, no trouble. And there is your father at the door!'

She hurried out to meet him; and little Bob in his comforter – he had need of it, poor fellow – came in. His tea was ready for him on the hob, and they all tried who should help him to it most. Then the two young Cratchits got upon his knees, and laid, each child, a little cheek against his face, as if they said, 'Don't mind it, father. Don't be grieved!'

Bob was very cheerful with them, and spoke pleasantly to all the family. He looked at the work upon the table, and praised the industry and speed of Mrs Cratchit and the girls. They would be done long before Sunday, he said.

'Sunday! You went today, then, Robert?' said his wife.

'Yes, my dear,' returned Bob. 'I wish you could have gone. It would have done you good to see how green a place it is. But you'll see it often. I promised him that I would walk there on a Sunday. My little, little child!' cried Bob. 'My little child!'

He broke down all at once. He couldn't help it. If he could have helped it, he and his child would have been farther apart, perhaps, than they were.

He left the room, and went upstairs into the room above, which was lighted cheerfully, and hung with Christmas. There was a chair set close beside the child, and there were signs of someone having been there lately. Poor Bob sat down in it, and when he had thought a little and composed himself, he kissed the little face. He was reconciled to what had happened, and went down again quite happy.

They drew about the fire, and talked, the girls and mother working still. Bob told them of the extraordinary kindness of Mr Scrooge's nephew, whom he had scarcely seen but once, and who, meeting him in the street that day, and seeing that he looked a little – 'just a little down, you know,' said Bob, enquired what had happened to distress him. 'On which,' said Bob, 'for he is the pleasantest-spoken gentleman you ever heard, I told him. "I am heartily sorry for it, Mr Cratchit," he said, "and heartily sorry for your good wife." By the by, how he ever knew *that* I don't know.'

'Knew what, my dear?'

'Why, that you were a good wife,' replied Bob.

'Everybody knows that,' said Peter.

'Very well observed, my boy!' cried Bob. 'I hope they do. "Heartily sorry," he said, "for your good wife. If I can be of service to you in any way," he said, giving me his card, "that's where I live. Pray come to me." Now, it wasn't,' cried Bob, 'for the sake of anything he might be able to do for us, so much as for his kind way, that this was quite delightful. It really seemed as if he had known our Tiny Tim, and felt with us.'

'I'm sure he's a good soul!' said Mrs Cratchit.

'You would be sure of it, my dear,' returned Bob, 'If you saw and spoke to him. I shouldn't be at all surprised – mark what I say! – if he got Peter a better situation.'

'Only hear that, Peter,' said Mrs Cratchit.

'And then,' cried one of the girls, 'Peter will be keeping company with someone, and setting up for himself.'

'Get along with you!' retorted Peter, grinning.

'It's just as likely as not,' said Bob, 'one of these days; though there's plenty of time for that, my dear. But, however and whenever we part from one another, I am sure we shall none of us forget poor Tiny Tim – shall we – or this first parting that there was among us?'

'Never, father!' cried they all.

'And I know,' said Bob, 'I know, my dears, that when we recollect how patient and how mild he was; although he was a little, little child; we shall not quarrel easily among ourselves, and forget poor Tiny Tim in doing it.'

'No, never, father!' they all cried again.

'I am very happy,' said little Bob, 'I am very happy!'

Mrs Cratchit kissed him, his daughters kissed him, the two young Cratchits kissed him, and Peter and himself shook hands. Spirit of Tiny Tim, thy childish essence was from God!

'Spectre,' said Scrooge, 'something informs me that our parting moment is at hand. I know it but I know not how. Tell me what man that was whom we saw lying dead?'

The ghost of Christmas Yet to Come conveyed him, as before – though at a different time, he thought: indeed there seemed no order in these latter visions, save that they were in the Future – into the resorts of business men, but showed him not himself. Indeed, the Spirit did not stay for anything, but went straight on, as to the end just now desired, until besought by Scrooge to tarry for a moment.

'This court,' said Scrooge, 'through which we hurry now, is where my place of occupation is, and has been for a length of time. I see the house. Let me behold what I shall be in days to come.'

The Spirit stopped; the hand was pointed elsewhere.

'The house is yonder,' Scrooge exclaimed. 'Why do you point away?'

The inexorable finger underwent no change.

Scrooge hastened to the window of his office, and looked in. It was an office still, but not his. The furniture was not the same, and the figure in the chair was not himself. The phantom pointed as before.

He joined it once again, and, wondering why and whither he had gone, accompanied it until they reached an iron gate. He paused to look round before entering.

A churchyard. Here, then, the wretched man, whose name he had now to learn, lay underneath the ground. It was a worthy place. Walled in by houses; overrun by grass and weeds, the growth of vegetation's death, not life; choked up with too much burying; fat with repleted appetite. A worthy place!

The Spirit stood among the graves, and pointed down to One. He advanced towards it trembling. The phantom was exactly as it had been, but he dreaded that he saw new meaning in its solemn shape.

'Before I draw nearer to that stone to which you point,' said Scrooge, 'answer me one question. Are these the shadows of the things that Will be, or are they shadows of the things that May be only?'

Still the ghost pointed downward to the grave by which it stood.

The last of the spirits the Ghost of Christmas Yet to Come

'Men's courses will foreshadow certain ends, to which, if persevered in, they must lead,' said Scrooge. 'But if the courses be departed from, the ends will change. Say it is thus with what you show me!'

The Spirit was immovable as ever.

Scrooge crept towards it, trembling as he went; and, following the finger, read upon the stone of the neglected grave his own name,

EBENEZER SCROOGE.

'Am *I* that man who lay upon the bed?' he cried upon his knees.

The finger pointed from the grave to him, and back again.

'No, Spirit! Oh no, no!'

The finger still was there.

'Spirit!' he cried, tight clutching at its robe, 'hear me! I am not the man I was. I will not be the man I must have been but for this intercourse. Why show me this, if I am past all hope?'

For the first time the hand appeared to shake.

'Good Spirit,' he pursued, as down upon the ground he fell before it, 'your nature intercedes for me, and pities me. Assure me that I yet may change these shadows you have shown me by an altered life?'

The kind hand trembled.

'I will honour Christmas in my heart, and try to keep it all the year. I will live in the Past, the Present, and the Future. The Spirits of all Three shall strive within me. I will not shut out the lessons that they teach. Oh, tell me I may sponge away the writing on this stone!'

In his agony he caught the spectral hand. It sought to free itself, but he was strong in his entreaty, and detained it. The Spirit stronger yet, repulsed him.

Holding up his hands in a last prayer to have his fate reversed, he saw an alteration in the phantom's hood and dress. It shrunk, collapsed, and dwindled down into a bedpost.

The End of It

Yes! and the bedpost was his own. The bed was his own, the room was his own. Best and happiest of all, the Time before him was his own, to make amends in!

'I will live in the Past, the Present, and the Future!' Scrooge repeated as he scrambled out of bed. 'The Spirits of all Three shall strive within me. O Jacob Marley! Heaven and the Christmastime be praised for this! I say it on my knees, old Jacob; on my knees!'

He was so fluttered and so glowing with his good intentions, that his broken voice would scarcely answer to his call. He had been sobbing violently in his conflict with the Spirit, and his face was wet with tears.

'They are not torn down,' cried Scrooge, folding one of his bed-curtains in his arms, 'They are not torn down, rings and all. They are here – I am here – the shadows of the things that would have been may be dispelled. They will be. I know they will!'

His hands were busy with his garments all this time: turning them inside out, putting them on upside down, tearing them, mislaying them, making them parties to every kind of extravagance.

'I don't know what to do!' cried Scrooge, laughing and crying in the same breath, and making a perfect Laocoön of himself with his stockings. 'I am as light as a feather, I am as happy as an angel, I am as merry as a schoolboy, I am as giddy as a drunken man. A merry Christmas to everybody! A happy New Year to all the world! Hallo here! Whoop! Hallo!'

He had frisked into the sitting-room; and was now standing there, perfectly winded.

'There's the saucepan that the gruel was in!' cried Scrooge, starting off again, and going round the fireplace. 'There's the door by which the ghost of Jacob Marley entered! There's the corner where the Ghost of Christmas Present sat! There's the window where I saw the wandering Spirits! It's all right, it's all true, it all happened. Ha, ha, ha!'

Really, for a man who had been out of practice for so many years, it was a splendid laugh, a most illustrious laugh. The father of a long, long line of brilliant laughs!

'I don't know what day of the month it is,' said Scrooge. 'I don't know how long I have been among the Spirits. I don't know anything. I'm quite a baby. Never mind. I don't care. I'd rather be a baby. Hallo! Whoop! Hallo here!'

He was checked in his transports by the churches ringing out the lustiest peals he had ever heard. Clash, clash, hammer; ding, dong, bell! Bell, dong, ding; hammer, clang, clash! Oh, glorious, glorious!

Running to the window, he opened it, and put out his head. No fog, no mist; clear, bright, jovial, stirring, cold; cold, piping for the blood to dance to; golden sunlight; heavenly sky; sweet fresh air; merry bells. Oh, glorious! Glorious!

'What's today?' cried Scrooge, calling downward to a boy in Sunday clothes, who perhaps had loitered in to look about him.

'Eh?' returned the boy with all his might of wonder.

'What's today, my fine fellow?' said Scrooge.

'Today!' replied the boy. 'Why, Christmas Day.'

'It's Christmas Day!' said Scrooge to himself. 'I haven't missed it. The Spirits have done it all in one night. They can do anything they like. Of course they can. Of course they can. Hallo, my fine fellow!'

'Hallo!' returned the boy.

'Do you know the poulterer's in the next street but one, at the corner?' Scrooge enquired.

'I should hope I did,' replied the lad.

'An intelligent boy!' said Scrooge. 'A remarkable boy! Do you know whether they've sold the prize turkey that was hanging up there? – Not the little prize turkey: the big one?'

'What! the one as big as me?' returned the boy.

'What a delightful boy!' said Scrooge. 'It's a pleasure to talk to him. Yes, my buck!'

'It's hanging there now,' replied the boy.

'Is it?' said Scrooge. 'Go and buy it.'

'Walk–er!' exclaimed the boy.

'No, no,' said Scrooge. 'I am in earnest. Go and buy it, and tell 'em to bring it here, that I may give them the directions where to take it. Come back with the man, and I'll give you a shilling. Come back with him in less than five minutes, and I'll give you half a crown!'

The boy was off like a shot. He must have had a steady hand at a trigger who could have got a shot off half as fast.

'I'll send it to Bob Cratchit's,' whispered Scrooge, rubbing his hands, and splitting with a laugh. 'He shan't know who sends it. It's twice the size of Tiny Tim. Joe Miller never made such a joke as sending it to Bob's will be!'

The hand in which he wrote the address was not a steady one; but write it he did, somehow, and went downstairs to open the street-door, ready for the coming of the poulterer's man. As he stood there, waiting his arrival, the knocker caught his eye.

'I shall love it as long as I live!' cried Scrooge, patting it with his hand. 'I scarcely ever looked at it before. What an honest expression it has in its face! It's a wonderful knocker! – Here's the turkey. Hallo! Whoop! How are you! Merry Christmas!'

It *was* a turkey! He never could have stood upon his legs, that bird. He would have snapped 'em short off in a minute, like sticks of sealing-wax.

'Why, it's impossible to carry that to Camden Town,' said Scrooge. 'You must have a cab.'

The chuckle with which he said this, and the chuckle with which he paid for the turkey, and the chuckle with which he paid for the cab, and the chuckle with which he recompensed the boy, were only to be exceeded by the chuckle with which he sat down breathless in his chair again, and chuckled till he cried.

Shaving was not an easy task, for his hand continued to shake very much; and shaving requires attention, even when you don't dance while you are at it. But if he had cut the end of his nose off, he would have put a piece of sticking-plaster over it, and been quite satisfied.

He dressed himself 'all in his best,' and at last got out into the streets. The people were by this time pouring forth, as he had seen them with the Ghost of Christmas Present; and, walking with his hands behind him, Scrooge regarded everyone with a delighted smile. He looked so irresistibly pleasant, in a word, that three or four good-humoured fellows said, 'Good-morning, sir! A merry Christmas to you!' And Scrooge said often afterwards that, of all the blithe sounds he had ever heard, those were the blithest in his ears.

He had not gone far when, coming on towards him, he beheld the portly gentleman who had walked into his counting-house the day before, and said, 'Scrooge and Marley's, I believe?' It sent a pang across his heart to think how this old gentleman would look upon him when they met; but he knew what path lay straight before him, and he took it.

'My dear sir,' said Scrooge, quickening his pace, and taking the old gentleman by both his hands, 'how do you do? I hope you succeeded yesterday. It was very kind of you. A merry Christmas to you, sir!'

'Mr Scrooge?'

'Yes,' said Scrooge. 'That is my name, and I fear it may not be pleasant to you. Allow me to ask your pardon. And will you have the goodness – ' Here Scrooge whispered in his ear.

'Lord bless me!' cried the gentleman, as if his breath were taken away. 'My dear Mr Scrooge, are you serious?'

'If you please,' said Scrooge. 'Not a farthing less. A great many back-payments are included in it, I assure you. Will you do me that favour?'

'My dear sir,' said the other, shaking hands with him, 'I don't know what to say to such munifi— '

'Don't say anything, please,' retorted Scrooge. 'Come and see me. Will you come and see me?'

'I will!' cried the old gentleman. And it was clear he meant to do it.

'Thankee,' said Scrooge. 'I am much obliged to you. I thank you fifty times. Bless you!'

He went to church, and walked about the streets, and watched the people hurrying to and fro, and patted the children on the head, and questioned beggars, and looked down into the kitchens of houses, and up to the window; and found that everything could yield him pleasure. He had never dreamed that any walk – that anything – could give him so much happiness. In the afternoon he turned his steps towards his nephew's house.

He passed the door a dozen times before he had the courage to go up and knock. But he made a dash and did it

'Is your master at home, my dear?' said Scrooge to the girl. Nice girl! Very.

'Yes, sir.'

'Where is he, my love?' said Scrooge.

'He's in the dining-room, sir, along with mistress. I'll show you upstairs, if you please.'

'Thankee. He knows me,' said Scrooge, with his hand already on the dining-room lock. 'I'll go in here, my dear.'

He turned it gently, and sidled his face in round the door. They were looking at the table (which was spread out in great array); for these young housekeepers are always nervous on such points, and like to see that everything is right.

'Fred!' said Scrooge.

Dear heart alive, how his niece by marriage started! Scrooge had forgotten, for the moment, about her sitting in the corner with the footstool, or he wouldn't have done it on any account.

'Why, bless my soul!' cried Fred, 'who's that?'

'It's I. Your uncle Scrooge. I have come to dinner. Will you let me in, Fred?'

Let him in! It is a mercy he didn't shake his arm off. He was at home in five minutes. Nothing could be heartier. His niece looked just the same. So did Topper when *he* came. So did the plump sister when *she* came. So did everyone when *they* came. Wonderful party, wonderful games, wonderful unanimity, won–der–ful happiness!

But he was early at the office next morning. Oh, he was early there! If he could only be there first, and catch Bob Cratchit coming late! That was the thing he had set his heart upon.

And he did it; yes, he did! The clock struck nine. No Bob. A quarter past. No Bob. He was full eighteen minutes and a half behind his time. Scrooge sat with his door wide open, that he might see him come into the tank.

His hat was off before he opened the door; his comforter too. He was on his stool in a jiffy, driving away with his pen, as if he were trying to overtake nine o'clock.

'Hallo!' growled Scrooge in his accustomed voice as near as he could feign it. 'What do you mean by coming here at this time of day?'

'I am very sorry, sir,' said Bob. 'I *am* behind my time.'

'You are!' repeated Scrooge. 'Yes, I think you are. Step this way, sir, if you please.'

'It's only once a year, sir,' pleaded Bob, appearing from the tank. 'It shall not be repeated. I was making rather merry yesterday, sir.'

'Now, I'll tell you what, my friend,' said Scrooge. 'I am not going to stand this sort of thing any longer. And therefore,' he continued, leaping from his stool, and giving Bob such a dig in the waistcoat that he staggered back into the tank again – 'and therefore I am about to raise your salary!'

Bob trembled, and got a little nearer to the ruler. He had a momentary

Over a Christmas bowl of smoking bishop

idea of knocking Scrooge down with it, holding him, and calling to the people in the court for help and a strait-waistcoat.

'A merry Christmas, Bob!' said Scrooge, with an earnestness that could not be mistaken, as he clapped him on the back. 'A merrier Christmas, Bob, my good fellow, than I have given you for many a year! I'll raise your salary, and endeavour to assist your struggling family, and we will discuss your affairs this very afternoon, over a Christmas bowl of smoking bishop, Bob! Make up the fires and buy another coal-scuttle before you dot another i, Bob Cratchit!'

Scrooge was better than his word. He did it all, and infinitely more; and to Tiny Tim, who did *not* die, he was a second father. He became as good a friend, as good a master, and as good a man as the good old City knew, or any other good old city, town, or borough in the good old world. Some people laughed to see the alteration in him, but he let them laugh, and little heeded them; for he was wise enough to know that nothing ever happened on this globe, for good, at which some people did not have their fill of laughter in the outset; and knowing that such as these would be blind anyway, he thought it quite as well that they should wrinkle up their eyes in grins as have the malady in less attractive forms. His own heart laughed, and that was quite enough for him.

He had no further intercourse with Spirits, but lived upon the Total-Abstinence Principle ever afterwards; and it was always said of him that he knew how to keep Christmas well, if any man alive possessed the knowledge. May that be truly said of us, and all of us! And so, as Tiny Tim observed, God bless us, every one!

THE CHIMES

*A Goblin Story of some Bells that rang an
Old Year out and a New Year in*

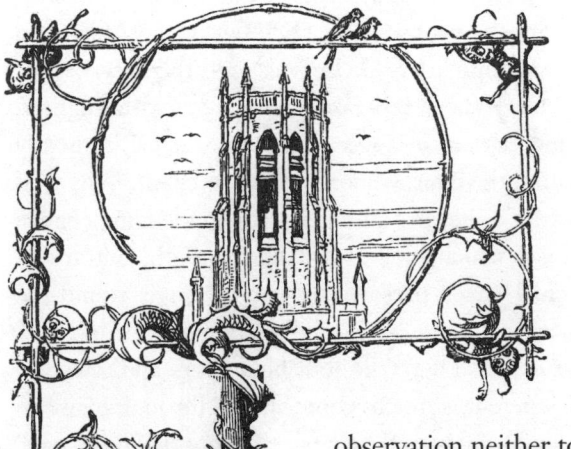

There are not many people – and as it is desirable that a story-teller and a story-reader should establish a mutual understanding as soon as possible, I beg it to be noticed that I confine this observation neither to young people nor to little people, but extend it to all conditions of people: little and big, young and old: yet growing up, or already growing down again – there are not, I say, many people who would care to sleep in a church. I don't mean at sermon-time in warm weather (when the thing has actually been done, once or twice), but in the night and alone. A great multitude of persons will be violently astonished, I know, by this position, in the broad bold Day. But it applies to Night. It must be argued by night. And I will undertake to maintain it successfully on any gusty winter's night appointed for the purpose, with any one opponent chosen from the rest, who will meet me singly in an old churchyard, before an old church door; and will previously empower me to lock him in, if needful to his satisfaction, until morning.

For the night-wind has a dismal trick of wandering round and round a building of that sort, and moaning as it goes; and of trying, with its unseen hand, the windows and the doors; and seeking out some crevices by which to enter. And when it has got in, as one not finding what it seeks, whatever that may be, it wails and howls to issue forth again: and not content with stalking through the aisles, and gliding round and round the pillars, and tempting the deep organ, soars up to the roof, and strives to rend the rafters: then flings itself despairingly upon the stones below, and passes, muttering, into the vaults. Anon, it comes up stealthily, and creeps along the walls seeming to read, in whispers, the Inscriptions sacred to the Dead. At some of these, it breaks out shrilly, as with laughter; and at others, moans and cries as if it were lamenting. It has a ghostly sound too, lingering within the altar; where it seems to chant, in its wild way, of Wrong and Murder done, and false gods worshipped; in defiance of the Tables of the Law, which look so fair and smooth, but are so flawed and broken. Ugh! Heaven preserve us, sitting snugly round the fire! It has an awful voice, that wind at Midnight, singing in a church!

But high up in the steeple! There the foul blast roars and whistles! High up in the steeple, where it is free to come and go through many an airy arch and loophole, and to twist and twine itself about the giddy stair, and twirl the groaning weathercock, and make the very tower shake and shiver! High up in the steeple, where the belfry is; and iron rails are ragged with rust; and sheets of lead and copper, shrivelled by the changing weather, crackle and heave beneath the unaccustomed tread; and birds stuff shabby nests into corners of old oaken joists and beams; and dust grows old and grey; and speckled spiders, indolent and fat with long security, swing idly to and fro in the vibration of the bells, and never loose their hold upon their thread-spun castles in the air, or climb up sailor-like in quick alarm, or drop upon the ground and ply a score of nimble legs to save a life! High up in the steeple of an old church, far above the light and murmur of the town and far below the flying clouds that shadow it, is the wild and dreary place at night: and high up in the steeple of an old church, dwelt the Chimes I tell of.

They were old Chimes, trust me. Centuries ago, these Bells had been baptised by bishops: so many centuries ago, that the register of their baptism was lost long, long before the memory of man: and no one knew their names. They had had their Godfathers and Godmothers, these Bells (for my own part, by the way, I would rather incur the responsibility of being Godfather to a Bell than a Boy): and had their silver mugs no doubt, besides. But Time had mowed down their sponsors, and Henry VIII had melted down their mugs: and they now hung, nameless and mugless, in the church tower.

Not speechless, though. Far from it. They had clear, loud, lusty, sounding voices, had these Bells; and far and wide they might be heard upon the wind. Much too sturdy Chimes were they, to be dependent on the pleasure of the wind, moreover; for, fighting gallantly against it when it took an adverse whim, they would pour their cheerful notes into a listening ear right royally; and bent on being heard, on stormy nights, by some poor mother watching a sick child, or some lone wife whose husband was at sea, they had been sometimes known to beat a blustering nor'wester; ay, 'all to fits,' as Toby Veck said; for though they chose to call him Trotty Veck, his name was Toby, and nobody could make it anything else either (except Tobias) without a special Act of Parliament;

Toby Veck

he having been as lawfully christened in his day as the Bells had been in theirs, though with not quite so much solemnity or public rejoicing.

For my part, I confess myself of Toby Veck's belief, for I am sure he had opportunities enough of forming a correct one. And whatever Toby Veck said, I say. And I take my stand by Toby Veck, although he *did* stand all day long (and weary work it was) just outside the church-door. In fact he was a ticket-porter, Toby Veck, and waited there for jobs.

And a breezy, goose-skinned, blue-nosed, red-eyed, stony-toed, tooth-chattering place it was, to wait in, in the wintertime, as Toby Veck well knew. The wind came tearing round the corner – especially the east wind – as if it had sallied forth, express, from the confines of the earth, to have a blow at Toby. And oftentimes it seemed to come upon him sooner than it had expected, for bouncing round the corner, and passing Toby, it would suddenly wheel round again, as if it cried, 'Why, here he is!' Incontinently his little apron would be caught up over his head like a naughty boy's garments, and his feeble little cane would be seen to wrestle and struggle unavailingly in his hand, and his legs would undergo tremendous agitation, and Toby himself all aslant, and facing now in this direction, now in that, would be so banged and buffeted, and tousled, and worried, and hustled, and lifted off his feet, as to render it a state of things but one degree removed from a positive miracle, that he wasn't carried up bodily into the air as a colony of frogs or snails or other very portable creatures sometimes are, and rained down again, to the great astonishment of the natives, on some strange corner of the world where ticket-porters are unknown.

But, windy weather, in spite of its using him so roughly, was, after all, a sort of holiday for Toby. That's the fact. He didn't seem to wait so long for a sixpence in the wind, as at other times; the having to fight with that boisterous element took off his attention, and quite freshened him up, when he was getting hungry and low-spirited. A hard frost too, or a fall of snow, was an Event; and it seemed to do him good, somehow or other – it would have been hard to say in what respect though, Toby! So wind and frost and snow, and perhaps a good stiff storm of hail, were Toby Veck's red-letter days.

Wet weather was the worst: the cold, damp, clammy wet, that wrapped him up like a moist greatcoat: the only kind of greatcoat Toby owned, or could have added to his comfort by dispensing with. Wet days, when the rain came slowly, thickly, obstinately down; when the street's throat, like his own, was choked with mist; when smoking umbrellas passed and repassed, spinning round and round like so many teetotums, as they knocked against each other on the crowded footway, throwing off a little whirlpool of uncomfortable sprinklings; when gutters brawled and water-spouts were full and noisy; when the wet from the projecting stones and ledges of the church fell drip, drip, drip, on Toby, making the wisp of straw on which he stood mere mud in no time; those were the days that tried him. Then indeed, you might see Toby looking anxiously out from his shelter in an angle of the church wall – such a meagre shelter that in summer time it never cast a shadow thicker than a good-sized walking stick upon the sunny pavement – with a disconsolate and lengthened face. But coming out, a minute afterwards, to warm himself by exercise; and trotting up and down some dozen times he would brighten even then, and go back more brightly to his niche.

They called him Trotty from his pace, which meant speed if it didn't make it. He could have Walked faster perhaps; most likely; but rob him of his trot, and Toby would have taken to his bed and died. It bespattered him with mud in dirty weather; it cost him a world of trouble; he could have walked with infinitely greater ease: but that was one reason for his clinging to it so tenaciously. A weak, small, spare old man, he was a very Hercules, this Toby, in his good intentions. He loved to earn his money. He delighted to believe – Toby was very poor, and couldn't well afford to part with a delight – that he was worth his salt. With a shilling or an eighteen-penny message or small parcel in hand, his courage, always high, rose higher. As he trotted on, he would call out to fast Postmen ahead of him, to get out of the way; devoutly believing that in the natural course of things he must inevitably overtake and run them down; and he had perfect faith – not often tested – in his being able to carry anything that man could lift.

Thus, even when he came out of his nook to warm himself on a wet day, Toby trotted. Making, with his leaky shoes, a crooked line of slushy footprints in the mire; and blowing on his chilly hands and rubbing them against each other, poorly defended from the searching cold by threadbare mufflers of grey worsted, with a private apartment only for the thumb, and a common room or tap for the rest of the fingers; Toby, with his knees bent and his cane beneath his arm, still trotted. Falling out into the road to look up at the belfry when the Chimes resounded. Toby trotted still.

He made this last excursion several times a day, for they were company to him; and when he heard their voices, he had an interest in glancing at their lodging-place, and thinking how they were moved, and what hammers beat upon them. Perhaps he was the more curious about these Bells, because there were points of resemblance between themselves and him. They hung there, in all weathers: with the wind and rain driving in upon them: facing only the outsides of all those houses; never getting any nearer to the blazing fires that gleamed and shone upon the windows, or came puffing out of the chimney tops; and incapable of participation in any of the good things that were constantly being handed, through the street doors and the area railings, to prodigious cooks. Faces came and went at many windows: sometimes pretty faces, youthful faces, pleasant faces: sometimes the reverse: but Toby knew no more (though he often speculated on these trifles, standing idle in the streets) whence they came, or where they went, or whether, when the lips moved, one kind word was said of him in all the year, than did the Chimes themselves.

Toby was not a casuist – that he knew of, at least – and I don't mean to say that when he began to take to the Bells, and to knit up his first rough acquaintance with them into something of a closer and more delicate woof, he passed through these considerations one by one, or held any formal review or great field-day in his thoughts. But what I mean to say, and do say is, that as the functions of Toby's body, his digestive organs for example, did of their own cunning, and by a great many operations of which he was altogether ignorant, and the knowledge of which would have astonished him very much, arrive at a certain end; so his mental faculties, without his privity or concurrence, set all these wheels and springs in motion, with a thousand others, when they worked to bring about his liking for the Bells.

And though I had said his love, I would not have recalled the word, though it would scarcely have expressed his complicated feeling. For, being but a simple man, he invested them with a strange and solemn character. They were so mysterious, often heard and never seen; so high up, so far off, so full of such a deep strong melody, that he regarded them with a species of awe; and sometimes when he looked up at the dark arched windows in the tower, he half expected to be beckoned to by something which was not a Bell, and yet was what he heard so often sounding in the Chimes. For all this, Toby scouted with indignation a certain flying rumour that the Chimes were haunted, as implying the possibility of their being connected with any Evil thing. In short, they were very often in his ears, and very often in his thoughts, but always in his good opinion; and he very often got such a crick in his neck by staring with his mouth wide open, at the steeple where they hung, that he was fain to take an extra trot or two, afterwards, to cure it.

The very thing he was in the act of doing one cold day, when the last drowsy sound of Twelve o'clock, just struck, was humming like a melodious monster of a Bee, and not by any means a busy Bee, all through the steeple!

'Dinner-time, eh!' said Toby, trotting up and down before the church. 'Ah!'

Toby's nose was very red, and his eyelids were very red, and he winked very much, and his shoulders were very near his ears, and his legs were very stiff; and altogether he was evidently a long way upon the frosty side of cool.

'Dinner-time, eh!' repeated Toby, using his right-hand muffler like an infantine boxing-glove, and punishing his chest for being cold. 'Ah–h–h–h!'

He took a silent trot, after that, for a minute or two.

'There's nothing,' said Toby, breaking forth afresh – but here he stopped short in his trot, and with a face of great interest and some alarm, felt his nose carefully all the way up. It was but a little way (not being much of a nose) and he had soon finished.

'I thought it was gone,' said Toby, trotting off again. 'It's all right, however. I am sure I couldn't blame it if it was to go. It has a precious hard service of it in the bitter weather, and precious little to look forward to: for I don't take snuff myself. It's a good deal tried, poor creetur, at the best of times; for when it *does* get hold of a pleasant whiff or so (which an't too often), it's generally from somebody else's dinner, a-coming home from the baker's.'

The reflection reminded him of that other reflection, which he had left unfinished.

'There's nothing,' said Toby, 'more regular in its coming round than dinner-time, and nothing less regular in its coming round than dinner. That's the great difference between 'em. It's took me a long time to find it out. I wonder whether it would be worth any gentleman's while, now, to buy that observation for the Papers; or the Parliament!'

Toby was only joking, for he gravely shook his head in self-depreciation.

'Why! Lord!' said Toby. 'The Papers is full of obserwations as it is; and so's the Parliament. Here's last week's paper, now;' taking a very dirty one from his pocket, and holding it from him at arm's length; 'full of obserwations! Full of obserwations! I like to know the news as well as any man,' said Toby, slowly; folding it a little smaller, and putting it in his pocket again: 'but it almost goes against the grain with me to read a paper now. It frightens me almost. I don't know what we poor people are coming to. Lord send we may be coming to something better in the New Year nigh upon us!'

'Why, father, father!' said a pleasant voice, hard by.

But Toby, not hearing it, continued to trot backwards and forwards: musing as he went, and talking to himself.

'It seems as if we can't go right, or do right, or be righted,' said Toby. 'I hadn't much schooling, myself, when I was young; and I can't make out whether we have any business on the face of the earth, or not. Sometimes I think we must have a little; and sometimes I think we must be intruding. I get so puzzled sometimes that I am not even able to make up my mind whether there is any good at all in us, or whether we are born bad. We seem to be dreadful things; we seem to give a deal of trouble; we are always being complained of and guarded against. One way or other, we fill the papers. Talk of a New Year!' said Toby, mournfully. 'I can bear up as well as another man at most times; better than a good many, for I am as strong as a lion, and all men an't; but supposing it should really be that we have no right to a New Year – supposing we really *are* intruding– '

'Why, father, father!' said the pleasant voice again.

Toby heard it this time; started; stopped; and shortening his sight, which had been directed a long way off as seeking for enlightenment in the very heart of the approaching year, found himself face to face with his own child, and looking close into her eyes.

Bright eyes they were. Eyes that would bear a world of looking in, before their depth was fathomed. Dark eyes, that reflected back the eyes which searched them; not flashingly, or at the owner's will, but with a clear, calm, honest, patient radiance, claiming kindred with that light which Heaven called into being. Eyes that were beautiful and true, and beaming with Hope. With Hope so young, and fresh; with Hope so buoyant, vigorous, and bright, despite the twenty years of work and poverty on which they had looked; that they became a voice to Trotty Veck, and said: 'I think we have some business here – a little!'

Trotty kissed the lips belonging to the eyes, and squeezed the blooming face between his hands.

'Why, Pet,' said Trotty. 'What's to do? I didn't expect you today, Meg.'

'Neither did I expect to come, father,' cried the girl, nodding her head and smiling as she spoke. 'But here I am! And not alone; not alone!'

'Why you don't mean to say,' observed Trotty, looking curiously at a covered basket which she carried in her hand, 'that you – '

'Smell it, father dear,' said Meg. 'Only smell it!'

Trotty was going to lift up the cover at once, in a great hurry, when she gaily interposed her hand.

'No, no, no,' said Meg, with the glee of a child. 'Lengthen it out a little. Let me just lift up the corner; just the lit–tle ti–ny cor–ner, you know,' said Meg, suiting the action to the word with the utmost gentleness, and speaking very softly, as if she were afraid of being overheard by something inside the basket; 'there. Now. What's that?'

Toby took the shortest possible sniff at the edge of the basket, and cried out in a rapture: 'Why it's hot!'

'It's burning hot!' cried Meg. 'Ha, ha, ha! It's scalding hot.'

'Ha, ha, ha!' roared Toby, with a sort of kick. 'It's scalding hot.'

'But what is it, father?' said Meg. 'Come! You haven't guessed what it is. And you must guess what it is. I can't think of taking it out, till you guess what it is. Don't be in such a hurry! Wait a minute! A little bit more of the cover. Now guess!'

Meg was in a perfect fright lest he should guess right too soon; shrinking away, as she held the basket towards him; curling up her pretty shoulders; stopping her ear with her hand, as if by so doing she could keep the right word out of Toby's lips; and laughing softly the whole time.

Meanwhile Toby, putting a hand on each knee, bent down his nose to the basket, and took a long inspiration at the lid; the grin upon his withered face expanding in the process, as if he were inhaling laughing gas.

'Ah! It's very nice,' said Toby. 'It an't – I suppose it an't Polonies?'

'No, no, no!' cried Meg, delighted. 'Nothing like Polonies!'

'No,' said Toby, after another sniff. 'It's – it's mellower than Polonies. It's very nice. It improves every moment. It's too decided for Trotters. An't it?'

Meg was in an ecstasy. He could not have gone wider of the mark than Trotters – except Polonies.

'Liver?' said Toby, communing with himself. 'No. There's a mildness about it that don't answer to liver. Pettitoes? No. It an't faint enough for pettitoes. It wants the stringiness of Cocks' heads. And I know it an't sausages. I'll tell you what it is. It's chitterlings!'

'No, it an't!' cried Meg, in a burst of delight. 'No, it an't!'

'Why, what am I a-thinking of!' said Toby, suddenly recovering a position as near the perpendicular as it was possible for him to assume. 'I shall forget my own name next. It's tripe!'

Tripe it was; and Meg, in high joy, protested he should say, in half a minute more, it was the best tripe ever stewed.

'And so,' said Meg, busying herself exultingly with the basket, 'I'll lay the cloth at once, father; for I have brought the tripe in a basin, and tied the basin up in a pocket-handkerchief; and if I like to be proud for once and spread that for a cloth, and call it a cloth, there's no law to prevent me; is there, father?'

'Not that I know of, my dear,' said Toby. 'But they're always a bringing up some new law or other.'

'And according to what I was reading you in the paper the other day, father; what the Judge said, you know; we poor people are supposed to know them all. Ha, ha! What a mistake! My goodness me, how clever they think us!'

'Yes, my dear,' cried Trotty; 'and they'd be very fond of any one of us that *did* know 'em all. He'd grow fat upon the work he'd get, that man and be popular with the gentlefolks in his neighbourhood. Very much so!'

'He'd eat his dinner with an appetite, whoever he was, if it smelt like this,' said Meg, cheerfully. 'Make haste, for there's a hot potato beside, and half a pint of fresh-drawn beer in a bottle. Where will you dine, father? On the Post, or on the Steps? Dear, dear, how grand we are. Two places to choose from!'

'The Steps today, my Pet,' said Trotty. 'Steps in dry weather. Posts in wet. There's a greater conveniency in the Steps at all times, because of the sitting down; but they're rheumatic in the damp.'

'Then here,' said Meg, clapping her hands, after a moment's bustle; 'here it is, all ready! And beautiful it looks! Come, father. Come!'

Since his discovery of the contents of the basket, Trotty had been standing looking at her – and had been speaking too – in an abstracted manner, which showed that though she was the object of his thoughts and eyes, to the exclusion even of tripe, he neither saw nor thought about her as she was at that moment, but had before him some imaginary rough sketch or drama of her future life. Roused, now, by her cheerful summons, he shook off a melancholy shake of the head which was just coming upon him, and trotted to her side. As he was stooping to sit down, the Chimes rang.

'Amen!' said Trotty, pulling off his hat and looking up towards them.

'Amen to the Bells, father?' cried Meg.

'They broke in like a grace, my dear,' said Trotty, taking his seat. 'They'd say a good one, I am sure, if they could. Many's the kind thing they say to me.'

'The Bells do, father?' laughed Meg, as she set the basin, and a knife and fork, before him. 'Well!'

'Seem to, my Pet,' said Trotty, falling to with great vigour. 'And where's the difference? If I hear 'em, what does it matter whether they speak it or not? Why bless you, my dear,' said Toby, pointing at the tower with his fork, and becoming more animated under the influence of dinner, 'how often have I heard them bells say, "Toby Veck, Toby Veck, keep a good heart Toby! Toby Veck, Toby Veck, keep a good heart Toby!" A million times? More!'

'Well, I never!' cried Meg.

She had, though – over and over again. For it was Toby's constant topic.

'When things is very bad,' said Trotty; 'very bad indeed, I mean; almost at the worst; then it's, "Toby Veck, Toby Veck, job coming soon, Toby! Toby Veck, Toby Veck, job coming soon, Toby!" That way.'

'And it comes – at last, father,' said Meg, with a touch of sadness in her pleasant voice.

'Always,' answered the unconscious Toby. 'Never fails'

While this discourse was holding, Trotty made no pause in his attack upon the savoury meat before him, but cut and ate, and cut and drank, and cut and chewed, and dodged about, from tripe to hot potato, and from hot potato back again to tripe, with an unctuous and unflagging relish. But happening now to look all round the street – in case anybody should be beckoning from any door or window, for a porter – his eyes, in coming back again, encountered Meg: sitting opposite to him, with her arms folded: and only busy in watching his progress with a smile of happiness.

'Why, Lord forgive me!' said Trotty, dropping his knife and fork. 'My dove! Meg! why didn't you tell me what a beast I was?'

'Father?'

'Sitting here,' said Trotty, in penitent explanation, 'cramming, and stuffing, and gorging myself; and you before me there, never so much as breaking your precious fast, nor wanting to, when – '

'But I have broken it, father,' interposed his daughter, laughing, 'all to bits. I have had my dinner.'

'Nonsense,' said Trotty. 'Two dinners in one day! It an't possible! You might as well tell me that two New Year's Days will come together, or that I have had a gold head all my life, and never changed it.'

'I have had my dinner, father, for all that,' said Meg, coming nearer to him. 'And if you'll go on with yours, I'll tell you how and where; and how your dinner came to be brought; and – and something else besides.'

Toby still appeared incredulous; but she looked into his face with her clear eyes, and laying her hand upon his shoulder, motioned him to go on while the meat was hot. So Trotty took up his knife and fork again, and went to work. But much more slowly than before and shaking his head, as if he were not at all pleased with himself.

'I had my dinner, father,' said Meg, after a little hesitation, 'with – with Richard. His dinner-time was early; and as he brought his dinner with him when he came to see me, we – we had it together, father.'

Trotty took a little beer, and smacked his lips. Then he said 'Oh!' – because she waited.

'And Richard says, father – ' Meg resumed. Then stopped.

'What does Richard say, Meg?' asked Toby.

'Richard says, father – ' Another stoppage.

'Richard's a long time saying it,' said Toby.

'He says then, father,' Meg continued, lifting up her eyes at last, and speaking in a tremble, but quite plainly; 'another year is nearly gone, and where is the use of waiting on from year to year, when it is so unlikely we shall ever be better off than we are now? He says we are poor now, father, and we shall be poor then; but we are young now, and years will make us old before we know it. He says that if we wait: people in our condition: until we see our way quite clearly, the way will be a narrow one indeed – the common way – the Grave, father.'

A bolder man than Trotty Veck must needs have drawn upon his boldness largely to deny it. Trotty held his peace.

'And how hard, father, to grow old, and die, and think we might have cheered and helped each other! How hard in all our lives to love each other; and to grieve, apart, to see each other working, changing, growing old and grey. Even if I got the better of it, and forgot him (which I never could), oh father dear, how hard to have a heart so full as mine is now, and live to have it slowly drained out every drop, without the recollection of one happy moment of a woman's life, to stay behind and comfort me, and make me better!'

Trotty sat quite still. Meg dried her eyes, and said more gaily: that is to say, with here a laugh, and there a sob, and here a laugh and sob together: 'So Richard says, father; as his work was yesterday made certain for some time to come, and as I love him and have loved him full three years – ah! longer than that, if he knew it! – will I marry him on New Year's Day; the best and happiest day, he says, in the whole year, and one that is almost sure to bring good fortune with it. It's a short notice, father – isn't it? – but I haven't my fortune to be settled, or my wedding dresses to be made, like the great ladies, father – have I? And he said so much, and said it in his way; so strong and earnest, and all the time so kind and gentle; that I said I'd come and talk to you, father. And as they paid the money for that work of mine this morning (unexpectedly, I am sure!), and as you have fared very poorly for a whole week, and as I couldn't help wishing there should be something to make this day a sort of holiday to you as well as a dear and happy day to me, father, I made a little treat and brought it to surprise you.'

'And see how he leaves it cooling on the step!' said another voice.

It was the voice of this same Richard, who had come upon them unobserved, and stood before the father and daughter: looking down upon them with a face as glowing as the iron on which his stout sledge-hammer daily rang. A handsome, well-made, powerful youngster he was; with eyes that sparkled like the red-hot droppings from a furnace fire; black hair that curled about his swarthy temples rarely; and a smile – a smile that bore out Meg's eulogium on his style of conversation.

'See how he leaves it cooling on the step!' said Richard. 'Meg don't know what he likes. Not she!'

Trotty, all action and enthusiasm, immediately reached up his hand to Richard, and was going to address him in a great hurry, when the house-door opened without any warning, and a footman very nearly put his foot in the tripe.

'Out of the ways here, will you! You must always go and be a settin' on our steps, must you! You can't go and give a turn to none of the neighbours never, can't you! *Will* you clear the road, or won't you?'

Strictly speaking, the last question was irrelevant, as they had already done it.

'What's the matter, what's the matter!' said the gentleman for whom the door was opened: coming out of the house at that kind of light-heavy pace – that peculiar compromise between a walk and a jog-trot – with which a gentleman upon the smooth downhill of life, wearing creaking boots, a watch-chain, and clean linen, *may* come out of his house: not only without any abatement of his dignity, but with an expression of having important and wealthy engagements elsewhere 'What's the matter What's the matter!'

'You're always a being begged, and prayed, upon your bended knees you are,' said the footman with great emphasis to Trotty Veck, 'to let our doorsteps be. Why don't you let 'em be? CAN'T you let 'em be?'

'There. That'll do, that'll do!' said the gentleman. 'Halloa there! Porter!' beckoning with his head to Trotty Veck. 'Come here. What's that? Your dinner?'

'Yes, sir,' said Trotty, leaving it behind him in a corner.

'Don't leave it there,' exclaimed the gentleman. 'Bring it here, bring it here. So! This is your dinner, is it?'

'Yes, sir,' repeated Trotty, looking, with a fixed eye and a watery mouth, at the piece of tripe he had reserved for a last delicious tit-bit; which the gentleman was now turning over and over on the end of the fork.

Two other gentlemen had come out with him. One was a low-spirited gentleman of middle age, of a meagre habit, and a disconsolate face; who kept his hands continually in the pockets of his scanty pepper-and-salt trousers, very large and dog's-eared from that custom; and was not particularly well brushed or washed. The other, a full-sized, sleek, well-conditioned gentleman, in a blue coat with bright buttons, and a white cravat. This gentleman had a very red face, as if an undue proportion of the blood in his body were squeezed up into his head; which perhaps accounted for his having also the appearance of being rather cold about the heart.

He who had Toby's meat upon the fork, called to the first one by the name of Filer; and they both drew near together. Mr Filer, being exceedingly short-sighted, was obliged to go so close to the remnant of Toby's dinner before he could make out what it was that Toby's heart leaped up into his mouth. But Mr Filer didn't eat it. 'This is a description of animal food, Alderman,' said Filer, making little punches in it, with

Mr Filer, being exceedingly short-sighted

a pencil-case, 'commonly known to the labouring population of this country, by the name of tripe.'

The Alderman laughed, and winked; for he was a merry fellow, Alderman Cute. Oh, and a sly fellow too! A knowing fellow. Up to everything. Not to be imposed upon. Deep in the people's hearts! He knew them, Cute did. I believe you!

'But who eats tripe?' said Mr Filer, looking round. 'Tripe is without an exception the least economical, and the most wasteful article of consumption that the markets of this country can by possibility produce. The loss upon a pound of tripe has been found to be, in the boiling, seven-eighths of a fifth more than the loss upon a pound of any other

animal substance whatever. Tripe is more expensive, properly understood, than the hothouse pineapple. Taking into account the number of
animals slaughtered yearly within the bills of mortality alone; and forming
a low estimate of the quantity of tripe which the carcases of those animals,
reasonably well butchered, would yield; I find that the waste on that
amount of tripe, if boiled, would victual a garrison of five hundred men
for five months of thirty-one days each, and a February over. The Waste,
the Waste!'

Trotty stood aghast, and his legs shook under him. He seemed to have
starved a garrison of five hundred men with his own hand.

'Who eats tripe?' said Mr Filer, warmly. 'Who eats tripe?'

Trotty made a miserable bow.

'You do, do you?' said Mr Filer. 'Then I'll tell you something. You
snatch your tripe, my friend, out of the mouths of widows and orphans.'

'I hope not, sir,' said Trotty, faintly. 'I'd sooner die of want!'

'Divide the amount of tripe before mentioned, Alderman,' said Mr
Filer, 'by the estimated number of existing widows and orphans, and the
result will be one pennyweight of tripe to each. Not a grain is left for that
man. Consequently, he's a robber.'

Trotty was so shocked, that it gave him no concern to see the Alderman
finish the tripe himself. It was a relief to get rid of it, anyhow.

'And what do you say?' asked the Alderman, jocosely, of the red-faced
gentleman in the blue coat. 'You have heard friend Filer. What do you
say?'

'What's it possible to say?' returned the gentleman. 'What *is* to be
said? Who can take any interest in a fellow like this,' meaning Trotty; 'in
such degenerate times as these? Look at him! What an object! The good
old times, the grand old times, the great old times! *Those* were the times
for a bold peasantry, and all that sort of thing. Those were the times for
every sort of thing, in fact. There's nothing nowadays. Ah!' sighed the
red-faced gentleman. 'The good old times, the good old times!'

The gentleman didn't specify what particular times he alluded to; nor
did he say whether he objected to the present times, from a disinterested
consciousness that they had done nothing very remarkable in producing
himself.

'The good old times, the good old times,' repeated the gentleman.
'What times they were! They were the only times. It's of no use talking
about any other times, or discussing what the people are in these times.

You don't call these, times, do you? I don't. Look into Strutt's Costumes, and see what a Porter used to be, in any of the good old English reigns.'

'He hadn't, in his very best circumstances, a shirt to his back, or a stocking to his foot; and there was scarcely a vegetable in all England for him to put into his mouth,' said Mr Filer. 'I can prove it, by tables.'

But still the red-faced gentleman extolled the good old times, the grand old times, the great old times. No matter what anybody else said, he still went turning round and round in one set form of words concerning them; as a poor squirrel turns and turns in its revolving cage; touching the mechanism, and trick of which, it has probably quite as distinct perceptions, as ever this red-faced gentleman had of his deceased Millennium.

It is possible that poor old Trotty's faith in these very vague Old Times was not entirely destroyed, for he felt vague enough, at that moment. One thing, however, was plain to him, in the midst of his distress; to wit, that however these gentlemen might differ in details, his misgivings of that morning, and of many other mornings, were well founded. 'No, no. We can't go right or do right,' thought Trotty in despair. 'There is no good in us. We are born bad!'

But Trotty had a father's heart within him; which had somehow got into his breast in spite of this decree; and he could not bear that Meg, in the blush of her brief joy, should have her fortune read by these wise gentlemen. 'God help her,' thought poor Trotty. 'She will know it soon enough.'

He anxiously signed, therefore, to the young smith, to take her away. But he was so busy, talking to her softly at a little distance, that he only became conscious of this desire, simultaneously with Alderman Cute. Now, the Alderman had not yet had his say, but *he* was a philosopher, too – practical, though! Oh, very practical! – and, as he had no idea of losing any portion of his audience, he cried 'Stop!'

'Now, you know,' said the Alderman, addressing his two friends, with a self-complacent smile upon his face which was habitual to him, 'I am a plain man, and a practical man; and I go to work in a plain practical way. That's my way. There is not the least mystery or difficulty in dealing with this sort of people if you only understand 'em, and can talk to 'em in their own manner. Now, you Porter! Don't you ever tell me or anybody else, my friend, that you haven't always enough to eat, and of the best; because I know better. I have tasted your tripe, you know, and you can't 'chaff' me. You understand what 'chaff' means, eh? That's the right word, isn't it? Ha, ha, ha! Lord bless you,' said the Alderman, turning to his friends again, 'it's the easiest thing on earth to deal with this sort of people, if you understand 'em.'

Famous man for the common people, Alderman Cute! Never out of temper with them! Easy, affable, joking, knowing gentleman!

'You see, my friend,' pursued the Alderman, 'there's a great deal of nonsense talked about Want – "hard up", you know that's the phrase, isn't it? ha! ha! ha! – and I intend to Put it Down. There's a certain amount of cant in vogue about Starvation, and I mean to Put it Down! That's all! Lord bless you,' said the Alderman, turning to his friends again, 'you may Put Down anything among this sort of people, if you only know the way to set about it!'

Trotty took Meg's hand and drew it through his arm. He didn't seem to know what he was doing though.

'Your daughter, eh?' said the Alderman, chucking her familiarly under the chin.

Always affable with the working classes, Alderman Cute! Knew what pleased them! Not a bit of pride!

'Where's her mother?' asked that worthy gentleman.

'Dead,' said Toby. 'Her mother got up linen; and was called to Heaven when She was born.'

'Not to get up linen *there*, I suppose,' remarked the Alderman pleasantly.

Toby might or might not have been able to separate his wife in Heaven from her old pursuits. But query: If Mrs Alderman Cute had gone to Heaven, would Mr Alderman Cute have pictured her as holding any state or station there?

'And you're making love to her, are you?' said Cute to the young smith.

'Yes,' returned Richard quickly, for he was nettled by the question. 'And we are going to be married on New Year's Day.'

'What do you mean!' cried Filer sharply. 'Married!'

'Why, yes, we're thinking of it, master,' said Richard. 'We're rather in a hurry, you see, in case it should be Put Down first.'

'Ah!' cried Filer, with a groan. 'Put *that* down indeed, Alderman, and you'll do something. Married! Married! The ignorance of the first principles of political economy on the part of these people; their improvidence; their wickedness; is, by Heavens! enough to – Now look at that couple, will you!'

Well! They were worth looking at. And marriage seemed as reasonable and fair a deed as they need have in contemplation.

'A man may live to be as old as Methusaleh,' said Mr Filer, 'and may labour all his life for the benefit of such people as those; and may heap up facts on figures, facts on figures, facts on figures, mountains high and dry; and he can no more hope to persuade 'em that they have no right or business to be married, than he can hope to persuade 'em that they have no earthly right or business to be born. And *that* we know they haven't. We reduced it to a mathematical certainty long ago.'

Alderman Cute was mightily diverted, and laid his right forefinger on the side of his nose, as much as to say to both his friends, 'Observe me, will you! Keep your eye on the practical man!' – and called Meg to him.

'Come here, my girl!' said Alderman Cute.

The young blood of her lover had been mounting, wrathfully, within the last few minutes; and he was indisposed to let her come. But, setting a constraint upon himself, he came forward with a stride as Meg approached, and stood beside her. Trotty kept her hand within his arm still, but looked from face to face as wildly as a sleeper in a dream.

'Now, I'm going to give you a word or two of good advice, my girl,' said the Alderman, in his nice easy way. 'It's my place to give advice, you know, because I'm a Justice. You know I'm a Justice, don't you?'

Meg timidly said, 'Yes.' But everybody knew Alderman Cute was a Justice! Oh dear, so active a Justice always! Who such a mote of brightness in the public eye, as Cute!

'You are going to be married, you say,' pursued the Alderman. 'Very unbecoming and indelicate in one of your sex! But never mind that. After you are married, you'll quarrel with your husband, and come to be a distressed wife. You may think not: but you will, because I tell you so. Now I give you fair warning, that I have made up my mind to Put distressed wives Down. So, don't be brought before me. You'll have children – boys. Those boys will grow up bad of course, and run wild in the streets, without shoes and stockings. Mind, my young friend! I'll convict 'em summarily, every one, for I am determined to Put boys without shoes and stockings, Down. Perhaps your husband will die young (most likely) and leave you with a baby. Then you'll be turned out of doors, and wander up and down the streets. Now, don't wander near me, my dear, for I am resolved to Put all wandering mothers Down. All young mothers, of all sorts and kinds, it's my determination to Put

Down. Don't think to plead illness as an excuse with me; or babies as an excuse with me; for all sick persons and young children (I hope you know the Church Service, but I'm afraid not) I am determined to Put Down. And if you attempt, desperately, and ungratefully, and impiously, and fraudulently attempt, to drown yourself, or hang yourself, I'll have no pity on you, for I have made up my mind to Put all suicide Down. If there is one thing,' said the Alderman, with his self-satisfied smile, 'on which I can be said to have made up my mind more than on another, it is to Put suicide Down. So don't try it on. That's the phrase, isn't it! Ha, ha! now we understand each other.'

Toby knew not whether to be agonised or glad to see that Meg had turned a deadly white, and dropped her lover's hand.

'As for you, you dull dog,' said the Alderman, turning with even increased cheerfulness and urbanity to the young smith, 'what are you thinking of being married for? What do you want to be married for, you silly fellow! If I was a fine, young, strapping chap like you, I should be ashamed of being milksop enough to pin myself to a woman's apron strings! Why, she'll be an old woman before you're a middle-aged man! And a pretty figure you'll cut then, with a draggle-tailed wife and a crowd of squalling children crying after you wherever you go!'

Oh, he knew how to banter the common people, Alderman Cute!

'There! Go along with you,' said the Alderman, 'and repent. Don't make such a fool of yourself as to get married on New Year's Day. You'll think very differently of it long before next New Year's Day; a trim young fellow like you, with all the girls looking after you. There! Go along with you!' They went along. Not arm in arm, or hand in hand, or interchanging bright glances: but she in tears, he gloomy and down-looking. Were these the hearts that had so lately made old Toby's leap up from its faintness? No, no. The Alderman (a blessing on his head!) had Put *them* Down.

'As you happen to be here,' said the Alderman to Toby, 'you shall carry a letter for me. Can you be quick? You're an old man.'

Toby, who had been looking after Meg, quite stupidly, made shift to murmur out that he was very quick, and very strong.

'How old are you?' enquired the Alderman.

'I'm over sixty, sir,' said Toby.

'Oh! This man's a great deal past the average age, you know,' cried Mr Filer, breaking in as if his patience would bear some trying, but this really was carrying matters a little too far.

'I feel I'm intruding, sir,' said Toby. 'I – I misdoubted it this morning. Oh dear me!'

The Alderman cut him short by giving him the letter from his pocket. Toby would have got a shilling too; but Mr Filer clearly showing that in that case he would rob a certain given number of persons of ninepence-halfpenny a-piece, he only got sixpence; and thought himself very well off to get that.

Then the Alderman gave an arm to each of his friends, and walked off in high feather; but he immediately came hurrying back alone as if he had forgotten something.

'Porter!' said the Alderman.

'Sir!' said Toby.

'Take care of that daughter of yours. She's much too handsome.'

'Even her good looks are stolen from somebody or other I suppose,' thought Toby, looking at the sixpence in his hand, and thinking of the tripe. 'She's been and robbed five hundred ladies of a bloom a-piece, I shouldn't wonder. It's very dreadful!'

'She's much too handsome, my man,' repeated the Alderman. 'The chances are, that she'll come to no good, I clearly see. Observe what I say. Take care of her!' With which, he hurried off again.

'Wrong every way. Wrong every way!' said Trotty, clasping his hands. 'Born bad. No business here!'

The Chimes came clashing in upon him as he said the words. Full, loud, and sounding – but with no encouragement. No, not a drop.

'The tune's changed,' cried the old man, as he listened. 'There's not a word of all that fancy in it. Why should there be? I have no business with the New Year nor with the old one neither. Let me die!'

Still the Bells, pealing forth their changes, made the very air spin. Put 'em down, Put 'em down! Good old Times, Good old Times! Facts and Figures, Facts and Figures! Put 'em down, Put 'em down! If they said anything they said this, till the brain of Toby reeled.

He pressed his bewildered head between his hands, as if to keep it from splitting asunder. A well-timed action, as it happened; for finding the letter in one of them, and being by that means reminded of his charge, he fell, mechanically, into his usual trot, and trotted off.

THE SECOND QUARTER

The letter Toby had received from Alderman Cute, was addressed to a great man in the great district of the town. The greatest district of the town. It must have been the greatest district of the town, because it was commonly called The World by its inhabitants. The letter positively seemed heavier in Toby's hand, than another letter. Not because the Alderman had sealed it with a very large coat of arms and no end of wax, but because of the weighty name on the superscription, and the ponderous amount of gold and silver with which it was associated.

'How different from us!' thought Toby, in all simplicity and earnestness, as he looked at the direction. 'Divide the lively turtles in the bills of mortality, by the number of gentlefolks able to buy 'em; and whose share does he take but his own! As to snatching tripe from anybody's mouth – he'd scorn it!'

With the involuntary homage due to such an exalted character, Toby interposed a corner of his apron between the letter and his fingers.

'His children,' said Trotty, and a mist rose before his eyes; 'his daughters – Gentlemen may win their hearts and marry them; they may be happy wives and mothers; they may be handsome like my darling M—e – '

He couldn't finish the name. The final letter swelled in his throat, to the size of the whole alphabet.

'Never mind,' thought Trotty 'I know what I mean. That's more than enough for me.' And with this consolatory rumination, trotted on.

It was a hard frost, that day. The air was bracing, crisp, and clear. The wintry sun, though powerless for warmth, looked brightly down upon the ice it was too weak to melt, and set a radiant glory there. At other times, Trotty might have learned a poor man's lesson from the wintry sun; but he was past that now.

The Year was Old that day. The patient Year had lived through the reproaches and misuses of its slanderers, and faithfully performed its work. Spring, summer, autumn, winter. It had laboured through the destined round, and now laid down its weary head to die. Shut out from hope, high impulse, active happiness, itself, but active messenger of many joys to others, it made appeal in its decline to have its toiling days and patient hours remembered, and to die in peace. Trotty might have read a poor man's allegory in the fading year; but he was past that now.

And only he? Or has the like appeal been ever made, by seventy years at once upon an English labourer's head, and made in vain!

The streets were full of motion, and the shops were decked out gaily. The New Year, like an Infant Heir to the whole world, was waited for, with welcomes, presents, and rejoicings. There were books and toys for the New Year, glittering trinkets for the New Year, dresses for the New Year, schemes of fortune for the New Year; new inventions to beguile it. Its life was parcelled out in almanacks and pocket-books; the coming of its moons, and stars, and tides, was known beforehand to the moment; all the workings of its seasons in their days and nights, were calculated with as much precision as Mr Filer could work sums in men and women.

The New Year, the New Year. Everywhere the New Year! The Old Year was already looked upon as dead; and its effects were selling cheap, like some drowned mariner's aboard ship. Its patterns were Last Year's and going at a sacrifice, before its breath was gone. Its treasures were mere dirt, beside the riches of its unborn successor!

Trotty had no portion, to his thinking, in the New Year or the Old.

'Put 'em down, Put 'em down! Facts and Figures, Facts and Figures! Good old Times, Good old Times! Put 'em down, Put 'em down!' – his trot went to that measure, and would fit itself to nothing else.

But even that one, melancholy as it was, brought him, in due time, to the end of his journey. To the mansion of Sir Joseph Bowley, Member of Parliament.

The door was opened by a Porter. Such a Porter! Not of Toby's order. Quite another thing. His place was the ticket though; not Toby's.

This Porter underwent some hard panting before he could speak; having breathed himself by coming incautiously out of his chair, without first taking time to think about it and compose his mind. When he had found his voice – which it took him some time to do, for it was a long way off, and hidden under a load of meat – he said in a fat whisper,

'Who's it from?'

Toby told him.

'You're to take it in, yourself,' said the Porter, pointing to a room at the end of a long passage, opening from the hall. 'Everything goes straight in on this day of the year. You're not a bit too soon, for the carriage is at the door now, and they have only come to town for a couple of hours, a' purpose.'

Toby wiped his feet (which were quite dry already) with great care, and took the way pointed out to him; observing as he went that it was an awfully grand house, but hushed and covered up, as if the family were in the country. Knocking at the room door, he was told to enter from within; and doing so found himself in a spacious library, where, at a table strewn with files and papers, were a stately lady in a bonnet; and a not very stately gentleman in black who wrote from her dictation; while another, and an older, and a much statelier gentleman, whose hat and cane were on the table, walked up and down, with one hand in his breast, and looked complacently from time to time at his own picture – full length; a very full length – hanging over the fireplace.

'What is this?' said the last-named gentleman. 'Mr Fish, will you have the goodness to attend?'

Mr Fish begged pardon, and taking the letter from Toby, handed it, with great respect.

'From Alderman Cute, Sir Joseph.'

'Is this all? Have you nothing else, Porter?' enquired Sir Joseph.

Toby replied in the negative.

'You have no bill or demand upon me; my name is Bowley, Sir Joseph Bowley; of any kind from anybody, have you?' said Sir Joseph. 'If you have, present it. There is a cheque-book by the side of Mr Fish. I allow nothing to be carried into the New Year. Every description of account is settled in this house at the close of the old one. So that if death was to – to – '

'To cut,' suggested Mr Fish.

'To sever, sir,' returned Sir Joseph, with great asperity, 'the cord of existence – my affairs would be found, I hope, in a state of preparation.'

'My dear Sir Joseph!' said the lady, who was greatly younger than the gentleman. 'How shocking!'

'My Lady Bowley,' returned Sir Joseph, floundering now and then, as in the great depth of his observations, 'at this season of the year we should think of – of – ourselves. We should look into our – our accounts. We should feel that every return of so eventful a period in human transactions, involves matters of deep moment between a man and his – and his banker.'

Sir Joseph delivered these words as if he felt the full morality of what he was saying; and desired that even Trotty should have an opportunity of being improved by such discourse. Possibly he had this end before him in still forbearing to break the seal of the letter, and in telling Trotty to wait where he was, a minute.

'You were desiring Mr Fish to say, my lady,' observed Sir Joseph.

'Mr Fish has said that, I believe,' returned his lady, glancing at the letter. 'But, upon my word, Sir Joseph, I don't think I can let it go after all. It is so very dear.'

'What is dear?' enquired Sir Joseph.

'That Charity, my love. They only allow two votes for a subscription of five pounds. Really monstrous!'

'My Lady Bowley,' returned Sir Joseph, 'you surprise me. Is the luxury of feeling in proportion to the number of votes; or is it, to a rightly constituted mind, in proportion to the number of applicants, and the wholesome state of mind to which their canvassing reduces them? Is there no excitement of the purest kind in having two votes to dispose of among fifty people?'

'Not to me, I acknowledge,' replied the lady. 'It bores one. Besides, one can't oblige one's acquaintance. But you are the Poor Man's Friend, you know, Sir Joseph. You think otherwise.'

'I *am* the Poor Man's Friend,' observed Sir Joseph, glancing at the poor man present. 'As such I may be taunted. As such I have been taunted. But I ask no other title.'

'Bless him for a noble gentleman!' thought Trotty.

'I don't agree with Cute here, for instance,' said Sir Joseph, holding out the letter. 'I don't agree with the Filer party. I don't agree with any party. My friend the Poor Man, has no business with anything of that sort, and nothing of that sort has any business with him. My friend the Poor Man, in my district, is my business. No man or body of men has any right to interfere between my friend and me. That is the ground I take. I assume a – a paternal character towards my friend. I say, "My good fellow, I will treat you paternally." '

Toby listened with great gravity, and began to feel more comfortable.

'Your only business, my good fellow,' pursued Sir Joseph, looking abstractly at Toby; 'your only business in life is with me. You needn't trouble yourself to think about anything. I will think for you; I know what is good for you; I am your perpetual parent. Such is the dispensation of an all-wise Providence! Now, the design of your creation is: not that you should swill, and guzzle, and associate your enjoyments, brutally, with food' – Toby thought remorsefully of the tripe – 'but that you should feel the Dignity of Labour; go forth erect into the cheerful morning air, and – and stop there. Live hard and temperately, be respectful, exercise your self-denial, bring up your family on next to nothing, pay your rent as regularly as the clock strikes, be punctual in your dealings (I set you a good example; you will find Mr Fish, my confidential secretary, with a cash-box before him at all times); and you may trust me to be your Friend and Father.'

'Nice children, indeed, Sir Joseph!' said the lady, with a shudder. 'Rheumatisms and fevers and crooked legs and asthmas and all kinds of horrors!'

'My lady,' returned Sir Joseph, with solemnity, 'not the less am I the Poor Man's Friend and Father. Not the less shall he receive encouragement at my hands. Every quarter-day he will be put in communication with Mr Fish. Every New Year's Day, myself and friends will drink his health. Once every year, myself and friends will address him with the deepest feeling. Once in his life, he may even perhaps receive; in public, in the presence of the gentry; a Trifle from a Friend. And when, upheld no more by these stimulants, and the Dignity of Labour, he sinks into his comfortable grave, then my lady' – here Sir Joseph blew his nose – 'I will be a Friend and Father – on the same terms – to his children.'

Toby was greatly moved.

'Oh! You have a thankful family, Sir Joseph!' cried his wife.

'My lady,' said Sir Joseph, quite majestically, 'Ingratitude is known to be the sin of that class. I expect no other return.'

'Ah! Born bad!' thought Toby. 'Nothing melts us.'

'What man can do, *I* do,' pursued Sir Joseph. 'I do my duty as the Poor Man's Friend and Father; and I endeavour to educate his mind, by inculcating on all occasions the one great moral lesson which that class requires. That is, entire Dependence on myself. They have no business whatever with – with themselves. If wicked and designing persons tell them otherwise, and they become impatient and discontented, and are guilty of insubordinate conduct and black-hearted ingratitude; which is undoubtedly the case; I am their Friend and Father still. It is so Ordained. It is in the nature of things.'

With that great sentiment, he opened the Alderman' s letter; and read it.

'Very polite and attentive, I am sure!' exclaimed Sir Joseph. 'My lady, the Alderman is so obliging as to remind me that he has had "the distinguished honour" – he is very good – of meeting me at the house of our mutual friend Deedles, the banker; and he does me the favour to enquire whether it will be agreeable to me to have Will Fern put down.'

'*Most* agreeable!' replied my Lady Bowley. 'The worst man among them! He has been committing a robbery, I hope?'

'Why no,' said Sir Joseph, referring to the letter. 'Not quite. Very near. Not quite. He came up to London, it seems, to look for employment (to better himself – that's his story), and being found at night asleep in a shed, was taken into custody and carried next morning before the Alderman. The Alderman observes (very properly) that he is determined to put this sort of thing down; and that if it will be agreeable to me to have Will Fern put down, he will be happy to begin with him.'

'Let him be made an example of, by all means,' returned the lady. 'Last winter, when I introduced pinking and eyelet-holing among the men and boys in the village, as a nice evening employment, and had the lines,

> Oh let us love our occupations,
> Bless the squire and his relations,
> Live upon our daily rations,
> And always know our proper stations,

set to music on the new system, for them to sing the while; this very Fern – I see him now – touched that hat of his, and said, "I humbly ask your pardon, my lady, but *an't* I something different from a great girl?" I expected it, of course; who can expect anything but insolence and ingratitude from that class of people! That is not to the purpose, however. Sir Joseph! Make an example of him!'

'Hem!' coughed Sir Joseph. 'Mr Fish, if you'll have the goodness to attend – '

Mr Fish immediately seized his pen, and wrote from Sir Joseph's dictation.

'Private. My dear sir. I am very much indebted to you for your courtesy in the matter of the man William Fern, of whom, I regret to add, I can say nothing favourable. I have uniformly considered myself in the light of his Friend and Father, but have been repaid (a common case I grieve to say) with ingratitude, and constant opposition to my plans. He is a turbulent and rebellious spirit. His character will not bear investigation. Nothing will persuade him to be happy when he might. Under these circumstances, it appears to me, I own, that when he comes before you again (as you informed me he promised to do tomorrow, pending your enquiries, and I think he may be so far relied upon), his committal for some short term as a Vagabond, would be a service to society, and would be a salutary example in a country where – for the sake of those who are, through good and evil report, the Friends and Fathers of the Poor, as well as with a view to that, generally speaking, misguided class themselves – examples are greatly needed. And I am,' and so forth.

'It appears,' remarked Sir Joseph when he had signed this letter, and Mr Fish was sealing it, 'as if this were Ordained: really. At the close of the year, I wind up my account and strike my balance, even with William Fern!'

Trotty, who had long ago relapsed, and was very low-spirited, stepped forward with a rueful face to take the letter.

'With my compliments and thanks,' said Sir Joseph. 'Stop!'

'Stop!' echoed Mr Fish.

'You have heard, perhaps,' said Sir Joseph, oracularly, 'certain remarks into which I have been led respecting the solemn period of time at which we have arrived, and the duty imposed upon us of settling our affairs, and being prepared. You have observed that I don't shelter myself behind my superior standing in society, but that Mr Fish – that gentleman – has a cheque-book at his elbow, and is in fact here, to enable me to turn over a perfectly new leaf, and enter on the epoch before us with a clean account. Now my friend, can you lay your hand upon your heart, and say that you also have made preparations for a New Year?'

'I am afraid sir,' stammered Trotty, looking meekly at him, 'that I am a – a – little behindhand with the world.'

'Behindhand with the world!' repeated Sir Joseph Bowley, in a tone of terrible distinctness.

'I am afraid, sir,' faltered Trotty, 'that there's a matter of ten or twelve shillings owing to Mrs Chickenstalker.'

'To Mrs Chickenstalker!' repeated Sir Joseph, in the same tone as before.

'A shop, sir,' exclaimed Toby, 'in the general line. Also a – a little money on account of rent. A very little, sir. It oughtn't to be owing, I know, but we have been hard put to it, indeed!'

Sir Joseph looked at his lady, and at Mr Fish, and at Trotty, one after another, twice all round. He then made a despondent gesture with both hands at once, as if he gave the thing up altogether.

'How a man, even among this improvident and impracticable race; an old man; a man grown grey; can look a New Year in the face, with his affairs in this condition; how he can lie down on his bed at night, and get up again in the morning, and – There!' he said, turning his back on Trotty. 'Take the letter. Take the letter!'

'I heartily wish it was otherwise, sir,' said Trotty, anxious to excuse himself. 'We have been tried very hard.'

Sir Joseph still repeating 'Take the letter, take the letter!' and Mr Fish not only saying the same thing, but giving additional force to the request by motioning the bearer to the door, he had nothing for it but to make his bow and leave the house. And in the street, poor Trotty pulled his worn old hat down on his head, to hide the grief he felt at getting no hold on the New Year, anywhere.

He didn't even lift his hat to look up at the Bell tower when he came to the old church on his return. He halted there a moment, from habit: and knew that it was growing dark, and that the steeple rose above him, indistinct and faint, in the murky air. He knew, too, that the Chimes would ring immediately; and that they sounded to his fancy, at such a time, like voices in the clouds. But he only made the more haste to deliver the Alderman's letter, and get out of the way before they began; for he dreaded to hear them tagging 'Friends and Fathers, Friends and Fathers,' to the burden they had rung out last.

Toby discharged himself of his commission, therefore, with all possible speed, and set off trotting homeward. But what with his pace, which was at best an awkward one in the street; and what with his hat, which didn't improve it; he trotted against somebody in less than no time, and was sent staggering out into the road.

'I beg your pardon, I'm sure!' said Trotty, pulling up his hat in great confusion, and between the hat and the torn lining, fixing his head into a kind of beehive. 'I hope I haven't hurt you.'

As to hurting anybody, Toby was not such an absolute Samson, but that he was much more likely to be hurt himself: and indeed, he had flown out into the road, like a shuttlecock. He had such an opinion of his own strength, however, that he was in real concern for the other party: and said again,

'I hope I haven't hurt you?'

The man against whom he had run; a sun-browned, sinewy, country-looking man, with grizzled hair, and a rough chin; stared at him for a moment, as if he suspected him to be in jest. But satisfied of his good faith, he answered: 'No, friend. You have not hurt me.'

'Nor the child, I hope?' said Trotty.

'Nor the child,' returned the man. 'I thank you kindly.'

As he said so, he glanced at a little girl he carried in his arms, asleep; and shading her face with the long end of the poor handkerchief he wore about his throat, went slowly on.

The tone in which he said 'I thank you kindly', penetrated Trotty's heart. He was so jaded and footsore, and so soiled with travel, and looked about him so forlorn and strange, that it was a comfort to him to be able to thank anyone: no matter for how little. Toby stood gazing after him as he plodded wearily away: with the child's arm clinging round his neck.

At the figure in the worn shoes – now the very shade and ghost of shoes – rough leather leggings, common frock, and broad slouched hat, Trotty stood gazing: blind to the whole street. And at the child's arm, clinging round its neck.

Before he merged into the darkness, the traveller stopped; and looking round, and seeing Trotty standing there yet, seemed undecided whether to return or go on. After doing first the one and then the other, he came back; and Trotty went half way to meet him.

'You can tell me, perhaps,' said the man with a faint smile, 'and if you can I am sure you will, and I'd rather ask you than another – where Alderman Cute lives.'

'Close at hand,' replied Toby. 'I'll show you his house with pleasure.'

'I was to have gone to him elsewhere tomorrow,' said the man, accompanying Toby, 'but I'm uneasy under suspicion, and want to clear myself, and to be free to go and seek my bread – I don't know where. So, maybe he'll forgive my going to his house tonight.'

'It's impossible,' cried Toby with a start, 'that your name's Fern!'

'Eh!' cried the other, turning on him in astonishment.

'Fern! Will Fern!' said Trotty.

'That's my name,' replied the other.

'Why then,' cried Trotty, seizing him by the arm, and looking cautiously round, 'for Heaven's sake don't go to him! Don't go to him! He'll put you down as sure as ever you were born. Here! come up this alley, and I'll tell you what I mean. Don't go to *him*.'

His new acquaintance looked as if he thought him mad; but he bore him company nevertheless. When they were shrouded from observation, Trotty told him what he knew, and what character he had received, and all about it.

The subject of his history listened to it with a calmness that surprised him. He did not contradict or interrupt it, once. He nodded his head now and then – more in corroboration of an old and worn-out story, it appeared, than in refutation of it; and once or twice threw back his hat, and passed his freckled hand over a brow, where every furrow he had ploughed seemed to have set its image in little. But he did no more.

'It's true enough in the main,' he said, 'master. I could sift grain from husk here and there, but let it be as 'tis. What odds? I have gone against his plans; to my misfortun'. I can't help it; I should do the like tomorrow. As to character, them gentlefolks will search and search, and pry and pry, and have it as free from spot or speck in us, afore they'll help us to a dry good word! Well! I hope they don't lose good opinion as easy as we do, or their lives is strict indeed, and hardly worth the keeping. For myself, master, I never took with that hand' – holding it before him – 'what wasn't my own; and never held it back from work, however hard, or poorly paid. Whoever can deny it, let him chop it off! But when work won't maintain me like a human creetur; when my living is so bad, that I am Hungry, out of doors and in; when I see a whole working life begin that way, go on that way, and end that way, without a chance or change; then I say to the gentlefolks, "Keep away from me! Let my cottage be. My doors is dark enough without your darkening of 'em more. Don't look for me to come up into the Park to help the show when there's a Birthday or a fine Speechmaking, or what not. Act your Plays and Games without me, and be welcome to 'em and enjoy 'em. We've nowt to do with one another. I'm best let alone!" '

Seeing that the child in his arms had opened her eyes, and was looking about her in wonder, he checked himself to say a word or two of foolish prattle in her ear, and stand her on the ground beside him. Then slowly winding one of her long tresses round and round his rough forefinger like a ring, while she hung about his dusty leg, he said to Trotty,

'I'm not a cross-grained man by natur', I believe; and easy satisfied, I'm sure. I bear no ill will against none of 'em: I only want to live like one of the Almighty's creeturs. I can't, I don't; and so there's a pit dug between me and them that can and do. There's others like me. You might tell 'em off by hundreds and by thousands, sooner than by ones.'

Trotty knew he spoke the Truth in this, and shook his head to signify as much.

'I've got a bad name this way,' said Fern; 'and I'm not likely, I'm afeared, to get a better. 'Tan't lawful to be out of sorts, and I AM out of sorts, though God knows I'd sooner bear a cheerful spirit if I could. Well! I don't know as this Alderman could hurt *me* much by sending me to gaol; but without a friend to speak a word for me, he might do it; and you see – !' pointing downward with his finger, at the child.

'She has a beautiful face,' said Trotty.

'Why yes!' replied the other in a low voice, as he gently turned it up with both his hands towards his own, and looked upon it steadfastly. 'I've thought so, many times. I've thought so, when my hearth was very cold, and cupboard very bare. I thought so t'other night, when we were taken like two thieves. But they – they shouldn't try the little face too often, should they, Lilian? That's hardly fair upon a man!'

He sank his voice so low, and gazed upon her with an air so stern and strange, that Toby, to divert the current of his thoughts, enquired if his wife were living.

'I never had one,' he returned, shaking his head. 'She's my brother's child: an orphan. Nine year old, though you'd hardly think it; but she's tired and worn out now. They'd have taken care on her, the Union; eight-and-twenty mile away from where we live; between four walls (as they took care of my old father when he couldn't work no more, though he didn't trouble 'em long) but I took her instead, and she's lived with me ever since. Her mother had a friend once, in London here. We are trying to find her, and to find work too; but it's a large place. Never mind. More room for us to walk about in, Lilly!'

Meeting the child's eyes with a smile which melted Toby more than tears, he shook him by the hand.

'I don't so much as know your name,' he said, 'but I've opened my heart free to you, for I'm thankful to you; with good reason. I'll take your advice, and keep clear of this – '

'Justice,' suggested Toby.

'Ah!' he said. 'If that's the name they give him. This Justice. And tomorrow will try whether there's better fortun' to be met with, somewheres near London. Good-night. A Happy New Year!'

'Stay!' cried Trotty, catching at his hand, as he relaxed his grip. 'Stay! The New Year never can be happy to me, if we part like this. The New Year never can be happy to me, if I see the child and you, go wandering away, you don't know where, without a shelter for your heads. Come home with me! I'm a poor man, living in a poor place; but I can give you lodging for one night and never miss it. Come home with me! Here! I'll take her!' cried Trotty, lifting up the child. 'A pretty one! I'd carry twenty times her weight, and never know I'd got it. Tell me if I go too quick for you. I'm very fast. I always was!' Trotty said this, taking about six of his trotting paces to one stride of his fatigued companion; and with his thin legs quivering again, beneath the load he bore.

'Why, she's as light,' said Trotty, trotting in his speech as well as in his gait; for he couldn't bear to be thanked, and dreaded a moment's pause; 'as light as a feather. Lighter than a Peacock's feather – a great deal lighter. Here we are, and here we go! Round this first turning to the right, Uncle Will, and past the pump, and sharp off up the passage to the left, right opposite the public-house. Here we are and here we go! Cross over, Uncle Will, and mind the kidney pieman at the corner! Here we are and here we go! Down the Mews here, Uncle Will, and stop at the black door, with 'T. Veck, Ticket Porter' wrote upon a board; and here we are and here we go, and here we are indeed, my precious Meg, surprising you!'

With which words Trotty, in a breathless state, set the child down before his daughter in the middle of the floor. The little visitor looked once at Meg; and doubting nothing in that face, but trusting everything she saw there; ran into her arms.

'Here we are and here we go!' cried Trotty, running round the room, and choking audibly. 'Here, Uncle Will! Here's a fire you know! Why don't you come to the fire? Oh here we are and here we go! Meg, my precious darling, where's the kettle? Here it is and here it goes, and it'll bile in no time!'

Trotty really had picked up the kettle somewhere or other in the course of his wild career, and now put it on the fire: while Meg, seating the child in a warm corner, knelt down on the ground before her, and pulled off her shoes, and dried her wet feet on a cloth. Ay, and she laughed at Trotty too – so pleasantly, so cheerfully, that Trotty could have blessed her where she kneeled: for he had seen that, when they entered, she was sitting by the fire in tears.

'Why, father!' said Meg. 'You're crazy tonight, I think. I don't know what the Bells would say to that. Poor little feet. How cold they are!'

'Oh, they're warmer now!' exclaimed the child. 'They're quite warm now.'

'No, no, no,' said Meg. 'We haven't rubbed 'em half enough. We're so busy. So busy! And when they're done, we'll brush out the damp hair; and when that's done, we'll bring some colour to the poor pale face with fresh water; and when that's done, we'll be so gay, and brisk, and happy – !'

The child, in a burst of sobbing, clasped her round the neck; caressed her fair cheek with its hand; and said, 'Oh Meg! oh dear Meg!'

Toby's blessing could have done no more. Who could do more!

'Why, father!' cried Meg, after a pause.

'Here I am and here I go, my dear.' said Trotty.

'Good Gracious me!' cried Meg. 'He's crazy! He's put the dear child's bonnet on the kettle, and hung the lid behind the door!'

'I didn't go to do it, my love,' said Trotty, hastily repairing this mistake. 'Meg, my dear?'

Meg looked towards him and saw that he had elaborately stationed himself behind the chair of their male visitor, where with many mysterious gestures he was holding up the sixpence he had earned.

'I see, my dear,' said Trotty, 'as I was coming in, half an ounce of tea lying somewhere on the stairs; and I'm pretty sure there was a bit of bacon too. As I don't remember where it was, exactly; I'll go myself and try to find 'em.'

With this inscrutable artifice, Toby withdrew to purchase the viands he had spoken of, for ready money, at Mrs Chickenstalker's; and presently came back, pretending he had not been able to find them, at first, in the dark.

'But here they are at last,' said Trotty, setting out the tea things, 'all correct! I was pretty sure it was tea, and a rasher. So it is. Meg, my pet, if you'll just make the tea, while your unworthy father toasts the bacon, we shall be ready, immediate. It's a curious circumstance,' said Trotty, proceeding in his cookery, with the assistance of the toasting-fork, 'curious, but well known to my friends, that I never care, myself, for rashers, nor for tea. I like to see other people enjoy 'em,' said Trotty, speaking very loud, to impress the fact upon his guest, 'but to me, as food, they're disagreeable.'

Yet Trotty sniffed the savour of the hissing bacon – ah! – as if he liked it; and when he poured the boiling water in the teapot, looked lovingly down into the depths of that snug cauldron, and suffered the fragrant steam to curl about his nose, and wreathe his head and face in a thick cloud. However, for all this, he neither ate nor drank, except at the very beginning, a mere morsel for form's sake, which he appeared to eat with infinite relish, but declared was perfectly uninteresting to him.

No. Trotty's occupation was, to see Will Fern and Lilian eat and drink; and so was Meg's. And never did spectators at a city dinner or court banquet find such high delight in seeing others feast: although it were a monarch or a pope: as those two did, in looking on that night. Meg smiled at Trotty, Trotty laughed at Meg. Meg shook her head, and made belief to clap her hands, applauding Trotty; Trotty conveyed, in dumb-show, unintelligible narratives of how and when and where he had found their visitors, to Meg; and they were happy. Very happy.

'Although,' thought Trotty, sorrowfully, as he watched Meg's face; 'that match is broken off, I see!'

'Now, I'll tell you what,' said Trotty after tea. 'The little one, she sleeps with Meg, I know.'

'With good Meg!' cried the child, caressing her. 'With Meg.'

'That's right,' said Trotty. 'And I shouldn't wonder if she kiss Meg's father, won't she? I'm Meg's father.'

Mightily delighted Trotty was, when the child went timidly towards him, and having kissed him, fell back upon Meg again.

'She's as sensible as Solomon,' said Trotty. 'Here we come and here we – no, we don't – I don't mean that – I – what was I saying, Meg, my precious?'

Meg looked towards their guest, who leaned upon her chair, and with his face turned from her, fondled the child's head, half hidden in her lap.

'To be sure,' said Toby. 'To be sure! I don't know what I'm rambling on about, tonight. My wits are wool-gathering, I think. Will Fern, you come along with me. You're tired to death, and broken down for want of rest. You come along with me.'

The man still played with the child's curls, still leaned upon Meg's chair, still turned away his face. He didn't speak, but in his rough coarse fingers, clenching and expanding in the fair hair of the child, there was an eloquence that said enough.

'Yes, yes,' said Trotty, answering unconsciously what he saw expressed in his daughter's face. 'Take her with you, Meg. Get her to bed. There! Now Will, I'll show you where you lie. It's not much of a place: only a loft: but, having a loft, I always say, is one of the great conveniences of living in a mews; and till this coach-house and stable gets a better let, we live here cheap. There's plenty of sweet hay up there, belonging to a neighbour; and it's as clean as hands, and Meg can make it. Cheer up! Don't give way. A new heart for a New Year, always!'

The hand released from the child's hair, had fallen, trembling, into Trotty's hand. So Trotty, talking without intermission, led him out as tenderly and easily as if he had been a child himself.

Returning before Meg, he listened for an instant at the door of her little chamber; an adjoining room. The child was murmuring a simple prayer before lying down to sleep; and when she had remembered Meg's name, 'Dearly, Dearly' – so her words ran – Trotty heard her stop and ask for his.

It was some short time before the foolish little old fellow could compose himself to mend the fire, and draw his chair to the warm hearth. But, when he had done so, and had trimmed the light, he took his newspaper from his pocket, and began to read. Carelessly at first, and skimming up and down the columns; but with an earnest and a sad attention, very soon.

For this same dreaded paper redirected Trotty's thoughts into the channel they had taken all that day, and which the day's events had so marked out and shaped. His interest in the two wanderers had set him on another course of thinking, and a happier one, for the time; but being alone again, and reading of the crimes and violences of the people, he relapsed into his former train.

In this mood, he came to an account (and it was not the first he had ever read) of a woman who had laid her desperate hands not only on her own life but on that of her young child. A crime so terrible, and so revolting to his soul, dilated with the love of Meg, that he let the journal drop, and fell back in his chair, appalled.

'Unnatural and cruel!' Toby cried. 'Unnatural and cruel! None but people who were bad at heart, born bad: who had no business on the earth; could do such deeds. It's too true, all I've heard today; too just, too full of proof. We're Bad!'

The Chimes took up the words so suddenly – burst out so loud, and clear, and sonorous – that the Bells seemed to strike him in his chair.

And what was that they said?

'Toby Veck, Toby Veck, waiting for you Toby! Toby Veck, Toby Veck, waiting for you Toby! Come and see us, come and see us, Drag him to us, drag him to us, Haunt and hunt him, haunt and hunt him, Break his slumbers, break his slumbers! Toby Veck, Toby Veck, door open wide Toby, Toby Veck, Toby Veck, door open wide Toby – ' then fiercely back to their impetuous strain again, and ringing in the very bricks and plaster on the walls.

Toby listened. Fancy, fancy! His remorse for having run away from them that afternoon! No, no. Nothing of the kind. Again, again, and yet a dozen times again. 'Haunt and hunt him, haunt and hunt him, Drag him to us, drag him to us!' Deafening the whole town!

'Meg,' said Trotty softly: tapping at her door. 'Do you hear anything?'

'I hear the Bells, father. Surely they're very loud tonight.'

'Is she asleep?' said Toby, making an excuse for peeping in.

'So peacefully and happily! I can't leave her yet though, father. Look how she holds my hand!'

'Meg,' whispered Trotty. 'Listen to the Bells!'

She listened, with her face towards him all the time. But it underwent no change. She didn't understand them.

Trotty withdrew, resumed his seat by the fire, and once more listened by himself. He remained here a little time.

It was impossible to bear it; their energy was dreadful.

'If the tower-door is really open,' said Toby, hastily laying aside his apron, but never thinking of his hat, 'what's to hinder me from going up into the steeple and satisfying myself? If it's shut, I don't want any other satisfaction. That's enough.'

He was pretty certain as he slipped out quietly into the street that he should find it shut and locked, for he knew the door well, and had so rarely seen it open, that he couldn't reckon above three times in all. It was a low arched portal, outside the church, in a dark nook behind a column; and had such great iron hinges, and such a monstrous lock, that there was more hinge and lock than door.

But what was his astonishment when, coming bareheaded to the church; and putting his hand into this dark nook, with a certain misgiving that it might be unexpectedly seized, and a shivering propensity to draw it back again; he found that the door, which opened outwards, actually stood ajar! He thought, on the first surprise, of going back; or of getting a light, or a companion; but his courage aided him immediately, and he determined to ascend alone.

'What have I to fear?' said Trotty. 'It's a church! Besides, the ringers may be there, and have forgotten to shut the door.'

So he went in; feeling his way as he went, like a blind man; for it was very dark. And very quiet, for the Chimes were silent.

The dust from the street had blown into the recess and lying there, heaped up, made it so soft and velvet-like to the foot that there was something startling even in that. The narrow stair was so close to the door, too, that he stumbled at the very first; and shutting the door upon himself, by striking it with his foot, and causing it to rebound back heavily, he couldn't open it again.

This was another reason, however, for going on. Trotty groped his

way, and went on. Up, up, up, and round and round; and up up, up; higher, higher, higher up! It was a disagreeable staircase for that groping work; so low and narrow, that his groping hand was always touching something; and it often felt so like a man or ghostly figure standing up erect and making room for him to pass without discovery, that he would rub the smooth wall upward searching for its face, and downward searching for its feet, while a chill tingling crept all over him. Twice or thrice, a door or niche broke the monotonous surface; and then it seemed a gap as wide as the whole church; and he felt on the brink of an abyss, and going to tumble headlong down; until he found the wall again.

Still up, up, up; and round and round; and up, up, up; higher, higher, higher up.

At length, the dull and stifling atmosphere began to freshen: presently to feel quite windy: presently it blew so strong, that he could hardly keep his legs. But he got to an arched window in the tower, breast high, and holding tight, looked down upon the housetops, on the smoking chimneys, on the blurr and blotch of lights (towards the place where Meg was wondering where he was and calling to him perhaps), all kneaded up together in a leaven of mist and darkness.

This was the belfry, where the ringers came. He had caught hold of one of the frayed ropes which hung down through apertures in the oaken roof. At first he started, thinking it was hair; then trembled at the very thought of waking the deep Bell. The Bells themselves were higher. Higher, Trotty, in his fascination, or in working out the spell upon him, groped his way. By ladders now, and toilsomely, for it was steep, and not too certain holding for the feet.

Up, up, up; and climb and clamber; up, up, up; higher, higher, higher up!

Until, ascending through the floor, and pausing with his head just raised above its beams, he came among the Bells. It was barely possible to make out their great shapes in the gloom; but there they were. Shadowy, and dark, and dumb.

A heavy sense of dread and loneliness fell instantly upon him, as he climbed into this airy nest of stone and metal. His head went round and round. He listened, and then raised a wild, 'Holloa.'

Holloa! was mournfully protracted by the echoes.

Giddy, confused, and out of breath, and frightened, Toby looked about him vacantly, and sank down in a swoon.

THE THIRD QUARTER

Black are the brooding clouds and troubled the deep waters, when the Sea of Thought, first heaving from a calm, gives up its Dead. Monsters uncouth and wild, arise in premature, imperfect resurrection; the several parts and shapes of different things are joined and mixed by chance; and when, and how, and by what wonderful degrees, each separates from each, and every sense and object of the mind resumes its usual form and lives again, no man – though every man is every day the casket of this type of the Great Mystery – can tell.

So, when and how the darkness of the night-black steeple changed to shining light; when and how the solitary tower was peopled with a myriad figures; when and how the whispered, 'Haunt and hunt him,' breathing monotonously through his sleep or swoon, became a voice exclaiming in the waking ears of Trotty, 'Break his slumbers;' when and how he ceased to have a sluggish and confused idea that such things were, companioning a host of others that were not; there are no dates or means to tell. But, awake and standing on his feet upon the boards where he had lately lain, he saw this Goblin Sight.

He saw the tower, whither his charmed footsteps had brought him, swarming with dwarf phantoms, spirits, elfin creatures of the Bells. He saw them leaping, flying, dropping, pouring from the Bells without a pause. He saw them, round him on the ground; above him, in the air; clambering from him, by the ropes below; looking down upon him, from the massive iron-girded beams; peeping in upon him, through the chinks and loopholes in the walls; spreading away and away from him in enlarging circles, as the water-ripples give place to a huge stone that suddenly comes splashing in among them. He saw them, of all aspects and all shapes. He saw them ugly, handsome, crippled, exquisitely formed. He saw them young, he saw them old, he saw them kind, he saw them cruel, he saw them merry, he saw them grim; he saw them dance, and heard them sing; he saw them tear their hair, and heard them howl. He saw the air thick with them. He saw them come and go, incessantly. He saw them riding downward, soaring upward, sailing off afar, perching near at hand, all restless and all violently active. Stone, and brick, and slate, and tile, became transparent to him as to them. He saw them in the houses, busy at the sleepers' beds. He saw them soothing people in their dreams; he saw them beating them with knotted whips; he saw them yelling in their ears; he saw them playing softest music on their pillows; he saw them cheering some with the songs of birds and the perfume of flowers; he saw them flashing awful faces on the troubled rest of others, from enchanted mirrors which they carried in their hands.

He saw these creatures, not only among sleeping men but waking also, active in pursuits irreconcilable with one another, and possessing or assuming natures the most opposite. He saw one buckling on innumerable wings to increase his speed; another loading himself with chains and weights to retard his. He saw some putting the hands of clocks forward, some putting the hands of clocks backward, some endeavouring to stop the clock entirely. He saw them representing, here a marriage ceremony, there a funeral; in this chamber an election, in that a ball; everywhere, restless and untiring motion.

Bewildered by the host of shifting and extraordinary figures, as well as by the uproar of the Bells, which all this while were ringing, Trotty clung to a wooden pillar for support, and turned his white face here and there, in mute and stunned astonishment.

As he gazed, the Chimes stopped. Instantaneous change! The whole swarm fainted! their forms collapsed, their speed deserted them; they sought to fly, but in the act of falling died and melted into air. No fresh supply succeeded them. One straggler leaped down pretty briskly from the surface of the Great Bell, and alighted on his feet, but he was dead and gone before he could turn round. Some few of the late company who had gambolled in the tower, remained there, spinning over and over a little longer; but these became at every turn more faint, and few, and feeble, and soon went the way of the rest. The last of all was one small hunchback, who had got into an echoing corner, where he twirled and twirled, and floated by himself a long time; showing such perseverance, that at last he dwindled to a leg and even to a foot, before he finally retired; but he vanished in the end, and then the tower was silent.

Then and not before, did Trotty see in every Bell a bearded figure of the bulk and stature of the Bell – incomprehensibly, a figure and the Bell itself. Gigantic, grave, and. darkly watchful of him, as he stood rooted to the ground.

Mysterious and awful figures! Resting on nothing; poised in the night air of the tower, with their draped and hooded heads merged in the dim roof; motionless and shadowy. Shadowy and dark, although he saw them by some light belonging to themselves – none else was there – each with its muffled hand upon its goblin mouth.

He could not plunge down wildly through the opening in the floor, for all power of motion had deserted him. Otherwise he would have done so – ay, would have thrown himself, headforemost, from the steeple-top, rather than have seen them watching him with eyes that would have waked and watched although the pupils had been taken out.

Again, again, the dread and terror of the lonely place, and of the wild and fearful night that reigned there, touched him like a spectral hand. His distance from all help; the long, dark, winding, ghost-beleaguered way that lay between him and the earth on which men lived; his being high, high, high, up there, where it had made him dizzy to see the birds fly in the day; cut off from all good people, who at such an hour were safe at home and sleeping in their beds; all this struck coldly through him, not as a reflection but a bodily sensation. Meantime his eyes and thoughts and fears, were fixed upon the watchful figures; which, rendered unlike any figures of this world by the deep gloom and shade enwrapping and enfolding them, as well as by their looks and forms and supernatural hovering above the floor, were nevertheless as plainly to be seen as were the stalwart oaken frames, cross-pieces, bars and beams, set up there to support the Bells. These hemmed them, in a very forest of hewn timber; from the entanglements, intricacies, and depths of which, as from among the boughs of a dead wood blighted for their phantom use, they kept their darksome and unwinking watch.

A blast of air – how cold and shrill! – came moaning through the tower. As it died away, the Great Bell, or the Goblin of the Great Bell, spoke.

'What visitor is this!' it said. The voice was low and deep, and Trotty fancied that it sounded in the other figures as well.

'I thought my name was called by the Chimes!' said Trotty, raising his hands in an attitude of supplication. 'I hardly know why I am here, or how I came. I have listened to the Chimes these many years. They have cheered me often.'

'And you have thanked them?' said the Bell.

'A thousand times!' cried Trotty.

'How?'

'I am a poor man,' faltered Trotty, 'and could only thank them in words.'

'And always so?' enquired the Goblin of the Bell. 'Have you never done us wrong in words?'

'No!' cried Trotty eagerly.

'Never done us foul, and false, and wicked wrong, in words?' pursued the Goblin of the Bell.

Trotty was about to answer, 'Never!' But he stopped, and was confused.

'The voice of Time,' said the phantom, 'cries to man, Advance! Time IS for his advancement and improvement; for his greater worth, his greater happiness, his better life; his progress onward to that goal within its knowledge and its view, and set there, in the period when Time and He began. Ages of darkness, wickedness, and violence, have come and gone: millions uncountable, have suffered, lived, and died: to point the way before him. Who seeks to turn him back, or stay him on his course, arrests a mighty engine which will strike the meddler dead; and be the fiercer and the wilder, ever, for its momentary check!'

'I never did so, to my knowledge, sir,' said Trotty. 'It was quite by accident if I did. I wouldn't go to do it, I'm sure.'

'Who puts into the mouth of Time, or of its servants,' said the Goblin of the Bell, 'a cry of lamentation for days which have had their trial and their failure, and have left deep traces of it which the blind may see – a cry that only serves the Present Time, by showing men how much it needs their help when any ears can listen to regrets for such a Past – who does this, does a wrong. And you have done that wrong to us, the Chimes.'

Trotty's first excess of fear was gone. But he had felt tenderly and gratefully towards the Bells, as you have seen; and when he heard himself arraigned as one who had offended them so weightily, his heart was touched with penitence and grief.

'If you knew,' said Trotty, clasping his hands earnestly – 'or perhaps you do know – if you know how often you have kept me company; how often you have cheered me up when I've been low; how you were quite the plaything of my little daughter Meg (almost the only one she ever had) when first her mother died, and she and me were left alone – you won't bear malice for a hasty word!'

'Who hears in us, the Chimes, one note bespeaking disregard, or stern regard, of any hope, or joy, or pain, or sorrow, of the many-sorrowed throng; who hears us make response to any creed that gauges human passions and affections, as it gauges the amount of miserable food on which humanity may pine and wither; does us wrong. That wrong you have done us!' said the Bell.

'I have!' said Trotty. 'Oh forgive me!'

'Who hears us echo the dull vermin of the earth: the Putters Down of crushed and broken natures, formed to be raised up higher than such maggots of the time can crawl or can conceive,' pursued the Goblin of the Bell: 'who does so, does us wrong. And you have done us wrong!'

'Not meaning it,' said Trotty. 'In my ignorance. Not meaning it!'

'Lastly and most of all,' pursued the Bell. 'Who turns his back upon the fallen and disfigured of his kind; abandons them as Vile; and does not trace and track with pitying eyes the unfenced precipice by which they fell from Good – grasping in their fall some tufts and shreds of that lost soil, and clinging to them still when bruised and dying in the gulf below; does wrong to Heaven and Man, to Time and to Eternity. And you have done that wrong!'

'Spare me,' cried Trotty, falling on his knees; 'for Mercy's sake!'

'Listen!' said the Shadow.

'Listen!' cried the other Shadows.

'Listen!' said a clear and childlike voice, which Trotty thought he recognised as having heard before.

The organ sounded faintly in the church below. Swelling by degrees, the melody ascended to the roof, and filled the choir and nave. Expanding more and more, it rose up, up; up, up; higher, higher, higher up; awakening agitated hearts within the bulky piles of oak, the hollow bells, the iron-bound doors, the stairs of solid stone; until the tower walls were insufficient to contain it, and it soared into the sky.

No wonder that an old man's breast could not contain a sound so vast and mighty. It broke from that weak prison in a rush of tears; and Trotty put his hands before his face.

'Listen!' said the Shadow.

'Listen!' said the other Shadows.

'Listen!' said the child's voice.

A solemn strain of blended voices rose into the tower.

It was a very low and mournful strain: a Dirge: and as he listened, Trotty heard his child among the singers.

'She is dead!' exclaimed the old man. 'Meg is dead! Her Spirit calls to me. I hear it!'

'The Spirit of your child bewails the dead, and mingles with the dead – dead hopes, dead fancies, dead imaginings of youth,' returned the Bell, 'but she is living. Learn from her life, a living truth. Learn from the creature dearest to your heart, how bad the Bad are born. See every bud and leaf plucked one by one from off the fairest stem, and know how bare and wretched it may be. Follow her! To desperation!'

Each of the shadowy figures stretched its right arm forth, and pointed downward.

'The Spirit of the Chimes is your companion,' said the figure. 'Go! It stands behind you!'

Trotty turned, and saw – the child! The child Will Fern had carried in the street; the child whom Meg had watched, but now, asleep!

'I carried her myself, tonight,' said Trotty. 'In these arms!'

'Show him what he calls himself,' said the dark figures, one and all.

The tower opened at his feet. He looked down, and beheld his own form, lying at the bottom on the outside: crushed and motionless.

'No more a living man!' cried Trotty. 'Dead!'

'Dead!' said the figures all together.

'Gracious Heaven! And the New Year – '

'Past,' said the figures.

'What!' he cried, shuddering. 'I missed my way, and coming on the outside of this tower in the dark, fell down – a year ago?'

'Nine years ago!' replied the figures.

As they gave the answer, they recalled their outstretched hands; and where their figures had been, there the Bells were.

And they rang; their time being come again. And once again, vast multitudes of phantoms sprang into existence; once again, were incoherently engaged, as they had been before; once again, faded on the stopping of the chimes; and dwindled into nothing.

'What are these?' he asked his guide. 'If I am not mad, what are these?'

'Spirits of the Bells. Their sound upon the air,' returned the child. 'They take such shapes and occupations as the hopes and thoughts of mortals, and the recollections they have stored up, give them.'

'And you,' said Trotty wildly. 'What are you?'

'Hush, hush!' returned the child. 'Look here!'

In a poor, mean room: working at the same kind of embroidery which he had often, often seen before her; Meg, his own dear daughter, was presented to his view. He made no effort to imprint his kisses on her face; he did not strive to clasp her to his loving heart; he knew that such endearments were for him no more. But he held his trembling breath; and brushed away the blinding tears that he might look upon her; that he might only see her.

Ah! Changed. Changed. The light of the clear eye, how dimmed. The bloom, how faded from the cheek. Beautiful she was, as she had ever been, but Hope, Hope, Hope, oh where was the fresh Hope that had spoken to him like a voice!

She looked up from her work, at a companion. Following her eyes, the old man started back.

In the woman grown, he recognised her at a glance. In the long silken hair, he saw the selfsame curls; around the lips, the child's expression lingering still. See! In the eyes, now turned enquiringly on Meg, there shone the very look that scanned those features when he brought her home.

Then what was this, beside him!

Looking with awe into its face, he saw a something reigning there: a lofty something, undefined and indistinct, which made it hardly more than a remembrance of that child – as yonder figure might be – yet it was the same: the same: and wore the dress.

Hark. They were speaking!

'Meg,' said Lilian, hesitating. 'How often you raise your head from your work to look at me?'

'Are my looks so altered, that they frighten you?' asked Meg.

'Nay, dear! But you smile at that, yourself! Why not smile, when you look at me, Meg?'

'I do so. Do I not?' she answered: smiling on her.

'Now you do,' said Lilian, 'but not usually. When you think I'm busy, and don't see you, you look so anxious and so doubtful, that I hardly like to raise my eyes. There is little cause for smiling in this hard and toilsome life, but you were once so cheerful.'

'Am I not now!' cried Meg, speaking in a tone of strange alarm, and rising to embrace her. 'Do *I* make our weary life more weary to you, Lilian!'

'You have been the only thing that made it life,' said Lilian, fervently kissing her; 'sometimes the only thing that made me care to live so, Meg. Such work, such work! So many hours, so many days, so many long, long nights of hopeless, cheerless, never-ending work – not to heap up riches, not to live grandly or gaily, not to live upon enough, however coarse; but to earn bare bread; to scrape together just enough to toil upon, and want upon, and keep alive in us the consciousness of our hard fate! Oh Meg, Meg!' she raised her voice, and twined her arms about her as she spoke, like one in pain. 'How can the cruel world go round, and bear to look upon such lives!'

'Lilly!' said Meg, soothing her, and putting back her hair from her wet face. 'Why Lilly! You! So pretty and so young!'

'Oh Meg!' she interrupted, holding her at arm's length, and looking in her face imploringly. 'The worst of all, the worst of all! Strike me old, Meg! Wither me and shrivel me, and free me from the dreadful thoughts that tempt me in my youth!'

Trotty turned to look upon his guide. But the Spirit of the child had taken flight. Was gone.

Neither did he himself remain in the same place; for Sir Joseph Bowley, Friend and Father of the Poor, held a great festivity at Bowley Hall, in honour of the natal day of Lady Bowley; and as Lady Bowley had been born on New Year's Day (which the local newspapers considered an especial pointing of the finger of Providence to number One as Lady Bowley's destined figure in Creation), it was on a New Year's Day that this festivity took place.

Bowley Hall was full of visitors. The red-faced gentleman was there, Mr Filer was there, the great Alderman Cute was there – Alderman

Cute had a sympathetic feeling with great people, and had considerably improved his acquaintance with Sir Joseph Bowley on the strength of his attentive letter: indeed had become quite a friend of the family since then – and many guests were there. Trotty's ghost was there, wandering about, poor phantom, drearily; and looking for its guide.

There was to be a great dinner in the Great Hall. At which Sir Joseph Bowley, in his celebrated character of Friend and Father of the Poor, was to make his great speech. Certain plum-puddings were to be eaten by his Friends and Children in another Hall first; and, at a given signal, Friends and Children flocking in among their Friends and Fathers, were to form a family assemblage, with not one manly eye therein unmoistened by emotion.

But there was more than this to happen. Even more than this. Sir Joseph Bowley, Baronet and Member of Parliament, was to play a match at skittles – real skittles – with his tenants.

'Which quite reminds one,' said Alderman Cute, 'of the days of old King Hal, stout King Hal, bluff King Hal. Ah. Fine character!'

'Very,' said Mr Filer, dryly. 'For marrying women and murdering 'em. Considerably more than the average number of wives by the by.'

'You'll marry the beautiful ladies, and not murder 'em, eh?' said Alderman Cute to the heir of Bowley, aged twelve. 'Sweet boy! We shall have this little gentleman in Parliament now,' said the Alderman, holding him by the shoulders, and looking as reflective as he could, 'before we know where we are. We shall hear of his successes at the poll; his speeches in the House; his overtures from Governments; his brilliant achievements of all kinds; ah! we shall make our little orations about him in the Common Council, I'll be bound; before we have time to look about us!'

'Oh, the difference of shoes and stockings!' Trotty thought. But his heart yearned towards the child, for the love of those same shoeless and stockingless boys, predestined (by the Alderman) to turn out bad, who might have been the children of poor Meg.

'Richard,' moaned Trotty, roaming among the company, to and fro; 'where is he? I can't find Richard! Where is Richard?'

Not likely to be there, if still alive! But Trotty's grief and solitude confused him; and he still went wandering among the gallant company, looking for his guide, and saying, 'Where is Richard? Show me Richard!'

He was wandering thus, when he encountered Mr Fish, the confidential Secretary: in great agitation.

'Bless my heart and soul!' cried Mr Fish. 'Where's Alderman Cute? Has anybody seen the Alderman?'

Seen the Alderman? Oh dear! Who could ever help seeing the Alderman? He was so considerate, so affable; he bore so much in mind the natural desire of folks to see him; that if he had a fault, it was the being constantly On View. And wherever the great people were, there, to be sure, attracted by the kindred sympathy between great souls, was Cute.

Several voices cried that he was in the circle round Sir Joseph. Mr Fish made way there; found him; and took him secretly into a window near at hand. Trotty joined them. Not of his own accord. He felt that his steps were led in that direction.

'My dear Alderman Cute,' said Mr Fish. 'A little more this way. The most dreadful circumstance has occurred. I have this moment received the intelligence. I think it will be best not to acquaint Sir Joseph with it till the day is over. You understand Sir Joseph, and will give me your opinion. The most frightful and deplorable event!'

'Fish!' returned the Alderman. 'Fish! My good fellow, what is the matter? Nothing revolutionary, I hope! No – no attempted interference with the magistrates?'

'Deedles, the banker,' gasped the Secretary. 'Deedles Brothers – who was to have been here today – high in office in the Goldsmiths' Company – '

'Not stopped!' exclaimed the Alderman. 'It can't be!'

'Shot himself.'

'Good God!'

'Put a double-barrelled pistol to his mouth, in his own counting-house,' said Mr Fish, 'and blew his brains out. No motive. Princely circumstances!'

'Circumstances!' exclaimed the Alderman. 'A man of noble fortune. One of the most respectable of men. Suicide, Mr Fish! By his own hand!'

'This very morning,' returned Mr Fish.

'Oh the brain, the brain!' exclaimed the pious Alderman, lifting up his hands. 'Oh the nerves, the nerves; the mysteries of this machine called Man! Oh the little that unhinges it: poor creatures that we are! Perhaps a dinner, Mr Fish. Perhaps the conduct of his son, who, I have heard, ran very wild, and was in the habit of drawing bills upon him without the least authority! A most respectable man. One of the most respectable men I ever knew! A lamentable instance, Mr Fish. A public calamity! I shall make a point of wearing the deepest mourning. A most respectable man! But there is One above. We must submit, Mr Fish. We must submit!'

What, Alderman! No word of Putting Down? Remember, Justice, your high moral boast and pride. Come, Alderman! Balance those scales. Throw me into this, the empty one, No Dinner, and Nature's founts in some poor woman, dried by starving misery and rendered obdurate to claims for which her offspring *has* authority in holy mother Eve. Weigh me the two, you Daniel going to judgement, when your day shall come! Weigh them, in the eyes of suffering thousands, audience (not unmindful) of the grim farce you play! Or supposing that you strayed from your five wits – it's not so far to go, but that it might be – and laid hands upon that throat of yours, warning your fellows (if you have a fellow) how they croak their comfortable wickedness to raving heads and stricken hearts. What then?

The words rose up in Trotty's breast, as if they had been spoken by some other voice within him. Alderman Cute pledged himself to Mr Fish that he would assist him in breaking the melancholy catastrophe to Sir Joseph, when the day was over. Then, before they parted, wringing Mr Fish's hand in bitterness of soul, he said, 'The most respectable of men!' And added that he hardly knew: not even he: why such afflictions were allowed on earth.

'It's almost enough to make one think, if one didn't know better,' said Alderman Cute, 'that at times some motion of a capsizing nature was going on in things, which affected the general economy of the social fabric. Deedles Brothers!'

The skittle-playing came off with immense success. Sir Joseph knocked the pins about quite skilfully; Master Bowley took an innings at a shorter distance also; and everybody said that now, when a Baronet and the Son of a Baronet played at skittles, the country was coming round again, as fast as it could come.

At its proper time, the Banquet was served up. Trotty involuntarily repaired to the Hall with the rest, for he felt himself conducted thither by some stronger impulse than his own free will. The sight was gay in the extreme; the ladies were very handsome; the visitors delighted, cheerful, and good-tempered. When the lower doors were opened, and the people flocked in, in their rustic dresses, the beauty of the spectacle was at its height; but Trotty only murmured more and more, 'Where is Richard! He should help and comfort her! I can't see Richard!'

There had been some speeches made; and Lady Bowley's health had been proposed; and Sir Joseph Bowley had returned thanks; and had made his great speech, showing by various pieces of evidence that he was the born Friend and Father, and so forth; and had given as a Toast, his Friends and Children, and the Dignity of Labour; when a slight disturbance at the bottom of the Hall attracted Toby's notice. After some confusion, noise, and opposition, one man broke through the rest, and stood forward by himself.

Not Richard. No. But one whom he had thought of, and had looked for, many times. In a scantier supply of light, he might have doubted the identity of that worn man, so old, and grey, and bent; but with a blaze of lamps upon his gnarled and knotted head, he knew Will Fern as soon as he stepped forth.

'What is this!' exclaimed Sir Joseph, rising. 'Who gave this man admittance? This is a criminal from prison! Mr Fish, sir, *will* you have the goodness – '

'A minute!' said Will Fern. 'A minute! My lady, you was born on this day along with a New Year. Get me a minute's leave to speak.'

She made some intercession for him. Sir Joseph took his seat again, with native dignity.

The ragged visitor – for he was miserably dressed – looked round upon the company, and made his homage to them with a humble bow.

'Gentlefolks!' he said. 'You've drunk the Labourer. Look at me!'

'Just come from jail,' said Mr Fish.

'Just come from jail,' said Will. 'And neither for the first time, nor the second, nor the third, nor yet the fourth.'

Mr Filer was heard to remark testily, that four times was over the average; and he ought to be ashamed of himself.

'Gentlefolks!' repeated Will Fern. 'Look at me! You see I'm at the worst. Beyond all hurt or harm; beyond your help; for the time when your kind words or kind actions could have done ME good' – he struck his hand upon his breast, and shook his head, 'is gone, with the scent of last year's beans or clover on the air. Let me say a word for these,' pointing to the labouring people in the Hall; 'and when you're met together, hear the real Truth spoke out for once.'

'There's not a man here,' said the host, 'who would have him for a spokesman.'

'Like enough, Sir Joseph. I believe it. Not the less true, perhaps, is

what I say. Perhaps that's a proof on it. Gentlefolks, I've lived many a year in this place. You may see the cottage from the sunk fence over yonder. I've seen the ladies draw it in their books, a hundred times. It looks well in a picter, I've heerd say; but there an't weather in picters, and maybe 'tis fitter for that, than for a place to live in. Well! I lived there. How hard – how bitter hard, I lived there, I won't say. Any day in the year, and every day, you can judge for your own selves.'

He spoke as he had spoken on the night when Trotty found him in the street. His voice was deeper and more husky, and had a trembling in it now and then; but he never raised it passionately, and seldom lifted it above the firm, stern level of the homely facts he stated.

' 'Tis harder than you think for, gentlefolks, to grow up decent:

commonly decent: in such a place. That I growed up a man and not a brute, says something for me – as I was then. As I am now, there's nothing can be said for me or done for me. I'm past it.'

'I am glad this man has entered,' observed Sir Joseph, looking round serenely. 'Don't disturb him. It appears to be Ordained. He is an Example: a living example. I hope and trust, and confidently expect, that it will not be lost upon my Friends here.'

'I dragged on,' said Fern, after a moment's silence. 'Somehow. Neither me nor any other man knows how; but so heavy, that I couldn't put a cheerful face upon it, or make believe that I was anything but what I was. Now gentlemen – you gentlemen that sits at Sessions – when you see a man with discontent writ on his face, you says to one another, "He's suspicious. I has my doubts," says you, "about Will Fern. Watch that fellow!" I don't say, gentlemen, it an't quite nat'ral, but I say 'tis so; and from that hour, whatever Will Fern does, or lets alone – all one – it goes against him.'

Alderman Cute stuck his thumbs in his waistcoat-pockets, and leaning back in his chair, and smiling, winked at a neighbouring chandelier. As much as to say, 'Of course! I told you so. The common cry! Lord bless you, we are up to all this sort of thing – myself and human nature.'

'Now, gentlemen,' said Will Fern, holding out his hands, and flushing for an instant in his haggard face, 'see how your laws are made to trap and hunt us when we're brought to this. I tries to live elsewhere. And I'm a vagabond. To jail with him! I comes back here. I goes a-nutting in your woods, and breaks – who don't? – a limber branch or two. To jail with him! One of your keepers sees me in the broad day, near my own patch of garden, with a gun. To jail with him! I has a nat'ral angry word with that man, when I'm free again. To jail with him! I cuts a stick. To jail with him! I eats a rotten apple or a turnip. To jail with him! It's twenty mile away; and coming back, I begs a trifle on the road. To jail with him! At last, the constable, the keeper – anybody – finds me anywhere, a-doing anything. To jail with him, for he's a vagrant, and a jail-bird known; and the jail's the only home he's got.'

The Alderman nodded sagaciously, as who should say, 'A very good home too!'

'Do I say this to serve MY cause!' cried Fern. 'Who can give me back my liberty, who can give me back my good name, who can give me back my innocent niece? Not all the Lords and Ladies in wide England. But gentlemen, gentlemen, dealing with other men like me, begin at the right end. Give us, in mercy, better homes when we're a-lying in our cradles; give us better food when we're a-working for our lives; give us kinder laws to bring us back when we're a-going wrong; and don't set Jail, Jail, Jail, afore us, everywhere we turn. There an't a condescension you can show the Labourer then, that he won't take, as ready and as grateful as a man can be; for, he has a patient, peaceful, willing heart. But you must put his rightful spirit in him first; for, whether he's a wreck and ruin such as me, or is like one of them that stand here now, his spirit is divided from you at this time. Bring it back, gentlefolks, bring it back! Bring it back, afore the day comes when even his Bible changes in his altered mind, and the words seem to him to read, as they have sometimes read in my own eyes – in Jail: "Whither thou goest, I can Not go; where thou lodgest, I do Not lodge; thy people are Not my people; Nor thy God my God!" '

A sudden stir and agitation took place in the Hall. Trotty thought at first, that several had risen to eject the man; and hence this change in its appearance. But another moment showed him that the room and all the company had vanished from his sight, and that his daughter was again before him, seated at her work. But in a poorer, meaner garret than before; and with no Lilian by her side.

The frame at which she had worked, was put away upon a shelf and covered up. The chair in which she had sat, was turned against the wall. A history was written in these little things, and in Meg's grief-worn face. Oh! who could fail to read it!

Meg strained her eyes upon her work until it was too dark to see the threads; and when the night closed in, she lighted her feeble candle and worked on. Still her old father was invisible about her; looking down upon her; loving her – how dearly loving her! – and talking to her in a tender voice about the old times, and the Bells. Though he knew, poor Trotty, though he knew she could not hear him.

A great part of the evening had worn away, when a knock came at her door. She opened it. A man was on the threshold. A slouching, moody, drunken sloven: wasted by intemperance and vice: and with his matted hair and unshorn beard in wild disorder: but with some traces on him, too, of having been a man of good proportion and good features in his youth.

He stopped until he had her leave to enter; and she, retiring a pace or two from the open door, silently and sorrowfully looked upon him. Trotty had his wish. He saw Richard.

'May I come in, Margaret?'

'Yes! Come in. Come in!'

It was well that Trotty knew him before he spoke; for with any doubt remaining on his mind, the harsh discordant voice would have persuaded him that it was not Richard but some other man.

There were but two chairs in the room. She gave him hers, and stood at some short distance from him, waiting to hear what he had to say.

He sat, however, staring vacantly at the floor; with a lustreless and stupid smile. A spectacle of such deep degradation, of such abject hopelessness, of such a miserable downfall, that she put her hands before her face and turned away, lest he should see how much it moved her.

Roused by the rustling of her dress, or some such trifling sound, he lifted his head, and began to speak as if there had been no pause since he entered.

'Still at work, Margaret? You work late.'

'I generally do.'

'And early?'

'And early.'

'So she said. She said you never tired; or never owned that you tired. Not all the time you lived together. Nor even when you fainted, between work and fasting. But I told you that, the last time I came.'

'You did,' she answered. 'And I implored you to tell me nothing more; and you made me a solemn promise, Richard, that you never would.'

'A solemn promise,' he repeated, with a drivelling laugh and vacant stare. 'A solemn promise. To be sure. A solemn promise!' Awakening, as it were, after a time; in the same manner as before; he said with sudden animation,

'How can I help it, Margaret? What am I to do? She has been to me again!'

'Again!' cried Meg, clasping her hands. 'Oh, does she think of me so often! Has she been again!'

'Twenty times again,' said Richard. 'Margaret, she haunts me. She comes behind me in the street, and thrusts it in my hand. I hear her foot upon the ashes when I'm at my work (ah, ha! that an't often), and before I can turn my head, her voice is in my ear, saying, "Richard, don't look round. For Heaven's love, give her this!" She brings it where I live; she sends it in letters; she taps at the window and lays it on the sill. What *can* I do? Look at it!'

He held out in his hand a little purse, and chinked the money it enclosed.

'Hide it,' said Meg. 'Hide it! When she comes again, tell her, Richard, that I love her in my soul. That I never lie down to sleep, but I bless her, and pray for her. That, in my solitary work, I never cease to have her in my thoughts. That she is with me, night and day. That if I died tomorrow, I would remember her with my last breath. But that I cannot look upon it!'

He slowly recalled his hand, and crushing the purse together, said with a kind of drowsy thoughtfulness: 'I told her so. I told her so, as plain as words could speak. I've taken this gift back and left it at her door, a dozen times since then. But when she came at last, and stood before me, face to face, what could I do?'

'You saw her!' exclaimed Meg. 'You saw her! Oh, Lilian, my sweet girl! Oh, Lilian, Lilian!'

'I saw her,' he went on to say, not answering, but engaged in the same slow pursuit of his own thoughts. 'There she stood: trembling! "How does she look, Richard? Does she ever speak of me? Is she thinner? My old place at the table: what's in my old place? And the frame she taught me our old work on – has she burnt it, Richard!" There she was. I heard her say it.'

Meg checked her sobs, and with the tears streaming from her eyes, bent over him to listen. Not to lose a breath.

With his arms resting on his knees; and stooping forward in his chair, as if what he said were written on the ground in some half legible character, which it was his occupation to decipher and connect; he went on.

' "Richard, I have fallen very low; and you may guess how much I have suffered in having this sent back, when I can bear to bring it in my hand to you. But you loved her once, even in my memory, dearly. Others stepped in between you; fears, and jealousies, and doubts, and vanities, estranged you from her; but you did love her, even in my memory!" I suppose I did,' he said, interrupting himself for a moment. 'I did! That's neither here nor there. "Oh Richard, if you ever did; if you have any memory for what is gone and lost, take it to her once more. Once more! Tell her how I begged and prayed. Tell her how I laid my head upon your shoulder, where her own head might have lain, and was so humble to you, Richard. Tell her that you looked into my face, and saw the beauty which she used to praise, all gone: all gone: and in its place, a poor, wan, hollow cheek, that she would weep to see. Tell her everything, and take it back, and she will not refuse again. She will not have the heart!"'

So he sat musing, and repeating the last words, until he woke again, and rose.

'You won't take it, Margaret.'

She shook her head, and motioned all entreaty to him to leave her.

'Good-night, Margaret.'

'Good-night!'

He turned to look upon her; struck by her sorrow, and perhaps by the pity for himself which trembled in her voice. It was a quick and rapid action; and for the moment some flash of his old bearing kindled in his form. In the next he went as he had come. Nor did this glimmer of a quenched fire seem to light him to a quicker sense of his debasement.

In any mood, in any grief, in any torture of the mind or body, Meg's work must be done. She sat down to her task, and plied it. Night, midnight. Still she worked.

She had a meagre fire, the night being very cold; and rose at intervals to mind it. The Chimes rang half-past twelve while she was thus engaged; and when they ceased she heard a gentle knocking at the door. Before she could so much as wonder who was there, at that unusual hour, it opened.

Oh Youth and Beauty, happy as ye should be, look at this! Oh Youth and Beauty, blest and blessing all within your reach, and working out the ends of your Beneficent Creator, look at this!

She saw the entering figure; screamed its name; cried 'Lilian!'

It was swift, and fell upon its knees before her: clinging to her dress.

'Up, dear! Up! Lilian! My own dearest!'

'Never more, Meg; never more! Here! Here! Close to you, holding to you, feeling your dear breath upon my face!'

'Sweet Lilian! Darling Lilian! Child of my heart – no mother's love can be more tender – lay your head upon my breast!'

'Never more, Meg. Never more! When I first looked into your face, you knelt before me. On my knees before you, let me die. Let it be here!'

'You have come back. My Treasure! We will live together, work together, hope together, die together!'

'Ah! Kiss my lips, Meg; fold your arms about me; press me to your bosom; look kindly on me; but don't raise me. Let it be here. Let me see the last of your dear face upon my knees!'

Oh Youth and Beauty, happy as ye should be, look at this! Oh Youth and Beauty, working out the ends of your Beneficent Creator, look at this!

'Forgive me, Meg! So dear, so dear! Forgive me! I know you do, I see you do, but say so, Meg!'

She said so, with her lips on Lilian's cheek. And with her arms twined round – she knew it now – a broken heart.

'His blessing on you, dearest love. Kiss me once more! He suffered her to sit beside His feet, and dry them with her hair. Oh Meg, what Mercy and Compassion!'

As she died, the Spirit of the child returning, innocent and radiant, touched the old man with its hand, and beckoned him away.

THE FOURTH
QUARTER

Some new remembrance of the ghostly figures in the Bell; some faint impression of the ringing of the Chimes; some giddy consciousness of having seen the swarm of phantoms reproduced and reproduced until the recollection of them lost itself in the confusion of their numbers; some hurried knowledge, how conveyed to him he knew not, that more years had passed; and Trotty, with the Spirit of the child attending him, stood looking on at mortal company.

Fat company, rosy-cheeked company, comfortable company. They were but two, but they were red enough for ten. They sat before a bright fire with a small low table between them; and unless the fragrance of hot tea and muffins lingered longer in that room than in most others, the table had seen service very lately. But all the cups and saucers being clean, and in their proper places in the corner cupboard; and the brass toasting-fork hanging in its usual nook, and spreading its four idle fingers out, as if it wanted to be measured for a glove; there remained no other visible tokens of the meal just finished, than such as purred and washed their whiskers in the person of the basking cat, and glistened in the gracious, not to say the greasy, faces of her patrons.

This cosy couple (married, evidently) had made a fair division of the fire between them, and sat looking at the glowing sparks that dropped into the grate; now nodding off into a doze; now waking up again when some hot fragment, larger than the rest, came rattling down, as if the fire were coming with it.

It was in no danger of sudden extinction, however; for it gleamed not only in the little room, and on the panes of window-glass in the door, and on the curtain half drawn across them, but in the little shop beyond. A little shop, quite crammed and choked with the abundance of its stock; a perfectly voracious little shop, with a maw as accommodating and full as any shark's. Cheese, butter, firewood, soap, pickles, matches, bacon, table-beer, peg-tops, sweetmeats, boys' kites, bird-seed, cold ham, birch brooms, hearth-stones, salt, vinegar, blacking, red-herrings, stationery, lard, mushroom-ketchup, staylaces, loaves of bread, shuttlecocks, eggs, and slate pencil: everything was fish that came to the net of this greedy little shop, and all these articles were in its net. How many other kinds of petty merchandise were there, it would be difficult to say; but balls of packthread, ropes of onions, pounds of candles, cabbage-nets, and brushes, hung in bunches from the ceiling, like extraordinary fruit; while various odd canisters emitting aromatic smells, established the veracity of the inscription over the outer door, which informed the public that the keeper of this little shop was a licensed dealer in tea, coffee, tobacco, pepper, and snuff.

Glancing at such of these articles as were visible in the shining of the blaze, and the less cheerful radiance of two smoky lamps which burnt but dimly in the shop itself, as though its plethora sat heavy on their lungs; and glancing, then, at one of the two faces by the parlour-fire; Trotty had small difficulty in recognising in the stout old lady, Mrs Chickenstalker: always inclined to corpulency, even in the days when he had known her as established in the general line, and having a small balance against him in her books.

The features of her companion were less easy to him. The great broad chin, with creases in it large enough to hide a finger in; the astonished eyes, that seemed to expostulate with themselves for sinking deeper and deeper into the yielding fat of the soft face; the nose afflicted with that disordered action of its functions which is generally termed The Snuffles;

the short thick throat and labouring chest, with other beauties of the like description; though calculated to impress the memory, Trotty could at first allot to nobody he had ever known: and yet he had some recollection of them too. At length, in Mrs Chickenstalker's partner in the general line, and in the crooked and eccentric line of life, he recognised the former porter of Sir Joseph Bowley; an apoplectic innocent, who had connected himself in Trotty's mind with Mrs Chickenstalker years ago, by giving him admission to the mansion where he had confessed his obligations to that lady, and drawn on his unlucky head such grave reproach.

Trotty had little interest in a change like this, after the changes he had seen; but association is very strong sometimes: and he looked involuntarily behind the parlour-door, where the accounts of credit customers were usually kept in chalk. There was no record of his name. Some names were there, but they were strange to him, and infinitely fewer than of old; from which he augured that the porter was an advocate of ready money transactions, and on coming into the business had looked pretty sharp after the Chickenstalker defaulters.

So desolate was Trotty, and so mournful for the youth and promise of his blighted child, that it was a sorrow to him, even to have no place in Mrs Chickenstalker's ledger.

'What sort of a night is it, Anne?' enquired the former porter of Sir Joseph Bowley, stretching out his legs before the fire, and rubbing as much of them as his short arms could reach: with an air that added, 'Here I am if it's bad, and I don't want to go out if it's good.'

'Blowing and sleeting hard,' returned his wife; 'and threatening snow. Dark. And very cold.'

'I'm glad to think we had muffins,' said the former porter, in the tone of one who had set his conscience at rest. 'It's a sort of night that's meant for muffins. Likewise crumpets. Also Sally Lunns.'

The former porter mentioned each successive kind of eatable, as if he were musingly summing up his good actions. After which he rubbed his fat legs as before, and jerking them at the knees to get the fire upon the yet unroasted parts, laughed as if somebody had tickled him.

'You're in spirits, Tugby, my dear,' observed his wife.

The firm was Tugby, late Chickenstalker.

'No,' said Tugby. 'No. Not particular. I'm a little elewated. The muffins came so pat!'

With that he chuckled until he was black in the face; and had so much ado to become any other colour, that his fat legs took the strangest excursions into the air. Nor were they reduced to anything like decorum until Mrs Tugby had thumped him violently on the back, and shaken him as if he were a great bottle.

'Good gracious, goodness, lord-a-mercy bless and save the man!' cried Mrs Tugby, in great terror. 'What's he doing?'

Mr Tugby wiped his eyes, and faintly repeated that he found himself a little elewated.

'Then don't be so again, that's a dear good soul,' said Mrs Tugby, 'if you don't want to frighten me to death, with your struggling and fighting!'

Mr Tugby said he wouldn't, but his whole existence was a fight; in which, if any judgement might be founded on the constantly-increasing shortness of his breath, and the deepening purple of his face, he was always getting the worst of it.

'So it's blowing, and sleeting, and threatening snow; and is dark, and very cold: is it, my dear?' said Mr Tugby, looking at the fire, and reverting to the cream and marrow of his temporary elevation.

'Hard weather indeed,' returned his wife, shaking her head.

'Ay, ay! Years,' said Mr Tugby, 'are like Christians in that respect. Some of 'em die hard; some of 'em die easy. This one hasn't many days to run, and is making a fight for it. I like him all the better. There's a customer, my love!'

Attentive to the rattling door, Mrs Tugby had already risen.

'Now then!' said that lady, passing out into the little shop. 'What's wanted? Oh! I beg your pardon, sir, I'm sure. I didn't think it was you.'

She made this apology to a gentleman in black, who, with his wristbands tucked up, and his hat cocked loungingly on one side, and his hands in his pockets, sat down astride on the table-beer barrel, and nodded in return.

'This is a bad business up stairs, Mrs Tugby,' said the gentleman. 'The man can't live.'

'Not the back-attic can't!' cried Tugby, coming out into the shop to join the conference.

'The back-attic, Mr Tugby,' said the gentleman, 'is coming down stairs fast; and will be below the basement very soon.'

Looking by turns at Tugby and his wife, he sounded the barrel with his knuckles for the depth of beer, and having found it, played a tune upon the empty part.

'The back-attic, Mr Tugby,' said the gentleman: Tugby having stood in silent consternation for some time: 'is Going.'

'Then,' said Tugby, turning to his wife, 'he must Go, you know, before he's Gone.'

'I don't think you can move him,' said the gentleman, shaking his head. 'I wouldn't take the responsibility of saying it could be done myself. You had better leave him where he is. He can't live long.'

'It's the only subject,' said Tugby, bringing the butter-scale down upon the counter with a crash, by weighing his fist on it, 'that we've ever had a word upon; she and me; and look what it comes to! He's going to die here, after all. Going to die upon the premises. Going to die in our house!'

'And where should he have died, Tugby?' cried his wife.

'In the workhouse,' he returned. 'What are workhouses made for?'

'Not for that,' said Mrs Tugby, with great energy. 'Not for that. Neither did I marry you for that. Don't think it, Tugby. I won't have it. I won't allow it. I'd be separated first, and never see your face again. When my widow's name stood over that door, as it did for many years: this house being known as Mrs Chickenstalker's far and wide, and never known but to its honest credit and its good report: when my widow's name stood over that door, Tugby, I knew him as a handsome, steady, manly, independent youth; I knew her as the sweetest-looking, sweetest-tempered girl, eyes ever saw; I knew her father (poor old creetur, he fell down from the steeple walking in his sleep, and killed himself), for the simplest, hardest-working, childest-hearted man, that ever drew the breath of life; and when I turn them out of house and home, may angels turn me out of Heaven. As they would! And serve me right!'

Her old face, which had been a plump and dimpled one before the changes which had come to pass, seemed to shine out of her as she said these words; and when she dried her eyes, and shook her head and her handkerchief at Tugby, with an expression of firmness which it was quite clear was not to be easily resisted, Trotty said, 'Bless her! Bless her!'

Then he listened, with a panting heart, for what should follow. Knowing nothing yet, but that they spoke of Meg.

If Tugby had been a little elevated in the parlour, he more than balanced that account by being not a little depressed in the shop, where he now stood staring at his wife, without attempting a reply; secretly conveying, however – either in a fit of abstraction or as a precautionary measure – all the money from the till into his own pockets, as he looked at her.

The gentleman upon the table-beer cask, who appeared to be some authorised medical attendant upon the poor, was far too well accustomed, evidently, to little differences of opinion between man and wife, to interpose any remark in this instance. He sat softly whistling, and turning little drops of beer out of the tap upon the ground, until there was a perfect calm: when he raised his head, and said to Mrs Tugby, late Chickenstalker: 'There's something interesting about the woman, even now. How did she come to marry him?'

'Why that,' said Mrs Tugby, taking a seat near him, 'is not the least cruel part of her story, sir. You see they kept company, she and Richard, many years ago. When they were a young and beautiful couple, everything was settled, and they were to have been married on a New Year's Day. But, somehow, Richard got it into his head, through what the gentlemen told him, that he might do better, and that he'd soon repent it, and that she wasn't good enough for him, and that a young man of spirit had no business to be married. And the gentlemen frightened her, and made her melancholy, and timid of his deserting her, and of her children coming to the gallows, and of its being wicked to be man and wife, and a good deal more of it. And in short, they lingered and lingered, and their trust in one another was broken, and so at last was the match. But the fault was his. She would have married him, sir, joyfully. I've seen her heart swell, many times afterwards, when he passed her in a proud and careless way; and never did a woman grieve more truly for a man, than she for Richard when he first went wrong.'

'Oh! he went wrong, did he?' said the gentleman, pulling out the vent-peg of the table-beer, and trying to peep down into the barrel through the hole.

'Well, sir, I don't know that he rightly understood himself, you see. I think his mind was troubled by their having broke with one another; and that but for being ashamed before the gentlemen, and perhaps for being uncertain too, how she might take it, he'd have gone through any suffering or trial to have had Meg's promise and Meg's hand again. That's my belief. He never said so; more's the pity! He took to drinking, idling, bad companions: all the fine resources that were to be so much better for him than the Home he might have had. He lost his looks, his character, his health, his strength, his friends, his work: everything!'

'He didn't lose everything, Mrs Tugby,' returned the gentleman, 'because he gained a wife; and I want to know how he gained her.'

'I'm coming to it, sir, in a moment. This went on for years and years; he sinking lower and lower; she enduring, poor thing, miseries enough to wear her life away. At last, he was so cast down, and cast out, that no one would employ or notice him; and doors were shut upon him, go where he would. Applying from place to place, and door to door; and coming for the hundredth time to one gentleman who had often and often tried him (he was a good workman to the very end); that gentleman, who knew his history, said, "I believe you are incorrigible; there is only one person in the world who has a chance of reclaiming you; ask me to trust you no more, until she tries to do it." Something like that, in his anger and vexation.'

'Ah!' said the gentleman. 'Well?'

'Well, sir, he went to her, and kneeled to her; said it was so; said it ever had been so; and made a prayer to her to save him.'

'And she – Don't distress yourself, Mrs Tugby.'

'She came to me that night to ask me about living here. "What he was once to me," she said, "is buried in a grave; side by side with what I was to him. But I have thought of this; and I will make the trial. In the hope of saving him; for the love of the light-hearted girl (you remember her) who was to have been married on a New Year's Day; and for the love of her Richard." And she said he had come to her from Lilian, and Lilian had trusted to him, and she never could forget that. So they were married; and when they came home here, and I saw them, I hoped that such prophecies as parted them when they were young, may not often fulfil themselves as they did in this case, or I wouldn't be the makers of them for a Mine of Gold.'

The gentleman got off the cask, and stretched himself, observing: 'I suppose he used her ill, as soon as they were married?'

'I don't think he ever did that,' said Mrs Tugby, shaking her head, and wiping her eyes. 'He went on better for a short time; but, his habits were too old and strong to be got rid of; he soon fell back a little; and was falling fast back, when his illness came so strong upon him. I think he has always felt for her. I am sure he has. I have seen him, in his crying fits and tremblings, try to kiss her hand; and I have heard him call her "Meg", and say it was her nineteenth birthday. There he has been lying, now, these weeks and months. Between him and her baby, she has not been able to do her old work; and by not being able to be regular, she has lost it, even if she could have done it. How they have lived, I hardly know!'

'I know,' muttered Mr Tugby; looking at the till, and round the shop, and at his wife; and rolling his head with immense intelligence. 'Like Fighting Cocks!'

He was interrupted by a cry – a sound of lamentation – from the upper story of the house. The gentleman moved hurriedly to the door.

'My friend,' he said, looking back, 'you needn't discuss whether he shall be removed or not. He has spared you that trouble, I believe.'

Saying so, he ran up stairs, followed by Mrs Tugby; while Mr Tugby panted and grumbled after them at leisure: being rendered more than commonly short-winded by the weight of the till, in which there had been an inconvenient quantity of copper. Trotty, with the child beside him, floated up the staircase like mere air.

'Follow her! Follow her! Follow her!' He heard the ghostly voices in the Bells repeat their words as he ascended. 'Learn it, from the creature dearest to your heart!'

It was over. It was over. And this was she, her father's pride and joy! This haggard, wretched woman, weeping by the bed, if it deserved that name, and pressing to her breast, and hanging down her head upon, an infant. Who can tell how spare, how sickly, and how poor an infant? Who can tell how dear!

'Thank God!' cried Trotty, holding up his folded hands. 'Oh, God be thanked! She loves her child!'

The gentleman, not otherwise hard-hearted or indifferent to such scenes, than that he saw them every day, and knew that they were figures of no moment in the Filer sums – mere scratches in the working of these calculations – laid his hand upon the heart that beat no more, and listened for the breath, and said, 'His pain is over. It's better as it is!' Mrs Tugby tried to comfort her with kindness. Mr Tugby tried philosophy.

'Come, come!' he said, with his hands in his pockets, 'you mustn't give way, you know. That won't do. You must fight up. What would have become of me if *I* had given way when I was porter; and we had as many as six runaway carriage-doubles at our door in one night! But I fell back upon my strength of mind, and didn't open it!'

Again Trotty heard the voices, saying, 'Follow her!' He turned towards his guide, and saw it rising from him, passing through the air. 'Follow her!' it said. And vanished.

He hovered round her; sat down at her feet; looked up into her face for one trace of her old self; listened for one note of her old pleasant voice. He flitted round the child: so wan, so prematurely old, so dreadful in its gravity, so plaintive in its feeble, mournful, miserable wail. He almost worshipped it. He clung to it as her only safeguard; as the last unbroken link that bound her to endurance. He set his father's hope and trust on the frail baby; watched her every look upon it as she held it in her arms; and cried a thousand times, 'She loves it! God be thanked, she loves it!'

He saw the woman tend her in the night; return to her when her grudging husband was asleep, and all was still; encourage her, shed tears with her, set nourishment before her. He saw the day come, and the night again; the day, the night; the time go by; the house of death relieved of death; the room left to herself and to the child; he heard it moan and cry; he saw it harass her, and tire her out, and when she slumbered in exhaustion, drag her back to consciousness, and hold her with its little hands upon the rack; but she was constant to it, gentle with it, patient with it. Patient! Was its loving mother in her inmost heart and soul, and had its Being knitted up with hers as when she carried it unborn.

All this time, she was in want: languishing away, in dire and pining want. With the baby in her arms, she wandered here and there, in quest of occupation; and with its thin face lying in her lap, and looking up in hers, did any work for any wretched sum: a day and night of labour for as many farthings as there were figures on the dial. If she had quarrelled with it; if she had neglected it; if she had looked upon it with a moment's hate; if, in the frenzy of an instant, she had struck it! No. His comfort was, She loved it always.

She told no one of her extremity, and wandered abroad in the day lest she should be questioned by her only friend: for any help she received from her hands, occasioned fresh disputes between the good woman and her husband; and it was new bitterness to be the daily cause of strife and discord, where she owed so much.

She loved it still. She loved it more and more. But a change fell on the aspect of her love. One night.

She was singing faintly to it in its sleep, and walking to and fro to hush it, when her door was softly opened, and a man looked in.

'For the last time,' he said.

'William Fern!'

'For the last time.'

He listened like a man pursued: and spoke in whispers.

'Margaret, my race is nearly run. I couldn't finish it, without a parting word with you. Without one grateful word.'

'What have you done?' she asked: regarding him with terror.

He looked at her, but gave no answer.

After a short silence, he made a gesture with his hand, as if he set her question by; as if he brushed it aside; and said, 'It's long ago, Margaret, now: but that night is as fresh in my memory as ever 'twas. We little thought, then,' he added, looking round, 'that we should ever meet like this. Your child, Margaret? Let me have it in my arms. Let me hold your child.'

He put his hat upon the floor, and took it. And he trembled, as he took it, from head to foot.

'Is it a girl?'

'Yes.'

He put his hand before its little face.

'See how weak I'm grown, Margaret, when I want the courage to look at it! Let her be a moment. I won't hurt her. It's long ago, but – What's her name?'

'Margaret,' she answered, quickly.

'I'm glad of that,' he said. 'I'm glad of that.'

He seemed to breathe more freely; and after pausing for an instant, took away his hand, and looked upon the infant's face. But covered it again, immediately.

'Margaret!' he said; and gave her back the child. 'It's Lilian's.'

'Lilian's!'

'I held the same face in my arms when Lilian's mother died and left her.'

'When Lilian's mother died and left her!' she repeated, wildly.

'How shrill you speak! Why do you fix your eyes upon me so? Margaret!'

She sank down in a chair, and pressed the infant to her breast, and wept over it. Sometimes, she released it from her embrace, to look anxiously in its face: then strained it to her bosom again. At those times: when she gazed upon it: then it was that something fierce and terrible began to mingle with her love. Then it was that her old father quailed.

'Follow her!' was sounded through the house. 'Learn it, from the creature dearest to your heart!'

'Margaret,' said Fern, bending over her, and kissing her upon the brow: 'I thank you for the last time. Good-night. Goodbye. Put your hand in mine, and tell me you'll forget me from this hour, and try to think the end of me was here.'

'What have you done!' she asked again.

'There'll be a Fire tonight,' he said, removing from her. 'There'll be Fires this wintertime, to light the dark nights, East, West, North and South. When you see the distant sky red, they'll be blazing. When you see the distant sky red, think of me no more; or if you do, remember what a Hell was lighted up inside of me, and think you see its flames reflected in the clouds. Good-night. Goodbye!'

She called to him; but he was gone. She sat down stupefied, until her infant roused her to a sense of hunger, cold, and darkness. She paced the room with it the livelong night, hushing it and soothing it. She said at intervals, 'Like Lilian, when her mother died and left her!' Why was her step so quick, her eye so wild, her love so fierce and terrible, whenever she repeated those words?

'But it is Love,' said Trotty. 'It is Love. She'll never cease to love it. My poor Meg!'

She dressed the child next morning with unusual care – ah vain expenditure of care upon such squalid robes! – and once more tried to find some means of life. It was the last day of the Old Year. She tried till night, and never broke her fast. She tried in vain.

She mingled with an abject crowd, who tarried in the snow, until it pleased some officer appointed to dispense the public charity (the lawful charity; not that once preached upon a Mount) to call them in, and question them, and say to this one, 'Go to such a place,' to that one, 'Come next week,' to make a football of another wretch, and pass him here and there, from hand to hand, from house to house, until he wearied and lay down to die; or started up and robbed, and so became a higher sort of criminal, whose claims allowed of no delay. Here, too, she failed.

She loved her child, and wished to have it lying on her breast. And that was quite enough.

It was night: a bleak, dark, cutting night: when, pressing the child close to her for warmth, she arrived outside the house she called her home. She was so faint and giddy, that she saw no one standing in the doorway until she was close upon it, and about to enter. Then she recognised the master of the house, who had so disposed himself – with his person it was not difficult – as to fill up the whole entry.

'Oh!' he said, softly. 'You have come back?'

She looked at the child, and shook her head.

'Don't you think you have lived here long enough without paying any rent? Don't you think that, without any money, you've been a pretty constant customer at this shop, now?' said Mr Tugby.

She repeated the same mute appeal.

'Suppose you try and deal somewhere else,' he said. 'And suppose you provide yourself with another lodging. Come! Don't you think you could manage it?'

She said, in a low voice, that it was very late. Tomorrow.

'Now I see what you want,' said Tugby; 'and what you mean. You know there are two parties in this house about you, and you delight in setting 'em by the ears. I don't want any quarrels; I'm speaking softly to avoid a quarrel; but if you don't go away, I'll speak out loud, and you shall cause words high enough to please you. But you shan't come in. That I am determined.'

She put her hair back with her hand, and looked in a sudden manner at the sky, and the dark lowering distance.

'This is the last night of an Old Year: and I won't carry ill-blood and quarrellings and disturbances into a New One, to please you nor anybody else,' said Tugby, who was quite a retail Friend and Father. 'I wonder you an't ashamed of yourself, to carry such practices into a New Year. If you haven't any business in the world, but to be always giving way, and always making disturbances between man and wife, you'd be better out of it. Go along with you.'

'Follow her! To desperation!'

Again the old man heard the voices. Looking up, he saw the figures hovering in the air, and pointing where she went, down the dark street.

'She loves it!' he exclaimed, in agonised entreaty for her. 'Chimes! she loves it still!'

'Follow her!' The shadows swept upon the track she had taken, like a cloud.

He joined in the pursuit; he kept close to her; he looked into her face. He saw the same fierce and terrible expression mingling with her love, and kindling in her eyes. He heard her say, 'Like Lilian! To be changed like Lilian!' and her speed redoubled.

Oh, for something to awaken her. For any sight, or sound, or scent, to call up tender recollections in a brain on fire! For any gentle image of the Past, to rise before her!

'I was her father! I was her father!' cried the old man, stretching out his hands to the dark shadows flying on above. 'Have mercy on her, and on me! Where does she go? Turn her back! I was her father!'

But they only pointed to her, as she hurried on; and said, 'To desperation! Learn it from the creature dearest to your heart!'

A hundred voices echoed it. The air was made of breath expended in those words. He seemed to take them in, at every gasp he drew. They were everywhere, and not to be escaped. And still she hurried on; the same light in her eyes, the same words in her mouth; 'Like Lilian! To be changed like Lilian!'

All at once she stopped.

'Now, turn her back!' exclaimed the old man, tearing his white hair. 'My child! Meg! Turn her back! Great Father, turn her back!'

In her own scanty shawl, she wrapped the baby warm. With her fevered hands, she smoothed its limbs, composed its face, arranged its mean attire. In her wasted arms she folded it, as though she never would resign it more. And with her dry lips, kissed it in a final pang, and last long agony of Love.

Putting its tiny hand up to her neck, and holding it there, within her dress: next to her distracted heart: she set its sleeping face against her: closely, steadily, against her: and sped onward to the River.

To the rolling River, swift and dim, where Winter Night sat brooding like the last dark thoughts of many who had sought a refuge there before her. Where scattered lights upon the banks gleamed sullen, red, and dull, as torches that were burning there, to show the way to Death. Where no abode of living people cast its shadow, on the deep, impenetrable, melancholy shade.

To the River! To that portal of Eternity, her desperate footsteps tended with the swiftness of its rapid waters running to the sea. He tried to touch her as she passed him, going down to its dark level; but the wild distempered form, the fierce and terrible love, the desperation that had left all human check or hold behind, swept by him like the wind.

He followed her. She paused a moment on the brink, before the dreadful plunge. He fell down on his knees, and in a shriek addressed the figures in the Bells now hovering above them.

'I have learnt it!' cried the old man. 'From the creature dearest to my heart! Oh, save her, save her!'

He could wind his fingers in her dress; could hold it! As the words escaped his lips, he felt his sense of touch return, and knew that he detained her.

The figures looked down steadfastly upon him.

'I have learnt it!' cried the old man. 'Oh, have mercy on me in this hour, if, in my love for her, so young and good, I slandered Nature in the breasts of mothers rendered desperate! Pity my presumption, wickedness, and ignorance, and save her!'

He felt his hold relaxing. They were silent still.

'Have mercy on her!' he exclaimed, 'as one in whom this dreadful crime has sprung from Love perverted; from the strongest, deepest love we fallen creatures know! Think what her misery must have been, when such seed bears such fruit! Heaven meant her to be good. There is no loving mother on the earth who might not come to this, if such a life had gone before. Oh, have mercy on my child, who, even at this pass, means mercy to her own, and dies herself, and perils her Immortal Soul, to save it!'

She was in his arms. He held her now. His strength was like a giant's.

'I see the Spirit of the Chimes among you!' cried the old man, singling out the child, and speaking in some inspiration, which their looks conveyed to him. 'I know that our inheritance is held in store for us by Time. I know there is a Sea of Time to rise one day, before which all who wrong us or oppress us will be swept away like leaves. I see it, on the flow! I know that we must trust and hope, and neither doubt ourselves, nor doubt the Good in one another. I have learnt it from the creature dearest to my heart. I clasp her in my arms again. Oh Spirits, merciful and good, I take your lesson to my breast along with her! Oh Spirits, merciful and good, I am grateful!'

He might have said more but the Bells; the old familiar Bells, his own dear, constant, steady friends, the Chimes; began to ring the joy-peals for a New Year, so lustily, so merrily, so happily, so gaily, that he leapt upon his feet, and broke the spell that bound him.

'And whatever you do, father,' said Meg, 'don't eat tripe again, without asking some doctor whether it's likely to agree with you; for how you *have* been going on, Good gracious!'

She was working with her needle, at the little table by the fire; dressing her simple gown with ribbons for her wedding. So quietly happy, so blooming and youthful, so full of beautiful promise, that he uttered a great cry as if it were an Angel in his house; then flew to clasp her in his arms.

But he caught his feet in the newspaper, which had fallen on the hearth; and somebody came rushing in between them.

'No!' cried the voice of this same somebody; a generous and jolly voice it was! 'Not even you. Not even you. The first kiss of Meg in the New Year is mine. Mine! I have been waiting outside the house, this hour, to hear the Bells and claim it. Meg, my precious prize, a happy year! A life of happy years, my darling wife!'

And Richard smothered her with kisses.

You never in all your life saw anything like Trotty after this. I don't care where you have lived or what you have seen; you never in your life saw anything at all approaching him! He sat down in his chair and beat his knees and cried; he sat down in his chair and beat his knees and laughed; he sat down in his chair and beat his knees and laughed and cried together; he got out of his chair and hugged Meg; he got out of his chair and hugged Richard; he got out of his chair and hugged them both at once; he kept running up to Meg, and squeezing her fresh face between his hands and kissing it, going from her backwards not to lose sight of it, and running up again like a figure in a magic lantern; and whatever he did, he was constantly sitting himself down in this chair, and never stopping in it for one single moment; being – that's the truth – beside himself with joy.

'And tomorrow's your wedding day, my pet!' cried Trotty. 'Your real, happy wedding-day!'

'Today!' cried Richard, shaking hands with him. 'Today. The Chimes are ringing in the New Year. Hear them!'

They WERE ringing! Bless their sturdy hearts, they WERE ringing! Great Bells as they were: melodious, deep-mouthed, noble Bells; cast in no common metal; made by no common founder; when had they ever chimed like that before!

'But today, my Pet,' said Trotty. 'You and Richard had some words today.'

'Because he's such a bad fellow, father,' said Meg. 'An't you, Richard? Such a headstrong, violent man! He'd have made no more of speaking his mind to that great Alderman, and putting *him* down I don't know where, than he would of – '

' – Kissing Meg,' suggested Richard. Doing it too!

'No. Not a bit more,' said Meg. 'But I wouldn't let him, father. Where would have been the use!'

'Richard my boy!' cried Trotty. 'You was turned up Trumps originally; and Trumps you must be, till you die! But you were crying by the fire tonight, my pet, when I came home! Why did you cry by the fire?'

'I was thinking of the years we've passed together, father. Only that. And thinking you might miss me, and be lonely.'

Trotty was backing off to that extraordinary chair again, when the child, who had been awakened by the noise, came running in half dressed.

'Why, here she is!' cried Trotty, catching her up. 'Here's little Lilian! Ha ha ha! Here we are and here we go! Oh, here we are and here we go again! And here we are and here we go! and Uncle Will too!' Stopping in his trot to greet him heartily. 'Oh, Uncle Will, the vision that I've had tonight, through lodging you! Oh, Uncle Will, the obligations that you've laid me under, by your coming, my good friend!'

Before Will Fern could make the least reply, a band of music burst into the room, attended by a lot of neighbours, screaming 'A Happy New Year, Meg!' 'A Happy Wedding!' 'Many of 'em!' and other fragmentary good wishes of that sort. The Drum (who was a private friend of Trotty's) then stepped forward, and said: 'Trotty Veck, my boy! It's got about, that your daughter is going to be married tomorrow. There an't a soul that knows you that don't wish you well, or that knows her and don't wish her well. Or that knows you both, and don't wish you both all the happiness the New Year can bring. And here we are, to play it in and dance it in, accordingly.'

Which was received with a general shout. The Drum was rather drunk, by the by; but never mind.

'What a happiness it is, I'm sure,' said Trotty, 'to be so esteemed! How kind and neighbourly you are! It's all along of my dear daughter. She deserves it!'

They were ready for a dance in half a second (Meg and Richard at the top); and the Drum was on the very brink of leathering away with all his power; when a combination of prodigious sounds was heard outside, and a good-humoured comely woman of some fifty years of age, or there-abouts, came running in, attended by a man bearing a stone pitcher of terrific size, and closely followed by the marrow-bones and cleavers, and the bells; not *the* Bells, but a portable collection, on a frame.

Trotty said, 'It's Mrs Chickenstalker!' And sat down, and beat his knees again.

'Married, and not tell me, Meg!' cried the good woman. 'Never! I couldn't rest on the last night of the Old Year without coming to wish you joy. I couldn't have done it, Meg. Not if I had been bedridden. So here I am; and as it's New Year's Eve, and the Eve of your Wedding too, my dear, I had a little flip made, and brought it with me.'

Mrs Chickenstalker's notion of a little flip, did honour to her character. The pitcher steamed and smoked and reeked like a volcano; and the man who had carried it, was faint.

'Mrs Tugby!' said Trotty, who had been going round and round her, in an ecstasy. 'I *should* say, Chickenstalker – Bless your heart and soul! A Happy New Year, and many of 'em! Mrs Tugby,' said Trotty when he had saluted her; 'I *should* say, Chickenstalker – This is William Fern and Lilian.'

The worthy dame, to his surprise, turned very pale and very red. 'Not Lilian Fern whose mother died in Dorsetshire!' said she. Her uncle answered, 'Yes,' and meeting hastily, they exchanged some hurried words together, of which the upshot was, that Mrs Chickenstalker shook him by both hands; saluted Trotty on his cheek again, of her own free will; and took the child to her capacious breast.

'Will Fern!' said Trotty, pulling on his right-hand muffler. 'Not the friend that you was hoping to find?'

'Ay!' returned Will, putting a hand on each of Trotty's shoulders. 'And like to prove a'most as good a friend, if that can be, as one I found.'

'Oh!' said Trotty. 'Please to play up there. Will you have the goodness!'

To the music of the band, the bells, the marrow-bones and cleavers, all at once; and while the Chimes were yet in lusty operation out of doors; Trotty, making Meg and Richard second couple, led off Mrs Chicken-stalker down the dance, and danced it in a step unknown before or since; founded on his own peculiar trot.

Had Trotty dreamed? Or are his joys and sorrows, and the actors in them, but a dream; himself a dream; the teller of this tale a dreamer, waking but now? If it be so, O Listener, dear to him in all his visions, try to bear in mind the stern realities from which these shadows come; and in your sphere – none is too wide, and none too limited for such an end – endeavour to correct, improve, and soften them. So may the New Year be a Happy one to You, Happy to many more whose Happiness depends on You! So may each Year be happier than the last, and not the meanest of our brethren or sisterhood debarred their rightful share, in what our Great Creator formed them to enjoy.

THE CRICKET ON THE HEARTH

A Fairy Tale of Home

CHIRP THE FIRST

The kettle began it! Don't tell me what Mrs Peerybingle said. I know better. Mrs Peerybingle may leave it on record to the end of time that she couldn't say which of them began it; but, I say the kettle did. I ought to know, I hope? The kettle began it, full five minutes by the little waxy-faced Dutch clock in the corner before the cricket uttered a chirp.

As if the clock hadn't finished striking, and the convulsive little Hay-maker at the top of it, jerking away right and left with a scythe in front of a Moorish palace, hadn't mowed down half an acre of imaginary grass before the cricket joined in at all!

Why, I am not naturally positive. Everyone knows that. I wouldn't set my own opinion against the opinion of Mrs Peerybingle, unless I were quite sure, on any account whatever. Nothing should induce me. But this is a question of fact. And the fact is, that the kettle began it, at least five minutes before the cricket gave any sign of being in existence. Contradict me: and I'll say ten.

Let me narrate exactly how it happened. I should have proceeded to do so, in my very first word, but for this plain consideration – if I am to tell a story I must begin at the beginning; and how is it possible to begin at the beginning without beginning at the kettle?

It appeared as if there were a sort of match, or trial of skill, you must understand, between the kettle and the cricket. And this is what led to it, and how it came about.

Mrs Peerybingle, going out into the raw twilight, and clicking over the wet stones in a pair of pattens that worked innumerable rough impressions of the first proposition in Euclid all about the yard – Mrs Peerybingle filled the kettle at the water-butt. Presently returning, less the pattens: and a good deal less, for they were tall and Mrs Peerybingle was but short: she set the kettle on the fire. In doing which she lost her temper, or mislaid it for an instant; for, the water – being uncomfortably cold, and in that slippy, slushy, sleety sort of state wherein it seems to penetrate through every kind of substance, patten rings included – had laid hold of Mrs Peerybingle's toes, and even splashed her legs. And when we rather plume ourselves (with reason too) upon our legs, and keep ourselves particularly neat in point of stockings, we find this, for the moment, hard to bear.

Besides, the kettle was aggravating and obstinate. It wouldn't allow itself to be adjusted on the top bar, it wouldn't hear of accommodating itself kindly to the knobs of coal; it would lean forward with a drunken air, and dribble, a very Idiot of a kettle, on the hearth. It was quarrelsome; and hissed and spluttered morosely at the fire. To sum up all, the lid, resisting Mrs Peerybingle's fingers, first of all turned topsy-turvy, and then, with an ingenious pertinacity deserving of a better cause, dived sideways in – down to the very bottom of the kettle. And the hull of the Royal George has never made half the monstrous resistance to coming out of the water, which the lid of that kettle employed against Mrs Peerybingle, before she got it up again.

It looked sullen and pig-headed enough, even then; carrying its handle with an air of defiance, and cocking its spout pertly and mockingly at Mrs Peerybingle, as if it said, 'I won't boil. Nothing shall induce me!'

But Mrs Peerybingle, with restored good humour, dusted her chubby little hands against each other, and sat down before the kettle: laughing. Meantime, the jolly blaze uprose and fell, flashing and gleaming on the little Haymaker at the top of the Dutch clock, until one might have thought he stood stock still before the Moorish palace, and nothing was in motion but the flame.

He was on the move, however; and had his spasms, two to the second, all right and regular. But his sufferings when the clock was going to strike were frightful to behold; and when a cuckoo looked out of a trap-door in the Palace, and gave note six times, it shook him, each time, like a spectral voice – or like a something wiry, plucking at his legs.

It was not until a violent commotion and a whirring noise among the weights and ropes below him had quite subsided, that this terrified Haymaker became himself again. Nor was he startled without reason; for these rattling, bony skeletons of clocks are very disconcerting in their operation, and I wonder very much how any set of men, but most of all how Dutchmen, can have had a liking to invent them. For there is a popular belief that Dutchmen love broad cases and much clothing for their own lower selves; and they might know better than to leave their clocks so very lank and unprotected, surely.

Now it was, you observe, that the kettle began to spend the evening. Now it was, that the kettle, growing mellow and musical, began to have irrepressible gurglings in its throat, and to indulge in short vocal snorts, which it checked in the bud, as if it hadn't quite made up its mind yet, to be good company. Now it was, that after two or three such vain attempts to stifle its convivial sentiments, it threw off all moroseness, all reserve, and burst into a stream of song so cosy and hilarious, as never maudlin nightingale yet formed the least idea of.

So plain, too! Bless you, you might have understood it like a book – better than some books you and I could name, perhaps. With its warm breath gushing forth in a light cloud which merrily and gracefully ascended a few feet, then hung about the chimney-corner as its own domestic Heaven, it trolled its song with that strong energy of cheerfulness, that its iron body hummed and stirred upon the fire; and the lid itself, the recently rebellious lid – such is the influence of a bright example – performed a sort of jig, and clattered like a deaf and dumb young cymbal that had never known the use of its twin brother.

That this song of the kettle's was a song of invitation and welcome to somebody out of doors; to somebody at that moment coming on, towards the snug small home and the crisp fire; there is no doubt whatever. Mrs Peerybingle knew it, perfectly, as she sat musing, before the hearth. It's a dark night, sang the kettle, and the rotten leaves are lying by the way; and above, all is mist and darkness, and below, all is mire and clay; and there's only one relief in all the sad and murky air; and I don't know that it is one, for it's nothing but a glare, of deep and angry crimson, where the sun and wind together, set a brand upon the clouds for being guilty of such weather; and the widest open country is a long dull streak of black; and there's hoar-frost on the finger-post, and thaw upon the track; and the ice it isn't water, and the water isn't free; and you couldn't say that anything is what it ought to be; but he's coming, coming, coming! –

And here, if you like, the cricket *did* chime in! with a chirrup, chirrup, chirrup of such magnitude, by way of chorus; with a voice, so astoundingly disproportionate to its size, as compared with the kettle; (size! you couldn't see it!) that if it had then and there burst itself like an overcharged gun: if it had fallen a victim on the spot, and chirruped its little body into fifty pieces: it would have seemed a natural and inevitable consequence, for which it had expressly laboured.

The kettle had had the last of its solo performance. It persevered with undiminished ardour; but the cricket took first fiddle and kept it. Good Heaven, how it chirped! Its shrill, sharp, piercing voice resounded through the house, and seemed to twinkle in the outer darkness like a Star. There was an indescribable little trill and tremble in it, at its loudest, which suggested its being carried off its legs, and made to leap again by its own intense enthusiasm. Yet they went very well together, the cricket and the kettle. The burden of the song was still the same; and louder, louder, louder still, they sang it in their emulation.

The fair little listener – for fair she was, and young: though something of what is called the dumpling shape; but I don't myself object to that – lighted a candle; glanced at the Haymaker on the top of the clock, who was getting in a pretty average crop of minutes; and looked out of the window, where she saw nothing, owing to the darkness, but her own face imaged in the glass. And my opinion is (and so would yours have been), that she might have looked a long way, and seen nothing half so agreeable. When she came back, and sat down in her former seat, the cricket and the kettle were still keeping it up, with a perfect fury of competition. The kettle's weak side clearly being that he didn't know when he was beat.

There was all the excitement of a race about it. Chirp, chirp, chirp! cricket a mile ahead. Hum, hum, hum–m–m! Kettle making play in the distance, like a great top. Chirp, chirp, chirp! Cricket round the corner. Hum, hum, hum–m–m! Kettle sticking to him in his own way; no idea of giving in. Chirp, chirp, chirp! Cricket fresher than ever. Hum, hum, hum–m–m! Kettle slow and steady. Chirp, chirp, chirp! Cricket going in to finish him. Hum, hum, hum–m–m! Kettle not to be finished. Until at last, they got so jumbled together, in the hurry-skurry, helter-skelter, of the match, that whether the kettle chirped and the cricket hummed, or the cricket chirped and the kettle hummed, or they both chirped and both hummed, it would have taken a clearer head than yours or mine to have decided with anything like certainty. But of this, there is no doubt: that the kettle and the cricket, at one and the same moment, and by some power of amalgamation best known to themselves, sent, each, his fireside song of comfort streaming into a ray of the candle that shone out through the window; and a long way down the lane. And this light, bursting on a certain person who, on the instant, approached towards it through the gloom, expressed the whole thing to him, literally in a twinkling, and cried 'Welcome home, old fellow! Welcome home, my Boy!'

This end attained, the kettle, being dead beat, boiled over, and was taken off the fire. Mrs Peerybingle then went running to the door, where, what with the wheels of a cart, the tramp of a horse, the voice of a man, the tearing in and out of an excited dog, and the surprising and mysterious appearance of a baby, there was soon the very-What's-his-name to pay.

Where the baby came from or how Mrs Peerybingle got hold of it in that flash of time, *I* don't know. But a live baby there was, in Mrs Peerybingle's arms; and a pretty tolerable amount of pride she seemed to have in it, when she was drawn gently to the fire, by a sturdy figure of a man, much taller and much older than herself; who had to stoop a long way down, to kiss her. But she was worth the trouble. Six foot six, with the lumbago, might have done it.

'Oh goodness, John!' said Mrs P. 'What a state you're in with the weather!'

He was something the worse for it, undeniably. The thick mist hung

in clots upon his eyelashes like candied thaw; and between the fog and fire together, there were rainbows in his very whiskers.

'Why, you see, Dot,' John made answer, slowly, as he unrolled a shawl from about his throat; and warmed his hands; 'it – it an't exactly summer weather. So, no wonder.'

'I wish you wouldn't call me Dot, John. I don't like it,' said Mrs Peerybingle: pouting in a way that clearly showed she *did* like it, very much.

'Why what else are you?' returned John, looking down upon her with a smile, and giving her waist as light a squeeze as his huge hand and arm could give. 'A dot and' – here he glanced at the baby – 'a dot and carry – I won't say it, for fear I should spoil it; but I was very near a joke. I don't know as ever I was nearer.' He was often near to something or other very clever, by his own account: this lumbering, slow, honest John; this John so heavy, but so light of spirit; so rough upon the surface, but so gentle at the core; so dull without, so quick within; so stolid, but so good! Oh Mother Nature, give thy children the true poetry of heart that hid itself in this poor carrier's breast – he was but a carrier by the way – and we can bear to have them talking prose, and leading lives of prose; and bear to bless Thee for their company!

It was pleasant to see Dot, with her little figure and her baby in her arms: a very doll of a baby: glancing with a coquettish thoughtfulness at the fire, and inclining her delicate little head just enough on one side to let it rest in an odd, half-natural, half-affected, wholly nestling and agreeable manner, on the great rugged figure of the carrier. It was pleasant to see him, with his tender awkwardness, endeavouring to adapt his rude support to her slight need, and make his burly middle-age a leaning-staff not inappropriate to her blooming youth. It was pleasant to observe how Tilly Slowboy, waiting in the background for the baby, took special cognisance (though in her earliest teens) of this grouping; and stood with her mouth and eyes wide open, and her head thrust forward, taking it in as if it were air. Nor was it less agreeable to observe how John the carrier, reference being made by Dot to the aforesaid baby, checked his hand when on the point of touching the infant, as if he thought he might crack it; and bending down, surveyed it from a safe distance, with a kind of puzzled pride: such as an amiable mastiff might be supposed to show, if he found himself, one day, the father of a young canary.

'An't he beautiful, John? Don't he look precious in his sleep?'

'Very precious,' said John. 'Very much so. He generally *is* asleep, ain't he?'

'Lor John! Good gracious no!'

'Oh,' said John, pondering. 'I thought his eyes was generally shut. Halloa!'

'Goodness John, how you startle one!'

'It an't right for him to turn 'em up in that way!' said the astonished carrier, 'is it? See how he's winking with both of 'em at once! And look at his mouth! why he's gasping like a gold and silver fish!'

'You don't deserve to be a father, you don't,' said Dot, with all the dignity of an experienced matron. 'But how should you know what little complaints children are troubled with, John! You wouldn't so much as know their names, you stupid fellow.' And when she had turned the baby over on her left arm, and had slapped its back as a restorative, she pinched her husband's ear, laughing.

'No,' said John, pulling off his outer coat. 'It's very true, Dot. I don't know much about it. I only know that I've been fighting pretty stiffly with the wind tonight. It's been blowing north-east straight into the cart, the whole way home.'

'Poor old man, so it has!' cried Mrs Peerybingle, instantly becoming very active. 'Here! Take the precious darling, Tilly, while I make myself of some use. Bless it, I could smother it with kissing it, I could! Hie then, good dog! Hie Boxer, boy! Only let me make the tea first, John; and then I'll help you with the parcels, like a busy bee. "How doth the little" – and all the rest of it, you know, John. Did you ever learn "how doth the little," when you went to school, John?'

'Not to quite know it,' John returned. 'I was very near it once. But I should only have spoilt it, I dare say.'

'Ha ha!' laughed Dot. She had the blithest little laugh you ever heard. 'What a dear old darling of a dunce you are, John, to be sure!'

Not at all disputing this position, John went out to see that the boy with the lantern, which had been dancing to and fro before the door and window, like a Will of the Wisp, took due care of the horse; who was fatter than you would quite believe, if I gave you his measure, and so old that his birthday was lost in the mists of antiquity. Boxer, feeling that his attentions were due to the family in general, and must be impartially distributed, dashed in and out with bewildering inconstancy; now describing a circle of short barks round the horse, where he was being rubbed down at the stable-door; now feigning to make savage rushes at his mistress, and facetiously bringing himself to sudden stops; now eliciting a shriek from Tilly Slowboy, in the low nursing-chair near the fire, by the unexpected application of his moist nose to her countenance; now exhibiting an obtrusive interest in the baby; now going round and round upon the hearth, and lying down as if he had established himself for the night; now getting up again, and taking that nothing of a fag-end of a tail of his, out into the weather, as if he had just remembered an appointment, and was off, at a round trot, to keep it.

'There! There's the teapot, ready on the hob!' said Dot; as briskly busy as a child at play at keeping house. 'And there's the cold knuckle of ham; and there's the butter; and there's the crusty loaf, and all. Here's the clothes-basket for the small parcels, John, if you've got any there – where are you, John? Don't let the dear child fall under the grate, Tilly, whatever you do.'

It may be noted of Miss Slowboy, in spite of her rejecting the caution with some vivacity, that she had a rare and surprising talent for getting this baby into difficulties: and had several times imperilled its short life, in a quiet way peculiarly her own. She was of a spare and straight shape,

this young lady, insomuch that her garments appeared to be in constant danger of sliding off those sharp pegs, her shoulders, on which they were loosely hung. Her costume was remarkable for the partial development, on all possible occasions, of some flannel vestment of a singular structure; also for affording glimpses, in the region of the back, of a corset or pair of stays in colour a dead-green. Being always in a state of gaping admiration at everything, and absorbed besides in the perpetual contemplation of her mistress's perfections and the baby's, Miss Slowboy, in her little errors of judgement, may be aid to have done equal honour to her head and to her heart; and though these did less honour to the baby's head, which they were the occasional means of bringing into contact with deal doors, dressers, stair-rails, bed-posts, and other foreign substances, still they were the honest results of Tilly Slowboy's constant astonishment at finding herself so kindly treated, and installed in such a comfortable home. For, the maternal and paternal Slowboy were alike unknown to fame, and Tilly had been bred by public charity, a Foundling; which word, though only differing from Fondling by one vowel's length, is very different in meaning, and expresses quite another thing.

To have seen little Mrs Peerybingle come back with her husband;

tugging at the clothes-basket, and making the most strenuous exertions to do nothing at all (for he carried it); would have amused you, almost as much as it amused him. It may have entertained the cricket too, for anything I know; but certainly, it now began to chirp again, vehemently.

'Heyday!' said John, in his slow way. 'It's merrier than ever, tonight, I think.'

'And it's sure to bring us good fortune, John! It always has done so. To have a cricket on the hearth, is the luckiest thing in all the world!'

John looked at her as if he had very nearly got the thought into his head, that she was his cricket in chief, and he quite agreed with her. But it was probably one of his narrow escapes, for he said nothing.

'The first time I heard its cheerful little note, John, was on that night when you brought me home – when you brought me to my new home here; its little mistress. Nearly a year ago. You recollect, John?'

Oh yes. John remembered. I should think so!

'Its chirp was such a welcome to me! It seemed so full of promise and encouragement. It seemed to say, you would be kind and gentle with me and would not expect (I had a fear of that, John, then) to find an old head on the shoulders of your foolish little wife.'

John thoughtfully patted one of the shoulders, and then the head, as though he would have said No, no; he had had no such expectation; he had been quite content to take them as they were. And really he had reason. They were very comely.

'It spoke the truth, John, when it seemed to say so; for you have ever been, I am sure, the best, the most considerate, the most affectionate of husbands to me. This has been a happy home, John; and I love the cricket for its sake!'

'Why so do I then,' said the carrier. 'So do I, Dot.'

'I love it for the many times I have heard it, and the many thoughts its harmless music has given me. Sometimes, in the twilight, when I felt a little solitary and down-hearted, John – before baby was here to keep me company and make the house gay – when I have thought how lonely you would be if I should die; how lonely I should be if I could know that you had lost me, dear; its chirp, chirp, chirp upon the hearth, has seemed to tell me of another little voice, so sweet, so very dear to me, before whose coming sound my trouble vanished like a dream. And when I used to fear – I did fear once, John; I was very young you know – that ours might prove to be an ill-assorted marriage: I being such a child, and you more like my guardian than my husband: and that you might not, however hard you tried, be able to learn to love me, as you hoped and prayed you might; its chirp, chirp, chirp has cheered me up again, and filled me with new trust and confidence. I was thinking of these things, dear, when I sat expecting you; and I love the cricket for their sake!'

'And so do I,' repeated John. 'But Dot? *I* hope and pray that I might learn to love you? How you talk! I had learnt that, long before I brought you here, to be the cricket's little mistress, Dot!'

She laid her hand, an instant, on his arm, and looked up at him with an agitated face, as if she would have told him something. Next moment she was down upon her knees before the basket; speaking in a sprightly voice, and busy with the parcels.

'There are not many of them tonight, John, but I saw some goods behind the cart, just now; and though they give more trouble, perhaps, still they pay as well; so we have no reason to grumble, have we? Besides, you have been delivering, I dare say, as you came along?'

'Oh yes,' John said. 'A good many.'

'Why what's this round box? Heart alive, John, it's a wedding-cake!'

'Leave a woman alone to find out that,' said John, admiringly. 'Now a man would never have thought of it! Whereas, it's my belief that if you was to pack a wedding cake up in a tea-chest, or a turn-up bedstead, or a pickled salmon keg, or any unlikely thing, a woman would be sure to find it out directly. Yes; I called for it at the pastrycook's.'

'And it weighs I don't know what – whole hundredweights!' cried Dot, making a great demonstration of trying to lift it. 'Whose is it, John? Where is it going?'

'Read the writing on the other side,' said John.

'Why, John! My goodness, John!'

'Ah! who'd have thought it!' John returned.

'You never mean to say,' pursued Dot, sitting on the floor and shaking her head at him, 'that it's Gruff and Tackleton the toymaker!'

John nodded.

Mrs Peerybingle nodded also, fifty times at least. Not in assent – in dumb and pitying amazement; screwing up her lips the while, with all their little force (they were never made for screwing up; I am clear of that), and looking the good carrier through and through, in her abstraction. Miss Slowboy, in the meantime, who had a mechanical power of reproducing scraps of current conversation for the delectation of the baby, with all the sense struck out of them, and all the nouns changed into the plural number, enquired aloud of that young creature, Was it Gruffs and Tackletons the toymakers then, and Would it call at pastry-cooks for wedding-cakes, and Did its mothers know the boxes when its fathers brought them homes; and so on.

'And that is really to come about!' said Dot. 'Why, she and I were girls at school together, John.'

He might have been thinking of her: or nearly thinking of her, perhaps: as she was in that same school time. He looked upon her with a thoughtful pleasure, but he made no answer.

'And he's as old! As unlike her! – Why, how many years older than you is Gruff and Tackleton, John?'

'How many more cups of tea shall I drink tonight at one sitting than Gruff and Tackleton ever took in four, I wonder!' replied John, good-humouredly, as he drew a chair to the round table, and began at the cold ham. 'As to eating, I eat but little; but that little I enjoy, Dot.'

Even this; his usual sentiment at meal times, one of his innocent delusions (for his appetite was always obstinate, and flatly contradicted him); awoke no smile in the face of his little wife, who stood among the parcels, pushing the cake-box slowly from her with her feet, and never once looked, though her eyes were cast down too, upon the dainty shoe she generally was so mindful of. Absorbed in thought, she stood there, heedless alike of the tea and John (although he called to her, and rapped the table with his knife to startle her), until he rose and touched her on the arm; when she looked at him for a moment, and hurried to her place behind the teaboard, laughing at her negligence. But not as she had laughed before. The manner and the music were quite changed.

The cricket, too, had stopped. Somehow the room was not so cheerful as it had been. Nothing like it.

'So these are all the parcels, are they, John?' she said: breaking a long silence, which the honest carrier had devoted to the practical illustration of one part of his favourite sentiment – certainly enjoying what he ate, if it couldn't be admitted that he ate but little. 'So these are all the parcels; are they, John?'

'That's all,' said John. 'Why – no – I – ' laying down his knife and fork, and taking a long breath. 'I declare – I've clean forgotten the old gentleman!'

'The old gentleman?'

'In the cart,' said John. 'He was asleep, among the straw, the last time

I saw him. I've very nearly remembered him, twice, since I came in; but he went out of my head again. Holloa! Yahip there! Rouse up! That's my hearty!'

John said these latter words outside the door, whither he had hurried with the candle in his hand.

Miss Slowboy, conscious of some mysterious reference to the Old Gentleman, and connecting in her mystified imagination certain associations of a religious nature with the phrase, was so disturbed, that hastily rising from the low chair by the fire to seek protection near the skirts of her mistress, and coming into contact as she crossed the doorway with an ancient stranger, she instinctively made a charge or butt at him with the only offensive instrument within her reach. This instrument happening to be the baby, great commotion and alarm ensued, which the sagacity of Boxer rather intended to increase; for that good dog, more thoughtful than its master, had, it seemed, been watching the old gentleman in his sleep lest he should walk off with a few young poplar trees that were tied up behind the cart; and he still attended on him very closely; worrying his gaiters in fact, and making dead sets at the buttons.

'You're such an undeniable good sleeper, sir,' said John, when tranquillity was restored; in the meantime the old gentleman had stood, bareheaded and motionless, in the centre of the room; 'that I have half a mind to ask you where the other six are: only that would be a joke, and I know I should spoil it. Very near though,' murmured the carrier, with a chuckle; 'very near!'

The stranger, who had long white hair; good features, singularly bold and well defined for an old man; and dark, bright, penetrating eyes; looked round with a smile, and saluted the carrier's wife by gravely inclining his head.

His garb was very quaint and odd – a long, long way behind the time. Its hue was brown, all over. In his hand he held a great brown club or walking-stick; and striking this upon the floor, it fell asunder, and became a chair. On which he sat down, quite composedly.

'There!' said the carrier, turning to his wife. 'That's the way I found him, sitting by the roadside! Upright as a milestone. And almost as deaf.'

'Sitting in the open air, John!'

'In the open air,' replied the carrier, 'just at dusk. "Carriage Paid," he said; and gave me eighteenpence. Then he got in. And there he is.'

'He's going, John, I think!'

Not at all. He was only going to speak.

'If you please, I was to be left till called for,' said the stranger, mildly. 'Don't mind me.'

With that, he took a pair of spectacles from one of his large pockets, and a book from another, and leisurely began to read. Making no more of Boxer than if he had been a house lamb!

The carrier and his wife exchanged a look of perplexity. The stranger raised his head; and glancing from the latter to the former, said: 'Your daughter, my good friend?'

'Wife,' returned John.

'Niece?' said the stranger.

'Wife,' roared John.

'Indeed?' observed the stranger. 'Surely? Very young!'

He quietly turned over, and resumed his reading. But before he could have read two lines, he again interrupted himself to say: 'baby, yours?'

John gave him a gigantic nod; equivalent to an answer in the affirmative, delivered through a speaking-trumpet.

'Girl?'

'Bo–o–oy!' roared John.

'Also very young, eh?'

Mrs Peerybingle instantly struck in. 'Two months and three da–ays! Vaccinated just six weeks ago–o! Took very fine–ly! Considered, by the doctor, a remarkably beautiful chi–ild! Equal to the general run of children at five months o–old! Takes notice, in a way quite won–derful. May seem impossible to you, but feels his legs already!'

Here the breathless little mother, who had been shrieking these short sentences into the old man's ear, until her pretty face was crimsoned, held up the baby before him as a stubborn and triumphant fact; while Tilly Slowboy, with a melodious cry of 'Ketcher, Ketcher' – which sounded like some unknown words, adapted to a popular sneeze – performed some cow-like gambols round that all-unconscious innocent.

'Hark! He's called for, sure enough,' said John. 'There's somebody at the door. Open it, Tilly.'

Before she could reach it, however, it was opened from without; being a primitive sort of door, with a latch that anyone could lift if he chose – and a good many people did choose, I can tell you; for all kinds of neighbours liked to have a cheerful word or two with the carrier, though he was no great talker himself. Being opened, it gave admission to a little, meagre, thoughtful, dingy-faced man, who seemed to have made himself a greatcoat from the sackcloth covering of some old box; for when he turned to shut the door, and keep the weather out, he disclosed upon the back of that garment, the inscription G & T in large black capitals. Also the word GLASS in bold characters.

'Good-evening, John!' said the little man. 'Good-evening, Mum. Good-evening, Tilly. Good-evening, Unbeknown! How's baby, Mum? Boxer's pretty well I hope?'

'All thriving, Caleb,' replied Dot. 'I am sure you need only look at the dear child, for one, to know that.'

'And I'm sure I need only look at you for another,' said Caleb.

He didn't look at her though; he had a wandering and thoughtful eye which seemed to be always projecting itself into some other time and place, no matter what he said; a description which will equally apply to his voice.

'Or at John for another,' said Caleb. 'Or at Tilly, as far as that goes. Or certainly at Boxer.'

'Busy just now, Caleb?' asked the carrier.

'Why, pretty well, John,' he returned, with the distraught air of a man who was casting about for the philosopher's stone, at least. 'Pretty much so. There's rather a run on Noah's Arks at present. I could have wished to improve upon the family, but I don't see how it's to be done at the price. It would be a satisfaction to one's mind, to make it clearer which was Shems and Hams and which was Wives. Flies an't on that scale neither, as compared with elephants you know! Ah! well! Have you got anything in the parcel line for me, John?'

The carrier put his hand into a pocket of the coat he had taken off; and brought out, carefully preserved in moss and paper, a tiny flowerpot.

'There it is!' he said, adjusting it with great care. 'Not so much as a leaf damaged. Full of buds!'

Caleb's dull eye brightened, as he took it, and thanked him.

'Dear, Caleb,' said the carrier. 'Very dear at this season.'

'Never mind that. It would be cheap to me, whatever it cost,' returned the little man. 'Anything else, John?'

'A small box,' replied the carrier. 'Here you are!'

' "For Caleb Plummer," said the little man, spelling out the direction. ' "With cash." With cash, John. I don't think it's for me.'

'With care,' returned the carrier, looking over his shoulder. 'Where do you make out cash?'

'Oh! To be sure!' said Caleb. 'It's all right. With care! Yes, yes; that's mine. It might have been with cash, indeed, if my dear boy in the golden South Americas had lived, John. You loved him like a son; didn't you? You needn't say you did. *I* know, of course. "Caleb Plummer. With care". Yes, yes, it's all right. It's a box of dolls' eyes for my daughter's work. I wish it was her own sight in a box, John.'

'I wish it was, or could be!' cried the carrier.

'Thank'ee,' said the little man. 'You speak very hearty. To think that she should never see the dolls – and them a-staring at her, so bold, all day long! That's where it cuts. What's the damage, John?'

'I'll damage you,' said John, 'if you enquire. Dot! Very near?'

'Well! it's like you to say so,' observed the little man. 'It's your kind way. Let me see. I think that's all.'

'I think not,' said the carrier. 'Try again.'

'Something for our governor, eh?' said Caleb, after pondering a little while. 'To be sure. That's what I came for; but my head's so running on them Arks and things! He hasn't been here, has he?'

'Not he,' returned the carrier. 'He's too busy, courting.'

'He's coming round though,' said Caleb; 'for he told me to keep on the near side of the road going home, and it was ten to one he'd take me up. I had better go, by the by. – You couldn't have the goodness to let me pinch Boxer's tail, Mum, for half a moment, could you?'

'Why, Caleb! what a question!'

'Oh never mind, Mum,' said the little man. 'He mightn't like it perhaps. There's a small order just come in, for barking dogs; and I should wish to go as close to Natur' as I could, for sixpence. That's all. Never mind Mum.'

It happened opportunely, that Boxer, without receiving the proposed stimulus, began to bark with great zeal. But as this implied the approach of some new visitor, Caleb, postponing his study from the life to a more convenient season, shouldered the round box, and took a hurried leave. He might have spared himself the trouble, for he met the visitor upon the threshold.

'Oh! You are here, are you? Wait a bit. I'll take you home. John Peerybingle, my service to you. More of my service to your pretty wife. Handsomer every day! Better too, if possible! And younger,' mused the speaker, in a low voice; 'that's the Devil of it!'

'I should be astonished at your paying compliments, Mr Tackleton,' said Dot, not with the best grace in the world; 'but for your condition.'

'You know all about it then?'

'I have got myself to believe it, somehow,' said Dot.

'After a hard struggle, I suppose?'

'Very.'

Tackleton the toy-merchant, pretty generally known as Gruff and Tackleton – for that was the firm, though Gruff had been bought out long ago; only leaving his name, and as some said his nature, according to its Dictionary meaning, in the business – Tackleton the toy-merchant, was a man whose vocation had been quite misunderstood by his parents and guardians. If they had made him a money lender, or a sharp Attorney, or a sheriff's officer, or a broker, he might have sown his discontented oats in his youth, and, after having had the full run of himself in ill-natured transactions, might have turned out amiable, at last, for the sake of a little freshness and novelty. But, cramped and chafing in the peaceable pursuit of toy-making, he was a domestic Ogre, who had been living on children all his life, and was their implacable enemy. He despised all toys; wouldn't have bought one for the world; delighted, in his malice, to insinuate grim expressions into the faces of brown-paper farmers who drove pigs to market, bellmen who advertised lost lawyers' consciences, moveable old ladies who darned stockings or carved pies; and other like samples of his stock in trade. In appalling masks; hideous, hairy, red-eyed jacks in boxes; vampire kites; demoniacal tumblers who wouldn't lie down, and were perpetually flying forward, to stare infants out of countenance; his soul perfectly revelled. They were his only relief, and safety-valve. He was great in such inventions. Anything suggestive of a pony-nightmare, was delicious to him. He had even lost money (and he took to that toy very kindly) by getting up goblin slides for magic-lanterns, whereon the powers of darkness were depicted as a sort of supernatural shellfish, with human faces. In intensifying the portraiture of giants, he had sunk quite a little capital; and, though no painter himself, he could indicate, for the instruction of his artists, with a piece of chalk, a certain furtive leer for the countenances of those monsters, which was safe to destroy the peace of mind of any young gentleman between the ages of six and eleven, for the whole Christmas or midsummer vacation.

What he was in toys, he was (as most men are) in all other things. You may easily suppose, therefore, that within the green cape, which reached down to the calves of his legs, there was buttoned up to the chin an uncommonly pleasant fellow; and that he was about as choice a spirit, and as agreeable a companion, as ever stood in a pair of bull-headed looking boots with mahogany-coloured tops.

Still, Tackleton, the toy-merchant, was going to be married. In spite of all this, he was going to be married. And to a young wife too; a beautiful young wife.

He didn't look much like a bridegroom, as he stood in the carrier's kitchen, with a twist in his dry face, and a screw in his body, and his hat jerked over the bridge of his nose, and his hands tucked down into the bottoms of his pockets, and his whole sarcastic ill-conditioned self peering out of one little corner of one little eye, like the concentrated essence of any number of ravens. But, a bridegroom he designed to be.

'In three days' time. Next Thursday. The last day of the first month in the year. That's my wedding-day,' said Tackleton.

Did I mention that he had always one eye wide open, and one eye nearly shut; and that the one eye nearly shut, was always the expressive eye? I don't think I did.

'That's my wedding-day!' said Tackleton, rattling his money.

'Why, it's our wedding-day too,' exclaimed the carrier.

'Ha ha!' laughed Tackleton. 'Odd! You're just such another couple. Just!'

The indignation of Dot at this presumptuous assertion is not to be described. What next? His imagination would compass the possibility of just such another baby, perhaps. The man was mad.

'I say! A word with you,' murmured Tackleton, nudging the carrier with his elbow, and taking him a little apart. 'You'll come to the wedding? We're in the same boat you know.'

'How in the same boat?' enquired the carrier.

'A little disparity, you know;' said Tackleton, with another nudge. 'Come and spend an evening with us, beforehand.'

'Why?' demanded John, astonished at this pressing hospitality.

'Why?' returned the other. 'That's a new way of receiving an invitation. Why, for pleasure; sociability, you know, and all that!'

'I thought you were never sociable,' said John, in his plain way.

'Tchah! It's of no use to be anything but free with you I see,' said Tackleton. 'Why, then, the truth is you have a – what tea-drinking people call a sort of a comfortable appearance together: you and your wife. We know better, you know, but – '

'No, we don't know better,' interposed John. 'What are you talking about?'

'Well! We *don't* know better, then,' said Tackleton. 'We'll agree that we don't. As you like; what does it matter? I was going to say, as you have that sort of appearance, your company will produce a favourable effect on Mrs Tackleton that will be. And, though I don't think your good lady's very friendly to me, in this matter, still she can't help herself from falling into my views, for there's a compactness and cosiness of appearance about her that always tells, even in an indifferent case. You'll say you'll come?'

'We have arranged to keep our wedding-day (as far as that goes) at home,' said John. 'We have made the promise to ourselves these six months. We think, you see, that home – '

'Bah! what's home?' cried Tackleton. 'Four walls and a ceiling! (Why don't you kill that cricket; *I* would! I always do. I hate their noise.) There are four walls and a ceiling at my house. Come to me!'

'You kill your crickets, eh?' said John.

'Scrunch 'em, sir,' returned the other, setting his heel heavily on the floor. 'You'll say you'll come? It's as much your interest as mine, you know, that the women should persuade each other that they're quiet and contented, and couldn't be better off. I know their way. Whatever one woman says, another woman is determined to clinch, always. There's that spirit of emulation among 'em, sir, that if your wife says to my wife, "I'm the happiest woman in the world, and mine's the best husband in the world, and I dote on him," my wife will say the same to yours, or more, and half believe it.'

'Do you mean to say she don't, then?' asked the carrier.

'Don't!' cried Tackleton, with a short, sharp laugh. 'Don't what?'

The carrier had had some faint idea of adding, 'dote upon you.' But happening to meet the half-closed eye as it twinkled upon him over the turned-up collar of the cape, which was within an ace of poking it out, he felt it such an unlikely part and parcel of anything to be doted on, that he substituted, 'that she don't believe it?'

'Ah you dog! You're joking,' said Tackleton.

But the carrier, though slow to understand the full drift of his meaning, eyed him in such a serious manner, that he was obliged to be a little more explanatory.

'I have the humour,' said Tackleton: holding up the fingers of his left hand, and tapping the forefinger, to imply 'there I am, Tackleton to wit'. 'I have the humour, sir, to marry a young wife and a pretty wife:' here he rapped his little finger, to express the bride; not sparingly, but sharply; with a sense of power. 'I'm able to gratify that humour and I do. It's my whim. But – now look there.'

He pointed to where Dot was sitting, thoughtfully, before the fire; leaning her dimpled chin upon her hand, and watching the bright blaze. The carrier looked at her, and then at him, and then at her, and then at him again.

'She honours and obeys, no doubt, you know,' said Tackleton; 'and that, as I am not a man of sentiment, is quite enough for *me*. But do you think there's anything more in it?'

'I think,' observed the carrier, 'that I should chuck any man out of window, who said there wasn't.'

'Exactly so,' returned the other with an unusual alacrity of assent. 'To be sure! Doubtless you would. Of course. I'm certain of it. Good-night. Pleasant dreams!'

The good carrier was puzzled, and made uncomfortable and uncertain, in spite of himself. He couldn't help showing it, in his manner.

'Good-night, my dear friend!' said Tackleton, compassionately. 'I'm off. We're exactly alike, in reality, I see. You won't give us tomorrow evening? Well! Next day you go out visiting, I know. I'll meet you there, and bring my wife that is to be. It'll do her good. You're agreeable? Thank'ee. What's that!'

It was a loud cry from the carrier's wife; a loud, sharp, sudden cry, that made the room ring, like a glass vessel. She had risen from her seat, and stood like one transfixed by terror and surprise. The stranger had advanced towards the fire to warm himself, and stood within a short stride of her chair. But quite still.

'Dot!' cried the carrier. 'Mary! Darling! What's the matter?'

They were all about her in a moment. Caleb, who had been dozing on the cake-box, in the first imperfect recovery of his suspended presence of mind seized Miss Slowboy by the hair of her head, but immediately apologised.

'Mary!' exclaimed the carrier, supporting her in his arms. 'Are you ill! What is it? Tell me, dear!'

She only answered by beating her hands together, and falling into a wild fit of laughter. Then, sinking from his grasp upon the ground, she covered her face with her apron, and wept bitterly. And then she laughed again, and then she cried again; and then, she said how cold it was, and suffered him to lead her to the fire, where she sat down as before. The old man standing, as before; quite still.

'I'm better, John,' she said. 'I'm quite well now – I – '

'John!' But John was on the other side of her. Why turn her face towards the strange old gentleman, as if addressing him! Was her brain wandering?

'Only a fancy, John dear – a kind of shock – a something coming suddenly before my eyes – I don't know what it was. It's quite gone; quite gone.'

'I'm glad it's gone,' muttered Tackleton, turning the expressive eye all round the room. 'I wonder where it's gone, and what it was. Humph! Caleb, come here! Who's that with the grey hair?'

'I don't know, sir,' returned Caleb in a whisper. 'Never see him before, in all my life. A beautiful figure for a nutcracker; quite a new model. With a screw-jaw opening down into his waistcoat, he'd be lovely.'

'Not ugly enough,' said Tackleton.

'Or for a firebox, either,' observed Caleb, in deep contemplation, 'what a model! Unscrew his head to put the matches in; turn him heels up'ards for the light; and what a firebox for a gentleman's mantelshelf, just as he stands!'

'Not half ugly enough,' said Tackleton. 'Nothing in him at all. Come! Bring that box! All right now, I hope?'

'Oh quite gone! Quite gone!' said the little woman waving him hurriedly away. 'Good-night!'

'Good-night,' said Tackleton. 'Good-night, John Peerybingle! Take care how you carry that box, Caleb. Let it fall, and I'll murder you! Dark as pitch, and weather worse than ever, eh? Good-night!'

So, with another sharp look round the room, he went out at the door; followed by Caleb with the wedding-cake on his head.

The carrier had been so much astounded by his little wife, and so busily engaged in soothing and tending her, that he had scarcely been conscious of the stranger's presence, until now, when he again stood there, their only guest.

'He don't belong to them, you see,' said John. 'I must give him a hint to go.'

'I beg your pardon, friend,' said the old gentleman, advancing to him; 'the more so, as I fear your wife has not been well; but the Attendant whom my infirmity,' he touched his ears and shook his head, 'renders almost indispensable, not having arrived, I fear there must be some mistake. The bad night which made the shelter of your comfortable cart (may I never have a worse!) so acceptable, is still as bad as ever. Would you, in your kindness, suffer me to rent a bed here?'

'Yes, yes,' cried Dot. 'Yes! Certainly!'

'Oh!' said the carrier, surprised by the rapidity of this consent. 'Well! I don't object; but still I'm not quite sure that – '

'Hush!' she interrupted. 'Dear John!'

'Why, he's stone deaf,' urged John.

'I know he is, but – Yes, sir, certainly. Yes! certainly! I'll make him up a bed, directly, John.'

As she hurried off to do it, the flutter of her spirits, and the agitation of her manner, were so strange, that the carrier stood looking after her, quite confounded.

'Did its mothers make it up a Beds then!' cried Miss Slowboy to the baby; 'and did its hair grow brown and curly, when its caps was lifted off, and frighten it, a precious pets, a sitting by the fires!'

With that unaccountable attraction of the mind to trifles, which is often incidental to a state of doubt and confusion, the carrier, as he walked slowly to and fro, found himself mentally repeating even these absurd words, many times. So many times that he got them by heart, and was still conning them over and over, like a lesson, when Tilly, after administering as much friction to the little bald head with her hand as she thought wholesome (according to the practice of nurses), had once more tied the baby's cap on.

'And frighten it a precious pets, a sitting by the fire. What frightened Dot, I wonder!' mused the carrier, pacing to and fro.

He scouted, from his heart, the insinuations of the toy-merchant, and yet they filled him with a vague, indefinite uneasiness; for Tackleton was quick and sly; and he had that painful sense, himself, of being a man of slow perception, that a broken hint was always worrying to him. He certainly had no intention in his mind of linking anything that Tackleton had said, with the unusual conduct of his wife; but the two subjects of reflection came into his mind together, and he could not keep them asunder.

The bed was soon made ready; and the visitor, declining all refreshment but a cup of tea, retired. Then Dot: quite well again, she said: quite well again: arranged the great chair in the chimney-corner for her husband; filled his pipe and gave it him; and took her usual little stool beside him on the hearth

She always *would* sit on that little stool; I think she must have had a kind of notion that it was a coaxing, wheedling, little stool.

She was, out and out, the very best filler of a pipe, I should say, in the four quarters of the globe. To see her put that chubby little finger in the bowl, and then blow down the pipe to clear the tube; and, when she had done so, affect to think that there was really something in the tube, and blow a dozen times, and hold it to her eye like a telescope, with a most provoking twist in her capital little face, as she looked down it; was quite a brilliant thing. As to the tobacco, she was perfect mistress of the subject; and her lighting of the pipe, with a wisp of paper, when the carrier had it in his mouth – going so very near his nose, and yet not scorching it – was Art: high Art, sir.

And the cricket and the kettle, turning up again, acknowledged it! The bright fire, blazing up again, acknowledged it! The little mower on the clock, in his unheeded work, acknowledged it! The carrier, in his smoothing forehead and expanding face, acknowledged it, the readiest of all. And as he soberly and thoughtfully puffed at his old pipe; and as the

Dutch clock ticked; and as the red fire gleamed; and as the cricket chirped; that genius of his hearth and home (for such the cricket was) came out, in fairy shape, into the room, and summoned many forms of Home about him. Dots of all ages, and all sizes, filled the chamber. Dots who were merry children, running on before him, gathering flowers, in the fields; coy Dots, half shrinking from, half yielding to, the pleading of his own rough image; newly-married Dots, alighting at the door, and taking wondering possession of the household keys; motherly little Dots, attended by fictitious Slowboys, bearing babies to be christened; matronly Dots, still young and blooming, watching Dots of daughters, as they danced at rustic balls; fat Dots, encircled and beset by troops of rosy grandchildren; withered Dots, who leaned on sticks, and tottered as they crept along. Old carriers too, appeared, with blind old Boxers lying at their feet; and newer carts with younger drivers ('Peerybingle Brothers' on the tilt); and sick old carriers, tended by the gentlest hands; and graves of dead and gone old carriers, green in the churchyard. And as the cricket showed him all these things – he saw them plainly, though his eyes were fixed upon the fire – the carrier's heart grew light and happy, and he thanked his household gods with all his might, and cared no more for Gruff and Tackleton than you do.

But what was that young figure of a man, which the same fair cricket set so near Her stool, and which remained there, singly and alone? Why did it linger still, so near her, with its arm upon the chimney-piece, ever repeating, 'Married! and not to me!'

Oh, Dot! Oh, failing Dot! There is no place for it in all your husband's visions; why has its shadow fallen on his hearth!

CHIRP THE SECOND

Caleb Plummer and his blind daughter lived all alone by themselves, as the storybooks say – and my blessing, with yours to back it I hope, on the storybooks, for saying anything in this workaday world! – Caleb Plummer and his blind daughter lived all alone by themselves, in a little cracked nutshell of a wooden house, which was, in truth, no better than a pimple on the prominent red-brick nose of Gruff and Tackleton. The premises of Gruff and Tackleton were the great feature of the street; but you might have knocked down Caleb Plummer's dwelling with a hammer or two, and carried off the pieces in a cart.

If anyone had done the dwelling-house of Caleb Plummer the honour to miss it after such an inroad, it would have been, no doubt, to commend its demolition as a vast improvement. It stuck to the premises of Gruff and Tackleton, like a barnacle to a ship's keel, or a snail to a door, or a little bunch of toadstools to the stem of a tree. But it was the germ from which the full-grown trunk of Gruff and Tackleton had sprung; and under its crazy roof, the Gruff before last had, in a small way, made toys for a generation of old boys and girls, who had played with them, and found them out, and broken them, and gone to sleep.

I have said that Caleb and his poor blind daughter lived here; I should have said that Caleb lived here, and his poor blind daughter somewhere else; in an enchanted home of Caleb's furnishing, where scarcity and shabbiness were not, and trouble never entered. Caleb was no sorcerer, but in the only magic art that still remains to us: the magic of devoted, deathless love: Nature had been the mistress of his study; and from her teaching, all the wonder came.

The blind girl never knew that ceilings were discoloured; walls blotched and bare of plaster here and there; high crevices unstopped and widening every day; beams mouldering and tending downward. The blind girl never knew that iron was rusting, wood rotting, paper peeling off; the very size, and shape, and true proportion of the dwelling, withering away. The blind girl never knew that ugly shapes of delf and earthenware were on the board; that sorrow and faintheartedness were in the house; that Caleb's scanty hairs were turning greyer and more grey, before her sightless face. The blind girl never knew they had a master, cold, exacting, and uninterested: never knew that Tackleton was Tackleton in short; but lived in the belief of an eccentric humourist who loved to have his jest with them; and who while he was the guardian angel of their lives, disdained to hear one word of thankfulness.

And all was Caleb's doing; all the doing of her simple father! But he too had a cricket on his hearth; and listening sadly to its music when the motherless blind child was very young, that spirit had inspired him with the thought that even her great deprivation might be almost changed into a blessing, and the girl made happy by these little means. For all the cricket tribe are potent spirits, even though the people who hold converse with them do not know it (which is frequently the case); and there are not in the unseen world, voices more gentle and more true; that may be so implicitly relied on, or that are so certain to give none but tenderest counsel; as the voices in which the spirits of the fireside and the hearth address themselves to human kind.

Caleb and his daughter were at work together in their usual working-room, which served them for their ordinary living-room as well; and a

strange place it was. There were houses in it, finished and unfinished, for dolls of all stations in life. Suburban tenements for dolls of moderate means; kitchens and single apartments for dolls of the lower classes; capital town residences for dolls of high estate. Some of these establish-ments were already furnished according to estimate, with a view to the convenience of dolls of limited income; others could be fitted on the most expensive scale, at a moment's notice, from whole shelves of chairs and tables, sofas, bedsteads, and upholstery. The nobility and gentry and public in general, for whose accommodation these tenements were designed, lay, here and there, in baskets, staring straight up at the ceiling; but in denoting their degrees in society, and confining them to their respective stations (which experience shows to be lamentably difficult in real life), the makers of these dolls had far improved on Nature, who is often froward and perverse; for they, not resting on such arbitrary marks as satin, cotton-print, and bits of rag, had superadded striking personal differences which allowed of no mistake. Thus, the doll-lady of distinction had wax limbs of perfect symmetry; but only she and her compeers; the next grade in the social scale being made of leather; and the next of coarse linen stuff. As to the common-people, they had just so many matches out of tinder-boxes for their arms and legs, and there they were – established in their sphere at once, beyond the possibility of getting out of it.

There were various other samples of his handicraft, besides dolls, in Caleb Plummer's room. There were Noah's Arks, in which the Birds and Beasts were an uncommonly tight fit, I assure you; though they could be crammed in, anyhow, at the roof, and rattled and shaken into the smallest compass. By a bold poetical license, most of these Noah's Arks had knockers on the doors; inconsistent appendages perhaps, as suggestive of morning callers and a postman, yet a pleasant finish to the outside of the building. There were scores of melancholy little carts which, when the wheels went round, performed most doleful music. Many small fiddles, drums, and other instruments of torture; no end of cannon, shields, swords, spears, and guns. There were little tumblers in red breeches, incessantly swarming up high obstacles of red-tape, and coming down, head first, on the other side; and there were innumerable old gentlemen of respectable, not to say venerable appearance, insanely flying over horizontal pegs, inserted, for the purpose, in their own street doors. There were beasts of all sorts; horses, in particular, of every breed, from the spotted barrel on four pegs, with a small tippet for a mane to the thoroughbred rocker on his highest mettle. As it would have been hard to count the dozens upon dozens of grotesque figures that were ever ready to commit all sorts of absurdities on the turning of a handle; so it would have been no easy task to mention any human folly, vice, or weakness, that had not its type, immediate or remote, in Caleb Plummer's room. And not in an exaggerated form; for very little handles will move men and women to as strange performances, as any toy was ever made to undertake.

In the midst of all these objects, Caleb and his daughter sat at work. The blind girl busy as a doll's dressmaker; Caleb painting and glazing the four pair front of a desirable family mansion.

The care imprinted in the lines of Caleb's face, and his absorbed and dreamy manner, which would have sat well on some alchemist or abstruse student, were at first sight an odd contrast to his occupation, and the trivialities about him. But trivial things, invented and pursued for bread, become very serious matters of fact; and, apart from this consideration, I am not at all prepared to say, myself, that if Caleb had been a Lord Chamberlain, or a Member of Parliament, or a lawyer, or even a great speculator, he would have dealt in toys one whit less whimsical; while I have a very great doubt whether they would have been as harmless.

'So you were out in the rain last night, father, in your beautiful, new, greatcoat,' said Caleb's daughter.

'In my beautiful new greatcoat,' answered Caleb, glancing towards a clothes-line in the room, on which the sackcloth garment previously described, was carefully hung up to dry.

'How glad I am you bought it, father!'

'And of such a tailor, too,' said Caleb. 'Quite a fashionable tailor. It's too good for me.'

The blind girl rested from her work, and laughed with delight. 'Too good, father! What can be too good for you?'

'I'm half ashamed to wear it though,' said Caleb, watching the effect of what he said, upon her brightening face; 'upon my word. When I hear the boys and people say behind me, "Halloa! Here's a swell!" I don't know which way to look. And when the beggar wouldn't go away last night; and, when I said I was a very common man, said, "No, your Honour! Bless your Honour, don't say that!" I was quite ashamed. I really felt as if I hadn't a right to wear it.'

Happy blind girl ! How merry she was, in her exultation!

'I see you, father,' she said, clasping her hands, 'as plainly, as if I had the eyes I never want when you are with me. A blue coat – '

'Bright blue,' said Caleb.

'Yes, yes! Bright blue!' exclaimed the girl, turning up her radiant face; 'the colour I can just remember in the blessed sky! You told me it was blue before! A bright blue coat – '

'Made loose to the figure,' suggested Caleb.

'Yes! Loose to the figure!' cried the blind girl , laughing heartily; 'and in it you, dear father, with your merry eye, your smiling face, your free step, and your dark hair: looking so young and handsome!'

'Halloa! Halloa!' said Caleb. 'I shall be vain, presently.'

'I think you are, already,' cried the blind girl , pointing at him, in her glee. 'I know you, father! Ha ha ha! I've found you out, you see!'

How different the picture in her mind, from Caleb, as he sat observing her! She had spoken of his free step. She was right in that. For years and years, he never once had crossed that threshold at his own slow pace, but with a footfall counterfeited for her ear; and never had he, when his heart was heaviest, forgotten the light tread that was to render her so cheerful and courageous!

Heaven knows! But I think Caleb's vague bewilderment of manner may have half originated in his having confused himself about himself and everything around him, for the love of his blind daughter. How could the little man be otherwise than bewildered, after labouring for so many years to destroy his own identity, and that of all the objects that had any bearing on it!

'There we are,' said Caleb, falling back a pace or two to form the better judgement of his work; 'as near the real thing as six-penn'orth of halfpence is to sixpence. What a pity that the whole front of the house opens at once! If there was only a staircase in it now, and regular doors to the rooms to go in at! But that's the worst of my calling, I'm always deluding myself, and swindling myself.'

'You are speaking quite softly. You are not tired, father?'

'Tired,' echoed Caleb, with a great burst of animation, 'what should tire me, Bertha? *I* was never tired. What does it mean?'

To give the greater force to his words, he checked himself in an involuntary imitation of two half-length stretching and yawning figures on the mantelshelf, who were represented as in one eternal state of weariness from the waist upwards; and hummed a fragment of a song. It was a Bacchanalian song, something about a sparkling bowl; and he sang it with an assumption of a devil-may-care voice, that made his face a thousand times more meagre and more thoughtful than ever.

'What! You're singing, are you?' said Tackleton, putting his head in, at the door. 'Go it! *I* can't sing.'

Nobody would have suspected him of it. He hadn't what is generally termed a singing face, by any means.

'I can't afford to sing,' said Tackleton. 'I'm glad you can. I hope you can afford to work too. Hardly time for both, I should think?'

'If you could only see him, Bertha, how he's winking at me!' whispered Caleb. 'Such a man to joke! you'd think, if you didn't know him, he was in earnest – wouldn't you now?'

The blind girl smiled, and nodded.

'The bird that can sing and won't sing, must be made to sing, they say,' grumbled Tackleton. 'What about the owl that can't sing, and oughtn't to sing, and will sing; is there anything that *he* should be made to do?'

'The extent to which he's winking at this moment!' whispered Caleb to his daughter. 'Oh, my gracious!'

'Always merry and light-hearted with us!' cried the smiling Bertha.

'Oh, you're there, are you?' answered Tackleton. 'Poor Idiot!'

He really did believe she was an Idiot; and he founded the belief, I can't say whether consciously or not, upon her being fond of him.

'Well! and being there – how are you?' said Tackleton; in his grudging way.

'Oh! well; quite well. And as happy as even you can wish me to be. As happy as you would make the whole world, if you could!'

'Poor Idiot!' muttered Tackleton. 'No gleam of reason. Not a gleam!'

The blind girl took his hand and kissed it; held it for a moment in her own two hands; and laid her cheek against it tenderly, before releasing it. There was such unspeakable affection and such fervent gratitude in the act, that Tackleton himself was moved to say, in a milder growl than usual: 'What's the matter now?'

'I stood it close beside my pillow when I went to sleep last night, and remembered it in my dreams. And when the day broke, and the glorious red sun – the *red* sun, father?'

'Red in the mornings and the evenings, Bertha,' said poor Caleb, with a woeful glance at his employer.

'When it rose, and the bright light I almost fear to strike myself against in walking, came into the room, I turned the little tree towards it, and blessed Heaven for making things so precious, and blessed you for sending them to cheer me!'

'Bedlam broke loose!' said Tackleton under his breath. 'We shall arrive at the strait-waistcoat and mufflers soon. We're getting on!'

Caleb, with his hands hooked loosely in each other, stared vacantly before him while his daughter spoke, as if he really were uncertain (I believe he was) whether Tackleton had done anything to deserve her thanks, or not. If he could have been a perfectly free agent, at that moment, required, on pain of death, to kick the toy-merchant, or fall at his feet, according to his merits, I believe it would have been an even chance which course he would have taken. Yet Caleb knew that with his own hands he had brought the little rose-tree home for her, so carefully; and that with his own lips he had forged the innocent deception which should help to keep her from suspecting how much, how very much, he every day denied himself, that she might be the happier.

'Bertha!' said Tackleton, assuming, for the nonce, a little cordiality. 'Come here.'

'Oh! I can come straight to you! You needn't guide me!' she rejoined.

'Shall I tell you a secret, Bertha?'

'If you will!' she answered, eagerly.

How bright the darkened face! How adorned with light, the listening head!

'This is the day on which little what's-her-name, the spoilt child; Peerybingle's wife; pays her regular visit to you – makes her fantastic picnic here; an't it?' said Tackleton, with a strong expression of distaste for the whole concern.

'Yes,' replied Bertha. 'This is the day.'

'I thought so!' said Tackleton. 'I should like to join the party.'

'Do you hear that, father!' cried the blind girl in an ecstasy.

'Yes, yes, I hear it,' murmured Caleb, with the fixed look of a sleep-walker; 'but I don't believe it. It's one of my lies, I've no doubt.'

'You see I – I want to bring the Peerybingles a little more into company with May Fielding,' said Tackleton. 'I am going to be married to May.'

'Married!' cried the blind girl , starting from him.

'She's such a confounded Idiot,' muttered Tackleton, 'that I was afraid she'd never comprehend me. Ah, Bertha! Married! Church, parson, clerk, beadle, glass-coach, bells, breakfast, bride-cake, favours, marrow-bones, cleavers, and all the rest of the tomfoolery. A wedding, you know; a wedding. Don't you know what a wedding is?'

'I know,' replied the blind girl , in a gentle tone. 'I understand!'

'Do you?' muttered Tackleton. 'It's more than I expected. Well! On that account I want to join the party, and to bring May and her mother. I'll send in a little something or other, before the afternoon. A cold leg of mutton, or some comfortable trifle of that sort. You'll expect me?'

'Yes,' she answered.

She had drooped her head, and turned away; and so stood, with her hands crossed, musing.

'I don't think you will,' muttered Tackleton, looking at her; 'for you seem to have forgotten all about it, already. Caleb!'

'I may venture to say I'm here, I suppose,' thought Caleb. 'sir!'

'Take care she don't forget what I've been saying to her.'

'*She* never forgets,' returned Caleb. 'It's one of the few things she an't clever in.'

'Every man thinks his own geese swans,' observed the toy-merchant, with a shrug. 'Poor devil!'

Having delivered himself of which remark, with infinite contempt, old Gruff and Tackleton withdrew.

Bertha remained where he had left her, lost in meditation. The gaiety had vanished from her downcast face, and it was very sad. Three or four times, she shook her head, as if bewailing some remembrance or some loss; but her sorrowful reflections found no vent in words.

It was not until Caleb had been occupied, some time, in yoking a team of horses to a wagon by the summary process of nailing the harness to the vital parts of their bodies, that she drew near to his working-stool, and sitting down beside him, said: 'Father, I am lonely in the dark. I want my eyes: my patient, willing eyes.'

'Here they are,' said Caleb. 'Always ready. They are more yours than mine, Bertha, any hour in the four and twenty. What shall your eyes do for you, dear?'

'Look round the room, father.'

'All right,' said Caleb. 'No sooner said than done, Bertha.'

'Tell me about it.'

'It's much the same as usual,' said Caleb. 'Homely, but very snug. The gay colours on the walls; the bright flowers on the plates and dishes; the shining wood, where there are beams or panels; the general cheerfulness and neatness of the building; make it very pretty.'

Cheerful and neat it was wherever Bertha's hands could busy themselves. But nowhere else were cheerfulness and neatness possible, in the old crazy shed which Caleb's fancy so transformed.

'You have your working dress on, and are not so gallant as when you wear the handsome coat?' said Bertha, touching him.

'Not quite so gallant,' answered Caleb. 'Pretty brisk though.'

'Father,' said the blind girl , drawing close to his side, and stealing one arm round his neck. 'Tell me something about May. She is very fair?'

'She is indeed,' said Caleb. And she was indeed. It was quite a rare thing to Caleb, not to have to draw on his invention.

'Her hair is dark,' said Bertha, pensively, 'darker than mine. Her voice is sweet and musical, I know. I have often loved to hear it. Her shape – '

'There's not a doll's in all the room to equal it,' said Caleb. 'And her eyes!' –

He stopped; for Bertha had drawn closer round his neck; and, from the arm that clung about him, came a warning pressure which he understood too well.

He coughed a moment, hammered for a moment, and then fell back upon the song about the sparkling bowl; his infallible resource in all such difficulties.

'Our friend, father; our benefactor. I am never tired you know of hearing about him – now was I, ever?' she said, hastily.

'Of course not,' answered Caleb. 'And with reason.'

'Ah! With how much reason!' cried the blind girl . With such fervency, that Caleb, though his motives were so pure, could not endure to meet her face; but dropped his eyes, as if she could have read in them his innocent deceit.

'Then tell me again about him, dear father,' said Bertha. 'Many times again! His face is benevolent, kind, and tender. Honest and true, I am sure it is. The manly heart that tries to cloak all favours with a show of roughness and unwillingness, beats in its every look and glance.'

'And makes it noble,' added Caleb in his quiet desperation.

'And makes it noble!' cried the blind girl . 'He is older than May, father.'

'Ye–es,' said Caleb, reluctantly. 'He's a little older than May. But that don't signify.'

'Oh father, yes! To be his patient companion in infirmity and age; to be his gentle nurse in sickness, and his constant friend in suffering and sorrow; to know no weariness in working for his sake; to watch him, tend him; sit beside his bed and talk to him, awake; and pray for him asleep; what privileges these would be! What opportunities for proving all her truth and her devotion to him! Would she do all this, dear father?'

'No doubt of it,' said Caleb.

'I love her, father; I can love her from my soul!' exclaimed the blind girl . And saying so, she laid her poor blind face on Caleb's shoulder, and so wept and wept, that he was almost sorry to have brought that tearful happiness upon her.

In the meantime, there had been a pretty sharp commotion at John Peerybingle's; for little Mrs Peerybingle naturally couldn't think of going anywhere without the baby; and to get the baby under weigh, took time. Not that there was much of the baby: speaking of it as a thing of weight and measure: but there was a vast deal to do about and about it, and it all had to be done by easy stages. For instance: when the baby was got, by hook and by crook, to a certain point of dressing, and you might have rationally supposed that another touch or two would finish him off, and turn him out a tip-top baby challenging the world, he was unexpectedly extinguished in a flannel cap, and hustled off to bed; where he simmered (so to speak) between two blankets for the best part of an hour. From this state of inaction he was then recalled, shining very much and roaring violently, to partake of – well! I would rather say, if you'll permit me to speak generally – of a slight repast. After which, he went to sleep again. Mrs Peerybingle took advantage of this interval, to make herself as smart in a small way as ever you saw anybody in all your life; and, during the same short truce, Miss Slowboy insinuated herself into a spencer of a fashion so surprising and ingenious, that it had no connection with herself, or anything else in the universe, but was a shrunken, dog's eared, independent fact, pursuing its lonely course without the least regard to anybody. By this time, the baby, being all alive again, was invested, by the united efforts of Mrs Peerybingle and Miss Slowboy, with a cream-coloured mantle for its body, and a sort of nankeen raised-pie for its head; and so in course of time they all three got down to the door, where the old horse had already taken more than the full value of his day's toll out of the Turnpike Trust, by tearing up the road with his impatient autographs – and whence Boxer might be dimly seen in the remote perspective, standing looking back, and tempting him to come on without orders.

As to a chair, or anything of that kind for helping Mrs Peerybingle into the cart, you know very little of John, I flatter myself, if you think *that* was necessary. Before you could have seen him lift her from the ground, there she was in her place, fresh and rosy, saying, 'John! How *can* you! Think of Tilly!'

If I might be allowed to mention a young lady's legs, on any terms, I would observe of Miss Slowboy's that there was a fatality about them which rendered them singularly liable to be grazed; and that she never effected the smallest ascent or descent, without recording the circumstance upon them with a notch, as Robinson Crusoe marked the days upon his wooden calendar. But as this might be considered ungenteel, I'll think of it.

'John? You've got the basket with the veal-and-ham pie and things; and the bottles of beer?' said Dot. 'If you haven't, you must turn round again, this very minute.'

'You're a nice little article,' returned the carrier, 'to be talking about turning round, after keeping me a full quarter of an hour behind my time.'

'I am sorry for it, John,' said Dot in a great bustle, 'but I really could not think of going to Bertha's – I would not do it, John, on any account – without the veal-and-ham pie and things, and the bottles of beer. Way!'

This monosyllable was addressed to the horse, who didn't mind it at all.

'Oh *do* way John!' said Mrs Peerybingle. 'Please!'

'It'll be time enough to do that,' returned John, 'when I begin to leave things behind me. The basket's here, safe enough.'

'What a hard-hearted monster you must be, John, not to have said so, at once, and save me such a turn! I declared I wouldn't go to Bertha's without the veal-and-ham pie and things, and the bottles of beer, for any money. Regularly once a fortnight ever since we have been married, John, have we made our little picnic there. If anything was to go wrong with it, I should almost think we were never to be lucky again.'

'It was a kind thought in the first instance,' said the carrier; 'and I honour you for it, little woman.'

'My dear John,' replied Dot, turning very red. 'Don't talk about honouring *me*. Good Gracious!'

'By the by – ' observed the carrier. 'That old gentleman – '

Again so visibly, and instantly embarrassed!

'He's an odd fish,' said the carrier, looking straight along the road before them. 'I can't make him out. I don't believe there's any harm in him.'

'None at all. I'm – I'm sure there's none at all.'

'Yes?' said the carrier, with his eyes attracted to her face by the great earnestness of her manner. 'I am glad you feel so certain of it, because it's a confirmation to me. It's curious that he should have taken it into his head to ask leave to go on lodging with us; an't it? Things come about so strangely.'

'So very strangely,' she rejoined in a low voice: scarcely audible.

'However, he's a good-natured old gentleman,' said John, 'and pays as a gentleman, and I think his word is to be relied upon, like a gentleman's. I had quite a long talk with him this morning: he can hear me better already, he says, as he gets more used to my voice. He told me a great deal about himself, and I told him a good deal about myself, and a rare lot of questions he asked me. I gave him information about my having two beats, you know, in my business; one day to the right from our house and back again; another day to the left from our house and back again (for he's a stranger and don't know the names of places about here); and he seemed quite pleased. "Why, then I shall be returning home tonight your way," he says, "when I thought you'd be coming in an exactly opposite direction. That's capital. I may trouble you for another lift perhaps, but I'll engage not to fall so sound asleep again." He *was* sound asleep, sure–ly! – Dot! what are you thinking of?'

'Thinking of, John? I – I was listening to you.'

'Oh! That's all right!' said the honest carrier. 'I was afraid, from the look of your face, that I had gone rambling on so long, as to set you thinking something else. I was very near it, I'll be bound.'

Dot making no reply, they jogged on, for some little time, in silence. But it was not easy to remain silent very long in John Peerybingle's cart, for everybody on the road had something to say; though it might only be 'How are you' and indeed it was very often nothing else, still, to give that back again in the right spirit of cordiality, required, not merely a nod and a smile, but as wholesome an action of the lungs withal, as a long-winded Parliamentary speech. Sometimes, passengers on foot, or horseback, plodded on a little way beside the cart, for the express purpose of having a chat; and then there was a great deal to be said, on both sides.

Then, Boxer gave occasion to more good-natured recognitions of and by the carrier, than half a dozen Christians could have done! Everybody knew him, all along the road – especially the fowls and pigs, who when they saw him approaching, with his body all on one side, and his ears

pricked up inquisitively, and hat knob of a tail making the most of itself in the air, immediately withdrew into remote back settlements, without waiting for the honour of a nearer acquaintance. He had business everywhere; going down all the turnings, looking into all the wells, bolting in and out of all the cottages, dashing into the midst of all the dame-Schools, fluttering all the pigeons, magnifying the tails of all the cats, and trotting into the public-houses like a regular customer. Wherever he went, somebody or other might have been heard to cry, 'Halloa! Here's Boxer!' and out came that somebody forthwith, accompanied by at least two or three other somebodies, to give John Peerybingle and his pretty wife, good-day.

The packages and parcels for the errand cart, were numerous; and there were many stoppages to take them in and give them out; which were not by any means the worst parts of the journey. Some people were so full of expectation about their parcels, and other people were so full of wonder about their parcels, and other people were so full of inexhaustible directions about their parcels, and John had such a lively interest in all the parcels, that it was as good as a play. Likewise, there were articles to carry, which required to be considered and discussed, and in reference to the adjustment and disposition of which, councils had to be holden by the carrier and the senders: at which Boxer usually assisted, in short fits of the closest attention, and long fits of tearing round and round the assembled sages and barking himself hoarse. Of all these little incidents, Dot was the amused and open-eyed spectatress from her chair in the cart; and as she sat there, looking on: a charming little portrait framed to admiration by the tilt: there was no lack of nudgings and glancings and whisperings and envyings among the younger men, I promise you. And this delighted John the carrier, beyond measure; for he was proud to have his little wife admired; knowing that she didn't mind it – that, if anything, she rather liked it perhaps.

The trip was a little foggy, to be sure, in the January weather; and was raw and cold. But who cared for such trifles? Not Dot, decidedly. Not Tilly Slowboy, for she deemed sitting in a cart, on any terms, to be the highest point of human joys; the crowning circumstance of earthly hopes. Not the baby, I'll be sworn; for it's not in baby nature to be warmer or more sound asleep, though its capacity is great in both respects, than that blessed young Peerybingle was, all the way.

You couldn't see very far in the fog, of course; but you could see a great deal, oh a great deal! It's astonishing how much you may see, in a thicker fog than that, if you will only take the trouble to look for it. Why, even to sit watching for the fairy-rings in the fields, and for the patches of hoar-frost still lingering in the shade, near hedges and by trees, was a pleasant occupation: to make no mention of the unexpected shapes in which the trees themselves came starting out of the mist, and glided into it again. The hedges were tangled and bare, and waved a multitude of blighted garlands in the wind; but there was no discouragement in this. It was agreeable to contemplate; for it made the fireside warmer in possession, and the summer greener in expectancy. The river looked chilly; but it was in motion, and moving at a good pace; which was a great point. The canal was rather slow and torpid; that must be admitted. Never mind. It would freeze the sooner when the frost set fairly in, and then there would be skating, and sliding; and the heavy old barges, frozen up somewhere, near a wharf, would smoke their rusty iron chimney-pipes all day, and have a lazy time of it.

In one place, there was a great mound of weeds or stubble burning; and they watched the fire, so white in the day time, flaring through the fog, with only here and there a dash of red in it, until, in consequence as she observed of the smoke 'getting up her nose,' Miss Slowboy choked – she could do anything of that sort, on the smallest provocation – and woke the baby, who wouldn't go to sleep again. But Boxer, who was in advance some quarter of a mile or so, had already passed the outposts of the town, and gained the corner of the street where Caleb and his daughter lived; and long before they reached the door, he and the blind girl were on the pavement waiting to receive them.

Boxer, by the way, made certain delicate distinctions of his own, in his communication with Bertha, which persuade me fully that he knew her to be blind. He never sought to attract her attention by looking at her, as he often did with other people, but touched her, invariably. What experience he could ever have had of blind people or blind dogs,

I don't know. He had never lived with a blind master; nor had Mr Boxer the elder, nor Mrs Boxer, nor any of his respectable family on either side, ever been visited with blindness, that I am aware of. He may have found it out for himself, perhaps, but he had got hold of it somehow; and therefore he had hold of Bertha too, by the skirt, and kept hold, until Mrs Peerybingle and the baby, and Miss Slowboy, and the basket, were all got safely within doors.

May Fielding was already come; and so was her mother – a little querulous chip of an old lady with a peevish face, who, in right of having preserved a waist like a bedpost, was supposed to be a most transcendent figure; and who, in consequence of having once been better off, or of labouring under an impression that she might have been, if something had happened which never did happen, and seemed to have never been particularly likely to come to pass – but it's all the same – was very genteel and patronising indeed. Gruff and Tackleton was also there, doing the agreeable, with the evident sensation of being as perfectly at home, and as unquestionably in his own element, as a fresh young salmon on the top of the Great Pyramid.

'May! My dear old friend!' cried Dot, running up to meet her. 'What a happiness to see you!'

Her old friend was, to the full, as hearty and as glad as she; and it really was, if you'll believe me, quite a pleasant sight to see them embrace. Tackleton was a man of taste, beyond all question. May was very pretty.

You know sometimes, when you are used to a pretty face, how, when it comes into contact and comparison with another pretty face, it seems for the moment to be homely and faded, and hardly to deserve the high opinion you have had of it. Now, this was not at all the case, either with Dot or May; for May's face set off Dot's, and Dot's face set off May's, so naturally and agreeably, that, as John Peerybingle was very near saying when he came into the room, they ought to have been born sisters – which was the only improvement you could have suggested.

Tackleton had brought his leg of mutton, and, wonderful to relate, a tart besides – but we don't mind a little dissipation when our brides are in the case; we don't get married every day – and in addition to these dainties, there were the veal-and-ham pie, and 'things,' as Mrs Peerybingle called them; which were chiefly nuts and oranges, and cakes, and such small deer. When the repast was set forth on the board, flanked by Caleb's contribution, which was a great wooden bowl of smoking potatoes (he was prohibited, by solemn compact, from producing any other viands), Tackleton led his intended mother-in-law to the post of honour. For the better gracing of this place at the high Festival, the majestic old soul had adorned herself with a cap, calculated to inspire the thoughtless with sentiments of awe. She also wore her gloves. But let us be genteel, or die!

Caleb sat next his daughter; Dot and her old schoolfellow were side by side; the good carrier took care of the bottom of the table. Miss Slowboy was isolated, for the time being, from every article of furniture but the chair she sat on, that she might have nothing else to knock the baby's head against.

As Tilly stared about her at the dolls and toys, they stared at her and at the company. The venerable old gentlemen at the street doors (who were all in full action) showed especial interest in the party; pausing occasionally before leaping, as if they were listening to the conversation: and then plunging wildly over and over, a great many times, without halting for breath – as in a frantic state of delight with the whole proceedings.

Certainly, if these old gentlemen were inclined to have a fiendish joy in the contemplation of Tackleton's discomfiture, they had good reason to be satisfied. Tackleton couldn't get on at all; and the more cheerful his intended bride became in Dot's society, the less he liked it, though he had brought them together for that purpose. For he was a regular dog in the manger, was Tackleton; and when they laughed, and he couldn't, he took it into his head, immediately, that they must be laughing at him.

'Ah, May!' said Dot. 'Dear, dear, what changes! To talk of those merry schooldays makes one young again.'

'Why, you an't particularly old, at any time; are you?' said Tackleton.

'Look at my sober plodding husband there,' returned Dot. 'He adds twenty years to my age at least. Don't you, John?'

'Forty,' John replied.

'How many *you'll* add to May's, I'm sure I don't know,' said Dot, laughing. 'But she can't be much less than a hundred years of age on her next birthday.'

'Ha ha!' laughed Tackleton. Hollow as a drum, that laugh though. And he looked as if he could have twisted Dot's neck: comfortably.

'Dear dear!' said Dot. 'Only to remember how we used to talk, at school, about the husbands we would choose. I don't know how young, and how handsome, and how gay, and how lively, mine was not to be! And as to May's – ! Ah dear! I don't know whether to laugh or cry, when I think what silly girls we were.'

May seemed to know which to do; for the colour flashed into her face, and tears stood in her eyes.

'Even the very persons themselves – real live young men – were fixed on sometimes,' said Dot. 'We little thought how things would come about. I never fixed on John I'm sure; I never so much as thought of him. And if I had told you, you were ever to be married to Mr Tackleton, why you'd have slapped me. Wouldn't you, May?'

Though May didn't say yes, she certainly didn't say no, or express no, by any means. Tackleton laughed – quite shouted, he laughed so loud. John Peerybingle laughed too, in his ordinary good-natured and contented manner; but his was a mere whisper of a laugh, to Tackleton's.

'You couldn't help yourselves, for all that. You couldn't resist us, you see,' said Tackleton. 'Here we are! Here we are! Where are your gay young bridegrooms now!'

'Some of them are dead,' said Dot; 'and some of them forgotten. Some of them, if they could stand among us at this moment, would not believe we were the same creatures; would not believe that what they saw and heard was real, and we *could* forget them so. No! they would not believe one word of it!'

'Why, Dot!' exclaimed the carrier. 'Little woman!'

She had spoken with such earnestness and fire, that she stood in need of some recalling to herself, without doubt. Her husband's check was very gentle, for he merely interfered, as he supposed, to shield old Tackleton; but it proved effectual, for she stopped, and said no more. There was an uncommon agitation, even in her silence, which the wary Tackleton, who had brought his half-shut eye to bear upon her, noted closely; and remembered to some purpose too, as you will see.

May uttered no word, good or bad, but sat quite still, with her eyes cast down; and made no sign of interest in what had passed. The good lady her mother now interposed: observing, in the first instance, that girls were girls, and bygones bygones, and that so long as young people were young and thoughtless, they would probably conduct themselves like young and thoughtless persons: with two or three other positions of a no less sound and incontrovertible character. She then remarked, in a devout spirit, that she thanked Heaven she had always found in her daughter May, a dutiful and obedient child; for which she took no credit to herself, though she had every reason to believe it was entirely owing to herself. With regard to Mr Tackleton she said, That he was in a moral point of view an undeniable individual; and That he was in an eligible point of view a son-in-law to be desired, no one in their senses could doubt. (She was very emphatic here.) With regard to the family into which he was so soon about, after some solicitation, to be admitted, she believed Mr Tackleton knew that, although reduced in purse, it had some pretensions to gentility; and if certain circumstances, not wholly unconnected, she would go so far as to say, with the indigo trade, but to which she would not more particularly refer, had happened differently, it might perhaps have been in possession of wealth. She then remarked that she would not allude to the past, and would not mention that her daughter had for some time rejected the suit of Mr Tackleton; and that she would not say a great many other things which she did say, at great length. Finally, she delivered it as the general result of her observation and experience, that those marriages in which there was least of what was romantically and sillily called love, were always the happiest; and that she anticipated the greatest possible amount of bliss – not rapturous bliss; but the solid, steady-going article – from the approaching nuptials. She concluded by informing the company that tomorrow was the day she had lived for, expressly; and that when it was over, she would desire nothing better than to be packed up and disposed of, in any genteel place of burial.

As these remarks were quite unanswerable: which is the happy property of all remarks that are sufficiently wide of the purpose: they changed the current of the conversation, and diverted the general attention to the veal-and-ham pie, the cold mutton, the potatoes, and the tart. In order that the bottled beer might not be slighted, John Peerybingle proposed tomorrow: the wedding day; and called upon them to drink a bumper to it, before he proceeded on his journey.

For you ought to know that he only rested there, and gave the old horse a bait. He had to go some four or five miles farther on; and when he returned in the evening, he called for Dot, and took another rest on his way home. This was the order of the day on all the picnic occasions, and had been, ever since their institution.

There were two persons present, beside the bride and bridegroom elect, who did but indifferent honour to the toast. One of these was Dot, too flushed and discomposed to adapt herself to any small occurrence of the moment; the other, Bertha, who rose up hurriedly, before the rest, and left the table.

'Goodbye!' said stout John Peerybingle, pulling on his dreadnought coat. 'I shall be back at the old time. Goodbye all!'

'Goodbye, John,' returned Caleb.

He seemed to say it by rote, and to wave his hand in the same unconscious manner; for he stood observing Bertha with an anxious wondering face, that never altered its expression.

'Goodbye, young shaver!' said the jolly carrier, bending down to kiss the child; which Tilly Slowboy, now intent upon her knife and fork, had deposited asleep (and strange to say, without damage) in a little cot of Bertha's furnishing; 'goodbye! Time will come, I suppose, when *you'll* turn out into the cold, my little friend, and leave your old father to enjoy his pipe and his rheumatics in the chimney-corner; eh? Where's Dot?'

'I'm here, John!' she said, starting.

'Come, come!' returned the carrier, clapping his sounding hands. 'Where's the pipe?'

'I quite forgot the pipe, John.'

Forgot the pipe! Was such a wonder ever heard of! She! Forgot the pipe!

'I'll – I'll fill it directly. It's soon done.'

But it was not so soon done, either. It lay in the usual place; the carrier's dreadnought pocket; with the little pouch, her own work, from which she was used to fill it; but her hand shook so, that she entangled it (and yet her hand was small enough to have come out easily, I am sure), and bungled terribly. The filling of the pipe and lighting it; those little offices in which I have commended her discretion, if you recollect; were vilely done, from first to last. During the whole process, Tackleton stood looking on maliciously with the half-closed eye; which, whenever it met hers – or caught it, for it can hardly be said to have ever met another eye:

rather being a kind of trap to snatch it up – augmented her confusion in a most remarkable degree.

'Why, what a clumsy Dot you are, this afternoon!' said John. 'I could have done it better myself, I verily believe!'

With these good-natured words, he strode away; and presently was heard, in company with Boxer, and the old horse, and the cart, making lively music down the road. What time the dreamy Caleb still stood, watching his blind daughter, with the same expression on his face.

'Bertha!' said Caleb, softly. 'What has happened? How changed you are, my darling, in a few hours – since this morning. *You* silent and dull all day! What is it? Tell me!'

'Oh father, father!' cried the blind girl , bursting into tears. 'Oh my hard, hard fate!'

Caleb drew his hand across his eyes before he answered her.

'But think how cheerful and how happy you have been, Bertha! How good, and how much loved, by many people.'

'That strikes me to the heart, dear father! Always so mindful of me! Always so kind to me!'

Caleb was very much perplexed to understand her.

'To be – to be blind, Bertha, my poor dear,' he faltered, 'is a great affliction; but – '

'I have never felt it!' cried the blind girl . 'I have never felt it, in its fullness. Never! I have sometimes wished that I could see you, or could see him; only once, dear father; only for one little minute; that I might know what it is I treasure up,' she laid her hands upon her breast, 'and hold here! That I might be sure I have it right! And sometimes (but then I was a child) I have wept, in my prayers at night, to think that when your images ascended from my heart to Heaven, they might not be the true resemblance of yourselves. But I have never had these feelings long. They have passed away and left me tranquil and contented.'

'And they will again,' said Caleb.

'But, father! Oh my good, gentle father, bear with me, if I am wicked!' said the blind girl. 'This is not the sorrow that so weighs me down!'

Her father could not choose but let his moist eyes overflow; she was so earnest and pathetic. But he did not understand her, yet.

'Bring her to me,' said Bertha. 'I cannot hold it closed and shut within myself. Bring her to me, father!'

She knew he hesitated, and said, 'May. Bring May!'

May heard the mention of her name, and coming quietly towards her, touched her on the arm. The blind girl turned immediately, and held her by both hands.

'Look into my face, dear heart, sweet heart!' said Bertha. 'Read it with your beautiful eyes, and tell me if the Truth is written on it.'

'Dear Bertha, Yes!'

The blind girl , still upturning the blank sightless face, down which the tears were coursing fast, addressed her in these words: 'There is not, in my soul, a wish or thought that is not for your good, bright May! There is not, in my soul, a grateful recollection stronger than the deep remembrance which is stored there, of the many times when, in the full pride of sight and beauty, you have had consideration for blind Bertha, even when we two were children, or when Bertha was as much a child as ever blindness can be! Every blessing on your head! Light upon your happy course! Not the less, my dear May;' and she drew towards her, in a closer grasp; 'not the less, my bird, because, today, the knowledge that you are to be His wife has wrung my heart almost to breaking! Father, May, Mary! oh forgive me that it is so, for the sake of all he has done to relieve the weariness of my dark life: and for the sake of the belief you have in me, when I call Heaven to witness that I could not wish him married to a wife more worthy of his goodness!'

While speaking, she had released May Fielding's hands, and clasped her garments in an attitude of mingled supplication and love. Sinking lower and lower down, as she proceeded in her strange confession, she dropped at last at the feet of her friend, and hid her blind face in the folds of her dress.

'Great Power!' exclaimed her father, smitten at one blow with the truth, 'have I deceived her from her cradle, but to break her heart at last!'

It was well for all of them that Dot, that beaming, useful, busy little Dot – for such she was, whatever faults she had, and however you may learn to hate her, in good time – it was well for all of them, I say, that she was there: or where this would have ended, it were hard to tell. But Dot, recovering her self-possession, interposed, before May could reply, or Caleb say another word.

'Come come, dear Bertha! come away with me! Give her your arm, May. So! How composed she is, you see, already; and how good it is of her to mind us,' said the cheery little woman, kissing her upon the forehead. 'Come away, dear Bertha! Come! and here's her good father will come with her; won't you, Caleb? To – be – sure!'

Well, well! she was a noble little Dot in such things, and it must have been an obdurate nature that could have withstood her influence. When she had got poor Caleb and his Bertha away, that they might comfort and console each other, as she knew they only could, she presently came bouncing back, – the saying is, as fresh as any daisy; *I* say fresher – to mount guard over that bridling little piece of consequence in the cap and gloves, and prevent the dear old creature from making discoveries.

'So bring me the precious baby, Tilly,' said she, drawing a chair to the fire; 'and while I have it in my lap, here's Mrs Fielding, Tilly, will tell me all about the management of babies, and put me right in twenty points where I'm as wrong as can be. Won't you, Mrs Fielding?'

Not even the Welsh Giant, who according to the popular expression, was so 'slow' as to perform a fatal surgical operation upon himself, in emulation of a juggling-trick achieved by his arch-enemy at breakfast-time; not even he fell half so readily into the Snare prepared for him, as the old lady did into this artful Pitfall. The fact of Tackleton having walked out; and furthermore, of two or three people having been talking together at a distance, for two minutes, leaving her to her own resources; was quite enough to have put her on her dignity, and the bewailment of that mysterious convulsion in the Indigo Trade, for four-and-twenty hours. But this becoming deference to her experience, on the part of the young mother, was so irresistible, that after a short affectation of humility, she began to enlighten her with the best grace in the world; and sitting bolt upright before the wicked Dot, she did, in half an hour, deliver more infallible domestic recipes and precepts, than would (if acted on) have utterly destroyed and done up that Young Peerybingle, though he had been an Infant Samson.

To change the theme, Dot did a little needlework – she carried the contents of a whole workbox in her pocket; however she contrived it, *I* don't know – then did a little nursing; then a little more needlework; then had a little whispering chat with May, while the old lady dozed; and so in little bits of bustle, which was quite her manner always, found it a very short afternoon. Then, as it grew dark, and as it was a solemn part of this Institution of the picnic that she should perform all Bertha's household tasks, she trimmed the fire, and swept the hearth, and set the tea-board out, and drew the curtain, and lighted a candle. Then, she played an air or two on a rude kind of harp, which Caleb had contrived for Bertha; and played them very well; for nature had made her delicate little ear as choice a one for music as it would have been for jewels, if she had had any to wear. By this time it was the established hour for having tea; and Tackleton came back again, to share the meal, and spend the evening.

Caleb and Bertha had returned some time before, and Caleb had sat down to his afternoon's work. But he couldn't settle to it, poor fellow, being anxious and remorseful for his daughter. It was touching to see him sitting idle on his working-stool, regarding her so wistfully; and always saying in his face, 'Have I deceived her from her cradle, but to break her heart!'

When it was night, and tea was done, and Dot had nothing more to do in washing up the cups and saucers; in a word – for I must come to it, and there is no use in putting it off – when the time drew nigh for expecting the carrier's return in every sound of distant wheels; her manner changed again; her colour came and went; and she was very restless. Not as good wives are, when listening for their husbands. No, no, no. It was another sort of restlessness from that.

Wheels heard. A horse's feet. The barking of a dog. The gradual approach of all the sounds. The scratching paw of Boxer at the door!

'Whose step is that!' cried Bertha, starting up.

'Whose step?' returned the carrier, standing in the portal, with his brown face ruddy as a winter berry from the keen night air. 'Why, mine.'

'The other step,' said Bertha. 'The man's tread behind you!'

'She is not to be deceived,' observed the carrier, laughing. 'Come along, sir. You'll be welcome, never fear!'

He spoke in a loud tone; and as he spoke, the deaf old gentleman entered.

'He's not so much a stranger, that you haven't seen him once, Caleb,' said the carrier. 'You'll give him house-room till we go?'

'Oh surely, John; and take it as an honour.'

'He's the best company on earth, to talk secrets in,' said John. 'I have reasonable good lungs, but he tries 'em, I can tell you. Sit down, sir. All friends here, and glad to see you!'

When he had imparted this assurance, in a voice that amply cor-roborated what he had said about his lungs, he added in his natural tone, 'A chair in the chimney-corner, and leave to sit quite silent and look pleasantly about him, is all he cares for. He's easily pleased.'

Bertha had been listening intently. She called Caleb to her side, when he had set the chair, and asked him, in a low voice, to describe their visitor. When he had done so (truly now; with scrupulous fidelity), she moved, for the first time since he had come in; and sighed; and seemed to have no further interest concerning him.

The carrier was in high spirits, good fellow that he was; and fonder of his little wife than ever.

'A clumsy Dot she was, this afternoon!' he said, encircling her with his rough arm, as she stood, removed from the rest; 'and yet I like her somehow. See yonder, Dot!'

He pointed to the old man. She looked down. I think she trembled.

'He's – ha–ha–ha! – he's full of admiration for you!' said the carrier.

'Talked of nothing else, the whole way here. Why, he's a brave old boy. I like him for it!'

'I wish he had had a better subject, John;' she said, with an uneasy glance about the room; at Tackleton especially.

'A better subject!' cried the jovial John. 'There's no such thing. Come! off with the greatcoat, off with the thick shawl, off with the heavy wrappers! and a cosy half-hour by the fire! My humble service, mistress. A game at cribbage, you and I? That's hearty. The cards and board, Dot. And a glass of beer here, if there's any left, small wife!'

His challenge was addressed to the old lady, who accepting it with gracious readiness, they were soon engaged upon the game. At first, the carrier looked about him sometimes, with a smile, or now and then called Dot to peep over his shoulder at his hand, and advise him on some knotty point. But his adversary being a rigid disciplinarian, and subject to an occasional weakness in respect of pegging more than she was entitled to, required such vigilance on his part, as left him neither eyes nor ears to spare. Thus, his whole attention gradually became absorbed upon the cards; and he thought of nothing else, until a hand upon his shoulder restored him to a consciousness of Tackleton.

'I am sorry to disturb you – but a word, directly.'

'I'm going to deal,' returned the carrier. 'It's a crisis.'

'It is,' said Tackleton. 'Come here, man!'

There was that in his pale face which made the other rise immediately, and ask him, in a hurry, what the matter was.

'Hush! John Peerybingle,' said Tackleton. 'I am sorry for this. I am indeed. I have been afraid of it. I have suspected it from the first.'

'What is it?' asked the carrier, with a frightened aspect.

'Hush! I'll show you, if you'll come with me.'

The carrier accompanied him, without another word. They went across a yard, where the stars were shining; and by a little side door, into Tackleton's own counting-house, where there was a glass window, commanding the ware-room: which was closed for the night. There was no light in the counting-house itself, but there were lamps in the long narrow ware-room; and consequently the window was bright.

'A moment!' said Tackleton. 'Can you bear to look through that window, do you think?'

'Why not?' returned the carrier.

'A moment more,' said Tackleton. 'Don't commit any violence. It's of no use. It's dangerous too. You're a strong-made man; and you might do murder before you know it.'

The carrier looked him in the face, and recoiled a step as if he had been struck. In one stride he was at the window, and he saw – Oh shadow on the hearth! Oh truthful cricket! Oh perfidious wife!

He saw her, with the old man; old no longer, but erect and gallant: bearing in his hand the false white hair that had won his way into their desolate and miserable home. He saw her listening to him, as he bent his head to whisper in her ear; and suffering him to clasp her round the waist, as they moved slowly down the dim wooden gallery towards the door by which they had entered it. He saw them stop, and saw her turn – to have the face, the face he loved so, so presented to his view! – and saw her, with her own hands, adjust the lie upon his head, laughing, as she did it, at his unsuspicious nature!

He clenched his strong right hand at first, as if it would have beaten down a lion. But opening it immediately again, he spread it out before the eyes of Tackleton (for he was tender of her, even then), and so, as they passed out, fell down upon a desk, and was as weak as any infant.

He was wrapped up to the chin, and busy with his horse and parcels, when she came into the room, prepared for going home.

'Now John, dear! Good-night, May! Good-night, Bertha!'

Could she kiss them? Could she be blithe and cheerful in her parting? Could she venture to reveal her face to them without a blush? Yes. Tackleton observed her closely; and she did all this.

Tilly was hushing the baby; and she crossed and recrossed Tackleton, a dozen times, repeating drowsily: 'Did the knowledge that it was to be its wifes, then, wring its hearts almost to breaking; and did its fathers deceive it from its cradles but to break its hearts at last!'

'Now Tilly, give me the baby. Good-night, Mr Tackleton. Where's John, for goodness' sake?'

'He's going to walk, beside the horse's head,' said Tackleton, who helped her to her seat.

'My dear John. Walk? Tonight?'

The muffled figure of her husband made a hasty sign in the affirmative; and the false stranger and the little nurse being in their places, the old horse moved off. Boxer, the unconscious Boxer, running on before, running back, running round and round the cart, and barking as triumphantly and merrily as ever.

When Tackleton had gone off likewise, escorting May and her mother home, poor Caleb sat down by the fire beside his daughter; anxious and remorseful at the core; and still saying in his wistful contemplation of her, 'Have I deceived her from her cradle, but to break her heart at last!'

The toys that had been set in motion for the baby, had all stopped and run down, long ago. In the faint light and silence, the imperturbably calm dolls; the agitated rocking-horses with distended eyes and nostrils; the old gentlemen at the street doors, standing, half doubled up, upon their failing knees and ankles; the wry-faced nutcrackers; the very beasts upon their way into the ark, in twos, like a boarding-school out walking; might have been imagined to be stricken motionless with fantastic wonder, at Dot being false, or Tackleton beloved, under any combination of circumstances.

CHIRP THE THIRD

The Dutch clock in the corner struck ten, when the carrier sat down by his fireside, so troubled and grief-worn that he seemed to scare the cuckoo, who, having cut his ten melodious announcements as short as possible, plunged back into the Moorish palace again, and clapped his little door behind him, as if the unwonted spectacle were too much for his feelings.

If the little haymaker had been armed with the sharpest of scythes, and had cut at every stroke into the carrier's heart, he never could have gashed and wounded it, as Dot had done.

It was a heart so full of love for her; so bound up and held together by innumerable threads of winning remembrance, spun from the daily working of her many qualities of endearment; it was a heart in which she had enshrined herself so gently and so closely; a heart so single and so earnest in its Truth: so strong in right, so weak in wrong: that it could cherish neither passion nor revenge at first, and had only room to hold the broken image of its Idol.

But slowly, slowly; as the carrier sat brooding on his hearth, now cold and dark; other and fiercer thoughts began to rise within him, as an angry wind comes rising in the night. The stranger was beneath his outraged roof. Three steps would take him to his chamber-door. One blow would beat it in. 'You might do murder before you know it,' Tackleton had said. How could it be Murder, if he gave the Villain time to grapple with him hand to hand! He was the younger man.

It was an ill-timed thought, bad for the dark mood of his mind. It was an angry thought, goading him to some avenging act, that should change the cheerful house into a haunted place which lonely travellers would dread to pass by night; and where the timid would see shadows struggling in the ruined windows when the moon was dim, and hear wild noises in the stormy weather.

He was the younger man! Yes, yes; some lover who had won the heart that *he* had never touched. Some lover of her early choice: of whom she had thought and dreamed: for whom she had pined and pined: when he had fancied her so happy by his side. Oh agony to think of it!

She had been above stairs with the baby, getting it to bed. As he sat brooding on the hearth, she came close beside him, without his knowledge – in the turning of the rack of his great misery, he lost all other sounds – and put her little stool at his feet. He only knew it, when he felt her hand upon his own, and saw her looking up into his face.

With wonder? No. It was his first impression, and he was fain to look at her again, to set it right. No, not with wonder. With an eager and enquiring look; but not with wonder. At first it was alarmed and serious; then it changed into a strange, wild, dreadful smile of recognition of his thoughts; then there was nothing but her clasped hands on her brow, and her bent head, and falling hair.

Though the power of omnipotence had been his to wield at that moment, he had too much of its diviner property of mercy in his breast, to have turned one feather's weight of it against her. But he could not bear to see her crouching down upon the little seat where he had often looked on her, with love and pride, so innocent and gay; and when she rose and left him, sobbing as she went, he felt it a relief to have the vacant place beside him rather than her so long cherished presence. This in itself was anguish keener than all: reminding him how desolate he was become, and how the great bond of his life was rent asunder.

The more he felt this, and the more he knew he could have better borne to see her lying prematurely dead before him with their little child upon her breast, the higher and the stronger rose his wrath against his enemy. He looked about him for a weapon.

There was a gun, hanging on the wall. He took it down, and moved a pace or two towards the door of the perfidious stranger's room. He knew the gun was loaded. Some shadowy idea that it was just to shoot this man like a Wild Beast, seized him, and dilated in his mind until it grew into a monstrous demon in complete possession of him, casting out all milder thoughts and setting up its undivided empire.

That phrase is wrong. Not casting out his milder thoughts, but artfully transforming them. Changing them into scourges to drive him on. Turning water into blood, love into hate, gentleness into blind ferocity. Her image, sorrowing, humbled, but still pleading to his tenderness and mercy with resistless power, never left his mind; but staying there, it urged him to the door; raised the weapon to his shoulder; fitted and nerved his finger to the trigger; and cried 'Kill him! In his bed!'

He reversed the gun to beat the stock upon the door; he already held it lifted in the air; some indistinct design was in his thoughts of calling out to him to fly, for God's sake, by the window –

When, suddenly, the struggling fire illumined the whole chimney with a glow of light; and the cricket on the hearth began to chirp!

No sound he could have heard; no human voice, not even hers; could so have moved and softened him. The artless words in which she had told him of her love for this same cricket, were once more freshly spoken; her trembling, earnest manner at the moment, was again before him; her pleasant voice – Oh, what a voice it was, for making household music at the fireside of an honest man! – thrilled through and through his better nature, and awoke it into life and action.

He recoiled from the door, like a man walking in his sleep, awakened

from a frightful dream; and put the gun aside. Clasping his hands before
his face, he then sat down again beside the fire, and found relief in tears.

The cricket on the hearth came out into the room, and stood in fairy
shape before him.

' "I love it," ' said the fairy voice, repeating what he well remembered,
' "for the many times I have heard it, and the many thoughts its harmless
music has given me." '

'She said so!' cried the carrier. 'True!'

' "This has been a happy home, John; and I love the cricket for its
sake!" '

'It has been, Heaven knows,' returned the carrier. 'She made it happy,
always, – until now.'

'So gracefully sweet-tempered; so domestic, joyful, busy, and light-
hearted!' said the voice.

'Otherwise I never could have loved her as I did,' returned the carrier.

The voice, correcting him, said 'do'.

The carrier repeated 'as I did.' But not firmly. His faltering tongue
resisted his control, and would speak in its own way, for itself and him.

The Figure, in an attitude of invocation, raised its hand and said: 'Upon your own hearth – '

'The hearth she has blighted,' interposed the carrier.

'The hearth she has – how often! – blessed and brightened,' said the cricket: 'the hearth which, but for her, were only a few stones and bricks and rusty bars, but which has been, through her, the Altar of your Home; on which you have nightly sacrificed some petty passion, selfishness, or care, and offered up the homage of a tranquil mind, a trusting nature, and an overflowing heart; so that the smoke from this poor chimney has gone upward with a better fragrance than the richest incense that is burnt before the richest shrines in all the gaudy temples of this world! – Upon your own hearth; in its quiet sanctuary; surrounded by its gentle influences and associations; hear her! Hear me! Hear everything that speaks the language of your hearth and home!'

'And pleads for her?' enquired the carrier.

'All things that speak the language of your hearth and home, *must* plead for her!' returned the cricket. 'For they speak the truth.'

And while the carrier, with his head upon his hands, continued to sit meditating in his chair, the presence stood beside him; suggesting his reflections by its power, and presenting them before him, as in a glass or picture. It was not a solitary presence. From the hearth-stone, from the chimney; from the clock, the pipe, the kettle, and the cradle; from the floor, the walls, the ceiling, and the stairs; from the cart without, and the cupboard within, and the household implements; from everything and every place with which she had ever been familiar, and with which she had ever entwined one recollection of herself in her unhappy husband's mind; fairies came trooping forth. Not to stand beside him as the cricket did, but to busy and bestir themselves. To do all honour to her image. To pull him by the skirts, and point to it when it appeared. To cluster round it, and embrace it, and strew flowers for it to tread on. To try to crown its fair head with their tiny hands. To show that they were fond of it and loved it; and that there was not one ugly, wicked, or accusatory creature to claim knowledge of it – none but their playful and approving selves.

His thoughts were constant to her image. It was always there.

She sat plying her needle, before the fire, and singing to herself. Such a blithe, thriving, steady little Dot! The fairy figures turned upon him all at once, by our consent, with one prodigious concentrated stare; and seemed to say 'Is this the light wife you are mourning for!'

There were sounds of gaiety outside: musical instruments, and noisy tongues, and laughter. A crowd of young merry-makers came pouring in; among whom were May Fielding and a score of pretty girls. Dot was the fairest of them all; as young as any of them too. They came to summon her to join their party. It was a dance. If ever little foot were made for dancing, hers was, surely. But she laughed, and shook her head, and pointed to her cookery on the fire, and her table ready spread: with an exulting defiance that rendered her more charming than she was before. And so she merrily dismissed them: nodding to her would-be partners, one by one, as they passed out, with a comical indifference, enough to make them go and drown themselves immediately if they were her admirers – and they must have been so, more or less; they couldn't help it. And yet indifference was not her character. Oh no! For presently, there came a certain carrier to the door; and bless her what a welcome she bestowed upon him!

Again the staring figures turned upon him all at once, and seemed to say, 'Is this the wife who has forsaken you!'

A shadow fell upon the mirror or the picture: call it what you will. A great shadow of the stranger, as he first stood underneath their roof; covering its surface, and blotting out all other objects. But the nimble fairies worked like bees to clear it off again; and Dot again was there. Still bright and beautiful.

Rocking her little baby in its cradle; singing to it softly; and resting her head upon a shoulder which had its counterpart in the musing figure by which the fairy cricket stood.

The night – I mean the real night: not going by fairy clocks – was wearing now; and in this stage of the carrier's thoughts, the moon burst out, and shone brightly in the sky. Perhaps some calm and quiet light had risen also, in his mind; and he could think more soberly of what had happened.

Although the shadow of the stranger fell at intervals upon the glass – always distinct, and big, and thoroughly defined – it never fell so darkly as at first. Whenever it appeared, the fairies uttered a general cry of consternation, and plied their little arms and legs, with inconceivable activity, to rub it out. And whenever they got at Dot again, and showed her to him once more, bright and beautiful, they cheered in the most inspiring manner.

They never showed her, otherwise than beautiful and bright, for they were household spirits to whom falsehood is annihilation; and being so, what Dot was there for them, but the one active, beaming, pleasant little creature who had been the light and sun of the carrier's home!

The fairies were prodigiously excited when they showed her, with the baby, gossiping among a knot of sage old matrons, and affecting to be wondrous old and matronly herself, and leaning in a staid, demure old way upon her husband's arm, attempting – she! such a bud of a little woman – to convey the idea of having abjured the vanities of the world in general, and of being the sort of person to whom it was no novelty at all to be a mother; yet in the same breath, they showed her, laughing at the carrier for being awkward, and pulling up his shirt-collar to make him smart, and mincing merrily about that very room to teach him how to dance.

They turned, and stared immensely at him when they showed her with the blind girl ; for though she carried cheerfulness and animation with her, wheresoever she went, she bore those influences into Caleb Plummer's home, heaped up and running over. The blind girl 's love for her, and trust in her, and gratitude to her; her own good busy way of setting Bertha's thanks aside; her dexterous little arts for filling up each moment of the visit in doing something useful to the house, and really working hard while feigning to make holiday; her bountiful provision of those standing delicacies, the veal-and-ham pie and the bottles of beer; her radiant little face arriving at the door, and taking leave; the wonderful expression in her whole self, from her neat foot to the crown of her head, of being a part of the establishment – a something necessary to it, which it couldn't be without; all this the fairies revelled in, and loved her for. And once again they looked upon him all at once, appealingly; and seemed to say, while some among them nestled in her dress and fondled her, 'Is this the Wife who has betrayed your confidence!'

More than once, or twice, or thrice, in the long thoughtful night, they showed her to him sitting on her favourite seat, with her bent head, her hands clasped on her brow, her falling hair. As he had seen her last. And when they found her thus, they neither turned nor looked upon him, but gathered close round her, and comforted and kissed her: and pressed on one another to show sympathy and kindness to her: and forgot him altogether.

Thus the night passed. The moon went down; the stars grew pale; the cold day broke; the sun rose. The carrier still sat, musing, in the chimney corner. He had sat there, with his head upon his hands, all night. All night the faithful cricket had been chirp, chirp, chirping on the hearth. All night he had listened to its voice. All night, the household fairies had been busy with him. All night, she had been amiable and blameless in the glass, except when that one shadow fell upon it.

He rose up when it was broad day, and washed and dressed himself. He couldn't go about his customary cheerful avocations; he wanted spirit for them; but it mattered the less, that it was Tackleton's wedding-day, and he had arranged to make his rounds by proxy. He had thought to have gone merrily to church with Dot. But such plans were at an end. It was their own wedding-day too. Ah! how little he had looked for such a close to such a year!

The carrier expected that Tackleton would pay him an early visit; and he was right. He had not walked to and fro before his own door, many minutes, when he saw the toy-merchant coming in his chaise along the road. As the chaise drew nearer, he perceived that Tackleton was dressed out sprucely, for his marriage: and had decorated his horse's head with flowers and favours.

The horse looked much more like a bridegroom than Tackleton: whose half-closed eye was more disagreeably expressive than ever. But the carrier took little heed of this. His thoughts had other occupation.

'John Peerybingle!' said Tackleton, with an air of condolence. 'My good fellow, how do you find yourself this morning?'

'I have had but a poor night, Master Tackleton,' returned the carrier, shaking his head: 'for I have been a good deal disturbed in my mind. But it's over now! Can you spare me half an hour or so, for some private talk?'

'I came on purpose,' returned Tackleton, alighting. 'Never mind the horse. He'll stand quiet enough, with the reins over this post, if you'll give him a mouthful of hay.'

The carrier having brought it from his stable and set it before him, they turned into the house.

'You are not married before noon?' he said, 'I think?'

'No,' answered Tackleton. 'Plenty of time. Plenty of time.'

When they entered the kitchen, Tilly Slowboy was rapping at the stranger's door; which was only removed from it by a few steps. One of her very red eyes (for Tilly had been crying all night long, because her mistress cried) was at the keyhole; and she was knocking very loud; and seemed frightened.

'If you please I can't make nobody hear,' said Tilly, looking round. 'I hope nobody an't gone and been and died if you please!'

This philanthropic wish, Miss Slowboy emphasised with various new raps and kicks at the door; which led to no result whatever.

'Shall I go?' said Tackleton. 'It's curious.'

The carrier, who had turned his face from the door, signed to him to go if he would.

So Tackleton went to Tilly Slowboy's relief; and he too kicked and knocked; and he too failed to get the least reply. But he thought of trying the handle of the door; and as it opened easily, he peeped in, looked in, went in; and soon came running out again.

'John Peerybingle,' said Tackleton, in his ear. 'I hope there has been nothing – nothing rash in the night.'

The carrier turned upon him quickly.

'Because he's gone!' said Tackleton; 'and the window's open. I don't see any marks – to be sure it's almost on a level with the garden: but I was afraid there might have been some – some scuffle. Eh?'

He nearly shut up the expressive eye altogether; he looked at him so hard. And he gave his eye, and his face, and his whole person, a sharp twist. As if he would have screwed the truth out of him.

'Make yourself easy,' said the carrier. 'He went into that room last night, without harm in word or deed from me; and no one has entered it since. He is away of his own free will. I'd go out gladly at that door, and beg my bread from house to house, for life, if I could so change the past that he had never come. But he has come and gone. And I have done with him!'

'Oh! – Well, I think he has got off pretty easy,' said Tackleton, taking a chair.

The sneer was lost upon the carrier, who sat down too: and shaded his face with his hand, for some little time, before proceeding.

'You showed me last night,' he said at length, 'my wife; my wife that I love; secretly – '

'And tenderly,' insinuated Tackleton.

'Conniving at that man's disguise, and giving him opportunities of meeting her alone. I think there's no sight I wouldn't have rather seen than that. I think there's no man in the world I wouldn't have rather had to show it me.'

'I confess to having had my suspicions always,' said Tackleton. 'And that has made me objectionable here, I know.'

'But as you did show it me,' pursued the carrier, not minding him; 'and as you saw her; my wife; my wife that I love' – his voice, and eye, and hand, grew steadier and firmer as he repeated these words: evidently in pursuance of a steadfast purpose – 'as you saw her at this disadvantage, it is right and just that you should also see with my eyes, and look into my breast, and know what my mind is, upon the subject. For it's settled,' said the carrier, regarding him attentively. 'And nothing can shake it now.'

Tackleton muttered a few general words of assent, about its being necessary to vindicate something or other; but he was overawed by the manner of his companion. Plain and unpolished as it was, it had a something dignified and noble in it, which nothing but the soul of generous Honour, dwelling in the man, could have imparted.

'I am a plain, rough man,' pursued the carrier, 'with very little to recommend me. I am not a clever man, as you very well know. I am not a young man. I loved my little Dot, because I had seen her grow up, from a child, in her father's house; because I knew how precious she was; because she had been my Life, for years and years. There's many men I can't compare with, who never could have loved my little Dot like me, I think!'

He paused, and softly beat the ground a short time with his foot, before resuming: 'I often thought that though I wasn't good enough for her, I should make her a kind husband, and perhaps know her value better than another; and in this way I reconciled it to myself, and came to think it might be possible that we should be married. And in the end, it came about, and we *were* married.'

'Hah!' said Tackleton, with a significant shake of his head.

'I had studied myself; I had had experience of myself; I knew how much I loved her, and how happy I should be,' pursued the carrier. 'But I had not – I feel it now – sufficiently considered her.'

'To be sure,' said Tackleton. 'Giddiness, frivolity, fickleness, love of admiration! Not considered! All left out of sight! Hah!'

'You had best not interrupt me,' said the carrier, with some sternness, 'till you understand me; and you're wide of doing so. If, yesterday, I'd have struck that man down at a blow, who dared to breathe a word against her; today I'd set my foot upon his face, if he was my brother!'

The toy-merchant gazed at him in astonishment. He went on in a softer tone: 'Did I consider,' said the carrier, 'that I took her; at her age, and with her beauty; from her young companions, and the many scenes of which she was the ornament; in which she was the brightest little star that ever shone; to shut her up from day to day in my dull house, and keep my tedious company? Did I consider how little suited I was to her sprightly humour, and how wearisome a plodding man like me must be, to one of her quick spirit; did I consider that it was no merit in me, or claim in me, that I loved her, when everybody must, who knew her? Never. I took advantage of her hopeful nature and her cheerful disposition; and I married her. I wish I never had! For her sake; not for mine!'

The toy-merchant gazed at him, without winking. Even the half-shut eye was open now.

'Heaven bless her!' said the carrier, 'for the cheerful constancy with which she tried to keep the knowledge of this from me! And Heaven help me, that, in my slow mind, I have not found it out before! Poor child! Poor Dot! *I* not to find it out, who have seen her eyes fill with tears, when such a marriage as our own was spoken of! I, who have seen the secret trembling on her lips a hundred times, and never suspected it, till last night! Poor girl! That I could ever hope she would be fond of me! That I could ever believe she was!'

'She made a show of it,' said Tackleton. 'She made such a show of it, that to tell you the truth it was the origin of my misgivings.'

And here he asserted the superiority of May Fielding, who certainly made no sort of show of being fond of *him*.

'She has tried,' said the poor carrier, with greater emotion than he had exhibited yet; 'I only now begin to know how hard she has tried; to be my dutiful and zealous wife. How good she has been; how much she has done; how brave and strong a heart she has; let the happiness I have known under this roof bear witness! It will be some help and comfort to me, when I am here alone.'

'Here alone?' said Tackleton. 'Oh! Then you do mean to take some notice of this?'

'I mean,' returned the carrier, 'to do her the greatest kindness, and make her the best reparation, in my power. I can release her from the daily pain of an unequal marriage, and the struggle to conceal it. She shall be as free as I can render her.'

'Make *her* reparation!' exclaimed Tackleton, twisting and turning his great ears with his hands. 'There must be something wrong here. You didn't say that, of course.'

The carrier set his grip upon the collar of the toy-merchant, and shook him like a reed.

'Listen to me!' he said. 'And take care that you hear me right. Listen to me. Do I speak plainly?'

'Very plainly indeed,' answered Tackleton.

'As if I meant it?'

'Very much as if you meant it.'

'I sat upon that hearth, last night, all night,' exclaimed the carrier. 'On the spot where she has often sat beside me, with her sweet face looking into mine. I called up her whole life, day by day; I had her dear self, in its every passage, in review before me. And upon my soul she is innocent, if there is one to judge the innocent and guilty!'

Staunch cricket on the hearth! Loyal household fairies!

'Passion and distrust have left me!' said the carrier; 'and nothing but my grief remains. In an unhappy moment some old lover, better suited to her tastes and years than I; forsaken, perhaps, for me, against her will; returned. In an unhappy moment: taken by surprise, and wanting time to think of what she did: she made herself a party to his treachery, by concealing it. Last night she saw him, in the interview we witnessed. It was wrong. But otherwise than this, she is innocent if there is truth on earth!'

'If that is your opinion – ' Tackleton began.

'So, let her go!' pursued the carrier. 'Go, with my blessing for the many happy hours she has given me, and my forgiveness for any pang she has caused me. Let her go, and have the peace of mind I wish her! She'll never hate me. She'll learn to like me better, when I'm not a drag upon her, and she wears the chain I have riveted, more lightly. This is the day on which I took her, with so little thought for her enjoyment, from her home. Today she shall return to it; and I will trouble her no more. Her father and mother will be here today – we had made a little plan for keeping it together – and they shall take her home. I can trust her, there, or anywhere. She leaves me without blame, and she will live so I am sure. If I should die – I may perhaps while she is still young; I have lost some courage in a few hours – she'll find that I remembered her, and loved her to the last! This is the end of what you showed me. Now, it's over!'

'Oh no, John, not over. Do not say it's over yet! Not quite yet. I have heard your noble words. I could not steal away, pretending to be ignorant of what has affected me with such deep gratitude. Do not say it's over, till the clock has struck again!'

She had entered shortly after Tackleton; and had remained there. She never looked at Tackleton, but fixed her eyes upon her husband. But she kept away from him, setting as wide a space as possible between them; and though she spoke with most impassioned earnestness, she went no nearer to him even then. How different in this, from her old self!

'No hand can make the clock which will strike again for me the hours that are gone,' replied the carrier, with a faint smile. 'But let it be so, if you will, my dear. It will strike soon. It's of little matter what we say. I'd try to please you in a harder case than that.'

'Well!' muttered Tackleton. 'I must be off, for when the clock strikes again, it'll be necessary for me to be upon my way to church. Good-morning, John Peerybingle. I'm sorry to be deprived of the pleasure of your company. Sorry for the loss, and the occasion of it too!'

'I have spoken plainly?' said the carrier, accompanying him to the door.

'Oh quite!'

'And you'll remember what I have said?'

'Why, if you compel me to make the observation,' said Tackleton; previously taking the precaution of getting into his chaise; 'I must say that it was so very unexpected, that I'm far from being likely to forget it.'

'The better for us both,' returned the carrier. 'Goodbye. I give you joy!'

'I wish I could give it to *you*,' said Tackleton. 'As I can't; thank'ee. Between ourselves (as I told you before, eh?) I don't much think I shall have the less joy in my married life, because May hasn't been too officious about me, and too demonstrative. Goodbye! Take care of yourself.'

The carrier stood looking after him until he was smaller in the distance than his horse's flowers and favours near at hand; and then, with a deep sigh, went strolling like a restless, broken man, among some neighbouring elms; unwilling to return until the clock was on the eve of striking.

His little wife, being left alone, sobbed piteously; but often dried her eyes and checked herself, to say how good he was, how excellent he was! and once or twice she laughed; so heartily, triumphantly, and incoherently (still crying all the time), that Tilly was quite horrified.

'Ow if you please don't!' said Tilly. 'It's enough to dead and bury the baby, so it is if you please.'

'Will you bring him sometimes, to see his father, Tilly,' enquired her mistress; drying her eyes; 'when I can't live here, and have gone to my old home?'

'Ow if you please don't!' cried Tilly, throwing back her head, and bursting out into a howl; she looked at the moment uncommonly like Boxer; 'Ow if you please don't! Ow, what has everybody gone and been and done with everybody, making everybody else so wretched! Ow–w–w–w!'

The soft-hearted Slowboy trailed off at this juncture, into such a deplorable howl: the more tremendous from its long suppression: that she must infallibly have awakened the baby, and frightened him into something serious (probably convulsions), if her eyes had not encountered Caleb Plummer, leading in his daughter. This spectacle restoring her to a sense of the proprieties, she stood for some few moments silent, with her mouth wide open: and then, posting off to the bed on which the baby lay asleep, danced in a weird, St Vitus manner on the floor, and at the same time rummaged with her face and head among the bedclothes: apparently deriving much relief from those extraordinary operations.

'Mary!' said Bertha. 'Not at the marriage!'

'I told her you would not be there, Mum,' whispered Caleb. 'I heard as much last night. But bless you,' said the little man, taking her tenderly by both hands, '*I* don't care for what they say; *I* don't believe them. There an't much of me, but that little should be torn to pieces sooner than I'd trust a word against you!'

He put his arms about her neck and hugged her, as a child might have hugged one of his own dolls.

'Bertha couldn't stay at home this morning,' said Caleb. 'She was afraid, I know, to hear the Bells ring: and couldn't trust herself to be so near them on their wedding-day. So we started in good time, and came here. I have been thinking of what I have done,' said Caleb, after a moment's pause; 'I have been blaming myself till I hardly knew what to do or where to turn, for the distress of mind I have caused her; and I've come to the conclusion that I'd better, if you'll stay with me, Mum, the while, tell her the truth. You'll stay with me the while?' he enquired, trembling from head to foot. 'I don't know what effect it may have upon her; I don't know what she'll think of me; I don't know that she'll ever care for her poor father afterwards. But it's best for her that she should be undeceived; and I must bear the consequences as I deserve!'

'Mary,' said Bertha, 'where is your hand! Ah! Here it is; here it is!' pressing it to her lips, with a smile, and drawing it through her arm. 'I heard them speaking softly among themselves, last night, of some blame against you. They were wrong.'

The carrier's wife was silent. Caleb answered for her.

'They were wrong,' he said.

'I knew it!' cried Bertha, proudly. 'I told them so. I scorned to hear a word! Blame *her* with justice!' she pressed the hand between her own, and the soft cheek against her face. 'No! I am not so blind as that.'

Her father went on one side of her, while Dot remained upon the other: holding her hand.

'I know you all,' said Bertha, 'better than you think. But none so well as her. Not even you, father. There is nothing half so real and so true about me, as she is. If I could be restored to sight this instant, and not a word were spoken, I could choose her from a crowd! My sister!'

'Bertha, my dear!' said Caleb, 'I have something on my mind I want to tell you, while we three are alone. Hear me kindly! I have a confession to make to you, my darling.'

'A confession, father?'

'I have wandered from the truth and lost myself, my child,' said Caleb, with a pitiable expression in his bewildered face. 'I have wandered from the truth, intending to be kind to you; and have been cruel.'

She turned her wonder-stricken face towards him, and repeated, 'Cruel!'

'He accuses himself too strongly, Bertha,' said Dot. 'You'll say so, presently. You'll be the first to tell him so.'

'He cruel to me!' cried Bertha, with a smile of incredulity.

'Not meaning it, my child,' said Caleb. 'But I have been; though I never suspected it, till yesterday. My dear blind daughter, hear me and forgive me! The world you live in, heart of mine, doesn't exist as I have represented it. The eyes you have trusted in, have been false to you.'

She turned her wonder-stricken face towards him still; but drew back, and clung closer to her friend.

'Your road in life was rough, my poor one,' said Caleb, 'and I meant to smooth it for you. I have altered objects, changed the characters of people, invented many things that never have been, to make you happier. I have had concealments from you, put deceptions on you, God forgive me! and surrounded you with fancies.'

'But living people are not fancies?' she said hurriedly, and turning very pale, and still retiring from him. 'You can't change them.'

'I have done so, Bertha,' pleaded Caleb. 'There is one person that you know, my dove – '

'Oh father! why do you say, I know?' she answered, in a tone of keen reproach. 'What and whom do I know! I who have no leader! I so miserably blind!'

In the anguish of her heart, she stretched out her hands, as if she were groping her way; then spread them, in a manner most forlorn and sad, upon her face.

'The marriage that takes place today,' said Caleb, 'is with a stern, sordid, grinding man. A hard master to you and me, my dear, for many years. Ugly in his looks, and in his nature. Cold and callous always. Unlike what I have painted him to you in everything, my child. In everything.'

'Oh why,' cried the blind girl , tortured, as it seemed, almost beyond endurance, 'why did you ever do this! Why did you ever fill my heart so full, and then come in like death, and tear away the objects of my love! Oh Heaven, how blind I am! How helpless and alone!'

Her afflicted father hung his head, and offered no reply but in his penitence and sorrow.

She had been but a short time in this passion of regret, when the cricket on the hearth, unheard by all but her, began to chirp. Not merrily, but in a low, faint, sorrowing way. It was so mournful, that her tears began to flow; and when the presence which had been beside the carrier all night, appeared behind her, pointing to her father, they fell down like rain.

She heard the cricket-voice more plainly soon; and was conscious, through her blindness, of the Presence hovering about her father.

'Mary,' said the blind girl , 'tell me what my home is. What it truly is.'

'It is a poor place, Bertha; very poor and bare indeed. The house will scarcely keep out wind and rain another winter. It is as roughly shielded from the weather, Bertha,' Dot continued in a low, clear voice, 'as your poor father in his sackcloth coat.'

The blind girl , greatly agitated, rose, and led the carrier's little wife aside.

'Those presents that I took such care of; that came almost at my wish, and were so dearly welcome to me,' she said, trembling; 'where did they come from? Did you send them?'

'No.'

'Who then?'

Dot saw she knew, already; and was silent. The blind girl spread her hands before her face again. But in quite another manner now.

'Dear Mary, a moment. One moment! More this way. Speak softly to me. You are true, I know. You'd not deceive me now; would you?'

'No, Bertha, indeed!'

'No, I am sure you would not. You have too much pity for me. Mary, look across the room to where we were just now; to where my father is – my father, so compassionate and loving to me – and tell me what you see.'

'I see,' said Dot, who understood her well; 'an old man sitting in a chair, and leaning sorrowfully on the back, with his face resting on his hand. As if his child should comfort him, Bertha.'

'Yes, yes. She will. Go on.'

'He is an old man worn with care and work. He is a spare, dejected, thoughtful, grey-haired man. I see him now, despondent and bowed down, and striving against nothing. But, Bertha, I have seen him many times before; and striving hard in many ways for one great sacred object. And I honour his grey head, and bless him!'

The blind girl broke away from her; and throwing herself upon her knees before him, took the grey head to her breast.

'It is my sight restored. It is my sight!' she cried. 'I have been blind, and now my eyes are open. I never knew him! To think I might have died, and never truly seen the father, who has been so loving to me!'

There were no words for Caleb's emotion.

'There is not a gallant figure on this earth,' exclaimed the blind girl , holding him in her embrace, 'that I would love so dearly, and would cherish so devotedly, as this! The greyer, and more worn, the dearer, father! Never let them say I am blind again. There's not a furrow in his face, there's not a hair upon his head, that shall be forgotten in my prayers and thanks to Heaven!'

Caleb managed to articulate 'My Bertha!'

'And in my blindness, I believed him,' said the girl, caressing him with tears of exquisite affection, 'to be so different! And having him beside me, day by day, so mindful of me always, never dreamed of this!'

'The fresh, smart father in the blue coat, Bertha,' said poor Caleb. 'He's gone!'

'Nothing is gone,' she answered. 'Dearest father, no! Everything is here – in you. The father that I loved so well; the father that I never loved enough, and never knew; the benefactor whom I first began to reverence and love, because he had such sympathy for me; All are here in you. Nothing is dead to me. The soul of all that was most dear to me is here – here, with the worn face, and the grey head. And I am NOT blind, father, any longer!'

Dot's whole attention had been concentrated, during this discourse, upon the father and daughter; but looking, now, towards the little Hay-maker in the Moorish meadow, she saw that the clock was within a few minutes of striking; and fell, immediately, into a nervous and excited state.

'Father,' said Bertha, hesitating. 'Mary.'

'Yes, my Mary,' returned Caleb. 'Here she is.'

'There is no change in *her*. You never told me anything of *her* that was not true?'

'I should have done it, my dear, I am afraid,' returned Caleb, 'if I could have made her better than she was. But I must have changed her for the worse, if I had changed her at all. Nothing could improve her, Bertha.'

Confident as the blind girl had been when she asked the question, her delight and pride in the reply, and her renewed embrace of Dot, were charming to behold.

'More changes than you think for, may happen though, my dear,' said Dot. 'Changes for the better, I mean; changes for great joy to some of us. You mustn't let them startle you too much, if any such should ever happen, and affect you? Are those wheels upon the road? You've a quick ear, Bertha. Are they wheels?'

'Yes. Coming very fast.'

'I – I – I know you have a quick ear,' said Dot, placing her hand upon her heart, and evidently talking on, as fast as she could, to hide its palpitating state, 'because I have noticed it often, and because you were so quick to find out that strange step last night. Though why you should have said, as I very well recollect you did say, Bertha, "Whose step is that!" and why you should have taken any greater observation of it than of any other step, I don't know. Though as I said just now, there are great changes in the world: great changes: and we can't do better than prepare ourselves to be surprised at hardly anything.'

Caleb wondered what this meant; perceiving that she spoke to him, no less than to his daughter. He saw her, with astonishment, so fluttered and distressed that she could scarcely breathe; and holding to a chair, to save herself from falling.

'They are wheels indeed!' she panted. 'Coming nearer! Nearer! Very close! And now you hear them stopping at the garden-gate! And now you hear a step outside the door – the same step, Bertha, is it not! – and now!' –

She uttered a wild cry of uncontrollable delight; and running up to Caleb put her hands upon his eyes, as a young man rushed into the room, and flinging away his hat to the air, came sweeping down upon them.

'Is it over?' cried Dot.

'Yes!'

'Happily over?'

'Yes!'

'Do you recollect the voice, dear Caleb? Did you ever hear the like of it before?' cried Dot.

'If my boy in the golden South Americas was alive – !' said Caleb, trembling.

'He is alive!' shrieked Dot, removing her hands from his eyes, and clapping them in ecstasy; 'look at him! See where he stands before you, healthy and strong! Your own dear son! Your own dear living, loving brother, Bertha!'

All honour to the little creature for her transports! All honour to her tears and laughter, when the three were locked in one another's arms! All honour to the heartiness with which she met the sunburnt sailor-fellow, with his dark streaming hair, half way, and never turned her rosy little mouth aside, but suffered him to kiss it, freely, and to press her to his bounding heart!

And honour to the cuckoo too – why not! – for bursting out of the trap-door in the Moorish palace like a housebreaker, and hiccoughing twelve times on the assembled company, as if he had got drunk for joy!

The carrier, entering, started back: and well he might: to find himself in such good company.

'Look, John!' said Caleb, exultingly, 'look here! My own boy from the golden South Americas! My own son! Him that you fitted out, and sent away yourself; him that you were always such a friend to!'

The carrier advanced to seize him by the hand; but recoiling, as some feature in his face awakened a remembrance of the deaf man in the cart, said: 'Edward! Was it you?'

'Now tell him all!' cried Dot. 'Tell him all, Edward; and don't spare me, for nothing shall make me spare myself in his eyes, ever again.'

'I was the man,' said Edward

'And could you steal, disguised, into the house of your old friend?' rejoined the carrier. 'There was a frank boy once – how many years is it, Caleb, since we heard that he was dead, and had it proved, we thought? – who never would have done that.'

'There was a generous friend of mine, once: more a father to me than a friend:' said Edward, 'who never would have judged me, or any other man unheard. You were he. So I am certain you will hear me now.'

The carrier, with a troubled glance at Dot, who still kept far away from him, replied, 'Well! that's but fair. I will.'

'You must know that when I left here, a boy,' said Edward, 'I was in love and my love was returned. She was a very young girl, who perhaps (you may tell me) didn't know her own mind. But I knew mine; and I had a passion for her.'

'You had!' exclaimed the carrier. 'You!'

'Indeed I had,' returned the other. 'And she returned it. I have ever since believed she did; and now I am sure she did.'

'Heaven help me!' said the carrier. 'This is worse than all.'

'Constant to her,' said Edward, 'and returning, full of hope, after many hardships and perils, to redeem my part of our old contract, I heard, twenty miles away, that she was false to me; that she had forgotten me; and had bestowed herself upon another and a richer man. I had no mind to reproach her; but I wished to see her, and to prove beyond dispute that this was true. I hoped she might have been forced into it, against her own desire and recollection. It would be small comfort, but it would be some, I thought: and on I came. That I might have the truth, the real truth; observing freely for myself, and judging for myself, without obstruction on the one hand, or presenting my own influence (if I had any) before her, on the other; I dressed myself unlike myself – you know how; and waited on the road – you know where. You had no suspicion of me; neither had – had she,' pointing to Dot, 'until I whispered in her ear at that fireside, and she so nearly betrayed me.'

'But when she knew that Edward was alive, and had come back,' sobbed Dot, now speaking for herself, as she had burned to do, all through this narrative; 'and when she knew his purpose, she advised him by all means to keep his secret close; for his old friend John Peerybingle was much too open in his nature, and too clumsy in all artifice – being a clumsy man in general,' said Dot, half laughing and half crying – 'to keep it for him. And when she – that's me, John,' sobbed the little woman – 'told him all, and how his sweetheart had believed him to be dead; and how she had at last been over- persuaded by her mother into a marriage which the silly, dear old thing called advantageous; and when she – that's me again, John – told him they were not yet married (though close upon it), and that it would be nothing but a sacrifice if it went on, for there was no love on her side; and when he went nearly mad with joy to hear it; then she – that's me again – said she would go between them, as she had often done before in old times, John, and would sound his sweetheart and be sure that what she – me again, John – said and thought was right. And it WAS right, John! And they were brought together, John! And they were married, John, an hour ago! And here's the bride! And Gruff and Tackleton may die a bachelor! And I'm a happy little woman, May, God bless you!'

She was an irresistible little woman, if that be anything to the purpose; and never so completely irresistible as in her present transports. There never were congratulations so endearing and delicious, as those she lavished on herself and on the bride.

Amid the tumult of emotions in his breast, the honest carrier had stood, confounded. Flying, now, towards her, Dot stretched out her hand to stop him, and retreated as before.

'No, John, no! Hear all! Don't love me any more, John, till you've heard every word I have to say. It was wrong to have a secret from you, John. I'm very sorry. I didn't think it any harm, till I came and sat down by you on the little stool last night; but when I knew by what was written in your face, that you had seen me walking in the gallery with Edward, and knew what you thought; I felt how giddy and how wrong it was. But oh, dear John, how could you, could you, think so!'

Little woman, how she sobbed again! John Peerybingle would have caught her in his arms. But no; she wouldn't let him.

'Don't love me yet, please John! Not for a long time yet! When I was sad about this intended marriage, dear, it was because I remembered May and Edward such young lovers; and knew that her heart was far away from Tackleton. You believe that, now. Don't you, John?'

John was going to make another rush at this appeal; but she stopped him again.

'No; keep there, please, John! When I laugh at you, as I sometimes do,

John; and call you clumsy, and a dear old goose, and names of that sort, it's because I love you John, so well; and take such pleasure in your ways; and wouldn't see you altered in the least respect to have you made a King tomorrow.'

'Hooroar!' said Caleb with unusual vigour. 'My opinion!'

'And when I speak of people being middle-aged, and steady, John, and pretend that we are a humdrum couple, going on in a jog-trot sort of way, it's only because I'm such a silly little thing, John, that I like, sometimes, to act a kind of play with baby, and all that: and make believe.'

She saw that he was coming; and stopped him again. But she was very nearly too late.

'No, don't love me for another minute or two, if you please, John! What I want most to tell you, I have kept to the last. My dear, good, generous John; when we were talking the other night about the cricket, I had it on my lips to say, that at first I did not love you quite so dearly as I do now; that when I first came home here, I was half afraid I mightn't learn to love you every bit as well as I hoped and prayed I might – being so very young, John. But, dear John, every day and hour, I loved you more and more. And if I could have loved you better than I do, the noble words I heard you say this morning, would have made me. But I can't. All the affection that I had (it was a great deal, John) I gave you, as you well deserve, long long ago, and I have no more left to give. Now, my dear husband, take me to your heart again! That's my home, John; and never, never think of sending me to any other!'

You never will derive so much delight from seeing a glorious little woman in the arms of a third party, as you would have felt if you had seen Dot run into the carrier's embrace. It was the most complete, unmitigated, soul-fraught little piece of earnestness that ever you beheld in all your days.

You may be sure the carrier was in a state of perfect rapture; and you may be sure Dot was likewise; and you may be sure they all were, inclusive of Miss Slowboy, who cried copiously for joy, and, wishing to include her young charge in the general interchange of congratulations, handed round the baby to everybody in succession, as if it were something to drink.

But now the sound of wheels was heard again outside the door; and somebody exclaimed that Gruff and Tackleton was coming back. Speedily that worthy gentleman appeared: looking warm and flustered.

'Why, what the Devil's this, John Peerybingle!' said Tackleton. 'There's some mistake. I appointed Mrs Tackleton to meet me at the church; and I'll swear I passed her on the road, on her way here. Oh! here she is! I beg your pardon, sir; I haven't the pleasure of knowing you; but if you can do me the favour to spare this young lady, she has rather a particular engagement this morning.'

'But I can't spare her,' returned Edward. 'I couldn't think of it.'

'What do you mean, you vagabond?' said Tackleton.

'I mean, that as I can make allowance for your being vexed,' returned the other, with a smile, 'I am as deaf to harsh discourse this morning, as I was to all discourse last night.'

The look that Tackleton bestowed upon him, and the start he gave!

'I am sorry, sir,' said Edward, holding out May's left hand, and especially the third finger; 'that the young lady can't accompany you to church; but as she has been there once, this morning, perhaps you'll excuse her.'

Tackleton looked hard at the third finger; and took a little piece of silver paper, apparently containing a ring, from his waistcoat pocket.

'Miss Slowboy,' said Tackleton. 'Will you have the kindness to throw that in the fire? Thank'ee.'

'It was a previous engagement: quite an old engagement: that prevented my wife from keeping her appointment with you, I assure you,' said Edward.

'Mr Tackleton will do me the justice to acknowledge that I revealed it to him faithfully; and that I told him, many times, I never could forget it,' said May, blushing.

'Oh certainly!' said Tackleton. 'Oh to be sure. Oh it's all right. It's quite correct. Mrs Edward Plummer, I infer?'

'That's the name,' returned the bridegroom.

'Ah, I shouldn't have known you, sir,' said Tackleton: scrutinising his face narrowly, and making a low bow. 'I give you joy, sir!'

'Thank'ee.'

'Mrs Peerybingle,' said Tackleton, turning suddenly to where she stood with her husband; 'I am sorry. You haven't done me a very great kindness, but, upon my life I am sorry. You are better than I thought you. John Peerybingle, I am sorry. You understand me; that's enough. It's quite correct, ladies and gentlemen all, and perfectly satisfactory. Good-morning!'

With these words he carried it off, and carried himself off too: merely stopping at the door, to take the flowers and favours from his horse's head, and to kick that animal once in the ribs, as a means of informing him that there was a screw loose in his arrangements.

Of course it became a serious duty now, to make such a day of it, as should mark these events for a high feast and festival in the Peerybingle calendar for evermore. Accordingly, Dot went to work to produce such an entertainment, as should reflect undying honour on the house and everyone concerned; and in a very short space of time, she was up to her dimpled elbows in flour, and whitening the carrier's coat, every time he came near her, by stopping him to give him a kiss. That good fellow washed the greens, and peeled the turnips, and broke the plates, and upset iron pots full of cold water on the fire, and made himself useful in all sorts of ways: while a couple of professional assistants, hastily called in from somewhere in the neighbourhood, as on a point of life or death, ran against each other in all the doorways and round all the corners; and everybody tumbled over Tilly Slowboy and the baby, everywhere. Tilly never came out in such force before. Her ubiquity was the theme of general admiration. She was a stumbling-block in the passage at five-and-twenty minutes past two; a mantrap in the kitchen at half-past two precisely; and a pitfall in the garret at five-and-twenty minutes to three. The baby's head was as it were, a test and touchstone for every description of matter, animal, vegetable, and mineral. Nothing was in use that day that didn't come, at some time or other, into close acquaintance with it.

Then, there was a great expedition set on foot to go and find out Mrs Fielding; and to be dismally penitent to that excellent gentlewoman; and to bring her back, by force if needful, to be happy and forgiving. And when the Expedition first discovered her, she would listen to no terms at all, but said, an unspeakable number of times, that ever she should have lived to see the day! and couldn't be got to say anything else, except 'Now carry me to the grave;' which seemed absurd, on account of her not being dead, or anything at all like it. After a time, she lapsed into a state of dreadful calmness, and observed, that when that unfortunate train of circumstances had occurred in the Indigo Trade, she had foreseen that she would be exposed, during her whole life, to every species of insult and contumely; and that she was glad to find it was the case; and begged they wouldn't trouble themselves about her,—for what was she? oh, dear! a nobody! – but would forget that such a being lived, and would take their course in life without her. From this bitterly sarcastic mood, she passed into an angry one, in which she gave vent to the remarkable expression that the worm would turn if trodden on; and after that, she yielded to a soft regret, and said, if they had only given her their confidence, what might she not have had it in her power to suggest! Taking advantage of this crisis in her feelings, the expedition embraced her; and she very soon had her gloves on, and was on her way to John Peerybingle's in a state of unimpeachable gentility; with a paper parcel at her side containing a cap of state, almost as tall, and quite as stiff, as a mitre.

Then, there were Dot's father and mother to come, in another little chaise; and they were behind their time; and fears were entertained; and there was much looking out for them down the road; and Mrs Fielding always would look in the wrong and morally impossible direction; and being apprised thereof, hoped she might take the liberty of looking where she pleased. At last they came: a chubby little couple, jogging along in a snug and comfortable little way that quite belonged to the Dot family: and Dot and her mother, side by side, were wonderful to see. They were so like each other.

Then, Dot's mother had to renew her acquaintance with May's mother; and May's mother always stood on her gentility; and Dot's mother never stood on anything but her active little feet. And old Dot: so to call Dot's father, I forgot it wasn't his right name, but never mind: took liberties, and shook hands at first sight, and seemed to think a cap but so much starch and muslin, and didn't defer himself at all to the Indigo Trade, but said there was no help for it now; and, in Mrs Fielding's summing up, was a good-natured kind of man—but coarse, my dear.

I wouldn't have missed Dot, doing the honours in her wedding-gown: my benison on her bright face! for any money. No! nor the good carrier, so jovial and so ruddy, at the bottom of the table. Nor the brown, fresh sailor-fellow, and his handsome wife. Nor anyone among them. To have missed the dinner would have been to miss as jolly and as stout a meal as man need eat; and to have missed the overflowing cups in which they drank The wedding-day, would have been the greatest miss of all.

After dinner, Caleb sang the song about the sparkling bowl! As I'm a living man: hoping to keep so, for a year or two: he sang it through.

And, by the by, a most unlooked-for incident occurred, just as he finished the last verse.

There was a tap at the door; and a man came staggering in, without saying with your leave, or by your leave, with something heavy on his head. Setting this down in the middle of the table, symmetrically in the centre of the nuts and apples, he said: 'Mr Tackleton's compliments, and as he hasn't got no use for the cake himself, p'raps you'll eat it.'

And with those words, he walked off.

There was some surprise among the company, as you may imagine. Mrs Fielding, being a lady of infinite discernment, suggested that the cake was poisoned, and related a narrative of a cake, which, within her knowledge, had turned a seminary for young ladies, blue. But she was overruled by acclamation; and the cake was cut by May, with much ceremony and rejoicing.

I don't think anyone had tasted it, when there came another tap at the door, and the same man appeared again, having under his arm a vast brown-paper parcel.

'Mr Tackleton's compliments, and he's sent a few toys for the Babby. They ain't ugly.'

After the delivery of which expressions, he retired again.

The whole party would have experienced great difficulty in finding words for their astonishment, even if they had had ample time to seek them. But they had none at all; for the messenger had scarcely shut the door behind him, when there came another tap, and Tackleton himself walked in.

'Mrs Peerybingle!' said the toy-merchant, hat in hand. 'I'm sorry. I'm more sorry than I was this morning. I have had time to think of it. John Peerybingle! I'm sour by disposition; but I can't help being sweetened, more or less, by coming face to face with such a man as you. Caleb! This unconscious little nurse gave me a broken hint last night, of which I have found the thread. I blush to think how easily I might have bound you and your daughter to me; and what a miserable idiot I was, when I took her for one! Friends, one and all, my house is very lonely tonight. I have not so much as a cricket on my hearth. I have scared them all away. Be gracious to me; let me join this happy party!'

He was at home in five minutes. You never saw such a fellow. What *had* he been doing with himself all his life, never to have known, before, his great capacity of being jovial! Or what had the fairies been doing with him, to have effected such a change!

'John! you won't send me home this evening, will you?' whispered Dot.

He had been very near it though!

There wanted but one living creature to make the party complete; and, in the twinkling of an eye, there he was: very thirsty with hard running, and engaged in hopeless endeavours to squeeze his head into a narrow pitcher. He had gone with the cart to its journey's end, very much disgusted with the absence of his master, and stupendously rebellious to the deputy. After lingering about the stable for some little time, vainly attempting to incite the old horse to the mutinous act of

returning on his own account, he had walked into the taproom and laid himself down before the fire. But suddenly yielding to the conviction that the deputy was a humbug, and must be abandoned, he had got up again, turned tail, and come home.

There was a dance in the evening. With which general mention of that recreation, I should have left it alone, if I had not some reason to suppose that it was quite an original dance, and one of a most uncommon figure. It was formed in an odd way; in this way.

Edward, that sailor-fellow – a good free dashing sort of a fellow he was – had been telling them various marvels concerning parrots, and mines, and Mexicans, and gold dust, when all at once he took it in his head to jump up from his seat and propose a dance; for Bertha's harp was there, and she had such a hand upon it as you seldom hear. Dot (sly little piece of affectation when she chose) said her dancing days were over; *I* think because the carrier was smoking his pipe, and she liked sitting by him, best. Mrs Fielding had no choice, of course, but to say her dancing days were over, after that; and everybody said the same, except May; May was ready.

So May and Edward get up, amid great applause, to dance alone; and Bertha plays her liveliest tune.

Well! if you'll believe me they have not been dancing five minutes, when suddenly the carrier flings his pipe away, takes Dot round the waist, dashes out into the room, and starts off with her, toe and heel, quite wonderfully. Tackleton no sooner sees this, than he skims across to Mrs Fielding, takes her round the waist, and follows suit. Old Dot no sooner sees this, than up he is, all alive, whisks off Mrs Dot in the middle of the dance, and is the foremost there. Caleb no sooner sees this, than he clutches Tilly Slowboy by both hands and goes off at score; Miss Slowboy, firm in the belief that diving hotly in among the other couples, and effecting any number of concussions with them, is your only principle of footing it.

Hark! how the cricket joins the music with its chirp, chirp, chirp; and how the kettle hums!

But what is this! Even as I listen to them, blithely, and turn towards Dot, for one last glimpse of a little figure very pleasant to me, she and the rest have vanished into air, and I am left alone. A cricket sings upon the hearth; a broken child's toy lies upon the ground; and nothing else remains.

THE BATTLE OF LIFE

A Love Story

PART THE FIRST

Once upon a time, it matters little when, and in stalwart England, it matters little where, a fierce battle was fought. It was fought upon a long summer day when the waving grass was green. Many a wild flower formed by the Almighty Hand to be a perfumed goblet for the dew, felt its enamelled cup fill high with blood that day, and shrinking dropped. Many an insect deriving its delicate colour from harmless leaves and herbs, was stained anew that day by dying men, and marked its frightened way with an unnatural track. The painted butterfly took blood into the air upon the edges of its wings. The stream ran red. The trodden ground became a quagmire, whence, from sullen pools collected in the prints of human feet and horses' hoofs, the one prevailing hue still lowered and glimmered at the sun.

Heaven keep us from a knowledge of the sights the moon beheld upon that field, when, coming up above the black line of distant rising-ground, softened and blurred at the edge by trees, she rose into the sky and looked upon the plain, strewn with upturned faces that had once at mothers' breasts sought mothers' eyes, or slumbered happily. Heaven keep us from a knowledge of the secrets whispered afterwards upon the tainted wind that blew across the scene of that day's work and that night's death and suffering! Many a lonely moon was bright upon the battle-ground, and many a star kept mournful watch upon it, and many a wind from every quarter of the earth blew over it, before the traces of the fight were worn away.

They lurked and lingered for a long time, but survived in little things, for Nature, far above the evil passions of men, soon recovered Her serenity, and smiled upon the guilty battleground as she had done before, when it was innocent. The larks sang high above it; the swallows skimmed and dipped and flitted to and fro; the shadows of the flying clouds pursued each other swiftly, over grass and corn and turnip-field and wood, and over roof and church-spire in the nestling town among the trees, away into the bright distance on the borders of the sky and earth, where the red sunsets faded. Crops were sown, and grew up, and were gathered in; the stream that had been crimsoned, turned a water-mill; men whistled at the plough; gleaners and haymakers were seen in quiet groups at work; sheep and oxen pastured; boys whooped and called, in fields, to scare away the birds; smoke rose from cottage chimneys; Sabbath bells rang peacefully; old people lived and died; the timid creatures of the field, and simple flowers of the bush and garden, grew and withered in their destined terms: and all upon the fierce and bloody battleground, where thousands upon thousands had been killed in the great fight.

But there were deep green patches in the growing corn at first, that people looked at awfully. Year after year they reappeared; and it was known that underneath those fertile spots, heaps of men and horses lay buried, indiscriminately, enriching the ground. The husbandmen who ploughed those places, shrank from the great worms abounding there; and the sheaves they yielded, were, for many a long year, called the Battle Sheaves, and set apart; and no one ever knew a Battle Sheaf to be among the last load at a Harvest Home. For a long time, every furrow that was turned, revealed some fragments of the fight. For a long time, there were wounded trees upon the battleground; and scraps of hacked and broken fence and wall, where deadly struggles had been made; and trampled parts where not a leaf or blade would grow. For a long time, no village girl would dress her hair or bosom with the sweetest flower from that field of death: and after many a year had come and gone, the berries growing there, were still believed to leave too deep a stain upon the hand that plucked them.

The Seasons in their course, however, though they passed as lightly as the summer clouds themselves, obliterated, in the lapse of time, even these remains of the old conflict; and wore away such legendary traces of it as the neighbouring people carried in their minds, until they dwindled into old wives' tales, dimly remembered round the winter fire, and waning every year. Where the wild flowers and berries had so long remained upon the stem untouched, gardens arose, and houses were built, and children played at battles on the turf. The wounded trees had long ago made Christmas logs, and blazed and roared away. The deep green patches were no greener now than the memory of those who lay in dust below. The ploughshare still turned up from time to time some rusty bits of metal, but it was hard to say what use they had ever served, and those who found them wondered and disputed. An old dinted corslet, and a helmet, had been hanging in the church so long, that the same weak half-blind old man who tried in vain to make them out above the whitewashed arch, had marvelled at them as a baby. If the host slain upon the field, could have been for a moment reanimated in the forms in which they fell, each upon the spot that was the bed of his untimely death, gashed and ghastly soldiers would have stared in, hundreds deep, at household door and window; and would have risen on the hearths of quiet homes; and would have been the garnered store of barns and granaries; and would have started up between the cradled infant and its nurse; and would have floated with the stream, and whirled round on the mill, and crowded the orchard, and burdened the meadow, and piled the rickyard high with dying men. So altered was the battleground, where thousands upon thousands had been killed in the great fight.

Nowhere more altered, perhaps, about a hundred years ago, than in one little orchard attached to an old stone house with a honeysuckle porch: where, on a bright autumn morning, there were sounds of music and laughter, and where two girls danced merrily together on the grass, while some half-dozen peasant women standing on ladders, gathering the apples from the trees, stopped in their work to look down, and share their enjoyment. It was a pleasant, lively, natural scene; a beautiful day, a retired spot; and the two girls, quite unconstrained and careless, danced in the very freedom and gaiety of their hearts.

If there were no such thing as display in the world, my private opinion is, and I hope you agree with me, that we might get on a great deal better than we do, and might be infinitely more agreeable company than we are. It was charming to see how these girls danced. They had no spectators but the apple-pickers on the ladders. They were very glad to please them, but they danced to please themselves (or at least you would have supposed so); and you could no more help admiring, than they could help dancing. How they did dance!

Not like opera-dancers. Not at all. And not like Madame Anybody's finished pupils. Not the least. It was not quadrille dancing, nor minuet dancing, nor even county-dance dancing. It was neither in the old style, nor the new style, nor the French style, nor the English style; though it may have been, by accident, a trifle in the Spanish style, which is a free and joyous one, I am told, deriving a delightful air of off-hand inspiration, from the chirping little castanets. As they danced among the orchard trees, and down the groves of stems and back again, and twirled each other lightly round and round, the influence of their airy motion seemed to spread and spread, in the sun-lighted scene, like an expanding circle in the water. Their streaming hair and fluttering skirts, the elastic grass beneath their feet, the boughs that rustled in the morning air – the flashing leaves, their speckled shadows on the soft green ground – the balmy wind that swept along the landscape, glad to turn the distant windmill, cheerily – everything between the two girls, and the man and team at plough upon the ridge of land, where they showed against the sky as if they were the last things in the world – seemed dancing too.

At last the younger of the dancing sisters, out of breath, and laughing gaily, threw herself upon a bench to rest. The other leaned against a tree hard by. The music, a wandering harp and fiddle, left off with a flourish, as if it boasted of its freshness; though, the truth is, it had gone at such a pace, and worked itself to such a pitch of competition with the dancing, that it never could have held on half a minute longer. The apple-pickers on the ladders raised a hum and murmur of applause, and then, in keeping with the sound, bestirred themselves to work again, like bees.

The more actively, perhaps, because an elderly gentleman, who was no other than Dr Jeddler himself – it was Dr Jeddler's house and orchard, you should know, and these were Dr Jeddler's daughters – came bustling out to see what was the matter, and who the deuce played music on his property, before breakfast. For he was a great philosopher, Dr Jeddler, and not very musical.

'Music and dancing *today!*' said the doctor, stopping short, and speaking to himself, 'I thought they dreaded today. But it's a world of contradictions. Why, Grace; why, Marion!' he added, aloud, 'is the world more mad than usual this morning?'

'Make some allowance for it, father, if it be,' replied his younger daughter, Marion, going close to him, and looking into his face, 'for it's somebody's birthday.'

'Somebody's birthday, Puss,' replied the doctor. 'Don't you know it's always somebody's birthday? Did you never hear how many new performers enter on this – ha! ha! ha! – it's impossible to speak gravely of it – on this preposterous and ridiculous business called Life, every minute?'

'No, father!'

'No, not you, of course; you're a woman – almost,' said the doctor. 'By the by,' and he looked into the pretty face, still close to his, 'I suppose it's *your* birthday.'

'No! Do you really, father?' cried his pet daughter, pursing up her red lips to be kissed.

'There! Take my love with it,' said the doctor, imprinting his upon them; 'and many happy returns of the – the idea! – of the day. The notion of wishing happy returns in such a farce as this,' said the doctor to himself, 'is good! Ha! ha! ha!'

Dr Jeddler was, as I have said, a great philosopher; and the heart and mystery of his philosophy was, to look upon the world as a gigantic practical joke: as something too absurd to be considered seriously, by any rational man. His system of belief had been, in the beginning, part and parcel of the battleground on which he lived; as you shall presently understand.

'Well! But how did you get the music?' asked the doctor. 'Poultry-stealers, of course. Where did the minstrels come from!'

'Alfred sent the music,' said his daughter Grace, adjusting a few simple flowers in her sister's hair, with which, in her admiration of that youthful beauty, she had herself adorned it half an hour before, and which the dancing had disarranged.

'Oh! Alfred sent the music, did he?' returned the doctor.

'Yes. He met it coming out of the town as he was entering early. The men are travelling on foot, and rested there last night; and as it was Marion's birthday, and he thought it would please her, he sent them on, with a pencilled note to me, saying that if I thought so too, they had come to serenade her.'

'Ay, ay,' said the doctor, carelessly, 'he always takes your opinion.'

'And my opinion being favourable,' said Grace, good-humouredly; and pausing for a moment to admire the pretty head she decorated, with her own thrown back; 'and Marion being in high spirits, and beginning to dance, I joined her: and so we danced to Alfred's music till we were out of breath And we thought the music all the gayer for being sent by Alfred. Didn't we, dear Marion?'

'Oh, I don't know, Grace. How you tease me about Alfred.'

'Tease you by mentioning your lover!' said her sister.

'I am sure I don't much care to have him mentioned,' said the wilful beauty, stripping the petals from some flowers she held, and scattering them on the ground. 'I am almost tired of hearing of him; and as to his being my lover – '

'Hush! Don't speak lightly of a true heart, which is all your own, Marion,' cried her sister, 'even in jest. There is not a truer heart than Alfred's in the world!'

'No – no,' said Marion, raising her eyebrows with a pleasant air of careless consideration, 'perhaps not. But I don't know that there's any great merit in that. I – I don't want him to be so very true. I never asked him. If he expects that I – But, dear Grace, why need we talk of him at all, just now!'

It was agreeable to see the graceful figures of the blooming sisters, twined together, lingering among the trees, conversing thus, with earnestness opposed to lightness, yet with love responding tenderly to love. And it was very curious indeed to see the younger sister's eyes suffused with tears; and something fervently and deeply felt, breaking through the wilfulness of what she said, and striving with it painfully.

The difference between them, in respect of age, could not exceed four years at most; but Grace, as often happens in such cases, when no mother watches over both (the doctor's wife was dead), seemed, in her gentle care of her young sister, and in the steadiness of her devotion to her, older than she was; and more removed, in course of nature, from all competition with her, or participation, otherwise than through her sympathy and true affection, in her wayward fancies, than their ages seemed to warrant. Great character of mother, that, even in this shadow, and faint reflection of it, purifies the heart, and raises the exalted nature nearer to the angels!

The doctor's reflections, as he looked after them, and heard the purport of their discourse, were limited, at first, to certain merry meditations on the folly of all loves and likings, and the idle imposition practised on themselves by young people, who believed, for a moment, that there could be anything serious in such bubbles, and were always undeceived – always!

But the home-adorning, self-denying qualities of Grace, and her sweet temper, so gentle and retiring, yet including so much constancy and bravery of spirit, seemed all expressed to him in the contrast between her quiet household figure and that of his younger and more beautiful child; and he was sorry for her sake – sorry for them both – that life should be such a very ridiculous business as it was.

The doctor never dreamed of enquiring whether his children, or either of them, helped in any way to make the scheme a serious one. But then he was a philosopher.

A kind and generous man by nature, he had stumbled, by chance, over that common philosopher's stone (much more easily discovered than the object of the alchemist's researches), which sometimes trips up kind and generous men, and has the fatal property of turning gold to dross, and every precious thing to poor account.

'Britain!' cried the doctor. 'Britain! Halloa!'

A small man, with an uncommonly sour and discontented face, emerged from the house, and returned to this call the unceremonious acknowledgement of, 'Now then!'

'Where's the breakfast table?' said the doctor.

'In the house,' returned Britain.

'Are you going to spread it out here, as you were told last night?' said the doctor. 'Don't you know that there are gentlemen coming? That there's business to be done this morning, before the coach comes by? That this is a very particular occasion?'

'I couldn't do anything, Dr Jeddler, till the women had done getting in the apples, could I?' said Britain, his voice rising with his reasoning, so that it was very loud at last.

'Well, have they done now?' returned the doctor, looking at his watch, and clapping his hands. 'Come! make haste! where's Clemency?'

'Here am I, mister,' said a voice from one of the ladders, which a pair of clumsy feet descended briskly. 'It's all done now. Clear away, gals. Everything shall be ready for you in half a minute, mister.'

With that she began to bustle about most vigorously; presenting, as she did so, an appearance sufficiently peculiar to justify a word of introduction.

She was about thirty years old; and had a sufficiently plump and cheerful face, though it was twisted up into an odd expression of tightness that made it comical. But the extraordinary homeliness of her gait and manner, would have superseded any face in the world. To say that she had two left legs, and somebody else's arms; and that all four limbs seemed to be out of joint, and to start from perfectly wrong places when they were set in motion; is to offer the mildest outline of the reality. To say that she was perfectly content and satisfied with these arrangements, and regarded them as being no business of hers, and took her arms and legs as they came, and allowed them to dispose of themselves just as it happened, is to render faint justice to her equanimity. Her dress was a prodigious pair of self-willed shoes, that never wanted to go where her feet went; blue stockings; a printed gown of many colours, and the most hideous pattern procurable for money; and a white apron. She always wore short sleeves, and always had, by some accident, grazed elbows, in which she took so lively an interest that she was continually trying to turn them round and get impossible views of them. In general, a little cap perched somewhere on her head; though it was rarely to be met with in the place usually occupied in other subjects, by that article of dress; but from head to foot she was scrupulously clean, and maintained a kind of dislocated tidiness. Indeed her laudable anxiety to be tidy and compact in her own conscience as well as in the public eye, gave rise to one of her most startling evolutions, which was to grasp herself sometimes by a sort of wooden handle (part of her clothing, and familiarly called a busk), and wrestle as it were with her garments, until they fell into a symmetrical arrangement.

Such, in outward form and garb, was Clemency Newcome; who was supposed to have unconsciously originated a corruption of her own Christian name, from Clementina (but nobody knew, for the deaf old mother, a very phenomenon of age, whom she had supported almost from a child, was dead, and she had no other relation); who now busied herself in preparing the table; and who stood, at intervals, with her bare red arms crossed, rubbing her grazed elbows with opposite hands, and staring at it very composedly, until she suddenly remembered something else it wanted and jogged off to fetch it.

'Here are them two lawyers a-coming, mister!' said Clemency, in a tone of no very great goodwill.

'Aha!' cried the doctor, advancing to the gate to meet them. 'Good-morning, good-morning! Grace, my dear! Marion! Here are Messrs Snitchey and Craggs. Where's Alfred?'

'He'll be back directly, father, no doubt,' said Grace. 'He had so much to do this morning in his preparations for departure, that he was up and out by daybreak. Good-morning, gentlemen.'

'Ladies!' said Mr Snitchey, 'for Self and Craggs,' who bowed, 'good-morning, miss,' to Marion, 'I kiss your hand.' Which he did. 'And I wish you' – which he might or might not, for he didn't look, at first sight, like a gentleman troubled with many warm outpourings of soul, in behalf of other people, 'a hundred happy returns of this auspicious day.'

'Ha, ha, ha!' laughed the doctor thoughtfully, with his hands in his pockets. 'The great farce in a hundred acts!'

'You wouldn't, I am sure,' said Mr Snitchey, standing a small pro-fessional blue bag against one leg of the table, 'cut the great farce short for this actress, at all events, Dr Jeddler.'

'No,' returned the doctor. 'God forbid! May she live to laugh at it, as long as she *can* laugh, and then say, with the French wit, "The farce is ended; draw the curtain." '

'The French wit,' said Mr Snitchey, peeping sharply into his blue bag, 'was wrong, Dr Jeddler; and your philosophy is altogether wrong, depend upon it, as I have often told you. Nothing serious in life! What do you call law?'

'A joke,' replied the doctor.

'Did you ever go to law?' asked Mr Snitchey, looking out of the blue bag.

'Never,' returned the doctor.

'If you ever do,' said Mr Snitchey, 'perhaps you'll alter that opinion.'

Craggs, who seemed to be represented by Snitchey, and to be conscious of little or no separate existence or personal individuality, offered a remark of his own in this place. It involved the only idea of which he did not stand seized and possessed in equal moieties with Snitchey; but he had some partners in it among the wise men of the world.

'It's made a great deal too easy,' said Mr Craggs.

'Law is?' asked the doctor.

'Yes,' said Mr Craggs, 'everything is. Everything appears to me to be made too easy, nowadays. It's the vice of these times. If the world is a joke (I am not prepared to say it isn't), it ought to be made a very difficult joke to crack. It ought to be as hard a struggle, sir, as possible. That's the intention. But it's being made far too easy. We are oiling the gates of life. They ought to be rusty. We shall have them beginning to turn, soon, with a smooth sound. Whereas they ought to grate upon their hinges, sir.'

Mr Craggs seemed positively to grate upon his own hinges, as he delivered this opinion; to which he communicated immense effect – being a cold, hard, dry man, dressed in grey and white, like a flint; with small twinkles in his eyes, as if something struck sparks out of them. The three natural kingdoms, indeed, had each a fanciful representative among this brotherhood of disputants: for Snitchey was like a magpie or a raven (only not so sleek), and the doctor had a streaked face like a winter-pippin, with here and there a dimple to express the peckings of the birds, and a very little bit of pigtail behind, that stood for the stalk.

As the active figure of a handsome young man, dressed for a journey, and followed by a porter, bearing several packages and baskets, entered the orchard at a brisk pace, and with an air of gaiety and hope that accorded well with the morning, these three drew together, like the brothers of the sister Fates, or like the Graces most effectually disguised, or like the three weird prophets on the heath, and greeted him.

'Happy returns, Alf,' said the doctor, lightly.

'A hundred happy returns of this auspicious day, Mr Heathfield,' said Snitchey, bowing low.

'Returns!' Craggs murmured in a deep voice, all alone.

'Why, what a battery!' exclaimed Alfred, stopping short, 'and one – two – three – all foreboders of no good, in the great sea before me. I am glad you are not the first I have met this morning: I should have taken it for a bad omen. But Grace was the first – sweet, pleasant Grace – so I defy you all!'

'If you please, mister, I was the first you know,' said Clemency Newcome. 'She was a-walking out here, before sunrise, you remember. I was in the house.'

'That's true! Clemency was the first,' said Alfred. 'So I defy you with Clemency.'

'Ha, ha, ha! – for Self and Craggs,' said Snitchey. 'What a defiance!'

'Not so bad a one as it appears, may be,' said Alfred, shaking hands heartily with the doctor, and also with Snitchey and Craggs, and then looking round. 'Where are the – Good Heavens!'

With a start, productive for the moment of a closer partnership between Jonathan Snitchey and Thomas Craggs than the subsisting articles of agreement in that wise contemplated, he hastily betook himself to where the sisters stood together, and – however, I needn't more particularly explain his manner of saluting Marion first, and Grace afterwards, than by hinting that Mr Craggs may possibly have considered it 'too easy'.

Perhaps to change the subject, Dr Jeddler made a hasty move towards the breakfast, and they all sat down at table. Grace presided; but so discreetly stationed herself, as to cut off her sister and Alfred from the rest of the company. Snitchey and Craggs sat at opposite corners, with the blue bag between them for safety; and the doctor took his usual position, opposite to Grace. Clemency hovered galvanically about the table, as waitress; and the melancholy Britain, at another and a smaller board, acted as Grand Carver of a round of beef, and a ham.

'Meat?' said Britain, approaching Mr Snitchey, with the carving knife and fork in his hands, and throwing the question at him like a missile.

'Certainly,' returned the lawyer.

'Do *you* want any?' to Craggs.

'Lean, and well done,' replied that gentleman.

Having executed these orders, and moderately supplied the doctor (he seemed to know that nobody else wanted anything to eat), he lingered as near the Firm as he decently could, watching, with an austere eye, their disposition of the viands, and but once relaxing the severe expression of his face. This was on the occasion of Mr Craggs, whose teeth were not of the best, partially choking, when he cried out with great animation, 'I thought he was gone!'

'Now Alfred,' said the doctor, 'for a word or two of business, while we are yet at breakfast.'

'While we are yet at breakfast,' said Snitchey and Craggs, who seemed to have no present idea of leaving off.

Although Alfred had not been breakfasting, and seemed to have quite enough business on his hands as it was, he respectfully answered: 'If you please, sir.'

'If anything could be serious,' the doctor began, 'in such a – '

'Farce as this, sir,' hinted Alfred.

'In such a farce as this,' observed the doctor, 'it might be this recurrence, on the eve of separation, of a double birthday, which is connected with many associations pleasant to us four, and with the recollection of a long and amicable intercourse. That's not to the purpose.'

'Ah! yes, yes, Dr Jeddler,' said the young man. 'It is to the purpose. Much to the purpose, as my heart bears witness this morning; and as yours does too, I know, if you would let it speak. I leave your house today; I cease to be your ward today; we part with tender relations stretching far behind us, that never can be exactly renewed, and with others dawning yet before us,' he looked down at Marion beside him, 'fraught with such considerations as I must not trust myself to speak of now. Come, come!' he added, rallying his spirits and the doctor at once, 'there's a serious grain in this large foolish dust-heap, doctor. Let us allow today that there is One.'

'Today!' cried the doctor. 'Hear him! Ha, ha, ha! Of all days in the foolish year. Why on this day, the great battle was fought on this ground. On this ground where we now sit, where I saw my two girls dance this morning, where the fruit has just been gathered for our eating from these trees, the roots of which are struck in Men, not earth – so many lives were lost, that within my recollection, generations afterwards, a church-yard full of bones, and dust of bones, and chips of cloven skulls, has been dug up from underneath our feet here. Yet not a hundred people in that battle knew for what they fought, or why; not a hundred of the inconsiderate rejoicers in the victory, why they rejoiced. Not half a hundred people were the better for the gain or loss. Not half a dozen men agree to this hour on the cause or merits; and nobody, in short, ever knew anything distinct about it, but the mourners of the slain. Serious, too!' said the doctor, laughing. 'Such a system!'

'But all this seems to me,' said Alfred, 'to be very serious.'

'Serious!' cried the doctor. 'If you allowed such things to be serious, you must go mad, or die, or climb up to the top of a mountain, and turn hermit.'

'Besides – so long ago,' said Alfred.

'Long ago!' returned the doctor. 'Do you know what the world has been doing, ever since? Do you know what else it has been doing? I don't!'

'It has gone to law a little,' observed Mr Snitchey, stirring his tea.

'Although the way out has been always made too easy,' said his partner.

'And you'll excuse my saying, doctor,' pursued Mr Snitchey, 'having been already put a thousand times in possession of my opinion, in the course of our discussions, that, in its having gone to law, and in its legal system altogether, I do observe a serious side – now, really, a something tangible, and with a purpose and intention in it – '

Clemency Newcome made an angular tumble against the table, occasioning a sounding clatter among the cups and saucers.

'Heyday! what's the matter there?' exclaimed the doctor.

'It's this evil-inclined blue bag,' said Clemency, 'always tripping up somebody!'

'With a purpose and intention in it, I was saying,' resumed Snitchey, 'that commands respect. Life a farce, Dr Jeddler? With law in it?'

The doctor laughed, and looked at Alfred.

'Granted, if you please, that war is foolish,' said Snitchey. 'There we agree. For example. Here's a smiling country,' pointing it out with his fork, 'once overrun by soldiers – trespassers every man of 'em – and laid waste by fire and sword. He, he, he! The idea of any man exposing himself, voluntarily, to fire and sword! Stupid, wasteful, positively ridiculous; you laugh at your fellow-creatures, you know, when you think of it! But take this smiling country as it stands. Think of the laws appertaining to real property; to the bequest and devise of real property; to the mortgage and redemption of real property; to leasehold, freehold, and copyhold estate; think,' said Mr Snitchey, with such great emotion that he actually smacked his lips, 'of the complicated laws relating to title and proof of title, with all the contradictory precedents and numerous Acts of Parliament connected with them; think of the infinite number of ingenious and interminable Chancery suits, to which this pleasant prospect may give rise; – and acknowledge, Dr Jeddler, that there is a green spot in the scheme about us! I believe,' said Mr Snitchey, looking at his partner, 'that I speak for Self and Craggs?'

Mr Craggs having signified assent, Mr Snitchey, somewhat freshened by his recent eloquence, observed that he would take a little more beef, and another cup of tea.

'I don't stand up for life in general,' he added, rubbing his hands and chuckling, 'it's full of folly; full of something worse. Professions of trust, and confidence, and unselfishness, and all that. Bah, bah, bah! We see what they're worth. But you mustn't laugh at life; you've got a game to play; a very serious game indeed! Everybody's playing against you, you know; and you're playing against them. Oh! it's a very interesting thing. There are deep moves upon the board. You must only laugh, Dr Jeddler, when you win; and then not much. He, he, he! And then not much,' repeated Snitchey, rolling his head and winking his eye; as if he would have added, 'you may do this instead!'

'Well, Alfred' cried the doctor, 'what do you say now?'

'I say, sir,' replied Alfred, 'that the greatest favour you could do me, and yourself too I am inclined to think, would be to try sometimes to forget this battlefield, and others like it, in that broader battlefield of Life on which the sun looks every day.'

'Really, I'm afraid that wouldn't soften his opinions, Mr Alfred,' said Snitchey. 'The combatants are very eager and very bitter in that same battle of Life. There's a great deal of cutting and slashing, and firing into people's heads from behind; terrible treading down, and trampling on; it's rather a bad business.'

'I believe, Mr Snitchey,' said Alfred, 'there are quiet victories and struggles, great sacrifices of self, and noble acts of heroism, in it – even in many of its apparent lightnesses and contradictions – not the less difficult to achieve, because they have no earthly chronicle or audience; done every day in nooks and corners, and in little households, and in men's and women's hearts – any one of which might reconcile the sternest man to such a world, and fill him with belief and hope in it, though two-fourths of its people were at war, and another fourth at law; and that's a bold word.'

Both the sisters listened keenly.

'Well, well!' said the doctor, 'I am too old to be converted, even by my friend Snitchey here, or my good spinster sister, Martha Jeddler; who had what she calls her domestic trials ages ago, and has led a sympathising life with all sorts of people ever since; and who is so much of your opinion (only she's less reasonable and more obstinate, being a woman), that we can't agree, and seldom meet. I was born upon this battlefield. I began, as a boy, to have my thoughts directed to the real history of a battlefield. Sixty years have gone over my head; and I have never seen the Christian world, including Heaven knows how many loving mothers and good enough girls, like mine here, anything but mad for a battlefield.

The same contradictions prevail in everything. One must either laugh or cry at such stupendous inconsistencies; and I prefer to laugh.'

Britain, who had been paying the profoundest and most melancholy attention to each speaker in his turn, seemed suddenly to decide in favour of the same preference, if a deep sepulchral sound that escaped him might be construed into a demonstration of risibility. His face, however, was so perfectly unaffected by it, both before and afterwards, that although one or two of the breakfast party looked round as being startled by a mysterious noise, nobody connected the offender with it.

Except his partner in attendance, Clemency Newcome; who, rousing him with one of those favourite joints, her elbows, enquired, in a reproachful whisper, what he laughed at.

'Not you!' said Britain.

'Who then?'

'Humanity,' said Britain. 'That's the joke.'

'What between master and them lawyers, he's getting more and more addle-headed every day!' cried Clemency, giving him a lunge with the other elbow, as a mental stimulant. 'Do you know where you are? Do you want to get warning?'

'I don't know anything,' said Britain, with a leaden eye and an immovable visage. 'I don't care for anything. I don't make out anything. I don't believe anything. And I don't want anything.'

Although this forlorn summary of his general condition may have been overcharged in an access of despondency, Benjamin Britain – sometimes called Little Britain, to distinguish him from Great; as we might say Young England, to express Old England with a difference – had defined his real state more accurately than might be supposed. For serving as a sort of man Miles to the doctor's Friar Bacon; and listening day after day to innumerable orations addressed by the doctor to various people, all tending to show that his very existence was at best a mistake and an absurdity, this unfortunate servitor had fallen, by degrees, into such an abyss of confused and contradictory suggestions from within and without, that Truth at the bottom of her well, was on the level surface as compared with Britain in the depths of his mystification. The only point he clearly comprehended, was, that the new element usually brought into these discussions by Snitchey and Craggs, never served to make them clearer, and always seemed to give the doctor a species of advantage and confirmation. Therefore he looked upon the Firm as one of the proximate causes of his state of mind, and held them in abhorrence accordingly.

'But this is not our business, Alfred,' said the doctor. 'Ceasing to be my ward (as you have said) today; and leaving us full to the brim of such learning as the Grammar School down here was able to give you, and your studies in London could add to that, and such practical knowledge as a dull old country doctor like myself could graft upon both; you are away, now, into the world. The first term of probation appointed by your poor father, being over, away you go now, your own master, to fulfil his second desire: and long before your three years' tour among the foreign schools of medicine is finished, you'll have forgotten us. Lord, you'll forget us easily in six months!'

'If I do – But you know better; why should I speak to you!' said Alfred, laughing.

'I don't know anything of the sort,' returned the doctor. 'What do you say, Marion?'

Marion, trifling with her teacup seemed to say – but she didn't say it – that he was welcome to forget them, if he could. Grace pressed the blooming face against her cheek, and smiled.

'I haven't been, I hope, a very unjust steward in the execution of my trust,' pursued the doctor; 'but I am to be, at any rate, formally discharged, and released, and what not, this morning; and here are our good friends Snitchey and Craggs, with a bagful of papers, and accounts, and documents, for the transfer of the balance of the trust fund to you (I wish it was a more difficult one to dispose of, Alfred, but you must get to be a great man and make it so), and other drolleries of that sort, which are to be signed, sealed, and delivered.'

'And duly witnessed, as by law required,' said Snitchey, pushing away his plate, and taking out the papers, which his partner proceeded to spread upon the table; 'and Self and Craggs having been co-trustees with you, doctor, in so far as the fund was concerned, we shall want your two servants to attest the signatures – can you read, Mrs Newcome?'

'I an't married, mister,' said Clemency.

'Oh, I beg your pardon. I should think not,' chuckled Snitchey, casting his eyes over her extraordinary figure. 'You *can* read?'

'A little,' answered Clemency.

'The marriage service, night and morning, eh?' observed the lawyer, jocosely.

'No,' said Clemency. 'Too hard. I only reads a thimble.'

'Read a thimble!' echoed Snitchey. 'What are you talking about, young woman?'

Clemency nodded. 'And a nutmeg-grater.'

'Why this is a lunatic! a subject for the Lord High Chancellor!' said Snitchey, staring at her.

'If possessed of any property,' stipulated Craggs.

Grace, however, interposing, explained that each of the articles in question bore an engraved motto, and so formed the pocket library of Clemency Newcome, who was not much given to the study of books.

'Oh, that's it, is it, Miss Grace!' said Snitchey.

'Yes, yes. Ha, ha, ha! I thought our friend was a idiot. She looks uncommonly like it,' he muttered, with a supercilious glance. 'And what does the thimble say, Mrs Newcome?'

'I an't married, mister,' observed Clemency.

'Well, Newcome. Will that do?' said the lawyer. 'What does the thimble say, Newcome?'

How Clemency, before replying to this question, held one pocket open, and looked down into its yawning depths for the thimble which wasn't there – and how she then held an opposite pocket open, and seeming to descry it, like a pearl of great price, at the bottom, cleared away such intervening obstacles as a handkerchief, an end of wax candle, a flushed apple, an orange, a lucky penny, a cramp bone, a padlock, a pair of scissors in a sheath, more expressively describable as promising young shears, a handful or so of loose beads, several balls of cotton, a needle-case, a cabinet collection of curl-papers, and a biscuit, all of which articles she entrusted individually and severally to Britain to hold – is of no consequence. Nor how, in her determination to grasp this pocket by the throat and keep it prisoner (for it had a tendency to swing and twist itself round the nearest corner), she assumed, and calmly maintained, an attitude apparently inconsistent with the human anatomy and the laws of gravity. It is enough that at last she triumphantly produced the thimble on her finger, and rattled the nutmeg-grater; the literature of both those trinkets being obviously in course of wearing out and wasting away, through excessive friction.

'That's the thimble, is it, young woman?' said Mr Snitchey, diverting himself at her expense. 'And what does the thimble say?'

'It says,' replied Clemency, reading slowly round it as if it were a tower, 'For–get and For–give.'

Snitchey and Craggs laughed heartily. 'So new!' said Snitchey. 'So easy!' said Craggs. 'Such a knowledge of human nature in it,' said Snitchey. 'So applicable to the affairs of life,' said Craggs.

'And the nutmeg-grater?' enquired the head of the Firm.

'The grater says,' returned Clemency, 'Do as you – wold – be – done by.'

'"Do, or you'll be done brown, you mean,"' said Mr Snitchey.

'I don't understand,' retorted Clemency, shaking her head vaguely. 'I an't no lawyer.'

'I am afraid that if she was, doctor,' said Mr Snitchey, turning to him suddenly, as if to anticipate any effect that might otherwise be consequent on this retort, 'she'd find it to be the golden rule of half her clients. They are serious enough in that – whimsical as your world is – and lay the blame on us afterwards. We, in our profession, are little else than mirrors after all, Mr Alfred; but we are generally consulted by angry and quarrelsome people, who are not in their best looks; and it's rather hard to quarrel with us if we reflect unpleasant aspects. I think,' said Mr Snitchey, 'that I speak for Self and Craggs?'

'Decidedly,' said Craggs.

'And so, if Mr Britain will oblige us with a mouthful of ink,' said Mr Snitchey, returning to the papers, 'we'll sign, seal, and deliver as soon as possible, or the coach will be coming past before we know where we are.'

If one might judge from his appearance, there was every probability of the coach coming past before Mr Britain knew where *he* was; for he stood in a state of abstraction, mentally balancing the doctor against the lawyers, and the lawyers against the doctor, and their clients against both; and engaged in feeble attempts to make the thimble and nutmeg-grater (a new idea to him) square with anybody's system of philosophy; and, in short, bewildering himself as much as ever his great namesake has done with theories and schools. But Clemency, who was his good Genius – though he had the meanest possible opinion of her understanding, by reason of her seldom troubling herself with abstract speculations, and being always at hand to do the right thing at the right time – having produced the ink in a twinkling, tendered him the further service of recalling him to himself by the application of her elbows; with which gentle flappers she so jogged his memory, in a more literal construction of that phrase than usual, that he soon became quite fresh and brisk.

How he laboured under an apprehension not uncommon to persons in his degree, to whom the use of pen and ink is an event, that he couldn't append his name to a document, not of his own writing, without committing himself in some shadowy manner, or somehow signing away vague and enormous sums of money; and how he approached the deeds under protest, and by dint of the doctor's coercion, and insisted on pausing to look at them before writing (the cramped hand, to say nothing of the phraseology, being so much Chinese to him), and also on turning them round to see whether there was anything fraudulent, underneath; and how, having signed his name, he became desolate as one who had parted with his property and rights; I want the time to tell. Also, how the blue bag containing his signature, afterwards had a mysterious interest for him, and he couldn't leave it; also, how Clemency Newcome, in an ecstasy of laughter at the idea of her own importance and dignity, brooded over the whole table with her two elbows like a spread eagle, and reposed her head upon her left arm as a preliminary to the formation of certain cabalistic characters, which required a deal of ink, and imaginary counterparts whereof she executed at the same time with her tongue. Also, how, having once tasted ink, she became thirsty in that regard, as tigers are said to be after tasting another sort of fluid, and wanted to sign everything, and put her name in all kinds of places. In brief, the doctor was discharged of his trust and all its responsibilities; and Alfred, taking it on himself, was fairly started on the journey of life.

'Britain!' said the doctor. 'Run to the gate, and watch for the coach. Time flies, Alfred!'

'Yes, sir, yes,' returned the young man, hurriedly. 'Dear Grace! a moment! Marion – so young and beautiful, so winning and so much admired, dear to my heart as nothing else in life is – remember! I leave Marion to you!'

'She has always been a sacred charge to me, Alfred. She is doubly so now. I will be faithful to my trust, believe me.'

'I do believe it, Grace. I know it well. Who could look upon your face, and hear your earnest voice, and not know it! Ah, good Grace! If I had your well-governed heart, and tranquil mind, how bravely I would leave this place today!'

'Would you?' she answered, with a quiet smile.

'And yet, Grace – Sister, seems the natural word.'

'Use it!' she said quickly. 'I am glad to hear it, call me nothing else.'

'And yet, sister, then,' said Alfred, 'Marion and I had better have your true and steadfast qualities serving us here, and making us both happier and better. I wouldn't carry them away, to sustain myself, if I could!'

'Coach upon the hilltop!' exclaimed Britain.

'Time flies, Alfred,' said the doctor.

Marion had stood apart, with her eyes fixed upon the ground; but this warning being given, her young lover brought her tenderly to where her sister stood, and gave her into her embrace.

'I have been telling Grace, dear Marion,' he said, 'that you are her charge; my precious trust at parting. And when I come back and reclaim you, dearest, and the bright prospect of our married life lies stretched before us, it shall be one of our chief pleasures to consult how we can make Grace happy; how we can anticipate her wishes; how we can show our gratitude and love to her; how we can return her something of the debt she will have heaped upon us.'

The younger sister had one hand in his; the other rested on her sister's neck. She looked into that sister's eyes, so calm, serene, and cheerful, with a gaze in which affection, admiration, sorrow, wonder, almost veneration were blended. She looked into that sister's face, as if it were the face of some bright angel. Calm, serene, and cheerful, it looked back on her and on her lover.

'And when the time comes, as it must one day,' said Alfred, – 'I wonder it has never come yet: but Grace knows best, for Grace is always right, – when *she* will want a friend to open her whole heart to, and to be to her something of what she has been to us – then, Marion, how faithful we will prove, and what delight to us to know that she; our dear good sister, loves and is loved again, as we would have her!'

Still the younger sister looked into her eyes, and turned not – even towards him. And still those honest eyes looked back, so calm, serene, and cheerful, on herself and on her lover.

'And when all that is past, and we are old, and living (as we must!) together – close together; talking often of old times,' said Alfred – 'these shall be our favourite times among them – this day most of all; and telling each other what we thought and felt, and hoped and feared, at parting; and how we couldn't bear to say goodbye – '

'Coach coming through the wood,' cried Britain.

'Yes! I am ready – and how we met again, so happily, in spite of all; we'll make this day the happiest in all the year, and keep it as a treble birthday. Shall we, dear?'

'Yes!' interposed the elder sister, eagerly, and with a radiant smile. 'Yes! Alfred, don't linger. There's no time. Say goodbye to Marion. And Heaven be with you!'

He pressed the younger sister to his heart. Released from his embrace, she again clung to her sister; and her eyes, with the same blended look, again sought those so calm, serene, and cheerful.

'Farewell, my boy!' said the doctor. 'To talk about any serious correspondence or serious affections, and engagements and so forth, in such a – ha, ha, ha! – you know what I mean – why that, of course, would be sheer nonsense. All I can say is, that if you and Marion should continue in the same foolish minds, I shall not object to have you for a son-in-law one of these days.'

'Over the bridge!' cried Britain.

'Let it come!' said Alfred, wringing the doctor's hand stoutly. 'Think of me sometimes, my old friend and guardian, as seriously as you can! Adieu, Mr Snitchey! Farewell, Mr Craggs!'

'Coming down the road!' cried Britain.

'A kiss of Clemency Newcome for long acquaintance' sake – shake hands, Britain – Marion, dearest heart, goodbye! Sister Grace! remember!'

The quiet houschold figure, and the face so beautiful in its serenity, were turned towards him in reply; but Marion's look and attitude remained unchanged.

The coach was at the gate. There was a bustle with the luggage. The coach drove away. Marion never moved.

'He waves his hat to you, my love,' said Grace. 'Your chosen husband, darling. Look!'

The younger sister raised her head, and, for a moment, turned it. Then turning back again, and fully meeting, for the first time, those calm eyes, fell sobbing on her neck.

'Oh, Grace. God bless you! But I cannot bear to see it, Grace! It breaks my heart.'

PART THE SECOND

Snitchey and Craggs had a snug little office on the old battleground, where they drove a snug little business, and fought a great many small pitched battles for a great many contending parties. Though it could hardly be said of these conflicts that they were running fights – for in truth they generally proceeded at a snail's pace – the part the Firm had in them came so far within that general denomination, that now they took a shot at this Plaintiff, and now aimed a chop at that Defendant, now made a heavy charge at an estate in Chancery, and now had some light skirmishing among an irregular body of small debtors, just as the occasion served, and the enemy happened to present himself. The Gazette was an important and profitable feature in some of their fields, as well as in fields of greater renown; and in most of the Actions wherein they showed their generalship, it was afterwards observed by the combatants that they had had great difficulty in making each other out, or in knowing with any degree of distinctness what they were about, in consequence of the vast amount of smoke by which they were surrounded.

The offices of Messrs Snitchey and Craggs stood convenient with an open door, down two smooth steps in the market-place; so that any angry farmer inclining towards hot water, might tumble into it at once. Their special council-chamber and hall of conference was an old back room up stairs, with a low dark ceiling, which seemed to be knitting its brows gloomily in the consideration of tangled points of law. It was furnished with some high-backed leathern chairs, garnished with great goggle-eyed brass nails, of which, every here and there, two or three had fallen out; or had been picked out, perhaps, by the wandering thumbs and forefingers of bewildered clients. There was a framed print of a great judge in it, every curl in whose dreadful wig had made a man's hair stand on end. Bales of papers filled the dusty closets, shelves, and tables; and round the wainscot there were tiers of boxes, padlocked and fireproof, with people's names painted outside, which anxious visitors felt them-selves, by a cruel enchantment, obliged to spell backwards and forwards,

and to make anagrams of, while they sat, seeming to listen to Snitchey and Craggs, without comprehending one word of what they said.

Snitchey and Craggs had each, in private life as in professional existence, a partner of his own. Snitchey and Craggs were the best friends in the world, and had a real confidence in one another; but Mrs Snitchey, by a dispensation not uncommon in the affairs of life, was, on principle, suspiciousof Mr Craggs; and Mrs Craggs was, on principle, suspicious of Mr Snitchey. 'Your Snitcheys indeed,' the latter lady would observe, sometimes, to Mr Craggs; using that imaginative plural as if in disparagement of an objectionable pair of pantaloons, or other articles not possessed of a singular number; 'I don't see what you want with your Snitcheys, for my part. You trust a great deal too much to your Snitcheys, *I* think, and I hope you may never find my words come true.' While Mrs Snitchey would observe to Mr Snitchey, of Craggs, 'that if ever he was led away by man he was led away by that man; and that if ever she read a double purpose in a mortal eye, she read that purpose in Craggs's eye.' Notwithstanding this, however, they were all very good friends in general: and Mrs Snitchey and Mrs Craggs maintained a close bond of alliance against 'the office', which they both considered a Blue chamber, and common enemy, full of dangerous (because unknown) machinations.

In this office, nevertheless, Snitchey and Craggs made honey for their several hives. Here sometimes they would linger, of a fine evening, at the window of their council-chamber overlooking the old battleground, and wonder (but that was generally at assize time, when much business had made them sentimental) at the folly of mankind, who couldn't always be at peace with one another, and go to law comfortably. Here days, and weeks, and months, and years, passed over them; their calendar, the gradually diminishing number of brass nails in the leathern chairs and the increasing bulk of papers on the tables. Here nearly three years' flight had thinned the one and swelled the other, since the breakfast in the orchard; when they sat together in consultation, at night.

Not alone; but with a man of thirty, or about that time of life, negligently dressed, and somewhat haggard in the face, but well-made, well-attired, and well-looking, who sat in the armchair of state, with one hand in his breast, and the other in his dishevelled hair, pondering moodily. Messrs Snitchey and Craggs sat opposite each other at a neighbouring desk. One of the fireproof boxes, unpadlocked and opened, was upon it; a part of its contents lay strewn upon the table, and the rest was then in course of passing through the hands of Mr Snitchey, who brought it to the candle, document by document, looked at ever paper singly, as he produced it, shook his head, and handed it to Mr Craggs, who looked it over also, shook his head and laid it down. Sometimes they would stop, and shaking their heads in concert, look towards the abstracted client; and the name on the box being Michael

Warden, Esquire, we may conclude from these premises that the name and the box were both his, and that the affairs of Michael Warden, Esquire, were in a bad way.

'That's all,' said Mr Snitchey, turning up the last paper. 'Really there's no other resource. No other resource.'

'All lost, spent, wasted, pawned, borrowed, and sold, eh?' said the client, looking up.

'All,' returned Mr Snitchey.

'Nothing else to be done, you say?'

'Nothing at all.'

The client bit his nails, and pondered again.

'And I am not even personally safe in England? You hold to that; do you?'

'In no part of the United Kingdom of Great Britain and Ireland,' replied Mr Snitchey.

'A mere prodigal son with no father to go back to, no swine to keep, and no husks to share with them? Eh?' pursued the client, rocking one leg over the other, and searching the ground with his eyes.

Mr Snitchey coughed, as if to deprecate the being supposed to participate in any figurative illustration of a legal position. Mr Craggs, as if to express that it was a partnership view of the subject, also coughed.

'Ruined at thirty!' said the client. 'Humph!'

'Not ruined, Mr Warden,' returned Snitchey. 'Not so bad as that. You have done a good deal towards it, I must say, but you are not ruined. A little nursing – '

'A little Devil,' said the client.

'Mr Craggs,' said Snitchey, 'will you oblige me with a pinch of snuff? Thank you, sir.'

As the imperturbable lawyer applied it to his nose, with great apparent relish and a perfect absorption of his attention in the proceeding, the client gradually broke into a smile, and, looking up, said: 'You talk of nursing. How long nursing?'

'How long nursing?' repeated Snitchey, dusting the snuff from his fingers, and making a slow calculation in his mind. 'For your involved estate, sir? In good hands? S and C's, say? Six or seven years.'

'To starve for six or seven years!' said the client with a fretful laugh, and an impatient change of his position.

'To starve for six or seven years, Mr Warden,' said Snitchey, 'would be very uncommon indeed. You might get another estate by showing yourself, the while. But we don't think you could do it – speaking for Self and Craggs – and consequently don't advise it.'

'What *do* you advise?'

'Nursing, I say,' repeated Snitchey. 'Some few years of nursing by Self and Craggs would bring it round. But to enable us to make terms, and hold terms, and you to keep terms, you must go away, you must live abroad. As to starvation, we could ensure you some hundreds a year to starve upon, even in the beginning, I dare say, Mr Warden.'

'Hundreds,' said the client. 'And I have spent thousands!'

'That,' retorted Mr Snitchey, putting the papers slowly back into the cast-iron box, 'there is no doubt about. No doubt a–bout,' he repeated to himself, as he thoughtfully pursued his occupation.

The lawyer very likely knew his man; at any rate his dry, shrewd whimsical manner, had a favourable influence upon the client's moody state, and disposed him to be more free and unreserved. Or perhaps the client knew *his* man, and had elicited such encouragement as he had received, to render some purpose he was about to disclose the more defensible in appearance. Gradually raising his head, he sat looking at his immovable adviser with a smile, which presently broke into a laugh.

'After all,' he said, 'my iron-headed friend – '

Mr Snitchey pointed out his partner. 'Self and – excuse me – Craggs.'

'I beg Mr Craggs's pardon,' said the client. 'After all, my iron-headed friends,' he leaned forward in his chair, and dropped his voice a little, 'you don't know half my ruin yet.'

Mr Snitchey stopped and stared at him. Mr Craggs also stared.

'I am not only deep in debt,' said the client, 'but I am deep in – '

'Not in love!' cried Snitchey.

'Yes!' said the client, falling back in his chair, and surveying the Firm with his hands in his pockets. 'Deep in love.'

'And not with an heiress, sir?' said Snitchey.

'Not with an heiress.'

'Nor a rich lady?'

'Nor a rich lady that I know of – except in beauty and merit.'

'A single lady, I trust?' said Mr Snitchey, with great expression.

'Certainly.'

'It's not one of Dr Jeddler's daughters?' said Snitchey, suddenly squaring his elbows on his knees, and advancing his face at least a yard.

'Yes!' returned the client.

'Not his younger daughter?' said Snitchey.

'Yes!' returned the client.

'Mr Craggs,' said Snitchey, much relieved, 'will you oblige me with another pinch of snuff? Thank you. I am happy to say it don't signify, Mr Warden; she's engaged, sir, she's bespoke. My partner can corroborate me. We know the fact.'

'We know the fact,' repeated Craggs.

'Why, so do I perhaps,' returned the client quietly. 'What of that! Are you men of the world, and did you never hear of a woman changing her mind?'

'There certainly have been actions for breach,' said Mr Snitchey, 'brought against both spinsters and widows, but, in the majority of cases – '

'Cases!' interposed the client, impatiently. 'Don't talk to me of cases. The general precedent is in a much larger volume than any of your law books. Besides, do you think I have lived six weeks in the doctor's house for nothing?'

'I think, sir,' observed Mr Snitchey, gravely addressing himself to his partner, 'that of all the scrapes Mr Warden's horses have brought him into at one time and another – and they have been pretty numerous, and pretty expensive, as none know better than himself and you and I – the worst scrape may turn out to be, if he talks in this way, his having been ever left by one of them at the doctor's garden wall, with three broken ribs, a snapped collarbone, and the Lord knows how many bruises. We didn't think so much of it, at the time when we knew he was going on well under the doctor's hands and roof; but it looks bad now, sir. Bad! It looks very bad. Dr Jeddler too – our client, Mr Craggs.'

'Mr Alfred Heathfield too – a sort of client, Mr Snitchey,' said Craggs.

'Mr Michael Warden too, a kind of client,' said the careless visitor, 'and no bad one either; having played the fool for ten or twelve years. However Mr Michael Warden has sown his wild oats now – there's their crop, in that box; and he means to repent and be wise. And in proof of it, Mr Michael Warden means, if he can, to marry Marion, the doctor's lovely daughter, and to carry her away with him.'

'Really, Mr Craggs,' Snitchey began.

'Really Mr Snitchey, and Mr Craggs, partners both,' said the client, interrupting him; 'you know your duty to your clients, and you know well enough, I am sure, that it is no part of it to interfere in a mere love affair, which I am obliged to confide to you. I am not going to carry the young lady off, without her own consent. There's nothing illegal in it. I never was Mr Heathfield's bosom friend. I violate no confidence of his. I love where he loves, and I mean to win where he would win, if I can.'

'He can't, Mr Craggs,' said Snitchey, evidently anxious and discomfited. 'He can't do it, sir. She dotes on Mr Alfred.'

'Does she?' returned the client.

'Mr Craggs, she dotes on him, sir,' persisted Snitchey.

'I didn't live six weeks, some few months ago, in the doctor's house for nothing; and I doubted that soon,' observed the client. 'She would have doted on him, if her sister could have brought it about; but I watched them. Marion avoided his name, avoided the subject: shrank from the least allusion to it, with evident distress.'

'Why should she, Mr Craggs, you know? Why should she, sir?' enquired Snitchey.

'I don't know why she should, though there are many likely reasons,' said the client, smiling at the attention and perplexity expressed in Mr Snitchey's shining eye, and at his cautious way of carrying on the conversation, and making himself informed upon the subject; 'but I know she does. She was very young when she made the engagement – if it may be called one, I am not even sure of that – and has repented of it, perhaps. Perhaps – it seems a foppish thing to say, but upon my soul I don't mean it in that light – she may have fallen in love with me, as I have fallen in love with her.'

'He, he! Mr Alfred, her old playfellow too, you remember Mr Craggs,' said Snitchey, with a disconcerted laugh; 'knew her almost from a baby!'

'Which makes it the more probable that she may be tired of his idea,' calmly pursued the client, 'and not indisposed to exchange it for the newer one of another lover, who presents himself (or is presented by his horse) under romantic circumstances; has the not unfavourable reputation – with a country girl – of having lived thoughtlessly and gaily, without doing much harm to anybody; and who, for his youth and figure, and so forth – this may seem foppish again, but upon my soul I don't mean it in that light – might perhaps pass muster in a crowd with Mr Alfred himself.'

There was no gainsaying the last clause, certainly; and Mr Snitchey, glancing at him, thought so. There was something naturally graceful and pleasant in the very carelessness of his air. It seemed to suggest, of his comely face and well-knit figure, that they might be greatly better if he chose: and that, once roused and made earnest (but he never had been earnest yet), he could be full of fire and purpose. 'A dangerous sort of libertine,' thought the shrewd lawyer, 'to seem to catch the spark he wants from a young lady's eyes.'

'Now, observe, Snitchey,' he continued, arising and taking him by the button, 'and Craggs,' taking him by the button also, and placing one partner on either side of him, so that neither might evade him. 'I don't ask you for any advice. You are right to keep quite aloof from all parties in such a matter, which is not one in which grave men like you could interfere, on any side. I am briefly going to review in half a dozen words, my position and intention, and then I shall leave it to you to do the best for me, in money matters, that you can: seeing, that, if I run away with the doctor's beautiful daughter (as I hope to do, and to become another man under her bright influence), it will be, for the moment more chargeable than running away alone. But I shall soon make all that up in an altered life.'

'I think it will be better not to hear this, Mr Craggs?' said Snitchey, looking at him across the client.

'I think not,' said Craggs – both listening attentively.

'Well! You needn't hear it,' replied their client. 'I'll mention it, however. I don't mean to ask the doctor's consent, because he wouldn't give it me. But I mean to do the doctor no wrong or harm, because (besides there being nothing serious in such trifles, as he says) I hope to rescue his child, my Marion, from what I see – *I know* – she dreads, and contemplates with misery: that is, the return of this old lover. If anything in the world is true, it is true that she dreads his return. Nobody is injured so far. I am so harried and worried here just now, that I lead the life of a flying-fish; skulk about in the dark, am shut out of my own house, and warned off my own grounds: but that house, and those grounds, and many an acre besides, will come back home one day, as you know and say; and Marion will probably be richer – on your showing, who are ever sanguine – ten years hence as my wife, than as the wife of Alfred Heathfield, whose return she dreads (remember that), and in whom or in any man, my passion is not surpassed. Who is injured yet? It is a fair case throughout. My right is as good as his, if she decide in my favour; and I will try my right by her alone. You will like to know no more after this, and I will tell you no more. Now you know my purpose, and wants. When must I leave here?'

'In a week,' said Snitchey. 'Mr Craggs? – '

'In something less, I should say,' responded Craggs.

'In a month,' said the client, after attentively watching the two faces. 'This day month. Today is Thursday. Succeed or fail, on this day month I go.'

'It's too long a delay,' said Snitchey; 'much too long. But let it be so. I thought he'd have stipulated for three,' he murmured to himself. 'Are you going? Good-night, sir.'

'Good-night!' returned the client, shaking hands with the Firm. 'You'll live to see me making a good use of riches yet. Henceforth, the star of my destiny is, Marion!'

'Take care of the stairs, sir,' replied Snitchey; 'for she don't shine there. Good-night!'

'Good-night!'

So they both stood at the stairhead with a pair of office-candles, watching him down; and when he had gone away, stood looking at each other.

'What do you think of all this, Mr Craggs?' said Snitchey.

Mr Craggs shook his head.

'It was our opinion, on the day when that release was executed, that there was something curious in the parting of that pair, I recollect,' said Snitchey.

'It was,' said Mr Craggs.

'Perhaps he deceives himself altogether,' pursued Mr Snitchey, locking up the fireproof box, and putting it away; 'or if he don't, a little bit of fickleness and perfidy is not a miracle, Mr Craggs. And yet I thought that pretty face was very true. Although,' said Mr Snitchey, putting on his greatcoat (for the weather was very cold), drawing on his gloves, and snuffing out one candle, 'that I had even seen her character becoming stronger and more resolved of late. More like her sister's.'

'Mrs Craggs was of the same opinion,' returned Craggs.

'I'd really give a trifle tonight,' observed Mr Snitchey, who was a good-natured man, 'if I could believe that Mr Warden was reckoning without his host; but light-headed, capricious, and unballasted as he is, he knows something of the world and its people (he ought to, for he has bought what he does know, dear enough); and I can't quite think that. We had better not interfere: we can do nothing, Mr Craggs, but keep quiet.'

'Nothing,' returned Craggs.

'Our friend the doctor makes light of such things,' said Mr Snitchey, shaking his head. 'I hope he mayn't stand in need of his philosophy. Our friend Alfred talks of the battle of life,' he shook his head again, 'I hope he mayn't be cut down early in the day. Have you got your hat, Mr Craggs? I am going to put the other candle out.'

Mr Craggs replying in the affirmative, Mr Snitchey suited the action to the word, and they groped their way out of the council-chamber: now as dark as the subject, or the law in general.

*   *   *

My story passes to a quiet little study, where, on that same night, the sisters and the hale old doctor sat by a cheerful fireside. Grace was working at her needle. Marion read aloud from a book before her. The doctor, in his dressing-gown and slippers, with his feet spread out upon the warm rug, leaned back in his easy-chair, and listened to the book, and looked upon his daughters.

They were very beautiful to look upon. Two better faces for a fireside, never made a fireside bright and sacred. Something of the difference between them had been softened down in three years' time; and enthroned upon the clear brow of the younger sister, looking through her eyes, and thrilling in her voice, was the same earnest nature that her own motherless youth had ripened in the elder sister long ago. But she still appeared at once the lovelier and weaker of the two; still seemed to rest her head upon her sister's breast, and put her trust in her, and look into her eyes for counsel and reliance. Those loving eyes, so calm, serene, and cheerful, as of old.

' "And being in her own home," ' read Marion, from the book; ' "her home made exquisitely dear by these remembrances, she now began to know that the great trial of her heart must soon come on, and could not be delayed. Oh, Home, our comforter and friend when others fall away, to part with whom, at any step between the cradle and the grave – " '

'Marion, my love!' said Grace.

'Why, Puss!' exclaimed her father, 'what's the matter?'

She put her hand upon the hand her sister stretched towards her, and read on; her voice still faltering and trembling, though she made an effort to command it when thus interrupted.

' "To part with whom, at any step between the cradle and the grave, is always sorrowful. Oh, Home, so true to us, so often slighted in return, be lenient to them that turn away from thee, and do not haunt their erring footsteps too reproachfully! Let no kind looks, no well-remembered smiles, be seen upon thy phantom face. Let no ray of affection, welcome, gentleness, forbearance, cordiality, shine from thy white head. Let no old loving word or tone rise up in judgement against thy deserter; but if thou can'st look harshly and severely, do, in mercy to the Penitent!'

'Dear Marion, read no more tonight,' said Grace – for she was weeping.

'I cannot,' she replied, and closed the book. 'The words seem all on fire!'

The doctor was amused at this; and laughed as he patted her on the head.

'What! overcome by a storybook!' said Dr Jeddler. 'Print and paper! Well, well, it's all one. It's as rational to make a serious matter of print and paper as of anything else. But dry your eyes, love, dry your eyes. I dare say the heroine has got home again long ago, and made it up all round – and if she hasn't, a real home is only four walls; and a fictitious one, mere rags and ink. What's the matter now?'

'It's only me, mister,' said Clemency, putting in her head at the door.

'And what's the matter with *you*?' said the doctor.

'Oh, bless you, nothing an't the matter with me,' returned Clemency – and truly too, to judge from her well-soaped face, in which there gleamed as usual the very soul of good humour, which, ungainly as she was, made her quite engaging. Abrasions on the elbows are not generally understood, it is true, to range within that class of personal charms called beauty-spots. But it is better, going through the world, to have the arms chafed in that narrow passage, than the temper: and Clemency's was sound and whole as any beauty's in the land.

'Nothing an't the matter with me,' said Clemency, entering, 'but – come a little closer, mister.'

The doctor, in some astonishment, complied with this invitation.

'You said I wasn't to give you one before them, you know,' said Clemency.

A novice in the family might have supposed, from her extraordinary ogling as she said it, as well as from a singular rapture or ecstasy which pervaded her elbows, as if she were embracing herself, that 'one,' in its most favourable interpretation, meant a chaste salute. Indeed the doctor himself seemed alarmed, for the moment; but quickly regained his composure, as Clemency, having had recourse to both her pockets – beginning with the right one, going away to the wrong one, and afterwards coming back to the right one again – produced a letter from the post office.

'Britain was riding by on a errand,' she chuckled, handing it to the doctor, 'and see the mail come in, and waited for it. There's A H in the corner. Mr Alfred's on his journey home, I bet. We shall have a wedding in the house – there was two spoons in my saucer this morning. Oh Luck, how slow he opens it!'

All this she delivered, by way of soliloquy, gradually rising higher and higher on tiptoe, in her impatience to hear the news, and making a corkscrew of her apron, and a bottle of her mouth. At last, arriving at a climax of suspense, and seeing the doctor still engaged in the perusal of the letter, she came down flat upon the soles of her feet again, and cast her apron, as a veil, over her head, in a mute despair, and inability to bear it any longer.

'Here! Girls!' cried the doctor. 'I can't help it: I never could keep a secret in my life. There are not many secrets, indeed, worth being kept in such a – Well! never mind that. Alfred's coming home, my dears, directly.'

'Directly!' exclaimed Marion.

'What! The storybook is soon forgotten!' said the doctor, pinching her cheek. 'I thought the news would dry those tears. Yes. "Let it be a surprise," he says, here. But I can't let it be a surprise. He must have a welcome.'

'Directly!' repeated Marion.

'Why, perhaps not what your impatience calls "directly",' returned the doctor; 'but pretty soon too. Let us see. Let us see. Today is Thursday, is it not? Then he promises to be here, this day month.'

'This day month!' repeated Marion, softly.

'A gay day and a holiday for us,' said the cheerful voice of her sister Grace, kissing her in congratulation. 'Long looked forward to, dearest, and come at last.'

She answered with a smile; a mournful smile, but full of sisterly affection: and as she looked in her sister's face, and listened to the quiet music of her voice, picturing the happiness of this return, her own face glowed with hope and joy.

And with a something else: a something shining more and more through all the rest of its expression: for which I have no name. It was not exultation, triumph, proud enthusiasm. They are not so calmly shown. It was not love and gratitude alone, though love and gratitude were part of it. It emanated from no sordid thought, for sordid thoughts do not light up the brow, and hover on the lips, and move the spirit, like a fluttered light, until the sympathetic figure trembles.

Dr Jeddler, in spite of his system of philosophy – which he was continually contradicting and denying in practice, but more famous philosophers have done that – could not help having as much interest in the return of his old ward and pupil, as if it had been a serious event. So he sat himself down in his easy-chair again, stretched out his slippered feet once more upon the rug, read the letter over and over a great many times, and talked it over more times still.

'Ah! The day was,' said the doctor, looking at the fire, 'when you and he, Grace, used to trot about arm-in-arm, in his holiday time, like a couple of walking dolls. You remember?'

'I remember,' she answered, with her pleasant laugh, and plying her needle busily.

'This day month, indeed?' mused the doctor. 'That hardly seems a twelvemonth ago. And where was my little Marion then!'

'Never far from her sister,' said Marion, cheerily, 'however little. Grace was everything to me, even when she was a young child herself.'

'True, Puss, true,' returned the doctor. 'She was a staid little woman, was Grace, and a wise housekeeper, and a busy, quiet, pleasant body; bearing with our humours and anticipating our wishes, and always ready to forget her own, even in those times. I never knew you positive or obstinate, Grace, my darling, even then on any subject but one.'

'I am afraid I have changed sadly for the worse, since,' laughed Grace, still busy at her work. 'What was that one, father?'

'Alfred, of course,' said the doctor. 'Nothing would serve you but you must be called Alfred's wife; so we called you Alfred's wife; and you liked it better, I believe (odd as it seems now), than being called a Duchess, if we could have made you one.'

'Indeed!' said Grace, placidly.

'Why, don't you remember?' enquired the doctor.

'I think I remember something of it,' she returned, 'but not much. It's so long ago.' And as she sat at work, she hummed the burden of an old song, which the doctor liked.

'Alfred will find a real wife soon,' she said, breaking off; 'and that will be a happy time indeed for all of us. My three years' trust is nearly at an end, Marion. It has been a very easy one. I shall tell Alfred, when I give you back to him, that you have loved him dearly all the time, and that he has never once needed my good services. May I tell him so, love?'

'Tell him, dear Grace,' replied Marion, 'that there never was a trust so generously, nobly, steadfastly discharged; and that I have loved *you*, all the time, dearer and dearer every day; and Oh! how dearly now!'

'Nay,' said her cheerful sister, returning her embrace, 'I can scarcely tell him that; we will leave my deserts to Alfred's imagination. It will be liberal enough, dear Marion; like your own.'

With that she resumed the work she had for a moment laid down, when her sister spoke so fervently: and with it the old song the doctor liked to hear. And the doctor, still reposing in his easy-chair, with his slippered feet stretched out before him on the rug, listened to the tune, and beat time on his knee with Alfred's letter, and looked at his two daughters, and thought that among the many trifles of the trifling world, these trifles were agreeable enough.

Clemency Newcome, in the meantime, having accomplished her mission and lingered in the room until she had made herself a party to the news, descended to the kitchen, where her co-adjutor, Mr Britain, was regaling after supper, surrounded by such a plentiful collection of bright pot-lids, well-scoured saucepans, burnished dinner-covers, gleaming kettles, and other tokens of her industrious habits, arranged upon the walls and shelves, that he sat as in the centre of a hall of mirrors. The majority did not give forth very flattering portraits of him, certainly; nor were they by any means unanimous in their reflections; as some made him very long-faced, others very broad-faced, some tolerably well-looking, others vastly ill- looking, according to their several manners of reflecting: which were as various, in respect of one fact, as those of so many kinds of men. But they all agreed that in the midst of them sat, quite at his ease, an individual with a pipe in his mouth, and a jug of beer at his elbow, who nodded condescendingly to Clemency, when she stationed herself at the same table.

'Well, Clemmy,' said Britain, 'how are you by this time, and what's the news?'

Clemency told him the news, which he received very graciously. A gracious change had come over Benjamin from head to foot. He was much broader, much redder, much more cheerful, and much jollier in all respects. It seemed as if his face had been tied up in a knot before, and was now untwisted and smoothed out.

'There'll be another job for Snitchey and Craggs, I suppose,' he observed, puffing slowly at his pipe. 'More witnessing for you and me, perhaps, Clemmy!'

'Lor!' replied his fair companion, with her favourite twist of her favourite joints. 'I wish it was me, Britain!'

'Wish what was you?'

'A-going to be married,' said Clemency.

Benjamin took his pipe out of his mouth and laughed heartily. 'Yes! you're a likely subject for that!' he said. 'Poor Clem!' Clemency for her part laughed as heartily as he, and seemed as much amused by the idea. 'Yes,' she assented, 'I'm a likely subject for that; an't I?'

'*You'll* never be married, you know,' said Mr Britain, resuming his pipe.

'Don't you think I ever shall though?' said Clemency, in perfect good faith.

Mr Britain shook his head. 'Not a chance of it!'

'Only think!' said Clemency. 'Well! – I suppose you mean to, Britain, one of these days; don't you?'

A question so abrupt, upon a subject so momentous, required consideration. After blowing out a great cloud of smoke, and looking at it with his head now on this side and now on that, as if it were actually the question, and he were surveying it in various aspects, Mr Britain replied that he wasn't altogether clear about it, but – ye–es – he thought he might come to that at last.

'I wish her joy, whoever she may be!' cried Clemency.

'Oh, she'll have that,' said Benjamin; 'safe enough.'

'But she wouldn't have led quite such a joyful life as she will lead, and wouldn't have had quite such a sociable sort of husband as she will have,' said Clemency, spreading herself half over the table, and staring retrospectively at the candle, 'if it hadn't been for – not that I went to do it, for it was accidental, I am sure – if it hadn't been for me; now would she, Britain?'

'Certainly not,' returned Mr Britain, by this time in that high state of appreciation of his pipe, when a man can open his mouth but a very little way for speaking purposes; and sitting luxuriously immovable in his chair, can afford to turn only his eyes towards a companion, and that very passively and gravely. 'Oh! I'm greatly beholden to you, you know, Clem.'

'Lor, how nice that is to think of!' said Clemency.

At the same time, bringing her thoughts as well as her sight to bear upon the candle-grease, and becoming abruptly reminiscent of its healing qualities as a balsam, she anointed her left elbow with a plentiful application of that remedy.

'You see I've made a good many investigations of one sort and another in my time,' pursued Mr Britain, with the profundity of a sage; 'having been always of an enquiring turn of mind; and I've read a good many books about the general Rights of things and Wrongs of things, for I went into the literary line myself, when I began life.'

'Did you though!' cried the admiring Clemency.

'Yes,' said Mr Britain; 'I was hid for the best part of two years behind a bookstall, ready to fly out if anybody pocketed a volume; and after that, I was light porter to a stay and mantua-maker, in which capacity I was employed to carry about, in oilskin baskets, nothing but deceptions – which soured my spirits and disturbed my confidence in human nature; and after that, I heard a world of discussions in this house, which soured my spirits fresh; and my opinion after all is, that, as a safe and comfortable sweetener of the same, and as a pleasant guide through life, there's nothing like a nutmeg-grater.'

Clemency was about to offer a suggestion, but he stopped her by anticipating it.

'Com–bined,' he added gravely, 'with a thimble.'

'Do as you would, you know, and cetrer, eh!' observed Clemency, folding her arms comfortably in her delight at this avowal, and patting her elbows. 'Such a short cut, an't it?'

'I'm not sure,' said Mr Britain, 'that it's what would be considered good philosophy. I've my doubts about that: but it wears well, and saves a quantity of snarling, which the genuine article don't always.'

'See how you used to go on once, yourself, you know!' said Clemency.

'Ah!' said Mr Britain. 'But the most extraordinary thing, Clemmy, is that I should live to be brought round, through you. That's the strange part of it. Through you! Why, I suppose you haven't so much as half an idea in your head.'

Clemency, without taking the least offence, shook it, and laughed, and hugged herself, and said, 'No, she didn't suppose she had.'

'I'm pretty sure of it,' said Mr Britain.

'Oh! I dare say you're right,' said Clemency. 'I don't pretend to none. I don't want any.'

Benjamin took his pipe from his lips, and laughed till the tears ran down his face. 'What a natural you are, Clemmy!' he said, shaking his head, with an infinite relish of the joke, and wiping his eyes. Clemency, without the smallest inclination to dispute it, did the like, and laughed as heartily as he.

'But I can't help liking you,' said Mr Britain; 'you're a regular good creature in your way; so shake hands, Clem. Whatever happens, I'll always take notice of you, and be a friend to you.'

'Will you?' returned Clemency. 'Well! that's very good of you.'

'Yes, yes,' said Mr Britain, giving her his pipe to knock the ashes out of; 'I'll stand by you. Hark! That's a curious noise!'

'Noise!' repeated Clemency.

'A footstep outside. Somebody dropping from the wall it sounded like,' said Britain. 'Are they all abed up stairs?'

'Yes, all abed by this time,' she replied.

'Didn't you hear anything?'

'No.'

They both listened, but heard nothing.

'I tell you what,' said Benjamin, taking down a lantern. 'I'll have a look round before I go to bed myself, for satisfaction's sake. Undo the door while I light this, Clemmy.'

Clemency complied briskly; but observed as she did so, that he would only have his walk for his pains, that it was all his fancy, and so forth. Mr Britain said 'very likely', but sallied out, nevertheless, armed with the poker, and casting the light of the lantern far and near in all directions.

'It's as quiet as a churchyard,' said Clemency, looking after him; 'and almost as ghostly too!'

Glancing back into the kitchen, she cried fearfully, as a light figure stole into her view, 'What's that!'

'Hush!' said Marion, in an agitated whisper. 'You have always loved me, have you not!'

'Loved you, child! You may be sure I have.'

'I am sure. And I may trust you, may I not? There is no one else just now, in whom I *can* trust.'

'Yes,' said Clemency, with all her heart.

'There is someone out there,' pointing to the door, 'whom I must see, and speak with, tonight. Michael Warden, for God's sake retire! Not now!'

Clemency started with surprise and trouble as, following the direction of the speaker's eyes, she saw a dark figure standing in the doorway.

'In another moment you may be discovered,' said Marion. 'Not now! Wait, if you can, in some concealment. I will come, presently.'

He waved his hand to her, and was gone.

'Don't go to bed. Wait here for me!' said Marion, hurriedly. 'I have been seeking to speak to you for an hour past. Oh, be true to me!'

Eagerly seizing her bewildered hand, and pressing it with both her own to her breast – an action more expressive, in its passion of entreaty, than the most eloquent appeal in words – Marion withdrew; as the light of the returning lantern flashed into the room.

'All still and peaceable. Nobody there. Fancy, I suppose,' said Mr Britain, as he locked and barred the door. 'One of the effects of having a lively imagination. Halloa! Why, what's the matter?'

Clemency, who could not conceal the effects of her surprise and concern, was sitting in a chair: pale, and trembling from head to foot.

'Matter!' she repeated, chafing her hands and elbows, nervously, and looking anywhere but at him. 'That's good in you, Britain, that is! After going and frightening one out of one's life with noises, and lanterns, and I don't know what all. Matter! Oh, yes!'

'If you're frightened out of your life by a lantern, Clemmy,' said Mr Britain, composedly blowing it out and hanging it up again, 'that apparition's very soon got rid of. But you're as bold as brass in general,' he said, stopping to observe her; 'and were, after the noise and the lantern too. What have you taken into your head? Not an idea, eh?'

But, as Clemency bade him good-night very much after her usual fashion, and began to bustle about with a show of going to bed herself immediately, Little Britain, after giving utterance to the original remark that it was impossible to account for a woman's whims, bade her good-night in return, and taking up his candle strolled drowsily away to bed.

When all was quiet, Marion returned.

'Open the door,' she said; 'and stand there close beside me, while I speak to him, outside.'

Timid as her manner was, it still evinced a resolute and settled purpose, such as Clemency could not resist. She softly unbarred the door: but before turning the key, looked round on the young creature waiting to issue forth when she should open it.

The face was not averted or cast down, but looking full upon her, in its pride of youth and beauty. Some simple sense of the slightness of the barrier that interposed itself between the happy home and honoured love of the fair girl, and what might be the desolation of that home, and shipwreck of its dearest treasure, smote so keenly on the tender heart of Clemency, and so filled it to overflowing with sorrow and compassion, that, bursting into tears, she threw her arms round Marion's neck.

'It's little that I know, my dear,' cried Clemency, 'very little; but I know that this should not be. Think of what you do!'

'I have thought of it many times,' said Marion, gently.

'Once more,' urged Clemency. 'Till tomorrow.'

Marion shook her head.

'For Mr Alfred's sake,' said Clemency, with homely earnestness. 'Him that you used to love so dearly, once!'

She hid her face, upon the instant, in her hands, repeating, 'Once!' as if it rent her heart.

'Let me go out,' said Clemency, soothing her. 'I'll tell him what you like. Don't cross the doorstep tonight. I'm sure no good will come of it. Oh, it was an unhappy day when Mr Warden was ever brought here! Think of your good father, darling: of your sister.'

'I have,' said Marion, hastily raising her head. 'You don't know what I do. I *must* speak to him. You are the best and truest friend in all the world for what you have said to me, but I must take this step. Will you go with me, Clemency,' she kissed her on her friendly face, 'or shall I go alone?'

Sorrowing and wondering, Clemency turned the key, and opened the door. Into the dark and doubtful night that lay beyond the threshold, Marion passed quickly, holding her by the hand.

In the dark night he joined her, and they spoke together earnestly and long: and the hand that held so fast by Clemency's, now trembled, now turned deadly cold, now clasped and closed on hers, in the strong feeling of the speech it emphasised unconsciously. When they returned he followed to the door; and pausing there a moment, seized the other hand, and pressed it to his lips. Then stealthily he withdrew.

The door was barred and locked again, and once again she stood beneath her father's roof. Not bowed down by the secret that she

brought there, though so young; but with that same expression on her face, for which I had no name before, and shining through her tears.

Again she thanked and thanked her humble friend, and trusted to her, as she said, with confidence, implicitly. Her chamber safely reached, she fell upon her knees; and with her secret weighing on her heart, could pray!

Could rise up from her prayers, so tranquil and serene, and bending over her fond sister in her slumber, look upon her face and smile: though sadly: murmuring, as she kissed her forehead, how that Grace had been a mother to her, ever, and she loved her as a child!

Could draw the passive arm about her neck when lying down to rest –

it seemed to cling there, of its own will, protectingly and tenderly even in sleep – and breathe upon the parted lips, God bless her!

Could sink into a peaceful sleep, herself; but for one dream, in which she cried out, in her innocent and touching voice, that she was quite alone, and they had all forgotten her.

*   *   *

A month soon passes, even at its tardiest pace. The month appointed to elapse between that night and the return, was quick of foot, and went by, like a vapour.

The day arrived. A raging winter day, that shook the old house, sometimes, as if it shivered in the blast. A day to make home doubly home. To give the chimney corner new delights. To shed a ruddier glow upon the faces gathered round the hearth; and draw each fireside group into a closer and more social league, against the roaring elements without. Such a wild winter day as best prepares the way for shut-out night; for curtained rooms, and cheerful looks; for music, laughter, dancing, light, and jovial entertainment!

All these the doctor had in store to welcome Alfred back. They knew that he could not arrive till night; and they would make the night air ring, he said, as he approached. All his old friends should congregate about him. He should not miss a face that he had known and liked. No! They should every one be there!

So, guests were bidden, and musicians were engaged, and tables spread, and floors prepared for active feet, and bountiful provision made, of every hospitable kind. Because it was the Christmas season, and his eyes were all unused to English holly and its sturdy green, the dancing room was garlanded and hung with it; and the red berries gleamed an English welcome to him, peeping from among the leaves.

It was a busy day for all of them: a busier day for none of them than Grace, who noiselessly presided everywhere, and was the cheerful mind of all the preparations. Many a time that day (as well as many a time within the fleeting month preceding it), did Clemency glance anxiously, and almost fearfully, at Marion. She saw her paler, perhaps, than usual; but there was a sweet composure on her face that made it lovelier than ever.

At night when she was dressed, and wore upon her head a wreath that Grace had proudly twined about it – its mimic flowers were Alfred's favourites, as Grace remembered when she chose them – that old expression, pensive, almost sorrowful, and yet so spiritual, high, and stirring, sat again upon her brow, enhanced a hundred-fold.

'The next wreath I adjust on this fair head, will be a marriage wreath,' said Grace; 'or I am no true prophet, dear.'

Her sister smiled, and held her in her arms.

'A moment, Grace. Don't leave me yet. Are you sure that I want nothing more?'

Her care was not for that. It was her sister's face she thought of, and her eyes were fixed upon it, tenderly.

'My art,' said Grace, 'can go no farther, dear girl; nor your beauty. I never saw you look so beautiful as now.'

'I never was so happy,' she returned.

'Ay, but there is greater happiness in store. In such another home, as cheerful and as bright as this looks now,' said Grace, 'Alfred and his young wife will soon be living.'

She smiled again. 'It is a happy home, Grace, in your fancy. I can see it in your eyes. I know it *will* be happy, dear. How glad I am to know it.'

'Well,' cried the doctor, bustling in. 'Here we are, all ready for Alfred, eh? He can't be here until pretty late – an hour or so before midnight – so there'll be plenty of time for making merry before he comes. He'll not find us with the ice unbroken. Pile up the fire here, Britain! Let it shine upon the holly till it winks again. It's a world of nonsense, Puss; true lovers and all the rest of it – all nonsense; but we'll be nonsensical with the rest of 'em, and give our true lover a mad welcome. Upon my word!' said the old doctor, looking at his daughters proudly, 'I'm not clear tonight, among other absurdities, but that I'm the father of two handsome girls.'

'All that one of them has ever done, or may do – may do, dearest father – to cause you pain or grief, forgive her,' said Marion: 'forgive her now, when her heart is full. Say that you forgive her. That you will forgive her. That she shall always share your love, and –' and the rest was not said, for her face was hidden on the old man's shoulder.

'Tut, tut, tut,' said the doctor, gently. 'Forgive! What have I to forgive? Heydey, if our true lovers come back to flurry us like this, we must hold 'em at a distance; we must send expresses out to stop 'em short upon the road, and bring 'em on a mile or two a day, until we're properly prepared to meet 'em. Kiss me, Puss. Forgive! Why, what a silly child you are. If you had vexed and crossed me fifty times a day, instead of not at all, I'd forgive you everything, but such a supplication. Kiss me again, Puss. There! Prospective and retrospective – a clear score between us. Pile up the fire here! Would you freeze the people on this bleak December night! Let us be light, and warm, and merry, or I'll not forgive some of you!'

So gaily the old doctor carried it! And the fire was piled up, and the lights were bright, and company arrived, and a murmuring of lively tongues began, and already there was a pleasant air of cheerful excitement stirring through all the house.

More and more company came flocking in. Bright eyes sparkled upon Marion; smiling lips gave her joy of his return; sage mothers fanned themselves, and hoped she mightn't be too youthful and inconstant for the quiet round of home; impetuous fathers fell into disgrace for too much exaltation of her beauty; daughters envied her; sons envied him; innumerable pairs of lovers profited by the occasion; all were interested, animated, and expectant.

Mr and Mrs Craggs came arm in arm, but Mrs Snitchey came alone. 'Why, what's become of *him*?' enquired the doctor.

The feather of a Bird of Paradise in Mrs Snitchey's turban, trembled as if the Bird of Paradise were alive again, when she said that doubtless Mr Craggs knew. *She* was never told.

'That nasty office,' said Mrs Craggs.

'I wish it was burnt down,' said Mrs Snitchey.

'He's – he's – there's a little matter of business that keeps my partner rather late,' said Mr Craggs, looking uneasily about him.

'Oh–h! Business. Don't tell me!' said Mrs Snitchey.

'*We* know what business means,' said Mrs Craggs.

But their not knowing what it meant, was perhaps the reason why Mrs Snitchey's Bird of Paradise feather quivered so portentously, and all the pendant bits on Mrs Craggs's earrings shook like little bells.

'I wonder *you* could come away, Mr Craggs,' said his wife.

'Mr Craggs is fortunate, I'm sure!' said Mrs Snitchey.

'That office so engrosses 'em,' said Mrs Craggs.

'A person with an office has no business to be married at all,' said Mrs Snitchey.

Then, Mrs Snitchey said, within herself, that that look of hers had pierced to Craggs's soul, and he knew it: and Mrs Craggs observed, to

Craggs, that 'his Snitcheys' were deceiving him behind his back, and he would find it out when it was too late.

Still, Mr Craggs, without much heeding these remarks, looked uneasily about him until his eye rested on Grace, to whom he immediately presented himself.

'Good-evening, Ma'am,' said Craggs. 'You look charmingly. Your – miss – your sister, Miss Marion, is she – '

'Oh she's quite well, Mr Craggs.'

'Yes – I – is she here?' asked Craggs.

'Here! Don't you see her yonder? Going to dance?' said Grace.

Mr Craggs put on his spectacles to see the better; looked at her through them, for some time; coughed; and put them, with an air of satisfaction, in their sheath again, and in his pocket.

Now the music struck up, and the dance commenced. The bright fire crackled and sparkled, rose and fell, as though it joined the dance itself, in right good fellowship. Sometimes it roared as if it would make music too. Sometimes it flashed and beamed as if it were the eye of the old room: it winked too, sometimes, like a knowing patriarch, upon the youthful whisperers in corners. Sometimes it sported with the holly-boughs; and, shining on the leaves by fits and starts, made them look as if they were in the cold winter night again, and fluttering in the wind. Sometimes its genial humour grew obstreperous, and passed all bounds; and then it cast into the room, among the twinkling feet, with a loud burst, a shower of harmless little sparks, and in its exultation leaped and bounded, like a mad thing, up the broad old chimney.

Another dance was near its close, when Mr Snitchey touched his partner, who was looking on, upon the arm.

Mr Craggs started, as if his familiar had been a spectre.

'Is he gone?' he asked.

'Hush! He has been with me,' said Snitchey, 'for three hours and more. He went over everything. He looked into all our arrangements for him, and was very particular indeed. He – Humph!'

The dance was finished. Marion passed close before him, as he spoke. She did not observe him, or his partner; but looked over her shoulder towards her sister in the distance, as she slowly made her way into the crowd, and passed out of their view.

'You see! All safe and well,' said Mr Craggs. 'He didn't recur to that subject, I suppose?'

'Not a word.'

'And is he really gone? Is he safe away?'

'He keeps to his word. He drops down the river with the tide in that shell of a boat of his, and so goes out to sea on this dark night – a daredevil he is – before the wind. There's no such lonely road anywhere else. That's one thing. The tide flows, he says, an hour before midnight about this time. I'm glad it's over.' Mr Snitchey wiped his forehead, which looked hot and anxious.

'What do you think,' said Mr Craggs, 'about – '

'Hush!' replied his cautious partner, looking straight before him. 'I understand you. Don't mention names, and don't let us seem to be talking secrets. I don't know what to think; and to tell you the truth, I don't care now. It's a great relief. His self-love deceived him, I suppose. Perhaps the young lady coquetted a little. The evidence would seem to point that way. Alfred not arrived?'

'Not yet,' said Mr Craggs. 'Expected every minute.'

'Good.' Mr Snitchey wiped his forehead again. 'It's a great relief. I haven't been so nervous since we've been in partnership. I intend to spend the evening now, Mr Craggs.'

Mrs Craggs and Mrs Snitchey joined them as he announced this intention.

The Bird of Paradise was in a state of extreme vibration; and the little bells were ringing quite audibly.

'It has been the theme of general comment, Mr Snitchey,' said Mrs Snitchey. 'I hope the office is satisfied.'

'Satisfied with what, my dear?' asked Mr Snitchey.

'With the exposure of a defenceless woman to ridicule and remark,' returned his wife. 'That is quite in the way of the office, *that* is.'

'I really, myself,' said Mrs Craggs, 'have been so long accustomed to connect the office with everything opposed to domesticity, that I am glad to know it as the avowed enemy of my peace. There is something honest in that, at all events.'

'My dear,' urged Mr Craggs, 'your good opinion is invaluable, but *I* never avowed that the office was the enemy of your peace.'

'No,' said Mrs Craggs, ringing a perfect peal upon the little bells. 'Not you, indeed. You wouldn't be worthy of the office, if you had the candour to.'

'As to my having been away tonight, my dear,' said Mr Snitchey, giving her his arm, 'the deprivation has been mine, I'm sure; but, as Mr Craggs knows – '

Mrs Snitchey cut this reference very short by hitching her husband to a distance, and asking him to look at that man. To do her the favour to look at him!

'At which man, my dear?' said Mr Snitchey.

'Your chosen companion; I'm no companion to you, Mr Snitchey.'

'Yes, yes, you are, my dear,' he interposed.

'No, no, I'm not,' said Mrs Snitchey, with a majestic smile. 'I know my station. Will you look at your chosen companion, Mr Snitchey; at your referee; at the keeper of your secrets; at the man you trust; at your other self, in short.'

The habitual association of Self with Craggs, occasioned Mr Snitchey to look in that direction.

'If you can look that man in the eye this night,' said Mrs Snitchey, 'and not know that you are deluded, practised upon: made the victim of his arts, and bent down prostrate to his will by some unaccountable fascination which it is impossible to explain, and against which no warning of mine is of the least avail: all I can say is – I pity you!'

At the very same moment Mrs Craggs was oracular on the cross subject. Was it possible, she said, that Craggs could so blind himself to his Snitcheys, as not to feel his true position? Did he mean to say that he had seen his Snitcheys come into that room, and didn't plainly see that there was reservation, cunning, treachery, in the man? Would he tell her that his very action, when he wiped his forehead and looked so stealthily about him, didn't show that there was something weighing on the conscience of his precious Snitcheys (if he had a conscience), that wouldn't bear the light? Did anybody but his Snitcheys come to festive entertainments like a burglar? – which, by the way, was hardly a clear illustration of the case, as he had walked in very mildly at the door. And would he still assert to her at noonday (it being nearly midnight), that his Snitcheys were to be justified through thick and thin, against all facts, and reason, and experience?

Neither Snitchey nor Craggs openly attempted to stem the current which had thus set in, but both were content to be carried gently along it, until its force abated; which happened at about the same time as a general movement for a country dance; when Mr Snitchey proposed himself as a partner to Mrs Craggs, and Mr Craggs gallantly offered himself to Mrs Snitchey; and after some such slight evasions as 'why don't you ask somebody else?' and 'you'll be glad, I know, if I decline' and 'I wonder you can dance out of the office' (but this jocosely now), each lady graciously accepted, and took her place.

It was an old custom among them, indeed, to do so, and to pair off, in like manner, at dinners and suppers; for they were excellent friends, and on a footing of easy familiarity. Perhaps the false Craggs and the wicked Snitchey were a recognised fiction with the two wives, as Doe and Roe, incessantly running up and down bailiwicks, were with the two husbands: or perhaps the ladies had instituted, and taken upon themselves, these two shares in the business, rather than be left out of it altogether. But certain it is, that each wife went as gravely and steadily to work in her vocation as her husband did in his: and would have considered it almost impossible for the Firm to maintain a successful and respectable existence, without her laudable exertions.

But now the Bird of Paradise was seen to flutter down the middle; and the little bells began to bounce and jingle in poussette; and the doctor's rosy face spun round and round, like an expressive pegtop highly varnished; and breathless Mr Craggs began to doubt already, whether country dancing had been made 'too easy', like the rest of life; and Mr Snitchey, with his nimble cuts and capers, footed it for Self and Craggs, and half a dozen more.

Now too, the fire took fresh courage, favoured by the lively wind the dance awakened, and burnt clear and high. It was the Genius of the room, and present everywhere. It shone in people's eyes, it sparkled in the jewels on the snowy necks of girls, it twinkled at their ears as if it whispered to them slyly, it flashed about their waists, it flickered on the ground and made it rosy for their feet, it bloomed upon the ceiling that its glow might set off their bright faces, and it kindled up a general illumination in Mrs Craggs's little belfry.

Now too, the lively air that fanned it, grew less gentle as the music quickened and the dance proceeded with new spirit; and a breeze arose that made the leaves and berries dance upon the wall, as they had often done upon the trees; and rustled in the room as if an invisible company of fairies, treading in the footsteps of the good substantial revellers, were whirling after them. Now too, no feature of the doctor's face could be distinguished as he spun and spun; and now there seemed a dozen Birds of Paradise in fitful flight; and now there were a thousand little bells at

work; and now a fleet of flying skirts was ruffled by a little tempest; when the music gave in, and the dance was over.

Hot and breathless as the doctor was, it only made him more impatient for Alfred's coming.

'Anything been seen, Britain? Anything been heard?'

'Too dark to see far, sir. Too much noise inside the house to hear.'

'That's right! The gayer welcome for him. How goes the time?'

'Just twelve, sir. He can't be long, sir.'

'Stir up the fire, and throw another log upon it,' said the doctor. 'Let him see his welcome blazing out upon the night – good boy! – as he comes along!'

He saw it – Yes! From the chaise he caught the light, as he turned the corner by the old church. He knew the room from which it shone. He saw the wintry branches of the old trees between the light and him. He knew that one of those trees rustled musically in the summertime at the window of Marion's chamber.

The tears were in his eyes. His heart throbbed so violently that he could hardly bear his happiness. How often he had thought of this time – pictured it under all circumstances – feared that it might never come – yearned, and wearied for it – far away!

Again the light! Distinct and ruddy; kindled, he knew, to give him welcome, and to speed him home. He beckoned with his hand, and waved his hat, and cheered out, loud, as if the light were they, and they could see and hear him, as he dashed towards them through the mud and mire, triumphantly.

Stop! He knew the doctor, and understood what he had done. He would not let it be a surprise to them. But he could make it one, yet, by going forward on foot. If the orchard gate were open, he could enter there; if not, the wall was easily climbed, as he knew of old; and he would be among them in an instant.

He dismounted from the chaise, and telling the driver – even that was not easy in his agitation – to remain behind for a few minutes, and then to follow slowly, ran on with exceeding swiftness, tried the gate, scaled the wall, jumped down on the other side, and stood panting in the old orchard.

There was a frosty rime upon the trees, which, in the faint light of the clouded moon, hung upon the smaller branches like dead garlands. Withered leaves crackled and snapped beneath his feet, as he crept softly on towards the house. The desolation of a winter night sat brooding on the earth, and in the sky. But the red light came cheerily towards him from the windows: figures passed and repassed there: and the hum and murmur of voices greeted his ear sweetly.

Listening for hers: attempting, as he crept on, to detach it from the rest, and half-believing that he heard it: he had nearly reached the door, when it was abruptly opened, and a figure coming out encountered his. It instantly recoiled with a half-suppressed cry.

'Clemency,' he said, 'don't you know me?'

'Don't come in,' she answered, pushing him back. 'Go away. Don't ask me why. Don't come in.'

'What is the matter?' he exclaimed.

'I don't know. I – I am afraid to think. Go back. Hark!'

There was a sudden tumult in the house. She put her hands upon her ears. A wild scream, such as no hands could shut out, was heard; and Grace – distraction in her looks and manner – rushed out at the door.

'Grace!' He caught her in his arms. 'What is it! Is she dead!'

She disengaged herself, as if to recognise his face, and fell down at his feet.

A crowd of figures came about them from the house. Among them was her father, with a paper in his hand.

'What is it!' cried Alfred, grasping his hair with his hands, and looking in an agony from face to face, as he bent upon his knee beside the insensible girl. 'Will no one look at me? Will no one speak to me? Does no one know me? Is there no voice among you all, to tell me what it is!'

There was a murmur among them. 'She is gone.'

'Gone!' he echoed.

'Fled, my dear Alfred!' said the doctor, in a broken voice, and with his hands before his face. 'Gone from her home and us. Tonight! She writes that she has made her innocent and blameless choice – entreats that we will forgive her – prays that we will not forget her – and is gone.'

'With whom? Where?'

He started up, as if to follow in pursuit, but when they gave way to let him pass, looked wildly round upon them, staggered back, and sank down in his former attitude, clasping one of Grace's cold hands in his own.

There was a hurried running to and fro, confusion, noise, disorder, and no purpose. Some proceeded to disperse themselves about the roads, and some took horse, and some got lights, and some conversed together, urging that there was no trace or track to follow. Some approached him kindly, with the view of offering consolation; some admonished him that Grace must be removed into the house, and that he prevented it. He never heard them, and he never moved.

The snow fell fast and thick. He looked up for a moment in the air, and thought that those white ashes strewn upon his hopes and misery, were suited to them well. He looked round on the whitening ground, and thought how Marion's footprints would be hushed and covered up, as soon as made, and even that remembrance of her blotted out. But he never felt the weather and he never stirred.

PART THE THIRD

The world had grown six years older since that night of the return. It was a warm autumn afternoon, and there had been heavy rain. The sun burst suddenly from among the clouds: and the old battleground, sparkling brilliantly and cheerfully at sight of it in one green place, flashed a responsive welcome there, which spread along the country side as if a joyful beacon had been lighted up, and answered from a thousand stations.

How beautiful the landscape kindling in the light, and that luxuriant influence passing on like a celestial presence, brightening everything! The wood, a sombre mass before, revealed its varied tints of yellow, green, brown, red; its different forms of trees, with raindrops glittering on their leaves and twinkling as they fell. The verdant meadowland, bright and glowing, seemed as if it had been blind a minute since, and now had found a sense of sight wherewith to look up at the shining sky. Cornfields, hedgerows, fences, homesteads, the clustered roofs, the steeple of the church, the stream, the watermill, all sprang out of the gloomy darkness, smiling. Birds sang sweetly, flowers raised their drooping heads, fresh scents arose from the invigorated ground; the blue expanse above, extended and diffused itself; already the sun's slanting rays pierced mortally the sullen bank of cloud that lingered in its flight; and a rainbow, spirit of all the colours that adorned the earth and sky, spanned the whole arch with its triumphant glory.

At such a time, one little roadside Inn, snugly sheltered behind a great elm-tree with a rare seat for idlers encircling its capacious bole, addressed a cheerful front towards the traveller, as a house of entertainment ought, and tempted him with many mute but significant assurances of a comfortable welcome. The ruddy signboard perched up in the tree, with its golden letters winking in the sun, ogled the passer-by from among the green leaves, like a jolly face, and promised good cheer. The horse-trough, full of clear fresh water, and the ground below it sprinkled with droppings of fragrant hay, made every horse that passed prick up his ears.

The crimson curtains in the lower rooms, and the pure white hangings in the little bedchambers above, beckoned, Come in! with every breath of air. Upon the bright green shutters, there were golden legends about beer and ale, and neat wines, and good beds; and an affecting picture of a brown jug frothing over at the top. Upon the window-sills were flowering plants in bright red pots, which made a lively show against the white front of the house; and in the darkness of the doorway there were streaks of light, which glanced off from the surfaces of bottles and tankards.

On the doorstep, appeared a proper figure of a landlord, too; for though he was a short man, he was round and broad, and stood with his hands in his pockets, and his legs just wide enough apart to express a mind at rest upon the subject of the cellar, and an easy confidence – too calm and virtuous to become a swagger – in the general resources of the Inn. The superabundant moisture, trickling from everything after the late rain, set him off well. Nothing near him was thirsty. Certain top-heavy dahlias, looking over the palings of his neat well-ordered garden, had swilled as much as they could carry – perhaps a trifle more – and may have been the worse for liquor; but the sweetbriar, roses, wall-flowers, the plants at the windows, and the leaves on the old tree, were in the beaming state of moderate company that had taken no more than was wholesome for them, and had served to develop their best qualities. Sprinkling dewy drops about them on the ground, they seemed profuse of innocent and sparkling mirth, that did good where it lighted, softening neglected corners which the steady rain could seldom reach, and hurting nothing.

This village inn had assumed, on being established, an uncommon sign. It was called the Nutmeg Grater. And underneath that household word, was inscribed, up in the tree, on the same flaming board, and in the like golden characters, By Benjamin Britain. At a second glance, and on a more minute examination of his face, you might have known that it was no other than Benjamin Britain himself who stood in the doorway – reasonably changed by time, but for the better; a very comfortable host indeed.

'Mrs B,' said Mr Britain, looking down the road, 'is rather late. It's teatime.'

As there was no Mrs Britain coming, he strolled leisurely out into the road and looked up at the house, very much to his satisfaction. 'It's just the sort of house,' said Benjamin, 'I should wish to stop at, if I didn't keep it.'

Then he strolled towards the garden paling, and took a look at the dahlias. They looked over at him, with a helpless, drowsy hanging of their heads: which bobbed again, as the heavy drops of wet dripped off them.

'You must be looked after,' said Benjamin. 'Memorandum, not to forget to tell her so. She's a long time coming!'

Mr Britain's better half seemed to be by so very much his better half, that his own moiety of himself was utterly cast away and helpless without her.

'She hadn't much to do, I think,' said Ben. 'There were a few little matters of business after market, but not many. Oh! here we are at last!'

A chaise-cart, driven by a boy, came clattering along the road: and seated in it, in a chair, with a large well-saturated umbrella spread out to dry behind her, was the plump figure of a matronly woman, with her bare arms folded across a basket which she carried on her knee, several other baskets and parcels lying crowded around her, and a certain bright good-nature in her face and contented awkwardness in her manner, as she jogged to and fro with the motion of her carriage, which smacked of old times, even in the distance. Upon her nearer approach, this relish of bygone days was not diminished; and when the cart stopped at the Nutmeg Grater door, a pair of shoes, alighting from it, slipped nimbly through Mr Britain's open arms, and came down with a substantial weight upon the pathway, which shoes could hardly have belonged to anyone but Clemency Newcome.

In fact they did belong to her, and she stood in them, and a rosy comfortable-looking soul she was: with as much soap on her glossy face as in times of yore, but with whole elbows now, that had grown quite dimpled in her improved condition.

'You're late, Clemmy!' said Mr Britain.

'Why, you see, Ben, I've had a deal to do!' she replied, looking busily after the safe removal into the house of all the packages and baskets; 'eight, nine, ten, – where's eleven? Oh! my basket's eleven! It's all right. Put the horse up, Harry, and if he coughs again give him a warm mash tonight. Eight, nine, ten. Why where's eleven? Oh I forgot, it's all right. How's the children, Ben?'

'Hearty, Clemmy, hearty.'

'Bless their precious faces!' said Mrs Britain, unbonneting her own round countenance (for she and her husband were by this time in the bar), and smoothing her hair with her open hands. 'Give us a kiss, old man.'

Mr Britain promptly complied.

'I think,' said Mrs Britain, applying herself to her pockets and drawing forth an immense bulk of thin books and crumpled papers, a very kennel of dogs'-ears: 'I've done everything. Bills all settled – turnips sold – brewer's account looked into and paid – 'bacco pipes ordered – seventeen pound four, paid into the bank – Dr Heathfield's charge for little Clem – you'll guess what that is – Dr Heathfield won't take nothing again, Ben.'

'I thought he wouldn't,' returned Britain.

'No. He says whatever family you was to have, Ben, he'd never put you to the cost of a halfpenny. Not if you was to have twenty.'

Mr Britain's face assumed a serious expression, and he looked hard at the wall.

'An't it kind of him?' said Clemency.

'Very,' returned Mr Britain. 'It's the sort of kindness that I wouldn't presume upon, on any account.'

'No,' retorted Clemency. 'Of course not. Then there's the pony – he fetched eight pound two; and that an't bad, is it?'

'It's very good,' said Ben.

'I'm glad you're pleased!' exclaimed his wife. 'I thought you would be; and I think that's all, and so no more at present from yours and cetrer, C. Britain. Ha, ha, ha! There! Take all the papers, and lock 'em up. Oh! Wait a minute. Here's a printed bill to stick on the wall. Wet from the printer's. How nice it smells!'

'What's this?' said Ben, looking over the document.

'I don't know,' replied his wife. 'I haven't read a word of it.'

' "To be sold by Auction," ' read the host of the Nutmeg Grater, ' "unless previously disposed of by private contract." '

'They always put that,' said Clemency.

'Yes, but they don't always put this,' he returned. 'Look here, "Mansion", &c. – "offices", &c., "shrubberies", &c., "ring fence", &c. "Messrs Snitchey and Craggs", &c., "ornamental portion of the unencumbered freehold property of Michael Warden, Esquire, intending to continue to reside abroad"!'

'Intending to continue to reside abroad!' repeated Clemency.

'Here it is,' said Britain. 'Look!'

'And it was only this very day that I heard it whispered at the old house, that better and plainer news had been half promised of her, soon!' said Clemency, shaking her head sorrowfully, and patting her elbows as if the recollection of old times unconsciously awakened her old habits. 'Dear, dear, dear! There'll be heavy hearts, Ben, yonder.'

Mr Britain heaved a sigh, and shook his head, and said he couldn't make it out: he had left off trying long ago. With that remark, he applied himself to putting up the bill just inside the bar window: and Clemency, after meditating in silence for a few moments, roused herself, cleared her thoughtful brow, and bustled off to look after the children.

Though the host of the Nutmeg Grater had a lively regard for his goodwife, it was of the old patronising kind; and she amused him mightily. Nothing would have astonished him so much, as to have known for certain from any third party, that it was she who managed the whole house, and made him, by her plain straightforward thrift, good-humour, honesty, and industry, a thriving man. So easy it is, in any degree of life (as the world very often finds it), to take those cheerful natures that never assert their merit, at their own modest valuation; and to conceive a flippant liking of people for their outward oddities and eccentricities, whose innate worth, if we would look so far, might make us blush in the comparison!

It was comfortable to Mr Britain, to think of his own condescension in having married Clemency. She was a perpetual testimony to him of the goodness of his heart, and the kindness of his disposition; and he felt that her being an excellent wife was an illustration of the old precept that virtue is its own reward.

He had finished wafering up the bill, and had locked the vouchers for her day's proceedings in the cupboard – chuckling all the time, over her capacity for business – when, returning with the news that the two Master Britains were playing in the coach-house, under the superintendence of one Betsey, and that little Clem was sleeping 'like a picture,' she sat down to tea, which had awaited her arrival on a little table. It was a very neat little bar, with the usual display of bottles and glasses; a sedate clock, right to the minute (it was half-past five); everything in its place, and everything furbished and polished up to the very utmost.

'It's the first time I've sat down quietly today, I declare,' said Mrs Britain, taking a long breath, as if she had sat down for the night; but getting up again immediately to hand her husband his tea, and cut him his bread and butter; 'how that bill does set me thinking of old times!'

'Ah!' said Mr Britain, handling his saucer like an oyster, and disposing of its contents on the same principle.

'That same Mr Michael Warden,' said Clemency, shaking her head at the notice of sale, 'lost me my old place.'

'And got you your husband,' said Mr Britain.

'Well! So he did,' retorted Clemency, 'and many thanks to him.'

'Man's the creature of habit,' said Mr Britain, surveying her, over his saucer. 'I had somehow got used to you, Clem; and I found I shouldn't be able to get on without you. So we went and got made man and wife. Ha, ha! We! Who'd have thought it!'

'Who indeed!' cried Clemency. 'It was very good of you, Ben.'

'No, no, no,' replied Mr Britain, with an air of self-denial. 'Nothing worth mentioning.'

'Oh yes it was, Ben,' said his wife, with great simplicity; 'I'm sure I think so; and am very much obliged to you. Ah!' looking again at the bill; 'when she was known to be gone, and out of reach, dear girl, I couldn't help telling – for her sake quite as much as theirs – what I knew, could I?'

'You told it, anyhow,' observed her husband.

'And Dr Jeddler,' pursued Clemency, putting down her teacup, and looking thoughtfully at the bill, 'in his grief and passion turned me out of house and home! I never have been so glad of anything in all my life, as that I didn't say an angry word to him, and hadn't an angry feeling towards him, even then; for he repented that truly, afterwards. How often he has sat in this room, and told me over and over again he was sorry for it! – the last time, only yesterday, when you were out. How often he has sat in this room and talked to me, hour after hour, about one thing and another, in which he made believe to be interested! – but only for the sake of the days that are gone away, and because he knows she used to like me, Ben!'

'Why, how did you ever come to catch a glimpse of that, Clem?' asked her husband; astonished that she should have a distinct perception of a truth which had only dimly suggested itself to his enquiring mind.

'I don't know I'm sure,' said Clemency, blowing her tea, to cool it. 'Bless you, I couldn't tell you if you was to offer me a reward of a hundred pound.'

He might have pursued this metaphysical subject but for her catching a glimpse of a substantial fact behind him, in the shape of a gentleman attired in mourning, and cloaked and booted like a rider on horseback, who stood at the bar-door. He seemed attentive to their conversation, and not at all impatient to interrupt it.

Clemency hastily rose at this sight. Mr Britain also rose and saluted the guest. 'Will you please to walk up stairs, sir? There's a very nice room up stairs, sir.'

'Thank you,' said the stranger, looking earnestly at Mr Britain's wife. 'May I come in here?'

'Oh, surely, if you like, sir,' returned Clemency, admitting him. 'What would you please to want, sir?'

The bill had caught his eye, and he was reading it.

'Excellent property that, sir,' observed Mr Britain.

He made no answer; but turning round, when he had finished reading, looked at Clemency with the same observant curiosity as before. 'You were asking me,' he said, still looking at her –

'What you would please to take, sir,' answered Clemency, stealing a glance at him in return.

'If you will let me have a draught of ale,' he said, moving to a table by the window, 'and will let me have it here, without being any interruption to your meal, I shall be much obliged to you.'

He sat down as he spoke, without any further parley, and looked out at the prospect. He was an easy, well-knit figure of a man in the prime of life. His face, much browned by the sun, was shaded by a quantity of dark hair; and he wore a moustache. His beer being set before him, he filled out a glass, and drank, good-humouredly, to the house; adding, as he put the tumbler down again: 'It's a new house, is it not?'

'Not particularly new, sir,' replied Mr Britain.

'Between five and six years old,' said Clemency: speaking very distinctly.

'I think I heard you mention Dr Jeddler's name, as I came in,' enquired the stranger. 'That bill reminds me of him; for I happen to know something of that story, by hearsay, and through certain connections of mine – Is the old man living?'

'Yes, he's living, sir,' said Clemency.

'Much changed?'

'Since when, sir?' returned Clemency, with remarkable emphasis and expression.

'Since his daughter – went away.'

'Yes! he's greatly changed since then,' said Clemency. 'He's grey and old, and hasn't the same way with him at all; but I think he's happy now. He has taken on with his sister since then, and goes to see her very often. That did him good directly. At first, he was sadly broken down; and it was enough to make one's heart bleed, to see him wandering about, railing at the world; but a great change for the better came over him after a year or two, and then he began to like to talk about his lost daughter, and to praise her, ay and the world too! and was never tired of saying, with the tears in his poor eyes, how beautiful and good she was. He had forgiven her then. That was about the same time as Miss Grace's marriage. Britain, you remember?'

Mr Britain remembered very well.

'The sister *is* married then,' returned the stranger. He paused for some time before he asked, 'To whom?'

Clemency narrowly escaped oversetting the tea-board, in her emotion at this question.

'Did *you* never hear?' she said.

'I should like to hear,' he replied, as he filled his glass again, and raised it to his lips.

'Ah! It would be a long story, if it was properly told,' said Clemency, resting her chin on the palm of her left hand, and supporting that elbow on her right hand, as she shook her head, and looked back through the intervening years, as if she were looking at a fire. 'It would be a long story, I am sure.'

'But told as a short one,' suggested the stranger.

'Told as a short one,' repeated Clemency in the same thoughtful tone, and without any apparent reference to him, or consciousness of having auditors, 'what would there be to tell? That they grieved together, and remembered her together, like a person dead; that they were so tender of her, never would reproach her, called her back to one another as she used to be, and found excuses for her? Everyone knows that. I'm sure *I* do. No one better,' added Clemency, wiping her eyes with her hand.

'And so,' suggested the stranger.

'And so,' said Clemency, taking him up mechanically, and without any change in her attitude or manner, 'they at last were married. They were married on her birthday – it comes round again tomorrow – very quiet, very humble like, but very happy. Mr Alfred said, one night when they were walking in the orchard, "Grace, shall our wedding-day be Marion's birthday?" And it was.'

'And they have lived happily together?' said the stranger.

'Ay,' said Clemency. 'No two people ever more so. They have had no sorrow but this.'

She raised her head as with a sudden attention to the circumstances under which she was recalling these events, and looked quickly at the stranger. Seeing that his face was turned toward the window, and that he seemed intent upon the prospect, she made some eager signs to her husband, and pointed to the bill, and moved her mouth as if she were repeating with great energy, one word or phrase to him over and over again. As she uttered no sound, and as her dumb motions like most of her gestures were of a very extraordinary kind, this unintelligible conduct reduced Mr Britain to the confines of despair. He stared at the table, at the stranger, at the spoons, at his wife – followed her pantomime with looks of deep amazement and perplexity – asked in the same language, was it property in danger, was it he in danger, was it she – answered her signals with other signals expressive of the deepest distress and confusion – followed the motions of her lips – guessed half aloud 'milk and water', 'monthly warning', 'mice and walnuts' – and couldn't approach her meaning.

Clemency gave it up at last, as a hopeless attempt; and moving her chair by very slow degrees a little nearer to the stranger, sat with her eyes apparently cast down but glancing sharply at him now and then, waiting until he should ask some other question. She had not to wait long; for he said, presently: 'And what is the after history of the young lady who went away? They know it, I suppose?'

Clemency shook her head. 'I've heard,' she said, 'that Dr Jeddler is thought to know more of it than he tells. Miss Grace has had letters from her sister, saying that she was well and happy, and made much happier by her being married to Mr Alfred: and has written letters back. But there's a mystery about her life and fortunes, altogether, which nothing has cleared up to this hour, and which – '

She faltered here, and stopped.

'And which – ' repeated the stranger.

'Which only one other person, I believe, could explain,' said Clemency, drawing her breath quickly.

'Who may that be?' asked the stranger.

'Mr Michael Warden!' answered Clemency, almost in a shriek; at once conveying to her husband what she would have had him understand before, and letting Michael Warden know that he was recognised.

'You remember me, sir?' said Clemency, trembling with emotion; 'I saw just now you did! You remember me, that night in the garden. I was with her!'

'Yes. You were,' he said.

'Yes, sir,' returned Clemency. 'Yes, to be sure. This is my husband, if you please. Ben, my dear Ben, run to Miss Grace – run to Mr Alfred – run somewhere, Ben! Bring somebody here, directly!'

'Stay!' said Michael Warden, quietly interposing himself between the door and Britain. 'What would you do?'

'Let them know that you are here, sir,' answered Clemency, clapping her hands in sheer agitation. 'Let them know that they may hear of her, from your own lips; let them know that she is not quite lost to them, but that she will come home again yet, to bless her father and her loving sister – even her old servant, even me,' she struck herself upon the breast with both hands, 'with a sight of her sweet face. Run, Ben, run!' And still she pressed him on towards the door, and still Mr Warden stood before it, with his hand stretched out, not angrily, but sorrowfully.

'Or perhaps,' said Clemency, running past her husband, and catching in her emotion at Mr Warden's cloak, 'perhaps she's here now; perhaps she's close by. I think from your manner she is. Let me see her, sir, if you please. I waited on her when she was a little child. I saw her grow to be the pride of all this place. I knew her when she was Mr Alfred's promised wife. I tried to warn her when you tempted her away. I know what her old home was when she was like the soul of it, and how it changed when she was gone and lost. Let me speak to her, if you please!'

He gazed at her with compassion, not unmixed with wonder: but he made no gesture of assent.

'I don't think she *can* know,' pursued Clemency, 'how truly they forgive her; how they love her; what joy it would be to them, to see her once more. She may be timorous of going home. Perhaps if she sees me, it may give her new heart. Only tell me truly, Mr Warden, is she with you?'

'She is not,' he answered, shaking his head.

This answer, and his manner, and his black dress, and his coming back so quietly, and his announced intention of continuing to live abroad, explained it all. Marion was dead.

He didn't contradict her; yes, she was dead! Clemency sat down, hid her face upon the table, and cried.

At that moment, a grey-headed old gentleman came running in quite out of breath, and panting so much that his voice was scarcely to be recognised as the voice of Mr Snitchey.

'Good Heaven, Mr Warden!' said the lawyer, taking him aside, 'what wind has blown – ' He was so blown himself, that he couldn't get on any further until after a pause, when he added, feebly, 'you here?'

'An ill wind, I am afraid,' he answered. 'If you could have heard what has just passed – how I have been besought and entreated to perform impossibilities – what confusion and affliction I carry with me!'

'I can guess it all. But why did you ever come here, my good sir?' retorted Snitchey.

'Come! How should I know who kept the house? When I sent my servant on to you, I strolled in here because the place was new to me; and

I had a natural curiosity in everything new and old, in these old scenes; and it was outside the town. I wanted to communicate with you first, before appearing there. I wanted to know what people would say to me. I see by your manner that you can tell me. If it were not for your confounded caution, I should have been possessed of everything long ago.'

'Our caution!' returned the lawyer. 'Speaking for Self and Craggs – deceased,' here Mr Snitchey, glancing at his hat-band, shook his head, 'how can you reasonably blame us, Mr Warden? It was understood between us that the subject was never to be renewed, and that it wasn't a subject on which grave and sober men like us (I made a note of your observations at the time) could interfere. Our caution too! When Mr Craggs, sir, went down to his respected grave in the full belief – '

'I had given a solemn promise of silence until I should return, whenever that might be,' interrupted Mr Warden; 'and I have kept it.'

'Well, sir, and I repeat it,' returned Mr Snitchey, 'we were bound to silence too. We were bound to silence in our duty towards ourselves, and in our duty towards a variety of clients, you among them, who were as close as wax. It was not our place to make enquiries of you on such a delicate subject. I had my suspicions, sir; but it is not six months since I have known the truth, and been assured that you lost her.'

'By whom?' enquired his client.

'By Dr Jeddler himself, sir, who at last reposed that confidence in me voluntarily. He, and only he, has known the whole truth, years and years.'

'And you know it?' said his client.

'I do, sir!' replied Snitchey; 'and I have also reason to know that it will be broken to her sister tomorrow evening. They have given her that promise. In the meantime, perhaps you'll give me the honour of your company at my house; being unexpected at your own. But, not to run the chance of any more such difficulties as you have had here, in case you should be recognised – though you're a good deal changed; I think I might have passed you myself, Mr Warden – we had better dine here, and walk on in the evening. It's a very good place to dine at, Mr Warden: your own property, by the by. Self and Craggs (deceased) took a chop here sometimes, and had it very comfortably served. Mr Craggs, sir,' said Snitchey, shutting his eyes tight for an instant, and opening them again, 'was struck off the roll of life too soon.'

'Heaven forgive me for not condoling with you,' returned Michael Warden, passing his hand across his forehead, 'but I'm like a man in a dream at present. I seem to want my wits. Mr Craggs – yes – I am very sorry we have lost Mr Craggs.' But he looked at Clemency as he said it, and seemed to sympathise with Ben, consoling her.

'Mr Craggs, sir,' observed Snitchey, 'didn't find life, I regret to say, as easy to have and to hold as his theory made it out, or he would have been among us now. It's a great loss to me. He was my right arm, my right leg, my right ear, my right eye, was Mr Craggs. I am paralytic without him. He bequeathed his share of the business to Mrs Craggs, her executors, administrators, and assigns. His name remains in the Firm to this hour. I try, in a childish sort of a way, to make believe, sometimes, that he's alive. You may observe that I speak for Self and Craggs – deceased sir – deceased,' said the tender-hearted attorney, waving his pocket-handkerchief.

Michael Warden, who had still been observant of Clemency, turned to Mr Snitchey when he ceased to speak, and whispered in his ear.

'Ah, poor thing!' said Snitchey, shaking his head. 'Yes. She was always very faithful to Marion. She was always very fond of her. Pretty Marion! Poor Marion! Cheer up, mistress – you *are* married now, you know, Clemency.'

Clemency only sighed, and shook her head.

'Well, well! Wait till tomorrow,' said the lawyer, kindly.

'Tomorrow can't bring back the dead to life, mister,' said Clemency, sobbing.

'No. It can't do that, or it would bring back Mr Craggs, deceased,' returned the lawyer. 'But it may bring some soothing circumstances; it may bring some comfort. Wait till tomorrow!'

So Clemency, shaking his proffered hand, said she would; and Britain, who had been terribly cast down at sight of his despondent wife (which was like the business hanging its head), said that was right; and Mr Snitchey and Michael Warden went up stairs; and there they were soon engaged in a conversation so cautiously conducted, that no murmur of it was audible above the clatter of plates and dishes, the hissing of the frying-pan, the bubbling of saucepans, the low monotonous waltzing of the jack – with a dreadful click every now and then as if it had met with some mortal accident to its head, in a fit of giddiness – and all the other preparations in the kitchen for their dinner.

*   *   *

Tomorrow was a bright and peaceful day; and nowhere were the autumn tints more beautifully seen, than from the quiet orchard of the doctor's house. The snows of many winter nights had melted from that ground, the withered leaves of many summer times had rustled there, since she had fled. The honeysuckle porch was green again, the trees cast bountiful and changing shadows on the grass, the landscape was as tranquil and serene as it had ever been; but where was she!

Not there. Not there. She would have been a stranger sight in her old home now, even than that home had been at first, without her. But a lady sat in the familiar place, from whose heart she had never passed away; in whose true memory she lived, unchanging, youthful, radiant with all promise and all hope; in whose affection – and it was a mother's now: there was a cherished little daughter playing by her side – she had no rival; no successor, upon whose gentle lips her name was trembling then.

The spirit of the lost girl looked out of those eyes. Those eyes of Grace, her sister, sitting with her husband in the orchard, on their wedding-day, and his and Marion's birthday.

He had not become a great man; he had not grown rich; he had not forgotten the scenes and friends of his youth: he had not fulfilled any one of the doctor's old predictions. But in his useful, patient, unknown visiting of poor men's homes; and in his watching of sick beds; and in his daily knowledge of the gentleness and goodness flowering the by-paths of the world, not to be trodden down beneath the heavy foot of poverty, but springing up, elastic, in its track, and making its way beautiful; he had better learned and proved, in each succeeding year, the truth of his old faith. The manner of his life, though quiet and remote, had shown him how often men still entertained angels, unawares, as in the olden time; and how the most unlikely forms – even some that were mean and ugly to the view, and poorly clad – became irradiated by the couch of sorrow, want, and pain, and changed to ministering spirits with a glory round their heads.

He lived to better purpose on the altered battleground perhaps, than if he had contended restlessly in more ambitious lists; and he was happy with his wife, dear Grace.

And Marion. Had *he* forgotten her?

'The time has flown, dear Grace,' he said, 'since then;' they had been talking of that night; 'and yet it seems a long long while ago. We count by changes and events within us. Not by years.'

'Yet we have years to count by, too, since Marion was with us,' returned Grace. 'Six times, dear husband, counting tonight as one, we have sat here on her birthday, and spoken together of that happy return, so eagerly expected and so long deferred. Ah when will it be! When will it be!'

Her husband attentively observed her, as the tears collected in her eyes; and drawing nearer, said: 'But Marion told you, in that farewell letter which she left for you upon your table, love, and which you read so often, that years must pass away before it *could* be. Did she not?'

She took a letter from her breast, and kissed it, and said, 'Yes.'

'That through those intervening years, however happy she might be, she would look forward to the time when you would meet again, and all would be made clear: and prayed you, trustfully and hopefully to do the same. The letter runs so, does it not, my dear?'

'Yes, Alfred.'

'And every other letter she has written since?'

'Except the last – some months ago – in which she spoke of you, and what you then knew, and what I was to learn tonight.'

He looked towards the sun, then fast declining, and said that the appointed time was sunset.

'Alfred!' said Grace, laying her hand upon his shoulder earnestly, 'there is something in this letter – this old letter, which you say I read so often – that I have never told you. But, tonight, dear husband, with that sunset drawing near, and all our life seeming to soften and become hushed with the departing day, I cannot keep it secret.'

'What is it, love?'

'When Marion went away, she wrote me, here, that you had once left her a sacred trust to me, and that now she left you, Alfred, such a trust in my hands: praying and beseeching me, as I loved her, and as I loved you, not to reject the affection she believed (she knew, she said) you would transfer to me when the new wound was healed, but to encourage and return it.'

' – And make me a proud, and happy man again, Grace. Did she say so?'

'She meant, to make myself so blest and honoured in your love,' was his wife's answer, as he held her in his arms.

'Hear me, my dear!' he said – 'No. Hear me so!' – and as he spoke, he gently laid the head she had raised, again upon his shoulder. 'I know why I have never heard this passage in the letter, until now. I know why no trace of it ever showed itself in any word or look of yours at that time. I know why Grace, although so true a friend to me, was hard to win to be my wife. And knowing it, my own! I know the priceless value of the heart I gird within my arms, and thank God for the rich possession!'

She wept, but not for sorrow, as he pressed her to his heart. After a brief space, he looked down at the child, who was sitting at their feet, playing with a little basket of flowers, and bade her look how golden and how red the sun was.

'Alfred,' said Grace, raising her head quickly at these words, 'the sun is going down. You have not forgotten what I am to know before it sets.'

'You are to know the truth of Marion's history, my love,' he answered.

'All the truth,' she said, imploringly. 'Nothing veiled from me, any more. That was the promise. Was it not?'

'It was,' he answered.

'Before the sun went down on Marion's birthday. And you see it, Alfred? It is sinking fast.'

He put his arm about her waist; and, looking steadily into her eyes, rejoined,

'That truth is not reserved so long for me to tell, dear Grace. It is to come from other lips.'

'From other lips!' she faintly echoed.

'Yes. I know your constant heart, I know how brave you are, I know that to you a word of preparation is enough. You have said, truly, that the time is come. It is. Tell me that you have present fortitude to bear a trial – a surprise – a shock: and the messenger is waiting at the gate.'

'What messenger?' she said. 'And what intelligence does he bring?'

'I am pledged,' he answered her, preserving his steady look, 'to say no more. Do you think you understand me?'

'I am afraid to think,' she said.

There was that emotion in his face, despite its steady gaze, which frightened her. Again she hid her own face on his shoulder, trembling, and entreated him to pause – a moment.

'Courage, my wife! When you have firmness to receive the messenger, the messenger is waiting at the gate. The sun is setting on Marion's birthday. Courage, courage, Grace!'

She raised her head, and, looking at him, told him she was ready. As she stood, and looked upon him going away, her face was so like Marion's as it had been in her later days at home, that it was wonderful to see. He took the child with him. She called her back – she bore the lost girl's name – and pressed her to her bosom. The little creature, being released again, sped after him, and Grace was left alone.

She knew not what she dreaded, or what hoped; but remained there, motionless, looking at the porch by which they had disappeared.

Ah! what was that, emerging from its shadow; standing on its threshold! That figure, with its white garments rustling in the evening air; its head laid down upon her father's breast, and pressed against it to his loving heart! Oh, God! was it a vision that came bursting from the old man's arms, and with a cry, and with a waving of its hands, and with a wild precipitation of itself upon her in its boundless love, sank down in her embrace!

'Oh, Marion, Marion! Oh, my sister! Oh, my heart's dear love! Oh, joy and happiness unutterable, so to meet again!'

It was no dream, no phantom conjured up by hope and fear, but Marion, sweet Marion! So beautiful, so happy, so unalloyed by care and trial, so elevated and exalted in her loveliness, that as the setting sun shone brightly on her upturned face, she might have been a spirit visiting the earth upon some healing mission.

Clinging to her sister, who had dropped upon a seat, and bent down over her: and smiling through her tears, and kneeling, close before her, with both arms twining round her, and never turning for an instant from her face: and with the glory of the setting sun upon her brow, and with the soft tranquillity of evening gathering around them: Marion at length broke silence; her voice, so calm, low, clear, and pleasant, well-tuned to the time.

'When this was my dear home, Grace, as it will be now, again – '

'Stay, my sweet love! A moment! Oh Marion, to hear you speak again.'

She could not bear the voice she loved so well, at first.

'When this was my dear home, Grace, as it will be now, again, I loved him from my soul. I loved him most devotedly. I would have died for him, though I was so young. I never slighted his affection in my secret breast, for one brief instant. It was far beyond all price to me. Although it is so long ago, and past and gone, and everything is wholly changed, I could not bear to think that you, who love so well, should think I did not truly love him once. I never loved him better, Grace, than when he left this very scene upon this very day. I never loved him better, dear one, than I did that night when I left here.'

Her sister, bending over her, could only look into her face, and hold her fast.

'But he had gained, unconsciously,' said Marion, with a gentle smile, 'another heart, before I knew that I had one to give him. That heart – yours, my sister – was so yielded up, in all its other tenderness, to me; was so devoted, and so noble; that it plucked its love away, and kept its secret from all eyes but mine – Ah! what other eyes were quickened by such tenderness and gratitude! – and was content to sacrifice itself to me. But I knew something of its depths. I knew the struggle it had made. I knew its high, inestimable worth to him, and his appreciation of it, let him love me as he would. I knew the debt I owed it. I had its great example every day before me. What you had done for me, I knew that I could do, Grace, if I would, for you. I never laid my head down on my pillow, but I prayed with tears to do it. I never laid my head down on my pillow, but I thought of Alfred's own words, on the day of his departure, and how truly he had said (for I knew that, by you) that there were victories gained every day, in struggling hearts, to which these fields of battle were as nothing. Thinking more and more upon the great endurance cheerfully sustained, and never known or cared for, that there must be every day and hour, in that great strife of which he spoke, my trial seemed to grow light and easy: and He who knows our hearts, my dearest, at this moment, and who knows there is no drop of bitterness or grief – of anything but unmixed happiness – in mine, enabled me to make the resolution that I never would be Alfred's wife. That he should be my brother, and your husband, if the course I took could bring that happy end to pass; but that I never would (Grace, I then loved him dearly, dearly!) be his wife.'

'Oh Marion! Oh Marion!'

'I had tried to seem indifferent to him;' and she pressed her sister's face against her own; 'but that was hard, and you were always his true advocate. I had tried to tell you of my resolution, but you would never hear me; you would never understand me. The time was drawing near for his return. I felt that I must act, before the daily intercourse between us was renewed. I knew that one great pang, undergone at that time, would save a lengthened agony to all of us. I knew that if I went away then, that end must follow which *has* followed, and which has made us both so happy, Grace! I wrote to good Aunt Martha, for a refuge in her house: I did not then tell her all, but something of my story, and she freely promised it. While I was contesting that step with myself, and with my love of you, and home, Mr Warden, brought here by an accident, became, for some time, our companion.'

'I have sometimes feared of late years, that this might have been,' exclaimed her sister, and her countenance was ashy-pale. 'You never loved him – and you married him in your self-sacrifice to me!'

'He was then,' said Marion, drawing her sister closer to her, 'on the eve of going secretly away for a long time. He wrote to me, after leaving here; told me what his condition and prospects really were; and offered me his hand. He told me he had seen I was not happy in the prospect of Alfred's return. I believe he thought my heart had no part in that contract; perhaps thought I might have loved him once, and did not then; perhaps thought that when I tried to seem indifferent, I tried to hide indifference – I cannot tell. But I wished that you should feel me wholly lost to Alfred – hopeless to him – dead. Do you understand me, love?'

Her sister looked into her face, attentively. She seemed in doubt.

'I saw Mr Warden, and confided in his honour; charged him with my secret, on the eve of his and my departure. He kept it. Do you understand me, dear?'

Grace looked confusedly upon her. She scarcely seemed to hear.

'My love, my sister!' said Marion, 'recall your thoughts a moment: listen to me. Do not look so strangely on me. There are countries, dearest, where those who would abjure a misplaced passion, or would strive against some cherished feeling of their hearts and conquer it, retire into a hopeless solitude, and close the world against themselves and worldly loves and hopes for ever. When women do so, they assume that name which is so dear to you and me, and call each other sisters. But there may be sisters, Grace, who, in the broad world out of doors, and underneath its free sky, and in its crowded places, and among its busy life, and trying to assist and cheer it and to do some good – learn the same lesson; and, with hearts still fresh and young, and open to all happiness and means of happiness, can say the battle is long past, the victory long won. And such a one am I! You understand me now?'

Still she looked fixedly upon her, and made no reply.

'Oh, Grace, dear Grace,' said Marion, clinging yet more tenderly and fondly to that breast from which she had been so long exiled, 'if you were not a happy wife and mother – if I had no little namesake here – if Alfred, my kind brother, were not your own fond husband – from whence could I derive the ecstasy I feel tonight! But as I left here, so I have returned.

My heart has known no other love, my hand has never been bestowed apart from it: I am still your maiden sister, unmarried, unbetrothed: your own old loving Marion, in whose affection you exist alone, and have no partner, Grace!'

She understood her now. Her face relaxed; sobs came to her relief; and falling on her neck, she wept and wept, and fondled her as if she were a child again.

When they were more composed, they found that the doctor, and his sister, good Aunt Martha, were standing near at hand, with Alfred.

'This is a weary day for me,' said good Aunt Martha, smiling through her tears, as she embraced her nieces; 'for I lose my dear companion in making you all happy; and what can you give me in return for my Marion?'

'A converted brother,' said the doctor.

'That's something, to be sure,' retorted Aunt Martha, 'in such a farce as –'

'No, pray don't,' said the doctor penitently.

'Well, I won't,' replied Aunt Martha. 'But I consider myself ill-used. I don't know what's to become of me without my Marion, after we have lived together half a dozen years.'

'You must come and live here, I suppose,' replied the doctor. 'We shan't quarrel now, Martha.'

'Or get married, aunt,' said Alfred.

'Indeed,' returned the old lady, 'I think it might be a good speculation if I were to set my cap at Michael Warden, who, I hear, is come home much the better for his absence, in all respects. But as I knew him when he was a boy, and I was not a very young woman then, perhaps he mightn't respond. So I'll make up my mind to go and live with Marion, when she marries, and until then (it will not be very long, I dare say) to live alone. What do you say, brother?'

'I've a great mind to say it's a ridiculous world altogether, and there's nothing serious in it,' observed the poor old doctor.

'You might take twenty affidavits of it if you chose, Anthony,' said his sister; 'but nobody would believe you with such eyes as those.'

'It's a world full of hearts,' said the doctor; hugging his younger daughter, and bending across her to hug Grace – for he couldn't separate the sisters; 'and a serious world, with all its folly – even with mine, which was enough to have swamped the whole globe; and a world on which the sun never rises, but it looks upon a thousand bloodless battles that are some set-off against the miseries and wickedness of battlefields; and a world we need be careful how we libel, Heaven forgive us, for it is a world of sacred mysteries, and its Creator only knows what lies beneath the surface of His lightest image!'

*   *   *

You would not be the better pleased with my rude pen, if it dissected and laid open to your view the transports of this family, long severed and now reunited. Therefore, I will not follow the poor doctor through his humbled recollection of the sorrow he had had, when Marion was lost to him; nor will I tell how serious he had found that world to be in which some love deep-anchored, is the portion of all human creatures; nor how such a trifle as the absence of one little unit in the great absurd account, had stricken him to the ground. Nor how, in compassion for his distress, his sister had, long ago, revealed the truth to him by slow degrees; and brought him to the knowledge of the heart of his self-banished daughter, and to that daughter's side.

Nor how Alfred Heathfield had been told the truth, too, in the course of that then current year; and Marion had seen him, and had promised him, as her brother, that on her birthday, in the evening, Grace should know it from her lips at last.

'I beg your pardon, doctor,' said Mr Snitchey, looking into the orchard, 'but have I liberty to come in?'

Without waiting for permission, he came straight to Marion, and kissed her hand, quite joyfully.

'If Mr Craggs had been alive, my dear Miss Marion,' said Mr Snitchey, 'he would have had great interest in this occasion. It might have suggested to him, Mr Alfred, that our life is not too easy, perhaps; that, taken altogether, it will bear any little smoothing we can give it; but Mr Craggs was a man who could endure to be convinced, sir. He was always open to conviction. If he were open to conviction, now, I – this is weakness. Mrs Snitchey, my dear,' – at his summons that lady appeared from behind the door, 'you are among old friends.'

Mrs Snitchey having delivered her congratulations, took her husband aside.

'One moment, Mr Snitchey,' said that lady. 'It is not in my nature to rake up the ashes of the departed.'

'No, my dear,' returned her husband.

'Mr Craggs is – '

'Yes, my dear, he is deceased,' said Mr Snitchey.

'But I ask you if you recollect,' pursued his wife, 'that evening of the ball. I only ask you that. If you do; and if your memory has not entirely failed you, Mr Snitchey; and if you are not absolutely in your dotage; I ask you to connect this time with that – to remember how I begged and prayed you, on my knees – '

'Upon your knees, my dear?' said Mr Snitchey.

'Yes,' said Mrs Snitchey, confidently, 'and you know it – to beware of that man – to observe his eye – and now to tell me whether I was right, and whether at that moment he knew secrets which he didn't choose to tell.'

'Mrs Snitchey,' returned her husband, in her ear, 'Madam. Did you ever observe anything in *my* eye?'

'No,' said Mrs Snitchey, sharply. 'Don't flatter yourself.'

'Because, ma'am, that night,' he continued, twitching her by the sleeve, 'it happens that we both knew secrets which we didn't choose to tell, and both knew just the same, professionally. And so the less you say about such things the better, Mrs Snitchey; and take this as a warning to have wiser and more charitable eyes another time. Miss Marion, I brought a friend of yours along with me. Here! mistress.'

Poor Clemency, with her apron to her eyes, came slowly in, escorted by her husband; the latter doleful with the presentiment, that if she abandoned herself to grief, the Nutmeg Grater was done for.

'Now, mistress,' said the lawyer, checking Marion as she ran towards her, and interposing himself between them, 'what's the matter with *you*?'

'The matter!' cried poor Clemency.

When, looking up in wonder, and in indignant remonstrance, and in the added emotion of a great roar from Mr Britain, and seeing that sweet face so well-remembered close before her, she stared, sobbed, laughed, cried, screamed, embraced her, held her fast, released her, fell on Mr Snitchey and embraced him (much to Mrs Snitchey's indignation), fell on the doctor and embraced him, fell on Mr Britain and embraced him, and concluded by embracing herself, throwing her apron over her head, and going into hysterics behind it.

A stranger had come into the orchard, after Mr Snitchey, and had remained apart, near the gate, without being observed by any of the group; for they had little spare attention to bestow, and that had been monopolised by the ecstasies of Clemency. He did not appear to wish to be observed, but stood alone, with downcast eyes; and there was an air of dejection about him (though he was a gentleman of a gallant appearance) which the general happiness rendered more remarkable.

None but the quick eyes of Aunt Martha, however, remarked him at all; but almost as soon as she espied him, she was in conversation with him. Presently, going to where Marion stood with Grace and her little namesake, she whispered something in Marion's ear, at which she started, and appeared surprised; but soon recovering from her confusion, she timidly approached the stranger, in Aunt Martha's company, and engaged in conversation with him too.

'Mr Britain,' said the lawyer, putting his hand in his pocket, and bringing out a legal-looking document, while this was going on, 'I congratulate you. You are now the whole and sole proprietor of that freehold tenement, at present occupied and held by yourself as a licensed tavern, or house of public entertainment, and commonly called or known by the sign of the Nutmeg Grater. Your wife lost one house, through my client Mr Michael Warden; and now gains another. I shall have the pleasure of canvassing you for the county, one of these fine mornings.'

'Would it make any difference in the vote if the sign was altered, sir?' asked Britain.

'Not in the least,' replied the lawyer.

'Then,' said Mr Britain, handing him back the conveyance, 'just clap in the words, "and Thimble", will you be so good; and I'll have the two mottoes painted up in the parlour, instead of my wife's portrait.'

'And let me,' said a voice behind them; it was the stranger's – Michael Warden's; 'let me claim the benefit of those inscriptions. Mr Heathfield and Dr Jeddler, I might have deeply wronged you both. That I did not, is no virtue of my own. I will not say that I am six years wiser than I was, or better. But I have known, at any rate, that term of self-reproach. I can urge no reason why you should deal gently with me. I abused the hospitality of this house and learnt my own demerits, with a shame I never have forgotten, yet with some profit too I would fain hope, from one,' he glanced at Marion, 'to whom I made my humble supplication for forgiveness, when I knew her merit and my deep unworthiness. In a few days I shall quit this place for ever. I entreat your pardon. Do as you would be done by! Forget and forgive!'

*   *   *

TIME – from whom I had the latter portion of this story, and with whom I have the pleasure of a personal acquaintance of some five-and-thirty-years' duration – informed me, leaning easily upon his scythe, that Michael Warden never went away again, and never sold his house, but opened it afresh, maintained a golden mean of hospitality, and had a wife, the pride and honour of that countryside, whose name was Marion. But as I have observed that Time confuses facts occasionally, I hardly know what weight to give to his authority.

THE HAUNTED MAN

And the Ghost's Bargain

CHAPTER 1

The Gift Bestowed

Everybody said so.

Far be it from me to assert that what everybody says must be true. Everybody is, often, as likely to be wrong as right. In the general experience, everybody has been wrong so often, and it has taken, in most instances, such a weary while to find out how wrong, that the authority is proved to be fallible. Everybody may sometimes be right; 'but *that's* no rule,' as the ghost of Giles Scroggins says in the ballad.

The dread word, ghost, recalls me.

Everybody said he looked like a haunted man. The extent of my present claim for everybody is that they were so far right. He did.

Who could have seen his hollow cheek; his sunken brilliant eye; his black-attired figure, indefinably grim, although well knit and well proportioned; his grizzled hair hanging, like tangled seaweed, about his face – as if he had been, through his whole life, a lonely mark for the chafing and beating of the great deep of humanity, but might have said he looked like a haunted man?

Who could have observed his manner, taciturn, thoughtful, gloomy, shadowed by habitual reserve, retiring always and jocund never, with a distraught air of reverting to a bygone place and time, or of listening to some old echoes in his mind, but might have said it was the manner of a haunted man?

Who could have heard his voice, slow-speaking, deep, and grave, with a natural fullness and melody in it which he seemed to set himself against and stop, but might have said it was the voice of a haunted man?

Who that had seen him in his inner chamber, part library and part laboratory – for he was, as the world knew, far and wide, a learned man in chemistry, and a teacher on whose lips and hands a crowd of aspiring ears and eyes hung daily – who that had seen him there, upon a winter night, alone, surrounded by his drugs and instruments and books; the shadow of his shaded lamp a monstrous beetle on the wall, motionless among a crowd of spectral shapes raised there by the flickering of the fire upon the quaint objects around him; some of these phantoms (the reflection of glass vessels that held liquids), trembling at heart like things that knew his power to uncombine them, and to give back their component parts to fire and vapour; who that had seen him then, his work done, and he pondering in his chair before the rusted grate and red flame, moving his thin mouth as if in speech, but silent as the dead, would not have said that the man seemed haunted and the chamber too?

Who might not, by a very easy flight of fancy, have believed that everything about him took this haunted tone, and that he lived on haunted ground?

His dwelling was so solitary and vaultlike – an old, retired part of an ancient endowment for students, once a brave edifice, planted in an open place, but now the obsolete whim of forgotten architects; smoke-age-and-weather-darkened, squeezed on every side by the overgrowing of the great city, and choked, like an old well, with stones and bricks; its small quadrangles, lying down in very pits formed by the streets and buildings, which, in course of time, had been constructed above its heavy chimney stacks; its old trees, insulted by the neighbouring smoke, which deigned to droop so low when it was very feeble and the weather very moody; its grass-plots, struggling with the mildewed earth to be grass, or to win any show of compromise; its silent pavements, unaccustomed to the tread of feet, and even to the observation of eyes, except when a stray face looked down from the upper world, wondering what nook it was; its sundial in a little bricked-up corner, where no sun had straggled for a hundred years, but where, in compensation for the sun's neglect, the snow would lie for weeks when it lay nowhere else, and the black east wind would spin like a huge humming-top, when in all other places it was silent and still.

His dwelling, at its heart and core – within doors – at his fireside – was so lowering and old, so crazy, yet so strong, with its worm-eaten beams of wood in the ceiling, and its sturdy floor shelving downward to the great oak chimney-piece; so environed and hemmed in by the pressure of the town, yet so remote in fashion, age, and custom; so quiet, yet so thundering with echoes when a distant voice was raised or a door was shut – echoes, not confined to the many low passages and empty rooms, but rumbling and grumbling till they were stifled in the heavy air of the forgotten crypt where the Norman arches were half-buried in the earth.

You should have seen him in his dwelling about twilight, in the dead wintertime.

When the wind was blowing, shrill and shrewd, with the going down of the blurred sun. When it was just so dark, as that the forms of things were indistinct and big – but not wholly lost. When sitters by the fire began to see wild faces and figures, mountains and abysses, ambuscades and armies, in the coals. When people in the streets bent down their heads and ran before the weather. When those who were obliged to meet it, were stopped at angry corners, stung by wandering snowflakes alighting on the lashes of their eyes – which fell too sparingly, and were blown away too quickly, to leave a trace upon the frozen ground. When windows of private houses closed up tight and warm. When lighted gas began to burst forth in the busy and the quiet streets, fast blackening otherwise. When stray pedestrians, shivering along the latter, looked down at the glowing fires in kitchens, and sharpened their sharp appetites by sniffing up the fragrance of whole miles of dinners.

When travellers by land were bitter cold, and looked wearily on gloomy landscapes, rustling and shuddering in the blast. When mariners at sea, outlying upon icy yards, were tossed and swung above the howling ocean dreadfully. When lighthouses, on rocks and headlands, showed solitary and watchful; and benighted seabirds breasted on against their ponderous lanterns, and fell dead. When little readers of storybooks, by the firelight, trembled to think of Cassim Baba cut into quarters, hanging in the Robbers' Cave, or had some small misgivings that the fierce little old woman, with the crutch, who used to start out of the box in the merchant Abudah's bedroom, might, one of these nights, be found upon the stairs, in the long, cold, dusky journey up to bed.

When, in rustic places, the last glimmering of daylight died away from the ends of avenues; and the trees, arching overhead, were sullen and black. When, in parks and woods, the high wet fern and sodden moss, and beds of fallen leaves, and trunks of trees, were lost to view, in masses of impenetrable shade. When mists arose from dyke, and fen, and river. When lights in old halls, and in cottage windows, were a cheerful sight. When the mill stopped, the wheelwright and the blacksmith shut their workshops, the turnpike-gate closed, the plough and harrow were left lonely in the fields, the labourer and team went home, and the striking of the church clock had a deeper sound than at noon, and the churchyard wicket would be swung no more that night.

When twilight everywhere released the shadows, prisoned up all day, that now closed in and gathered like mustering swarms of ghosts. When they stood lowering, in corners of rooms, and frowned out from behind half-opened doors. When they had full possession of unoccupied apartments. When they danced upon the floors, and walls, and ceilings of inhabited chambers, while the fire was low, and withdrew like ebbing waters when it sprang into a blaze. When they fantastically mocked the shapes of household objects, making the nurse an ogress, the rocking-horse a monster, the wondering child, half-scared and half-amused, a stranger to itself – the very tongs upon the hearth, a straddling giant with his arms akimbo, evidently smelling the blood of Englishmen, and wanting to grind people's bones to make his bread.

When these shadows brought into the minds of older people other thoughts, and showed them different images. When they stole from their retreats, in the likenesses of forms and faces from the past, from the grave, from the deep, deep gulf, where the things that might have been, and never were, are always wandering.

When he sat, as already mentioned, gazing at the fire. When, as it rose and fell, the shadows went and came. When he took no heed of them, with his bodily eyes; but, let them come or let them go, looked fixedly at the fire. You should have seen him, then.

When the sounds that had arisen with the shadows, and come out of their lurking-places at the twilight summons, seemed to make a deeper stillness all about him. When the wind was rumbling in the chimney, and sometimes crooning, sometimes howling, in the house. When the old trees outside were so shaken and beaten, that one querulous old rook, unable to sleep, protested now and then, in a feeble, dozy, high-up 'Caw!' When, at intervals, the window trembled, the rusty vane upon the turret-top complained, the clock beneath it recorded that another quarter of an hour was gone, or the fire collapsed and fell in with a rattle.

When a knock came at his door, in short, as he was sitting so, and roused him.

'Who's that?' said he. 'Come in!'

Surely there had been no figure leaning on the back of his chair; no face looking over it. It is certain that no gliding footstep touched the floor, as he lifted up his head, with a start, and spoke. And yet there was no mirror in the room on whose surface his own form could have cast its shadow for a moment; and Something had passed darkly and gone!

'I'm humbly fearful, sir,' said a fresh-coloured busy man, holding the door open with his foot for the admission of himself and a wooden tray he carried, and letting it go again by very gentle and careful degrees, when he and the tray had got in, lest it should close noisily, 'that it's a good bit past the time tonight. But Mrs William has been taken off her legs so often – '

'By the wind? Ay! I have heard it rising.'

' – By the wind, sir – that it's a mercy she got home at all. Oh dear, yes. Yes. It was by the wind, Mr Redlaw. By the wind.'

He had, by this time, put down the tray for dinner, and was employed in lighting the lamp, and spreading a cloth on the table. From this employment he desisted in a hurry, to stir and feed the fire, and then resumed it; the lamp he had lighted, and the blaze that rose under his hand, so quickly changing the appearance of the room, that it seemed as if the mere coming in of his fresh red face and active manner had made the pleasant alteration.

'Mrs William is of course subject at any time, sir, to be taken off her balance by the elements. She is not formed superior to *that*.'

'No,' returned Mr Redlaw good-naturedly, though abruptly.

'No, sir. Mrs William may be taken off her balance by Earth; as for example, last Sunday week, when sloppy and greasy, and she going out to tea with her newest sister-in-law, and having a pride in herself, and wishing to appear perfectly spotless though pedestrian. Mrs William may be taken off her balance by Air; as being once over-persuaded by a friend to try a swing at Peckham Fair, which acted on her constitution instantly like a steamboat. Mrs William may be taken off her balance by Fire; as on a false alarm of engines at her mother's, when she went two miles in her nightcap. Mrs William may be taken off her balance by Water; as at Battersea, when rowed into the piers by her young nephew, Charley Swidger junior, aged twelve, which had no idea of boats whatever. But these are elements. Mrs William must be taken out of elements for the strength of *her* character to come into play.'

As he stopped for a reply, the reply was, 'Yes,' in the same tone as before.

'Yes, sir. Oh dear, yes!' said Mr Swidger, still proceeding with his preparations, and checking them off as he made them. 'That's where it is, sir. That's what I always say myself, sir. Such a many of us Swidgers! – Pepper. Why there's my father, sir, superannuated keeper and custodian of this Institution, eigh–ty-seven year old. He's a Swidger! – Spoon.'

'True, William,' was the patient and abstracted answer, when he stopped again.

'Yes, sir,' said Mr Swidger. 'That's what I always say, sir. You may call him the trunk of the tree! – Bread. Then you come to his successor, my unworthy self – Salt – and Mrs William, Swidgers both. – Knife and fork. Then you come to all my brothers and their families, Swidgers, man and woman, boy and girl. Why, what with cousins, uncles, aunts, and relationships of this, that, and t'other degree, and what-not-degree, and marriages, and lyings-in, the Swidgers – Tumbler – might take hold of hands, and make a ring round England!'

Receiving no reply at all here, from the thoughtful man whom he addressed, Mr William approached him nearer, and made a feint of accidentally knocking the table with a decanter, to rouse him. The moment he succeeded, he went on, as if in great alacrity of acquiescence.

'Yes, sir! That's just what I say myself, sir. Mrs William and me have often said so. "There's Swidgers enough," we say, "without *our* voluntary contributions" – Butter. In fact, sir, my father is a family in himself – Castors – to take care of; and it happens all for the best that we have no child of our own, though it's made Mrs William rather quiet-like, too. Quite ready for the fowl and mashed potatoes, sir? Mrs William said she'd dish in ten minutes when I left the Lodge.'

'I am quite ready,' said the other, waking as from a dream, and walking slowly to and fro.

'Mrs William has been at it again, sir!' said the keeper, as he stood warming a plate at the fire, and pleasantly shading his face with it. Mr Redlaw stopped in his walking, and an expression of interest appeared in him.

'What I always say myself, sir. She will do it! There's a motherly feeling in Mrs William's breast that must and will have went.'

'What has she done?'

'Why, sir, not satisfied with being a sort of mother to all the young gentlemen that come up from a variety of parts, to attend your courses of lectures at this ancient foundation – it's surprising how stone-chaney catches the heat this frosty weather, to be sure!' Here he turned the plate, and cooled his fingers.

'Well?' said Mr Redlaw.

'That's just what I say myself, sir,' returned Mr William, speaking over his shoulder, as if in ready and delighted assent. 'That's exactly where it is, sir! There ain't one of our students but appears to regard Mrs William in that light. Every day, right through the course, they puts their heads into the Lodge, one after another, and have all got something to tell her, or something to ask her. "Swidge" is the appellation by which they speak of Mrs William in general, among themselves, I'm told; but that's what I say, sir. Better be called ever so far out of your name, if it's done in real liking, than have it made ever so much of, and not cared about! What's a name for? To know a person by. If Mrs William is known by something better than her name – I allude to Mrs William's qualities and disposition – never mind her name, though it *is* Swidger, by rights. Let 'em call her Swidge, Widge, Bridge – Lord! London Bridge, Blackfriars, Chelsea, Putney, Waterloo or Hammersmith Suspension – if they like.'

The close of this triumphant oration brought him and the plate to the table, upon which he half laid and half dropped it, with a lively sense of its being thoroughly heated, just as the subject of his praises entered the room, bearing another tray and a lantern, and followed by a venerable old man with long grey hair.

Mrs William, like Mr William, was a simple, innocent-looking person, in whose smooth cheeks the cheerful red of her husband's official waist-coat was very pleasantly repeated. But whereas Mr William's light hair stood on end all over his head, and seemed to draw his eyes up with it in an excess of bustling readiness for anything, the dark brown hair of Mrs William was carefully smoothed down, and waved away under a trim tidy cap, in the most exact and quiet manner imaginable. Whereas Mr William's very trousers hitched themselves up at the ankles, as if it were not in their iron-grey nature to rest without looking about them, Mrs William's neatly-flowered skirts – red and white, like her own pretty face – were as composed and orderly, as if the very wind that blew so hard out of doors could not disturb one of their folds. Whereas his coat had something of a fly-away and half-off appearance about the collar and breast, her little bodice was so placid and neat, that there should have been protection for her, in it, had she needed any, with the roughest people. Who could have had the heart to make so calm a bosom swell with grief, or throb with fear, or mutter with a thought of shame! To whom would its repose and peace have not appealed against disturbance, like the innocent slumber of a child!

'Punctual, of course, Milly,' said her husband, relieving her of the tray, 'or it wouldn't be you. Here's Mrs William, sir! – He looks lonelier than ever tonight,' whispering to his wife, as he was taking the tray, 'and ghostlier altogether.'

Without any show of hurry or noise, or any show of herself even, she was so calm and quiet, Milly set the dishes she had brought upon the table – Mr William, after much clattering and running about, having only gained possession of a butter-boat of gravy, which he stood ready to serve.

'What is that the old man has in his arms?' asked Mr Redlaw, as he sat down to his solitary meal.

'Holly, sir,' replied the quiet voice of Milly.

'That's what I say myself, sir,' interposed Mr William, striking in with the butter-boat. 'Berries is so seasonable to the time of year! Brown gravy!'

'Another Christmas come, another year gone!' murmured the chemist, with a gloomy sigh. 'More figures in the lengthening sum of recollection that we work and work at to our torment, till Death idly jumbles all together, and rubs all out. So, Philip!' breaking off, and raising his voice as he addressed the old man, standing apart, with his glistening burden in his arms, from which the quiet Mrs William took small branches, which she noiselessly trimmed with her scissors, and decorated the room with, while her aged father-in-law looked on much interested in the ceremony.

'My duty to you, sir,' returned the old man. 'Should have spoke before, sir, but know your ways, Mr Redlaw – proud to say – and wait till spoke to! Merry Christmas, sir, and

Happy New Year, and many of 'em. Have had a pretty many of 'em myself – ha, ha! – and may take the liberty of wishing 'em. I'm eighty-seven!'

'Have you had so many that were merry and happy?' asked the other.

'Ay, sir, ever so many,' returned the old man.

'Is his memory impaired with age? It is to be expected now,' said Mr Redlaw, turning to the son, and speaking lower.

'Not a morsel of it, sir,' replied Mr William. 'That's exactly what I say myself, sir. There never was such a memory as my father's. He's the most wonderful man in the world. He don't know what forgetting means. It's the very observation I'm always making to Mrs William, sir, if you'll believe me!'

Mr Swidger, in his polite desire to seem to acquiesce at all events, delivered this as if there were no iota of contradiction in it, and it were all said in unbounded and unqualified assent.

The chemist pushed his plate away, and, rising from the table, walked across the room to where the old man stood looking at a little sprig of holly in his hand.

'It recalls the time when many of those years were old and new, then?' he said, observing him attentively, and touching him on the shoulder. 'Does it?'

'Oh many, many!' said Philip, half awaking from his reverie. 'I'm eighty-seven!'

'Merry and happy, was it?' asked the chemist in a low voice. 'Merry and happy, old man?'

'Maybe as high as that, no higher,' said the old man, holding out his hand a little way above the level of his knee, and looking retrospectively at his questioner, 'when I first remember 'em! Cold, sunshiny day it was, out a-walking: when someone – it was my mother as sure as you stand there, though I don't know what her blessed face was like, for she took ill and died that Christmastime – told me they were food for birds. The pretty little fellow thought – that's me, you understand – that birds' eyes were so bright, perhaps, because the berries that they lived on in the winter were so bright. I recollect that. And I'm eighty-seven!'

'Merry and happy!' mused the other, bending his dark eyes upon the stooping figure, with a smile of compassion. 'Merry and happy and remember well?'

'Ay, ay, ay!' resumed the old man, catching the last words. 'I remember 'em well in my school time, year after year, and all the merrymaking that used to come along with them. I was a strong chap then, Mr Redlaw; and, if you'll believe me, hadn't my match at football within ten mile. Where's my son William? Hadn't my match at football, William, within ten mile!'

'That's what I always say, father!' returned the son promptly, and with great respect. 'You are a Swidger, if ever there was one of the family!'

'Dear!' said the old man, shaking his head as he again looked at the holly. 'His mother – my son William's my youngest son – and I, have sat among 'em all, boys and girls, little children and babies, many a year, when the berries like these were not shining half so bright all round us, as their bright faces. Many of 'em are gone; she's gone; and my son George (our eldest, who was her pride more than all the rest!) is fallen very low: but I can see them, when I look here, alive and healthy, as they used to be in those days; and I can see him, thank God, in his innocence. It's a blessed thing to me, at eighty-seven.'

The keen look that had been fixed upon him with so much earnestness, had gradually sought the ground.

'When my circumstances got to be not so good as formerly, through not being honestly dealt by, and I first come here to be custodian,' said the old man, ' – which was upwards of fifty years ago – where's my son William? More than half a century ago, William!'

'That's what I say, father,' replied the son, as promptly and dutifully as before, 'that's exactly where it is. Two times ought's an ought, and twice five ten, and there's a hundred of 'em.'

'It was quite a pleasure to know that one of our founders – or more correctly speaking,' said the old man, with a great glory in his subject and his knowledge of it, 'one of the learned gentlemen that helped endow us in Queen Elizabeth's time, for we were founded afore her day – left in his will, among the other bequests he made us, so much to buy holly, for garnishing the walls and windows, come Christmas. There was something homely and friendly in it. Being but strange here, then, and coming at Christmastime, we took a liking for his very picter that hangs in what used to be, anciently, afore our ten poor gentlemen commuted for an annual stipend in money, our great Dinner Hall. A sedate gentleman in a peaked beard, with a ruff round his neck, and a scroll below him, in old English letters, "Lord! keep my memory green!" You know all about him, Mr Redlaw?'

'I know the portrait hangs there, Philip.'

'Yes, sure, it's the second on the right, above the panelling. I was going to say – he has helped to keep *my* memory green, I thank him; for going round the building every year, as I'm a doing now, and freshening up the bare rooms with these branches and berries, freshens up my bare old brain. One year brings back another, and that year another, and those others numbers! At last, it seems to me as if the birth-time of our Lord was the birth-time of all I have ever had affection for, or mourned for, or delighted in – and they're a pretty many, for I'm eighty-seven!'

'Merry and happy,' murmured Redlaw to himself.

The room began to darken strangely.

'So you see, sir,' pursued old Philip, whose hale wintry cheek had warmed into a ruddier glow, and whose blue eyes had brightened while he spoke, 'I have plenty to keep, when I keep this present season. Now, where's my quiet Mouse? Chattering's the sin of my time of life, and there's half the building to do yet, if the cold don't freeze us first, or the wind don't blow us away, or the darkness don't swallow us up.'

The quiet Mouse had brought her calm face to his side and silently taken his arm, before he finished speaking.

'Come away, my dear,' said the old man. 'Mr Redlaw won't settle to his dinner, otherwise, till it's cold as the winter. I hope you'll excuse me rambling on, sir, and I wish you good-night, and, once again, a merry – '

'Stay!' said Mr Redlaw, resuming his place at the table, more, it would have seemed from his manner, to reassure the old keeper, than in any remembrance of his own appetite. 'Spare me another moment, Philip. William, you were going to tell me something to your excellent wife's honour. It will not be disagreeable to her to hear you praise her. What was it?'

'Why, that's where it is, you see, sir,' returned Mr William Swidger, looking towards his wife in considerable embarrassment. 'Mrs William's got her eye upon me.'

'But you're not afraid of Mrs William's eye?'

'Why, no, sir,' returned Mr Swidger, 'that's what I say myself. It wasn't made to be afraid of. It wouldn't have been made so mild, if that was the intention. But I wouldn't like to – Milly! – him, you know. Down in the Buildings.'

Mr William, standing behind the table, and rummaging disconcertedly among the objects upon it, directed persuasive glances at Mrs William, and secret jerks of his head and thumb at Mr Redlaw, as alluring her towards him.

'Him, you know, my love,' said Mr William. 'Down in the Buildings. Tell, my dear! You're the works of Shakespeare in comparison with myself. Down in the Buildings, you know, my love – Student.'

'Student?' repeated Mr Redlaw, raising his head.

'That's what I say, sir!' cried Mr William, in the utmost animation of assent. 'If it wasn't the poor student down in the Buildings, why should you wish to hear it from Mrs William's lips? Mrs William, my dear – Buildings.'

'I didn't know,' said Milly, with a quiet frankness, free from any haste or confusion, 'that William had said anything about it, or I wouldn't have come. I asked him not to. It's a sick young gentleman, sir – and very poor, I am afraid – who is too ill to go home this holiday-time, and lives, unknown to anyone, in but a common kind of lodging for a gentleman, down in Jerusalem Buildings. That's all, sir.'

'Why have I never heard of him?' said the chemist, rising hurriedly. 'Why has he not made his situation known to me? Sick! give me my hat and cloak. Poor! – what house? – what number?'

'Oh, you mustn't go there, sir,' said Milly, leaving her father-in-law, and calmly confronting him with her collected little face and folded hands.

'Not go there?'

'Oh dear, no!' said Milly, shaking her head as at a most manifest and self-evident impossibility. 'It couldn't be thought of!'

'What do you mean? Why not?'

'Why, you see, sir,' said Mr William Swidger, persuasively and con-fidentially, 'that's what I say. Depend upon it, the young gentleman would never have made his situation known to one of his own sex. Mrs William has got into his confidence, but that's quite different. They all confide in Mrs William; they all trust *her*. A man, sir, couldn't have got a whisper out of him; but woman, sir, and Mrs William combined!'

'There is good sense and delicacy in what you say, William,' returned Mr Redlaw, observant of the gentle and composed face at his shoulder. And laying his finger on his lip, he secretly put his purse into her hand.

'Oh dear no, sir!' cried Milly, giving it back again. 'Worse and worse! Couldn't be dreamed of!'

Such a staid matter-of-fact housewife she was, and so unruffled by the momentary haste of this rejection, that, an instant afterwards, she was tidily picking up a few leaves which had strayed from between her scissors and her apron, when she had arranged the holly.

Finding, when she rose from her stooping posture, that Mr Redlaw was still regarding her with doubt and astonishment, she quietly repeated – looking about, the while, for any other fragments that might have escaped her observation – 'Oh dear no, sir! He said that of all the world he would not be known to you, or receive help from you – though he is a student in your class. I have made no terms of secrecy with you, but I trust to your honour completely.'

'Why did he say so?'

'Indeed I can't tell, sir,' said Milly, after thinking a little, 'because I am not at all clever, you know; and I wanted to be useful to him in making things neat and comfortable about him, and employed myself that way. But I know he is poor, and lonely, and I think he is somehow neglected too. How dark it is!'

The room had darkened more and more. There was a very heavy gloom and shadow gathering behind the chemist's chair.

'What more about him?' he asked.

'He is engaged to be married when he can afford it,' said Milly, 'and is studying, I think, to qualify himself to earn a living. I have seen, a long time, that he has studied hard and denied himself much. How very dark it is!'

'It's turned colder, too,' said the old man, rubbing his hands. 'There's a chill and dismal feeling in the room. Where's my son William? William, my boy, turn the lamp, and rouse the fire!'

Milly's voice resumed, like quiet music very softly played: 'He muttered in his broken sleep yesterday afternoon, after talking to me' (this was to herself) 'about someone dead, and some great wrong done that could never be forgotten; but whether to him or to another person, I don't know. Not *by* him, I am sure.'

'And, in short, Mrs William, you see – which she wouldn't say herself, Mr Redlaw, if she was to stop here till the new year after this next one – ' said Mr William, coming up to him to speak in his ear, 'has done him worlds of good! Bless you, worlds of good! All at home just the same as ever – my father made as snug and comfortable – not a crumb of litter to be found in the house, if you were to offer fifty pound ready money for it – Mrs William apparently never out of the way – yet Mrs William backwards and forwards, backwards and forwards, up and down, up and down, a mother to him!'

The room turned darker and colder, and the gloom and shadow gathering behind the chair was heavier.

'Not content with this, sir, Mrs William goes and finds, this very night, when she was coming home (why it's not above a couple of hours ago), a creature more like a young wild beast than a young child, shivering upon a doorstep. What does Mrs William do but brings it home to dry it, and feed it, and keep it till our old Bounty of food and flannel is given away, on Christmas morning! If it ever felt a fire before, it's as much as ever it did; for it's sitting in the old Lodge chimney, staring at ours as if its ravenous eyes would never shut again. It's sitting there, at least,' said Mr William, correcting himself, on reflection, 'unless it's bolted!'

'Heaven keep her happy!' said the chemist aloud, 'and you too, Philip! and you, William! I must consider what to do in this. I may desire to see this student, I'll not detain you longer now. Good-night!'

'I thank'ee, sir, I thank'ee!' said the old man, 'for Mouse, and for my son William, and for myself. Where's my son William? William, you take the lantern and go on first, through them long dark passages, as you did last year and the year afore. Ha, ha! I remember though I'm eighty-seven! "Lord keep my memory green!" It's a very good prayer, Mr Redlaw, that of the learned gentleman in the peaked beard, with a ruff round his neck – hangs up, second on the right above the panelling, in what used to be, afore our ten poor gentlemen commuted, our great Dinner Hall. "Lord keep my memory green!" It's very good and pious, sir. Amen! Amen!'

As they passed out and shut the heavy door, which, however carefully withheld, fired a long train of thundering reverberations when it shut at last, the room turned darker.

As he fell a musing in his chair alone, the healthy holly withered on the wall, and dropped – dead branches.

As the gloom and shadow thickened behind him, in that place where it had been gathering so darkly, it took, by slow degrees – or out of it there came, by some unreal, unsubstantial process – not to be traced by any human sense – an awful likeness of himself!

Ghastly and cold, colourless in its leaden face and hands, but with his features, and his bright eyes, and his grizzled hair, and dressed in the gloomy shadow of his dress, it came into his terrible appearance of

existence, motionless, without a sound. As *he* leaned his arm upon the elbow of his chair, ruminating before the fire, *it* leaned upon the chair-back, close above him, with its appalling copy of his face looking where his face looked, and bearing the expression his face bore.

This, then, was the Something that had passed and gone already. This was the dread companion of the haunted man!

It took, for some moments, no more apparent heed of him, than he of it. The Christmas waits were playing somewhere in the distance, and, through his thoughtfulness, he seemed to listen to the music. It seemed to listen too.

At length he spoke; without moving or lifting up his face.

'Here again!' he said.

'Here again,' replied the phantom.

'I see you in the fire,' said the haunted man; 'I hear you in music, in the wind, in the dead stillness of the night.'

The phantom moved its head, assenting.

'Why do you come, to haunt me thus?'

'I come as I am called,' replied the ghost.

'No. Unbidden,' exclaimed the chemist.

'Unbidden be it,' said the spectre. 'It is enough I am here.'

Hitherto the light of the fire had shone on the two faces – if the dread lineaments behind the chair might be called a face – both addressed towards it, as at first, and neither looking at the other. But, now, the haunted man turned, suddenly, and stared upon the ghost. The ghost, as sudden in its motion, passed to before the chair, and stared on him.

The living man, and the animated image of himself dead, might so have looked, the one upon the other. An awful survey, in a lonely and remote part of an empty old pile of building, on a winter night, with the loud wind going by upon its journey of mystery – whence, or whither, no man knowing since the world began – and the stars, in unimaginable millions, glittering through it, from eternal space, where the world's bulk is as a grain, and its hoary age is infancy.

'Look upon me!' said the spectre. 'I am he, neglected in my youth, and miserably poor, who strove and suffered, and still strove and suffered, until I hewed out knowledge from the mine where it was buried, and made rugged steps thereof, for my worn feet to rest and rise on.'

'I *am* that man,' returned the chemist.

'No mother's self-denying love,' pursued the phantom, 'no father's counsel, aided *me*. A stranger came into my father's place when I was but a child, and I was easily an alien from my mother's heart. My parents, at the best, were of that sort whose care soon ends, and whose duty is soon done; who cast their offspring loose, early, as birds do theirs; and, if they do well, claim the merit; and, if ill, the pity.'

It paused, and seemed to tempt and goad him with its look, and with the manner of its speech, and with its smile.

'I am he,' pursued the phantom, 'who, in this struggle upward, found a friend. I made him – won him – bound him to me! We worked together, side by side. All the love and confidence that in my earlier youth had had no outlet, and found no expression, I bestowed on him.'

'Not all,' said Redlaw, hoarsely.

'No, not all,' returned the phantom. 'I had a sister.'

The haunted man, with his head resting on his hands, replied, 'I had!' The phantom, with an evil smile, drew closer to the chair, and resting its chin upon its folded hands, its folded hands upon the back, and looking down into his face with searching eyes, that seemed instinct with fire, went on: 'Such glimpses of the light of home as I had ever known, had streamed from her. How young she was, how fair, how loving! I took her to the first poor roof that I was master of, and made it rich. She came into the darkness of my life, and made it bright – She is before me!'

'I saw her, in the fire, but now I hear her in music, in the wind, in the dead stillness of the night,' returned the haunted man.

'*Did* he love her?' said the phantom, echoing his contemplative tone. 'I think he did, once. I am sure he did. Better had she loved him less – less secretly, less dearly, from the shallower depths of a more divided heart!'

'Let me forget it!' said the chemist, with an angry motion of his hand. 'Let me blot it from my memory!'

The spectre, without stirring, and with its unwinking, cruel eyes still fixed upon his face, went on: 'A dream, like hers, stole upon my own life.'

'It did,' said Redlaw.

'A love, as like hers,' pursued the phantom, 'as my inferior nature might cherish, arose in my own heart. I was too poor to bind its object to my fortune then, by any thread of promise or entreaty. I loved her far too well, to seek to do it. But, more than ever I had striven in my life, I strove to climb. Only an inch gained, brought me something nearer to the height. I toiled up! In the late pauses of my labour at that time – my sister (sweet companion!) still sharing with me the expiring embers and the cooling hearth – when day was breaking, what pictures of the future did I see!'

'I saw them, in the fire, but now,' he murmured. 'They come back to me in music, in the wind, in the dead stillness of the night, in the revolving years.'

' – Pictures of my own domestic life, in after-time, with her who was the inspiration of my toil. Pictures of my sister, made the wife of my dear friend, on equal terms – for he had some inheritance, we none – pictures of our sobered age and mellowed happiness, and of the golden links, extending back so far, that should bind us, and our children, in a radiant garland,' said the phantom.

'Pictures,' said the haunted man, 'that were delusions. Why is it my doom to remember them too well!'

'Delusions,' echoed the phantom in its changeless voice, and glaring on him with its changeless eyes. 'For my friend (in whose breast my confidence was locked as in my own), passing between me and the centre of the system of my hopes and struggles, won her to himself, and shattered my frail universe. My sister, doubly dear, doubly devoted, doubly cheerful in my home, lived on to see me famous, and my old ambition so rewarded when its spring was broken, and then –'

'Then died,' he interposed. 'Died, gentle as ever; happy; and with no concern but for her brother. Peace!'

The phantom watched him silently.

'Remembered!' said the haunted man, after a pause. 'Yes. So well remembered, that even now, when years have passed, and nothing is more idle or more visionary to me than the boyish love so long outlived, I think of it with sympathy, as if it were a younger brother's or a son's. Sometimes I even wonder when her heart first inclined to him, and how it had been affected towards me. – Not lightly, once, I think. – But that is nothing. Early unhappiness, a wound from a hand I loved and trusted, and a loss that nothing can replace, outlive such fancies.'

'Thus,' said the phantom, 'I bear within me a Sorrow and a Wrong. Thus I prey upon myself. Thus, memory is my curse; and, if I could forget my sorrow and my wrong, I would!'

'Mocker!' said the chemist, leaping up, and making, with a wrathful hand, at the throat of his other self. 'Why have I always that taunt in my ears?'

'Forbear!' exclaimed the spectre in an awful voice. 'Lay a hand on Me, and die!'

He stopped midway, as if its words had paralysed him, and stood looking on it. It had glided from him; it had its arm raised high in warning; and a smile passed over its unearthly features, as it reared its dark figure in triumph.

'If I could forget my sorrow and my wrong, I would,' the ghost repeated. 'If I could forget my sorrow and my wrong, I would!'

'Evil spirit of myself,' returned the haunted man, in a low, trembling tone, 'my life is darkened by that incessant whisper.'

'It is an echo,' said the phantom.

'If it be an echo of my thoughts – as now, indeed, I know it is,' rejoined the haunted man, 'why should I, therefore, be tormented? It is not a selfish thought. I suffer it to range beyond myself. All men and women have their sorrows – most of them their wrongs; ingratitude, and sordid jealousy, and interest, besetting all degrees of life. Who would not forget their sorrows and their wrongs?'

'Who would not, truly, and be the happier and better for it?' said the phantom.

'These revolutions of years, which we commemorate,' proceeded Redlaw, 'what do *they* recall! Are there any minds in which they do not reawaken some sorrow, or some trouble? What is the remembrance of the old man who was here tonight? A tissue of sorrow and trouble.'

'But common natures,' said the phantom, with its evil smile upon its glassy face, 'unenlightened minds and ordinary spirits, do not feel or reason on these things like men of higher cultivation and profounder thought.'

'Tempter,' answered Redlaw, 'whose hollow look and voice I dread more than words can express, and from whom some dim foreshadowing of greater fear is stealing over me while I speak, I hear again an echo of my own mind.'

'Receive it as a proof that I am powerful,' returned the ghost. 'Hear what I offer! Forget the sorrow, wrong, and trouble you have known!'

'Forget them!' he repeated.

'I have the power to cancel their remembrance – to leave but very faint, confused traces of them, that will die out soon,' returned the spectre. 'Say! Is it done?'

'Stay!' cried the haunted man, arresting by a terrified gesture the uplifted hand. 'I tremble with distrust and doubt of you; and the dim fear you cast upon me deepens into a nameless horror I can hardly bear. I would not deprive myself of any kindly recollection, or any sympathy that is good for me, or others. What shall I lose, if I assent to this? What else will pass from my remembrance?'

'No knowledge; no result of study; nothing but the intertwisted chain of feelings and associations, each in its turn dependent on, and nourished by, the banished recollections. Those will go.'

'Are they so many?' said the haunted man, reflecting in alarm.

'They have been wont to show themselves in the fire, in music, in the wind, in the dead stillness of the night, in the revolving years,' returned the phantom scornfully.

'In nothing else?'

The phantom held its peace.

But having stood before him, silent, for a little while, it moved towards the fire; then stopped.

'Decide!' it said, 'before the opportunity is lost!'

'A moment! I call heaven to witness,' said the agitated man, 'that I have never been a hater of my kind – never morose, indifferent, or hard, to anything around me. If, living here alone, I have made too much of all that was and might have been, and too little of what is, the evil, I believe, has fallen on me, and not on others. But, if there were poison in my body, should I not, possessed of antidotes and knowledge how to use them, use them? If there be poison in my mind, and through this fearful shadow I can cast it out, shall I not cast it out?'

'Say,' said the spectre, 'is it done?'

'A moment longer!' he answered hurriedly. '*I would forget it if I could!* Have I thought that, alone, or has it been the thought of thousands upon thousands, generation after generation? All human memory is fraught with sorrow and trouble. My memory is as the memory of other men, but other men have not this choice. Yes, I close the bargain. Yes! I will forget my sorrow, wrong, and trouble!'

'Say,' said the spectre, 'is it done?'

'It is!'

'It is. And take this with you, man whom I here renounce! The gift that I have given, you shall give again, go where you will. Without recovering yourself the power that you have yielded up, you shall henceforth destroy its like in all whom you approach. Your wisdom has discovered that the memory of sorrow, wrong, and trouble is the lot of all mankind, and that mankind would be the happier, in its other memories, without it. Go! Be its benefactor! Freed from such remembrance, from this hour, carry involuntarily the blessing of such freedom with you. Its diffusion is inseparable and inalienable from you. Go! Be happy in the good you have won, and in the good you do!'

The phantom, which had held its bloodless hand above him while it spoke, as if in some unholy invocation, or some ban; and which had gradually advanced its eyes so close to his that he could see how they did not participate in the terrible smile upon its face, but were a fixed, unalterable, steady horror; melted before him and was gone.

As he stood rooted to the spot, possessed by fear and wonder, and imagining he heard repeated in melancholy echoes, dying away fainter and fainter, the words, 'Destroy its like in all whom you approach!' a shrill cry reached his ears. It came, not from the passages beyond the door, but from another part of the old building, and sounded like the cry of someone in the dark who had lost the way.

He looked confusedly upon his hands and limbs, as if to be assured of his identity, and then shouted in reply, loudly and wildly; for there was a strangeness and terror upon him, as if he too were lost.

The cry responding, and being nearer, he caught up the lamp, and raised a heavy curtain in the wall, by which he was accustomed to pass into and out of the theatre where he lectured – which adjoined his room. Associated with youth and animation, and a high amphitheatre of faces which his entrance charmed to interest in a moment, it was a ghostly place when all this life was faded out of it, and stared upon him like an emblem of Death.

'Halloa!' he cried. 'Halloa! This way! Come to the light!' When, as he held the curtain with one hand, and with the other raised the lamp and tried to pierce the gloom that filled the place, something rushed past him into the room like a wildcat, and crouched down in a corner.

'What is it?' he said, hastily.

He might have asked, 'What is it?' even had he seen it well, as presently he did when he stood looking at it gathered up in its corner.

A bundle of tatters, held together by a hand, in size and form almost an infant's, but in its greedy, desperate little clutch, a bad old man's. A face rounded and smoothed by some half-dozen years, but pinched and twisted by the experiences of a life. Bright eyes, but not youthful. Naked feet, beautiful in their childish delicacy – ugly in the blood and dirt that cracked upon them. A baby savage, a young monster, a child who had never been a child, a creature who might live to take the outward form of man, but who, within, would live and perish a mere beast.

Used, already, to be worried and hunted like a beast, the boy crouched down as he was looked at, and looked back again, and interposed his arm to ward off the expected blow.

'I'll bite,' he said, 'if you hit me!'

The time had been, and not many minutes since, when such a sight as this would have wrung the chemist's heart. He looked upon it now, coldly; but with a heavy effort to remember something – he did not know what – he asked the boy what he did there, and whence he came.

'Where's the woman?' he replied. 'I want to find the woman.'

'Who?'

'The woman. Her that brought me here, and set me by the large fire. She was so long gone, that I went to look for her, and lost myself. I don't want you. I want the woman.'

He made a spring, so suddenly, to get away, that the dull sound of his naked feet upon the floor was near the curtain, when Redlaw caught him by his rags.

'Come! you let me go!' muttered the boy, struggling, and clenching his teeth. 'I've done nothing to you. Let me go, will you, to the woman!'

'That is not the way. There is a nearer one,' said Redlaw, detaining him, in the same blank effort to remember some association that ought, of right, to bear upon this monstrous object. 'What is your name?'

'Got none.'

'Where do you live?'

'Live! What's that?'

The boy shook his hair from his eyes to look at him for a moment, and then, twisting round his legs and wrestling with him, broke again into his repetition of, 'You let me go, will you? I want to find the woman.'

The chemist led him to the door. 'This way,' he said, looking at him still confusedly, but with repugnance and avoidance, growing out of his coldness. 'I'll take you to her.'

The sharp eyes in the child's head, wandering round the room, lighted on the table where the remnants of the dinner were.

'Give me some of that!' he said, covetously.

'Has she not fed you?'

'I shall be hungry again tomorrow, shan't I? Ain't I hungry every day?'

Finding himself released, he bounded at the table like some small animal of prey, and hugging to his breast bread and meat, and his own rags, all together, said: 'There! Now take me to the woman!'

As the chemist, with a newborn dislike to touch him, sternly motioned him to follow, and was going out of the door, he trembled and stopped.

'The gift that I have given, you shall give again, go where you will!'

The phantom's words were blowing in the wind, and the wind blew chill upon him.

'I'll not go there, tonight,' he murmured faintly. 'I'll go nowhere tonight. Boy! straight down this long-arched passage, and past the great dark door into the yard – you see the fire shining on the window there.'

'The woman's fire?' enquired the boy.

He nodded, and the naked feet had sprung away. He came back with his lamp, locked his door hastily, and sat down in his chair, covering his face like one who was frightened at himself.

For now he was, indeed, alone. Alone, alone.

CHAPTER 2

The Gift Diffused

A small man sat in a small parlour, partitioned off from a small shop by a small screen, pasted all over with small scraps of newspapers. In company with the small man, was almost any amount of small children you may please to name – at least it seemed so; they made, in that very limited sphere of action, such an imposing effect, in point of numbers.

Of these small fry, two had, by some strong machinery, been got into bed in a corner, where they might have reposed snugly enough in the sleep of innocence, but for a constitutional propensity to keep awake, and also to scuffle in and out of bed. The immediate occasion of these predatory dashes at the waking world, was the construction of an oyster-shell wall in a corner, by two other youths of tender age; on which fortification the two in bed made harassing descents (like those accursed Picts and Scots who beleaguer the early historical studies of most young Britons), and then withdrew to their own territory.

In addition to the stir attendant on these inroads, and the retorts of the invaded, who pursued hotly, and made lunges at the bedclothes under which the marauders took refuge, another little boy, in another little bed, contributed his mite of confusion to the family stock, by casting his boots upon the waters; in other words, by launching these and several small objects, inoffensive in themselves, though of a hard substance considered as missiles, at the disturbers of his repose – who were not slow to return these compliments.

Besides which, another little boy – the biggest there, but still little – was tottering to and fro, bent on one side, and considerably affected in his knees by the weight of a large baby, which he was supposed by a fiction that obtains sometimes in sanguine families, to be hushing to sleep. But oh! the inexhaustible regions of contemplation and watchfulness into which this baby's eyes were then only beginning to compose themselves to stare, over his unconscious shoulder!

It was a very Moloch of a baby, on whose insatiate altar the whole existence of this particular young brother was offered up, a daily sacrifice. Its personality may be said to have consisted in its never being quiet, in any one place, for five consecutive minutes, and never going to sleep when required. 'Tetterby's baby' was as well known in the neighbourhood as the postman or the pot-boy. It roved from doorstep to doorstop, in the arms of little Johnny Tetterby, and lagged heavily at the rear of troops of juveniles who followed the Tumblers or the Monkey, and came up, all on one side, a little too late for everything that was attractive, from Monday morning until Saturday night. Wherever childhood congregated to play, there was little Moloch making Johnny fag and toil. Wherever Johnny desired to stay, little Moloch became fractious, and would not remain. Whenever Johnny wanted to go out, Moloch was asleep, and must be watched. Whenever Johnny wanted to stay at home, Moloch was awake, and must be taken out. Yet Johnny was verily persuaded that it was a faultless baby, without its peer in the realm of England, and was quite content to catch meek glimpses of things in general from behind its skirts, or over its limp flapping bonnet, and to go staggering about with it like a very little porter with a very large parcel, which was not directed to anybody, and could never be delivered anywhere.

The small man who sat in the small parlour, making fruitless attempts to read his newspaper peaceably in the midst of this disturbance, was the father of the family, and the chief of the firm described in the inscription over the little shop front, by the name and title of A. Tetterby and Co., Newsmen. Indeed, strictly speaking, he was the only personage answering to that designation, as Co. was a mere poetical abstraction, altogether baseless and impersonal.

Tetterby's was the corner shop in Jerusalem Buildings. There was a good show of literature in the window, chiefly consisting of picture-newspapers out of date, and serial pirates, and footpads. Walking-sticks, likewise, and marbles, were included in the stock in trade. It had once extended into the light confectionery line; but it would seem that those elegancies of life were not in demand about Jerusalem Buildings, for nothing connected with that branch of commerce remained in the window, except a sort of small glass lantern containing a languishing mass of bull's-eyes, which had melted in the summer and congealed in the winter until all hope of ever getting them out, or of eating them without eating the lantern too, was gone for ever. Tetterby's had tried its hand at several things. It had once made a feeble little dart at the toy business; for in another lantern, there was a heap of minute wax dolls, all sticking together upside down, in the direst confusion, with their feet on one another's heads, and a precipitate of broken arms and legs at the bottom. It had made a move in the millinery direction, which a few dry, wiry bonnet-shapes remained in a corner of the window to attest. It had fancied that a living might lie hidden in the tobacco trade, and had stuck up a representation of a native of each of the three integral portions of the British Empire, in the act of consuming that fragrant weed, with a poetic legend attached, importing that united in one cause they sat and joked; one chewed tobacco, one took snuff, one smoked: but nothing seemed to have come of it except flies. Time had been when it had put a forlorn trust in imitative jewellery, for in one pane of glass there was a card of cheap seals, and another of pencil-cases, and a mysterious black amulet of inscrutable intention, labelled ninepence. But, to that hour Jerusalem Buildings had bought none of them. In short, Tetterby's had tried so hard to get a livelihood out of Jerusalem Buildings in one way or other, and appeared to have done so indifferently in all, that the best position in the firm was too evidently Co.'s, Co., as a bodiless creation, being untroubled with the vulgar inconveniences of hunger and thirst, being chargeable neither to the poor's-rates nor the assessed taxes, and having no young family to provide for.

Tetterby himself, however, in his little parlour, as already mentioned, having the presence of a young family impressed upon his mind in a manner too clamorous to be disregarded, or to comport with the quiet perusal of a newspaper, laid down his paper, wheeled, in his distraction, a few times round the parlour, like an undecided carrier-pigeon, made an ineffectual rush at one or two flying little figures in bed-gowns that skimmed past him, and then, bearing suddenly down upon the only unoffending member of the family, boxed the ears of little Moloch's nurse.

'You bad boy!' said Mr Tetterby, 'haven't you any feeling for your poor father after the fatigues and anxieties of a hard winter's day, since five o'clock in the morning, but must you wither his rest, and corrode his latest intelligence, with *your* wicious tricks? Isn't it enough, sir, that your brother 'Dolphus is toiling and moiling in the fog and cold, and you rolling in the lap of luxury with a – with a baby, and everything you can wish for,' said Mr Tetterby, heaping this up as a great climax of blessings, 'but must you make a wilderness of home, and maniacs of your parents?

Must you, Johnny? Hey?' At each interrogation, Mr Tetterby made a feint of boxing his ears again, but thought better of it, and held his hand.

'Oh, father!' whimpered Johnny, 'when I wasn't doing anything, I'm sure, but taking such care of Sally, and getting her to sleep. Oh, father!'

'I wish my little woman would come home!' said Mr Tetterby, relenting and repenting, 'I only wish my little woman would come home! I ain't fit to deal with 'em. They make my head go round, and get the better of me. Oh, Johnny! Isn't it enough that your dear mother has provided you with that sweet sister?' indicating Moloch; 'isn't it enough that you were seven boys before, without a ray of gal, and that your dear mother went through what she *did* go through, on purpose that you might all of you have a little sister, but must you so behave yourself as to make my head swim?'

Softening more and more, as his own tender feelings and those of his injured son were worked on, Mr Tetterby concluded by embracing him, and immediately breaking away to catch one of the real delinquents. A reasonably good start occurring, he succeeded, after a short but smart run, and some rather severe cross-country work under and over the bedsteads, and in and out among the intricacies of the chairs, in capturing this infant, whom he condignly punished, and bore to bed. This example had a powerful and, apparently, mesmeric influence on him of the boots, who instantly fell into a deep sleep, though he had been, but a moment before, broad awake, and in the highest possible feather. Nor was it lost upon the two young architects, who retired to bed, in an adjoining closet, with great privacy and speed. The comrade of the Intercepted One also shrinking into his nest with similar discretion, Mr Tetterby, when he paused for breath, found himself unexpectedly in a scene of peace.

'My little woman herself,' said Mr Tetterby, wiping his flushed face, 'could hardly have done it better! I only wish my little woman had had it to do, I do indeed!'

Mr Tetterby sought upon his screen for a passage appropriate to be impressed upon his children's minds on the occasion, and read the following. ' "It is an undoubted fact that all remarkable men have had remarkable mothers, and have respected them in after life as their best friends." Think of your own remarkable mother, my boys,' said Mr Tetterby, 'and know her value while she is still among you!'

He sat down again in his chair by the fire, and composed himself, cross-legged, over his newspaper.

'Let anybody, I don't care who it is, get out of bed again,' said Tetterby, as a general proclamation, delivered in a very soft-hearted manner, 'and astonishment will be the portion of that respected contemporary!' – which expression Mr Tetterby selected from his screen. 'Johnny, my child, take care of your only sister, Sally; for she's the brightest gem that ever sparkled on your early brow.'

Johnny sat down on a little stool, and devotedly crushed himself beneath the weight of Moloch.

'Ah, what a gift that baby is to you, Johnny!' said his father, 'and how thankful you ought to be! "It is not generally known," Johnny,' he was now referring to the screen again, ' "but it is a fact ascertained, by accurate calculations, that the following immense percentage of babies never attain to two years old; that is to say – " '

'Oh, don't, father, please!' cried Johnny. 'I can't bear it, when I think of Sally.'

Mr Tetterby desisting, Johnny, with a profounder sense of his trust, wiped his eyes, and hushed his sister.

'Your brother 'Dolphus,' said his father, poking the fire, 'is late tonight, Johnny, and will come home like a lump of ice. What's got your precious mother?'

'Here's mother, and 'Dolphus too, father!' exclaimed Johnny, 'I think.'

'You're right!' returned his father, listening. 'Yes, that's the footstep of my little woman.'

The process of induction, by which Mr Tetterby had come to the conclusion that his wife was a little woman, was his own secret. She would have made two editions of himself very easily. Considered as an individual, she was rather remarkable for being robust and portly, but considered with reference to her husband, her dimensions became magnificent. Nor did they assume a less imposing proportion, when studied with reference to the size of her seven sons, who were but diminutive. In the case of Sally, however, Mrs Tetterby had asserted herself, at last; as nobody knew better than the victim Johnny, who weighed and measured that exacting idol every hour in the day.

Mrs Tetterby, who had been marketing, and carried a basket, threw back her bonnet and shawl, and sitting down, fatigued, commanded Johnny to bring his sweet charge to her straightway, for a kiss. Johnny having complied, and gone back to his stool and again crushed himself, Master Adolphus Tetterby, who had by this time unwound his torso out of a prismatic comforter, apparently interminable, requested the same favour. Johnny having again complied, and again gone back to his stool, and again crushed himself, Mr Tetterby, struck by a sudden thought, preferred the same claim on his own parental part. The satisfaction of this third desire completely exhausted the sacrifice, who had hardly breath enough left to get back to his stool, crush himself again, and pant at his relations.

'Whatever you do, Johnny,' said Mrs Tetterby, shaking her head, 'take care of her, or never look your mother in the face again.'

'Nor your brother,' said Adolphus.

'Nor your father, Johnny,' added Mr Tetterby.

Johnny, much affected by this conditional renunciation of him looked down at Moloch's eyes to see that they were all right, so far, and skilfully patted her back (which was uppermost), and rocked her with his foot.

'Are you wet, 'Dolphus, my boy?' said his father. 'Come and take my chair, and dry yourself.'

'No, father, thank'ee,' said Adolphus, smoothing himself down with his hands. 'I an't very wet, I don't think. Does my face shine much, father?'

'Well, it does look waxy, my boy,' returned Mr Tetterby.

'It's the weather, father,' said Adolphus, polishing his cheeks on the worn sleeve of his jacket. 'What with rain, and sleet, and wind, and snow, and fog, my face gets quite brought out into a rash sometimes. And shines, it does – oh, don't it, though!'

Master Adolphus was also in the newspaper line of life, being employed, by a more thriving firm than his father and Co., to vend newspapers at a railway station, where his chubby little person, like a shabbily-disguised Cupid, and his shrill little voice (he was not much more than ten years old), were as well known as the hoarse panting of the locomotives, running in and out. His juvenility might have been at some loss for a harmless outlet, in his early application to traffic, but for a fortunate discovery he made of a means of entertaining himself, and of dividing the long day into stages of interest, without neglecting business. This ingenious invention, remarkable, like many great discoveries, for its simplicity, consisted in varying the first vowel in the word 'paper', and substituting, in its stead, at different periods of the day, all the other vowels in grammatical suc-cession. Thus, before daylight in the wintertime, he went to and fro, in his little oilskin cap and cape, and his big comforter, piercing the heavy air with his cry of 'Morn–ing Pa–per!' which, about an hour before noon, changed to 'Morn–ing Pep–per!' which at about two, changed to 'Morn–ing Pip–per!' which, in a couple of hours, changed to 'Morn–ing Pop–per!' and so declined with the sun into 'Eve–ning Pup–per!' to the great relief and comfort of this young gentleman's spirits.

Mrs Tetterby, his lady-mother, who had been sitting with her bonnet and shawl thrown back, as aforesaid, thoughtfully turning her wedding-ring round and round upon her finger, now rose, and divesting herself of her out-of-door attire, began to lay the cloth for supper.

'Ah, dear me, dear me, dear me!' said Mrs Tetterby. 'That's the way the world goes!'

'Which is the way the world goes, my dear?' asked Mr Tetterby, looking round.

'Oh, nothing,' said Mrs Tetterby.

Mr Tetterby elevated his eyebrows, folded his newspaper afresh, and carried his eyes up it, and down it, and across it, but was wandering in his attention, and not reading it.

Mrs Tetterby, at the same time, laid the cloth, but rather as if she were punishing the table than preparing the family supper, hitting it unnecessarily hard with the knives and forks, slapping it with the plates, dinting it with the salt-cellar, and coming heavily down upon it with the loaf.

'Ah, dear me, dear me, dear me!' said Mrs Tetterby. 'That's the way the world goes!'

'My duck,' returned her husband, looking round again, 'you said that before. Which is the way the world goes?'

'Oh, nothing!' said Mrs Tetterby.

'Sophia!' remonstrated her husband, 'you said that before, too.'

'Well, I'll say it again if you like,' returned Mrs Tetterby. 'Oh nothing – there! And again if you like, oh nothing – there! And again if you like, oh nothing – now then!'

Mr Tetterby brought his eye to bear upon the partner of his bosom, and said, in mild astonishment: 'My little woman, what has put you out?'

'I'm sure *I* don't know,' she retorted. 'Don't ask me. Who said I was put out at all! *I* never did.'

Mr Tetterby gave up the perusal of his newspaper as a bad job, and, taking a slow walk across the room with his hands behind him, and his shoulders raised – his gait according perfectly with the resignation of his manner – addressed himself to his two eldest offspring.

'Your supper will be ready in a minute, 'Dolphus,' said Mr Tetterby. 'Your mother has been out in the wet, to the cook's shop, to buy it. It was very good of your mother so to do. You shall get some supper too, very soon, Johnny. Your mother's pleased with you, my man, for being so attentive to your precious sister.'

Mrs Tetterby, without any remark, but with a decided subsidence of her animosity towards the table, finished her preparations, and took, from her ample basket, a substantial slab of hot pease pudding wrapped in paper, and a basin covered with a saucer, which, on being uncovered, sent forth an odour so agreeable, that the three pair of eyes in the two beds opened wide and fixed themselves upon the banquet. Mr Tetterby, without regarding this tacit invitation to be seated, stood repeating, slowly, 'Yes, yes, your supper will be ready in a minute, 'Dolphus – your mother went out in the wet, to the cook's shop, to buy it. It was very good of your mother so to do' – until Mrs Tetterby, who had been exhibiting sundry tokens of contrition behind him, caught him round the neck, and wept.

'Oh, 'Dolphus!' said Mrs Tetterby, 'how could I go and behave so?'

This reconciliation affected Adolphus the younger and Johnny to that degree that they both, as with one accord, raised a dismal cry, which had the effect of immediately shutting up the round eyes in the beds, and utterly routing the two remaining little Tetterbys, just then stealing in from the adjoining closet to see what was going on in the eating way.

'I am sure, 'Dolphus,' sobbed Mrs Tetterby, 'coming home, I had no more idea than a child unborn –'

Mr Tetterby seemed to dislike this figure of speech and observed, 'Say than the baby, my dear.'

' – Had no more idea than the baby,' said Mrs Tetterby. 'Johnny, don't look at me, but look at her, or she'll fall out of your lap and be killed, and then you'll die in agonies of a broken heart, and serve you right – No more idea I hadn't than that darling of being cross when I came home; but somehow, 'Dolphus –' Mrs Tetterby paused, and again turned her wedding-ring round and round upon her finger.

'I see!' said Mr Tetterby. 'I understand! My little woman was put out. Hard times, and hard weather, and hard work, make it trying now and then. I see, bless your soul! No wonder! 'Dolf, my man,' continued Mr Tetterby, exploring the basin with a fork, 'here's your mother been and bought, at the cook's shop, besides pease pudding, a whole knuckle of a lovely roast leg of pork, with lots of crackling left upon it, and with seasoning gravy and mustard quite unlimited. Hand in your plate, my boy, and begin while it's simmering.'

Master Adolphus, needing no second summons, received his portion with eyes rendered moist by appetite, and withdrawing to his particular stool, fell upon his supper, tooth and nail. Johnny was not forgotten, but received his rations on bread, lest he should, in a flush of gravy, trickle any on the baby. He was required, for similar reasons, to keep his pudding, when not on active service, in his pocket.

There might have been more pork on the knucklebone – which knucklebone the carver at the cook's shop had assuredly not forgotten in carving for previous customers – but there was no stint of seasoning, and that is an accessory dreamily suggesting pork, and pleasantly cheating the sense of taste. The pease pudding, too, the gravy and mustard, like the Eastern rose in respect of the nightingale, if they were not absolutely pork, had lived near it; so, upon the whole, there was the flavour of a middle-sized pig. It was irresistible to the Tetterbys in bed, who, though professing to slumber peacefully, crawled out when unseen by their parents, and silently appealed to their brothers for any gastronomic token of fraternal affection. They, not hard of heart, presenting scraps in return, it resulted that a party of light skirmishers in nightgowns were careering about the parlour all through supper, which harassed Mr Tetterby exceedingly, and once or twice imposed upon him the necessity of a charge, before which these guerrilla troops retired in all directions and in great confusion.

Mrs Tetterby did not enjoy her supper. There seemed to be something on Mrs Tetterby's mind. At one time she laughed without reason, and at another time she cried without reason, and at last she laughed and cried together in a manner so very unreasonable that her husband was confounded.

'My little woman,' said Mr Tetterby, 'if the world goes that way, it appears to go the wrong way, and to choke you.'

'Give me a drop of water,' said Mrs Tetterby, struggling with herself, 'and don't speak to me for the present, or take any notice of me. Don't do it!'

Mr Tetterby having administered the water, turned suddenly on the unlucky Johnny (who was full of sympathy), and demanded why he was wallowing there, in gluttony and idleness, instead of coming forward with the baby, that the sight of her might revive his mother. Johnny immediately approached, borne down by its weight; but Mrs Tetterby holding out her hand to signify that she was not in a condition to bear that trying appeal to her feelings, he was interdicted from advancing another inch, on pain of perpetual hatred from all his dearest connections; and accordingly retired to his stool again, and crushed himself as before.

After a pause, Mrs Tetterby said she was better now, and began to laugh.

'My little woman,' said her husband, dubiously, 'are you quite sure you're better? Or are you, Sophia, about to break out in a fresh direction?'

'No, 'Dolphus, no,' replied his wife, 'I'm quite myself.' With that, settling her hair, and pressing the palms of her hands upon her eyes, she laughed again.

'What a wicked fool I was, to think so for a moment!' said Mrs

Tetterby. 'Come nearer, 'Dolphus, and let me ease my mind, and tell you what I mean. Let me tell you all about it.'

Mr Tetterby bringing his chair closer, Mrs Tetterby laughed again, gave him a hug, and wiped her eyes.

'You know, 'Dolphus, my dear,' said Mrs Tetterby, 'that when I was single, I might have given myself away in several directions. At one time, four after me at once; two of them were sons of Mars.'

'We're all sons of Ma's, my dear,' said Mr Tetterby, 'jointly with Pa's.'

'I don't mean that,' replied his wife, 'I mean soldiers – sergeants.'

'Oh!' said Mr Tetterby.

'Well, 'Dolphus, I'm sure I never think of such things now, to regret them; and I'm sure I've got as good a husband, and would do as much to prove that I was fond of him, as – '

'As any little woman in the world,' said Mr Tetterby. 'Very good. *Very good.*'

If Mr Tetterby had been ten feet high, he could not have expressed a gentler consideration for Mrs Tetterby's fury-like stature; and if Mrs Tetterby had been two feet high, she could not have felt it more appropriately her due.

'But you see, 'Dolphus,' said Mrs Tetterby, 'this being Christmastime, when all people who can make holiday, and when all people who have got money like to spend some, I did, somehow, get a little out of sorts when I was in the streets just now. There were so many things to be sold – such delicious things to eat, such fine things to look at, such delightful things to have – and there was so much calculating and calculating necessary, before I durst lay out a sixpence for the commonest thing; and the basket was so large, and wanted so much in it: and my stock of money was so small, and would go such a little way – you hate me, don't you, 'Dolphus?'

'Not quite,' said Mr Tetterby, 'as yet.'

'Well! I'll tell you the whole truth,' pursued his wife, penitently, 'and then perhaps you will. I felt all this, so much, when I was trudging about in the cold, and when I saw a lot of other calculating faces and large baskets trudging about, too, that I began to think whether I mightn't have done better, and been happier, if – I – hadn't – ' the wedding-ring went round again, and Mrs Tetterby shook her downcast head as she turned it.

'I see,' said her husband quietly; 'if you hadn't married at all, or if you had married somebody else?'

'Yes,' sobbed Mrs Tetterby. 'That's really what I thought. Do you hate me now, 'Dolphus?'

'Why no,' said Mr Tetterby, 'I don't find that I do, as yet.'

Mrs Tetterby gave him a thankful kiss, and went on.

'I begin to hope you won't, now, 'Dolphus, though I am afraid I haven't told you the worst. I can't think what came over me. I don't know whether I was ill, or mad, or what I was, but I couldn't call up anything that seemed to bind us to each other, or to reconcile me to my fortune. All the pleasures and enjoyments we had ever had – *they* seemed so poor and insignificant, I hated them. I could have trodden on them. And I could think of nothing else, except our being poor, and the number of mouths there were at home.'

'Well, well, my dear,' said Mr Tetterby, shaking her hand encouragingly, 'that's truth, after all. We *are* poor, and there *are* a number of mouths at home here.'

'Ah! but, Dolf, Dolf!' cried his wife, laying her hands upon his neck, 'my good, kind, patient fellow, when I had been at home a very little while – how different! Oh, Dolf, dear, how different it was! I felt as if there was a rush of recollection on me, all at once, that softened my hard heart and filled it up till it was bursting. All our struggles for a livelihood, all our cares and wants since we have been married, all the times of sickness, all the hours of watching, we have ever had, by one another, or by the children, seemed to speak to me, and say that they had made us one, and that I never might have been, or could have been, or would have been, any other than the wife and mother I am. Then, the cheap enjoyments that I could have trodden on so cruelly, got to be so precious to me – Oh so priceless, and dear! – that I couldn't bear to think how much I had wronged them; and I said, and say again a hundred times, how could I ever behave so, 'Dolphus, how could I ever have the heart to do it!'

The good woman, quite carried away by her honest tenderness and remorse, was weeping with all her heart, when she started up with a scream, and ran behind her husband. Her cry was so terrified, that the children started from their sleep and from their beds, and clung about her. Nor did her gaze belie her voice, as she pointed to a pale man in a black cloak who had come into the room.

'Look at that man! Look there! What does he want?'

'My dear,' returned her husband, 'I'll ask him if you'll let me go. What's the matter? How you shake!'

'I saw him in the street, when I was out just now. He looked at me, and stood near me. I am afraid of him.'

'Afraid of him! Why?'

'I don't know why – I – stop! husband!' for he was going towards the stranger.

She had one hand pressed upon her forehead, and one upon her breast, and there was a peculiar fluttering all over her, and a hurried unsteady motion of her eyes, as if she had lost something.

'Are you ill, my dear?'

'What is it that is going from me again?' she muttered, in a low voice. 'What *is* this that is going away?'

Then she abruptly answered: 'Ill? No, I am quite well,' and stood looking vacantly at the floor.

Her husband, who had not been altogether free from the infection of her fear at first, and whom the present strangeness of her manner did not tend to reassure, addressed himself to the pale visitor in the black cloak, who stood still, and whose eyes were bent upon the ground.

'What may be your pleasure, sir,' he asked, 'with us?'

'I fear that my coming in unperceived,' returned the visitor, 'has alarmed you; but you were talking and did not hear me.'

'My little woman says – perhaps you heard her say it,' returned Mr Tetterby, 'that it's not the first time you have alarmed her tonight.'

'I am sorry for it. I remember to have observed her, for a few moments only, in the street. I had no intention of frightening her.'

As he raised his eyes in speaking, she raised hers. It was extraordinary to see what dread she had of him, and with what dread he observed it – and yet how narrowly and closely.

'My name,' he said, 'is Redlaw. I come from the old college hard by. A young gentleman who is a student there lodges in your house, does he not?'

'Mr Denham?' said Tetterby.

'Yes.'

It was a natural action, and so slight as to be hardly noticeable; but the little man, before speaking again, passed his hand across his forehead, and looked quickly round the room, as though he were sensible of some change in its atmosphere. The chemist, instantly transferring to him the look of dread he had directed towards the wife, stepped back, and his face turned paler.

'The gentleman's room,' said Tetterby, 'is upstairs, sir. There's a more convenient private entrance; but as you have come in here, it will save your going out into the cold, if you'll take this little staircase,' showing one communicating directly with the parlour, 'and go up to him that way, if you wish to see him.'

'Yes, I wish to see him,' said the chemist. 'Can you spare a light?'

The watchfulness of his haggard look, and the inexplicable distrust that darkened it, seemed to trouble Mr Tetterby. He paused; and looking fixedly at him in return, stood for a minute or so, like a man stupefied, or fascinated.

At length he said, 'I'll light you, sir, if you'll follow me.'

'No,' replied the chemist, 'I don't wish to be attended, or announced to him. He does not expect me. I would rather go alone. Please to give me the light, if you can spare it, and I'll find the way.'

In the quickness of his expression of this desire, and in taking the candle from the newsman, he touched him on the breast. Withdrawing his hand hastily, almost as though he had wounded him by accident (for he did not know in what part of himself his new power resided, or how it was communicated, or how the manner of its reception varied in different persons), he turned and ascended the stair.

But when he reached the top, he stopped and looked down. The wife was standing in the same place, twisting her ring round and round upon her finger. The husband, with his head bent forward on his breast, was musing heavily and sullenly. The children, still clustering about the mother, gazed timidly after the visitor, and nestled together when they saw him looking down.

'Come!' said the father, roughly. 'There's enough of this. Go to bed here!'

'The place is inconvenient and small enough,' the mother added, 'without you. Get to bed!'

The whole brood, scared and sad, crept away; little Johnny and the baby lagging last. The mother, glancing contemptuously round the sordid room, and tossing from her the fragments of their meal, stopped on the threshold of her task of clearing the table, and sat down, pondering idly and dejectedly. The father betook himself to the chimney-corner, and impatiently raking the small fire together, bent over it as if he would monopolise it all. They did not interchange a word.

The chemist, paler than before, stole upward like a thief; looking back upon the change below, and dreading equally to go on or return.

'What have I done!' he said, confusedly. 'What am I going to do!'

'To be the benefactor of mankind,' he thought he heard a voice reply.

He looked round, but there was nothing there; and a passage now shutting out the little parlour from his view, he went on, directing his eyes before him at the way he went.

'It is only since last night,' he muttered gloomily, 'that I have remained shut up, and yet all things are strange to me. I am strange to myself. I am here, as in a dream. What interest have I in this place, or in any place that I can bring to my remembrance? My mind is going blind!'

There was a door before him, and he knocked at it. Being invited, by a voice within, to enter, he complied.

'Is that my kind nurse?' said the voice. 'But I need not ask her. There is no one else to come here.'

It spoke cheerfully, though in a languid tone, and attracted his attention to a young man lying on a couch, drawn before the chimney-piece, with the back towards the door. A meagre scanty stove, pinched and hollowed like a sick man's cheeks, and bricked into the centre of a hearth that it could scarcely warm, contained the fire, to which his face was turned. Being so near the windy house-top, it wasted quickly, and with a busy sound, and the burning ashes dropped down fast.

'They chink when they shoot out here,' said the student, smiling; 'so, according to the gossips, they are not coffins, but purses. I shall be well and rich yet, someday, if it please God, and shall live, perhaps, to love a daughter Milly, in remembrance of the kindest nature and the gentlest heart in the world.'

He put up his hand as if expecting her to take it but, being weakened, he lay still, with his face resting on his other hand, and did not turn round.

The chemist glanced about the room – at the student's books and papers, piled upon a table in a corner, where they, and his extinguished reading-lamp, now prohibited and put away, told of the attentive hours that had gone before this illness, and perhaps caused it – at such signs of his old health and freedom, as the out-of-door attire that hung idle on the wall – at those remembrances of other and less solitary scenes, the little miniatures upon the chimney-piece, and the drawing of home – at that token of his emulation, perhaps, in some sort, of his personal attachment too, the framed engraving of himself, the looker-on. The time had been, only yesterday, when not one of these objects, in its remotest association of interest with the living figure before him, would have been lost on Redlaw. Now, they were but objects; or, if any gleam of such connection shot upon him, it perplexed, and not enlightened him, as he stood looking round with a dull wonder.

The student, recalling the thin hand which had remained so long untouched, raised himself on the couch, and turned his head.

'Mr Redlaw!' he exclaimed, and started up.

Redlaw put out his arm.

'Don't come nearer to me. I will sit here. Remain you, where you are!'

He sat down on a chair near the door, and having glanced at the young man standing leaning with his hand upon the couch, spoke with his eyes averted towards the ground.

'I heard, by an accident, by what accident is no matter, that one of my class was ill and solitary. I received no other description of him, than that he lived in this street. Beginning my enquiries at the first house in it, I have found him.'

'I have been ill, sir,' returned the student, not merely with a modest hesitation, but with a kind of awe of him, 'but am greatly better. An attack of fever – of the brain, I believe – has weakened me, but I am much better. I cannot say I have been solitary, in my illness, or I should forget the ministering hand that has been near me.'

'You are speaking of the keeper's wife,' said Redlaw.

'Yes.' The student bent his head, as if he rendered her some silent homage.

The chemist, in whom there was a cold, monotonous apathy, which rendered him more like a marble image on the tomb of the man who had started from his dinner yesterday at the first mention of this student's case, than the breathing man himself, glanced again at the student leaning with his hand upon the couch, and looked upon the ground, and in the air, as if for light for his blinded mind.

'I remembered your name,' he said, 'when it was mentioned to me downstairs, just now; and I recollect your face. We have held but very little personal communication together?'

'Very little.'

'You have retired and withdrawn from me, more than any of the rest, I think?'

The student signified assent.

'And why?' said the chemist; not with the least expression of interest, but with a moody, wayward kind of curiosity. 'Why? How comes it that you have sought to keep especially from me, the knowledge of your remaining here, at this season, when all the rest have dispersed, and of your being ill? I want to know why this is?'

The young man, who had heard him with increasing agitation, raised his downcast eyes to his face, and clasping his hands together, cried with sudden earnestness and with trembling lips: 'Mr Redlaw! You have discovered me. You know my secret!'

'Secret?' said the chemist, harshly. '*I* know?'

'Yes! Your manner, so different from the interest and sympathy which endear you to so many hearts, your altered voice, the constraint there is in everything you say, and in your looks,' replied the student, 'warn me that you know me. That you would conceal it, even now, is but a proof to me (God knows I need none!) of your natural kindness, and of the bar there is between us.'

A vacant and contemptuous laugh was all his answer.

'But, Mr Redlaw,' said the student, 'as a just man, and a good man, think how innocent I am, except in name and descent, of participation in any wrong inflicted on you, or in any sorrow you have borne.'

'Sorrow!' said Redlaw, laughing. 'Wrong! What are those to me?'

'For heaven's sake,' entreated the shrinking student, 'do not let the mere interchange of a few words with me change you like this, sir! Let me pass again from your knowledge and notice. Let me occupy my old reserved and distant place among those whom you instruct. Know me only by the name I have assumed, and not by that of Longford – '

'Longford!' exclaimed the other.

He clasped his head with both his hands, and for a moment turned upon the young man his own intelligent and thoughtful face. But the light passed from it, like the sunbeam of an instant, and it clouded as before.

'The name my mother bears, sir,' faltered the young man, 'the name she took, when she might, perhaps, have taken one more honoured. Mr Redlaw,' hesitating, 'I believe I know that history. Where my information halts, my guesses at what is wanting may supply something not remote from the truth. I am the child of a marriage that has not proved itself a well-assorted or a happy one. From infancy, I have heard you spoken of with honour and respect – with something that was almost reverence. I have heard of such devotion, of such fortitude and tenderness, of such rising up against the obstacles which press men down, that my fancy, since I learnt my little lesson from my mother, has shed a lustre on your name. At last, a poor student myself, from whom could I learn but you?'

Redlaw, unmoved, unchanged, and looking at him with a staring frown, answered by no word or sign.

'I cannot say,' pursued the other, 'I should try in vain to say, how much it has impressed me, and affected me, to find the gracious traces of the past in that certain power of winning gratitude and confidence which is associated among us students (among the humblest of us, most) with Mr Redlaw's generous name. Our ages and positions are so different, sir, and I am so accustomed to regard you from a distance, that I wonder at my own presumption when I touch, however lightly, on that theme. But to one who – I may say, who felt no common interest in my mother once – it may be something to hear, now that all is past, with what indescribable feelings of affection I have, in my obscurity, regarded him; with what pain and reluctance I have kept aloof from his encouragement, when a word of it would have made me rich; yet now I have felt it fit that I should hold my course, content to know him, and to be unknown. Mr Redlaw,' said the student, faintly, 'what I would have said, I have said ill, for my strength is strange to me as yet; but for anything unworthy in this fraud of mine, forgive me, and for all the rest forget me!'

The staring frown remained on Redlaw's face, and yielded to no other expression until the student, with these words, advanced towards him, as if to touch his hand, when he drew back and cried to him: 'Don't come nearer to me!'

The young man stopped, shocked by the eagerness of his recoil, and by the sternness of his repulsion; and he passed his hand, thoughtfully, across his forehead.

'The past is past,' said the chemist. 'It dies like the brutes. Who talks to me of its traces in my life? He raves or lies! What have I to do with your distempered dreams? If you want money here it is. I came to offer it; and that is all I came for. There can be nothing else that brings me here,' he muttered, holding his head again, with both his hands. 'There can be nothing else, and yet – '

He had tossed his purse upon the table. As he fell into this dim cogitation with himself, the student took it up, and held it out to him.

'Take it back, sir,' he said proudly, though not angrily. 'I wish you could take from me, with it, the remembrance of your words and offer.'

'You do?' he retorted, with a wild light in his eyes. 'You do?'

'I do!'

The chemist went close to him, for the first time, and took the purse, and turned him by the arm, and looked him in the face.

'There is sorrow and trouble in sickness, is there not?' he demanded, with a laugh.

The wondering student answered, 'Yes.'

'In its unrest, in its anxiety, in its suspense, in all its train of physical and mental miseries?' said the chemist, with a wild unearthly exultation. 'All best forgotten, are they not?'

The student did not answer, but again passed his hand, confusedly, across his forehead. Redlaw still held him by the sleeve, when Milly's voice was heard outside.

'I can see very well now,' she said, 'thank you, Dolf. Don't cry, dear. Father and mother will be comfortable again, tomorrow, and home will be comfortable too. A gentleman with him, is there!'

Redlaw released his hold, as he listened.

'I have feared, from the first moment,' he murmured to himself, 'to meet her. There is a steady quality of goodness in her, that I dread to influence. I may be the murderer of what is tenderest and best within her bosom.'

She was knocking at the door.

'Shall I dismiss it as an idle foreboding, or still avoid her?' he muttered, looking uneasily around.

She was knocking at the door again.

'Of all the visitors who could come here,' he said, in a hoarse alarmed voice, turning to his companion, 'this is the one I should desire most to avoid. Hide me!'

The student opened a frail door in the wall, communicating, where the garret-roof began to slope towards the floor, with a small inner room. Redlaw passed in hastily and shut it after him.

The student then resumed his place upon the couch, and called to her to enter.

'Dear Mr Edmund,' said Milly, looking round, 'they told me there was a gentleman here.'

'There is no one here but I.'

'There has been someone?'

'Yes, yes, there has been someone.'

She put her little basket on the table, and went up to the back of the couch, as if to take the extended hand – but it was not there. A little surprised, in her quiet way, she leaned over to look at his face, and gently touched him on the brow.

'Are you quite as well tonight? Your head is not so cool as in the afternoon.'

'Tut!' said the student, petulantly, 'very little ails me.'

A little more surprise, but no reproach, was expressed in her face as she withdrew to the other side of the table, and took a small packet of needlework from her basket. But she laid it down again, on second thoughts, and going noiselessly about the room, set everything exactly in its place, and in the neatest order; even to the cushions on the couch, which she touched with so light a hand, that he hardly seemed to know it, as he lay looking at the fire. When all this was done, and she had swept the hearth, she sat down, in her modest little bonnet, to her work, and was quietly busy on it directly.

'It's the new muslin curtain for the window, Mr Edmund,' said Milly, stitching away as she talked. 'It will look very clean and nice, though it costs very little, and will save your eyes, too, from the light. My William says the room should not be too light just now, when you are recovering so well, or the glare might make you giddy.'

He said nothing; but there was something so fretful and impatient in his change of position, that her quick fingers stopped, and she looked at him anxiously.

'The pillows are not comfortable,' she said, laying down her work and rising. 'I will soon put them right.'

'They are very well,' he answered. 'Leave them alone, pray. You make so much of everything.'

He raised his head to say this, and looked at her so thanklessly, that,

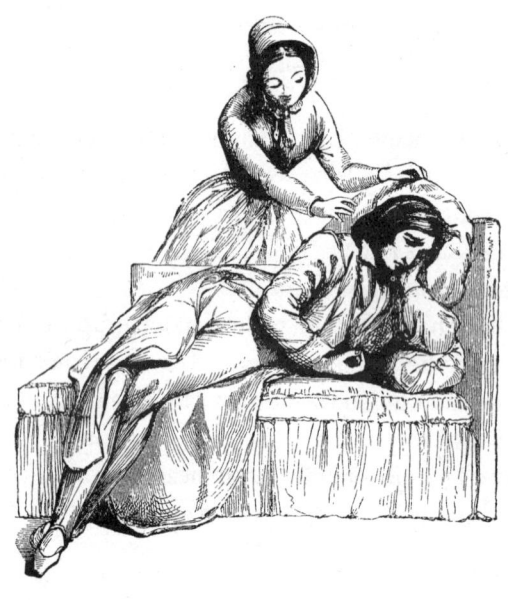

after he had thrown himself down again, she stood timidly pausing. However, she resumed her seat, and her needle, without having directed even a murmuring look towards him, and was soon as busy as before.

'I have been thinking, Mr Edmund, that you have been often thinking of late, when I have been sitting by, how true the saying is, that adversity is a good teacher. Health will be more precious to you, after this illness, than it has ever been. And years hence, when this time of year comes round, and you remember the days when you lay here sick, alone, that the knowledge of your illness might not afflict those who are dearest to you, your home will be doubly dear and doubly blest. Now, isn't that a good, true thing?'

She was too intent upon her work, and too earnest in what she said, and too composed and quiet altogether, to be on the watch for any look he might direct towards her in reply; so the shaft of his ungrateful glance fell harmless, and did not wound her.

'Ah!' said Milly, with her pretty head inclining thoughtfully on one side, as she looked down, following her busy fingers with her eyes. 'Even on me – and I am very different from you, Mr Edmund, for I have no learning, and don't know how to think properly – this view of such things has made a great impression, since you have been lying ill. When I have seen you so touched by the kindness and attention of the poor people downstairs, I have felt that you thought even that experience some repayment for the loss of health, and I have read in your face, as plain as if it was a book, that but for some trouble and sorrow we should never know half the good there is about us.'

His getting up from the couch, interrupted her, or she was going on to say more.

'We needn't magnify the merit, Mrs William,' he rejoined slightingly. 'The people downstairs will be paid in good time, I dare say, for any little extra service they may have rendered me; and perhaps they anticipate no less. I am much obliged to you, too.'

Her fingers stopped, and she looked at him.

'I can't be made to feel the more obliged by your exaggerating the case,' he said. 'I am sensible that you have been interested in me, and I say I am much obliged to you. What more would you have?'

Her work fell on her lap, as she still looked at him walking to and fro with an intolerant air, and stopping now and then.

'I say again, I am much obliged to you. Why weaken my sense of what is your due in obligation, by preferring enormous claims upon me? Trouble, sorrow, affliction, adversity! One might suppose I had been dying a score of deaths here!'

'Do you believe, Mr Edmund,' she asked, rising and going nearer to him, 'that I spoke of the poor people of the house, with any reference to myself? To me?' laying her hand upon her bosom with a simple and innocent smile of astonishment.

'Oh! I think nothing about it, my good creature,' he returned. 'I have had an indisposition, which your solicitude – observe! I say solicitude – makes a great deal more of, than it merits; and it's over, and we can't perpetuate it.'

He coldly took a book, and sat down at the table.

She watched him for a little while, until her smile was quite gone, and then, returning to where her basket was, said gently: 'Mr Edmund, would you rather be alone?'

'There is no reason why I should detain you here,' he replied.

'Except –' said Milly, hesitating, and showing her work.

'Oh! the curtain,' he answered, with a supercilious laugh. 'That's not worth staying for.'

She made up the little packet again, and put it in her basket. Then, standing before him with such an air of patient entreaty that he could not choose but look at her, she said: 'If you should want me, I will come back willingly. When you did want me, I was quite happy to come; there was no merit in it. I think you must be afraid, that, now you are getting well, I may be troublesome to you; but I should not have been, indeed. I should have come no longer than your weakness and confinement lasted. You owe me nothing; but it is right that you should deal as justly by me as if I was a lady – even the very lady that you love; and if you suspect me of meanly making much of the little I have tried to do to comfort your sickroom, you do yourself more wrong than ever you can do me. That is why I am sorry. That is why I am very sorry.'

If she had been as passionate as she was quiet, as indignant as she was calm, as angry in her look as she was gentle, as loud of tone as she was low and clear, she might have left no sense of her departure in the room, compared with that which fell upon the lonely student when she went away.

He was gazing drearily upon the place where she had been, when Redlaw came out of his concealment, and came to the door.

'When sickness lays its hand on you again,' he said, looking fiercely back at him, ' – may it be soon! – Die here! Rot here!'

'What have you done?' returned the other, catching at his cloak. 'What change have you wrought in me? What curse have you brought upon me? Give me back myself!'

'Give me back *myself!*' exclaimed Redlaw like a madman. 'I am infected! I am infectious! I am charged with poison for my own mind, and the minds of all mankind. Where I felt interest, compassion, sympathy, I am turning into stone. Selfishness and ingratitude spring up in my blighting footsteps. I am only so much less base than the wretches whom I make so, that in the moment of their transformation I can hate them.'

As he spoke – the young man still holding to his cloak – he cast him off, and struck him: then, wildly hurried out into the night air where the wind was blowing, the snow falling, the cloud-drift sweeping on, the moon dimly shining; and where, blowing in the wind, falling with the snow, drifting with the clouds, shining in the moonlight, and heavily looming in the darkness, were the phantom's words, 'The gift that I have given, you shall give again, go where you will!'

Whither he went, he neither knew nor cared, so that he avoided company. The change he felt within him made the busy streets a desert, and himself a desert, and the multitude around him, in their manifold endurances and ways of life, a mighty waste of sand, which the winds tossed into unintelligible heaps and made a ruinous confusion of. Those traces in his breast which the phantom had told him would 'die out soon' were not, as yet, so far upon their way to death but that he understood enough of what he was, and what he made of others, to desire to be alone.

This put it in his mind – he suddenly bethought himself, as he was going along, of the boy who had rushed into his room. And then he recollected, that of those with whom he had communicated since the phantom's disappearance, that boy alone had shown no sign of being changed.

Monstrous and odious as the wild thing was to him, he determined to seek it out, and prove if this were really so; and also to seek it with another intention, which came into his thoughts at the same time.

So, resolving with some difficulty where he was, he directed his steps back to the old college, and to that part of it where the general porch was, and where, alone, the pavement was worn by the tread of the students' feet.

The keeper's house stood just within the iron gates, forming a part of the chief quadrangle. There was a little cloister outside, and from that sheltered place he knew he could look in at the window of their ordinary room, and see who was within. The iron gates were shut, but his hand was familiar with the fastening, and drawing it back by thrusting in his wrist between the bars, he passed through softly, shut it again, and crept up to the window, crumbling the thin crust of snow with his feet.

The fire, to which he had directed the boy last night, shining brightly through the glass, made an illuminated place upon the ground. Instinctively avoiding this, and going round it, he looked in at the window. At first, he thought that there was no one there, and that the blaze was reddening only the old beams in the ceiling and the dark walls; but peering in more narrowly he saw the object of his search coiled asleep before it on the floor. He passed quickly to the door, opened it, and went in.

The creature lay in such a fiery heat, that, as the chemist stooped to rouse him, it scorched his head. So soon as he was touched, the boy, not half awake, clutching his rags together with the instinct of flight upon him, half rolled and half ran into a distant corner of the room, where, heaped upon the ground, he stuck his foot out to defend himself.

'Get up!' said the chemist. 'You have not forgotten me?'

'You let me alone!' returned the boy. 'This is the woman's house – not yours.'

The chemist's steady eye controlled him somewhat, or inspired him with enough submission to be raised upon his feet, and looked at.

'Who washed them, and put those bandages where they were bruised and cracked?' asked the chemist, pointing to their altered state.

'The woman did.'

'And is it she who has made you cleaner in the face, too?'

'Yes, the woman.'

Redlaw asked these questions to attract his eyes towards himself, and with the same intent now held him by the chin, and threw his wild hair back, though he loathed to touch him. The boy watched his eyes keenly, as if he thought it needful to his own defence, not knowing what he might do next; and Redlaw could see well that no change came over him.

'Where are they?' he enquired.

'The woman's out.'

'I know she is. Where is the old man with the white hair, and his son?'

'The woman's husband, d'ye mean?' enquired the boy.

'Ay. Where are those two?'

'Out. Something's the matter, somewhere. They were fetched out in a hurry, and told me to stop here.'

'Come with me,' said the chemist, 'and I'll give you money.'

'Come where? and how much will you give?'

'I'll give you more shillings than you ever saw, and bring you back soon. Do you know your way to where you came from?'

'You let me go,' returned the boy, suddenly twisting out of his grasp. 'I'm not a-going to take you there. Let me be, or I'll heave some fire at you!'

He was down before it, and ready, with his savage little hand, to pluck the burning coals out.

What the chemist had felt, in observing the effect of his charmed influence stealing over those with whom he came in contact, was not nearly equal to the cold vague terror with which he saw this baby monster put it at defiance. It chilled his blood to look on the immovable impenetrable thing, in the likeness of a child, with its sharp malignant face turned up to his, and its almost infant hand, ready at the bars.

'Listen, boy!' he said. 'You shall take me where you please, so that you take me where the people are very miserable or very wicked. I want to do them good, and not to harm them. You shall have money, as I have told you, and I will bring you back. Get up! Come quickly!' He made a hasty step towards the door, afraid of her returning.

'Will you let me walk by myself, and never hold me, nor yet touch me?' said the boy, slowly withdrawing the hand with which he threatened, and beginning to get up.

'I will!'

'And let me go before, behind, or anyways I like?'

'I will!'

'Give me some money first then, and I'll go.'

The chemist laid a few shillings, one by one, in his extended hand. To count them was beyond the boy's knowledge, but he said 'one', every time, and avariciously looked at each as it was given, and at the donor. He had nowhere to put them, out of his hand, but in his mouth; and he put them there.

Redlaw then wrote with his pencil on a leaf of his pocketbook that the boy was with him, and laying it on the table, signed to him to follow. Keeping his rags together, as usual, the boy complied, and went out with his bare head and his naked feet into the winter night.

Preferring not to depart by the iron gate by which he had entered, where they were in danger of meeting her whom he so anxiously avoided, the chemist led the way through some of those passages among which the boy had lost himself, and by that portion of the building where he lived, to a small door of which he had the key. When they got into the street, he stopped to ask his guide – who instantly retreated from him – if he knew where they were.

The savage thing looked here and there, and at length, nodding his head, pointed in the direction he designed to take. Redlaw going on at once, he followed, something less suspiciously; shifting his money from his mouth into his hand, and back again into his mouth, and stealthily rubbing it bright upon his shreds of dress, as he went along.

Three times, in their progress, they were side by side. Three times they stopped, being side by side. Three times the chemist glanced down at his face, and shuddered as it forced upon him one reflection.

The first occasion was when they were crossing an old churchyard, and Redlaw stopped among the graves, utterly at a loss how to connect them with any tender, softening or consolatory thought.

The second was when the breaking forth of the moon induced him to look up at the heavens, where he saw her in her glory, surrounded by a host of stars he still knew by the names and histories which human science has appended to them; but where he saw nothing else he had been wont to see, felt nothing he had been wont to feel, in looking up there, on a bright night.

The third was when he stopped to listen to a plaintive strain of music, but could only hear a tune, made manifest to him by the dry mechanism of the instruments and his own ears, with no address to any mystery within him, without a whisper in it of the past, or of the future, powerless upon him as the sound of last year's running water, or the rushing of last year's wind.

At each of these three times, he saw with horror that, in spite of the vast intellectual distance between them, and their being unlike each other in all physical respects, the expression on the boy's face was the expression on his own.

They journeyed on for some time – now through such crowded places, that he often looked over his shoulder thinking he had lost his guide, but generally finding him within his shadow on his other side; now by ways so quiet, that he could have counted his short, quick, naked footsteps coming on behind – until they arrived at a ruinous collection of houses, and the boy touched him and stopped.

'In there!' he said, pointing out one house where there were scattered lights in the windows, and a dim lantern in the doorway, with 'Lodgings for Travellers' painted on it.

Redlaw looked about him; from the houses, to the waste piece of ground on which the houses stood, or rather did not altogether tumble down, unfenced, undrained, unlighted, and bordered by a sluggish ditch; from that, to the sloping line of arches, part of some neighbouring viaduct or bridge with which it was surrounded, and which lessened gradually, towards them, until the last but one was a mere kennel for a dog, the last a plundered little heap of bricks; from that, to the child, close to him, cowering and trembling with the cold, and limping on one little foot, while he coiled the other round his leg to warm it, yet staring at all these things with that frightful littleness of expression so apparent in his face, that Redlaw started from him.

'In there!' said the boy, pointing out the house again. 'I'll wait.'

'Will they let me in?' asked Redlaw.

'Say you're a doctor,' he answered with a nod. 'There's plenty ill here.'

Looking back on his way to the house-door, Redlaw saw him trail himself upon the dust and crawl within the shelter of the smallest arch, as if he were a rat. He had no pity for the thing, but he was afraid of it; and when it looked out of its den at him, he hurried to the house as a retreat.

'Sorrow, wrong and trouble,' said the chemist, with a painful effort at some more distinct remembrance, 'at least haunt this place, darkly. He can do no harm, who brings forgetfulness of such things here!'

With these words, he pushed the yielding door, and went in.

There was a woman sitting on the stairs, either asleep or forlorn, whose head was bent down on her hands and knees. As it was not easy to pass without treading on her, and as she was perfectly regardless of his near approach, he stopped, and touched her on the shoulder. Looking up she showed him quite a young face, but one whose bloom and promise were all swept away, as if the haggard winter should unnaturally kill the spring.

With little or no show of concern on his account, she moved nearer to the wall to leave him a wider passage.

'What are you?' said Redlaw, pausing, with his hand upon the broken stair-rail.

'What do you think I am?' she answered, showing him her face again.

He looked upon the ruined Temple of God, so lately made, so soon disfigured; and something, which was not compassion – for the springs in which a true compassion for such miseries has its rise, were dried up in his breast – but which was nearer to it, for the moment, than any feeling that had lately struggled into the darkening, but not yet wholly darkened, night of his mind – mingled a touch of softness with his next words.

'I am come here to give relief, if I can,' he said. 'Are you thinking of any wrong?'

She frowned at him, and then laughed; and then her laugh prolonged itself into a shivering sigh, as she dropped her head again, and hid her fingers in her hair.

'Are you thinking of a wrong?' he asked once more.

'I am thinking of my life,' she said, with a momentary look at him.

He had a perception that she was one of many, and that he saw the type of thousands, when he saw her, drooping at his feet.

'What are your parents?' he demanded.

'I had a good home once. My father was a gardener, far away, in the country.'

'Is he dead?'

'He's dead to me. All such things are dead to me. You a gentleman, and not know that!' She raised her eyes again, and laughed at him.

'Girl!' said Redlaw, sternly, 'before this death, of all such things, was brought about, was there no wrong done to you? In spite of all that you can do, does no remembrance of wrong cleave to you? Are there not times upon times when it is misery to you?'

So little of what was womanly was left in her appearance, that now, when she burst into tears, he stood amazed. But he was more amazed, and much disquieted, to note that in her awakened recollection of this wrong, the first trace of her old humanity and frozen tenderness appeared to show itself.

He drew a little off, and in doing so, observed that her arms were black, her face cut, and her bosom bruised.

'What brutal hand has hurt you so?' he asked.

'My own. I did it myself!' she answered quickly.

'It is impossible.'

'I'll swear I did! He didn't touch me. I did it to myself in a passion, and threw myself down here. He wasn't near me. He never laid a hand upon me!'

In the white determination of her face, confronting him with this untruth, he saw enough of the last perversion and distortion of good surviving in that miserable breast, to be stricken with remorse that he had ever come near her.

'Sorrow, wrong and trouble!' he muttered, turning his fearful gaze away. 'All that connects her with the state from which she has fallen, has those roots! In the name of God, let me go by!'

Afraid to look at her again, afraid to touch her, afraid to think of having sundered the last thread by which she held upon the mercy of heaven, he gathered his cloak about him, and glided swiftly up the stairs.

Opposite to him, on the landing, was a door, which stood partly open, and which, as he ascended, a man with a candle in his hand, came forward from within to shut. But this man, on seeing him, drew back, with much emotion in his manner, and, as if by a sudden impulse, mentioned his name aloud.

In the surprise of such a recognition there, he stopped, endeavouring to recollect the wan and startled face. He had no time to consider it, for, to his yet greater amazement, old Philip came out of the room, and took him by the hand.

'Mr Redlaw,' said the old man, 'this is like you, this is like you, sir! you have heard of it, and have come after us to render any help you can. Ah, too late, too late!'

Redlaw, with a bewildered look, submitted to be led into the room. A man lay there, on a truckle-bed, and William Swidger stood at the bedside.

'Too late!' murmured the old man, looking wistfully into the chemist's face; and the tears stole down his cheeks.

'That's what I say, father,' interposed his son in a low voice. 'That's where it is, exactly. To keep as quiet as ever we can while he's a-dozing, is the only thing to do. You're right, father!'

Redlaw paused at the bedside, and looked down on the figure that was stretched upon the mattress. It was that of a man, who should have been in the vigour of his life, but on whom it was not likely the sun would ever shine again. The vices of his forty or fifty years' career had so branded him, that, in comparison with their effects upon his face, the heavy hand of Time upon the old man's face who watched him had been merciful and beautifying.

'Who is this?' asked the chemist, looking round.

'My son George, Mr Redlaw,' said the old man, wringing his hands. 'My eldest son, George, who was more his mother's pride than all the rest!'

Redlaw's eyes wandered from the old man's grey head, as he laid it down upon the bed, to the person who had recognised him, and who had kept aloof, in the remotest corner of the room. He seemed to be about his own age; and although he knew no such hopeless decay, and broken man as he appeared to be, there was something in the turn of his figure, as he stood with his back towards him, and now went out at the door, that made him pass his hand uneasily across his brow.

'William,' he said in a gloomy whisper, 'who is that man?'

'Why you see, sir,' returned Mr William, 'that's what I say, myself. Why should a man ever go and gamble, and the like of that, and let himself down inch by inch till he can't let himself down any lower!'

'Has he done so?' asked Redlaw, glancing after him with the same uneasy action as before.

'Just exactly that, sir,' returned William Swidger, 'as I'm told. He knows a little about medicine, sir, it seems; and having been wayfaring towards London with my unhappy brother that you see here,' Mr William passed

his coat-sleeve across his eyes, 'and being lodging upstairs for the night –
what I say, you see, is that strange companions come together here
sometimes – he looked in to attend upon him, and came for us at his
request. What a mournful spectacle, sir! But that's where it is. It's enough
to kill my father!'

Redlaw looked up, at these words, and, recalling where he was and
with whom, and the spell he carried with him – which his surprise had
obscured – retired a little, hurriedly, debating with himself whether to
shun the house that moment, or remain.

Yielding to a certain sullen doggedness, which it seemed to be a part of
his condition to struggle with, he argued for remaining.

'Was it only yesterday,' he said, 'when I observed the memory of this
old man to be a tissue of sorrow and trouble, and shall I be afraid,
tonight, to shake it? Are such remembrances as I can drive away, so
precious to this dying man that I need fear for him? No! I'll stay here.'

But he stayed, in fear and trembling none the less for these words; and,
shrouded in his black cloak with his face turned from them, stood away
from the bedside, listening to what they said, as if he felt himself a demon
in the place.

'Father!' murmured the sick man, rallying a little from his stupor.

'My boy! My son George!' said old Philip.

'You spoke, just now, of my being mother's favourite, long ago. It's a
dreadful thing to think now, of long ago!'

'No, no, no,' returned the old man. 'Think of it. Don't say it's dreadful.
It's not dreadful to me, my son.'

'It cuts you to the heart, father.' For the old man's tears were falling on
him.

'Yes, yes,' said Philip, 'so it does; but it does me good. It's a heavy
sorrow to think of that time, but it does me good, George. Oh, think of it
too, think of it too, and your heart will be softened more and more!
Where's my son William? William, my boy, your mother loved him
dearly to the last, and with her latest breath said, "Tell him I forgave him,
blessed him, and prayed for him." Those were her words to me. I have
never forgotten them, and I'm eighty-seven!'

'Father!' said the man upon the bed, 'I am dying, I know. I am so far
gone that I can hardly speak, even of what my mind most runs on. Is
there any hope for me beyond this bed?'

'There is hope,' returned the old man, 'for all who are softened and penitent. There is hope for all such. Oh!' he exclaimed, clasping his hands and looking up, 'I was thankful, only yesterday, that I could remember this unhappy son when he was an innocent child. But what a comfort it is, now, to think that even God himself has that remembrance of him!'

Redlaw spread his hands upon his face, and shrank, like a murderer.

'Ah!' feebly moaned the man upon the bed. 'The waste since then, the waste of life since then!'

'But he was a child once,' said the old man. 'He played with children. Before he lay down on his bed at night, and fell into his guiltless rest, he said his prayers at his poor mother's knee. I have seen him do it, many a time; and seen her lay his head upon her breast, and kiss him. Sorrowful as it was to her and me, to think of this, when he went so wrong, and when our hopes and plans for him were all broken, this gave him still a hold upon us, that nothing else could have given. Oh, Father, so much better than the fathers upon earth! Oh, Father, so much more afflicted by the errors of Thy children! take this wanderer back! Not as he is, but as he was then, let him cry to Thee, as he has so often seemed to cry to us!'

As the old man lifted up his trembling hands, the son, for whom he made the supplication, laid his sinking head against him for support and comfort, as if he were indeed the child of whom he spoke.

When did man ever tremble, as Redlaw trembled, in the silence that ensued! He knew it must come upon them, knew that it was coming fast.

'My time is very short, my breath is shorter,' said the sick man, supporting himself on one arm, and with the other groping in the air, 'and I remember there is something on my mind concerning the man who was here just now. Father and William – wait! – is there really anything in black, out there?'

'Yes, yes, it is real,' said his aged father.

'Is it a man?'

'What I say myself, George,' interposed his brother, bending kindly over him. 'It's Mr Redlaw.'

'I thought I had dreamed of him. Ask him to come here.'

The chemist, whiter than the dying man, appeared before him. Obedient to the motion of his hand, he sat upon the bed.

'It has been so ripped up, tonight, sir,' said the sick man, laying his hand upon his heart, with a look in which the mute, imploring agony of his condition was concentrated, 'by the sight of my poor old father, and the thought of all the trouble I have been the cause of, and all the wrong and sorrow lying at my door, that –'

Was it the extremity to which he had come, or was it the dawning of another change, that made him stop?

' – that what I can do right with my mind running on so much, so fast, I'll try to do. There was another man here. Did you see him?'

Redlaw could not reply by any word; for when he saw that fatal sign he knew so well now, of the wandering hand upon the forehead, his voice died at his lips. But he made some indication of assent.

'He is penniless, hungry and destitute. He is completely beaten down, and has no resource at all. Look after him! Lose no time! I know he has it in his mind to kill himself.'

It was working. It was on his face. His face was changing, hardening, deepening in all its shades, and losing all its sorrow.

'Don't you remember? Don't you know him?' he pursued.

He shut his face out for a moment, with the hand that again wandered over his forehead, and then it lowered on Redlaw, reckless, ruffianly and callous.

'Why, damn you!' he said, scowling round, 'what have you been doing to me here! I have lived bold, and I mean to die bold. To the devil with you!'

And so lay down upon his bed, and put his arms up, over his head and ears, as resolute from that time to keep out all access, and to die in his indifference.

If Redlaw had been struck by lightning, it could not have struck him from the bedside with a more tremendous shock. But the old man, who had left the bed while his son was speaking to him, now returning, avoided it quickly likewise, and with abhorrence.

'Where's my boy William?' said the old man hurriedly. 'William, come away from here. We'll go home.'

'Home, father!' returned William. 'Are you going to leave your own son?'

'Where's my own son?' replied the old man.

'Where? why, there!'

'That's no son of mine,' said Philip, trembling with resentment. 'No such wretch as that has any claim on me. My children are pleasant to look at, and they wait upon me, and get my meat and drink ready, and are useful to me. I've a right to it! I'm eighty-seven!'

'You're old enough to be no older,' murmured William, looking at him grudgingly, with his hands in his pockets. 'I don't know what good you are, myself. We could have a deal more pleasure without you.'

'*My* son, Mr Redlaw!' said the old man. 'My son, too! The boy talking to me of my son! Why, what has he ever done to give me any pleasure, I should like to know?'

'I don't know what you have ever done to give me any pleasure,' said William, sulkily.

'Let me think,' said the old man. 'For how many Christmas times running, have I sat in my warm place, and never had to come out in the cold night air; and have made good cheer, without being disturbed by any such uncomfortable, wretched sight as him there? Is it twenty, William?'

'Nigher forty, it seems,' he muttered. 'Why, when I look at my father, sir, and come to think of it,' addressing Redlaw, with an impatience and irritation that were quite new, 'I'm whipped if I can see anything in him but a calendar of ever so many years of eating and drinking, and making himself comfortable, over and over again.'

'I – I'm eighty-seven,' said the old man, rambling on, childishly and weakly, 'and I don't know as I ever was much put out by anything. I'm not going to begin now, because of what he calls my son. He's not my son. I've had a power of pleasant times. I recollect once – no I don't – no, it's broken off. It was something about a game of cricket and a friend of mine, but it's somehow broken off. I wonder who he was – I suppose I liked him? And I wonder what became of him – I suppose he died? But I don't know. And I don't care, neither; I don't care a bit.'

In his drowsy chuckling, and the shaking of his head, he put his hands into his waistcoat pockets. In one of them he found a bit of holly (left there, probably, last night), which he now took out, and looked at.

'Berries, eh?' said the old man. 'Ah! It's a pity they're not good to eat. I recollect, when I was a little chap about as high as that, and out a-walking with – let me see – who was I out a-walking with? – no, I don't remember how that was. I don't remember as I ever walked with anyone particular, or cared for anyone, or anyone for me. Berries, eh? There's good cheer when there's berries. Well; I ought to have my share of it, and to be waited on, and kept warm and comfortable; for I'm eighty-seven, and a poor old man. I'm eigh–ty-seven. Eigh–ty-seven!'

The drivelling, pitiable manner in which, as he repeated this, he nibbled at the leaves, and spat the morsels out; the cold, uninterested eye with which his youngest son (so changed) regarded him; the determined apathy with which his eldest son lay hardened in his sin, impressed themselves no more on Redlaw's observation – for he broke his way from the spot to which his feet seemed to have been planted, and ran out of the house.

His guide came crawling forth from his place of refuge, and was ready for him before he reached the arches.

'Back to the woman's?' he enquired.

'Back, quickly!' answered Redlaw. 'Stop nowhere on the way!'

For a short distance the boy went on before; but their return was more like a flight than a walk, and it was as much as his bare feet could do to keep pace with the chemist's rapid strides. Shrinking from all who passed, shrouded in his cloak, and keeping it drawn closely about him, as though there were mortal contagion in any fluttering touch of his garments, he made no pause until they reached the door by which they had come out. He unlocked it with his key, went in, accompanied by the boy, and hastened through the dark passages to his own chamber.

The boy watched him as he made the door fast, and withdrew behind the table when he looked round.

'Come!' he said. 'Don't you touch me! You've not brought me here to take my money away?'

Redlaw threw some more upon the ground. He flung his body on it immediately, as if to hide it from him, lest the sight of it should tempt him to reclaim it; and not until he saw him seated by his lamp, with his face hidden in his hands, did he begin furtively to pick it up. When he had done so, he crept near the fire, and sitting down in a great chair before it, took from his breast some broken scraps of food, and fell to munching, and to staring at the blaze, and now and then to glancing at his shillings, which he kept clenched up in a bunch, in one hand.

'And this,' said Redlaw, gazing on him with increased repugnance and fear, 'is the only one companion I have left on earth!'

How long it was before he was aroused from his contemplation of this creature, whom he dreaded so – whether half an hour, or half the night – he knew not. But the stillness of the room was broken by the boy (whom he had seen listening) starting up, and running towards the door.

'Here's the woman coming!' he exclaimed.

The chemist stopped him on his way, at the moment when she knocked.

'Let me go to her, will you?' said the boy.

'Not now,' returned the chemist. 'Stay here. Nobody must pass in or out of the room now – Who's that?'

'It's I, sir,' cried Milly. 'Pray, sir, let me in!'

'No! not for the world!' he said.

'Mr Redlaw, Mr Redlaw, pray, sir, let me in.'

'What is the matter?' he said, holding the boy.

'The miserable man you saw, is worse, and nothing I can say will wake him from his terrible infatuation. William's father has turned childish in a moment. William himself is changed. The shock has been too sudden for him; I cannot understand him; he is not like himself. Oh, Mr Redlaw, pray advise me, help me!'

'No! No! No!' he answered.

'Mr Redlaw! Dear sir! George has been muttering, in his doze, about the man you saw there, who, he fears, will kill himself.'

'Better he should do it than come near me!'

'He says, in his wandering, that you know him; that he was your friend once, long ago; that he is the ruined father of a student here – my mind misgives me, of the young gentleman who has been ill. What is to be done? How is he to be followed? How is he to be saved? Mr Redlaw, pray, oh, pray, advise me! Help me!'

All this time he held the boy, who was half-mad to pass him and let her in.

'Phantoms! Punishers of impious thoughts!' cried Redlaw, gazing round in anguish, 'Look upon me! From the darkness of my mind, let the glimmering of contrition that I know is there, shine up, and show my misery! In the material world, as I have long taught, nothing can be spared; no step or atom in the wondrous structure could be lost, without a blank being made in the great universe. I know, now, that it is the same with good and evil, happiness and sorrow, in the memories of men. Pity me! Relieve me!'

There was no response, but her, 'Help me, help me, let me in!' and the boy's struggling to get to her.

'Shadow of myself! Spirit of my darker hours!' cried Redlaw, in distraction. 'Come back, and haunt me day and night, but take this gift away! Or, if it must still rest with me, deprive me of the dreadful power of giving it to others. Undo what I have done. Leave me benighted, but restore the day to those whom I have cursed. As I have spared this woman from the first, and as I never will go forth again, but will die here, with no hand to tend me, save this creature who is proof against me – hear me!'

The only reply still was the boy struggling to get to her, while he held him back, and the cry, increasing in its energy, 'Help! let me in. He was your friend once, how shall he be followed, how shall he be saved? They are all changed, there is no one else to help me, pray, pray, let me in!'

CHAPTER 3

The Gift Reversed

Night was still heavy in the sky. On open plains, from hilltops, and from the decks of solitary ships at sea, a distant low-lying line, that promised by and by to change to light, was visible in the dim horizon; but its promise was remote and doubtful, and the moon was striving with the night-clouds busily.

The shadows upon Redlaw's mind succeeded thick and fast to one another, and obscured its light as the night-clouds hovered between the moon and earth, and kept the latter veiled in darkness. Fitful and uncertain as the shadows which the night-clouds cast, were their concealments from him, and imperfect revelations to him; and, like the night-clouds still, if the clear light broke forth for a moment, it was only that they might sweep over it, and make the darkness deeper than before.

Without, there was a profound and solemn hush upon the ancient pile of building, and its buttresses and angles made dark shapes of mystery upon the ground, which now seemed to retire into the smooth white snow and now seemed to come out of it, as the moon's path was more or less beset. Within, the chemist's room was indistinct and murky, by the light of the expiring lamp; a ghostly silence had succeeded to the knocking and the voice outside; nothing was audible but, now and then, a low sound among the whitened ashes of the fire as of its yielding up its last breath. Before it on the ground the boy lay fast asleep. In his chair, the chemist sat, as he had sat there since the calling at his door had ceased – like a man turned to stone.

At such a time, the Christmas music he had heard before, began to play. He listened to it at first, as he had listened in the churchyard; but presently – it playing still, and being borne towards him on the night air, in a low, sweet, melancholy strain – he rose, and stood stretching his hands about him, as if there were some friend approaching within his reach, on whom his desolate touch might rest, yet do no harm. As he did this, his face became less fixed and wondering; a gentle trembling came upon him; and at last his eyes filled with tears, and he put his hands before them, and bowed down his head.

His memory of sorrow, wrong and trouble had not come back to him; he knew that it was not restored; he had no passing belief or hope that it was. But some dumb stir within him made him capable, again, of being moved by what was hidden, afar off, in the music. If it were only that it told him sorrowfully the value of what he had lost, he thanked heaven for it with a fervent gratitude.

As the last chord died upon his ear, he raised his head to listen to its lingering vibration. Beyond the boy, so that his sleeping figure lay at his feet, the phantom stood immovable and silent, with its eyes upon him.

Ghastly it was, as it had ever been, but not so cruel and relentless in its aspect – or he thought or hoped so, as he looked upon it, trembling. It was not alone, but in its shadowy hand it held another hand.

And whose was that? Was the form that stood beside it indeed Milly's, or but her shade and picture? The quiet head was bent a little, as her manner was, and her eyes were looking down, as if in pity, on the sleeping child. A radiant light fell on her face, but did not touch the phantom; for, though close beside her, it was dark and colourless as ever.

'Spectre!' said the chemist, newly troubled as he looked, 'I have not been stubborn or presumptuous in respect of her. Oh, do not bring her here. Spare me that!'

'This is but a shadow,' said the phantom; 'when the morning shines seek out the reality whose image I present before you.'

'Is it my inexorable doom to do so?' cried the chemist.

'It is,' replied the phantom.

'To destroy her peace, her goodness; to make her what I am myself, and what I have made of others!'

'I have said "seek her out",' returned the phantom. 'I have said no more.'

'Oh, tell me,' exclaimed Redlaw, catching at the hope which he fancied might lie hidden in the words. 'Can I undo what I have done?'

'No,' returned the phantom.

'I do not ask for restoration to myself,' said Redlaw. 'What I abandoned, I abandoned of my own free will, and have justly lost. But for those to whom I have transferred the fatal gift; who never sought it; who unknowingly received a curse of which they had no warning, and which they had no power to shun; can I do nothing?'

'Nothing,' said the phantom.

'If I cannot, can anyone?'

The phantom, standing like a statue, kept his gaze upon him for a while; then turned its head suddenly, and looked upon the shadow at its side.

'Ah! Can she?' cried Redlaw, still looking upon the shade.

The phantom released the hand it had retained till now, and softly raised its own with a gesture of dismissal. Upon that, her shadow, still preserving the same attitude, began to move or melt away.

'Stay,' cried Redlaw with an earnestness to which he could not give enough expression. 'For a moment! As an act of mercy! I know that some change fell upon me when those sounds were in the air just now. Tell me, have I lost the power of harming her? May I go near her without dread? Oh, let her give me any sign of hope!'

The phantom looked upon the shade as he did – not at him – and gave no answer.

'At least, say this – has she, henceforth, the consciousness of any power to set right what I have done?'

'She has not,' the phantom answered.

'Has she the power bestowed on her without the consciousness?'

The phantom answered: 'Seek her out.' And her shadow slowly vanished.

They were face to face again, and looking on each other, as intently and awfully as at the time of the bestowal of the gift, across the boy who still lay on the ground between them, at the phantom's feet.

'Terrible instructor,' said the chemist, sinking on his knee before it, in an attitude of supplication, 'by whom I was renounced, but by whom I am revisited (in which, and in whose milder aspect, I would fain believe I have a gleam of hope), I will obey without enquiry, praying that the cry I have sent up in the anguish of my soul has been, or will be, heard, in behalf of those whom I have injured beyond human reparation. But there is one thing – '

'You speak to me of what is lying here,' the phantom interposed, and pointed with its finger to the boy.

'I do,' returned the chemist. 'You know what I would ask. Why has this child alone been proof against my influence, and why, why, have I detected in its thoughts a terrible companionship with mine?'

'This,' said the phantom, pointing to the boy, 'is the last, completest illustration of a human creature, utterly bereft of such remembrances as you have yielded up. No softening memory of sorrow, wrong or trouble enters here, because this wretched mortal from his birth has been abandoned to a worse condition than the beasts, and has, within his knowledge, no one contrast, no humanising touch, to make a grain of such a memory spring up in his hardened breast. All within this desolate creature is barren wilderness. All within the man bereft of what you have resigned is the same barren wilderness. Woe to such a man! Woe, tenfold, to the nation that shall count its monsters such as this, lying here, by hundreds and by thousands!'

Redlaw shrank, appalled, from what he heard.

'There is not,' said the phantom, 'one of these – not one – but sows a harvest that mankind must reap. From every seed of evil in this boy, a field of grain is grown that shall be gathered in, and garnered up, and sown again in many places in the world, until regions are overspread with wickedness enough to raise the waters of another Deluge. Open and unpunished murder in a city's streets would be less guilty in its daily toleration, than one such spectacle as this.'

It seemed to look down upon the boy in his sleep. Redlaw, too, looked down upon him with a new emotion.

'There is not a father,' said the phantom, 'by whose side in his daily or his nightly walk, these creatures pass; there is not a mother among all the ranks of loving mothers in this land; there is no one risen from the state of childhood, but shall be responsible in his or her degree for this enormity. There is not a country throughout the earth on which it would not bring a curse. There is no religion upon earth that it would not deny; there is no people upon earth it would not put to shame.'

The chemist clasped his hands, and looked, with trembling fear and pity from the sleeping boy to the phantom, standing above him with its finger pointing down.

'Behold, I say,' pursued the spectre, 'the perfect type of what it was your choice to be. Your influence is powerless here, because from this child's bosom you can banish nothing. His thoughts have been in "terrible companionship" with yours, because you have gone down to his unnatural level. He is the growth of man's indifference; you are the growth of man's presumption. The beneficent design of heaven is, in each case, overthrown, and from the two poles of the immaterial world you come together.'

The chemist stooped upon the ground beside the boy, and, with the same kind of compassion for him that he now felt for himself, covered him as he slept, and no longer shrank from him with abhorrence or indifference.

Soon, now, the distant line on the horizon brightened, the darkness faded, the sun rose red and glorious, and the chimney stacks and gables of the ancient building gleamed in the clear air, which turned the smoke and vapour of the city into a cloud of gold. The very sundial in his shady corner, where the wind was used to spin with such unwindy constancy, shook off the finer particles of snow that had accumulated on his dull old face in the night, and looked out at the little white wreaths eddying round and round him. Doubtless some blind groping of the morning made its way down into the forgotten crypt so cold and earthy, where the Norman arches were half buried in the ground, and stirred the dull sap in the lazy vegetation hanging to the walls, and quickened the slow principle of life within the little world of wonderful and delicate creation which existed there, with some faint knowledge that the sun was up.

The Tetterbys were up, and doing. Mr Tetterby took down the shutters of the shop, and, strip by strip, revealed the treasures of the window to the eyes, so proof against their seductions, of Jerusalem Buildings. Adolphus had been out so long already, that he was halfway on to 'Morning Pepper'. Five small Tetterbys, whose ten round eyes were much inflamed by soap and friction, were in the tortures of a cool wash in the back kitchen; Mrs Tetterby presiding. Johnny, who was pushed and hustled through his toilet with great rapidity when Moloch chanced to be in an exacting frame of mind (which was always the case), staggered up and down with his charge before the shop door, under greater difficulties than usual; the weight of Moloch being much increased by a complication of defences against the cold, composed of knitted worsted-work, and forming a complete suit of chain-armour, with a head-piece and blue gaiters.

It was a peculiarity of this baby to be always cutting teeth. Whether they never came, or whether they came and went away again, is not in evidence; but it had certainly cut enough, on the showing of Mrs Tetterby, to make a handsome dental provision for the sign of the Bull and Mouth. All sorts of objects were impressed for the rubbing of its gums, notwithstanding that it always carried, dangling at its waist (which was immediately under its chin), a bone ring, large enough to have represented the rosary of a young nun. Knife-handles, umbrella-tops, the heads of walking-sticks selected from the stock, the fingers of the family in general, but especially of Johnny, nutmeg-graters, crusts, the handles of doors, and the cool knobs on the tops of pokers, were among the commonest instruments indiscriminately applied for this baby's relief. The amount of electricity that must have been rubbed out of it in a week, is not to be calculated. Still Mrs Tetterby always said 'it was coming through, and then the child would be herself!' and still it never did come through, and the child continued to be somebody else.

The tempers of the little Tetterbys had sadly changed with a few

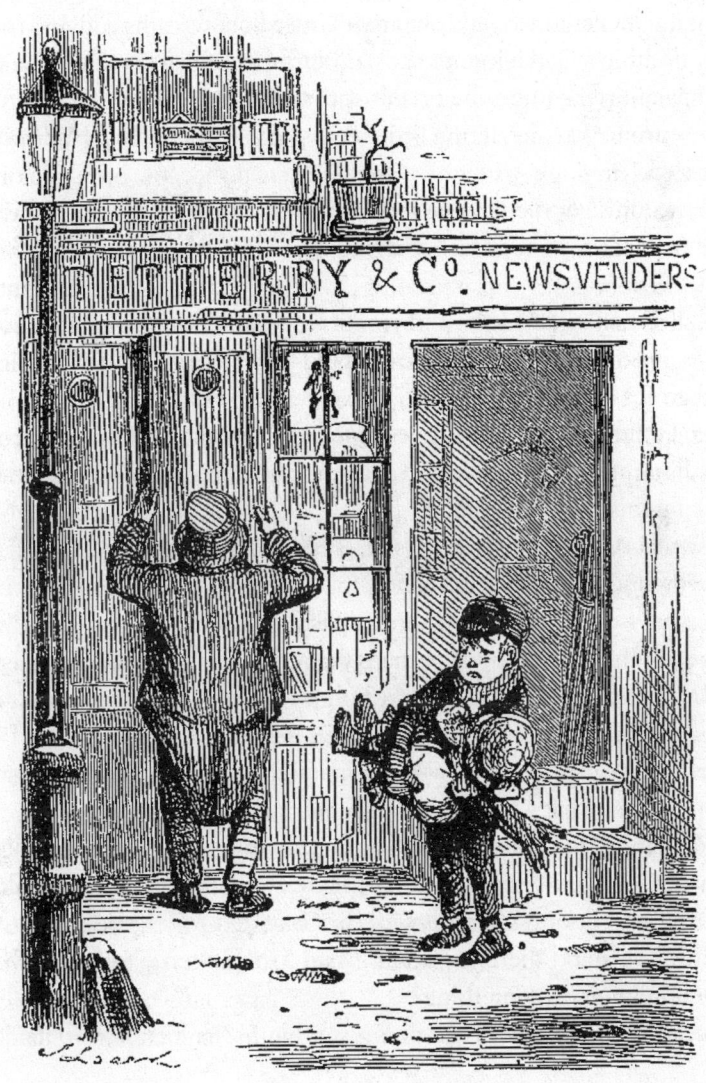

hours. Mr and Mrs Tetterby themselves were not more altered than their offspring. Usually they were an unselfish, good-natured, yielding little race, sharing short commons when it happened (which was pretty often) contentedly and even generously, and taking a great deal of enjoyment out of a very little meat. But they were fighting now, not only for the soap and water, but even for the breakfast which was yet in perspective. The hand of every little Tetterby was against the other little Tetterbys; and even Johnny's hand – the patient, much-enduring and devoted Johnny – rose against the baby! Yes, Mrs Tetterby, going to the door by mere accident, saw him viciously pick out a weak place in the suit of armour where a slap would tell, and slap that blessed child.

Mrs Tetterby had him into the parlour by the collar, in that same flash of time, and repaid him the assault with usury thereto.

'You brute, you murdering little boy,' said Mrs Tetterby. 'Had you the heart to do it?'

'Why don't her teeth come through, then,' retorted Johnny, in a loud rebellious voice, 'instead of bothering me? How would you like it yourself?'

'Like it, sir!' said Mrs Tetterby, relieving him of his dishonoured load.

'Yes, like it,' said Johnny. 'How would you? Not at all. If you was me, you'd go for a soldier. I will, too. There an't no babies in the army.'

Mr Tetterby, who had arrived upon the scene of action, rubbed his chin thoughtfully, instead of correcting the rebel, and seemed rather struck by this view of a military life.

'I wish I was in the army myself, if the child's in the right,' said Mrs Tetterby, looking at her husband, 'for I have no peace of my life here. I'm a slave – a Virginia slave:' some indistinct association with their weak descent on the tobacco trade perhaps suggested this aggravated expression to Mrs Tetterby. 'I never have a holiday, or any pleasure at all, from year's end to year's end! Why, Lord bless and save the child,' said Mrs Tetterby, shaking the baby with an irritability hardly suited to so pious an aspiration, 'what's the matter with her now?'

Not being able to discover, and not rendering the subject much clearer by shaking it, Mrs Tetterby put the baby away in a cradle, and, folding her arms, sat rocking it angrily with her foot.

'How you stand there, Dolphus,' said Mrs Tetterby to her husband. 'Why don't you do something?'

'Because I don't care about doing anything,' Mr Tetterby replied.

'I am sure I don't,' said Mrs Tetterby.

'I'll take my oath I don't,' said Mr Tetterby.

A diversion arose here among Johnny and his five younger brothers, who, in preparing the family breakfast table, had fallen to skirmishing for the temporary possession of the loaf, and were buffeting one another with great heartiness; the smallest boy of all, with precocious discretion, hovering outside the knot of combatants, and harassing their legs. Into the midst of this fray, Mr and Mrs Tetterby both precipitated themselves with great ardour, as if such ground were the only ground on which they could now agree; and having, with no visible remains of their late soft-heartedness, laid about them without any lenity, and done much execution, resumed their former relative positions.

'You had better read your paper than do nothing at all,' said Mrs Tetterby.

'What's there to read in a paper?' returned Mr Tetterby, with excessive discontent.

'What?' said Mrs Tetterby. 'Police.'

'It's nothing to me,' said Tetterby. 'What do I care what people do, or are done to?'

'Suicides,' suggested Mrs Tetterby.

'No business of mine,' replied her husband.

'Births, deaths and marriages, are those nothing to you?' said Mrs Tetterby.

'If the births were all over for good, and all today; and the deaths were all to begin to come off tomorrow; I don't see why it should interest me, till I thought it was a-coming to my turn,' grumbled Tetterby. 'As to marriages, I've done it myself. I know quite enough about them.'

To judge from the dissatisfied expression of her face and manner, Mrs Tetterby appeared to entertain the same opinions as her husband; but she opposed him, nevertheless, for the gratification of quarrelling with him.

'Oh, you're a consistent man,' said Mrs Tetterby, 'an't you? You, with the screen of your own making there, made of nothing else but bits of newspapers, which you sit and read to the children by the half-hour together!'

'Say used to, if you please;' returned her husband. 'You won't find me doing so any more. I'm wiser now.'

'Bah! wiser, indeed!' said Mrs Tetterby. 'Are you better?'

The question sounded some discordant note in Mr Tetterby's breast. He ruminated dejectedly, and passed his hand across and across his forehead.

'Better!' murmured Mr Tetterby. 'I don't know as any of us are better, or happier either. Better, is it?'

He turned to the screen, and faced about it with his finger, until he found a certain paragraph of which he was in quest.

'This used to be one of the family favourites, I recollect,' said Tetterby, in a forlorn and stupid way, 'and used to draw tears from the children, and make 'em good if there was any little bickering or discontent among 'em, next to the story of the robin redbreasts in the wood. "Melancholy case of destitution. Yesterday a small man, with a baby in his arms, and surrounded by half a dozen ragged little ones, of various ages between ten and two, the whole of whom were evidently in a famishing condition, appeared before the worthy magistrate, and made the following recital" – Ha! I don't understand it, I'm sure,' said Tetterby; 'I don't see what it has got to do with us.'

'How old and shabby he looks,' said Mrs Tetterby, watching him. 'I never saw such a change in a man. Ah! dear me, dear me, dear me, it was a sacrifice!'

'What was a sacrifice?' her husband sourly enquired.

Mrs Tetterby shook her head; and without replying in words, raised a complete sea-storm about the baby, by her violent agitation of the cradle.

'If you mean your marriage was a sacrifice, my good woman – ' said her husband.

'I *do* mean it,' said his wife.

'Why, then I mean to say,' pursued Mr Tetterby, as sulkily and surlily as she, 'that there are two sides to that affair; and that I was the sacrifice; and that I wish the sacrifice hadn't been accepted.'

'I wish it hadn't, Tetterby, with all my heart and soul I do assure you,' said his wife. 'You can't wish it more than I do, Tetterby.'

'I don't know what I saw in her,' muttered the newsman, 'I'm sure – certainly, if I saw anything, it's not there now. I was thinking so, last night, after supper, by the fire. She's fat, she's ageing, she won't bear comparison with most other women.'

'He's common-looking, he has no air with him, he's small, he's beginning to stoop, and he's getting bald,' muttered Mrs Tetterby.

'I must have been half out of my mind when I did it,' muttered Mr Tetterby.

'My senses must have forsook me. That's the only way in which I can explain it to myself,' said Mrs Tetterby, with elaboration.

In this mood they sat down to breakfast. The little Tetterbys were not habituated to regard that meal in the light of a sedentary occupation, but discussed it as a dance or trot, rather resembling a savage ceremony, in the occasional shrill whoops, and brandishings of bread and butter, with which it was accompanied, as well as in the intricate filings off into the street and back again, and the hoppings up and down the doorsteps, which were incidental to the performance. In the present instance, the contentions between these Tetterby children for the milk-and-water jug, common to all, which stood upon the table, presented so lamentable an instance of angry passions risen very high indeed, that it was an outrage on the memory of Dr Watts. It was not until Mr Tetterby had driven the whole herd out at the front door, that a moment's peace was secured; and even that was broken by the discovery that Johnny had surreptitiously come back, and was at that instant choking in the jug like a ventriloquist, in his indecent and rapacious haste.

'These children will be the death of me at last!' said Mrs Tetterby, after banishing the culprit. 'And the sooner the better, I think.'

'Poor people,' said Mr Tetterby, 'ought not to have children at all. They give *us* no pleasure.'

He was at that moment taking up the cup which Mrs Tetterby had rudely pushed towards him, and Mrs Tetterby was lifting her own cup to her lips, when they were both stopped, as if they were transfixed.

'Here! Mother! Father!' cried Johnny, running into the room. 'Here's Mrs William coming down the street!'

And if ever, since the world began, a young boy took a baby from a cradle with the care of an old nurse, and hushed and soothed it tenderly, and tottered away with it cheerfully, Johnny was that boy, and Moloch was that baby, as they went out together!

Mr Tetterby put down his cup; Mrs Tetterby put down her cup.

Mr Tetterby rubbed his forehead; Mrs Tetterby rubbed hers. Mr Tetterby's face began to smooth and brighten; Mrs Tetterby's began to smooth and brighten.

'Why, Lord forgive me,' said Mr Tetterby to himself, 'what evil tempers have I been giving way to? What has been the matter here?'

'How could I ever treat him ill again, after all I said and felt last night!' sobbed Mrs Tetterby, with her apron to her eyes.

'Am I a brute,' said Mr Tetterby, 'or is there any good in me at all? Sophia! My little woman!'

' 'Dolphus dear,' returned his wife.

'I – I've been in a state of mind,' said Mr Tetterby, 'that I can't abear to think of, Sophy.'

'Oh! It's nothing to what I've been in, Dolf,' cried his wife in a great burst of grief.

'My Sophia,' said Mr Tetterby, 'don't take on. I never shall forgive myself. I must have nearly broke your heart, I know.'

'No, Dolf, no. It was me! Me!' cried Mrs Tetterby.

'My little woman,' said her husband, 'don't. You make me reproach myself dreadful, when you show such a noble spirit. Sophia, my dear, you don't know what I thought. I showed it bad enough, no doubt; but what I thought, my little woman!'

'Oh, dear Dolf, don't! Don't!' cried his wife.

'Sophia,' said Mr Tetterby, 'I must reveal it. I couldn't rest in my conscience unless I mentioned it. My little woman – '

'Mrs William's very nearly here!' screamed Johnny at the door.

'My little woman, I wondered how,' gasped Mr Tetterby, supporting himself by his chair, 'I wondered how I had ever admired you – I forgot the precious children you have brought about me, and thought you didn't look as slim as I could wish. I – I never gave a recollection,' said Mr Tetterby, with severe self-accusation, 'to the cares you've had as my wife, and along of me and mine, when you might have had hardly any with another man, who got on better and was luckier than me (anybody might have found such a man easily I am sure); and I quarrelled with you for having aged a little in the rough years you have lightened for me. Can you believe it, my little woman? I hardly can myself.'

Mrs Tetterby, in a whirlwind of laughing and crying, caught his face within her hands, and held it there.

'Oh, Dolf!' she cried. 'I am so happy that you thought so; I am so grateful that you thought so! For I thought that you were common-looking, Dolf; and so you are, my dear, and may you be the commonest of all sights in my eyes, till you close them with your own good hands. I thought that you were small; and so you are, and I'll make much of you because you are, and more of you because I love my husband. I thought that you began to stoop; and so you do, and you shall lean on me, and I'll do all I can to keep you up. I thought there was no air about you; but there is, and it's the air of home, and that's the purest and the best there is, and God bless home once more, and all belonging to it, Dolf!'

'Hurrah! Here's Mrs William!' cried Johnny.

So she was, and all the children with her; and as she came in, they kissed her, and kissed one another, and kissed the baby, and kissed their father and mother, and then ran back and flocked and danced about her, trooping on with her in triumph.

Mr and Mrs Tetterby were not a bit behindhand in the warmth of their reception. They were as much attracted to her as the children were; they ran towards her, kissed her hands, pressed round her, could not receive her ardently or enthusiastically enough. She came among them like the spirit of all goodness, affection, gentle consideration, love and domesticity.

'What! are *you* all so glad to see me, too, this bright Christmas morning?' said Milly, clapping her hands in a pleasant wonder. 'Oh dear, how delightful this is!'

More shouting from the children, more kissing, more trooping round her, more happiness, more love, more joy, more honour, on all sides, than she could bear.

'Oh dear!' said Milly, 'what delicious tears you make me shed. How can I ever have deserved this! What have I done to be so loved?'

'Who can help it!' cried Mr Tetterby.

'Who can help it!' cried Mrs Tetterby.

'Who can help it!' echoed the children, in a joyful chorus. And they danced and trooped about her again, and clung to her, and laid their rosy faces against her dress, and kissed and fondled it, and could not fondle it, or her, enough.

'I never was so moved,' said Milly, drying her eyes, 'as I have been this morning I must tell you, as soon as I can speak. Mr Redlaw came to me at sunrise, and with a tenderness in his manner, more as if I had been his darling daughter than myself, implored me to go with him to where William's brother George is lying ill. We went together, and all the way along he was so kind, and so subdued, and seemed to put such trust and hope in me, that I could not help crying with pleasure. When we got to the house, we met a woman at the door (somebody had bruised and hurt her, I am afraid) who caught me by the hand, and blessed me as I passed.'

'She was right!' said Mr Tetterby. Mrs Tetterby said she was right. All the children cried out that she was right.

'Ah, but there's more than that,' said Milly. 'When we got upstairs, into the room, the sick man who had lain for hours in a state from which no effort could rouse him, rose up in his bed, and, bursting into tears, stretched out his arms to me, and said that he had led a misspent life, but that he was truly repentant now in his sorrow for the past, which was all as plain to him as a great prospect, from which a dense black cloud had cleared away, and that he entreated me to ask his poor old father for his pardon and his blessing, and to say a prayer beside his bed. And when I did so, Mr Redlaw joined in it so fervently, and then so thanked and thanked me, and thanked heaven, that my heart quite overflowed, and I could have done nothing but sob and cry, if the sick man had not begged me to sit down by him – which made me quiet of course. As I sat there, he held my hand in his until he sank in a doze; and even then, when I withdrew my hand to leave him to come here (which Mr Redlaw was very earnest indeed in wishing me to do), his hand felt for mine, so that someone else was obliged to take my place and make believe to give him my hand back. Oh dear, oh dear,' said Milly, sobbing. 'How thankful and how happy I should feel, and do feel, for all this!'

While she was speaking, Redlaw had come in, and after pausing for a moment to observe the group of which she was the centre, had silently ascended the stairs. Upon those stairs he now appeared again; remaining there, while the young student passed him, and came running down.

'Kind nurse, gentlest, best of creatures,' he said, falling on his knee to her, and catching at her hand, 'forgive my cruel ingratitude!'

'Oh dear, oh dear!' cried Milly innocently, 'here's another of them! Oh dear, here's somebody else who likes me. What shall I ever do!'

The guileless, simple way in which she said it, and in which she put her hands before her eyes and wept for very happiness, was as touching as it was delightful.

'I was not myself,' he said. 'I don't know what it was – it was some consequence of my disorder perhaps – I was mad. But I am so no longer. Almost as I speak, I am restored. I heard the children crying out your name, and the shade passed from me at the very sound of it. Oh don't weep! Dear Milly, if you could read my heart, and only knew with what affection and what grateful homage it is glowing, you would not let me see you weep. It is such deep reproach.'

'No, no,' said Milly, 'it's not that. It's not indeed. It's joy. It's wonder that you should think it necessary to ask me to forgive so little, and yet it's pleasure that you do.'

'And will you come again? and will you finish the little curtain?'

'No,' said Milly, drying her eyes, and shaking her head. 'You won't care for *my* needlework now.'

'Is it forgiving me, to say that?'

She beckoned him aside, and whispered in his ear.

'There is news from your home, Mr Edmund.'

'News? How?'

'Either your not writing when you were very ill, or the change in your handwriting when you began to be better, created some suspicion of the truth; however that is – but you're sure you'll not be the worse for any news, if it's not bad news?'

'Sure.'

'Then there's someone come!' said Milly.

'My mother?' asked the student, glancing round involuntarily towards Redlaw, who had come down from the stairs.

'Hush! No,' said Milly.

'It can be no one else.'

'Indeed?' said Milly, 'are you sure?'

'It is not – ' Before he could say more, she put her hand upon his mouth.

'Yes it is!' said Milly. 'The young lady (she is very like the miniature, Mr Edmund, but she is prettier) was too unhappy to rest without satisfying her doubts, and came up, last night, with a little servant-maid. As you always dated your letters from the college, she came there; and before I saw Mr Redlaw this morning, I saw her. She likes me too!' said Milly. 'Oh dear, that's another!'

'This morning! Where is she now?'

'Why, she is now,' said Milly, advancing her lips to his ear, 'in my little parlour in the Lodge, and waiting to see you.'

He pressed her hand, and was darting off, but she detained him.

'Mr Redlaw is much altered, and has told me this morning that his memory is impaired. Be very considerate to him, Mr Edmund; he needs that from us all.'

The young man assured her, by a look, that her caution was not ill-bestowed; and as he passed the chemist on his way out, bent respectfully and with an obvious interest before him.

Redlaw returned the salutation courteously and even humbly, and looked after him as he passed on. He drooped his head upon his hand too, as trying to reawaken something he had lost. But it was gone.

The abiding change that had come upon him since the influence of the music, and the phantom's reappearance, was that now he truly felt how much he had lost, and could compassionate his own condition, and contrast it, clearly, with the natural state of those who were around him. In this, an interest in those who were around him was revived, and a meek, submissive sense of his calamity was bred, resembling that which sometimes obtains in age, when its mental powers are weakened, without insensibility or sullenness being added to the list of its infirmities.

He was conscious that, as he redeemed, through Milly, more and more of the evil he had done, and as he was more and more with her, this change ripened itself within him. Therefore, and because of the attachment she inspired him with (but without other hope), he felt that he was quite dependent on her, and that she was his staff in his affliction.

So, when she asked him whether they should go home now, to where the old man and her husband were, and he readily replied 'yes' – being anxious in that regard – he put his arm through hers, and walked beside her; not as if he were the wise and learned man to whom the wonders of Nature were an open book, and hers were the uninstructed mind, but as if their two positions were reversed, and he knew nothing, and she all.

He saw the children throng about her, and caress her, as he and she went away together thus, out of the house; he heard the ringing of their laughter, and their merry voices; he saw their bright faces, clustering around him like flowers; he witnessed the renewed contentment and affection of their parents; he breathed the simple air of their poor home, restored to its tranquillity, he thought of the unwholesome blight he had shed upon it, and might, but for her, have been diffusing then; and perhaps it is no wonder that he walked submissively beside her, and drew her gentle bosom nearer to his own.

When they arrived at the Lodge, the old man was sitting in his chair in the chimney-corner, with his eyes fixed on the ground, and his son was leaning against the opposite side of the fireplace, looking at him. As she came in at the door, both started, and turned round towards her, and a radiant change came upon their faces.

'Oh dear, dear, dear, they are all pleased to see me like the rest!' cried

Milly, clapping her hands in an ecstasy, and stopping short. 'Here are two more!'

Pleased to see her! Pleasure was no word for it. She ran into her husband's arms, thrown wide open to receive her, and he would have been glad to have her there with her head lying on his shoulder, through the short winter's day. But the old man couldn't spare her. He had arms for her too, and he locked her in them.

'Why, where has my quiet Mouse been all this time?' said the old man. 'She has been a long while away. I find that it's impossible for me to get on without Mouse. I – where's my son William? – I fancy I have been dreaming, William.'

'That's what I say myself, father,' returned his son. 'I have been in an ugly sort of dream, I think – How are you, father? Are you pretty well?'

'Strong and brave, my boy,' returned the old man.

It was quite a sight to see Mr William shaking hands with his father, and patting him on the back, and rubbing him gently down with his hand, as if he could not possibly do enough to show an interest in him.

'What a wonderful man you are, father! – How are you, father? Are you really pretty hearty, though?' said William, shaking hands with him again, and patting him again, and rubbing him gently down again.

'I never was fresher or stouter in my life, my boy.'

'What a wonderful man you are, father! But that's exactly where it is,' said Mr William, with enthusiasm. 'When I think of all that my father's gone through, and all the chances and changes, and sorrows and troubles, that have happened to him in the course of his long life, and under which his head has grown grey, and years upon years have gathered on it, I feel as if we couldn't do enough to honour the old gentleman, and make his old age easy – How are you, father? Are you really pretty well, though?'

Mr William might never have left off repeating this enquiry, and shaking hands with him again, and patting him again, and rubbing him down again, if the old man had not espied the chemist, whom until now he had not seen.

'I ask your pardon, Mr Redlaw,' said Philip, 'but didn't know you were here, sir, or should have made less free. It reminds me, Mr Redlaw, seeing you here on a Christmas morning of the time when you was a student yourself, and worked so hard that you was backwards and forwards in our Library even at Christmastime. Ha! ha! I'm old enough to remember that; and I remember it right well, I do, though I'm eighty-seven. It was after you left here that my poor wife died. You remember my poor wife, Mr Redlaw?'

The chemist answered yes.

'Yes,' said the old man. 'She was a dear creetur. I recollect you come here one Christmas morning with a young lady – I ask your pardon, Mr Redlaw, but I think it was a sister you was very much attached to.'

The chemist looked at him, and shook his head. 'I had a sister,' he said vacantly. He knew no more.

'One Christmas morning,' pursued the old man, 'that you come here with her – and it began to snow, and my wife invited the young lady to walk in, and sit by the fire that is always a-burning on Christmas Day in what used to be, before our ten poor gentlemen commuted, our great Dinner Hall. I was there; and I recollect, as I was stirring up the blaze for the young lady to warm her pretty feet by, she read the scroll out loud, that is underneath that picter. "Lord, keep my memory green!" She and my poor wife fell a-talking about it; and it's a strange thing to think of, now, that they both said (both being so unlike to die) that it was a good prayer, and that it was one they would put up very earnestly, if they were called away young, with reference to those who were dearest to them. "My brother," says the young lady – "My husband," says my poor wife – "Lord, keep his memory of me green, and do not let me be forgotten!" '

Tears more painful, and more bitter than he had ever shed in all his life, coursed down Redlaw's face. Philip, fully occupied in recalling his story, had not observed him until now, nor Milly's anxiety that he should not proceed.

'Philip!' said Redlaw, laying his hand upon his arm, 'I am a stricken man, on whom the hand of Providence has fallen heavily, although deservedly. You speak to me, my friend, of what I cannot follow; my memory is gone.'

'Merciful Power!' cried the old man.

'I have lost my memory of sorrow, wrong and trouble,' said the chemist, 'and with that I have lost all man would remember!'

To see old Philip's pity for him, to see him wheel his own great chair for him to rest in, and look down upon him with a solemn sense of his bereavement, was to know, in some degree, how precious to old age such recollections are.

The boy came running in, and ran to Milly.

'Here's the man,' he said, 'in the other room. I don't want *him*.'

'What man does he mean?' asked Mr William.

'Hush!' said Milly.

Obedient to a sign from her, he and his old father softly withdrew. As they went out, unnoticed, Redlaw beckoned to the boy to come to him.

'I like the woman best,' he answered, holding to her skirts.

'You are right,' said Redlaw, with a faint smile. 'But you needn't fear to come to me. I am gentler than I was. Of all the world, to you, poor child!'

The boy still held back at first, but yielding little by little to her urging, he consented to approach, and even to sit down at his feet. As Redlaw laid his hand upon the shoulder of the child, looking on him with compassion and a fellow-feeling, he put out his other hand to Milly.

She stooped down on that side of him, so that she could look into his face, and after silence, said: 'Mr Redlaw, may I speak to you?'

'Yes,' he answered, fixing his eyes upon her. 'Your voice and music are the same to me.'

'May I ask you something?'

'What you will.'

'Do you remember what I said, when I knocked at your door last night? About one who was your friend once, and who stood on the verge of destruction?'

'Yes. I remember,' he said, with some hesitation.

'Do you understand it?'

He smoothed the boy's hair – looking at her fixedly the while – and shook his head.

'This person,' said Milly, in her clear, soft voice, which her mild eyes, looking at him, made clearer and softer, 'I found soon afterwards. I went back to the house, and, with heaven's help, traced him. I was not too soon. A very little and I should have been too late.'

He took his hand from the boy, and laying it on the back of that hand of hers, whose timid and yet earnest touch addressed him no less appealingly than her voice and eyes, looked more intently on her.

'He *is* the father of Mr Edmund, the young gentleman we saw just now. His real name is Longford. You recollect the name?'

'I recollect the name.'

'And the man?'

'No, not the man. Did he ever wrong me?'

'Yes!'

'Ah! Then it's hopeless – hopeless.'

He shook his head, and softly beat upon the hand he held, as though mutely asking her commiseration.

'I did not go to Mr Edmund last night – ' said Milly – 'You will listen to me just the same as if you did remember all?'

'To every syllable you say.'

' – both, because I did not know, then, that this really was his father, and because I was fearful of the effect of such intelligence upon him, after his illness, if it should be. Since I have known who this person is, I have not gone either; but that is for another reason. He has long been separated from his wife and son – has been a stranger to his home almost from this son's infancy, I learn from him – and has abandoned and deserted what he should have held most dear. In all that time he has been falling from the state of a gentleman, more and more, until –' she rose up, hastily, and going out for a moment, returned, accompanied by the wreck that Redlaw had beheld last night.

'Do you know me?' asked the chemist.

'I should be glad,' returned the other, 'and that is an unwonted word for me to use, if I could answer no.'

The chemist looked at the man standing in self-abasement and degradation before him, and would have looked longer, in an ineffectual struggle for enlightenment, but that Milly resumed her late position by his side, and attracted his attentive gaze to her own face.

'See how low he is sunk, how lost he is!' she whispered, stretching out her arm towards him, without looking from the chemist's face. 'If you could remember all that is connected with him, do you not think it would move your pity to reflect that one you ever loved (do not let us mind how long ago, or in what belief that he has forfeited), should come to this?'

'I hope it would,' he answered. 'I believe it would.' His eyes wandered to the figure standing near the door, but came back speedily to her, on whom he gazed intently, as if he strove to learn some lesson from every tone of her voice, and every beam of her eyes.

'I have no learning, and you have much,' said Milly; 'I am not urged to think, and you are always thinking. May I tell you why it seems to me a good thing for us to remember wrong that has been done us?'

'Yes.'

'That we may forgive it.'

'Pardon me, great heaven!' said Redlaw, lifting up his eyes, 'for having thrown away thine own high attribute!'

'And if,' said Milly, 'if your memory should one day be restored, as we will hope and pray it may be, would it not be a blessing to you to recall at once a wrong and its forgiveness?'

He looked at the figure by the door, and fastened his attentive eyes on her again; a ray of clearer light appeared to him to shine into his mind from her bright face.

'He cannot go to his abandoned home. He does not seek to go there. He knows that he could only carry shame and trouble to those he has so cruelly neglected; and that the best reparation he can make them now, is to avoid them. A very little money carefully bestowed, would remove him to some distant place, where he might live and do no wrong, and make such atonement as is left within his power for the wrong he has done. To the unfortunate lady who is his wife, and to his son, this would be the best and kindest boon that their best friend could give them – one too that they need never know of; and to him, shattered in reputation, mind and body, it might be salvation.'

He took her head between his hands, and kissed it, and said: 'It shall be done. I trust to you to do it for me, now and secretly, and to tell him that I would forgive him, if I were so happy as to know for what.'

As she rose, and turned her beaming face towards the fallen man, implying that her mediation had been successful, he advanced a step, and without raising his eyes, addressed himself to Redlaw. 'You are so generous,' he said, ' – you ever were – that you will try to banish your rising sense of retribution in the spectacle that is before you. I do not try to banish it from myself, Redlaw. If you can, believe me.'

The chemist entreated Milly, by a gesture, to come nearer to him; and, as he listened, looked in her face, as if to find in it the clue to what he heard.

'I am too decayed a wretch to make professions; I recollect my own career too well, to array any such before you. But from the day on which I made my first step downward, in dealing falsely by you, I have gone down with a certain, steady, doomed progression. That, I say.'

Redlaw, keeping her close at his side, turned his face towards the speaker, and there was sorrow in it. Something like mournful recognition too.

'I might have been another man, my life might have been another life, if I had avoided that first fatal step. I don't know that it would have been. I claim nothing for the possibility. Your sister is at rest, and better than she would have been with me, if I had continued even what you thought me: even what I once supposed myself to be.'

Redlaw made a hasty motion with his hand, as if he would have put that subject on one side.

'I speak,' the other went on, 'like a man taken from the grave. I should have made my own grave, last night, had it not been for this blessed hand.'

'Oh dear, he likes me too!' sobbed Milly under her breath. 'That's another!'

'I could not have put myself in your way, last night, even for bread. But, today, my recollection of what has been is so strongly stirred, and is presented to me, I don't know how, so vividly, that I have dared to come at her suggestion, and to take your bounty, and to thank you for it, and to beg you, Redlaw, in your dying hour, to be as merciful to me in your thoughts, as you are in your deeds.'

He turned towards the door, and stopped a moment on his way forth.

'I hope my son may interest you, for his mother's sake. I hope he may deserve to do so. Unless my life should be preserved a long time, and I should know that I have not misused your aid, I shall never look upon him more.'

Going out, he raised his eyes to Redlaw for the first time. Redlaw, whose steadfast gaze was fixed upon him, dreamily held out his hand. He returned and touched it – little more – with both his own; and bending down his head, went slowly out.

In the few moments that elapsed, while Milly silently took him to the gate, the chemist dropped into his chair, and covered his face with his hands. Seeing him thus, when she came back accompanied by her husband and his father (who were both greatly concerned for him), she avoided disturbing him or permitting him to be disturbed; and kneeled down near the chair to put some warm clothing on the boy.

'That's exactly where it is. That's what I always say, father!' exclaimed her admiring husband. 'There's a motherly feeling in Mrs William's breast that must and will have went!'

'Ay, ay,' said the old man; 'you're right. My son William's right!'

'It happens all for the best, Milly dear, no doubt,' said Mr William, tenderly, 'that we have no children of our own; and yet I sometimes wish you had one to love and cherish. Our little dead child that you built such hopes upon, and that never breathed the breath of life – it has made you quiet-like, Milly.'

'I am very happy in the recollection of it, William dear,' she answered. 'I think of it every day.'

'I was afraid you thought of it a good deal.'

'Don't say, afraid; it is a comfort to me; it speaks to me in so many ways. The innocent thing that never lived on earth is like an angel to me, William.'

'You are like an angel to father and me,' said Mr William, softly. 'I know that.'

'When I think of all those hopes I built upon it, and the many times I sat and pictured to myself the little smiling face upon my bosom that never lay there, and the sweet eyes turned up to mine that never opened to the light,' said Milly, 'I can feel a greater tenderness, I think, for all the disappointed hopes in which there is no harm. When I see a beautiful child in its fond mother's arms, I love it all the better, thinking that my child might have been like that, and might have made my heart as proud and happy.'

Redlaw raised his head, and looked towards her.

'All through life, it seems by me,' she continued, 'to tell me something. For poor neglected children, my little child pleads as if it were alive, and had a voice I knew, with which to speak to me. When I hear of youth in suffering or shame, I think that my child might have come to that, perhaps, and that God took it from me in his mercy. Even in age and grey hair, such as father's, it is present: saying that it too might have lived to be old, long and long after you and I were gone, and to have needed the respect and love of younger people.'

Her quiet voice was quieter than ever, as she took her husband's arm, and laid her head against it.

'Children love me so, that sometimes I half fancy – it's a silly fancy, William – they have some way I don't know of of feeling for my little child, and me, and understanding why their love is precious to me. If I have been quiet since, I have been more happy, William, in a hundred ways. Not least happy, dear, in this – that even when my little child was born and dead but a few days, and I was weak and sorrowful, and could not help grieving a little, the thought arose, that if I tried to lead a good life, I should meet in heaven a bright creature, who would call me, Mother!'

Redlaw fell upon his knees, with a loud cry.

'O Thou,' he said, 'who, through the teaching of pure love, hast graciously restored me to the memory which was the memory of Christ upon the Cross, and of all the good who perished in His cause, receive my thanks, and bless her!'

Then, he folded her to his heart; and Milly, sobbing more than ever, cried, as she laughed, 'He is come back to himself! He likes me very much indeed, too! Oh, dear, dear, dear me, here's another!'

Then, the student entered, leading by the hand a lovely girl, who was afraid to come. And Redlaw so changed towards him, seeing in him and his youthful choice the softened shadow of that chastening passage in his own life, to which, as to a shady tree, the dove so long imprisoned in his solitary ark might fly for rest and company, fell upon his neck, entreating them to be his children.

Then, as Christmas is a time in which, of all times in the year, the memory of every remediable sorrow, wrong and trouble in the world around us should be active with us, not less than our own experiences, for all good, he laid his hand upon the boy, and, silently calling Him to witness who laid His hand on children in old time, rebuking, in the majesty of His prophetic knowledge, those who kept them from Him, vowed to protect him, teach him, and reclaim him.

Then, he gave his right hand cheerily to Philip, and said that they would that day hold a Christmas dinner in what used to be, before the ten poor gentlemen commuted, their great Dinner Hall; and that they would bid to it as many of that Swidger family, who, his son had told him, were so numerous that they might join hands and make a ring round England, as could be brought together on so short a notice.

And it was that day done. There were so many Swidgers there, grown up and children, that an attempt to state them in round numbers might engender doubts, in the distrustful, of the veracity of this history. Therefore the attempt shall not be made. But there they were, by dozens and scores – and there was good news and good hope there, ready for them, of George, who had been visited again by his father and brother, and by Milly, and again left in a quiet sleep. There, present at the dinner, too, were the Tetterbys, including young Adolphus, who arrived in his prismatic comforter in good time for the beef. Johnny and the baby were too late, of course, and came in all on one side, the one exhausted, the other in a supposed state of double-tooth; but that was customary, and not alarming.

It was sad to see the child who had no name or lineage, watching the other children as they played, not knowing how to talk with them, or sport with them, and more strange to the ways of childhood than a rough dog. It was sad, though in a different way, to see what an instinctive knowledge the youngest children there had of his being different from all the rest, and how they made timid approaches to him with soft words and touches, and with little presents, that he might not be unhappy. But he kept by Milly, and began to love her – that was another, as she said! – and, as they all liked her dearly, they were glad of that, and when they saw him peeping at them from behind her chair, they were pleased that he was so close to it.

All this, the chemist, sitting with the student and his bride that was to be, and Philip, and the rest, saw.

Some people have said since that he only thought what has been herein set down; others, that he read it in the fire, one winter night about the twilight time; others, that the ghost was but the representation of his gloomy thoughts, and Milly the embodiment of his better wisdom. *I* say nothing.

– Except this. That as they were assembled in the old Hall, by no other light than that of a great fire (having dined early), the shadows once more stole out of their hiding-places, and danced about the room, showing the children marvellous shapes and faces on the walls, and gradually changing what was real and familiar there to what was wild and magical. But that there was one thing in the Hall to which the eyes of Redlaw, and of Milly and her husband, and of the old man, and of the student and his bride that was to be, were often turned, which the shadows did not obscure or change. Deepened in its gravity by the firelight, and gazing from the darkness of the panelled wall like life, the sedate face in the portrait, with the beard and ruff, looked down at them from under its verdant wreath of holly, as they looked up at it; and clear and plain below, as if a voice had uttered them, were the words,

𝕷ord, keep my memory green.

CHRISTMAS GHOSTS

I like to come home at Christmas. We all do, or we all *should*. We all come home, or ought to come home, for a short holiday – the longer, the better – from the great boarding-school, where we are for ever working at our arithmetical slates, to take, and give a rest. As to going a-visiting, where can we not go, if we will; where have we not been, when we would; starting our fancy from our Christmas Tree!

Away into the winter prospect. There are many such upon the tree! On, by low-lying, misty grounds, through fens and fogs, up long hills, winding dark as caverns between thick plantations, almost shutting out the sparkling stars; so, out on broad heights, until we stop at last, with sudden silence, at an avenue. The gate-bell has a deep, half-awful sound in the frosty air; the gate swings open on its hinges; and, as we drive up to a great house, the glancing lights grow larger in the windows, and the opposing rows of trees seem to fall solemnly back on either side, to give us place. At intervals, all day, a frightened hare has shot across this whitened turf; or the distant clatter of a herd of deer trampling the hard frost, has, for the minute, crushed the silence too. Their watchful eyes beneath the fern may be shining now, if we could see them, like the icy dewdrops on the leaves; but they are still, and all is still. And so, the lights growing larger, and the trees falling back before us, and closing up again behind us, as if to forbid retreat, we come to the house.

There is probably a smell of roasted chestnuts and other good comfortable things all the time, for we are telling Winter Stories – Ghost Stories, or more shame for us – round the Christmas fire; and we have never stirred, except to draw a little nearer to it. But, no matter for that. We come to the house, and it is an old house, full of great chimneys where wood is burnt on ancient dogs upon the hearth, and grim portraits (some of them with grim legends, too) lour distrustfully from the oaken panels of the walls. We are a middle-aged nobleman, and we make a generous supper with our host and hostess and their guests – it being Christmastime, and the old house full of company – and then we go to bed. Our room is a very old room. It is hung with tapestry. We don't like the portrait of a cavalier in green, over the fireplace. There are great black beams in the ceiling, and there is a great black bedstead, supported at the foot by two great black figures, who seem to have come off a couple of tombs in the old baronial church in the park, for our particular accommodation. But, we are not a superstitious nobleman, and we don't mind. Well! we dismiss our servant, lock the door, and sit before the fire in our dressing-gown, musing about a great many things. At length we go to bed. Well! we can't sleep. We toss and tumble, and can't sleep. The embers on the hearth burn fitfully and make the room look ghostly. We can't help peeping out over the counterpane at the two black figures and the cavalier – that wicked-looking cavalier – in green. In the flickering light they seem to advance and retire: which, though we are not by any means a superstitious nobleman, is not agreeable. Well! we get nervous – more and more nervous. We say, 'This is very foolish, but we can't stand this; we'll pretend to be ill, and knock up somebody.' Well! we are just going to do it, when the locked door opens, and there comes in a young woman, deadly pale, and with long fair hair, who glides to the fire, and sits down in the chair we have left there, wringing her hands. Then, we notice that her clothes are wet. Our tongue cleaves to the roof of our mouth, and we can't speak; but, we observe her accurately. Her clothes are wet; her long hair is dabbled with moist mud; she is dressed in the fashion of two hundred years ago; and she has at her girdle a bunch of rusty keys. Well! there she sits, and we can't even faint, we are in such a state about it. Presently she gets up, and tries all the locks in the room with the rusty keys, which won't fit one of them; then, she fixes her eyes on the portrait of the cavalier in green, and says, in a low, terrible voice, 'The stags know it!' After that, she wrings her hands again, passes the bedside, and goes out at the door. We hurry on our dressing-gown, seize our pistols (we always travel with pistols), and are following, when we find the door locked. We turn the key, look out into the dark gallery; no one there. We wander away, and try to find our servant. Can't be done. We pace the gallery till daybreak; then return to our deserted room, fall asleep, and are awakened by our servant (nothing ever haunts him) and the shining sun. Well! we make a wretched breakfast, and all the company say we look queer. After breakfast, we go over the house with our host, and then we take him to the portrait of the cavalier in green, and then it all comes out. He was false to a young housekeeper once attached to that family, and famous for her beauty, who drowned herself in a pond, and whose body was discovered, after a long time, because the stags refused to drink of the water. Since which, it has been whispered that she traverses the house at midnight (but goes especially to that room where the cavalier in green was wont to sleep), trying the old locks with the rusty keys. Well! we tell our host of what we have seen, and a shade comes over his features, and he begs it may be hushed up; and so it is. But, it's all true; and we said so, before we died (we are dead now) to many responsible people.

There is no end to the old houses, with resounding galleries, and dismal state-bedchambers, and haunted wings shut up for many years, through which we may ramble, with an agreeable creeping up our back, and encounter any number of ghosts, but (it is worthy of remark perhaps) reducible to a very few general types and classes; for, ghosts have little originality, and 'walk' in a beaten track. Thus, it comes to pass, that a certain room in a certain old hall, where a certain bad lord, baronet, knight, or gentleman, shot himself, has certain planks in the floor from which the blood *will not* be taken out. You may scrape and scrape, as the present owner has done, or plane and plane, as his father did, or scrub and scrub, as his grandfather did, or burn and burn with strong acids, as his great- grandfather did, but, there the blood will still be – no redder and no paler – no more and no less – always just the same. Thus, in such another house there is a haunted door, that never will keep open; or another door that never will keep shut, or a haunted sound of a spinning-wheel, or a hammer, or a footstep, or a cry, or a sigh, or a horse's tramp, or the rattling of a chain. Or else, there is a turret-clock, which, at the midnight hour, strikes thirteen when the head of the family is going to die; or a shadowy, immovable black carriage which at such a time is always seen by somebody, waiting near the great gates in the stable-yard. Or thus, it came to pass how Lady Mary went to pay a visit at a large wild house in the Scottish Highlands, and, being fatigued with her long journey, retired to bed early, and innocently said, next morning, at the breakfast-table, 'How odd, to have so late a party last night, in this remote place, and not to tell me of it, before I went to bed!' Then, everyone asked Lady Mary what she meant? Then, Lady Mary replied, 'Why, all night long, the carriages were driving round and round the terrace, underneath my window!' Then, the owner of the house turned pale, and so did his Lady, and Charles Macdoodle of Macdoodle signed to Lady Mary to say no more, and everyone was silent. After breakfast, Charles Macdoodle told Lady Mary that it was a tradition in the family that those rumbling carriages on the terrace betokened death. And so it proved, for, two months afterwards, the Lady of the mansion died. And Lady Mary, who was a Maid of Honour at Court, often told this story to the old Queen Charlotte; by this token that the old King always said, 'Eh, eh? What, what? Ghosts, ghosts? No such thing, no such thing!' And never left off saying so, until he went to bed.

Or, a friend of somebody's whom most of us know, when he was a young man at college, had a particular friend, with whom he made the compact that, if it were possible for the Spirit to return to this earth after its separation from the body, he of the twain who first died, should reappear to the other. In course of time, this compact was forgotten by our friend; the two young men having progressed in life, and taken diverging paths that were wide asunder. But, one night, many years afterwards, our friend being in the North of England, and staying for the night in an inn, on the Yorkshire Moors, happened to look out of bed; and there, in the moonlight, leaning on a bureau near the window, steadfastly regarding him, saw his old college friend! The appearance being solemnly addressed, replied, in a kind of whisper, but very audibly, 'Do not come near me. I am dead. I am here to redeem my promise. I come from another world, but may not disclose its secrets!' Then, the whole form becoming paler, melted, as it were, into the moonlight, and faded away.

Or, there was the daughter of the first occupier of the picturesque Elizabethan house, so famous in our neighbourhood. You have heard about her? No! Why, *she* went out one summer evening at twilight, when she was a beautiful girl, just seventeen years of age, to gather flowers in the garden; and presently came running, terrified, into the hall to her father, saying, 'Oh, dear father, I have met myself!' He took her in his arms, and told her it was fancy, but she said, 'Oh no! I met myself in the broad walk, and I was pale and gathering withered flowers, and I turned my head, and held them up!' And, that night, she died; and a picture of her story was begun, though never finished, and they say it is somewhere in the house to this day, with its face to the wall.

Or, the uncle of my brother's wife was riding home on horseback, one mellow evening at sunset, when, in a green lane close to his own house, he saw a man standing before him, in the very centre of a narrow way. 'Why does that man in the cloak stand there!' he thought. 'Does he want me to ride over him?' But the figure never moved. He felt a strange sensation at seeing it so still, but slackened his trot and rode forward. When he was so close to it, as almost to touch it with his stirrup, his horse shied, and the figure glided up the bank, in a curious, unearthly manner – backward, and without seeming to use its feet – and was gone. The uncle of my brother's wife, exclaiming, 'Good Heaven! It's my cousin Harry, from Bombay!' put spurs to his horse, which was suddenly in a profuse sweat, and, wondering at such strange behaviour, dashed round to the front of his house. There, he saw the same figure, just passing in at the long French window of the drawing-room, opening on the ground. He threw his bridle to a servant, and hastened in after it. His sister was sitting there, alone. 'Alice, where's my cousin Harry?' 'Your cousin Harry, John?' 'Yes. From Bombay. I met him in the lane just now, and saw him enter here, this instant.' Not a creature had been seen by anyone; and in that hour and minute, as it afterwards appeared, this cousin died in India.

Or, it was a certain sensible old maiden lady, who died at ninety-nine, and retained her faculties to the last, who really did see the Orphan Boy; a story which has often been incorrectly told, but, of which the real truth is this – because it is, in fact, a story belonging to our family – and she was a connection of our family. When she was about forty years of age, and still an uncommonly fine woman (her lover died young, which was the reason why she never married, though she had many offers), she went to stay at a place in Kent, which her brother, an Indian-Merchant, had newly bought. There was a story that this place had once been held in trust by the guardian of a young boy; who was himself the next heir, and who killed the young boy by harsh and cruel treatment. She knew nothing of that. It has been said that there was a cage in her bedroom in which the guardian used to put the boy. There was no such thing. There was only a closet. She went to bed, made no alarm whatever in the night, and in the morning said composedly to her maid when she came in, 'Who is the pretty forlorn-looking child who has been peeping out of that closet all night?' The maid replied by giving a loud scream, and instantly decamping. She was surprised; but she was a woman of remarkable strength of mind, and she dressed herself and went downstairs, and closeted herself with her brother. 'Now, Walter,' she said, 'I have been disturbed all night by a pretty, forlorn-looking boy, who has been constantly peeping out of that closet in my room, which I can't open. This is some trick.' 'I am afraid not, Charlotte,' said he, 'for it is the legend of the house. It is the Orphan Boy. What did he do?' 'He opened the door softly,' said she, 'and peeped out. Sometimes, he came a step or two into the room. Then, I called to him, to encourage him, and he shrank, and shuddered, and crept in again, and shut the door.' 'The closet has no communication, Charlotte,' said her brother, 'with any other part of the house, and it's nailed up.' This was undeniably true, and it took two carpenters a whole forenoon to get it open, for examination. Then, she was satisfied that she had seen the Orphan Boy. But the wild and terrible part of the story is that he was also seen by three of her brother's sons, in succession, who all died young. On the occasion of each child being taken ill, he came home in a heat, twelve hours before, and said, Oh, Mamma, he had been playing under a particular oak tree, in a certain meadow, with a strange boy – a pretty, forlorn-looking boy, who was very timid, and made signs! From fatal experience, the parents came to know that this was the Orphan Boy, and that the course of that child whom he chose for his little playmate was surely run.

THE QUEER CHAIR

The Bagman's Story

One winter's evening, about five o'clock, just as it began to grow dusk, a man in a gig might have been seen urging his tired horse along the road which leads across Marlborough Downs, in the direction of Bristol. I say he might have been seen, and I have no doubt he would have been, if anybody but a blind man had happened to pass that way; but the weather was so bad, and the night so cold and wet, that nothing was out but the water, and so the traveller jogged along in the middle of the road, lonesome and dreary enough. If any bagman of that day could have caught sight of the little neck-or-nothing sort of gig, with a clay-coloured body and red wheels, and the vixenish ill-tempered fast-going bay mare that looked like a cross between a butcher's horse and a twopenny post-office pony, he would have known at once that this traveller could have been no other than Tom Smart, of the great house of Bilson and Slum, Cateaton Street, City. However, as there was no bagman to look on, nobody knew anything at all about the matter; and so Tom Smart and his clay-coloured gig with the red wheels, and the vixenish mare with the fast pace, went on together keeping the secret among them: and nobody was a bit the wiser.

There are many pleasanter places even in this dreary world than Marlborough Downs when it blows hard; and if you throw in beside, a gloomy winter's evening, a miry and sloppy road, and a pelting fall of heavy rain, and try the effect, by way of experiment, in your own proper person, you will experience the full force of this observation.

The wind blew – not up the road or down it, though that's bad enough, but sheer across it, sending the rain slanting down like the lines they used to rule in the copybooks at school, to make the boys slope well. For a moment it would die away, and the traveller would begin to delude himself into the belief that, exhausted with its previous fury, it had quietly lain itself down to rest, when, whoo! he would hear it growling and whistling in the distance, and on it would come rushing over the hilltops, and sweeping along the plain, gathering sound and strength as it drew nearer, until it dashed with a heavy gust against horse and man, driving the sharp rain into their ears and its cold damp breath into their very bones; and past them it would scour, far, far away, with a stunning roar, as if in ridicule of their weakness and triumphant in the consciousness of its own strength and power.

The bay mare splashed away, through the mud and water, with drooping ears; now and then tossing her head as if to express her disgust at this very ungentlemanly behaviour of the elements, but keeping a good pace notwithstanding, until a gust of wind, more furious than any that had yet assailed them, caused her to stop suddenly and plant her four feet firmly against the ground, to prevent her being blown over. It's a special mercy that she did this, for if she *had* been blown over, the vixenish mare was so light, and the gig was so light, and Tom Smart such a light weight into the bargain, that they must infallibly have all gone rolling over and over together, until they reached the confines of earth, or until the wind fell; and in either case the probability is that neither the vixenish mare, nor the clay-coloured gig with the red wheels, nor Tom Smart, would ever have been fit for service again.

'Well, damn my straps and whiskers,' says Tom Smart (Tom sometimes had an unpleasant knack of swearing), 'Damn my straps and whiskers,' says Tom, 'if this ain't pleasant, blow me!'

You'll very likely ask me why, as Tom Smart had been pretty well blown already, he expressed this wish to be submitted to the same process again. I can't say – all I know is that Tom Smart said so – or at least he always told my uncle he said so, and it's just the same thing.

'Blow me,' says Tom Smart; and the mare neighed as if she were precisely of the same opinion.

'Cheer up, old girl,' said Tom, patting the bay mare on the neck with the end of his whip. 'It won't do pushing on, such a night as this; the first house we come to we'll put up at, so the faster you go the sooner it's over. Soho, old girl – gently – gently.'

Whether the vixenish mare was sufficiently well acquainted with the tones of Tom's voice to comprehend his meaning, or whether she found it colder standing still than moving on, of course I can't say. But I can say that Tom had no sooner finished speaking, than she pricked up her ears, and started forward at a speed which made the clay-coloured gig rattle till you would have supposed every one of the red spokes were going to fly out on the turf of Marlborough Downs; and even Tom, whip as he was, couldn't stop or check her pace, until she drew up, of her own accord, before a roadside inn on the right-hand side of the way, about half a quarter of a mile from the end of the Downs.

Tom cast a hasty glance at the upper part of the house as he threw the reins to the hostler, and stuck the whip in the box. It was a strange old place, built of a kind of shingle, inlaid, as it were, with crossbeams, with gabled-topped windows projecting completely over the pathway and a low door with a dark porch, and a couple of steep steps leading down into the house, instead of the modern fashion of half a dozen shallow ones leading up to it. It was a comfortable-looking place though, for there was a strong cheerful light in the bar-window, which shed a bright ray across the road, and even lighted up the hedge on the other side; and there was a red flickering light in the opposite window, one moment but faintly discernible, and the next gleaming strongly through the drawn curtains, which intimated that a rousing fire was blazing within. Marking these little evidences with the eye of an experienced traveller, Tom dismounted with as much agility as his half-frozen limbs would permit, and entered the house.

In less than five minutes' time, Tom was ensconced in the room opposite the bar – the very room where he had imagined the fire blazing – before a substantial matter-of-fact roaring fire, composed of something short of a bushel of coals, and wood enough to make half a dozen decent gooseberry bushes, piled halfway up the chimney, and roaring and crackling with a sound that of itself would have warmed the heart of any reasonable man. This was comfortable, but this was not all, for a smartly-dressed girl, with a bright eye and a neat ankle, was laying a very clean white cloth on the table; and as Tom sat with his slippered feet on the fender, and his back to the open door, he saw a charming prospect of the bar reflected in the glass over the chimney-piece, with delightful rows of green bottles and gold labels, together with jars of pickles and preserves, and cheeses and boiled hams, and rounds of beef arranged on shelves in the most tempting and delicious array. Well, this was comfortable too; but even this was not all – for in the bar, seated at tea at the nicest possible little table, drawn close up before the brightest possible little fire, was a buxom widow of somewhere about eight-and-forty or thereabouts, with a face as comfortable as the bar, who was evidently the landlady of the house, and the supreme ruler over all these agreeable possessions. There was only one drawback to the beauty of the whole picture, and that was a tall man – a very tall man – in a brown coat and bright basket buttons, and black whiskers and wavy black hair, who was seated at tea with the widow, and who it required no great penetration to discover was in a fair way of persuading her to be a widow no longer, but to confer upon him the privilege of sitting down in that bar for and during the whole remainder of the term of his natural life.

Tom Smart was by no means of an irritable or envious disposition, but somehow or other the tall man with the brown coat and the bright basket buttons did rouse what little gall he had in his composition, and did make him feel extremely indignant: the more especially as he could now and then observe, from his seat before the glass, certain little affectionate familiarities passing between the tall man and the widow, which sufficiently denoted that the tall man was as high in favour as he was in size. Tom was fond of hot punch – I may venture to say he was *very* fond of hot punch – and after he had seen the vixenish mare well fed and well littered down, and had eaten every bit of the nice little hot dinner which the widow tossed up for him with her own hands, he just ordered a tumbler of it, by way of experiment. Now, if there was one thing in the whole range of domestic art which the widow could manufacture better than another, it was this identical article; and the first tumbler was adapted to Tom Smart's taste with such peculiar nicety that he ordered a second with the least possible delay. Hot punch is a pleasant thing, gentlemen – an extremely pleasant thing under any circumstances – but in that snug old parlour, before the roaring fire, with the wind blowing outside till every timber in the old house creaked again, Tom Smart found it perfectly delightful. He ordered another tumbler, and then another – I am not quite certain whether he didn't order another after that – but the more he drank of the hot punch, the more he thought of the tall man.

'Confound his impudence!' said Tom to himself, 'what business has he in that snug bar? Such an ugly villain too!' said Tom. 'If the widow had any taste, she might surely pick up some better fellow than that.' Here Tom's eye wandered from the glass on the chimney-piece, to the glass on the table; and as he felt himself become gradually sentimental, he emptied the fourth tumbler of punch and ordered a fifth.

Tom Smart, gentlemen, had always been very much attached to the public line. It had long been his ambition to stand in a bar of his own, in a green coat, knee-cords, and tops. He had a great notion of taking the chair at convivial dinners, and he had often thought how well he could preside in a room of his own in the talking way, and what a capital example he could set to his customers in the drinking compartment. All these things passed rapidly through Tom's mind as he sat drinking the hot punch by the roaring fire, and he felt very justly and properly indignant that the tall man should be in a fair way of keeping such an excellent house, while he, Tom Smart, was as far from it as ever. So, after deliberating over the last two tumblers, whether he hadn't a perfect right to pick a quarrel with the tall man for having contrived to get into the good graces of the buxom widow, Tom Smart at last arrived at the satisfactory conclusion that he was a very ill-used and persecuted individual, and had better go to bed.

Up a wide and ancient staircase the smart girl preceded Tom, shading the chamber candle with her hand, to protect it from the currents of air which in such a rambling old place might have found plenty of room to disport themselves in, without blowing the candle out, but which did blow it out nevertheless; thus affording Tom's enemies an opportunity of asserting that it was he, and not the wind, who extinguished the candle, and that while he pretended to be blowing it alight again, he was in fact kissing the girl. Be this as it may, another light was obtained, and Tom was conducted through a maze of rooms, and a labyrinth of passages, to the apartment which had been prepared for his reception, where the girl bade him good-night and left him alone.

It was a good large room with big closets, and a bed which might have served for a whole boarding-school, to say nothing of a couple of oaken presses that would have held the baggage of a small army; but what struck Tom's fancy most was a strange, grim-looking high-backed chair, carved in the most fantastic manner, with a flowered damask cushion, and the round knobs at the bottom of the legs carefully tied up in red cloth, as if it had got the gout in its toes. Of any other queer chair, Tom would only have thought it *was* a queer chair, and there would have been an end of the matter; but there was something about this particular chair, and yet he couldn't tell what it was, so odd and so unlike any other piece of furniture he had ever seen, that it seemed to fascinate him. He sat down before the fire, and stared at the old chair for half an hour; deuce take the chair, it was such a strange old thing, he couldn't take his eyes off it.

'Well,' said Tom, slowly undressing himself, and staring at the old chair all the while, which stood with a mysterious aspect by the bedside, 'I never saw such a rum concern as that in all my days. Very odd,' said Tom, who had got rather sage with the hot punch. 'Very odd.' Tom shook his head with an air of profound wisdom, and looked at the chair again. He couldn't make anything of it though, so he got into bed, covered himself up warm, and fell asleep.

In about half an hour, Tom woke up, with a start, from a confused dream of tall men and tumblers of punch: and the first object that presented itself to his waking imagination was the queer chair.

'I won't look at it any more,' said Tom to himself, and he squeezed his eyelids together, and tried to persuade himself he was going to sleep again. No use; nothing but queer chairs danced before his eyes, kicking up their legs, jumping over each other's backs, and playing all kinds of antics.

'I may as well see one real chair, as two or three complete sets of false ones,' said Tom, bringing out his head from under the bedclothes. There it was, plainly discernible by the light of the fire, looking as provoking as ever.

Tom gazed at the chair; and, suddenly as he looked at it, a most extraordinary change seemed to come over it. The carving of the back gradually assumed the lineaments and expression of an old shrivelled human face; the damask cushion became an antique, flapped waistcoat; the round knobs grew into a couple of feet, encased in red cloth slippers; and the old chair looked like a very ugly old man of the previous century, with his arms akimbo. Tom sat up in bed, and rubbed his eyes to dispel the illusion. No. The chair was an ugly old gentleman; and what was more, he was winking at Tom Smart.

Tom was naturally a headlong, careless sort of dog, and he had had five tumblers of hot punch into the bargain; so, although he was a little startled at first, he began to grow rather indignant when he saw the old gentleman winking and leering at him with such an impudent air. At length he resolved he wouldn't stand it; and as the old face still kept winking away as fast as ever, Tom said, in a very angry tone: 'What the devil are you winking at me for?'

'Because I like it, Tom Smart,' said the chair; or the old gentleman, whichever you like to call him. He stopped winking though, when Tom spoke, and began grinning like a superannuated monkey.

'How do you know my name, old nutcracker face!' enquired Tom Smart, rather staggered – though he pretended to carry it off so well.

'Come, come, Tom,' said the old gentleman, 'that's not the way to address solid Spanish mahogany. Dam'me, you couldn't treat me with less respect if I was veneered.' When the old gentleman said this, he looked so fierce that Tom began to be frightened.

'I didn't mean to treat you with any disrespect, sir,' said Tom; in a much humbler tone than he had spoken in at first.

'Well, well,' said the old fellow, 'perhaps not – perhaps not. Tom – '

'Sir – '

'I know everything about you, Tom; everything. You're very poor, Tom.'

'I certainly am,' said Tom Smart. 'But how came you to know that?'

'Never mind that,' said the old gentleman; 'you're much too fond of punch, Tom.'

Tom Smart was just on the point of protesting that he hadn't tasted a drop since his last birthday, but when his eye encountered that of the old gentleman, he looked so knowing that Tom blushed, and was silent.

'Tom,' said the old gentleman, 'the widow's a fine woman – remarkably fine woman – eh, Tom?' Here the old fellow screwed up his eyes, cocked up one of his wasted little legs, and looked altogether so unpleasantly amorous, that Tom was quite disgusted with the levity of his behaviour – at his time of life, too!

'I am her guardian, Tom,' said the old gentleman.

'Are you?' enquired Tom Smart.

'I knew her mother, Tom,' said the old fellow; 'and her grandmother. She was very fond of me – made me this waistcoat, Tom.'

'Did she?' said Tom Smart.

'And these shoes,' said the old fellow, lifting up one of the red-cloth mufflers; 'but, don't mention it, Tom. I shouldn't like to have it known that she was so much attached to me. It might occasion some unpleasantness in the family.' When the old rascal said this, he looked so extremely impertinent, that, as Tom Smart afterwards declared, he could have sat upon him without remorse.

'I have been a great favourite among the women in my time, Tom,' said the profligate old debauchee; 'hundreds of fine women have sat in my lap for hours together. What do you think of that, you dog, eh!' The old gentleman was proceeding to recount some other exploits of his youth, when he was seized with such a violent fit of creaking that he was unable to proceed.

'Just serves you right, old boy,' thought Tom Smart; but he didn't say anything.

'Ah!' said the old fellow, 'I am a good deal troubled with this now. I am getting old, Tom, and have lost nearly all my rails. I have had an operation performed, too – a small piece let into my back and I found it a severe trial, Tom.'

'I dare say you did, sir,' said Tom Smart.

'However,' said the old gentleman, 'that's not the point. Tom! I want you to marry the widow.'

'Me, sir!' said Tom.

'You,' said the old gentleman.

'Bless your reverend locks,' said Tom (he had a few scattered horse-hairs left), 'bless your reverend locks, she wouldn't have me.' And Tom sighed involuntarily, as he thought of the bar.

'Wouldn't she?' said the old gentleman, firmly.

'No, no,' said Tom; 'there's somebody else in the wind. A tall man – a confoundedly tall man – with black whiskers.'

'Tom,' said the old gentleman; 'she will never have him.'

'Won't she?' said Tom. 'If you stood in the bar, old gentleman, you'd tell another story.'

'Pooh, pooh,' said the old gentleman. 'I know all about that.'

'About what?' said Tom.

'The kissing behind the door, and all that sort of thing, Tom,' said the old gentleman. And here he gave another impudent look, which made Tom very wroth, because as you all know, gentlemen, to hear an old fellow, who ought to know better, talking about these things, is very unpleasant – nothing more so.

'I know all about that, Tom,' said the old gentleman. 'I have seen it done very often in my time, Tom, between more people than I should like to mention to you; but it never came to anything after all.'

'You must have seen some queer things,' said Tom with an inquisitive look.

'You may say that, now,' replied the old fellow, with a very complicated wink. 'I am the last of my family, Tom,' said the old gentleman, with a melancholy sigh.

'Was it a large one?' enquired Tom Smart.

'There were twelve of us, Tom,' said the old gentleman; 'fine straight-backed, handsome fellows as you'd wish to see. None of your modern abortions – all with arms, and with a degree of polish, though I say it that should not, which would have done your heart good to behold.'

'And what's become of the others, sir?' asked Tom Smart.

The old gentleman applied his elbow to his eye as he replied, 'Gone,

Tom, gone. We had hard service, Tom, and they hadn't all my constitution. They got rheumatic about the legs and arms, and went into kitchens and other hospitals; and one of 'em, with long service and hard usage, positively lost his senses: he got so crazy that he was obliged to be burnt. Shocking thing that, Tom.'

'Dreadful!' said Tom Smart.

The old fellow paused for a few minutes, apparently struggling with his feelings of emotion, and then said: 'However, Tom, I am wandering from the point. This tall man, Tom, is a rascally adventurer. The moment he married the widow, he would sell off all the furniture, and run away. What would be the consequence? She would be deserted and reduced to ruin, and I should catch my death of cold in some broker's shop.'

'Yes, but –'

'Don't interrupt me,' said the old gentleman. 'Of you, Tom, I entertain a very different opinion; for I well know that if you once settled yourself in a public-house, you would never leave it, as long as there was anything to drink within its walls.'

'I am very much obliged to you for your good opinion, sir,' said Tom Smart.

'Therefore,' resumed the old gentleman, in a dictatorial tone, 'you shall have her, and he shall not.'

'What is to prevent it?' said Tom Smart, eagerly.

'This disclosure,' replied the old gentleman; 'he is already married.'

'How can I prove it?' said Tom, starting half out of bed.

The old gentleman untucked his arm from his side, and having pointed to one of the oaken presses, immediately replaced it in its old position.

'He little thinks,' said the old gentleman, 'that in the right-hand pocket of a pair of trousers in that press, he has left a letter, entreating him to return to his disconsolate wife, with six – mark me, Tom – six babes, and all of them small ones.'

As the old gentleman solemnly uttered these words, his features grew less and less distinct, and his figure more shadowy. A film came over Tom Smart's eyes. The old man seemed gradually blending into the chair, the damask waistcoat to resolve into a cushion, the red slippers to shrink into little red cloth bags. The light faded gently away, and Tom Smart fell back on his pillow, and dropped asleep.

Morning aroused Tom from the lethargic slumber into which he had fallen on the disappearance of the old man. He sat up in bed, and for some minutes vainly endeavoured to recall the events of the preceding night. Suddenly they rushed upon him. He looked at the chair; it was a fantastic grim-looking piece of furniture, certainly, but it must have been a remarkably ingenious and lively imagination that could have discovered any resemblance between it and an old man.

'How are you, old boy?' said Tom. He was bolder in the daylight – most men are.

The chair remained motionless, and spoke not a word.

'Miserable morning,' said Tom. No. The chair would not be drawn into conversation.

'Which press did you point to? – can you tell me that?' said Tom. Devil a word, gentlemen, the chair would say.

'It's not much trouble to open it anyhow,' said Tom, getting out of bed very deliberately. He walked up to one of the presses. The key was in the lock; he turned it, and opened the door. There was a pair of trousers there. He put his hand into the pocket and drew forth the identical letter the old gentleman had described!

'Queer sort of thing, this,' said Tom Smart; looking first at the chair and then at the press, and then at the letter, and then at the chair again. 'Very queer,' said Tom. But, as there was nothing in either to lessen the queerness, he thought he might as well dress himself and settle the tall man's business at once – just to put him out of his misery.

Tom surveyed the rooms he passed through on his way downstairs with the scrutinising eye of a landlord; thinking it not impossible, that before long, they and their contents would be his property. The tall man was standing in the snug little bar, with his hands behind him, quite at home. He grinned vacantly at Tom. A casual observer might have supposed he did it only to show his white teeth; but Tom Smart thought that a consciousness of triumph was passing through the place where the tall man's mind would have been, if he had had any. Tom laughed in his face; and summoned the landlady.

'Good-morning, ma'am,' said Tom Smart, closing the door of the little parlour as the widow entered.

'Good-morning, sir,' said the widow. 'What will you take for breakfast, sir?'

Tom was thinking how he should open the case, so he made no answer.

'There's a very nice ham,' said the widow, 'and a beautiful cold larded fowl. Shall I send 'em in, sir?'

These words roused Tom from his reflections. His admiration of the widow increased as she spoke. Thoughtful creature! Comfortable provider!

'Who is that gentleman in the bar, ma'am?' enquired Tom.

'His name is Jinkins, sir,' said the widow, slightly blushing.

'He's a tall man,' said Tom.

'He is a very fine man,' replied the widow, 'and a very nice gentleman.'

'Ah!' said Tom.

'Is there anything more you want, sir?' enquired the widow, rather puzzled by Tom's manner.

'Why, yes,' said Tom. 'My dear ma'am, will you have the kindness to sit down for one moment?'

The widow looked much amazed but she sat down, and Tom sat down too, close beside her. I don't know how it happened, gentlemen – indeed my uncle used to tell me that Tom Smart said *he* didn't know how it happened either – but somehow or other the palm of Tom's hand fell upon the back of the widow's hand, and remained there while he spoke.

'My dear ma'am,' said Tom Smart – he had always a great notion of committing the amiable – 'My dear ma'am, you deserve a very excellent husband; you do indeed.'

'Lor, sir!' said the widow – as well she might: Tom's mode of commencing the conversation being rather unusual, not to say startling; the fact of his never having set eyes upon her before the previous night, being taken into consideration. 'Lor, sir!'

'I scorn to flatter, my dear ma'am,' said Tom Smart. 'You deserve a very admirable husband, and whoever he is, he'll be a very lucky man.' As Tom said this his eye involuntarily wandered from the widow's face, to the comforts around him.

The widow looked more puzzled than ever, and made an effort to rise. Tom gently pressed her hand, as if to detain her, and she kept her seat. Widows, gentlemen, are not usually timorous, as my uncle used to say.

'I am sure I am very much obliged to you, sir, for your good opinion,' said the buxom landlady, half laughing; 'and if ever I marry again – '

'*If*,' said Tom Smart, looking very shrewdly out of the right-hand corner of his left eye. '*If* – '

'Well,' said the widow, laughing outright this time. '*When* I do, I hope I shall have as good a husband as you describe.'

'Jinkins to wit,' said Tom.

'Lor, sir!' exclaimed the widow.

'Oh, don't tell me,' said Tom, 'I know him.'

'I am sure nobody who knows him, knows anything bad of him,' said the widow, bridling up at the mysterious air with which Tom had spoken.

'Hem!' said Tom Smart.

The widow began to think it was high time to cry, so she took out her handkerchief, and enquired whether Tom wished to insult her: whether he thought it like a gentleman to take away the character of another gentleman behind his back; why, if he had got anything to say, he didn't say it to the man, like a man, instead of terrifying a poor weak woman in that way; and so forth.

'I'll say it to him fast enough,' said Tom, 'only I want you to hear it first.'

'What is it?' enquired the widow, looking intently in Tom's countenance.

'I'll astonish you,' said Tom, putting his hand in his pocket.

'If it is that he wants money,' said the widow, 'I know that already, and you needn't trouble yourself.'

'Pooh, nonsense, that's nothing,' said Tom Smart. '*I* want money. 'Tain't that.'

'Oh, dear, what can it be?' exclaimed the poor widow.

'Don't be frightened,' said Tom Smart. He slowly drew forth the letter, and unfolded it. 'You won't scream?' said Tom doubtfully.

'No, no,' replied the widow; 'let me see it.'

'You won't go fainting away, or any of that nonsense?' said Tom.

'No, no,' returned the widow, hastily.

'And don't run out, and blow him up,' said Tom, 'because I'll do all that for you; you had better not exert yourself.'

'Well, well,' said the widow, 'let me see it.'

'I will,' replied Tom Smart; and, with these words, he placed the letter in the widow's hand.

Gentlemen, I have heard my uncle say that Tom Smart said the widow's lamentations when she heard the disclosure would have pierced a heart of stone. Tom was certainly very tender-hearted, but they pierced his, to the very core. The widow rocked herself to and fro, and wrung her hands.

'Oh, the deception and villainy of man!' said the widow.

'Frightful, my dear ma'am; but compose yourself,' said Tom Smart.

'Oh, I can't compose myself,' shrieked the widow. 'I shall never find anyone else I can love so much!'

'Oh yes, you will, my dear soul,' said Tom Smart, letting fall a shower of the largest sized tears, in pity for the widow's misfortunes. Tom Smart, in the energy of his compassion, had put his arm round the widow's waist; and the widow, in a passion of grief, had clasped Tom's hand. She looked up in Tom's face, and smiled through her tears. Tom looked down in hers, and smiled through his.

I never could find out, gentlemen, whether Tom did or did not kiss the widow at that particular moment. He used to tell my uncle he didn't, but I have my doubts about it. Between ourselves, gentlemen, I rather think he did.

At all events, Tom kicked the very tall man out at the front door half an hour after, and married the widow a month after. And he used to drive about the country, with the clay-coloured gig with red wheels, and the vixenish mare with the fast pace, till he gave up business many years afterwards, and went to France with his wife; and then the old house was pulled down.

A MADMAN'S
MANUSCRIPT

'Yes! – a madman's! How that word would have struck to my heart, many years ago! How it would have roused the terror that used to come upon me sometimes, sending the blood hissing and tingling through my veins, till the cold dew of fear stood in large drops upon my skin and my knees knocked together with fright! I like it now though. It's a fine name. Show me the monarch whose angry frown was ever feared like the glare of a madman's eye – whose cord and axe were ever half so sure as a madman's grip. Ho! ho! It's a grand thing to be mad! to be peeped at like a wild lion through the iron bars – to gnash one's teeth and howl, through the long still night, to the merry ring of a heavy chain – and to roll and twine among the straw, transported with such brave music. Hurrah for the madhouse! Oh, it's a rare place!

'I remember days when I was *afraid* of being mad; when I used to start from my sleep, and fall upon my knees, and pray to be spared from the curse of my race; when I rushed from the sight of merriment or happiness, to hide myself in some lonely place and spend the weary hours in watching the progress of the fever that was to consume my brain. I knew that madness was mixed up with my very blood, and the marrow of my bones! that one generation had passed away without the pestilence appearing among them, and that I was the first in whom it would revive. I knew it *must* be so: that so it always had been, and so it ever would be: and when I cowered in some obscure corner of a crowded room, and saw men whisper, and point, and turn their eyes towards me, I knew they were telling each other of the doomed madman; and I slunk away again to mope in solitude.

'I did this for years; long, long years they were. The nights here are long sometimes – very long; but they are nothing to the restless nights, and dreadful dreams I had at that time. It makes me cold to remember them. Large dusky forms with sly and jeering faces crouched in the corners of the room, and bent over my bed at night, tempting me to madness. They told me in low whispers that the floor of the old house in which my father's father died, was stained with his own blood, shed by his own hand in raging madness. I drove my fingers into my ears, but they screamed into my head till the room rang with it, that in one generation before him the madness slumbered, but that his grandfather had lived for years with his hands fettered to the ground, to prevent his tearing himself to pieces. I knew they told the truth – I knew it well. I had found it out years before, though they had tried to keep it from me. Ha! ha! I was too cunning for them, madman as they thought me.

'At last it came upon me, and I wondered how I could ever have feared it. I could go into the world now, and laugh and shout with the best among them. I knew I was mad, but they did not even suspect it. How I used to hug myself with delight when I thought of the fine trick I was playing them after their old pointing and leering when I was not mad but only dreading that I might one day become so! And how I used to laugh for joy when I was alone and thought how well I kept my secret, and how quickly my kind friends would have fallen from me if they had known the truth. I could have screamed with ecstasy when I dined alone with some fine roaring fellow to think how pale he would have turned and how fast he would have run if he had known that the dear friend who sat close to him, sharpening a bright, glittering knife, was a madman with all the power and half the will to plunge it in his heart. Oh, it was a merry life!

'Riches became mine, wealth poured in upon me, and I rioted in pleasures enhanced a thousandfold to me by the consciousness of my well-kept secret. I inherited an estate. The law – the eagle-eyed law itself – had been deceived and had handed over disputed thousands to a madman's hands. Where was the wit of the sharp-sighted men of sound mind? Where the dexterity of the lawyers eager to discover a flaw? The madman's cunning had overreached them all.

'I had money. How I was courted! I spent it profusely. How I was praised! How those three proud, overbearing brothers humbled themselves before me! The old, white-headed father, too – such deference – such respect – such devoted friendship – he worshipped me! The old man had a daughter, and the young men a sister; and all the five were poor. I was rich; and when I married the girl, I saw a smile of triumph play upon the faces of her needy relatives, as they thought of their well-planned scheme, and their fine prize. It was for me to smile. To smile! To laugh outright, and tear my hair, and roll upon the ground with shrieks of merriment. They little thought they had married her to a madman.

'Stay. If they had known it, would they have saved her? A sister's happiness against her husband's gold. The lightest feather I blow into the air, against the gay chain that ornaments my body!

'In one thing I was deceived with all my cunning. If I had not been mad – for though we madmen are sharp-witted enough, we get bewildered sometimes – I should have known that the girl would rather have been placed, stiff and cold, in a dull leaden coffin than borne an envied bride to my rich, glittering house. I should have known that her heart was with the dark-eyed boy whose name I once heard her breathe in her troubled sleep; and that she had been sacrificed to me, to relieve the poverty of the old, white-headed man and the haughty brothers.

'I don't remember forms or faces now, but I know the girl was beautiful. I *know* she was; for in the bright moonlight nights, when I start up from my sleep, and all is quiet about me, I see, standing still and motionless in one corner of this cell, a slight and wasted figure with long black hair, which, streaming down her back, stirs with no earthly wind, and eyes that fix their gaze on me, and never wink or close. Hush! the blood chills at my heart as I write it down – that form is *hers*; the face is very pale, and the eyes are glassy bright; but I know them well. That figure never moves; it never frowns and mouths as others do, that fill this place sometimes; but it is much more dreadful to me, even than the spirits that tempted me many years ago – it comes fresh from the grave; and is so very deathlike.

'For nearly a year I saw that face grow paler; for nearly a year I saw the tears steal down the mournful cheeks, and never knew the cause. I found it out at last though. They could not keep it from me long. She had never liked me: I had never thought she did; she despised my wealth, and hated the splendour in which she lived: but I had not expected that. She loved another. This I had never thought of. Strange feelings came over me, and thought, forced upon me by some secret power, whirled round and round my brain. I did not hate her though I hated the boy she still wept for. I pitied – yes, I pitied – the wretched life to which her cold and selfish relations had doomed her. I knew that she could not live long; but the thought that before her death she might give birth to some ill-fated being, destined to hand down madness to its offspring, determined me. I resolved to kill her.

'For many weeks I thought of poison, and then of drowning, and then of fire. A fine sight, the grand house in flames, and the madman's wife smouldering away to cinders. Think of the jest of a large reward, too, and of some sane man swinging in the wind for a deed he never did, and all through a madman's cunning! I thought often of this, but I gave it up at last. Oh! the pleasure of stropping the razor day after day, feeling the sharp edge, and thinking of the gash one stroke of its thin, bright edge would make!

'At last the old spirits who had been with me so often before whispered in my ear that the time was come, and thrust the open razor into my hand. I grasped it firmly, rose softly from the bed, and leaned over my sleeping wife. Her face was buried in her hands. I withdrew them softly, and they fell listlessly on her bosom. She had been weeping, for the traces of the tears were still wet upon her cheek. Her face was calm and placid; and even as I looked upon it, a tranquil smile lighted up her pale features. I laid my hand softly on her shoulder. She started – it was only a passing dream. I leaned forward again. She screamed, and woke.

'One motion of my hand, and she would never again have uttered cry or sound. But I was startled, and drew back. Her eyes were fixed on mine. I knew not how it was, but they cowed and frightened me; and I quailed beneath them. She rose from the bed, still gazing fixedly and steadily on me. I trembled; the razor was in my hand, but I could not move. She made towards the door. As she neared it, she turned, and withdrew her eyes from my face. The spell was broken. I bounded forward, and clutched her by the arm. Uttering shriek upon shriek, she sank upon the ground.

'Now I could have killed her without a struggle; but the house was alarmed. I heard the tread of footsteps on the stairs. I replaced the razor in its usual drawer, unfastened the door, and called loudly for assistance.

'They came, and raised her, and placed her on the bed. She lay bereft of animation for hours; and when life, look and speech returned, her senses had deserted her, and she raved wildly and furiously.

'Doctors were called in – great men who rolled up to my door in easy carriages, with fine horses and gaudy servants. They were at her bedside for weeks. They had a great meeting, and consulted together in low and solemn voices in another room. One, the cleverest and most celebrated among them, took me aside, and bidding me prepare for the worst, told me – me, the madman! – that my wife was mad. He stood close beside me at an open window, his eyes looking in my face, and his hand laid upon my arm. With one effort, I could have hurled him into the street beneath. It would have been rare sport to have done it; but my secret was at stake, and I let him go. A few days after, they told me I must place her under some restraint: I must provide a keeper for her. *I!* I went into the open fields where none could hear me, and laughed till the air resounded with my shouts!

'She died next day. The white-headed old man followed her to the grave, and the proud brothers dropped a tear over the insensible corpse of her whose sufferings they had regarded in her lifetime with muscles of iron. All this was food for my secret mirth, and I laughed behind the white handkerchief which I held up to my face, as we rode home, till the tears came into my eyes.

'But though I had carried my object and killed her, I was restless and disturbed, and I felt that before long my secret must be known. I could not hide the wild mirth and joy which boiled within me, and made me, when I was alone at home, jump up and beat my hands together, and dance round and round, and roar aloud. When I went out, and saw the busy crowds hurrying about the streets; or the theatre, and heard the sound of music, and beheld the people dancing, I felt such glee, that I could have rushed among them, and torn them to pieces, limb from limb, and howled in transport. But I ground my teeth, and struck my feet upon the floor, and drove my sharp nails into my hands. I kept it down; and no one knew I was a madman yet.

'I remember – though it's one of the last things I *can* remember: for now I mix up realities with my dreams, and having so much to do, and being always hurried here, have no time to separate the two from some strange confusion in which they get involved – I remember how I let it out at last. Ha! ha! I think I see their frightened looks now, and feel the ease with which I flung them from me, and dashed my clenched fist into their white faces, and then flew like the wind, and left them screaming and shouting far behind. The strength of a giant comes upon me when I think of it. There – see how this iron bar bends beneath my furious wrench. I could snap it like a twig, only there are long galleries here with many doors – I don't think I could find my way along them; and even if I could, I know there are iron gates below which they keep locked and barred. They know what a clever madman I have been, and they are proud to have me here, to show.

'Let me see: yes, I had been out. It was late at night when I reached home, and found the proudest of the three proud brothers waiting to see me – urgent business he said: I recollect it well. I hated that man with all a madman's hate. Many and many a time had my fingers longed to tear him. They told me he was there. I ran swiftly upstairs. He had a word to say to me. I dismissed the servants. It was late, and we were alone together – *for the first time*.

'I kept my eyes carefully from him at first, for I knew what he little thought – and I gloried in the knowledge – that the light of madness gleamed from them like fire. We sat in silence for a few minutes. He spoke at last. My recent dissipation, and strange remarks, made so soon after his sister's death, were an insult to her memory. Coupling together many circumstances which had at first escaped his observation, he thought I had not treated her well. He wished to know whether he was right in inferring that I meant to cast a reproach upon her memory, and a disrespect upon her family. It was due to the uniform he wore to demand this explanation.

'This man had a commission in the army – a commission purchased with my money, and his sister's misery! This was the man who had been foremost in the plot to ensnare me and grasp my wealth. This was the man who had been the main instrument in forcing his sister to wed me; well knowing that her heart was given to that puling boy. Due to *his* uniform! The livery of his degradation! I turned my eyes upon him – I could not help it – but I spoke not a word.

'I saw the sudden change that came upon him beneath my gaze. He was a bold man but the colour faded from his face, and he drew back in his chair. I dragged mine nearer to him; and as I laughed – I was very merry then – I saw him shudder. I felt the madness rising within me. He was afraid of me.

' "You were very fond of your sister when she was alive," I said. "Very."

'He looked uneasily round him, and I saw his hand grasp the back of his chair; but he said nothing.

' "You villain," said I, "I found you out; I discovered your hellish plots against me; I know her heart was fixed on someone else before you compelled her to marry me. I know it – I know it."

'He jumped suddenly from his chair, brandishing it aloft, and bid me stand back – for I took care to be getting closer to him all the time I spoke.

'I screamed rather than talked, for I felt tumultuous passions eddying through my veins, and the old spirits whispering and taunting me to tear his heart out.

' "Damn you," said I, starting up, and rushing upon him. "I killed her. I am a madman. Down with you. Blood. Blood! I will have it!"

'I turned aside with one blow the chair he hurled at me in his terror, and closed with him; and with a heavy crash we rolled upon the floor together.

'It was a fine struggle that; for he was a tall, strong man, fighting for his life: and I, a powerful madman, thirsting to destroy him. I knew no strength could equal mine, and I was right. Right again, though a madman! His struggles grew fainter. I knelt upon his chest, and clasped his brawny throat firmly with both hands. His face grew purple; his eyes were starting from his head, and with protruded tongue, he seemed to mock me. I squeezed the tighter.

'The door was suddenly burst open with a loud noise, and a crowd of people rushed forward, crying aloud to each other to secure the madman.

'My secret was out; and my only struggle now was for liberty and freedom. I gained my feet before a hand was on me, threw myself among my assailants and cleared my way with my strong arm, as if I bore a hatchet in my hand, and hewed them down before me. I gained the door, dropped over the banisters, and in an instant was in the street.

'Straight and swift I ran, and no one dared to stop me. I heard the noise of feet behind, and redoubled my speed. It grew fainter and fainter in the distance, and at length died away altogether; but on I bounded, through marsh and rivulet, over fence and wall, with a wild shout which was taken up by the strange beings that flocked around me on every side, and swelled the sound, till it pierced the air. I was borne upon the arms of demons who swept along upon the wind, and bore down bank and hedge before them, and spun me round and round with a rustle and a speed that made my head swim, until at last they threw me from them with a violent shock, and I fell heavily upon the earth. When I woke I found myself here – here in this grey cell, where the sunlight seldom comes, and the moon steals in, in rays which only serve to show the dark shadows about me, and that silent figure in its old corner. When I lie awake, I can sometimes hear strange shrieks and cries from distant parts of this large place. What they are, I know not; but they neither come from that pale form, nor does it regard them. For from the first shades of dusk till the earliest light of morning, it still stands motionless in the same place, listening to the music of my iron chain, and watching my gambols on my straw bed.'

THE GOBLINS WHO
STOLE A SEXTON

In an old abbey town, down in this part of the country, a long, long, while ago – so long, that the story must be a true one, because our great-grandfathers implicitly believed it – there officiated as sexton and grave-digger in the churchyard, one Gabriel Grub. It by no means follows that because a man is a sexton, and constantly surrounded by the emblems of mortality, therefore he should be a morose and melancholy man; your undertakers are the merriest fellows in the world; and I once had the honour of being on intimate terms with a mute, who in private life, and off duty, was as comical and jocose a little fellow as ever chirped out a devil-may-care song, without a hitch in his memory, or drained off the contents of a good stiff glass without stopping for breath. But, not-withstanding these precedents to the contrary, Gabriel Grub was an ill-conditioned, cross-grained, surly fellow – a morose and lonely man, who consorted with nobody but himself, and an old wicker bottle which fitted into his large deep waistcoat pocket – and who eyed each merry face, as it passed him by, with such a deep scowl of malice and ill-humour, as it was difficult to meet without feeling something the worse for.

A little before twilight, one Christmas Eve, Gabriel shouldered his spade, lighted his lantern, and betook himself towards the old church-yard; for he had got a grave to finish by next morning, and, feeling very low, he thought it might raise his spirits, perhaps, if he went on with his work at once. As he went his way, up the ancient street, he saw the cheerful light of the blazing fires gleam through the old casements, and heard the loud laugh and the cheerful shouts of those who were assembled around them; he marked the bustling preparations for next day's cheer, and smelt the numerous savoury odours consequent thereupon, as they steamed up from the kitchen windows in clouds. All this was gall and wormwood to the heart of Gabriel Grub; and when groups of children bounded out of the houses, tripped across the road, and were met, before they could knock at the opposite door, by half a dozen curly-headed little rascals who crowded round them as they flocked upstairs to spend the evening in their Christmas games, Gabriel smiled grimly, and clutched the handle of his spade with a firmer grasp, as he thought of measles, scarlet-fever, thrush, whooping-cough, and a good many other sources of consolation besides.

In this happy frame of mind, Gabriel strode along: returning a short, sullen growl to the good-humoured greetings of such of his neighbours as now and then passed him: until he turned into the dark lane which led to the churchyard. Now, Gabriel had been looking forward to reaching the dark lane, because it was, generally speaking, a nice, gloomy, mournful place, into which the townspeople did not much care to go, except in broad daylight, and when the sun was shining; consequently, he was not a little indignant to hear a young urchin roaring out some jolly song about a merry Christmas, in this very sanctuary, which had been called Coffin Lane ever since the days of the old abbey, and the time of the shaven-headed monks. As Gabriel walked on, and the voice drew nearer, he found it proceeded from a small boy, who was hurrying along, to join one of the little parties in the old street, and who, partly to keep himself company, and partly to prepare himself for the occasion, was shouting out the song at the highest pitch of his lungs. So Gabriel waited until the boy came up, and then dodged him into a corner, and rapped him over the head with his lantern five or six times, to teach him to modulate his voice. And as the boy hurried away with his hand to his head, singing quite a different sort of tune, Gabriel Grub chuckled very heartily to himself, and entered the churchyard, locking the gate behind him.

He took off his coat, put down his lantern, and getting into the unfinished grave, worked at it for an hour or so, with right good will. But the earth was hardened with the frost, and it was no very easy matter to break it up, and shovel it out; and although there was a moon, it was a very young one, and shed little light upon the grave, which was in the shadow of the church. At any other time, these obstacles would have made Gabriel Grub very moody and miserable, but he was so well pleased with having stopped the small boy's singing that he took little heed of the scanty progress he had made, and looked down into the grave, when he had finished work for the night, with grim satisfaction: murmuring as he gathered up his things:

> 'Brave lodgings for one, brave lodgings for one,
> A few feet of cold earth, when life is done;
> A stone at the head, a stone at the feet,
> A rich, juicy meal for the worms to eat;

Rank grass over head, and damp clay around,
Brave lodgings for one, these, in holy ground!

'Ho! Ho!' laughed Gabriel Grub, as he sat himself down on a flat tombstone which was a favourite resting-place of his; and drew forth his wicker bottle. 'A coffin at Christmas! A Christmas Box. Ho! ho! ho!'

'Ho! ho! ho!' repeated a voice which sounded close behind him.

Gabriel paused, in some alarm, in the act of raising the wicker bottle to his lips: and looked round. The bottom of the oldest grave about him was not more still and quiet than the churchyard in the pale moonlight. The cold hoar-frost glistened on the tombstones, and sparkled like rows of gems, among the stone carvings of the old church. The snow lay hard and crisp upon the ground; and spread over the thickly-strewn mounds of earth so white and smooth a cover that it seemed as if corpses lay there, hidden only by their winding sheets. Not the faintest rustle broke the profound tranquillity of the solemn scene. Sound itself appeared to be frozen up, all was so cold and still.

'It was the echoes,' said Gabriel Grub, raising the bottle to his lips again.

'It was *not*,' said a deep voice.

Gabriel started up, and stood rooted to the spot with astonishment and terror; for his eyes rested on a form that made his blood run cold.

Seated on an upright tombstone, close to him, was a strange unearthly figure, whom Gabriel felt at once was no being of this world. His long fantastic legs which might have reached the ground, were cocked up, and crossed after a quaint, fantastic fashion; his sinewy arms were bare; and his hands rested on his knees. On his short round body, he wore a close covering, ornamented with small slashes; a short cloak dangled at his back; the collar was cut into curious peaks, which served the goblin in lieu of ruff or neckerchief, and his shoes curled at his toes into long points. On his head, he wore a broad-brimmed sugar-loaf hat, garnished with a single feather. The hat was covered with the white frost; and the goblin looked as if he had sat on the same tombstone very comfortably for two or three hundred years. He was sitting perfectly still; his tongue was put out, as if in derision; and he was grinning at Gabriel Grub with such a grin as only a goblin could call up.

'It was *not* the echoes,' said the goblin.

Gabriel Grub was paralysed, and could make no reply.

'What do you do here on Christmas Eve?' said the goblin sternly.

'I came to dig a grave, sir,' stammered Gabriel Grub.

'What man wanders among graves and churchyards on such a night as this?' cried the goblin.

'Gabriel Grub! Gabriel Grub!' screamed a wild chorus of voices that seemed to fill the churchyard. Gabriel looked fearfully round – nothing was to be seen.

'What have you got in that bottle?' said the goblin.

'Hollands, sir,' replied the sexton, trembling more than ever; for he had bought it off the smugglers, and he thought that perhaps his questioner might be in the excise department of the goblins.

'Who drinks Hollands alone, and in a churchyard, on such a night as this?' said the goblin.

'Gabriel Grub! Gabriel Grub!' exclaimed the wild voices again.

The goblin leered maliciously at the terrified sexton, and then raising his voice, exclaimed: 'And who, then, is our fair and lawful prize?'

To this enquiry the invisible chorus replied, in a strain that sounded like the voices of many choristers singing to the mighty swell of the old church organ – a strain that seemed borne to the sexton's ears upon a wild wind, and to die away as it passed onward; but the burden of the reply was still the same, 'Gabriel Grub! Gabriel Grub!'

The goblin grinned a broader grin than before, as he said, 'Well, Gabriel, what do you say to this?'

The sexton gasped for breath.

'What do you think of this, Gabriel?' said the goblin, kicking up his feet in the air on either side of the tombstone, and looking at the turned-up points with as much complacency as if he had been contemplating the most fashionable pair of Wellingtons in all Bond Street.

'It's – it's – very curious, sir,' replied the sexton, half dead with fright; 'very curious, and very pretty, but I think I'll go back and finish my work, sir, if you please.'

'Work!' said the goblin, 'what work?'

'The grave, sir; making the grave,' stammered the sexton.

'Oh, the grave, eh?' said the goblin. 'Who makes graves at a time when all other men are merry, and takes a pleasure in it?'

Again the mysterious voices replied, 'Gabriel Grub! Gabriel Grub!'

'I'm afraid my friends want you, Gabriel,' said the goblin, thrusting his tongue further into his cheek than ever – and a most astonishing tongue it was – 'I'm afraid my friends want you, Gabriel,' said the goblin.

'Under favour, sir,' replied the horror-stricken sexton, 'I don't think they can, sir; they don't know me, sir; I don't think the gentlemen have ever seen me, sir.'

'Oh yes they have,' replied the goblin; 'we know the man with the sulky face and grim scowl, that came down the street tonight, throwing his evil looks at the children, and grasping his burying spade the tighter. We know the man who struck the boy in the envious malice of his heart, because the boy could be merry, and he could not. We know him, we know him.'

Here the goblin gave a loud shrill laugh, which the echoes returned twentyfold: and throwing his legs up in the air, stood upon his head, or rather upon the very point of his sugar-loaf hat, on the narrow edge of the tombstone: whence he threw a somersault with extraordinary agility right to the sexton's feet, at which he planted himself in the attitude in which tailors generally sit upon the shop-board.

'I – I – am afraid I must leave you, sir,' said the sexton, making an effort to move.

'Leave us!' said the goblin, 'Gabriel Grub going to leave us? Ho! ho! ho!'

As the goblin laughed, the sexton observed, for one instant, a brilliant illumination within the windows of the church, as if the whole building were lighted up; it disappeared, the organ pealed forth a lively air, and whole troops of goblins, the very counterpart of the first one, poured into the churchyard, and began playing at leap-frog with the tombstones: never stopping for an instant to take breath, but 'overing' the highest among them, one after the other, with the most marvellous dexterity. The first goblin was a most astonishing leaper, and none of the others could come near him; even in the extremity of his terror, the sexton could not help observing that while his friends were content to leap over the common-sized gravestones, the first one took the family vaults, iron railings and all, with as much ease as if they had been so many street-posts.

At last the game reached to a most exciting pitch; the organ played quicker and quicker; and the goblins leaped faster and faster, coiling themselves up, rolling head over heels upon the ground, and bounding over the tombstones like footballs. The sexton's brain whirled round with the rapidity of the motion he beheld, and his legs reeled beneath him, as the spirits flew before his eyes: when the goblin king, suddenly darting towards him, laid his hand upon his collar, and sank with him through the earth.

When Gabriel Grub had had time to catch his breath, which the rapidity of his descent had for the moment taken away, he found himself in what appeared to be a large cavern, surrounded on all sides by crowds of goblins, ugly and grim; in the centre of the room, on an elevated seat, was stationed his friend of the churchyard; and close beside him stood Gabriel Grub himself, without power of motion.

'Cold tonight,' said the king of the goblins, 'very cold. A glass of something warm, here!'

At this command, half a dozen officious goblins, with a perpetual smile upon their faces, whom Gabriel Grub imagined to be courtiers, on that account, hastily disappeared, and presently returned with a goblet of liquid fire, which they presented to the king.

'Ah!' cried the goblin, whose cheeks and throat were transparent as he tossed down the flame, 'This warms one, indeed! Bring a bumper of the same, for Mr Grub.'

It was in vain for the unfortunate sexton to protest that he was not in the habit of taking anything warm at night; one of the goblins held him while another poured the blazing liquid down his throat; the whole assembly screeched with laughter as he coughed and choked, and wiped away the tears which gushed plentifully from his eyes, after swallowing the burning draught.

'And now,' said the king, fantastically poking the taper corner of his sugar-loaf hat into the sexton's eye, and thereby occasioning him the most exquisite pain: 'And now, show the man of misery and gloom a few of the pictures from our own great storehouse!'

As the goblin said this, a thick cloud which obscured the remoter end of the cavern rolled gradually away and disclosed, apparently at a great distance, a small and scantily furnished, but neat and clean apartment. A crowd of little children were gathered round a bright fire, clinging to their mother's gown, and gambolling around her chair. The mother occasionally rose, and drew aside the window-curtain, as if to look for some expected object: a frugal meal was placed near the fire. A knock was heard at the door: the mother opened it, and the children crowded round her, and clapped their hands for joy, as their father entered. He was wet and weary, and shook the snow from his garments as the children crowded round him, and seizing his cloak, hat, stick and gloves, with busy zeal, ran with them from the room. Then, as he sat down to his meal before the fire, the children climbed about his knee, and the mother sat by his side, and all seemed happiness and comfort.

But a change came upon the view, almost imperceptibly. The scene was altered to a small bedroom, where the fairest and youngest child was dying; the roses had fled from his cheek, and the light from his eye; and even as the sexton looked upon him with an interest he had never felt or known before, he died. His young brothers and sisters crowded round his little bed, and seized his tiny hand, so cold and heavy, but they shrank back from its touch, and looked with awe on his infant face; for calm and tranquil as it was, and sleeping in rest and peace as the beautiful child seemed to be, they saw that he was dead, and they knew that he was an angel looking down upon, and blessing, them from a bright and happy heaven.

Again the light cloud passed across the picture, and again the subject changed. The father and mother were old and helpless now, and the number of those about them was diminished more than half; but content and cheerfulness sat on every face, and beamed in every eye as they crowded round the fireside, and told and listened to old stories of earlier and bygone days. Slowly and peacefully, the father sank into the grave, and, soon after, the sharer of all his cares and troubles followed him to a place of rest. The few who yet survived them knelt by their tomb, and watered the green turf which covered it with their tears; then rose, and turned away: sadly and mournfully, but not with bitter cries, or despairing lamentations, for they knew that they should one day meet again; and once more they mixed with the busy world, and their content and cheerfulness was restored. The cloud settled upon the picture and concealed it from the sexton's view.

'What do you think of *that*?' said the goblin, turning his large face towards Gabriel Grub.

Gabriel murmured out something about its being very pretty, and looked somewhat ashamed, as the goblin bent his fiery eyes upon him.

'*You* a miserable man!' said the goblin, in a tone of excessive contempt. 'You!' He appeared disposed to add more, but indignation choked his utterance, so he lifted up one of his very pliable legs, and flourishing it above his head a little, to insure his aim, administered a good sound kick to Gabriel Grub; immediately after which all the goblins in waiting crowded round the wretched sexton, and kicked him without mercy: according to the established and invariable custom of courtiers upon earth, who kick whom royalty kicks, and hug whom royalty hugs.

'Show him some more!' said the king of the goblins.

At these words, the cloud was dispelled, and a rich and beautiful landscape was disclosed to view – there is just such another, to this day, within half a mile of the old abbey town. The sun shone from out the clear blue sky, the water sparkled beneath his rays, and the trees looked greener, and the flowers more gay, beneath his cheering influence. The water rippled on, with a pleasant sound; the trees rustled in the light wind that murmured among their leaves; the birds sang upon the boughs; and the lark carolled on high her welcome to the morning. Yes, it was morning; the bright, balmy morning of summer; the minutest leaf, the smallest blade of grass, was instinct with life. The ant crept forth to her daily toil, the butterfly fluttered and basked in the warm rays of the sun; myriads of insects spread their transparent wings, and revelled in their brief but happy existence. Man walked forth, elated with the scene, and all was brightness and splendour.

'*You* a miserable man!' said the king of the goblins, in a more contemptuous tone than before. And again the king of the goblins gave his leg a flourish; again it descended on the shoulders of the sexton; and again the attendant goblins imitated the example of their chief.

Many a time the cloud went and came, and many a lesson it taught to Gabriel Grub, who, although his shoulders smarted with pain from the frequent applications of the goblins' feet, looked on with an interest that nothing could diminish. He saw that men who worked hard, and earned their scanty bread with lives of labour, were cheerful and happy; and that to the most ignorant, the sweet face of nature was a never-failing source of cheerfulness and joy. He saw those who had been delicately nurtured, and tenderly brought up, cheerful under privations, and superior to suffering that would have crushed many of a rougher grain, because they bore within their own bosoms the materials of happiness, contentment, and peace. He saw that women, the tenderest and most fragile of all God's creatures, were the oftenest superior to sorrow, adversity, and distress; and he saw that it was because they bore, in their own hearts, an inexhaustible well-spring of affection and devotion. Above all, he saw that men like himself, who snarled at the mirth and cheerfulness of others, were the foulest weeds on the fair surface of the earth; and setting all the good of the world against the evil, he came to the conclusion that it was a very decent and respectable sort of world after all. No sooner had he formed it, than the cloud which closed over the last picture, seemed to settle on his senses, and lull him to repose. One by one, the goblins faded from his sight; and as the last one disappeared, he sank to sleep.

The day had broken when Gabriel Grub awoke, and found himself lying, at full length, on the flat gravestone in the churchyard, with the wicker bottle lying empty by his side, and his coat, spade and lantern, all well whitened by last night's frost, scattered on the ground. The stone on which he had first seen the goblin seated, stood bolt upright before him, and the grave at which he had worked, the night before, was not far off.

At first, he began to doubt the reality of his adventures, but the acute pain in his shoulders when he attempted to rise, assured him that the kicking of the goblins was certainly not ideal. He was staggered again by observing no traces of footsteps in the snow on which the goblins had played at leap-frog with the gravestones, but he speedily accounted for this circumstance when he remembered that, being spirits, they would leave no visible impression behind them. So Gabriel Grub got on his feet as well as he could for the pain in his back, and brushing the frost off his coat, put it on, and turned his face towards the town.

But he was an altered man, and he could not bear the thought of returning to a place where his repentance would be scoffed at, and his reformation disbelieved. He hesitated for a few moments, and then turned away to wander where he might, and seek his bread elsewhere.

The lantern, the spade and the wicker bottle were found, that day, in the churchyard. There were a great many speculations about the sexton's fate, at first, but it was speedily determined that he had been carried away by the goblins; and there were not wanting some very credible witnesses who had distinctly seen him whisked through the air on the back of a chestnut horse, blind of one eye, with the hindquarters of a lion and the tail of a bear. At length all this was devoutly believed; and the new sexton used to exhibit to the curious, for a trifling emolument, a good-sized piece of the church weathercock which had been accidentally picked up by himself in the churchyard a year or two afterwards.

Unfortunately, these stories were somewhat disturbed by the unlooked-for reappearance of Gabriel Grub himself, some ten years afterwards, a ragged, contented, rheumatic old man. He told his story to the clergyman, and also to the mayor; and in course of time it began to be received, as a matter of history, in which form it has continued down to this very day. The believers in the weathercock tale, having misplaced their confidence once, were not easily prevailed upon to part with it again, so they looked as wise as they could, shrugged their shoulders, touched their foreheads, and murmured something about Gabriel Grub having drunk all the Hollands, and then fallen asleep on the flat tombstone; and they affected to explain what he supposed he had witnessed in the goblins' cavern by saying that he had seen the world and grown wiser. But this opinion, which was by no means a popular one at any time, gradually died off; and be the matter how it may, as Gabriel Grub was afflicted with rheumatism to the end of his days, this story has at least one moral, if it teach no better one – and that is, that if a man turn sulky and drink by himself at Christmas time, he may make up his mind to be not a bit the better for it: let the spirits be never so good, or let them be even as many degrees beyond proof, as those which Gabriel Grub saw in the goblins' cavern.

THE GHOSTS OF
THE MAIL

The Story of the Bagman's Uncle

'My uncle, gentlemen,' said the bagman, 'was one of the merriest, pleasantest, cleverest fellows that ever lived. I wish you had known him, gentlemen. On second thoughts, gentlemen, I *don't* wish you had known him, for if you had, you would have been all, by this time, in the ordinary course of nature, if not dead, at all events so near it as to have taken to stopping at home and giving up company: which would have deprived me of the inestimable pleasure of addressing you at this moment. Gentlemen, I wish your fathers and mothers had known my uncle. They would have been amazingly fond of him, especially your respectable mothers; I know they would. If any two of his numerous virtues predominated over the many that adorned his character, I should say they were his mixed punch and his after-supper song. Excuse my dwelling on these melancholy recollections of departed worth; you won't see a man like my uncle every day in the week.'

*   *   *

I have always considered it a great point in my uncle's character, gentle-men, that he was the intimate friend and companion of Tom Smart, of the great house of Bilson and Slum, Cateaton Street, City. My uncle collected for Tiggin and Welps, but for a long time he went pretty near the same journey as Tom; and the very first night they met, my uncle took a fancy for Tom, and Tom took a fancy for my uncle. They made a bet of a new hat, before they had known each other half an hour, who should brew the best quart of punch and drink it the quickest. My uncle was judged to have won the making, but Tom Smart beat him in the drinking by about half a salt-spoon-full. They took another quart apiece to drink each other's health in, and were staunch friends ever afterwards. There's a destiny in these things, gentlemen; we can't help it.

In the personal appearance, my uncle was a trifle shorter than the middle size; he was a thought stouter too, than the ordinary run of people, and perhaps his face might be a shade redder. He had the jolliest face you ever saw, gentlemen: something like Punch, with a handsomer nose and chin; his eyes were always twinkling and sparkling with good humour; and a smile – not one of your unmeaning wooden grins, but a real, merry, hearty, good-tempered smile – was perpetually on his countenance. He was pitched out of his gig once, and knocked, head first, against a milestone. There he lay, stunned, and so cut about the face with some gravel which had been heaped up alongside it that, to use my uncle's own strong expression, if his mother could have revisited the earth, she wouldn't have known him. Indeed, when I come to think of the matter, gentlemen, I feel pretty sure she wouldn't, for she died when my uncle was two years and seven months old, and I think it's very likely that, even without the gravel, his top-boots would have puzzled the good lady not a little: to say nothing of his jolly red face. However, there he lay, and I have heard my uncle say, many a time, that the man said who picked him up that he was smiling as merrily as if he had tumbled out for a treat, and that after they had bled him, the first faint glimmerings of returning animation were his jumping up in bed, bursting out into a loud laugh, kissing the young woman who held the basin, and demanding a mutton chop and a pickled walnut. He was very fond of pickled walnuts, gentle-men. He said he always found that, taken without vinegar, they relished the beer.

My uncle's great journey was in the fall of the leaf, at which time he collected debts, and took orders, in the north: going from London to Edinburgh, from Edinburgh to Glasgow, from Glasgow back to Edin-burgh, and thence to London by the smack. You are to understand that his second visit to Edinburgh was for his own pleasure. He used to go back for a week, just to look up his old friends; and what with breakfasting with this one, lunching with that, dining with a third, and supping with another, a pretty tight week he used to make of it. I don't know whether any of you, gentlemen, ever partook of a real substantial hospitable Scotch breakfast, and then went out to a slight lunch of a bushel of oysters, a dozen or so of bottled ale, and a noggin or two of whiskey to close up with. If you ever did, you will agree with me that it requires a pretty strong head to go out to dinner and supper afterwards.

But, bless your hearts and eyebrows, all this sort of thing was nothing to my uncle! He was so well seasoned, that it was mere child's play. I have heard him say that he could see the Dundee people out, any day, and walk home afterwards without staggering; and yet the Dundee people have as strong heads and as strong punch, gentlemen, as you are likely to meet with between the poles. I have heard of a Glasgow man and a

Dundee man drinking against each other for fifteen hours at a sitting. They were both suffocated, as nearly as could be ascertained, at the same moment, but with this trifling exception, gentlemen, they were not a bit the worse for it.

One night, within four-and-twenty hours of the time when he had settled to take shipping for London, my uncle supped at the house of a very old friend of his, a Baillie Mac something and four syllables after it, who lived in the old town of Edinburgh. There were the baillie's wife and the baillie's three daughters, and the baillie's grown-up son, and three or four stout, bushy eyebrowed, canny old Scotch fellows that the baillie had got together to do honour to my uncle and help to make merry. It was a glorious supper. There were kippered salmon, and finnan haddocks, and a lamb's head, and a haggis – a celebrated Scotch dish, gentlemen, which my uncle used to say always looked to him, when it came to table, very much like a cupid's stomach – and a great many other things besides that I forget the names of, but very good things notwithstanding. The lassies were pretty and agreeable; the baillie's wife was one of the best creatures that ever lived; and my uncle was in thoroughly good cue. The consequence of which was that the young ladies tittered and giggled, and the old lady laughed out loud, and the baillie and the other old fellows roared till they were red in the face, the whole mortal time. I don't quite recollect how many tumblers of whiskey toddy each man drank after supper; but this I know, that about one o'clock in the morning, the baillie's grown-up son became insensible while attempting the first verse of 'Willie brewed a peck o'maut'; and he having been, for half an hour before, the only other man visible above the mahogany, it occurred to my uncle that it was almost time to think about going: especially as drinking had set in at seven o'clock, in order that he might get home at a decent hour. But, thinking it might not be quite polite to go just then, my uncle voted himself into the chair, mixed another glass, rose to propose his own health, addressed himself in a neat and complimentary speech, and drank the toast with great enthusiasm. Still nobody woke; so my uncle took a little drop more – neat this time to prevent the toddy from disagreeing with him – and, laying violent hands on his hat, sallied forth into the street.

It was a wild gusty night when my uncle closed the baillie's door, and settling his hat firmly on his head, to prevent the wind from taking it, thrust his hands into his pockets, and looking upward, took a short survey of the state of the weather. The clouds were drifting over the moon at their giddiest speed: at one time wholly obscuring her; at another, suffering her to burst forth in full splendour and shed her light on all the objects around; anon, driving over her again, with increased velocity, and shrouding everything in darkness. 'Really, this won't do,' said my uncle, addressing himself to the weather, as if he felt himself personally offended. 'This is not at all the kind of thing for my voyage. It will not do, at any price,' said my uncle very impressively. Having repeated this, several times, he recovered his balance with some difficulty – for he was rather giddy with looking up into the sky so long – and walked merrily on.

The baillie's house was in the Canongate, and my uncle was going to the other end of Leith Walk, rather better than a mile's journey. On either side of him, there shot up against the dark sky, tall gaunt straggling houses, with time-stained fronts, and windows that seemed to have shared the lot of eyes in mortals, and to have grown dim and sunken with age. Six, seven, eight storeys high, were the houses; storey piled above storey, as children build with cards – throwing their dark shadows over the roughly paved road, and making the dark night darker. A few oil lamps were scattered at long distances, but they only served to mark the dirty entrance to some narrow close, or to show where a common stair communicated, by steep and intricate windings, with the various flats above. Glancing at all these things with the air of a man who had seen them too often before to think them worthy of much notice now, my uncle walked up the middle of the street, with a thumb in each waistcoat pocket, indulging from time to time in various snatches of song, chanted forth with such good will and spirit that the quiet honest folk started from their first sleep and lay trembling in bed till the sound died away in the distance; when, satisfying themselves that it was only some drunken ne'er-do-weel finding his way home, they covered themselves up warm and fell asleep again.

I am particular in describing how my uncle walked up the middle of the street, with his thumbs in his waistcoat pockets, gentlemen, because as he often used to say (and with great reason too) there is nothing at all extraordinary in this story, unless you distinctly understand at the beginning that he was not by any means of a marvellous or romantic turn.

Gentlemen, my uncle walked on with his thumbs in his waistcoat pockets, taking the middle of the street to himself, and singing, now a verse of a love song, and then a verse of a drinking one, and when he was tired of both, whistling melodiously, until he reached the North Bridge, which, at this point, connects the old and new towns of Edinburgh. Here he stopped for a minute to look at the strange irregular clusters of lights piled one above the other, and twinkling afar off so high that they looked like stars, gleaming from the castle walls on the one side and the Calton Hill on the other, as if they illuminated veritable castles in the air; while the old picturesque town slept heavily on, in gloom and darkness below: its palace and chapel of Holyrood, guarded day and night, as a friend of my uncle's used to say, by old Arthur's Seat, towering, surly and dark, like some gruff genius, over the ancient city he has watched so long. I say, gentlemen, my uncle stopped here, for a minute, to look about him; and then, paying a compliment to the weather which had a little cleared up, though the moon was sinking, walked on again, as royally as before; keeping the middle of the road with great dignity, and looking as if he would very much like to meet with somebody who would dispute possession of it with him. There was nobody at all disposed to contest the point, as it happened; and so, on he went, with his thumbs in his waistcoat pockets, like a lamb.

When my uncle reached the end of Leith Walk, he had to cross a pretty large piece of waste ground which separated him from a short street which he had to turn down, to go direct to his lodging. Now, in this piece of waste ground, there was, at that time, an enclosure belonging to some wheelwright who contracted with the Post Office for the purchase of old worn-out mail coaches; and my uncle, being very fond of coaches, old, young or middle-aged, all at once took it into his head to step out of his road for no other purpose than to peep between the palings at these mails – about a dozen of which, he remembered to have seen, crowded together in a very forlorn and dismantled state, inside. My uncle was a very enthusiastic, emphatic sort of person, gentlemen; so, finding that he could not obtain a good peep between the palings, he got over them, and sitting himself quietly down on an old axle tree, began to contemplate the mail coaches with a deal of gravity.

There might be a dozen of them, or there might be more – my uncle was never quite certain on this point, and being a man of scrupulous veracity about numbers, didn't like to say – but there they stood, all huddled together in the most desolate condition imaginable. The doors had been torn from their hinges and removed; the linings had been stripped off: only a shred hanging here and there by a rusty nail; the lamps were gone, the poles had long since vanished, the ironwork was rusty, the paint was worn away; the wind whistled through the chinks in the bare woodwork; and the rain, which had collected on the roofs, fell drop by drop into the insides with a hollow and melancholy sound. They were the decaying skeletons of departed mails, and in that lonely place, at that time of night, they looked chill and dismal.

My uncle rested his head upon his hands, and thought of the busy bustling people who had rattled about, years before, in the old coaches, and were now as silent and changed; he thought of the numbers of people to whom one of those crazy mouldering vehicles had borne, night after night, for many years, and through all weathers, the anxiously expected intelligence, the eagerly looked-for remittance, the promised assurance of health and safety, the sudden announcement of sickness and death. The merchant, the lover, the wife, the widow, the mother, the schoolboy, the very child who tottered to the door at the postman's knock – how had they all looked forward to the arrival of the old coach. And where were they all now!

Gentlemen, my uncle used to say that he thought all this at the time, but I rather suspect he learnt it out of some book afterwards, for he distinctly stated that he fell into a kind of doze, as he sat on the old axle tree looking at the decayed mail coaches, and that he was suddenly awakened by some deep church bell striking two. Now, my uncle was never a fast thinker, and if he had thought all these things, I am quite certain it would have taken him till full half-past two o'clock, at the very least. I am, therefore, decidedly of the opinion, gentlemen, that my uncle fell into a kind of doze, without having thought about anything at all.

Be this as it may, a church bell struck two. My uncle woke, rubbed his eyes, and jumped up in astonishment.

In one instant after the clock struck two, the whole of this deserted and quiet spot had become a scene of most extraordinary life and animation. The mail coach doors were on their hinges, the lining was replaced, the ironwork was as good as new, the paint was restored, the lamps were alight, cushions and greatcoats were on every coach-box, porters were thrusting parcels into every boot, guards were stowing away letter bags, hostlers were dashing pails of water against the renovated wheels; numbers of men were rushing about, fixing poles into every coach; passengers arrived, portmanteaus were handed up, horses were put to; in short, it was perfectly clear that every mail there was to be off directly. Gentlemen, my uncle opened his eyes so wide at all this that, to the very last moment of

his life, he used to wonder how it fell out that he had ever been able to shut 'em again.

'Now then!' said a voice, as my uncle felt a hand on his shoulder, 'You're booked for one inside. You'd better get in.'

'*I* booked!' said my uncle, turning round.

'Yes, certainly.'

My uncle, gentlemen, could say nothing; he was so very much astonished. The queerest thing of all was that although there was such a crowd of persons, and although fresh faces were pouring in, every moment, there was no telling where they came from. They seemed to start up, in some strange manner, from the ground, or the air, and disappear in the same way. When a porter had put his luggage in the coach, and received his fare, he turned round and was gone; and before my uncle had well begun to wonder what had become of him, half a dozen fresh ones started up, and staggered along under the weight of the parcels which seemed big enough to crush them. The passengers were all dressed so oddly too! Large, broad-skirted laced coats with great cuffs and no collars; and wigs, gentlemen – great formal wigs with a tie behind. My uncle could make nothing of it.

'Now, *are* you going to get in?' said the person who had addressed my uncle before. He was dressed as a mail guard, with a wig on his head and most enormous cuffs to his coat, and had a lantern in one hand, and a huge blunderbuss in the other, which he was going to stow away in his little arms-chest. '*Are* you going to get in, Jack Martin?' said the guard, holding the lantern to my uncle's face.

'Hallo!' said my uncle, falling back a step or two. 'That's familiar!'

'It's so on the waybill,' replied the guard.

'Isn't there a "Mister" before it?' said my uncle. For he felt, gentlemen, that for a guard he didn't know to call him Jack Martin was a liberty which the Post Office wouldn't have sanctioned if they had known it.

'No, there is not,' rejoined the guard coolly.

'Is the fare paid?' enquired my uncle.

'Of course it is,' rejoined the guard.

'It is, is it?' said my uncle. 'Then here goes! Which coach?'

'This,' said the guard, pointing to an old-fashioned Edinburgh and London Mail, which had the steps down, and the door open. 'Stop! Here are the other passengers. Let them get in first.'

As the guard spoke, there all at once appeared, right in front of my uncle, a young gentleman in a powdered wig and a sky-blue coat trimmed with silver, made very full and broad in the skirts, which were lined with buckram. Tiggin and Welps were in the printed calico and waistcoat piece line, gentlemen, so my uncle knew all the materials at once. He wore knee breeches, and a kind of leggings rolled up over his silk stockings, and shoes with buckles; he had ruffles at his wrists, a three-cornered hat on his head, and a long taper sword by his side. The flaps of his waistcoat came halfway down his thighs, and the ends of his cravat reached to his waist. He stalked gravely to the coach-door, pulled off his hat, and held it above his head at arm's length: cocking his little finger in the air at the same time, as some affected people do when they take a cup of tea. Then he drew his feet together, and made a low grave bow, and then put out his left hand. My uncle was just going to step forward, and shake it heartily, when he perceived that these attentions were directed, not towards him, but to a young lady who just then appeared at the foot of the steps, attired in an old-fashioned green velvet dress with a long waist and stomacher. She had no bonnet on her head, gentlemen, which was muffled in a black silk hood, but she looked round for an instant as she prepared to get into the coach, and such a beautiful face as she disclosed my uncle had never seen – not even in a picture. She got into the coach, holding up her dress with one hand and, as my uncle always said with a round oath, when he told the story, he wouldn't have believed it possible that legs and feet could have been brought to such a state of perfection unless he had seen them with his own eyes.

But, in this one glimpse of the beautiful face, my uncle saw that the young lady cast an imploring look upon him, and that she appeared terrified and distressed. He noticed, too, that the young fellow in the powdered wig, notwithstanding his show of gallantry, which was all very fine and grand, clasped her tight by the wrist when she got in, and followed himself immediately afterwards. An uncommonly ill-looking fellow, in a close brown wig and a plum-coloured suit, wearing a very large sword, and boots up to his hips, belonged to the party; and when he sat himself down next to the young lady, who shrank into a corner at his approach, my uncle was confirmed in his original impression that something dark and mysterious was going forward, or, as he always said to himself, that 'there was a screw loose somewhere'. It's quite surprising how quickly he made up his mind to help the lady at any peril, if she needed help.

'Death and lightning!' exclaimed the young gentleman, laying his hand upon his sword as my uncle entered the coach.

'Blood and thunder!' roared the other gentleman. With this, he whipped his sword out, and made a lunge at my uncle without further ceremony. My uncle had no weapon about him, but with great dexterity he snatched the ill-looking gentleman's three-cornered hat from his head, and, receiving the point of his sword right through the crown, squeezed the sides together, and held it tight.

'Pink him behind!' cried the ill-looking gentleman to his companion, as he struggled to regain his sword.

'He had better not,' cried my uncle, displaying the heel of one of his shoes, in a threatening manner. 'I'll kick his brains out, if he has any, or fracture his skull if he hasn't.' Exerting all his strength, at this moment, my uncle wrenched the ill-looking man's sword from his grasp, and flung it clean out of the coach-window: upon which the younger gentleman vociferated, 'Death and lightning!' again, and laid his hand upon the hilt of his sword, in a very fierce manner, but didn't draw it. Perhaps, gentlemen, as my uncle used to say with a smile, perhaps he was afraid of alarming the lady.

'Now, gentlemen,' said my uncle, taking his seat deliberately, 'I don't want to have any death, with or without lightning, in a lady's presence, and we have had quite blood and thundering enough for one journey; so, if you please, we'll sit in our places like quiet insides. Here, guard, pick up that gentleman's carving-knife.'

As quickly as my uncle said the words, the guard appeared at the coach-window, with the gentleman's sword in his hand. He held up his lantern, and looked earnestly in my uncle's face, as he handed it in; when, by its light, my uncle saw, to his great surprise, that an immense crowd of mail coach guards swarmed round the window, every one of whom had his eyes earnestly fixed upon him too. He had never seen such a sea of white faces, red bodies, and earnest eyes, in all his born days.

'This is the strangest sort of thing I ever had anything to do with,' thought my uncle. 'Allow me to return you your hat, sir.'

The ill-looking gentleman received his three-cornered hat in silence, looked at the hole in the middle with an enquiring air, and finally stuck it on the top of his wig with a solemnity the effect of which was a trifle impaired by his sneezing violently at the moment, and jerking it off again.

'All right!' cried the guard with the lantern, mounting into his little seat behind. Away they went. My uncle peeped out of the coach-window as they emerged from the yard, and observed that the other mails, with coachmen, guards, horses, and passengers, complete, were driving round and round in circles, at a slow trot of about five miles an hour. My uncle burnt with indignation, gentlemen. As a commercial man, he felt that the mail bags were not to be trifled with, and he resolved to memorialise the Post Office on the subject, the very instant he reached London.

At present, however, his thoughts were occupied with the young lady who sat in the farthest corner of the coach, with her face muffled closely in her hood; the gentleman with the sky-blue coat sitting opposite her; the other man in the plum-coloured suit, by her side, the both watching her intently. If she so much as rustled the folds of her hood, he could hear the ill-looking man clap his hand upon his sword, and could tell by the other's breathing (it was so dark he couldn't see his face) that he was looking as big as if he were going to devour her at a mouthful. This roused my uncle more and more, and he resolved, come what come might, to see the end of it. He had a great admiration for bright eyes, and sweet faces, and pretty legs and feet; in short, he was fond of the whole sex. It runs in our family, gentlemen – so am I.

Many were the devices which my uncle practised to attract the lady's attention, or at all events, to engage the mysterious gentlemen in conversation. They were all in vain; the gentlemen wouldn't talk, and the lady didn't dare. He thrust his head out of the coach-window at intervals, and bawled out to know why they didn't go faster? But he called till he was hoarse; nobody paid the least attention to him. He leant back in the coach, and thought of the beautiful face, and the feet and legs. This answered better; it whiled away the time, and kept him from wondering where he was going, and how it was that he found himself in such an odd situation. Not that this would have worried him much, anyway – he was a mighty free and easy, roving, devil-may-care sort of person, was my uncle, gentlemen.

All of a sudden the coach stopped. 'Hallo!' said my uncle. 'What's in the wind now?'

'Alight here,' said the guard, letting down the steps.

'Here?' cried my uncle.

'Here,' rejoined the guard.

'I'll do nothing of the sort,' said my uncle.

'Very well, then stop where you are,' said the guard.

'I will,' said my uncle.

'Do,' said the guard.

The other passengers had regarded this colloquy with great attention, and, finding that my uncle was determined not to alight, the younger man squeezed past him, to hand the lady out. At this moment, the ill-looking man was inspecting the hole in the crown of his three-cornered hat. As the young lady brushed past, she dropped one of her gloves into my uncle's hand, and softly whispered, with her lips so close to his face that he felt her warm breath on his nose, the single word 'Help!' Gentlemen, my uncle leaped out of the coach at once, with such violence that it rocked on the springs again.

'Oh! You've thought better of it, have you?' said the guard when he saw my uncle standing on the ground.

My uncle looked at the guard for a few seconds, in some doubt whether it wouldn't be better to wrench his blunderbuss from him, fire it in the face of the man with the big sword, knock the rest of the company over the head with the stock, snatch up the young lady, and go off in the smoke. On second thoughts, however, he abandoned this plan, as being a shade too melodramatic in the execution, and followed the two mysterious men, who, keeping the lady between them, were now entering an old house in front of which the coach had stopped. They turned into the passage, and my uncle followed.

Of all the ruinous and desolate places my uncle had ever beheld, this was the most so. It looked as if it had once been a large house of entertainment; but the roof had fallen in, in many places, and the stairs were steep, rugged, and broken. There was a huge fireplace in the room into which they walked, and the chimney was blackened with smoke; but no warm blaze lighted it up now. The white feathery dust of burnt wood was still strewn over the hearth, but the stove was cold, and all was dark and gloomy.

'Well,' said my uncle, as he looked about him, 'a mail travelling at the rate of six miles and a half an hour, and stopping for an indefinite time at such a hole as this, is rather an irregular sort of proceeding, I fancy. This shall be made known. I'll write to the papers.'

My uncle said this in a pretty loud voice, and in an open unreserved sort of manner, with the view of engaging the two strangers in conversation if he could. But, neither of them took any more notice of him than whispering to each other, and scowling at him as they did so. The lady was at the farther end of the room, and once she ventured to wave her hand, as if beseeching my uncle's assistance.

At length the two strangers advanced a little, and the conversation began in earnest.

'You don't know this is a private room, I suppose, fellow?' said the gentleman in sky-blue.

'No, I do not, fellow,' rejoined my uncle. 'Only if this is a private room specially ordered for the occasion, I should think the public room must be a *very* comfortable one'; with this my uncle sat himself down in a high-backed chair, and took such an accurate measure of the gentleman, with his eyes, that Tiggin and Welps could have supplied him with printed calico for a suit, and not an inch too much or too little, from the estimate alone.

'Quit this room,' said both the men together, grasping their swords.

'Eh?' said my uncle, not at all appearing to comprehend their meaning.

'Quit the room, or you are a dead man,' said the ill-looking fellow with the large sword, drawing it at the same time and flourishing it in the air.

'Down with him!' cried the gentleman in sky-blue, drawing his sword also, and falling back two or three yards. 'Down with him!' The lady gave a loud scream.

Now, my uncle was always remarkable for great boldness, and great presence of mind. All the time that he had appeared so indifferent to what was going on, he had been looking slyly about, for some missile or weapon of defence, and at the very instant when the swords were drawn, he espied, standing in the chimney corner, an old basket-hilted rapier, in a rusty scabbard. At one bound, my uncle caught it in his hand, drew it, flourished it gallantly above his head, called aloud to the lady to keep out of the way, hurled the chair at the man in sky-blue, and the scabbard at the man in plum-colour, and taking advantage of the confusion, fell upon them both, pell-mell.

Gentlemen, there is an old story – none the worse for being true – regarding a fine young Irish gentleman, who being asked if he could play the fiddle, replied he had no doubt he could, but he couldn't exactly say, for certain, because he had never tried. This is not inapplicable to my uncle and his fencing. He had never had a sword in his hand before, except once when he played Richard III at a private theatre: upon which occasion it was arranged with Richmond that he was to be run through, from behind, without showing fight at all. But here he was, cutting and slashing with two experienced swordsmen: thrusting and guarding and poking and slicing, and acquitting himself in the most manful and dexterous manner possible, although up to that time he had never been aware that he had the least notion of the science. It only shows how true the old saying is, that a man never knows what he can do, till he tries, gentlemen.

The noise of the combat was terrific; each of the three combatants swearing like troopers, and their swords clashing with as much noise as if all the knives and steels in Newport market were rattling together, at the same time. When it was at its very height, the lady (to encourage my uncle most probably) withdrew her hood entirely from her face, and disclosed a countenance of such dazzling beauty that he would have fought against fifty men to win one smile from it and die. He had done wonders before, but now he began to powder away like a raving mad giant.

At this very moment, the gentleman in sky-blue turning round, and seeing the young lady with her face uncovered, vented an exclamation of rage and jealousy, and, turning his weapon against her beautiful bosom, pointed a thrust at her heart, which caused my uncle to utter a cry of apprehension that made the building ring. The lady stepped lightly aside, and snatching the young man's sword from his hand before he had recovered his balance, drove him to the wall, and running it through him, and the panelling, up to the very hilt, pinned him there, hard and fast. It was a splendid example. My uncle, with a loud shout of triumph, and a strength that was irresistible, made his adversary retreat in the same direction, and plunging the old rapier into the very centre of a large red flower in the pattern of his waistcoat, nailed him beside his friend; there they both stood, gentlemen, jerking their arms and legs about, in agony, like the toy-shop figures that are moved by a piece of packthread. My uncle always said, afterwards, that this was one of the surest means he knew of for disposing of an enemy; but it was liable to one objection on the ground of expense, inasmuch as it involved the loss of a sword for every man disabled.

'The mail, the mail!' cried the lady, running up to my uncle and throwing her beautiful arms round his neck; 'we may yet escape.'

'May!' cried my uncle; 'why, my dear, there's nobody else to kill, is there?' My uncle was rather disappointed, gentlemen, for he thought a little quiet bit of lovemaking would be agreeable after the slaughtering, if it were only to change the subject.

'We have not an instant to lose here,' said the young lady. 'He' (pointing to the young gentleman in sky-blue) 'is the only son of the powerful Marquess of Filletoville.'

'Well, then, my dear, I'm afraid he'll never come to the title,' said my uncle, looking coolly at the young gentleman as he stood fixed up against the wall, in the cockchafer fashion I have described. 'You have cut off the entail, my love.'

'I have been torn from my home and friends by these villains,' said the young lady, her features glowing with indignation. 'That wretch would have married me by violence in another hour.'

'Confound his impudence!' said my uncle, bestowing a very contemptuous look on the dying heir of Filletoville.

'As you may guess from what you have seen,' said the young lady, 'the party were prepared to murder me if I appealed to anyone for assistance. If their accomplices find us here, we are lost. Two minutes hence may be too late. The mail!' With these words, overpowered by her feelings, and the exertion of sticking the young Marquess of Filletoville, she sank into my uncle's arms. My uncle caught her up, and bore her to the housedoor. There stood the mail, with four long-tailed, flowing-maned, black horses, ready harnessed; but no coachman, no guard, no hostler even, at the horses' heads.

Gentlemen, I hope I do no injustice to my uncle's memory when I express my opinion that, although he was a bachelor, he *had* held some ladies in his arms before this time; I believe indeed, that he had rather a habit of kissing barmaids; and I know, that in one or two instances, he had been seen by credible witnesses to hug a landlady in a very perceptible manner. I mention the circumstance, to show what a very uncommon sort of person this beautiful young lady must have been to have affected my uncle in the way she did; he used to say that as her long dark hair trailed over his arm, and her beautiful dark eyes fixed themselves upon his face when she recovered, he felt so strange and nervous that his legs trembled beneath him. But who can look in a sweet soft pair of dark eyes without feeling queer? *I* can't, gentlemen. I am afraid to look at some eyes I know, and that's the truth of it.

'You will never leave me,' murmured the young lady.

'Never,' said my uncle. And he meant it too.

'My dear preserver!' exclaimed the young lady. 'My dear, kind, brave preserver!'

'Don't,' said my uncle, interrupting her.

'Why?' enquired the young lady.

'Because your mouth looks so beautiful when you speak,' rejoined my uncle, 'that I'm afraid I shall be rude enough to kiss it.'

The young lady put up her hand as if to caution my uncle not to do so and said – no, she didn't say anything – she smiled. When you are looking at a pair of the most delicious lips in the world, and see them gently break into a roguish smile – if you are very near them, and nobody else by – you cannot better testify your admiration of their beautiful form and colour than by kissing them at once. My uncle did so, and I honour him for it.

'Hark!' cried the young lady, starting. 'The noise of wheels and horses!'

'So it is,' said my uncle, listening. He had a good ear for wheels, and the trampling of hoofs; but there appeared to be so many horses and carriages rattling towards them, from a distance, that it was impossible to form a guess at their number. The sound was like that of fifty breaks, with six blood cattle in each.

'We are pursued!' cried the young lady, clasping her hands. 'We are pursued. I have no hope but in you!'

There was such an expression of terror in her beautiful face, that my uncle made up his mind at once. He lifted her into the coach, told her not to be frightened, pressed his lips to hers once more, and then advising her to draw up the window to keep the cold air out, mounted to the box.

'Stay, love,' cried the young lady.

'What's the matter?' said my uncle, from the coach-box.

'I want to speak to you,' said the young lady; 'only a word. Only one word, dearest.'

'Must I get down?' enquired my uncle. The lady made no answer, but she smiled again. Such a smile, gentlemen! It beat the other one, all to nothing. My uncle descended from his perch in a twinkling.

'What is it, my dear?' said my uncle, looking in at the coach-window. The lady happened to bend forward at the same time, and my uncle thought she looked more beautiful than she had done yet. He was very close to her just then, gentlemen, so he really ought to know.

'What is it, my dear?' said my uncle.

'Will you never love anyone but me, never marry anyone beside?' said the young lady.

My uncle swore a great oath that he never would marry anybody else, and the young lady drew in her head, and pulled up the window. He jumped upon the box, squared his elbows, adjusted the ribands, seized the whip which lay on the roof, gave one flick to the off leader, and away went the four long-tailed flowing-maned black horses, at fifteen good English miles an hour, with the old mail coach behind them. Whew! How they tore along!

The noise behind grew louder. The faster the old mail went, the faster came the pursuers – men, horses, dogs, were leagued in the pursuit. The noise was frightful, but, above all, rose the voice of the young lady, urging my uncle on, and shrieking, 'Faster! Faster!'

They whirled past the dark trees, as feathers would be swept before a hurricane. Houses, gates, churches, haystacks, objects of every kind they shot by, with a velocity and noise like roaring waters suddenly let loose. Still the noise of pursuit grew louder, and still my uncle could hear the young lady wildly screaming, 'Faster! Faster!'

My uncle plied whip and rein, and the horses flew onward till they were white with foam; and yet the noise behind increased; and yet the young lady cried, 'Faster! Faster!' My uncle gave a loud stamp on the boot in the energy of the moment, and – found that it was grey morning, and he was sitting in the wheelwright's yard, on the box of an old Edinburgh mail, shivering with the cold and wet and stamping his feet to warm them. He got down, and looked eagerly inside for the beautiful young lady. Alas! There was neither door nor seat to the coach. It was a mere shell.

Of course, my uncle knew very well that there was some mystery in the matter, and that everything had passed exactly as he used to relate it. He remained staunch to the great oath he had sworn to the beautiful young lady: refusing several eligible landladies on her account, and dying a bachelor at last. He always said what a curious thing it was that he should have found out, by such a mere accident as his climbing over the palings, that the ghosts of mail coaches and horses, guards, coachmen and passengers were in the habit of making journeys regularly every night. He used to add, that he believed he was the only living person who had ever been taken as a passenger on one of these excursions. And I think he was right, gentlemen – at least, I never heard of any other.

*   *   *

'I wonder what these ghosts of mail coaches carry in their bags,' said the landlord, who had listened to the whole story with profound attention.

'The dead letters, of course,' said the bagman.

'Oh, ah! To be sure,' rejoined the landlord. 'I never thought of that.'

BARON KOËLDWETHOUT'S
APPARITION

'The Baron Von Koëldwethout, of Grogzwig in Germany, was as likely a young baron as you would wish to see. I needn't say that he lived in a castle, because that's of course; neither need I say that he lived in an old castle; for what German baron ever lived in a new one? There were many strange circumstances connected with this venerable building, among which not the least startling and mysterious were that when the wind blew, it rumbled in the chimneys or even howled among the trees in the neighbouring forest; and that when the moon shone, she found her way through certain small loopholes in the wall, and actually made some parts of the wide halls and galleries quite light, while she left others in gloomy shadow. I believe that one of the baron's ancestors, being short of money, had inserted a dagger in a gentleman who called one night to ask his way, and it was supposed that these miraculous occurrences took place in consequence. And yet I hardly know how that could have been, either, because the baron's ancestor, who was an amiable man, felt very sorry afterwards for having been so rash, and laying violent hands upon a quantity of stone and timber which belonged to a weaker baron, built a chapel as an apology, and so took a receipt from heaven in full of all demands.

'Talking of the baron's ancestor puts me in mind of the baron's great claims to respect on the score of his pedigree. I am afraid to say, I am sure, how many ancestors the baron had; but I know that he had a great many more than any other man of his time; and I only wish that he had lived in these latter days, that he might have done more. It is a very hard thing upon the great men of past centuries, that they should have come into the world so soon, because a man who was born three or four hundred years ago cannot reasonably be expected to have had as many relations before him as a man who is born now. The last man, whoever he is – and he may be a cobbler or some low vulgar dog for aught we know – will have a longer pedigree than the greatest nobleman now alive; and I contend that this is not fair.

'Well, but the Baron Von Koëldwethout of Grogzwig! He was a fine swarthy fellow, with dark hair and large moustaches, who rode a-hunting in clothes of Lincoln green, with russet boots on his feet, and a bugle slung over his shoulder like the guard of a long stage. When he blew his bugle, four-and-twenty other gentleman of inferior rank, in Lincoln green a little coarser, and russet boots with a little thicker soles, turned out directly; and away galloped the whole train, with spears in their hands like lacquered area railings, to hunt down the boars, or perhaps encounter a bear: in which latter case the baron killed him first, and greased his whiskers with him afterwards.

'This was a merry life for the Baron of Grogzwig, and a merrier still for the baron's retainers, who drank Rhine wine every night till they fell under the table, and then had the bottles on the floor, and called for pipes. Never were such jolly, roystering, rollicking, merrymaking blades as the jovial crew of Grogzwig.

'But the pleasures of the table, or the pleasures of under the table, require a little variety; especially when the same five-and-twenty people sit daily down to the same board to discuss the same subjects, and tell the same stories. The baron grew weary, and wanted excitement. He took to quarrelling with his gentlemen, and tried kicking two or three of them every day after dinner. This was a pleasant change at first; but it became monotonous after a week or so, and the baron felt quite out of sorts, and cast about, in despair, for some new amusement.

'One night, after a day's sport in which he had outdone Nimrod or Gillingwater, and slaughtered "another fine bear", and brought him home in triumph, the Baron Von Koëldwethout sat moodily at the head of his table, eyeing the smoky roof of the hall with a discontented aspect. He swallowed huge bumpers of wine, but, the more he swallowed, the more he frowned. The gentlemen who had been honoured with the dangerous distinction of sitting on his right and left, imitated him to a miracle in the drinking and frowned at each other.

' "I will!" cried the baron suddenly, smiting the table with his right hand, and twirling his moustache with his left. "Fill to the Lady of Grogzwig!"

'The four-and-twenty Lincoln greens turned pale, with the exception of their four-and-twenty noses, which were unchangeable.

' "I said, to the Lady of Grogzwig," repeated the baron, looking round the board.

' "To the Lady of Grogzwig!" shouted the Lincoln greens; and down their four-and-twenty throats went four-and-twenty imperial pints of such rare old hock, that they smacked their eight-and-forty lips, and winked again.

' "The fair daughter of the Baron Von Swillenhausen," said Koëldwethout, condescending to explain. "We will demand her in marriage of her father ere the sun goes down tomorrow. If he refuse our suit, we will cut off his nose."

'A hoarse murmur arose from the company; every man touched first the hilt of his sword, and then the tip of his nose, with appalling significance.

'What a pleasant thing filial piety is to contemplate! If the daughter of the Baron Von Swillenhausen had pleaded a preoccupied heart, or fallen at her father's feet and corned them in salt tears, or only fainted away, and complimented the old gentleman in frantic ejaculations, the odds are a hundred to one but Swillenhausen's castle would have been turned out at window, or rather the baron turned out at window, and the castle demolished. The damsel held her peace, however, when an early messenger bore the request of Von Koëldwethout next morning, and modestly retired to her chamber, from the casement of which she watched the coming of the suitor and his retinue. She was no sooner assured that the horseman with the large moustaches was her proffered husband than she hastened to her father's presence, and expressed her readiness to sacrifice herself to secure his peace. The venerable baron caught his child to his arms, and shed a wink of joy.

'There was great feasting at the castle that day. The four-and-twenty Lincoln greens of Von Koëldwethout exchanged vows of eternal friendship with twelve Lincoln greens of Von Swillenhausen, and promised the old baron that they would drink his wine "till all was blue" – meaning, probably, until their whole countenances had acquired the same tint as their noses. Everybody slapped everybody else's back when the time for parting came; and the Baron Von Koëldwethout and his followers rode gaily home.

'For six mortal weeks the bears and boars had a holiday. The houses of Koëldwethout and Swillenhausen were united; the spears rusted; and the baron's bugle grew hoarse for lack of blowing.

'Those were great times for the four-and-twenty; but, alas! their high and palmy days had taken boots to themselves, and were already walking off.

' "My dear," said the baroness.

' "My love," said the baron.

' "Those coarse, noisy men – "

' "Which, ma'am?" said the baron, starting.

'The baroness pointed from the window at which they stood to the courtyard beneath, where the unconscious Lincoln greens were taking a copious stirrup-cup preparatory to issuing forth after a boar or two.

' "My hunting train, ma'am," said the baron.

' "Disband them, love," murmured the baroness.

' "Disband them!" cried the baron in amazement.

' "To please me, love," replied the baroness.

' "To please the devil, ma'am," answered the baron.

'Whereupon the baroness uttered a great cry and swooned away at the baron's feet.

'What could the baron do? He called for the lady's maid and roared for the doctor; and then, rushing into the yard, kicked the two Lincoln greens who were the most used to it, and cursing the others all round, bade them go . . . But never mind where. I don't know the German for it, or I would put it delicately that way.

'It is not for me to say by what means, or by what degrees, some wives manage to keep down some husbands as they do, although I may have my private opinion on the subject, and may think that no Member of Parliament ought to be married, inasmuch as three married members out of every four must vote according to their wives' consciences (if there be such things), and not according to their own. All I need say, just now, is that the Baroness Von Koëldwethout somehow or other acquired great control over the Baron Von Koëldwethout, and that, little by little, and bit by bit, and day by day, and year by year the baron got the worst of some disputed question, or was slyly unhorsed from some old hobby; and that, by the time he was a fat hearty fellow of forty-eight or thereabouts he had no feasting, no revelry, no hunting train, and no hunting – nothing, in short, that he liked, or used to have, and that, although he was as fierce as a lion, and as bold as brass, he was decidedly snubbed and put down, by his own lady, in his own castle of Grogzwig.

'Nor was this the whole extent of the baron's misfortunes. About a year after his nuptials, there came into the world a lusty young baron, in whose honour a great many fireworks were let off, and a great many dozens of bottles drunk; but next year there came a young baroness, and next year another young baron, and so on, every year, either a baron or baroness (and one year both together) until the baron found himself the father of a small family of twelve. Upon every one of these anniversaries the venerable Baroness Von Swillenhausen was nervously sensitive for the well-being of her child, the Baroness Von Koëldwethout; and although it was not found that the good lady ever did anything material towards contributing to her child's recovery, still she made it a point of duty to be as nervous as possible at the castle of Grogzwig, and to divide her time between moral observations on the baron's housekeeping, and bewailing the hard lot of her unhappy daughter. And if the Baron of Grogzwig, a little hurt and irritated at this, took heart, and ventured to suggest that his wife was at least no worse off than the wives of other barons, the Baroness Von Swillenhausen begged all persons to take notice that nobody but she sympathised with her dear daughter's sufferings: upon which her relations and friends remarked that to be sure she did cry a great deal more than her son-in-law, and that, if there were a hardhearted brute alive, it was that Baron of Grogzwig.

'The poor baron bore it all as long as he could, and, when he could bear it no longer, lost his appetite and his spirits, and sat himself gloomily and dejectedly down. But there were worse troubles yet in store for him, and, as they came on, his melancholy and sadness increased. Times changed. He got into debt. The Grogzwig coffers ran low, though the Swillenhausen family had looked upon them as inexhaustible; and just when the baroness was on the point of making a thirteenth addition to the family pedigree, Von Koëldwethout discovered that he had no means of replenishing them.

' "I don't see what is to be done," said the baron. "I think I'll kill myself."

'This was a bright idea. The baron took an old hunting knife from a cupboard hard by, and having sharpened it on his boot, made what boys call "an offer" at his throat.

' "Hem!" said the baron, stopping short. "Perhaps it's not sharp enough."

'The baron sharpened it again and made another offer, when his hand was arrested by a loud screaming among the young barons and baronesses, who had a nursery in an upstairs tower, with iron bars outside the windows, to prevent their tumbling out into the moat.

' "If I had been a bachelor," said the baron, sighing, "I might have done it fifty times over without being interrupted. Hallo! Put a flask of wine and the largest pipe in the little vaulted room behind the hall."

'One of the domestics, in a very kind manner, executed the baron's order in the course of half an hour or so, and Von Koëldwethout, being apprised thereof, strode to the vaulted room, the walls of which, being of dark shining wood, gleamed in the light of the blazing logs which were piled upon the hearth. The bottle and pipe were ready, and, upon the whole, the place looked very comfortable.

' "Leave the lamp," said the baron.

' "Anything else, my lord?" enquired the domestic.

' "The room," replied the baron. The domestic obeyed, and the baron locked the door.

' "I'll smoke a last pipe," said the baron, "and then I'll be off." So putting the knife upon the table till he wanted it, and tossing off a goodly measure of wine, the Lord of Grogzwig threw himself back in his chair, stretched his legs out before the fire, and puffed away.

'He thought about a great many things – about his present troubles and past days of bachelorship, and about the Lincoln greens, long since dispersed up and down the country, no one knew whither; with the exception of two who had been unfortunately beheaded, and four who had killed themselves with drinking. His mind was running upon bears and boars, when, in the process of draining his glass to the bottom, he raised his eyes, and saw, for the first time and with unbounded astonishment, that he was not alone.

'No, he was not; for, on the opposite side of the fire there sat with folded arms a wrinkled hideous figure, with deeply-sunk and bloodshot eyes and an immensely long cadaverous face shadowed by jagged and matted locks of coarse black hair. He wore a kind of tunic of a dull bluish colour, which, the baron observed, on regarding it attentively, was clasped or ornamented down the front with coffin handles. His legs, too, were encased in coffin plates as though in armour; and over his left shoulder he wore a short dusky cloak, which seemed made of a remnant of some pall. He took no notice of the baron, but was intently eyeing the fire.

' "Halloa!" said the baron, stamping his foot to attract attention.

' "Halloa!" replied the stranger, moving his eyes towards the baron, but not his face or himself. "What now?"

' "What now!" replied the baron, nothing daunted by his hollow voice and lustreless eyes. "*I* should ask that question. How did you get here?"

' "Through the door," replied the figure.

' "What are you?" says the baron.

' "A man," replied the figure.

' "I don't believe it," says the baron.

' "Disbelieve it, then," says the figure.

' "I will," replied the baron.

'The figure looked at the bold Baron of Grogzwig for some time, and then said familiarly, "There's no coming over you, I see. I am not a man!"

' "What are you, then?" asked the baron.

' "A genius," replied the figure.

' "You don't look much like one," returned the baron scornfully.

' "I am the Genius of Despair and Suicide," said the apparition. "Now you know me."

'With these words the apparition turned towards the baron, as if composing himself for a talk – and what was very remarkable was that he threw his cloak aside, and displaying a stake, which was run through the centre of his body, pulled it out with a jerk, and laid it on the table as composedly as if it had been a walking-stick.

' "Now," said the figure, glancing at the hunting knife, "are you ready for me?"

' "Not quite," rejoined the baron, "I must finish this pipe first."

' "Look sharp, then," said the figure.

' "You seem in a hurry," said the baron.

' "Why, yes, I am," answered the figure; "they're doing a pretty brisk business in my way over in England and France just now, and my time is a good deal taken up."

' "Do you drink?" said the baron, touching the bottle with the bowl of his pipe.

' "Nine times out of ten, and then very hard," rejoined the figure drily.

' "Never in moderation?" asked the baron.

' "Never," replied the figure with a shudder; "that breeds cheerfulness."

'The baron took another look at his new friend, whom he thought an uncommonly queer customer, and at length enquired whether he took any active part in such little proceedings as that which he had in contemplation.

' "No," replied the figure evasively; "but I am always present."

' "Just to see fair play, I suppose?" said the baron.

' "Just that," replied the figure, playing with his stake and examining the ferrule. "Be as quick as you can, will you? for there's a young gentleman who is afflicted with too much money and leisure wanting me now, I find."

' "Going to kill himself because he has too much money!" exclaimed the baron, quite tickled. "Ha! ha! that's a good one." (This was the first time the baron had laughed for many a long day.)

' "I say," expostulated the figure, looking very much scared; "don't do that again."

' "Why not?" demanded the baron.

' "Because it gives me pain all over," replied the figure. "Sigh as much as you please: that does me good."

'The baron sighed mechanically at the mention of the word; the figure, brightening up again, handed him the hunting knife with most winning politeness.

' "It's not a bad idea, though," said the baron, feeling the edge of the weapon; "a man killing himself because he has too much money."

' "Pooh!" said the apparition petulantly, "no better than a man's killing himself because he has none or little."

'Whether the genius unintentionally committed himself in saying this, or whether he thought the baron's mind was so thoroughly made up that it didn't matter what he said, I have no means of knowing. I only know that the baron stopped his hand all of a sudden, opened his eyes wide and looked as if quite a new light had come upon him for the first time.

' "Why, certainly," said Von Koëldwethout, "nothing is too bad to be retrieved."

' "Except empty coffers," cried the genius.

' "Well; but they may be one day filled again," said the baron.

' "Scolding wives," snarled the genius.

' "Oh! They may be made quiet," said the baron.

' "Thirteen children," shouted the genius.

' "Can't all go wrong, surely," said the baron.

'The genius was evidently growing very savage with the baron for holding these opinions all at once; but he tried to laugh it off and said if he would let him know when he had left off joking he should feel obliged to him.

' "But I am not joking; I was never farther from it," remonstrated the baron.

' "Well, I am glad to hear that," said the genius, looking very grim, "because a joke, without any figure of speech, *is* the death of me. Come! Quit this dreary world at once."

' "I don't know," said the baron, playing with the knife: "it's a dreary one certainly, but I don't think yours is much better, for you have not the appearance of being particularly comfortable. That puts me in mind – what security have I that I shall be any the better for going out of the world after all?" he cried, starting up; "I never thought of that."

' "Dispatch!" cried the figure, gnashing his teeth.

' "Keep off!" said the baron. "I'll brood over miseries no longer, but put a good face on the matter, and try the fresh air and the bears again; and, if that don't do, I'll talk to the baroness soundly, and cut the Von Swillenhausens dead."

With this, the baron fell into his chair, and laughed so loud and boisterously that the room rang with it.

'The figure fell back a pace or two, regarding the baron meanwhile with a look of intense terror, and, when he had ceased, caught up the stake, plunged it violently into his body, uttered a frightful howl, and disappeared.

'Von Koëldwethout never saw it again. Having once made up his mind to action, he soon brought the baroness and the Von Swillenhausens to reason, and died many years afterwards: not a rich man that I am aware of, but certainly a happy one: leaving behind him a numerous family, who had been carefully educated in bear and boar hunting under his own personal eye. And my advice to all men is, that if ever they become hipped and melancholy from similar causes (as very many men do), they look at both sides of the question, applying a magnifying glass to the best one; and if they still feel tempted to retire without leave, that they smoke a large pipe and drink a full bottle first, and profit by the laudable example of the Baron of Grogzwig.'

TO BE READ AT DUSK

One, two, three, four, five. There were five of them.

Five couriers, sitting on a bench outside the convent on the summit of the Great St Bernard in Switzerland, looking at the remote heights, stained by the setting sun, as if a mighty quantity of red wine had been broached upon the mountain top, and had not yet had time to sink into the snow.

This is not my simile. It was made for the occasion by the stoutest courier, who was a German. None of the others took any more notice of it than they took of me, sitting on another bench on the other side of the convent door, smoking my cigar, like them, and – also like them – looking at the reddened snow, and at the lonely shed hard by, where the bodies of belated travellers, dug out of it, slowly wither away, knowing no corruption in that cold region.

The wine upon the mountain top soaked in as we looked; the mountain became white; the sky, a very dark blue; the wind rose; and the air turned piercing cold. The five couriers buttoned their rough coats. There being no safer man to imitate in all such proceedings than a courier, I buttoned mine.

The mountain in the sunset had stopped the five couriers in a conversation. It is a sublime sight, likely to stop conversation. The mountain being now out of the sunset, they resumed. Not that I had heard any part of their previous discourse; for indeed, I had not then broken away from the American gentleman, in the travellers' parlour of the convent, who, sitting with his face to the fire, had undertaken to realise to me the whole progress of events which had led to the accumulation by the Honourable Ananias Dodger of one of the largest acquisitions of dollars ever made in our country.

'My God!' said the Swiss courier, speaking in French, which I do not hold (as some authors appear to do) to be such an all-sufficient excuse for a naughty word that I have only to write it in that language to make it innocent: 'if you talk of ghosts – '

'But I *don't* talk of ghosts,' said the German.

'Of what then?' asked the Swiss.

'If I knew of what then,' said the German, 'I should probably know a great deal more.'

It was a good answer, I thought, and it made me curious. So, I moved my position to that corner of my bench which was nearest to them, and leaning my back against the convent wall, heard perfectly, without appearing to attend.

'Thunder and lightning!' said the German, warming, 'when a certain man is coming to see you unexpectedly, and without his own knowledge, sends some invisible messenger to put the idea of him into your head all day, what do you call that? When you walk along a crowded street – at Frankfurt, Milan, London, Paris – and think that a passing stranger is like your friend Heinrich, and then that another passing stranger is like your friend Heinrich, and so begin to have a strange foreknowledge that presently you'll meet your friend Heinrich – which you do, though you believed him at Trieste – what do you call *that*?'

'It's not uncommon, either,' murmured the Swiss and the other three.

'Uncommon!' said the German. 'It's as common as cherries in the Black Forest. It's as common as macaroni at Naples. And Naples reminds me! When the old Marchesa Senzanima shrieks at a card-party on the Chiaja – as I heard and saw her, for it happened in a Bavarian family of mine, and I was overlooking the service that evening – I say, when the old Marchesa starts up at the card-table, white through her rouge, and cries, "My sister in Spain is dead! I felt her cold touch on my back!" – and when that sister *is* dead at the moment – what do you call that?'

'Or when the blood of San Gennaro liquefies at the request of the clergy as all the world knows that it does regularly once a year, in my native city,' said the Neapolitan courier after a pause, with a comical look, 'what do you call that?'

'*That*!' cried the German. 'Well, I think I know a name for that.'

'Miracle?' said the Neapolitan, with the same sly face.

The German merely smoked and laughed; and they all smoked and laughed.

'Bah!' said the German, presently. 'I speak of things that really do happen. When I want to see the conjurer, I pay to see a professed one, and have my money's worth. Very strange things do happen without ghosts. Ghosts! Giovanni Baptista, tell your story of the English bride. There's no ghost in that, but something full as strange. Will any man tell me what?'

As there was a silence among them, I glanced around. He whom I took to be Baptista was lighting a fresh cigar. He presently went on to speak. He was a Genoese, as I judged.

'The story of the English bride?' said he. '*Basta!* one ought not to call so slight a thing a story. Well, it's all one. But it's true. Observe me well, gentlemen, it's true. That which glitters is not always gold; but what I am going to tell, is true.'

He repeated this more than once.

* * *

Ten years ago, I took my credentials to an English gentleman at Long's Hotel, in Bond Street, London, who was about to travel – it might be for one year, it might be for two. He approved of them; likewise of me. He was pleased to make enquiry. The testimony that he received was favourable. He engaged me by the six months, and my entertainment was generous.

He was young, handsome, very happy. He was enamoured of a fair young English lady, with a sufficient fortune, and they were going to be married. It was the wedding-trip, in short, that we were going to take. For three months' rest in the hot weather (it was early summer then) he had hired an old place on the Riviera, at an easy distance from my city, Genoa, on the road to Nice. Did I know that place? Yes; I told him I knew it well. It was an old palace with great gardens. It was a little bare, and it was a little dark and gloomy, being close surrounded by trees; but it was spacious, ancient, grand, and on the seashore. He said it had been so described to him exactly, and he was well pleased that I knew it. For its being a little bare of furniture, all such places were. For its being a little gloomy, he had hired it principally for the gardens, and he and my mistress would pass the summer weather in their shade.

'So all goes well, Baptista?' said he.

'Indubitably, *signore*; very well.'

We had a travelling chariot for our journey, newly built for us, and in all respects complete. All we had was complete; we wanted for nothing. The marriage took place. They were happy. *I* was happy, seeing all so bright, being so well situated, going to my own city, teaching my language in the rumble to the maid, *la bella* Carolina, whose heart was gay with laughter: who was young and rosy.

The time flew. But I observed – listen to this, I pray! (and here the courier dropped his voice) – I observed my mistress sometimes brooding in a manner very strange; in a frightened manner; in an unhappy manner; with a cloudy, uncertain alarm upon her. I think that I began to notice this when I was walking up hills by the carriage side, and master had gone on in front. At any rate, I remember that it impressed itself upon my mind one evening in the South of France, when she called to me to call master back; and when he came back, and walked for a long way, talking encouragingly and affectionately to her, with his hand upon the open window, and hers in it. Now and then he laughed in a merry way, as if he were bantering her out of something. By and by she laughed, and then all went well again.

It was curious. I asked *la bella* Carolina, the pretty little one, Was mistress unwell? – No. Out of spirits? – No. Fearful of bad roads, or brigands? – No. And what made it more mysterious was, the pretty little one would not look at me in giving answer, but *would* look at the view.

But, one day she told me the secret.

'If you must know,' said Carolina, 'I find, from what I have overheard, that mistress is haunted.'

'How haunted?'

'By a dream.'

'What dream?'

'By a dream of a face. For three nights before her marriage, she saw a face in a dream – always the same face, and only one.'

'A terrible face?'

'No. The face of a dark, remarkable-looking man in black, with black hair and a grey moustache – a handsome man except for a reserved and secret air. Not a face she ever saw, or at all like a face she ever saw. Doing nothing in the dream but looking at her fixedly, out of darkness.'

'Does the dream come back?'

'Never. The recollection of it is all her trouble.'

'And why does it trouble her?'

Carolina shook her head.

'That's master's question,' said *la bella*. 'She don't know. She wonders why, herself. But I heard her tell him, only last night, that if she was to find a picture of that face in our Italian house (which she is afraid she will) she did not know how she could ever bear it.'

Upon my word I was fearful after this (said the Genoese courier) of our coming to the old *palazzo*, lest some such ill-starred picture should happen to be there. I knew there were many there; and, as we got nearer and nearer to the place, I wished the whole gallery in the crater of Vesuvius. To mend the matter, it was a stormy dismal evening when we, at last, approached that part of the Riviera. It thundered; and the thunder of my city and its environs, rolling among the high hills, is very loud. The lizards ran in and out of the chinks in the broken stone wall of the garden, as if they were frightened; the frogs bubbled and croaked their loudest; the sea-wind moaned, and the wet trees dripped; and the lightning – body of San Lorenzo, how it lightened!

We all know what an old palace in or near Genoa is – how time and the sea air have blotted it – how the drapery painted on the outer walls has peeled off in great flakes of plaster – how the lower windows are darkened with rusty bars of iron – how the courtyard is overgrown with grass – how the outer buildings are dilapidated – how the whole pile seems devoted to ruin. Our *palazzo* was one of the true kind. It had been shut up close for months. Months? Years! – it had an earthy smell, like a tomb. The scent of the orange trees on the broad back terrace, and of the lemons ripening on the wall, and of some shrubs that grew around a broken fountain, had got into the house somehow, and had never been able to get out again. There was, in every room, an aged smell, grown faint with confinement. It pined in all the cupboards and drawers. In the little rooms of communication between great rooms, it was stifling. If you turned a picture – to come back to the pictures – there it still was, clinging to the wall behind the frame, like a sort of bat.

The lattice-blinds were close shut, all over the house. There were two ugly grey old women in the house, to take care of it; one of them with a spindle, who stood winding and mumbling in the doorway, and who would as soon have let in the devil as the air. Master, mistress, *la bella* Carolina and I went all through the *palazzo*. I went first, though I have named myself last, opening the windows and the lattice-blinds, and shaking down on myself splashes of rain, and scraps of mortar, and now and then a dozing mosquito, or a monstrous, fat, blotchy Genoese spider.

When I had let the evening light into a room, master, mistress and *la bella* Carolina entered. Then, we looked round at all the pictures, and I went forward again into another room. Mistress secretly had great fear of meeting with the likeness of that face – we all had; but there was no such thing. The Madonna and Bambino, San Francisco, San Sebastiano, Venus, Santa Caterina, Angels, Brigands, Friars, Temples at Sunset, Battles, White Horses, Forests, Apostles, Doges, all my old acquaintances many times repeated? – yes. Dark handsome man in black, reserved and secret, with black hair and grey moustache, looking fixedly at mistress out of darkness? – no.

At last we got through all the rooms and all the pictures, and came out into the gardens. They were pretty well kept, being rented by a gardener, and were large and shady. In one place there was a rustic theatre, open to the sky; the stage a green slope; the coulisses, three entrances upon a side, sweet-smelling, leafy screens. Mistress moved her bright eyes, even there, as if she looked to see the face come in upon the scene; but all was well.

'Now, Clara,' master said, in a low voice, 'you see that it is nothing? You are happy.'

Mistress was much encouraged. She soon accustomed herself to that grim *palazzo*, and would sing, and play the harp, and copy the old pictures, and stroll with master under the green trees and vines all day. She was beautiful. He was happy. He would laugh and say to me, mounting his horse for his morning ride before the heat, 'All goes well, Baptista!'

'Yes, *signore*, thank God, very well.'

We kept no company. I took *la bella* to the *duomo* and *annunciata*, to the café, to the opera, to the village *festa*, to the public garden, to the day theatre, to the *marionetti*. The pretty little one was charmed with all she saw. She learnt Italian – heavens! miraculously! Was mistress quite forgetful of that dream? I asked Carolina sometimes. Nearly, said *la bella* – almost. It was wearing out.

One day master received a letter, and called me.

'Baptista!'

'*Signore!*'

'A gentleman who is presented to me will dine here today. He is called the Signor Dellombra. Let me dine like a prince.'

It was an odd name. I did not know that name. But, there had been many noblemen and gentlemen pursued by Austria on political suspicions, lately, and some names had changed. Perhaps this was one. *Altro!* Dellombra was as good a name to me as another.

When the Signor Dellombra came to dinner (said the Genoese courier in the low voice, into which he had subsided once before), I showed him into the reception-room, the great *sala* of the old *palazzo*. Master received him with cordiality, and presented him to mistress. As she rose, her faced changed, she gave a cry, and fell upon the marble floor.

Then I turned my head to the Signor Dellombra, and saw that he was dressed in black, and had a reserved and secret air, and was a dark remarkable-looking man, with black hair and a grey moustache.

Master raised mistress in his arms, and carried her to her own room, where I sent *la bella* Carolina straight. *La bella* told me afterwards that mistress was nearly terrified to death, and that she wandered in her mind about her dream all night.

Master was vexed and anxious – almost angry, and yet full of solicitude. The Signor Dellombra was a courtly gentleman, and spoke with great respect and sympathy of mistress's being so ill. The African wind had been blowing for some days (they had told him at his hotel of the Maltese Cross), and he knew that it was often hurtful. He hoped the beautiful lady would recover soon. He begged permission to retire, and to renew his visit when he should have the happiness of hearing that she was better. Master would not allow of this, and they dined alone.

He withdrew early. Next day he called at the gate, on horseback, to enquire for mistress. He did so two or three times in that week.

What I observed myself, and what *la bella* Carolina told me, united to explain to me that master had now set his mind on curing mistress of her fanciful terror. He was all kindness, but he was sensible and firm. He reasoned with her that to encourage such fancies was to invite melancholy, if not madness. That it rested with herself to be herself. That if she once resisted her strange weakness, so successfully as to receive the Signor Dellombra as an English lady would receive any other guest, it was for ever conquered. To make an end, the *signore* came again, and mistress received him without marked distress (though with constraint and apprehension still), and the evening passed serenely. Master was so delighted with this change, and so anxious to confirm it, that the Signor Dellombra became a constant guest. He was accomplished in pictures, books and music; and his society in any grim *palazzo* would have been welcome.

I used to notice, many times, that mistress was not quite recovered. She would cast down her eyes and droop her head, before the Signor Dellombra, or would look at him with a terrified and fascinated glance as if his presence had some evil influence or power upon her. Turning from her to him, I used to see him in the shaded gardens, or the large half-lighted *sala*, looking, as I might say, 'fixedly upon her out of darkness'. But, truly, I had not forgotten *la bella* Carolina's words describing the face in the dream.

After his second visit I heard master say, 'Now, see, my dear Clara, it's over! Dellombra has come and gone, and your apprehension is broken like glass.'

'Will he – will he ever come again?' asked mistress.

'Again? Why, surely, over and over again! Are you cold?' (She shivered.)

'No, dear – but – he terrifies me: are you sure that he need come again?'

'The surer for the question, Clara!' replied master, cheerfully.

But, he was very hopeful of her complete recovery now, and grew more and more so every day. She was beautiful. He was happy.

'All goes well, Baptista?' he would say to me again.

'Yes, *signore*, thank God; very well.'

We were all (said the Genoese courier, constraining himself to speak a little louder), we were all at Rome for the carnival. I had been out, all day, with a Sicilian, a friend of mine, and a courier, who was there with an English family. As I returned at night to our hotel, I met the little Carolina, who never stirred from home alone, running distractedly along the Corso.

'Carolina! What's the matter?'

'Oh, Baptista! Oh, for the Lord's sake! where is my mistress?'

'Mistress, Carolina?'

'Gone since morning – told me, when master went out on his day's journey, not to call her, for she was tired with not resting in the night (having been in pain) and would lie in bed until the evening; then get up refreshed. She is gone! – she is gone! Master has come back, broke down the door, and she is gone! My beautiful, my good, my innocent mistress!'

The pretty little one so cried, and raved, and tore herself that I could not have held her, but for her swooning on my arm as if she had been shot. Master came up – in manner, face or voice no more the master that I knew than I was he. He took me (I laid the little one upon her bed in the hotel, and left her with the chamber-women), in a carriage, furiously through the darkness, across the desolate *campagna*. When it was day, we stopped at a miserable post-house, only to find that all the horses had been hired twelve hours ago, and sent away in different directions – sent away, mark me! by the Signor Dellombra, who had passed there in a carriage, with a frightened English lady crouching in one corner.

I never heard (said the Genoese courier, drawing a long breath) that she was ever traced beyond that spot. All I know is that she vanished into infamous oblivion, with the dreaded face beside her that she had seen in her dream.

* * *

'What do you call *that*?' said the German courier, triumphantly. 'Ghosts! There are no ghosts *there*! What do you call this, that I am going to tell you? Ghosts! There are no ghosts *here*!'

* * *

I took an engagement once (pursued the German courier) with an English gentleman, elderly and a bachelor, to travel through my country, my Fatherland. He was a merchant who traded with my country and knew the language, but who had never been there since he was a boy – as I judge, some sixty years before.

His name was James, and he had a twin-brother John, also a bachelor. Between these brothers there was a great affection. They were in business together, at Goodman's Fields, but they did not live together. Mr James dwelt in Poland Street, turning out of Oxford Street, London; Mr John resided by Epping Forest.

Mr James and I were to start for Germany in about a week. The exact day depended on business. Mr John came to Poland Street (where I was staying in the house), to pass that week with Mr James. But, he said to his brother on the second day, 'I don't feel very well, James. There's not much the matter with me; but I think I am a little gouty. I'll go home and put myself under the care of my old housekeeper, who understands my ways. If I get quite better, I'll come back and see you before you go. If I don't feel well enough to resume my visit where I leave it off, why *you* will come and see *me* before you go.' Mr James, of course, said he would, and they shook hands – both hands, as they always did – and Mr John ordered out his old-fashioned chariot and rumbled home.

It was on the second night after that – that is to say, the fourth in the week – when I was awoke out of my sound sleep by Mr James coming into my bedroom in his flannel-gown, with a lighted candle. He sat upon the side of my bed, and looking at me, said, 'Wilhelm, I have reason to think I have got some strange illness upon me.'

I then perceived that there was a very unusual expression in his face.

'Wilhelm,' said he, 'I am not afraid or ashamed to tell you what I might be afraid or ashamed to tell another man. You come from a sensible

country, where mysterious things are enquired into and are not settled to
have been weighed and measured – or to have been unweighable and
unmeasurable – or in either case to have been completely disposed of, for
all time – ever so many years ago. I have just now seen the phantom of my
brother.'

I confess (said the German courier) that it gave me a little tingling of
the blood to hear it.

'I have just now seen,' Mr James repeated, looking full at me, that I
might see how collected he was, 'the phantom of my brother John. I was
sitting up in bed, unable to sleep, when it came into my room, in a white
dress, and regarding me earnestly, passed up to the end of the room,
glanced at some papers on my writing-desk, turned, and, still looking
earnestly at me as it passed the bed, went out at the door. Now I am not
in the least mad, and am not in the least disposed to invest that phantom
with any external existence out of myself. I think it is a warning to me
that I am ill; and I think I had better be bled.'

I got out of bed directly (said the German courier) and began to get on
my clothes, begging him not to be alarmed, and telling him that I would
go myself to the doctor. I was just ready, when we heard a loud knocking
and ringing at the street door. My room being an attic at the back, and
Mr James's being the second-floor room in the front, we went down to
his room, and put up the window, to see what was the matter.

'Is that Mr James?' said a man below, falling back to the opposite side
of the way to look up.

'It is,' said Mr James, 'and you are my brother's man, Robert.'

'Yes, sir. I am sorry to say, sir, that Mr John is ill. He is very bad, sir. It
is even feared that he may be lying at the point of death. He wants to see
you, sir. I have a chaise here. Pray come to him. Pray lose no time.'

Mr James and I looked at one another. 'Wilhelm,' said he, 'this is
strange. I wish you to come with me!' I helped him to dress, partly there
and partly in the chaise; and no grass grew under the horses' iron shoes
between Poland Street and the Forest.

Now, mind! (said the German courier) I went with Mr James into his
brother's room, and I saw and heard myself what follows.

His brother lay upon his bed, at the upper end of a long bedchamber.
His old housekeeper was there, and others were there: I think three
others were there, if not four, and they had been with him since early in
the afternoon. He was in white, like the figure – necessarily so, because

he had his nightdress on. He looked like the figure – necessarily so, because he looked earnestly at his brother when he saw him come into the room.

But, when his brother reached the bedside, he slowly raised himself in bed, and looking full upon him, said these words: *'James, you have seen me before, tonight – and you know it!'*

And so died!

*   *   *

I waited, when the German courier ceased, to hear something said of this strange story. The silence was unbroken. I looked round, and the five couriers were gone: so noiselessly that the ghostly mountain might have absorbed them into its eternal snows. By this time, I was by no means in a mood to sit alone in that awful scene, with the chill air coming solemnly upon me – or, if I may tell the truth, to sit alone anywhere. So I went back into the convent parlour, and, finding the American gentleman still disposed to relate the biography of the Honourable Ananias Dodger, heard it all out.

THE GHOST IN THE
BRIDE'S CHAMBER

The house was a genuine old house of a very quaint description, teeming with old carvings, and beams, and panels, and having an excellent old staircase, with a gallery or upper staircase, cut off from it by a curious fence-work of old oak, or of the old Honduras Mahogany wood. It was, and is, and will be, for many a long year to come, a remarkably picturesque house; and a certain grave mystery lurking in the depth of the old mahogany panels, as if they were so many deep pools of dark water – such, indeed, as they had been much among when they were trees – gave it a very mysterious character after nightfall.

When Mr Goodchild and Mr Idle had first alighted at the door, and stepped into the sombre handsome old hall, they had been received by half a dozen noiseless old men in black, all dressed exactly alike, who glided up the stairs with the obliging landlord and waiter – but without appearing to get into their way, or to mind whether they did or no – and who had filed off to the right and left on the old staircase, as the guests entered their sitting-room. It was then broad, bright day. But, Mr Good-child had said, when their door was shut, 'Who on earth are those old men?' And afterwards, both on going out and coming in, he had noticed that there were no old men to be seen.

Neither had the old men, or any one of the old men, reappeared since. The two friends had passed a night in the house, but had seen nothing more of the old men. Mr Goodchild, in rambling about it, had looked along passages, and glanced in at doorways, but had encountered no old men; neither did it appear that any old men were, by any member of the establishment, missed or expected.

Another odd circumstance impressed itself on their attention. It was that the door of their sitting-room was never left untouched for a quarter of an hour. It was opened with hesitation, opened with confidence, opened a little way, opened a good way, always clapped-to again without a word of explanation. They were reading, they were writing, they were eating, they were drinking, they were talking, they were dozing; the door was always opened at an unexpected moment, and they looked towards it, and it was clapped-to again, and nobody was to be seen. When this had happened fifty times or so, Mr Goodchild had said to his companion, jestingly: 'I begin to think, Tom, there was something wrong with those six old men.'

Night had come again, and they had been writing for two or three hours: writing, in short, a portion of the lazy notes from which these lazy sheets are taken. They had left off writing, and glasses were on the table between them. The house was closed and quiet. Around the head of Thomas Idle, as he lay upon his sofa, hovered light wreaths of fragrant smoke. The temples of Francis Goodchild, as he leaned back in his chair, with his two hands clasped behind his head, and his legs crossed, were similarly decorated.

They had been discussing several idle subjects of speculation, not omitting the strange old men, and were still so occupied, when Mr Goodchild abruptly changed his attitude to wind up his watch. They were just becoming drowsy enough to be stopped in their talk by any such slight check. Thomas Idle, who was speaking at the moment, paused and said, 'How goes it?'

'One,' said Goodchild.

As if he had ordered one old man, and the order were promptly executed (truly, all orders were so, in that excellent hotel), the door opened, and one old man stood there.

He did not come in, but stood with the door in his hand.

'One of the six, Tom, at last!' said Mr Goodchild, in a surprised whisper. 'Sir, your pleasure?'

'Sir, *your* pleasure?' said the one old man.

'I didn't ring.'

'The bell did,' said the one old man.

He said *bell*, in a deep strong way, that would have expressed the church bell.

'I had the pleasure, I believe, of seeing you yesterday?' said Goodchild.

'I cannot undertake to say for certain,' was the grim reply of the one old man.

'I think you saw me? Did you not?'

'Saw *you*?' said the old man. 'Oh yes, I saw *you*. But I see many who never see me.'

A chilled, slow, earthy, fixed old man. A cadaverous old man of measured speech. An old man who seemed as unable to wink as if his eyelids had been nailed to his forehead. An old man whose eyes – two spots of fire – had no more motion than if they had been connected with the back of his skull by screws driven through it, and riveted and bolted outside, among his grey hairs.

The night had turned so cold, to Mr Goodchild's sensations, that he shivered. He remarked lightly, and half apologetically, 'I think somebody is walking over my grave.'

'No,' said the weird old man, 'there is no one there.'

Mr Goodchild looked at Idle, but Idle lay with his head enwreathed in smoke.

'No one there?' said Goodchild.

'There is no one at your grave, I assure you,' said the old man.

He had come in and shut the door and he now sat down. He did not bend himself to sit as other people do, but seemed to sink bolt upright, as if in water, until the chair stopped him.

'My friend, Mr Idle,' said Goodchild, extremely anxious to introduce a third person into the conversation.

'I am,' said the old man, without looking at him, 'at Mr Idle's service.'

'If you are an old inhabitant of this place – ' Francis Goodchild resumed.

'Yes.'

'Perhaps you can decide a point my friend and I were in doubt upon, this morning. They hang condemned criminals at the castle, I believe?'

'*I* believe so,' said the old man.

'Are their faces turned towards that noble prospect?'

'Your face is turned,' replied the old man, 'to the castle wall. When you are tied up, you see its stones expanding and contracting violently, and a similar expansion and contraction seem to take place in your own head and breast. Then, there is a rush of fire and an earthquake, and the castle springs into the air, and you tumble down a precipice.'

His cravat seemed to trouble him. He put his hand to his throat, and moved his neck from side to side. He was an old man of a swollen character of face, and his nose was immovably hitched up on one side, as if by a little hook inserted in that nostril. Mr Goodchild felt exceedingly uncomfortable, and began to think the night was hot, and not cold.

'A strong description, sir,' he observed.

'A strong sensation,' the old man rejoined.

Again, Mr Goodchild looked to Mr Thomas Idle; but Thomas lay on his back with his face attentively turned towards the one old man, and made no sign. At this time Mr Goodchild believed that he saw threads of fire stretch from the old man's eyes to his own, and there attach themselves. (Mr Goodchild writes the present account of his experience, and, with the utmost solemnity, protests that he had the strongest sensation upon him of being forced to look at the old man along those two fiery films, from that moment.)

'I must tell it to you,' said the old man, with a ghastly and a stony stare.

'What?' asked Francis Goodchild.

'You know where it took place. Yonder!'

Whether he pointed to the room above, or to the room below, or to any room in that old house, or to a room in some other old house in that old town, Mr Goodchild was not, nor is, nor ever can be, sure. He was confused by the circumstances that the right forefinger of the one old man seemed to dip itself in one of the threads of fire, light itself, and make a fiery start in the air, as it pointed somewhere. Having pointed somewhere, it went out.

'You know she was a bride,' said the old man.

'I know they still send up bride-cake,' Mr Goodchild faltered. 'This is a very oppressive air.'

'She was a bride,' said the old man. 'She was a fair, flaxen-haired, large-eyed girl, who had no character, no purpose. A weak, credulous, incapable, helpless nothing. Not like her mother. No, no. It was her father whose character she reflected.

'Her mother had taken care to secure everything to herself, for her own life, when the father of this girl (a child at that time) died – of sheer helplessness; no other disorder – and then he renewed the acquaintance that had once subsisted between the mother and him. He had been put aside for the flaxen-haired, large-eyed man (or nonentity) with money. He could overlook that for money. He wanted compensation in money.

'So, he returned to the side of that woman the mother, made love to her again, danced attendance on her, and submitted himself to her whims. She wreaked upon him every whim she had, or could invent. He bore it. And the more he bore, the more he wanted compensation in money, and the more he was resolved to have it.

'But lo! Before he got it, she cheated him. In one of her imperious states, she froze, and never thawed again. She put her hands to her head one night, uttered a cry, stiffened, lay in that attitude certain hours, and died. Again he had got no compensation from her in money, yet. Blight and murrain on her! Not a penny.

'He had hated her throughout that second pursuit, and had longed for retaliation on her. He now counterfeited her signature to an instrument, leaving all she had to leave to her daughter – ten years old then – to whom the property passed absolutely, and appointed himself the daughter's guardian. When he slid it under the pillow of the bed on which she lay, he bent down in the deaf ear of death, and whispered: "Mistress Pride, I have determined a long time that, dead or alive, you must make me compensation in money."

'So, now there were only two left. Which two were he and the fair flaxen-haired, large-eyed foolish daughter, who afterwards became the bride.

'He put her to school. In a secret, dark, oppressive, ancient house, he put her to school with a watchful and unscrupulous woman. "My worthy lady," he said, "here is a mind to be formed; will you help me to form it?" She accepted the trust. For which she, too, wanted compensation in money, and had it.

'The girl was formed in the fear of him, and in the conviction, that there was no escape from him. She was taught, from the first, to regard him as her future husband – the man who must marry her – the destiny that overshadowed her – the appointed certainty that could never be evaded. The poor fool was soft white wax in their hands, and took the impression that they put upon her. It hardened with time. It became a part of herself. Inseparable from herself and only to be torn away from her by tearing life away from her.

'Eleven years she had lived in the dark house and its gloomy garden. He was jealous of the very light and air getting to her, and they kept her close. He stopped the wide chimneys, shaded the little windows, left the strong-stemmed ivy to wander where it would over the house-front, the moss to accumulate on the untrimmed fruit trees in the red-walled garden, the weeds to overrun its green and yellow walks. He surrounded her with images of sorrow and desolation. He caused her to be filled with fears of the place and of the stories that were told of it, and then on pretext of correcting them, to be left in it in solitude, or made to shrink about it in the dark. When her mind was most depressed and fullest of terrors, then he would come out of one of the hiding-places from which he overlooked her and present himself as her sole recourse.

'Thus, by being from her childhood the one embodiment her life presented to her of power to coerce and power to relieve, power to bind and power to loose, the ascendency over her weakness was secured. She was twenty-one years and twenty-one days old when he brought her home to the gloomy house, his half-witted, frightened, and submissive bride of three weeks.

'He had dismissed the governess by that time – what he had left to do, he could best do alone – and they came back, upon a rainy night, to the scene of her long preparation.

'She turned to him upon the threshold, as the rain was dripping from the porch, and said: "Oh sir, it is the death-watch ticking for me!"

' "Well!" he answered. "And if it were?"

' "Oh sir!" she returned to him, "look kindly on me, and be merciful to me! I beg your pardon. I will do anything you wish, if you will only forgive me!"

'That had become the poor fool's constant song: "I beg your pardon," and "Forgive me!"

'She was not worth hating; he felt nothing but contempt for her. But she had long been in the way, and he had long been weary, and the work was near its end, and had to be worked out.

' "You fool," he said. "Go up the stairs!"

'She obeyed very quickly, murmuring, "I will do anything you wish!" When he came into the bride's chamber, having been a little retarded by the heavy fastenings of the great door (for they were alone in the house, and he had arranged that the people who attended on them should come and go in the day), he found her withdrawn to the furthest corner, and there standing pressed against the panelling as if she would have shrunk through it: her flaxen hair all wild about her face, and her large eyes staring at him in vague terror.

' "What are you afraid of? Come and sit down by me."

' "I will do anything you wish. I beg your pardon, sir. Forgive me!" Her monotonous tune as usual.

' "Ellen, here is a writing that you must write out tomorrow, in your own hand. You may as well be seen by others, busily engaged upon it. When you have written it all fairly, and corrected all mistakes, call in any two people there may be about the house, and sign your name to it before them. Then, put it in your bosom to keep it safe, and when I sit here again tomorrow night, give it to me."

' "I will do it all, with the greatest care. I will do anything you wish."

' "Don't shake and tremble, then."

' "I will try my utmost not to do it – if you will only forgive me!"

'Next day, she sat down at her desk, and did as she had been told. He often passed in and out of the room, to observe her, and always saw her slowly and laboriously writing: repeating to herself the words she copied, in appearance quite mechanically, and without caring or endeavouring to comprehend them, so that she did her task. He saw her follow the directions she had received, in all particulars; and at night, when they were alone again in the same bride's chamber, and he drew his chair to the hearth, she timidly approached him from her distant seat, took the paper from her bosom, and gave it into his hand.

'It secured all her possessions to him, in the event of her death. He put her before him, face to face, that he might look at her steadily; and he asked her, in so many plain words, neither fewer nor more, did she know that?

'There were spots of ink upon the bosom of her white dress, and they made her face look whiter and her eyes look larger as she nodded her head. There were spots of ink upon the hand with which she stood before him nervously plaiting and folding her white skirts.

'He took her by the arm, and looked her, yet more closely and steadily, in the face. "Now, die! I have done with you."

'She shrank, and uttered a low, suppressed cry.

' "I am not going to kill you. I will not endanger my life for yours. Die!"

'He sat before her in the gloomy bride's chamber, day after day, night after night, looking the word at her when he did not utter it. As often as her large unmeaning eyes were raised from the hands in which she rocked her head to the stern figure sitting with crossed arms and knitted forehead in the chair, they read in it, "Die!" When she dropped asleep in exhaustion, she was called back to shuddering consciousness by the whisper, "Die!" When she fell upon her old entreaty to be pardoned, she was answered, "Die!" When she had out-watched and out-suffered the long night, and the rising sun flamed into the sombre room, she heard it hailed with, "Another day and not dead?"

'It was done, upon a windy morning, before sunrise. He computed the time to be half-past four; but his forgotten watch had run down and he could not be sure. She had broken away from him in the night with loud and sudden cries – the first of that kind to which she had given vent – and he had had to put his hands over her mouth. Since then, she had been quiet in the corner of the panelling where she had sunk down; and he had left her and had gone back with his folded arms and his knitted forehead to his chair.

'Paler in the pale light, more colourless than ever in the leaden dawn, he saw her coming, trailing herself along the floor towards him – a white wreck of hair, and dress, and wild eyes, pushing itself on by an irresolute and bending hand.

' "Oh, forgive me! I will do anything. Oh, sir, pray tell me I may live!"
' "Die!"
' "Are you so resolved? Is there no hope for me?"
' "Die!"

'Her large eyes strained themselves with wonder and fear; wonder and fear changed to reproach; reproach to blank nothing. It was done. He was not at first so sure it was done, but that the morning sun was hanging jewels in her hair – he saw the diamond, emerald and ruby, glittering among it in little points, as he stood looking down at her – when he lifted her and laid her on her bed.

'She was soon laid in the ground. And now they were all gone, and he had compensated himself well.

'He had a mind to travel. Not that he meant to waste his money, for he was a pinching man and liked his money dearly (like nothing else, indeed), but that he had grown tired of the desolate house and wished to turn his back upon it and have done with it. But, the house was worth money, and money must not be thrown away. He determined to sell it before he went. That it might look the less wretched and bring a better price, he hired some labourers to work in the overgrown garden: to cut out the dead wood, trim the ivy that dropped in heavy masses over the windows and gables, and clear the walks in which the weeds were growing mid-leg high.

'He worked, himself, along with them. He worked later than they did, and, one evening at dusk, was left working alone with his billhook in his hand. One autumn evening, when the bride was five weeks dead, "It grows too dark to work longer," he said to himself. "I must give over for the night."

'He detested the house, and was loath to enter it. He looked at the dark porch waiting for him like a tomb, and felt that it was an accursed house. Near to the porch, and near to where he stood, was a tree whose branches waved before the old bay window of the bride's chamber, where it had been done. The tree swung suddenly, and made him start. It swung again, although the night was still. Looking up into it, he saw a figure among the branches.

'It was the figure of a young man. The face looked down, as he looked up; the branches cracked and swayed; the figure rapidly descended, and slid upon its feet before him. A slender youth of about her age, with long light brown hair.

' "What thief are you?" he said, seizing the youth by the collar.

'The young man, in shaking himself free, swung him a blow with his arm across the face and throat. They closed, but the young man got from him and stepped back, crying, with great eagerness and horror, "Don't touch me! I would as lieve be touched by the devil!"

'He stood still, with his billhook in his hand, looking at the young man. For the young man's look was the counterpart of her last look, and he had not expected ever to see that again.

' "I am no thief. Even if I were, I would not have a coin of your wealth, if it would buy me the Indies. You murderer!"

' "What!"

' "I climbed it," said the young man, pointing up into the tree, "for the first time, nigh four years ago. I climbed it, to look at her. I saw her. I spoke to her. I have climbed it, many a time, to watch and listen for her. I was a boy, hidden among its leaves, when from that bay window she gave me this!"

'He showed a tress of flaxen hair, tied with a mourning ribbon.

' "Her life," said the young man, "was a life of mourning. She gave me this, as a token of it, and a sign that she was dead to everyone but you. If I had been older, if I had seen her sooner, I might have saved her from you. But she was fast in the web when I first climbed the tree, and what could I do then to break it!"

'In saying these words, he burst into a fit of sobbing and crying: weakly at first, then passionately.

' "Murderer! I climbed the tree on the night when you brought her back. I heard her, from the tree, speak of the death-watch at the door. I was three times in the tree while you were shut up with her, slowly killing her. I saw her, from the tree, lie dead upon her bed. I have watched you, from the tree, for proofs and traces of your guilt. The manner of it is a mystery to me yet, but I will pursue you until you have rendered up your life to the hangman. You shall never, until then, be rid of me. I loved her! I can know no relenting towards you. Murderer! I loved her!"

GHOST STORIES

'The youth was bareheaded, his hat having fluttered away in his descent from the tree. He moved towards the gate. He had to pass – him – to get to it. There was breadth for two old-fashioned carriages abreast; and the youth's abhorrence, openly expressed in every feature of his face and limb of his body, and very hard to bear, had verge enough to keep itself at a distance in. He (by which I mean the other) had not stirred hand or feet since he had stood still to look at the boy. He faced round, now, to follow him with his eyes. As the back of the bare light-brown head was turned to him, he saw a red curve stretch from his hand to it. He knew, before he threw the billhook, where it had alighted – I say, had alighted, and not would alight; for, to his clear perception the thing was done before he did it. It cleft the head, and it remained there, and the boy lay on his face.

'He buried the body in the night, at the foot of the tree. As soon as it was light in the morning, he worked at turning up all the ground near the tree, and hacking and hewing at the neighbouring bushes and under-growth. When the labourers came, there was nothing suspicious, and nothing suspected.

'But, he had, in a moment, defeated all his precautions, and destroyed the triumph of the scheme he had so long concerted, and so successfully worked out. He had got rid of the bride, and had acquired her fortune without endangering his life; but now, for a death by which he had gained nothing, he had evermore to live with a rope around his neck.

'Beyond this, he was chained to the house of gloom and horror, which he could not endure. Being afraid to sell it or to quit it, lest discovery should be made, he was forced to live in it. He hired two old people, man and wife, for his servants; and dwelt in it, and dreaded it. His great difficulty, for a long time, was the garden. Whether he should keep it trim, whether he should suffer it to fall into its former state of neglect, what would be the least likely way of attracting attention to it?

'He took the middle course of gardening, himself, in his evening leisure, and of then calling the old serving-man to help him; but, of never letting him work there alone. And he made himself an arbour over against the tree, where he could sit and see that it was safe.

'As the seasons changed, and the tree changed, his mind perceived dangers that were always changing. In the leafy time, he perceived that the upper boughs were growing into the form of the young man – that they made the shape of him exactly, sitting in a forked branch swinging in the wind. In the time of the falling leaves he perceived that they came down from the tree, forming tell-tale letters on the path, or that they had a tendency to heap themselves into a churchyard mound above the grave. In the winter, when the tree was bare, he perceived that the boughs swung at him the ghost of the blow the young man had given, and that they threatened him openly. In the spring, when sap was mounting in the trunk, he asked himself, were the dried-up particles of blood mounting with it – to make out, more obviously this year than last, the leaf-screened figure of the young man, swinging in the wind?

'However, he turned his money over and over, and still over. He was in the dark trade, the gold-dust trade, and most secret trades that yielded great returns. In ten years, he had turned his money over so many times that the traders and shippers who had dealings with him absolutely did not lie – for once – when they declared that he had increased his fortune twelve hundred per cent.

'He possessed his riches one hundred years ago, when people could be lost easily. He had heard who the youth was, from hearing of the search that was made after him; but, it died away, and the youth was forgotten.

'The annual round of changes in the tree had been repeated ten times since the night of the burial at its foot, when there was a great thunderstorm over this place. It broke at midnight, and raged until morning. The first intelligence he heard from his old serving-man that morning was that the tree had been struck by lightning.

'It had been riven down the stem, in a very surprising manner, and the stem lay in two blighted shafts: one resting against the house, and one against a portion of the old red garden-wall in which its fall had made a gap. The fissure went down the tree to a little above the earth, and there stopped. There was great curiosity to see the tree, and, with most of his former fears revived, he sat in his arbour – grown quite an old man – watching the people who came to see it.

'They quickly began to come, in such dangerous numbers that he closed his garden-gate and refused to admit any more. But there were certain men of science who travelled from a distance to examine the tree, and, in an evil hour, he let them in – blight and murrain on them, let them in!

'They wanted to dig up the ruin by the roots, and closely examine it, and the earth about it. Never, while he lived! They offered money for it. They! Men of science, whom he could have bought by the gross, with a scratch of his pen! He showed them the garden-gate again, and locked and barred it.

'But they were bent on doing what they wanted to do, and they bribed the old serving-man – a thankless wretch who regularly complained, when he received his wages, of being underpaid – and they stole into the garden by night with their lanterns, picks, and shovels, and fell to at the tree. He was lying in a turret room on the other side of the house (the bride's chamber had been unoccupied ever since), but he soon dreamed of picks and shovels, and got up.

'He came to an upper window on that side, whence he could see their lanterns, and them, and the loose earth in a heap which he had himself disturbed and put back when it was last turned to the air. It was found. They had that minute lighted on it. They were all bending over it. One of them said, "The skull is fractured"; and another, "See here the bones"; said another, "See here the clothes"; and then the first struck in again, and said, "A rusty billhook!"

'He became sensible, next day, that he was already put under a strict watch, and that he could go nowhere without being followed. Before a week was out he was taken and laid in hold. The circumstances were gradually pieced together against him, with a desperate malignity, and an appalling ingenuity. But, see the justice of men and how it was extended to him! He was further accused of having poisoned that girl in the bride's chamber. He, who had carefully and expressly avoided imperilling a hair of his head for her, and who had seen her die of her own incapacity!'

'There was doubt for which of the two murders he should be first tried; but, the real one was chosen, and he was found guilty, and cast for death. Bloodthirsty wretches! They would have made him guilty of any-thing, so set they were upon having his life.

'His money could do nothing to save him, and he was hanged. *I* am he, and I was hanged at Lancaster Castle, with my face to the wall, a hundred years ago!'

*   *   *

At this terrific announcement, Mr Goodchild tried to rise and cry out. But, the two fiery lines extending from the old man's eyes to his own, kept him down, and he could not utter a sound. His sense of hearing, however, was acute, and he could hear the clock strike two. No sooner had he heard the clock strike two, than he saw before him two old men!

Two.

The eyes of each, connected with his eyes by two films of fire: each, exactly like the other; each, addressing him at precisely one and the same instant; each, gnashing the same teeth in the same head, with the same twitched nostril above them, and the same suffused expression around it. Two old men. Differing in nothing, equally distinct to the sight, the copy no fainter than the original, the second as real as the first.

'At what time,' said the two old men, 'did you arrive at the door below?'

'At six.'

'And there were six old men upon the stairs!'

Mr Goodchild having wiped the perspiration from his brow, or tried to do it, the two old men proceeded in one voice, and in the singular number: 'I had been anatomised, but had not yet had my skeleton put together and re-hung on an iron hook, when it began to be whispered that the bride's chamber was haunted. It *was* haunted, and I was there.

'*We* were there. She and I were there. I, in the chair upon the hearth; she, a white wreck again, trailing itself towards me on the floor. But, I was the speaker no more, and the one word that she said to me from midnight until dawn was, "Live!"

'The youth was there, likewise. In the tree outside the window. Coming and going in the moonlight, as the tree bent and gave. He has, ever since, been there, peeping in at me in my torment; revealing to me by snatches, in the pale light and slatey shadows, where he comes and goes, bareheaded – a billhook standing edgewise in his hair.

'In the bride's chamber, every night from midnight until dawn – one month in the year excepted, as I am going to tell you – he hides in the tree, and she comes towards me on the floor; always approaching; never coming nearer; always visible as if by moonlight, whether the moon shines or no; always saying, from midnight until dawn, her one word, "Live!"

'But, in the month wherein I was forced out of this life – this present month of thirty days – the bride's chamber is empty and quiet. Not so my old dungeon. Not so the rooms where I was restless and afraid, ten years. Both are fitfully haunted then. At one in the morning, I am what you saw me when the clock struck that hour – one old man. At two in the morning, I am two old men. At three, I am three. By twelve noon, I am twelve old men. One for every hundred per cent of old gain. Every one of the twelve, with twelve times my old power of suffering and agony. From that hour until twelve at night, I, twelve old men in anguish and fearful forebodings, wait for the coming of the executioner. At twelve at night, I, twelve old men turned off, swing invisible outside Lancaster Castle, with twelve faces to the wall!

'When the bride's chamber was first haunted, it was known to me that this punishment would never cease until I could make its nature, and my story, known to two living men together. I waited for the coming of two living men together into the bride's chamber, years upon years. It was infused into my knowledge (of the means I am ignorant) that if two living men, with their eyes open, could be in the bride's chamber at one in the morning, they would see me sitting in my chair.

'At length, the whispers that the room was spiritually troubled, brought two men to try the adventure. I was scarcely struck upon the hearth at midnight (I come there as if the lightning blasted me into being), when I heard them ascending the stairs. Next, I saw them enter. One of them was a bold, gay, active man, in the prime of life, some five and forty years of age; the other, a dozen years younger. They brought provisions with them in a basket, and bottles. A young woman accompanied them, with wood and coals for the lighting of the fire. When he had lighted it, the bold, gay, active man accompanied her along the gallery outside the room, to see her safely down the staircase, and came back laughing.

'He locked the door, examined the chamber, put out the contents of the basket on the table before the fire – little recking of me, in my appointed station on the hearth close to him – and filled the glasses, and ate and drank. His companion did the same, and was as cheerful and confident as he: though he was the leader. When they had supped, they laid pistols on the table, turned to the fire, and began to smoke their pipes of foreign make.

'They had travelled together, and had been much together, and had an abundance of subjects in common. In the midst of their talking and laughing, the younger man made a reference to the leader's being always ready for any adventure; that one, or any other.

'He replied in these words: "Not quite so, Dick; if I am afraid of nothing else, I am afraid of myself."

'His companion, who seemed to grow a little dull, asked him in what sense? How?

' "Why, thus," he returned. "Here is a ghost to be disproved. Well! I cannot answer for what my fancy might do if I were alone here, or what tricks my senses might play with me if they had me to themselves. But, in company with another man, and especially with you, Dick, I would consent to out-face all the ghosts that were ever told of in the universe."

' "I had not the vanity to suppose that I was of so much importance tonight," said the other.

' "Of so much," rejoined the leader, more seriously than he had spoken yet, "that I would, for the reason I have given, on no account have undertaken to pass the night here alone."

'It was within a few minutes of one. The head of the younger man had drooped when he made his last remark, and it drooped lower now.

' "Keep awake, Dick!" said the leader, gaily. "The small hours are the worst."

He tried, but his head drooped again.

' "Dick!" urged the leader. "Keep awake!"

' "I can't," he indistinctly muttered. "I don't know what strange influence is stealing over me. I can't."

'His companion looked at him with a sudden horror, and I, in my different way, felt a new horror also; it was on the stroke of one, and I felt that the second watcher was yielding to me, and that the curse was upon me that I must send him to sleep.

' "Get up and walk, Dick!" cried the leader. "Try!"

'It was in vain to go behind the slumberer's chair and shake him. One o'clock sounded, and I was present to the elder man, and he stood transfixed before me.

'To him alone, I was obliged to relate my story, without hope of benefit. To him alone, I was an awful phantom making a quite useless confession. I foresee it will ever be the same. The two living men together will never come to release me. When I appear, the senses of one of the two will be locked in sleep; he will neither see nor hear me; my communication will ever be made to a solitary listener, and will ever be unserviceable. Woe! Woe! Woe!'

As the two old men, with these words, wrung their hands, it shot into Mr Goodchild's mind that he was in the terrible situation of being virtually alone with the spectre, and that Mr Idle's immovability was explained by his having been charmed asleep at one o'clock. In the terror of this sudden discovery which produced an indescribable dread, he struggled so hard to get free from the four fiery threads, that he snapped them, after he had pulled them out to a great width. Being then out of bonds, he caught up Mr Idle from the sofa and rushed downstairs with him.

THE HAUNTED HOUSE

THE MORTALS IN THE HOUSE

Under none of the accredited ghostly circumstances, and environed by none of the conventional ghostly surroundings, did I first make acquaintance with the house which is the subject of this Christmas piece. I saw it in the daylight, with the sun upon it. There was no wind, no rain, no lightning, no thunder, no awful or unwonted circumstance, of any kind, to heighten its effect. More than that: I had come to it direct from a railway station: it was not more than a mile distant from the railway station; and, as I stood outside the house, looking back upon the way I had come, I could see the goods train running smoothly along the embankment in the valley. I will not say that everything was utterly commonplace, because I doubt if anything can be that, except to utterly commonplace people – and there my vanity steps in; but, I will take it on myself to say that anybody might see the house as I saw it, any fine autumn morning.

The manner of my lighting on it was this.

I was travelling towards London out of the North, intending to stop by the way, to look at the house. My health required a temporary residence in the country; and a friend of mine who knew that, and who had happened to drive past the house, had written to me to suggest it as a likely place. I had got into the train at midnight, and had fallen asleep, and had woke up and had sat looking out of window at the brilliant Northern Lights in the sky, and had fallen asleep again, and had woke up again to find the night gone, with the usual discontented conviction on me that I hadn't been to sleep at all; upon which question, in the first imbecility of that condition, I am ashamed to believe that I would have done wager by battle with the man who sat opposite me. That opposite man had had, through the night – as that opposite man always has – several legs too many, and all of them too long. In addition to this unreasonable conduct (which was only to be expected of him), he had had a pencil and a pocketbook, and had been perpetually listening and taking notes. It had appeared to me that these aggravating notes related to the jolts and bumps of the carriage, and I should have resigned myself to his taking them, under a general supposition that he was in the civil-engineering way of life, if he had not sat staring straight over my head whenever he listened. He was a goggle-eyed gentleman of a perplexed aspect, and his demeanour became unbearable.

It was a cold, dead morning (the sun not being up yet), and when I had out-watched the paling light of the fires of the iron country, and the curtain of heavy smoke that hung at once between me and the stars and between me and the day, I turned to my fellow traveller and said, 'I *beg* your pardon, sir, but do you observe anything particular in me?' For, really, he appeared to be taking down either my travelling-cap or my hair with a minuteness that was a liberty.

The goggle-eyed gentleman withdrew his eyes from behind me, as if the back of the carriage were a hundred miles off, and said, with a lofty look of compassion for my insignificance, 'In you, sir? – B.'

'B, sir?' said I, growing warm.

'I have nothing to do with you, sir,' returned the gentleman; 'pray let me listen – O.'

He enunciated this vowel after a pause, and noted it down.

At first I was alarmed, for an Express lunatic and no communication with the guard is a serious position. The thought came to my relief that the gentleman might be what is popularly called a Rapper: one of a sect for (some of) whom I have the highest respect, but whom I don't believe in. I was going to ask him the question, when he took the bread out of my mouth.

'You will excuse me,' said the gentleman contemptuously, 'if I am too much in advance of common humanity to trouble myself at all about it. I have passed the night – as indeed I pass the whole of my time now – in spiritual intercourse.'

'Oh!' said I, something snappishly.

'The conferences of the night began,' continued the gentleman, turning several leaves of his notebook, 'with this message: "Evil communications corrupt good manners." '

'Sound,' said I; 'but, absolutely new?'

'New from spirits,' returned the gentleman.

I could only repeat my rather snappish 'Oh!' and ask if I might be favoured with the last communication.

' "A bird in the hand," ' said the gentleman, reading his last entry with great solemnity, ' "is worth two in the bosh." '

'Truly I am of the same opinion,' said I; 'but shouldn't it be bush?'

'It came to me, bosh,' returned the gentleman.

The gentleman then informed me that the spirit of Socrates had delivered this special revelation in the course of the night. 'My friend, I hope you are pretty well. There are two in this railway carriage. How do you do? There are seventeen thousand four hundred and seventy-nine spirits here, but you cannot see them. Pythagoras is here. He is not at liberty to mention it, but hopes you like travelling.' Galileo likewise had dropped in, with this scientific intelligence. 'I am glad to see you, *amico. Come sta?* Water will freeze when it is cold enough. *Addio!*' In the course of the night, also, the following phenomena had occurred. Bishop Butler had insisted on spelling his name, 'Bubler', for which offence against orthography and good manners he had been dismissed as out of temper. John Milton (suspected of wilful mystification) had repudiated the authorship of *Paradise Lost*, and had introduced, as joint authors of that poem, two unknown gentlemen, respectively named Grungers and Scadgingtone. And Prince Arthur, nephew of King John of England, had described himself as tolerably comfortable in the seventh circle, where he was learning to paint on velvet, under the direction of Mrs Trimmer and Mary Queen of Scots.

If this should meet the eye of the gentleman who favoured me with these disclosures, I trust he will excuse my confessing that the sight of the rising sun, and the contemplation of the magnificent order of the vast universe, made me impatient of them. In a word, I was so impatient of them, that I was mightily glad to get out at the next station, and to exchange these clouds and vapours for the free air of heaven.

By that time it was a beautiful morning. As I walked away among such leaves as had already fallen from the golden, brown and russet trees; and as I looked around me on the wonders of creation, and thought of the steady, unchanging and harmonious laws by which they are sustained; the gentleman's spiritual intercourse seemed to me as poor a piece of journey-work as ever this world saw. In which heathen state of mind, I came within view of the house, and stopped to examine it attentively.

It was a solitary house; standing in a sadly neglected garden: a pretty even square of some two acres. It was a house of about the time of George II; as stiff, as cold, as formal, and in as bad taste, as could possibly be desired by the most loyal admirer of the whole quartet of Georges. It was uninhabited, but had, within a year or two, been cheaply repaired to render it habitable; I say cheaply, because the work had been done in a surface manner, and was already decaying as to the paint and plaster, though the colours were fresh. A lopsided board drooped over the garden wall, announcing that it was 'to let on very reasonable terms, well furnished'. It was much too closely and heavily shadowed by trees, and, in particular, there were six tall poplars before the front windows, which were excessively melancholy, and the site of which had been extremely ill chosen.

It was easy to see that it was an avoided house – a house that was shunned by the village, to which my eye was guided by a church spire some half a mile off – a house that nobody would take. And the natural inference was that it had the reputation of being a haunted house.

No period within the four-and-twenty hours of day and night is so solemn to me as the early morning. In the summertime, I often rise very early, and repair to my room to do a day's work before breakfast, and I am always on those occasions deeply impressed by the stillness and solitude around me. Besides that there is something awful in the being surrounded by familiar faces asleep – in the knowledge that those who are dearest to us and to whom we are dearest, are profoundly unconscious of us, in an impassive state, anticipative of that mysterious condition to which we are all tending – the stopped life, the broken threads of yesterday, the deserted seat, the closed book, the unfinished and abandoned occupation, all are images of death. The tranquillity of the hour is the tranquillity of death. The colour and the chill have the same association. Even a certain air that familiar household objects take upon them when they first emerge from the shadows of the night into the morning, of being newer, and as they used to be long ago, has its counterpart in the subsidence of the worn face of maturity or age, in death, into the old youthful look. Moreover, I once saw the apparition of my father, at this hour. He was alive and well, and nothing ever came of it, but I saw him in the daylight, sitting with his back towards me, on a seat that stood beside my bed. His head was resting on his hand, and whether he was slumbering or grieving, I could not discern. Amazed to see him there, I sat up, moved my position, leaned out of bed, and watched him. As he did not move, I spoke to him more than once. As he did not move then, I became alarmed and laid my hand upon his shoulder, as I thought – and there was no such thing.

For all these reasons, and for others less easily and briefly statable, I find the early morning to be my most ghostly time. Any house would be more or less haunted, to me, in the early morning; and a haunted house could scarcely address me to greater advantage than then.

I walked on into the village, with the desertion of this house upon my mind, and I found the landlord of the little inn sanding his doorstep. I bespoke breakfast, and broached the subject of the house.

'Is it haunted?' I asked.

The landlord looked at me, shook his head, and answered, 'I say nothing.'

'Then it *is* haunted?'

'Well!' cried the landlord, in an outburst of frankness that had the appearance of desperation – 'I wouldn't sleep in it.'

'Why not?'

'If I wanted to have all the bells in a house ring, with nobody to ring 'em; and all the doors in a house bang, with nobody to bang 'em; and all sorts of feet treading about, with no feet there; why, then,' said the landlord, 'I'd sleep in that house.'

'Is anything seen there?'

The landlord looked at me again, and then, with his former appearance of desperation, called down his stable-yard for 'Ikey!'

The call produced a high-shouldered young fellow, with a round red face, a short crop of sandy hair, a very broad humorous mouth, a turned-up nose, and a great sleeved waistcoat of purple bars, with mother-of-pearl buttons, that seemed to be growing upon him, and to be in a fair way – if it were not pruned – of covering his head and over running his boots.

'This gentleman wants to know,' said the landlord, 'if anything's seen at the Poplars.'

' 'Ooded woman with a howl,' said Ikey, in a state of great freshness.

'Do you mean a cry?'

'I mean a bird, sir.'

'A hooded woman with an owl. Dear me! Did you ever see her?'

'I seen the howl.'

'Never the woman?'

'Not so plain as the howl, but they always keeps together.'

'Has anybody ever seen the woman as plainly as the owl?'

'Lord bless you, sir! Lots.'

'Who?'

'Lord bless you, sir! Lots.'

'The general-dealer opposite, for instance, who is opening his shop?'

'Perkins? Bless you, Perkins wouldn't go a-nigh the place. No!' observed the young man, with considerable feeling; 'he an't over-wise, an't Perkins, but he an't such a fool as *that*.'

(Here, the landlord murmured his confidence in Perkins's knowing better.)

'Who is – or who was – the hooded woman with the owl? Do you know?'

'Well!' said Ikey, holding up his cap with one hand while he scratched his head with the other, 'they say, in general, that she was murdered, and the howl he 'ooted the while.'

This very concise summary of the facts was all I could learn, except that a young man, as hearty and likely a young man as ever I see, had been took with fits and held down in 'em, after seeing the hooded woman. Also, that a personage, dimly described as 'a hold chap, a sort of one-eyed tramp, answering to the name of Joby, unless you challenged him as Greenwood, and then he said, "Why not? and even if so, mind your own business," ' had encountered the hooded woman, a matter of five or six times. But I was not materially assisted by these witnesses: inasmuch as the first was in California, and the last was, as Ikey said (and he was confirmed by the landlord), anywheres.

Now, although I regard with a hushed and solemn fear, the mysteries, between which and this state of existence is interposed the barrier of the great trial and change that fall on all the things that live; and although I have not the audacity to pretend that I know anything of them; I can no more reconcile the mere banging of doors, ringing of bells, creaking of boards, and suchlike insignificances, with the majestic beauty and pervading analogy of all the Divine rules that I am permitted to under-stand, than I had been able, a little while before, to yoke the spiritual intercourse of my fellow-traveller to the chariot of the rising sun. More-over, I had lived in two haunted houses – both abroad. In one of these, an old Italian palace, which bore the reputation of being very badly haunted indeed, and which had recently been twice abandoned on that account, I lived eight months, most tranquilly and pleasantly: notwith-standing that the house had a score of mysterious bedrooms, which were never used, and possessed, in one large room in which I sat reading, times out of number at all hours, and next to which I slept, a haunted chamber of the first pretensions. I gently hinted these considerations to the landlord. And as to this particular house having a bad name, I reasoned with him, Why, how many things had bad names undeservedly, and how easy it was to give bad names, and did he not think that if he and I were persistently to whisper in the village that any weird-looking old drunken tinker of the neighbourhood had sold himself to the devil, he would come in time to be suspected of that commercial venture! All this wise talk was perfectly ineffective with the landlord, I am bound to confess, and was as dead a failure as ever I made in my life.

To cut this part of the story short, I was piqued about the haunted house, and was already half resolved to take it. So, after breakfast, I got the keys from Perkins's brother-in-law (a whip- and harness-maker, who keeps the Post Office, and is under submission to a most rigorous wife of the Doubly Seceding Little Emmanuel persuasion), and went up to the house, attended by my landlord and by Ikey.

Within, I found it, as I had expected, transcendently dismal. The slowly changing shadows waved on it from the heavy trees, were doleful in the last degree; the house was ill-placed, ill-built, ill-planned and ill-fitted. It was damp, it was not free from dry rot, there was a flavour of rats in it, and it was the gloomy victim of that indescribable decay which settles on all the work of man's hands whenever it is not turned to man's account. The kitchens and offices were too large, and too remote from each other. Above stairs and below, waste tracts of passage intervened between patches of fertility represented by rooms; and there was a mouldy old well with a green growth upon it, hiding like a murderous trap, near the bottom of the back-stairs, under the double row of bells. One of these bells was labelled, on a black background in faded white letters, master b. This, they told me, was the bell that rang the most.

'Who was Master B?' I asked. 'Is it known what he did while the owl hooted?'

'Rang the bell,' said Ikey.

I was rather struck by the prompt dexterity with which this young man pitched his fur cap at the bell, and rang it himself. It was a loud, unpleasant bell, and made a very disagreeable sound. The other bells were inscribed according to the names of the rooms to which their wires were conducted, as: 'Picture Room', 'Double Room', 'Clock Room', and the like. Following Master B's bell to its source, I found that young gentleman to have had but indifferent third-class accommodation in a triangular cabin under the cock-loft, with a corner fireplace which Master B must have been exceedingly small if he were ever able to warm himself at, and a corner chimney-piece like a pyramidal staircase to the ceiling for Tom Thumb. The papering of one side of the room had dropped down bodily, with fragments of plaster adhering to it, and almost blocked up the door. It appeared that Master B, in his spiritual condition, always made a point of pulling the paper down. Neither the landlord nor Ikey could suggest why he made such a fool of himself.

Except that the house had an immensely large rambling loft at the top, I made no other discoveries. It was moderately well furnished, but sparely. Some of the furniture – say a third – was as old as the house; the rest was of various periods within the last half century. I was referred to a corn-chandler in the market-place of the county town to treat for the house. I went that day, and I took it for six months.

It was just the middle of October when I moved in with my maiden sister (I venture to call her eight-and-thirty, she is so very handsome, sensible and engaging). We took with us a deaf stable-man, my blood-hound Turk, two women servants, and a young person called an Odd Girl. I have reason to record of the attendant last enumerated, who was one of the Saint Lawrence's Union Female Orphans, that she was a fatal mistake and a disastrous engagement.

The year was dying early, the leaves were falling fast, it was a raw cold day when we took possession, and the gloom of the house was most depressing. The cook (an amiable woman, but of a weak turn of intellect) burst into tears on beholding the kitchen, and requested that her silver watch might be delivered over to her sister (2 Tuppintock's Gardens, Liggs's Walk, Clapham Rise), in the event of anything happening to her from the damp. Streaker, the housemaid, feigned cheerfulness, but was the greater martyr. The Odd Girl, who had never been in the country, alone was pleased, and made arrangements for sowing an acorn in the garden outside the scullery window, and rearing an oak.

We went, before dark, through all the natural – as opposed to super-natural – miseries incidental to our state. Dispiriting reports ascended (like the smoke) from the basement in volumes, and descended from the upper rooms. There was no rolling-pin, there was no salamander (which failed to surprise me, for I don't know what it is), there was nothing in the house, what there was, was broken, the last people must have lived like pigs, what could the meaning of the landlord be? Through these distresses, the Odd Girl was cheerful and exemplary. But within four hours after dark we had got into a supernatural groove, and the Odd Girl had seen 'Eyes' and was in hysterics.

My sister and I had agreed to keep the haunting strictly to ourselves, and my impression was, and still is, that I had not left Ikey, when he helped to unload the cart, alone with the women, or any one of them, for one minute. Nevertheless, as I say, the Odd Girl had 'seen Eyes' (no other explanation could ever be drawn from her) before nine, and by ten o'clock had had as much vinegar applied to her as would pickle a handsome salmon.

I leave a discerning public to judge of my feelings, when, under these untoward circumstances, at about half-past ten o'clock Master B's bell began to ring in a most infuriated manner, and Turk howled until the house resounded with his lamentations!

I hope I may never again be in a state of mind so unchristian as the mental frame in which I lived for some weeks, respecting the memory of Master B. Whether his bell was rung by rats, or mice, or bats, or wind, or what other accidental vibration, or sometimes by one cause, sometimes another, and sometimes by collusion, I don't know; but, certain it is, that it did ring two nights out of three, until I conceived the happy idea of twisting Master B's neck – in other words, breaking his bell short off – and silencing that young gentleman, as to my experience and belief, for ever.

But, by that time, the Odd Girl had developed such improving powers of catalepsy, that she had become a shining example of that very inconvenient disorder. She would stiffen, like a Guy Fawkes endowed with unreason, on the most irrelevant occasions. I would address the servants in a lucid manner, pointing out to them that I had painted Master B's room and balked the paper, and taken Master B's bell away and balked the ringing, and if they could suppose that that confounded boy had lived and died to clothe himself with no better behaviour than would most unquestionably have brought him and the sharpest particles of a birch-broom into close acquaintance in the present imperfect state of existence, could they also suppose a mere poor human being, such as I was, capable by those contemptible means of counteracting and limiting the powers of the disembodied spirits of the dead, or of any spirits? I say I would become emphatic and cogent, not to say rather complacent, in such an address, when it would all go for nothing by reason of the Odd Girl's suddenly stiffening from the toes upward, and glaring among us like a parochial petrifaction.

Streaker the housemaid, too, had an attribute of a most discomfiting nature. I am unable to say whether she was of an unusually lymphatic temperament, or what else was the matter with her, but this young woman became a mere distillery for the production of the largest and most transparent tears I ever met with. Combined with these characteristics, was a peculiar tenacity of hold in those specimens, so that they didn't fall, but hung upon her face and nose. In this condition, and mildly and deplorably shaking her head, her silence would throw me more heavily than the Admirable Crichton could have done in a verbal disputation for a purse of money. Cook, likewise, always covered me with confusion, as with a garment, by neatly winding up the session with the protest that the 'ouse was wearing her out, and by meekly repeating her last wishes regarding her silver watch.

As to our nightly life, the contagion of suspicion and fear was among us, and there is no such contagion under the sky. Hooded woman? According to the accounts, we were in a perfect convent of hooded women. Noises? With that contagion downstairs, I myself have sat in the dismal parlour, listening, until I have heard so many and such strange noises, that they would have chilled my blood if I had not warmed it by dashing out to make discoveries. Try this in bed in the dead of the night; try this at your own comfortable fireside, in the life of the night. You can fill any house with noises, if you will, until you have a noise for every nerve in your nervous system.

I repeat; the contagion of suspicion and fear was among us, and there is no such contagion under the sky. The women (their noses in a chronic state of excoriation from smelling-salts) were always primed and loaded for a swoon, and ready to go off with hair-triggers. The two older despatched the Odd Girl on all expeditions that were considered doubly hazardous, and she always established the reputation of such adventures by coming back cataleptic. If Cook or Streaker went overhead after dark, we knew we should presently hear a bump on the ceiling; and this took place so constantly, that it was as if a fighting man were engaged to go about the house, administering a touch of his art which I believe is called the Auctioneer, to every domestic he met with.

It was in vain to do anything. It was in vain to be frightened, for the moment in one's own person, by a real owl, and then to show the owl. It was in vain to discover, by striking an accidental discord on the piano, that Turk always howled at particular notes and combinations. It was in vain to be a Rhadamanthus with the bells, and if an unfortunate bell rang without leave, to have it down inexorably and silence it. It was in vain to fire up chimneys, let torches down the well, charge furiously into suspected rooms and recesses. We changed servants, and it was no better. The new set ran away, and a third set came, and it was no better. At last our comfortable housekeeping got to be so disorganised and wretched that I one night dejectedly said to my sister, 'Patty, I begin to despair of our getting people to go on with us here, and I think we must give this up.'

My sister, who is a woman of immense spirit, replied, 'No, John, don't give it up. Don't be beaten, John. There is another way.'

'And what is that?' said I.

'John,' returned my sister, 'if we are not to be driven out of this house, and that for no reason whatever that is apparent to you or me, we must help ourselves and take the house wholly and solely into our own hands.'

'But the servants,' said I.

'Have no servants,' said my sister, boldly.

Like most people in my grade of life, I had never thought of the possibility of going on without those faithful obstructions. The notion was so new to me when suggested, that I looked very doubtful.

'We know they come here to be frightened and infect one another, and we know they are frightened and do infect one another,' said my sister.

'With the exception of Bottles,' I observed, in a meditative tone. (The deaf stable-man. I kept him in my service, and still keep him, as a phenomenon of moroseness not to be matched in England.)

'To be sure, John,' assented my sister; 'except Bottles. And what does that go to prove? Bottles talks to nobody, and hears nobody unless he is absolutely roared at, and what alarm has Bottles ever given or taken! None.'

This was perfectly true; the individual in question having retired, every night at ten o'clock, to his bed over the coach-house, with no other company than a pitchfork and a pail of water. That the pail of water would have been over me, and the pitchfork through me, if I had put myself without announcement in Bottles' way after that minute, I had deposited in my own mind as a fact worth remembering. Neither had Bottles ever taken the least notice of any of our many uproars. An imperturbable and speechless man, he had sat at his supper, with Streaker present in a swoon, and the Odd Girl marble, and had only put another potato in his cheek, or profited by the general misery to help himself to beef-steak pie.

'And so,' continued my sister, 'I exempt Bottles. And considering, John, that the house is too large, and perhaps too lonely, to be kept well in hand by Bottles, you, and me, I propose that we cast about among out friends for a certain selected number of the most reliable and willing – form a Society here for three months – wait upon ourselves and one another – live cheerfully and socially – and see what happens.'

I was so charmed with my sister, that I embraced her on the spot, and went into her plan with the greatest ardour.

We were then in the third week of November; but, we took our measures so vigorously, and were so well seconded by the friends in whom we confided, that there was still a week of the month unexpired, when our party all came down together merrily, and mustered in the haunted house.

I will mention, in this place, two small changes that I made while my sister and I were yet alone. It occurring to me as not improbable that Turk howled in the house at night partly because he wanted to get out of it, I stationed him in his kennel outside, but unchained: and I seriously warned the village that any man who came in his way must not expect to leave him without a rip in his own throat. I then casually asked Ikey if he were a judge of a gun? On his saying, 'Yes, sir, I knows a good gun when I sees her,' I begged the favour of his stepping up to the house and looking at mine.

'*She's* a true one, sir,' said Ikey, after inspecting a double-barrelled rifle that I bought in New York a few years ago. 'No mistake about her, sir.'

'Ikey,' said I, 'don't mention it; I have seen something in this house.'

'No, sir?' he whispered, greedily opening his eyes. ''Ooded lady, sir?'

'Don't be frightened,' said I. 'It was a figure rather like you.'

'Lord, sir?'

'Ikey!' said I, shaking hands with him warmly: I may say affectionately; 'if there is any truth in these ghost-stories, the greatest service I can do you is to fire at that figure. And I promise you, by heaven and earth, I will do it with this gun if I see it again!'

The young man thanked me, and took his leave with some little precipitation, after declining a glass of liquor. I imparted my secret to him, because I had never quite forgotten his throwing his cap at the bell; because I had, on another occasion, noticed something very like a fur cap lying not far from the bell, one night when it had burst out ringing; and because I had remarked that we were at our ghostliest whenever he came up in the evening to comfort the servants. Let me do Ikey no injustice. He was afraid of the house, and believed in its being haunted; and yet he would play false on the haunting side, so surely as he got an opportunity. The Odd Girl's case was exactly similar. She went about the house in a state of real terror, and yet lied monstrously and wilfully, and invented many of the alarms she spread, and made many of the sounds we heard. I had had my eye on the two, and I know it. It is not necessary for me, here, to account for this preposterous state of mind; I content myself with remarking that it is familiarly known to every intelligent man who has had fair medical, legal, or other watchful experience; that it is as well established and as common a state of mind as any with which observers are acquainted; and that it is one of the first elements, above all others, rationally to be suspected in, and strictly looked for, and separated from, any question of this kind.

To return to our party. The first thing we did when we were all assembled was to draw lots for bedrooms. That done, and every bedroom, and, indeed, the whole house, having been minutely examined by the whole body, we allotted the various household duties, as if we had been on a gypsy party, or a yachting party, or a hunting party, or were ship-wrecked. I then recounted the floating rumours concerning the hooded lady, the owl and Master B with others, still more filmy, which had floated about during our occupation, relative to some ridiculous old ghost of the female gender who went up and down carrying the ghost of a round table; and also to an impalpable jackass, whom nobody was ever able to catch. Some of these ideas I really believe our people below had communicated to one another in some diseased way, without conveying them in words. We then gravely called one another to witness that we were not there to be deceived, or to deceive – which we considered pretty much the same thing – and that, with a serious sense of responsibility, we would be strictly true to one another, and would strictly follow out the truth. The understanding was established that anyone who heard unusual noises in the night and who wished to trace them should knock at my door; lastly, that on Twelfth Night, the last night of holy Christmas, all our individual experiences since that then present hour of our coming together in the haunted house should be brought to light for the good of all; and that we would hold our peace on the subject till then, unless on some remarkable provocation to break silence.

We were, in number and in character, as follows. First – to get my sister and myself out of the way – there were we two. In the drawing of lots, my sister drew her own room, and I drew Master B's. Next, there was our first cousin John Herschel, so called after the great astronomer: than whom I suppose a better man at a telescope does not breathe. With him, was his wife: a charming creature to whom he had been married in the previous spring. I thought it (under the circumstances) rather imprudent to bring her, because there is no knowing what even a false alarm may do at such a time: but I suppose he knew his own business best, and I must say that if she had been my wife, I never could have left her endearing and bright face behind. They drew the Clock Room. Alfred Starling, an uncommonly agreeable young fellow of eight-and-twenty for whom I have the greatest liking, was in the Double Room; mine, usually, and designated by that name from having a dressing-room within it, with two large and cumbersome windows, which no wedges *I* was ever able to make would keep from shaking in any weather, wind or no wind. Alfred is a young fellow who pretends to be 'fast' (another word for loose, as I understand the term), but who is much too good and sensible for that nonsense, and who would have distinguished himself before now, if his father had not unfortunately left him a small independence of two hundred a year, on the strength of which his only occupation in life has been to spend six. I am in hopes, however, that his banker may break, or that he may enter into some speculation guaranteed to pay twenty per cent; for I am convinced that if he could only be ruined, his fortune is made. Belinda Bates, bosom friend of my sister, and a most intellectual, amiable and delightful girl, got the Picture Room. She has a fine genius for poetry, combined with real business earnestness, and 'goes in' – to use an expression of Alfred's – for Woman's mission, Woman's rights, Woman's wrongs, and everything that is woman's with a capital W, or is not and ought to be, or is and ought not to be. 'Most praiseworthy, my dear, and heaven prosper you!' I whispered to her on the first night of my taking leave of her at the Picture-Room door, 'but don't overdo it. And in respect of the great necessity there is, my darling, for more employments being within the reach of Woman than our civilisation has as yet assigned to her, don't fly at the unfortunate men, even those men who are at first sight in your way, as if they were the natural oppressors of your sex; for, trust me, Belinda, they do sometimes spend their wages among wives and daughters, sisters, mothers, aunts and grandmothers; and the play is, really, not *all* Wolf and Red Riding-Hood, but has other parts in it.' However, I digress.

Belinda, as I have mentioned, occupied the Picture Room. We had but three other chambers: the Corner Room, the Cupboard Room and the Garden Room. My old friend, Jack Governor, 'slung his hammock', as he called it, in the Corner Room. I have always regarded Jack as the finest-looking sailor that ever sailed. He is grey now, but as handsome as he was a quarter of a century ago – nay, handsomer. A portly, cheery, well-built figure of a broad-shouldered man, with a frank smile, a brilliant dark eye, and a rich dark eyebrow. I remember those under darker hair, and they look all the better for their silver setting. He has been wherever his Union namesake flies, has Jack, and I have met old shipmates of his, away in the Mediterranean and on the other side of the Atlantic, who have beamed and brightened at the casual mention of his name, and have cried, 'You know Jack Governor? Then you know a prince of men!' That he is! And so unmistakably a naval officer, that if you were to meet him coming out of an Eskimo snow-hut in seal's skin, you would be vaguely persuaded he was in full naval uniform.

Jack once had that bright clear eye of his on my sister; but it fell out that he married another lady and took her to South America, where she died. This was a dozen years ago or more. He brought down with him to our haunted house a little cask of salt beef; for, he is always convinced that all salt beef not of his own pickling, is mere carrion, and invariably, when he goes to London, packs a piece in his portmanteau. He had also volunteered to bring with him one 'Nat Beaver', an old comrade of his, captain of a merchantman. Mr Beaver, with a thickset wooden face and figure, and apparently as hard as a block all over, proved to be an intelligent man, with a world of watery experiences in him, and great practical knowledge. At times, there was a curious nervousness about him, apparently the lingering result of some old illness; but, it seldom lasted many minutes. He got the Cupboard Room, and lay there next to Mr Undery, my friend and solicitor who came down, in an amateur capacity, 'to go through with it', as he said, and who plays whist better than the whole Law List, from the red cover at the beginning to the red cover at the end.

I never was happier in my life, and I believe it was the universal feeling among us. Jack Governor, always a man of wonderful resources, was chief cook, and made some of the best dishes I ever ate, including unapproachable curries. My sister was pastrycook and confectioner. Starling and I were cook's mate, turn and turn about, and on special occasions the chief cook 'pressed' Mr Beaver. We had a great deal of outdoor sport and exercise, but nothing was neglected within, and there was no ill-humour or misunderstanding among us, and our evenings were so delightful that we had at least one good reason for being reluctant to go to bed.

We had a few night alarms in the beginning. On the first night I was knocked up by Jack with a most wonderful ship's lantern in his hand, like the gills of some monster of the deep, who informed me that he 'was going aloft to the main truck', to have the weathercock down. It was a stormy night and I remonstrated; but Jack called my attention to its making a sound like a cry of despair, and said somebody would be 'hailing a ghost' presently, if it wasn't done. So, up to the top of the house, where I could hardly stand for the wind, we went, accompanied by Mr Beaver; and there Jack, lantern and all, with Mr Beaver after him, swarmed up to the top of a cupola, some two dozen feet above the chimneys, and stood upon nothing particular, coolly knocking the weathercock off, until they both got into such good spirits with the wind and the height, that I thought they would never come down. Another night, they turned out again, and had a chimney-cowl off. Another night, they cut a sobbing and gulping water pipe away. Another night, they found out something else. On several occasions, they both, in the coolest manner, simultaneously dropped out of their respective bedroom windows, hand over hand by their counterpanes, to 'overhaul' something mysterious in the garden.

The engagement among us was faithfully kept, and nobody revealed anything. All we knew was, if anyone's room was haunted, no one looked the worse for it.

When I established myself in the triangular garret which had gained so distinguished a reputation, my thoughts naturally turned to Master B. My speculations about him were uneasy and manifold. Whether his Christian name was Benjamin, Bissextile (from his having been born in Leap Year), Bartholomew or Bill. Whether the initial letter belonged to his family name, and that was Baxter, Black, Brown, Barker, Buggins, Baker or Bird. Whether he was a foundling, and had been baptised B. Whether he was a lion-hearted boy, and B was short for Briton, or for bull. Whether he could possibly have been kith and kin to an illustrious lady who brightened my own childhood, and had come of the blood of the brilliant Mother Bunch?

With these profitless meditations I tormented myself much. I also carried the mysterious letter into the appearance and pursuits of the deceased, wondering whether he dressed in blue, wore boots (he couldn't have been bald), was a boy of brains, liked books, was good at bowling, had any skill as a boxer, even in his buoyant boyhood bathed from a bathing-machine at Bognor, Bangor, Bournemouth, Brighton or Broadstairs, like a bounding billiard ball?

So, from the first, I was haunted by the letter B.

It was not long before I remarked that I never by any hazard had a dream of Master B, or of anything belonging to him. But, the instant I awoke from sleep, at whatever hour of the night, my thoughts took him up, and roamed away, trying to attach his initial letter to something that would fit it and keep it quiet.

For six nights I had been worried thus in Master B's room, when I began to perceive that things were going wrong.

The first appearance that presented itself was early in the morning when it was but just daylight and no more. I was standing shaving at my glass, when I suddenly discovered, to my consternation and amazement, that I was shaving – not myself – I am fifty – but a boy. Apparently Master B!

I trembled and looked over my shoulder; nothing there. I looked again in the glass, and distinctly saw the features and expression of a boy, who was shaving, not to get rid of a beard, but to get one. Extremely troubled in my mind, I took a few turns in the room, and went back to the looking-glass, resolved to steady my hand and complete the operation in which I had been disturbed. Opening my eyes, which I had shut while recovering my firmness, I now met in the glass, looking straight at me, the eyes of a young man of four- or five-and-twenty. Terrified by this new ghost, I closed my eyes, and made a strong effort to recover myself. Opening them again, I saw, shaving his cheek in the glass, my father, who has long been dead. Nay, I even saw my grandfather too, whom I never did see in my life.

Although naturally much affected by these remarkable visitations, I determined to keep my secret until the time agreed upon for the present general disclosure. Agitated by a multitude of curious thoughts, I retired to my room that night prepared to encounter some new experience of a spectral character. Nor was my preparation needless, for, waking from an uneasy sleep at exactly two o'clock in the morning, what were my feelings to find that I was sharing my bed with the skeleton of Master B!

I sprang up, and the skeleton sprang up also. I then heard a plaintive voice saying, 'Where am I? What is become of me?' and, looking hard in that direction, perceived the ghost of Master B.

The young spectre was dressed in an obsolete fashion: or rather, was not so much dressed as put into a case of inferior pepper-and-salt cloth, made horrible by means of shining buttons. I observed that these buttons went, in a double row, over each shoulder of the young ghost, and appeared to descend his back. He wore a frill round his neck. His right hand (which I distinctly noticed to be inky) was laid upon his stomach; connecting this action with some feeble pimples on his countenance, and his general air of nausea, I concluded this ghost to be the ghost of a boy who had habitually taken a great deal too much medicine.

'Where am I?' said the little spectre, in a pathetic voice. 'And why was I born in the Calomel days, and why did I have all that Calomel given me?'

I replied, with sincere earnestness, that upon my soul I couldn't tell him.

'Where is my little sister?' said the ghost, 'and where my angelic little wife, and where is the boy I went to school with?'

I entreated the phantom to be comforted, and above all things to take heart respecting the loss of the boy he went to school with. I represented to him that probably that boy never did, within human experience, come out well, when discovered. I urged that I myself had, in later life, turned up several boys whom I went to school with, and none of them had at all answered. I expressed my humble belief that that boy never did answer. I represented that he was a mythic character, a delusion, and a snare. I recounted how, the last time I found him, I found him at a dinner party behind a wall of white cravat, with an inconclusive opinion on every possible subject, and a power of silent boredom absolutely titanic. I related how, on the strength of our having been together at 'Old Doylance's', he had asked himself to breakfast with me (a social offence of the largest magnitude); how, fanning my weak embers of belief in Doylance's boys, I had let him in; and how he had proved to be a fearful wanderer about the earth, pursuing the race of Adam with inexplicable notions concerning the currency, and with a proposition that the Bank of England should, on pain of being abolished, instantly strike off and circulate God knows how many thousand millions of ten-and-sixpenny notes.

The ghost heard me in silence, and with a fixed stare. 'Barber!' it apostrophised me when I had finished.

'Barber?' I repeated – for I am not of that profession.

'Condemned,' said the ghost, 'to shave a constant change of customers – now, me – now, a young man – now, thyself as thou art – now, thy father – now, thy grandfather; condemned, too, to lie down with a skeleton every night, and to rise with it every morning – '

(I shuddered on hearing this dismal announcement.)

'Barber! Pursue me!'

I had felt, even before the words were uttered, that I was under a spell to pursue the phantom. I immediately did so, and was in Master B's room no longer.

Most people know what long and fatiguing night journeys had been forced upon the witches who used to confess, and who, no doubt, told the exact truth – particularly as they were always assisted with leading questions, and the torture was always ready. I asseverate that, during my occupation of Master B's room, I was taken by the ghost that haunted it on expeditions fully as long and wild as any of those. Assuredly, I was presented to no shabby old man with a goat's horns and tail (something between Pan and an old clothes-man), holding conventional receptions, as stupid as those of real life and less decent; but, I came upon other things which appeared to me to have more meaning.

Confident that I speak the truth and shall be believed, I declare without hesitation that I followed the ghost, in the first instance on a broomstick, and afterwards on a rocking-horse. The very smell of the animal's paint – especially when I brought it out, by making him warm – I am ready to swear to. I followed the ghost, afterwards, in a hackney coach, an institution with the peculiar smell of which the present generation is unacquainted, but to which I am again ready to swear as a combination of stable, dog with the mange, and very old bellows. (In this, I appeal to previous generations to confirm or refute me.) I pursued the phantom, on a headless donkey: at least, upon a donkey who was so interested in the state of his stomach that his head was always down there, investigating it; on ponies, expressly born to kick up behind; on roundabouts and swings, from fairs; in the first cab – another forgotten institution where the fare regularly got into bed and was tucked up with the driver.

Not to trouble you with a detailed account of all my travels in pursuit of the ghost of Master B, which were longer and more wonderful than those of Sinbad the Sailor, I will confine myself to one experience from which you may judge of many.

I was marvellously changed. I was myself; yet not myself. I was conscious of something within me, which has been the same all through my life, and which I have always recognised under all its phases and varieties as never altering, and yet I was not the I who had gone to bed in Master B's room. I had the smoothest of faces and the shortest of legs, and I had taken another creature like myself, also with the smoothest of faces and the shortest of legs, behind a door, and was confiding to him a proposition of the most astounding nature.

This proposition was, that we should have a seraglio.

The other creature assented warmly. He had no notion of respectability, neither had I. It was the custom of the East, it was the way of the good Caliph Haroun Alraschid (let me have the corrupted name again for once, it is so scented with sweet memories!), the usage was highly laudable and most worthy of imitation. 'Oh, yes! Let us,' said the other creature with a jump, 'have a seraglio.'

It was not because we entertained the faintest doubts of the meritorious character of the Oriental establishment we proposed to import that we perceived it must be kept a secret from Miss Griffin. It was because we knew Miss Griffin to be bereft of human sympathies, and incapable of appreciating the greatness of the great Haroun. Mystery impenetrably shrouded from Miss Griffin then, let us entrust it to Miss Bule.

We were ten in Miss Griffin's establishment by Hampstead Ponds; eight ladies and two gentlemen. Miss Bule, whom I judge to have attained the ripe age of eight or nine, took the lead in society. I opened the subject to her in the course of the day, and proposed that she should become the Favourite.

Miss Bule, after struggling with diffidence so natural to, and charming in, her adorable sex, expressed herself as flattered by the idea but wished to know how it was proposed to provide for Miss Pipson? Miss Bule – who was understood to have vowed towards that young lady, a friendship, halves, and no secrets, until death, on the *Church Service and Lessons*, complete in two volumes with case and lock – Miss Bule said she could not, as the friend of Pipson, disguise from herself, or me, that Pipson was not one of the common.

Now, Miss Pipson, having curly light hair and blue eyes (which was my idea of anything mortal and feminine that was called fair), I promptly replied that I regarded Miss Pipson in the light of a Fair Circassian.

'And what then?' Miss Bule pensively asked.

I replied that she must be inveigled by a merchant, brought to me veiled, and purchased as a slave.

(The other creature had already fallen into the second male place in the state, and was set apart for Grand Vizier. He afterwards resisted this disposal of events, but had his hair pulled until he yielded.)

'Shall I not be jealous?' Miss Bule enquired, casting down her eyes.

'Zobeide, no,' I replied; 'you will ever be the favourite sultana; the first place in my heart, and on my throne, will be ever yours.'

Miss Bule, upon that assurance, consented to propound the idea to her seven beautiful companions. It occurring to me, in the course of the same day, that we knew we could trust a grinning and good-natured soul called Tabby, who was the serving drudge of the house, and had no more figure than one of the beds, and upon whose face there was always more or less black-lead, I slipped into Miss Bule's hand after supper a little note to that effect: dwelling on the black-lead as being in a manner deposited by the finger of Providence, pointing Tabby out for Mesrour, the celebrated chief of the Blacks of the Hareem.

There were difficulties in the formation of the desired institution, as there are in all combinations. The other creature showed himself of a low character, and, when defeated in aspiring to the throne, pretended to have conscientious scruples about prostrating himself before the Caliph; wouldn't call him Commander of the Faithful; spoke of him slightingly and inconsistently as a mere 'chap'; said he, the other creature, 'wouldn't play' – Play! – and was otherwise coarse and offensive. This meanness of disposition was, however, put down by the general indignation of an united seraglio, and I became blessed in the smiles of eight of the fairest of the daughters of men.

The smiles could only be bestowed when Miss Griffin was looking another way, and only then in a very wary manner, for there was a legend among the followers of the Prophet that she saw with a little round ornament in the middle of the pattern on the back of her shawl. But every day after dinner, for an hour, we were all together, and then the Favourite and the rest of the royal hareem competed who should most beguile the leisure of the Serene Haroun reposing from the cares of state – which were generally, as in most affairs of state, of an arithmetical character, the Commander of the Faithful being a fearful boggler at a sum.

On these occasions, the devoted Mesrour, chief of the Blacks of the Hareem, was always in attendance (Miss Griffin usually ringing for that officer, at the same time, with great vehemence), but never acquitted himself in a manner worthy of his historical reputation. In the first place, his bringing a broom into the divan of the Caliph, even when Haroun wore on his shoulders the red robe of anger (Miss Pipson's pelisse), though it might be got over for the moment, was never to be quite satisfactorily accounted for. In the second place, his breaking out into grinning exclamations of 'Lork you pretties!' was neither Eastern nor respectful. In the third place, when specially instructed to say 'Bismillah!' he always said 'Hallelujah!' This officer, unlike his class, was too good-humoured altogether, kept his mouth open far too wide, expressed approbation to an incongruous extent, and even once – it was on the occasion of the purchase of the Fair Circassian for five hundred thousand purses of gold, and cheap, too – embraced the Slave, the Favourite, and the Caliph, all round. (Parenthetically let me say God bless Mesrour, and may there have been sons and daughters on that tender bosom, softening many a hard day since!)

Miss Griffin was a model of propriety, and I am at a loss to imagine what the feelings of the virtuous woman would have been if she had known, when she paraded us down the Hampstead Road two and two, that she was walking with a stately step at the head of polygamy and Islam. I believe that a mysterious and terrible joy with which the contemplation of Miss Griffin, in this unconscious state, inspired us, and a grim sense prevalent among us that there was a dreadful power in our knowledge of what Miss Griffin (who knew all things that could be learnt out of a book) didn't know, were the mainspring of the preservation of our secret. It was wonderfully kept, but was once upon the verge of self-betrayal. The danger and escape occurred upon a Sunday. We were all ten ranged in a conspicuous part of the gallery at church, with Miss Griffin at our head – as we were every Sunday advertising the establishment in an unsecular sort of way – when the description of Solomon in his domestic glory happened to be read. The moment that monarch was thus referred to, conscience whispered to me, 'Thou, too, Haroun!' The officiating minister had a cast in his eye, and it assisted conscience by giving him the appearance of reading personally at me. A crimson blush, attended by a fearful perspiration, suffused my features. The Grand Vizier became more dead than alive, and the whole seraglio reddened as if the sunset of Baghdad shone direct upon their lovely faces. At this portentous time the awful Griffin rose, and balefully surveyed the children of Islam. My own impression was that church and state had entered into a conspiracy with Miss Griffin to expose us, and that we should all be put into white sheets and exhibited in the centre aisle. But, so Westerly – if I may be allowed the expression as opposite to Eastern associations – was Miss Griffin's sense of rectitude, that she merely suspected apples, and we were saved.

I have called the seraglio united. Upon the question, solely, whether the Commander of the Faithful durst exercise a right of kissing in that sanctuary of the palace were its peerless inmates divided. Zobeide asserted a counter-right in the Favourite to scratch, and the Fair Circassian put her face, for refuge, into a green baize bag, originally designed for books. On the other hand, a young antelope of transcendent beauty from the fruitful plains of Camden Town (whence she had been brought, by traders, in the half-yearly caravan that crossed the intermediate desert after the holidays), held more liberal opinions, but stipulated for limiting the benefit of them to that dog, and son of a dog, the Grand Vizier – who had no rights, and was not in question. At length, the difficulty was compromised by the installation of a very youthful slave as deputy.

She, raised upon a stool, officially received upon her cheeks the salutes intended by the gracious Haroun for other sultanas, and was privately rewarded from the coffers of the Ladies of the Hareem.

And now it was, at the full height of enjoyment of my bliss, that I became heavily troubled. I began to think of my mother, and what she would say to my taking home at midsummer eight of the most beautiful of the daughters of men, but all unexpected. I thought of the number of beds we made up at our house, of my father's income, and of the baker, and my despondency redoubled. The seraglio and malicious Vizier, divining the cause of their lord's unhappiness, did their utmost to augment it. They professed unbounded fidelity, and declared that they would live and die with him. Reduced to the utmost wretchedness by these protestations of attachment, I lay awake, for hours at a time, ruminating on my frightful lot. In my despair, I think I might have taken an early opportunity of falling on my knees before Miss Griffin, avowing my resemblance to Solomon, and praying to be dealt with according to the outraged laws of my country, if an unthought-of means of escape had not opened before me.

One day, we were out walking, two and two – on which occasion the Vizier had his usual instructions to take note of the boy at the turnpike, and if he profanely gazed (which he always did) at the beauties of the Hareem, to have him bowstrung in the course of the night – and it happened that our hearts were veiled in gloom. An unaccountable action on the part of the antelope had plunged the state into disgrace. That charmer, on the representation that the previous day was her birthday, and that vast treasures had been sent in a hamper for its celebration (both baseless assertions), had secretly but most pressingly invited thirty-five neighbouring princes and princesses to a ball and supper: with a special stipulation that they were 'not to be fetched till twelve'. This wandering of the antelope's fancy led to the surprising arrival at Miss Griffin's door, in divers equipages and under various escorts, of a great company in full dress, who were deposited on the top step in a flush of high expectancy, and who were dismissed in tears. At the beginning of the double knocks attendant on these ceremonies, the antelope had retired to a back attic, and bolted herself in; and at every new arrival, Miss Griffin had gone so much more and more distracted, that at last she had been seen to tear her front. Ultimate capitulation on the part of the offender, had been followed by solitude in the linen-closet, bread and water and a lecture to all, of vindictive length, in which Miss Griffin had used expressions: firstly, 'I believe you all of you knew of it'; secondly, 'Every one of you is as wicked as another'; thirdly, 'A pack of little wretches'.

Under these circumstances, we were walking drearily along, and I especially, with my Musulman responsibilities heavy on me, was in a very low state of mind, when a strange man accosted Miss Griffin, and, after walking on at her side for a little while and talking with her, looked at me. Supposing him to be a minion of the law, and that my hour was come, I instantly ran away, with the general purpose of making for Egypt.

The whole seraglio cried out, when they saw me making off as fast as my legs would carry me (I had an impression that the first turning on the left, and round by the public-house, would be the shortest way to the Pyramids), Miss Griffin screamed after me, the faithless Vizier ran after me, and the boy at the turnpike dodged me into a corner, like a sheep, and cut me off. Nobody scolded me when I was taken and brought back; Miss Griffin only said, with a stunning gentleness, this was very curious! Why had I run away when the gentleman looked at me?

If I had had any breath to answer with, I dare say I should have made no answer: having no breath, I certainly made none. Miss Griffin and the strange man took me between them, and walked me back to the palace in a sort of state; but not at all (as I couldn't help feeling, with astonishment) in culprit state.

When we got there, we went into a room by ourselves, and Miss Griffin called in to her assistance Mesrour, chief of the dusky guards of the hareem. Mesrour, on being whispered to, began to shed tears.

'Bless you, my precious!' said that officer, turning to me: 'your pa's took bitter bad!'

I asked, with a fluttered heart, 'Is he very ill?'

'Lord temper the wind to you, my lamb!' said the good Mesrour, kneeling down, that I might have a comforting shoulder for my head to rest on, 'your pa's dead!'

Haroun Alraschid took to flight at the words; the seraglio vanished; from that moment I never again saw one of the eight of the fairest of the daughters of men.

I was taken home, and there was debt at home as well as death, and we had a sale there. My own little bed was so superciliously looked upon by a power unknown to me, hazily called 'The Trade', that a brass coal-scuttle, a roasting-jack and a birdcage were obliged to be put into it to make a lot of it, and then it went for a song. So I heard mentioned, and I wondered what song, and thought what a dismal song it must have been to sing!

Then, I was sent to a great, cold, bare, school of big boys; where everything to eat and wear was thick and clumpy, without being enough; where everybody, large and small, was cruel; where the boys knew all about the sale before I got there, and asked me what I had fetched, and who had bought me, and hooted at me, 'Going, going, gone!' I never whispered in that wretched place that I had been Haroun, or had had a seraglio: for, I knew that if I mentioned my reverses, I should be so worried, that I should have to drown myself in the muddy pond near the playground, which looked like the beer.

Ah me, ah me! No other ghost has haunted the boy's room, my friends, since I have occupied it, than the ghost of my own childhood, the ghost of my own innocence, the ghost of my own airy belief. Many a time have I pursued the phantom: never with this man's stride of mine to come up with it, never with these man's hands of mine to touch it, never more to this man's heart of mine to hold it in its purity. And here you see me working out, as cheerfully and thankfully as I may, my doom of shaving in the glass a constant change of customers, and of lying down and rising up with the skeleton allotted to me for my mortal companion.

THE TRIAL FOR MURDER

To be Taken with a Grain of Salt

I have always noticed a prevalent want of courage, even among persons of superior intelligence and culture, as to imparting their own psychological experiences when those have been of a strange sort. Almost all men are afraid that what they could relate in such wise would find no parallel or response in a listener's internal life, and might be suspected or laughed at. A truthful traveller, who should have seen some extraordinary creature in the likeness of a sea-serpent, would have no fear of mentioning it; but the same traveller, having had some singular presentiment, impulse, vagary of thought, vision (so-called), dream, or other remarkable mental impression, would hesitate considerably before he would own to it. To this reticence I attribute much of the obscurity in which such subjects are involved. We do not habitually communicate our experiences of these subjective things as we do our experiences of objective creation. The consequence is that the general stock of experience in this regard appears exceptional, and really is so, in respect of being miserably imperfect.

In what I am going to relate, I have no intention of setting up, opposing, or supporting, any theory whatever. I know the history of the bookseller in Berlin. I have studied the case of the wife of a late Astronomer Royal as related by Sir David Brewster, and I have followed the minutest details of a much more remarkable case of spectral illusion occurring within my private circle of friends. It may be necessary to state, as to this last, that the sufferer (a lady) was in no degree, however distant, related to me. A mistaken assumption on that head might suggest an explanation of a part of my own case – but only a part – which would be wholly without foundation. It cannot be referred to my inheritance of any developed peculiarity, nor had I ever before any at all similar experience, nor have I ever had any at all similar experience since.

It does not signify how many years ago, or how few, a certain murder was committed in England which attracted great attention. We hear more than enough of murderers as they rise in succession to their atrocious eminence, and I would bury the memory of this particular brute, if I could, as his body was buried in Newgate Jail. I purposely abstain from giving any direct clue to the criminal's individuality.

When the murder was first discovered, no suspicion fell – or I ought rather to say, for I cannot be too precise in my facts, it was nowhere publicly hinted that any suspicion fell – on the man who was afterwards brought to trial. As no reference was at that time made to him in the newspapers, it is obviously impossible that any description of him can at that time have been given in the newspapers. It is essential that this fact be remembered.

Unfolding at breakfast my morning paper, containing the account of that first discovery, I found it to be deeply interesting, and I read it with close attention. I read it twice, if not three times. The discovery had been made in a bedroom, and, when I laid down the paper, I was aware of a flash – rush, flow – I do not know what to call it, no word I can find is satisfactorily descriptive, in which I seemed to see that bedroom passing through my room, like a picture impossibly painted on a running river. Though almost instantaneous in its passing, it was perfectly clear; so clear that I distinctly, and with a sense of relief, observed the absence of the dead body from the bed.

It was in no romantic place that I had this curious sensation, but in chambers in Piccadilly, very near to the corner of St James's Street. It was entirely new to me. I was in my easy-chair at the moment, and the sensation was accompanied with a peculiar shiver which started the chair from its position. (But it is to be noted that the chair ran easily on castors.) I went to one of the windows (there are two in the room, and the room is on the second floor) to refresh my eyes with the moving objects down in Piccadilly. It was a bright autumn morning, and the street was sparkling and cheerful. The wind was high. As I looked out, it brought down from the park a quantity of fallen leaves, which a gust took, and whirled into a spiral pillar. As the pillar fell and the leaves dispersed, I saw two men on the opposite side of the way, going from west to east. They were one behind the other. The foremost man often looked back over his shoulder. The second man followed him, at a distance of some thirty paces, with his right hand menacingly raised. First, the singularity and steadiness of this threatening gesture in so public a thoroughfare attracted my attention; and next, the more remarkable circumstance that nobody heeded it. Both men threaded their way among the other passengers with a smoothness hardly consistent even with the action of walking on a pavement; and no single creature, that I could see, gave them place, touched them, or looked after them. In passing before my windows, they both stared up at me. I saw their two faces very distinctly, and I knew that

I could recognise them anywhere. Not that I had consciously noticed anything very remarkable in either face, except that the man who went first had an unusually lowering appearance, and that the face of the man who followed him was of the colour of impure wax.

I am a bachelor, and my valet and his wife constitute my whole establishment. My occupation is in a certain branch bank, and I wish that my duties as head of a department were as light as they are popularly supposed to be. They kept me in town that autumn, when I stood in need of change. I was not ill, but I was not well. My reader is to make the most that can be reasonably made of my feeling jaded, having a depressing sense upon me of a monotonous life, and being 'slightly dyspeptic'. I am assured by my renowned doctor that my real state of health at that time justifies no stronger description, and I quote his own from his written answer to my request for it.

As the circumstances of the murder, gradually unravelling, took stronger and stronger possession of the public mind, I kept them away from mine by knowing as little about them as was possible in the midst of the universal excitement. But I knew that a verdict of wilful murder had been found against the suspected murderer, and that he had been committed to Newgate for trial. I also knew that his trial had been postponed over one Sessions of the Central Criminal Court, on the ground of general prejudice and want of time for the preparation of the defence. I may further have known, but I believe I did not, when, or about when, the Sessions to which his trial stood postponed would come on.

My sitting-room, bedroom and dressing-room are all on one floor. With the last there is no communication but through the bedroom. True, there is a door in it, once communicating with the staircase; but a part of the fitting of my bath has been – and had then been for some years – fixed across it. At the same period, and as a part of the same arrangement, the door had been nailed up and canvassed over.

I was standing in my bedroom late one night, giving some directions to my servant before he went to bed. My face was towards the only available door of communication with the dressing-room, and it was closed. My servant's back was towards that door. While I was speaking to him, I saw it open, and a man look in, who very earnestly and mysteriously beckoned to me. That man was the man who had gone second of the two along Piccadilly, and whose face was of the colour of impure wax.

The figure, having beckoned, drew back, and closed the door. With no longer pause than was made by my crossing the bedroom, I opened the dressing-room door, and looked in. I had a lighted candle already in my hand. I felt no inward expectation of seeing the figure in the dressing-room, and I did not see it there.

Conscious that my servant stood amazed, I turned round to him, and said, 'Derrick, could you believe that in my cool senses I fancied I saw a – '

As I there laid my hand upon his breast, with a sudden start he trembled violently, and said, 'Oh Lord, yes, sir! A dead man beckoning!'

Now I do not believe that this John Derrick, my trusty and attached servant for more than twenty years, had any impression whatever of having seen any such figure, until I touched him. The change in him was so startling, when I touched him, that I fully believe he derived his impression in some occult manner from me at that instant.

I bade John Derrick bring some brandy, and I gave him a dram, and was glad to take one myself. Of what had preceded that night's phenomenon, I told him not a single word. Reflecting on it, I was absolutely certain that I had never seen that face before, except on the one occasion in Piccadilly. Comparing its expression when beckoning at the door with its expression when it had stared up at me as I stood at my window, I came to the conclusion that on the first occasion it had sought to fasten itself upon my memory, and that on the second occasion it had made sure of being immediately remembered.

I was not very comfortable that night, though I felt a certainty, difficult to explain, that the figure would not return. At daylight I fell into a heavy sleep, from which I was awakened by John Derrick's coming to my bedside with a paper in his hand.

This paper, it appeared, had been the subject of an altercation at the door between its bearer and my servant. It was a summons to me to serve upon a jury at the forthcoming Sessions at the Central Criminal Court at the Old Bailey. I had never before been summoned on such a jury, as John Derrick well knew. He believed – I am not certain at this hour whether with reason or otherwise – that that class of jurors were customarily chosen on a lower qualification than mine, and he had at first refused to accept the summons. The man who served it had taken the matter very coolly. He had said that my attendance or non-attendance was nothing to him; there the summons was; and I should deal with it at my own peril, and not at his.

For a day or two I was undecided whether to respond to this call, or take no notice of it. I was not conscious of the slightest mysterious bias, influence or attraction one way or other. Of that I am as strictly sure as of every other statement that I make here. Ultimately I decided, as a break in the monotony of my life, that I would go.

The appointed morning was a raw morning in the month of November. There was a dense brown fog in Piccadilly, and it became positively black and in the last degree oppressive east of Temple Bar. I found the passages and staircases of the courthouse flaringly lighted with gas, and the court itself similarly illuminated. I *think* that, until I was conducted by officers into the old court and saw its crowded state, I did not know that the murderer was to be tried that day. I *think* that, until I was so helped into the old court with considerable difficulty, I did not know into which of the two courts sitting my summons would take me. But this must not be received as a positive assertion, for I am not completely satisfied in my mind on either point.

I took my seat in the place appropriated to jurors in waiting, and I looked about the court as well as I could through the cloud of fog and breath that was heavy in it. I noticed the black vapour hanging like a murky curtain outside the great windows, and I noticed the stifled sound of wheels on the straw or tan that was littered in the street; also, the hum of the people gathered there, which a shrill whistle, or a louder song or hail than the rest, occasionally pierced. Soon afterwards the judges, two in number, entered, and took their seats. The buzz in the court was awfully hushed. The direction was given to put the murderer to the bar. He appeared there. And in that same instant I recognised in him the first of the two men who had gone down Piccadilly.

If my name had been called then, I doubt if I could have answered it audibly. But it was called about sixth or eighth in the panel, and I was by that time able to say, 'Here!' Now, observe. As I stepped into the box, the prisoner, who had been looking on attentively, but with no sign of concern, became violently agitated, and beckoned to his attorney. The prisoner's wish to challenge me was so manifest, that it occasioned a pause, during which the attorney, with his hand upon the dock, whispered with his client, and shook his head. I afterwards had it from that gentleman, that the prisoner's first affrighted words to him were, 'At all hazards, challenge that man!' But that, as he would give no reason for it, and admitted that he had not even known my name until he heard it called and I appeared, it was not done.

Both on the ground already explained, that I wish to avoid reviving the unwholesome memory of that murderer, and also because a detailed account of his long trial is by no means indispensable to my narrative, I shall confine myself closely to such incidents in the ten days and nights during which we, the jury, were kept together, as directly bear on my own curious personal experience. It is in that, and not in the murderer, that I seek to interest my reader. It is to that, and not to a page of the *Newgate Calendar*, that I beg attention.

I was chosen foreman of the jury. On the second morning of the trial, after evidence had been taken for two hours (I heard the church clocks strike), happening to cast my eyes over my brother jurymen, I found an inexplicable difficulty in counting them. I counted them several times, yet always with the same difficulty. In short, I made them one too many.

I touched the brother juryman whose place was next me, and I whispered to him, 'Oblige me by counting us.'

He looked surprised by the request, but turned his head and counted. 'Why,' says he, suddenly, 'we are thirt–; but no, it's not possible. No. We are twelve.'

According to my counting that day, we were always right in detail, but in the gross we were always one too many. There was no appearance – no figure – to account for it; but I had now an inward foreshadowing of the figure that was surely coming.

The jury were housed at the London Tavern. We all slept in one large room on separate tables, and we were constantly in the charge and under the eye of the officer sworn to hold us in safe-keeping. I see no reason for suppressing the real name of that officer. He was intelligent, highly polite and obliging, and (I was glad to hear) much respected in the City. He had an agreeable presence, good eyes, enviable black whiskers and a fine sonorous voice. His name was Mr Harker.

When we turned into our twelve beds at night, Mr Harker's bed was drawn across the door. On the night of the second day, not being disposed to lie down, and seeing Mr Harker sitting on his bed, I went and sat beside him, and offered him a pinch of snuff. As Mr Harker's hand touched mine in taking it from my box, a peculiar shiver crossed him, and he said, 'Who is this?'

Following Mr Harker's eyes, and looking along the room, I saw again the figure I expected – the second of the two men who had gone down Piccadilly. I rose, and advanced a few steps; then stopped, and looked round at Mr Harker. He was quite unconcerned, laughed, and said in a pleasant way, 'I thought for a moment we had a thirteenth juryman, without a bed. But I see it is the moonlight.'

Making no revelation to Mr Harker, but inviting him to take a walk with me to the end of the room, I watched what the figure did. It stood for a few moments by the bedside of each of my eleven brother jurymen, close to the pillow. It always went to the right-hand side of the bed, and always passed out crossing the foot of the next bed. It seemed, from the action of the head, merely to look down pensively at each recumbent figure. It took no notice of me, or of my bed, which was that nearest to Mr Harker's. It seemed to go out where the moonlight came in, through a high window, as by an aerial flight of stairs.

Next morning at breakfast, it appeared that everybody present had dreamed of the murdered man last night, except myself and Mr Harker.

I now felt as convinced that the second man who had gone down Piccadilly was the murdered man (so to speak), as if it had been borne into my comprehension by his immediate testimony. But even this took place, and in a manner for which I was not at all prepared.

On the fifth day of the trial, when the case for the prosecution was drawing to a close, a miniature of the murdered man, missing from his bedroom upon the discovery of the deed, and afterwards found in a hiding place where the murderer had been seen digging, was put in evidence. Having been identified by the witness under examination, it was handed up to the bench, and thence handed down to be inspected by the jury. As an officer in a black gown was making his way with it across to me, the figure of the second man who had gone down Piccadilly impetuously started from the crowd, caught the miniature from the officer, and gave it to me with his own hands, at the same time saying, in a low and hollow tone – before I saw the miniature, which was in a locket – 'I was younger then, and my face was not then drained of blood.' It also came between me and the brother juryman to whom I would have given the miniature, and between him and the brother juryman to whom he would have given it, and so passed it on through the whole of our number, and back into my possession. Not one of them, however, detected this.

At table, and generally when we were shut up together in Mr Harker's custody, we had from the first naturally discussed the day's proceedings a good deal. On that fifth day, the case for the prosecution being closed, and we having that side of the question in a completed shape before us, our discussion was more animated and serious. Among our number was a vestryman – the densest idiot I have ever seen at large – who met the plainest evidence with the most preposterous objections, and who was sided with by two flabby parochial parasites; all the three empanelled from a district so delivered over to fever that they ought to have been upon their own trial for five hundred murders. When these mischievous blockheads were at their loudest, which was towards midnight, while some of us were already preparing for bed, I again saw the murdered man. He stood grimly behind them, beckoning to me. On my going towards them, and striking into the conversation, he immediately retired. This was the beginning of a separate series of appearances, confined to that long room in which we were confined. Whenever a knot of my brother jurymen laid their heads together, I saw the head of the murdered man among theirs. Whenever their comparison of notes was going against him, he would solemnly and irresistibly beckon to me.

It will be borne in mind that down to the production of the miniature, on the fifth day of the trial, I had never seen the appearance in court. Three changes occurred now that we entered on the case for the defence. Two of them I will mention together, first. The figure was now in court continually, and it never there addressed itself to me, but always to the person who was speaking at the time. For instance: the throat of the murdered man had been cut straight across. In the opening speech for the defence, it was suggested that the deceased might have cut his own throat. At that very moment, the figure, with its throat in the dreadful condition referred to (this it had concealed before), stood at the speaker's elbow, motioning across and across its windpipe, now with the right hand, now with the left, vigorously suggesting to the speaker himself the impossibility of such a wound having been self-inflicted by either hand. For another instance: a witness to character, a woman, deposed to the prisoner's being the most amiable of mankind. The figure in that instant stood on the floor before her, looking her full in the face, and pointing out the prisoner's evil countenance with an extended arm and an out-stretched finger.

The third change now to be added impressed me strongly as the most marked and striking of all. I do not theorise upon it; I accurately state it, and there leave it. Although the appearance was not itself perceived by those whom it addressed, its coming close to such persons was invariably attended by some trepidation or disturbance on their part. It seemed to me as if it were prevented, by laws to which I was not amenable, from fully revealing itself to others, and yet as if it could invisibly, dumbly and darkly overshadow their minds. When the leading counsel for the defence suggested that hypothesis of suicide, and the figure stood at the learned gentleman's elbow, frightfully sawing at its severed throat, it is undeniable that the counsel faltered in his speech, lost for a few seconds the thread of his ingenious discourse, wiped his forehead with his handkerchief, and turned extremely pale. When the witness to character was confronted by the appearance, her eyes most certainly did follow the direction of its pointed finger, and rest in great hesitation and trouble upon the prisoner's face. Two additional illustrations will suffice. On the eighth day of the trial, after the pause which was every day made early in the afternoon for a few minutes' rest and refreshment, I came back into court with the rest of the jury some little time before the return of the judges. Standing up in the box and looking about me, I thought the figure was not there, until, chancing to raise my eyes to the gallery, I saw it bending forward, and leaning over a very decent woman, as if to assure itself whether the judges had resumed their seats or not. Immediately afterwards that woman screamed, fainted, and was carried out. So with the venerable, sagacious and patient judge who conducted the trial. When the case was over, and he settled himself and his papers to sum up, the murdered man, entering by the judges' door, advanced to his lordship's desk, and looked eagerly over his shoulder at the pages of his notes which he was turning. A change came over his lordship's face; his hand stopped; the peculiar shiver, that I knew so well, passed over him; he faltered, 'Excuse me, gentlemen, for a few moments. I am somewhat oppressed by the vitiated air'; and did not recover until he had drunk a glass of water.

Through all the monotony of six of those interminable ten days – the same judges and others on the bench, the same murderer in the dock, the same lawyers at the table, the same tones of question and answer rising to the roof of the court, the same scratching of the judge's pen, the same ushers going in and out, the same lights kindled at the same hour when there was no longer any natural light of day, the same foggy curtain outside the great windows when it was foggy, the same rain pattering and dripping when it was rainy, the same footmarks of turnkeys and prisoner day after day on the same sawdust, the same keys locking and unlocking the same heavy doors – through all the wearisome monotony which made me feel as if I had been foreman of the jury for a vast period of time, and Piccadilly had flourished coevally with Babylon, the murdered man never lost one trace of his distinctness in my eyes, nor was he at any moment less distinct than anybody else. I must not omit, as a matter of fact, that I never once saw the appearance which I call by the name of the murdered man look at the murderer. Again and again I wondered, 'Why does he not?' But he never did.

Nor did he look at me, after the production of the miniature, until the last closing minutes of the trial arrived. We retired to consider, at seven minutes before ten at night. The idiotic vestryman and his two parochial parasites gave us so much trouble that we twice returned into court to beg to have certain extracts from the judge's notes reread. Nine of us had not the smallest doubt about those passages, neither, I believe, had anyone in the court; the dunderhead triumvirate, however, having no idea but obstruction, disputed them for that very reason. At length we prevailed, and finally the jury returned into court at ten minutes past twelve.

The murdered man at that time stood directly opposite the jury-box, on the other side of the court. As I took my place, his eyes rested on me with great attention; he seemed satisfied, and slowly shook a great grey veil, which he carried on his arm for the first time, over his head and whole form. As I gave in our verdict, 'Guilty', the veil collapsed, all was gone, and his place was empty.

The murderer, being asked by the judge, according to usage, whether he had anything to say before sentence of death should be passed upon him, indistinctly muttered something which was described in the leading newspapers of the following day as 'a few rambling, incoherent and half-audible words, in which he was understood to complain that he had not had a fair trial, because the foreman of the jury was prepossessed against him'. The remarkable declaration that he really made was this: 'My Lord, I knew I was a doomed man, when the foreman of my jury came into the box. My Lord, I knew he would never let me off, because before I was taken, he somehow got to my bedside in the night, woke me, and put a rope round my neck.'

THE SIGNALMAN

'Halloa! Below there!'

When he heard a voice thus calling to him, he was standing at the door of his box, with a flag in his hand, furled round its short pole. One would have thought, considering the nature of the ground, that he could not have doubted from what quarter the voice came; but instead of looking up to where I stood on the top of the steep cutting nearly over his head, he turned himself about, and looked down the line. There was something remarkable in his manner of doing so, though I could not have said for my life what. But I know it was remarkable enough to attract my notice, even though his figure was foreshortened and shadowed, down in the deep trench, and mine was high above him, so steeped in the glow of an angry sunset that I had shaded my eyes with my hand before I saw him at all.

'Halloa! Below!'

From looking down the line, he turned himself about again, and raising his eyes, saw my figure high above him.

'Is there any path by which I can come down and speak to you?'

He looked up at me without replying, and I looked down at him without pressing him too soon with a repetition of my idle question. Just then there came a vague vibration in the earth and air, quickly changing into a violent pulsation, and an oncoming rush that caused me to start back, as though it had force to draw me down. When such vapour as rose to my height from this rapid train had passed me, and was skimming away over the landscape, I looked down again, and saw him refurling the flag he had shown while the train went by.

I repeated my enquiry. After a pause, during which he seemed to regard me with fixed attention, he motioned with his rolled-up flag towards a point on my level, some two or three hundred yards distant. I called down to him, 'All right!' and made for that point. There, by dint of looking closely about me, I found a rough zigzag descending path notched out, which I followed.

The cutting was extremely deep, and unusually precipitate. It was made through a clammy stone, that became oozier and wetter as I went down. For these reasons, I found the way long enough to give me time to recall a singular air of reluctance or compulsion with which he had pointed out the path.

When I came down low enough upon the zigzag descent to see him again, I saw that he was standing between the rails on the way by which the train had lately passed, in an attitude as if he were waiting for me to appear. He had his left hand at his chin, and that left elbow rested on his right hand, crossed over his breast. His attitude was one of such expectation and watchfulness that I stopped a moment, wondering at it.

I resumed my downward way, and stepping out upon the level of the railroad, and drawing nearer to him, saw that he was a dark sallow man, with a dark beard and rather heavy eyebrows. His post was in as solitary and dismal a place as ever I saw. On either side, a dripping-wet wall of jagged stone, excluding all view but a strip of sky; the perspective one way only a crooked prolongation of this great dungeon; the shorter per-spective in the other direction terminating in a gloomy red light, and the gloomier entrance to a black tunnel, in whose massive architecture there was a barbarous, depressing and forbidding air. So little sunlight ever found its way to this spot, that it had an earthy, deadly smell; and so much cold wind rushed through it, that it struck chill to me, as if I had left the natural world.

Before he stirred, I was near enough to him to have touched him. Not even then removing his eyes from mine, he stepped back one step, and lifted his hand.

This was a lonesome post to occupy (I said), and it had riveted my attention when I looked down from up yonder. A visitor was a rarity, I should suppose; not an unwelcome rarity, I hoped? In me, he merely saw a man who had been shut up within narrow limits all his life, and who, being at last set free, had a newly-awakened interest in these great works. To such purpose I spoke to him; but I am far from sure of the terms I used; for, besides that I am not happy in opening any conversation, there was something in the man that daunted me.

He directed a most curious look towards the red light near the tunnel's mouth, and looked all about it, as if something were missing from it, and then looked at me.

That light was part of his charge? Was it not?

He answered in a low voice, 'Don't you know it is?'

The monstrous thought came into my mind, as I perused the fixed eyes and the saturnine face, that this was a spirit, not a man. I have speculated since, whether there may have been infection in his mind.

In my turn, I stepped back. But in making the action, I detected in his eyes some latent fear of me. This put the monstrous thought to flight.

'You look at me,' I said, forcing a smile, 'as if you had a dread of me.'

'I was doubtful,' he returned, 'whether I had seen you before.'

'Where?'

He pointed to the red light he had looked at.

'There?' I said.

Intently watchful of me, he replied (but without sound), 'Yes.'

'My good fellow, what should I do there? However, be that as it may, I never was there, you may swear.'

'I think I may,' he rejoined. 'Yes; I am sure I may.'

His manner cleared, like my own. He replied to my remarks with readiness, and in well-chosen words. Had he much to do there? Yes; that was to say, he had enough responsibility to bear; but exactness and watchfulness were what was required of him, and of actual work – manual labour – he had next to none. To change that signal, to trim those lights, and to turn this iron handle now and then, was all he had to do under that head. Regarding those many long and lonely hours of which I seemed to make so much, he could only say that the routine of his life had shaped itself into that form, and he had grown used to it. He had taught himself a language down here, if only to know it by sight, and to have formed his own crude ideas of its pronunciation, could be called learning it. He had also worked at fractions and decimals, and tried a little algebra; but he was, and had been as a boy, a poor hand at figures. Was it necessary for him when on duty always to remain in that channel of damp air, and could he never rise into the sunshine between those high stone walls? Why, that depended upon times and circumstances. Under some conditions there would be less upon the line than under others, and the same held good as to certain hours of the day and night. In bright weather, he did choose occasions for getting a little above these lower shadows; but, being at all times liable to be called by his electric bell, and at such times listening for it with redoubled anxiety, the relief was less than I would suppose.

He took me into his box, where there was a fire, a desk for an official book in which he had to make certain entries, a telegraphic instrument with its dial, face and needles, and the little bell of which he had spoken.

On my trusting that he would excuse the remark that he had been well educated, and (I hoped I might say without offence) perhaps educated above that station, he observed that instances of slight incongruity in such wise would rarely be found wanting among large bodies of men; that he had heard it was so in workhouses, in the police force, even in that last desperate resource, the army; and that he knew it was so, more or less, in any great railway staff. He had been, when young (if I could believe it, sitting in that hut – he scarcely could), a student of natural philosophy, and had attended lectures; but he had run wild, misused his opportunities, gone down and never risen again. He had no complaint to offer about that. He had made his bed, and he lay upon it. It was far too late to make another.

All that I have here condensed he said in a quiet manner, with his grave dark regards divided between me and the fire. He threw in the word 'sir' from time to time, and especially when he referred to his youth, as though to request me to understand that he claimed to be nothing but what I found him. He was several times interrupted by the little bell, and had to read off messages, and send replies. Once he had to stand without the door, and display a flag as a train passed, and make some verbal communication to the driver. In the discharge of his duties, I observed him to be remarkably exact and vigilant, breaking off his discourse at a syllable, and remaining silent until what he had to do was done.

In a word, I should have set this man down as one of the safest of men to be employed in that capacity, but for the circumstance that while he was speaking to me he twice broke off with a fallen colour, turned his face towards the little bell when it did not ring, opened the door of the hut (which was kept shut to exclude the unhealthy damp), and looked out towards the red light near the mouth of the tunnel. On both of those occasions, he came back to the fire with the inexplicable air upon him which I had remarked, without being able to define, when we were so far asunder.

Said I, when I rose to leave him, 'You almost make me think that I have met with a contented man.'

(I am afraid I must acknowledge that I said it to lead him on.)

'I believe I used to be so,' he rejoined, in the low voice in which he had first spoken; 'but I am troubled, sir, I am troubled.'

He would have recalled the words if he could. He had said them, however, and I took them up quickly.

'With what? What is your trouble?'

'It is very difficult to impart, sir. It is very, very difficult to speak of. If ever you make me another visit, I will try to tell you.'

'But I expressly intend to make you another visit. Say, when shall it be?'

'I go off early in the morning, and I shall be on again at ten tomorrow night, sir.'

'I will come at eleven.'

He thanked me, and went out at the door with me. 'I'll show my white light, sir,' he said, in his peculiar low voice, ''till you have found the way up. When you have found it, don't call out! And when you are at the top, don't call out!'

His manner seemed to make the place strike colder to me, but I said no more than, 'Very well.'

'And when you come down tomorrow night, don't call out! Let me ask you a parting question. What made you cry, "Halloa! Below there!" tonight?'

'Heaven knows,' said I. 'I cried something to that effect – '

'Not to that effect, sir. Those were the very words. I know them well.'

'I admit those were the very words. I said them, no doubt, because I saw you below.'

'For no other reason?'

'What other reason could I possibly have?'

'You had no feeling that they were conveyed to you in any supernatural way?'

'No.'

He wished me good-night, and held up his light. I walked by the side of the down line of rails (with a very disagreeable sensation of a train coming behind me) until I found the path. It was easier to mount than to descend, and I got back to my inn without any adventure.

Punctual to my appointment, I placed my foot on the first notch of the zigzag next night, as the distant clocks were striking eleven. He was waiting for me at the bottom, with his white light on. 'I have not called out,' I said, when we came close together; 'may I speak now?' 'By all means, sir.' 'Good-night, then, and here's my hand.' 'Good-night, sir, and here's mine.' With that we walked side by side to his box, entered it, closed the door, and sat down by the fire.

'I have made up my mind, sir,' he began, bending forward as soon as we were seated, and speaking in a tone but a little above a whisper, 'that you shall not have to ask me twice what troubles me. I took you for someone else yesterday evening. That troubles me.'

'That mistake?'

'No. That someone else.'

'Who is it?'

'I don't know.'

'Like me?'

'I don't know. I never saw the face. The left arm is across the face, and the right arm is waved – violently waved. This way.'

I followed his action with my eyes, and it was the action of an arm gesticulating, with the utmost passion and vehemence, 'For God's sake, clear the way!'

'One moonlight night,' said the man, 'I was sitting here, when I heard a voice cry, "Halloa! Below there!" I started up, looked from that door, and saw this someone else standing by the red light near the tunnel, waving as I just now showed you. The voice seemed hoarse with shouting, and it cried, "Look out! Look out!" And then again, "Halloa! Below there! Look out!" I caught up my lamp, turned it on red, and ran towards the figure, calling, "What's wrong? What has happened? Where?" It stood just outside the blackness of the tunnel. I advanced so close upon it that I wondered at its keeping the sleeve across its eyes. I ran right up at it, and had my hand stretched out to pull the sleeve away, when it was gone.'

'Into the tunnel?' said I.

'No. I ran on into the tunnel, five hundred yards. I stopped, and held my lamp above my head, and saw the figures of the measured distance, and saw the wet stains stealing down the walls and trickling through the arch. I ran out again faster than I had run in (for I had a mortal abhorrence of the place upon me), and I looked all round the red light with my own red light, and I went up the iron ladder to the gallery atop of it, and I came down again, and ran back here. I telegraphed both ways, "An alarm has been given. Is anything wrong?" The answer came back, both ways, "All well."'

Resisting the slow touch of a frozen finger tracing out my spine, I showed him how that this figure must be a deception of his sense of sight; and how that figures, originating in disease of the delicate nerves that minister to the functions of the eye, were known to have often troubled patients, some of whom had become conscious of the nature of their affliction, and had even proved it by experiments upon themselves. 'As to an imaginary cry,' said I, 'do but listen for a moment to the wind in this unnatural valley while we speak so low, and to the wild harp it makes of the telegraph wires.'

That was all very well, he returned, after we had sat listening for a while, and he ought to know something of the wind and the wires – he who so often passed long winter nights there, alone and watching. But he would beg to remark that he had not finished.

I asked his pardon, and he slowly added these words, touching my arm, 'Within six hours after the appearance, the memorable accident on this line happened, and within ten hours the dead and wounded were brought along through the tunnel over the spot where the figure had stood.'

A disagreeable shudder crept over me, but I did my best against it. It was not to be denied, I rejoined, that this was a remarkable coincidence, calculated deeply to impress his mind. But it was unquestionable that remarkable coincidences did continually occur, and they must be taken into account in dealing with such a subject. Though to be sure I must admit, I added (for I thought I saw that he was going to bring the objection to bear upon me), men of common sense did not allow much for coincidences in making the ordinary calculations of life.

He again begged to remark that he had not finished.

I again begged his pardon for being betrayed into interruptions.

'This,' he said, again laying his hand upon my arm, and glancing over his shoulder with hollow eyes, 'was just a year ago. Six or seven months passed, and I had recovered from the surprise and shock, when one morning, as the day was breaking, I, standing at the door, looked towards the red light and saw the spectre again.' He stopped, with a fixed look at me.

'Did it cry out?'

'No. It was silent.'

'Did it wave its arm?'

'No. It leaned against the shaft of the light, with both hands before the face. Like this.'

Once more I followed his action with my eyes. It was an action of mourning. I have seen such an attitude in stone figures on tombs.

'Did you go up to it?'

'I came in and sat down, partly to collect my thoughts, partly because it had turned me faint. When I went to the door again, daylight was above, and the ghost was gone.'

'But nothing followed? Nothing came of this?'

He touched me on the arm with his forefinger twice or thrice, giving a ghastly nod each time: 'That very day, as a train came out of the tunnel, I noticed, at a carriage window on my side, what looked like a confusion of hands and heads, and something waved. I saw it just in time to signal the driver, Stop! He shut off, and put his brake on, but the train drifted past here a hundred and fifty yards or more. I ran after it, and, as I went along, heard terrible screams and cries. A beautiful young lady had died instantaneously in one of the compartments, and was brought in here, and laid down on this floor between us.'

Involuntarily I pushed my chair back, as I looked from the boards at which he pointed to himself.

'True, sir, True. Precisely as it happened, so I tell it you.'

I could think of nothing to say to any purpose, and my mouth was very dry. The wind and the wires took up the story with a long lamenting wail.

He resumed. 'Now, sir, mark this, and judge how my mind is troubled. The spectre came back a week ago. Ever since, it has been there, now and again, by fits and starts.'

'At the light?'

'At the danger-light.'

'What does it seem to do?'

He repeated, if possible with increased passion and vehemence, that former gesticulation of, 'For God's sake, clear the way!'

Then he went on. 'I have no peace or rest from it. It calls to me, for many minutes together, in an agonised manner, "Below there! Look out! Look out!" It stands waving to me. It rings my little bell – '

I caught at that. 'Did it ring your bell yesterday evening when I was here, and you went to the door?'

'Twice.'

'Why, see,' said I, 'how your imagination misleads you. My eyes were on the bell, and my ears were open to the bell, and if I am a living man, it did *not* ring at those times. No, nor at any other time, except when it was rung in the natural course of physical things by the station communicating with you.'

He shook his head. 'I have never made a mistake as to that yet, sir. I have never confused the spectre's ring with the man's. The ghost's ring is a strange vibration in the bell that it derives from nothing else, and I have not asserted that the bell stirs to the eye. I don't wonder that you failed to hear it. But *I* heard it.'

'And did the spectre seem to be there, when you looked out?'

'It *was* there.'

'Both times?'

He repeated firmly, 'Both times.'

'Will you come to the door with me, and look for it now?'

He bit his underlip as though he were somewhat unwilling, but arose. I opened the door, and stood on the step, while he stood in the doorway. There was the danger-light. There was the dismal mouth of the tunnel. There were the high, wet stone walls of the cutting. There were the stars above them.

'Do you see it?' I asked him, taking particular note of his face. His eyes were prominent and strained, but not very much more so, perhaps, than my own had been when I had directed them earnestly towards the same spot.

'No,' he answered, 'it is not there.'

'Agreed,' said I.

We went in again, shut the door, and resumed our seats. I was thinking how best to improve this advantage, if it might be called one, when he took up the conversation in such a matter-of-course way, so assuming that there could be no serious question of fact between us, that I felt myself placed in the weakest of positions.

'By this time you will fully understand, sir,' he said, 'that what troubles me so dreadfully is the question, What does the spectre mean?'

I was not sure, I told him, that I did fully understand.

'What is its warning against?' he said, ruminating, with his eyes on the fire, and only by times turning them on me. 'What is the danger? Where is the danger? There is danger overhanging somewhere on the line. Some dreadful calamity will happen. It is not to be doubted this third time, after what has gone before. But surely this is a cruel haunting of *me*. What can *I* do?'

He pulled out his handkerchief, and wiped the drops from his heated forehead.

'If I telegraphed danger on either side of me, or on both, I can give no reason for it,' he went on, wiping the palms of his hands. 'I should get into trouble, and do no good. They would think I was mad. This is the way it would work: Message – "Danger! Take care!" Answer – "What Danger? Where?" Message – "Don't know. But, for God's sake, take care!" They would displace me. What else could they do?'

His pain of mind was most pitiable to see. It was the mental torture of a conscientious man, oppressed beyond endurance by an unintelligible responsibility involving life.

'When it first stood under the danger-light,' he went on, putting his dark hair back from his head, and drawing his hands outward across and across his temples in an extremity of feverish distress, 'why not tell me where that accident was to happen – if it must happen? Why not tell me how it could be averted – if it could have been averted? When on its second coming it hid its face, why not tell me, instead, "She is going to die. Let them keep her at home"? If it came, on those two occasions, only to show me that its warnings were true, and so to prepare me for the third, why not warn me plainly now? And I, Lord help me! A mere poor signalman on this solitary station! Why not go to somebody with credit to be believed, and power to act?'

When I saw him in this state, I saw that for the poor man's sake, as well as for the public safety, what I had to do for the time was to compose his mind. Therefore, setting aside all question of reality or unreality between us, I represented to him that whoever thoroughly discharged his duty must do well, and that at least it was his comfort that he understood his duty, though he did not understand these confounding appearances. In this effort I succeeded far better than in the attempt to reason him out of his conviction. He became calm; the occupations incidental to his post as the night advanced began to make larger demands on his attention: and I left him at two in the morning. I had offered to stay through the night, but he would not hear of it.

That I more than once looked back at the red light as I ascended the pathway, that I did not like the red light, and that I should have slept but poorly if my bed had been under it, I see no reason to conceal. Nor did I like the two sequences of the accident and the dead girl. I see no reason to conceal that either.

But what ran most in my thoughts was the consideration how ought I to act, having become the recipient of this disclosure? I had proved the man to be intelligent, vigilant, painstaking and exact; but how long might he remain so, in his state of mind? Though in a subordinate position, still he held a most important trust, and would I (for instance) like to stake my own life on the chances of his continuing to execute it with precision?

Unable to overcome a feeling that there would be something treacherous in my communicating what he had told me to his superiors in the company, without first being plain with himself and proposing a middle course to him, I ultimately resolved to offer to accompany him (otherwise keeping his secret for the present) to the wisest medical practitioner we could hear of in those parts, and to take his opinion. A change in his time of duty would come round next night, he had apprised me, and he would be off an hour or two after sunrise, and on again soon after sunset. I had appointed to return accordingly.

Next evening was a lovely evening, and I walked out early to enjoy it. The sun was not yet quite down when I traversed the field path near the top of the deep cutting. I would extend my walk for an hour, I said to myself, half an hour on and half an hour back, and it would then be time to go to my signalman's box.

Before pursuing my stroll, I stepped to the brink and mechanically looked down, from the point from which I had first seen him. I cannot describe the thrill that seized upon me when, close at the mouth of the tunnel, I saw the appearance of a man, with his left sleeve across his eyes, passionately waving his right arm.

The nameless horror that oppressed me passed in a moment, for in a moment I saw that this appearance of a man was a man indeed, and that there was a little group of other men, standing at a short distance, to whom he seemed to be rehearsing the gesture he made. The danger-light was not yet lighted. Against its shaft, a little low hut, entirely new to me, had been made of some wooden supports and tarpaulin. It looked no bigger than a bed.

With an irresistible sense that something was wrong, with a flashing self-reproachful fear that fatal mischief had come of my leaving the man there, and causing no one to be sent to overlook or correct what he did, I descended the notched path with all the speed I could make.

'What is the matter?' I asked the men.

'Signalman killed this morning, sir. '

'Not the man belonging to that box?'

'Yes, sir.'

'Not the man I know?'

'You will recognise him, sir, if you knew him,' said the man who spoke for the others, solemnly uncovering his own head and raising the end of the tarpaulin, 'for his face is quite composed.'

'Oh, how did this happen, how did this happen?' I asked, turning from one to another as the hut closed in again.

'He was cut down by an engine, sir. No man in England knew his work better. But somehow he was not clear of the outer rail. It was just at broad day. He had struck the light, and had the lamp in his hand. As the engine came out of the tunnel, his back was towards her, and she cut him down. That man drove her, and was showing how it happened. Show the gentleman, Tom.'

The man, who wore rough dark dress, stepped back to his former place at the mouth of the tunnel.

'Coming round the curve in the tunnel, sir,' he said, 'I saw him at the end, like as if I saw him down a perspective-glass. There was no time to check speed, and I knew him to be very careful. As he didn't seem to take heed of the whistle, I shut it off when we were running down upon him, and called to him as loud as I could call.'

'What did you say?'

'I said, "Below there! Look out! Look out! For God's sake, clear the way!" '

I started.

'Ah! it was a dreadful time, sir. I never left off calling to him. I put this arm before my eyes not to see, and I waved this arm to the last; but it was no use.'

* * *

Without prolonging the narrative to dwell on any one of its curious circumstances more than on any other, I may, in closing it, point out the coincidence that the warning of the engine-driver included, not only the words which the unfortunate signalman had repeated to me as haunting him, but also the words which I myself – not he – had attached, and that only in my own mind, to the gesticulation he had imitated.

THE LAWYER AND
THE GHOST

I knew a man – let me see – forty years ago now – who took an old, damp, rotten set of chambers, in one of the most ancient inns, that had been shut up and empty for years and years before. There were lots of old women's stories about the place, and it certainly was very far from being a cheerful one; but he was poor, and the rooms were cheap, and that would have been quite a sufficient reason for him, if they had been ten times worse than they really were.

He was obliged to take some mouldering fixtures that were on the place, and, among the rest, was a great lumbering wooden press for papers, with large glass doors, and a green curtain inside; a pretty useless thing for him, for he had no papers to put in it; and as to his clothes, he carried them about with him, and that wasn't very hard work, either.

Well, he had moved in all his furniture – it wasn't quite a truck-full – and had sprinkled it about the room, so as to make the four chairs look as much like a dozen as possible, and was sitting down before the fire at night, drinking the first glass of two gallons of whisky he had ordered on credit, wondering whether it would ever be paid for, and if so, in how many years' time, when his eyes encountered the glass doors of the wooden press.

'Ah,' says he, 'if I hadn't been obliged to take that ugly article at the old broker's valuation, I might have got something comfortable for the money. I'll tell you what it is, old fellow,' he said, speaking aloud to the press, having nothing else to speak to, 'if it wouldn't cost more to break up your old carcass, than it would ever be worth afterward, I'd have a fire out of you in less than no time.'

He had hardly spoken the words, when a sound resembling a faint groan, appeared to issue from the interior of the case. It startled him at first, but thinking, on a moment's reflection, that it must be some young fellow in the next chamber, who had been dining out, he put his feet on the fender, and raised the poker to stir the fire.

At that moment, the sound was repeated; and one of the glass doors slowly opening, disclosed a pale and emaciated figure in soiled and worn apparel, standing erect in the press. The figure was tall and thin, and the countenance expressive of care and anxiety; but there was something in the hue of the skin, and the gaunt and unearthly appearance of the whole form, which no being of this world was ever seen to exhibit.

'Who are you?' said the new tenant, turning very pale; poising the poker in his hand, however, and taking a very decent aim at the countenance of the figure. 'Who are you?'

'Don't throw that poker at me,' replied the form; 'if you hurled it with ever so sure an aim, it would pass through me, without resistance, and expend its force on the wood behind. I am a spirit.'

'And pray, what do you want here?' faltered the tenant.

'In this room,' replied the apparition, 'my worldly ruin was worked, and I and my children beggared. In this press, the papers in a long, long suit, which accumulated for years, were deposited. In this room, when I had died of grief, and long-deferred hope, two wily harpies divided the wealth for which I had contested during a wretched existence, and of which, at last, not one farthing was left for my unhappy descendants. I terrified them from the spot, and since that day have prowled by night – the only period at which I can revisit the earth – about the scenes of my long-protracted misery. This apartment is mine: leave it to me.'

'If you insist upon making your appearance here,' said the tenant, who had had time to collect his presence of mind during this prosy statement of the ghost's, 'I shall give up possession with the greatest pleasure; but I should like to ask you one question, if you will allow me.'

'Say on,' said the apparition sternly.

'Well,' said the tenant, 'I don't apply the observation personally to you, because it is equally applicable to most of the ghosts I ever heard of; but it does appear to me somewhat inconsistent, that when you have an opportunity of visiting the fairest spots of earth – for I suppose space is nothing to you – you should always return exactly to the very places where you have been most miserable.'

'Egad, that's very true; I never thought of that before,' said the ghost.

'You see, sir,' pursued the tenant, 'this is a very uncomfortable room. From the appearance of that press, I should be disposed to say that it is not wholly free from bugs; and I really think you might find much more comfortable quarters: to say nothing of the climate of London, which is extremely disagreeable.'

'You are very right, sir,' said the ghost politely, 'it never struck me till now; I'll try a change of air directly' – and, in fact, he began to vanish as he spoke; his legs, indeed, had quite disappeared.

'And if, sir,' said the tenant, calling after him, 'if you *would* have the goodness to suggest to the other ladies and gentlemen who are now engaged in haunting old empty houses, that they might be much more comfortable elsewhere, you will confer a very great benefit on society.'

'I will,' replied the ghost; 'we must be dull fellows – very dull fellows, indeed; I can't imagine how we can have been so stupid.'

With these words, the spirit disappeared; and what is rather remarkable, he never came back again.

FOUR GHOST STORIES

THE FIRST STORY

Some few years ago a well-known English artist received a commission from Lady F— to paint a portrait of her husband. It was settled that he should execute the commission at F— Hall, in the country, because his engagements were too many to permit his entering upon a fresh work till the London season should be over. As he happened to be on terms of intimate acquaintance with his employers, the arrangement was satisfactory to all concerned, and on the 13th of September he set out in good heart to perform his engagement.

He took the train for the station nearest to F— Hall, and found himself, when first starting, alone in a carriage. His solitude did not, however, continue long. At the first station out of London, a young lady entered the carriage, and took the corner opposite to him. She was very delicate-looking, with a remarkable blending of sweetness and sadness in her countenance, which did not fail to attract the notice of a man of observation and sensibility. For some time neither uttered a syllable. But at length the gentleman made the remarks usual under such circumstances, on the weather and the country, and, the ice being broken, they entered into conversation. They spoke of painting. The artist was much surprised by the intimate knowledge the young lady seemed to have of himself and his doings. He was quite certain that he had never seen her before. His surprise was by no means lessened when she suddenly enquired whether he could make, from recollection, the likeness of a person whom he had seen only once, or at most twice? He was hesitating what to reply, when she added, 'Do you think, for example, that you could paint me from recollection?'

He replied that he was not quite sure, but that perhaps he could.

'Well,' she said, 'look at me again. You may have to take a likeness of me.'

He complied with this odd request, and she asked, rather eagerly, 'Now, do you think you could?'

'I think so,' he replied; 'but I cannot say for certain.' At this moment the train stopped. The young lady rose from her seat, smiled in a friendly manner on the painter, and bade him goodbye; adding, as she quitted the carriage, 'We shall meet again soon.' The train rattled off, and Mr H— (the artist) was left to his own reflections.

The station was reached in due time, and Lady F—'s carriage was there to meet the expected guest. It carried him to the place of his destination, one of 'the stately homes of England', after a pleasant drive, and deposited him at the hall door, where his host and hostess were standing to receive him. A kind greeting passed, and he was shown to his room: for the dinner-hour was close at hand.

Having completed his toilet, and descended to the drawing-room, Mr H— was much surprised, and much pleased, to see, seated on one of the ottomans, his young companion of the railway carriage. She greeted him with a smile and a bow of recognition. She sat by his side at dinner, spoke to him two or three times, mixed in the general conversation, and seemed perfectly at home. Mr H— had no doubt of her being an intimate friend of his hostess. The evening passed away pleasantly. The conversation turned a good deal upon the fine arts in general, and on painting in particular, and Mr H— was entreated to show some of the sketches he had brought down with him from London. He readily produced them, and the young lady was much interested in them.

At a late hour the party broke up, and its members retired to their several apartments.

Next morning, early, Mr H— was tempted by the bright sunshine to leave his room and stroll out into the park. The drawing-room opened into the garden; passing through it, he enquired of a servant who was busy arranging the furniture whether the young lady had come down yet?

'What young lady, sir?' asked the man, with an appearance of surprise.

'The young lady who dined here last night.'

'No young lady dined here last night, sir,' replied the man, looking fixedly at him.

The painter said no more: thinking within himself that the servant was either very stupid or had a very bad memory. So, leaving the room, he sauntered out into the park.

He was returning to the house, when his host met him, and the usual morning salutations passed between them.

'Your fair young friend has left you?' observed the artist.

'What young friend?' enquired the lord of the manor.

'The young lady who dined here last night,' returned Mr H—.

'I cannot imagine to whom you refer,' replied the gentleman, very greatly surprised.

'Did not a young lady dine and spend the evening here yesterday?' persisted Mr H—, who in his turn was beginning to wonder.

'No,' replied his host; 'most certainly not. There was no one at table but yourself, my lady, and I.'

The subject was never reverted to after this occasion, yet our artist could not bring himself to believe that he was labouring under a delusion. If the whole were a dream, it was a dream in two parts. As surely as the young lady had been his companion in the railway carriage, so surely she had sat beside him at the dinner-table. Yet she did not come again; and everybody in the house, except himself, appeared to be ignorant of her existence.

He finished the portrait on which he was engaged, and returned to London.

For two whole years he followed up his profession: growing in reputation, and working hard. Yet he never all the while forgot a single lineament in the fair young face of his fellow-traveller. He had no clue by which to discover where she had come from, or who she was. He often thought of her, but spoke to no one about her. There was a mystery about the matter which imposed silence on him. It was wild, strange, utterly unaccountable.

Mr H— was called by business to Canterbury. An old friend of his – whom I will call Mr Wylde – resided there. Mr H—, being anxious to see him, and having only a few hours at his disposal, wrote as soon as he reached the hotel, begging Mr Wylde to call upon him there. At the time appointed the door of his room opened, and Mr Wylde was announced. He was a complete stranger to the artist; and the meeting between the two was a little awkward. It appeared, on explanation, that Mr H—'s friend had left Canterbury some time before; that the gentleman now face to face with the artist was another Mr Wylde; that the note intended for the absentee had been given to him; and that he had obeyed the summons, supposing some business matter to be the cause of it.

The first coldness and surprise dispelled, the two gentlemen entered into a more friendly conversation; for Mr H— had mentioned his name, and it was not a strange one to his visitor. When they had conversed a little while, Mr Wylde asked Mr H— whether he had ever painted, or

could undertake to paint, a portrait from mere description? Mr H—
replied, never.

'I ask you this strange question,' said Mr Wylde, 'because, about two
years ago, I lost a dear daughter. She was my only child, and I loved her
dearly. Her loss was a heavy affliction to me, and my regrets are the
deeper that I have no likeness of her. You are a man of unusual genius. If
you could paint me a portrait of my child, I should be very grateful.'

Mr Wylde then described the features and appearance of his daughter,
and the colour of her eyes and hair, and tried to give an idea of the
expression of her face. Mr H— listened attentively, and, feeling great
sympathy with his grief, made a sketch. He had no thought of its being
like, but hoped the bereaved father might possibly think it so. But the
father shook his head on seeing the sketch, and said, 'No, it was not at all
like.' Again the artist tried, and again he failed. The features were pretty
well, but the expression was not hers; and the father turned away from it,
thanking Mr H— for his kind endeavours, but quite hopeless of any
successful result. Suddenly a thought struck the painter; he took another
sheet of paper, made a rapid and vigorous sketch, and handed it to his
companion. Instantly, a bright look of recognition and pleasure lighted
up the father's face, and he exclaimed, 'That is she! Surely you must have
seen my child, or you never could have made so perfect a likeness!'

'When did your daughter die?' enquired the painter, with agitation.

'Two years ago; on the 13th of September. She died in the afternoon,
after a few days' illness.'

Mr H— pondered, but said nothing. The image of that fair young face
was engraven on his memory as with a diamond's point, and her strangely
prophetic words were now fulfilled.

A few weeks after, having completed a beautiful full-length portrait of
the young lady, he sent it to her father, and the likeness was declared, by
all who had ever seen her, to be perfect.

THE SECOND STORY

Among the friends of my family was a young Swiss lady, who, with an only brother, had been left an orphan in her childhood. She was brought up, as well as her brother, by an aunt; and the children, thus thrown very much upon each other, became very strongly attached. At the age of twenty-two the youth got some appointment in India, and the terrible day drew near when they must part. I need not describe the agony of persons so circumstanced. But the mode in which these two sought to mitigate the anguish of separation was singular. They agreed that if either should die before the young man's return, the dead should appear to the living.

The youth departed. The young lady by and by married a Scotch gentleman, and quitted her home, to be the light and ornament of his. She was a devoted wife, but she never forgot her brother. She corresponded with him regularly, and her brightest days in all the year were those which brought letters from India.

One cold winter's day, two or three years after her marriage, she was seated at work near a large bright fire, in her own bedroom upstairs. It was about midday, and her room was full of light. She was very busy, when some strange impulse caused her to raise her head and look round. The door was slightly open, and, near the large antique bed, stood a figure, which she, at a glance, recognised as that of her brother. With a cry of delight she started up, and ran forward to meet him, exclaiming, 'Oh, Henry! How could you surprise me so! You never told me you were coming!' But he waved his hand sadly, in a way that forbade approach, and she remained rooted to the spot. He advanced a step towards her, and said, in a low soft voice, 'Do you remember our agreement? I have come to fulfil it;' and approaching nearer he laid his hand on her wrist. It was icy cold, and the touch made her shiver. Her brother smiled, a faint sad smile, and, again waving his hand, turned and left the room.

When the lady recovered from a long swoon there was a mark on her wrist, which never left it to her dying day. The next mail from India brought a letter, informing her that her brother had died on the very day, and at the very hour, when he presented himself to her in her room.

THE THIRD STORY

Overhanging the waters of the Firth of Forth there lived, a good many years ago, a family of old standing in the kingdom of Fife: frank, hospitable and hereditary Jacobites. It consisted of the squire, or laird – a man well advanced in years – his wife, three sons and four daughters. The sons were sent out into the world, but not into the service of the reigning family. The daughters were all young and unmarried, and the eldest and the youngest were much attached to each other. They slept in the same room, shared the same bed, and had no secrets one from the other. It chanced that among the visitors to the old house there came a young naval officer, whose gun-brig often put in to the neighbouring harbours. He was well received, and between him and the elder of the two sisters a tender attachment sprang up.

But the prospect of such an alliance did not quite please the lady's mother, and, without being absolutely told that it should never take place, the lovers were advised to separate. The plea urged was that they could not then afford to marry, and that they must wait for better times. Those were times when parental authority – at all events in Scotland – was like the decree of fate, and the lady felt that she had nothing left to do but to say farewell to her lover. Not so he. He was a fine gallant fellow, and, taking the old lady at her word, he determined to do his utmost to push his worldly fortunes.

There was war at that time with some northern power – I think with Prussia – and the lover, who had interest at the Admiralty, applied to be sent to the Baltic. He obtained his wish. Nobody interfered to prevent the young people from taking a tender farewell of each other, and he full of hope, and she desponding, they parted. It was settled that he should write by every opportunity; and twice a week – on the post-days at the neighbouring village – the younger sister would mount her pony and ride in for letters. There was much hidden joy over every letter that arrived. And often and often the sisters would sit at the window a whole winter's night listening to the roar of the sea among the rocks, and hoping and praying that each light, as it shone far away, might be the signal-lamp hung at the masthead to apprise them that the gun-brig was coming. So weeks stole on in hope deferred, and there came a lull in the correspondence. Post-day after post-day brought no letters from the Baltic, and the agony of the sisters, especially of the betrothed, became almost unbearable.

They slept, as I have said, in the same room, and their window looked down well-nigh into the waters of the Firth. One night, the younger sister was awakened by the heavy moanings of the elder. They had taken to burning a candle in their room, and placing it in the window: thinking, poor girls, that it would serve as a beacon to the brig. She saw by its light that her sister was tossing about, and was greatly disturbed in her sleep. After some hesitation she determined to awaken the sleeper, who sprang up with a wild cry, and, pushing back her long hair with her hands, exclaimed, 'What have you done, what have you done!' Her sister tried to soothe her, and asked tenderly if anything had alarmed her. 'Alarmed!' she answered, still very wildly. 'No! But I saw him! He entered at that door, and came near the foot of the bed. He looked very pale, and his hair was wet. He was just going to speak to me, when you drove him away. Oh what have you done, what have you done!'

I do not believe that her lover's ghost really appeared, but the fact is certain that the next mail from the Baltic brought intelligence that the gun-brig had gone down in a gale of wind, with all on board.

THE FOURTH STORY

When my mother was a girl about eight or nine years old, and living in Switzerland, the Count R— of Holstein, coming to Switzerland for his health, took a house at Vevay, with the intention of remaining there for two or three years. He soon became acquainted with my mother's parents, and between him and them acquaintance ripened into friendship. They met constantly, and liked each other more and more. Knowing the count's intentions respecting his stay in Switzerland, my grandmother was much surprised by receiving from him one morning a short hurried note, informing her that urgent and unexpected business obliged him to return that very day to Germany. He added that he was very sorry to go, but that he must go; and he ended by bidding her farewell, and hoping they might meet again someday. He quitted Vevay that evening, and nothing more was heard of him or his mysterious business.

A few years after this departure, my grandmother and one of her sons went to spend some time at Hamburg. Count R—, hearing that they were there, went to see them, and brought them to his castle at Breitenburg, where they were to stay a few days. It was a wild but beautiful district, and the castle, a huge pile, was a relic of the feudal times, which, like most old places of the sort, was said to be haunted. Never having heard the story upon which this belief was founded, my grandmother entreated the count to tell it. After some little hesitation and demur, he consented: 'There is a room in this house,' he began, 'in which no one is ever able to sleep. Noises are heard in it continually, which have never been accounted for, and which sound like the ceaseless turning over and upsetting of furniture. I have had the room emptied, I have had the old floor taken up and a new one laid down, but nothing would stop the noises. At last, in despair, I have had it walled up. The story attached to the room is this.'

Some hundreds of years ago, there lived in this castle a countess, whose charity to the poor and kindness to all people were unbounded. She was known far and wide as 'the good Countess R—' and everybody loved her. The room in question was her room. One night, she was awakened from her sleep by a voice near her; and looking out of bed, she saw, by the faint light of her lamp, a little tiny man, about a foot in height, standing near her bedside. She was greatly surprised, but he spoke, and said, 'Good Countess of R—, I have come to ask you to be godmother to my child. Will you consent?' She said she would, and he told her that he would come and fetch her in a few days, to attend the christening; with those words he vanished out of the room.

Next morning, recollecting the incidents of the night, the countess came to the conclusion that she had had an odd dream, and thought no more of the matter. But, about a fortnight afterwards, when she had well-nigh forgotten the dream, she was again roused at the same hour and by the same small individual, who said he had come to claim the fulfilment of her promise. She rose, dressed herself, and followed her tiny guide down the stairs of the castle. In the centre of the courtyard there was, and still is, a large square well, very deep, and stretching underneath the building nobody knew how far. Having reached the side of this well, the little man blindfolded the countess, and bidding her not fear, but follow him, descended some unknown stairs. This was for the countess a strange and novel position, and she felt uncomfortable; but she determined at all hazards to see the adventure to the end, and descended bravely. They reached the bottom, and when her guide removed the bandage from her eyes, she found herself in a room full of small people like himself. The christening was performed, the countess stood godmother, and at the conclusion of the ceremony, as the lady was about to say goodbye, the mother of the baby took a handful of wood shavings which lay in a corner, and put them into her visitor's apron.

'You have been very kind, good Countess of R—,' she said, 'in coming to be godmother to my child, and your kindness shall not go unrewarded. When you rise tomorrow, these shavings will have turned into metal, and out of them you must immediately get made two fishes and thirty silberlingen (a German coin). When you get them back, take great care of them, for so long as they all remain in your family everything will prosper with you; but, if one of them ever gets lost, then you will have troubles without end.' The countess thanked her, and bade them all farewell. Having again covered her eyes, the little man led her out of the well, and landed her safe in her own courtyard, where he removed the bandage, and she never saw him more.

Next morning the countess awoke with a confused notion of some extraordinary dream. While at her toilet, she recollected all the incidents quite plainly, and racked her brain for some cause which might account for it. She was so employed when, stretching out her hand for her apron, she was astounded to find it tied up, and, within the folds, a number of metal shavings. How came they there? Was it a reality? Had she not dreamed of the little man and the christening? She told the story to the members of her family at breakfast, who all agreed that whatever the token might mean, it should not be disregarded. It was therefore settled that the fishes and the silberlingen should be made, and carefully kept among the archives of the family. Time passed; everything prospered with the house of R——. The King of Denmark loaded them with honours and benefits, and gave the count high office in his household. For many years all went well with them.

Suddenly, to the consternation of the family, one of the fishes disappeared, and though strenuous efforts were made to discover what had become of it, they all failed. From this time everything went wrong. The count then living, had two sons; while out hunting together, one killed the other; whether accidentally or not, is uncertain, but, as the youths were known to be perpetually disagreeing, the case seemed doubtful. This was the beginning of sorrows. The king, hearing what had occurred, thought it necessary to deprive the count of the office he held. Other misfortunes followed. The family fell into discredit. Their lands were sold, or forfeited to the crown; till little was left but the old castle of Breitenburg and the narrow domain which surrounded it. This deteriorating process went on through two or three generations, and, to add to all other misfortunes, there was always in the family one mad member.

*   *   *

'And now,' continued the count, 'comes the strange part of the mystery. I had never placed much faith in these mysterious little relics, and I regarded the story in connection with them as a fable. I should have continued in this belief, but for a very extraordinary circumstance. You remember my sojourn in Switzerland a few years ago, and how abruptly it terminated? Well. Just before leaving Holstein, I had received a curious wild letter from some knight in Norway, saying that he was very ill, but that he could not die without first seeing and conversing with me. I thought the man mad, because I had never heard of him before, and he could have no possible business to transact with me. So, throwing the letter aside, I did not give it another thought.

'My correspondent, however, was not satisfied. He wrote again. My agent, who in my absence opened and answered my letters, told him that I was in Switzerland for my health, and that if he had anything to say, he had better say it in writing, as I could not possibly travel so far as Norway.

'This, however, did not satisfy the knight. He wrote a third time, beseeching me to come to him, and declaring that what he had to tell me was of the utmost importance to us both. My agent was so struck by the earnest tone of the letter, that he forwarded it to me: at the same time advising me not to refuse the entreaty. This was the cause of my sudden departure from Vevay, and I shall never cease to rejoice that I did not persist in my refusal.

'I had a long and weary journey, and once or twice I felt sorely tempted to stop short, but some strange impulse kept me going. I had to traverse well-nigh the whole of Norway; often for days on horseback, riding over wild moorland, heathery bogs, mountains and crags and lonely places, and ever at my left the rocky coast, lashed and torn by the surging waters.

'At last, after some fatigue and hardship, I reached the village named in the letter, on the northern coast of Norway. The knight's castle – a large round tower – was built on a small island off the coast, and communicated with the land by a drawbridge. I arrived there, late at night, and must admit that I felt misgivings when I crossed the bridge by the lurid glare of torchlight, and heard the dark waters surging under me. The gate was opened by a man, who as soon as I entered closed it behind me. My horse was taken from me, and I was led up to the knight's room. It was a small circular apartment, nearly at the top of the tower, and scantily furnished. There, on a bed, lay the old knight, evidently at the point of death. He tried to rise as I entered, and gave me such a look of gratitude and relief that it repaid me for my pains.

' "I cannot thank you sufficiently, Count of R—," said he, "for granting my request. Had I been in a state to travel I should have gone to you; but that was impossible, and I could not die without first seeing you. My business is short, though important. Do you know this?" And he drew from under his pillow, my long-lost fish. Of course I knew it; and he went on. "How long it has been in this house, I do not know, nor by what means it came here, nor, till quite lately, was I at all aware to whom it rightfully belonged. It did not come here in my time, nor in my father's time, and who brought it is a mystery. When I fell ill, and my recovery was pronounced to be impossible, I heard one night, a voice telling me that I should not die till I had restored the fish to the Count R— of Breitenburg. I did not know you: I had never heard of you; and at first I took no heed of the voice. But it came again, every night, until at length in despair I wrote to you. Then the voice stopped. Your answer came, and again I heard the warning, that I must not die till you arrived. At last I heard that you were coming, and I have no language in which to thank you for your kindness. I feel sure I could not have died without seeing you."

'That night the old man died. I waited to bury him, and then returned home, bringing my recovered treasure with me. It was carefully restored to its place. That same year, my eldest brother, whom you know to have been the inmate of a lunatic asylum for years, died, and I became the owner of this place. Last year, to my great surprise, I received a kind letter from the King of Denmark, restoring to me the office which my fathers once held. This year, I have been named governor to his eldest son, and the king has returned a great part of the confiscated property; so that the sun of prosperity seems to shine once more upon the house of Breitenburg. Not long ago, I sent one of the silberlingen to Paris, and another to Vienna, in order that they might be analysed, and the metal of which they are composed made known to me; but no one is able to decide that point.'

Thus ended the Count of R—'s story, after which he led his eager listener to the place where these precious articles were kept, and showed them to her.

THE PORTRAIT-PAINTER'S STORY

There was lately published in these pages* a paper entitled 'Four Ghost Stories'. The first of those stories related the strange experience of a well-known English artist, Mr H—. On the publication of that account, Mr H— himself addressed the Editor of this journal – to his great surprise – and forwarded to him his own narrative of the occurrences in question. As Mr H— wrote, without any concealment, in his own name in full, and from his own studio in London, and as there was no possible doubt of his being a real existing person and a responsible gentleman, it became a duty to read his communication attentively. And great injustice having been unconsciously done to it, in the version published as the first of the 'Four Ghost Stories', it follows here exactly as received. It is, of course, published with the sanction and authority of Mr H—, and Mr H— has himself corrected the proofs. Entering on no theory of our own towards the explanation of any part of this remarkable narrative, we hare prevailed on Mr H— to present it without any introductory remarks whatever. It only remains to add that no one has for a moment stood between us and Mr H— in this matter. The whole communication is at first hand. On seeing the article, 'Four Ghost Stories', Mr H— frankly and good humouredly wrote, 'I am the Mr H—, the living man, of whom mention is made; how my story has been picked up, I do not know, but it is correctly told. I have it by me, written by myself, and here it is.'

*   *   *

I am a painter. One morning in May 1858, I was seated in my studio at my usual occupation. At an earlier hour than that at which visits are usually made, I received one from a friend whose acquaintance I had made some year or two previously in Richmond Barracks, Dublin. My acquaintance was a captain in the 3rd West York Militia, and from the hospitable manner in which I had been received while a guest with that regiment, as well as from the intimacy that existed between us personally, it was incumbent on me to offer my visitor suitable refreshments; consequently, two o'clock found us well occupied in conversation, cigars, and a decanter of sherry. About that hour a ring at the bell reminded me of an engagement I had made with a model, or a young person who, having a pretty face and neck, earned a livelihood by sitting for artists. Not being in the humour for work, I arranged with her to come on the following day, promising, of course, to remunerate her for her loss of time, and she went away. In about five minutes she returned, and, speaking to me privately, stated that she had looked forward to the money for the day's sitting, and would be inconvenienced by the want of it; would I let her have a part? There being no difficulty on this point, she again went. Close to the street in which I live there is another of a very similar name, and persons who are not familiar with my address often go to it by mistake. The model's way lay directly through it, and, on arriving there, she was accosted by a lady and gentleman, who asked if she could inform them where I lived? They had forgotten my right address, and were endeavouring to find me by enquiring of persons whom they met; in a few more minutes they were shown into my room.

My new visitors were strangers to me. They had seen a portrait I had painted, and wished for likenesses of themselves and their children. The price I named did not deter them, and they asked to look round the studio to select the style and size they should prefer. My friend of the 3rd West York, with infinite address and humour, took upon himself the office of showman, dilating on the merits of the respective works in a manner that the diffidence that is expected in a professional man when speaking of his own productions would not have allowed me to adopt. The inspection proving satisfactory, they asked whether I could paint the pictures at their house in the country, and there being no difficulty on this point, an engagement was made for the following autumn, subject to my writing to fix the time when I might be able to leave town for the purpose. This being adjusted, the gentleman gave me his card, and they left. Shortly afterwards my friend went also, and on looking for the first time at the card left by the strangers, I was somewhat disappointed to find that though it contained the name of Mr and Mrs Kirkbeck, there was no address. I tried to find it by looking at the Court Guide, but it contained no such name, so I put the card in my writing-desk, and forgot for a time the entire transaction.

Autumn came, and with it a series of engagements I had made in the north of England. Towards the end of September 1858, I was one of a dinner-party at a country-house on the confines of Yorkshire and Lincolnshire. Being a stranger to the family, it was by a mere accident that I was at the house at all. I had arranged to pass a day and a night with a friend in the neighbourhood who was intimate at the house, and had received an invitation, and the dinner occurring on the evening in question, I had been asked to accompany him. The party was a numerous one, and as the meal approached its termination, and was about to subside into the dessert, the conversation became general. I should here mention that my hearing is defective, at some times more so than at others, and on this particular evening I was extra deaf – so much so that the conversation only reached me in the form of a continued din. At one instant, however, I heard a word distinctly pronounced, though it was uttered by a person at a considerable distance from me, and that word was Kirkbeck. In the business of the London season I had forgotten all about the visitors of the spring, who had left their card without the address. The word reaching me under such circumstances, arrested my attention, and immediately recalled the transaction to my remembrance. On the first opportunity that offered, I asked a person whom I was conversing with if a family of the name in question was resident in the neighbourhood. I was told in reply that a Mr Kirkbeck lived at A—, at the farther end of the county. The next morning I wrote to this person, saying that I believed he called at my studio in the spring, and had made an arrangement with me, which I was prevented fulfilling by there being no address on his card; furthermore, that I should shortly be in his neighbourhood on my return from the north, but should I be mistaken in addressing him, I begged he would not trouble himself to reply to my note. I gave as my address, The Post Office, York. On applying there three days afterwards, I received a note from Mr Kirkbeck, stating that he was very glad he had heard from me, and that if I would call on my return, he would arrange about the pictures; he also told me to write a day before I proposed coming, that he might not otherwise engage himself. It was ultimately arranged that I should go to his house the succeeding Saturday, stay till Monday morning, transact afterwards what matters I had to attend to in London, and return in a fortnight to execute the commissions.

The day having arrived for my visit, directly after breakfast I took my place in the morning train from York to London. The train would stop at Doncaster, and after that at Retford junction, where I should have to get out in order to take the line through Lincoln to A—. The day was cold, wet, foggy, and in every way as disagreeable as I have ever known a day to be in an English October. The carriage in which I was seated had no other occupant than myself, but at Doncaster a lady got in. My place was back to the engine and next to the door. As that is considered the ladies' seat, I offered it to her; she, however, very graciously declined it, and took the corner opposite, saying, in a very agreeable voice, that she liked to feel the breeze on her cheek The next few minutes were occupied in locating herself. There was the cloak to be spread under her, the skirts of the dress to be arranged, the gloves to be tightened, and such other trifling arrangements of plumage as ladies are wont to make before settling themselves comfortably at church or elsewhere, the last and most important being the placing back over her hat the veil that concealed her features. I could then see that the lady was young, certainly not more than two- or three-and-twenty; but being moderately tall, rather robust in make, and decided in expression, she might have been two or three years younger. I suppose that her complexion would be termed a medium one: her hair being of a bright brown, or auburn, while her eyes and rather decidedly marked eyebrows were nearly black. The colour of her cheek was of that pale transparent hue that sets off to such advantage large expressive eyes, and an equable firm expression of mouth. On the whole, the ensemble was rather handsome than beautiful, her expression having that agreeable depth and harmony about it that rendered her face and features, though not strictly regular, infinitely more attractive than if they had been modelled upon the strictest rules of symmetry.

It is no small advantage on a wet day and a dull long journey to have an agreeable companion, one who can converse, and whose conversation has sufficient substance in it to make one forget the length and the dreariness of the journey. In this respect I had no deficiency to complain of, the lady being decidedly and agreeably conversational. When she had settled herself to her satisfaction, she asked to be allowed to look at my *Bradshaw*, and not being a proficient in that difficult work, she requested my aid in ascertaining at what time the train passed through Retford again on its way back from London to York. The conversation turned afterwards on general topics, and, somewhat to my surprise, she led it into such particular subjects as I might be supposed to be more especially familiar with; indeed, I could not avoid remarking that her entire manner, while it was anything but forward, was that of one who had either known me personally or by report. There was in her manner a kind of confidential reliance when she listened to me that is not usually accorded to a stranger, and sometimes she actually seemed to refer to different circumstances with which I had been connected in times past. After about three-quarters of an hour's conversation the train arrived at Retford, where I was to change carriages. On my alighting and wishing her good-morning, she made a slight movement of the hand as if she meant me to shake it, and on my doing so she said, by way of adieu, 'I dare say we shall meet again'; to which I replied, 'I hope that we shall all meet again,' and so parted, she going on the line towards London, and I through Lincolnshire to A——. The remainder of the journey was cold, wet and dreary. I missed the agreeable conversation, and tried to supply its place with a book I had brought with me from York, and *The Times* newspaper, which I had procured at Retford. But the most disagreeable journey comes to an end at last, and half-past five in the evening found me at the termination of mine. A carriage was waiting for me at the station, where Mr Kirkbeck was also expected by the same train, but as he did not appear it was concluded he would come by the next – half an hour later, accordingly, the carriage drove away with myself only.

The family being from home at the moment, and the dinner hour being seven, I went at once to my room to unpack and to dress; having completed these operations, I descended to the drawing-room. It probably wanted some time to the dinner hour, as the lamps were not lighted, but in their place a large blazing fire threw a flood of light into every corner of the room, and more especially over a lady who, dressed in deep black, was standing by the chimney-piece warming a very handsome foot on the edge of the fender. Her face being turned away from the door by which I had entered, I did not at first see her features; on my advancing into the middle of the room, however, the foot was immediately withdrawn, and she turned round to accost me, when, to my profound astonishment, I perceived that it was none other than my companion in the railway carriage. She betrayed no surprise at seeing me; on the contrary, with one of those agreeable joyous expressions that make the plainest woman appear beautiful, she accosted me with, 'I said we should meet again.'

My bewilderment at the moment almost deprived me of utterance. I knew of no railway or other means by which she could have come. I had certainly left her in a London train, and had seen it start, and the only conceivable way in which she could have come was by going on to Peterborough and then returning by a branch to A—, a circuit of about ninety miles. As soon as my surprise enabled me to speak, I said that I wished I had come by the same conveyance as herself.

'That would have been rather difficult,' she rejoined.

At this moment the servant came with the lamps, and informed me that his master had just arrived and would be down in a few minutes.

The lady took up a book containing some engravings, and having singled one out (a portrait of Lady —), asked me to look at it well and tell her whether I thought it like her.

I was engaged trying to get up an opinion, when Mr and Mrs Kirkbeck entered, and shaking me heartily by the hand, apologised for not being at home to receive me; the gentleman ending by requesting me to take Mrs Kirkbeck in to dinner.

The lady of the house having taken my arm, we marched on. I certainly hesitated a moment to allow Mr Kirkbeck to pass on first with the mysterious lady in black, but Mrs Kirkbeck not seeming to understand it, we passed on at once. The dinner-party consisting of us four only, we fell into our respective places at the table without difficulty, the mistress and master of the house at the top and bottom, the lady in black and myself on each side. The dinner passed much as is usual on such occasions. I, having to play the guest, directed my conversation principally, if not exclusively, to my host and hostess, and I cannot call to mind that I or anyone else once addressed the lady opposite. Seeing this, and remembering something that looked like a slight want of attention to her on coming into the dining-room, I at once concluded that she was the governess. I observed, however, that she made an excellent dinner; she seemed to appreciate both the beef and the tart as well as a glass of claret afterwards; probably she had had no luncheon, or the journey had given her an appetite.

The dinner ended, the ladies retired, and after the usual port, Mr Kirkbeck and I joined them in the drawing-room. By this time, however, a much larger party had assembled. Brothers and sisters-in-law had come in from their residences in the neighbourhood, and several children, with Miss Hardwick, their governess, were also introduced to me. I saw at once that my supposition as to the lady in black being the governess was incorrect. After passing the time necessarily occupied in complimenting the children, and saying something to the different persons to whom I was introduced, I found myself again engaged in conversation with the lady of the railway carriage, and as the topic of the evening had referred principally to portrait-painting, she continued the subject.

'Do you think you could paint my portrait?' the lady enquired.

'Yes, I think I could, if I had the opportunity.'

'Now, look at my face well; do you think you should recollect my features?'

'Yes, I am sure I should never forget your features.'

'Of course I might have expected you to say that; but do you think you could do me from recollection?'

'Well, if it be necessary, I will try: but can't you give me any sittings?'

'No, quite impossible; it could not be. It is said that the print I showed to you before dinner is like me; do you think so?'

'Not much,' I replied: 'it has not your expression. If you can give me only one sitting, it would be better than none.'

'No; I don't see how it could be.'

The evening being by this time rather far advanced, and the chamber candles being brought in, on the plea of being rather tired, she shook me heartily by the hand, and wished me good-night. My mysterious acquaintance caused me no small pondering during the night. I had never been introduced to her, I had not seen her speak to anyone during the entire evening, not even to wish them good-night – how she got across the country was an inexplicable mystery. Then, why did she wish me to paint her from memory, and why could she not give me even one sitting? Finding the difficulties of a solution to these questions rather increase upon me, I made up my mind to defer further consideration of them till breakfast-time, when I supposed the matter would receive some elucidation.

The breakfast now came, but with it no lady in black. The breakfast over, we went to church, came home to luncheon, and so on through the day, but still no lady, neither any reference to her. I then concluded that she must be some relative, who had gone away early in the morning to visit another member of the family living close by. I was much puzzled, however, by no reference whatever being made to her, and finding no opportunity of leading any part of my conversation with the family towards the subject, I went to bed the second night more puzzled than ever. On the servant coming in in the morning, I ventured to ask him the name of the lady who dined at the table on the Saturday evening, to which he answered: 'A lady, sir? No lady, only Mrs Kirkbeck, sir.'

'Yes, the lady that sat opposite me dressed in black?'

'Perhaps, Miss Hardwick, the governess, sir?'

'No, not Miss Hardwick; she came down afterwards.'

'No lady as I see, sir.'

'Oh dear me, yes, the lady dressed in black that was in the drawing-room when I arrived, before Mr Kirkbeck came home?'

The man looked at me with surprise as if he doubted my sanity, and only answered, 'I never see any lady, sir,' and then left.

The mystery now appeared more impenetrable than ever – I thought it over in every possible aspect, but could come to no conclusion upon it. Breakfast was early that morning, in order to allow of my catching the morning train to London. The same cause also slightly hurried us, and allowed no time for conversation beyond that having direct reference to the business that brought me there; so, after arranging to return to paint the portraits on that day three weeks, I made my adieus, and took my departure for town.

It is only necessary for me to refer to my second visit to that house in order to state that I was assured most positively, both by Mr and Mrs Kirkbeck, that no fourth person dined at the table on the Saturday evening in question. Their recollection was clear on the subject, as they had debated whether they should ask Miss Hardwick, the governess, to take the vacant seat, but had decided not to do so; neither could they recall to mind any such person as I described in the whole circle of their acquaintance.

Some weeks passed. It was close upon Christmas. The light of a short winter day was drawing to a close, and I was seated at my table, writing letters for the evening post. My back was towards the folding-doors leading into the room in which my visitors usually waited. I had been engaged some minutes in writing, when, without hearing or seeing anything, I became aware that a person had come through the folding-doors, and was then standing beside me. I turned, and beheld the lady of the railway carriage. I suppose that my manner indicated that I was somewhat startled, as the lady, after the usual salutation, said, 'Pardon me for disturbing you. You did not hear me come in.' Her manner, though it was more quiet and subdued than I had known it before, was hardly to be termed grave, still less sorrowful. There was a change, but it was that kind of change only which may often be observed from the frank impulsiveness of an intelligent young lady, to the composure of self-possession of that same young lady when she is either betrothed or has recently become a matron. She asked me whether I had made any attempt at a likeness of her. I was obliged to confess that I had not. She regretted it much, as she wished one for her father. She had brought an engraving (a portrait of Lady M— A—) with her that she thought would assist me. It was like the one she had asked my opinion upon at the house in Lincolnshire. It had always been considered very like her, and she would leave it with me. Then (putting her hand impressively on my arm) she added, 'I really would be most thankful and grateful to you if you would do it' (and, if I recollect rightly, she added), '*as much depended on it.*'

Seeing she was so much in earnest, I took up my sketchbook, and by the dim light that was still remaining began to make a rapid pencil sketch of her. On observing my doing so, however, instead of giving me what assistance she was able, she turned away under pretence of looking at the pictures around the room, occasionally passing from one to another so as to enable me to catch a momentary glimpse of her features. In this manner I made two hurried but rather expressive sketches of her, which being all that the declining light would allow me to do, I shut my book, and she prepared to leave. This time, instead of the usual, 'Good-morning,' she wished me an impressively pronounced, 'Goodbye,' firmly holding rather than shaking my hand while she said it. I accompanied her to the door, outside of which she seemed rather to fade into the darkness than to pass through it. But I refer this impression to my own fancy.

I immediately enquired of the servant why she had not announced the visitor to me. She stated that she was not aware there had been one, and that anyone who had entered must have done so when she had left the street door open about half an hour previously, while she went across the road for a moment.

Soon after this occurred I had to fulfil an engagement at a house near Bosworth Field, in Leicestershire. I left town on a Friday, having sent some pictures, that were too large to take with me, by the luggage train a week previously, in order that they might be at the house on my arrival and occasion me no loss of time in waiting for them. On getting to the house, however, I found that they had not been heard of, and on enquiring at the station, it was stated that a case similar to the one I described had passed through and gone on to Leicester, where it probably still was. It being Friday, and past the hour for the post, there was no possibility of getting a letter to Leicester before Monday morning, as the luggage office would be closed there on the Sunday; consequently, I could in no case expect the arrival of the pictures before the succeeding Tuesday or Wednesday. The loss of three days would be a serious one; therefore, to avoid it, I suggested to my host that I should leave immediately to transact some business in South Staffordshire, as I should be obliged to attend to it before my return to town, and if I could see about it in the vacant interval thus thrown upon my hands, it would be saving me some amount of time after my visit to his house was concluded. This arrangement meeting with his ready assent, I hastened to the Atherstone station on the Trent Valley Railway. By reference to *Bradshaw*, I found that my route lay through Litchfield, where I was to change carriages for S—, in Staffordshire. I was just in time for the train that would put me down at Litchfield at eight in the evening, and a train was announced to start from Litchfield for S— at ten minutes after eight, answering, as I concluded, to the train in which I was about to travel. I therefore saw no reason to doubt but that I should get to my journey's end the same night; but on my arriving at Litchfield. I found my plans entirely frustrated. The train arrived punctually, and I got out intending to wait on the platform for the arrival of the carriages for the other line. I found, however, that though the two lines crossed at Litchfield, they did not communicate with each other, the Litchfield station on the Trent Valley line being on one side of the town, and the Litchfield station on the South Staffordshire line on the other. I also found that there was not time to get to the other station so as to catch the train the same evening; indeed, the train had just that moment passed on a lower level beneath my feet, and to get to the other side of the town, where it would stop for two minutes only, was out of the question. There was, therefore, nothing for it but to put up at the Swan Hotel for the night. I have an especial dislike to passing an evening at an hotel in a country town. Dinner at such places I never take, as I had rather go without than have such as I am likely to get. Books are never to be had, the country newspapers do not interest me. *The Times* I have spelt through on my journey. The society I am likely to meet have few ideas in common with myself. Under such circumstances, I usually resort to a meat tea to while away the time, and when that is over, occupy myself in writing letters.

This was the first time I had been in Litchfield, and while waiting for the tea, it occurred to me how, on two occasions within the past six months, I had been on the point of coming to that very place, at one time to execute a small commission for an old acquaintance, resident there, and another, to get the materials for a picture I proposed painting of an incident in the early life of Dr Johnson. I should have come on each of these occasions had not other arrangements diverted my purpose and caused me to postpone the journey indefinitely. The thought, however, would occur to me, 'How strange! Here I am at Litchfield, by no intention of my own, though I have twice tried to get here and been balked.' When I had done tea, I thought I might as well write to an acquaintance I had known some years previously, and who lived in the Cathedral Close, asking him to come and pass an hour or two with me. Accordingly, I rang for the waitress and asked, 'Does Mr Lute live in Lichfield?'

'Yes, sir.'

'Cathedral Close?'

'Yes, sir.'

'Can I send a note to him?'

'Yes, sir.'

I wrote the note, saying where I was, and asking if he would come for an hour or two and talk over old matters. The note was taken; in about twenty minutes a person of gentlemanly appearance, and in what might be termed advanced middle age, entered the room with my note in his hand, saying that I had sent him a letter, he presumed, by mistake, as he did not know my name. Seeing instantly that he was not the person I intended to write to, I apologised, and asked whether there was not another Mr Lute living in Litchfield?

'No, there was none other.'

Certainly, I rejoined, my friend must have given me his right address, for I had written to him on other occasions here. He was a fair young man, he succeeded to an estate in consequence of his uncle having been killed while hunting with the Quorn hounds, and he married about two years since a lady of the name of Fairbairn.

The stranger very composedly replied, 'You are speaking of Mr Clyne; he did live in the Cathedral Close, but he has now gone away.'

The stranger was right, and in my surprise I exclaimed, 'Oh dear, to be sure, that is the name; what could have made me address you instead? I really beg your pardon; my writing to you, and unconsciously guessing your name, is one of the most extraordinary and unaccountable things I ever did. Pray pardon me.'

He continued very quietly, 'There is no need of apology; it happens that you are the very person I most wished to see. You are a painter, and I want you to paint a portrait of my daughter; can you come to my house immediately for the purpose?'

I was rather surprised at finding myself known by him, and the turn matters had taken being so entirely unexpected, I did not at the moment feel inclined to undertake the business; I therefore explained how I was situate, stating that I had only the next day and Monday at my disposal. He, however, pressed me so earnestly that I arranged to do what I could for him in those two days, and having put up my baggage, and arranged other matters, I accompanied him to his house. During the walk home he scarcely spoke a word, but his taciturnity seemed only a continuance of his quiet composure at the inn. On our arrival he introduced me to his daughter Maria, and then left the room. Maria Lute was a fair and a decidedly handsome girl of about fifteen; her manner was, however, in advance of her years, and evinced that self-possession, and, in the favourable sense of the term, that womanliness, that is only seen at such an early age in girls that have been left motherless, or from other causes thrown much on their own resources.

She had evidently not been informed of the purpose of my coming, and only knew that I was to stay there for the night; she therefore excused herself for a few moments, that she might give the requisite directions to the servants as to preparing my room. When she returned, she told me that I should not see her father again that evening, the state of his health having obliged him to retire for the night, but she hoped I should be able to see him sometime on the morrow. In the meantime, she hoped I would make myself quite at home, and call for anything I wanted. She, herself, was sitting in the drawing-room, but perhaps I should like to smoke and take something; if so, there was a fire in the housekeeper's room, and she would come and sit with me, as she expected the medical attendant every minute, and he would probably stay to smoke, and take something. As the little lady seemed to recommend this course, I readily complied. I did not smoke, or take anything, but sat down by the fire, when she immediately joined me. She conversed well and readily, and with a command of language singular in a person so young. Without being disagreeably inquisitive, or putting any question to me, she seemed desirous of learning the business that had brought me to the house. I told her that her father wished me to paint either her portrait or that of a sister of hers, if she had one.

She remained silent and thoughtful for a moment, and then seemed to comprehend it at once. She told me that a sister of hers, an only one, to whom her father was devotedly attached, died near four months previously; that her father had never yet recovered from the shock of her death. He had often expressed the most earnest wish for a portrait of her; indeed, it was his one thought, and she hoped, if something of the kind could be done, it would improve his health. Here she hesitated, stammered, and burst into tears. After a while she continued, 'It is no use hiding from you what you must very soon be aware of. Papa is insane – he has been so ever since dear Caroline was buried. He says he is always seeing dear Caroline, and he is subject to fearful delusions. The doctor says he cannot tell how much worse he may be, and that everything dangerous, like knives or razors, are to be kept out of his reach. It was necessary you should not see him again this evening, as he was unable to converse properly, and I fear the same may be the case tomorrow; but perhaps you can stay over Sunday, and I may be able to assist you in doing what he wishes.' I asked whether they had any materials for making a likeness – a photograph, a sketch, or anything else for me to go from. No, they had nothing. 'Could she describe her clearly?' She thought she could; and there was a print that was very much like her, but she had mislaid it. I mentioned that with such disadvantages, and in such an absence of materials, I did not anticipate a satisfactory result. I had painted portraits under such circumstances, but their success much depended upon the powers of description of the persons who were to assist me by their recollection; in some instances I had attained a certain amount of success, but in most the result was quite a failure. The medical attendant came, but I did not see him. I learnt, however, that he ordered a strict watch to be kept on his patient till he came again the next morning. Seeing the state of things, and how much the little lady had to attend to, I retired early to bed. The next morning I heard that her father was decidedly better; he had enquired earnestly on waking whether I was really in the house, and at breakfast-time he sent down to say that he hoped nothing would prevent my making an attempt at the portrait immediately, and he expected to be able to see me in the course of the day.

Directly after breakfast I set to work, aided by such description as the sister could give me. I tried again and again, but without success, or, indeed, the least prospect of it. The features, I was told, were separately like, but the expression was not. I toiled on the greater part of the day with no better result. The different studies I made were taken up to the invalid, but the same answer was always returned – no resemblance. I had exerted myself to the utmost, and, in fact, was not a little fatigued by so doing – a circumstance that the little lady evidently noticed, as she expressed herself most grateful for the interest she could see I took in the matter, and referred the unsuccessful result entirely to her want of powers of description. She also said it was so provoking. She had a print – a portrait of a lady – that was so like, but it had gone – she had missed it from her book for three weeks past. It was the more disappointing, as she was sure it would have been of such great assistance. I asked if she could tell me who the print was of, as if I knew, I could easily procure one in London. She answered, Lady M— A—. Immediately the name was uttered the whole scene of the lady of the railway carriage presented itself to me. I had my sketchbook in my portmanteau upstairs, and, by a fortunate chance, fixed in it was the print in question, with the two pencil sketches. I instantly brought them down, and showed them to Maria Lute. She looked at them for a moment, turned her eyes full upon me, and said slowly, and with something like fear in her manner, 'Where did you get these?' Then quicker, and without waiting for my answer, 'Let me take them instantly to papa.' She was away ten minutes, or more; when she returned, her father came with her. He did not wait for salutations, but said, in a tone and manner I had not observed in him before, 'I was right all the time; it was you that I saw with her, and these sketches are from her, and from no one else. I value them more than all my possessions, except this dear child.' The daughter also assured me that the print I had brought to the house must be the one taken from the book about three weeks before, in proof of which she pointed out to me the gum marks at the back, which exactly corresponded with those left on the blank leaf. From the moment the father saw these sketches his mental health returned.

I was not allowed to touch either of the pencil drawings in the sketchbook, as it was feared I might injure them; but an oil picture from them was commenced immediately, the father sitting by me hour after hour, directing my touches, conversing rationally, and indeed cheerfully, while he did so. He avoided direct reference to his delusions, but from time to time led the conversation to the manner in which I had originally obtained the sketches. The doctor came in the evening, and, after extolling the particular treatment he had adopted, pronounced his patient decidedly, and he believed permanently, improved.

The next day being Sunday, we all went to church. The father, for the first time since his bereavement. During a walk which he took with me after luncheon, he again approached the subject of the sketches, and after some seeming hesitation as to whether he should confide in me or not, said, 'Your writing to me by name, from the inn at Litchfield, was one of those inexplicable circumstances that I suppose it is impossible to clear up. I knew you, however, directly I saw you; when those about me considered that my intellect was disordered, and that I spoke incoherently, it was only because I saw things that they did not. Since her death, I know, with a certainty that nothing will ever disturb, that at different times I have been in the actual and visible presence of my dear daughter that is gone – oftener, indeed, just after her death than latterly. Of the many times that this has occurred, I distinctly remember once seeing her in a railway carriage, speaking to a person seated opposite; who that person was I could not ascertain, as my position seemed to be immediately behind him. I next saw her at a dinner-table, with others, and amongst those others unquestionably I saw yourself. I afterwards learnt that at that time I was considered to be in one of my longest and most violent paroxysms, as I continued to see her speaking to you, in the midst of a large assembly, for some hours. Again I saw her, standing by your side, while you were engaged in either writing or drawing. I saw her once again afterwards, but the next time I saw you was in the inn parlour.'

The picture was proceeded with the next day, and on the day after the face was completed, and I afterwards brought it with me to London to finish.

I have often seen Mr Lute since that period; his health is perfectly re-established, and his manner and conversation are as cheerful as can be expected within a few years of so great a bereavement.

The portrait now hangs in his bedroom, with the print and the two sketches by the side, and written beneath is: 'C. L., 13th September 1858, aged 22'.

THE SEVEN TRAVELLERS

In the Old City of Rochester

Strictly speaking, there were only six poor travellers; but, being a traveller myself, though an idle one, and being withal as poor as I hope to be, I brought the number up to seven. This word of explanation is due at once, for what says the inscription over the quaint old door?

RICHARD WATTS, Esq.
by his Will, dated 22 Aug. 1579,
founded this Charity
for Six poor Travellers,
who not being ROGUES, or PROCTORS,
May receive gratis for one Night,
Lodging, Entertainment,
and Fourpence each.

It was in the ancient little city of Rochester in Kent, of all the good days in the year upon a Christmas Eve, that I stood reading this inscription over the quaint old door in question. I had been wandering about the neighbouring cathedral, and had seen the tomb of Richard Watts, with the effigy of worthy Master Richard starting out of it like a ship's figurehead; and I had felt that I could do no less, as I gave the verger his fee, than enquire the way to Watts's Charity. The way being very short and very plain, I had come prosperously to the inscription and the quaint old door.

'Now,' said I to myself, as I looked at the knocker, 'I know I am not a proctor; I wonder whether I am a rogue!'

Upon the whole, though conscience reproduced two or three pretty faces which might have had smaller attraction for a moral Goliath than they had had for me, who am but a Tom Thumb in that way, I came to the conclusion that I was not a rogue. So, beginning to regard the establishment as in some sort my property, bequeathed to me and divers co-legatees, share and share alike, by the Worshipful Master Richard Watts, I stepped backward into the road to survey my inheritance.

I found it to be a clean white house, of a staid and venerable air, with the quaint old door already three times mentioned (an arched door), choice little long low lattice-windows, and a roof of three gables. The silent High Street of Rochester is full of gables, with old beams and timbers carved into strange faces. It is oddly garnished with a queer old clock that projects over the pavement out of a grave red brick building, as if time carried on business there, and hung out his sign. Sooth to say, he did an active stroke of work in Rochester, in the old days of the Romans, and the Saxons, and the Normans; and down to the times of King John, when the rugged castle – I will not undertake to say how many hundreds of years old then – was abandoned to the centuries of weather which have so defaced the dark apertures in its walls, that the ruin looks as if the rooks and daws had pecked its eyes out.

I was very well pleased, both with my property and its situation. While I was yet surveying it with growing content, I espied, at one of the upper lattices which stood open, a decent body, of a wholesome matronly appearance, whose eyes I caught inquiringly addressed to mine. They said so plainly, 'Do you wish to see the house?' that I answered aloud, 'Yes, if you please.' And within a minute the old door opened, and I bent my head, and went down two steps into the entry.

'This,' said the matronly presence, ushering me into a low room on the right, 'is where the travellers sit by the fire, and cook what bits of suppers they buy with their fourpences.'

'O! Then they have no entertainment?' said I. For the inscription over the outer door was still running in my head, and I was mentally repeating, in a kind of tune, 'Lodging, entertainment, and fourpence each.'

'They have a fire provided for 'em,' returned the matron – a mighty civil person, not, as I could make out, overpaid; 'and these cooking utensils. And this what's painted on a board is the rules for their behaviour. They have their fourpences when they get their tickets from the steward over the way – for I don't admit 'em myself, they must get their tickets first – and sometimes one buys a rasher of bacon, and another a herring, and another a pound of potatoes, or what not. Sometimes two or three of 'em will club their fourpences together, and make a supper that way. But not much of anything is to be got for fourpence, at present, when provisions is so dear.'

'True indeed,' I remarked. I had been looking about the room, admiring its snug fireside at the upper end, its glimpse of the street through the low mullioned window, and its beams overhead. 'It is very comfortable,' said I.

'Ill-conwenient,' observed the matronly presence.

I liked to hear her say so; for it showed a commendable anxiety to execute in no niggardly spirit the intentions of Master Richard Watts. But the room was really so well adapted to its purpose that I protested, quite enthusiastically, against her disparagement.

'Nay, ma'am,' said I, 'I am sure it is warm in winter and cool in summer. It has a look of homely welcome and soothing rest. It has a remarkably cosy fireside, the very blink of which, gleaming out into the street upon a winter night, is enough to warm all Rochester's heart. And as to the convenience of the six poor travellers – '

'I don't mean them,' returned the presence. 'I speak of its being an ill-conwenience to myself and my daughter, having no other room to sit in of a night.'

This was true enough, but there was another quaint room of corresponding dimensions on the opposite side of the entry: so I stepped across to it, through the open doors of both rooms, and asked what this chamber was for.

'This,' returned the presence, 'is the board room. Where the gentlemen meet when they come here.'

Let me see. I had counted from the street six upper windows besides these on the ground-story. Making a perplexed calculation in my mind, I rejoined, 'Then the six poor travellers sleep upstairs?'

My new friend shook her head. 'They sleep,' she answered, 'in two little outer galleries at the back, where their beds has always been, ever since the charity was founded. It being so very ill-conwenient to me as things is at present, the gentlemen are going to take off a bit of the back-yard, and make a slip of a room for 'em there, to sit in before they go to bed.'

'And then the six poor travellers,' said I, 'will be entirely out of the house?'

'Entirely out of the house,' assented the presence, comfortably smoothing her hands. 'Which is considered much better for all parties, and much more conwenient.'

I had been a little startled, in the cathedral, by the emphasis with which the effigy of Master Richard Watts was bursting out of his tomb; but I began to think, now, that it might be expected to come across the High Street some stormy night, and make a disturbance here.

Howbeit, I kept my thoughts to myself, and accompanied the presence to the little galleries at the back. I found them on a tiny scale, like the galleries in old inn-yards; and they were very clean.

While I was looking at them, the matron gave me to understand that the prescribed number of poor travellers were forthcoming every night from year's end to year's end; and that the beds were always occupied. My questions upon this, and her replies, brought us back to the board room so essential to the dignity of 'the gentlemen', where she showed me the printed accounts of the charity hanging up by the window. From them I gathered that the greater part of the property bequeathed by the Worshipful Master Richard Watts for the maintenance of this foundation was, at the period of his death, mere marsh-land; but that, in course of time, it had been reclaimed and built upon, and was very considerably increased in value. I found, too, that about a thirtieth part of the annual revenue was now expended on the purposes commemorated in the inscription over the door; the rest being handsomely laid out in Chancery, law expenses, collectorship, receivership, poundage, and other appendages of management, highly complimentary to the importance of the six poor travellers. In short, I made the not entirely new discovery that it may be said of an establishment like this, in dear old England, as of the fat oyster in the American story, that it takes a good many men to swallow it whole.

'And pray, ma'am,' said I, sensible that the blankness of my face began to brighten as the thought occurred to me, 'could one see these travellers?'

'Well!' she returned dubiously, 'no!'

'Not tonight, for instance!' said I.

'Well!' she returned more positively, 'No. Nobody ever asked to see them, and nobody ever did see them.'

As I am not easily balked in a design when I am set upon it, I urged to the good lady that this was Christmas Eve; that Christmas comes but once a year – which is unhappily too true, for when it begins to stay with us the whole year round we shall make this earth a very different place; that I was possessed by the desire to treat the travellers to a supper and a temperate glass of hot wassail; that the voice of fame had been heard in that land, declaring my ability to make hot wassail; that if I were permitted to hold the feast, I should be found conformable to reason, sobriety, and good hours; in a word, that I could be merry and wise myself, and had been even known at a pinch to keep others so, although I was decorated with no badge or medal, and was not a brother, orator, apostle, saint, or prophet of any denomination whatever. In the end I prevailed, to my great joy. It was settled that at nine o'clock that night a turkey and a piece of roast beef should smoke upon the board; and that I, faint and unworthy minister for once of Master Richard Watts, should preside as the Christmas supper host of the six poor travellers.

I went back to my inn to give the necessary directions for the turkey and roast beef, and, during the remainder of the day, could settle to nothing for thinking of the poor travellers. When the wind blew hard against the windows – it was a cold day, with dark gusts of sleet alternating with periods of wild brightness, as if the year were dying fitfully – I pictured them advancing towards their resting-place along various cold roads, and felt delighted to think how little they foresaw the supper that awaited them. I painted their portraits in my mind, and indulged in little heightening touches. I made them footsore; I made them weary; I made them carry packs and bundles; I made them stop by finger-posts and milestones, leaning on their bent sticks, and looking wistfully at what was written there; I made them lose their way; and filled their five wits with apprehensions of lying out all night, and being frozen to death. I took up my hat, and went out, climbed to the top of the Old Castle, and looked over the windy hills that slope down to the Medway, almost believing that I could descry some of my travellers in the distance. After it fell dark, and the cathedral bell was heard in the invisible steeple – quite a bower of frosty rime when I had last seen it – striking five, six, seven, I became so full of my travellers that I could eat no dinner, and felt constrained to watch them still in the red coals of my fire. They were all arrived by this time, I thought, had got their tickets, and were gone in. There my pleasure was dashed by the reflection that probably some travellers had come too late and were shut out.

After the cathedral bell had struck eight, I could smell a delicious savour of turkey and roast beef rising to the window of my adjoining bedroom, which looked down into the inn-yard just where the lights of the kitchen reddened a massive fragment of the castle wall. It was high time to make the wassail now; therefore I had up the materials (which, together with their proportions and combinations, I must decline to impart, as the only secret of my own I was ever known to keep), and made a glorious jorum. Not in a bowl; for a bowl anywhere but on a shelf is a low superstition, fraught with cooling and slopping; but in a brown earthenware pitcher, tenderly suffocated, when full, with a coarse cloth.

It being now upon the stroke of nine, I set out for Watts's Charity, carrying my brown beauty in my arms. I would trust Ben, the waiter, with untold gold; but there are strings in the human heart which must never be sounded by another, and drinks that I make myself are those strings in mine.

The travellers were all assembled, the cloth was laid, and Ben had brought a great billet of wood, and had laid it artfully on the top of the fire, so that a touch or two of the poker after supper should make a roaring blaze. Having deposited my brown beauty in a red nook of the hearth, inside the fender, where she soon began to sing like an ethereal cricket, diffusing at the same time odours as of ripe vineyards, spice forests, and orange groves – I say, having stationed my beauty in a place of security and improvement, I introduced myself to my guests by shaking hands all round, and giving them a hearty welcome.

I found the party to be thus composed. Firstly, myself. Secondly, a very decent man indeed, with his right arm in a sling, who had a certain clean agreeable smell of wood about him, from which I judged him to have something to do with shipbuilding. Thirdly, a little sailor-boy, a mere child, with a profusion of rich dark brown hair, and deep womanly-looking eyes. Fourthly, a shabby-genteel personage in a threadbare black suit, and apparently in very bad circumstances, with a dry suspicious look; the absent buttons on his waistcoat eked out with red tape; and a bundle of extraordinarily tattered papers sticking out of an inner breast-pocket. Fifthly, a foreigner by birth, but an Englishman in speech, who carried his pipe in the band of his hat, and lost no time in telling me, in an easy, simple, engaging way, that he was a watchmaker from Geneva, and travelled all about the Continent, mostly on foot, working as a journey-man, and seeing new countries – possibly (I thought) also smuggling a watch or so, now and then. Sixthly, a little widow, who had been very pretty and was still very young, but whose beauty had been wrecked in some great misfortune, and whose manner was remarkably timid, scared, and solitary. Seventhly and lastly, a traveller of a kind familiar to my boyhood, but now almost obsolete – a book-pedlar, who had a quantity of pamphlets and numbers with him, and who presently boasted that he could repeat more verses in an evening than he could sell in a twelve-month.

All these I have mentioned in the order in which they sat at table. I presided, and the matronly presence faced me. We were not long in taking our places, for the supper had arrived with me, in the following procession:

Myself with the pitcher.
Ben with beer.
Inattentive boy with hot plates (1).
Inattentive boy with hot plates (2).
THE TURKEY.
Female carrying sauces to be heated on the spot.
THE BEEF.
Man with tray on his head, containing vegetables and sundries.
Volunteer hostler from hotel, grinning,
and rendering no assistance.

As we passed along the High Street, comet-like, we left a long tail of fragrance behind us which caused the public to stop, sniffing in wonder. We had previously left at the corner of the inn-yard a wall-eyed young man connected with the fly department, and well accustomed to the sound of a railway whistle which Ben always carries in his pocket, whose instructions were, so soon as he should hear the whistle blown, to dash into the kitchen, seize the hot plum-pudding and mince-pies, and speed with them to Watts's Charity, where they would be received (he was further instructed) by the sauce-female, who would be provided with brandy in a blue state of combustion.

All these arrangements were executed in the most exact and punctual manner. I never saw a finer turkey, finer beef, or greater prodigality of sauce and gravy; – and my travellers did wonderful justice to everything set before them. It made my heart rejoice to observe how their wind- and frost-hardened faces softened in the clatter of plates and knives and forks, and mellowed in the fire and supper heat. While their hats and caps and wrappers, hanging up, a few small bundles on the ground in a corner, and in another corner three or four old walking-sticks, worn down at the end to mere fringe, linked this smug interior with the bleak outside in a golden chain.

When supper was done, and my brown beauty had been elevated on the table, there was a general requisition to me to 'take the corner'; which suggested to me comfortably enough how much my friends here made of a fire – for when had I ever thought so highly of the corner, since the days when I connected it with Jack Horner? However, as I declined, Ben, whose touch on all convivial instruments is perfect, drew the table apart, and instructing my travellers to open right and left on either side of me, and form round the fire, closed up the centre with myself and my chair, and preserved the order we had kept at table. He had already, in a tranquil manner, boxed the ears of the inattentive boys until they had been by imperceptible degrees boxed out of the room; and he now rapidly skirmished the sauce-female into the High Street, disappeared, and softly closed the door.

This was the time for bringing the poker to bear on the billet of wood. I tapped it three times, like an enchanted talisman, and a brilliant host of merrymakers burst out of it, and sported off by the chimney – rushing up the middle in a fiery country dance, and never coming down again. Meanwhile, by their sparkling light, which threw our lamp into the shade, I filled the glasses, and gave my Travellers, 'Christmas! Christmas Eve! my friends, when the shepherds, who were poor travellers, too, in their way, heard the angels sing, "On earth, peace. Goodwill towards men!" '

I don't know who was the first among us to think that we ought to take hands as we sat, in deference to the toast, or whether any one of us anticipated the others, but at any rate we all did it. We then drank to the memory of the good Master Richard Watts. And I wish his ghost may never have had worse usage under that roof than it had from us.

It was the witching time for storytelling. 'Our whole life, travellers,' said I, 'is a story more or less intelligible – generally less; but we shall read it by a clearer light when it is ended. I, for one, am so divided this night between fact and fiction, that I scarce know which is which. Shall I beguile the time by telling you a story as we sit here?'

They all answered, yes. I had little to tell them, but I was bound by my own proposal. Therefore, after looking for awhile at the spiral column of smoke wreathing up from my brown beauty, through which I could have almost sworn I saw the effigy of Master Richard Watts less startled than usual, I fired away.

The Story of Richard Doubledick

In the year one thousand seven hundred and ninety-nine, a relative of mine came limping down, on foot, to this town of Chatham. I call it this town, because if anybody present knows to a nicety where Rochester ends and Chatham begins, it is more than I do. He was a poor traveller, with not a farthing in his pocket. He sat by the fire in this very room, and he slept one night in a bed that will be occupied tonight by some one here.

My relative came down to Chatham to enlist in a cavalry regiment, if a cavalry regiment would have him; if not, to take King George's shilling from any corporal or sergeant who would put a bunch of ribbons in his hat. His object was to get shot; but he thought he might as well ride to death as be at the trouble of walking.

My relative's Christian name was Richard, but he was better known as Dick. He dropped his own surname on the road down, and took up that of Doubledick. He was passed as Richard Doubledick; age, twenty- two; height, five foot ten; native place, Exmouth, which he had never been near in his life. There was no cavalry in Chatham when he limped over the bridge here with half a shoe to his dusty feet, so he enlisted into a regiment of the line, and was glad to get drunk and forget all about it.

You are to know that this relative of mine had gone wrong, and run wild. His heart was in the right place, but it was sealed up. He had been betrothed to a good and beautiful girl, whom he had loved better than she – or perhaps even he – believed; but in an evil hour he had given her cause to say to him solemnly, 'Richard, I will never marry another man. I will live single for your sake, but Mary Marshall's lips' – her name was Mary Marshall – 'never address another word to you on earth. Go, Richard! Heaven forgive you!' This finished him. This brought him down to Chatham. This made him Private Richard Doubledick, with a determination to be shot.

There was not a more dissipated and reckless soldier in Chatham barracks, in the year one thousand seven hundred and ninety-nine, than Private Richard Doubledick. He associated with the dregs of every regiment; he was as seldom sober as he could be, and was constantly under punishment. It became clear to the whole barracks that Private Richard Doubledick would very soon be flogged.

Now the captain of Richard Doubledick's company was a young gentleman not above five years his senior, whose eyes had an expression in them which affected Private Richard Doubledick in a very remarkable way. They were bright, handsome, dark eyes – what are called laughing eyes generally, and, when serious, rather steady than severe – but they were the only eyes now left in his narrowed world that Private Richard Doubledick could not stand. Unabashed by evil report and punishment, defiant of everything else and everybody else, he had but to know that those eyes looked at him for a moment, and he felt ashamed. He could not so much as salute Captain Taunton in the street like any other officer. He was reproached and confused – troubled by the mere possibility of the captain's looking at him. In his worst moments, he would rather turn back, and go any distance out of his way, than encounter those two handsome, dark, bright eyes.

One day, when Private Richard Doubledick came out of the Black Hole, where he had been passing the last eight-and-forty hours, and in which retreat he spent a good deal of his time, he was ordered to betake himself to Captain Taunton's quarters. In the stale and squalid state of a man just out of the Black Hole, he had less fancy than ever for being seen by the captain; but he was not so mad yet as to disobey orders, and consequently went up to the terrace overlooking the parade-ground, where the officers' quarters were; twisting and breaking in his hands, as he went along, a bit of the straw that had formed the decorative furniture of the Black Hole.

'Come in!' cried the captain, when he had knocked with his knuckles at the door. Private Richard Doubledick pulled off his cap, took a stride forward, and felt very conscious that he stood in the light of the dark, bright eyes.

There was a silent pause. Private Richard Doubledick had put the straw in his mouth, and was gradually doubling it up into his windpipe and choking himself.

'Doubledick,' said the captain, 'do you know where you are going to?'

'To the Devil, sir?' faltered Doubledick.

'Yes,' returned the captain. 'And very fast.'

Private Richard Doubledick turned the straw of the Black Hole in his month, and made a miserable salute of acquiescence.

'Doubledick,' said the captain, 'since I entered his Majesty's service, a boy of seventeen, I have been pained to see many men of promise going that road; but I have never been so pained to see a man make the shameful journey as I have been, ever since you joined the regiment, to see you.'

Private Richard Doubledick began to find a film stealing over the floor at which he looked; also to find the legs of the captain's breakfast-table turning crooked, as if he saw them through water.

'I am only a common soldier, sir,' said he. 'It signifies very little what such a poor brute comes to.'

'You are a man,' returned the captain, with grave indignation, 'of education and superior advantages; and if you say that, meaning what you say, you have sunk lower than I had believed. How low that must be, I leave you to consider, knowing what I know of your disgrace, and seeing what I see.'

'I hope to get shot soon, sir,' said Private Richard Doubledick; 'and then the regiment and the world together will be rid of me.'

The legs of the table were becoming very crooked. Doubledick, looking up to steady his vision, met the eyes that had so strong an influence over him. He put his hand before his own eyes, and the breast of his disgrace-jacket swelled as if it would fly asunder.

'I would rather,' said the young captain, 'see this in you, Doubledick, than I would see five thousand guineas counted out upon this table for a gift to my good mother. Have you a mother?'

'I am thankful to say she is dead, sir.'

'If your praises,' returned the captain, 'were sounded from mouth to mouth through the whole regiment, through the whole army, through the whole country, you would wish she had lived to say, with pride and joy, "He is my son!"'

'Spare me, sir,' said Doubledick. 'She would never have heard any good of me. She would never have had any pride and joy in owning herself my mother. Love and compassion she might have had, and would have always had, I know but not – Spare me, sir! I am a broken wretch, quite at your mercy!' And he turned his face to the wall, and stretched out his imploring hand.

'My friend – ' began the captain.

'God bless you, sir!' sobbed Private Richard Doubledick.

'You are at the crisis of your fate. Hold your course unchanged a little longer, and you know what must happen. I know even better than you can imagine, that, after that has happened, you are lost. No man who could shed those tears could bear those marks.'

'I fully believe it, sir,' in a low, shivering voice said Private Richard Doubledick.

'But a man in any station can do his duty,' said the young captain, 'and, in doing it, can earn his own respect, even if his case should be so very unfortunate and so very rare that he can earn no other man's. A common soldier, poor brute though you called him just now, has this advantage in the stormy times we live in, that he always does his duty before a host of sympathising witnesses. Do you doubt that he may so do it as to be extolled through a whole regiment, through a whole army, through a whole country? Turn while you may yet retrieve the past, and try.'

'I will! I ask for only one witness, sir,' cried Richard, with a bursting heart.

'I understand you. I will be a watchful and a faithful one.'

I have heard from Private Richard Doubledick's own lips, that he dropped down upon his knee, kissed that officer's hand, arose, and went out of the light of the dark, bright eyes, an altered man.

In that year, one thousand seven hundred and ninety-nine, the French were in Egypt, in Italy, in Germany, where not? Napoleon Bonaparte had likewise begun to stir against us in India, and most men could read the signs of the great troubles that were coming on. In the very next year, when we formed an alliance with Austria against him, Captain Taunton's regiment was on service in India. And there was not a finer noncommissioned officer in it – no, nor in the whole line – than Corporal Richard Doubledick.

In eighteen hundred and one, the Indian army were on the coast of Egypt. Next year was the year of the proclamation of the short peace, and they were recalled. It had then become well known to thousands of men, that wherever Captain Taunton, with the dark, bright eyes, led, there, close to him, ever at his side, firm as a rock, true as the sun, and brave as Mars, would be certain to be found, while life beat in their hearts, that famous soldier, Sergeant Richard Doubledick.

Eighteen hundred and five, besides being the great year of Trafalgar, was a year of hard fighting in India. That year saw such wonders done by a sergeant-major, who cut his way single-handed through a solid mass of men, recovered the colours of his regiment, which had been seized from the hand of a poor boy shot through the heart, and rescued his wounded captain, who was down, and in a very jungle of horses' hoofs and sabres – saw such wonders done, I say, by this brave sergeant-major, that he was specially made the bearer of the colours he had won; and Ensign Richard Doubledick had risen from the ranks.

Sorely cut up in every battle, but always reinforced by the bravest of men – for the fame of following the old colours, shot through and through, which Ensign Richard Doubledick had saved, inspired all breasts – this regiment fought its way through the Peninsular War, up to the investment of Badajos in eighteen hundred and twelve. Again and again it had been cheered through the British ranks until the tears had sprung into men's eyes at the mere hearing of the mighty British voice, so exultant in their valour; and there was not a drummer-boy but knew the legend, that wherever the two friends, Major Taunton, with the dark, bright eyes, and Ensign Richard Doubledick, who was devoted to him, were seen to go, there the boldest spirits in the English army became wild to follow.

One day, at Badajos – not in the great storming, but in repelling a hot sally of the besieged upon our men at work in the trenches, who had given way – the two officers found themselves hurrying forward, face to face, against a party of French infantry, who made a stand. There was an officer at their head, encouraging his men – a courageous, handsome, gallant officer of five-and-thirty, whom Doubledick saw hurriedly, almost momentarily, but saw well. He particularly noticed this officer waving his sword, and rallying his men with an eager and excited cry, when they fired in obedience to his gesture, and Major Taunton dropped.

It was over in ten minutes more, and Doubledick returned to the spot where he had laid the best friend man ever had on a coat spread upon the wet clay. Major Taunton's uniform was opened at the breast, and on his shirt were three little spots of blood.

'Dear Doubledick,' said he, 'I am dying.'

'For the love of Heaven, no!' exclaimed the other, kneeling down beside him, and passing his arm round his neck to raise his head. 'Taunton! My preserver, my guardian angel, my witness! Dearest, truest, kindest of human beings! Taunton! For God's sake!'

The bright, dark eyes – so very, very dark now, in the pale face – smiled upon him; and the hand he had kissed thirteen years ago laid itself fondly on his breast.

'Write to my mother. You will see home again. Tell her how we became friends. It will comfort her, as it comforts me.'

He spoke no more, but faintly signed for a moment towards his hair as it fluttered in the wind. The ensign understood him. He smiled again when he saw that, and, gently turning his face over on the supporting arm as if for rest, died, with his hand upon the breast in which he had revived a soul.

No dry eye looked on Ensign Richard Doubledick that melancholy day. He buried his friend on the field, and became a lone, bereaved man. Beyond his duty he appeared to have but two remaining cares in life – one, to preserve the little packet of hair he was to give to Taunton's mother; the other, to encounter that French officer who had rallied the men under whose fire Taunton fell. A new legend now began to circulate among our troops; and it was, that when he and the French officer came face to face once more, there would be weeping in France.

The war went on – and through it went the exact picture of the French officer on the one side, and the bodily reality upon the other – until the Battle of Toulouse was fought. In the returns sent home appeared these words: 'Severely wounded, but not dangerously, Lieutenant Richard Doubledick.'

At midsummer-time, in the year eighteen hundred and fourteen, Lieutenant Richard Doubledick, now a browned soldier, seven-and-thirty years of age, came home to England invalided. He brought the hair with him, near his heart. Many a French officer had he seen since that day; many a dreadful night, in searching with men and lanterns for his wounded, had he relieved French officers lying disabled; but the mental picture and the reality had never come together.

Though he was weak and suffered pain, he lost not an hour in getting down to Frome in Somersetshire, where Taunton's mother lived. In the sweet, compassionate words that naturally present themselves to the mind tonight, 'he was the only son of his mother, and she was a widow'.

It was a Sunday evening, and the lady sat at her quiet garden-window, reading the Bible; reading to herself, in a trembling voice, that very passage in it, as I have heard him tell. He heard the words: 'Young man, I say unto thee, arise!'

He had to pass the window; and the bright, dark eyes of his debased time seemed to look at him. Her heart told her who he was; she came to the door quickly, and fell upon his neck.

'He saved me from ruin, made me a human creature, won me from infamy and shame. O, God for ever bless him! As he will, he will!'

'He will!' the lady answered. 'I know he is in heaven!' Then she piteously cried, 'But O, my darling boy, my darling boy!'

Never from the hour when Private Richard Doubledick enlisted at Chatham had the private, corporal, sergeant, sergeant-major, ensign, or lieutenant breathed his right name, or the name of Mary Marshall, or a word of the story of his life, into any ear except his reclaimer's. That previous scene in his existence was closed. He had firmly resolved that his expiation should be to live unknown; to disturb no more the peace that had long grown over his old offences; to let it be revealed, when he was dead, that he had striven and suffered, and had never forgotten; and then, if they could forgive him and believe him – well, it would be time enough – time enough!

But that night, remembering the words he had cherished for two years, 'Tell her how we became friends. It will comfort her, as it comforts me,' he related everything. It gradually seemed to him as if in his maturity he had recovered a mother; it gradually seemed to her as if in her bereavement she had found a son. During his stay in England, the quiet garden into which he had slowly and painfully crept, a stranger, became the boundary of his home; when he was able to rejoin his regiment in the spring, he left the garden, thinking this was indeed the first time he had ever turned his face towards the old colours with a woman's blessing!

He followed them – so ragged, so scarred and pierced now, that they would scarcely hold together – to Quatre Bras and Ligny. He stood beside them, in an awful stillness of many men, shadowy through the mist and drizzle of a wet June forenoon, on the field of Waterloo. And down to that hour the picture in his mind of the French officer had never been compared with the reality.

The famous regiment was in action early in the battle, and received its first check in many an eventful year, when he was seen to fall. But it swept on to avenge him, and left behind it no such creature in the world of consciousness as Lieutenant Richard Doubledick.

Through pits of mire, and pools of rain; along deep ditches, once roads, that were pounded and ploughed to pieces by artillery, heavy waggons, tramp of men and horses, and the struggle of every wheeled thing that could carry wounded soldiers; jolted among the dying and the dead, so disfigured by blood and mud as to be hardly recognisable for humanity;

undisturbed by the moaning of men and the shrieking of horses, which, newly taken from the peaceful pursuits of life, could not endure the sight of the stragglers lying by the wayside, never to resume their toilsome journey; dead, as to any sentient life that was in it, and yet alive – the form that had been Lieutenant Richard Doubledick, with whose praises England rang, was conveyed to Brussels. There it was tenderly laid down in hospital; and there it lay, week after week, through the long bright summer days, until the harvest, spared by war, had ripened and was gathered in.

Over and over again the sun rose and set upon the crowded city; over and over again the moonlight nights were quiet on the plains of Waterloo: and all that time was a blank to what had been Lieutenant Richard Doubledick. Rejoicing troops marched into Brussels, and marched out; brothers and fathers, sisters, mothers, and wives, came thronging thither, drew their lots of joy or agony, and departed; so many times a day the bells rang; so many times the shadows of the great buildings changed; so many lights sprang up at dusk; so many feet passed here and there upon the pavements; so many hours of sleep and cooler air of night succeeded: indifferent to all, a marble face lay on a bed, like the face of a recumbent statue on the tomb of Lieutenant Richard Doubledick.

Slowly labouring, at last, through a long heavy dream of confused time and place, presenting faint glimpses of army surgeons whom he knew, and of faces that had been familiar to his youth – dearest and kindest among them, Mary Marshall's, with a solicitude upon it more like reality than anything he could discern – Lieutenant Richard Doubledick came back to life. To the beautiful life of a calm autumn evening sunset, to the peaceful life of a fresh quiet room with a large window standing open; a balcony beyond, in which were moving leaves and sweet-smelling flowers; beyond, again, the clear sky, with the sun full in his sight, pouring its golden radiance on his bed.

It was so tranquil and so lovely that he thought he had passed into another world. And he said in a faint voice, 'Taunton, are you near me?'

A face bent over him. Not his, his mother's.

'I came to nurse you. We have nursed you many weeks. You were moved here long ago. Do you remember nothing?'

'Nothing.'

The lady kissed his cheek, and held his hand, soothing him.

'Where is the regiment? What has happened? Let me call you mother. What has happened, mother?'

'A great victory, dear. The war is over, and the regiment was the bravest in the field.'

His eyes kindled, his lips trembled, he sobbed, and the tears ran down his face. He was very weak, too weak to move his hand.

'Was it dark just now?' he asked presently.

'No.'

'It was only dark to me? Something passed away, like a black shadow. But as it went, and the sun – O the blessed sun, how beautiful it is! – touched my face, I thought I saw a light white cloud pass out at the door. Was there nothing that went out?'

She shook her head, and in a little while he fell asleep, she still holding his hand, and soothing him.

From that time, he recovered. Slowly, for he had been desperately wounded in the head, and had been shot in the body, but making some little advance every day. When he had gained sufficient strength to converse as he lay in bed, he soon began to remark that Mrs Taunton always brought him back to his own history. Then he recalled his preserver's dying words, and thought, 'It comforts her.'

One day he awoke out of a sleep, refreshed, and asked her to read to him. But the curtain of the bed, softening the light, which she always drew back when he awoke, that she might see him from her table at the bedside where she sat at work, was held undrawn; and a woman's voice spoke, which was not hers.

'Can you bear to see a stranger?' it said softly. 'Will you like to see a stranger?'

'Stranger!' he repeated. The voice awoke old memories, before the days of Private Richard Doubledick.

'A stranger now, but not a stranger once,' it said in tones that thrilled him. 'Richard, dear Richard, lost through so many years, my name – '

He cried out her name, 'Mary,' and she held him in her arms, and his head lay on her bosom.

'I am not breaking a rash vow, Richard. These are not Mary Marshall's lips that speak. I have another name.'

She was married.

'I have another name, Richard. Did you ever hear it?'

'Never!'

He looked into her face, so pensively beautiful, and wondered at the smile upon it through her tears.

'Think again, Richard. Are you sure you never heard my altered name?'

'Never!'

'Don't move your head to look at me, dear Richard. Let it lie here, while I tell my story. I loved a generous, noble man; loved him with my whole heart; loved him for years and years; loved him faithfully, devotedly; loved him without hope of return; loved him, knowing nothing of his highest qualities – not even knowing that he was alive. He was a brave soldier. He was honoured and beloved by thousands of thousands, when the mother of his dear friend found me, and showed me that in all his triumphs he had never forgotten me. He was wounded in a great battle. He was brought, dying, here, into Brussels. I came to watch and tend him, as I would have joyfully gone, with such a purpose, to the dreariest ends of the earth. When he knew no one else, he knew me. When he suffered most, he bore his sufferings barely murmuring, content to rest his head where yours rests now. When he lay at the point of death, he married me, that he might call me Wife before he died. And the name, my dear love, that I took on that forgotten night – '

'I know it now!' he sobbed. 'The shadowy remembrance strengthens. It is come back. I thank Heaven that my mind is quite restored! My Mary, kiss me; lull this weary head to rest, or I shall die of gratitude. His parting words were fulfilled. I see home again!'

Well! They were happy. It was a long recovery, but they were happy through it all. The snow had melted on the ground, and the birds were singing in the leafless thickets of the early spring, when those three were first able to ride out together, and when people flocked about the open carriage to cheer and congratulate Captain Richard Doubledick.

But even then it became necessary for the captain, instead of returning to England, to complete his recovery in the climate of southern France. They found a spot upon the Rhône, within a ride of the old town of Avignon, and within view of its broken bridge, which was all they could desire; they lived there, together, six months; then returned to England. Mrs Taunton, growing old after three years – though not so old as that her bright, dark eyes were dimmed – and remembering that her strength had been benefited by the change, resolved to go back for a year to those parts. So she went with a faithful servant, who had often carried her son in his arms; and she was to be rejoined and escorted home, at the year's end, by Captain Richard Doubledick.

She wrote regularly to her children (as she called them now), and they to her. She went to the neighbourhood of Aix; and there, in their own château near the farmer's house she rented, she grew into intimacy with a family belonging to that part of France. The intimacy began in her often meeting among the vineyards a pretty child, a girl with a most compassionate heart, who was never tired of listening to the solitary English lady's stories of her poor son and the cruel wars. The family were as gentle as the child, and at length she came to know them so well that she accepted their invitation to pass the last month of her residence abroad under their roof. All this intelligence she wrote home, piecemeal as it came about, from time to time; and at last enclosed a polite note, from the head of the château, soliciting, on the occasion of his approaching mission to that neighbourhood, the honour of the company of *cet homme si justement célèbre*, Monsieur le Capitaine Richard Doubledick.

Captain Doubledick, now a hardy, handsome man in the full vigour of life, broader across the chest and shoulders than he had ever been before, dispatched a courteous reply, and followed it in person. Travelling through all that extent of country after three years of Peace, he blessed the better days on which the world had fallen. The corn was golden, not drenched in unnatural red; was bound in sheaves for food, not trodden underfoot by men in mortal fight. The smoke rose up from peaceful hearths, not blazing ruins. The carts were laden with the fair fruits of the earth, not with wounds and death. To him who had so often seen the terrible reverse, these things were beautiful indeed; and they brought him in a softened spirit to the old château near Aix upon a deep blue evening.

It was a large château of the genuine old ghostly kind, with round towers, and extinguishers, and a high leaden roof, and more windows than Aladdin's Palace. The lattice blinds were all thrown open after the heat of the day, and there were glimpses of rambling walls and corridors within. Then there were immense outbuildings fallen into partial decay, masses of dark trees, terrace-gardens, balustrades; tanks of water, too weak to play and too dirty to work; statues, weeds, and thickets of iron railing that seemed to have overgrown themselves like the shrubberies, and to have branched out in all manner of wild shapes. The entrance doors stood open, as doors often do in that country when the heat of the day is past; and the captain saw no bell or knocker, and walked in.

He walked into a lofty stone hall, refreshingly cool and gloomy after the glare of a southern day's travel. Extending along the four sides of this hall was a gallery, leading to suites of rooms; and it was lighted from the top. Still no bell was to be seen.

'Faith,' said the captain halting, ashamed of the clanking of his boots, 'this is a ghostly beginning!'

He started back, and felt his face turn white. In the gallery, looking down at him, stood the French officer – the officer whose picture he had carried in his mind so long and so far. Compared with the original, at last – in every lineament how like it was!

He moved, and disappeared, and Captain Richard Doubledick heard his steps coming quickly down into the hall. He entered through an archway. There was a bright, sudden look upon his face, much such a look as it had worn in that fatal moment.

Monsieur le Capitaine Richard Doubledick? Enchanted to receive him! A thousand apologies! The servants were all out in the air. There was a little fête among them in the garden. In effect, it was the fête day of my daughter, the little cherished and protected of Madame Taunton.

He was so gracious and so frank that Monsieur le Capitaine Richard Doubledick could not withhold his hand. 'It is the hand of a brave Englishman,' said the French officer, retaining it while he spoke. 'I could respect a brave Englishman, even as my foe, how much more as my friend! I also am a soldier.'

'He has not remembered me, as I have remembered him; he did not take such note of my face, that day, as I took of his,' thought Captain Richard Doubledick. 'How shall I tell him?'

The French officer conducted his guest into a garden and presented him to his wife, an engaging and beautiful woman, sitting with Mrs Taunton in a whimsical old-fashioned pavilion. His daughter, her fair young face beaming with joy, came running to embrace him; and there was a boy-baby to tumble down among the orange trees on the broad steps, in making for his father's legs. A multitude of children visitors were dancing to sprightly music; and all the servants and peasants about the château were dancing too. It was a scene of innocent happiness that might have been invented for the climax of the scenes of peace which had soothed the captain's journey.

He looked on, greatly troubled in his mind, until a resounding bell rang, and the French officer begged to show him his rooms. They went upstairs into the gallery from which the officer had looked down; and Monsieur le Capitaine Richard Doubledick was cordially welcomed to a grand outer chamber, and a smaller one within, all clocks and draperies, and hearths, and brazen dogs, and tiles, and cool devices, and elegance, and vastness.

'You were at Waterloo,' said the French officer.

'I was,' said Captain Richard Doubledick. 'And at Badajos.'

Left alone with the sound of his own stern voice in his ears, he sat down to consider, What shall I do, and how shall I tell him? At that time, unhappily, many deplorable duels had been fought between English and French officers, arising out of the recent war; and these duels, and how to avoid this officer's hospitality, were the uppermost thought in Captain Richard Doubledick's mind.

He was thinking, and letting the time run out in which he should have dressed for dinner, when Mrs Taunton spoke to him outside the door, asking if he could give her the letter he had brought from Mary. 'His mother, above all,' the captain thought. 'How shall I tell her?'

'You will form a friendship with your host, I hope,' said Mrs Taunton, whom he hurriedly admitted, 'that will last for life. He is so true-hearted and so generous, Richard, that you can hardly fail to esteem one another. If he had been spared,' she kissed (not without tears) the locket in which she wore his hair, 'he would have appreciated him with his own magnanimity, and would have been truly happy that the evil days were past which made such a man his enemy.'

She left the room; and the captain walked, first to one window, whence he could see the dancing in the garden, then to another window, whence he could see the smiling prospect and the peaceful vineyards.

'Spirit of my departed friend,' said he, 'is it through thee these better thoughts are rising in my mind? Is it thou who hast shown me, all the way I have been drawn to meet this man, the blessings of the altered time? Is it thou who hast sent thy stricken mother to me, to stay my angry hand? Is it from thee the whisper comes, that this man did his duty as thou didst – and as I did, through thy guidance, which has wholly saved me here on earth – and that he did no more?'

He sat down, with his head buried in his hands, and, when he rose up, made the second strong resolution of his life – that neither to the French officer, nor to the mother of his departed friend, nor to any soul, while either of the two was living, would he breathe what only he knew. And when he touched that French officer's glass with his own, that day at dinner, he secretly forgave him in the name of the divine forgiver of injuries.

Here I ended my story as the first poor traveller. But, if I had told it now, I could have added that the time has since come when the son of Major Richard Doubledick, and the son of that French officer, friends as their fathers were before them, fought side by side in one cause, with their respective nations, like long-divided brothers whom the better times have brought together, fast united.

3

The Road

My story being finished, and the Wassail too, we broke up as the cathedral bell struck twelve. I did not take leave of my travellers that night; for it had come into my head to reappear, in conjunction with some hot coffee, at seven in the morning.

As I passed along the High Street, I heard the waits at a distance, and struck off to find them. They were playing near one of the old gates of the city, at the corner of a wonderfully quaint row of red brick tenements, which the clarionet obligingly informed me were inhabited by the minor-canons. They had odd little porches over the doors, like sounding-boards over old pulpits; and I thought I should like to see one of the minor-canons come out upon his top stop, and favour us with a little Christmas discourse about the poor scholars of Rochester; taking for his text the words of his master relative to the devouring of widows' houses.

The clarionet was so communicative, and my inclinations were (as they generally are) of so vagabond a tendency, that I accompanied the waits across an open green called the Vines, and assisted – in the French sense – at the performance of two waltzes, two polkas, and three Irish melodies, before I thought of my inn any more. However, I returned to it then, and found a fiddle in the kitchen, and Ben, the wall-eyed young man, and two chambermaids, circling round the great deal table with the utmost animation.

I had a very bad night. It cannot have been owing to the turkey or the beef – and the Wassail is out of the question – but in every endeavour that I made to get to sleep I failed most dismally. I was never asleep; and in whatsoever unreasonable direction my mind rambled, the effigy of Master Richard Watts perpetually embarrassed it.

In a word, I only got out of the Worshipful Master Richard Watts's way by getting out of bed in the dark at six o'clock, and tumbling, as my custom is, into all the cold water that could be accumulated for the purpose. The outer air was dull and cold enough in the street, when I came down there; and the one candle in our supper-room at Watts's Charity looked as pale in the burning as if it had had a bad night too. But my travellers had all slept soundly, and they took to the hot coffee, and the piles of bread-and-butter, which Ben had arranged like deals in a timberyard, as kindly as I could desire.

While it was yet scarcely daylight, we all came out into the street together, and there shook hands. The widow took the little sailor towards Chatham, where he was to find a steamboat for Sheerness; the lawyer, with an extremely knowing look, went his own way, without committing himself by announcing his intentions; two more struck off by the cathedral and old castle for Maidstone; and the book-pedlar accompanied me over the bridge. As for me, I was going to walk by Cobham Woods, as far upon my way to London as I fancied.

When I came to the stile and footpath by which I was to diverge from the main road, I bade farewell to my last remaining Poor Traveller, and pursued my way alone. And now the mists began to rise in the most beautiful manner, and the sun to shine; and as I went on through the bracing air, seeing the hoarfrost sparkle everywhere, I felt as if all nature shared in the joy of the great Birthday.

Going through the woods, the softness of my tread upon the mossy ground and among the brown leaves enhanced the Christmas sacredness by which I felt surrounded. As the whitened stems environed me, I thought how the Founder of the time had never raised his benignant hand, save to bless and heal, except in the case of one unconscious tree. By Cobham Hall, I came to the village, and the churchyard where the dead had been quietly buried, 'in the sure and certain hope' which Christmas time inspired. What children could I see at play, and not be loving of, recalling who had loved them! No garden that I passed was out of unison with the day, for I remembered that the tomb was in a garden, and that 'she, supposing him to be the gardener', had said, 'Sir, if thou have borne him hence, tell me where thou hast laid him, and I will take him away.' In time, the distant river with the ships came full in view, and with it pictures of the poor fishermen, mending their nets, who arose and followed him – of the teaching of the people from a ship pushed off a little way from shore, by reason of the multitude – of a majestic figure walking on the water, in the loneliness of night. My very shadow on the ground was eloquent of Christmas; for did not the people lay their sick where the mere shadows of the men who had heard and seen him might fall as they passed along?

Thus Christmas begirt me, far and near, until I had come to Blackheath, and had walked down the long vista of gnarled old trees in Greenwich Park, and was being steam-rattled through the mists now closing in once more, towards the lights of London. Brightly they shone, but not so brightly as my own fire, and the brighter faces around it, when we came together to celebrate the day. And there I told of worthy Master Richard Watts, and of my supper with the six poor travellers who were neither rogues nor proctors, and from that hour to this I have never seen one of them again.

DR MARIGOLD

I am a cheap jack, and my own father's name was Willum Marigold. It was in his lifetime supposed by some that his name was William, but my own father always consistently said, No, it was Willum. On which point I content myself with looking at the argument this way: If a man is not allowed to know his own name in a free country, how much is he allowed to know in a land of slavery? As to looking at the argument through the medium of the Register, Willum Marigold come into the world before Registers come up much – and went out of it too. They wouldn't have been greatly in his line neither, if they had chanced to come up before him.

I was born on the Queen's highway, but it was the King's at that time. A doctor was fetched to my own mother by my own father, when it took place on a common; and in consequence of his being a very kind gentleman, and accepting no fee but a tea-tray, I was named Doctor, out of gratitude and compliment to him. There you have me. Dr Marigold.

I am at present a middle-aged man of a broadish build, in cords, leggings, and a sleeved waistcoat the strings of which is always gone behind. Repair them how you will, they go like fiddle-strings. You have been to the theatre, and you have seen one of the wiolin-players screw up his wiolin, after listening to it as if it had been whispering the secret to him that it feared it was out of order, and then you have heard it snap. That's as exactly similar to my waistcoat as a waistcoat and a wiolin can be like one another.

I am partial to a white hat, and I like a shawl round my neck wore loose and easy. Sitting down is my favourite posture. If I have a taste in point of personal jewellery, it is mother-of-pearl buttons. There you have me again, as large as life.

The doctor having accepted a tea-tray, you'll guess that my father was a cheap jack before me. You are right. He was. It was a pretty tray. It represented a large lady going along a serpentining uphill gravel-walk, to attend a little church. Two swans had likewise come astray with the same intentions. When I call her a large lady, I don't mean in point of breadth, for there she fell below my views, but she more than made it up in height; her height and slimness was – in short *the* height of both.

I often saw that tray, after I was the innocently smiling cause (or more likely screeching one) of the doctor's standing it up on a table against the wall in his consulting-room. Whenever my own father and mother were in that part of the country, I used to put my head (I have heard my own mother say it was flaxen curls at that time, though you wouldn't know an old hearth-broom from it now till you come to the handle, and found it wasn't me) in at the doctor's door, and the doctor was always glad to see me, and said, 'Aha, my brother practitioner! Come in, little MD. How are your inclinations as to sixpence?'

You can't go on for ever, you'll find, nor yet could my father nor yet my mother. If you don't go off as a whole when you are about due, you're liable to go off in part, and two to one your head's the part. Gradually my father went off his, and my mother went off hers. It was in a harmless way, but it put out the family where I boarded them. The old couple, though retired, got to be wholly and solely devoted to the cheap jack business, and were always selling the family off. Whenever the cloth was laid for dinner, my father began rattling the plates and dishes, as we do in our line when we put up crockery for a bid, only he had lost the trick of it, and mostly let 'em drop and broke 'em. As the old lady had been used to sit in the cart, and hand the articles out one by one to the old gentleman on the footboard to sell, just in the same way she handed him every item of the family's property, and they disposed of it in their own imaginations from morning to night. At last the old gentleman, lying bedridden in the same room with the old lady, cries out in the old patter, fluent, after having been silent for two days and nights:

> 'Now here, my jolly companions every one – which the
> Nightingale club in a village was held,
> At the sign of the Cabbage and Shears,
> Where the singers no doubt would have greatly excelled,
> But for want of taste, voices and ears –

now, here, my jolly companions, every one, is a working model of a used-up old cheap jack, without a tooth in his head, and with a pain in every bone: so like life that it would be just as good if it wasn't better, just as bad if it wasn't worse, and just as new if it wasn't worn out. Bid for the working model of the old cheap jack, who has drunk more gunpowder-tea with the ladies in his time than would blow the lid off a washer-woman's copper, and carry it as many thousands of miles higher than the moon as naught nix naught, divided by the national debt, carry nothing to the poor-rates, three under, and two over. Now, my hearts of oak and men of straw, what do you say for the lot? Two shillings, a shilling, tenpence, eightpence, sixpence, fourpence. Twopence? Who said two-pence? The gentleman in the scarecrow's hat? I am ashamed of the gentleman in the scarecrow's hat. I really am ashamed of him for his want of public spirit. Now I'll tell you what I'll do with you. Come! I'll throw you in a working model of a old woman that was married to the old cheap jack so long ago that upon my word and honour it took place in Noah's Ark, before the unicorn could get in to forbid the banns by blowing a tune upon his horn. There now! Come! What do you say for both? I'll tell you what I'll do with you. I don't bear you malice for being so backward. Here! If you make me a bid that'll only reflect a little credit on your town, I'll throw you in a warming-pan for nothing, and lend you a toasting-fork for life. Now come; what do you say after that splendid offer? Say two pound, say thirty shillings, say a pound, say ten shillings, say five, say two and six. You don't say even two and six? You say two and three? No. You shan't have the lot for two and three. I'd sooner give it to you, if you was good-looking enough. Here! Missis! Chuck the old man and woman into the cart, put the horse to, and drive 'em away and bury 'em!' Such were the last words of Willum Marigold, my own father, and they were carried out, by him and by his wife, my own mother, on one and the same day, as I ought to know, having followed as mourner.

My father had been a lovely one in his time at the cheap jack work, as his dying observations went to prove. But I top him. I don't say it because it's myself, but because it has been universally acknowledged by all that has had the means of comparison. I have worked at it. I have measured myself against other public speakers – Members of Parliament, platforms, pulpits, counsel learned in the law – and where I have found 'em good, I have took a bit of imagination from 'em, and where I have found 'em bad, I have let 'em alone. Now I'll tell you what. I mean to go down into my grave declaring that of all the callings ill used in Great Britain, the cheap jack calling is the worst used. Why ain't we a profession? Why ain't we endowed with privileges? Why are we forced to take out a hawker's licence, when no such thing is expected of the political hawkers? Where's the difference betwixt us? Except that we are cheap jacks and they are dear jacks, *I* don't see any difference but what's in our favour.

For look here! Say it's election time. I am on the footboard of my cart in the market-place, on a Saturday night. I put up a general miscellaneous lot. I say: 'Now here, my free and independent woters, I'm a going to give you such a chance as you never had in all your born days, nor yet the days preceding. Now I'll show you what I am a going to do with you. Here's a pair of razors that'll shave you closer than the board of guardians; here's a flat-iron worth its weight in gold; here's a frying-pan artificially flavoured with essence of beefsteaks to that degree that you've only got for the rest of your lives to fry bread and dripping in it and there you are replete with animal food; here's a genuine chronometer watch in such a solid silver case that you may knock at the door with it when you come home late from a social meeting, and rouse your wife and family, and save up your knocker for the postman; and here's half-a-dozen dinner plates that you may play the cymbals with to charm baby when it's fractious. Stop! I'll throw in another article, and I'll give you that, and it's a rolling-pin; and if the baby can only get it well into its mouth when its teeth is coming and rub the gums once with it, they'll come through double, in a fit of laughter equal to being tickled. Stop again! I'll throw you in another article, because I don't like the looks of you, for you haven't the appearance of buyers unless I lose by you, and because I'd rather lose than not take money tonight, and that's a looking-glass in which you may see how ugly you look when you don't bid. What do you say now? Come! Do you say a pound? Not you, for you haven't got it. Do you say ten shillings? Not you, for you owe more to the tallyman. Well then, I'll tell you what I'll do with you. I'll heap 'em all on the footboard of the cart – there they are! razors, flat watch, dinner plates, rolling-pin, and away for four shillings, and I'll give you sixpence for your trouble!' This is me, the cheap jack. But on the Monday morning, in the same market-place, comes the dear jack on the hustings – *his* cart – and, what does *he* say? 'Now my free and independent woters, I am a going to give you such a chance' (he begins just like me) 'as you never had in all your born days, and that's the chance of sending myself to Parliament. Now I'll tell you what I am a going to do for you. Here's the interests of this magnificent town promoted above all the rest of the civilised and uncivilised earth. Here's your railways carried, and your neighbours' railways jockeyed. Here's all your sons in the Post-office. Here's Britannia smiling on you. Here's the eyes of Europe on you. Here's uniwersal prosperity for you, repletion of animal food, golden cornfields, gladsome homesteads, and rounds of applause from your own hearts, all in one lot, and that's myself. Will you take me as I stand? You won't? Well, then, I'll tell you what I'll do with you. Come now! I'll throw you in anything you ask for. There! Church-rates, abolition of more malt tax, no malt tax, uniwersal education to the highest mark, or uniwersal ignorance to the lowest, total abolition of flogging in the army or a dozen for every private once a month all round, wrongs of men or rights of women – only say which it shall be, take 'em or leave 'em, and I'm of your opinion altogether, and the lot's your own on your own terms. There! You won't take it yet! Well, then, I'll tell you what I'll do with you. Come! You *are* such free and independent woters, and I am so proud of you – you *are* such a noble and enlightened constituency, and I *am* so ambitious of the honour and dignity of being your member, which is by far the highest level to which the wings of the human mind can soar – that I'll tell you what I'll do with you. I'll throw you in all the public-houses in your magnificent town for nothing. Will that content you? It won't? You won't take the lot yet? Well, then, before I put the horse in and drive away, and make the offer to the next most magnificent town that can be discovered, I'll tell you what I'll do. Take the lot, and I'll drop two thousand pound in the streets of your magnificent town for them to pick up that can. Not enough? Now look here. This is the very furthest that I'm a going to. I'll make it two thousand five hundred. And still you won't? Here, missis! Put the horse – no, stop half a moment, I shouldn't like to turn my back upon you neither for a trifle, I'll make it two thousand seven hundred and fifty pound. There! Take the lot on your own terms, and I'll count out two thousand seven hundred and fifty pound on the footboard of the cart, to be dropped in the streets of your magnificent town for them to pick up that can. What do you say? Come now! You won't do better, and you may do worse. You take it? Hooray! Sold again, and got the seat!'

These dear jacks soap the people shameful, but we cheap jacks don't. We tell 'em the truth about themselves to their faces, and scorn to court 'em. As to wenturesomeness in the way of puffing up the lots, the dear jacks beat us hollow. It is considered in the cheap jack calling, that better patter can be made out of a gun than any article we put up from the cart, except a pair of spectacles. I often hold forth about a gun for a quarter of an hour, and feel as if I need never leave off. But when I tell 'em what the gun can do, and what the gun has brought down, I never go half so far as the dear jacks do when they make speeches in praise of *their* guns – their great guns that set 'em on to do it. Besides, I'm in business for myself: I ain't sent down into the market-place to order, as they are. Besides, again, my guns don't know what I say in their laudation, and their guns do, and the whole concern of 'em have reason to be sick and ashamed all round. These are some of my arguments for declaring that the cheap jack calling is treated ill in Great Britain, and for turning warm when I think of the other jacks in question setting themselves up to pretend to look down upon it.

I courted my wife from the footboard of the cart. I did indeed. She was a Suffolk young woman, and it was in Ipswich market-place right opposite the corn-chandler's shop. I had noticed her up at a window last Saturday that was, appreciating highly. I had took to her, and I had said to myself, 'If not already disposed of, I'll have that lot.' Next Saturday that come, I pitched the cart on the same pitch, and I was in very high feather indeed, keeping 'em laughing the whole of the time, and getting off the goods briskly. At last I took out of my waistcoat-pocket a small lot wrapped in soft paper, and I put it this way (looking up at the window where she was). 'Now here, my blooming English maidens, is an article, the last article of the present evening's sale, which I offer to only you, the lovely Suffolk Dumplings biling over with beauty, and I won't take a bid of a thousand pounds for from any man alive. Now what is it? Why, I'll tell you what it is. It's made of fine gold, and it's not broke, though there's a hole in the middle of it, and it's stronger than any fetter that ever was forged, though it's smaller than any finger in my set of ten. Why ten? Because, when my parents made over my property to me, I tell you true, there was twelve sheets, twelve towels, twelve tablecloths, twelve knives, twelve forks, twelve tablespoons, and twelve teaspoons, but my set of fingers was two short of a dozen, and could never since be matched. Now what else is it? Come, I'll tell you. It's a hoop of solid gold, wrapped in a silver curl-paper, that I myself took off the shining locks of the ever beautiful old lady in Threadneedle Street, London city; I wouldn't tell you so if I hadn't the paper to show, or you mightn't believe it even of me. Now what else is it? It's a mantrap and a handcuff, the parish stocks and a leg-lock, all in gold and all in one. Now what else is it? It's a wedding-ring. Now I'll tell you what I'm a going to do with it. I'm not a going to offer this lot for money; but I mean to give it to the next of you beauties that laughs, and I'll pay her a visit tomorrow morning at exactly half after nine o'clock as the chimes go, and I'll take her out for a walk to put up the banns.' She laughed, and got the ring handed up to her. When I called in the morning, she says, 'O dear! It's never you, and you never mean it?' 'It's ever me,' says I, 'and I am ever yours, and I ever mean it.' So we got married, after being put up three times – which, by the bye, is quite in the cheap jack way again, and shows once more how the cheap jack customs pervade society.

She wasn't a bad wife, but she had a temper. If she could have parted with that one article at a sacrifice, I wouldn't have swopped her away in exchange for any other woman in England. Not that I ever did swop her away, for we lived together till she died, and that was thirteen year. Now, my lords and ladies and gentlefolks all, I'll let you into a secret, though you won't believe it. Thirteen year of temper in a palace would try the worst of you, but thirteen year of temper in a cart would try the best of you. You are kept so very close to it in a cart, you see. There's thousands of couples among you getting on like sweet ile upon a whetstone in houses five and six pairs of stairs high, that would go to the Divorce Court in a cart. Whether the jolting makes it worse, I don't undertake to decide; but in a cart it does come home to you, and stick to you. Wiolence in a cart is *so* wiolent, and aggrawation in a cart is *so* aggrawating.

We might have had such a pleasant life! A roomy cart, with the large goods hung outside, and the bed slung underneath it when on the road, an iron pot and a kettle, a fireplace for the cold weather, a chimney for the smoke, a hanging-shelf and a cupboard, a dog and a horse. What more do you want? You draw off upon a bit of turf in a green lane or by the roadside, you hobble your old horse and turn him grazing, you light your fire upon the ashes of the last visitors, you cook your stew, and you wouldn't call the Emperor of France your father. But have a temper in the cart, flinging language and the hardest goods in stock at you, and where are you then? Put a name to your feelings.

My dog knew as well when she was on the turn as I did. Before she broke out, he would give a howl, and bolt. How he knew it, was a mystery to me; but the sure and certain knowledge of it would wake him up out of his soundest sleep, and he would give a howl, and bolt. At such times I wished I was him.

The worst of it was, we had a daughter born to us, and I love children with all my heart. When she was in her furies she beat the child. This got to be so shocking, as the child got to be four or five year old, that I have many a time gone on with my whip over my shoulder, at the old horse's head, sobbing and crying worse than ever little Sophy did. For how could

I prevent it? Such a thing is not to be tried with such a temper – in a cart – without coming to a fight. It's in the natural size and formation of a cart to bring it to a fight. And then the poor child got worse terrified than before, as well as worse hurt generally, and her mother made complaints to the next people we lighted on, and the word went round, 'Here's a wretch of a cheap jack been a beating his wife.'

Little Sophy was such a brave child! She grew to be quite devoted to her poor father, though he could do so little to help her. She had a wonderful quantity of shining dark hair, all curling natural about her. It is quite astonishing to me now, that I didn't go tearing mad when I used to see her run from her mother before the cart, and her mother catch her by this hair, and pull her down by it, and beat her.

Such a brave child I said she was! Ah! with reason.

'Don't you mind next time, father dear,' she would whisper to me, with her little face still flushed, and her bright eyes still wet; 'if I don't cry out, you may know I am not much hurt. And even if I do cry out, it will only be to get mother to let go and leave off.' What I have seen the little spirit bear – for me – without crying out!

Yet in other respects her mother took great care of her. Her clothes were always clean and neat, and her mother was never tired of working at 'em. Such is the inconsistency in things. Our being down in the marsh country in unhealthy weather, I consider the cause of Sophy's taking bad low fever; but however she took it, once she got it she turned away from her mother for evermore, and nothing would persuade her to be touched by her mother's hand. She would shiver and say, 'No, no, no,' when it was offered at, and would hide her face on my shoulder, and hold me tighter round the neck.

The cheap jack business had been worse than ever I had known it, what with one thing and what with another (and not least with railroads, which will cut it all to pieces, I expect, at last), and I was run dry of money. For which reason, one night at that period of little Sophy's being so bad, either we must have come to a deadlock for victuals and drink, or I must have pitched the cart as I did.

I couldn't get the dear child to lie down or leave go of me, and indeed I hadn't the heart to try, so I stepped out on the footboard with her holding round my neck. They all set up a laugh when they see us, and one chuckle-headed Joskin (that I hated for it) made the bidding, 'Tuppence for her!'

'Now, you country boobies,' says I, feeling as if my heart was a heavy weight at the end of a broken sashline, 'I give you notice that I am a going to charm the money out of your pockets, and to give you so much more than your money's worth that you'll only persuade yourselves to draw your Saturday night's wages ever again arterwards by the hopes of meeting me to lay 'em out with, which you never will, and why not? Because I've made my fortunes by selling my goods on a large scale for seventy-five per cent less than I give for 'em, and I am consequently to be elevated to the House of Peers next week, by the title of the Duke of Cheap and Markis Jackaloorul. Now let's know what you want tonight, and you shall have it. But first of all, shall I tell you why I have got this little girl round my neck? You don't want to know? Then you shall. She belongs to the fairies. She's a fortune-teller. She can tell me all about you in a whisper, and can put me up to whether you're going to buy a lot or leave it. Now do you want a saw? No, she says you don't, because you're too clumsy to use one. Else here's a saw which would be a lifelong blessing to a handy man, at four shillings, at three and six, at three, at two and six, at two, at eighteen-pence. But none of you shall have it at any price, on account of your well-known awkwardness, which would make it manslaughter. The same objection applies to this set of three planes which I won't let you have neither, so don't bid for 'em. Now I am a going to ask her what you do want.' (Then I whispered, 'Your head burns so, that I am afraid it hurts you bad, my pet,' and she answered, without opening her heavy eyes, 'Just a little, father.') 'O! This little fortune-teller says it's a memorandum-book you want. Then why didn't you mention it? Here it is. Look at it. Two hundred superfine hot-pressed wire-wove pages – if you don't believe me, count 'em – ready ruled for your expenses, an everlastingly pointed pencil to put 'em down with, a double-bladed penknife to scratch 'em out with, a book of printed tables to calculate your income with, and a camp-stool to sit down upon while you give your mind to it! Stop! And an umbrella to keep the moon off when you give your mind to it on a pitch-dark night. Now I won't ask you how much for the lot, but how little? How little are you thinking of? Don't be ashamed to mention it, because my fortune-teller knows already.' (Then making believe to whisper, I kissed her – and she kissed me.) 'Why, she says you are thinking of as little as three and threepence! I couldn't have believed it, even of you, unless she told me. Three and threepence! And a set of printed tables in the lot that'll calculate your income up to forty thousand a year! With an income of forty thousand a year, you grudge three and sixpence. Well then, I'll tell you my opinion. I so despise the threepence, that I'd sooner take three shillings. There. For three shillings, three shillings, three shillings! Gone. Hand 'em over to the lucky man.'

As there had been no bid at all, everybody looked about and grinned at everybody, while I touched little Sophy's face and asked her if she felt faint, or giddy. 'Not very, father. It will soon be over.' Then turning from the pretty patient eyes, which were opened now, and seeing nothing but grins across my lighted grease-pot, I went on again in my cheap jack style. 'Where's the butcher?' (My sorrowful eye had just caught sight of a fat young butcher on the outside of the crowd.) 'She says the good luck is the butcher's. Where is he?' Everybody handed on the blushing butcher to the front, and there was a roar, and the butcher felt himself obliged to put his hand in his pocket, and take the lot. The party so picked out, in general, does feel obliged to take the lot – good four times out of six. Then we had another lot, the counterpart of that one, and sold it sixpence cheaper, which is always wery much enjoyed. Then we had the spectacles. It ain't a special profitable lot, but I put 'em on, and I see what the Chancellor of the Exchequer is going to take off the taxes, and I see what the sweetheart of the young woman in the shawl is doing at home, and I see what the Bishops has got for dinner, and a deal more that seldom fails to fetch 'em up in their spirits; and the better their spirits, the better their bids. Then we had the ladies' lot – the teapot, tea-caddy, glass sugar-basin, half a dozen spoons, and caudle-cup – and all the time I was making similar excuses to give a look or two and say a word or two to my poor child. It was while the second ladies' lot was holding 'em enchained that I felt her lift herself a little on my shoulder, to look across the dark street. 'What troubles you, darling?' 'Nothing troubles me, father. I am not at all troubled. But don't I see a pretty churchyard over there?' 'Yes, my dear.' 'Kiss me twice, dear father, and lay me down to rest upon that churchyard grass so soft and green.' I staggered back into the cart with her head dropped on my shoulder, and I says to her mother, 'Quick. Shut the door! Don't let those laughing people see!' 'What's the matter?' she cries. 'O woman, woman,' I tells her, 'you'll never catch my little Sophy by her hair again, for she has flown away from you!'

Maybe those were harder words than I meant 'em; but from that time forth my wife took to brooding, and would sit in the cart or walk beside it, hours at a stretch, with her arms crossed, and her eyes looking on the ground. When her furies took her (which was rather seldomer than before) they took her in a new way, and she banged herself about to that extent that I was forced to hold her. She got none the better for a little drink now and then, and through some years I used to wonder, as I plodded along at the old horse's head, whether there was many carts upon the road that held so much dreariness as mine, for all my being looked up to as the king of the cheap jacks. So sad our lives went on till one summer evening, when, as we were coming into Exeter, out of the farther West of England, we saw a woman beating a child in a cruel manner, who screamed, 'Don't beat me! O mother, mother, mother!' Then my wife stopped her ears, and ran away like a wild thing, and next day she was found in the river.

Me and my dog were all the company left in the cart now; and the dog learned to give a short bark when they wouldn't bid, and to give another and a nod of his head when I asked him, 'Who said half a crown? Are you the gentleman, sir, that offered half a crown?' He attained to an immense height of popularity, and I shall always believe taught himself entirely out of his own head to growl at any person in the crowd that bid as low as sixpence. But he got to be well on in years, and one night when I was conwulsing York with the spectacles, he took a conwulsion on his own account upon the very footboard by me, and it finished him.

Being naturally of a tender turn, I had dreadful lonely feelings on me arter this. I conquered 'em at selling times, having a reputation to keep (not to mention keeping myself), but they got me down in private, and rolled upon me. That's often the way with us public characters. See us on the footboard, and you'd give pretty well anything you possess to be us. See us off the footboard, and you'd add a trifle to be off your bargain. It was under those circumstances that I come acquainted with a giant. I might have been too high to fall into conversation with him, had it not been for my lonely feelings. For the general rule is, going round the country, to draw the line at dressing up. When a man can't trust his getting a living to his undisguised abilities, you consider him below your sort. And this giant when on view figured as a Roman.

He was a languid young man, which I attribute to the distance betwixt his extremities. He had a little head and less in it, he had weak eyes and weak knees, and altogether you couldn't look at him without feeling that there was greatly too much of him both for his joints and his mind. But he was an amiable though timid young man (his mother let him out, and spent the money), and we come acquainted when he was walking to ease the horse betwixt two fairs. He was called Rinaldo di Velasco, his name being Pickleson.

This giant, otherwise Pickleson, mentioned to me under the seal of confidence that, beyond his being a burden to himself, his life was made a burden to him by the cruelty of his master towards a stepdaughter who was deaf and dumb. Her mother was dead, and she had no living soul to take her part, and was used most hard. She travelled with his master's caravan only because there was nowhere to leave her, and this giant, otherwise Pickleson, did go so far as to believe that his master often tried to lose her. He was such a very languid young man, that I don't know how long it didn't take him to get this story out, but it passed through his defective circulation to his top extremity in course of time.

When I heard this account from the giant, otherwise Pickleson, and likewise that the poor girl had beautiful long dark hair, and was often pulled down by it and beaten, I couldn't see the giant through what stood in my eyes. Having wiped 'em, I give him sixpence (for he was kept as short as he was long), and he laid it out in two three-penn'orths of gin-and-water, which so brisked him up, that he sang the 'Favourite Comic of Shivery Shakey, ain't it cold?' – a popular effect which his master had tried every other means to get out of him as a Roman wholly in vain.

His master's name was Mim, a wery hoarse man, and I knew him to speak to. I went to that Fair as a mere civilian, leaving the cart outside the town, and I looked about the back of the vans while the performing was going on, and at last, sitting dozing against a muddy cartwheel, I come upon the poor girl who was deaf and dumb. At the first look I might almost have judged that she had escaped from the Wild Beast Show; but at the second I thought better of her, and thought that if she was more cared for and more kindly used she would be like my child. She was just the same age that my own daughter would have been, if her pretty head had not fell down upon my shoulder that unfortunate night.

To cut it short, I spoke confidential to Mim while he was beating the gong outside betwixt two lots of Pickleson's publics, and I put it to him, 'She lies heavy on your own hands; what'll you take for her?' Mim was a most ferocious swearer. Suppressing that part of his reply which was much the longest part, his reply was, 'A pair of braces.' 'Now I'll tell you,' says I, 'what I'm a going to do with you. I'm a going to fetch you half-a-dozen pair of the primest braces in the cart, and then to take her away with me.' Says Mim (again ferocious), 'I'll believe it when I've got the goods, and no sooner.' I made all the haste I could, lest he should think twice of it, and the bargain was completed, which Pickleson he was thereby so relieved in his mind that he come out at his little back door, longways like a serpent, and give us 'Shivery Shakey' in a whisper among the wheels at parting.

It was happy days for both of us when Sophy and me began to travel in the cart. I at once give her the name of Sophy, to put her ever towards me in the attitude of my own daughter. We soon made out to begin to understand one another, through the goodness of the Heavens, when she knowed that I meant true and kind by her. In a very little time she was wonderful fond of me. You have no idea what it is to have anybody wonderful fond of you, unless you have been got down and rolled upon by the lonely feelings that I have mentioned as having once got the better of me.

You'd have laughed – or the rewerse – it's according to your disposition – if you could have seen me trying to teach Sophy. At first I was helped – you'd never guess by what – milestones. I got some large alphabets in a box, all the letters separate on bits of bone, and saying we was going to WINDSOR, I give her those letters in that order, and then at every milestone I showed her those same letters in that same order again, and pointed towards the abode of royalty. Another time I give her CART, and then chalked the same upon the cart. Another time I give her DR MARIGOLD, and hung a corresponding inscription outside my waistcoat. People that met us might stare a bit and laugh, but what did *I* care, if she caught the idea? She caught it after long patience and trouble, and then we did begin to get on swimmingly, I believe you! At first she was a little given to consider me the cart, and the cart the abode of royalty, but that soon wore off.

We had our signs, too, and they was hundreds in number. Sometimes she would sit looking at me and considering hard how to communicate with me about something fresh – how to ask me what she wanted explained – and then she was (or I thought she was; what does it signify?) so like my child with those years added to her, that I half-believed it was herself, trying to tell me where she had been to up in the skies, and what she had seen since that unhappy night when she flied away. She had a pretty face, and now that there was no one to drag at her bright dark hair, and it was all in order, there was a something touching in her looks that made the cart most peaceful and most quiet, though not at all melancholy.

[N.B. In the cheap jack patter, we generally sound it lemon jolly, and it gets a laugh.]

The way she learnt to understand any look of mine was truly surprising. When I sold of a night, she would sit in the cart unseen by them outside, and would give a eager look into my eyes when I looked in, and would hand me straight the precise article or articles I wanted. And then she would clap her hands, and laugh for joy. And as for me, seeing her so bright, and remembering what she was when I first lighted on her, starved and beaten and ragged, leaning asleep against the muddy cartwheel, it give me such heart that I gained a greater height of reputation than ever, and I put Pickleson down (by the name of Mim's Travelling Giant otherwise Pickleson) for a fypunnote in my will.

This happiness went on in the cart till she was sixteen year old. By which time I began to feel not satisfied that I had done my whole duty by her, and to consider that she ought to have better teaching than I could give her. It drew a many tears on both sides when I commenced explaining my views to her; but what's right is right, and you can't neither by tears nor laughter do away with its character.

So I took her hand in mine, and I went with her one day to the Deaf and Dumb Establishment in London, and when the gentleman come to speak to us, I says to him: 'Now I'll tell you what I'll do with you, sir. I am nothing but a cheap jack, but of late years I have laid by for a rainy day notwithstanding. This is my only daughter (adopted), and you can't produce a deafer nor a dumber. Teach her the most that can be taught her in the shortest separation that can be named – state the figure for it – and I am game to put the money down. I won't bate you a single farthing, sir, but I'll put down the money here and now, and I'll thankfully throw you in a pound to take it. There!' The gentleman smiled, and then, 'Well, well,' says he, 'I must first know what she has learned already. How do you communicate with her?' Then I showed him, and she wrote in printed writing many names of things and so forth; and we held some sprightly conversation, Sophy and me, about a little story in a book which the gentleman showed her, and which she was able to read. 'This is most extraordinary,' says the gentleman; 'is it possible that you have been her only teacher?' 'I have been her only teacher, sir,' I says, 'besides herself.' 'Then,' says the gentleman, and more acceptable words was never spoke to me, 'you're a clever fellow, and a good fellow.' This he makes known to Sophy, who kisses his hands, claps her own, and laughs and cries upon it.

We saw the gentleman four times in all, and when he took down my name and asked how in the world it ever chanced to be Doctor, it come out that he was own nephew by the sister's side, if you'll believe me, to the very doctor that I was called after. This made our footing still easier, and he says to me: 'Now, Marigold, tell me what more do you want your adopted daughter to know?'

'I want her, sir, to be cut off from the world as little as can be, considering her deprivations, and therefore to be able to read whatever is wrote with perfect ease and pleasure.'

'My good fellow,' urges the gentleman, opening his eyes wide, 'why I can't do that myself!'

I took his joke, and gave him a laugh (knowing by experience how flat you fall without it), and I mended my words accordingly.

'What do you mean to do with her afterwards?' asks the gentleman, with a sort of a doubtful eye. 'To take her about the country?'

'In the cart, sir, but only in the cart. She will live a private life, you understand, in the cart. I should never think of bringing her infirmities before the public. I wouldn't make a show of her for any money.'

The gentleman nodded, and seemed to approve.

'Well,' says he, 'can you part with her for two years?'

'To do her that good – yes, sir.'

'There's another question,' says the gentleman, looking towards her – 'can she part with you for two years?'

I don't know that it was a harder matter of itself (for the other was hard enough to me), but it was harder to get over. However, she was pacified to it at last, and the separation betwixt us was settled. How it cut up both of us when it took place, and when I left her at the door in the dark of an evening, I don't tell. But I know this; remembering that night, I shall never pass that same establishment without a heartache and a swelling in the throat; and I couldn't put you up the best of lots in sight of it with my usual spirit – no, not even the gun, nor the pair of spectacles – for five hundred pound reward from the Secretary of State for the Home Department, and throw in the honour of putting my legs under his mahogany arterwards.

Still, the loneliness that followed in the cart was not the old loneliness, because there was a term put to it, however long to look forward to; and because I could think, when I was any ways down, that she belonged to me and I belonged to her. Always planning for her coming back, I bought in a few months' time another cart, and what do you think I planned to do with it? I'll tell you. I planned to fit it up with shelves and books for her reading, and to have a seat in it where I could sit and see her read, and think that I had been her first teacher. Not hurrying over the job, I had the fittings knocked together in contriving ways under my own inspection, and here was her bed in a berth with curtains, and there was her reading-table, and here was her writing-desk, and elsewhere was her books in rows upon rows, picters and no picters, bindings and no bindings, gilt-edged and plain, just as I could pick 'em up for her in lots up and down the country –

> North and South and West and East,
> Winds liked best and winds liked least,
> Here and there and gone astray,
> Over the hills and far away.

And when I had got together pretty well as many books as the cart would neatly hold, a new scheme come into my head, which, as it turned out, kept my time and attention a good deal employed, and helped me over the two years' stile.

Without being of an awaricious temper, I like to be the owner of things. I shouldn't wish, for instance, to go partners with yourself in the cheap jack cart. It's not that I mistrust you, but that I'd rather know it was mine. Similarly, very likely you'd rather know it was yours. Well! A kind of a jealousy began to creep into my mind when I reflected that all those books would have been read by other people long before they was read by her. It seemed to take away from her being the owner of 'em like. In this way, the question got into my head: Couldn't I have a book new-made express for her, which she should be the first to read?

It pleased me, that thought did; and as I never was a man to let a thought sleep (you must wake up all the whole family of thoughts you've got and burn their nightcaps, or you won't do in the cheap jack line), I set to work at it. Considering that I was in the habit of changing so much about the country, and that I should have to find out a literary character here to make a deal with, and another literary character there to make a deal with, as opportunities presented, I hit on the plan that this same book should be a general miscellaneous lot – like the razors, flat-iron, chronometer watch, dinner plates, rolling-pin, and looking-glass – and shouldn't be offered as a single indiwidual article, like the spectacles or the gun. When I had come to that conclusion, I come to another, which shall likewise be yours.

Often had I regretted that she never had heard me on the footboard, and that she never could hear me. It ain't that *I* am vain, but that *you* don't like to put your own light under a bushel. What's the worth of your reputation, if you can't convey the reason for it to the person you most wish to value it? Now I'll put it to you. Is it worth sixpence, fippence, fourpence, threepence, twopence, a penny, a halfpenny, a farthing? No, it ain't. Not worth a farthing. Very well, then. My conclusion was that I would begin her book with some account of myself. So that, through reading a specimen or two of me on the footboard, she might form an idea of my merits there. I was aware that I couldn't do myself justice. A man can't write his eye (at least *I* don't know how to), nor yet can a man write his voice, nor the rate of his talk, nor the quickness of his action, nor his general spicy way. But he can write his turns of speech, when he is a public speaker – and indeed I have heard that he very often does, before he speaks 'em.

Well! Having formed that resolution, then come the question of a name. How did I hammer that hot iron into shape? This way. The most difficult explanation I had ever had with her was, how I come to be called Doctor, and yet was no Doctor. After all, I felt that I had failed of getting it correctly into her mind, with my utmost pains. But trusting to her improvement in the two years, I thought that I might trust to her understanding it when she should come to read it as put down by my own hand. Then I thought I would try a joke with her and watch how it took, by which of itself I might fully judge of her understanding it. We had first discovered the mistake we had dropped into, through her having asked me to prescribe for her when she had supposed me to be a Doctor in a medical point of view; so thinks I, 'Now, if I give this book the name of my Prescriptions, and if she catches the idea that my only Prescriptions are for her amusement and interest – to make her laugh in a pleasant way, or to make her cry in a pleasant way – it will be a delightful proof to both of us that we have got over our difficulty.' It fell out to absolute perfection. For when she saw the book, as I had it got up – the printed and pressed book – lying on her desk in her cart, and saw the title, *Dr Marigold's Prescriptions*, she looked at me for a moment with astonishment, then fluttered the leaves, then broke out a laughing in the charmingest way, then felt her pulse and shook her head, then turned the pages pretending to read them most attentive, then kissed the book to me, and put it to her bosom with both her hands. I never was better pleased in all my life!

But let me not anticipate. (I take that expression out of a lot of romances I bought for her. I never opened a single one of 'em – and I have opened many – but I found the romancer saying 'let me not anticipate'. Which being so, I wonder why he did anticipate, or who asked him to it.) Let me not, I say, anticipate. This same book took up all my spare time. It was no play to get the other articles together in the general miscellaneous lot, but when it come to my own article! There! I couldn't have believed the blotting, nor yet the buckling to at it, nor the patience over it. Which again is like the footboard. The public have no idea.

At last it was done, and the two years' time was gone after all the other time before it, and where it's all gone to, who knows? The new cart was finished – yellow outside, relieved with wermilion and brass fittings – the old horse was put in it, a new 'un and a boy being laid on for the cheap jack cart – and I cleaned myself up to go and fetch her. Bright cold weather it was, cart-chimneys smoking, carts pitched private on a piece of waste ground over at Wandsworth, where you may see 'em from the Sou'western Railway when not upon the road. (Look out of the right-hand window going down.)

'Marigold,' says the gentleman, giving his hand hearty, 'I am very glad to see you.'

'Yet I have my doubts, sir,' says I, 'if you can be half as glad to see me as I am to see you.'

'The time has appeared so long – has it, Marigold?'

'I won't say that, sir, considering its real length; but – '

'What a start, my good fellow!'

Ah! I should think it was! Grown such a woman, so pretty, so intelligent, so expressive! I knew then that she must be really like my child, or I could never have known her, standing quiet by the door.

'You are affected,' says the gentleman in a kindly manner.

'I feel, sir,' says I, 'that I am but a rough chap in a sleeved waistcoat.'

'I feel,' says the gentleman, 'that it was you who raised her from misery and degradation, and brought her into communication with her kind. But why do we converse alone together, when we can converse so well with her? Address her in your own way.'

'I am such a rough chap in a sleeved waistcoat, sir,' says I, 'and she is such a graceful woman, and she stands so quiet at the door!'

'*Try* if she moves at the old sign,' says the gentleman.

They had got it up together o' purpose to please me! For when I give her the old sign, she rushed to my feet, and dropped upon her knees, holding up her hands to me with pouring tears of love and joy; and when I took her hands and lifted her, she clasped me round the neck, and lay there; and I don't know what a fool I didn't make of myself, until we all three settled down into talking without sound, as if there was a something soft and pleasant spread over the whole world for us.

* * *

[A portion is here omitted from the text, having reference to the sketches contributed by other writers; but the reader will be pleased to have what follows retained in a note:

'Now I'll tell you what I am a-going to do with you. I am a-going to offer you the general miscellaneous lot, her own book, never read by anybody else but me, added to and completed by me after her first reading of it, eight-and-forty printed pages, six-and-ninety columns, Whiting's own work, Beaufort House to wit, thrown off by the steam-ingine, best of paper, beautiful green wrapper, folded like clean linen come home from the clear-starcher's, and so exquisitely stitched that, regarded as a piece of needlework alone, it's better than the sampler of a seamstress undergoing a competitive examination for starvation before the Civil Service Commissioners – and I offer the lot for what? For eight pound? Not so much. For six pound? Less. For four pound. Why, I hardly expect you to believe me, but that's the sum. Four pound! The stitching alone cost half as much again. Here's forty-eight original pages, ninety-six original columns, for four pound. You want more for the money? Take it. Three whole pages of advertisements of thrilling interest thrown in for nothing. Read 'em and believe 'em. More? My best of wishes for your merry Christmases and your happy New Years, your long lives and your true prosperities. Worth twenty pound good if they are delivered as I send them. Remember! Here's a final prescription added, "To be taken for life," which will tell you how the cart broke down, and where the journey ended. You think four pound too much? And still you think so? Come! I'll tell you what then. Say four pence, and keep the secret.']

* * *

So every item of my plan was crowned with success. Our reunited life was more than all that we had looked forward to. Content and joy went with us as the wheels of the two carts went round, and the same stopped with us when the two carts stopped. I was as pleased and as proud as a Pug-Dog with his muzzle black-leaded for a evening party, and his tail extra curled by machinery.

But I had left something out of my calculations. Now, what had I left out? To help you to guess I'll say, a figure. Come. Make a guess and guess right. Nought? No. Nine? No. Eight? No. Seven? No. Six? No. Five? No. Four? No. Three? No. Two? No. One? No. Now I'll tell you what I'll do with you. I'll say it's another sort of figure altogether. There. Why then, says you, it's a mortal figure. No, nor yet a mortal figure. By such means you got yourself penned into a corner, and you can't help guessing a *im*mortal figure. That's about it. Why didn't you say so sooner?

Yes. It was a immortal figure that I had altogether left out of my calculations. Neither man's, nor woman's, but a child's. Girl's or boy's? Boy's. 'I, says the sparrow with my bow and arrow.' Now you have got it.

We were down at Lancaster, and I had done two nights more than fair average business (though I cannot in honour recommend them as a quick audience) in the open square there, near the end of the street where Mr Sly's King's Arms and Royal Hotel stands. Mim's travelling giant, otherwise Pickleson, happened at the self-same time to be trying it on in the town. The genteel lay was adopted with him. No hint of a van. Green baize alcove leading up to Pickleson in a Auction Room. Printed poster, 'Free list suspended, with the exception of that proud boast of an enlightened country, a free press. Schools admitted by private arrangement. Nothing to raise a blush in the cheek of youth or shock the most fastidious.' Mim swearing most horrible and terrific, in a pink calico pay-place, at the slackness of the public. Serious handbill in the shops, importing that it was all but impossible to come to a right understanding of the history of David without seeing Pickleson.

I went to the auction room in question, and I found it entirely empty of everything but echoes and mouldiness, with the single exception of Pickleson on a piece of red drugget. This suited my purpose, as I wanted a private and confidential word with him, which was: 'Pickleson. Owing much happiness to you, I put you in my will for a fypunnote; but, to save trouble, here's fourpunten down, which may equally suit your views, and let us so conclude the transaction.' Pickleson, who up to that remark had had the dejected appearance of a long Roman rushlight that couldn't anyhow get lighted, brightened up at his top extremity, and made his acknowledgements in a way which (for him) was parliamentary eloquence. He likewise did add, that, having ceased to draw as a Roman, Mim had made proposals for his going in as a conwerted Indian giant worked upon by the dairyman's daughter. This, Pickleson, having no acquaintance with the tract named after that young woman, and not being willing to couple gag with his serious views, had declined to do, thereby leading to words and the total stoppage of the unfortunate young man's beer. All of which, during the whole of the interview, was confirmed by the ferocious growling of Mim down below in the pay-place, which shook the giant like a leaf.

But what was to the present point in the remarks of the travelling giant, otherwise Pickleson, was this: 'Dr Marigold,' – I give his words without a hope of conweying their feebleness – 'who is the strange young man that hangs about your carts?' – 'The strange young *man?*' I gives him back, thinking that he meant her, and his languid circulation had dropped a syllable. 'Doctor,' he returns, with a pathos calculated to draw a tear from even a manly eye, 'I am weak, but not so weak yet as that I don't know my words. I repeat them, Doctor. The strange young man.' It then appeared that Pickleson, being forced to stretch his legs (not that they wanted it) only at times when he couldn't be seen for nothing, to wit in the dead of the night and towards daybreak, had twice seen hanging about my carts, in that same town of Lancaster where I had been only two nights, this same unknown young man.

It put me rather out of sorts. What it meant as to particulars I no more foreboded then than you forebode now, but it put me rather out of sorts. Howsoever, I made light of it to Pickleson, and I took leave of Pickleson, advising him to spend his legacy in getting up his stamina, and to continue to stand by his religion. Towards morning I kept a look out for the strange young man, and – what was more – I saw the strange young man. He was well dressed and well looking. He loitered very nigh my carts, watching them like as if he was taking care of them, and soon after daybreak turned and went away. I sent a hail after him, but he never started or looked round, or took the smallest notice.

We left Lancaster within an hour or two, on our way towards Carlisle. Next morning, at daybreak, I looked out again for the strange young man. I did not see him. But next morning I looked out again, and there he was once more. I sent another hail after him, but as before he gave not the slightest sign of being any ways disturbed. This put a thought into my head. Acting on it I watched him in different manners and at different times not necessary to enter into, till I found that this strange young man was deaf and dumb.

The discovery turned me over, because I knew that a part of that establishment where she had been was allotted to young men (some of them well off), and I thought to myself, 'If she favours him, where am I? and where is all that I have worked and planned for?' Hoping – I must confess to the selfishness – that she might *not* favour him, I set myself to find out. At last I was by accident present at a meeting between them in the open air, looking on leaning behind a fir tree without their knowing of it. It was a moving meeting for all the three parties concerned. I knew every syllable that passed between them as well as they did. I listened with my eyes, which had come to be as quick and true with deaf and dumb conversation as my ears with the talk of people that can speak. He was a-going out to China as clerk in a merchant's house, which his father had been before him. He was in circumstances to keep a wife, and he wanted her to marry him and go along with him. She persisted, no. He asked if she didn't love him. Yes, she loved him dearly, dearly; but she could never disappoint her beloved, good, noble, generous, and I-don't-know-what-all father (meaning me, the cheap jack in the sleeved waistcoat) and she would stay with him, Heaven bless him! though it was to break her heart. Then she cried most bitterly, and that made up my mind.

While my mind had been in an unsettled state about her favouring this young man, I had felt that unreasonable towards Pickleson, that it was well for him he had got his legacy down. For I often thought, 'If it hadn't been for this same weak-minded giant, I might never have come to trouble my head and wex my soul about the young man.' But, once that I knew she loved him – once that I had seen her weep for him – it was a different thing. I made it right in my mind with Pickleson on the spot, and I shook myself together to do what was right by all.

She had left the young man by that time (for it took a few minutes to get me thoroughly well shook together), and the young man was leaning against another of the fir trees – of which there was a cluster – with his face upon his arm. I touched him on the back. Looking up and seeing me, he says, in our deaf-and-dumb talk, 'Do not be angry.'

'I am not angry, good boy. I am your friend. Come with me.'

I left him at the foot of the steps of the library cart, and I went up alone. She was drying her eyes.

'You have been crying, my dear.'

'Yes, father.'

'Why?'

'A headache.'

'Not a heartache?'

'I said a headache, father.'

'Dr Marigold must prescribe for that headache.'

She took up the book of my prescriptions, and held it up with a forced smile; but seeing me keep still and look earnest, she softly laid it down again, and her eyes were very attentive.

'The prescription is not there, Sophy.'

'Where is it?'

'Here, my dear.'

I brought her young husband in, and I put her hand in his, and my only farther words to both of them were these: 'Dr Marigold's last prescription. To be taken for life.' After which I bolted.

When the wedding come off, I mounted a coat (blue, and bright buttons), for the first and last time in all my days, and I give Sophy away with my own hand. There were only us three and the gentleman who had had charge of her for those two years. I give the wedding dinner of four in the library cart. Pigeon-pie, a leg of pickled pork, a pair of fowls, and suitable garden stuff. The best of drinks. I give them a speech, and the gentleman give us a speech, and all our jokes told, and the whole went off like a skyrocket. In the course of the entertainment I explained to Sophy that I should keep the library cart as my living-cart when not upon the road, and that I should keep all her books for her just as they stood, till she come back to claim them. So she went to China with her young husband, and it was a parting sorrowful and heavy, and I got the boy I had another service; and so as of old, when my child and wife were gone, I went plodding along alone, with my whip over my shoulder, at the old horse's head.

Sophy wrote me many letters, and I wrote her many letters. About the end of the first year she sent me one in an unsteady hand: 'Dearest father, not a week ago I had a darling little daughter, but I am so well that they let me write these words to you. Dearest and best father, I hope my child may not be deaf and dumb, but I do not yet know.' When I wrote back, I hinted the question; but as Sophy never answered that question, I felt it to be a sad one, and I never repeated it. For a long time our letters were regular, but then they got irregular, through Sophy's husband being moved to another station, and through my being always on the move. But we were in one another's thoughts, I was equally sure, letters or no letters.

Five years, odd months, had gone since Sophy went away. I was still the King of the cheap jacks, and at a greater height of popularity than ever. I had had a first-rate autumn of it, and on the twenty-third of December, one thousand eight hundred and sixty-four, I found myself at Uxbridge, Middlesex, clean sold out. So I jogged up to London with the old horse, light and easy, to have my Christmas Eve and Christmas Day alone by the fire in the library cart, and then to buy a regular new stock of goods all round, to sell 'em again and get the money.

I am a neat hand at cookery, and I'll tell you what I knocked up for my Christmas Eve dinner in the library cart. I knocked up a beefsteak-pudding for one, with two kidneys, a dozen oysters, and a couple of mushrooms thrown in. It's a pudding to put a man in good humour with everything, except the two bottom buttons of his waistcoat. Having relished that pudding and cleared away, I turned the lamp low, and sat down by the light of the fire, watching it as it shone upon the backs of Sophy's books.

Sophy's books so brought Sophy's self, that I saw her touching face quite plainly, before I dropped off dozing by the fire. This may be a reason why Sophy, with her deaf-and-dumb child in her arms, seemed to stand silent by me all through my nap. I was on the road, off the road, in all sorts of places,

> North and South and West and East,
> Winds liked best and winds liked least,
> Here and there and gone astray,
> Over the hills and far away,

and still she stood silent by me, with her silent child in her arms. Even when I woke with a start, she seemed to vanish, as if she had stood by me in that very place only a single instant before.

I had started at a real sound, and the sound was on the steps of the cart. It was the light hurried tread of a child, coming clambering up. That tread of a child had once been so familiar to me, that for half a moment I believed I was a-going to see a little ghost.

But the touch of a real child was laid upon the outer handle of the door, and the handle turned, and the door opened a little way, and a real child peeped in. A bright little comely girl with large dark eyes.

Looking full at me, the tiny creature took off her mite of a straw hat, and a quantity of dark curls fell about her face. Then she opened her lips, and said in a pretty voice,

'Grandfather!'

'Ah, my God!' I cries out. 'She can speak!'

'Yes, dear grandfather. And I am to ask you whether there was ever anyone that I remind you of?'

In a moment Sophy was round my neck, as well as the child, and her husband was a-wringing my hand with his face hid, and we all had to shake ourselves together before we could get over it. And when we did begin to get over it, and I saw the pretty child a-talking, pleased and quick and eager and busy, to her mother, in the signs that I had first taught her mother, the happy and yet pitying tears fell rolling down my face.

SOMEBODY'S LUGGAGE

CHAPTER I

His Leaving it till Called for

The writer of these humble lines being a waiter, and having come of a family of waiters, and owning at the present time five brothers who are all waiters, and likewise an only sister who is a waitress, would wish to offer a few words respecting his calling; first having the pleasure of hereby in a friendly manner offering the dedication of the same unto *Joseph*, much respected head waiter at the Slamjam Coffee House, London, EC, than which an individual more eminently deserving of the name of man, or a more amenable honour to his own head and heart, whether considered in the light of a waiter or regarded as a human being, do not exist.

In case confusion should arise in the public mind (which it is open to confusion on many subjects) respecting what is meant or implied by the term waiter, the present humble lines would wish to offer an explanation. It may not be generally known that the person as goes out to wait is *not* a waiter. It may not be generally known that the hand as is called in extra, at the Freemasons' Tavern, or the London, or the Albion, or otherwise, is *not* a waiter. Such hands may be took on for public dinners by the bushel (and you may know them by their breathing with difficulty when in attendance, and taking away the bottle ere yet it is half out); but such are not waiters. For you cannot lay down the tailoring, or the shoemaking, or the brokering, or the green-grocering, or the pictorial-periodicalling, or the second-hand wardrobe, or the small fancy businesses – you cannot lay down those lines of life at your will and pleasure by the half-day or evening, and take up waitering. You may suppose you can, but you cannot; or you may go so far as to say you do, but you do not. Nor yet can you lay down the gentleman's-service when stimulated by prolonged incompatibility on the part of cooks (and here it may be remarked that cooking and incompatibility will be mostly found united), and take up waitering. It has been ascertained that what a gentleman will sit meek under, at home, he will not bear out of doors, at the Slamjam or any similar establishment. Then, what is the inference to be drawn respecting true waitering? You must be bred to it. You must be born to it.

Would you know how born to it, fair reader – if of the adorable female sex? Then learn from the biographical experience of one that is a waiter in the sixty-first year of his age.

You were conveyed – ere yet your dawning powers were otherwise developed than to harbour vacancy in your inside – you were conveyed, by surreptitious means, into a pantry adjoining the Admiral Nelson, civic and general dining-rooms, there to receive by stealth that healthful sustenance which is the pride and boast of the British female constitution. Your mother was married to your father (himself a distant waiter) in the profoundest secrecy; for a waitress known to be married would ruin the best of businesses – it is the same as on the stage. Hence your being smuggled into the pantry, and that – to add to the infliction – by an unwilling grandmother. Under the combined influence of the smells of roast and boiled, and soup, and gas, and malt liquors, you partook of your earliest nourishment; your unwilling grandmother sitting prepared to catch you when your mother was called and dropped you; your grand-mother's shawl ever ready to stifle your natural complainings; your innocent mind surrounded by uncongenial cruets, dirty plates, dish-covers, and cold gravy; your mother calling down the pipe for veals and porks, instead of soothing you with nursery rhymes. Under these untoward circumstances you were early weaned. Your unwilling grand–mother, ever growing more unwilling as your food assimilated less, then contracted habits of shaking you till your system curdled, and your food would not assimilate at all. At length she was no longer spared, and could have been thankfully spared much sooner. When your brothers began to appear in succession, your mother retired, left off her smart dressing (she had previously been a smart dresser), and her dark ringlets (which had previously been flowing), and haunted your father late of nights, lying in wait for him, through all weathers, up the shabby court which led to the back door of the Royal Old Dust-Bin (said to have been so named by George IV), where your father was head. But the Dust-Bin was going down then, and your father took but little – excepting from a liquid point of view. Your mother's object in those visits was of a housekeeping character, and you was set on to whistle your father out. Sometimes he came out, but generally not. Come or not come, however, all that part of his existence which was unconnected with open waitering was kept a close secret, and was acknowledged by your mother to be a close secret, and you and your mother flitted about the court, close secrets both of you, and would scarcely have confessed under torture that you knew your father, or that your father had any name than Dick (which wasn't his name, though he was never known by any other), or that he had kith or kin or chick or child. Perhaps the attraction of this mystery, combined with your father's having a damp compartment, to himself, behind a leaky cistern, at the Dust-Bin – a sort of a cellar compartment, with a sink in it, and a smell, and a plate-rack, and a bottle-rack, and three windows that didn't match each other or anything else, and no daylight – caused your young mind to feel convinced that you must grow up to be a waiter too; but you did feel convinced of it, and so did all your brothers, down to your sister. Every one of you felt convinced that you was born to the waitering. At this stage of your career, what was your feelings one day when your father came home to your mother in open broad daylight – of itself an act of Madness on the part of a waiter – and took to his bed (leastwise, your mother and family's bed), with the statement that his eyes were devilled kidneys. Physicians being in vain, your father expired, after repeating at intervals for a day and a night, when gleams of reason and old business fitfully illuminated his being, 'Two and two is five. And three is sixpence.' Interred in the parochial department of the neighbouring churchyard, and accompanied to the grave by as many waiters of long standing as could spare the morning time from their soiled glasses (namely, one), your bereaved form was attired in a white neckankecher, and you was took on from motives of benevolence at the George and Gridiron, theatrical and supper. Here, supporting nature on what you found in the plates (which was as it happened, and but too often thoughtlessly, immersed in mustard), and on what you found in the glasses (which rarely went beyond driblets and lemon), by night you dropped asleep standing, till you was cuffed awake, and by day was set to polishing every individual article in the coffee-room. Your couch being sawdust; your counterpane being ashes of cigars. Here, frequently hiding a heavy heart under the smart tie of your white neckankecher (or correctly speaking lower down and more to the left), you picked up the rudiments of knowledge from an extra, by the name of Bishops, and by calling plate-washer, and gradually elevating your mind with chalk on the back of the corner-box partition, until such time as you used the inkstand when it was out of hand, attained to manhood, and to be the waiter that you find yourself.

I could wish here to offer a few respectful words on behalf of the calling so long the calling of myself and family, and the public interest in which is but too often very limited. We are not generally understood. No, we are not. Allowance enough is not made for us. For, say that we ever show a little drooping listlessness of spirits, or what might be termed indifference or apathy. Put it to yourself what would your own state of mind be, if you was one of an enormous family every member of which except you was always greedy, and in a hurry. Put it to yourself that you was regularly replete with animal food at the slack hours of one in the day and again at nine o'clock., and that the repleter you was, the more voracious all your fellow-creatures came in. Put it to yourself that it was your business, when your digestion was well on, to take a personal interest and sympathy in a hundred gentlemen fresh and fresh (say, for the sake of argument, only a hundred), whose imaginations was given up to grease and fat and gravy and melted butter, and abandoned to questioning you about cuts of this, and dishes of that – each of 'em going on as if him and you and the bill of fare was alone in the world. Then look what you are expected to know. You are never out, but they seem to think you regularly attend everywhere. 'What's this, Christopher, that I hear about the smashed excursion train?' 'How are they doing at the Italian Opera, Christopher?' 'Christopher, what are the real particulars of this business at the Yorkshire Bank?' Similarly a ministry gives me more trouble than it gives the Queen. As to Lord Palmerston, the constant and wearing connection into which I have been brought with his lordship during the last few years is deserving of a pension. Then look at the hypocrites we are made, and the lies (white, I hope) that are forced upon us! Why must a sedentary-pursuited waiter be considered to be a judge of horseflesh, and to have a most tremendous interest in horse-training and racing? Yet it would be half our little incomes out of our pockets if we didn't take on to have those sporting tastes. It is the same (inconceivable why!) with farming. Shooting, equally so. I am sure that so regular as the months of August, September, and October come round, I am ashamed of myself in my own private bosom for the way in which I make believe to care whether or not the grouse is strong on the wing (much their wings, or drumsticks either, signifies to me, uncooked!), and whether the partridges is plentiful among the turnips, and whether the pheasants is shy or bold, or anything else you please to mention. Yet you may see me, or any other waiter of my standing, holding on by the back of the box, and leaning over a gentleman with his purse out and his bill before him, discussing these points in a confidential tone of voice, as if my happiness in life entirely depended on 'em.

I have mentioned our little incomes. Look at the most unreasonable point of all, and the point on which the greatest injustice is done us! Whether it is owing to our always carrying so much change in our right-hand trousers-pocket, and so many halfpence in our coat-tails, or whether it is human nature (which I were loth to believe), what is meant by the everlasting fable that head waiters is rich? How did that fable get into circulation? Who first put it about, and what are the facts to establish the unblushing statement? Come forth, thou slanderer, and refer the public to the waiter's will in Doctors' Commons supporting thy malignant hiss! Yet this is so commonly dwelt upon – especially by the screws who give waiters the least – that denial is vain; and we are obliged, for our credit's sake, to carry our heads as if we were going into a business, when of the two we are much more likely to go into a union. There was formerly a screw as frequented the Slamjam ere yet the present writer had quitted that establishment on a question of teaing his assistant staff out of his own pocket, which screw carried the taunt to its bitterest height. Never soaring above threepence, and as often as not grovelling on the earth a penny lower, he yet represented the present writer as a large holder of consols, a lender of money on mortgage, a capitalist. He has been over-heard to dilate to other customers on the allegation that the present writer put out thousands of pounds at interest in distilleries and breweries. 'Well, Christopher,' he would say (having grovelled his lowest on the earth, half a moment before), 'looking out for a house to open, eh? Can't find a business to be disposed of on a scale as is up to your resources, humph?' To such a dizzy precipice of falsehood has this misrepresent-ation taken wing, that the well-known and highly respected Old Charles, long eminent at the West Country Hotel, and by some considered the father of the waitering, found himself under the obligation to fall into it through so many years that his own wife (for he had an unbeknown old lady in that capacity towards himself) believed it! And what was the consequence? When he was borne to his grave on the shoulders of six picked waiters, with six more for change, six more acting as pallbearers, all keeping step in a pouring shower without a dry eye visible, and a concourse only inferior to royalty, his pantry and lodgings was equally ransacked high and low for property, and none was found! How could it be found, when, beyond his last monthly collection of walking-sticks, umbrellas, and pocket-handkerchiefs (which happened to have been not yet disposed of, though he had ever been through life punctual in clearing off his collections by the month), there was no property existing? Such, however, is the force of this universal libel, that the widow of Old Charles, at the present hour an inmate of the Almshouses of the Cork-Cutters' Company, in Blue Anchor Road (identified sitting at the door of one of 'em, in a clean cap and a Windsor armchair, only last Monday), expects John's hoarded wealth to be found hourly! Nay, ere yet he had succumbed to the grisly dart, and when his portrait was painted in oils life-size, by subscription of the frequenters of the West Country, to hang over the coffee-room chimney-piece, there were not wanting those who contended that what is termed the accessories of such a portrait ought to be the Bank of England out of window, and a strongbox on the table. And but for better-regulated minds contending for a bottle and screw and the attitude of drawing – and carrying their point – it would have been so handed down to posterity.

I am now brought to the title of the present remarks. Having, I hope without offence to any quarter, offered such observations as I felt it my duty to offer, in a free country which has ever dominated the seas, on the general subject, I will now proceed to wait on the particular question.

At a momentous period of my life, when I was off, so far as concerned notice given, with a House that shall be nameless – for the question on which I took my departing stand was a fixed charge for waiters, and no House as commits itself to that eminently un-English act of more than foolishness and baseness shall be advertised by me – I repeat, at a momentous crisis, when I was off with a House too mean for mention, and not yet on with that to which I have ever since had the honour of being attached in the capacity of head, I was casting about what to do next. Then it were that proposals were made to me on behalf of my present establishment. Stipulations were necessary on my part, emendations were necessary on my part: in the end, ratifications ensued on both sides, and I entered on a new career.

We are a bed business, and a coffee-room business. We are not a general dining business, nor do we wish it. In consequence, when diners drop in, we know what to give 'em as will keep 'em away another time. We are a private room or family business also; but coffee-room principal. Me and the directory and the writing materials and cetrer occupy a place to ourselves – a place fended off up a step or two at the end of the coffee-room, in what I call the good old-fashioned style. The good old-fashioned style is, that whatever you want, down to a wafer, you must be olely and solely dependent on the head waiter for. You must put yourself a new-born child into his hands. There is no other way in which a business untinged with Continental vice can be conducted. (It were bootless to add, that if languages is required to be jabbered and English is not good enough, both families and gentlemen had better go somewhere else.)

When I began to settle down in this right-principled and well-conducted house, I noticed, under the bed in No. 24B (which it is up a angle off the staircase, and usually put off upon the lowly-minded), a heap of things in a corner. I asked our head chambermaid in the course of the day, 'What are them things in 24B?'

To which she answered with a careless air, 'Somebody's luggage.'

Regarding her with a eye not free from severity, I says, 'Whose luggage?'

Evading my eye, she replied, 'Lor! How should *I* know!'

Being, it may be right to mention, a female of some pertness, though acquainted with her business.

A head waiter must be either head or tail. He must be at one extremity or the other of the social scale. He cannot be at the waist of it, or anywhere else but the extremities. It is for him to decide which of the extremities.

On the eventful occasion under consideration, I give Mrs Pratchett so distinctly to understand my decision, that I broke her spirit as towards myself, then and there, and for good. Let not inconsistency be suspected on account of my mentioning Mrs Pratchett as 'Mrs', and having formerly remarked that a waitress must not be married. Readers are respectfully requested to notice that Mrs Pratchett was not a waitress, but a chamber-maid. Now a chambermaid *may* be married; if head, generally is married – or says so. It comes to the same thing as expressing what is customary. (N.B. Mr Pratchett is in Australia, and his address there is 'the Bush'.)

Having took Mrs Pratchett down as many pegs as was essential to the future happiness of all parties, I requested her to explain herself.

'For instance,' I says, to give her a little encouragement, 'who is somebody?'

'I give you my sacred honour, Mr Christopher,' answers Pratchett, 'that I haven't the faintest notion.'

But for the manner in which she settled her cap-strings, I should have doubted this; but in respect of positiveness it was hardly to be discriminated from an affidavit.

'Then you never saw him?' I followed her up with.

'Nor yet,' said Mrs Pratchett, shutting her eyes and making as if she had just took a pill of unusual circumference – which gave a remarkable force to her denial – 'nor yet any servant in this house. All have been changed, Mr Christopher, within five year, and somebody left his luggage here before then.'

Enquiry of Miss Martin yielded (in the language of the Bard of A1) 'confirmation strong'. So it had really and truly happened. Miss Martin is the young lady at the bar as makes out our bills; and though higher than I could wish considering her station, is perfectly well-behaved.

Farther investigations led to the disclosure that there was a bill against this Luggage to the amount of two sixteen six. The Luggage had been lying under the bedstead of 24B over six year. The bedstead is a four-poster, with a deal of old hanging and valance, and is, as I once said, probably connected with more than 24Bs – which I remember my hearers was pleased to laugh at, at the time.

I don't know why – when *do* we know why? – but this Luggage laid heavy on my mind. I fell a wondering about Somebody, and what he had got and been up to. I couldn't satisfy my thoughts why he should leave so much Luggage against so small a bill. For I had the Luggage out within a day or two and turned it over, and the following were the items: – A black portmanteau, a black bag, a desk, a dressing-case, a brown-paper parcel, a hatbox, and an umbrella strapped to a walking-stick. It was all very dusty and fluey. I had our porter up to get under the bed and fetch it out; and though he habitually wallows in dust – swims in it from morning to night, and wears a close-fitting waistcoat with black calimanco sleeves for the purpose – it made him sneeze again, and his throat was that hot with it that it was obliged to be cooled with a drink of Allsopp's draft.

The Luggage so got the better of me, that instead of having it put back when it was well dusted and washed with a wet cloth – previous to which it was so covered with feathers that you might have thought it was turning into poultry, and would by and by begin to lay – I say, instead of having it put back, I had it carried into one of my places downstairs. There from time to time I stared at it and stared at it, till it seemed to grow big and grow little, and come forward at me and retreat again, and go through all manner of performances resembling intoxication. When this had lasted weeks – I may say months, and not be far out – I one day thought of asking Miss Martin for the particulars of the two sixteen six total. She was so obliging as to extract it from the books – it dating before her time – and here follows a true copy:

Coffee-Room. 1856. No. 4.	£	s.	d.
Feb. 2d,			
Pen and paper	0	0	6
Port Negus	0	2	0
Ditto	0	2	0
Pen and paper	0	0	6
Tumbler broken	0	2	6
Brandy	0	2	0
Pen and paper	0	0	6
Anchovy toast	0	2	6
Pen and paper	0	0	6
Bed	0	3	0
Feb. 3d,			
Pen and paper	0	0	6
Breakfast	0	2	6
Broiled ham	0	2	0
Eggs	0	1	0
Watercresses	0	1	0
Shrimps	0	1	0
Pen and paper	0	0	6
Blotting-paper	0	0	6
Messenger to Paternoster Row and back	0	1	6
Again, when no answer	0	1	6
Brandy	0	2	0
Devilled pork chop	0	2	0
Pens and paper	0	1	0
Messenger to Albemarle Street and back	0	1	0
Again (detained), when no answer	0	1	6
Salt-cellar broken	0	3	6
Large liqueur-glass orange brandy	0	1	6
Dinner, soup, fish, joint, and bird	0	7	6
Bottle old East India Brown	0	8	0
Pen and paper	0	0	6
	£2	16	6

Mem.: January 1st, 1857. He went out after dinner, directing Luggage to be ready when he called for it. Never called.

*   *   *

So far from throwing a light upon the subject, this bill appeared to me, if I may so express my doubts, to involve it in a yet more lurid halo. Speculating it over with the mistress, she informed me that the Luggage had been advertised in the master's time as being to be sold after such and such a day to pay expenses, but no farther steps had been taken. (I may here remark, that the mistress is a widow in her fourth year. The master was possessed of one of those unfortunate constitutions in which spirits turns to water, and rises in the ill-starred victim.)

My speculating it over, not then only, but repeatedly, sometimes with the mistress, sometimes with one, sometimes with another, led up to the mistress's saying to me – whether at first in joke or in earnest, or half joke and half earnest, it matters not: 'Christopher, I am going to make you a handsome offer.'

(If this should meet her eye – a lovely blue – may she not take it ill my mentioning that if I had been eight or ten year younger, I would have done as much by her! That is, I would have made her a offer. It is for others than me to denominate it a handsome one.)

'Christopher, I am going to make you a handsome offer.'

'Put a name to it, ma'am.'

'Look here, Christopher. Run over the articles of Somebody's Luggage. You've got it all by heart, I know.'

'A black portmanteau, ma'am, a black bag, a desk, a dressing-case, a brown-paper parcel, a hatbox, and an umbrella strapped to a walking-stick.'

'All just as they were left. Nothing opened, nothing tampered with.'

'You are right, ma'am. All locked but the brown-paper parcel, and that sealed.'

The mistress was leaning on Miss Martin's desk at the bar-window, and she taps the open book that lays upon the desk – she has a pretty-made hand to be sure – and bobs her head over it and laughs.

'Come,' says she, 'Christopher. Pay me Somebody's bill, and you shall have Somebody's Luggage.'

I rather took to the idea from the first moment; but,

'It mayn't be worth the money,' I objected, seeming to hold back.

'That's a lottery,' says the mistress, folding her arms upon the book – it ain't her hands alone that's pretty made, the observation extends right up her arms. 'Won't you venture two pound sixteen shillings and sixpence in the lottery? Why, there's no blanks!' says the mistress; laughing and bobbing her head again, 'you *must* win. If you lose, you must win! All prizes in this lottery! Draw a blank, and remember, gentlemen-sportsmen, you'll still be entitled to a black portmanteau, a black bag, a desk, a dressing-case, a sheet of brown paper, a hatbox, and an umbrella strapped to a walking-stick!'

To make short of it, Miss Martin come round me, and Mrs Pratchett come round me, and the mistress she was completely round me already, and all the women in the house come round me, and if it had been Sixteen two instead of Two sixteen, I should have thought myself well out of it. For what can you do when they do come round you?

So I paid the money – down – and such a laughing as there was among 'em! But I turned the tables on 'em regularly, when I said: 'My family-name is Blue-Beard. I'm going to open Somebody's Luggage all alone in the Secret Chamber, and not a female eye catches sight of the contents!'

Whether I thought proper to have the firmness to keep to this, don't signify, or whether any female eye, and if any, how many, was really present when the opening of the Luggage came off. Somebody's Luggage is the question at present: Nobody's eyes, nor yet noses.

What I still look at most, in connection with that Luggage, is the extraordinary quantity of writing-paper, and all written on! And not our paper neither – not the paper charged in the bill, for we know our paper – so he must have been always at it. And he had crumpled up this writing of his, everywhere, in every part and parcel of his Luggage. There was writing in his dressing-case, writing in his boots, writing among his shaving-tackle, writing in his hatbox, writing folded away down among the very whalebones of his umbrella.

His clothes wasn't bad, what there was of 'em. His dressing-case was poor – not a particle of silver stopper – bottle apertures with nothing in 'em, like empty little dog-kennels – and a most searching description of tooth-powder diffusing itself around, as under a deluded mistake that all the chinks in the fittings was divisions in teeth. His clothes I parted with, well enough, to a second-hand dealer not far from St Clement's Danes, in the Strand – him as the officers in the army mostly dispose of their uniforms to, when hard pressed with debts of honour, if I may judge from their coats and epaulettes diversifying the window with their backs towards the public. The same party bought in one lot the portmanteau, the bag, the desk, the dressing-case, the hatbox, the umbrella, strap, and walking-stick. On my remarking that I should have thought those articles not quite in his line, he said: 'No more ith a man'th grandmother, Mithter Chrithtopher; but if any man will bring hith grandmother here, and offer her at a fair trifle below what the'll feth with good luck when the'th thcoured and turned – I'll buy her!'

These transactions brought me home, and, indeed, more than home, for they left a goodish profit on the original investment. And now there remained the writings; and the writings I particular wish to bring under the candid attention of the reader.

I wish to do so without postponement, for this reason. That is to say, namely, viz. i.e., as follows, thus: – Before I proceed to recount the mental sufferings of which I became the prey in consequence of the writings, and before following up that harrowing tale with a statement of the wonderful and impressive catastrophe, as thrilling in its nature as unlooked for in any other capacity, which crowned the ole and filled the cup of unexpectedness to overflowing, the writings themselves ought to stand forth to view. Therefore it is that they now come next. One word to introduce them, and I lay down my pen (I hope, my unassuming pen) until I take it up to trace the gloomy sequel of a mind with something on it.

He was a smeary writer, and wrote a dreadful bad hand. Utterly regardless of ink, he lavished it on every undeserving object – on his clothes, his desk, his hat, the handle of his toothbrush, his umbrella. Ink was found freely on the coffee-room carpet by No. 4 table, and two blots was on his restless couch. A reference to the document I have given entire will show that on the morning of the third of February, eighteen fifty-six, he procured his no less than fifth pen and paper. To whatever deplorable act of ungovernable composition he immolated those materials obtained from the bar, there is no doubt that the fatal deed was committed in bed, and that it left its evidences but too plainly, long afterwards, upon the pillowcase.

He had put no heading to any of his writings. Alas! Was he likely to have a heading without a head, and where was *his* head when he took such things into it? In some cases, such as his boots, he would appear to have hid the writings; thereby involving his style in greater obscurity. But his boots was at least pairs – and no two of his writings can put in any claim to be so regarded. Here follows (not to give more specimens) what was found in

CHAPTER 2

His Boots

'Eh! well then, Monsieur Mutuel! What do I know, what can I say? I assure you that he calls himself Monsieur the Englishman.'

'Pardon. But I think it is impossible,' said Monsieur Mutuel – a spectacled, snuffy, stooping old gentleman in carpet shoes and a cloth cap with a peaked shade, a loose blue frock-coat reaching to his heels, a large limp white shirt-frill, and cravat to correspond – that is to say, white was the natural colour of his linen on Sundays, but it toned down with the week.

'It is,' repeated Monsieur Mutuel, his amiable old walnut-shell countenance very walnut-shelly indeed as he smiled and blinked in the bright morning sunlight – 'it is, my cherished Madame Bouclet, I think, impossible!'

'Hey!' (with a little vexed cry and a great many tosses of her head). 'But it is not impossible that you are a pig!' retorted Madame Bouclet, a compact little woman of thirty-five or so. 'See then – look there – read! "On the second floor Monsieur L'Anglais". Is it not so?'

'It is so,' said Monsieur Mutuel.

'Good. Continue your morning walk. Get out!' Madame Bouclet dismissed him with a lively snap of her fingers.

The morning walk of Monsieur Mutuel was in the brightest patch that the sun made in the Grande Place of a dull old fortified French town. The manner of his morning walk was with his hands crossed behind him; an umbrella, in figure the express image of himself, always in one hand; a snuffbox in the other. Thus, with the shuffling gait of the elephant (who really does deal with the very worst trousers-maker employed by the zoological world, and who appeared to have recommended him to Monsieur Mutuel), the old gentleman sunned himself daily when sun was to be had – of course, at the same time sunning a red ribbon at his buttonhole; for was he not an ancient Frenchman?

Being told by one of the angelic sex to continue his morning walk and get out, Monsieur Mutuel laughed a walnut-shell laugh, pulled off his cap at arm's length with the hand that contained his snuffbox, kept it off for a considerable period after he had parted from Madame Bouclet, and continued his morning walk and got out, like a man of gallantry as he was.

The documentary evidence to which Madame Bouclet had referred Monsieur Mutuel was the list of her lodgers, sweetly written forth by her own nephew and bookkeeper, who held the pen of an angel, and posted up at the side of her gateway, for the information of the police: 'Au second, M. L'Anglais, proprietaire'. On the second floor, Mr the Englishman, man of property. So it stood; nothing could be plainer.

Madame Bouclet now traced the line with her forefinger, as it were to confirm and settle herself in her parting snap at Monsieur Mutuel, and so placing her right hand on her hip with a defiant air, as if nothing should ever tempt her to unsnap that snap, strolled out into the place to glance up at the windows of Mr the Englishman. That worthy happening to be looking out of window at the moment, Madame Bouclet gave him a graceful salutation with her head, looked to the right and looked to the left to account to him for her being there, considered for a moment, like one who accounted to herself for somebody she had expected not being there, and re-entered her own gateway. Madame Bouclet let all her house giving on the place in furnished flats or floors, and lived up the yard behind in company with Monsieur Bouclet her husband (great at billiards), an inherited brewing business, several fowls, two carts, a nephew, a little dog in a big kennel, a grapevine, a counting-house, four horses, a married sister (with a share in the brewing business), the husband and two children of the married sister, a parrot, a drum (performed on by the little boy of the married sister), two billeted soldiers, a quantity of pigeons, a fife (played by the nephew in a ravishing manner), several domestics and supernumeraries, a perpetual flavour of coffee and soup, a terrific range of artificial rocks and wooden precipices at least four feet high, a small fountain, and half-a-dozen large sunflowers.

Now the Englishman, in taking his appartement – or, as one might say on our side of the Channel, his set of chambers – had given his name, correct to the letter, Langley. But as he had a British way of not opening his mouth very wide on foreign soil, except at meals, the brewery had been able to make nothing of it but L'Anglais. So Mr the Englishman he had become and he remained.

'Never saw such a people!' muttered Mr the Englishman, as he now looked out of window. 'Never did, in my life!'

This was true enough, for he had never before been out of his own country – a right little island, a tight little island, a bright little island, a show-fight little island, and full of merit of all sorts; but not the whole round world.

'These chaps,' said Mr the Englishman to himself, as his eye rolled over the place, sprinkled with military here and there, 'are no more like soldiers – ' Nothing being sufficiently strong for the end of his sentence, he left it unended.

This again (from the point of view of his experience) was strictly correct; for though there was a great agglomeration of soldiers in the town and neighbouring country, you might have held a grand review and field-day of them every one, and looked in vain among them all for a soldier choking behind his foolish stock, or a soldier lamed by his ill-fitting shoes, or a soldier deprived of the use of his limbs by straps and buttons, or a soldier elaborately forced to be self-helpless in all the small affairs of life. A swarm of brisk, bright, active, bustling, handy, odd, skirmishing fellows, able to turn cleverly at anything, from a siege to soup, from great guns to needles and thread, from the broadsword exercise to slicing an onion, from making war to making omelettes, was all you would have found.

What a swarm! From the Great Place under the eye of Mr the English-man, where a few awkward squads from the last conscription were doing the goose-step – some members of those squads still as to their bodies, in the chrysalis peasant-state of Blouse, and only military butterflies as to their regimentally clothed legs – from the Great Place, away outside the fortifications, and away for miles along the dusty roads, soldiers swarmed. All day long, upon the grass-grown ramparts of the town, practising soldiers trumpeted and bugled; all day long, down in angles of dry trenches, practising soldiers drummed and drummed. Every forenoon, soldiers burst out of the great barracks into the sandy gymnasium-ground hard by, and flew over the wooden horse, and hung on to flying ropes, and dangled upside-down between parallel bars, and shot themselves off wooden platforms – splashes, sparks, coruscations, showers of soldiers. At every corner of the town-wall, every guardhouse, every gateway, every sentry-box, every drawbridge, every reedy ditch, and rushy dike, soldiers, soldiers, soldiers. And the town being pretty well all wall, guardhouse, gateway, sentry-box, drawbridge, reedy ditch, and rushy dike, the town was pretty well all soldiers.

What would the sleepy old town have been without the soldiers, seeing that even with them it had so overslept itself as to have slept its echoes hoarse, its defensive bars and locks and bolts and chains all rusty, and its ditches stagnant! From the days when Vauban engineered it to that perplexing extent that to look at it was like being knocked on the head with it, the stranger becoming stunned and stertorous under the shock of its incomprehensibility – from the days when Vauban made it the express incorporation of every substantive and adjective in the art of military engineering, and not only twisted you into it and twisted you out of it, to the right, to the left, opposite, under here, over there, in the dark, in the dirt, by the gateway, archway, covered way, dry way, wet way, fosse, portcullis, drawbridge, sluice, squat tower, pierced wall, and heavy battery, but likewise took a fortifying dive under the neighbouring country, and came to the surface three or four miles off, blowing out incomprehensible mounds and batteries among the quiet crops of chicory and beetroot – from those days to these the town had been asleep, and dust and rust and must had settled on its drowsy arsenals and magazines, and grass had grown up in its silent streets.

On market-days alone, its Great Place suddenly leaped out of bed. On market-days, some friendly enchanter struck his staff upon the stones of the Great Place, and instantly arose the liveliest booths and stalls, and sittings and standings, and a pleasant hum of chaffering and huckstering from many hundreds of tongues, and a pleasant, though peculiar, blending of colours – white caps, blue blouses, and green vegetables – and at last the knight destined for the adventure seemed to have come in earnest, and all the Vaubanois sprang up awake. And now, by long, low-lying avenues of trees, jolting in white-hooded donkey-cart, and on donkey-back, and in tumbril and waggon, and cart and cabriolet, and afoot with barrow and burden – and along the dikes and ditches and canals, in little peak-prowed country boats – came peasant-men and women in flocks and crowds, bringing articles for sale. And here you had boots and shoes, and sweetmeats and stuffs to wear, and here (in the cool shade of the town hall) you had milk and cream and butter and cheese, and here you had fruits and onions and carrots, and all things needful for your soup, and here you had poultry and flowers and protesting pigs, and here new shovels, axes, spades, and billhooks for your farming work, and here huge mounds of bread, and here your unground grain in sacks, and here your children's dolls, and here the cake-seller, announcing his wares by beat and roll of drum. And hark! fanfaronade of trumpets, and here into the Great Place, resplendent in an open carriage, with four gorgeously attired servitors up behind, playing horns, drums, and cymbals, rolled 'the daughter of a physician' in massive golden chains and ear-rings, and blue-feathered hat, shaded from the admiring sun by two immense umbrellas of artificial roses, to dispense (from motives of philanthropy) that small and pleasant dose which had cured so many thousands! Toothache, earache, headache, heartache, stomachache, debility, nervousness, fits, fainting, fever, ague, all equally cured by the small and pleasant dose of the great physician's great daughter! The process was this – she, the daughter of a physician, proprietress of the superb equipage you now admired with its confirmatory blasts of trumpet, drum, and cymbal, told you so: On the first day after taking the small and pleasant dose, you would feel no particular influence beyond a most harmonious sensation of indescribable and irresistible joy; on the second day you would be so astonishingly better that you would think yourself changed into somebody else; on the third day you would be entirely free from disorder, whatever its nature and however long you had had it, and would seek out the physician's daughter to throw yourself at her feet, kiss the hem of her garment, and buy as many more of the small and pleasant doses as by the sale of all your few effects you could obtain; but she would be inaccessible – gone for herbs to the Pyramids of Egypt – and you would be (though cured) reduced to despair! Thus would the physician's daughter drive her trade (and briskly too), and thus would the buying and selling and mingling of tongues and colours continue, until the changing sunlight, leaving the physician's daughter in the shadow of high roofs, admonished her to jolt out westward, with a departing effect of gleam and glitter on the splendid equipage and brazen blast. And now the enchanter struck his staff upon the stones of the Great Place once more, and down went the booths, the sittings and standings, and vanished the merchandise, and with it the barrows, donkeys, donkey-carts, and tumbrils, and all other things on wheels and feet, except the slow scavengers with unwieldy carts and meagre horses clearing up the rubbish, assisted by the sleek town pigeons, better plumped out than on non-market-days. While there was yet an hour or two to wane before the autumn sunset, the loiterer outside town-gate and drawbridge, and postern and double-ditch, would see the last white-hooded cart lessening in the avenue of lengthening shadows of trees, or the last country boat, paddled by the last market-woman on her way home, showing black upon the reddening, long, low, narrow dike between him and the mill; and as the paddle-parted scum and weed closed over the boat's track, he might be comfortably sure that its sluggish rest would be troubled no more until next market-day.

As it was not one of the Great Place's days for getting out of bed, when Mr the Englishman looked down at the young soldiers practising the goose-step there, his mind was left at liberty to take a military turn.

'These fellows are billeted everywhere about,' said he; 'and to see them lighting the people's fires, boiling the people's pots, minding the people's babies, rocking the people's cradles, washing the people's greens, and making themselves generally useful, in every sort of unmilitary way, is most ridiculous! Never saw such a set of fellows – never did in my life!'

All perfectly true again. Was there not Private Valentine in that very house, acting as sole housemaid, valet, cook, steward, and nurse, in the family of his captain, Monsieur le Capitaine de la Cour – cleaning the floors, making the beds, doing the marketing, dressing the captain, dressing the dinners, dressing the salads, and dressing the baby, all with equal readiness? Or, to put him aside, he being in loyal attendance on his chief, was there not Private Hyppolite, billeted at the perfumer's two hundred yards off, who, when not on duty, volunteered to keep shop while the fair perfumeress stepped out to speak to a neighbour or so, and laughingly sold soap with his war-sword girded on him? Was there not Emile, billeted at the clock-maker's, perpetually turning to of an evening, with his coat off, winding up the stock? Was there not Eugene, billeted at the tinman's, cultivating, pipe in mouth, a garden four feet square, for the tinman, in the little court, behind the shop, and extorting the fruits of the earth from the same, on his knees, with the sweat of his brow? Not to multiply examples, was there not Baptiste, billeted on the poor water-carrier, at that very instant sitting on the pavement in the sunlight, with his martial legs asunder, and one of the water-carrier's spare pails between them, which (to the delight and glory of the heart of the water-carrier coming across the place from the fountain, yoked and burdened) he was painting bright-green outside and bright-red within? Or, to go no farther than the barber's at the very next door, was there not Corporal Theophile –

'No,' said Mr the Englishman, glancing down at the barber's, 'he is not there at present. There's the child, though.'

A mere mite of a girl stood on the steps of the barber's shop, looking across the place. A mere baby, one might call her, dressed in the close white linen cap which small French country children wear (like the children in Dutch pictures), and in a frock of homespun blue, that had no shape except where it was tied round her little fat throat. So that, being naturally short and round all over, she looked, behind, as if she had been cut off at her natural waist, and had had her head neatly fitted on it.

'There's the child, though.'

To judge from the way in which the dimpled hand was rubbing the eyes, the eyes had been closed in a nap, and were newly opened. But they seemed to be looking so intently across the place, that the Englishman looked in the same direction.

'O!' said he presently. 'I thought as much. The corporal's there.'

The corporal, a smart figure of a man of thirty, perhaps a thought under the middle size, but very neatly made – a sunburnt corporal with a brown peaked beard – faced about at the moment, addressing voluble words of instruction to the squad in hand. Nothing was amiss or awry about the corporal. A lithe and nimble corporal, quite complete, from the sparkling dark eyes under his knowing uniform cap to his sparkling white gaiters. The very image and presentment of a corporal of his country's army, in the line of his shoulders, the line of his waist, the broadest line of his bloomer trousers, and their narrowest line at the calf of his leg.

Mr the Englishman looked on, and the child looked on, and the corporal looked on (but the last-named at his men), until the drill ended a few minutes afterwards, and the military sprinkling dried up directly, and was gone. Then said Mr the Englishman to himself, 'Look here! By George!' And the corporal, dancing towards the barber's with his arms wide open, caught up the child, held her over his head in a flying attitude, caught her down again, kissed her, and made off with her into the barber's house.

Now Mr the Englishman had had a quarrel with his erring and disobedient and disowned daughter, and there was a child in that case too. Had not his daughter been a child, and had she not taken angel-flights above his head as this child had flown above the corporal's?

'He's a "National Participled" fool!' said the Englishman, and shut his window.

But the windows of the house of memory, and the windows of the house of mercy, are not so easily closed as windows of glass and wood. They fly open unexpectedly; they rattle in the night; they must be nailed up. Mr the Englishman had tried nailing them, but had not driven the nails quite home. So he passed but a disturbed evening and a worse night.

By nature a good-tempered man? No; very little gentleness, confounding the quality with weakness. Fierce and wrathful when crossed? Very, and stupendously unreasonable. Moody? Exceedingly so. Vindictive? Well; he had had scowling thoughts that he would formally curse his daughter, as he had seen it done on the stage. But remembering that the real Heaven is some paces removed from the mock one in the great chandelier of the theatre, he had given that up.

And he had come abroad to be rid of his repudiated daughter for the rest of his life. And here he was.

At bottom, it was for this reason, more than for any other, that Mr the Englishman took it extremely ill that Corporal Theophile should be so devoted to little Bebelle, the child at the barber's shop. In an unlucky moment he had chanced to say to himself, 'Why, confound the fellow, he is not her father!' There was a sharp sting in the speech which ran into him suddenly, and put him in a worse mood. So he had National Participled the unconscious corporal with most hearty emphasis, and had made up his mind to think no more about such a mountebank.

But it came to pass that the corporal was not to be dismissed. If he had known the most delicate fibres of the Englishman's mind, instead of knowing nothing on earth about him, and if he had been the most obstinate corporal in the Grand Army of France, instead of being the most obliging, he could not have planted himself with more determined immovability plump in the midst of all the Englishman's thoughts. Not only so, but he seemed to be always in his view. Mr the Englishman had but to look out of window, to look upon the corporal with little Bebelle. He had but to go for a walk, and there was the corporal walking with Bebelle. He had but to come home again, disgusted, and the corporal and Bebelle were at home before him. If he looked out at his back windows early in the morning, the corporal was in the barber's back yard, washing and dressing and brushing Bebelle. If he took refuge at his front windows, the corporal brought his breakfast out into the place, and shared it there with Bebelle. Always corporal and always Bebelle. Never corporal without Bebelle. Never Bebelle without corporal.

Mr the Englishman was not particularly strong in the French language as a means of oral communication, though he read it very well. It is with languages as with people – when you only know them by sight, you are apt to mistake them; you must be on speaking terms before you can be said to have established an acquaintance.

For this reason, Mr the Englishman had to gird up his loins considerably before he could bring himself to the point of exchanging ideas with Madame Bouclet on the subject of this corporal and this Bebelle. But Madame Bouclet looking in apologetically one morning to remark, that, O Heaven! she was in a state of desolation because the lamp-maker had not sent home that lamp confided to him to repair, but that truly he was a lamp-maker against whom the whole world shrieked out, Mr the Englishman seized the occasion.

'Madame, that baby – '

'Pardon, monsieur. That lamp.'

'No, no, that little girl.'

'But, pardon!' said Madame Bouclet, angling for a clew, 'one cannot light a little girl, or send her to be repaired.'

'The little girl – at the house of the barber.'

'Ah-h-h!' cried Madame Bouclet, suddenly catching the idea with her delicate little line and rod. 'Little Bebelle? Yes, yes, yes! And her friend the corporal? Yes, yes, yes, yes! So genteel of him – is it not?'

'He is not – ?'

'Not at all; not at all! He is not one of her relations. Not at all!'

'Why, then, he – '

'Perfectly!' cried Madame Bouclet, 'you are right, monsieur. It is so genteel of him. The less relation, the more genteel. As you say.'

'Is she – ?'

'The child of the barber?' Madame Bouclet whisked up her skilful little line and rod again. 'Not at all, not at all! She is the child of – in a word, of no one.'

'The wife of the barber, then – ?'

'Indubitably. As you say. The wife of the barber receives a small stipend to take care of her. So much by the month. Eh, then! It is without doubt very little, for we are all poor here.'

'You are not poor, madame.'

'As to my lodgers,' replied Madame Bouclet, with a smiling and a gracious bend of her head, 'no. As to all things else, so-so.'

'You flatter me, madame.'

'Monsieur, it is you who flatter me in living here.'

Certain fishy gasps on Mr the Englishman's part, denoting that he was about to resume his subject under difficulties, Madame Bouclet observed him closely, and whisked up her delicate line and rod again with triumphant success.

'O no, monsieur, certainly not. The wife of the barber is not cruel to the poor child, but she is careless. Her health is delicate, and she sits all day, looking out at window. Consequently, when the corporal first came, the poor little Bebelle was much neglected.'

'It is a curious – ' began Mr the Englishman.

'Name? That Bebelle? Again you are right, monsieur. But it is a playful name for Gabrielle.'

'And so the child is a mere fancy of the corporal's?' said Mr the Englishman, in a gruffly disparaging tone of voice.

'Eh, well!' returned Madame Bouclet, with a pleading shrug: 'one must love something. Human nature is weak.'

('Devilish weak,' muttered the Englishman, in his own language.)

'And the corporal,' pursued Madame Bouclet, 'being billeted at the barber's – where he will probably remain a long time, for he is attached to the general – and finding the poor unowned child in need of being loved, and finding himself in need of loving – why, there you have it all, you see!'

Mr the Englishman accepted this interpretation of the matter with an indifferent grace, and observed to himself, in an injured manner, when he was again alone: 'I shouldn't mind it so much, if these people were not such a' – National Participled – 'sentimental people!'

There was a cemetery outside the town, and it happened ill for the reputation of the Vaubanois, in this sentimental connection, that he took a walk there that same afternoon. To be sure there were some wonderful things in it (from the Englishman's point of view), and of a certainty in all Britain you would have found nothing like it. Not to mention the fanciful flourishes of hearts and crosses in wood and iron, that were planted all over the place, making it look very like a firework-ground, where a most splendid pyrotechnic display might be expected after dark, there were so many wreaths upon the graves, embroidered, as it might be, 'To my mother', 'To my daughter', 'To my father', 'To my brother', 'To my sister', 'To my friend', and those many wreaths were in so many stages of elaboration and decay, from the wreath of yesterday, all fresh colour and bright beads, to the wreath of last year, a poor mouldering wisp of straw! There were so many little gardens and grottos made upon graves, in so many tastes, with plants and shells and plaster figures and porcelain pitchers, and so many odds and ends! There were so many tributes of remembrance hanging up, not to be discriminated by the closest inspection from little round waiters, whereon were depicted in glowing lines either a lady or a gentleman with a white pocket-hand-kerchief out of all proportion, leaning, in a state of the most faultless mourning and most profound affliction, on the most architectural and gorgeous urn! There were so many surviving wives who had put their names on the tombs of their deceased husbands, with a blank for the date of their own departure from this weary world; and there were so many surviving husbands who had rendered the same homage to their deceased wives; and out of the number there must have been so many who had long ago married again! In fine, there was so much in the place that would have seemed more frippery to a stranger, save for the consideration that the lightest paper flower that lay upon the poorest heap of earth was never touched by a rude hand, but perished there, a sacred thing!

'Nothing of the solemnity of death here,' Mr the Englishman had been going to say, when this last consideration touched him with a mild appeal, and on the whole he walked out without saying it. 'But these people are,' he insisted, by way of compensation, when he was well outside the gate, 'they are so' – Participled – 'sentimental!'

His way back lay by the military gymnasium-ground. And there he passed the corporal glibly instructing young soldiers how to swing them-selves over rapid and deep watercourses on their way to glory, by means of a rope, and himself deftly plunging off a platform, and flying a hundred feet or two, as an encouragement to them to begin. And there he also passed, perched on a crowning eminence (probably the corporal's careful hands), the small Bebelle, with her round eyes wide open, surveying the proceeding like a wondering sort of blue and white bird.

'If that child was to die,' this was his reflection as he turned his back and went his way – 'and it would almost serve the fellow right for making such a fool of himself – I suppose we should have him sticking up a wreath and a waiter in that fantastic burying-ground.'

Nevertheless, after another early morning or two of looking out of window, he strolled down into the place, when the corporal and Bebelle were walking there, and touching his hat to the corporal (an immense achievement), wished him Good-day.

'Good-day, monsieur.'

'This is a rather pretty child you have here,' said Mr the Englishman, taking her chin in his hand, and looking down into her astonished blue eyes.

'Monsieur, she is a very pretty child,' returned the corporal, with a stress on his polite correction of the phrase.

'And good?' said the Englishman.

'And very good. Poor little thing!'

'Hah!' The Englishman stooped down and patted her cheek, not without awkwardness, as if he were going too far in his conciliation. 'And what is this medal round your neck, my little one?'

Bebelle having no other reply on her lips than her chubby right fist, the corporal offered his services as interpreter.

'Monsieur demands, what is this, Bebelle?'

'It is the Holy Virgin,' said Bebelle.

'And who gave it you?' asked the Englishman.

'Theophile.'

'And who is Theophile?'

Bebelle broke into a laugh, laughed merrily and heartily, clapped her chubby hands, and beat her little feet on the stone pavement of the place.

'He doesn't know Theophile! Why, he doesn't know anyone! He doesn't know anything!' Then, sensible of a small solecism in her manners, Bebelle twisted her right hand in a leg of the corporal's bloomer trousers, and, laying her cheek against the place, kissed it.

'Monsieur Theophile, I believe?' said the Englishman to the corporal.

'It is I, monsieur.'

'Permit me.' Mr the Englishman shook him heartily by the hand and turned away. But he took it mighty ill that old Monsieur Mutuel in his patch of sunlight, upon whom he came as he turned, should pull off his cap to him with a look of pleased approval. And he muttered, in his own tongue, as he returned the salutation, 'Well, walnut-shell! And what business is it of *yours*?'

Mr the Englishman went on for many weeks passing but disturbed evenings and worse nights, and constantly experiencing that those aforesaid windows in the houses of memory and mercy rattled after dark, and that he had very imperfectly nailed them up. Likewise, he went on for many weeks daily improving the acquaintance of the corporal and Bebelle. That is to say, he took Bebelle by the chin, and the corporal by the hand, and offered Bebelle sous and the corporal cigars, and even got the length of changing pipes with the corporal and kissing Bebelle. But he did it all in a shamefaced way, and always took it extremely ill that Monsieur Mutuel in his patch of sunlight should note what he did. Whenever that seemed to be the case, he always growled in his own tongue, 'There you are again, walnut-shell! What business is it of yours?'

In a word, it had become the occupation of Mr the Englishman's life to look after the corporal and little Bebelle, and to resent old Monsieur Mutuel's looking after *him*. An occupation only varied by a fire in the town one windy night, and much passing of water-buckets from hand to hand (in which the Englishman rendered good service), and much beating of drums – when all of a sudden the corporal disappeared.

Next, all of a sudden, Bebelle disappeared.

She had been visible a few days later than the corporal – sadly deteriorated as to washing and brushing – but she had not spoken when addressed by Mr the Englishman, and had looked scared and had run away. And now it would seem that she had run away for good. And there lay the Great Place under the windows, bare and barren.

In his shamefaced and constrained way, Mr the Englishman asked no question of anyone, but watched from his front windows and watched from his back windows, and lingered about the place, and peeped in at the barber's shop, and did all this and much more with a whistling and tune-humming pretence of not missing anything, until one afternoon when Monsieur Mutuel's patch of sunlight was in shadow, and when, according to all rule and precedent, he had no right whatever to bring his red ribbon out of doors, behold here he was, advancing with his cap already in his hand twelve paces off!

Mr the Englishman had got as far into his usual objurgation as, 'What bu-si –' when he checked himself.

'Ah, it is sad, it is sad! Helas, it is unhappy, it is sad!' Thus old Monsieur Mutuel, shaking his grey head.

'What busin – at least, I would say, what do you mean, Monsieur Mutuel?'

'Our corporal. Helas, our dear corporal!'

'What has happened to him?'

'You have not heard?'

'No.'

'At the fire. But he was so brave, so ready. Ah, too brave, too ready!'

'May the Devil carry you away!' the Englishman broke in impatiently; 'I beg your pardon – I mean me – I am not accustomed to speak French – go on, will you?'

'And a falling beam – '

'Good God!' exclaimed the Englishman. 'It was a private soldier who was killed?'

'No. A corporal, the same corporal, our dear corporal. Beloved by all his comrades. The funeral ceremony was touching – penetrating. Monsieur the Englishman, your eyes fill with tears.'

'What bu-si – '

'Monsieur the Englishman, I honour those emotions. I salute you with profound respect. I will not obtrude myself upon your noble heart.'

Monsieur Mutuel – a gentleman in every thread of his cloudy linen, under whose wrinkled hand every grain in the quarter of an ounce of poor snuff in his poor little tin box became a gentleman's property – Monsieur Mutuel passed on, with his cap in his hand.

'I little thought,' said the Englishman, after walking for several minutes, and more than once blowing his nose, 'when I was looking round that cemetery – I'll go there!'

Straight he went there, and when he came within the gate he paused, considering whether he should ask at the lodge for some direction to the grave. But he was less than ever in a mood for asking questions, and he thought, 'I shall see something on it to know it by.'

In search of the corporal's grave he went softly on, up this walk and down that, peering in, among the crosses and hearts and columns and obelisks and tombstones, for a recently disturbed spot. It troubled him now to think how many dead there were in the cemetery – he had not thought them a tenth part so numerous before – and after he had walked and sought for some time, he said to himself, as he struck down a new vista of tombs, 'I might suppose that every one was dead but I.'

Not every one. A live child was lying on the ground asleep. Truly he had found something on the corporal's grave to know it by, and the something was Bebelle.

With such a loving will had the dead soldier's comrades worked at his resting-place, that it was already a neat garden. On the green turf of the garden Bebelle lay sleeping, with her cheek touching it. A plain, unpainted little wooden cross was planted in the turf, and her short arm embraced this little cross, as it had many a time embraced the corporal's neck. They had put a tiny flag (the flag of France) at his head, and a laurel garland.

Mr the Englishman took off his hat, and stood for a while silent. Then, covering his head again, he bent down on one knee, and softly roused the child.

'Bebelle! My little one!'

Opening her eyes, on which the tears were still wet, Bebelle was at first frightened; but seeing who it was, she suffered him to take her in his arms, looking steadfastly at him.

'You must not lie here, my little one. You must come with me.'

'No, no. I can't leave Theophile. I want the good dear Theophile.'

'We will go and seek him, Bebelle. We will go and look for him in England. We will go and look for him at my daughter's, Bebelle.'

'Shall we find him there?'

'We shall find the best part of him there. Come with me, poor forlorn little one. Heaven is my witness,' said the Englishman, in a low voice, as, before he rose, he touched the turf above the gentle corporal's breast, 'that I thankfully accept this trust!'

It was a long way for the child to have come unaided. She was soon asleep again, with her embrace transferred to the Englishman's neck. He looked at her worn shoes, and her galled feet, and her tired face, and believed that she had come there every day.

He was leaving the grave with the slumbering Bebelle in his arms, when he stopped, looked wistfully down at it, and looked wistfully at the other graves around. 'It is the innocent custom of the people,' said Mr the Englishman, with hesitation. 'I think I should like to do it. No one sees.'

Careful not to wake Bebelle as he went, he repaired to the lodge where such little tokens of remembrance were sold, and bought two wreaths. One, blue and white and glistening silver, 'To my friend'; one of a soberer red and black and yellow, 'To my friend'. With these he went back to the grave, and so down on one knee again. Touching the child's lips with the brighter wreath, he guided her hand to hang it on the cross; then hung his own wreath there. After all, the wreaths were not far out of keeping with the little garden. To my friend. To my friend.

Mr the Englishman took it very ill when he looked round a street corner into the Great Place, carrying Bebelle in his arms, that old Mutuel should be there airing his red ribbon. He took a world of pains to dodge the worthy Mutuel, and devoted a surprising amount of time and trouble to skulking into his own lodging like a man pursued by Justice. Safely arrived there at last, he made Bebelle's toilet with as accurate a remembrance as he could bring to bear upon that work of the way in which he had often seen the poor corporal make it, and having given her to eat and drink, laid her down on his own bed. Then he slipped out into the barber's shop, and after a brief interview with the barber's wife, and a brief recourse to his purse and card-case, came back again with the whole of Bebelle's personal property in such a very little bundle that it was quite lost under his arm.

As it was irreconcilable with his whole course and character that he should carry Bebelle off in state, or receive any compliments or congratulations on that feat, he devoted the next day to getting his two portmanteaus out of the house by artfulness and stealth, and to comporting himself in every particular as if he were going to run away – except, indeed, that he paid his few debts in the town, and prepared a letter to leave for Madame Bouclet, enclosing a sufficient sum of money in lieu of notice. A railway train would come through at midnight, and by that train he would take away Bebelle to look for Theophile in England and at his forgiven daughter's.

At midnight, on a moonlight night, Mr the Englishman came creeping forth like a harmless assassin, with Bebelle on his breast instead of a dagger. Quiet the Great Place, and quiet the never-stirring streets; closed the cafes; huddled together motionless their billiard balls, drowsy the guard or sentinel on duty here and there; lulled for the time, by sleep, even the insatiate appetite of the office of town-dues.

Mr the Englishman left the place behind, and left the streets behind, and left the civilian-inhabited town behind, and descended down among the military works of Vauban, hemming all in. As the shadow of the first heavy arch and postern fell upon him and was left behind, as the shadow of the second heavy arch and postern fell upon him and was left behind, as his hollow tramp over the first drawbridge was succeeded by a gentler sound, as his hollow tramp over the second drawbridge was succeeded by a gentler sound, as he overcame the stagnant ditches one by one, and passed out where the flowing waters were and where the moonlight, so the dark shades and the hollow sounds and the unwholesomely locked currents of his soul were vanquished and set free. See to it, Vaubans of your own hearts, who gird them in with triple walls and ditches, and with bolt and chain and bar and lifted bridge – raze those fortifications, and lay them level with the all-absorbing dust, before the night cometh when no hand can work!

All went prosperously, and he got into an empty carriage in the train, where he could lay Bebelle on the seat over against him, as on a couch, and cover her from head to foot with his mantle. He had just drawn himself up from perfecting this arrangement, and had just leaned back in his own seat contemplating it with great satisfaction, when he became aware of a curious appearance at the open carriage window – a ghostly little tin box floating up in the moonlight, and hovering there.

He leaned forward, and put out his head. Down among the rails and wheels and ashes, Monsieur Mutuel, red ribbon and all!

'Excuse me, Monsieur the Englishman,' said Monsieur Mutuel, holding up his box at arm's length, the carriage being so high and he so low; 'but I shall reverence the little box for ever, if your so generous hand will take a pinch from it at parting.'

Mr the Englishman reached out of the window before complying, and – without asking the old fellow what business it was of his – shook hands and said, 'Adieu! God bless you!'

'And, Mr the Englishman, God bless *you!*' cried Madame Bouclet, who was also there among the rails and wheels and ashes. 'And God will bless you in the happiness of the protected child now with you. And God will bless you in your own child at home. And God will bless you in your own remembrances. And this from me!'

He had barely time to catch a bouquet from her hand, when the train was flying through the night. Round the paper that enfolded it was bravely written (doubtless by the nephew who held the pen of an angel), 'Homage to the friend of the friendless'.

'Not bad people, Bebelle!' said Mr the Englishman, softly drawing the mantle a little from her sleeping face, that he might kiss it, 'though they are so – '

Too 'sentimental' himself at the moment to be able to get out that word, he added nothing but a sob, and travelled for some miles, through the moonlight, with his hand before his eyes.

CHAPTER 3

His Brown-Paper Parcel

My works are well known. I am a young man in the art line. You have seen my works many a time, though it's fifty thousand to one if you have seen me. You say you don't want to see me? You say your interest is in my works, and not in me? Don't be too sure about that. Stop a bit.

Let us have it down in black and white at the first go off, so that there may be no unpleasantness or wrangling afterwards. And this is looked over by a friend of mine, a ticket writer, that is up to literature. I am a young man in the art line – in the fine-art line. You have seen my works over and over again, and you have been curious about me, and you think you have seen me. Now, as a safe rule, you never have seen me, and you never do see me, and you never will see me. I think that's plainly put – and it's what knocks me over.

If there's a blighted public character going, I am the party.

It has been remarked by a certain (or an uncertain) philosopher, that the world knows nothing of its greatest men. He might have put it plainer if he had thrown his eye in my direction. He might have put it, that while the world knows something of them that apparently go in and win, it knows nothing of them that really go in and don't win. There it is again in another form – and that's what knocks me over.

Not that it's only myself that suffers from injustice, but that I am more alive to my own injuries than to any other man's. Being, as I have mentioned, in the fine-art line, and not the philanthropic line, I openly admit it. As to company in injury, I have company enough. Who are you passing every day at your competitive excruciations? The fortunate candidates whose heads and livers you have turned upside down for life? Not you. You are really passing the crammers and coaches. If your principle is right, why don't you turn out tomorrow morning with the keys of your cities on velvet cushions, your musicians playing, and your flags flying, and read addresses to the crammers and coaches on your bended knees, beseeching them to come out and govern you? Then, again, as to your public business of all sorts, your financial statements and your budgets; the public knows much, truly, about the real doers of all that! Your nobles and right honourables are first-rate men? Yes, and so is a goose a first-rate bird. But I'll tell you this about the goose; – you'll find his natural flavour disappointing, without stuffing.

Perhaps I am soured by not being popular? But suppose I *am* popular. Suppose my works never fail to attract. Suppose that, whether they are exhibited by natural light or by artificial, they invariably draw the public. Then no doubt they are preserved in some collection? No, they are not; they are not preserved in any collection. Copyright? No, nor yet copyright. Anyhow they must be somewhere? Wrong again, for they are often nowhere.

Says you, 'At all events, you are in a moody state of mind, my friend.' My answer is, I have described myself as a public character with a blight upon him – which fully accounts for the curdling of the milk in *that* coconut.

Those that are acquainted with London are aware of a locality on the Surrey side of the River Thames, called the Obelisk, or, more generally, the Obstacle. Those that are not acquainted with London will also be aware of it, now that I have named it. My lodging is not far from that locality. I am a young man of that easy disposition, that I lie abed till it's absolutely necessary to get up and earn something, and then I lie abed again till I have spent it.

It was on an occasion when I had had to turn to with a view to victuals, that I found myself walking along the Waterloo Road, one evening after dark, accompanied by an acquaintance and fellow-lodger in the gas-fitting way of life. He is very good company, having worked at the theatres, and, indeed, he has a theatrical turn himself, and wishes to be brought out in the character of Othello; but whether on account of his regular work always blacking his face and hands more or less, I cannot say.

'Tom,' he says, 'what a mystery hangs over you!'

'Yes, Mr Click' – the rest of the house generally give him his name, as being first, front, carpeted all over, his own furniture, and if not mahogany, an out-and-out imitation – 'yes, Mr Click, a mystery does hang over me.'

'Makes you low, you see, don't it?' says he, eyeing me sideways.

'Why, yes, Mr Click, there are circumstances connected with it that have,' I yielded to a sigh, 'a lowering effect.'

'Gives you a touch off the misanthrope too, don't it?' says he. 'Well, I'll tell you what. If I was you, I'd shake it off.'

'If I was you, I would, Mr Click; but, if you was me, you wouldn't.'

'Ah!' says he, 'there's something in that.'

When we had walked a little further, he took it up again by touching me on the chest.

'You see, Tom, it seems to me as if, in the words of the poet who wrote the domestic drama of the Stranger, you had a silent sorrow there.'

'I have, Mr Click.'

'I hope, Tom,' lowering his voice in a friendly way, 'it isn't coining, or smashing?'

'No, Mr Click. Don't be uneasy.'

'Nor yet forg – ' Mr Click checked himself, and added, 'counterfeiting anything, for instance?'

'No, Mr Click. I am lawfully in the art line – fine-art line – but I can say no more.'

'Ah! Under a species of star? A kind of malignant spell? A sort of a gloomy destiny? A cankerworm pegging away at your vitals in secret, as well as I make it out?' said Mr Click, eyeing me with some admiration.

I told Mr Click that was about it, if we came to particulars; and I thought he appeared rather proud of me.

Our conversation had brought us to a crowd of people, the greater part struggling for a front place from which to see something on the pavement, which proved to be various designs executed in coloured chalks on the pavement stones, lighted by two candles stuck in mud sconces. The subjects consisted of a fine fresh salmon's head and shoulders, supposed to have been recently sent home from the fishmonger's; a moonlight night at sea (in a circle); dead game; scrollwork; the head of a hoary hermit engaged in devout contemplation; the head of a pointer smoking a pipe; and a cherubim, his flesh creased as in infancy, going on a horizontal errand against the wind. All these subjects appeared to me to be exquisitely done.

On his knees on one side of this gallery, a shabby person of modest appearance who shivered dreadfully (though it wasn't at all cold), was engaged in blowing the chalk-dust off the moon, toning the outline of the back of the hermit's head with a bit of leather, and fattening the down-stroke of a letter or two in the writing. I have forgotten to mention that writing formed a part of the composition, and that it also – as it appeared to me – was exquisitely done. It ran as follows, in fine round characters:

An honest man is the noblest work of God.

1 2 3 4 5 6 7 8 9 0.

Pounds s. d.

Employment in an office is humbly requested.

Honour the Queen. Hunger is a sharp thorn.

Chip chop, cherry chop, fol de rol de ri do.

Astronomy and mathematics.

I do this to support my family.

Murmurs of admiration at the exceeding beauty of this performance went about among the crowd. The artist, having finished his touching (and having spoilt those places), took his seat on the pavement, with his knees crouched up very nigh his chin; and halfpence began to rattle in.

'A pity to see a man of that talent brought so low; ain't it?' said one of the crowd to me.

'What he might have done in the coach-painting, or house-decorating!' said another man, who took up the first speaker because I did not.

'Why, he writes – alone – like the Lord Chancellor!' said another man.

'Better,' said another. 'I know his writing. He couldn't support his family this way.'

Then, a woman noticed the natural fluffiness of the hermit's hair, and another woman, her friend, mentioned of the salmon's gills that you could almost see him gasp. Then, an elderly country gentleman stepped forward and asked the modest man how he executed his work? And the modest man took some scraps of brown paper with colours in 'em out of his pockets, and showed them. Then a fair-complexioned donkey, with sandy hair and spectacles, asked if the hermit was a portrait? To which the modest man, casting a sorrowful glance upon it, replied that it was, to a certain extent, a recollection of his father. This caused a boy to yelp out, 'Is the Pinter a smoking the pipe your mother?' who was immediately shoved out of view by a sympathetic carpenter with his basket of tools at his back.

At every fresh question or remark the crowd leaned forward more eagerly, and dropped the halfpence more freely, and the modest man gathered them up more meekly. At last, another elderly gentleman came to the front, and gave the artist his card, to come to his office tomorrow, and get some copying to do. The card was accompanied by sixpence, and the artist was profoundly grateful, and, before he put the card in his hat, read it several times by the light of his candles to fix the address well in his mind, in case he should lose it. The crowd was deeply interested by this last incident, and a man in the second row with a gruff voice growled to the artist, 'You've got a chance in life now, ain't you?' The artist answered (sniffing in a very low-spirited way, however), 'I'm thankful to hope so.' Upon which there was a general chorus of 'You are all right,' and the halfpence slackened very decidedly.

I felt myself pulled away by the arm, and Mr Click and I stood alone at the corner of the next crossing.

'Why, Tom,' said Mr Click, 'what a horrid expression of face you've got!'

'Have I?' says I.

'Have you?' says Mr Click. 'Why, you looked as if you would have his blood.'

'Whose blood?'

'The artist's.'

'The artist's?' I repeated. And I laughed, frantically, wildly, gloomily, incoherently, disagreeably. I am sensible that I did. I know I did.

Mr Click stared at me in a scared sort of a way, but said nothing until we had walked a street's length. He then stopped short, and said, with excitement on the part of his forefinger: 'Thomas, I find it necessary to be plain with you. I don't like the envious man. I have identified the cankerworm that's pegging away at *your* vitals, and it's envy, Thomas.'

'Is it?' says I.

'Yes, it is,' says be. 'Thomas, beware of envy. It is the green-eyed monster which never did and never will improve each shining hour, but quite the reverse. I dread the envious man, Thomas. I confess that I am afraid of the envious man, when he is so envious as you are. Whilst you contemplated the works of a gifted rival, and whilst you heard that rival's praises, and especially whilst you met his humble glance as he put that card away, your countenance was so malevolent as to be terrific. Thomas, I have heard of the envy of them that follows the fine-art line, but I never believed it could be what yours is. I wish you well, but I take my leave of you. And if you should ever got into trouble through knifeing – or say, garotting – a brother artist, as I believe you will, don't call me to character, Thomas, or I shall be forced to injure your case.'

Mr Click parted from me with those words, and we broke off our acquaintance.

I became enamoured. Her name was Henrietta. Contending with my easy disposition, I frequently got up to go after her. She also dwelt in the neighbourhood of the Obstacle, and I did fondly hope that no other would interpose in the way of our union.

To say that Henrietta was volatile is but to say that she was woman. To say that she was in the bonnet-trimming is feebly to express the taste which reigned predominant in her own.

She consented to walk with me. Let me do her the justice to say that she did so upon trial. 'I am not,' said Henrietta, 'as yet prepared to regard you, Thomas, in any other light than as a friend; but as a friend I am willing to walk with you, on the understanding that softer sentiments may flow.'

We walked.

Under the influence of Henrietta's beguilements, I now got out of bed daily. I pursued my calling with an industry before unknown, and it cannot fail to have been observed at that period, by those most familiar with the streets of London, that there was a larger supply. But hold! The time is not yet come!

One evening in October I was walking with Henrietta, enjoying the cool breezes wafted over Vauxhall Bridge. After several slow turns, Henrietta gaped frequently (so inseparable from woman is the love of excitement), and said, 'Let's go home by Grosvenor Place, Piccadilly, and Waterloo' – localities, I may state for the information of the stranger and the foreigner, well known in London, and the last a bridge.

'No. Not by Piccadilly, Henrietta,' said I.

'And why not Piccadilly, for goodness' sake?' said Henrietta.

Could I tell her? Could I confess to the gloomy presentiment that overshadowed me? Could I make myself intelligible to her? No.

'I don't like Piccadilly, Henrietta.'

'But I do,' said she. 'It's dark now, and the long rows of lamps in Piccadilly after dark are beautiful. I *will* go to Piccadilly!'

Of course we went. It was a pleasant night, and there were numbers of people in the streets. It was a brisk night, but not too cold, and not damp. Let me darkly observe, it was the best of all nights – *for the purpose*.

As we passed the garden wall of the royal palace, going up Grosvenor Place, Henrietta murmured: 'I wish I was a queen!'

'Why so, Henrietta?'

'I would make *you* something,' said she, and crossed her two hands on my arm, and turned away her head.

Judging from this that the softer sentiments alluded to above had begun to flow, I adapted my conduct to that belief. Thus happily we passed on into the detested thoroughfare of Piccadilly. On the right of that thoroughfare is a row of trees, the railing of the Green Park, and a fine broad eligible piece of pavement.

'Oh my!' cried Henrietta presently. 'There's been an accident!'

I looked to the left, and said, 'Where, Henrietta?'

'Not there, stupid!' said she. 'Over by the park railings. Where the crowd is. Oh no, it's not an accident, it's something else to look at! What's them lights?'

She referred to two lights twinkling low amongst the legs of the assemblage: two candles on the pavement.

'Oh, do come along!' cried Henrietta, skipping across the road with me. I hung back, but in vain. 'Do let's look!'

Again, designs upon the pavement. Centre compartment, Mt Vesuvius going it (in a circle), supported by four oval compartments, severally representing a ship in heavy weather, a shoulder of mutton attended by two cucumbers, a golden harvest with distant cottage of proprietor, and a knife and fork after nature; above the centre compartment a bunch of grapes, and over the whole a rainbow. The whole, as it appeared to me, exquisitely done.

The person in attendance on these works of art was in all respects, shabbiness excepted, unlike the former personage. His whole appearance and manner denoted briskness. Though threadbare, he expressed to the crowd that poverty had not subdued his spirit, or tinged with any sense of shame this honest effort to turn his talents to some account. The writing which formed a part of his composition was conceived in a similarly cheerful tone. It breathed the following sentiments:

> The writer is poor, but not despondent.
> To a British public he appeals.
> Honour to our brave Army!
> And also to our gallant Navy.
> 1234567890 £ s. d. ABCDEFG
> *Britons strike* the writer in common chalks would
> be grateful for any suitable employment *Home! Hurrah!*

The whole of this writing appeared to me to be exquisitely done.

But this man, in one respect like the last, though seemingly hard at it with a great show of brown paper and rubbers, was only really fattening the down-stroke of a letter here and there, or blowing the loose chalk off the rainbow, or toning the outside edge of the shoulder of mutton. Though he did this with the greatest confidence, he did it (as it struck me) in so ignorant a manner, and so spoilt everything he touched, that when he began upon the purple smoke from the chimney of the distant cottage of the proprietor of the golden harvest (which smoke was beautifully soft), I found myself saying aloud, without considering of it: 'Let that alone, will you?'

'Halloa!' said the man next me in the crowd, jerking me roughly from him with his elbow, 'why didn't you send a telegram? If we had known you was coming, we'd have provided something better for you. You understand the man's work better than he does himself, don't you? Have you made your will? You're too clever to live long.'

'Don't be hard upon the gentleman, sir,' said the person in attendance on the works of art, with a twinkle in his eye as he looked at me; 'he may chance to be an artist himself. If so, sir, he will have a fellow-feeling with me, sir, when I' – he adapted his action to his words as he went on, and gave a smart slap of his hands between each touch, working himself all the time about and about the composition – 'when I lighten the bloom of my grapes – shade off the orange in my rainbow – dot the i of my Britons – throw a yellow light into my cow-cum-*ber* – insinuate another morsel of fat into my shoulder of mutton – dart another zigzag flash of lightning at my ship in distress!'

He seemed to do this so neatly, and was so nimble about it, that the halfpence came flying in.

'Thanks, generous public, thanks!' said the professor. 'You will stimulate me to further exertions. My name will be found in the list of British painters yet. I shall do better than this, with encouragement. I shall indeed.'

'You never can do better than that bunch of grapes,' said Henrietta. 'Oh, Thomas, them grapes!'

'Not better than *that*, lady? I hope for the time when I shall paint anything but your own bright eyes and lips equal to life.'

'(Thomas, did you ever?) But it must take a long time, sir,' said Henrietta, blushing, 'to paint equal to that.'

'I was 'prenticed to it, miss,' said the young man, smartly touching up the composition – ' 'prenticed to it in the caves of Spain and Portingale, ever so long and two year over.'

There was a laugh from the crowd; and a new man who had worked himself in next me, said, 'He's a smart chap, too; ain't he?'

'And what a eye!' exclaimed Henrietta softly.

'Ah! He need have a eye,' said the man.

'Ah! He just need,' was murmured among the crowd.

'He couldn't come that 'ere burning mountain without a eye,' said the man. He had got himself accepted as an authority, somehow, and everybody looked at his finger as it pointed out Vesuvius. 'To come that effect in a general illumination would require a eye; but to come it with two dips – why, it's enough to blind him!'

That impostor, pretending not to have heard what was said, now winked to any extent with both eyes at once, as if the strain upon his sight was too much, and threw back his long hair – it was very long – as if to cool his fevered brow. I was watching him doing it, when Henrietta suddenly whispered, 'Oh, Thomas, how horrid you look!' and pulled me out by the arm.

Remembering Mr Click's words, I was confused when I retorted, 'What do you mean by horrid?'

'Oh gracious! Why, you looked,' said Henrietta, 'as if you would have his blood.'

I was going to answer, 'So I would, for twopence – from his nose,' when I checked myself and remained silent.

We returned home in silence. Every step of the way, the softer sentiments that had flowed, ebbed twenty mile an hour. Adapting my conduct to the ebbing, as I had done to the flowing, I let my arm drop limp, so as she could scarcely keep hold of it, and I wished her such a cold good-night at parting, that I keep within the bounds of truth when I characterise it as a rasper.

In the course of the next day I received the following document:

Henrietta informs Thomas that my eyes are open to you. I must ever wish you well, but walking and us is separated by an unfarmable abyss. One so malignant to superiority – Oh that look at him! – can never never conduct

HENRIETTA

P.S. – To the altar.

Yielding to the easiness of my disposition, I went to bed for a week, after receiving this letter. During the whole of such time, London was bereft of the usual fruits of my labour. When I resumed it, I found that Henrietta was married to the artist of Piccadilly.

Did I say to the artist? What fell words were those, expressive of what a galling hollowness, of what a bitter mockery! I – I – I – am the artist. I was the real artist of Piccadilly, I was the real artist of the Waterloo Road, I am the only artist of all those pavement-subjects which daily and nightly arouse your admiration. I do 'em, and I let 'em out. The man you behold with the papers of chalks and the rubbers, touching up the down-strokes of the writing and shading off the salmon, the man you give the credit to, the man you give the money to, hires – yes! and I live to tell it! – hires those works of art of me, and brings nothing to 'em but the candles.

Such is genius in a commercial country. I am not up to the shivering, I am not up to the liveliness, I am not up to the wanting-employment-in-an-office move; I am only up to originating and executing the work. In consequence of which you never see me; you think you see me when you see somebody else, and that somebody else is a mere commercial character. The one seen by self and Mr Click in the Waterloo Road can only write a single word, and that I taught him, and it's *multiplication* – which you may see him execute upside down, because he can't do it the natural way. The one seen by self and Henrietta by the Green Park railings can just smear into existence the two ends of a rainbow, with his cuff and a rubber – if very hard put upon making a show – but he could no more come the arch of the rainbow, to save his life, than he could come the moonlight, fish, volcano, shipwreck, mutton, hermit, or any of my most celebrated effects.

To conclude as I began: if there's a blighted public character going, I am the party. And often as you have seen, do see, and will see, my works, it's fifty thousand to one if you'll ever see me, unless, when the candles are burnt down and the commercial character is gone, you should happen to notice a neglected young man perseveringly rubbing out the last traces of the pictures, so that nobody can renew the same. That's me.

CHAPTER 4

His Wonderful End

It will have been, ere now, perceived that I sold the foregoing writings. From the fact of their being printed in these pages, the inference will, ere now, have been drawn by the reader (may I add, the gentle reader?) that I sold them to one who never yet –

Having parted with the writings on most satisfactory terms – for, in opening negotiations with the present journal, was I not placing myself in the hands of one of whom it may be said, in the words of another – I resumed my usual functions. But I too soon discovered that peace of mind had fled from a brow which, up to that time, time had merely took the hair off, leaving an unruffled expanse within.

It were superfluous to veil it – the brow to which I allude is my own.

Yes, over that brow uneasiness gathered like the sable wing of the fabled bird, as – as no doubt will be easily identified by all right-minded individuals. If not, I am unable, on the spur of the moment, to enter into particulars of him. The reflection that the writings must now inevitably get into print, and that he might yet live and meet with them, sat like the hag of night upon my jaded form. The elasticity of my spirits departed. Fruitless was the bottle, whether wine or medicine. I had recourse to both, and the effect of both upon my system was witheringly lowering.

In this state of depression, into which I subsided when I first began to revolve what could I ever say if he – the unknown – was to appear in the coffee-room and demand reparation, I one forenoon in this last November received a turn that appeared to be given me by the finger of fate and conscience, hand in hand. I was alone in the coffee-room, and had just poked the fire into a blaze, and was standing with my back to it, trying whether heat would penetrate with soothing influence to the voice within, when a young man in a cap, of an intelligent countenance, though requiring his hair cut, stood before me.

'Mr Christopher, the head waiter?'

'The same.'

The young man shook his hair out of his vision – which it impeded – to a packet from his breast, and handing it over to me, said, with his eye (or did I dream?) fixed with a lambent meaning on me, 'The proofs.'

Although I smelt my coat-tails singeing at the fire, I had not the power to withdraw them. The young man put the packet in my faltering grasp, and repeated – let me do him the justice to add, with civility: 'The proofs. A. Y. R.'

With those words he departed.

A.Y.R.? And You Remember. Was that his meaning? At Your Risk. Were the letters short for *that* reminder? Anticipate Your Retribution. Did they stand for *that* warning? Outdacious Youth Repent? But no; for that, a O was happily wanting, and the vowel here was a A.

I opened the packet, and found that its contents were the foregoing writings printed just as the reader (may I add the discerning reader?) peruses them. In vain was the reassuring whisper – A.Y.R., All the Year Round – it could not cancel the proofs. Too appropriate name. The proofs of my having sold the writings.

My wretchedness daily increased. I had not thought of the risk I ran, and the defying publicity I put my head into, until all was done, and all was in print. Give up the money to be off the bargain and prevent the publication, I could not. My family was down in the world, Christmas was coming on, a brother in the hospital and a sister in the rheumatics could not be entirely neglected. And it was not only ins in the family that had told on the resources of one unaided waitering; outs were not wanting. A brother out of a situation, and another brother out of money to meet an acceptance, and another brother out of his mind, and another brother out at New York (not the same, though it might appear so), had really and truly brought me to a stand till I could turn myself round. I got worse and worse in my meditations, constantly reflecting 'The proofs', and reflecting that when Christmas drew nearer, and the proofs were published, there could be no safety from hour to hour but that He might confront me in the coffee-room, and in the face of day and his country demand his rights.

The impressive and unlooked-for catastrophe towards which I dimly pointed the reader (shall I add, the highly intellectual reader?) in my first remarks now rapidly approaches.

It was November still, but the last echoes of the Guy Foxes had long ceased to reverberate. We was slack – several joints under our average mark, and wine, of course, proportionate. So slack had we become at last, that Beds Nos. 26, 27, 28 and 31, having took their six o'clock dinners, and dozed over their respective pints, had drove away in their respective hansoms for their respective night mail-trains and left us empty.

I had took the evening paper to No. 6 table – which is warm and most to be preferred – and, lost in the all-absorbing topics of the day, had dropped into a slumber. I was recalled to consciousness by the well-known intimation, 'Waiter!' and replying, 'Sir!' found a gentleman standing at No. 4 table. The reader (shall I add, the observant reader?) will please to notice the locality of the gentleman – *at No. 4 table*.

He had one of the newfangled uncollapsable bags in his hand (which I am against, for I don't see why you shouldn't collapse, while you are about it, as your fathers collapsed before you), and he said: 'I want to dine, waiter. I shall sleep here tonight.'

'Very good, sir. What will you take for dinner, sir?'

'Soup, bit of codfish, oyster sauce, and the joint.'

'Thank you, sir.'

I rang the chambermaid's bell; and Mrs Pratchett marched in, according to custom, demurely carrying a lighted flat candle before her, as if she was one of a long public procession, all the other members of which was invisible.

In the meanwhile the gentleman had gone up to the mantelpiece, right in front of the fire, and had laid his forehead against the mantelpiece (which it is a low one, and brought him into the attitude of leapfrog), and had heaved a tremenjous sigh. His hair was long and lightish; and when he laid his forehead against the mantelpiece, his hair all fell in a dusty fluff together over his eyes; and when he now turned round and lifted up his head again, it all fell in a dusty fluff together over his ears. This give him a wild appearance, similar to a blasted heath.

'O! The chambermaid. Ah!' He was turning something in his mind. 'To be sure. Yes. I won't go upstairs now, if you will take my bag. It will be enough for the present to know my number. – Can you give me 24B?'

(O Conscience, what a adder art thou!)

Mrs Pratchett allotted him the room, and took his bag to it. He then went back before the fire, and fell a biting his nails.

'Waiter!' biting between the words, 'give me', bite, 'pen and paper; and in five minutes', bite, 'let me have, if you please', bite, 'a', bite, 'messenger'.

Unmindful of his waning soup, he wrote and sent off six notes before he touched his dinner. Three were City; three West-End. The City letters were to Cornhill, Ludgate Hill, and Farringdon Street. The West-End letters were to Great Marlborough Street, New Burlington Street, and Piccadilly. Everybody was systematically denied at every one of the six places, and there was not a vestige of any answer. Our light porter whispered to me, when he came back with that report, 'All booksellers.'

But before then he had cleared off his dinner, and his bottle of wine. He now – mark the concurrence with the document formerly given in full! – knocked a plate of biscuits off the table with his agitated elber (but without breakage), and demanded boiling brandy-and-water.

Now fully convinced that it was himself, I perspired with the utmost freedom. When he became flushed with the heated stimulant referred to, he again demanded pen and paper, and passed the succeeding two hours in producing a manuscript which he put in the fire when completed. He then went up to bed, attended by Mrs Pratchett. Mrs Pratchett (who was aware of my emotions) told me, on coming down, that she had noticed his eye rolling into every corner of the passages and staircase, as if in search of his Luggage, and that, looking back as she shut the door of 24B, she perceived him with his coat already thrown off immersing himself bodily under the bedstead, like a chimley-sweep before the application of machinery.

The next day – I forbear the horrors of that night – was a very foggy day in our part of London, insomuch that it was necessary to light the coffee-room gas. We was still alone, and no feverish words of mine can do justice to the fitfulness of his appearance as he sat at No. 4 table, increased by there being something wrong with the meter.

Having again ordered his dinner, he went out, and was out for the best part of two hours. Enquiring on his return whether any of the answers had arrived, and receiving an unqualified negative, his instant call was for mulligatawny, the cayenne pepper, and orange brandy.

Feeling that the mortal struggle was now at hand, I also felt that I must be equal to him, and with that view resolved that whatever he took I would take. Behind my partition, but keeping my eye on him over the curtain, I therefore operated on mulligatawny, cayenne pepper, and orange brandy. And at a later period of the day, when he again said, 'Orange brandy,' I said so too, in a lower tone, to George, my second lieutenant (my first was absent on leave), who acts between me and the bar.

Throughout that awful day he walked about the coffee-room continually. Often he came close up to my partition, and then his eye rolled within, too evidently in search of any signs of his Luggage. Half-past six came, and I laid his cloth. He ordered a bottle of old Brown. I likewise ordered a bottle of old Brown. He drank his. I drank mine (as nearly as my duties would permit) glass for glass against his. He topped with coffee and a small glass. I topped with coffee and a small glass. He dozed. I dozed. At last, 'Waiter!' – and he ordered his bill. The moment was now at hand when we two must be locked in the deadly grapple.

Swift as the arrow from the bow, I had formed my resolution; in other words, I had hammered it out between nine and nine. It was, that I would be the first to open up the subject with a full acknowledgement, and would offer any gradual settlement within my power. He paid his bill (doing what was right by attendance) with his eye rolling about him to the last for any tokens of his Luggage. One only time our gaze then met, with the lustrous fixedness (I believe I am correct in imputing that character to it?) of the well-known basilisk. The decisive moment had arrived.

With a tolerable steady hand, though with humility, I laid the proofs before him.

'Gracious heavens!' he cries out, leaping up, and catching hold of his hair. 'What's this? Print!'

'Sir,' I replied, in a calming voice, and bending forward, 'I humbly acknowledge to being the unfortunate cause of it. But I hope, sir, that when you have heard the circumstances explained, and the innocence of my intentions – '

To my amazement, I was stopped short by his catching me in both his arms, and pressing me to his breastbone; where I must confess to my face (and particular, nose) having undergone some temporary vexation from his wearing his coat buttoned high up, and his buttons being uncommon hard.

'Ha, ha, ha!' he cries, releasing me with a wild laugh, and grasping my hand. 'What is your name, my benefactor?'

'My name, sir' (I was crumpled, and puzzled to make him out), 'is Christopher; and I hope, sir, that, as such, when you've heard my ex – '

'In print!' he exclaims again, dashing the proofs over and over as if he was bathing in them. – 'In print!! O Christopher! Philanthropist! Nothing can recompense you – but what sum of money would be acceptable to you?'

I had drawn a step back from him, or I should have suffered from his buttons again.

'Sir, I assure you, I have been already well paid, and – '

. 'No, no, Christopher! Don't talk like that! What sum of money would be acceptable to you, Christopher? Would you find twenty pounds acceptable, Christopher?'

However great my surprise, I naturally found words to say, 'Sir, I am not aware that the man was ever yet born without more than the average amount of water on the brain as would not find twenty pounds acceptable. But – extremely obliged to you, sir, I'm sure'; for he had tumbled it out of his purse and crammed it in my hand in two bank-notes; 'but I could wish to know, sir, if not intruding, how I have merited this liberality?'

'Know then, my Christopher,' he says, 'that from boyhood's hour I have unremittingly and unavailingly endeavoured to get into print. Know, Christopher, that all the booksellers alive – and several dead – have refused to put me into print. Know, Christopher, that I have written unprinted reams. But they shall be read to you, my friend and brother. You sometimes have a holiday?'

Seeing the great danger I was in, I had the presence of mind to answer, 'Never!' To make it more final, I added, 'Never! Not from the cradle to the grave.'

'Well,' says he, thinking no more about that, and chuckling at his proofs again. 'But I am in print! The first flight of ambition emanating from my father's lowly cot is realised at length! The golden bow' – he was getting on – 'struck by the magic hand, has emitted a complete and perfect sound! When did this happen, my Christopher?'

'Which happen, sir?'

'This,' he held it out at arm's length to admire it – 'this Per-rint.'

When I had given him my detailed account of it, he grasped me by the hand again, and said: 'Dear Christopher, it should be gratifying to you to know that you are an instrument in the hands of Destiny. Because you *are*.'

A passing Something of a melancholy cast put it into my head to shake it, and to say, 'Perhaps we all are.'

'I don't mean that,' he answered; 'I don't take that wide range; I confine myself to the special case. Observe me well, my Christopher! Hopeless of getting rid, through any effort of my own, of any of the manuscripts among my Luggage – all of which, send them where I would, were always coming back to me – it is now some seven years since I left that Luggage here, on the desperate chance, either that the too, too faithful manuscripts would come back to me no more, or that someone less accursed than I might give them to the world. You follow me, my Christopher?'

'Pretty well, sir.' I followed him so far as to judge that he had a weak head, and that the orange, the boiling, and old Brown combined was beginning to tell. (The old Brown, being heady, is best adapted to seasoned cases.)

'Years elapsed, and those compositions slumbered in dust. At length, destiny, choosing her agent from all mankind, sent you here, Christopher, and lo! the casket was burst asunder, and the giant was free!'

He made hay of his hair after he said this, and he stood a-tiptoe.

'But,' he reminded himself in a state of excitement, 'we must sit up all night, my Christopher. I must correct these proofs for the press. Fill all the inkstands, and bring me several new pens.'

He smeared himself and he smeared the proofs, the night through, to that degree that when Sol gave him warning to depart (in a four-wheeler), few could have said which was them, and which was him, and which was blots. His last instructions was, that I should instantly run and take his corrections to the office of the present journal. I did so. They most likely will not appear in print, for I noticed a message being brought round from Beauford Printing House, while I was a-throwing this concluding statement on paper, that the ole resources of that establishment was unable to make out what they meant. Upon which a certain gentleman in the company, as I will not more particularly name, laughed, and put the corrections in the fire.

THREE DETECTIVE ANECDOTES

1

A Pair of Gloves

'It's a singler story, sir,' said Inspector Wield, of the Detective Police, who, in company with Sergeants Dornton and Mith, paid us another twilight visit, one July evening; 'and I've been thinking you might like to know it.

'It's concerning the murder of the young woman, Eliza Grimwood, some years ago, over in the Waterloo Road. She was commonly called the Countess, because of her handsome appearance and her proud way of carrying of herself; and when I saw the poor Countess (I had known her well to speak to), lying dead, with her throat cut, on the floor of her bedroom, you'll believe me that a variety of reflections calculated to make a man rather low in his spirits, came into my head.

'That's neither here nor there. I went to the house the morning after the murder, and examined the body, and made a general observation of the bedroom where it was. Turning down the pillow of the bed with my hand, I found, underneath it, a pair of gloves. A pair of gentleman's dress gloves, very dirty; and inside the lining, the letters TR, and a cross.

'Well, sir, I took them gloves away, and I showed 'em to the magistrate, over at Union Hall, before whom the case was. He says, "Wield," he says, "there's no doubt this is a discovery that may lead to something very important; and what you have got to do, Wield, is, to find out the owner of these gloves."

'I was of the same opinion, of course, and I went at it immediately. I looked at the gloves pretty narrowly, and it was my opinion that they had been cleaned. There was a smell of sulphur and rosin about 'em, you know, which cleaned gloves usually have, more or less. I took 'em over to a friend of mine at Kennington, who was in that line, and I put it to him. "What do you say now? Have these gloves been cleaned?" "These gloves have been cleaned," says he. "Have you any idea who cleaned them?" says I. "Not at all," says he; "I've a very distinct idea who *didn't* clean 'em, and that's myself. But I'll tell you what, Wield, there ain't above eight or nine reg'lar glove-cleaners in London," – there were not, at that time, it seems – "and I think I can give you their addresses, and you may find out, by that means, who did clean 'em." Accordingly, he gave me the directions, and I went here, and I went there, and I looked up this man, and I looked up that man; but, though they all agreed that the gloves had been cleaned, I couldn't find the man, woman, or child, that had cleaned that aforesaid pair of gloves.

'What with this person not being at home, and that person being expected home in the afternoon, and so forth, the enquiry took me three days. On the evening of the third day, coming over Waterloo Bridge from the Surrey side of the river, quite beat, and very much vexed and disappointed, I thought I'd have a shilling's worth of entertainment at the Lyceum Theatre to freshen myself up. So I went into the pit, at half-price, and I sat myself down next to a very quiet, modest sort of young man. Seeing I was a stranger (which I thought it just as well to appear to be) he told me the names of the actors on the stage, and we got into conversation. When the play was over, we came out together, and I said, "We've been very companionable and agreeable, and perhaps you wouldn't object to a drain?" "Well, you're very good," says he; "*I shouldn't* object to a drain." Accordingly, we went to a public-house, near the theatre, sat ourselves down in a quiet room upstairs on the first floor, and called for a pint of half-and-half, apiece, and a pipe.

'Well, sir, we put our pipes aboard, and we drank our half-and-half, and sat a-talking, very sociably, when the young man says, "You must excuse me stopping very long," he says, "because I'm forced to go home in good time. I must be at work all night." "At work all night?" says I. "You ain't a baker?" "No," he says, laughing, "I ain't a baker." "I thought not," says I, "you haven't the looks of a baker." "No," says he, "I'm a glove-cleaner."

'I never was more astonished in my life, than when I heard them words come out of his lips. "You're a glove-cleaner, are you?" says I. "Yes," he says, "I am." "Then, perhaps," says I, taking the gloves out of my pocket, "you can tell me who cleaned this pair of gloves? It's a rum story," I says. "I was dining over at Lambeth, the other day, at a free-and-easy – quite promiscuous – with a public company – when some gentleman, he left these gloves behind him! Another gentleman and me, you see, we laid a wager of a sovereign, that I wouldn't find out who they belonged to. I've spent as much as seven shillings already, in trying to discover; but, if you could help me, I'd stand another seven and welcome. You see there's TR and a cross, inside." "I see," he says. "Bless you, I know these gloves very well! I've seen dozens of pairs belonging to the same party." "No?" says I. "Yes," says he. "Then you know who cleaned 'em?" says I. "Rather so," says he. "My father cleaned 'em."

'"Where does your father live?" says I. "Just round the corner," says the young man, "near Exeter Street, here. He'll tell you who they belong to, directly." "Would you come round with me now?" says I. "Certainly," says he, "but you needn't tell my father that you found me at the play, you know, because he mightn't like it." "All right!" We went round to the place, and there we found an old man in a white apron, with two or three daughters, all rubbing and cleaning away at lots of gloves, in a front parlour. "Oh, Father!" says the young man, "here's a person been and made a bet about the ownership of a pair of gloves, and I've told him you can settle it." "Good-evening, sir," says I to the old gentleman. "Here's the gloves your son speaks of. Letters TR, you see, and a cross." "Oh yes," he says, "I know these gloves very well; I've cleaned dozens of pairs of 'em. They belong to Mr Trinkle, the great upholsterer in Cheapside." "Did you get 'em from Mr Trinkle, direct," says I, "if you'll excuse my asking the question?" "No," says he; "Mr Trinkle always sends 'em to Mr Phibbs's, the haberdasher's, opposite his shop, and the haberdasher sends 'em to me." "Perhaps *you* wouldn't object to a drain?" says I. "Not in the least!" says he. So I took the old gentleman out, and had a little more talk with him and his son, over a glass, and we parted excellent friends.

'This was late on a Saturday night. First thing on the Monday morning, I went to the haberdasher's shop, opposite Mr Trinkle's, the great upholsterer's in Cheapside. "Mr Phibbs in the way?" "My name is Phibbs." "Oh! I believe you sent this pair of gloves to be cleaned?" "Yes, I did, for young Mr Trinkle over the way. There he is in the shop!" "Oh! that's him in the shop, is it? Him in the green coat?" "The same individual." "Well, Mr Phibbs, this is an unpleasant affair; but the fact is, I am Inspector Wield of the Detective Police, and I found these gloves under the pillow of the young woman that was murdered the other day, over in the Waterloo Road!" "Good Heaven!" says he. "He's a most respectable young man, and if his father was to hear of it, it would be the ruin of him!" "I'm very sorry for it," says I, "but I must take him into custody." "Good Heaven!" says Mr Phibbs, again; "can nothing be done?" "Nothing," says I. "Will you allow me to call him over here," says he, "that his father may not see it done?" "I don't object to that," says I; "but unfortunately, Mr Phibbs, I can't allow of any communication between you. If any was attempted, I should have to interfere directly. Perhaps you'll beckon him over here?" Mr Phibbs went to the door and beckoned, and the young fellow came across the street directly; a smart, brisk young fellow.

' "Good-morning, sir," says I. "Good-morning, sir," says he. "Would you allow me to enquire, sir," says I, "if you ever had any acquaintance with a party of the name of Grimwood?" "Grimwood! Grimwood!" says he. "No!" "You know the Waterloo Road?" "Oh! of course I know the Waterloo Road!" "Happen to have heard of a young woman being murdered there?" "Yes, I read it in the paper, and very sorry I was to read it." "Here's a pair of gloves belonging to you, that I found under her pillow the morning afterwards!"

'He was in a dreadful state, sir; a dreadful state! "Mr Wield," he says, "upon my solemn oath I never was there. I never so much as saw her, to my knowledge, in my life!" "I am very sorry," says I. "To tell you the truth; I don't think you *are* the murderer, but I must take you to Union Hall in a cab. However, I think it's a case of that sort, that, at present, at all events, the magistrate will hear it in private."

'A private examination took place, and then it came out that this young man was acquainted with a cousin of the unfortunate Eliza Grimwood, and that, calling to see this cousin a day or two before the murder, he left these gloves upon the table. Who should come in, shortly afterwards, but Eliza Grimwood! "Whose gloves are these?" she says, taking 'em up. "Those are Mr Trinkle's gloves," says her cousin. "Oh!" says she, "they are very dirty, and of no use to him, I am sure. I shall take 'em away for my girl to clean the stoves with." And she put 'em in her pocket. The girl had used 'em to clean the stoves, and, I have no doubt, had left 'em lying on the bedroom mantelpiece, or on the drawers, or somewhere; and her mistress, looking round to see that the room was tidy, had caught 'em up and put 'em under the pillow where I found 'em.

'That's the story, sir.'

The Artful Touch

'One of the most *beautiful* things that ever was done, perhaps,' said Inspector Wield, emphasising the adjective, as preparing us to expect dexterity or ingenuity rather than strong interest, 'was a move of Sergeant Witchem's. It was a lovely idea!

'Witchem and me were down at Epsom one Derby Day, waiting at the station for the swell mob. As I mentioned, when we were talking about these things before, we are ready at the station when there's races, or an agricultural show, or a chancellor sworn in for an university, or Jenny Lind, or anything of that sort; and as the swell mob come down, we send 'em back again by the next train. But some of the swell mob, on the occasion of this Derby that I refer to, so far kidded us as to hire a horse and shay; start away from London by Whitechapel, and miles round; come into Epsom from the opposite direction; and go to work, right and left, on the course, while we were waiting for 'em at the Rail. That, however, ain't the point of what I'm going to tell you.

'While Witchem and me were waiting at the station, there comes up one Mr Tatt; a gentleman formerly in the public line, quite an amateur detective in his way, and very much respected. "Halloa, Charley Wield," he says. "What are you doing here? On the look out for some of your old friends?" "Yes, the old move, Mr Tatt." "Come along," he says, "you and Witchem, and have a glass of sherry." "We can't stir from the place," says I, "till the next train comes in; but after that, we will with pleasure." Mr Tatt waits, and the train comes in, and then Witchem and me go off with him to the hotel. Mr Tatt he's got up quite regardless of expense, for the occasion; and in his shirt-front there's a beautiful diamond prop, cost him fifteen or twenty pound – a very handsome pin indeed. We drink our sherry at the bar, and have had our three or four glasses, when Witchem cries suddenly, "Look out, Mr Wield! stand fast!" and a dash is made into the place by the swell mob – four of 'em – that have come down as I tell you, and in a moment Mr Tatt's prop is gone! Witchem, he cuts 'em off at the door, I lay about me as hard as I can, Mr Tatt shows fight like a good 'un, and there we are, all down together, heads and heels, knocking about on the floor of the bar – perhaps you never see such a scene of confusion! However, we stick to our men (Mr Tatt being as good as any officer), and we take 'em all, and carry 'em off to the station. The station's full of people, who have been took on the course; and it's a precious piece of work to get 'em secured. However, we do it at last, and we search 'em; but nothing's found upon 'em, and they're locked up; and a pretty state of heat we are in by that time, I assure you!

'I was very blank over it, myself, to think that the prop had been passed away; and I said to Witchem, when we had set 'em to rights, and were cooling ourselves along with Mr Tatt, "We don't take much by *this* move, anyway, for nothing's found upon 'em, and it's only the braggadocia, after all." "What do you mean, Mr Wield?" says Witchem. "Here's the diamond pin!" and in the palm of his hand there it was, safe and sound! "Why, in the name of wonder," says me and Mr Tatt, in astonishment, "how did you come by that?" "I'll tell you how I come by it," says he. "I saw which of 'em took it; and when we were all down on the floor together, knocking about, I just gave him a little touch on the back of his hand, as I knew his pal would; and he thought it *was* his pal; and gave it me!" It was beautiful, beau–ti–ful!

'Even that was hardly the best of the case, for that chap was tried at the quarter sessions at Guildford. You know what quarter sessions are, sir. Well, if you'll believe me, while them slow justices were looking over the Acts of Parliament, to see what they could do to him, I'm blowed if he didn't cut out of the dock before their faces! He cut out of the dock, sir, then and there; swam across a river; and got up into a tree to dry himself. In the tree he was took – an old woman having seen him climb up – and Witchem's artful touch transported him!'

The Sofa

'What young men will do, sometimes, to ruin themselves and break their friends' hearts,' said Sergeant Dornton, 'it's surprising! I had a case at Saint Blank's Hospital which was of this sort. A bad case, indeed, with a bad end!

'The secretary, and the house-surgeon, and the treasurer, of Saint Blank's Hospital, came to Scotland Yard to give information of numerous robberies having been committed on the students. The students could leave nothing in the pockets of their greatcoats, while the greatcoats were hanging at the hospital, but it was almost certain to be stolen. Property of various descriptions was constantly being lost; and the gentlemen were naturally uneasy about it, and anxious, for the credit of the institution, that the thief or thieves should be discovered. The case was entrusted to me, and I went to the hospital.

' "Now, gentlemen," said I, after we had talked it over; "I understand this property is usually lost from one room."

'Yes, they said. It was.

' "I should wish, if you please," said I, "to see the room."

'It was a good-sized bare room downstairs, with a few tables and forms in it, and a row of pegs, all round, for hats and coats.

' "Next, gentlemen," said I, "do you suspect anybody?"

'Yes, they said. They did suspect somebody. They were sorry to say, they suspected one of the porters.

' "I should like," said I, "to have that man pointed out to me, and to have a little time to look after him."

'He was pointed out, and I looked after him, and then I went back to the hospital, and said, "Now, gentlemen, it's not the porter. He's, unfortunately for himself, a little too fond of drink, but he's nothing worse. My suspicion is, that these robberies are committed by one of the students; and if you'll put me a sofa into that room where the pegs are – as there's no closet – I think I shall be able to detect the thief. I wish the sofa, if you please, to be covered with chintz, or something of that sort, so that I may lie on my chest, underneath it, without being seen."

'The sofa was provided, and next day at eleven o'clock, before any of the students came, I went there, with those gentlemen, to get underneath it. It turned out to be one of those old-fashioned sofas with a great crossbeam at the bottom, that would have broken my back in no time if I could ever have got below it. We had quite a job to break all this away in the time; however, I fell to work, and they fell to work, and we broke it out, and made a clear place for me. I got under the sofa, lay down on my chest, took out my knife, and made a convenient hole in the chintz to look through. It was then settled between me and the gentlemen that when the students were all up in the wards, one of the gentlemen should come in, and hang up a greatcoat on one of the pegs. And that that greatcoat should have, in one of the pockets, a pocketbook containing marked money.

'After I had been there some time, the students began to drop into the room, by ones, and twos, and threes, and to talk about all sorts of things, little thinking there was anybody under the sofa – and then to go upstairs. At last there came in one who remained until he was alone in the room by himself. A tallish, good-looking young man of one or two and twenty, with a light whisker. He went to a particular hat-peg, took off a good hat that was hanging there, tried it on, hung his own hat in its place, and hung that hat on another peg, nearly opposite to me. I then felt quite certain that he was the thief, and would come back by and by.

'When they were all upstairs, the gentleman came in with the greatcoat. I showed him where to hang it, so that I might have a good view of it; and he went away; and I lay under the sofa on my chest, for a couple of hours or so, waiting.

'At last, the same young man came down. He walked across the room, whistling – stopped and listened – took another walk and whistled – stopped again, and listened – then began to go regularly round the pegs, feeling in the pockets of all the coats. When he came to the greatcoat, and felt the pocketbook, he was so eager and so hurried that he broke the strap in tearing it open. As he began to put the money in his pocket, I crawled out from under the sofa, and his eyes met mine.

'My face, as you may perceive, is brown now, but it was pale at that time, my health not being good; and looked as long as a horse's. Besides which, there was a great draught of air from the door, underneath the sofa, and I had tied a handkerchief round my head; so what I looked like, altogether, I don't know. He turned blue – literally blue – when he saw me crawling out, and I couldn't feel surprised at it.

' "I am an officer of the Detective Police," said I, "and have been lying here, since you first came in this morning. I regret, for the sake of yourself and your friends, that you should have done what you have; but this case is complete. You have the pocketbook in your hand and the money upon you; and I must take you into custody!"

'It was impossible to make out any case in his behalf, and on his trial he pleaded guilty. How or when he got the means I don't know; but while he was awaiting his sentence, he poisoned himself in Newgate.'

We enquired of this officer, on the conclusion of the foregoing anecdote, whether the time appeared long, or short, when he lay in that constrained position under the sofa?

'Why, you see, sir,' he replied, 'if he hadn't come in, the first time, and I had not been quite sure he was the thief, and would return, the time would have seemed long. But, as it was, I being dead certain of my man, the time seemed pretty short.'

NO THOROUGHFARE

by Charles Dickens and Wilkie Collins

THE OVERTURE

Day of the month and year, November the thirtieth, one thousand eight hundred and thirty-five. London time by the great clock of Saint Paul's, ten at night. All the lesser London churches strain their metallic throats. Some, flippantly begin before the heavy bell of the great cathedral; some, tardily begin three, four, half a dozen, strokes behind it; all are in sufficiently near accord, to leave a resonance in the air, as if the winged father who devours his children, had made a sounding sweep with his gigantic scythe in flying over the city.

What is this clock lower than most of the rest, and nearer to the ear, that lags so far behind tonight as to strike into the vibration alone? This is the clock of the Hospital for Foundling Children. Time was, when the foundlings were received without question in a cradle at the gate. Time is, when enquiries are made respecting them, and they are taken as by favour from the mothers who relinquish all natural knowledge of them and claim to them for evermore.

The moon is at the full, and the night is fair with light clouds. The day has been otherwise than fair, for slush and mud, thickened with the droppings of heavy fog, lie black in the streets. The veiled lady who flutters up and down near the postern-gate of the Hospital for Foundling Children has need to be well shod tonight.

She flutters to and fro, avoiding the stand of hackney-coaches, and often pausing in the shadow of the western end of the great quadrangle wall, with her face turned towards the gate. As above her there is the purity of the moonlit sky, and below her there are the defilements of the pavement, so may she, haply, be divided in her mind between two vistas of reflection or experience. As her footprints crossing and recrossing one another have made a labyrinth in the mire, so may her track in life have involved itself in an intricate and unravellable tangle.

The postern-gate of the Hospital for Foundling Children opens, and a young woman comes out. The lady stands aside, observes closely, sees that the gate is quietly closed again from within, and follows the young woman.

Two or three streets have been traversed in silence before she, following close behind the object of her attention, stretches out her hand and touches her. Then the young woman stops and looks round, startled.

'You touched me last night, and, when I turned my head, you would not speak. Why do you follow me like a silent ghost?'

'It was not,' returned the lady, in a low voice, 'that I would not speak, but that I could not when I tried.'

'What do you want of me? I have never done you any harm?'

'Never.'

'Do I know you?'

'No.'

'Then what can you want of me?'

'Here are two guineas in this paper. Take my poor little present, and I will tell you.'

Into the young woman's face, which is honest and comely, comes a flush as she replies: 'There is neither grown person nor child in all the large establishment that I belong to, who hasn't a good word for Sally. I am Sally. Could I be so well thought of, if I was to be bought?'

'I do not mean to buy you; I mean only to reward you very slightly.'

Sally firmly, but not ungently, closes and puts back the offering hand. 'If there is anything I can do for you, ma'am, that I will not do for its own sake, you are much mistaken in me if you think that I will do it for money. What is it you want?'

'You are one of the nurses or attendants at the hospital; I saw you leave tonight and last night.'

'Yes, I am. I am Sally.'

'There is a pleasant patience in your face which makes me believe that very young children would take readily to you.'

'God bless 'em! So they do.'

The lady lifts her veil, and shows a face no older than the nurse's. A face far more refined and capable than hers, but wild and worn with sorrow.

'I am the miserable mother of a baby lately received under your care. I have a prayer to make to you.'

Instinctively respecting the confidence which has drawn aside the veil, Sally – whose ways are all ways of simplicity and spontaneity – replaces it, and begins to cry.

'You will listen to my prayer?' the lady urges. 'You will not be deaf to the agonised entreaty of such a broken suppliant as I am?'

'O dear, dear, dear!' cries Sally. 'What shall I say, or can say! Don't talk of prayers. Prayers are to be put up to the Good Father of All, and not to nurses and such. And there! I am only to hold my place for half a year longer, till another young woman can be trained up to it. I am going to be married. I shouldn't have been out last night, and I shouldn't have been out tonight, but that my Dick (he is the young man I am going to be married to) lies ill, and I help his mother and sister to watch him. Don't take on so, don't take on so!'

'O good Sally, dear Sally,' moans the lady, catching at her dress entreatingly. 'As you are hopeful, and I am hopeless; as a fair way in life is before you, which can never, never, be before me; as you can aspire to become a respected wife, and as you can aspire to become a proud mother, as you are a living loving woman, and must die; for *God's* sake hear my distracted petition!'

'Deary, deary, deary *me!*' cries Sally, her desperation culminating in the pronoun, 'what am I ever to do? And there! See how you turn my own words back upon me. I tell you I am going to be married, on purpose to make it clearer to you that I am going to leave, and therefore couldn't help you if I would, Poor Thing, and you make it seem to my own self as if I was cruel in going to be married and not helping you. It ain't kind. Now, is it kind, Poor Thing?'

'Sally! Hear me, my dear. My entreaty is for no help in the future. It applies to what is past. It is only to be told in two words.'

'There! This is worse and worse,' cries Sally, 'supposing that I understand what two words you mean.'

'You do understand. What are the names they have given my poor baby? I ask no more than that. I have read of the customs of the place. He has been christened in the chapel, and registered by some surname in the book. He was received last Monday evening. What have they called him?'

Down upon her knees in the foul mud of the by-way into which they have strayed – an empty street without a thoroughfare giving on the dark gardens of the hospital – the lady would drop in her passionate entreaty, but that Sally prevents her.

'Don't! Don't! You make me feel as if I was setting myself up to be good. Let me look in your pretty face again. Put your two hands in mine. Now, promise. You will never ask me anything more than the two words?'

'Never! Never!'

'You will never put them to a bad use, if I say them?'

'Never! Never!'

'Walter Wilding.'

The lady lays her face upon the nurse's breast, draws her close in her embrace with both arms, murmurs a blessing and the words, 'Kiss him for me!' and is gone.

* * *

Day of the month and year, the first Sunday in October, one thousand eight hundred and forty-seven. London time by the great clock of Saint Paul's, half-past one in the afternoon. The clock of the Hospital for Foundling Children is well up with the cathedral today. Service in the chapel is over, and the foundling children are at dinner.

There are numerous lookers-on at the dinner, as the custom is. There are two or three governors, whole families from the congregation, smaller groups of both sexes, individual stragglers of various degrees. The bright autumnal sun strikes freshly into the wards; and the heavy-framed windows through which it shines, and the panelled walls on which it strikes, are such windows and such walls as pervade Hogarth's pictures. The girls' refectory (including that of the younger children) is the principal attraction. Neat attendants silently glide about the orderly and silent tables; the lookers-on move or stop as the fancy takes them; comments in whispers on face such a number from such a window are not unfrequent; many of the faces are of a character to fix attention. Some of the visitors from the outside public are accustomed visitors. They have established a speaking acquaintance with the occupants of particular seats at the tables, and halt at those points to bend down and say a word or two. It is no disparagement to their kindness that those points are generally points where personal attractions are. The monotony of the long spacious rooms and the double lines of faces is agreeably relieved by these incidents, although so slight.

A veiled lady, who has no companion, goes among the company. It would seem that curiosity and opportunity have never brought her there before. She has the air of being a little troubled by the sight, and, as she goes the length of the tables, it is with a hesitating step and an uneasy manner. At length she comes to the refectory of the boys. They are so much less popular than the girls that it is bare of visitors when she looks in at the doorway.

But just within the doorway, chances to stand, inspecting, an elderly female attendant: some order of matron or housekeeper. To whom the lady addresses natural questions: As, how many boys? At what age are they usually put out in life? Do they often take a fancy to the sea? So, lower and lower in tone until the lady puts the question: 'Which is Walter Wilding?'

Attendant's head shaken. Against the rules.

'You know which is Walter Wilding?'

So keenly does the attendant feel the closeness with which the lady's eyes examine her face, that she keeps her own eyes fast upon the floor, lest by wandering in the right direction they should betray her.

'I know which is Walter Wilding, but it is not my place, ma'am, to tell names to visitors.'

'But you can show me without telling me.'

The lady's hand moves quietly to the attendant's hand. Pause and silence.

'I am going to pass round the tables,' says the lady's interlocutor, without seeming to address her. 'Follow me with your eyes. The boy that I stop at and speak to, will not matter to you. But the boy that I touch, will be Walter Wilding. Say nothing more to me, and move a little away.'

Quickly acting on the hint, the lady passes on into the room, and looks about her. After a few moments, the attendant, in a staid official way, walks down outside the line of tables commencing on her left hand. She goes the whole length of the line, turns, and comes back on the inside. Very slightly glancing in the lady's direction, she stops, bends forward, and speaks. The boy whom she addresses, lifts his head and replies. Good humouredly and easily, as she listens to what he says, she lays her hand upon the shoulder of the next boy on his right. That the action may be well noted, she keeps her hand on the shoulder while speaking in return, and pats it twice or thrice before moving away. She completes her tour of the tables, touching no one else, and passes out by a door at the opposite end of the long room.

Dinner is done, and the lady, too, walks down outside the line of tables commencing on her left hand, goes the whole length of the line, turns, and comes back on the inside. Other people have strolled in, fortunately for her, and stand sprinkled about. She lifts her veil, and, stopping at the touched boy, asks how old he is?

'I am twelve, ma'am,' he answers, with his bright eyes fixed on hers.

'Are you well and happy?'

'Yes, ma'am.'

'May you take these sweetmeats from my hand?'

'If you please to give them to me.'

In stooping low for the purpose, the lady touches the boy's face with her forehead and with her hair. Then, lowering her veil again, she passes on, and passes out without looking back.

ACT ONE

The Curtain Rises

In a courtyard in the City of London, which was No Thoroughfare either for vehicles or foot-passengers; a courtyard diverging from a steep, a slippery, and a winding street connecting Tower Street with the Middlesex shore of the Thames; stood the place of business of Wilding & Co., Wine Merchants. Probably as a jocose acknowledgement of the obstructive character of this main approach, the point nearest to its base at which one could take the river (if so inodorously minded) bore the appellation Break-Neck-Stairs. The courtyard itself had likewise been descriptively entitled in old time, Cripple Corner.

Years before the year one thousand eight hundred and sixty-one, people had left off taking boat at Break-Neck-Stairs, and watermen had ceased to ply there. The slimy little causeway had dropped into the river by a slow process of suicide, and two or three stumps of piles and a rusty iron mooring-ring were all that remained of the departed Break-Neck glories. Sometimes, indeed, a laden coal barge would bump itself into the place, and certain laborious heavers, seemingly mud-engendered, would arise, deliver the cargo in the neighbourhood, shove off, and vanish; but at most times the only commerce of Break-Neck-Stairs arose out of the conveyance of casks and bottles, both full and empty, both to and from the cellars of Wilding & Co., Wine Merchants. Even that commerce was but occasional, and through three-fourths of its rising tides the dirty indecorous drab of a river would come solitarily oozing and lapping at the rusty ring, as if it had heard of the Doge and the

Adriatic, and wanted to be married to the great conserver of its filthiness, the Right Honourable the Lord Mayor.

Some two hundred and fifty yards on the right, up the opposite hill (approaching it from the low ground of Break-Neck-Stairs) was Cripple Corner. There was a pump in Cripple Corner, there was a tree in Cripple Corner. All Cripple Corner belonged to Wilding and Co., Wine Merchants. Their cellars burrowed under it, their mansion towered over it. It really had been a mansion in the days when merchants inhabited the City, and had a ceremonious shelter to the doorway without visible support, like the sounding-board over an old pulpit. It had also a number of long narrow strips of window, so disposed in its grave brick front as to render it symmetrically ugly. It had also, on its roof, a cupola with a bell in it.

'When a man at five-and-twenty can put his hat on, and can say "This hat covers the owner of this property and of the business which is transacted on this property," I consider, Mr Bintrey, that, without being boastful, he may be allowed to be deeply thankful. I don't know how it may appear to you, but so it appears to me.'

Thus Mr Walter Wilding to his man of law, in his own counting-house; taking his hat down from its peg to suit the action to the word, and hanging it up again when he had done so, not to overstep the modesty of nature.

An innocent, open-speaking, unused-looking man, Mr Walter Wilding, with a remarkably pink and white complexion, and a figure much too bulky for so young a man, though of a good stature. With crispy curling brown hair, and amiable bright blue eyes. An extremely communicative man: a man with whom loquacity was the irrestrainable outpouring of contentment and gratitude. Mr Bintrey, on the other hand, a cautious man, with twinkling beads of eyes in a large overhanging bald head, who inwardly but intensely enjoyed the comicality of openness of speech, or hand, or heart.

'Yes,' said Mr Bintrey. 'Yes. Ha, ha!'

A decanter, two wine glasses, and a plate of biscuits, stood on the desk.

'You like this forty-five-year-old port wine?' said Mr Wilding.

'Like it?' repeated Mr Bintrey. 'Rather, sir!'

'It's from the best corner of our best forty-five-year-old bin,' said Mr Wilding.

'Thank you, sir,' said Mr Bintrey. 'It's most excellent.'

He laughed again, as he held up his glass and ogled it, at the highly ludicrous idea of giving away such wine.

'And now,' said Wilding, with a childish enjoyment in the discussion of affairs, 'I think we have got everything straight, Mr Bintrey.'

'Everything straight,' said Bintrey.

'A partner secured – '

'Partner secured,' said Bintrey.

'A housekeeper advertised for – '

'Housekeeper advertised for,' said Bintrey, ' "apply personally at Cripple Corner, Great Tower Street, from ten to twelve" – tomorrow, by the by.'

'My late dear mother's affairs wound up – '

'Wound up,' said Bintrey.

'And all charges paid.'

'And all charges paid,' said Bintrey, with a chuckle: probably occasioned by the droll circumstance that they had been paid without a haggle.

'The mention of my late dear mother,' Mr Wilding continued, his eyes filling with tears and his pocket-handkerchief drying them, 'unmans me still, Mr Bintrey. You know how I loved her; you (her lawyer) know how she loved me. The utmost love of mother and child was cherished between us, and we never experienced one moment's division or un-happiness from the time when she took me under her care. Thirteen years in all! Thirteen years under my late dear mother's care, Mr Bintrey, and eight of them her confidentially acknowledged son! You know the story, Mr Bintrey, who but you, sir!' Mr Wilding sobbed and dried his eyes, without attempt at concealment, during these remarks.

Mr Bintrey enjoyed his comical port, and said, after rolling it in his mouth: 'I know the story.'

'My late dear mother, Mr Bintrey,' pursued the wine-merchant, 'had been deeply deceived, and had cruelly suffered. But on that subject my late dear mother's lips were for ever sealed. By whom deceived, or under what circumstances, Heaven only knows. My late dear mother never betrayed her betrayer.'

'She had made up her mind,' said Mr Bintrey, again turning his wine on his palate, 'and she could hold her peace.' An amused twinkle in his eyes pretty plainly added – 'A devilish deal better than *you* ever will!'

' "Honour," said Mr Wilding, sobbing as he quoted from the com-mandments, "thy father and thy mother, that thy days may be long in the land." When I was in the Foundling, Mr Bintrey, I was at such a loss how to do it, that I apprehended my days would be short in the land. But I afterwards came to honour my mother deeply, profoundly. And I honour and revere her memory. For seven happy years, Mr Bintrey,' pursued Wilding, still with the same innocent catching in his breath, and the same unabashed tears, 'did my excellent mother article me to my predecessors in this business, Pebbleson Nephew. Her affectionate forethought likewise apprenticed me to the Vintners' Company, and made me in time a free Vintner, and – and – everything else that the best of mothers could desire. When I came of age, she bestowed her inherited share in this business upon me; it was her money that afterwards bought out Pebbleson Nephew, and painted in Wilding and Co.; it was she who left me everything she possessed, but the mourning ring you wear. And yet, Mr Bintrey,' with a fresh burst of honest affection, 'she is no more. It is little over half a year since she came into the Corner to read on that doorpost with her own eyes, WILDING & CO., WINE MERCHANTS. And yet she is no more!'

'Sad. But the common lot, Mr Wilding,' observed Bintrey. 'At some time or other we must all be no more.' He placed the forty-five-year-old port wine in the universal condition, with a relishing sigh.

'So now, Mr Bintrey,' pursued Wilding, putting away his pocket-handkerchief, and smoothing his eyelids with his fingers, 'now that I can no longer show my love and honour for the dear parent to whom my heart was mysteriously turned by Nature when she first spoke to me, a strange lady, I sitting at our Sunday dinner-table in the Foundling, I can at least show that I am not ashamed of having been a Foundling, and that I, who never knew a father of my own, wish to be a father to all in my employment. Therefore,' continued Wilding, becoming enthusiastic in his loquacity, 'therefore, I want a thoroughly good housekeeper to undertake this dwelling-house of Wilding and Co., Wine Merchants, Cripple Corner, so that I may restore in it some of the old relations betwixt employer and employed! So that I may live in it on the spot where my money is made! So that I may daily sit at the head of the table at which the people in my employment eat together, and may eat of the same roast and boiled, and drink of the same beer! So that the people in my employment may lodge under the same roof with me! So that we may one and all – I beg your pardon, Mr Bintrey, but that old singing in my head has suddenly come on, and I shall feel obliged if you will lead me to the pump.'

Alarmed by the excessive pinkness of his client, Mr Bintrey lost not a moment in leading him forth into the courtyard. It was easily done; for the counting-house in which they talked together opened on to it, at one side of the dwelling-house. There the attorney pumped with a will, obedient to a sign from the client, and the client laved his head and face with both hands, and took a hearty drink. After these remedies, he declared himself much better.

'Don't let your good feelings excite you,' said Bintrey, as they returned to the counting-house, and Mr Wilding dried himself on a jack-towel behind an inner door.

'No, no. I won't,' he returned, looking out of the towel. 'I won't. I have not been confused, have I?'

'Not at all. Perfectly clear.'

'Where did I leave off, Mr Bintrey?'

'Well, you left off – but I wouldn't excite myself, if I was you, by taking it up again just yet.'

'I'll take care. I'll take care. The singing in my head came on at where, Mr Bintrey?'

'At roast, and boiled, and beer,' answered the lawyer – 'prompting lodging under the same roof – and one and all – '

'Ah! And one and all singing in the head together – '

'Do you know, I really *would not* let my good feelings excite me, if I was you,' hinted the lawyer again, anxiously. 'Try some more pump.'

'No occasion, no occasion. All right, Mr Bintrey. And one and all forming a kind of family! You see, Mr Bintrey, I was not used in my childhood to that sort of individual existence which most individuals have led, more or less, in their childhood. After that time I became absorbed in my late dear mother. Having lost her, I find that I am more fit for being one of a body than one by myself one. To be that, and at the same time to do my duty to those dependent on me, and attach them to me, has a patriarchal and pleasant air about it. I don't know how it may appear to you, Mr Bintrey, but so it appears to me.'

'It is not I who am all-important in the case, but you,' returned Bintrey. 'Consequently, how it may appear to me is of very small importance.'

'It appears to me,' said Mr Wilding, in a glow, 'hopeful, useful, delightful!'

'Do you know,' hinted the lawyer again, 'I really would not ex – '

'I am not going to. Then there's Handel.'

'There's who?' asked Bintrey.

'Handel, Mozart, Haydn, Kent, Purcell, Dr Arne, Greene, Mendelssohn. I know the choruses to those anthems by heart. Foundling Chapel Collection. Why shouldn't we learn them together?'

'Who learn them together?' asked the lawyer, rather shortly.

'Employer and employed.'

'Ay, ay,' returned Bintrey, mollified; as if he had half expected the answer to be, Lawyer and client. 'That's another thing.'

'Not another thing, Mr Bintrey! The same thing. A part of the bond among us. We will form a choir in some quiet church near the Corner here, and, having sung together of a Sunday with a relish, we will come home and take an early dinner together with a relish. The object that I have at heart now is, to get this system well in action without delay, so that my new partner may find it founded when he enters on his partnership.'

'All good be with it!' exclaimed Bintrey, rising. 'May it prosper! Is Joey Ladle to take a share in Handel, Mozart, Haydn, Kent, Purcell, Doctor Arne, Greene, and Mendelssohn?'

'I hope so.'

'I wish them all well out of it,' returned Bintrey, with much heartiness. 'Goodbye, sir.'

They shook hands and parted. Then (first knocking with his knuckles for leave) entered to Mr Wilding from a door of communication between his private counting-house and that in which his clerks sat, the head cellarman of the cellars of Wilding and Co., Wine Merchants, and erst head cellarman of the cellars of Pebbleson Nephew. The Joey Ladle in question. A slow and ponderous man, of the drayman order of human architecture, dressed in a corrugated suit and bibbed apron, apparently a composite of doormat and rhinoceros-hide.

'Respecting this same boarding and lodging, Young Master Wilding,' said he.

'Yes, Joey?'

'Speaking for myself, Young Master Wilding – and I never did speak and I never do speak for no one else – I don't want no boarding nor yet no lodging. But if you wish to board me and to lodge me, take me. I can peck as well as most men. Where I peck ain't so high a object with me as What I peck. Nor even so high a object with me as How Much I peck. Is all to live in the house, Young Master Wilding? The two other cellarmen, the three porters, the two 'prentices, and the odd men?'

'Yes. I hope we shall all be an united family, Joey.'

'Ah!' said Joey. 'I hope they may be.'

'They? Rather say we, Joey.'

Joey Ladle shook his held. 'Don't look to me to make we on it, Young Master Wilding, not at my time of life and under the circumstances which has formed my disposition. I have said to Pebbleson Nephew many a time, when they have said to me, "Put a livelier face upon it, Joey" – I have said to them, "Gentlemen, it is all wery well for you that has been accustomed to take your wine into your systems by the conwivial channel of your throttles, to put a lively face upon it; but," I says, "I have been accustomed to take *my* wine in at the pores of the skin, and, took that way, it acts different. It acts depressing. It's one thing, gentlemen," I says to Pebbleson Nephew, "to charge your glasses in a dining-room with a Hip Hurrah and a Jolly Companions Every One, and it's another thing to be charged yourself, through the pores, in a low dark cellar and a mouldy atmosphere. It makes all the difference betwixt bubbles and wapours," I tells Pebbleson Nephew. And so it do. I've been a cellarman my life through, with my mind fully given to the business. What's the consequence? I'm as muddled a man as lives – you won't find a muddleder man than me – nor yet you won't find my equal in molloncolly. Sing of Filling the bumper fair, Every drop you sprinkle, O'er the brow of care, Smooths away a wrinkle? Yes. P'raps so. But try filling yourself through the pores, underground, when you don't want to it!'

'I am sorry to hear this, Joey. I had even thought that you might join a singing-class in the house.'

'Me, sir? No, no, Young Master Wilding, you won't catch Joey Ladle muddling the Armony. A pecking-machine, sir, is all that I am capable of proving myself, out of my cellars; but that you're welcome to, if you think it is worth your while to keep such a thing on your premises.'

'I do, Joey.'

'Say no more, sir. The Business's word is my law. And you're a going to take Young Master George Vendale partner into the old Business?'

'I am, Joey.'

'More changes, you see! But don't change the name of the Firm again. Don't do it, Young Master Wilding. It was bad luck enough to make it Yourself and Co. Better by far have left it Pebbleson Nephew that good luck always stuck to. You should never change luck when it's good, sir.'

'At all events, I have no intention of changing the name of the House again, Joey.'

'Glad to hear it, and wish you good-day, Young Master Wilding. But you had better by half,' muttered Joey Ladle inaudibly, as he closed the door and shook his head, 'have let the name alone from the first. You had better by half have followed the luck instead of crossing it.'

Enter the Housekeeper

The wine merchant sat in his dining-room next morning, to receive the personal applicants for the vacant post in his establishment. It was an old-fashioned wainscoted room; the panels ornamented with festoons of flowers carved in wood; with an oaken floor, a well-worn Turkey carpet, and dark mahogany furniture, all of which had seen service and polish under Pebbleson Nephew. The great sideboard had assisted at many business-dinners given by Pebbleson Nephew to their connection, on the principle of throwing sprats overboard to catch whales; and Pebbleson Nephew's comprehensive three-sided plate-warmer, made to fit the whole front of the large fireplace, kept watch beneath it over a sarcophagus-shaped cellaret that had in its time held many a dozen of Pebbleson Nephew's wine. But the little rubicund old bachelor with a pigtail, whose portrait was over the sideboard (and who could easily be identified as decidedly Pebbleson and decidedly not Nephew), had retired into another sarcophagus, and the plate-warmer had grown as cold as he. So, the golden and black griffins that supported the candelabra, with black balls in their mouths at the end of gilded chains, looked as if in their old age they had lost all heart for playing at ball, and were dolefully exhibiting their chains in the missionary line of enquiry, whether they had not earned emancipation by this time, and were not griffins and brothers.

Such a Columbus of a morning was the summer morning, that it discovered Cripple Corner. The light and warmth pierced in at the open windows, and irradiated the picture of a lady hanging over the chimney-piece, the only other decoration of the walls.

'My mother at five-and-twenty,' said Mr Wilding to himself, as his eyes enthusiastically followed the light to the portrait's face, 'I hang up here, in order that visitors may admire my mother in the bloom of her youth and beauty. My mother at fifty I hang in the seclusion of my own chamber, as a remembrance sacred to me. O! It's you, Jarvis!'

These latter words he addressed to a clerk who had tapped at the door, and now looked in.

'Yes, sir. I merely wished to mention that it's gone ten, sir, and that there are several females in the counting-house.'

'Dear me!' said the wine merchant, deepening in the pink of his complexion and whitening in the white, 'are there several? So many as several? I had better begin before there are more. I'll see them one by one, Jarvis, in the order of their arrival.'

Hastily entrenching himself in his easy-chair at the table behind a great inkstand, having first placed a chair on the other side of the table opposite his own seat, Mr Wilding entered on his task with considerable trepidation.

He ran the gauntlet that must be run on any such occasion. There were the usual species of profoundly unsympathetic women, and the usual species of much too sympathetic women. There were buccaneering widows who came to seize him, and who griped umbrellas under their arms, as if each umbrella were he, and each griper had got him. There were towering maiden ladies who had seen better days, and who came armed with clerical testimonials to their theology, as if he were Saint Peter with his keys. There were gentle maiden ladies who came to marry him. There were professional housekeepers, like noncommissioned officers, who put him through his domestic exercise, instead of submitting themselves to catechism. There were languid invalids, to whom salary was not so much an object as the comforts of a private hospital. There were sensitive creatures who burst into tears on being addressed, and had to be restored with glasses of cold water. There were some respondents who came two together, a highly promising one and a wholly unpromising one: of whom the promising one answered all questions charmingly, until it would at last appear that she was not a candidate at all, but only the friend of the unpromising one, who had glowered in absolute silence and apparent injury.

At last, when the good wine merchant's simple heart was failing him, there entered an applicant quite different from all the rest. A woman, perhaps fifty, but looking younger, with a face remarkable for placid cheerfulness, and a manner no less remarkable for its quiet expression of equability of temper. Nothing in her dress could have been changed to her advantage. Nothing in the noiseless self-possession of her manner could have been changed to her advantage. Nothing could have been in better unison with both, than her voice when she answered the question:

'What name shall I have the pleasure of noting down?' with the words, 'My name is Sarah Goldstraw. Mrs Goldstraw. My husband has been dead many years, and we had no family.'

Half-a-dozen questions had scarcely extracted as much to the purpose from anyone else. The voice dwelt so agreeably on Mr Wilding's ear as he made his note, that he was rather long about it. When he looked up again, Mrs Goldstraw's glance had naturally gone round the room, and now returned to him from the chimney-piece. Its expression was one of frank readiness to be questioned, and to answer straight.

'You will excuse my asking you a few questions?' said the modest wine merchant.

'O, surely, sir. Or I should have no business here.'

'Have you filled the station of housekeeper before?'

'Only once. I have lived with the same widow lady for twelve years. Ever since I lost my husband. She was an invalid, and is lately dead: which is the occasion of my now wearing black.'

'I do not doubt that she has left you the best credentials?' said Mr Wilding.

'I hope I may say, the very best. I thought it would save trouble, sir, if I wrote down the name and address of her representatives, and brought it with me.' Laying a card on the table.

'You singularly remind me, Mrs Goldstraw,' said Wilding, taking the card beside him, 'of a manner and tone of voice that I was once acquainted with. Not of an individual – I feel sure of that, though I cannot recall what it is I have in my mind – but of a general bearing. I ought to add, it was a kind and pleasant one.'

She smiled, as she rejoined: 'At least, I am very glad of that, sir.'

'Yes,' said the wine merchant, thoughtfully repeating his last phrase, with a momentary glance at his future housekeeper, 'it was a kind and pleasant one. But that is the most I can make of it. Memory is sometimes like a half-forgotten dream. I don't know how it may appear to you, Mrs Goldstraw, but so it appears to me.'

Probably it appeared to Mrs Goldstraw in a similar light, for she quietly assented to the proposition. Mr Wilding then offered to put himself at once in communication with the gentlemen named upon the card: a firm of proctors in Doctors' Commons. To this, Mrs Goldstraw thankfully assented. Doctors' Commons not being far off, Mr Wilding suggested the feasibility of Mrs Goldstraw's looking in again, say in three hours' time. Mrs Goldstraw readily undertook to do so. In fine, the result of Mr Wilding's enquiries being eminently satisfactory, Mrs Goldstraw was that afternoon engaged (on her own perfectly fair terms) to come tomorrow and set up her rest as housekeeper in Cripple Corner.

The Housekeeper Speaks

On the next day Mrs Goldstraw arrived, to enter on her domestic duties.

Having settled herself in her own room, without troubling the servants, and without wasting time, the new housekeeper announced herself as waiting to be favoured with any instructions which her master might wish to give her. The wine merchant received Mrs Goldstraw in the dining-room, in which he had seen her on the previous day; and, the usual preliminary civilities having passed on either side, the two sat down to take counsel together on the affairs of the house.

'About the meals, sir?' said Mrs Goldstraw. 'Have I a large, or a small, number to provide for?'

'If I can carry out a certain old-fashioned plan of mine,' replied Mr Wilding, 'you will have a large number to provide for. I am a lonely single man, Mrs Goldstraw; and I hope to live with all the persons in my employment as if they were members of my family. Until that time comes, you will only have me, and the new partner whom I expect immediately, to provide for. What my partner's habits may be, I cannot yet say. But I may describe myself as a man of regular hours, with an invariable appetite that you may depend upon to an ounce.'

'About breakfast, sir?' asked Mrs Goldstraw. 'Is there anything particular – ?'

She hesitated, and left the sentence unfinished. Her eyes turned slowly away from her master, and looked towards the chimney-piece. If she had been a less excellent and experienced housekeeper, Mr Wilding might have fancied that her attention was beginning to wander at the very outset of the interview.

'Eight o'clock is my breakfast-hour,' he resumed. 'It is one of my virtues to be never tired of broiled bacon, and it is one of my vices to be habitually suspicious of the freshness of eggs.' Mrs Goldstraw looked back at him, still a little divided between her master's chimney-piece and her master. 'I take tea,' Mr Wilding went on; 'and I am perhaps rather nervous and fidgety about drinking it, within a certain time after it is made. If my tea stands too long – '

He hesitated, on his side, and left the sentence unfinished. If he had not been engaged in discussing a subject of such paramount interest to himself as his breakfast, Mrs Goldstraw might have fancied that his attention was beginning to wander at the very outset of the interview.

'If your tea stands too long, sir – ?' said the housekeeper, politely taking up her master's lost thread.

'If my tea stands too long,' repeated the wine merchant mechanically, his mind getting farther and farther away from his breakfast, and his eyes fixing themselves more and more enquiringly on his housekeeper's face. 'If my tea – Dear, dear me, Mrs Goldstraw! what *is* the manner and tone of voice that you remind me of? It strikes me even more strongly today, than it did when I saw you yesterday. What can it be?'

'What can it be?' repeated Mrs Goldstraw.

She said the words, evidently thinking while she spoke them of something else. The wine merchant, still looking at her enquiringly, observed that her eyes wandered towards the chimney-piece once more. They fixed on the portrait of his mother, which hung there, and looked at it with that slight contraction of the brow which accompanies a scarcely conscious effort of memory.

Mr Wilding remarked, 'My late dear mother, when she was five-and-twenty.'

Mrs Goldstraw thanked him with a movement of the head for being at the pains to explain the picture, and said, with a cleared brow, that it was the portrait of a very beautiful lady.

Mr Wilding, falling back into his former perplexity, tried once more to recover that lost recollection, associated so closely, and yet so undiscoverably, with his new housekeeper's voice and manner.

'Excuse my asking you a question which has nothing to do with me or my breakfast,' he said. 'May I enquire if you have ever occupied any other situation than the situation of housekeeper?'

'O yes, sir. I began life as one of the nurses at the Foundling.'

'Why, that's it!' cried the wine merchant, pushing back his chair. 'By heaven! Their manner is the manner you remind me of!'

In an astonished look at him, Mrs Goldstraw changed colour, checked herself, turned her eyes upon the ground, and sat still and silent.

'What is the matter?' asked Mr Wilding.

'Do I understand that you were in the Foundling, sir?'

'Certainly. I am not ashamed to own it.'

'Under the name you now bear?'

'Under the name of Walter Wilding.'

'And the lady – ?' Mrs Goldstraw stopped short with a look at the portrait which was now unmistakably a look of alarm.

'You mean my mother,' interrupted Mr Wilding.

'Your – mother,' repeated the housekeeper, a little constrainedly, 'removed you from the Foundling? At what age, sir?'

'At between eleven and twelve years old. It's quite a romantic adventure, Mrs Goldstraw.'

He told the story of the lady having spoken to him, while he sat at dinner with the other boys in the Foundling, and of all that had followed in his innocently communicative way. 'My poor mother could never have discovered me,' he added, 'if she had not met with one of the matrons who pitied her. The matron consented to touch the boy whose name was "Walter Wilding" as she went round the dinner-tables – and so my mother discovered me again, after having parted from me as an infant at the Foundling doors.'

At those words Mrs Goldstraw's hand, resting on the table, dropped helplessly into her lap. She sat, looking at her new master, with a face that had turned deadly pale, and with eyes that expressed an unutterable dismay.

'What does this mean?' asked the wine merchant. 'Stop!' he cried. 'Is there something else in the past time which I ought to associate with you? I remember my mother telling me of another person at the Foundling, to whose kindness she owed a debt of gratitude. When she first parted with me, as an infant, one of the nurses informed her of the name that had been given to me in the institution. You were that nurse?'

'God forgive me, sir – I was that nurse!'

'God forgive you?'

'We had better get back, sir (if I may make so bold as to say so), to my duties in the house,' said Mrs Goldstraw. 'Your breakfast-hour is eight. Do you lunch, or dine, in the middle of the day?'

The excessive pinkness which Mr Bintrey had noticed in his client's face began to appear there once more. Mr Wilding put his hand to his head, and mastered some momentary confusion in that quarter, before he spoke again.

'Mrs Goldstraw,' he said, 'you are concealing something from me!'

The housekeeper obstinately repeated, 'Please to favour me, sir, by saying whether you lunch, or dine, in the middle of the day?'

'I don't know what I do in the middle of the day. I can't enter into my household affairs, Mrs Goldstraw, till I know why you regret an act of kindness to my mother, which she always spoke of gratefully to the end of her life. You are not doing me a service by your silence. You are agitating me, you are alarming me, you are bringing on the singing in my head.'

His hand went up to his head again, and the pink in his face deepened by a shade or two.

'It's hard, sir, on just entering your service,' said the housekeeper, 'to say what may cost me the loss of your good will. Please to remember, end how it may, that I only speak because you have insisted on my speaking, and because I see that I am alarming you by my silence. When I told the poor lady, whose portrait you have got there, the name by which her infant was christened in the Foundling, I allowed myself to forget my duty, and dreadful consequences, I am afraid, have followed from it. I'll tell you the truth, as plainly as I can. A few months from the time when I had informed the lady of her baby's name, there came to our institution in the country another lady (a stranger), whose object was to adopt one of our children. She brought the needful permission with her, and after looking at a great many of the children, without being able to make up her mind, she took a sudden fancy to one of the babies – a boy – under my care. Try, pray try, to compose yourself, sir! It's no use disguising it any longer. The child the stranger took away was the child of that lady whose portrait hangs there!'

Mr Wilding started to his feet. 'Impossible!' he cried out, vehemently. 'What are you talking about? What absurd story are you telling me now? There's her portrait! Haven't I told you so already? The portrait of my mother!'

'When that unhappy lady removed you from the Foundling, in after years,' said Mrs Goldstraw, gently, 'she was the victim, and you were the victim, sir, of a dreadful mistake.'

He dropped back into his chair. 'The room goes round with me,' he said. 'My head! my head!' The housekeeper rose in alarm, and opened the windows. Before she could get to the door to call for help, a sudden burst of tears relieved the oppression which had at first almost appeared to threaten his life. He signed entreatingly to Mrs Goldstraw not to leave him. She waited until the paroxysm of weeping had worn itself out. He raised his head as he recovered himself, and looked at her with the angry unreasoning suspicion of a weak man.

'Mistake?' he said, wildly repeating her last word. 'How do I know you are not mistaken yourself?'

'There is no hope that I am mistaken, sir. I will tell you why, when you are better fit to hear it.'

'Now! now!'

The tone in which he spoke warned Mrs Goldstraw that it would be cruel kindness to let him comfort himself a moment longer with the vain hope that she might be wrong. A few words more would end it, and those few words she determined to speak.

'I have told you,' she said, 'that the child of the lady whose portrait hangs there, was adopted in its infancy, and taken away by a stranger. I am as certain of what I say as that I am now sitting here, obliged to distress you, sir, sorely against my will. Please to carry your mind on, now, to about three months after that time. I was then at the Foundling, in London, waiting to take some children to our institution in the country. There was a question that day about naming an infant – a boy – who had just been received. We generally named them out of the Directory. On this occasion, one of the gentlemen who managed the hospital happened to be looking over the register. He noticed that the name of the baby who had been adopted ("Walter Wilding") was scratched out – for the reason, of course, that the child had been removed for good from our care. "Here's a name to let," he said. "Give it to the new foundling who has been received today." The name was given, and the child was christened. You, sir, were that child.'

The wine merchant's head dropped on his breast. 'I was that child!' he said to himself, trying helplessly to fix the idea in his mind. 'I was that child!'

'Not very long after you had been received into the institution, sir,' pursued Mrs Goldstraw, 'I left my situation there, to be married. If you will remember that, and if you can give your mind to it, you will see for yourself how the mistake happened. Between eleven and twelve years passed before the lady, whom you have believed to be your mother, returned to the Foundling, to find her son, and to remove him to her own home. The lady only knew that her infant had been called "Walter Wilding". The matron who took pity on her, could but point out the only "Walter Wilding" known in the institution. I, who might have set the matter right, was far away from the Foundling and all that belonged to it. There was nothing – there was really nothing that could prevent this terrible mistake from taking place. I feel for you – I do indeed, sir! You must think – and with reason – that it was in an evil hour that I came here (innocently enough, I'm sure), to apply for your house-keeper's place. I feel as if I was to blame – I feel as if I ought to have had more self-command. If I had only been able to keep my face from showing you what that portrait and what your own words put into my mind, you need never, to your dying day, have known what you know now.'

Mr Wilding looked up suddenly. The inbred honesty of the man rose in protest against the housekeeper's last words. His mind seemed to steady itself, for the moment, under the shock that had fallen on it.

'Do you mean to say that you would have concealed this from me if you could?' he exclaimed.

'I hope I should always tell the truth, sir, if I was asked,' said Mrs Goldstraw. 'And I know it is better for *me* that I should not have a secret of this sort weighing on my mind. But is it better for *you*? What use can it serve now – ?'

'What use? Why, good Lord! if your story is true – '

'Should I have told it, sir, as I am now situated, if it had not been true?'

'I beg your pardon,' said the wine merchant. 'You must make allowance for me. This dreadful discovery is something I can't realise even yet. We loved each other so dearly – I felt so fondly that I was her son. She died, Mrs Goldstraw, in my arms – she died blessing me as only a mother *could* have blessed me. And now, after all these years, to be told she was *not* my mother! O me, O me! I don't know what I am saying!' he cried, as the impulse of self-control under which he had spoken a moment since, flickered, and died out. 'It was not this dreadful grief – it was something else that I had it in my mind to speak of. Yes, yes. You surprised me – you wounded me just now. You talked as if you would have hidden this from me, if you could. Don't talk in that way again. It would have been a crime to have hidden it. You mean well, I know. I don't want to distress you – you are a kind-hearted woman. But you don't remember what my position is. She left me all that I possess, in the firm persuasion that I was her son. I am not her son. I have taken the place, I have innocently got the inheritance of another man. He must be found! How do I know he is not at this moment in misery, without bread to eat? He must be found! My only hope of bearing up against the shock that has fallen on me, is the hope of doing something which *she* would have approved. You must know more, Mrs Goldstraw, than you have told me yet. Who was the stranger who adopted the child? You must have heard the lady's name?'

'I never heard it, sir. I have never seen her, or heard of her, since.'

'Did she say nothing when she took the child away? Search your memory. She must have said something.'

'Only one thing, sir, that I can remember. It was a miserably bad season, that year; and many of the children were suffering from it. When she took the baby away, the lady said to me, laughing, "Don't be alarmed about his health. He will be brought up in a better climate than this – I am going to take him to Switzerland." '

'To Switzerland? What part of Switzerland?'

'She didn't say, sir.'

'Only that faint clue!' said Mr Wilding. 'And a quarter of a century has passed since the child was taken away! What am I to do?'

'I hope you won't take offence at my freedom, sir,' said Mrs Goldstraw; 'but why should you distress yourself about what is to be done? He may not be alive now, for anything you know. And, if he is alive, it's not likely he can be in any distress. The lady who adopted him was a bred and born lady – it was easy to see that. And she must have satisfied them at the Foundling that she could provide for the child, or they would never have let her take him away. If I was in your place, sir – please to excuse my saying so – I should comfort myself with remembering that I had loved that poor lady whose portrait you have got there – truly loved her as my mother, and that she had truly loved me as her son. All she gave to you, she gave for the sake of that love. It never altered while she lived; and it won't alter, I'm sure, as long as *you* live. How can you have a better right, sir, to keep what you have got than that?'

Mr Wilding's immovable honesty saw the fallacy in his housekeeper's point of view at a glance.

'You don't understand me,' he said. 'It's *because* I loved her that I feel it a duty – a sacred duty – to do justice to her son. If he is a living man, I must find him: for my own sake, as well as for his. I shall break down under this dreadful trial, unless I employ myself – actively, instantly employ myself – in doing what my conscience tells me ought to be done. I must speak to my lawyer; I must set my lawyer at work before I sleep tonight.' He approached a tube in the wall of the room, and called down through it to the office below. 'Leave me for a little, Mrs Goldstraw,' he resumed; 'I shall be more composed, I shall be better able to speak to you later in the day. We shall get on well – I hope we shall get on well together – in spite of what has happened. It isn't your fault; I know it isn't your fault. There! there! shake hands; and – and do the best you can in the house – I can't talk about it now.'

The door opened as Mrs Goldstraw advanced towards it; and Mr Jarvis appeared.

'Send for Mr Bintrey,' said the wine merchant. 'Say I want to see him directly.'

The clerk unconsciously suspended the execution of the order, by announcing 'Mr Vendale', and showing in the new partner in the firm of Wilding and Co.

'Pray excuse me for one moment, George Vendale,' said Wilding. 'I have a word to say to Jarvis. Send for Mr Bintrey,' he repeated – 'send at once.'

Mr Jarvis laid a letter on the table before he left the room.

'From our correspondents at Neuchatel, I think, sir. The letter has got the Swiss postmark.'

New Characters on the Scene

The words, 'the Swiss postmark', following so soon upon the house-keeper's reference to Switzerland, wrought Mr Wilding's agitation to such a remarkable height, that his new partner could not decently make a pretence of letting it pass unnoticed.

'Wilding,' he asked hurriedly, and yet stopping short and glancing around as if for some visible cause of his state of mind: 'what is the matter?'

'My good George Vendale,' returned the wine merchant, giving his hand with an appealing look, rather as if he wanted help to get over some obstacle, than as if he gave it in welcome or salutation: 'my good George Vendale, so much is the matter, that I shall never be myself again. It is impossible that I can ever be myself again. For, in fact, I am not myself.'

The new partner, a brown-cheeked handsome fellow, of about his own age, with a quick determined eye and an impulsive manner, retorted with natural astonishment: 'Not yourself?'

'Not what I supposed myself to be,' said Wilding.

'What, in the name of wonder, *did* you suppose yourself to be that you are not?' was the rejoinder, delivered with a cheerful frankness, inviting confidence from a more reticent man. 'I may ask without impertinence, now that we are partners.'

'There again!' cried Wilding, leaning back in his chair, with a lost look at the other. 'Partners! I had no right to come into this business. It was never meant for me. My mother never meant it should be mine. I mean, his mother meant it should be his – if I mean anything – or if I am anybody.'

'Come, come,' urged his partner, after a moment's pause, and taking possession of him with that calm confidence which inspires a strong nature when it honestly desires to aid a weak one. 'Whatever has gone wrong, has gone wrong through no fault of yours, I am very sure. I was not in this counting-house with you, under the old *regime*, for three years, to doubt you, Wilding. We were not younger men than we are, together, for that. Let me begin our partnership by being a serviceable partner, and setting right whatever is wrong. Has that letter anything to do with it?'

'Hah!' said Wilding, with his hand to his temple. 'There again! My head! I was forgetting the coincidence. The Swiss postmark.'

'At a second glance I see that the letter is unopened, so it is not very likely to have much to do with the matter,' said Vendale, with comforting composure. 'Is it for you, or for us?'

'For us,' said Wilding.

'Suppose I open it and read it aloud, to get it out of our way?'

'Thank you, thank you.'

'The letter is only from our champagne-making friends, the house at Neuchatel.

'DEAR SIR – We are in receipt of yours of the 28th ult., informing us that you have taken your Mr Vendale into partnership, whereon we beg you to receive the assurance of our felicitations. Permit us to embrace the occasion of specially commanding to you M. Jules Obenreizer.

'Impossible!'

Wilding looked up in quick apprehension, and cried, 'Eh?'

'Impossible sort of name,' returned his partner, slightly – 'Obenreizer.

' – of specially commanding to you M. Jules Obenreizer, of Soho Square, London (north side), henceforth fully accredited as our agent, and who has already had the honour of making the acquaintance of your Mr Vendale, in his (said M. Obenreizer's) native country, Switzerland.

'To be sure! pooh pooh, what have I been thinking of! I remember now; "when travelling with his niece".'

'With his – ?' Vendale had so slurred the last word, that Wilding had not heard it.

'When travelling with his niece. Obenreizer's niece,' said Vendale, in a somewhat superfluously lucid manner. 'Niece of Obenreizer. (I met them in my first Swiss tour, travelled a little with them, and lost them for two years; met them again, my Swiss tour before last, and have lost them ever since.) Obenreizer. Niece of Obenreizer. To be sure! Possible sort of name, after all! "M. Obenreizer is in possession of our absolute confidence, and we do not doubt you will esteem his merits." Duly signed by the House, "Defresnier et Cie". Very well. I undertake to see M. Obenreizer presently, and clear him out of the way. That clears the Swiss postmark out of the way. So now, my dear Wilding, tell me what I can clear out of *your* way, and I'll find a way to clear it.'

More than ready and grateful to be thus taken charge of, the honest wine merchant wrung his partner's hand, and, beginning his tale by pathetically declaring himself an impostor, told it.

'It was on this matter, no doubt, that you were sending for Bintrey when I came in?' said his partner, after reflecting.

'It was.'

'He has experience and a shrewd head; I shall be anxious to know his opinion. It is bold and hazardous in me to give you mine before I know his, but I am not good at holding back. Plainly, then, I do not see these circumstances as you see them. I do not see your position as you see it. As to your being an impostor, my dear Wilding, that is simply absurd, because no man can be that without being a consenting party to an imposition. Clearly you never were so. As to your enrichment by the lady who believed you to be her son, and whom you were forced to believe, on her showing, to be your mother, consider whether that did not arise out of the personal relations between you. You gradually became much attached to her; she gradually became much attached to you. It was on you, personally you, as I see the case, that she conferred these worldly advantages; it was from her, personally her, that you took them.'

'She supposed me,' objected Wilding, shaking his head, 'to have a natural claim upon her, which I had not.'

'I must admit that,' replied his partner, 'to be true. But if she had made the discovery that you have made, six months before she died, do you think it would have cancelled the years you were together, and the tenderness that each of you had conceived for the other, each on increasing knowledge of the other?'

'What I think,' said Wilding, simply but stoutly holding to the bare fact, 'can no more change the truth than it can bring down the sky. The truth is that I stand possessed of what was meant for another man.'

'He may be dead,' said Vendale.

'He may be alive,' said Wilding. 'And if he is alive, have I not – innocently, I grant you innocently – robbed him of enough? Have I not robbed him of all the happy time that I enjoyed in his stead? Have I not robbed him of the exquisite delight that filled my soul when that dear lady,' stretching his hand towards the picture, 'told me she was my mother? Have I not robbed him of all the care she lavished on me? Have I not even robbed him of all the devotion and duty that I so proudly gave to her? Therefore it is that I ask myself, George Vendale, and I ask you, where is he? What has become of him?'

'Who can tell!'

'I must try to find out who can tell. I must institute enquiries. I must never desist from prosecuting enquiries. I will live upon the interest of my share – I ought to say his share – in this business, and will lay up the rest for him. When I find him, I may perhaps throw myself upon his generosity; but I will yield up all to him. I will, I swear. As I loved and honoured her,' said Wilding, reverently kissing his hand towards the picture, and then covering his eyes with it. 'As I loved and honoured her, and have a world of reasons to be grateful to her!' And so broke down again.

His partner rose from the chair he had occupied, and stood beside him with a hand softly laid upon his shoulder. 'Walter, I knew you before today to be an upright man, with a pure conscience and a fine heart. It is very fortunate for me that I have the privilege to travel on in life so near to so trustworthy a man. I am thankful for it. Use me as your right hand, and rely upon me to the death. Don't think the worse of me if I protest to you that my uppermost feeling at present is a confused, you may call it an unreasonable, one. I feel far more pity for the lady and for you, because you did not stand in your supposed relations, than I can feel for the unknown man (if he ever became a man), because he was unconsciously displaced. You have done well in sending for Mr Bintrey. What I think will be a part of his advice, I know is the whole of mine. Do not move a step in this serious matter precipitately. The secret must be kept among us with great strictness, for to part with it lightly would be to invite fraudulent claims, to encourage a host of knaves, to let loose a flood of perjury and plotting. I have no more to say now, Walter, than to remind you that you sold me a share in your business, expressly to save yourself from more work than your present health is fit for, and that I bought it expressly to do work, and mean to do it.'

With these words, and a parting grip of his partner's shoulder that gave them the best emphasis they could have had, George Vendale betook himself presently to the counting-house, and presently afterwards to the address of M. Jules Obenreizer.

As he turned into Soho Square, and directed his steps towards its north side, a deepened colour shot across his sun-browned face, which Wilding, if he had been a better observer, or had been less occupied with his own trouble, might have noticed when his partner read aloud a certain passage in their Swiss correspondent's letter, which he had not read so distinctly as the rest.

A curious colony of mountaineers has long been enclosed within that small flat London district of Soho. Swiss watchmakers, Swiss silver-chasers, Swiss jewellers, Swiss importers of Swiss musical boxes and Swiss toys of various kinds, draw close together there. Swiss professors of music, painting, and languages; Swiss artificers in steady work; Swiss couriers, and other Swiss servants chronically out of place; industrious Swiss laundresses and clear-starchers; mysteriously existing Swiss of both sexes; Swiss creditable and Swiss discreditable; Swiss to be trusted by all means, and Swiss to be trusted by no means; these diverse Swiss particles are attracted to a centre in the district of Soho. Shabby Swiss eating-houses, coffee-houses, and lodging-houses, Swiss drinks and dishes, Swiss service for Sundays, and Swiss schools for weekdays, are all to be found there. Even the native-born English taverns drive a sort of broken-English trade; announcing in their windows Swiss whets and drams, and sheltering in their bars Swiss skirmishes of love and animosity on most nights in the year.

When the new partner in Wilding and Co. rang the bell of a door bearing the blunt inscription OBENREIZER on a brass plate – the inner door of a substantial house, whose ground story was devoted to the sale of Swiss clocks – he passed at once into domestic Switzerland. A white-tiled stove for wintertime filled the fireplace of the room into which he was shown, the room's bare floor was laid together in a neat pattern of several ordinary woods, the room had a prevalent air of surface bareness and much scrubbing; and the little square of flowery carpet by the sofa, and the velvet chimney-board with its capacious clock and vases of artificial flowers, contended with that tone, as if, in bringing out the whole effect, a Parisian had adapted a dairy to domestic purposes.

Mimic water was dropping off a mill-wheel under the clock. The visitor had not stood before it, following it with his eyes, a minute, when M. Obenreizer, at his elbow, startled him by saying, in very good English, very slightly clipped: 'How do you do? So glad!'

'I beg your pardon. I didn't hear you come in.'

'Not at all! Sit, please.'

Releasing his visitor's two arms, which he had lightly pinioned at the elbows by way of embrace, M. Obenreizer also sat, remarking, with a smile: 'You are well? So glad!' and touching his elbows again.

'I don't know,' said Vendale, after exchange of salutations, 'whether you may yet have heard of me from your House at Neuchatel?'

'Ah, yes!'

'In connection with Wilding and Co.?'

'Ah, surely!'

'Is it not odd that I should come to you, in London here, as one of the firm of Wilding and Co., to pay the firm's respects?'

'Not at all! What did I always observe when we were on the mountains? We call them vast; but the world is so little. So little is the world, that one cannot keep away from persons. There are so few persons in the world, that they continually cross and re-cross. So very little is the world, that one cannot get rid of a person. Not,' touching his elbows again, with an ingratiatory smile, 'that one would desire to get rid of you.'

'I hope not, M. Obenreizer.'

'Please call me, in your country, Mr. I call myself so, for I love your country. If I *could* be English! But I am born. And you? Though descended from so fine a family, you have had the condescension to come into trade? Stop though. Wines? Is it trade in England or profession? Not fine art?'

'Mr Obenreizer,' returned Vendale, somewhat out of countenance, 'I was but a silly young fellow, just of age, when I first had the pleasure of travelling with you, and when you and I and Mademoiselle your niece – who is well?'

'Thank you. Who is well.'

' – Shared some slight glacier dangers together. If, with a boy's vanity,

I rather vaunted my family, I hope I did so as a kind of introduction of myself. It was very weak, and in very bad taste; but perhaps you know our English proverb, "Live and Learn".

'You make too much of it,' returned the Swiss. 'And what the devil! After all, yours *was* a fine family.'

George Vendale's laugh betrayed a little vexation as he rejoined: 'Well! I was strongly attached to my parents, and when we first travelled together, Mr Obenreizer, I was in the first flush of coming into what my father and mother left me. So I hope it may have been, after all, more youthful openness of speech and heart than boastfulness.'

'All openness of speech and heart! No boastfulness!' cried Obenreizer. 'You tax yourself too heavily. You tax yourself, my faith! as if you was your Government taxing you! Besides, it commenced with me. I remember, that evening in the boat upon the lake, floating among the reflections of the mountains and valleys, the crags and pine woods, which were my earliest remembrance, I drew a word-picture of my sordid childhood. Of our poor hut, by the waterfall which my mother showed to travellers; of the cowshed where I slept with the cow; of my idiot half-brother always sitting at the door, or limping down the pass to beg; of my half-sister always spinning, and resting her enormous goitre on a great stone; of my being a famished naked little wretch of two or three years, when they were men and women with hard hands to beat me, I, the only child of my father's second marriage – if it even was a marriage. What more natural than for you to compare notes with me, and say, "We are as one by age; at that same time I sat upon my mother's lap in my father's carriage, rolling through the rich English streets, all luxury surrounding me, all squalid poverty kept far from me. Such is *my* earliest remembrance as opposed to yours!" '

Mr Obenreizer was a black-haired young man of a dark complexion, through whose swarthy skin no red glow ever shone. When colour would have come into another cheek, a hardly discernible beat would come into his, as if the machinery for bringing up the ardent blood were there, but the machinery were dry. He was robustly made, well proportioned, and had handsome features. Many would have perceived that some surface change in him would have set them more at their ease with him, without being able to define what change. If his lips could have been made much thicker, and his neck much thinner, they would have found their want supplied.

But the great Obenreizer peculiarity was, that a certain nameless film would come over his eyes – apparently by the action of his own will – which would impenetrably veil, not only from those tellers of tales, but from his face at large, every expression save one of attention. It by no means followed that his attention should be wholly given to the person with whom he spoke, or even wholly bestowed on present sounds and objects. Rather, it was a comprehensive watchfulness of everything he had in his own mind, and everything that he knew to be, or suspected to be, in the minds of other men.

At this stage of the conversation, Mr Obenreizer's film came over him.

'The object of my present visit,' said Vendale, 'is, I need hardly say, to assure you of the friendliness of Wilding and Co., and of the goodness of your credit with us, and of our desire to be of service to you. We hope shortly to offer you our hospitality. Things are not quite in train with us yet, for my partner, Mr Wilding, is reorganising the domestic part of our establishment, and is interrupted by some private affairs. You don't know Mr Wilding, I believe?'

Mr Obenreizer did not.

'You must come together soon. He will be glad to have made your acquaintance, and I think I may predict that you will be glad to have made his. You have not been long established in London, I suppose, Mr Obenreizer?'

'It is only now that I have undertaken this agency.'

'Mademoiselle your niece – is – not married?'

'Not married.'

George Vendale glanced about him, as if for any tokens of her.

'She has been in London?'

'She *is* in London.'

'When, and where, might I have the honour of recalling myself to her remembrance?'

Mr Obenreizer, discarding his film and touching his visitor's elbows as before, said lightly: 'Come upstairs.'

Fluttered enough by the suddenness with which the interview he had sought was coming upon him after all, George Vendale followed upstairs. In a room over the chamber he had just quitted – a room also Swiss-appointed – a young lady sat near one of three windows, working at an embroidery-frame; and an older lady sat with her face turned close to another white-tiled stove (though it was summer, and the stove was not lighted), cleaning gloves. The young lady wore an unusual quantity of fair bright hair, very prettily braided about a rather rounder white fore-head than the average English type, and so her face might have been a shade – or say a light – rounder than the average English face, and her figure slightly rounder than the figure of the average English girl at nineteen. A remarkable indication of freedom and grace of limb, in her quiet attitude, and a wonderful purity and freshness of colour in her dimpled face and bright grey eyes, seemed fraught with mountain air. Switzerland too, though the general fashion of her dress was English, peeped out of the fanciful bodice she wore, and lurked in the curious clocked red stocking, and in its little silver-buckled shoe. As to the elder lady, sitting with her feet apart upon the lower brass ledge of the stove, supporting a lap-full of gloves while she cleaned one stretched on her left hand, she was a true Swiss impersonation of another kind; from the breadth of her cushion-like back, and the ponderosity of her respectable legs (if the word be admissible), to the black velvet band tied tightly round her throat for the repression of a rising tendency to goitre; or, higher still, to her great copper-coloured gold ear-rings; or, higher still, to her headdress of black gauze stretched on wire.

'Miss Marguerite,' said Obenreizer to the young lady, 'do you recollect this gentleman?'

'I think,' she answered, rising from her seat, surprised and a little confused: 'it is Mr Vendale?'

'I think it is,' said Obenreizer, dryly. 'Permit me, Mr Vendale. Madame Dor.'

The elder lady by the stove, with the glove stretched on her left hand, like a glover's sign, half got up, half looked over her broad shoulder, and wholly plumped down again and rubbed away.

'Madame Dor,' said Obenreizer, smiling, 'is so kind as to keep me free from stain or tear. Madame Dor humours my weakness for being always neat, and devotes her time to removing every one of my specks and spots.'

Madame Dor, with the stretched glove in the air, and her eyes closely scrutinising its palm, discovered a tough spot in Mr Obenreizer at that instant, and rubbed hard at him. George Vendale took his seat by the embroidery-frame (having first taken the fair right hand that his entrance had checked), and glanced at the gold cross that dipped into the bodice, with something of the devotion of a pilgrim who had reached his shrine at last. Obenreizer stood in the middle of the room with his thumbs in his waistcoat-pockets, and became filmy.

'He was saying downstairs, Miss Obenreizer,' observed Vendale, 'that the world is so small a place, that people cannot escape one another. I have found it much too large for me since I saw you last.'

'Have you travelled so far, then?' she enquired.

'Not so far, for I have only gone back to Switzerland each year; but I could have wished – and indeed I have wished very often – that the little world did not afford such opportunities for long escapes as it does. If it had been less, I might have found my follow-travellers sooner, you know.'

The pretty Marguerite coloured, and very slightly glanced in the direction of Madame Dor.

'You find us at length, Mr Vendale. Perhaps you may lose us again.'

'I trust not. The curious coincidence that has enabled me to find you, encourages me to hope not.'

'What is that coincidence, sir, if you please?' A dainty little native touch in this turn of speech, and in its tone, made it perfectly captivating, thought George Vendale, when again he noticed an instantaneous glance towards Madame Dor. A caution seemed to be conveyed in it, rapid flash though it was; so he quietly took heed of Madame Dor from that time forth.

'It is that I happen to have become a partner in a house of business in London, to which Mr Obenreizer happens this very day to be expressly recommended: and that, too, by another house of business in Switzerland, in which (as it turns out) we both have a commercial interest. He has not told you?'

'Ah!' cried Obenreizer, striking in, filmless. 'No. I had not told Miss Marguerite. The world is so small and so monotonous that a surprise is worth having in such a little jog-trot place. It is as he tells you, Miss Marguerite. He, of so fine a family, and so proudly bred, has condescended to trade. To trade! Like us poor peasants who have risen from ditches!'

A cloud crept over the fair brow, and she cast down her eyes.

'Why, it is good for trade!' pursued Obenreizer, enthusiastically. 'It ennobles trade! It is the misfortune of trade, it is its vulgarity, that any low people – for example, we poor peasants – may take to it and climb by it. See you, my dear Vendale!' He spoke with great energy. 'The father of Miss Marguerite, my eldest half-brother, more than two times your age or mine, if living now, wandered without shoes, almost without rags, from that wretched pass – wandered – wandered – got to be fed with the mules and dogs at an inn in the main valley far away – got to be Boy there – got to be Ostler – got to be Waiter – got to be Cook – got to be Landlord. As Landlord, he took me (could he take the idiot beggar his brother, or the spinning monstrosity his sister?) to put as pupil to the famous watchmaker, his neighbour and friend. His wife dies when Miss Marguerite is born. What is his will, and what are his words to me, when he dies, she being between girl and woman? "All for Marguerite, except so much by the year for you. You are young, but I make her your ward, for you were of the obscurest and the poorest peasantry, and so was I, and so was her mother; we were abject peasants all, and you will remember it." The thing is equally true of most of my countrymen, now in trade in this your London quarter of Soho. Peasants once; low-born drudging Swiss peasants. Then how good and great for trade': here, from having been warm, he became playfully jubilant, and touched the young wine merchant's elbows again with his light embrace: 'to be exalted by gentlemen.'

'I do not think so,' said Marguerite, with a flushed cheek, and a look away from the visitor, that was almost defiant. 'I think it is as much exalted by us peasants.'

'Fie, fie, Miss Marguerite,' said Obenreizer. 'You speak in proud England.'

'I speak in proud earnest,' she answered, quietly resuming her work, 'and I am not English, but a Swiss peasant's daughter.'

There was a dismissal of the subject in her words, which Vendale could not contend against. He only said in an earnest manner, 'I most heartily agree with you, Miss Obenreizer, and I have already said so, as Mr Obenreizer will bear witness,' which he by no means did, 'in this house.'

Now, Vendale's eyes were quick eyes, and sharply watching Madame Dor by times, noted something in the broad back view of that lady. There was considerable pantomimic expression in her glove-cleaning. It had been very softly done when he spoke with Marguerite, or it had altogether stopped, like the action of a listener. When Obenreizer's peasant-speech came to an end, she rubbed most vigorously, as if applauding it. And once or twice, as the glove (which she always held before her a little above her face) turned in the air, or as this finger went down, or that went up, he even fancied that it made some telegraphic communication to Obenreizer:

whose back was certainly never turned upon it, though he did not seem at all to heed it.

Vendale observed too, that in Marguerite's dismissal of the subject twice forced upon him to his misrepresentation, there was an indignant treatment of her guardian which she tried to check: as though she would have flamed out against him, but for the influence of fear. He also observed – though this was not much – that he never advanced within the distance of her at which he first placed himself: as though there were limits fixed between them. Neither had he ever spoken of her without the prefix 'Miss', though whenever he uttered it, it was with the faintest trace of an air of mockery. And now it occurred to Vendale for the first time that something curious in the man, which he had never before been able to define, was definable as a certain subtle essence of mockery that eluded touch or analysis. He felt convinced that Marguerite was in some sort a prisoner as to her free will – though she held her own against those two combined, by the force of her character, which was nevertheless inadequate to her release. To feel convinced of this, was not to feel less disposed to love her than he had always been. In a word, he was desperately in love with her, and thoroughly determined to pursue the opportunity which had opened at last.

For the present, he merely touched upon the pleasure that Wilding and Co. would soon have in entreating Miss Obenreizer to honour their establishment with her presence – a curious old place, though a bachelor house withal – and so did not protract his visit beyond such a visit's ordinary length. Going downstairs, conducted by his host, he found the Obenreizer counting-house at the back of the entrance-hall, and several shabby men in outlandish garments hanging about, whom Obenreizer put aside that he might pass, with a few words in *patois*.

'Countrymen,' he explained, as he attended Vendale to the door. 'Poor compatriots. Grateful and attached, like dogs! Goodbye. To meet again. So glad!'

Two more light touches on his elbows dismissed him into the street.

Sweet Marguerite at her frame, and Madame Dor's broad back at her telegraph, floated before him to Cripple Corner. On his arrival there, Wilding was closeted with Bintrey. The cellar doors happening to be open, Vendale lighted a candle in a cleft stick, and went down for a cellarous stroll. Graceful Marguerite floated before him faithfully, but Madame Dor's broad back remained outside.

The vaults were very spacious, and very old. There had been a stone crypt down there, when bygones were not bygones; some said, part of a monkish refectory; some said, of a chapel; some said, of a Pagan temple. It was all one now. Let who would make what he liked of a crumbled pillar and a broken arch or so. Old Time had made what he liked of it, and was quite indifferent to contradiction.

The close air, the musty smell, and the thunderous rumbling in the streets above, as being out of the routine of ordinary life, went well enough with the picture of pretty Marguerite holding her own against those two. So Vendale went on until, at a turning in the vaults, he saw a light like the light he carried.

'O! You are here, are you, Joey?'

'Oughtn't it rather to go, "O! *You're* here, are you, Master George?" For it's my business to be here. But it ain't yourn.'

'Don't grumble, Joey.'

'O! *I* don't grumble,' returned the cellarman. 'If anything grumbles, it's what I've took in through the pores; it ain't me. Have a care as something in you don't begin a grumbling, Master George. Stop here long enough for the wapours to work, and they'll be at it.'

His present occupation consisted of poking his head into the bins, making measurements and mental calculations, and entering them in a rhinoceros-hide-looking notebook, like a piece of himself.

'They'll be at it,' he resumed, laying the wooden rod that he measured with across two casks, entering his last calculation, and straightening his back, 'trust 'em! And so you've regularly come into the business, Master George?'

'Regularly. I hope you don't object, Joey?'

'*I* don't, bless you. But wapours objects that you're too young. You're both on you too young.'

'We shall get over that objection day by day, Joey.'

'Ay, Master George; but I shall day by day get over the objection that I'm too old, and so I shan't be capable of seeing much improvement in you.'

The retort so tickled Joey Ladle that he grunted forth a laugh and delivered it again, grunting forth another laugh after the second edition of 'improvement in you'.

'But what's no laughing matter, Master George,' he resumed, straightening his back once more, 'is, that young Master Wilding has gone and changed the luck. Mark my words. He has changed the luck, and he'll find it out. *I* ain't been down here all my life for nothing! *I* know by what I notices down here, when it's a-going to rain, when it's a-going to hold up, when it's a-going to blow, when it's a-going to be calm. *I* know, by what I notices down here, when the luck's changed, quite as well.'

'Has this growth on the roof anything to do with your divination?' asked Vendale, holding his light towards a gloomy ragged growth of dark fungus, pendent from the arches with a very disagreeable and repellent effect. 'We are famous for this growth in this vault, aren't we?'

'We are, Master George,' replied Joey Ladle, moving a step or two away, 'and if you'll be advised by me, you'll let it alone.'

Taking up the rod just now laid across the two casks, and faintly moving the languid fungus with it, Vendale asked, 'Ay, indeed? Why so?'

'Why, not so much because it rises from the casks of wine, and may leave you to judge what sort of stuff a cellarman takes into himself when he walks in the same all the days of his life, nor yet so much because at a stage of its growth it's maggots, and you'll fetch 'em down upon you,' returned Joey Ladle, still keeping away, 'as for another reason, Master George.'

'What other reason?'

'(I wouldn't keep on touchin' it, if I was you, sir.) I'll tell you if you'll come out of the place. First, take a look at its colour, Master George.'

'I am doing so.'

'Done, sir. Now, come out of the place.'

He moved away with his light, and Vendale followed with his. When Vendale came up with him, and they were going back together, Vendale, eyeing him as they walked through the arches, said: 'Well, Joey? The colour.'

'Is it like clotted blood, Master George?'

'Like enough, perhaps.'

'More than enough, I think,' muttered Joey Ladle, shaking his head solemnly.

'Well, say it is like; say it is exactly like. What then?'

'Master George, they do say – '

'Who?'

'How should I know who?' rejoined the cellarman, apparently much exasperated by the unreasonable nature of the question. 'Them! Them as says pretty well everything, you know. How should I know who They are, if you don't?'

'True. Go on.'

'They do say that the man that gets by any accident a piece of that dark growth right upon his breast, will, for sure and certain, die by murder.'

As Vendale laughingly stopped to meet the cellarman's eyes, which he had fastened on his light while dreamily saying those words, he suddenly became conscious of being struck upon his own breast by a heavy hand. Instantly following with his eyes the action of the hand that struck him – which was his companion's – he saw that it had beaten off his breast a web or clot of the fungus even then floating to the ground.

For a moment he turned upon the cellarman almost as scared a look as the cellarman turned upon him. But in another moment they had reached the daylight at the foot of the cellar-steps, and before he cheerfully sprang up them, he blew out his candle and the superstition together.

Exit Wilding

On the morning of the next day, Wilding went out alone, after leaving a message with his clerk. 'If Mr Vendale should ask for me,' he said, 'or if Mr Bintrey should call, tell them I am gone to the Foundling.' All that his partner had said to him, all that his lawyer, following on the same side, could urge, had left him persisting unshaken in his own point of view. To find the lost man, whose place he had usurped, was now the paramount interest of his life, and to enquire at the Foundling was plainly to take the first step in the direction of discovery. To the Foundling, accordingly, the wine merchant now went.

The once familiar aspect of the building was altered to him, as the look of the portrait over the chimney-piece was altered to him. His one dearest association with the place which had sheltered his childhood had been broken away from it for ever. A strange reluctance possessed him, when he stated his business at the door. His heart ached as he sat alone in the waiting-room while the Treasurer of the institution was being sent for to see him. When the interview began, it was only by a painful effort that he could compose himself sufficiently to mention the nature of his errand.

The Treasurer listened with a face which promised all needful attention, and promised nothing more.

'We are obliged to be cautious,' he said, when it came to his turn to speak, 'about all enquiries which are made by strangers.'

'You can hardly consider me a stranger,' answered Wilding, simply. 'I was one of your poor lost children here, in the bygone time.'

The Treasurer politely rejoined that this circumstance inspired him with a special interest in his visitor. But he pressed, nevertheless, for that visitor's motive in making his enquiry. Without further preface, Wilding told him his motive, suppressing nothing. The Treasurer rose, and led the way into the room in which the registers of the institution were kept. 'All the information which our books can give is heartily at your service,' he said. 'After the time that has elapsed, I am afraid it is the only information we have to offer you.'

The books were consulted, and the entry was found expressed as follows:

3d March, 1836. Adopted, and removed from the Foundling Hospital, a male infant, named Walter Wilding. Name and condition of the person adopting the child – Mrs Jane Ann Miller, widow. Address – Lime Tree Lodge, Groombridge Wells. References – the Reverend John Harker, Groombridge Wells; and Messrs Giles, Jeremie, and Giles, bankers, Lombard Street.

'Is that all?' asked the wine merchant. 'Had you no after-communication with Mrs Miller?'

'None – or some reference to it must have appeared in this book.'

'May I take a copy of the entry?'

'Certainly! You are a little agitated. Let me make a copy for you.'

'My only chance, I suppose,' said Wilding, looking sadly at the copy, 'is to enquire at Mrs Miller's residence, and to try if her references can help me?'

'That is the only chance I see at present,' answered the Treasurer. 'I heartily wish I could have been of some further assistance to you.'

With those farewell words to comfort him Wilding set forth on the journey of investigation which began from the Foundling doors. The first stage to make for, was plainly the house of business of the bankers in Lombard Street. Two of the partners in the firm were inaccessible to chance-visitors when he asked for them. The third, after raising certain inevitable difficulties, consented to let a clerk examine the ledger marked with the initial letter 'M'. The account of Mrs Miller, widow, of Groombridge Wells, was found. Two long lines, in faded ink, were drawn across it; and at the bottom of the page there appeared this note: 'Account closed, September 30th, 1837'.

So the first stage of the journey was reached – and so it ended in No Thoroughfare! After sending a note to Cripple Corner to inform his partner that his absence might be prolonged for some hours, Wilding took his place in the train, and started for the second stage on the journey – Mrs Miller's residence at Groombridge Wells.

Mothers and children travelled with him; mothers and children met each other at the station; mothers and children were in the shops when he entered them to enquire for Lime Tree Lodge. Everywhere, the nearest and dearest of human relations showed itself happily in the happy light of day. Everywhere, he was reminded of the treasured delusion from which he had been awakened so cruelly – of the lost memory which had passed from him like a reflection from a glass.

Enquiring here, enquiring there, he could hear of no such place as Lime Tree Lodge. Passing a house-agent's office, he went in wearily, and put the question for the last time. The house-agent pointed across the street to a dreary mansion of many windows, which might have been a manufactory, but which was an hotel. 'That's where Lime Tree Lodge stood, sir,' said the man, 'ten years ago.'

The second stage reached, and No Thoroughfare again!

But one chance was left. The clerical reference, Mr Harker, still remained to be found. Customers coming in at the moment to occupy the house-agent's attention, Wilding went down the street, and entering a bookseller's shop, asked if he could be informed of the Reverend John Harker's present address.

The bookseller looked unaffectedly shocked and astonished, and made no answer.

Wilding repeated his question.

The bookseller took up from his counter a prim little volume in a binding of sober grey. He handed it to his visitor, open at the title-page. Wilding read: 'The martyrdom of the Reverend John Harker in New Zealand. Related by a former member of his flock.'

Wilding put the book down on the counter. 'I beg your pardon,' he said, thinking a little, perhaps, of his own present martyrdom while he spoke. The silent bookseller acknowledged the apology by a bow. Wilding went out.

Third and last stage, and No Thoroughfare for the third and last time.

There was nothing more to be done; there was absolutely no choice but to go back to London, defeated at all points. From time to time on the return journey, the wine merchant looked at his copy of the entry in the Foundling Register. There is one among the many forms of despair – perhaps the most pitiable of all – which persists in disguising itself as hope. Wilding checked himself in the act of throwing the useless morsel of paper out of the carriage window. 'It may lead to something yet,' he thought. 'While I live, I won't part with it. When I die, my executors shall find it sealed up with my will.'

Now, the mention of his will set the good wine merchant on a new track of thought, without diverting his mind from its engrossing subject. He must make his will immediately.

The application of the phrase No Thoroughfare to the case had originated with Mr Bintrey. In their first long conference following the discovery, that sagacious personage had a hundred times repeated, with an obstructive shake of the head, 'No Thoroughfare, sir, No Thorough- fare. My belief is that there is no way out of this at this time of day, and my advice is, make yourself comfortable where you are.'

In the course of the protracted consultation, a magnum of the forty- five-year-old port wine had been produced for the wetting of Mr Bintrey's legal whistle; but the more clearly he saw his way through the wine, the more emphatically he did not see his way through the case; repeating as often as he set his glass down empty, 'Mr Wilding, No Thoroughfare. Rest and be thankful.'

It is certain that the honest wine merchant's anxiety to make a will originated in profound conscientiousness; though it is possible (and quite consistent with his rectitude) that he may unconsciously have derived some feeling of relief from the prospect of delegating his own difficulty to two other men who were to come after him. Be that as it may, he pursued his new track of thought with great ardour, and lost no time in begging George Vendale and Mr Bintrey to meet him in Cripple Corner and share his confidence.

'Being all three assembled with closed doors,' said Mr Bintrey, addressing the new partner on the occasion, 'I wish to observe, before our friend (and my client) entrusts us with his further views, that I have endorsed what I understand from him to have been your advice, Mr Vendale, and what would be the advice of every sensible man. I have told him that he positively must keep his secret. I have spoken with Mrs Goldstraw, both in his presence and in his absence; and if anybody is to be trusted (which is a very large IF), I think she is to be trusted to that extent. I have pointed out to our friend (and my client), that to set on foot random enquiries would not only be to raise the Devil, in the likeness of all the swindlers in the kingdom, but would also be to waste the estate. Now, you see, Mr Vendale, our friend (and my client) does not desire to waste the estate, but, on the contrary, desires to husband it for what he considers – but I can't say I do – the rightful owner, if such rightful owner should ever be found. I am very much mistaken if he ever will be, but never mind that. Mr Wilding and I are, at least, agreed that the estate is not to be wasted. Now, I have yielded to Mr Wilding's desire to keep an advertisement at intervals flowing through the newspapers, cautiously inviting any person who may know anything about that adopted infant, taken from the Foundling Hospital, to come to my office; and I have pledged myself that such advertisement shall regularly appear. I have gathered from our friend (and my client) that I meet you here today to take his instructions, not to give him advice. I am prepared to receive his instructions, and to respect his wishes; but you will please observe that this does not imply my approval of either as a matter of professional opinion.'

Thus Mr Bintrey; talking quite as much *at* Wilding as *to* Vendale. And yet, in spite of his care for his client, he was so amused by his client's Quixotic conduct, as to eye him from time to time with twinkling eyes, in the light of a highly comical curiosity.

'Nothing,' observed Wilding, 'can be clearer. I only wish my head were as clear as yours, Mr Bintrey.'

'If you feel that singing in it coming on,' hinted the lawyer, with an alarmed glance, 'put it off. – I mean the interview.'

'Not at all, I thank you,' said Wilding. 'What was I going to – '

'Don't excite yourself, Mr Wilding,' urged the lawyer.

'No; I *wasn't* going to,' said the wine merchant. 'Mr Bintrey and George Vendale, would you have any hesitation or objection to become my joint trustees and executors, or can you at once consent?'

'*I* consent,' replied George Vendale, readily.

'*I* consent,' said Bintrey, not so readily.

'Thank you both. Mr Bintrey, my instructions for my last will and testament are short and plain. Perhaps you will now have the goodness to take them down. I leave the whole of my real and personal estate, without any exception or reservation whatsoever, to you two, my joint trustees and executors, in trust to pay over the whole to the true Walter Wilding, if he shall be found and identified within two years after the day of my death. Failing that, in trust to you two to pay over the whole as a benefaction and legacy to the Foundling Hospital.'

'Those are all your instructions, are they, Mr Wilding?' demanded Bintrey, after a blank silence, during which nobody had looked at anybody.

'The whole.'

'And as to those instructions, you have absolutely made up your mind, Mr Wilding?'

'Absolutely, decidedly, finally.'

'It only remains,' said the lawyer, with one shrug of his shoulders, 'to get them into technical and binding form, and to execute and attest. Now, does that press? Is there any hurry about it? You are not going to die yet, sir.'

'Mr Bintrey,' answered Wilding, gravely, 'when I am going to die is within other knowledge than yours or mine. I shall be glad to have this matter off my mind, if you please.'

'We are lawyer and client again,' rejoined Bintrey, who, for the nonce, had become almost sympathetic. 'If this day week – here, at the same hour – will suit Mr Vendale and yourself, I will enter in my diary that I attend you accordingly.'

The appointment was made, and in due sequence, kept. The will was formally signed, sealed, delivered, and witnessed, and was carried off by Mr Bintrey for safe storage among the papers of his clients, ranged in their respective iron boxes, with their respective owners' names outside, on iron tiers in his consulting-room, as if that legal sanctuary were a condensed Family Vault of Clients.

With more heart than he had lately had for former subjects of interest, Wilding then set about completing his patriarchal establishment, being much assisted not only by Mrs Goldstraw but by Vendale too: who, perhaps, had in his mind the giving of an Obenreizer dinner as soon as possible. Anyhow, the establishment being reported in sound working order, the Obenreizers, guardian and ward, were asked to dinner, and Madame Dor was included in the invitation. If Vendale had been over head and ears in love before – a phrase not to be taken as implying the faintest doubt about it – this dinner plunged him down in love ten thousand fathoms deep. Yet, for the life of him, he could not get one word alone with charming Marguerite. So surely as a blessed moment seemed to come, Obenreizer, in his filmy state, would stand at Vendale's elbow, or the broad back of Madame Dor would appear before his eyes. That speechless matron was never seen in a front view, from the moment of her arrival to that of her departure – except at dinner. And from the instant of her retirement to the drawing-room, after a hearty participation in that meal, she turned her face to the wall again.

Yet, through four or five delightful though distracting hours, Marguerite was to be seen, Marguerite was to be heard, Marguerite was to be occasionally touched. When they made the round of the old dark cellars, Vendale led her by the hand; when she sang to him in the lighted room at night, Vendale, standing by her, held her relinquished gloves, and would have bartered against them every drop of the forty-five-year-old, though it had been forty-five times forty-five years old, and its nett price forty-five times forty-five pounds per dozen. And still, when she was gone, and a great gap of an extinguisher was clapped on Cripple Corner, he tormented himself by wondering, Did she think that he admired her! Did she think that he adored her! Did she suspect that she had won him, heart and soul! Did she care to think at all about it! And so, Did she and Didn't she, up and down the gamut, and above the line and below the line, dear, dear! Poor restless heart of humanity! To think that the men who were mummies thousands of years ago, did the same, and ever found the secret how to be quiet after it!

'What do you think, George,' Wilding asked him next day, 'of Mr Obenreizer? (I won't ask you what you think of Miss Obenreizer.)'

'I don't know,' said Vendale, 'and I never did know, what to think of him.'

'He is well informed and clever,' said Wilding.

'Certainly clever.'

'A good musician.' (He had played very well, and sung very well, overnight.)

'Unquestionably a good musician.'

'And talks well.'

'Yes,' said George Vendale, ruminating, 'and talks well. Do you know, Wilding, it oddly occurs to me, as I think about him, that he doesn't keep silence well!'

'How do you mean? He is not obtrusively talkative.'

'No, and I don't mean that. But when he is silent, you can hardly help vaguely, though perhaps most unjustly, mistrusting him. Take people whom you know and like. Take anyone you know and like.'

'Soon done, my good fellow,' said Wilding. 'I take you.'

'I didn't bargain for that, or foresee it,' returned Vendale, laughing. 'However, take me. Reflect for a moment. Is your approving knowledge of my interesting face mainly founded (however various the momentary expressions it may include) on my face when I am silent?'

'I think it is,' said Wilding.

'I think so too. Now, you see, when Obenreizer speaks – in other words, when he is allowed to explain himself away – he comes out right enough; but when he has not the opportunity of explaining himself away, he comes out rather wrong. Therefore it is, that I say he does not keep silence well. And passing hastily in review such faces as I know, and don't trust, I am inclined to think, now I give my mind to it, that none of them keep silence well.'

This proposition in Physiognomy being new to Wilding, he was at first slow to admit it, until asking himself the question whether Mrs Goldstraw kept silence well, and remembering that her face in repose decidedly invited trustfulness, he was as glad as men usually are to believe what they desire to believe.

But, as he was very slow to regain his spirits or his health, his partner, as another means of setting him up – and perhaps also with contingent Obenreizer views – reminded him of those musical schemes of his in connection with his family, and how a singing-class was to be formed in the house, and a choir in a neighbouring church. The class was established speedily, and, two or three of the people having already some musical knowledge, and singing tolerably, the choir soon followed. The latter was led, and chiefly taught, by Wilding himself: who had hopes of converting his dependants into so many Foundlings, in respect of their capacity to sing sacred choruses.

Now, the Obenreizers being skilled musicians, it was easily brought to pass that they should be asked to join these musical unions. Guardian and ward consenting, or guardian consenting for both, it was necessarily brought to pass that Vendale's life became a life of absolute thraldom and enchantment. For, in the mouldy Christopher Wren church on Sundays, with its dearly beloved brethren assembled and met together, five-and-twenty strong, was not that Her voice that shot like light into the darkest places, thrilling the walls and pillars as though they were pieces of his heart! What time, too, Madame Dor in a corner of the high pew, turning her back upon everybody and everything, could not fail to be ritualistically right at some moment of the service; like the man whom the doctors recommended to get drunk once a month, and who, that he might not overlook it, got drunk every day.

But, even those seraphic Sundays were surpassed by the Wednesday concerts established for the patriarchal family. At those concerts she would sit down to the piano and sing them, in her own tongue, songs of her own land, songs calling from the mountain-tops to Vendale, 'Rise above the grovelling level country; come far away from the crowd; pursue me as I mount higher; higher, higher, melting into the azure distance; rise to my supremest height of all, and love me here!' Then would the pretty bodice, the clocked stocking, and the silver-buckled shoe be, like the broad forehead and the bright eyes, fraught with the spring of a very chamois, until the strain was over.

Not even over Vendale himself did these songs of hers cast a more potent spell than over Joey Ladle in his different way. Steadily refusing to muddle the harmony by taking any share in it, and evincing the supremest contempt for scales and suchlike rudiments of music – which, indeed, seldom captivate mere listeners – Joey did at first give up the whole business for a bad job, and the whole of the performers for a set of howling dervishes. But, descrying traces of unmuddled harmony in a part-song one day, he gave his two under-cellarmen faint hopes of getting on towards something in course of time. An anthem of Handel's led to further encouragement from him: though he objected that that great musician must have been down in some of them foreign cellars pretty much, for to go and say the same thing so many times over; which, took it in how you might, he considered a certain sign of your having took it in somehow. On a third occasion, the public appearance of Mr Jarvis with a flute, and of an odd man with a violin, and the performance of a duet by the two, did so astonish him that, solely of his own impulse and motion, he became inspired with the words, 'Ann Koar!' repeatedly pronouncing them as if calling in a familiar manner for some lady who had distinguished herself in the orchestra. But this was his final testimony to the merits of his mates, for, the instrumental duet being performed at the first Wednesday concert, and being presently followed by the voice of Marguerite Obenreizer, he sat with his mouth wide open, entranced, until she had finished; when, rising in his place with much solemnity, and prefacing what he was about to say with a bow that specially included Mr Wilding in it, he delivered himself of the gratifying sentiment: 'Arter that, ye may all on ye get to bed!' And ever afterwards declined to render homage in any other words to the musical powers of the family.

Thus began a separate personal acquaintance between Marguerite Obenreizer and Joey Ladle. She laughed so heartily at his compliment, and yet was so abashed by it, that Joey made bold to say to her, after the concert was over, he hoped he wasn't so muddled in his head as to have took a liberty? She made him a gracious reply, and Joey ducked in return.

'You'll change the luck time about, miss,' said Joey, ducking again. 'It's such as you in the place that can bring round the luck of the place.'

'Can I? Round the luck?' she answered, in her pretty English, and with a pretty wonder. 'I fear I do not understand. I am so stupid.'

'Young Master Wilding, miss,' Joey explained confidentially, though not much to her enlightenment, 'changed the luck, afore he took in young Master George. So I say, and so they'll find. Lord! Only come into the place and sing over the luck a few times, miss, and it won't be able to help itself!'

With this, and with a whole brood of ducks, Joey backed out of the presence. But Joey being a privileged person, and even an involuntary conquest being pleasant to youth and beauty, Marguerite merrily looked out for him next time.

'Where is my Mr Joey, please?' she asked Vendale.

So Joey was produced, and shaken hands with, and that became an institution.

Another institution arose in this wise. Joey was a little hard of hearing. He himself said it was 'wapours', and perhaps it might have been; but whatever the cause of the effect, there the effect was, upon him. On this first occasion he had been seen to sidle along the wall, with his left hand to his left ear, until he had sidled himself into a seat pretty near the singer, in which place and position he had remained, until addressing to his friends the amateurs the compliment before mentioned. It was observed on the following Wednesday that Joey's action as a pecking machine was impaired at dinner, and it was rumoured about the table that this was explainable by his high-strung expectations of Miss Obenreizer's singing, and his fears of not getting a place where he could hear every note and syllable. The rumour reaching Wilding's ears, he in his good nature called Joey to the front at night before Marguerite began. Thus the institution came into being that on succeeding nights, Marguerite, running her hands over the keys before singing, always said to

Vendale, 'Where is my Mr Joey, please?' and that Vendale always brought him forth, and stationed him near by. That he should then, when all eyes were upon him, express in his face the utmost contempt for the exertions of his friends and confidence in Marguerite alone, whom he would stand contemplating, not unlike the rhinoceros out of the spelling-book, tamed and on his hind legs, was a part of the institution. Also that when he remained after the singing in his most ecstatic state, some bold spirit from the back should say, 'What do you think of it, Joey?' and he should be goaded to reply, as having that instant conceived the retort, 'Arter that ye may all on ye get to bed!' These were other parts of the institution.

But, the simple pleasures and small jests of Cripple Corner were not destined to have a long life. Underlying them from the first was a serious matter, which every member of the patriarchal family knew of, but which, by tacit agreement, all forbore to speak of. Mr Wilding's health was in a bad way.

He might have overcome the shock he had sustained in the one great affection of his life, or he might have overcome his consciousness of being in the enjoyment of another man's property; but the two together were too much for him. A man haunted by twin ghosts, he became deeply depressed. The inseparable spectres sat at the board with him, ate from his platter, drank from his cup, and stood by his bedside at night. When he recalled his supposed mother's love, he felt as though he had stolen it. When he rallied a little under the respect and attachment of his dependants, he felt as though he were even fraudulent in making them happy, for that should have been the unknown man's duty and gratification.

Gradually, under the pressure of his brooding mind, his body stooped, his step lost its elasticity, his eyes were seldom lifted from the ground. He knew he could not help the deplorable mistake that had been made, but he knew he could not mend it; for the days and weeks went by, and no one claimed his name or his possessions. And now there began to creep over him a cloudy consciousness of often-recurring confusion in his head. He would unaccountably lose, sometimes whole hours, sometimes a whole day and night. Once, his remembrance stopped as he sat at the head of the dinner-table, and was blank until daybreak. Another time, it stopped as he was beating time to their singing, and went on again when he and his partner were walking in the courtyard by the light of the moon, half the night later. He asked Vendale (always full of consideration, work, and help) how this was? Vendale only replied, 'You have not been quite well; that's all.' He looked for explanation into the faces of his people. But they would put it off with 'Glad to see you looking so much better, sir'; or 'Hope you're doing nicely now, sir'; in which was no information at all.

At length, when the partnership was but five months old, Walter Wilding took to his bed, and his housekeeper became his nurse.

'Lying here, perhaps you will not mind my calling you Sally, Mrs Goldstraw?' said the poor wine merchant.

'It sounds more natural to me, sir, than any other name, and I like it better.'

'Thank you, Sally. I think, Sally, I must of late have been subject to fits. Is that so, Sally? Don't mind telling me now.'

'It has happened, sir.'

'Ah! That is the explanation!' he quietly remarked. 'Mr Obenreizer, Sally, talks of the world being so small that it is not strange how often the same people come together, and come together at various places, and in various stages of life. But it does seem strange, Sally, that I should, as I may say, come round to the Foundling to die.'

He extended his hand to her, and she gently took it.

'You are not going to die, dear Mr Wilding.'

'So Mr Bintrey said, but I think he was wrong. The old child-feeling is coming back upon me, Sally. The old hush and rest, as I used to fall asleep.'

After an interval he said, in a placid voice, 'Please kiss me, Nurse,' and, it was evident, believed himself to be lying in the old dormitory.

As she had been used to bend over the fatherless and motherless children, Sally bent over the fatherless and motherless man, and put her lips to his forehead, murmuring: 'God bless you!'

'God bless you!' he replied, in the same tone.

After another interval, he opened his eyes in his own character, and said: 'Don't move me, Sally, because of what I am going to say; I lie quite easily. I think my time is come, I don't know how it may appear to you, Sally, but – '

Insensibility fell upon him for a few minutes; he emerged from it once more.

' – I don't know how it may appear to you, Sally, but so it appears to me.'

When he had thus conscientiously finished his favourite sentence, his time came, and he died.

ACT TWO

Vendale Makes Love

The summer and the autumn passed. Christmas and the New Year were at hand.

As executors honestly bent on performing their duty towards the dead, Vendale and Bintrey had held more than one anxious consultation on the subject of Wilding's will. The lawyer had declared, from the first, that it was simply impossible to take any useful action in the matter at all. The only obvious enquiries to make, in relation to the lost man, had been made already by Wilding himself; with this result, that time and death together had not left a trace of him discoverable. To advertise for the claimant to the property, it would be necessary to mention particulars – a course of proceeding which would invite half the impostors in England to present themselves in the character of the true Walter Wilding. 'If we find a chance of tracing the lost man, we will take it. If we don't, let us meet for another consultation on the first anniversary of Wilding's death.' So Bintrey advised. And so, with the most earnest desire to fulfil his dead friend's wishes, Vendale was fain to let the matter rest for the present.

Turning from his interest in the past to his interest in the future, Vendale still found himself confronting a doubtful prospect. Months on months had passed since his first visit to Soho Square – and through all that time, the one language in which he had told Marguerite that he loved her was the language of the eyes, assisted, at convenient opportunities, by the language of the hand.

What was the obstacle in his way? The one immovable obstacle which had been in his way from the first. No matter how fairly the opportunities looked, Vendale's efforts to speak with Marguerite alone ended invariably in one and the same result. Under the most accidental circumstances, in the most innocent manner possible, Obenreizer was always in the way.

With the last days of the old year came an unexpected chance of spending an evening with Marguerite, which Vendale resolved should be a chance of speaking privately to her as well. A cordial note from

Obenreizer invited him, on New Year's Day, to a little family dinner in Soho Square. 'We shall be only four,' the note said. 'We shall be only two,' Vendale determined, 'before the evening is out!'

New Year's Day, among the English, is associated with the giving and receiving of dinners, and with nothing more. New Year's Day, among the foreigners, is the grand opportunity of the year for the giving and receiving of presents. It is occasionally possible to acclimatise a foreign custom. In this instance Vendale felt no hesitation about making the attempt. His one difficulty was to decide what his New Year's gift to Marguerite should be. The defensive pride of the peasant's daughter – morbidly sensitive to the inequality between her social position and his – would be secretly roused against him if he ventured on a rich offering. A gift, which a poor man's purse might purchase, was the one gift that could be trusted to find its way to her heart, for the giver's sake. Stoutly resisting temptation, in the form of diamonds and rubies, Vendale bought a brooch of the filagree-work of Genoa – the simplest and most unpretending ornament that he could find in the jeweller's shop.

He slipped his gift into Marguerite's hand as she held it out to welcome him on the day of the dinner.

'This is your first New Year's Day in England,' he said. 'Will you let me help to make it like a New Year's Day at home?'

She thanked him, a little constrainedly, as she looked at the jeweller's box, uncertain what it might contain. Opening the box, and discovering the studiously simple form under which Vendale's little keepsake offered itself to her, she penetrated his motive on the spot. Her face turned on him brightly, with a look which said, 'I own you have pleased and flattered me.' Never had she been so charming, in Vendale's eyes, as she was at that moment. Her winter dress – a petticoat of dark silk, with a bodice of black velvet rising to her neck, and enclosing it softly in a little circle of swansdown – heightened, by all the force of contrast, the dazzling fairness of her hair and her complexion. It was only when she turned aside from him to the glass, and, taking out the brooch that she wore, put his New Year's gift in its place, that Vendale's attention wandered far enough away from her to discover the presence of other persons in the room. He now became conscious that the hands of Obenreizer were affectionately in possession of his elbows. He now heard the voice of Obenreizer thanking him for his attention to Marguerite, with the faintest possible ring of mockery in its tone. ('Such a simple present, dear sir! and showing such nice tact!') He now discovered, for the first time, that there was one other guest, and but one, besides himself, whom Obenreizer presented as a compatriot and friend. The friend's face was mouldy, and the friend's figure was fat. His age was suggestive of the autumnal period of human life. In the course of the evening he developed two extraordinary capacities. One was a capacity for silence; the other was a capacity for emptying bottles.

Madame Dor was not in the room. Neither was there any visible place reserved for her when they sat down to table. Obenreizer explained that it was 'the good Dor's simple habit to dine always in the middle of the day. She would make her excuses later in the evening.' Vendale wondered whether the good Dor had, on this occasion, varied her domestic employment from cleaning Obenreizer's gloves to cooking Obenreizer's dinner. This at least was certain – the dishes served were, one and all, as achievements in cookery, high above the reach of the rude elementary art of England. The dinner was unobtrusively perfect. As for the wine, the eyes of the speechless friend rolled over it, as in solemn ecstasy. Sometimes he said 'Good!' when a bottle came in full; and sometimes he said 'Ah!' when a bottle went out empty – and there his contributions to the gaiety of the evening ended.

Silence is occasionally infectious. Oppressed by private anxieties of their own, Marguerite and Vendale appeared to feel the influence of the speechless friend. The whole responsibility of keeping the talk going rested on Obenreizer's shoulders, and manfully did Obenreizer sustain it. He opened his heart in the character of an enlightened foreigner, and sang the praises of England. When other topics ran dry, he returned to this inexhaustible source, and always set the stream running again as copiously as ever. Obenreizer would have given an arm, an eye, or a leg to have been born an Englishman. Out of England there was no such institution as a home, no such thing as a fireside, no such object as a beautiful woman. His dear Miss Marguerite would excuse him, if he accounted for *her* attractions on the theory that English blood must have mixed at some former time with their obscure and unknown ancestry. Survey this English nation, and behold a tall, clean, plump, and solid people! Look at their cities! What magnificence in their public buildings! What admirable order and propriety in their streets! Admire their laws, combining the eternal principle of justice with the other eternal principle of pounds, shillings, and pence; and applying the product to all civil injuries, from an injury to a man's honour, to an injury to a man's nose! You have ruined my daughter – pounds, shillings, and pence! You have knocked me down with a blow in my face – pounds, shillings, and pence! Where was the material prosperity of such a country as *that* to stop? Obenreizer, projecting himself into the future, failed to see the end of it. Obenreizer's enthusiasm entreated permission to exhale itself, English fashion, in a toast. Here is our modest little dinner over, here is our frugal dessert on the table, and here is the admirer of England conforming to national customs, and making a speech! A toast to your white cliffs of Albion, Mr Vendale! to your national virtues, your charming climate, and your fascinating women! to your Hearths, to your Homes, to your Habeas Corpus, and to all your other institutions! In one word – to England! Heep-heep-heep! hooray!'

Obenreizer's voice had barely chanted the last note of the English cheer, the speechless friend had barely drained the last drop out of his glass, when the festive proceedings were interrupted by a modest tap at the door. A woman-servant came in, and approached her master with a little note in her hand. Obenreizer opened the note with a frown; and, after reading it with an expression of genuine annoyance, passed it on to his compatriot and friend. Vendale's spirits rose as he watched these proceedings. Had he found an ally in the annoying little note? Was the long-looked-for chance actually coming at last?

'I am afraid there is no help for it?' said Obenreizer, addressing his fellow-countryman. 'I am afraid we must go.'

The speechless friend handed back the letter, shrugged his heavy shoulders, and poured himself out a last glass of wine. His fat fingers lingered fondly round the neck of the bottle. They pressed it with a little amatory squeeze at parting. His globular eyes looked dimly, as through an intervening haze, at Vendale and Marguerite. His heavy articulation laboured, and brought forth a whole sentence at a birth. 'I think,' he said, 'I should have liked a little more wine.' His breath failed him after that effort; he gasped, and walked to the door.

Obenreizer addressed himself to Vendale with an appearance of the deepest distress.

'I am so shocked, so confused, so distressed,' he began. 'A misfortune has happened to one of my compatriots. He is alone, he is ignorant of your language – I and my good friend, here, have no choice but to go and help him. What can I say in my excuse? How can I describe my affliction at depriving myself in this way of the honour of your company?'

He paused, evidently expecting to see Vendale take up his hat and retire. Discerning his opportunity at last, Vendale determined to do nothing of the kind. He met Obenreizer dexterously, with Obenreizer's own weapons.

'Pray don't distress yourself,' he said. 'I'll wait here with the greatest pleasure till you come back.'

Marguerite blushed deeply, and turned away to her embroidery-frame in a corner by the window. The film showed itself in Obenreizer's eyes, and the smile came something sourly to Obenreizer's lips. To have told Vendale that there was no reasonable prospect of his coming back in good time, would have been to risk offending a man whose favourable opinion was of solid commercial importance to him. Accepting his defeat with the best possible grace, he declared himself to be equally honoured and delighted by Vendale's proposal. 'So frank, so friendly, so English!' He bustled about, apparently looking for something he wanted, disappeared for a moment through the folding-doors communicating with the next room, came back with his hat and coat, and protesting that he would return at the earliest possible moment, embraced Vendale's elbows, and vanished from the scene in company with the speechless friend.

Vendale turned to the corner by the window, in which Marguerite had placed herself with her work. There, as if she had dropped from the ceiling, or come up through the floor – there, in the old attitude, with her face to the stove – sat an Obstacle that had not been foreseen, in the person of Madame Dor! She half got up, half looked over her broad shoulder at Vendale, and plumped down again. Was she at work? Yes. Cleaning Obenreizer's gloves, as before? No; darning Obenreizer's stockings.

The case was now desperate. Two serious considerations presented themselves to Vendale. Was it possible to put Madame Dor into the stove? The stove wouldn't hold her. Was it possible to treat Madame Dor, not as a living woman, but as an article of furniture? Could the mind be brought to contemplate this respectable matron purely in the light of a chest of drawers, with a black gauze held-dress accidentally left on the top of it? Yes, the mind could be brought to do that. With a comparatively trifling effort, Vendale's mind did it. As he took his place on the old-fashioned window-seat, close by Marguerite and her embroidery, a slight movement appeared in the chest of drawers, but no remark issued from it. Let it be remembered that solid furniture is not easy to move, and that it has this advantage in consequence – there is no fear of upsetting it.

Unusually silent and unusually constrained – with the bright colour fast fading from her face, with a feverish energy possessing her fingers – the pretty Marguerite bent over her embroidery, and worked as if her life depended on it. Hardly less agitated himself, Vendale felt the importance of leading her very gently to the avowal which he was eager to make – to the other sweeter avowal still, which he was longing to hear. A woman's love is never to be taken by storm; it yields insensibly to a system of gradual approach. It ventures by the roundabout way, and listens to the low voice. Vendale led her memory back to their past meetings when they were travelling together in Switzerland. They revived the impressions, they recalled the events, of the happy bygone time. Little by little, Marguerite's constraint vanished. She smiled, she was interested, she looked at Vendale, she grew idle with her needle, she made false stitches in her work. Their voices sank lower and lower; their faces bent nearer and nearer to each other as they spoke. And Madame Dor? Madame Dor behaved like an angel. She never looked round; she never said a word; she went on with Obenreizer's stockings. Pulling each stocking up tight over her left arm, and holding that arm aloft from time to time, to catch the light on her work, there were moments – delicate and indescribable moments – when Madame Dor appeared to be sitting upside down, and contemplating one of her own respectable legs, elevated in the air. As the minutes wore on, these elevations followed each other at longer and longer intervals. Now and again, the black gauze headdress nodded, dropped forward, recovered itself. A little heap of stockings slid softly from Madame Dor's lap, and remained unnoticed on the floor. A prodigious ball of worsted followed the stockings, and rolled lazily under the table. The black gauze headdress nodded, dropped forward, recovered itself, nodded again, dropped forward again, and recovered itself no more. A composite sound, partly as of the purring of an immense cat, partly as of the planing of a soft board, rose over the hushed voices of the lovers, and hummed at regular intervals through the room. Nature and Madame Dor had combined together in Vendale's interests. The best of women was asleep.

Marguerite rose to stop – not the snoring – let us say, the audible repose of Madame Dor. Vendale laid his hand on her arm, and pressed her back gently into her chair.

'Don't disturb her,' he whispered. 'I have been waiting to tell you a secret. Let me tell it now.'

Marguerite resumed her seat. She tried to resume her needle. It was useless; her eyes failed her; her hand failed her; she could find nothing.

'We have been talking,' said Vendale, 'of the happy time when we first met, and first travelled together. I have a confession to make. I have been concealing something. When we spoke of my first visit to Switzerland, I told you of all the impressions I had brought back with me to England – except one. Can you guess what that one is?'

Her eyes looked steadfastly at the embroidery, and her face turned a little away from him. Signs of disturbance began to appear in her neat velvet bodice, round the region of the brooch. She made no reply. Vendale pressed the question without mercy.

'Can you guess what the one Swiss impression is which I have not told you yet?'

Her face turned back towards him, and a faint smile trembled on her lips.

'An impression of the mountains, perhaps?' she said slyly.

'No; a much more precious impression than that.'

'Of the lakes?'

'No. The lakes have not grown dearer and dearer in remembrance to me every day. The lakes are not associated with my happiness in the present, and my hopes in the future. Marguerite! all that makes life worth having hangs, for me, on a word from your lips. Marguerite! I love you!'

Her head drooped as he took her hand. He drew her to him, and looked at her. The tears escaped from her downcast eyes, and fell slowly over her cheeks.

'O, Mr Vendale,' she said sadly, 'it would have been kinder to have kept your secret. Have you forgotten the distance between us? It can never, never be!'

'There can be but one distance between us, Marguerite – a distance of your making. My love, my darling, there is no higher rank in goodness, there is no higher rank in beauty, than yours! Come! whisper the one little word which tells me you will be my wife!'

She sighed bitterly. 'Think of your family,' she murmured; 'and think of mine!'

Vendale drew her a little nearer to him.

'If you dwell on such an obstacle as that,' he said, 'I shall think but one thought – I shall think I have offended you.'

She started, and looked up. 'O, no!' she exclaimed innocently. The instant the words passed her lips, she saw the construction that might be placed on them. Her confession had escaped her in spite of herself. A lovely flush of colour overspread her face. She made a momentary effort to disengage herself from her lover's embrace. She looked up at him entreatingly. She tried to speak. The words died on her lips in the kiss that Vendale pressed on them. 'Let me go, Mr Vendale!' she said faintly.

'Call me George.'

She laid her head on his bosom. All her heart went out to him at last. 'George!' she whispered.

'Say you love me!'

Her arms twined themselves gently round his neck. Her lips, timidly touching his cheek, murmured the delicious words – 'I love you!'

In the moment of silence that followed, the sound of the opening and closing of the house-door came clear to them through the wintry stillness of the street.

Marguerite started to her feet.

'Let me go!' she said. 'He has come back!'

She hurried from the room, and touched Madame Dor's shoulder in passing. Madame Dor woke up with a loud snort, looked first over one shoulder and then over the other, peered down into her lap, and discovered neither stockings, worsted, nor darning-needle in it. At the same moment, footsteps became audible ascending the stairs. 'Mon Dieu!' said Madame Dor, addressing herself to the stove, and trembling violently. Vendale picked up the stockings and the ball, and huddled them all back in a heap over her shoulder. 'Mon Dieu!' said Madame Dor, for the second time, as the avalanche of worsted poured into her capacious lap.

The door opened, and Obenreizer came in. His first glance round the room showed him that Marguerite was absent.

'What!' he exclaimed, 'my niece is away? My niece is not here to entertain you in my absence? This is unpardonable. I shall bring her back instantly.'

Vendale stopped him.

'I beg you will not disturb Miss Obenreizer,' he said. 'You have returned, I see, without your friend?'

'My friend remains, and consoles our afflicted compatriot. A heart-rending scene, Mr Vendale! The household goods at the pawnbroker's – the family immersed in tears. We all embraced in silence. My admirable friend alone possessed his composure. He sent out, on the spot, for a bottle of wine.'

'Can I say a word to you in private, Mr Obenreizer?'

'Assuredly.' He turned to Madame Dor. 'My good creature, you are sinking for want of repose. Mr Vendale will excuse you.'

Madame Dor rose, and set forth sideways on her journey from the stove to bed. She dropped a stocking. Vendale picked it up for her, and opened one of the folding-doors. She advanced a step, and dropped three more stockings. Vendale stooping to recover them as before, Obenreizer interfered with profuse apologies, and with a warning look at Madame Dor. Madame Dor acknowledged the look by dropping the whole of the stockings in a heap, and then shuffling away panic-stricken from the scene of disaster. Obenreizer swept up the complete collection fiercely in both hands. 'Go!' he cried, giving his prodigious handful a preparatory swing in the air. Madame Dor said, 'Mon Dieu,' and vanished into the next room, pursued by a shower of stockings.

'What must you think, Mr Vendale,' said Obenreizer, closing the door, 'of this deplorable intrusion of domestic details? For myself, I blush at it. We are beginning the New Year as badly as possible; everything has gone wrong tonight. Be seated, pray – and say, what may I offer you? Shall we pay our best respects to another of your noble English institutions? It is my study to be, what you call, jolly. I propose a grog.'

Vendale declined the grog with all needful respect for that noble institution.

'I wish to speak to you on a subject in which I am deeply interested,' he said. 'You must have observed, Mr Obenreizer, that I have, from the first, felt no ordinary admiration for your charming niece?'

'You are very good. In my niece's name, I thank you.'

'Perhaps you may have noticed, latterly, that my admiration for Miss Obenreizer has grown into a tenderer and deeper feeling – ?'

'Shall we say friendship, Mr Vendale?'

'Say love – and we shall be nearer to the truth.'

Obenreizer started out of his chair. The faintly discernible beat, which was his nearest approach to a change of colour, showed itself suddenly in his cheeks.

'You are Miss Obenreizer's guardian,' pursued Vendale. 'I ask you to confer upon me the greatest of all favours – I ask you to give me her hand in marriage.'

Obenreizer dropped back into his chair. 'Mr Vendale,' he said, 'you petrify me.'

'I will wait,' rejoined Vendale, 'until you have recovered yourself.'

'One word before I recover myself. You have said nothing about this to my niece?'

'I have opened my whole heart to your niece. And I have reason to hope – '

'What!' interposed Obenreizer. 'You have made a proposal to my niece, without first asking for my authority to pay your addresses to her?' He struck his hand on the table, and lost his hold over himself for the first time in Vendale's experience of him. 'Sir!' he exclaimed, indignantly, 'what sort of conduct is this? As a man of honour, speaking to a man of honour, how can you justify it?'

'I can only justify it as one of our English institutions,' said Vendale quietly. 'You admire our English institutions. I can't honestly tell you, Mr Obenreizer, that I regret what I have done. I can only assure you that I have not acted in the matter with any intentional disrespect towards yourself. This said, may I ask you to tell me plainly what objection you see to favouring my suit?'

'I see this immense objection,' answered Obenreizer, 'that my niece and you are not on a social equality together. My niece is the daughter of a poor peasant; and you are the son of a gentleman. You do us an honour,' he added, lowering himself again gradually to his customary polite level, 'which deserves, and has, our most grateful acknowledgements. But the inequality is too glaring; the sacrifice is too great. You English are a proud people, Mr Vendale. I have observed enough of this country to see that such a marriage as you propose would be a scandal here. Not a hand would be held out to your peasant-wife; and all your best friends would desert you.'

'One moment,' said Vendale, interposing on his side. 'I may claim, without any great arrogance, to know more of my country people in general, and of my own friends in particular, than you do. In the estimation of everybody whose opinion is worth having, my wife herself would be the one sufficient justification of my marriage. If I did not feel certain – observe, I say certain – that I am offering her a position which she can accept without so much as the shadow of a humiliation – I would never (cost me what it might) have asked her to be my wife. Is there any other obstacle that you see? Have you any personal objection to me?'

Obenreizer spread out both his hands in courteous protest. 'Personal objection!' he exclaimed. 'Dear sir, the bare question is painful to me.'

'We are both men of business,' pursued Vendale, 'and you naturally expect me to satisfy you that I have the means of supporting a wife. I can explain my pecuniary position in two words. I inherit from my parents a fortune of twenty thousand pounds. In half of that sum I have only a life-interest, to which, if I die, leaving a widow, my widow succeeds. If I die, leaving children, the money itself is divided among them, as they come of age. The other half of my fortune is at my own disposal, and is invested in the wine-business. I see my way to greatly improving that business. As it stands at present, I cannot state my return from my capital embarked at more than twelve hundred a year. Add the yearly value of my life-interest – and the total reaches a present annual income of fifteen hundred pounds. I have the fairest prospect of soon making it more. In the meantime, do you object to me on pecuniary grounds?'

Driven back to his last entrenchment, Obenreizer rose, and took a turn backwards and forwards in the room. For the moment, he was plainly at a loss what to say or do next.

'Before I answer that last question,' he said, after a little close consideration with himself, 'I beg leave to revert for a moment to Miss Marguerite. You said something just now which seemed to imply that she returns the sentiment with which you are pleased to regard her?'

'I have the inestimable happiness,' said Vendale, 'of knowing that she loves me.'

Obenreizer stood silent for a moment, with the film over his eyes, and the faintly perceptible beat becoming visible again in his cheeks.

'If you will excuse me for a few minutes,' he said, with ceremonious politeness, 'I should like to have the opportunity of speaking to my niece.' With those words, he bowed, and quitted the room.

Left by himself, Vendale's thoughts (as a necessary result of the interview, thus far) turned instinctively to the consideration of Obenreizer's motives. He had put obstacles in the way of the courtship; he was now putting obstacles in the way of the marriage – a marriage offering advantages which even his ingenuity could not dispute. On the face of it, his conduct was incomprehensible. What did it mean?

Seeking, under the surface, for the answer to that question – and remembering that Obenreizer was a man of about his own age; also, that Marguerite was, strictly speaking, his half-niece only – Vendale asked himself, with a lover's ready jealousy, whether he had a rival to fear, as well as a guardian to conciliate. The thought just crossed his mind, and no more. The sense of Marguerite's kiss still lingering on his cheek reminded him gently that even the jealousy of a moment was now a treason to *her*.

On reflection, it seemed most likely that a personal motive of another kind might suggest the true explanation of Obenreizer's conduct. Marguerite's grace and beauty were precious ornaments in that little household. They gave it a special social attraction and a special social importance. They armed Obenreizer with a certain influence in reserve, which he could always depend upon to make his house attractive, and which he might always bring more or less to bear on the forwarding of his own private ends. Was he the sort of man to resign such advantages as were here implied, without obtaining the fullest possible compensation for the loss? A connection by marriage with Vendale offered him solid advantages, beyond all doubt. But there were hundreds of men in London with far greater power and far wider influence than Vendale possessed. Was it possible that this man's ambition secretly looked higher than the highest prospects that could be offered to him by the alliance now proposed for his niece? As the question passed through Vendale's mind, the man himself reappeared – to answer it, or not to answer it, as the event might prove.

A marked change was visible in Obenreizer when he resumed his place. His manner was less assured, and there were plain traces about his mouth of recent agitation which had not been successfully composed. Had he said something, referring either to Vendale or to himself, which had raised Marguerite's spirit, and which had placed him, for the first time, face to face with a resolute assertion of his niece's will? It might or might not be. This only was certain – he looked like a man who had met with a repulse.

'I have spoken to my niece,' he began. 'I find, Mr Vendale, that even your influence has not entirely blinded her to the social objections to your proposal.'

'May I ask,' returned Vendale, 'if that is the only result of your interview with Miss Obenreizer?'

A momentary flash leapt out through the Obenreizer film.

'You are master of the situation,' he answered, in a tone of sardonic submission. 'If you insist on my admitting it, I do admit it in those words. My niece's will and mine used to be one, Mr Vendale. You have come between us, and her will is now yours. In my country, we know when we are beaten, and we submit with our best grace. I submit, with my best grace, on certain conditions. Let us revert to the statement of your pecuniary position. I have an objection to you, my dear sir – a most amazing, a most audacious objection, from a man in my position to a man in yours.'

'What is it?'

'You have honoured me by making a proposal for my niece's hand. For the present (with best thanks and respects), I beg to decline it.'

'Why?'

'Because you are not rich enough.'

The objection, as the speaker had foreseen, took Vendale completely by surprise. For the moment he was speechless.

'Your income is fifteen hundred a year,' pursued Obenreizer. 'In my miserable country I should fall on my knees before your income, and say, "What a princely fortune!" In wealthy England, I sit as I am, and say, "A modest independence, dear sir; nothing more. Enough, perhaps, for a wife in your own rank of life who has no social prejudices to conquer. Not more than half enough for a wife who is a meanly born foreigner, and who has all your social prejudices against her." Sir! if my niece is ever to marry you, she will have what you call uphill work of it in taking her place at starting. Yes, yes; this is not your view, but it remains, immovably remains, my view for all that. For my niece's sake, I claim that this uphill work shall be made as smooth as possible. Whatever material advantages she can have to help her, ought, in common justice, to be hers. Now, tell me, Mr Vendale, on your fifteen hundred a year can your wife have a house in a fashionable quarter, a footman to open her door, a butler to wait at her table, and a carriage and horses to drive about in? I see the answer in your face – your face says, No. Very good. Tell me one more thing, and I have done. Take the mass of your educated, accomplished, and lovely country-women, is it, or is it not, the fact that a lady who has a house in a fashionable quarter, a footman to open her door, a butler to wait at her table, and a carriage and horses to drive about in, is a lady who has gained four steps, in female estimation, at starting? Yes? or No?'

'Come to the point,' said Vendale. 'You view this question as a question of terms. What are your terms?'

'The lowest terms, dear sir, on which you can provide your wife with those four steps at starting. Double your present income – the most rigid economy cannot do it in England on less. You said just now that you expected greatly to increase the value of your business. To work – and increase it! I am a good devil after all! On the day when you satisfy me, by plain proofs, that your income has risen to three thousand a year, ask me for my niece's hand, and it is yours.'

'May I enquire if you have mentioned this arrangement to Miss Obenreizer?'

'Certainly. She has a last little morsel of regard still left for me, Mr Vendale, which is not yours yet; and she accepts my terms. In other words, she submits to be guided by her guardian's regard for her welfare, and by her guardian's superior knowledge of the world.' He threw himself back in his chair, in firm reliance on his position, and in full possession of his excellent temper.

Any open assertion of his own interests, in the situation in which Vendale was now placed, seemed to be (for the present at least) hopeless. He found himself literally left with no ground to stand on. Whether Obenreizer's objections were the genuine product of Obenreizer's own view of the case, or whether he was simply delaying the marriage in the hope of ultimately breaking it off altogether – in either of these events, any present resistance on Vendale's part would be equally useless. There was no help for it but to yield, making the best terms that he could on his own side.

'I protest against the conditions you impose on me,' he began.

'Naturally,' said Obenreizer; 'I dare say I should protest, myself, in your place.'

'Say, however,' pursued Vendale, 'that I accept your terms. In that case, I must be permitted to make two stipulations on my part. In the first place, I shall expect to be allowed to see your niece.'

'Aha! to see my niece? and to make her in as great a hurry to be married as you are yourself? Suppose I say, No? you would see her perhaps without my permission?'

'Decidedly!'

'How delightfully frank! How exquisitely English! You shall see her, Mr Vendale, on certain days, which we will appoint together. What next?'

'Your objection to my income,' proceeded Vendale, 'has taken me completely by surprise. I wish to be assured against any repetition of that surprise. Your present views of my qualification for marriage require me to have an income of three thousand a year. Can I be certain, in the future, as your experience of England enlarges, that your estimate will rise no higher?'

'In plain English,' said Obenreizer, 'you doubt my word?'

'Do you purpose to take *my* word for it when I inform you that I have doubled my income?' asked Vendale. 'If my memory does not deceive me, you stipulated, a minute since, for plain proofs?'

'Well played, Mr Vendale! You combine the foreign quickness with the English solidity. Accept my best congratulations. Accept, also, my written guarantee.'

He rose; seated himself at a writing-desk at a side-table, wrote a few lines, and presented them to Vendale with a low bow. The engagement was perfectly explicit, and was signed and dated with scrupulous care.

'Are you satisfied with your guarantee?'

'I am satisfied.'

'Charmed to hear it, I am sure. We have had our little skirmish – we have really been wonderfully clever on both sides. For the present our affairs are settled. I bear no malice. You bear no malice. Come, Mr Vendale, a good English shake hands.'

Vendale gave his hand, a little bewildered by Obenreizer's sudden transitions from one humour to another.

'When may I expect to see Miss Obenreizer again?' he asked, as he rose to go.

'Honour me with a visit tomorrow,' said Obenreizer, 'and we will settle it then. Do have a grog before you go! No? Well! well! we will reserve the grog till you have your three thousand a year, and are ready to be married. Aha! When will that be?'

'I made an estimate, some months since, of the capacities of my business,' said Vendale. 'If that estimate is correct, I shall double my present income – '

'And be married!' added Obenreizer.

'And be married,' repeated Vendale, 'within a year from this time. Good-night.'

Vendale Makes Mischief

When Vendale entered his office the next morning, the dull commercial routine at Cripple Corner met him with a new face. Marguerite had an interest in it now! The whole machinery which Wilding's death had set in motion, to realise the value of the business – the balancing of ledgers, the estimating of debts, the taking of stock, and the rest of it – was now transformed into machinery which indicated the chances for and against a speedy marriage. After looking over results, as presented by his accountant, and checking additions and subtractions, as rendered by the clerks, Vendale turned his attention to the stocktaking department next, and sent a message to the cellars, desiring to see the report.

The cellarman's appearance, the moment he put his head in at the door of his master's private room, suggested that something very extraordinary must have happened that morning. There was an approach to alacrity in Joey Ladle's movements! There was something which actually simulated cheerfulness in Joey Ladle's face.

'What's the matter?' asked Vendale. 'Anything wrong?'

'I should wish to mention one thing,' answered Joey. 'Young Mr Vendale, I have never set myself up for a prophet.'

'Who ever said you did?'

'No prophet, as far as I've heard tell of that profession,' proceeded Joey, 'ever lived principally underground. No prophet, whatever else he might take in at the pores, ever took in wine from morning to night, for a number of years together. When I said to young Master Wilding, respecting his changing the name of the firm, that one of these days he might find he'd changed the luck of the firm – did I put myself forward as a prophet? No, I didn't. Has what I said to him come true? Yes, it has. In the time of Pebbleson Nephew, Young Mr Vendale, no such thing was ever known as a mistake made in a consignment delivered at these doors. There's a mistake been made now. Please to remark that it happened before Miss Margaret came here. For which reason it don't go against what I've said respecting Miss Margaret singing round the luck. Read that, sir,' concluded Joey, pointing attention to a special passage in the report, with a forefinger which appeared to be in process of taking in through the pores nothing more remarkable than dirt. 'It's foreign to my nature to crow over the house I serve, but I feel it a kind of solemn duty to ask you to read that.'

Vendale read as follows: – 'Note, respecting the Swiss champagne. An irregularity has been discovered in the last consignment received from the firm of Defresnier and Co.' Vendale stopped, and referred to a memorandum-book by his side. 'That was in Mr Wilding's time,' he said. 'The vintage was a particularly good one, and he took the whole of it. The Swiss champagne has done very well, hasn't it?'

'I don't say it's done badly,' answered the cellarman. 'It may have got sick in our customers' bins, or it may have bust in our customers' hands. But I don't say it's done badly with us.'

Vendale resumed the reading of the note: 'We find the number of the cases to be quite correct by the books. But six of them, which present a slight difference from the rest in the brand, have been opened, and have been found to contain a red wine instead of champagne. The similarity in the brands, we suppose, caused a mistake to be made in sending the consignment from Neuchatel. The error has not been found to extend beyond six cases.'

'Is that all!' exclaimed Vendale, tossing the note away from him.

Joey Ladle's eye followed the flying morsel of paper drearily.

'I'm glad to see you take it easy, sir,' he said. 'Whatever happens, it will be always a comfort to you to remember that you took it easy at first. Sometimes one mistake leads to another. A man drops a bit of orange-peel on the pavement by mistake, and another man treads on it by mistake, and there's a job at the hospital, and a party crippled for life. I'm glad you take it easy, sir. In Pebbleson Nephew's time we shouldn't have taken it easy till we had seen the end of it. Without desiring to crow over the house, Young Mr Vendale, I wish you well through it. No offence, sir,' said the cellarman, opening the door to go out, and looking in again ominously before he shut it. 'I'm muddled and molloncolly, I grant you. But I'm an old servant of Pebbleson Nephew, and I wish you well through them six cases of red wine.'

Left by himself, Vendale laughed, and took up his pen. 'I may as well send a line to Defresnier and Company,' he thought, 'before I forget it.' He wrote at once in these terms:

DEAR SIRS – We are taking stock, and a trifling mistake has been discovered in the last consignment of champagne sent by your house to ours. Six of the cases contain red wine – which we hereby return to you. The matter can easily be set right, either by your sending us six cases of the champagne, if they can be produced, or, if not, by your crediting us with the value of six cases on the amount last paid (five hundred pounds) by our firm to yours. Your faithful servants,

WILDING & CO.

This letter despatched to the post, the subject dropped at once out of Vendale's mind. He had other and far more interesting matters to think of. Later in the day he paid the visit to Obenreizer which had been agreed on between them. Certain evenings in the week were set apart which he was privileged to spend with Marguerite – always, however, in the presence of a third person. On this stipulation Obenreizer politely but positively insisted. The one concession he made was to give Vendale his choice of who the third person should be. Confiding in past experience, his choice fell unhesitatingly upon the excellent woman who mended Obenreizer's stockings. On hearing of the responsibility entrusted to her, Madame Dor's intellectual nature burst suddenly into a new stage of development. She waited till Obenreizer's eye was off her – and then she looked at Vendale, and dimly winked.

The time passed – the happy evenings with Marguerite came and went. It was the tenth morning since Vendale had written to the Swiss firm, when the answer appeared, on his desk, with the other letters of the day:

DEAR SIRS – We beg to offer our excuses for the little mistake which has happened. At the same time, we regret to add that the statement of our error, with which you have favoured us, has led to a very unexpected discovery. The affair is a most serious one for you and for us.

The particulars are as follows: Having no more champagne of the vintage last sent to you, we made arrangements to credit your firm to the value of six cases, as suggested by yourself. On taking this step, certain forms observed in our mode of doing business necessitated a reference to our bankers' book, as well as to our ledger. The result is a moral certainty that no such remittance as you mention can have reached our house, and a literal certainty that no such remittance has been paid to our account at the bank.

It is needless, at this stage of the proceedings, to trouble you with details. The money has unquestionably been stolen in the course of its transit from you to us. Certain peculiarities which we observe, relating to the manner in which the fraud has been perpetrated, lead us to conclude that the thief may have calculated on being able to pay the missing sum to our bankers, before an inevitable discovery followed the annual striking of our balance. This would not have happened, in the usual course, for another three months. During that period, but for your letter, we might have remained perfectly unconscious of the robbery that has been committed.

We mention this last circumstance, as it may help to show you that we have to do, in this case, with no ordinary thief. Thus far we have not even a suspicion of who that thief is. But we believe you will assist us in making some advance towards discovery, by examining the receipt (forged, of course) which has no doubt purported to come to you from our house. Be pleased to look and see whether it is a receipt entirely in manuscript, or whether it is a numbered and printed form which merely requires the filling in of the amount. The settlement of this apparently trivial question is, we assure you, a matter of vital importance. Anxiously awaiting your reply, we remain, with high esteem and consideration,

DEFRESNIER & CIE

Vendale had the letter on his desk, and waited a moment to steady his mind under the shock that had fallen on it. At the time of all others when it was most important to him to increase the value of his business, that business was threatened with a loss of five hundred pounds. He thought of Marguerite, as he took the key from his pocket and opened the iron chamber in the wall in which the books and papers of the firm were kept.

He was still in the chamber, searching for the forged receipt, when he was startled by a voice speaking close behind him.

'A thousand pardons,' said the voice; 'I am afraid I disturb you.'

He turned, and found himself face to face with Marguerite's guardian.

'I have called,' pursued Obenreizer, 'to know if I can be of any use. Business of my own takes me away for some days to Manchester and Liverpool. Can I combine any business of yours with it? I am entirely at your disposal, in the character of commercial traveller for the firm of Wilding and Co.'

'Excuse me for one moment,' said Vendale; 'I will speak to you directly.' He turned round again, and continued his search among the papers. 'You come at a time when friendly offers are more than usually precious to me,' he resumed. 'I have had very bad news this morning from Neuchatel.'

'Bad news,' exclaimed Obenreizer. 'From Defresnier and Company?'

'Yes. A remittance we sent to them has been stolen. I am threatened with a loss of five hundred pounds. What's that?'

Turning sharply, and looking into the room for the second time, Vendale discovered his envelope case overthrown on the floor, and Obenreizer on his knees picking up the contents.

'All my awkwardness,' said Obenreizer. 'This dreadful news of yours startled me; I stepped back – ' He became too deeply interested in collecting the scattered envelopes to finish the sentence.

'Don't trouble yourself,' said Vendale. 'The clerk will pick the things up.'

'This dreadful news!' repeated Obenreizer, persisting in collecting the envelopes. 'This dreadful news!'

'If you will read the letter,' said Vendale, 'you will find I have exaggerated nothing. There it is, open on my desk.'

He resumed his search, and in a moment more discovered the forged receipt. It was on the numbered and printed form, described by the Swiss firm. Vendale made a memorandum of the number and the date. Having replaced the receipt and locked up the iron chamber, he had leisure to notice Obenreizer, reading the letter in the recess of a window at the far end of the room.

'Come to the fire,' said Vendale. 'You look perished with the cold out there. I will ring for some more coals.'

Obenreizer rose, and came slowly back to the desk. 'Marguerite will be as sorry to hear of this as I am,' he said, kindly. 'What do you mean to do?'

'I am in the hands of Defresnier and Company,' answered Vendale. 'In my total ignorance of the circumstances, I can only do what they recommend. The receipt which I have just found, turns out to be the numbered and printed form. They seem to attach some special importance to its discovery. You have had experience, when you were in the Swiss house, of their way of doing business. Can you guess what object they have in view?'

Obenreizer offered a suggestion.

'Suppose I examine the receipt?' he said.

'Are you ill?' asked Vendale, startled by the change in his face, which now showed itself plainly for the first time. 'Pray go to the fire. You seem to be shivering – I hope you are not going to be ill?'

'Not I!' said Obenreizer. 'Perhaps I have caught cold. Your English climate might have spared an admirer of your English institutions. Let me look at the receipt.'

Vendale opened the iron chamber. Obenreizer took a chair, and drew it close to the fire. He held both hands over the flames. 'Let me look at the receipt,' he repeated, eagerly, as Vendale reappeared with the paper in his hand. At the same moment a porter entered the room with a fresh supply of coals. Vendale told him to make a good fire. The man obeyed the order with a disastrous alacrity. As he stepped forward and raised the scuttle, his foot caught in a fold of the rug, and he discharged his entire cargo of coals into the grate. The result was an instant smothering of the flame, and the production of a stream of yellow smoke, without a visible morsel of fire to account for it.

'Imbecile!' whispered Obenreizer to himself, with a look at the man which the man remembered for many a long day afterwards.

'Will you come into the clerks' room?' asked Vendale. 'They have a stove there.'

'No, no. No matter.'

Vendale handed him the receipt. Obenreizer's interest in examining it appeared to have been quenched as suddenly and as effectually as the fire itself. He just glanced over the document, and said, 'No; I don't understand it! I am sorry to be of no use.'

'I will write to Neuchatel by tonight's post,' said Vendale, putting away the receipt for the second time. 'We must wait, and see what comes of it.'

'By tonight's post,' repeated Obenreizer. 'Let me see. You will get the answer in eight or nine days' time. I shall be back before that. If I can be of any service, as commercial traveller, perhaps you will let me know between this and then. You will send me written instructions? My best thanks. I shall be most anxious for your answer from Neuchatel. Who knows? It may be a mistake, my dear friend, after all. Courage! courage! courage!' He had entered the room with no appearance of being pressed for time. He now snatched up his hat, and took his leave with the air of a man who had not another moment to lose.

Left by himself, Vendale took a turn thoughtfully in the room.

His previous impression of Obenreizer was shaken by what he had heard and seen at the interview which had just taken place. He was disposed, for the first time, to doubt whether, in this case, he had not been a little hasty and hard in his judgement on another man.

Obenreizer's surprise and regret, on hearing the news from Neuchatel, bore the plainest marks of being honestly felt – not politely assumed for the occasion. With troubles of his own to encounter, suffering, to all appearance, from the first insidious attack of a serious illness, he had looked and spoken like a man who really deplored the disaster that had fallen on his friend. Hitherto Vendale had tried vainly to alter his first opinion of Marguerite's guardian, for Marguerite's sake. All the generous instincts in his nature now combined together and shook the evidence which had seemed unanswerable up to this time. 'Who knows?' he thought. 'I may have read that man's face wrongly, after all.'

The time passed – the happy evenings with Marguerite came and went. It was again the tenth morning since Vendale had written to the Swiss firm; and again the answer appeared on his desk with the other letters of the day:

DEAR SIR – My senior partner, M. Defresnier, has been called away, by urgent business, to Milan. In his absence (and with his full concurrence and authority), I now write to you again on the subject of the missing five hundred pounds.

Your discovery that the forged receipt is executed upon one of our numbered and printed forms has caused inexpressible surprise and distress to my partner and to myself. At the time when your remittance was stolen, but three keys were in existence opening the strongbox in which our receipt-forms are invariably kept. My partner had one key; I had the other. The third was in the possession of a gentleman who, at that period, occupied a position of trust in our house. We should as soon have thought of suspecting one of ourselves as of suspecting this person. Suspicion now points at him, nevertheless. I cannot prevail on myself to inform you who the person is, so long as there is the shadow of a chance that he may come innocently out of the enquiry which must now be instituted. Forgive my silence; the motive of it is good.

The form our investigation must now take is simple enough. The handwriting of your receipt must be compared, by competent persons whom we have at our disposal, with certain specimens of handwriting in our possession. I cannot send you the specimens for business reasons, which, when you hear them, you are sure to approve. I must beg you to send me the receipt to Neuchatel – and, in making this request, I must accompany it by a word of necessary warning.

If the person, at whom suspicion now points, really proves to be the person who has committed this forgery and theft, I have reason to fear that circumstances may have already put him on his guard. The only evidence against him is the evidence in your hands, and he will move heaven and earth to obtain and destroy it. I strongly urge you not to trust the receipt to the post. Send it to me, without loss of time, by a private hand, and choose nobody for your messenger but a person long established in your own employment, accustomed to travelling, capable of speaking French; a man of courage, a man of honesty, and, above all things, a man who can be trusted to let no stranger scrape acquaintance with him on the route. Tell no one – absolutely no one – but your messenger of the turn this matter has now taken. The safe transit of the receipt may depend on your interpreting *literally* the advice which I give you at the end of this letter.

I have only to add that every possible saving of time is now of the last importance. More than one of our receipt-forms is missing – and it is impossible to say what new frauds may not be committed if we fail to lay our hands on the thief.

Your faithful servant

ROLLAND (*Signing for Defresnier and Cie*)

Who was the suspected man? In Vendale's position, it seemed useless to enquire.

Who was to be sent to Neuchatel with the receipt? Men of courage and men of honesty were to be had at Cripple Corner for the asking. But where was the man who was accustomed to foreign travelling, who could speak the French language, and who could be really relied on to let no stranger scrape acquaintance with him on his route? There was but one man at hand who combined all those requisites in his own person, and that man was Vendale himself.

It was a sacrifice to leave his business; it was a greater sacrifice to leave Marguerite. But a matter of five hundred pounds was involved in the pending enquiry; and a literal interpretation of M. Rolland's advice was insisted on in terms which there was no trifling with. The more Vendale thought of it, the more plainly the necessity faced him, and said, 'Go!'

As he locked up the letter with the receipt, the association of ideas reminded him of Obenreizer. A guess at the identity of the suspected man looked more possible now. Obenreizer might know.

The thought had barely passed through his mind, when the door opened, and Obenreizer entered the room.

'They told me at Soho Square you were expected back last night,' said Vendale, greeting him. 'Have you done well in the country? Are you better?'

A thousand thanks. Obenreizer had done admirably well; Obenreizer was infinitely better. And now, what news? Any letter from Neuchatel?

'A very strange letter,' answered Vendale. 'The matter has taken a new turn, and the letter insists – without excepting anybody – on my keeping our next proceedings a profound secret.'

'Without excepting anybody?' repeated Obenreizer. As he said the words, he walked away again, thoughtfully, to the window at the other end of the room, looked out for a moment, and suddenly came back to Vendale. 'Surely they must have forgotten?' he resumed, 'or they would have excepted me?'

'It is Monsieur Rolland who writes,' said Vendale. 'And, as you say, he must certainly have forgotten. That view of the matter quite escaped me. I was just wishing I had you to consult, when you came into the room. And here I am tried by a formal prohibition, which cannot possibly have been intended to include you. How very annoying!'

Obenreizer's filmy eyes fixed on Vendale attentively.

'Perhaps it is more than annoying!' he said. 'I came this morning not only to hear the news, but to offer myself as messenger, negotiator – what you will. Would you believe it? I have letters which oblige me to go to Switzerland immediately. Messages, documents, anything – I could have taken them all to Defresnier and Rolland for you.'

'You are the very man I wanted,' returned Vendale. 'I had decided, most unwillingly, on going to Neuchatel myself, not five minutes since, because I could find no one here capable of taking my place. Let me look at the letter again.'

He opened the strong room to get at the letter. Obenreizer, after first glancing round him to make sure that they were alone, followed a step or two and waited, measuring Vendale with his eye. Vendale was the tallest man, and unmistakably the strongest man also of the two. Obenreizer turned away, and warmed himself at the fire.

Meanwhile, Vendale read the last paragraph in the letter for the third time. There was the plain warning – there was the closing sentence, which insisted on a literal interpretation of it. The hand, which was leading Vendale in the dark, led him on that condition only. A large sum was at stake: a terrible suspicion remained to be verified. If he acted on his own responsibility, and if anything happened to defeat the object in view, who would be blamed? As a man of business, Vendale had but one course to follow. He locked the letter up again.

'It is most annoying,' he said to Obenreizer – 'it is a piece of forgetfulness on Monsieur Rolland's part which puts me to serious inconvenience, and places me in an absurdly false position towards you. What am I to do? I am acting in a very serious matter, and acting entirely in the dark. I have no choice but to be guided, not by the spirit, but by the letter of my instructions. You understand me, I am sure? You know, if I had not been fettered in this way, how gladly I should have accepted your services?'

'Say no more!' returned Obenreizer. 'In your place I should have done the same. My good friend, I take no offence. I thank you for your compliment. We shall be travelling companions, at any rate,' added Obenreizer. 'You go, as I go, at once?'

'At once. I must speak to Marguerite first, of course!'

'Surely! surely! Speak to her this evening. Come, and pick me up on the way to the station. We go together by the mail train tonight?'

'By the mail train tonight.'

*　　*　　*

It was later than Vendale had anticipated when he drove up to the house in Soho Square. Business difficulties, occasioned by his sudden departure, had presented themselves by dozens. A cruelly large share of the time which he had hoped to devote to Marguerite had been claimed by duties at his office which it was impossible to neglect.

To his surprise and delight, she was alone in the drawing-room when he entered it.

'We have only a few minutes, George,' she said. 'But Madame Dor has been good to me – and we can have those few minutes alone.' She threw her arms round his neck, and whispered eagerly, 'Have you done anything to offend Mr Obenreizer?'

'I!' exclaimed Vendale, in amazement.

'Hush!' she said, 'I want to whisper it. You know the little photograph I have got of you. This afternoon it happened to be on the chimney-piece. He took it up and looked at it – and I saw his face in the glass. I know you have offended him! He is merciless; he is revengeful; he is as secret as the grave. Don't go with him, George – don't go with him!'

'My own love,' returned Vendale, 'you are letting your fancy frighten you! Obenreizer and I were never better friends than we are at this moment.'

Before a word more could be said, the sudden movement of some ponderous body shook the floor of the next room. The shock was followed by the appearance of Madame Dor. 'Obenreizer,' exclaimed this excellent person in a whisper, and plumped down instantly in her regular place by the stove.

Obenreizer came in with a courier's bag strapped over his shoulder. 'Are you ready?' he asked, addressing Vendale. 'Can I take anything for you? You have no travelling-bag. I have got one. Here is the compartment for papers, open at your service.'

'Thank you,' said Vendale. 'I have only one paper of importance with me; and that paper I am bound to take charge of myself. Here it is,' he added, touching the breast-pocket of his coat, 'and here it must remain till we get to Neuchatel.'

As he said those words, Marguerite's hand caught his, and pressed it significantly. She was looking towards Obenreizer. Before Vendale could look, in his turn, Obenreizer had wheeled round, and was taking leave of Madame Dor.

'Adieu, my charming niece!' he said, turning to Marguerite next. 'En route, my friend, for Neuchatel!' He tapped Vendale lightly over the breast-pocket of his coat and led the way to the door.

Vendale's last look was for Marguerite. Marguerite's last words to him were, 'Don't go!'

ACT THREE

In the Valley

It was about the middle of the month of February when Vendale and Obenreizer set forth on their expedition. The winter being a hard one, the time was bad for travellers. So bad was it that these two travellers, coming to Strasbourg, found its great inns almost empty. And even the few people they did encounter in that city, who had started from England or from Paris on business journeys towards the interior of Switzerland, were turning back.

Many of the railroads in Switzerland that tourists pass easily enough now, were almost or quite impracticable then. Some were not begun; more were not completed. On such as were open, there were still large gaps of old road where communication in the winter season was often stopped; on others, there were weak points where the new work was not safe, either under conditions of severe frost, or of rapid thaw. The running of trains on this last class was not to be counted on in the worst time of the year, was contingent upon weather, or was wholly abandoned through the months considered the most dangerous.

At Strasbourg there were more travellers' stories afloat, respecting the difficulties of the way further on, than there were travellers to relate them. Many of these tales were as wild as usual; but the more modestly marvellous did derive some colour from the circumstance that people were indisputably turning back. However, as the road to Basle was open, Vendale's resolution to push on was in no wise disturbed. Obenreizer's resolution was necessarily Vendale's, seeing that he stood at bay thus desperately: He must be ruined, or must destroy the evidence that Vendale carried about him, even if he destroyed Vendale with it.

The state of mind of each of these two fellow-travellers towards the other was this. Obenreizer, encircled by impending ruin through Vendale's quickness of action, and seeing the circle narrowed every hour by Vendale's energy, hated him with the animosity of a fierce cunning lower animal. He had always had instinctive movements in his breast against him; perhaps, because of that old sore of gentleman and peasant; perhaps, because of the openness of his nature; perhaps, because of his better looks; perhaps, because of his success with Marguerite; perhaps, on all those grounds, the two last not the least. And now he saw in him, besides, the hunter who was tracking him down. Vendale, on the other hand, always contending generously against his first vague mistrust, now felt bound to contend against it more than ever: reminding himself, 'He is Marguerite's guardian. We are on perfectly friendly terms; he is my companion of his own proposal, and can have no interested motive in sharing this undesirable journey.' To which pleas in behalf of Obenreizer, chance added one consideration more, when they came to Basle after a journey of more than twice the average duration.

They had had a late dinner, and were alone in an inn room there, overhanging the Rhine: at that place rapid and deep, swollen and loud. Vendale lounged upon a couch, and Obenreizer walked to and fro: now, stopping at the window, looking at the crooked reflection of the town lights in the dark water (and peradventure thinking, 'If I could fling him into it!'); now, resuming his walk with his eyes upon the floor.

'Where shall I rob him, if I can? Where shall I murder him, if I must?' So, as he paced the room, ran the river, ran the river, ran the river.

The burden seemed to him, at last, to be growing so plain, that he stopped; thinking it as well to suggest another burden to his companion.

'The Rhine sounds tonight,' he said with a smile, 'like the old waterfall at home. That waterfall which my mother showed to travellers (I told you of it once). The sound of it changed with the weather, as does the sound of all falling waters and flowing waters. When I was pupil of the watchmaker, I remembered it as sometimes saying to me for whole days, "Who are you, my little wretch? Who are you, my little wretch?" I remembered it as saying, other times, when its sound was hollow, and storm was coming up the pass: "Boom, boom, boom. Beat him, beat him, beat him." Like my mother enraged – if she was my mother.'

'If she was?' said Vendale, gradually changing his attitude to a sitting one. 'If she was? Why do you say "if"?'

'What do I know?' replied the other negligently, throwing up his hands and letting them fall as they would. 'What would you have? I am so obscurely born, that how can I say? I was very young, and all the rest of the family were men and women, and my so-called parents were old. Anything is possible of a case like that.'

'Did you ever doubt – '

'I told you once, I doubt the marriage of those two,' he replied, throwing up his hands again, as if he were throwing the unprofitable subject away. 'But here I am in Creation. *I* come of no fine family. What does it matter?'

'At least you are Swiss,' said Vendale, after following him with his eyes to and fro.

'How do I know?' he retorted abruptly, and stopping to look back over his shoulder. 'I say to you, at least you are English. How do you know?'

'By what I have been told from infancy.'

'Ah! I know of myself that way.'

'And,' added Vendale, pursuing the thought that he could not drive back, 'by my earliest recollections.'

'I also. I know of myself that way – if that way satisfies.'

'Does it not satisfy you?'

'It must. There is nothing like "it must" in this little world. It must. Two short words those, but stronger than long proof or reasoning.'

'You and poor Wilding were born in the same year. You were nearly of an age,' said Vendale, again thoughtfully looking after him as he resumed his pacing up and down.

'Yes. Very nearly.'

Could Obenreizer be the missing man? In the unknown associations of things, was there a subtler meaning than he himself thought, in that theory so often on his lips about the smallness of the world? Had the Swiss letter presenting him followed so close on Mrs Goldstraw's revelation concerning the infant who had been taken away to Switzerland, because he was that infant grown a man? In a world where so many depths lie unsounded, it might be. The chances, or the laws – call them either – that had wrought out the revival of Vendale's own acquaintance with Obenreizer, and had ripened it into intimacy, and had brought them here together this present winter night, were hardly less curious; while read by such a light, they were seen to cohere towards the furtherance of a continuous and an intelligible purpose.

Vendale's awakened thoughts ran high while his eyes musingly followed Obenreizer pacing up and down the room, the river ever running to the tune: 'Where shall I rob him, if I can? Where shall I murder him, if I must?' The secret of his dead friend was in no hazard from Vendale's lips; but just as his friend had died of its weight, so did he in his lighter succession feel the burden of the trust, and the obligation to follow any clue, however obscure. He rapidly asked himself, would he like this man to be the real Wilding? No. Argue down his mistrust as he might, he was unwilling to put such a substitute in the place of his late guileless, outspoken childlike partner. He rapidly asked himself, would he like this man to be rich? No. He had more power than enough over Marguerite as it was, and wealth might invest him with more. Would he like this man to be Marguerite's guardian, and yet proved to stand in no degree of relationship towards her, however disconnected and distant? No. But these were not considerations to come between him and fidelity to the dead. Let him see to it that they passed him with no other notice than the knowledge that they *had* passed him, and left him bent on the discharge of a solemn duty. And he did see to it, so soon that he followed his companion with ungrudging eyes, while he still paced the room; that companion, whom he supposed to be moodily reflecting on his own birth, and not on another man's – least of all what man's – violent death.

The road in advance from Basle to Neuchatel was better than had been represented. The latest weather had done it good. Drivers, both of horses and mules, had come in that evening after dark, and had reported nothing more difficult to be overcome than trials of patience, harness, wheels, axles, and whipcord. A bargain was soon struck for a carriage and horses, to take them on in the morning, and to start before daylight.

'Do you lock your door at night when travelling?' asked Obenreizer, standing warming his hands by the wood fire in Vendale's chamber, before going to his own.

'Not I. I sleep too soundly.'

'You are so sound a sleeper?' he retorted, with an admiring look. 'What a blessing!'

'Anything but a blessing to the rest of the house,' rejoined Vendale, 'if I had to be knocked up in the morning from the outside of my bedroom door.'

'I, too,' said Obenreizer, 'leave open my room. But let me advise you, as a Swiss who knows: always, when you travel in my country, put your papers – and, of course, your money – under your pillow. Always the same place.'

'You are not complimentary to your countrymen,' laughed Vendale.

'My countrymen,' said Obenreizer, with that light touch of his friend's elbows by way of good-night and benediction, 'I suppose are like the majority of men. And the majority of men will take what they can get. Adieu! At four in the morning.'

'Adieu! At four.'

Left to himself, Vendale raked the logs together, sprinkled over them the white wood-ashes lying on the hearth, and sat down to compose his thoughts. But they still ran high on their latest theme, and the running of the river tended to agitate rather than to quiet them. As he sat thinking, what little disposition he had had to sleep departed. He felt it hopeless to lie down yet, and sat dressed by the fire. Marguerite, Wilding, Obenreizer, the business he was then upon, and a thousand hopes and doubts that had nothing to do with it, occupied his mind at once. Everything seemed to have power over him but slumber. The departed disposition to sleep kept far away.

He had sat for a long time thinking, on the hearth, when his candle burned down and its light went out. It was of little moment; there was light enough in the fire. He changed his attitude, and, leaning his arm on the chair-back, and his chin upon that hand, sat thinking still.

But he sat between the fire and the bed, and, as the fire flickered in the play of air from the fast-flowing river, his enlarged shadow fluttered on the white wall by the bedside. His attitude gave it an air, half of mourning and half of bending over the bed imploring. His eyes were observant of it, when he became troubled by the disagreeable fancy that it was like Wilding's shadow, and not his own.

A slight change of place would cause it to disappear. He made the change, and the apparition of his disturbed fancy vanished. He now sat in the shade of a little nook beside the fire, and the door of the room was before him.

It had a long cumbrous iron latch. He saw the latch slowly and softly rise. The door opened a very little, and came to again, as though only the air had moved it. But he saw that the latch was out of the hasp.

The door opened again very slowly, until it opened wide enough to admit someone. It afterwards remained still for a while, as though cautiously held open on the other side. The figure of a man then entered, with its face turned towards the bed, and stood quiet just within the door. Until it said, in a low half-whisper, at the same time taking one stop forward: 'Vendale!'

'What now?' he answered, springing from his seat; 'who is it?'

It was Obenreizer, and he uttered a cry of surprise as Vendale came upon him from that unexpected direction. 'Not in bed?' he said, catching him by both shoulders with an instinctive tendency to a struggle. 'Then something *is* wrong!'

'What do you mean?' said Vendale, releasing himself.

'First tell me; you are not ill?'

'Ill? No.'

'I have had a bad dream about you. How is it that I see you up and dressed?'

'My good fellow, I may as well ask you how it is that I see *you* up and undressed?'

'I have told you why. I have had a bad dream about you. I tried to rest after it, but it was impossible. I could not make up my mind to stay where I was without knowing you were safe; and yet I could not make up my mind to come in here. I have been minutes hesitating at the door. It is so easy to laugh at a dream that you have not dreamed. Where is your candle?'

'Burnt out.'

'I have a whole one in my room. Shall I fetch it?'

'Do so.'

His room was very near, and he was absent for but a few seconds. Coming back with the candle in his hand, he kneeled down on the hearth and lighted it. As he blew with his breath a charred billet into flame for the purpose, Vendale, looking down at him, saw that his lips were white and not easy of control.

'Yes!' said Obenreizer, setting the lighted candle on the table, 'it was a bad dream. Only look at me!'

His feet were bare; his red-flannel shirt was thrown back at the throat, and its sleeves were rolled above the elbows; his only other garment, a pair of under pantaloons or drawers, reaching to the ankles, fitted him close and tight. A certain lithe and savage appearance was on his figure, and his eyes were very bright.

'If there had been a wrestle with a robber, as I dreamed,' said Obenreizer, 'you see, I was stripped for it.'

'And armed too,' said Vendale, glancing at his girdle.

'A traveller's dagger, that I always carry on the road,' he answered carelessly, half drawing it from its sheath with his left hand, and putting it back again. 'Do you carry no such thing?'

'Nothing of the kind.'

'No pistols?' said Obenreizer, glancing at the table, and from it to the untouched pillow.

'Nothing of the sort.'

'You Englishmen are so confident! You wish to sleep?'

'I have wished to sleep this long time, but I can't do it.'

'I neither, after the bad dream. My fire has gone the way of your candle. May I come and sit by yours? Two o'clock! It will so soon be four, that it is not worth the trouble to go to bed again.'

'I shall not take the trouble to go to bed at all, now,' said Vendale; 'sit here and keep me company, and welcome.'

Going back to his room to arrange his dress, Obenreizer soon returned in a loose cloak and slippers, and they sat down on opposite sides of the hearth. In the interval Vendale had replenished the fire from the wood-basket in his room, and Obenreizer had put upon the table a flask and cup from his.

'Common cabaret brandy, I am afraid,' he said, pouring out; 'bought upon the road, and not like yours from Cripple Corner. But yours is exhausted; so much the worse. A cold night, a cold time of night, a cold country, and a cold house. This may be better than nothing; try it.'

Vendale took the cup, and did so.

'How do you find it?'

'It has a coarse after-flavour,' said Vendale, giving back the cup with a slight shudder, 'and I don't like it.'

'You are right,' said Obenreizer, tasting, and smacking his lips; 'it *has* a coarse after-flavour, and *I* don't like it. Booh! It burns, though!' He had flung what remained in the cup upon the fire.

Each of them leaned an elbow on the table, reclined his head upon his hand, and sat looking at the flaring logs. Obenreizer remained watchful and still; but Vendale, after certain nervous twitches and starts, in one of which he rose to his feet and looked wildly about him, fell into the strangest confusion of dreams. He carried his papers in a leather case or pocketbook, in an inner breast-pocket of his buttoned travelling-coat; and whatever he dreamed of, in the lethargy that got possession of him, something importunate in those papers called him out of that dream, though he could not wake from it. He was berated on the steppes of Russia (some shadowy person gave that name to the place) with Marguerite; and yet the sensation of a hand at his breast, softly feeling the outline of the pocketbook as he lay asleep before the fire, was present to him. He was shipwrecked in an open boat at sea, and having lost his clothes, had no other covering than an old sail; and yet a creeping hand, tracing outside all the other pockets of the dress he actually wore, for papers, and finding none answer its touch, warned him to rouse himself. He was in the ancient vault at Cripple Corner, to which was transferred the very bed substantial and present in that very room at Basle; and Wilding (not dead, as he had supposed, and yet he did not wonder much) shook him, and whispered, 'Look at that man! Don't you see he has risen, and is turning the pillow? Why should he turn the pillow, if not to seek those papers that are in your breast? Awake!' And yet he slept, and wandered off into other dreams.

Watchful and still, with his elbow on the table, and his head upon that hand, his companion at length said: 'Vendale! We are called. Past four!' Then, opening his eyes, he saw, turned sideways on him, the filmy face of Obenreizer.

'You have been in a heavy sleep,' he said. 'The fatigue of constant travelling and the cold!'

'I am broad awake now,' cried Vendale, springing up, but with an unsteady footing. 'Haven't you slept at all?'

'I may have dozed, but I seem to have been patiently looking at the fire. Whether or no, we must wash, and breakfast, and turn out. Past four, Vendale; past four!'

It was said in a tone to rouse him, for already he was half asleep again. In his preparation for the day, too, and at his breakfast, he was often virtually asleep while in mechanical action. It was not until the cold dark day was closing in, that he had any distincter impressions of the ride than jingling bells, bitter weather, slipping horses, frowning hillsides, bleak woods, and a stoppage at some wayside house of entertainment, where they had passed through a cow-house to reach the travellers' room above. He had been conscious of little more, except of Obenreizer sitting thoughtful at his side all day, and eyeing him much.

But when he shook off his stupor, Obenreizer was not at his side. The carriage was stopping to bait at another wayside house; and a line of long narrow carts, laden with casks of wine, and drawn by horses with a quantity of blue collar and headgear, were baiting too. These came from the direction in which the travellers were going, and Obenreizer (not thoughtful now, but cheerful and alert) was talking with the foremost driver. As Vendale stretched his limbs, circulated his blood, and cleared off the lees of his lethargy, with a sharp run to and fro in the bracing air, the line of carts moved on: the drivers all saluting Obenreizer as they passed him.

'Who are those?' asked Vendale.

'They are our carriers – Defresnier and Company's,' replied Obenreizer. 'Those are our casks of wine.' He was singing to himself, and lighting a cigar.

'I have been drearily dull company today,' said Vendale. 'I don't know what has been the matter with me.'

'You had no sleep last night; and a kind of brain-congestion frequently comes, at first, of such cold,' said Obenreizer. 'I have seen it often. After all, we shall have our journey for nothing, it seems.'

'How for nothing?'

'The house is at Milan. You know, we are a wine house at Neuchatel, and a silk house at Milan? Well, Silk happening to press of a sudden, more than wine, Defresnier was summoned to Milan. Rolland, the other partner, has been taken ill since his departure, and the doctors will allow him to see no one. A letter awaits you at Neuchatel to tell you so. I have it from our chief carrier whom you saw me talking with. He was surprised to see me, and said he had that word for you if he met you. What do you do? Go back?'

'Go on,' said Vendale.

'On?'

'On? Yes. Across the Alps, and down to Milan.'

Obenreizer stopped in his smoking to look at Vendale, and then smoked heavily, looked up the road, looked down the road, looked down at the stones in the road at his feet.

'I have a very serious matter in charge,' said Vendale; 'more of these missing forms may be turned to as bad account, or worse: I am urged to lose no time in helping the house to take the thief; and nothing shall turn me back.'

'No?' cried Obenreizer, taking out his cigar to smile, and giving his hand to his fellow-traveller. 'Then nothing shall turn *me* back. Ho, driver! Despatch. Quick there! Let us push on!'

They travelled through the night. There had been snow, and there was a partial thaw, and they mostly travelled at a foot-pace, and always with many stoppages to breathe the splashed and floundering horses. After an hour's broad daylight, they drew rein at the inn-door at Neuchatel, having been some eight-and-twenty hours in conquering some eighty English miles.

When they had hurriedly refreshed and changed, they went together to the house of business of Defresnier and Company. There they found the letter which the wine-carrier had described, enclosing the tests and comparisons of handwriting essential to the discovery of the forger. Vendale's determination to press forward, without resting, being already taken, the only question to delay them was by what pass could they cross the Alps? Respecting the state of the two passes of the St Gotthard and the Simplon, the guides and mule-drivers differed greatly; and both passes were still far enough off, to prevent the travellers from having the benefit of any recent experience of either. Besides which, they well knew that a fall of snow might altogether change the described conditions in a single hour, even if they were correctly stated. But, on the whole, the Simplon appearing to be the hopefuller route, Vendale decided to take it. Obenreizer bore little or no part in the discussion, and scarcely spoke.

To Geneva, to Lausanne, along the level margin of the lake to Vevay, so into the winding valley between the spurs of the mountains, and into the valley of the Rhône. The sound of the carriage-wheels, as they rattled on, through the day, through the night, became as the wheels of a great clock, recording the hours. No change of weather varied the journey, after it had hardened into a sullen frost. In a sombre-yellow sky, they saw the Alpine ranges; and they saw enough of snow on nearer and much lower hilltops and hillsides, to sully, by contrast, the purity of lake, torrent, and waterfall, and make the villages look discoloured and dirty. But no snow fell, nor was there any snowdrift on the road. The stalking along the valley of more or less of white mist, changing on their hair and dress into icicles, was the only variety between them and the gloomy sky. And still by day, and still by night, the wheels. And still they rolled, in the hearing of one of them, to the burden, altered from the burden of the Rhine: 'The time is gone for robbing him alive, and I must murder him.'

They came, at length, to the poor little town of Brieg, at the foot of the Simplon. They came there after dark, but yet could see how dwarfed men's works and men became with the immense mountains towering over them. Here they must lie for the night; and here was warmth of fire, and lamp, and dinner, and wine, and after-conference resounding, with guides and drivers. No human creature had come across the pass for four days. The snow above the snow-line was too soft for wheeled carriage, and not hard enough for sledge. There was snow in the sky. There had been snow in the sky for days past, and the marvel was that it had not fallen, and the certainty was that it must fall. No vehicle could cross. The journey might be tried on mules, or it might be tried on foot; but the best guides must be paid danger-price in either case, and that, too, whether they succeeded in taking the two travellers across, or turned for safety and brought them back.

In this discussion, Obenreizer bore no part whatever. He sat silently smoking by the fire until the room was cleared and Vendale referred to him.

'Bah! I am weary of these poor devils and their trade,' he said, in reply. 'Always the same story. It is the story of their trade today, as it was the story of their trade when I was a ragged boy. What do you and I want? We want a knapsack each, and a mountain-staff each. We want no guide; we should guide him; he would not guide us. We leave our portmanteaus here, and we cross together. We have been on the mountains together before now, and I am mountain-born, and I know this pass – pass! – rather high road! – by heart. We will leave these poor devils, in pity, to trade with others; but they must not delay us to make a pretence of earning money. Which is all they mean.'

Vendale, glad to be quit of the dispute, and to cut the knot: active, adventurous, bent on getting forward, and therefore very susceptible to the last hint: readily assented. Within two hours, they had purchased what they wanted for the expedition, had packed their knapsacks, and lay down to sleep.

At break of day, they found half the town collected in the narrow street to see them depart. The people talked together in groups; the guides and drivers whispered apart, and looked up at the sky; no one wished them a good journey.

As they began the ascent, a gleam of run shone from the otherwise unaltered sky, and for a moment turned the tin spires of the town to silver.

'A good omen!' said Vendale (though it died out while he spoke). 'Perhaps our example will open the pass on this side.'

'No; we shall not be followed,' returned Obenreizer, looking up at the sky and back at the valley. 'We shall be alone up yonder.'

On the Mountain

The road was fair enough for stout walkers, and the air grew lighter and easier to breathe as the two ascended. But the settled gloom remained as it had remained for days back. Nature seemed to have come to a pause. The sense of hearing, no less than the sense of sight, was troubled by having to wait so long for the change, whatever it might be, that impended. The silence was as palpable and heavy as the lowering clouds – or rather cloud, for there seemed to be but one in all the sky, and that one covering the whole of it.

Although the light was thus dismally shrouded, the prospect was not obscured. Down in the valley of the Rhône behind them, the stream could be traced through all its many windings, oppressively sombre and solemn in its one leaden hue, a colourless waste. Far and high above them, glaciers and suspended avalanches overhung the spots where they must pass, by and by; deep and dark below them on their right, were awful precipice and roaring torrent; tremendous mountains arose in every vista. The gigantic landscape, uncheered by a touch of changing light or a solitary ray of sun, was yet terribly distinct in its ferocity. The hearts of two lonely men might shrink a little, if they had to win their way for miles and hours among a legion of silent and motionless men – mere men like themselves – all looking at them with fixed and frowning front. But how much more, when the legion is of Nature's mightiest works, and the frown may turn to fury in an instant!

As they ascended, the road became gradually more rugged and difficult. But the spirits of Vendale rose as they mounted higher, leaving so much more of the road behind them conquered. Obenreizer spoke little, and held on with a determined purpose. Both, in respect of agility and endurance, were well qualified for the expedition. Whatever the born mountaineer read in the weather-tokens that was illegible to the other, he kept to himself.

'Shall we get across today?' asked Vendale.

'No,' replied the other. 'You see how much deeper the snow lies here than it lay half a league lower. The higher we mount the deeper the snow will lie. Walking is half wading even now. And the days are so short! If we get as high as the fifth refuge, and lie tonight at the hospice, we shall do well.'

'Is there no danger of the weather rising in the night,' asked Vendale, anxiously, 'and snowing us up?'

'There is danger enough about us,' said Obenreizer, with a cautious glance onward and upward, 'to render silence our best policy. You have heard of the Bridge of the Ganther?'

'I have crossed it once.'

'In the summer?'

'Yes; in the travelling season.'

'Yes; but it is another thing at this season'; with a sneer, as though he were out of temper. 'This is not a time of year, or a state of things, on an Alpine pass, that you gentlemen holiday-travellers know much about.'

'You are my guide,' said Vendale, good-humouredly. 'I trust to you.'

'I am your guide,' said Obenreizer, 'and I will guide you to your journey's end. There is the bridge before us.'

They had made a turn into a desolate and dismal ravine, where the snow lay deep below them, deep above them, deep on every side. While speaking, Obenreizer stood pointing at the bridge, and observing Vendale's face, with a very singular expression on his own.

'If I, as guide, had sent you over there, in advance, and encouraged you to give a shout or two, you might have brought down upon yourself tons and tons and tons of snow, that would not only have struck you dead, but buried you deep, at a blow.'

'No doubt,' said Vendale.

'No doubt. But that is not what I have to do, as guide. So pass silently. Or, going as we go, our indiscretion might else crush and bury *me*. Let us get on!'

There was a great accumulation of snow on the bridge; and such enormous accumulations of snow overhung them from protecting masses of rock, that they might have been making their way through a stormy sky of white clouds. Using his staff skilfully, sounding as he went, and looking upward, with bent shoulders, as it were to resist the mere idea of a fall from above, Obenreizer softly led. Vendale closely followed. They were yet in the midst of their dangerous way, when there came a mighty rush, followed by a sound as of thunder. Obenreizer clapped his hand on Vendale's mouth and pointed to the track behind them. Its aspect had been wholly changed in a moment. An avalanche had swept over it, and plunged into the torrent at the bottom of the gulf below.

Their appearance at the solitary inn not far beyond this terrible bridge, elicited many expressions of astonishment from the people shut up in the house. 'We stay but to rest,' said Obenreizer, shaking the snow from his dress at the fire. 'This gentleman has very pressing occasion to get across; tell them, Vendale.'

'Assuredly, I have very pressing occasion. I must cross.'

'You hear, all of you. My friend has very pressing occasion to get across, and we want no advice and no help. I am as good a guide, my fellow-countrymen, as any of you. Now, give us to eat and drink.'

In exactly the same way, and in nearly the same words, when it was coming on dark and they had struggled through the greatly increased difficulties of the road, and had at last reached their destination for the night, Obenreizer said to the astonished people of the hospice, gathering about them at the fire, while they were yet in the act of getting their wet shoes off, and shaking the snow from their clothes: 'It is well to understand one another, friends all. This gentleman – '

' – Has,' said Vendale, readily taking him up with a smile, 'very pressing occasion to get across. Must cross.'

'You hear? – has very pressing occasion to get across, must cross. We want no advice and no help. I am mountain-born, and act as guide. Do not worry us by talking about it, but let us have supper, and wine, and bed.'

All through the intense cold of the night, the same awful stillness. Again at sunrise, no sunny tinge to gild or redden the snow. The same interminable waste of deathly white; the same immovable air; the same monotonous gloom in the sky.

'Travellers!' a friendly voice called to them from the door, after they were afoot, knapsack on back and staff in hand, as yesterday; 'recollect! There are five places of shelter, near together, on the dangerous road before you; and there is the wooden cross, and there is the next hospice. Do not stray from the track. If the *Tourmente* comes on, take shelter instantly!'

'The trade of these poor devils!' said Obenreizer to his friend, with a contemptuous backward wave of his hand towards the voice. 'How they stick to their trade! You Englishmen say we Swiss are mercenary. Truly, it does look like it.'

They had divided between the two knapsacks such refreshments as they had been able to obtain that morning, and as they deemed it prudent to take. Obenreizer carried the wine as his share of the burden; Vendale, the bread and meat and cheese, and the flask of brandy.

They had for some time laboured upward and onward through the snow – which was now above their knees in the track, and of unknown depth elsewhere – and they were still labouring upward and onward through the most frightful part of that tremendous desolation, when snow began to fall. At first, but a few flakes descended slowly and steadily. After a little while the fall grew much denser, and suddenly it began without apparent cause to whirl itself into spiral shapes. Instantly ensuing upon this last change, an icy blast came roaring at them, and every sound and force imprisoned until now was let loose.

One of the dismal galleries through which the road is carried at that perilous point, a cave eked out by arches of great strength, was near at hand. They struggled into it, and the storm raged wildly. The noise of the wind, the noise of the water, the thundering down of displaced masses of rock and snow, the awful voices with which not only that gorge but every gorge in the whole monstrous range seemed to be suddenly endowed, the darkness as of night, the violent revolving of the snow which beat and broke it into spray and blinded them, the madness of everything around insatiate for destruction, the rapid substitution of furious violence for unnatural calm, and hosts of appalling sounds for silence: these were things, on the edge of a deep abyss, to chill the blood, though the fierce wind, made actually solid by ice and snow, had failed to chill it.

Obenreizer, walking to and fro in the gallery without ceasing, signed to Vendale to help him unbuckle his knapsack. They could see each other, but could not have heard each other speak. Vendale complying, Obenreizer produced his bottle of wine, and poured some out, motioning Vendale to take that for warmth's sake, and not brandy. Vendale again complying, Obenreizer seemed to drink after him, and the two walked backwards and forwards side by side; both well knowing that to rest or sleep would be to die.

The snow came driving heavily into the gallery by the upper end at which they would pass out of it, if they ever passed out; for greater dangers lay on the road behind them than before. The snow soon began to choke the arch. An hour more, and it lay so high as to block out half the returning daylight. But it froze hard now, as it fell, and could be clambered through or over. The violence of the mountain storm was gradually yielding to steady snowfall. The wind still raged at intervals, but not incessantly; and when it paused, the snow fell in heavy flakes.

They might have been two hours in their frightful prison, when

Obenreizer, now crunching into the mound, now creeping over it with his head bowed down and his body touching the top of the arch, made his way out. Vendale followed close upon him, but followed without clear motive or calculation. For the lethargy of Basle was creeping over him again, and mastering his senses.

How far he had followed out of the gallery, or with what obstacles he had since contended, he knew not. He became roused to the knowledge that Obenreizer had set upon him, and that they were struggling desperately in the snow. He became roused to the remembrance of what his assailant carried in a girdle. He felt for it, drew it, struck at him, struggled again, struck at him again, cast him off, and stood face to face with him.

'I promised to guide you to your journey's end,' said Obenreizer, 'and I have kept my promise. The journey of your life ends here. Nothing can prolong it. You are sleeping as you stand.'

'You are a villain. What have you done to me?'

'You are a fool. I have drugged you. You are doubly a fool, for I drugged you once before upon the journey, to try you. You are trebly a fool, for I am the thief and forger, and in a few moments I shall take those proofs against the thief and forger from your insensible body.'

The entrapped man tried to throw off the lethargy, but its fatal hold upon him was so sure that, even while he heard those words, he stupidly wondered which of them had been wounded, and whose blood it was that he saw sprinkled on the snow.

'What have I done to you,' he asked, heavily and thickly, 'that you should be – so base – a murderer?'

'Done to me? You would have destroyed me, but that you have come to your journey's end. Your cursed activity interposed between me, and the time I had counted on in which I might have replaced the money. Done to me? You have come in my way – not once, not twice, but again and again and again. Did I try to shake you off in the beginning, or no? You were not to be shaken off. Therefore you die here.'

Vendale tried to think coherently, tried to speak coherently, tried to pick up the iron-shod staff he had let fall; failing to touch it, tried to stagger on without its aid. All in vain, all in vain! He stumbled, and fell heavily forward on the brink of the deep chasm.

Stupefied, dozing, unable to stand upon his feet, a veil before his eyes, his sense of hearing deadened, he made such a vigorous rally that, supporting himself on his hands, he saw his enemy standing calmly over him, and heard him speak. 'You call me murderer,' said Obenreizer, with a grim laugh. 'The name matters very little. But at least I have set my life against yours, for I am surrounded by dangers, and may never make my way out of this place. The *Tourmente* is rising again. The snow is on the whirl. I must have the papers now. Every moment has my life in it.'

'Stop!' cried Vendale, in a terrible voice, staggering up with a last flash of fire breaking out of him, and clutching the thievish hands at his breast, in both of his. 'Stop! Stand away from me! God bless my Marguerite! Happily she will never know how I died. Stand off from me, and let me look at your murderous face. Let it remind me – of something – left to say.'

The sight of him fighting so hard for his senses, and the doubt whether he might not for the instant be possessed by the strength of a dozen men, kept his opponent still. Wildly glaring at him, Vendale faltered out the broken words: 'It shall not be – the trust – of the dead – betrayed by me – reputed parents – misinherited fortune – see to it!'

As his head dropped on his breast, and he stumbled on the brink of the chasm as before, the thievish hands went once more, quick and busy, to his breast. He made a convulsive attempt to cry 'No!' desperately rolled himself over into the gulf; and sank away from his enemy's touch, like a phantom in a dreadful dream.

* * *

The mountain storm raged again, and passed again. The awful mountain-voices died away, the moon rose, and the soft and silent snow fell.

Two men and two large dogs came out at the door of the hospice. The men looked carefully around them, and up at the sky. The dogs rolled in the snow, and took it into their mouths, and cast it up with their paws.

One of the men said to the other: 'We may venture now. We may find them in one of the five refuges.' Each fastened on his back a basket; each took in his hand a strong spiked pole; each girded under his arms a looped end of a stout rope, so that they were tied together.

Suddenly the dogs desisted from their gambols in the snow, stood looking down the ascent, put their noses up, put their noses down, became greatly excited, and broke into a deep loud bay together.

The two men looked in the faces of the two dogs. The two dogs looked, with at least equal intelligence, in the faces of the two men.

'*Au secours*, then! Help! To the rescue!' cried the two men. The two dogs, with a glad, deep, generous bark, bounded away.

'Two more mad ones!' said the men, stricken motionless, and looking away in the moonlight. 'Is it possible in such weather! And one of them a woman!'

Each of the dogs had the corner of a woman's dress in its mouth, and drew her along. She fondled their heads as she came up, and she came up through the snow with an accustomed tread. Not so the large man with her, who was spent and winded.

'Dear guides, dear friends of travellers! I am of your country. We seek two gentlemen crossing the pass, who should have reached the hospice this evening.'

'They have reached it, ma'amselle.'

'Thank Heaven! O thank Heaven!'

'But, unhappily, they have gone on again. We are setting forth to seek them even now. We had to wait until the *Tourmente* passed. It has been fearful up here.'

'Dear guides, dear friends of travellers! Let me go with you. Let me go with you for the love of *God*! One of those gentlemen is to be my husband. I love him, O, so dearly. O so dearly! You see I am not faint, you see I am not tired. I am born a peasant girl. I will show you that I know well how to fasten myself to your ropes. I will do it with my own hands. I will swear to be brave and good. But let me go with you, let me go with you! If any mischance should have befallen him, my love would find him, when nothing else could. On my knees, dear friends of travellers! By the love your dear mothers had for your fathers!'

The good rough fellows were moved. 'After all,' they murmured to one another, 'she speaks but the truth. She knows the ways of the mountains. See how marvellously she has come here. But as to Monsieur there, ma'amselle?'

'Dear Mr Joey,' said Marguerite, addressing him in his own tongue, 'you will remain at the house, and wait for me; will you not?'

'If I know'd which o' you two recommended it,' growled Joey Ladle, eyeing the two men with great indignation, 'I'd fight you for sixpence, and give you half-a-crown towards your expenses. No, miss. I'll stick by you as long as there's any sticking left in me, and I'll die for you when I can't do better.'

The state of the moon rendering it highly important that no time should be lost, and the dogs showing signs of great uneasiness, the two men quickly took their resolution. The rope that yoked them together was exchanged for a longer one; the party were secured, Marguerite second, and the cellarman last; and they set out for the refuges. The actual distance of those places was nothing: the whole five, and the next hospice to boot, being within two miles; but the ghastly way was whitened out and sheeted over.

They made no miss in reaching the gallery where the two had taken shelter. The second storm of wind and snow had so wildly swept over it since, that their tracks were gone. But the dogs went to and fro with their noses down, and were confident. The party stopping, however, at the further arch, where the second storm had been especially furious, and where the drift was deep, the dogs became troubled, and went about and about, in quest of a lost purpose.

The great abyss being known to lie on the right, they wandered too much to the left, and had to regain the way with infinite labour through a deep field of snow. The leader of the line had stopped it, and was taking note of the landmarks, when one of the dogs fell to tearing up the snow a little before them. Advancing and stooping to look at it, thinking that someone might be overwhelmed there, they saw that it was stained, and that the stain was red.

The other dog was now seen to look over the brink of the gulf, with his forelegs straightened out, lest he should fall into it, and to tremble in every limb. Then the dog who had found the stained snow joined him, and then they ran to and fro, distressed and whining. Finally, they both stopped on the brink together, and setting up their heads, howled dolefully.

'There is someone lying below,' said Marguerite.

'I think so,' said the foremost man. 'Stand well inward, the two last, and let us look over.'

The last man kindled two torches from his basket, and handed them forward. The leader taking one, and Marguerite the other, they looked down; now shading the torches, now moving them to the right or left, now raising them, now depressing them, as moonlight far below contended with black shadows. A piercing cry from Marguerite broke a long silence.

'My God! On a projecting point, where a wall of ice stretches forward over the torrent, I see a human form!'

'Where, ma'amselle, where?'

'See, there! On the shelf of ice below the dogs!'

The leader, with a sickened aspect, drew inward, and they were all silent. But they were not all inactive, for Marguerite, with swift and skilful fingers, had detached both herself and him from the rope in a few seconds.

'Show me the baskets. These two are the only ropes?'

'The only ropes here, ma'amselle; but at the hospice – '

'If he is alive – I know it is my lover – he will be dead before you can return. Dear guides! Blessed friends of travellers! Look at me. Watch my hands. If they falter or go wrong, make me your prisoner by force. If they are steady and go right, help me to save him!'

She girded herself with a cord under the breast and arms, she formed it into a kind of jacket, she drew it into knots, she laid its end side by side with the end of the other cord, she twisted and twined the two together, she knotted them together, she set her foot upon the knots, she strained them, she held them for the two men to strain at.

'She is inspired,' they said to one another.

'By the Almighty's mercy!' she exclaimed. 'You both know that I am by far the lightest here. Give me the brandy and the wine, and lower me down to him. Then go for assistance and a stronger rope. You see that when it is lowered to me – look at this about me now – I can make it fast and safe to his body. Alive or dead, I will bring him up, or die with him. I love him passionately. Can I say more?'

They turned to her companion, but he was lying senseless on the snow.

'Lower me down to him,' she said, taking two little kegs they had brought, and hanging them about her, 'or I will dash myself to pieces! I am a peasant, and I know no giddiness or fear; and this is nothing to me, and I passionately love him. Lower me down!'

'Ma'amselle, ma'amselle, he must be dying or dead.'

'Dying or dead, my husband's head shall lie upon my breast, or I will dash myself to pieces.'

They yielded, overborne. With such precautions as their skill and the circumstances admitted, they let her slip from the summit, guiding herself down the precipitous icy wall with her hand, and they lowered down, and lowered down, and lowered down, until the cry came up: 'Enough!'

'Is it really he, and is he dead?' they called down, looking over.

The cry came up: 'He is insensible; but his heart beats. It beats against mine.'

'How does he lie?'

The cry came up: 'Upon a ledge of ice. It has thawed beneath him, and it will thaw beneath me. Hasten. If we die, I am content.'

One of the two men hurried off with the dogs at such topmost speed as he could make; the other set up the lighted torches in the snow, and applied himself to recovering the Englishman. Much snow-chafing and some brandy got him on his legs, but delirious and quite unconscious where he was.

The watch remained upon the brink, and his cry went down continually: 'Courage! They will soon be here. How goes it?' And the cry came up: 'His heart still beats against mine. I warm him in my arms. I have cast off the rope, for the ice melts under us, and the rope would separate me from him; but I am not afraid.'

The moon went down behind the mountain tops, and all the abyss lay in darkness. The cry went down: 'How goes it?' The cry came up: 'We are sinking lower, but his heart still beats against mine.'

At length the eager barking of the dogs, and a flare of light upon the snow, proclaimed that help was coming on. Twenty or thirty men, lamps, torches, litters, ropes, blankets, wood to kindle a great fire, restoratives and stimulants, came in fast. The dogs ran from one man to another, and from this thing to that, and ran to the edge of the abyss, dumbly entreating Speed, speed, speed!

The cry went down: 'Thanks to God, all is ready. How goes it?'

The cry came up: 'We are sinking still, and we are deadly cold. His heart no longer beats against mine. Let no one come down, to add to our weight. Lower the rope only.'

The fire was kindled high, a great glare of torches lighted the sides of the precipice, lamps were lowered, a strong rope was lowered. She could be seen passing it round him, and making it secure.

The cry came up into a deathly silence: 'Raise! Softly!' They could see her diminished figure shrink, as he was swung into the air.

They gave no shout when some of them laid him on a litter, and others lowered another strong rope. The cry again came up into a deathly silence: 'Raise! Softly!' But when they caught her at the brink, then they shouted, then they wept, then they gave thanks to Heaven, then they kissed her feet, then they kissed her dress, then the dogs caressed her, licked her icy hands, and with their honest faces warmed her frozen bosom!

She broke from them all, and sank over him on his litter, with both her loving hands upon the heart that stood still.

The Clock-Lock

The pleasant scene was Neuchatel; the pleasant month was April; the pleasant place was a notary's office; the pleasant person in it was the notary: a rosy, hearty, handsome old man, chief notary of Neuchatel, known far and wide in the canton as Maitre Voigt. Professionally and personally, the notary was a popular citizen. His innumerable kindnesses and his innumerable oddities had for years made him one of the recognised public characters of the pleasant Swiss town. His long brown frock-coat and his black skullcap, were among the institutions of the place: and he carried a snuffbox which, in point of size, was popularly believed to be without a parallel in Europe.

There was another person in the notary's office, not so pleasant as the notary. This was Obenreizer.

An oddly pastoral kind of office it was, and one that would never have answered in England. It stood in a neat back yard, fenced off from a pretty flower-garden. Goats browsed in the doorway, and a cow was within half-a-dozen feet of keeping company with the clerk. Maitre Voigt's room was a bright and varnished little room, with panelled walls, like a toy-chamber. According to the seasons of the year, roses, sunflowers, hollyhocks, peeped in at the windows. Maitre Voigt's bees hummed through the office all the summer, in at this window and out at that, taking it frequently in their day's work, as if honey were to be made from Maitre Voigt's sweet disposition. A large musical box on the chimney-piece often trilled away at the Overture to Fra Diavolo, or a selection from William Tell, with a chirruping liveliness that had to be stopped by force on the entrance of a client, and irrepressibly broke out again the moment his back was turned.

'Courage, courage, my good fellow!' said Maitre Voigt, patting Obenreizer on the knee, in a fatherly and comforting way. 'You will begin a new life tomorrow morning in my office here.'

Obenreizer – dressed in mourning, and subdued in manner – lifted his hand, with a white handkerchief in it, to the region of his heart. 'The gratitude is here,' he said. 'But the words to express it are not here.'

'Ta-ta-ta! Don't talk to me about gratitude!' said Maitre Voigt. 'I hate to see a man oppressed. I see you oppressed, and I hold out my hand to you by instinct. Besides, I am not too old yet, to remember my young days. Your father sent me my first client. (It was on a question of half an acre of vineyard that seldom bore any grapes.) Do I owe nothing to your father's son? I owe him a debt of friendly obligation, and I pay it to you. That's rather neatly expressed, I think,' added Maitre Voigt, in high good humour with himself. 'Permit me to reward my own merit with a pinch of snuff!'

Obenreizer dropped his eyes to the ground, as though he were not even worthy to see the notary take snuff.

'Do me one last favour, sir,' he said, when he raised his eyes. 'Do not act on impulse. Thus far, you have only a general knowledge of my position. Hear the case for and against me, in its details, before you take me into your office. Let my claim on your benevolence be recognised by your sound reason as well as by your excellent heart. In *that* case, I may hold up my head against the bitterest of my enemies, and build myself a new reputation on the ruins of the character I have lost.'

'As you will,' said Maitre Voigt. 'You speak well, my son. You will be a fine lawyer one of these days.'

'The details are not many,' pursued Obenreizer. 'My troubles begin with the accidental death of my late travelling companion, my lost dear friend Mr Vendale.'

'Mr Vendale,' repeated the notary. 'Just so. I have heard and read of the name, several times within these two months. The name of the unfortunate English gentleman who was killed on the Simplon. When you got that scar upon your cheek and neck.'

' – From my own knife,' said Obenreizer, touching what must have been an ugly gash at the time of its infliction.

'From your own knife,' assented the notary, 'and in trying to save him. Good, good, good. That was very good. Vendale. Yes. I have several times, lately, thought it droll that I should once have had a client of that name.'

'But the world, sir,' returned Obenreizer, 'is *so* small!' Nevertheless he made a mental note that the notary had once had a client of that name.

'As I was saying, sir, the death of that dear travelling comrade begins my troubles. What follows? I save myself. I go down to Milan. I am received with coldness by Defresnier and Company. Shortly afterwards, I am discharged by Defresnier and Company. Why? They give no reason why. I ask, do they assail my honour? No answer. I ask, what is the imputation against me? No answer. I ask, where are their proofs against me? No answer. I ask, what am I to think? The reply is, "M. Obenreizer is free to think what he will. What M. Obenreizer thinks, is of no importance to Defresnier and Company." And that is all.'

'Perfectly. That is all,' asserted the notary, taking a large pinch of snuff.

'But is that enough, sir?'

'That is not enough,' said Maitre Voigt. 'The House of Defresnier are my fellow-townsmen – much respected, much esteemed – but the House of Defresnier must not silently destroy a man's character. You can rebut assertion. But how can you rebut silence?'

'Your sense of justice, my dear patron,' answered Obenreizer, 'states in a word the cruelty of the case. Does it stop there? No. For, what follows upon that?'

'True, my poor boy,' said the notary, with a comforting nod or two; 'your ward rebels upon that.'

'Rebels is too soft a word,' retorted Obenreizer. 'My ward revolts from me with horror. My ward defies me. My ward withdraws herself from my authority, and takes shelter (Madame Dor with her) in the house of that English lawyer, Mr Bintrey, who replies to your summons to her to submit herself to my authority, that she will not do so.'

' – And who afterwards writes,' said the notary, moving his large snuffbox to look among the papers underneath it for the letter, 'that he is coming to confer with me.'

'Indeed?' replied Obenreizer, rather checked. 'Well, sir. Have I no legal rights?'

'Assuredly, my poor boy,' returned the notary. 'All but felons have their legal rights.'

'And who calls me felon?' said Obenreizer, fiercely.

'No one. Be calm under your wrongs. If the House of Defresnier would call you felon, indeed, we should know how to deal with them.'

While saying these words, he had handed Bintrey's very short letter to Obenreizer, who now read it and gave it back.

'In saying,' observed Obenreizer, with recovered composure, 'that he is coming to confer with you, this English lawyer means that he is coming to deny my authority over my ward.'

'You think so?'

'I am sure of it. I know him. He is obstinate and contentious. You will tell me, my dear sir, whether my authority is unassailable, until my ward is of age?'

'Absolutely unassailable.'

'I will enforce it. I will make her submit herself to it. For,' said Obenreizer, changing his angry tone to one of grateful submission, 'I owe it to you, sir; to you, who have so confidingly taken an injured man under your protection, and into your employment.'

'Make your mind easy,' said Maitre Voigt. 'No more of this now, and no thanks! Be here tomorrow morning, before the other clerk comes – between seven and eight. You will find me in this room; and I will myself initiate you in your work. Go away! go away! I have letters to write. I won't hear a word more.'

Dismissed with this generous abruptness, and satisfied with the favourable impression he had left on the old man's mind, Obenreizer was at leisure to revert to the mental note he had made that Maitre Voigt once had a client whose name was Vendale.

'I ought to know England well enough by this time'; so his meditations ran, as he sat on a bench in the yard; 'and it is not a name I ever encountered there, except – ' he looked involuntarily over his shoulder – 'as *his* name. Is the world so small that I cannot get away from him, even now when he is dead? He confessed at the last that he had betrayed the trust of the dead, and misinherited a fortune. And I was to see to it. And I was to stand off, that my face might remind him of it. Why *my* face, unless it concerned *me*? I am sure of his words, for they have been in my ears ever since. Can there be anything bearing on them, in the keeping of this old idiot? Anything to repair my fortunes, and blacken his memory? He dwelt upon my earliest remembrances, that night at Basle. Why, unless he had a purpose in it?'

Maitre Voigt's two largest he-goats were butting at him to butt him out of the place, as if for that disrespectful mention of their master. So he got up and left the place. But he walked alone for a long time on the border of the lake, with his head drooped in deep thought.

Between seven and eight next morning, he presented himself again at the office. He found the notary ready for him, at work on some papers which had come in on the previous evening. In a few clear words, Maitre Voigt explained the routine of the office, and the duties Obenreizer would be expected to perform. It still wanted five minutes to eight, when the preliminary instructions were declared to be complete.

'I will show you over the house and the offices,' said Maitre Voigt, 'but I must put away these papers first. They come from the municipal authorities, and they must be taken special care of.'

Obenreizer saw his chance, here, of finding out the repository in which his employer's private papers were kept.

'Can't I save you the trouble, sir?' he asked. 'Can't I put those documents away under your directions?'

Maitre Voigt laughed softly to himself; closed the portfolio in which the papers had been sent to him; handed it to Obenreizer.

'Suppose you try,' he said. 'All my papers of importance are kept yonder.'

He pointed to a heavy oaken door, thickly studded with nails, at the lower end of the room. Approaching the door, with the portfolio, Obenreizer discovered, to his astonishment, that there were no means whatever of opening it from the outside. There was no handle, no bolt, no key, and (climax of passive obstruction!) no keyhole.

'There is a second door to this room?' said Obenreizer, appealing to the notary.

'No,' said Maitre Voigt. 'Guess again.'

'There is a window?'

'Nothing of the sort. The window has been bricked up. The only way in, is the way by that door. Do you give it up?' cried Maitre Voigt, in high triumph. 'Listen, my good fellow, and tell me if you hear nothing inside?'

Obenreizer listened for a moment, and started back from the door.

'I know!' he exclaimed. 'I heard of this when I was apprenticed here at the watchmaker's. Perrin Brothers have finished their famous clock-lock at last – and you have got it?'

'Bravo!' said Maitre Voigt. 'The clock-lock it is! There, my son! There you have one more of what the good people of this town call "Daddy Voigt's follies". With all my heart! Let those laugh who win. No thief can steal my keys. No burglar can pick my lock. No power on earth, short of a battering-ram or a barrel of gunpowder, can move that door, till my little sentinel inside – my worthy friend who goes "Tick, tick", as I tell him – says, "Open!" The big door obeys the little tick, tick, and the little tick, tick, obeys *me*. That!' cried Daddy Voigt, snapping his fingers, 'for all the thieves in Christendom!'

'May I see it in action?' asked Obenreizer. 'Pardon my curiosity, dear sir! You know that I was once a tolerable worker in the clock trade.'

'Certainly you shall see it in action,' said Maitre Voigt. 'What is the time now? One minute to eight. Watch, and in one minute you will see the door open of itself.'

In one minute, smoothly and slowly and silently, as if invisible hands had set it free, the heavy door opened inward, and disclosed a dark chamber beyond. On three sides, shelves filled the walls, from floor to ceiling. Arranged on the shelves, were rows upon rows of boxes made in the pretty inlaid woodwork of Switzerland, and bearing inscribed on their fronts (for the most part in fanciful coloured letters) the names of the notary's clients.

Maitre Voigt lighted a taper, and led the way into the room.

'You shall see the clock,' he said proudly. 'I possess the greatest curiosity in Europe. It is only a privileged few whose eyes can look at it. I give the privilege to your good father's son – you shall be one of the favoured few who enter the room with me. See! here it is, on the right-hand wall at the side of the door.'

'An ordinary clock,' exclaimed Obenreizer. 'No! Not an ordinary clock. It has only one hand.'

'Aha!' said Maitre Voigt. 'Not an ordinary clock, my friend. No, no. That one hand goes round the dial. As I put it, so it regulates the hour at which the door shall open. See! The hand points to eight. At eight the door opened, as you saw for yourself.'

'Does it open more than once in the four-and-twenty hours?' asked Obenreizer.

'More than once?' repeated the notary, with great scorn. 'You don't know my good friend, tick-tick! He will open the door as often as I ask him. All he wants is his directions, and he gets them here. Look below the dial. Here is a half-circle of steel let into the wall, and here is a hand (called the regulator) that travels round it, just as *my* hand chooses. Notice, if you please, that there are figures to guide me on the half-circle of steel. Figure 1 means: Open once in the four-and-twenty hours. Figure 2 means: Open twice; and so on to the end. I set the regulator every morning, after I have read my letters, and when I know what my day's work is to be. Would you like to see me set it now? What is today?

Wednesday. Good! This is the day of our rifle-club; there is little business to do; I grant a half-holiday. No work here today, after three o'clock. Let us first put away this portfolio of municipal papers. There! No need to trouble tick-tick to open the door until eight tomorrow. Good! I leave the dial-hand at eight; I put back the regulator to 1; I close the door; and closed the door remains, past all opening by anybody, till tomorrow morning at eight.'

Obenreizer's quickness instantly saw the means by which he might make the clock-lock betray its master's confidence, and place its master's papers at his disposal.

'Stop, sir!' he cried, at the moment when the notary was closing the door. 'Don't I see something moving among the boxes – on the floor there?'

(Maitre Voigt turned his back for a moment to look. In that moment, Obenreizer's ready hand put the regulator on, from the figure '1' to the figure '2'. Unless the notary looked again at the half-circle of steel, the door would open at eight that evening, as well as at eight next morning, and nobody but Obenreizer would know it.)

'There is nothing!' said Maitre Voigt. 'Your troubles have shaken your nerves, my son. Some shadow thrown by my taper; or some poor little beetle, who lives among the old lawyer's secrets, running away from the light. Hark! I hear your fellow-clerk in the office. To work! to work! and build today the first step that leads to your new fortunes!'

He good-humouredly pushed Obenreizer out before him; extinguished the taper, with a last fond glance at his clock which passed harmlessly over the regulator beneath; and closed the oaken door.

At three, the office was shut up. The notary and everybody in the notary's employment, with one exception, went to see the rifle-shooting. Obenreizer had pleaded that he was not in spirits for a public festival. Nobody knew what had become of him. It was believed that he had slipped away for a solitary walk.

The house and offices had been closed but a few minutes, when the door of a shining wardrobe in the notary's shining room opened, and Obenreizer stepped out. He walked to a window, unclosed the shutters, satisfied himself that he could escape unseen by way of the garden, turned back into the room, and took his place in the notary's easy-chair. He was locked up in the house, and there were five hours to wait before eight o'clock came.

He wore his way through the five hours: sometimes reading the books and newspapers that lay on the table: sometimes thinking: sometimes walking to and fro. Sunset came on. He closed the window-shutters before he kindled a light. The candle lighted, and the time drawing nearer and nearer, he sat, watch in hand, with his eyes on the oaken door.

At eight, smoothly and softly and silently the door opened.

One after another, he read the names on the outer rows of boxes. No such name as Vendale! He removed the outer row, and looked at the row behind. These were older boxes, and shabbier boxes. The four first that he examined, were inscribed with French and German names. The fifth bore a name which was almost illegible. He brought it out into the room, and examined it closely. There, covered thickly with time-stains and dust, was the name: 'Vendale'.

The key hung to the box by a string. He unlocked the box, took out four loose papers that were in it, spread them open on the table, and began to read them. He had not so occupied a minute, when his face fell from its expression of eagerness and avidity, to one of haggard astonishment and disappointment. But, after a little consideration, he copied the papers. He then replaced the papers, replaced the box, closed the door, extinguished the candle, and stole away.

As his murderous and thievish footfall passed out of the garden, the steps of the notary and someone accompanying him stopped at the front door of the house. The lamps were lighted in the little street, and the notary had his door-key in his hand.

'Pray do not pass my house, Mr Bintrey,' he said. 'Do me the honour to come in. It is one of our town half-holidays – our Tir – but my people will be back directly. It is droll that you should ask your way to the hotel of me. Let us eat and drink before you go there.'

'Thank you; not tonight,' said Bintrey. 'Shall I come to you at ten tomorrow?'

'I shall be enchanted, sir, to take so early an opportunity of redressing the wrongs of my injured client,' returned the good notary.

'Yes,' retorted Bintrey; 'your injured client is all very well – but – a word in your ear.'

He whispered to the notary and walked off. When the notary's house-keeper came home, she found him standing at his door motionless, with the key still in his hand, and the door unopened.

Obenreizer's Victory

The scene shifts again – to the foot of the Simplon, on the Swiss side.

In one of the dreary rooms of the dreary little inn at Brieg, Mr Bintrey and Maitre Voigt sat together at a professional council of two. Mr Bintrey was searching in his despatch-box. Maitre Voigt was looking towards a closed door, painted brown to imitate mahogany, and communicating with an inner room.

'Isn't it time he was here?' asked the notary, shifting his position, and glancing at a second door at the other end of the room, painted yellow to imitate deal.

'He *is* here,' answered Bintrey, after listening for a moment.

The yellow door was opened by a waiter, and Obenreizer walked in.

After greeting Maitre Voigt with a cordiality which appeared to cause the notary no little embarrassment, Obenreizer bowed with grave and distant politeness to Bintrey. 'For what reason have I been brought from Neuchatel to the foot of the mountain?' he enquired, taking the seat which the English lawyer had indicated to him.

'You shall be quite satisfied on that head before our interview is over,' returned Bintrey. 'For the present, permit me to suggest proceeding at once to business. There has been a correspondence, Mr Obenreizer, between you and your niece. I am here to represent your niece.'

'In other words, you, a lawyer, are here to represent an infraction of the law.'

'Admirably put!' said Bintrey. 'If all the people I have to deal with were only like you, what an easy profession mine would be! I am here to represent an infraction of the law – that is your point of view. I am here to make a compromise between you and your niece – that is my point of view.'

'There must be two parties to a compromise,' rejoined Obenreizer. 'I decline, in this case, to be one of them. The law gives me authority to control my niece's actions, until she comes of age. She is not yet of age; and I claim my authority.'

At this point Maitre attempted to speak. Bintrey silenced him with a compassionate indulgence of tone and manner, as if he was silencing a favourite child.

'No, my worthy friend, not a word. Don't excite yourself unnecessarily; leave it to me.' He turned, and addressed himself again to

Obenreizer. 'I can think of nothing comparable to you, Mr Obenreizer, but granite – and even that wears out in course of time. In the interests of peace and quietness – for the sake of your own dignity – relax a little. If you will only delegate your authority to another person whom I know of, that person may be trusted never to lose sight of your niece, night or day!'

'You are wasting your time and mine,' returned Obenreizer. 'If my niece is not rendered up to my authority within one week from this day, I invoke the law. If you resist the law, I take her by force.'

He rose to his feet as he said the last word. Maitre Voigt looked round again towards the brown door which led into the inner room.

'Have some pity on the poor girl,' pleaded Bintrey. 'Remember how lately she lost her lover by a dreadful death! Will nothing move you?'

'Nothing.'

Bintrey, in his turn, rose to his feet, and looked at Maitre Voigt. Maitre Voigt's hand, resting on the table, began to tremble. Maitre Voigt's eyes remained fixed, as if by irresistible fascination, on the brown door. Obenreizer, suspiciously observing him, looked that way too.

'There is somebody listening in there!' he exclaimed, with a sharp backward glance at Bintrey.

'There are two people listening,' answered Bintrey.

'Who are they?'

'You shall see.'

With this answer, he raised his voice and spoke the next words – the two common words which are on everybody's lips, at every hour of the day: 'Come in!'

The brown door opened. Supported on Marguerite's arm – his sun-burnt colour gone, his right arm bandaged and clung over his breast – Vendale stood before the murderer, a man risen from the dead.

In the moment of silence that followed, the singing of a caged bird in the courtyard outside was the one sound stirring in the room. Maitre Voigt touched Bintrey, and pointed to Obenreizer. 'Look at him!' said the notary, in a whisper.

The shock had paralysed every movement in the villain's body, but the movement of the blood. His face was like the face of a corpse. The one vestige of colour left in it was a livid purple streak which marked the course of the scar where his victim had wounded him on the cheek and neck. Speechless, breathless, motionless alike in eye and limb, it seemed as if, at the sight of Vendale, the death to which he had doomed Vendale had struck him where he stood.

'Somebody ought to speak to him,' said Maitre Voigt. 'Shall I?'

Even at that moment Bintrey persisted in silencing the notary, and in keeping the lead in the proceedings to himself. Checking Maitre Voigt by a gesture, he dismissed Marguerite and Vendale in these words: – 'The object of your appearance here is answered,' he said. 'If you will withdraw for the present, it may help Mr Obenreizer to recover himself.'

It did help him. As the two passed through the door and closed it behind them, he drew a deep breath of relief. He looked round him for the chair from which he had risen, and dropped into it.

'Give him time!' pleaded Maitre Voigt.

'No,' said Bintrey. 'I don't know what use he may make of it if I do.' He turned once more to Obenreizer, and went on. 'I owe it to myself,' he said – 'I don't admit, mind, that I owe it to you – to account for my appearance in these proceedings, and to state what has been done under my advice, and on my sole responsibility. Can you listen to me?'

'I can listen to you.'

'Recall the time when you started for Switzerland with Mr Vendale,' Bintrey begin. 'You had not left England four-and-twenty hours before your niece committed an act of imprudence which not even your penetration could foresee. She followed her promised husband on his journey, without asking anybody's advice or permission, and without any better companion to protect her than a cellarman in Mr Vendale's employment.'

'Why did she follow me on the journey? and how came the cellarman to be the person who accompanied her?'

'She followed you on the journey,' answered Bintrey, 'because she suspected there had been some serious collision between you and Mr Vendale, which had been kept secret from her; and because she rightly believed you to be capable of serving your interests, or of satisfying your enmity, at the price of a crime. As for the cellarman, he was one, among the other people in Mr Vendale's establishment, to whom she had applied (the moment your back was turned) to know if anything had happened between their master and you. The cellarman alone had something to tell her. A senseless superstition, and a common accident which had happened to his master, in his master's cellar, had connected Mr Vendale in this man's mind with the idea of danger by murder. Your niece surprised him into a confession, which aggravated tenfold the terrors that possessed her. Aroused to a sense of the mischief he had done, the man, of his own accord, made the one atonement in his power. "If my master is in danger, miss," he said, "it's my duty to follow him, too; and it's more than my duty to take care of *you*." The two set forth together – and, for once, a superstition has had its use. It decided your niece on taking the journey; and it led the way to saving a man's life. Do you understand me, so far?'

'I understand you, so far.'

'My first knowledge of the crime that you had committed,' pursued Bintrey, 'came to me in the form of a letter from your niece. All you need know is that her love and her courage recovered the body of your victim, and aided the after-efforts which brought him back to life. While he lay helpless at Brieg, under her care, she wrote to me to come out to him. Before starting, I informed Madame Dor that I knew Miss Obenreizer to be safe, and knew where she was. Madame Dor informed me, in return, that a letter had come for your niece, which she knew to be in your handwriting. I took possession of it, and arranged for the forwarding of any other letters which might follow. Arrived at Brieg, I found Mr Vendale out of danger, and at once devoted myself to hastening the day of reckoning with you. Defresnier and Company turned you off on suspicion; acting on information privately supplied by me. Having stripped you of your false character, the next thing to do was to strip you of your authority over your niece. To reach this end, I not only had no scruple in digging the pitfall under your feet in the dark – I felt a certain professional pleasure in fighting you with your own weapons. By my advice the truth has been carefully concealed from you up to this day. By my advice the trap into which you have walked was set for you (you know why, now, as well as I do) in this place. There was but one certain way of shaking the devilish self-control which has hitherto made you a formidable man. That way has been tried, and (look at me as you may) that way has succeeded. The last thing that remains to be done,' concluded Bintrey, producing two little slips of manuscript from his despatch-box, 'is to set your niece free. You have attempted murder, and you have committed forgery and theft. We have the evidence ready against you in both cases. If you are convicted as a felon, you know as well as I do what becomes of your authority over your niece. Personally, I should have preferred taking that way out of it. But considerations are pressed on me which I am not able to resist, and this interview must end, as I have told you already, in a compromise. Sign those lines, resigning all authority over Miss Oben-reizer, and pledging yourself never to be seen in England or in Switzer-land again; and I will sign an indemnity which secures you against further proceedings on our part.'

Obenreizer took the pen in silence, and signed his niece's release. On receiving the indemnity in return, he rose, but made no movement to leave the room. He stood looking at Maitre Voigt with a strange smile gathering at his lips, and a strange light flashing in his filmy eyes.

'What are you waiting for?' asked Bintrey.

Obenreizer pointed to the brown door. 'Call them back,' he answered. 'I have something to say in their presence before I go.'

'Say it in my presence,' retorted Bintrey. 'I decline to call them back.'

Obenreizer turned to Maitre Voigt. 'Do you remember telling me that you once had an English client named Vendale?' he asked.

'Well,' answered the notary. 'And what of that?'

'Maitre Voigt, your clock-lock has betrayed you.'

'What do you mean?'

'I have read the letters and certificates in your client's box. I have taken copies of them. I have got the copies here. Is there, or is there not, a reason for calling them back?'

For a moment the notary looked to and fro, between Obenreizer and Bintrey, in helpless astonishment. Recovering himself, he drew his brother-lawyer aside, and hurriedly spoke a few words close at his ear. The face of Bintrey – after first faithfully reflecting the astonishment on the face of Maitre Voigt – suddenly altered its expression. He sprang, with the activity of a young man, to the door of the inner room, entered it, remained inside for a minute, and returned followed by Marguerite and Vendale. 'Now, Mr Obenreizer,' said Bintrey, 'the last move in the game is yours. Play it.'

'Before I resign my position as that young lady's guardian,' said Oben-reizer, 'I have a secret to reveal in which she is interested. In making my disclosure, I am not claiming her attention for a narrative which she, or any other person present, is expected to take on trust. I am possessed of written proofs, copies of originals, the authenticity of which Maitre Voigt himself can attest. Bear that in mind, and permit me to refer you, at starting, to a date long past – the month of February, in the year one thousand eight hundred and thirty-six.'

'Mark the date, Mr Vendale,' said Bintrey.

'My first proof,' said Obenreizer, taking a paper from his pocketbook. 'Copy of a letter, written by an English lady (married) to her sister, a widow. The name of the person writing the letter I shall keep suppressed until I have done. The name of the person to whom the letter is written I am willing to reveal. It is addressed to "Mrs Jane Anne Miller, of Groombridge Wells, England".'

Vendale started, and opened his lips to speak. Bintrey instantly stopped him, as he had stopped Maitre Voigt. 'No,' said the pertinacious lawyer. 'Leave it to me.'

Obenreizer went on: 'It is needless to trouble you with the first half of the letter,' he said. 'I can give the substance of it in two words. The writer's position at the time is this. She has been long living in Switzerland with her husband – obliged to live there for the sake of her husband's health. They are about to move to a new residence on the Lake of Neuchatel in a week, and they will be ready to receive Mrs Miller as visitor in a fortnight from that time. This said, the writer next enters into an important domestic detail. She has been childless for years – she and her husband have now no hope of children; they are lonely; they want an interest in life; they have decided on adopting a child. Here the important part of the letter begins; and here, therefore, I read it to you word for word.'

He folded back the first page of the letter and read as follows. 'Will you help us, my dear sister, to realise our new project? As English people, we wish to adopt an English child. This may be done, I believe, at the Foundling: my husband's lawyers in London will tell you how. I leave the choice to you, with only these conditions attached to it – that the child is to be an infant under a year old, and is to be a boy. Will you pardon the trouble I am giving you, for my sake; and will you bring our adopted child to us, with your own children, when you come to Neuchatel?

'I must add a word as to my husband's wishes in this matter. He is resolved to spare the child whom we make our own any future mortification and loss of self-respect which might be caused by a discovery of his true origin. He will bear my husband's name, and he will be brought up in the belief that he is really our son. His inheritance of what we have to leave will be secured to him – not only according to the laws of England in such cases, but according to the laws of Switzerland also; for we have lived so long in this country, that there is a doubt whether we may not be considered as domiciled, in Switzerland. The one precaution left to take is to prevent any after-discovery at the Foundling. Now, our name is a very uncommon one; and if we appear on the register of the institution as the persons adopting the child, there is just a chance that something might result from it. Your name, my dear, is the name of thousands of other people; and if you will consent to appear on the register, there need be no fear of any discoveries in that quarter. We are moving, by the doctor's orders, to a part of Switzerland in which our circumstances are quite unknown; and you, as I understand, are about to engage a new nurse for the journey when you come to see us. Under these circumstances, the child may appear as my child, brought back to me under my sister's care. The only servant we take with us from our old home is my own maid, who can be safely trusted. As for the lawyers in England and in Switzerland, it is their profession to keep secrets – and we may feel quite easy in that direction. So there you have our harmless little conspiracy! Write by return of post, my love, and tell me you will join it.'

*   *   *

'Do you still conceal the name of the writer of that letter?' asked Vendale.

'I keep the name of the writer till the last,' answered Obenreizer, 'and I proceed to my second proof – a mere slip of paper this time, as you see. Memorandum given to the Swiss lawyer, who drew the documents referred to in the letter I have just read, expressed as follows: – "Adopted from the Foundling Hospital of England, 3d March, 1836, a male infant, called, in the institution, Walter Wilding. Person appearing on the register, as adopting the child, Mrs Jane Anne Miller, widow, acting in this matter for her married sister, domiciled in Switzerland." Patience!' resumed Obenreizer, as Vendale, breaking loose from Bintrey, started to his feet. 'I shall not keep the name concealed much longer. Two more little slips of paper, and I have done. Third proof! Certificate of Dr Ganz, still living in practice at Neuchatel, dated July, 1838. The doctor certifies (you shall read it for yourselves directly), first, that he attended the adopted child in its infant maladies; second, that, three months before the date of the certificate, the gentleman adopting the child as his son died; third, that on the date of the certificate, his widow and her maid, taking the adopted child with them, left Neuchatel on their return to England. One more link now added to this, and my chain of evidence is complete. The maid remained with her mistress till her mistress's death, only a few years since. The maid can swear to the identity of the adopted infant, from his childhood to his youth – from his youth to his manhood, as he is now. There is her address in England – and there, Mr Vendale, is the fourth, and final proof!'

'Why do you address yourself to *me*?' said Vendale, as Obenreizer threw the written address on the table.

Obenreizer turned on him, in a sudden frenzy of triumph.

'*Because you are the man!* If my niece marries you, she marries a bastard, brought up by public charity. If my niece marries you, she marries an impostor, without name or lineage, disguised in the character of a gentleman of rank and family.'

'Bravo!' cried Bintrey. 'Admirably put, Mr Obenreizer! It only wants one word more to complete it. She marries – thanks entirely to your exertions – a man who inherits a handsome fortune, and a man whose origin will make him prouder than ever of his peasant-wife. George Vendale, as brother-executors, let us congratulate each other! Our dear dead friend's last wish on earth is accomplished. We have found the lost Walter Wilding. As Mr Obenreizer said just now – you are the man!'

The words passed by Vendale unheeded. For the moment he was conscious of but one sensation; he heard but one voice. Marguerite's hand was clasping his. Marguerite's voice was whispering to him: 'I never loved you, George, as I love you now!'

The Curtain Falls

May Day. There is merrymaking in Cripple Corner, the chimneys smoke, the patriarchal dining-hall is hung with garlands, and Mrs Goldstraw, the respected housekeeper, is very busy. For, on this bright morning the young master of Cripple Corner is married to its young mistress, far away: to wit, in the little town of Brieg, in Switzerland, lying at the foot of the Simplon Pass where she saved his life.

The bells ring gaily in the little town of Brieg, and flags are stretched across the street, and rifle shots are heard, and sounding music from brass instruments. Streamer-decorated casks of wine have been rolled out under a gay awning in the public way before the inn, and there will be free feasting and revelry. What with bells and banners, draperies hanging from windows, explosion of gunpowder, and reverberation of brass music, the little town of Brieg is all in a flutter, like the hearts of its simple people.

It was a stormy night last night, and the mountains are covered with snow. But the sun is bright today, the sweet air is fresh, the tin spires of the little town of Brieg are burnished silver, and the Alps are ranges of far-off white cloud in a deep blue sky.

The primitive people of the little town of Brieg have built a greenwood arch across the street, under which the newly married pair shall pass in triumph from the church. It is inscribed, on that side, 'Honour and Love to Marguerite Vendale', for the people are proud of her to enthusiasm. This greeting of the bride under her new name is affectionately meant as a surprise, and therefore the arrangement has been made that she, unconscious why, shall be taken to the church by a tortuous back way. A scheme not difficult to carry into execution in the crooked little town of Brieg.

So, all things are in readiness, and they are to go and come on foot. Assembled in the inn's best chamber, festively adorned, are the bride and bridegroom, the Neuchatel notary, the London lawyer, Madame Dor, and a certain large mysterious Englishman, popularly known as Monsieur Zhoe-Ladelle. And behold Madame Dor, arrayed in a spotless pair of gloves of her own, with no hand in the air, but both hands clasped round the neck of the bride; to embrace whom Madame Dor has turned her broad back on the company, consistent to the last.

'Forgive me, my beautiful,' pleads Madame Dor, 'for that I ever was his she-cat!'

'She-cat, Madame Dor?'

'Engaged to sit watching my so charming mouse,' are the explanatory words of Madame Dor, delivered with a penitential sob.

'Why, you were our best friend! George, dearest, tell Madame Dor. Was she not our best friend?'

'Undoubtedly, darling. What should we have done without her?'

'You are both so generous,' cries Madame Dor, accepting consolation, and immediately relapsing. 'But I commenced as a she-cat.'

'Ah! But like the cat in the fairy-story, good Madame Dor,' says Vendale, saluting her cheek, 'you were a true woman. And, being a true woman, the sympathy of your heart was with true love.'

'I don't wish to deprive Madame Dor of her share in the embraces that are going on,' Mr Bintrey puts in, watch in hand, 'and I don't presume to offer any objection to your having got yourselves mixed together, in the corner there, like the three Graces. I merely remark that I think it's time we were moving. What are *your* sentiments on that subject, Mr Ladle?'

'Clear, sir,' replies Joey, with a gracious grin. 'I'm clearer altogether, sir, for having lived so many weeks upon the surface. I never was half so long upon the surface afore, and it's done me a power of good. At Cripple Corner, I was too much below it. Atop of the Simpleton, I was a deal too high above it. I've found the medium here, sir. And if ever I take it in convivial, in all the rest of my days, I mean to do it this day, to the toast of "Bless 'em both".'

'I, too!' says Bintrey. 'And now, Monsieur Voigt, let you and me be two men of Marseilles, and *allons, marchons*, arm-in-arm!'

They go down to the door, where others are waiting for them, and they go quietly to the church, and the happy marriage takes place. While the ceremony is yet in progress, the notary is called out. When it is finished, he has returned, is standing behind Vendale, and touches him on the shoulder.

'Go to the side door, one moment, Monsieur Vendale. Alone. Leave Madame to me.'

At the side door of the church, are the same two men from the hospice. They are snow-stained and travel-worn. They wish him joy, and then each lays his broad hand upon Vendale's breast, and one says in a low voice, while the other steadfastly regards him: 'It is here, monsieur. Your litter. The very same.'

'My litter is here? Why?'

'Hush! For the sake of Madame. Your companion of that day – '

'What of him?'

The man looks at his comrade, and his comrade takes him up. Each keeps his hand laid earnestly on Vendale's breast.

'He had been living at the first refuge, monsieur, for some days. The weather was now good, now bad.'

'Yes?'

'He arrived at our hospice the day before yesterday, and, having refreshed himself with sleep on the floor before the fire, wrapped in his cloak, was resolute to go on, before dark, to the next hospice. He had a great fear of that part of the way, and thought it would be worse tomorrow.'

'Yes?'

'He went on alone. He had passed the gallery when an avalanche – like that which fell behind you near the Bridge of the Ganther – '

'Killed him?'

'We dug him out, suffocated and broken all to pieces! But, monsieur, as to Madame. We have brought him here on the litter, to be buried. We must ascend the street outside. Madame must not see. It would be an accursed thing to bring the litter through the arch across the street, until Madame has passed through. As you descend, we who accompany the litter will set it down on the stones of the street the second to the right, and will stand before it. But do not let Madame turn her head towards the street the second to the right. There is no time to lose. Madame will be alarmed by your absence. Adieu!'

Vendale returns to his bride, and draws her hand through his arm. A pretty procession awaits them at the main door of the church. They take their station in it, and descend the street amidst the ringing of the bells, the firing of the guns, the waving of the flags, the playing of the music, the shouts, the smiles, and tears, of the excited town. Heads are uncovered as she passes, hands are kissed to her, all the people bless her. 'Heaven's benediction on the dear girl! See where she goes in her youth and beauty; she who so nobly saved his life!'

Near the corner of the street the second to the right, he speaks to her, and calls her attention to the windows on the opposite side. The corner well passed, he says: 'Do not look round, my darling, for a reason that I have,' and turns his head. Then, looking back along the street, he sees the litter and its bearers passing up alone under the arch, as he and she and their marriage train go down towards the shining valley.

THE HOLLY TREE

FIRST BRANCH

Myself

I have kept one secret in the course of my life. I am a bashful man. Nobody would suppose it, nobody ever does suppose it, nobody ever did suppose it, but I am naturally a bashful man. This is the secret which I have never breathed until now.

I might greatly move the reader by some account of the innumerable places I have not been to, the innumerable people I have not called upon or received, the innumerable social evasions I have been guilty of, solely because I am by original constitution and character a bashful man. But I will leave the reader unmoved, and proceed with the object before me.

That object is to give a plain account of my travels and discoveries in the Holly Tree Inn; in which place of good entertainment for man and beast I was once snowed up.

It happened in the memorable year when I parted for ever from Angela Leath, whom I was shortly to have married, on making the discovery that she preferred my bosom friend. From our schooldays I had freely admitted Edwin, in my own mind, to be far superior to myself; and, though I was grievously wounded at heart, I felt the preference to be natural, and tried to forgive them both. It was under these circumstances that I resolved to go to America – on my way to the Devil.

Communicating my discovery neither to Angela nor to Edwin, but resolving to write each of them an affecting letter conveying my blessing and forgiveness, which the steam-tender for shore should carry to the post when I myself should be bound for the New World, far beyond recall – I say, locking up my grief in my own breast, and consoling myself as I could with the prospect of being generous, I quietly left all I held dear, and started on the desolate journey I have mentioned.

The dead wintertime was in full dreariness when I left my chambers for ever, at five o'clock in the morning. I had shaved by candlelight, of course, and was miserably cold, and experienced that general all-pervading sensation of getting up to be hanged which I have usually found inseparable from untimely rising under such circumstances.

How well I remember the forlorn aspect of Fleet Street when I came out of the Temple! The street-lamps flickering in the gusty north-east wind, as if the very gas were contorted with cold; the white-topped houses; the bleak, star-lighted sky; the market people and other early stragglers, trotting to circulate their almost frozen blood; the hospitable light and warmth of the few coffee-shops and public-houses that were open for such customers; the hard, dry, frosty rime with which the air was charged (the wind had already beaten it into every crevice), and which lashed my face like a steel whip.

It wanted nine days to the end of the month, and end of the year. The Post-office packet for the United States was to depart from Liverpool, weather permitting, on the first of the ensuing month, and I had the intervening time on my hands. I had taken this into consideration, and had resolved to make a visit to a certain spot (which I need not name) on the farther borders of Yorkshire. It was endeared to me by my having first seen Angela at a farmhouse in that place, and my melancholy was gratified by the idea of taking a wintry leave of it before my expatriation. I ought to explain, that, to avoid being sought out before my resolution should have been rendered irrevocable by being carried into full effect, I had written to Angela overnight, in my usual manner, lamenting that urgent business, of which she should know all particulars by and by – took me unexpectedly away from her for a week or ten days.

There was no Northern Railway at that time, and in its place there were stage coaches; which I occasionally find myself, in common with some other people, affecting to lament now, but which everybody dreaded as a very serious penance then. I had secured the box-seat on the fastest of these, and my business in Fleet Street was to get into a cab with my portmanteau, so to make the best of my way to the Peacock at Islington, where I was to join this coach. But when one of our Temple watchmen, who carried my portmanteau into Fleet Street for me, told me about the huge blocks of ice that had for some days past been floating in the river, having closed up in the night, and made a walk from the Temple Gardens over to the Surrey shore, I began to ask myself the question, whether the box-seat would not be likely to put a sudden and a frosty end to my unhappiness. I was heart-broken, it is true, and yet I was not quite so far gone as to wish to be frozen to death.

When I got up to the Peacock – where I found everybody drinking hot purl, in self-preservation – I asked if there were an inside seat to spare. I then discovered that, inside or out, I was the only passenger. This gave me a still livelier idea of the great inclemency of the weather, since that coach always loaded particularly well. However, I took a little purl (which I found uncommonly good), and got into the coach. When I was seated, they built me up with straw to the waist, and, conscious of making a rather ridiculous appearance, I began my journey.

It was still dark when we left the Peacock. For a little while, pale, uncertain ghosts of houses and trees appeared and vanished, and then it was hard, black, frozen day. People were lighting their fires; smoke was mounting straight up high into the rarefied air; and we were rattling for Highgate Archway over the hardest ground I have ever heard the ring of iron shoes on. As we got into the country, everything seemed to have grown old and grey. The roads, the trees, thatched roofs of cottages and homesteads, the ricks in farmers' yards. Outdoor work was abandoned, horse-troughs at roadside inns were frozen hard, no stragglers lounged about, doors were close shut, little turnpike houses had blazing fires inside, and children (even turnpike people have children, and seem to like them) rubbed the frost from the little panes of glass with their chubby arms, that their bright eyes might catch a glimpse of the solitary coach going by. I don't know when the snow begin to set in; but I know that we were changing horses somewhere when I heard the guard remark, that 'the old lady up in the sky was picking her geese pretty hard today'. Then, indeed, I found the white down falling fast and thick.

The lonely day wore on, and I dozed it out, as a lonely traveller does. I was warm and valiant after eating and drinking – particularly after dinner; cold and depressed at all other times. I was always bewildered as to time and place, and always more or less out of my senses. The coach and horses seemed to execute in chorus Auld Lang Syne, without a moment's intermission. They kept the time and tune with the greatest regularity, and rose into the swell at the beginning of the refrain, with a precision that worried me to death. While we changed horses, the guard and coachman went stumping up and down the road, printing off their shoes in the snow, and poured so much liquid consolation into themselves without being any the worse for it, that I began to confound them, as it darkened again, with two great white casks standing on end. Our horses tumbled down in solitary places, and we got them up – which was the pleasantest variety *I* had, for it warmed me. And it snowed and snowed, and still it snowed, and never left off snowing. All night long we went on in this manner. Thus we came round the clock, upon the Great North Road, to the performance of Auld Lang Syne by day again. And it snowed and snowed, and still it snowed, and never left off snowing.

I forget now where we were at noon on the second day, and where we ought to have been; but I know that we were scores of miles behindhand, and that our case was growing worse every hour. The drift was becoming prodigiously deep; landmarks were getting snowed out; the road and the fields were all one; instead of having fences and hedgerows to guide us, we went crunching on over an unbroken surface of ghastly white that might sink beneath us at any moment and drop us down a whole hillside. Still the coachman and guard – who kept together on the box, always in council, and looking well about them – made out the track with astonishing sagacity.

When we came in sight of a town, it looked, to my fancy, like a large drawing on a slate, with abundance of slate-pencil expended on the churches and houses where the snow lay thickest. When we came within a town, and found the church clocks all stopped, the dial-faces choked with snow, and the inn-signs blotted out, it seemed as if the whole place were overgrown with white moss. As to the coach, it was a mere snowball; similarly, the men and boys who ran along beside us to the town's end, turning our clogged wheels and encouraging our horses, were men and boys of snow; and the bleak wild solitude to which they at last dismissed us was a snowy Sahara. One would have thought this enough: notwithstanding which, I pledge my word that it snowed and snowed, and still it snowed, and never left off snowing.

We performed Auld Lang Syne the whole day; seeing nothing, out of towns and villages, but the track of stoats, hares, and foxes, and sometimes of birds. At nine o'clock at night, on a Yorkshire moor, a cheerful burst from our horn, and a welcome sound of talking, with a glimmering and moving about of lanterns, roused me from my drowsy state. I found that we were going to change.

They helped me out, and I said to a waiter, whose bare head became as white as King Lear's in a single minute, 'What inn is this?'

'The Holly Tree, sir,' said he.

'Upon my word, I believe,' said I, apologetically, to the guard and coachman, 'that I must stop here.'

Now the landlord, and the landlady, and the ostler, and the post-boy, and all the stable authorities, had already asked the coachman, to the wide-eyed interest of all the rest of the establishment, if he meant to go on. The coachman had already replied, 'Yes, he'd take her through it,' – meaning by Her the coach – 'if so be as George would stand by him.' George was the guard, and he had already sworn that he would stand by him. So the helpers were already getting the horses out.

My declaring myself beaten, after this parley, was not an announcement without preparation. Indeed, but for the way to the announcement being smoothed by the parley, I more than doubt whether, as an innately bashful man, I should have had the confidence to make it. As it was, it received the approval even of the guard and coachman. Therefore, with many confirmations of my inclining, and many remarks from one bystander to another, that the gentleman could go for'ard by the mail tomorrow, whereas tonight he would only be froze, and where was the good of a gentleman being froze – ah, let alone buried alive (which latter clause was added by a humorous helper as a joke at my expense, and was extremely well received), I saw my portmanteau got out stiff, like a frozen body; did the handsome thing by the guard and coachman; wished them good-night and a prosperous journey; and, a little ashamed of myself, after all, for leaving them to fight it out alone, followed the landlord, landlady, and waiter of the Holly Tree upstairs.

I thought I had never seen such a large room as that into which they showed me. It had five windows, with dark red curtains that would have absorbed the light of a general illumination; and there were complications of drapery at the top of the curtains, that went wandering about the wall in a most extraordinary manner. I asked for a smaller room, and they told me there was no smaller room.

They could screen me in, however, the landlord said. They brought a great old japanned screen, with natives (Japanese, I suppose) engaged in a variety of idiotic pursuits all over it; and left me roasting whole before an immense fire.

My bedroom was some quarter of a mile off, up a great staircase at the end of a long gallery; and nobody knows what a misery this is to a bashful man who would rather not meet people on the stairs. It was the grimmest room I have ever had the nightmare in; and all the furniture, from the four posts of the bed to the two old silver candlesticks, was tall, high-shouldered, and spindle-waisted. Below, in my sitting-room, if I looked round my screen, the wind rushed at me like a mad bull; if I stuck to my armchair, the fire scorched me to the colour of a new brick. The chimney-piece was very high, and there was a bad glass – what I may call a wavy glass – above it, which, when I stood up, just showed me my anterior phrenological developments – and these never look well, in any subject, cut short off at the eyebrow. If I stood with my back to the fire, a gloomy vault of darkness above and beyond the screen insisted on being looked at; and, in its dim remoteness, the drapery of the ten curtains of the five windows went twisting and creeping about, like a nest of gigantic worms.

I suppose that what I observe in myself must be observed by some other men of similar character in *themselves*; therefore I am emboldened to mention, that, when I travel, I never arrive at a place but I immediately want to go away from it. Before I had finished my supper of broiled fowl and mulled port, I had impressed upon the waiter in detail my arrangements for departure in the morning. Breakfast and bill at eight. Fly at nine. Two horses, or, if needful, even four.

Tired though I was, the night appeared about a week long. In cases of nightmare, I thought of Angela, and felt more depressed than ever by the reflection that I was on the shortest road to Gretna Green. What had *I* to do with Gretna Green? I was not going *that* way to the Devil, but by the American route, I remarked in my bitterness.

In the morning I found that it was snowing still, that it had snowed all night, and that I was snowed up. Nothing could get out of that spot on the moor, or could come at it, until the road had been cut out by labourers from the market-town. When they might cut their way to the Holly Tree nobody could tell me.

It was now Christmas Eve. I should have had a dismal Christmastime of it anywhere, and consequently that did not so much matter; still, being snowed up was like dying of frost, a thing I had not bargained for. I felt very lonely. Yet I could no more have proposed to the landlord and landlady to admit me to their society (though I should have liked it – very much) than I could have asked them to present me with a piece of plate. Here my great secret, the real bashfulness of my character, is to be observed. Like most bashful men, I judge of other people as if they were bashful too. Besides being far too shamefaced to make the proposal myself, I really had a delicate misgiving that it would be in the last degree disconcerting to them.

Trying to settle down, therefore, in my solitude, I first of all asked what books there were in the house. The waiter brought me a *Book of Roads*, two or three old newspapers, a little song-book, terminating in a collection of Toasts and Sentiments, a little jest-book, an odd volume of *Peregrine Pickle*, and the *Sentimental Journey*. I knew every word of the two last already, but I read them through again, then tried to hum all the songs (Auld Lang Syne was among them); went entirely through the jokes – in which I found a fund of melancholy adapted to my state of mind; proposed all the toasts, enunciated all the sentiments, and mastered the papers. The latter had nothing in them but stock advertisements, a meeting about a county rate, and a highway robbery. As I am a greedy reader, I could not make this supply hold out until night; it was exhausted by teatime. Being then entirely cast upon my own resources, I got through an hour in considering what to do next. Ultimately, it came into my head (from which I was anxious by any means to exclude Angela and Edwin), that I would endeavour to recall my experience of inns, and would try how long it lasted me. I stirred the fire, moved my chair a little to one side of the screen – not daring to go far, for I knew the wind was waiting to make a rush at me, I could hear it growling – and began.

My first impressions of an inn dated from the nursery; consequently I went back to the nursery for a starting-point, and found myself at the knee of a sallow woman with a fishy eye, an aquiline nose, and a green gown, whose speciality was a dismal narrative of a landlord by the road-side, whose visitors unaccountably disappeared for many years, until it was discovered that the pursuit of his life had been to convert them into pies. For the better devotion of himself to this branch of industry, he had constructed a secret door behind the head of the bed; and when the visitor (oppressed with pie) had fallen asleep, this wicked landlord would look softly in with a lamp in one hand and a knife in the other, would cut his throat, and would make him into pies; for which purpose he had coppers, underneath a trap-door, always boiling; and rolled out his pastry in the dead of the night. Yet even he was not insensible to the stings of conscience, for he never went to sleep without being heard to mutter, 'Too much pepper!' which was eventually the cause of his being brought to justice. I had no sooner disposed of this criminal than there started up another of the same period, whose profession was originally house-breaking; in the pursuit of which art he had had his right ear chopped off one night, as he was burglariously getting in at a window, by a brave and lovely servant-maid (whom the aquiline-nosed woman, though not at all answering the description, always mysteriously implied to be herself). After several years, this brave and lovely servant-maid was married to the landlord of a country inn; which landlord had this remarkable characteristic, that he always wore a silk nightcap, and never would on any consideration take it off. At last, one night, when he was fast asleep, the brave and lovely woman lifted up his silk nightcap on the right side, and found that he had no ear there; upon which she sagaciously perceived that he was the clipped housebreaker, who had married her with the intention of putting her to death. She immediately heated the poker and terminated his career, for which she was taken to King George upon his throne, and received the compliments of royalty on her great discretion and valour. This same narrator, who had a ghoulish pleasure, I have long been persuaded, in terrifying me to the utmost confines of my reason, had another authentic anecdote within her own experience, founded, I now believe, upon *Raymond and Agnes, or the Bleeding Nun*. She said it happened to her brother-in-law, who was immensely rich – which my father was not; and immensely tall – which my father was not. It was always a point with this ghoul to present my clearest relations and friends to my youthful mind under circumstances of disparaging contrast. The brother-in-law was riding once through a forest on a magnificent horse (we had no magnificent horse at our house), attended by a favourite and valuable Newfoundland dog (we had no dog), when he found himself benighted, and came to an inn. A dark woman opened the door, and he asked her if he could have a bed there. She answered yes, and put his horse in the stable, and took him into a room where there were two dark men. While he was at supper, a parrot in the room began to talk, saying, 'Blood, blood! Wipe up the blood!' Upon which one of the dark men wrung the parrot's neck, and said he was fond of roasted parrots, and he meant to have this one for breakfast in the morning. After eating and drinking heartily, the immensely rich, tall brother-in-law went up to bed; but he was rather vexed, because they had shut his dog in the stable, saying that they never allowed dogs in the house. He sat very quiet for more than an hour, thinking and thinking, when, just as his candle was burning out, he heard a scratch at the door. He opened the door, and there was the Newfoundland dog! The dog came softly in, smelt about him, went straight to some straw in the corner which the dark men had said covered apples, tore the straw away, and disclosed two sheets steeped in blood. Just at that moment the candle went out, and the brother-in-law, looking through a chink in the door, saw the two dark men stealing upstairs; one armed with a dagger that long (about five feet); the other carrying a chopper, a sack, and a spade. Having no remembrance of the close of this adventure, I suppose my faculties to have been always so frozen with terror at this stage of it, that the power of listening stagnated within me for some quarter of an hour.

These barbarous stories carried me, sitting there on the Holly Tree hearth, to the roadside inn, renowned in my time in a sixpenny book with a folding plate, representing in a central compartment of oval form the portrait of Jonathan Bradford, and in four corner compartments four incidents of the tragedy with which the name is associated – coloured with a hand at once so free and economical, that the bloom of Jonathan's complexion passed without any pause into the breeches of the ostler, and, smearing itself off into the next division, became rum in a bottle. Then I remembered how the landlord was found at the murdered traveller's bedside, with his own knife at his feet, and blood upon his hand; how he was hanged for the murder, notwithstanding his protestation that he had indeed come there to kill the traveller for his saddle-bags, but had been stricken motionless on finding him already slain; and how the ostler, years afterwards, owned the deed. By this time I had made myself quite uncomfortable. I stirred the fire, and stood with my back to it as long as I could bear the heat, looking up at the darkness beyond the screen, and at the wormy curtains creeping in and creeping out, like the worms in the ballad of Alonzo the Brave and the Fair Imogene.

There was an inn in the cathedral town where I went to school, which had pleasanter recollections about it than any of these. I took it next. It was the inn where friends used to put up, and where we used to go to see parents, and to have salmon and fowls, and be tipped. It had an ecclesiastical sign – the Mitre – and a bar that seemed to be the next best thing to a bishopric, it was so snug. I loved the landlord's youngest daughter to distraction – but let that pass. It was in this inn that I was cried over by my rosy little sister, because I had acquired a black eye in a fight. And though she had been, that Holly Tree night, for many a long year where all tears are dried, the Mitre softened me yet.

'To be continued tomorrow,' said I, when I took my candle to go to bed. But my bed took it upon itself to continue the train of thought that night. It carried me away, like the enchanted carpet, to a distant place (though still in England), and there, alighting from a stage-coach at another inn in the snow, as I had actually done some years before, I repeated in my sleep a curious experience I had really had there. More than a year before I made the journey in the course of which I put up at that inn, I had lost a very near and dear friend by death. Every night since, at home or away from home, I had dreamed of that friend; sometimes as still living; sometimes as returning from the world of shadows to comfort me; always as being beautiful, placid, and happy, never in association with any approach to fear or distress. It was at a lonely inn in a wide moorland place, that I halted to pass the night. When I had looked from my bedroom window over the waste of snow on which the moon was shining, I sat down by my fire to write a letter. I had always, until that hour, kept it within my own breast that I dreamed every night of the dear lost one. But in the letter that I wrote I recorded the circumstance, and added that I felt much interested in proving whether the subject of my dream would still be faithful to me, travel-tired, and in that remote place. No. I lost the beloved figure of my vision in parting with the secret. My sleep has never looked upon it since, in sixteen years, but once. I was in Italy, and awoke (or seemed to awake), the well-remembered voice distinctly in my ears, conversing with it. I entreated it, as it rose above my bed and soared up to the vaulted roof of the old room, to answer me a question I had asked touching the Future Life. My hands were still outstretched towards it as it vanished, when I heard a bell ringing by the garden wall, and a voice in the deep stillness of the night calling on all good Christians to pray for the souls of the dead; it being All Souls' Eve.

To return to the Holly Tree. When I awoke next day, it was freezing hard, and the lowering sky threatened more snow. My breakfast cleared away, I drew my chair into its former place, and, with the fire getting so much the better of the landscape that I sat in twilight, resumed my inn remembrances.

That was a good inn down in Wiltshire where I put up once, in the days of the hard Wiltshire ale, and before all beer was bitterness. It was on the skirts of Salisbury Plain, and the midnight wind that rattled my lattice window came moaning at me from Stonehenge. There was a hanger-on at that establishment (a supernaturally preserved Druid I believe him to have been, and to be still), with long white hair, and a flinty blue eye always looking afar off; who claimed to have been a shepherd, and who seemed to be ever watching for the reappearance, on the verge of the horizon, of some ghostly flock of sheep that had been mutton for many ages. He was a man with a weird belief in him that no one could count the stones of Stonehenge twice, and make the same number of them; likewise, that anyone who counted them three times nine times, and then stood in the centre and said, 'I dare!' would behold a tremendous apparition, and be stricken dead. He pretended to have seen a bustard (I suspect him to have been familiar with the dodo), in manner following: He was out upon the plain at the close of a late autumn day, when he dimly discerned, going on before him at a curious fitfully bounding pace, what he at first supposed to be a gig-umbrella that had been blown from some conveyance, but what he presently believed to be a lean dwarf man upon a little pony. Having followed this object for some distance without gaining on it, and having called to it many times without receiving any answer, he pursued it for miles and miles, when, at length coming up with it, he discovered it to be the last bustard in Great Britain, degenerated into a wingless state, and running along the ground. Resolved to capture him or perish in the attempt, he closed with the bustard; but the bustard, who had formed a counter-resolution that he should do neither, threw him, stunned him, and was last seen making off due west. This weird main, at that stage of metempsychosis, may have been a sleepwalker or an enthusiast or a robber; but I awoke one night to find him in the dark at my bedside, repeating the Athanasian Creed in a terrific voice. I paid my bill next day, and retired from the county with all possible precipitation.

That was not a commonplace story which worked itself out at a little inn in Switzerland, while I was staying there. It was a very homely place, in a village of one narrow zigzag street, among mountains, and you went in at the main door through the cow-house, and among the mules and the dogs and the fowls, before ascending a great bare staircase to the rooms; which were all of unpainted wood, without plastering or papering – like rough packing-cases. Outside there was nothing but the straggling street, a little toy church with a copper-coloured steeple, a pine forest, a torrent, mists, and mountain-sides. A young man belonging to this inn had disappeared eight weeks before (it was wintertime), and was supposed to have had some undiscovered love affair, and to have gone for a soldier. He had got up in the night, and dropped into the village street from the loft in which he slept with another man; and he had done it so quietly, that his companion and fellow-labourer had heard no movement when he was awakened in the morning, and they said, 'Louis, where is Henri?' They looked for him high and low, in vain, and gave him up. Now, outside this inn, there stood, as there stood outside every dwelling in the village, a stack of firewood; but the stack belonging to the inn was higher than any of the rest, because the inn was the richest house, and burnt the most fuel. It began to be noticed, while they were looking high and low, that a Bantam cock, part of the live stock of the inn, put himself wonderfully out of his way to get to the top of this wood-stack; and that he would stay there for hours and hours, crowing, until he appeared in danger of splitting himself. Five weeks went on – six weeks – and still this terrible Bantam, neglecting his domestic affairs, was always on the top of the wood-stack, crowing the very eyes out of his head. By this time it was perceived that Louis had become inspired with a violent animosity towards the terrible Bantam, and one morning he was seen by a woman, who sat nursing her goitre at a little window in a gleam of sun, to catch up a rough billet of wood, with a great oath, hurl it at the terrible Bantam crowing on the wood-stack, and bring him down dead. Hereupon the woman, with a sudden light in her mind, stole round to the back of the wood-stack, and, being a good climber, as all those women are, climbed up, and soon was seen upon the summit, screaming, looking down the hollow within, and crying, 'Seize Louis, the murderer! Ring the church bell! Here is the body!' I saw the murderer that day, and I saw him as I sat by my fire at the Holly Tree Inn, and I see him now, lying shackled with cords on the stable litter, among the mild eyes and the smoking breath of the cows, waiting to be taken away by the police, and stared at by the fearful village. A heavy animal – the dullest animal in the stables – with a stupid head, and a lumpish face devoid of any trace of insensibility, who had been, within the knowledge of the murdered youth, an embezzler of certain small moneys belonging to his master, and who had taken this hopeful mode of putting a possible accuser out of his way. All of which he confessed next day, like a sulky wretch who couldn't be troubled any more, now that they had got hold of him, and meant to make an end of him. I saw him once again, on the day of my departure from the inn. In that canton the headsman still does his office with a sword; and I came upon this murderer sitting bound, to a chair, with his eyes bandaged, on a scaffold in a little market-place. In that instant, a great sword (loaded with quicksilver in the thick part of the blade) swept round him like a gust of wind or fire, and there was no such creature in the world. My wonder was, not that he was so suddenly dispatched, but that any head was left unreaped, within a radius of fifty yards of that tremendous sickle.

That was a good inn, too, with the kind, cheerful landlady and the honest landlord, where I lived in the shadow of Mont Blanc, and where one of the apartments has a zoological papering on the walls, not so accurately joined but that the elephant occasionally rejoices in a tiger's hind legs and tail, while the lion puts on a trunk and tusks, and the bear, moulting as it were, appears as to portions of himself like a leopard. I made several American friends at that inn, who all called Mont Blanc Mount Blank – except one good-humoured gentleman, of a very sociable nature, who became on such intimate terms with it that he spoke of it familiarly as 'Blank'; observing, at breakfast, 'Blank looks pretty tall this morning'; or considerably doubting in the courtyard in the evening, whether there warn't some go-ahead naters in our country, sir, that would make out the top of Blank in a couple of hours from first start – now!

Once I passed a fortnight at an inn in the North of England, where I was haunted by the ghost of a tremendous pie. It was a Yorkshire pie, like a fort – an abandoned fort with nothing in it; but the waiter had a fixed idea that it was a point of ceremony at every meal to put the pie on the table. After some days I tried to hint, in several delicate ways, that I considered the pie done with; as, for example, by emptying fag-ends of glasses of wine into it; putting cheese-plates and spoons into it, as into a basket; putting wine-bottles into it, as into a cooler; but always in vain, the pie being invariably cleaned out again and brought up as before. At last, beginning to be doubtful whether I was not the victim of a spectral illusion, and whether my health and spirits might not sink under the horrors of an imaginary pie, I cut a triangle out of it, fully as large as the musical instrument of that name in a powerful orchestra. Human provision could not have foreseen the result – but the waiter mended the pie. With some effectual species of cement, he adroitly fitted the triangle in again, and I paid my reckoning and fled.

The Holly Tree was getting rather dismal. I made an overland expedition beyond the screen, and penetrated as far as the fourth window. Here I was driven back by stress of weather. Arrived at my winter-quarters once more, I made up the fire, and took another inn.

It was in the remotest part of Cornwall. A great annual miners' feast was being holden at the inn, when I and my travelling companions presented ourselves at night among the wild crowd that were dancing before it by torchlight. We had had a breakdown in the dark, on a stony morass some miles away; and I had the honour of leading one of the unharnessed post-horses. If any lady or gentleman, on perusal of the present lines, will take any very tall post-horse with his traces hanging about his legs, and will conduct him by the bearing-rein into the heart of a country dance of a hundred and fifty couples, that lady or gentleman will then, and only then, form an adequate idea of the extent to which that post-horse will tread on his conductor's toes. Over and above which, the post-horse, finding three hundred people whirling about him, will probably rear, and also lash out with his hind legs, in a manner incompatible with dignity or self-respect on his conductor's part. With such little drawbacks on my usually impressive aspect, I appeared at this Cornish inn, to the unutterable wonder of the Cornish miners. It was full, and twenty times full, and nobody could be received but the post-horse – though to get rid of that noble animal was something. While my fellow-travellers and I were discussing how to pass the night and so much of the next day as must intervene before the jovial blacksmith and the jovial wheelwright would be in a condition to go out on the morass and mend the coach, an honest man stepped forth from the crowd and proposed his unlet floor of two rooms, with supper of eggs and bacon, ale and punch. We joyfully accompanied him home to the strangest of clean houses, where we were well entertained to the satisfaction of all parties. But the novel feature of the entertainment was, that our host was a chair-maker, and that the chairs assigned to us were mere frames, altogether without bottoms of any sort; so that we passed the evening on perches. Nor was this the absurdest consequence; for when we unbent at supper, and anyone of us gave way to laughter, he forgot the peculiarity of his position, and instantly disappeared. I myself, doubled up into an attitude from which self-extrication was impossible, was taken out of my frame, like a clown in a comic pantomime who has tumbled into a tub, five times by the taper's light during the eggs and bacon.

The Holly Tree was fast reviving within me a sense of loneliness. I began to feel conscious that my subject would never carry on until I was dug out. I might be a week here – weeks!

There was a story with a singular idea in it, connected with an inn I once passed a night at in a picturesque old town on the Welsh border. In a large double-bedded room of this inn there had been a suicide committed by poison, in one bed, while a tired traveller slept unconscious in the other. After that time, the suicide bed was never used, but the other constantly was; the disused bedstead remaining in the room empty, though as to all other respects in its old state. The story ran, that whosoever slept in this room, though never so entire a stranger, from never so far off, was invariably observed to come down in the morning with an impression that he smelt laudanum, and that his mind always turned upon the subject of suicide; to which, whatever kind of man he might be, he was certain to make some reference if he conversed with anyone. This went on for years, until it at length induced the landlord to take the disused bedstead down, and bodily burn it – bed, hangings, and all. The strange influence (this was the story) now changed to a fainter one, but never changed afterwards. The occupant of that room, with occasional but very rare exceptions, would come down in the morning, trying to recall a forgotten dream he had had in the night. The landlord, on his mentioning his perplexity, would suggest various commonplace subjects, not one of which, as he very well knew, was the true subject. But the moment the landlord suggested 'poison', the traveller started, and cried, 'Yes!' He never failed to accept that suggestion, and he never recalled any more of the dream.

This reminiscence brought the Welsh inns in general before me; with the women in their round hats, and the harpers with their white beards (venerable, but humbugs, I am afraid), playing outside the door while I took my dinner. The transition was natural to the Highland inns, with the oatmeal bannocks, the honey, the venison steaks, the trout from the loch, the whisky, and perhaps (having the materials so temptingly at hand) the Athol brose. Once was I coming south from the Scottish Highlands in hot haste, hoping to change quickly at the station at the bottom of a certain wild historical glen, when these eyes did with mortification see the landlord come out with a telescope and sweep the whole prospect for the horses; which horses were away picking up their own living, and did not heave in sight under four hours. Having thought of the loch-trout, I was taken by quick association to the anglers' inns of England (I have assisted at innumerable feats of angling by lying in the bottom of the boat, whole summer days, doing nothing with the greatest perseverance; which I have generally found to be as effectual towards the taking of fish as the finest tackle and the utmost science), and to the pleasant white, clean, flower-pot-decorated bedrooms of those inns, overlooking the river, and the ferry, and the green island, and the church-spire, and the country bridge; and to the peerless Emma with the bright eyes and the pretty smile, who waited, bless her! with a natural grace that would have converted Blue-Beard. Casting my eyes upon my Holly Tree fire, I next discerned among the glowing coals the pictures of a score or more of those wonderful English posting-inns which we are all so sorry to have lost, which were so large and so comfortable, and which were such monuments of British submission to rapacity and extortion. He who would see these houses pining away, let him walk from Basingstoke, or even Windsor, to London, by way of Hounslow, and moralise on their perishing remains; the stables crumbling to dust; unsettled labourers and wanderers bivouacking in the outhouses; grass growing in the yards; the rooms, where erst so many hundred beds of down were made up, let off to Irish lodgers at eighteenpence a week; a little ill-looking beer-shop shrinking in the tap of former days, burning coach-house gates for firewood, having one of its two windows bunged up, as if it had received punishment in a fight with the railroad; a low, bandy-legged, brick-making bulldog standing in the doorway. What could I next see in my fire so naturally as the new railway-house of these times near the dismal country station; with nothing particular on draught but cold air and damp, nothing worth mentioning in the larder but new mortar, and no business doing beyond a conceited affectation of luggage in the hall? Then I came to the inns of Paris, with the pretty apartment of four pieces up one hundred and seventy-five waxed stairs, the privilege of ringing the bell all day long without influencing anybody's mind or body but your own, and the not-too-much-for-dinner, considering the price. Next to the provincial inns of France, with the great church-tower rising above the courtyard, the horse-bells jingling merrily up and down the street beyond, and the clocks of all descriptions in all the rooms, which are never right, unless taken at the precise minute when, by getting exactly twelve hours too fast or too slow, they unintentionally become so. Away I went, next, to the lesser roadside inns of Italy; where all the dirty clothes in the house (not in wear) are always lying in your anteroom; where the mosquitoes make a raisin pudding of your face in summer, and the cold bites it blue in winter; where you get what you can, and forget what you can't: where I should again like to be boiling my tea in a pocket-handkerchief dumpling, for want of a teapot. So to the old palace inns and old monastery inns, in towns and cities of the same bright country;

with their massive quadrangular staircases, whence you may look from among clustering pillars high into the blue vault of heaven; with their stately banqueting-rooms, and vast refectories; with their labyrinths of ghostly bedchambers, and their glimpses into gorgeous streets that have no appearance of reality or possibility. So to the close little inns of the malaria districts, with their pale attendants, and their peculiar smell of never letting in the air. So to the immense fantastic inns of Venice, with the cry of the gondolier below, as he skims the corner; the grip of the watery odours on one particular little bit of the bridge of your nose (which is never released while you stay there); and the great bell of St Mark's Cathedral tolling midnight. Next I put up for a minute at the restless inns upon the Rhine, where your going to bed, no matter at what hour, appears to be the tocsin for everybody else's getting up; and where, in the *table-d'hôte* room at the end of the long table (with several Towers of Babel on it at the other end, all made of white plates), one knot of stoutish men, entirely dressed in jewels and dirt, and having nothing else upon them, *will* remain all night, clinking glasses, and singing about the river that flows, and the grape that grows, and Rhine wine that beguiles, and Rhine woman that smiles and hi drink drink my friend and ho drink drink my brother, and all the rest of it. I departed thence, as a matter of course, to other German inns, where all the eatables are soddened down to the same flavour, and where the mind is disturbed by the apparition of hot puddings, and boiled cherries, sweet and slab, at awfully unexpected periods of the repast. After a draught of sparkling beer from a foaming glass jug, and a glance of recognition through the windows of the student beer-houses at Heidelberg and elsewhere, I put out to sea for the inns of America, with their four hundred beds apiece, and their eight or nine hundred ladies and gentlemen at dinner every day. Again I stood in the bar-rooms thereof, taking my evening cobbler, julep, sling, or cocktail. Again I listened to my friend the General – whom I had known for five minutes, in the course of which period he had made me intimate for life with two Majors, who again had made me intimate for life with three Colonels, who again had made me brother to twenty-two civilians – again, I say, I listened to my friend the General, leisurely expounding the resources of the establishment, as to gentlemen's morning-room, sir; ladies' morning-room, sir; gentlemen's evening-room, sir; ladies' evening-room, sir; ladies' and gentlemen's evening reuniting-room, sir; music-room, sir; reading-room, sir; over four hundred sleeping-rooms, sir; and the entire planned and finited within twelve calendar months from the first clearing off of the old encumbrances on the plot, at a cost of five hundred thousand dollars, sir. Again I found, as to my individual way of thinking, that the greater, the more gorgeous, and the more dollarous the establishment was, the less desirable it was. Nevertheless, again I drank my cobbler, julep, sling, or cocktail, in all goodwill, to my friend the General, and my friends the Majors, Colonels, and civilians all; full well knowing that, whatever little motes my beamy eyes may have descried in theirs, they belong to a kind, generous, large-hearted, and great people.

I had been going on lately at a quick pace to keep my solitude out of my mind; but here I broke down for good, and gave up the subject. What was I to do? What was to become of me? Into what extremity was I submissively to sink? Supposing that, like Baron Trenck, I looked out for a mouse or spider, and found one, and beguiled my imprisonment by training it? Even that might be dangerous with a view to the future. I might be so far gone when the road did come to be cut through the snow, that, on my way forth, I might burst into tears, and beseech, like the prisoner who was released in his old age from the Bastille, to be taken back again to the five windows, the ten curtains, and the sinuous drapery.

A desperate idea came into my head. Under any other circumstances I should have rejected it; but, in the strait at which I was, I held it fast. Could I so far overcome the inherent bashfulness which withheld me from the landlord's table and the company I might find there, as to call up the Boots, and ask him to take a chair – and something in a liquid form – and talk to me? I could, I would, I did.

The Boots

Where had he been in his time? he repeated, when I asked him the question. Lord, he had been everywhere! And what had he been? Bless you, he had been everything you could mention a'most!

Seen a good deal? Why, of course he had. I should say so, he could assure me, if I only knew about a twentieth part of what had come in his way. Why, it would be easier for him, he expected, to tell what he hadn't seen than what he had. Ah! A deal, it would.

What was the curiousest thing he had seen? Well! He didn't know. He couldn't momently name what was the curiousest thing he had seen – unless it was a unicorn, and he see *him* once at a fair. But supposing a young gentleman not eight year old was to run away with a fine young woman of seven, might I think *that* a queer start? Certainly. Then that was a start as he himself had had his blessed eyes on, and he had cleaned the shoes they run away in – and they was so little that he couldn't get his hand into 'em.

Master Harry Walmers's father, you see, he lived at the Elmses, down away by Shooter's Hill there, six or seven miles from Lunnon. He was a gentleman of spirit, and good-looking, and held his head up when he walked, and had what you may call fire about him. He wrote poetry, and he rode, and he ran, and he cricketed, and he danced, and he acted, and he done it all equally beautiful. He was uncommon proud of Master Harry as was his only child; but he didn't spoil him neither. He was a gentleman that had a will of his own and a eye of his own, and that would be minded. Consequently, though he made quite a companion of the fine bright boy, and was delighted to see him so fond of reading his fairy books, and was never tired of hearing him say my name is Norval, or hearing him sing his songs about 'Young May Moons is beaming love', and 'When he as adores thee has left but the name, and that'; still he kept the command over the child, and the child *was* a child, and it's to be wished more of 'em was!

How did Boots happen to know all this? Why, through being under-gardener. Of course he couldn't be under-gardener, and be always about, in the summertime, near the windows on the lawn, a mowing, and sweeping, and weeding, and pruning, and this and that, without getting acquainted with the ways of the family. Even supposing Master Harry hadn't come to him one morning early, and said, 'Cobbs, how should you spell Norah, if you was asked?' and then began cutting it in print all over the fence.

He couldn't say he had taken particular notice of children before that; but really it was pretty to see them two mites a going about the place together, deep in love. And the courage of the boy! Bless your soul, he'd have throwed off his little hat, and tucked up his little sleeves, and gone in at a lion, he would, if they had happened to meet one, and she had been frightened of him. One day he stops, along with her, where Boots was hoeing weeds in the gravel, and says, speaking up, 'Cobbs,' he says, 'I like *you*.' 'Do you, sir? I'm proud to hear it.' 'Yes, I do, Cobbs. Why do I like you, do you think, Cobbs?' 'Don't know, Master Harry, I am sure.' 'Because Norah likes you, Cobbs.' 'Indeed, sir? That's very gratifying.' 'Gratifying, Cobbs? It's better than millions of the brightest diamonds to be liked by Norah.' 'Certainly, sir.' 'You're going away, ain't you, Cobbs?' 'Yes, sir.' 'Would you like another situation, Cobbs?' 'Well, sir, I shouldn't object, if it was a good inn.' 'Then, Cobbs,' says he, 'you shall be our head gardener when we are married.' And he tucks her, in her little sky-blue mantle, under his arm, and walks away.

Boots could assure me that it was better than a picter, and equal to a play, to see them babies, with their long, bright, curling hair, their sparkling eyes, and their beautiful light tread, a rambling about the garden, deep in love. Boots was of opinion that the birds believed they was birds, and kept up with 'em, singing to please 'em. Sometimes they would creep under the tulip tree, and would sit there with their arms round one another's necks, and their soft cheeks touching, a reading about the Prince and the Dragon, and the good and bad enchanters, and the king's fair daughter. Sometimes he would hear them planning about having a house in a forest, keeping bees and a cow, and living entirely on milk and honey. Once he came upon them by the pond, and heard Master Harry say, 'Adorable Norah, kiss me, and say you love me to distraction, or I'll jump in head-foremost.' And Boots made no question he would have done it if she hadn't complied. On the whole, Boots said it had a tendency to make him feel as if he was in love himself – only he didn't exactly know who with.

'Cobbs,' said Master Harry, one evening, when Cobbs was watering the flowers, 'I am going on a visit, this present midsummer, to my grandmamma's at York.'

'Are you indeed, sir? I hope you'll have a pleasant time. I am going into Yorkshire, myself, when I leave here.'

'Are you going to your grandmamma's, Cobbs?'

'No, sir. I haven't got such a thing.'

'Not as a grandmamma, Cobbs?'

'No, sir.'

The boy looked on at the watering of the flowers for a little while, and then said, 'I shall be very glad indeed to go, Cobbs – Norah's going.'

'You'll be all right then, sir,' says Cobbs, 'with your beautiful sweetheart by your side.'

'Cobbs,' returned the boy, flushing, 'I never let anybody joke about it, when I can prevent them.'

'It wasn't a joke, sir,' says Cobbs, with humility – 'wasn't so meant.'

'I am glad of that, Cobbs, because I like you, you know, and you're going to live with us. – Cobbs!'

'Sir.'

'What do you think my grandmamma gives me when I go down there?'

'I couldn't so much as make a guess, sir.'

'A Bank of England five-pound note, Cobbs.'

'Whew!' says Cobbs, 'that's a spanking sum of money, Master Harry.'

'A person could do a good deal with such a sum of money as that – couldn't a person, Cobbs?'

'I believe you, sir!'

'Cobbs,' said the boy, 'I'll tell you a secret. At Norah's house, they have been joking her about me, and pretending to laugh at our being engaged – pretending to make game of it, Cobbs!'

'Such, sir,' says Cobbs, 'is the depravity of human nature.'

The boy, looking exactly like his father, stood for a few minutes with his glowing face towards the sunset, and then departed with, 'Goodnight, Cobbs. I'm going in.'

If I was to ask Boots how it happened that he was a-going to leave that place just at that present time, well, he couldn't rightly answer me. He did suppose he might have stayed there till now if he had been any ways inclined. But, you see, he was younger then, and he wanted change. That's what he wanted – change. Mr Walmers, he said to him when he gave him notice of his intentions to leave, 'Cobbs,' he says, 'have you anythink to complain of? I make the enquiry because if I find that any of my people really has anythink to complain of, I wish to make it right if I can.' 'No, sir,' says Cobbs; 'thanking you, sir, I find myself as well sitiwated here as I could hope to be anywheres. The truth is, sir, that I'm a-going to seek my fortun'.' 'O, indeed, Cobbs!' he says; 'I hope you may find it.' And Boots could assure me – which he did, touching his hair with his bootjack, as a salute in the way of his present calling – that he hadn't found it yet.

Well, sir! Boots left the Elmses when his time was up, and Master Harry, he went down to the old lady's at York, which old lady would have given that child the teeth out of her head (if she had had any), she was so wrapped up in him. What does that infant do – for infant you may call him and be within the mark – but cut away from that old lady's with his Norah, on a expedition to go to Gretna Green and be married!

Sir, Boots was at this identical Holly Tree inn (having left it several times since to better himself, but always come back through one thing or another), when, one summer afternoon, the coach drives up, and out of the coach gets them two children. The guard says to our governor, 'I don't quite make out these little passengers, but the young gentleman's words was, that they was to be brought here.' The young gentleman gets out; hands his lady out; gives the guard something for himself; says to our governor, 'We're to stop here tonight, please. Sitting-room and two bedrooms will be required. Chops and cherry-pudding for two!' and tucks her, in her sky-blue mantle, under his arm, and walks into the house much bolder than brass.

Boots leaves me to judge what the amazement of that establishment was, when these two tiny creatures all alone by themselves was marched into the Angel – much more so, when he, who had seen them without their seeing him, give the governor his views of the expedition they was upon. 'Cobbs,' says the governor, 'if this is so, I must set off myself to York, and quiet their friends' minds. In which case you must keep your eye upon 'em, and humour 'em, till I come back. But before I take these measures, Cobbs, I should wish you to find from themselves whether your opinion is correct.' 'Sir, to you,' says Cobbs, 'that shall be done directly.'

So Boots goes upstairs to the Angel, and there he finds Master Harry on a enormous sofa – immense at any time, but looking like the Great Bed of Ware, compared with him – a drying the eyes of Miss Norah with his pocket-hankecher. Their little legs was entirely off the ground, of course, and it really is not possible for Boots to express to me how small them children looked.

'It's Cobbs! It's Cobbs!' cries Master Harry, and comes running to him, and catching hold of his hand. Miss Norah comes running to him on t'other side and catching hold of his t'other hand, and they both jump for joy.

'I see you a getting out, sir,' says Cobbs. 'I thought it was you. I thought I couldn't be mistaken in your height and figure. What's the object of your journey, sir? – Matrimonial?'

'We are going to be married, Cobbs, at Gretna Green,' returned the boy. 'We have run away on purpose. Norah has been in rather low spirits, Cobbs; but she'll be happy, now we have found you to be our friend.'

'Thank you, sir, and thank you, miss,' says Cobbs, 'for your good opinion. *Did* you bring any luggage with you, sir?'

If I will believe Boots when he gives me his word and honour upon it, the lady had got a parasol, a smelling-bottle, a round and a half of cold buttered toast, eight peppermint drops, and a hairbrush – seemingly a doll's. The gentleman had got about half a dozen yards of string, a knife, three or four sheets of writing-paper folded up surprising small, a orange, and a Chaney mug with his name upon it.

'What may be the exact natur of your plans, sir?' says Cobbs.

'To go on,' replied the boy – which the courage of that boy was something wonderful! – 'in the morning, and be married tomorrow.'

'Just so, sir,' says Cobbs. 'Would it meet your views, sir, if I was to accompany you?'

When Cobbs said this, they both jumped for joy again, and cried out, 'Oh, yes, yes, Cobbs! Yes!'

'Well, sir,' says Cobbs. 'If you will excuse my having the freedom to give an opinion, what I should recommend would be this. I'm acquainted with a pony, sir, which, put in a pheayton that I could borrow, would take you and Mrs Harry Walmers, Junior (myself driving, if you approved), to the end of your journey in a very short space of time. I am not altogether sure, sir, that this pony will be at liberty tomorrow, but even if you had to wait over tomorrow for him, it might be worth your while. As to the small account here, sir, in case you was to find yourself running at all short, that don't signify; because I'm a part proprietor of this inn, and it could stand over.'

Boots assures me that when they clapped their hands, and jumped for joy again, and called him 'Good Cobbs!' and 'Dear Cobbs!' and bent across him to kiss one another in the delight of their confiding hearts, he felt himself the meanest rascal for deceiving 'em that ever was born.

'Is there anything you want just at present, sir?' says Cobbs, mortally ashamed of himself.

'We should like some cakes after dinner,' answered Master Harry, folding his arms, putting out one leg, and looking straight at him, 'and two apples – and jam. With dinner we should like to have toast-and-water. But Norah has always been accustomed to half a glass of currant wine at dessert. And so have I.'

'It shall be ordered at the bar, sir,' says Cobbs; and away he went.

Boots has the feeling as fresh upon him at this minute of speaking as he had then, that he would far rather have had it out in half-a-dozen rounds with the governor than have combined with him; and that he wished with all his heart there was any impossible place where those two babies could make an impossible marriage, and live impossibly happy ever afterwards. However, as it couldn't be, he went into the governor's plans, and the governor set off for York in half an hour.

The way in which the women of that house – without exception – every one of 'em – married *and* single – took to that boy when they heard the story, Boots considers surprising. It was as much as he could do to keep 'em from dashing into the room and kissing him. They climbed up all sorts of places, at the risk of their lives, to look at him through a pane of glass. They was seven deep at the keyhole. They was out of their minds about him and his bold spirit.

In the evening, Boots went into the room to see how the runaway couple was getting on. The gentleman was on the window-seat, supporting the lady in his arms. She had tears upon her face, and was lying, very tired and half asleep, with her head upon his shoulder.

'Mrs Harry Walmers, Junior, fatigued, sir?' says Cobbs.

'Yes, she is tired, Cobbs; but she is not used to be away from home, and she has been in low spirits again. Cobbs, do you think you could bring a biffin, please?'

'I ask your pardon, sir,' says Cobbs. 'What was it you – ?'

'I think a Norfolk biffin would rouse her, Cobbs. She is very fond of them.'

Boots withdrew in search of the required restorative, and when he brought it in, the gentleman handed it to the lady, and fed her with a spoon, and took a little himself; the lady being heavy with sleep, and rather cross. 'What should you think, sir,' says Cobbs, 'of a chamber candlestick?' The gentleman approved; the chambermaid went first, up the great staircase; the lady, in her sky-blue mantle, followed, gallantly escorted by the gentleman; the gentleman embraced her at her door, and retired to his own apartment, where Boots softly locked him up.

Boots couldn't but feel with increased acuteness what a base deceiver he was, when they consulted him at breakfast (they had ordered sweet milk-and-water, and toast and currant jelly, overnight) about the pony. It really was as much as he could do, he don't mind confessing to me, to look them two young things in the face, and think what a wicked old father of lies he had grown up to be. Howsomever, he went on a lying like a Trojan about the pony. He told 'em that it did so unfortunately happen that the pony was half clipped, you see, and that he couldn't be taken out in that state, for fear it should strike to his inside. But that he'd be finished clipping in the course of the day, and that tomorrow morning at eight o'clock the pheayton would be ready. Boots's view of the whole case, looking back on it in my room, is, that Mrs Harry Walmers, Junior, was beginning to give in. She hadn't had her hair curled when she went to bed, and she didn't seem quite up to brushing it herself, and its getting in her eyes put her out. But nothing put out Master Harry. He sat behind his breakfast-cup, a tearing away at the jelly, as if he had been his own father.

After breakfast, Boots is inclined to consider that they drawed soldiers – at least, he knows that many such was found in the fireplace, all on horseback. In the course of the morning, Master Harry rang the bell – it was surprising how that there boy did carry on – and said, in a sprightly way, 'Cobbs, is there any good walks in this neighbourhood?'

'Yes, sir,' says Cobbs. 'There's Love Lane.'

'Get out with you, Cobbs!' – that was that there boy's expression – 'you're joking.'

'Begging your pardon, sir,' says Cobbs, 'there really is Love Lane. And a pleasant walk it is, and proud shall I be to show it to yourself and Mrs Harry Walmers, Junior.'

'Norah, dear,' said Master Harry, 'this is curious. We really ought to see Love Lane. Put on your bonnet, my sweetest darling, and we will go there with Cobbs.'

Boots leaves me to judge what a beast he felt himself to be, when that young pair told him, as they all three jogged along together, that they had made up their minds to give him two thousand guineas a year as head-gardener, on accounts of his being so true a friend to 'em. Boots could have wished at the moment that the earth would have opened and swallowed him up, he felt so mean, with their beaming eyes a looking at him, and believing him. Well, sir, he turned the conversation as well as he could, and he took 'em down Love Lane to the water-meadows, and there Master Harry would have drowned himself in half a moment more, a getting out a water-lily for her – but nothing daunted that boy. Well, sir, they was tired out. All being so new and strange to 'em, they was tired as tired could be. And they laid down on a bank of daisies, like the children in the wood, leastways meadows, and fell asleep.

Boots don't know – perhaps I do – but never mind, it don't signify either way – why it made a man fit to make a fool of himself to see them two pretty babies a lying there in the clear still sunny day, not dreaming half so hard when they was asleep as they done when they was awake. But, Lord! when you come to think of yourself, you know, and what a game you have been up to ever since you was in your own cradle, and what a poor sort of a chap you are, and how it's always either Yesterday with you, or else Tomorrow, and never Today, that's where it is!

Well, sir, they woke up at last, and then one thing was getting pretty clear to Boots, namely, that Mrs Harry Walmers, Junior's, temper was on the move. When Master Harry took her round the waist, she said he 'teased her so'; and when he says, 'Norah, my young May Moon, your Harry tease you?' she tells him, 'Yes; and I want to go home!'

A biled fowl, and baked bread-and-butter pudding, brought Mrs Walmers up a little; but Boots could have wished, he must privately own to me, to have seen her more sensible of the woice of love, and less abandoning of herself to currants. However, Master Harry, he kept up, and his noble heart was as fond as ever. Mrs Walmers turned very sleepy about dusk, and began to cry. Therefore, Mrs Walmers went off to bed as per yesterday; and Master Harry ditto repeated.

About eleven or twelve at night comes back the governor in a chaise, along with Mr Walmers and a elderly lady. Mr Walmers looks amused and very serious, both at once, and says to our missis, 'We are much indebted to you, ma'am, for your kind care of our little children, which we can never sufficiently acknowledge. Pray, ma'am, where is my boy?' Our missis says, 'Cobbs has the dear child in charge, sir. Cobbs, show Forty!' Then he says to Cobbs, 'Ah, Cobbs, I am glad to see *you*! I understood you was here!' And Cobbs says, 'Yes, sir. Your most obedient, sir.'

I may be surprised to hear Boots say it, perhaps; but Boots assures me that his heart beat like a hammer, going upstairs. 'I beg your pardon, sir,' says he, while unlocking the door; 'I hope you are not angry with Master Harry. For Master Harry is a fine boy, sir, and will do you credit and honour.' And Boots signifies to me, that, if the fine boy's father had contradicted him in the daring state of mind in which he then was, he thinks he should have 'fetched him a crack', and taken the consequences.

But Mr Walmers only says, 'No, Cobbs. No, my good fellow. Thank you!' And, the door being opened, goes in.

Boots goes in too, holding the light, and he sees Mr Walmers go up to the bedside, bend gently down, and kiss the little sleeping face. Then he stands looking at it for a minute, looking wonderfully like it (they do say he ran away with Mrs Walmers); and then he gently shakes the little shoulder.

'Harry, my dear boy! Harry!'

Master Harry starts up and looks at him. Looks at Cobbs too. Such is the honour of that mite, that he looks at Cobbs, to see whether he has brought him into trouble.

'I am not angry, my child. I only want you to dress yourself and come home.'

'Yes, pa.'

Master Harry dresses himself quickly. His breast begins to swell when he has nearly finished, and it swells more and more as he stands, at last, a looking at his father: his father standing a looking at him, the quiet image of him.

'Please may I' – the spirit of that little creatur, and the way he kept his rising tears down! – 'please, dear pa – may I – kiss Norah before I go?'

'You may, my child.'

So he takes Master Harry in his hand, and Boots leads the way with the candle, and they come to that other bedroom, where the elderly lady is seated by the bed, and poor little Mrs Harry Walmers, Junior, is fast asleep. There the father lifts the child up to the pillow, and he lays his little face down for an instant by the little warm face of poor unconscious little Mrs Harry Walmers, Junior, and gently draws it to him – a sight so touching to the chambermaids who are peeping through the door, that one of them calls out, 'It's a shame to part 'em!' But this chambermaid was always, as Boots informs me, a soft-hearted one. Not that there was any harm in that girl. Far from it.

Finally, Boots says, that's all about it. Mr Walmers drove away in the chaise, having hold of Master Harry's hand. The elderly lady and Mrs Harry Walmers, Junior, that was never to be (she married a Captain long afterwards, and died in India), went off next day. In conclusion, Boots put it to me whether I hold with him in two opinions: firstly, that there are not many couples on their way to be married who are half as innocent of guile as those two children; secondly, that it would be a jolly good thing for a great many couples on their way to be married, if they could only be stopped in time, and brought back separately.

THIRD BRANCH

The Bill

I had been snowed up a whole week. The time had hung so lightly on my hands, that I should have been in great doubt of the fact but for a piece of documentary evidence that lay upon my table.

The road had been dug out of the snow on the previous day, and the document in question was my bill. It testified emphatically to my having eaten and drunk, and warmed myself, and slept among the sheltering branches of the Holly Tree, seven days and nights.

I had yesterday allowed the road twenty-four hours to improve itself, finding that I required that additional margin of time for the completion of my task. I had ordered my bill to be upon the table, and a chaise to be at the door, 'at eight o'clock tomorrow evening'. It was eight o'clock tomorrow evening when I buckled up my travelling writing-desk in its leather case, paid my bill, and got on my warm coats and wrappers. Of course, no time now remained for my travelling on to add a frozen tear to the icicles which were doubtless hanging plentifully about the farmhouse where I had first seen Angela. What I had to do was to get across to Liverpool by the shortest open road, there to meet my heavy baggage and embark. It was quite enough to do, and I had not an hour too much time to do it in.

I had taken leave of all my Holly Tree friends – almost, for the time being, of my bashfulness too – and was standing for half a minute at the inn door watching the ostler as he took another turn at the cord which tied my portmanteau on the chaise, when I saw lamps coming down towards the Holly Tree. The road was so padded with snow that no wheels were audible; but all of us who were standing at the inn door saw lamps coming on, and at a lively rate too, between the walls of snow that had been heaped up on either side of the track. The chambermaid instantly divined how the case stood, and called to the ostler, 'Tom, this is a Gretna job!' The ostler, knowing that her sex instinctively scented a marriage, or anything in that direction, rushed up the yard bawling, 'Next four out!' and in a moment the whole establishment was thrown into commotion.

I had a melancholy interest in seeing the happy man who loved and was beloved; and therefore, instead of driving off at once, I remained at the inn door when the fugitives drove up. A bright-eyed fellow, muffled in a mantle, jumped out so briskly that he almost overthrew me. He turned to apologise, and, by heaven, it was Edwin!

'Charley!' said he, recoiling. 'Gracious powers, what do you do here?'

'Edwin,' said I, recoiling, 'gracious powers, what do *you* do here?' I struck my forehead as I said it, and an insupportable blaze of light seemed to shoot before my eyes.

He hurried me into the little parlour (always kept with a slow fire in it and no poker), where posting company waited while their horses were putting to, and, shutting the door, said: 'Charley, forgive me!'

'Edwin!' I returned. 'Was this well? When I loved her so dearly! When I had garnered up my heart so long!' I could say no more.

He was shocked when he saw how moved I was, and made the cruel observation, that he had not thought I should have taken it so much to heart.

I looked at him. I reproached him no more. But I looked at him. 'My dear, dear Charley,' said he, 'don't think ill of me, I beseech you! I know you have a right to my utmost confidence, and, believe me, you have ever had it until now. I abhor secrecy. Its meanness is intolerable to me. But I and my dear girl have observed it for your sake.'

He and his dear girl! It steeled me.

'You have observed it for my sake, sir?' said I, wondering how his frank face could face it out so.

'Yes! – and Angela's,' said he.

I found the room reeling round in an uncertain way, like a labouring humming-top. 'Explain yourself,' said I, holding on by one hand to an armchair.

'Dear old darling Charley!' returned Edwin, in his cordial manner, 'consider! When you were going on so happily with Angela, why should I compromise you with the old gentleman by making you a party to our engagement, and (after he had declined my proposals) to our secret intention? Surely it was better that you should be able honourably to say, "He never took counsel with me, never told me, never breathed a word of it." If Angela suspected it, and showed me all the favour and support she could – God bless her for a precious creature and a priceless wife! – I couldn't help that. Neither I nor Emmeline ever told her, any more than we told you. And for the same good reason, Charley; trust me, for the same good reason, and no other upon earth!'

Emmeline was Angela's cousin. Lived with her. Had been brought up with her. Was her father's ward. Had property.

'Emmeline is in the chaise, my dear Edwin!' said I, embracing him with the greatest affection.

'My good fellow!' said he, 'do you suppose I should be going to Gretna Green without her?'

I ran out with Edwin, I opened the chaise door, I took Emmeline in my arms, I folded her to my heart. She was wrapped in soft white fur, like the snowy landscape: but was warm, and young, and lovely. I put their leaders to with my own hands, I gave the boys a five-pound note apiece, I cheered them as they drove away, I drove the other way myself as hard as I could pelt.

I never went to Liverpool, I never went to America, I went straight back to London, and I married Angela. I have never until this time, even to her, disclosed the secret of my character, and the mistrust and the mistaken journey into which it led me. When she, and they, and our eight children and their seven – I mean Edwin and Emmeline's, whose oldest girl is old enough now to wear white for herself, and to look very like her mother in it – come to read these pages, as of course they will, I shall hardly fail to be found out at last. Never mind! I can bear it. I began at the Holly Tree, by idle accident, to associate the Christmas time of year with human interest, and with some enquiry into, and some care for, the lives of those by whom I find myself surrounded. I hope that I am none the worse for it, and that no one near me or afar off is the worse for it. And I say, May the green Holly Tree flourish, striking its roots deep into our English ground, and having its germinating qualities carried by the birds of Heaven all over the world!

A HOUSE TO LET

Over the Way

I had been living at Tunbridge Wells and nowhere else, going on for ten years, when my medical man – very clever in his profession, and the prettiest player I ever saw in my life of a hand at long whist, which was a noble and a princely game before short was heard of – said to me, one day, as he sat feeling my pulse on the actual sofa which my poor dear sister Jane worked before her spine came on, and laid her on a board for fifteen months at a stretch – the most upright woman that ever lived – said to me, 'What we want, ma'am, is a fillip.'

'Good gracious, goodness gracious, Dr Towers!' says I, quite startled at the man, for he was so christened himself: 'don't talk as if you were alluding to people's names; but say what you mean.'

'I mean, my dear ma'am, that we want a little change of air and scene.'

'Bless the man!' said I; 'does he mean we or me!'

'I mean you, ma'am.'

'Then Lard forgive you, Dr Towers,' I said; 'why don't you get into a habit of expressing yourself in a straightforward manner, like a loyal subject of our gracious Queen Victoria, and a member of the Church of England?'

Towers laughed, as he generally does when he has fidgeted me into any of my impatient ways – one of my states, as I call them – and then he began, –

'Tone, ma'am, tone, is all you require!' He appealed to Trottle, who just then came in with the coal-scuttle, looking, in his nice black suit, like an amiable man putting on coals from motives of benevolence.

Trottle (whom I always call my right hand) has been in my service two-and-thirty years. He entered my service, far away from England. He is the best of creatures, and the most respectable of men; but, opinionated.

'What you want, ma'am,' says Trottle, making up the fire in his quiet and skilful way, 'is tone.'

'Lard forgive you both!' says I, bursting out a-laughing; 'I see you are in a conspiracy against me, so I suppose you must do what you like with me, and take me to London for a change.'

For some weeks Towers had hinted at London, and consequently I was prepared for him. When we had got to this point, we got on so expeditiously, that Trottle was packed off to London next day but one, to find some sort of place for me to lay my troublesome old head in.

Trottle came back to me at the Wells after two days' absence, with accounts of a charming place that could be taken for six months certain, with liberty to renew on the same terms for another six, and which really did afford every accommodation that I wanted.

'Could you really find no fault at all in the rooms, Trottle?' I asked him.

'Not a single one, ma'am. They are exactly suitable to you. There is not a fault in them. There is but one fault outside of them.'

'And what's that?'

'They are opposite a house to let.'

'O!' I said, considering of it. 'But is that such a very great objection?'

'I think it my duty to mention it, ma'am. It is a dull object to look at. Otherwise, I was so greatly pleased with the lodging that I should have closed with the terms at once, as I had your authority to do.'

Trottle thinking so highly of the place, in my interest, I wished not to disappoint him. Consequently I said: 'The empty house may let, perhaps.'

'O, dear no, ma'am,' said Trottle, shaking his head with decision; 'it won't let. It never does let, ma'am.'

'Mercy me! Why not?'

'Nobody knows, ma'am. All I have to mention is, ma'am, that the house won't let!'

'How long has this unfortunate house been to let, in the name of fortune?' said I.

'Ever so long,' said Trottle. 'Years.'

'Is it in ruins?'

'It's a good deal out of repair, ma'am, but it's not in ruins.'

The long and the short of this business was, that next day I had a pair of post-horses put to my chariot – for, I never travel by railway: not that I have anything to say against railways, except that they came in when I was too old to take to them; and that they made ducks and drakes of a few turnpike-bonds I had – and so I went up myself, with Trottle in the rumble, to look at the inside of this same lodging, and at the outside of this same house.

As I say, I went and saw for myself. The lodging was perfect. That, I was sure it would be; because Trottle is the best judge of comfort I know.

The empty house was an eyesore; and that I was sure it would be too, for the same reason. However, setting the one thing against the other, the good against the bad, the lodging very soon got the victory over the house. My lawyer, Mr Squares, of Crown Office Row, Temple, drew up an agreement; which his young man jabbered over so dreadfully when he read it to me, that I didn't understand one word of it except my own name; and hardly that, and I signed it, and the other party signed it, and, in three weeks' time, I moved my old bones, bag and baggage, up to London.

For the first month or so, I arranged to leave Trottle at the Wells. I made this arrangement, not only because there was a good deal to take care of in the way of my schoolchildren and pensioners, and also of a new stove in the hall to air the house in my absence, which appeared to me calculated to blow up and burst; but, likewise because I suspect Trottle (though the steadiest of men, and a widower between sixty and seventy) to be what I call rather a Philanderer. I mean, that when any friend comes down to see me and brings a maid, Trottle is always remarkably ready to show that maid the Wells of an evening; and that I have more than once noticed the shadow of his arm, outside the room door nearly opposite my chair, encircling that maid's waist on the landing, like a tablecloth brush.

Therefore, I thought it just as well, before any London Philandering took place, that I should have a little time to look round me, and to see what girls were in and about the place. So, nobody stayed with me in my new lodging at first after Trottle had established me there safe and sound, but Peggy Flobbins, my maid; a most affectionate and attached woman, who never was an object of Philandering since I have known her, and is not likely to begin to become so after nine-and-twenty years next March.

It was the fifth of November when I first breakfasted in my new rooms. The Guys were going about in the brown fog, like magnified monsters of insects in table-beer, and there was a Guy resting on the doorsteps of the house to let. I put on my glasses, partly to see how the boys were pleased with what I sent them out by Peggy, and partly to make sure that she didn't approach too near the ridiculous object, which of course was full of sky-rockets, and might go off into bangs at any moment. In this way it happened that the first time I ever looked at the house to let, after I became its opposite neighbour, I had my glasses on.

And this might not have happened once in fifty times, for my sight is uncommonly good for my time of life; and I wear glasses as little as I can, for fear of spoiling it.

I knew already that it was a ten-roomed house, very dirty, and much dilapidated; that the area-rails were rusty and peeling away, and that two or three of them were wanting, or half-wanting; that there were broken panes of glass in the windows, and blotches of mud on other panes, which the boys had thrown at them; that there was quite a collection of stones in the area, also proceeding from those young mischiefs; that there were games chalked on the pavement before the house, and likenesses of ghosts chalked on the street-door; that the windows were all darkened by rotting old blinds, or shutters, or both; that the bills 'To Let', had curled up, as if the damp air of the place had given them cramps; or had dropped down into corners, as if they were no more. I had seen all this on my first visit, and I had remarked to Trottle, that the lower part of the black board about terms was split away; that the rest had become illegible, and that the very stone of the doorsteps was broken across. Notwithstanding, I sat at my breakfast table on that please-to-remember-the-fifth-of-November morning, staring at the house through my glasses, as if I had never looked at it before.

All at once – in the first-floor window on my right – down in a low corner, at a hole in a blind or a shutter – I found that I was looking at a secret eye. The reflection of my fire may have touched it and made it shine; but, I saw it shine and vanish.

The eye might have seen me, or it might not have seen me, sitting there in the glow of my fire – you can take which probability you prefer, without offence – but something struck through my frame, as if the sparkle of this eye had been electric, and had flashed straight at me. It had such an effect upon me, that I could not remain by myself, and I rang for Flobbins, and invented some little jobs for her, to keep her in the room. After my breakfast was cleared away, I sat in the same place with my glasses on, moving my head, now so, and now so, trying whether, with the shining of my fire and the flaws in the window glass, I could reproduce any sparkle seeming to be up there, that was like the sparkle of an eye. But no; I could make nothing like it. I could make ripples and crooked lines in the front of the house to let, and I could even twist one window up and loop it into another; but, I could make no eye, nor anything like an eye. So I convinced myself that I really had seen an eye.

Well, to be sure I could not get rid of the impression of this eye, and it troubled me and troubled me, until it was almost a torment. I don't think I was previously inclined to concern my head much about the opposite house; but, after this eye, my head was full of the house; and I thought of little else than the house, and I watched the house, and I talked about the house, and I dreamed of the house. In all this, I fully believe now, there was a good Providence. But, you will judge for yourself about that, by and by.

My landlord was a butler, who had married a cook, and set up house-keeping. They had not kept house longer than a couple of years, and they knew no more about the house to let than I did. Neither could I find out anything concerning it among the tradespeople or otherwise; further than what Trottle had told me at first. It had been empty, some said six years, some said eight, some said ten. It never did let, they all agreed, and it never would let.

I soon felt convinced that I should work myself into one of my states about the house; and I soon did. I lived for a whole month in a flurry, that was always getting worse. Towers's prescriptions, which I had brought to London with me, were of no more use than nothing. In the cold winter sunlight, in the thick winter fog, in the black winter rain, in the white winter snow, the house was equally on my mind. I have heard, as everybody else has, of a spirit's haunting a house; but I have had my own personal experience of a house's haunting a spirit; for that house haunted mine.

In all that month's time, I never saw anyone go into the house nor come out of the house. I supposed that such a thing must take place sometimes, in the dead of the night, or the glimmer of the morning; but, I never saw it done. I got no relief from having my curtains drawn when it came on dark, and shutting out the house. The eye then began to shine in my fire.

I am a single old woman. I should say at once, without being at all afraid of the name, I am an old maid; only that I am older than the phrase would express. The time was when I had my love-trouble, but, it is long and long ago. He was killed at sea (dear Heaven rest his blessed head!) when I was twenty-five. I have all my life, since ever I can remember, been deeply fond of children. I have always felt such a love for them, that I have had my sorrowful and sinful times when I have fancied something must have gone wrong in my life – something must have been turned aside from its original intention I mean – or I should have been the proud and happy mother of many children, and a fond old grandmother this day. I have soon known better in the cheerfulness and contentment that God has blessed me with and given me abundant reason for; and yet I have had to dry my eyes even then, when I have thought of my dear, brave, hopeful, handsome, bright-eyed Charley, and the trust meant to cheer me with. Charley was my youngest brother, and he went to India. He married there, and sent his gentle little wife home to me to be confined, and she was to go back to him, and the baby was to be left with me, and I was to bring it up. It never belonged to this life. It took its silent place among the other incidents in my story that might have been, but never were. I had hardly time to whisper to her 'Dead my own!' or she to answer, 'Ashes to ashes, dust to dust! O lay it on my breast and comfort Charley!' when she had gone to seek her baby at Our Saviour's feet. I went to Charley, and I told him there was nothing left but me, poor me; and I lived with Charley, out there, several years. He was a man of fifty, when he fell asleep in my arms. His face had changed to be almost old and a little stern; but, it softened, and softened when I laid it down that I might cry and pray beside it; and, when I looked at it for the last time, it was my dear, untroubled, handsome, youthful Charley of long ago.

I was going on to tell that the loneliness of the house to let brought back all these recollections, and that they had quite pierced my heart one evening, when Flobbins, opening the door, and looking very much as if she wanted to laugh but thought better of it, said: 'Mr Jabez Jarber, ma'am!'

Upon which Mr Jarber ambled in, in his usual absurd way, saying: 'Sophonisba!'

Which I am obliged to confess is my name. A pretty one and proper one enough when it was given to me: but, a good many years out of date now, and always sounding particularly high-flown and comical from his lips. So I said, sharply: 'Though it is Sophonisba, Jarber, you are not obliged to mention it, that *I* see.'

In reply to this observation, the ridiculous man put the tips of my five right-hand fingers to his lips, and said again, with an aggravating accent on the third syllable: 'Sophon*i*sba!'

I don't burn lamps, because I can't abide the smell of oil, and wax candles belonged to my day. I hope the convenient situation of one of my tall old candlesticks on the table at my elbow will be my excuse for saying, that if he did that again, I would chop his toes with it. (I am sorry to add that when I told him so, I knew his toes to be tender.) But, really, at my time of life and at Jarber's, it is too much of a good thing. There is an orchestra still standing in the open air at the Wells, before which, in the presence of a throng of fine company, I have walked a minuet with Jarber. But, there is a house still standing, in which I have worn a pinafore, and had a tooth drawn by fastening a thread to the tooth and the door-handle, and toddling away from the door. And how should I look now, at my years, in a pinafore, or having a door for my dentist?

Besides, Jarber always was more or less an absurd man. He was sweetly dressed, and beautifully perfumed, and many girls of my day would have given their ears for him; though I am bound to add that he never cared a fig for them, or their advances either, and that he was very constant to me. For, he not only proposed to me before my love-happiness ended in sorrow, but afterwards too: not once, nor yet twice: nor will we say how many times. However many they were, or however few they were, the last time he paid me that compliment was immediately after he had presented me with a digestive dinner-pill stuck on the point of a pin. And I said on that occasion, laughing heartily, 'Now, Jarber, if you don't know that two people whose united ages would make about a hundred and fifty, have got to be old, I do; and I beg to swallow this nonsense in the form of this pill' (which I took on the spot), 'and I request to hear no more of it.'

After that, he conducted himself pretty well. He was always a little squeezed man, was Jarber, in little sprigged waistcoats; and he had always little legs and a little smile, and a little voice, and little roundabout ways. As long as I can remember him he was always going little errands for people, and carrying little gossip. At this present time when he called me 'Sophonisba!' he had a little old-fashioned lodging in that new neighbourhood of mine. I had not seen him for two or three years, but I had heard that he still went out with a little perspective-glass and stood on doorsteps in Saint James's Street, to see the nobility go to Court; and went in his little cloak and goloshes outside Willis's rooms to see them go to Almack's; and caught the frightfullest colds, and got himself trodden upon by coachmen and linkmen, until he went home to his landlady a mass of bruises, and had to be nursed for a month.

Jarber took off his little fur-collared cloak, and sat down opposite me, with his little cane and hat in his hand.

'Let us have no more Sophonisbaing, if *you* please, Jarber,' I said. 'Call me Sarah. How do you do? I hope you are pretty well.'

'Thank you. And you?' said Jarber.

'I am as well as an old woman can expect to be.'

Jarber was beginning: 'Say, not old, Sophon – ' but I looked at the candlestick, and he left off; pretending not to have said anything.

'I am infirm, of course,' I said, 'and so are you. Let us both be thankful it's no worse.'

'Is it possible that you look worried?' said Jarber.

'It is very possible. I have no doubt it is the fact.'

'And what has worried my Soph – , soft-hearted friend,' said Jarber.

'Something not easy, I suppose, to comprehend. I am worried to death by a house to let, over the way.'

Jarber went with his little tiptoe step to the window-curtains, peeped out, and looked round at me.

'Yes,' said I, in answer: 'that house.'

After peeping out again, Jarber came back to his chair with a tender air, and asked: 'How does it worry you – , Sarah?'

'It is a mystery to me,' said I. 'Of course every house *is* a mystery, more or less; but, something that I don't care to mention' (for truly the eye was so slight a thing to mention that I was more than half ashamed of it), 'has made that house so mysterious to me, and has so fixed it in my mind, that I have had no peace for a month. I foresee that I shall have no peace, either, until Trottle comes to me, next Monday.'

I might have mentioned before, that there is a long-standing jealousy between Trottle and Jarber; and that there is never any love lost between those two.

'*Trottle*,' petulantly repeated Jarber, with a little flourish of his cane; 'how is *Trottle* to restore the lost peace of Sarah?'

'He will exert himself to find out something about the house. I have fallen into that state about it, that I really must discover by some means or other, good or bad, fair or foul, how and why it is that that house remains to let.'

'And why Trottle? Why not,' putting his little hat to his heart; 'why not, Jarber?'

'To tell you the truth, I have never thought of Jarber in the matter. And now I do think of Jarber, through your having the kindness to suggest him – for which I am really and truly obliged to you – I don't think he could do it.'

'Sarah!'

'I think it would be too much for you, Jarber.'

'Sarah!'

'There would be coming and going, and fetching and carrying, Jarber, and you might catch cold.'

'Sarah! What can be done by Trottle, can be done by me. I am on terms of acquaintance with every person of responsibility in this parish. I am intimate at the Circulating Library. I converse daily with the Assessed Taxes. I lodge with the Water Rate. I know the Medical Man. I lounge habitually at the house agent's. I dine with the churchwardens. I move to the guardians. Trottle! A person in the sphere of a domestic, and totally unknown to society!'

'Don't be warm, Jarber. In mentioning Trottle, I have naturally relied on my right-hand, who would take any trouble to gratify even a whim of his old mistress's. But, if you can find out anything to help to unravel the mystery of this house to let, I shall be fully as much obliged to you as if there was never a Trottle in the land.'

Jarber rose and put on his little cloak. A couple of fierce brass lions held it tight round his little throat; but a couple of the mildest hares might have done that, I am sure. 'Sarah,' he said, 'I go. Expect me on Monday evening, the sixth, when perhaps you will give me a cup of tea; – may I ask for no green? Adieu!'

This was on a Thursday, the second of December. When I reflected that Trottle would come back on Monday, too, I had my misgivings as to the difficulty of keeping the two powers from open warfare, and indeed I was more uneasy than I quite like to confess. However, the empty house swallowed up that thought next morning, as it swallowed up most other thoughts now, and the house quite preyed upon me all that day, and all the Saturday.

It was a very wet Sunday: raining and blowing from morning to night. When the bells rang for afternoon church, they seemed to ring in the commotion of the puddles as well as in the wind, and they sounded very loud and dismal indeed, and the street looked very dismal indeed, and the house looked dismallest of all.

I was reading my prayers near the light, and my fire was growing in the darkening window-glass, when, looking up, as I prayed for the fatherless children and widows and all who were desolate and oppressed – I saw the eye again. It passed in a moment, as it had done before; but, this time, I was inwardly more convinced that I had seen it.

Well to be sure, I *had* a night that night! Whenever I closed my own eyes, it was to see eyes. Next morning, at an unreasonably, and I should have said (but for that railroad) an impossibly early hour, comes Trottle. As soon as he had told me all about the Wells, I told him all about the house. He listened with as great interest and attention as I could possibly wish, until I came to Jabez Jarber, when he cooled in an instant, and became opinionated.

'Now, Trottle,' I said, pretending not to notice, 'when Mr Jarber comes back this evening, we must all lay our heads together.'

'I should hardly think that would be wanted, ma'am; Mr Jarber's head is surely equal to anything.'

Being determined not to notice, I said again, that we must all lay our heads together.

'Whatever you order, ma'am, shall be obeyed. Still, it cannot be doubted, I should think, that Mr Jarber's head is equal, if not superior, to any pressure that can be brought to bear upon it.'

This was provoking; and his way, when he came in and out all through the day, of pretending not to see the house to let, was more provoking still. However, being quite resolved not to notice, I gave no sign whatever that I did notice. But, when evening came, and he showed in Jarber, and, when Jarber wouldn't be helped off with his cloak, and poked his cane into cane chair-backs and china ornaments and his own eye, in trying to unclasp his brazen lions of himself (which he couldn't do, after all), I could have shaken them both.

As it was, I only shook the teapot, and made the tea. Jarber had brought from under his cloak, a roll of paper, with which he had triumphantly pointed over the way, like the Ghost of Hamlet's Father appearing to the late Mr Kemble, and which he had laid on the table.

'A discovery?' said I, pointing to it, when he was seated, and had got his teacup. – 'Don't go, Trottle.'

'The first of a series of discoveries,' answered Jarber. 'Account of a former tenant, compiled from the Water Rate, and Medical Man.'

'Don't go, Trottle,' I repeated. For, I saw him making imperceptibly to the door.

'Begging your pardon, ma'am, I might be in Mr Jarber's way?'

Jarber looked that he decidedly thought he might be. I relieved myself with a good angry croak, and said – always determined not to notice: 'Have the goodness to sit down, if you please, Trottle. I wish you to hear this.'

Trottle bowed in the stiffest manner, and took the remotest chair he could find. Even that, he moved close to the draught from the keyhole of the door.

'Firstly,' Jarber began, after sipping his tea, 'would my Sophon – '

'Begin again, Jarber,' said I.

'Would you be much surprised, if this house to let should turn out to be the property of a relation of your own?'

'I should indeed be very much surprised.'

'Then it belongs to your first cousin (I learn, by the way, that he is ill at this time) George Forley.'

'Then that is a bad beginning. I cannot deny that George Forley stands in the relation of first cousin to me; but I hold no communication with him. George Forley has been a hard, bitter, stony father to a child now dead. George Forley was most implacable and unrelenting to one of his two daughters who made a poor marriage. George Forley brought all the weight of his hand to bear as heavily against that crushed thing, as he brought it to bear lightly, favouringly, and advantageously upon her sister, who made a rich marriage. I hope that, with the measure George Forley meted, it may not be measured out to him again. I will give George Forley no worse wish.'

I was strong upon the subject, and I could not keep the tears out of my eyes; for, that young girl's was a cruel story, and I had dropped many a tear over it before.

'The house being George Forley's,' said I, 'is almost enough to account for there being a Fate upon it, if Fate there is. Is there anything about George Forley in those sheets of paper?'

'Not a word.'

'I am glad to hear it. Please to read on. Trottle, why don't you come nearer? Why do you sit mortifying yourself in those arctic regions? Come nearer.'

'Thank you, ma'am; I am quite near enough to Mr Jarber.'

Jarber rounded his chair, to get his back full to my opinionated friend and servant, and, beginning to read, tossed the words at him over his (Jabez Jarber's) own ear and shoulder.

He read what follows:

The Manchester Marriage

Mr and Mrs Openshaw came from Manchester to London and took the house to let. He had been, what is called in Lancashire, a salesman for a large manufacturing firm, who were extending their business, and opening a warehouse in London; where Mr Openshaw was now to superintend the business. He rather enjoyed the change of residence; having a kind of curiosity about London, which he had never yet been able to gratify in his brief visits to the metropolis. At the same time he had an odd, shrewd, contempt for the inhabitants; whom he had always pictured to himself as fine, lazy people; caring nothing but for fashion and aristocracy, and lounging away their days in Bond Street, and such places; ruining good English, and ready in their turn to despise him as a provincial. The hours that the men of business kept in the city scandalised him too; accustomed as he was to the early dinners of Manchester folk, and the consequently far longer evenings. Still, he was pleased to go to London; though he would not for the world have confessed it, even to himself, and always spoke of the step to his friends as one demanded of him by the interests of his employers, and sweetened to him by a considerable increase of salary. His salary indeed was so liberal that he might have been justified in taking a much larger house than this one, had he not thought himself bound to set an example to Londoners of how little a Manchester man of business cared for show. Inside, however, he furnished the house with an unusual degree of comfort, and, in the winter time, he insisted on keeping up as large fires as the grates would allow, in every room where the temperature was in the least chilly. Moreover, his northern sense of hospitality was such, that, if he were at home, he could hardly suffer a visitor to leave the house without forcing meat and drink upon him. Every servant in the house was well warmed, well fed, and kindly treated; for their master scorned all petty saving in aught that conduced to comfort; while he amused himself by following out all his accustomed habits and individual ways in defiance of what any of his new neighbours might think.

His wife was a pretty, gentle woman, of suitable age and character. He was forty-two, she thirty-five. He was loud and decided; she soft and yielding. They had two children or rather, I should say, she had two; for the elder, a girl of eleven, was Mrs Openshaw's child by Frank Wilson her first husband. The younger was a little boy, Edwin, who could just prattle, and to whom his father delighted to speak in the broadest and most unintelligible Lancashire dialect, in order to keep up what he called the true Saxon accent.

Mrs Openshaw's Christian-name was Alice, and her first husband had been her own cousin. She was the orphan niece of a sea-captain in Liverpool: a quiet, grave little creature, of great personal attraction when she was fifteen or sixteen, with regular features and a blooming complexion. But she was very shy, and believed herself to be very stupid and awkward; and was frequently scolded by her aunt, her own uncle's second wife. So when her cousin, Frank Wilson, came home from a long absence at sea, and first was kind and protective to her; secondly, attentive and thirdly, desperately in love with her, she hardly knew how to be grateful enough to him. It is true she would have preferred his remaining in the first or second stages of behaviour; for his violent love puzzled and frightened her. Her uncle neither helped nor hindered the love affair though it was going on under his own eyes. Frank's stepmother had such a variable temper, that there was no knowing whether what she liked one day she would like the next, or not. At length she went to such extremes of crossness, that Alice was only too glad to shut her eyes and rush blindly at the chance of escape from domestic tyranny offered her by a marriage with her cousin; and, liking him better than anyone in the world except her uncle (who was at this time at sea) she went off one morning and was married to him; her only bridesmaid being the housemaid at her aunt's. The consequence was, that Frank and his wife went into lodgings, and Mrs Wilson refused to see them, and turned away Norah, the warm-hearted housemaid; whom they accordingly took into their service. When Captain Wilson returned from his voyage, he was very cordial with the young couple, and spent many an evening at their lodgings; smoking his pipe, and sipping his grog; but he told them that, for quietness' sake, he could not ask them to his own house; for his wife was bitter against them. They were not very unhappy about this.

The seed of future unhappiness lay rather in Frank's vehement, passionate disposition; which led him to resent his wife's shyness and want of demonstration as failures in conjugal duty. He was already tormenting himself, and her too, in a slighter degree, by apprehensions and imaginations of what might befall her during his approaching absence at sea. At last he went to his father and urged him to insist upon Alice's being once more received under his roof; the more especially as there was now a prospect of her confinement while her husband was away on his voyage. Captain Wilson was, as he himself expressed it, 'breaking up', and unwilling to undergo the excitement of a scene; yet he felt that what his son said was true. So he went to his wife. And before Frank went to sea, he had the comfort of seeing his wife installed in her old little garret in his father's house. To have placed her in the one best spare room was a step beyond Mrs Wilson's powers of submission or generosity. The worst part about it, however, was that the faithful Norah had to be dismissed. Her place as housemaid had been filled up; and, even had it not, she had forfeited Mrs Wilson's good opinion for ever. She comforted her young master and mistress by pleasant prophecies of the time when they would have a household of their own; of which, in whatever service she might be in the meantime, she should be sure to form part. Almost the last action Frank Wilson did, before setting sail, was going with Alice to see Norah once more at her mother's house. And then he went away.

Alice's father-in-law grew more and more feeble as winter advanced. She was of great use to her stepmother in nursing and amusing him; and, although there was anxiety enough in the household, there was perhaps more of peace than there had been for years; for Mrs Wilson had not a bad heart, and was softened by the visible approach of death to one whom she loved, and touched by the lonely condition of the young creature, expecting her first confinement in her husband's absence. To this relenting mood Norah owed the permission to come and nurse Alice when her baby was born, and to remain to attend on Captain Wilson.

Before one letter had been received from Frank (who had sailed for the East Indies and China), his father died. Alice was always glad to remember that he had held her baby in his arms, and kissed and blessed it before his death. After that, and the consequent examination into the state of his affairs, it was found that he had left far less property than people had been led by his style of living to imagine; and, what money there was, was all settled upon his wife, and at her disposal after her death. This did not signify much to Alice, as Frank was now first mate of his ship, and, in another voyage or two, would be captain. Meanwhile he had left her some hundreds (all his savings) in the bank.

It became time for Alice to hear from her husband. One letter from the Cape she had already received. The next was to announce his arrival in India. As week after week passed over, and no intelligence of the ship's arrival reached the office of the owners, and the Captain's wife was in the same state of ignorant suspense as Alice herself, her fears grew most oppressive. At length the day came when, in reply to her enquiry at the Shipping Office, they told her that the owners had given up hope of ever hearing more of the Betsy-Jane, and had sent in their claim upon the underwriters. Now that he was gone for ever, she first felt a yearning, longing love for the kind cousin, the dear friend, the sympathising protector, whom she should never see again – first felt a passionate desire to show him his child, whom she had hitherto rather craved to have all to herself – her own sole possession. Her grief was, however, noiseless, and quiet – rather to the scandal of Mrs Wilson; who bewailed her stepson as if he and she had always lived together in perfect harmony, and who evidently thought it her duty to burst into fresh tears at every strange face she saw; dwelling on his poor young widow's desolate state, and the helplessness of the fatherless child, with an unction, as if she liked the excitement of the sorrowful story.

So passed away the first days of Alice's widowhood. By and by things subsided into their natural and tranquil course. But, as if this young creature was always to be in some heavy trouble, her ewe-lamb began to be ailing, pining and sickly. The child's mysterious illness turned out to be some affection of the spine likely to affect health; but not to shorten life – at least so the doctors said. But the long dreary suffering of one whom a mother loves as Alice loved her only child, is hard to look forward to. Only Norah guessed what Alice suffered; no one but God knew.

And so it fell out, that when Mrs Wilson, the elder, came to her one day in violent distress, occasioned by a very material diminution in the value of the property that her husband had left her – a diminution which made her income barely enough to support herself, much less Alice – the latter could hardly understand how anything which did not touch health or life could cause such grief; and she received the intelligence with irritating composure. But when, that afternoon, the little sick child was brought in, and the grandmother – who after all loved it well – began a fresh moan over her losses to its unconscious ears – saying how she had planned to consult this or that doctor, and to give it this or that comfort or luxury in after yearn but that now all chance of this had passed away – Alice's heart was touched, and she drew near to Mrs Wilson with unwonted caresses, and, in a spirit not unlike to that of Ruth, entreated, that come what would, they might remain together. After much discussion in succeeding days, it was arranged that Mrs Wilson should take a house in Manchester, furnishing it partly with what furniture she had, and providing the rest with Alice's remaining two hundred pounds. Mrs Wilson was herself a Manchester woman, and naturally longed to return to her native town. Some connections of her own at that time required lodgings, for which they were willing to pay pretty handsomely. Alice undertook the active superintendence and superior work of the household. Norah, willing faithful Norah, offered to cook, scour, do anything in short, so that, she might but remain with them.

The plan succeeded. For some years their first lodgers remained with them, and all went smoothly – with the one sad exception of the little girl's increasing deformity. How that mother loved that child, is not for words to tell!

Then came a break of misfortune. Their lodgers left, and no one succeeded to them. After some months they had to remove to a smaller house; and Alice's tender conscience was torn by the idea that she ought not to be a burden to her mother-in-law, but ought to go out and seek her own maintenance. And leave her child! The thought came like the sweeping boom of a funeral bell over her heart.

By and by, Mr Openshaw came to lodge with them. He had started in life as the errand-boy and sweeper-out of a warehouse; had struggled up through all the grades of employment in the place, fighting his way through the hard striving Manchester life with strong pushing energy of character. Every spare moment of time had been sternly given up to self-teaching. He was a capital accountant, a good French and German scholar, a keen, far-seeing tradesman; understanding markets, and the bearing of events, both near and distant, on trade: and yet, with such vivid attention to present details, that I do not think he ever saw a group of flowers in the fields without thinking whether their colours would, or would not, form harmonious contrasts in the coming spring muslins and prints. He went to debating societies, and threw himself with all his heart and soul into politics; esteeming, it must be owned, every man a fool or a knave who differed from him, and overthrowing his opponents rather by the loud strength of his language than the calm strength of his logic. There was something of the Yankee in all this. Indeed his theory ran parallel to the famous Yankee motto – 'England flogs creation, and Manchester flogs England.' Such a man, as may be fancied, had had no time for falling in love, or any such nonsense. At the age when most young men go through their courting and matrimony, he had not the means of keeping a wife, and was far too practical to think of having one. And now that he was in easy circumstances, a rising man, he considered women almost as encumbrances to the world, with whom a man had better have as little to do as possible. His first impression of Alice was indistinct, and he did not care enough about her to make it distinct. 'A pretty yea-nay kind of woman', would have been his description of her, if he had been pushed into a corner. He was rather afraid, in the beginning, that her quiet ways arose from a listlessness and laziness of character which would have been exceedingly discordant to his active energetic nature. But, when he found out the punctuality with which his wishes were attended to, and her work was done; when he was called in the morning at the very stroke of the clock, his shaving-water scalding hot, his fire bright, his coffee made exactly as his peculiar fancy dictated (for he was a man who had his theory about everything, based upon what he knew of science, and often perfectly original) – then he began to think: not that Alice had any peculiar merit; but that he had got into remarkably good lodgings: his restlessness wore away, and he began to consider himself as almost settled for life in them.

Mr Openshaw had been too busy, all his life, to be introspective. He did not know that he had any tenderness in his nature; and if he had become conscious of its abstract existence, he would have considered it as a manifestation of disease in some part of his nature. But he was decoyed into pity unawares; and pity led on to tenderness. That little helpless child – always carried about by one of the three busy women of the house, or else patiently threading coloured beads in the chair from which, by no effort of its own, could it ever move; the great grave blue eyes, full of serious, not uncheerful, expression, giving to the small delicate face a look beyond its years; the soft plaintive voice dropping out but few words, so unlike the continual prattle of a child – caught Mr Openshaw's attention in spite of himself. One day – he half scorned himself for doing so – he cut short his dinner-hour to go in search of some toy which should take the place of those eternal beads. I forget what he bought; but, when he gave the present (which he took care to do in a short abrupt manner, and when no one was by to see him), he was almost thrilled by the flash of delight that came over that child's face, and could not help all through that afternoon going over and over again the picture left on his memory, by the bright effect of unexpected joy on the little girl's face. When he returned home, he found his slippers placed by his sitting-room fire; and even more careful attention paid to his fancies than was habitual in those model lodgings. When Alice had taken the last of his tea-things away – she had been silent as usual till then – she stood for an instant with the door in her hand. Mr Openshaw looked as if he were deep in his book, though in fact he did not see a line; but was heartily wishing the woman would be gone, and not make any palaver of gratitude. But she only said: 'I am very much obliged to you, sir. Thank you very much,' and was gone, even before he could send her away with a 'There, my good woman, that's enough!'

For some time longer he took no apparent notice of the child. He even hardened his heart into disregarding her sudden flush of colour, and little timid smile of recognition, when he saw her by chance. But, after all, this could not last for ever; and, having a second time given way to tenderness, there was no relapse. The insidious enemy having thus entered his heart, in the guise of compassion to the child, soon assumed the more dangerous form of interest in the mother. He was aware of this change of feeling, despised himself for it, struggled with it, nay, internally yielded to it and cherished it, long before he suffered the slightest expression of it, by word, action, or look, to escape him. He watched Alice's docile obedient ways to her stepmother; the love which she had inspired in the rough Norah (roughened by the wear and tear of sorrow and years); but above all, he saw the wild, deep, passionate affection existing between her and her child. They spoke little to anyone else, or when anyone else was by; but, when alone together, they talked, and murmured, and cooed, and chattered so continually, that Mr Openshaw first wondered what they could find to say to each other, and next became irritated because they were always so grave and silent with him. All this time, he was perpetually devising small new pleasures for the child. His thoughts ran, in a pertinacious way, upon the desolate life before her; and often he came back from his day's work loaded with the very thing Alice had been longing for, but had not been able to procure. One time it was a little chair for drawing the little sufferer along the streets, and many an evening that ensuing summer Mr Openshaw drew her along himself, regardless of the remarks of his acquaintances. One day in autumn he put down his newspaper, as Alice came in with the breakfast, and said, in as indifferent a voice as he could assume: 'Mrs Frank, is there any reason why we two should not put up our horses together?'

Alice stood still in perplexed wonder. What did he mean? He had resumed the reading of his newspaper, as if he did not expect any answer; so she found silence her safest course, and went on quietly arranging his breakfast without another word passing between them. Just as he was leaving the house, to go to the warehouse as usual, he turned back and put his head into the bright, neat, tidy kitchen, where all the women breakfasted in the morning: 'You'll think of what I said, Mrs Frank' (this was her name with the lodgers), 'and let me have your opinion upon it tonight.'

Alice was thankful that her mother and Norah were too busy talking together to attend much to this speech. She determined not to think about it at all through the day; and, of course, the effort not to think made her think all the more. At night she sent up Norah with his tea. But Mr Openshaw almost knocked Norah down as she was going out at the door, by pushing past her and calling out 'Mrs Frank!' in an impatient voice, at the top of the stairs.

Alice went up, rather than seem to have affixed too much meaning to his words.

'Well, Mrs Frank,' he said, 'what answer? Don't make it too long; for I have lots of office-work to get through tonight.'

'I hardly know what you meant, sir,' said truthful Alice.

'Well! I should have thought you might have guessed. You're not new at this sort of work, and I am. However, I'll make it plain this time. Will you have me to be thy wedded husband, and serve me, and love me, and honour me, and all that sort of thing? Because if you will, I will do as much by you, and be a father to your child – and that's more than is put in the prayer-book. Now, I'm a man of my word; and what I say, I feel; and what I promise, I'll do. Now, for your answer!'

Alice was silent. He began to make the tea, as if her reply was a matter of perfect indifference to him; but, as soon as that was done, he became impatient.

'Well?' said he.

'How long, sir, may I have to think over it?'

'Three minutes!' (looking at his watch). 'You've had two already – that makes five. Be a sensible woman, say Yes, and sit down to tea with me, and we'll talk it over together; for, after tea, I shall be busy; say No' (he hesitated a moment to try and keep his voice in the same tone), 'and I shan't say another word about it, but pay up a year's rent for my rooms tomorrow, and be off. Time's up! Yes or no?'

'If you please, sir – you have been so good to little Ailsie – '

'There, sit down comfortably by me on the sofa, and let us have our tea together. I am glad to find you are as good and sensible as I took for.'

And this was Alice Wilson's second wooing.

Mr Openshaw's will was too strong, and his circumstances too good, for him not to carry all before him. He settled Mrs Wilson in a comfortable house of her own, and made her quite independent of lodgers. The little that Alice said with regard to future plans was in Norah's behalf.

'No,' said Mr Openshaw. 'Norah shall take care of the old lady as long as she lives; and, after that, she shall either come and live with us, or, if she likes it better, she shall have a provision for life – for your sake, missus. No one who has been good to you or the child shall go unrewarded. But even the little one will be better for some fresh stuff about her. Get her a bright, sensible girl as a nurse: one who won't go rubbing her with calf's-foot jelly as Norah does; wasting good stuff outside that ought to go in, but will follow doctors' directions; which, as you must see pretty clearly by this time, Norah won't; because they give the poor little wench pain. Now, I'm not above being nesh for other folks myself. I can stand a good blow, and never change colour; but, set me in the operating-room in the infirmary, and I turn as sick as a girl. Yet, if need were, I would hold the little wench on my knees while she screeched with pain, if it were to do her poor back good. Nay, nay, wench! keep your white looks for the time when it comes – I don't say it ever will. But this I know, Norah will spare the child and cheat the doctor if she can. Now, I say, give the bairn a year or two's chance, and then, when the pack of doctors have done their best – and, maybe, the old lady has gone – we'll have Norah back, or do better for her.'

The pack of doctors could do no good to little Ailsie. She was beyond their power. But her father (for so he insisted on being called, and also on Alice's no longer retaining the appellation of Mama, but becoming henceforward Mother), by his healthy cheerfulness of manner, his clear decision of purpose, his odd turns and quirks of humour, added to his real strong love for the helpless little girl, infused a new element of brightness and confidence into her life; and, though her back remained the same, her general health was strengthened, and Alice – never going beyond a smile herself – had the pleasure of seeing her child taught to laugh.

As for Alice's own life, it was happier than it had ever been. Mr Openshaw required no demonstration, no expressions of affection from her. Indeed, these would rather have disgusted him. Alice could love deeply, but could not talk about it. The perpetual requirement of loving words, looks, and caresses, and misconstruing their absence into absence of love, had been the great trial of her former married life. Now, all went on clear and straight, under the guidance of her husband's strong sense, warm heart, and powerful will. Year by year their worldly prosperity increased. At Mrs Wilson's death, Norah came back to them, as nurse to the newly born little Edwin; into which post she was not installed without a pretty strong oration on the part of the proud and happy father; who declared that if he found out that Norah ever tried to screen the boy by a falsehood, or to make him nesh either in body or mind, she should go that very day. Norah and Mr Openshaw were not on the most thoroughly cordial terms; neither of them fully recognising or appreciating the other's best qualities.

This was the previous history of the Lancashire family who had now removed to London, and had come to occupy the house.

They had been there about a year, when Mr Openshaw suddenly informed his wife that he had determined to heal long-standing feuds, and had asked his uncle and aunt Chadwick to come and pay them a visit and see London. Mrs Openshaw had never seen this uncle and aunt of her husband's. Years before she had married him, there had been a quarrel. All she knew was, that Mr Chadwick was a small manufacturer in a country town in South Lancashire. She was extremely pleased that the breach was to be healed, and began making preparations to render their visit pleasant.

They arrived at last. Going to see London was such an event to them, that Mrs Chadwick had made all new linen fresh for the occasion – from nightcaps downwards; and, as for gowns, ribbons, and collars, she might have been going into the wilds of Canada where never a shop is, so large was her stock. A fortnight before the day of her departure for London, she had formally called to take leave of all her acquaintance; saying she should need all the intermediate time for packing up. It was like a second wedding in her imagination; and, to complete the resemblance which an entirely new wardrobe made between the two events, her husband brought her back from Manchester, on the last market-day before they set off, a gorgeous pearl and amethyst brooch, saying, 'Lunnon should see that Lancashire folks knew a handsome thing when they saw it.'

For some time after Mr and Mrs Chadwick arrived at the Openshaws', there was no opportunity for wearing this brooch; but at length they obtained an order to see Buckingham Palace, and the spirit of loyalty demanded that Mrs Chadwick should wear her best clothes in visiting the abode of her sovereign. On her return, she hastily changed her dress; for Mr Openshaw had planned that they should go to Richmond, drink tea and return by moonlight. Accordingly, about five o'clock, Mr and Mrs Openshaw and Mr and Mrs Chadwick set off.

The housemaid and cook sat below, Norah hardly knew where. She was always engrossed in the nursery, in tending her two children, and in sitting by the restless, excitable Ailsie till she fell asleep. By and by, the housemaid Bessy tapped gently at the door. Norah went to her, and they spoke in whispers.

'Nurse! there's someone downstairs wants you.'

'Wants me! Who is it?'

'A gentleman – '

'A gentleman? Nonsense!'

'Well! a man, then, and he asks for you, and he rung at the front door bell, and has walked into the dining room.'

'You should never have let him,' exclaimed Norah, 'master and missus out – '

'I did not want him to come in; but when he heard you lived here, he walked past me, and sat down on the first chair, and said, "Tell her to come and speak to me." There is no gas lighted in the room, and supper is all set out.'

'He'll be off with the spoons!' exclaimed Norah, putting the housemaid's fear into words, and preparing to leave the room, first, however, giving a look to Ailsie, sleeping soundly and calmly.

Downstairs she went, uneasy fears stirring in her bosom. Before she entered the dining-room she provided herself with a candle, and, with it in her hand, she went in, looking round her in the darkness for her visitor.

He was standing up, holding by the table. Norah and he looked at each other; gradual recognition coming into their eyes.

'Norah?' at length he asked.

'Who are you?' asked Norah, with the sharp tones of alarm and incredulity. 'I don't know you': trying, by futile words of disbelief, to do away with the terrible fact before her.

'Am I so changed?' he said, pathetically. 'I dare say I am. But, Norah, tell me!' he breathed hard, 'where is my wife? Is she – is she alive?'

He came nearer to Norah, and would have taken her hand; but she backed away from him; looking at him all the time with staring eyes, as if he were some horrible object. Yet he was a handsome, bronzed, good-looking fellow, with beard and moustache, giving him a foreign-looking aspect; but his eyes! there was no mistaking those eager, beautiful eyes – the very same that Norah had watched not half an hour ago, till sleep stole softly over them.

'Tell me, Norah – I can bear it – I have feared it so often. Is she dead?' Norah still kept silence. 'She is dead!' He hung on Norah's words and looks, as if for confirmation or contradiction.

'What shall I do?' groaned Norah. 'O, sir! why did you come? how did you find me out? where have you been? We thought you dead, we did, indeed!' She poured out words and questions to gain time, as if time would help her.

'Norah! answer me this question, straight, by yes or no – Is my wife dead?'

'No, she is not!' said Norah, slowly and heavily.

'O what a relief! Did she receive my letters? But perhaps you don't know. Why did you leave her? Where is she? O Norah, tell me all quickly!'

'Mr Frank!' said Norah at last, almost driven to bay by her terror lest her mistress should return at any moment, and find him there – unable to consider what was best to be done or said– rushing at something decisive, because she could not endure her present state: 'Mr Frank! we never heard a line from you, and the shipowners said you had gone down, you and every one else. We thought you were dead, if ever man was, and poor Miss Alice and her little sick, helpless child! O, sir, you must guess it,' cried the poor creature at last, bursting out into a passionate fit of crying, 'for indeed I cannot tell it. But it was no one's fault. God help us all this night!'

Norah had sat down. She trembled too much to stand. He took her hands in his. He squeezed them hard, as if by physical pressure, the truth could be wrung out.

'Norah!' This time his tone was calm, stagnant as despair. 'She has married again!'

Norah shook her head sadly. The grasp slowly relaxed. The man had fainted.

There was brandy in the room. Norah forced some drops into Mr Frank's mouth, chafed his hands, and – when mere animal life returned, before the mind poured in its flood of memories and thoughts – she lifted him up, and rested his head against her knees. Then she put a few crumbs of bread taken from the supper-table, soaked in brandy, into his mouth. Suddenly he sprang to his feet.

'Where is she? Tell me this instant.' He looked so wild, so mad, so desperate, that Norah felt herself to be in bodily danger; but her time of dread had gone by. She had been afraid to tell him the truth, and then she had been a coward. Now, her wits were sharpened by the sense of his desperate state. He must leave the house. She would pity him afterwards; but now she must rather command and upbraid; for he must leave the house before her mistress came home. That one necessity stood clear before her.

'She is not here; that is enough for you to know. Nor can I say exactly where she is' (which was true to the letter if not to the spirit). 'Go away, and tell me where to find you tomorrow, and I will tell you all. My master and mistress may come back at any minute, and then what would become of me with a strange man in the house?'

Such an argument was too petty to touch his excited mind.

'I don't care for your master and mistress. If your master is a man, he must feel for me, poor shipwrecked sailor that I am – kept for years a prisoner amongst savages, always, always, always thinking of my wife and my home – dreaming of her by night, talking to her, though she could not hear, by day. I loved her more than all heaven and earth put together. Tell me where she is, this instant, you wretched woman, who salved over her wickedness to her, as you do to me.'

The clock struck ten. Desperate positions require desperate measures.

'If you will leave the house now, I will come to you tomorrow and tell you all. What is more, you shall see your child now. She lies sleeping upstairs. O, sir, you have a child, you do not know that as yet – a little weakly girl – with just a heart and soul beyond her years. We have reared her up with such care. We watched her, for we thought for many a year she might die any day, and we tended her, and no hard thing has come near her, and no rough word has ever been said to her. And now you come and will take her life into your hand, and will crush it. Strangers to her have been kind to her; but her own father – Mr Frank, I am her nurse, and I love her, and I tend her, and I would do anything for her that I could. Her mother's heart beats as hers beats; and, if she suffers a pain, her mother trembles all over. If she is happy, it is her mother that smiles and is glad. If she is growing stronger, her mother is healthy: if she dwindles, her mother languishes. If she dies – well, I don't know: it is not every one can lie down and die when they wish it. Come upstairs, Mr Frank, and see your child. Seeing her will do good to your poor heart. Then go away, in God's name, just this one night – tomorrow, if need be, you can do anything – kill us all if you will, or show yourself – a great grand man, whom God will bless for ever and ever. Come, Mr Frank, the look of a sleeping child is sure to give peace.'

She led him upstairs; at first almost helping his steps, till they came near the nursery door. She had almost forgotten the existence of little Edwin. It struck upon her with affright as the shaded light fell upon the other cot; but she skilfully threw that corner of the room into darkness, and let the light fall on the sleeping Ailsie. The child had thrown down the coverings, and her deformity, as she lay with her back to them, was plainly visible through her slight nightgown. Her little face, deprived of the lustre of her eyes, looked wan and pinched, and had a pathetic expression in it, even as she slept. The poor father looked and looked with hungry, wistful eyes, into which the big tears came swelling up slowly, and dropped heavily down, as he stood trembling and shaking all over. Norah was angry with herself for growing impatient of the length of time that long lingering gaze lasted. She thought that she waited for full half an hour before Frank stirred. And then – instead of going away – he sank down on his knees by the bedside, and buried his face in the clothes. Little Ailsie stirred uneasily. Norah pulled him up in terror. She could afford no more time even for prayer in her extremity of fear; for surely the next moment would bring her mistress home. She took him forcibly by the arm; but, as he was going, his eye lighted on the other bed: he stopped. Intelligence came back into his face. His hands clenched.

'His child?' he asked.

'Her child,' replied Norah. 'God watches over him,' said she instinctively; for Frank's looks excited her fears, and she needed to remind herself of the Protector of the helpless.

'God has not watched over me,' he said, in despair; his thoughts apparently recoiling on his own desolate, deserted state. But Norah had no time for pity. Tomorrow she would be as compassionate as her heart prompted. At length she guided him downstairs and shut the outer door and bolted it – as if by bolts to keep out facts.

Then she went back into the dining-room and effaced all traces of his presence as far as she could. She went upstairs to the nursery and sat there, her head on her hand, thinking what was to come of all this misery. It seemed to her very long before they did return; yet it was hardly eleven o'clock. She so heard the loud, hearty Lancashire voices on the stairs; and, for the first time, she understood the contrast of the desolation of the poor man who had so lately gone forth in lonely despair.

It almost put her out of patience to see Mrs Openshaw come in, calmly smiling, handsomely dressed, happy, easy, to enquire after her children.

'Did Ailsie go to sleep comfortably?' she whispered to Norah.

'Yes.'

Her mother bent over her, looking at her slumbers with the soft eyes of love. How little she dreamed who had looked on her last! Then she went to Edwin, with perhaps less wistful anxiety in her countenance, but more of pride. She took off her things, to go down to supper. Norah saw her no more that night.

Beside the door into the passage, the sleeping-nursery opened out of Mr and Mrs Openshaw's room, in order that they might have the children more immediately under their own eyes. Early the next summer morning Mrs Openshaw was awakened by Ailsie's startled call of 'Mother! mother!' She sprang up, put on her dressing-gown, and went to her child. Ailsie was only half awake, and in a not uncommon state of terror.

'Who was he, mother? Tell me!'

'Who, my darling? No one is here. You have been dreamings, love. Waken up quite. See, it is broad daylight.'

'Yes,' said Ailsie, looking round her; then clinging to her mother, said, 'but a man was here in the night, mother.'

'Nonsense, little goose. No man has ever come near you!'

'Yes, he did. He stood there. Just by Norah. A man with hair and a beard. And he knelt down and said his prayers. Norah knows he was here, mother' (half angrily, as Mrs Openshaw shook her head in smiling incredulity).

'Well! we will ask Norah when she comes,' said Mrs Openshaw, soothingly. 'But we won't talk any more about him now. It is not five o'clock; it is too early for you to get up. Shall I fetch you a book and read to you?'

'Don't leave me, mother,' said the child, clinging to her. So Mrs Openshaw sat on the bedside talking to Ailsie, and telling her of what they had done at Richmond the evening before, until the little girl's eyes slowly closed and she once more fell asleep.

'What was the matter?' asked Mr Openshaw, as his wife returned to bed.

'Ailsie wakened up in a fright, with some story of a man having been in the room to say his prayers – a dream, I suppose.' And no more was said at the time.

Mrs Openshaw had almost forgotten the whole affair when she got up about seven o'clock. But, by and by, she heard a sharp altercation going on in the nursery. Norah was speaking angrily to Ailsie, a most unusual thing. Both Mr and Mrs Openshaw listened in astonishment.

'Hold your tongue, Ailsie! let me hear none of your dreams; never let me hear you tell that story again!' Ailsie began to cry.

Mr Openshaw opened the door of communication before his wife could say a word.

'Norah, come here!'

The nurse stood at the door, defiant. She perceived she had been heard, but she was desperate.

'Don't let me hear you speak in that manner to Ailsie again,' he said sternly, and shut the door.

Norah was infinitely relieved; for she had dreaded some questioning; and a little blame for sharp speaking was what she could well bear, if cross-examination was let alone.

Downstairs they went, Mr Openshaw carrying Ailsie; the sturdy Edwin coming step by step, right foot foremost, always holding his mother's hand. Each child was placed in a chair by the breakfast-table, and then Mr and Mrs Openshaw stood together at the window, awaiting their visitors' appearance and making plans for the day. There was a pause. Suddenly Mr Openshaw turned to Ailsie, and said: 'What a little goosy somebody is with her dreams, waking up poor, tired mother in the middle of the night with a story of a man being in the room.'

'Father! I'm sure I saw him,' said Ailsie, half crying. 'I don't want to make Norah angry; but I was not asleep, for all she says I was. I had been asleep – and I awakened up quite wide awake though I was so frightened. I kept my eyes nearly shut, and I saw the man quite plain. A great brown man with a beard. He said his prayers. And then he looked at Edwin. And then Norah took him by the arm and led him away, after they had whispered a bit together.'

'Now, my little woman must be reasonable,' said Mr Openshaw, who was always patient with Ailsie. 'There was no man in the house last night at all. No man comes into the house, as you know, if you think; much less goes up into the nursery. But sometimes we dream something has happened, and the dream is so like reality, that you are not the first person, little woman, who has stood out that the thing has really happened.'

'But, indeed it was not a dream!' said Ailsie, beginning to cry.

Just then Mr and Mrs Chadwick came down, looking grave and discomposed. All during breakfast time they were silent and uncomfortable. As soon as the breakfast things were taken away, and the children had been carried upstairs, Mr Chadwick began in an evidently preconcerted manner to enquire if his nephew was certain that all his servants were honest; for, that Mrs Chadwick had that morning missed a very valuable brooch, which she had worn the day before. She remembered taking it off when she came home from Buckingham Palace. Mr Openshaw's face contracted into hard lines: grew like what it was before he had known his wife and her child. He rang the bell even before his uncle had done speaking. It was answered by the housemaid.

'Mary, was anyone here last night while we were away?'

'A man, sir, came to speak to Norah.'

'To speak to Norah! Who was he? How long did he stay?'

'I'm sure I can't tell, sir. He came – perhaps about nine. I went up to tell Norah in the nursery, and she came down to speak to him. She let him out, sir. She will know who he was, and how long he stayed.'

She waited a moment to be asked any more questions, but she was not, so she went away.

A minute afterwards Openshaw made as though he were going out of the room; but his wife laid her hand on his arm: 'Do not speak to her before the children,' she said, in her low, quiet voice. 'I will go up and question her.'

'No! I must speak to her. You must know,' said he, turning to his uncle and aunt, 'my missus has an old servant, as faithful as ever woman was, I do believe, as far as love goes – but, at the same time, who does not always speak truth, as even the missus must allow. Now, my notion is, that this Norah of ours has been come over by some good-for-nothing chap (for she's at the time o' life when they say women pray for husbands – "any, good Lord, any") and has let him into our house, and the chap has made off with your brooch, and m'appen many another thing beside. It's only saying that Norah is soft-hearted, and does not stick at a white lie – that's all, missus.'

It was curious to notice how his tone, his eyes, his whole face changed as he spoke to his wife; but he was the resolute man through all. She knew better than to oppose him; so she went upstairs, and told Norah her master wanted to speak to her, and that she would take care of the children in the meanwhile.

Norah rose to go without a word. Her thoughts were these: 'If they tear me to pieces they shall never know through me. He may come – and then just Lord have mercy upon us all: for some of us are dead folk to a certainty. But he shall do it; not me.'

You may fancy, now, her look of determination as she faced her master alone in the dining-room; Mr and Mrs Chadwick having left the affair in their nephew's hands, seeing that he took it up with such vehemence.

'Norah! Who was that man that came to my house last night?'

'Man, sir!' As if infinitely surprised; but it was only to gain time.

'Yes; the man whom Mary let in; whom she went upstairs to the nursery to tell you about; whom you came down to speak to; the same chap, I make no doubt, whom you took into the nursery to have your talk out with; whom Ailsie saw, and afterwards dreamed about; thinking, poor wench! she saw him say his prayers, when nothing, I'll be bound, was farther from his thoughts; who took Mrs Chadwick's brooch, value ten pounds. Now, Norah! Don't go off! I am as sure as that my name's Thomas Openshaw, that you knew nothing of this robbery. But I do think you've been imposed on, and that's the truth. Some good-for-nothing chap has been making up to you, and you've been just like all other women, and have turned a soft place in your heart to him; and he came last night a-lovyering, and you had him up in the nursery, and he made use of his opportunities, and made off with a few things on his way down! Come, now, Norah: it's no blame to you, only you must not be such a fool again. Tell us,' he continued, 'what name he gave you, Norah? I'll be bound it was not the right one; but it will be a clue for the police.'

Norah drew herself up. 'You may ask that question, and taunt me with my being single, and with my credulity, as you will, Master Openshaw. You'll get no answer from me. As for the brooch, and the story of theft and burglary; if any friend ever came to see me (which I defy you to prove, and deny), he'd be just as much above doing such a thing as you yourself, Mr Openshaw, and more so, too; for I'm not at all sure as everything you have is rightly come by, or would be yours long, if every man had his own.' She meant, of course, his wife; but he understood her to refer to his property in goods and chattels.

'Now, my good woman,' said he, 'I'll just tell you truly, I never trusted you out and out; but my wife liked you, and I thought you had many a good point about you. If you once begin to sauce me, I'll have the police to you, and get out the truth in a court of justice, if you'll not tell it me quietly and civilly here. Now the best thing you can do is quietly to tell me who the fellow is. Look here! a man comes to my house; asks for you; you take him upstairs; a valuable brooch is missing next day; we know that you, and Mary, and cook, are honest; but you refuse to tell us who the man is. Indeed you've told one lie already about him, saying no one was here last night. Now I just put it to you, what do you think a policeman would say to this, or a magistrate? A magistrate would soon make you tell the truth, my good woman.'

'There's never the creature born that should get it out of me,' said Norah. 'Not unless I choose to tell.'

'I've a great mind to see,' said Mr Openshaw, growing angry at the defiance. Then, checking himself, he thought before he spoke again: 'Norah, for your missus's sake I don't want to go to extremities. Be a sensible woman, if you can. It's no great disgrace, after all, to have been taken in. I ask you once more – as a friend – who was this man whom you let into my house last night?'

No answer. He repeated the question in an impatient tone. Still no answer. Norah's lips were set in determination not to speak.

'Then there is but one thing to be done. I shall send for a policeman.'

'You will not,' said Norah, starting forwards. 'You shall not, sir! No policeman shall touch me. I know nothing of the brooch, but I know this:

ever since I was four-and-twenty I have thought more of your wife than of myself: ever since I saw her, a poor motherless girl put upon in her uncle's house, I have thought more of serving her than of serving myself! I have cared for her and her child, as nobody ever cared for me. I don't cast blame on you, sir, but I say it's ill giving up one's life to anyone; for, at the end, they will turn round upon you, and forsake you. Why does not my missus come herself to suspect me? Maybe she is gone for the police? But I don't stay here, either for police, or magistrate, or master. You're an unlucky lot. I believe there's a curse on you. I'll leave you this very day. Yes! I leave that poor Ailsie, too. I will! No good will ever come to you!'

Mr Openshaw was utterly astonished at this speech; most of which was completely unintelligible to him, as may easily be supposed. Before he could make up his mind what to say, or what to do, Norah had left the room. I do not think he had ever really intended to send for the police to this old servant of his wife's; for he had never for a moment doubted her perfect honesty. But he had intended to compel her to tell him who the man was, and in this he was baffled. He was, consequently, much irritated. He returned to his uncle and aunt in a state of great annoyance and perplexity, and told them he could get nothing out of the woman; that some man had been in the house the night before; but that she refused to tell who he was. At this moment his wife came in, greatly agitated, and asked what had happened to Norah; for that she had put on her things in passionate haste, and had left the house.

'This looks suspicious,' said Mr Chadwick. 'It is not the way in which an honest person would have acted.'

Mr Openshaw kept silence. He was sorely perplexed. But Mrs Openshaw turned round on Mr Chadwick with a sudden fierceness no one ever saw in her before.

'You don't know Norah, uncle! She is gone because she is deeply hurt at being suspected. O, I wish I had seen her – that I had spoken to her myself. She would have told me anything.' Alice wrung her hands.

'I must confess,' continued Mr Chadwick to his nephew, in a lower voice, 'I can't make you out. You used to be a word and a blow, and oftenest the blow first; and now, when there is every cause for suspicion, you just do nought. Your missus is a very good woman, I grant; but she may have been put upon as well as other folk, I suppose. If you don't send for the police, I shall.'

'Very well,' replied Mr Openshaw, surlily. 'I can't clear Norah. She won't clear herself, as I believe she might if she would. Only I wash my hands of it; for I am sure the woman herself is honest, and she's lived a long time with my wife, and I don't like her to come to shame.'

'But she will then be forced to clear herself. That, at any rate, will be a good thing.'

'Very well, very well! I am heart-sick of the whole business. Come, Alice, come up to the babies; they'll be in a sore way. I tell you, uncle!' he said, turning round once more to Mr Chadwick, suddenly and sharply, after his eye had fallen on Alice's wan, tearful, anxious face; 'I'll have none sending for the police after all. I'll buy my aunt twice as handsome a brooch this very day; but I'll not have Norah suspected, and my missus plagued. There's for you.'

He and his wife left the room. Mr Chadwick quietly waited till he was out of hearing, and then said to his wife: 'For all Tom's heroics, I'm just quietly going for a detective, wench. Thou need'st know nought about it.'

He went to the police-station, and made a statement of the case. He was gratified by the impression which the evidence against Norah seemed to make. The men all agreed in his opinion, and steps were to be immediately taken to find out where she was. Most probably, as they suggested, she had gone at once to the man, who, to all appearance, was her lover. When Mr Chadwick asked how they would find her out? they smiled, shook their heads, and spoke of mysterious but infallible ways and means. He returned to his nephew's house with a very comfortable opinion of his own sagacity. He was met by his wife with a penitent face: 'O master, I've found my brooch! It was just sticking by its pin in the flounce of my brown silk, that I wore yesterday. I took it off in a hurry, and it must have caught in it; and I hung up my gown in the closet. Just now, when I was going to fold it up, there was the brooch! I'm very vexed, but I never dreamt but what it was lost!'

Her husband muttering something very like 'Confound thee and thy brooch too! I wish I'd never given it thee,' snatched up his hat, and rushed back to the station; hoping to be in time to stop the police from searching for Norah. But a detective was already gone off on the errand.

Where was Norah? Half mad with the strain of the fearful secret, she had hardly slept through the night for thinking what must be done. Upon this terrible state of mind had come Ailsie's questions, showing that she had seen the Man, as the unconscious child called her father. Lastly came the suspicion of her honesty. She was little less than crazy as she ran upstairs and dashed on her bonnet and shawl; leaving all else, even her purse, behind her. In that house she would not stay. That was all she knew or was clear about. She would not even see the children again, for fear it should weaken her. She feared above everything Mr Frank's return to claim his wife. She could not tell what remedy there was for a sorrow so tremendous, for her to stay to witness. The desire of escaping from the coming event was a stronger motive for her departure than her soreness about the suspicions directed against her; although this last had been the final goad to the course she took. She walked away almost at headlong speed; sobbing as she went, as she had not dared to do during the past night for fear of exciting wonder in those who might hear her. Then she stopped. An idea came into her mind that she would leave London altogether, and betake herself to her native town of Liverpool. She felt in her pocket for her purse, as she drew near the Euston Square station with this intention. She had left it at home. Her poor head aching, her eyes swollen with crying, she had to stand still, and think, as well as she could, where next she should bend her steps. Suddenly the thought flashed into her mind that she would go and find out poor Mr Frank. She had been hardly kind to him the night before, though her heart had bled for him ever since. She remembered his telling her as she enquired for his address, almost as she had pushed him out of the door, of some hotel in a street not far distant from Euston Square. Thither she went: with what intention she hardly knew, but to assuage her conscience by telling him how much she pitied him. In her present state she felt herself unfit to counsel, or restrain, or assist, or do ought else but sympathise and weep. The people of the inn said such a person had been there; had arrived only the day before; had gone out soon after his arrival, leaving his luggage in their care; but had never come back. Norah asked for leave to sit down, and await the gentleman's return. The landlady – pretty secure in the deposit of luggage against any probable injury – showed her into a room, and quietly locked the door on the outside. Norah was utterly worn out, and fell asleep – a shivering, starting, uneasy slumber, which lasted for hours.

The detective, meanwhile, had come up with her some time before she entered the hotel, into which he followed her. Asking the landlady to detain her for an hour or so, without giving any reason beyond showing his authority (which made the landlady applaud herself a good deal for having locked her in), he went back to the police-station to report his proceedings. He could have taken her directly; but his object was, if possible, to trace out the man who was supposed to have committed the robbery. Then he heard of the discovery of the brooch; and consequently did not care to return.

Norah slept till even the summer evening began to close in. Then up. Someone was at the door. It would be Mr Frank; and she dizzily pushed back her ruffled grey hair, which had fallen over her eyes, and stood looking to see him. Instead, there came in Mr Openshaw and a policeman.

'This is Norah Kennedy,' said Mr Openshaw.

'O, sir,' said Norah, 'I did not touch the brooch; indeed I did not. O, sir, I cannot live to be thought so badly of'; and very sick and faint, she suddenly sank down on the ground. To her surprise, Mr Openshaw raised her up very tenderly. Even the policeman helped to lay her on the sofa; and, at Mr Openshaw's desire, he went for some wine and sandwiches; for the poor gaunt woman lay there almost as if dead with weariness and exhaustion.

'Norah!' said Mr Openshaw, in his kindest voice, 'the brooch is found. It was hanging to Mrs Chadwick's gown. I beg your pardon. Most truly I beg your pardon, for having troubled you about it. My wife is almost broken-hearted. Eat, Norah – or, stay, first drink this glass of wine,' said he, lifting her head, pouring a little down her throat.

As she drank, she remembered where she was, and who she was waiting for. She suddenly pushed Mr Openshaw away, saying, 'O, sir, you must go. You must not stop a minute. If he comes back he will kill you.'

'Alas, Norah! I do not know who "he" is. But someone is gone away who will never come back: someone who knew you, and whom I am afraid you cared for.'

'I don't understand you, sir,' said Norah, her master's kind and sorrowful manner bewildering her yet more than his words. The policeman had left the room at Mr Openshaw's desire, and they two were alone.

'You know what I mean, when I say someone is gone who will never come back. I mean that he is dead!'

'Who?' said Norah, trembling all over.

'A poor man has been found in the Thames this morning, drowned.'

'Did he drown himself?' asked Norah, solemnly.

'God only knows,' replied Mr Openshaw, in the same tone. 'Your name and address at our house, were found in his pocket: that, and his purse, were the only things, that were found upon him. I am sorry to say it, my poor Norah; but you are required to go and identify him.'

'To what?' asked Norah.

'To say who it is. It is always done, in order that some reason may be discovered for the suicide – if suicide it was. I make no doubt he was the man who came to see you at our house last night. It is very sad, I know.' He made pauses between each little clause, in order to try and bring back her senses; which he feared were wandering – so wild and sad was her look.

'Master Openshaw,' said she, at last, 'I've a dreadful secret to tell you – only you must never breathe it to anyone, and you and I must hide it away for ever. I thought to have done it all by myself, but I see I cannot. Yon poor man – yes! the dead, drowned creature is, I fear, Mr Frank, my mistress's first husband!'

Mr Openshaw sat down, as if shot. He did not speak; but, after a while, he signed to Norah to go on.

'He came to me the other night – when – God be thanked – you were all away at Richmond. He asked me if his wife was dead or alive. I was a brute, and thought more of your all coming home than of his sore trial: spoke out sharp, and said she was married again, and very content and happy: I all but turned him away: and now he lies dead and cold!'

'God forgive me!' said Mr Openshaw.

'God forgive us all!' said Norah. 'Yon poor man needs forgiveness perhaps less than anyone among us. He had been among the savages – shipwrecked – I know not what – and he had written letters which had never reached my poor missus.'

'He saw his child!'

'He saw her – yes! I took him up, to give his thoughts another start; for I believed he was going mad on my hands. I came to seek him here, as I more than half promised. My mind misgave me when I heard he had never come in. O, sir! it must be him!'

Mr Openshaw rang the bell. Norah was almost too much stunned to wonder at what he did. He asked for writing materials, wrote a letter, and then said to Norah: 'I am writing to Alice, to say I shall be unavoidably absent for a few days; that I have found you; that you are well, and send her your love, and will come home tomorrow. You must go with me to the Police Court; you must identify the body: I will pay high to keep name and details out of the papers.'

'But where are you going, sir?'

He did not answer her directly. Then he said: 'Norah! I must go with you, and look on the face of the man whom I have so injured – unwittingly, it is true; but it seems to me as if I had killed him. I will lay his head in the grave, as if he were my only brother: and how he must have hated me! I cannot go home to my wife till all that I can do for him is done. Then I go with a dreadful secret on my mind. I shall never speak of it again, after these days are over. I know you will not, either.' He shook hands with her: and they never named the subject again, the one to the other.

Norah went home to Alice the next day. Not a word was said on the cause of her abrupt departure a day or two before. Alice had been charged by her husband in his letter not to allude to the supposed theft of the brooch; so she, implicitly obedient to those whom she loved both by nature and habit, was entirely silent on the subject, only treated Norah with the most tender respect, as if to make up for unjust suspicion.

Nor did Alice enquire into the reason why Mr Openshaw had been absent during his uncle and aunt's visit, after he had once said that it was unavoidable. He came back, grave and quiet; and, from that time forth, was curiously changed. More thoughtful, and perhaps less active; quite as decided in conduct, but with new and different rules for the guidance of that conduct. Towards Alice he could hardly be more kind than he had always been; but he now seemed to look upon her as someone sacred and to be treated with reverence, as well as tenderness. He throve in business, and made a large fortune, one half of which was settled upon her.

*   *   *

Long years after these events – a few months after her mother died, Ailsie and her 'father' (as she always called Mr Openshaw) drove to a cemetery a little way out of town, and she was carried to a certain mound by her maid, who was then sent back to the carriage. There was a headstone, with F.W. and a date. That was all. Sitting by the grave, Mr Openshaw told her the story; and for the sad fate of that poor father whom she had never seen, he shed the only tears she ever saw fall from his eyes.

*   *   *

'A most interesting story, all through,' I said, as Jarber folded up the first of his series of discoveries in triumph. 'A story that goes straight to the heart – especially at the end. But' – I stopped, and looked at Trottle.

Trottle entered his protest directly in the shape of a cough.

'Well!' I said, beginning to lose my patience. 'Don't you see that I want you to speak, and that I don't want you to cough?'

'Quite so, ma'am,' said Trottle, in a state of respectful obstinacy which would have upset the temper of a saint. 'Relative, I presume, to this story, ma'am?'

'Yes, yes!' said Jarber. 'By all means let us hear what this good man has to say.'

'Well, sir,' answered Trottle, 'I want to know why the house over the way doesn't let, and I don't exactly see how your story answers the question. That's all I have to say, sir.'

I should have liked to contradict my opinionated servant, at that moment. But, excellent as the story was in itself, I felt that he had hit on the weak point, so far as Jarber's particular purpose in reading it was concerned.

'And that is what you have to say, is it?' repeated Jarber. 'I enter this room announcing that I have a series of discoveries, and you jump instantly to the conclusion that the first of the series exhausts my resources. Have I your permission, dear lady, to enlighten this obtuse person, if possible, by reading number two?'

'My work is behindhand, ma'am,' said Trottle, moving to the door, the moment I gave Jarber leave to go on.

'Stop where you are,' I said, in my most peremptory manner, 'and give Mr Jarber his fair opportunity of answering your objection now you have made it.'

Trottle sat down with the look of a martyr, and Jarber began to read with his back turned on the enemy more decidedly than ever.

Going into Society

At one period of its reverses, the house fell into the occupation of a showman. He was found registered as its occupier, on the parish books of the time when he rented the house, and there was therefore no need of any clue to his name. But, he himself was less easy to be found; for, he had led a wandering life, and settled people had lost sight of him, and people who plumed themselves on being respectable were shy of admitting that they had ever known anything of him. At last, among the marsh lands near the river's level, that lie about Deptford and the neighbouring market-gardens, a grizzled personage in velveteen, with a face so cut up by varieties of weather that he looked as if he had been tattooed, was found smoking a pipe at the door of a wooden house on wheels. The wooden house was laid up in ordinary for the winter, near the mouth of a muddy creek; and everything near it, the foggy river, the misty marshes, and the steaming market-gardens, smoked in company with the grizzled man. In the midst of this smoking party, the funnel-chimney of the wooden house on wheels was not remiss, but took its pipe with the rest in a companionable manner.

On being asked if it were he who had once rented the house to let, grizzled velveteen looked surprised, and said yes. Then his name was Magsman? That was it, Toby Magsman – which lawfully christened Robert; but called in the line, from a infant, Toby. There was nothing agin Toby Magsman, he believed? If there was suspicion of such – mention it!

There was no suspicion of such, he might rest assured. But, some enquiries were making about that house, and would he object to say why he left it?

Not at all; why should he? He left it, along of a dwarf.

Along of a dwarf?

Mr Magsman repeated, deliberately and emphatically, Along of a dwarf.

Might it be compatible with Mr Magsman's inclination and convenience to enter, as a favour, into a few particulars?

Mr Magsman entered into the following particulars.

It was a long time ago, to begin with; – afore lotteries and a deal more was done away with. Mr Magsman was looking about for a good pitch, and he see that house, and he says to himself, 'I'll have you, if you're to be had. If money'll get you, I'll have you.'

The neighbours cut up rough, and made complaints; but Mr Magsman don't know what they *would* have had. It was a lovely thing. First of all, there was the canvass, representin the picter of the giant, in Spanish trunks and a ruff, who was himself half the height of the house, and was run up with a line and pulley to a pole on the roof, so that his 'ed was coeval with the parapet. Then, there was the canvass, representin the picter of the albina lady, showing her white air to the Army and Navy in correct uniform. Then, there was the canvass, representin the picter of the Wild Indian a scalpin a member of some foreign nation. Then, there was the canvass, representin the picter of a child of a British Planter, seized by two boa constrictors – not that *we* never had no child, nor no constrictors neither. Similarly, there was the canvass, representin the picter of the wild ass of the prairies – not that *we* never had no wild asses, nor wouldn't have had 'em at a gift. Last, there was the canvass, representin the picter of the dwarf, and like him too (considerin), with George IV in such a state of astonishment at him as His Majesty couldn't with his utmost politeness and stoutness express. The front of the house was so covered with canvasses, that there wasn't a spark of daylight ever visible on that side. 'Magsman's Amusements', fifteen foot long by two foot high, ran over the front door and parlour winders. The passage was an arbour of green baize and garden stuff. A barrel-organ performed there unceasing. And as to respectability – if threepence ain't respectable, what is?

But, the dwarf is the principal article at present, and he was worth the money. He was wrote up as 'Major Tpschoffki of the Imperial Bulgraderian Brigade'. Nobody couldn't pronounce the name, and it never was intended anybody should. The public always turned it, as a regular rule, into Chopski. In the line he was called Chops; partly on that account, and partly because his real name, if he ever had any real name (which was very dubious), was Stakes.

He was a uncommon small man, he really was. Certainly not so small as he was made out to be, but where *is* your dwarf as is? He was a most uncommon small man, with a most uncommon large 'ed; and what he had inside that 'ed, nobody ever knowed but himself: even supposin himself to have ever took stock of it, which it would have been a stiff job for even him to do.

The kindest little man as never growed! Spirited, but not proud. When he travelled with the spotted baby – though he knowed himself to be a nat'ral dwarf, and knowed the baby's spots to be put upon him artificial, he nursed that baby like a mother. You never heerd him give a ill-name to a giant. He *did* allow himself to break out into strong language respectin the fat lady from Norfolk; but that was an affair of the 'art; and when a man's 'art has been trifled with by a lady, and the preference giv to a Indian, he ain't master of his actions.

He was always in love, of course; every human nat'ral phenomenon is. And he was always in love with a large woman; I never knowed the dwarf as could be got to love a small one. Which helps to keep 'em the curiosities they are.

One sing'ler idea he had in that 'ed of his, which must have meant something, or it wouldn't have been there. It was always his opinion that he was entitled to property. He never would put his name to anything. He had been taught to write, by the young man without arms, who got his living with his toes (quite a writing master *he* was, and taught scores in the line), but Chops would have starved to death, afore he'd have gained a bit of bread by putting his hand to a paper. This is the more curious to bear in mind, because *he* had no property, nor hope of property, except his house and a sarser. When I say his house, I mean the box, painted and got up outside like a reg'lar six-roomer, that he used to creep into, with a diamond ring (or quite as good to look at) on his forefinger, and ring a little bell out of what the public believed to be the drawing-room winder. And when I say a sarser, I mean a Chaney sarser in which he made a collection for himself at the end of every entertainment. His cue for that, he took from me: 'Ladies and gentlemen, the little man will now walk three times round the Cairawan, and retire behind the curtain.' When he said anything important, in private life, he mostly wound it up with this form of words, and they was generally the last thing he said to me at night afore he went to bed.

He had what I consider a fine mind – a poetic mind. His ideas respectin his property never come upon him so strong as when he sat upon a barrel-organ and had the handle turned. Arter the wibration had run through him a little time, he would screech out, 'Toby, I feel my property coming – grind away! I'm counting my guineas by thousands, Toby – grind away! Toby, I shall be a man of fortun! I feel the Mint a jingling in me, Toby, and I'm swelling out into the Bank of England!' Such is the influence of music on a poetic mind. Not that he was partial to any other music but a barrel-organ; on the contrary, hated it.

He had a kind of a everlasting grudge agin the Public: which is a thing you may notice in many phenomenons that get their living out of it. What riled him most in the nater of his occupation was, that it kep him out of society. He was continiwally saying, 'Toby, my ambition is, to go into society. The curse of my position towards the public is, that it keeps me hout of society. This don't signify to a low beast of a Indian; he an't formed for society. This don't signify to a spotted baby; *he* an't formed for society. – I am.'

Nobody never could make out what Chops done with his money. He had a good salary, down on the drum every Saturday as the day came round, besides having the run of his teeth – and he was a woodpecker to eat – but all dwarfs are. The sarser was a little income, bringing him in so many halfpence that he'd carry 'em for a week together, tied up in a pocket-handkercher. And yet he never had money. And it couldn't be the fat lady from Norfolk, as was once supposed; because it stands to reason that when you have a animosity towards a Indian, which makes you grind your teeth at him to his face, and which can hardly hold you from Goosing him audible when he's going through his war-dance – it stands to reason you wouldn't under them circumstances deprive yourself, to support that Indian in the lap of luxury.

Most unexpected, the mystery come out one day at Egham Races. The Public was shy of bein pulled in, and Chops was ringin his little bell out of his drawing-room winder, and was snarlin to me over his shoulder as he kneeled down with his legs out at the backdoor – for he couldn't be shoved into his house without kneeling down, and the premises wouldn't accommodate his legs – was snarlin, 'Here's a precious public for you; why the devil don't they tumble up?' when a man in the crowd holds up a carrier-pigeon, and cries out, 'If there's any person here as has got a ticket, the lottery's just drawed, and the number as has come up for the great prize is three, seven, forty-two! Three, seven, forty-two!' I was giving the man to the Furies myself, for calling off the public's attention – for the public will turn away, at any time, to look at anything in preference to the thing showed 'em; and if you doubt it, get 'em together for any indiwidual purpose on the face of the earth, and send only two people in late, and see if the whole company an't far more interested in takin particular notice of them two than of you – I say, I wasn't best pleased with the man for callin out, and wasn't blessin him in my own mind, when I see Chops's little bell fly out of winder at a old lady, and he gets up and kicks his box over, exposin the whole secret, and he catches hold of the calves of my legs and he says to me, 'Carry me into the wan, Toby, and throw a pail of water over me or I'm a dead man, for I've come into my property!'

Twelve thousand odd hundred pound, was Chops's winnins. He had bought a half-ticket for the twenty-five-thousand prize, and it had come up. The first use he made of his property, was, to offer to fight the Wild Indian for five hundred pound a side, him with a poisoned darnin-needle and the Indian with a club; but the Indian being in want of backers to that amount, it went no further.

Arter he had been mad for a week – in a state of mind, in short, in which, if I had let him sit on the organ for only two minutes, I believe he would have bust – but we kep the organ from him – Mr Chops come round, and behaved liberal and beautiful to all. He then sent for a young man he knowed, as had a wery genteel appearance and was a Bonnet at a gaming-booth (most respectable brought up, father havin been imminent in the livery stable line but unfort'nate in a commercial crisis, through paintin a old grey, ginger-bay, and sellin him with a pedigree), and Mr Chops said to this Bonnet, who said his name was Normandy, which it wasn't: 'Normandy, I'm a goin into society. Will you go with me?'

Says Normandy: 'Do I understand you, Mr Chops, to hintimate that the 'ole of the expenses of that move will be borne by yourself?'

'Correct,' says Mr Chops. 'And you shall have a princely allowance too.'

The Bonnet lifted Mr Chops upon a chair, to shake hands with him, and replied in poetry, with his eyes seemingly full of tears:

> 'My boat is on the shore,
> And my bark is on the sea,
> And I do not ask for more,
> But I'll go – along with thee.'

They went into society, in a chay and four greys with silk jackets. They took lodgings in Pall Mall, London, and they blazed away.

In consequence of a note that was brought to Bartlemy Fair in the autumn of next year by a servant, most wonderful got up in milk-white cords and tops, I cleaned myself and went to Pall Mall, one evening appinted. The gentlemen was at their wine arter dinner, and Mr Chops's eyes was more fixed in that 'ed of his than I thought good for him. There was three of 'em (in company, I mean), and I knowed the third well. When last met, he had on a white Roman shirt, and a bishop's mitre covered with leopard-skin, and played the clarionet all wrong, in a band at a Wild Beast Show.

This gent took on not to know me, and Mr Chops said: 'Gentlemen, this is a old friend of former days': and Normandy looked at me through a eyeglass, and said, 'Magsman, glad to see you!' – which I'll take my oath he wasn't. Mr Chops, to git him convenient to the table, had his chair on a throne (much of the form of George IV's in the canvass), but he hardly appeared to me to be King there in any other pint of view, for his two gentlemen ordered about like Emperors. They was all dressed like May Day – gorgeous! – And as to wine, they swam in all sorts.

I made the round of the bottles, first separate (to say I had done it), and then mixed 'em all together (to say I had done it), and then tried two of 'em as half and half, and then t'other two. Altogether, I passed a pleasin evenin, but with a tendency to feel muddled, until I considered it good manners to get up and say, 'Mr Chops, the best of friends must part, I thank you for the wariety of foreign drains you have stood so 'ansome, I looks towards you in red wine, and I takes my leave.' Mr Chops replied, 'If you'll just hitch me out of this over your right arm, Magsman, and carry me downstairs, I'll see you out.' I said I couldn't think of such a thing, but he would have it, so I lifted him off his throne. He smelt strong of Maideary, and I couldn't help thinking as I carried him down that it was like carrying a large bottle full of wine, with a rayther ugly stopper, a good deal out of proportion.

When I set him on the doormat in the hall, he kep me close to him by holding on to my coat-collar, and he whispers: 'I ain't 'appy, Magsman.'

'What's on your mind, Mr Chops?'

'They don't use me well. They an't grateful to me. They puts me on the mantelpiece when I won't have in more Champagne-wine, and they locks me in the sideboard when I won't give up my property.'

'Get rid of 'em, Mr Chops.'

'I can't. We're in society together, and what would society say?'

'Come out of society!' says I.

'I can't. You don't know what you're talking about. When you have once gone into society, you mustn't come out of it.'

'Then if you'll excuse the freedom, Mr Chops,' were my remark, shaking my head grave, 'I think it's a pity you ever went in.'

Mr Chops shook that deep 'ed of his, to a surprisin extent, and slapped it half a dozen times with his hand, and with more wice than I thought were in him. Then, he says, 'You're a good fellow, but you don't understand. Good-night, go along. Magsman, the little man will now walk three times round the Cairawan, and retire behind the curtain.' The last I see of him on that occasion was his tryin, on the extremest werge of insensibility, to climb up the stairs, one by one, with his hands and knees. They'd have been much too steep for him, if he had been sober; but he wouldn't be helped.

It warn't long after that, that I read in the newspaper of Mr Chops's being presented at court. It was printed, 'It will be recollected' – and I've noticed in my life, that it is sure to be printed that it *will* be recollected, whenever it won't – 'that Mr Chops is the individual of small stature, whose brilliant success in the last state lottery attracted so much attention.' Well, I says to myself, Such is life! He has been and done it in earnest at last. He has astonished George IV!

(On account of which, I had that canvass new-painted, him with a bag of money in his hand, a presentin it to George IV, and a lady in Ostrich Feathers fallin in love with him in a bag-wig, sword, and buckles correct.)

I took the house as is the subject of present enquiries – though not the honour of bein acquainted – and I run Magsman's Amusements in it thirteen months – sometimes one thing, sometimes another, sometimes nothin particular, but always all the canvasses outside. One night, when we had played the last company out, which was a shy company, through its raining Heavens hard, I was takin a pipe in the one pair back along with the young man with the toes, which I had taken on for a month (though he never drawed – except on paper), and I heard a kickin at the street door. 'Halloa!' I says to the young man, 'what's up!' He rubs his eyebrows with his toes, and he says, 'I can't imagine, Mr Magsman' – which he never could imagine nothin, and was monotonous company.

The noise not leavin off, I laid down my pipe, and I took up a candle, and I went down and opened the door. I looked out into the street; but nothin could I see, and nothin was I aware of, until I turned round quick, because some creetur run between my legs into the passage. There was Mr Chops!

'Magsman,' he says, 'take me, on the old terms, and you've got me; if it's done, say done!'

I was all of a maze, but I said, 'Done, sir.'

'Done to your done, and double done!' says he. 'Have you got a bit of supper in the house?'

Bearin in mind them sparklin warieties of foreign drains as we'd guzzled away at in Pall Mall, I was ashamed to offer him cold sassages and gin-and-water; but he took 'em both and took 'em free; havin a chair for his table, and sittin down at it on a stool, like hold times. I, all of a maze all the while.

It was arter he had made a clean sweep of the sassages (beef, and to the best of my calculations two pound and a quarter), that the wisdom as was in that little man began to come out of him like prespiration.

'Magsman,' he says, 'look upon me! You see afore you, One as has both gone into society and come out.'

'O! You *are* out of it, Mr Chops? How did you get out, sir?'

'Sold out!' says he. You never saw the like of the wisdom as his 'ed expressed, when he made use of them two words.

'My friend Magsman, I'll impart to you a discovery I've made. It's wallable; it's cost twelve thousand five hundred pound; it may do you good in life – The secret of this matter is, that it ain't so much that a person goes into society, as that society goes into a person.'

Not exactly keepin up with his meanin, I shook my head, put on a deep look, and said, 'You're right there, Mr Chops.'

'Magsman,' he says, twitchin me by the leg, 'society has gone into me, to the tune of every penny of my property.'

I felt that I went pale, and though nat'rally a bold speaker, I couldn't hardly say, 'Where's Normandy?'

'Bolted. With the plate,' said Mr Chops.

'And t'other one?' meaning him as formerly wore the bishop's mitre.

'Bolted. With the jewels,' said Mr Chops.

I sat down and looked at him, and he stood up and looked at me.

'Magsman,' he says, and he seemed to myself to get wiser as he got hoarser; 'Society, taken in the lump, is all dwarfs. At the court of St James's, they was all a doing my old business – all a goin three times round the Cairawan, in the hold court-suits and properties. Elsewheres, they was most of 'em ringin their little bells out of make-believes. Everywheres, the sarser was a goin round. Magsman, the sarser is the uniwersal institution!'

I perceived, you understand, that he was soured by his misfortunes, and I felt for Mr Chops.

'As to Fat Ladies,' he says, giving his head a tremendious one agin the wall, 'there's lots of *them* in society, and worse than the original. *Hers* was a outrage upon taste – simply a outrage upon taste – awakenin contempt – carryin its own punishment in the form of a Indian.' Here he giv himself another tremendious one. 'But *theirs*, Magsman, *theirs* is mercenary outrages. Lay in Cashmeer shawls, buy bracelets, strew 'em and a lot of 'andsome fans and things about your rooms, let it be known that you give away like water to all as come to admire, and the Fat Ladies that don't exhibit for so much down upon the drum, will come from all the pints of the compass to flock about you, whatever you are. They'll drill holes in your 'art, Magsman, like a cullender. And when you've no more left to give, they'll laugh at you to your face, and leave you to have your bones picked dry by Wulturs, like the dead wild ass of the prairies that you deserve to be!' Here he giv himself the most tremendious one of all, and dropped.

I thought he was gone. His 'ed was so heavy, and he knocked it so hard, and he fell so stoney, and the sassagerial disturbance in him must have been so immense, that I thought he was gone. But, he soon come round with care, and he sat up on the floor, and he said to me, with wisdom comin out of his eyes, if ever it come: 'Magsman! The most material difference between the two states of existence through which your unhappy friend has passed'; he reached out his poor little hand, and his tears dropped down on the moustachio which it was a credit to him to have done his best to grow, but it is not in mortals to command success – 'the difference this. When I was out of society, I was paid light for being seen. When I went into society, I paid heavy for being seen. I prefer the former, even if I wasn't forced upon it. Give me out through the trumpet, in the hold way, tomorrow.'

Arter that, he slid into the line again as easy as if he had been iled all over. But the organ was kep from him, and no allusions was ever made, when a company was in, to his property. He got wiser every day; his views of society and the public was luminous, bewilderin, awful; and his 'ed got bigger and bigger as his wisdom expanded it.

He took well, and pulled 'em in most excellent for nine weeks. At the expiration of that period, when his 'ed was a sight, he expressed one evenin, the last Company havin been turned out, and the door shut, a wish to have a little music.

'Mr Chops,' I said (I never dropped the 'Mr' with him; the world might do it, but not me); 'Mr Chops, are you sure as you are in a state of mind and body to sit upon the organ?'

His answer was this: 'Toby, when next met with on the tramp, I forgive her and the Indian. And I am.'

It was with fear and trembling that I began to turn the handle; but he sat like a lamb. It will be my belief to my dying day, that I see his 'ed expand as he sat; you may therefore judge how great his thoughts was. He sat out all the changes, and then he come off.

'Toby,' he says, with a quiet smile, 'the little man will now walk three times round the Cairawan, and retire behind the curtain.'

When we called him in the morning, we found him gone into a much better society than mine or Pall Mall's. I give Mr Chops as comfortable a funeral as lay in my power, followed myself as Chief, and had the George IV canvass carried first, in the form of a banner. But, the house was so dismal arterwards, that I giv it up, and took to the wan again.

*   *   *

'I don't triumph,' said Jarber, folding up the second manuscript, and looking hard at Trottle. 'I don't triumph over this worthy creature. I merely ask him if he is satisfied now?'

'How can he be anything else?' I said, answering for Trottle, who sat obstinately silent. 'This time, Jarber, you have not only read us a delightfully amusing story, but you have also answered the question about the house. Of course it stands empty now. Who would think of taking it after it had been turned into a caravan?' I looked at Trottle, as I said those last words, and Jarber waved his hand indulgently in the same direction.

'Let this excellent person speak,' said Jarber. 'You were about to say, my good man?'

'I only wished to ask, sir,' said Trottle doggedly, 'if you could kindly oblige me with a date or two in connection with that last story?'

'A date!' repeated Jarber. 'What does the man want with dates!'

'I should be glad to know, with great respect,' persisted Trottle, 'if the person named Magsman was the last tenant who lived in the house. It's my opinion – if I may be excused for giving it – that he most decidedly was not.'

With those words, Trottle made a low bow, and quietly left the room.

There is no denying that Jarber, when we were left together, looked sadly discomposed. He had evidently forgotten to enquire about dates; and, in spite of his magnificent talk about his series of discoveries, it was quite as plain that the two stories he had just read, had really and truly exhausted his present stock. I thought myself bound, in common gratitude, to help him out of his embarrassment by a timely suggestion. So I proposed that he should come to tea again, on the next Monday evening, the thirteenth, and should make such enquiries in the meantime, as might enable him to dispose triumphantly of Trottle's objection.

He gallantly kissed my hand, made a neat little speech of acknowledgement, and took his leave. For the rest of the week I would not encourage Trottle by allowing him to refer to the house at all. I suspected he was making his own enquiries about dates, but I put no questions to him.

On Monday evening, the thirteenth, that dear unfortunate Jarber came, punctual to the appointed time. He looked so terribly harassed, that he was really quite a spectacle of feebleness and fatigue. I saw, at a glance, that the question of dates had gone against him, that Mr Magsman had not been the last tenant of the house, and that the reason of its emptiness was still to seek.

'What I have gone through,' said Jarber, 'words are not eloquent enough to tell. O Sophonisba, I have begun another series of discoveries! Accept the last two as stories laid on your shrine; and wait to blame me for leaving your curiosity unappeased, until you have heard number three.'

Number three looked like a very short manuscript, and I said as much. Jarber explained to me that we were to have some poetry this time. In the course of his investigations he had stepped into the circulating library, to seek for information on the one important subject. All the library-people knew about the house was, that a female relative of the last tenant, as they believed, had, just after that tenant left, sent a little manuscript poem to them which she described as referring to events that had actually passed in the house; and which she wanted the proprietor of the library to publish. She had written no address on her letter; and the proprietor had kept the manuscript ready to be given back to her (the publishing of poems not being in his line) when she might call for it. She had never called for it; and the poem had been lent to Jarber, at his express request, to read to me.

Before he began, I rang the bell for Trottle; being determined to have him present at the new reading, as a wholesome check on his obstinacy.

To my surprise Peggy answered the bell, and told me, that Trottle had stepped out without saying where. I instantly felt the strongest possible conviction that he was at his old tricks: and that his stepping out in the evening, without leave, meant – philandering.

Controlling myself on my visitor's account, I dismissed Peggy, stifled my indignation, and prepared, as politely as might be, to listen to Jarber.

Three Evenings in the House – Number One

1

Yes, it look'd dark and dreary,
That long and narrow street:
Only the sound of the rain,
And the tramp of passing feet,
The duller glow of the fire,
And gathering mists of night
To mark how slow and weary
The long day's cheerless flight!

2

Watching the sullen fire,
Hearing the dreary rain,
Drop after drop, run down
On the darkening window-pane;
Chill was the heart of Bertha,
Chill as that winter day –
For the star of her life had risen
Only to fade away.

3

The voice that had been so strong
To bid the snare depart,
The true and earnest will,
And the calm and steadfast heart,
Were now weigh'd down by sorrow,
Were quivering now with pain;
The clear path now seem'd clouded,
And all her grief in vain.

4

Duty, Right, Truth, who promised
To help and save their own,
Seem'd spreading wide their pinions
To leave her there alone.
So, turning from the present
To well-known days of yore,
She call'd on them to strengthen
And guard her soul once more.

5

She thought how in her girlhood
Her life was given away,
The solemn promise spoken
She kept so well today;
How to her brother Herbert
She had been help and guide,
And how his artist-nature
On her calm strength relied.

6

How through life's fret and turmoil
The passion and fire of art
In him was soothed and quicken'd
By her true sister heart;
How future hopes had always
Been for his sake alone;
And now, what strange new feeling
Possess'd her as its own?

7

Her home; each flower that breathed there;
The wind's sigh, soft and low;
Each trembling spray of ivy;
The river's murmuring flow;
The shadow of the forest;
Sunset, or twilight dim;
Dear as they were, were dearer
By leaving them for him.

8

And each year as it found her
In the dull, feverish town,
Saw self still more forgotten,
And selfish care kept down
By the calm joy of evening
That brought him to her side,
To warn him with wise counsel,
Or praise with tender pride.

9

Her heart, her life, her future,
Her genius, only meant
Another thing to give him,
And be therewith content.
Today, what words had stirr'd her,
Her soul could not forget?
What dream had fill'd her spirit
With strange and wild regret?

10

To leave him for another:
Could it indeed be so?
Could it have cost such anguish
To bid this vision go?
Was this her faith? Was Herbert
The second in her heart?
Did it need all this struggle
To bid a dream depart?

11

And yet, within her spirit
A far-off land was seen;
A home, which might have held her;
A love, which might have been;
And Life: not the mere being
Of daily ebb and flow,
But Life itself had claim'd her,
And she had let it go!

12

Within her heart there echo'd
Again the well-known tune
That promised this bright future,
And ask'd her for its own:
Then words of sorrow, broken
By half-reproachful pain;
And then a farewell, spoken
In words of cold disdain.

13

Where now was the stern purpose
That nerved her soul so long?
Whence came the words she utter'd,
So hard, so cold, so strong?
What right had she to banish
A hope that God had given?
Why must she choose earth's portion,
And turn aside from Heaven?

14

Today! Was it this morning?
If this long, fearful strife
Was but the work of hours,
What would be years of life?
Why did a cruel Heaven
For such great suffering call?
And why – O, still more cruel! –
Must her own words do all?

15

Did she repent? O Sorrow!
Why do we linger still
To take thy loving message,
And do thy gentle will?
See, her tears fall more slowly;
The passionate murmurs cease,
And back upon her spirit
Flow strength, and love, and peace.

16

The fire burns more brightly,
The rain has passed away,
Herbert will see no shadow
Upon his home today;
Only that Bertha greets him
With doubly tender care,
Kissing a fonder blessing
Down on his golden hair.

Three Evenings in the House – Number Two

1

The studio is deserted,
Palette and brush laid by,
The sketch rests on the easel,
The paint is scarcely dry;
And silence – who seems always
Within her depths to bear
The next sound that will utter –
Now holds a dumb despair.

2

So Bertha feels it: listening
With breathless, stony fear,
Waiting the dreadful summons
Each minute brings more near:
When the young life, now ebbing,
Shall fail, and pass away
Into that mighty shadow
Who shrouds the house today.

3

But why – when the sick chamber
Is on the upper floor –
Why dares not Bertha enter
Within the close-shut door?

If he – her all – her Brother,
Lies dying in that gloom,
What strange mysterious power
Has sent her from the room?

4

It is not one week's anguish
That can have changed her so;
Joy has not died here lately,
Struck down by one quick blow;
But cruel months have needed
Their long relentless chain,
To teach that shrinking manner
Of helpless, hopeless pain.

5

The struggle was scarce over
Last Christmas Eve had brought:
The fibres still were quivering
Of the one wounded thought,
When Herbert – who, unconscious,
Had guessed no inward strife –
Bade her, in pride and pleasure,
Welcome his fair young wife.

6

Bade her rejoice, and smiling,
Although his eyes were dim,
Thank'd God he thus could pay her
The care she gave to him.
This fresh bright life would bring her
A new and joyous fate –
O Bertha, check the murmur
That cries, Too late! too late!

7

Too late! Could she have known it
A few short weeks before,
That his life was completed,
And needing hers no more,

She might – O sad repining!
What 'might have been', forget;
'It was not,' should suffice us
To stifle vain regret.

8

He needed her no longer,
Each day it grew more plain;
First with a startled wonder,
Then with a wondering pain.
Love: why, his wife best gave it;
Comfort: durst Bertha speak?
Counsel: when quick resentment
Flush'd on the young wife's cheek.

9

No more long talks by firelight
Of childish times long past,
And dreams of future greatness
Which he must reach at last;
Dreams, where her purer instinct
With truth unerring told
Where was the worthless gilding,
And where refined gold.

10

Slowly, but surely ever,
Dora's poor jealous pride,
Which she call'd love for Herbert,
Drove Bertha from his side;
And, spite of nervous effort
To share their alter'd life,
She felt a check to Herbert,
A burden to his wife.

11

This was the least; for Bertha
Fear'd, dreaded, *knew* at length,
How much his nature owed her
Of truth, and power, and strength;

And watch'd the daily failing
Of all his nobler part:
Low aims, weak purpose, telling
In lower, weaker art.

12

And now, when he is dying,
The last words she could hear
Must not be hers, but given
The bride of one short year.
The last care is another's;
The last prayer must not be
The one they learnt together
Beside their mother's knee.

13

Summon'd at last: she kisses
The clay-cold stiffening hand;
And, reading pleading efforts
To make her understand,
Answers, with solemn promise,
In clear but trembling tone,
To Dora's life henceforward
She will devote her own.

14

Now all is over. Bertha
Dares not remain to weep,
But soothes the frightened Dora
Into a sobbing sleep.
The poor weak child will need her:
O, who can dare complain,
When God sends a new Duty
To comfort each new Pain!

Three Evenings in the House – Number Three

1

The house is all deserted
In the dim evening gloom,
Only one figure passes
Slowly from room to room;
And, pausing at each doorway,
Seems gathering up again
Within her heart the relics
Of bygone joy and pain.

2

There is an earnest longing
In those who onward gaze,
Looking with weary patience
Towards the coming days.
There is a deeper longing,
More sad, more strong, more keen:
Those know it who look backward,
And yearn for what has been.

3

At every hearth she pauses,
Touches each well-known chair;
Gazes from every window,
Lingers on every stair.
What have these months brought Bertha
Now one more year is past?
This Christmas Eve shall tell us,
The third one and the last.

4

The wilful, wayward Dora,
In those first weeks of grief,
Could seek and find in Bertha
Strength, soothing, and relief.

And Bertha – last sad comfort
True woman-heart can take –
Had something still to suffer
And do for Herbert's sake.

5

Spring, with her western breezes,
From Indian islands bore
To Bertha news that Leonard
Would seek his home once more.
What was it – joy, or sorrow?
What were they – hopes, or fears?
That flush'd her cheeks with crimson,
And fill'd her eyes with tears?

6

He came. And who so kindly
Could ask and hear her tell
Herbert's last hours; for Leonard
Had known and loved him well.
Daily he came; and Bertha,
Poor weary heart, at length,
Weigh'd down by other's weakness,
Could rest upon his strength.

7

Yet not the voice of Leonard
Could her true care beguile,
That turn'd to watch, rejoicing,
Dora's reviving smile.
So, from that little household
The worst gloom pass'd away,
The one bright hour of evening
Lit up the livelong day.

8

Days passed. The golden summer
In sudden heat bore down
Its blue, bright, glowing sweetness
Upon the scorching town.

And sights and sounds of country
Came in the warm soft tune
Sung by the honey'd breezes
Borne on the wings of June.

9

One twilight hour, but earlier
Than usual, Bertha thought
She knew the fresh sweet fragrance
Of flowers that Leonard brought;
Through open'd doors and windows
It stole up through the gloom,
And with appealing sweetness
Drew Bertha from her room.

10

Yes, he was there; and pausing
Just near the open'd door,
To check her heart's quick beating,
She heard – and paused still more –
His low voice Dora's answers –
His pleading – Yes, she knew
The tone – the words – the accents:
She once had heard them too.

11

'Would Bertha blame her?' Leonard's
Low, tender answer came:
'Bertha was far too noble
To think or dream of blame.'
'And was he sure he loved her?'
'Yes, with the one love given
Once in a lifetime only,
With one soul and one heaven!'

12

Then came a plaintive murmur –
'Dora had once been told
That he and Bertha – '
'Dearest, Bertha is far too cold

To love; and I, my Dora,
If once I fancied so,
It was a brief delusion,
And over – long ago.'

13

Between the Past and Present,
On that bleak moment's height,
She stood. As some lost traveller
By a quick flash of light
Seeing a gulf before him,
With dizzy, sick despair,
Reels to clutch backward, but to find
A deeper chasm there.

14

The twilight grew still darker,
The fragrant flowers more sweet,
The stars shone out in heaven,
The lamps gleam'd down the street;
And hours pass'd in dreaming
Over their new-found fate,
Ere they could think of wondering
Why Bertha was so late.

15

She came, and calmly listen'd;
In vain they strove to trace
If Herbert's memory shadow'd
In grief upon her face.
No blame, no wonder show'd there,
No feeling could be told;
Her voice was not less steady,
Her manner not more cold.

16

They could not hear the anguish
That broke in words of pain
Through that calm summer midnight –
'My Herbert – mine again!'

Yes, they have once been parted,
But this day shall restore
The long lost one: she claims him:
'My Herbert – mine once more!'

17

Now Christmas Eve returning,
Saw Bertha stand beside
The altar, greeting Dora,
Again a smiling bride;
And now the gloomy evening
Sees Bertha pale and worn,
Leaving the house for ever,
To wander out forlorn.

18

Forlorn – nay, not so. Anguish
Shall do its work at length;
Her soul, pass'd through the fire,
Shall gain still purer strength.
Somewhere there waits for Bertha
An earnest noble part;
And, meanwhile, God is with her –
God, and her own true heart!

* * *

I could warmly and sincerely praise the little poem, when Jarber had done reading it; but I could not say that it tended in any degree towards clearing up the mystery of the empty house.

Whether it was the absence of the irritating influence of Trottle, or whether it was simply fatigue, I cannot say, but Jarber did not strike me, that evening, as being in his usual spirits. And though he declared that he was not in the least daunted by his want of success thus far, and that he was resolutely determined to make more discoveries, he spoke in a languid absent manner, and shortly afterwards took his leave at rather an early hour.

When Trottle came back, and when I indignantly taxed him with Philandering, he not only denied the imputation, but asserted that he had been employed on my service, and, in consideration of that, boldly asked for leave of absence for two days, and for a morning to himself afterwards, to complete the business, in which he solemnly declared that I was interested. In remembrance of his long and faithful service to me, I did violence to myself, and granted his request. And he, on his side, engaged to explain himself to my satisfaction, in a week's time, on Monday evening the twentieth.

A day or two before, I sent to Jarber's lodgings to ask him to drop in to tea. His landlady sent back an apology for him that made my hair stand on end. His feet were in hot water; his head was in a flannel petticoat; a green shade was over his eyes; the rheumatism was in his legs; and a mustard-poultice was on his chest. He was also a little feverish, and rather distracted in his mind about Manchester Marriages, a Dwarf, and Three Evenings, or Evening Parties – his landlady was not sure which – in an empty house, with the Water Rate unpaid.

Under these distressing circumstances, I was necessarily left alone with Trottle. His promised explanation began, like Jarber's discoveries, with the reading of a written paper. The only difference was that Trottle introduced his manuscript under the name of a report.

Trottle's Report

The curious events related in these pages would, many of them, most likely never have happened, if a person named Trottle had not presumed, contrary to his usual custom, to think for himself.

The subject on which the person in question had ventured, for the first time in his life, to form an opinion purely and entirely his own, was one which had already excited the interest of his respected mistress in a very extraordinary degree. Or, to put it in plainer terms still, the subject was no other than the mystery of the empty house.

Feeling no sort of objection to set a success of his own, if possible, side by side with a failure of Mr Jarber's, Trottle made up his mind, one Monday evening, to try what he could do, on his own account, towards clearing up the mystery of the empty house. Carefully dismissing from his mind all nonsensical notions of former tenants and their histories, and keeping the one point in view steadily before him, he started to reach it in the shortest way, by walking straight up to the house, and bringing himself face to face with the first person in it who opened the door to him.

It was getting towards dark, on Monday evening, the thirteenth of the month, when Trottle first set foot on the steps of the house. When he knocked at the door, he knew nothing of the matter which he was about to investigate, except that the landlord was an elderly widower of good fortune, and that his name was Forley. A small beginning enough for a man to start from, certainly!

On dropping the knocker, his first proceeding was to look down cautiously out of the corner of his right eye, for any results which might show themselves at the kitchen-window. There appeared at it immediately the figure of a woman, who looked up inquisitively at the stranger on the steps, left the window in a hurry, and came back to it with an open letter in her hand, which she held up to the fading light. After looking over the letter hastily for a moment or so, the woman disappeared once more.

Trottle next heard footsteps shuffling and scraping along the bare hall of the house. On a sudden they ceased, and the sound of two voices – a shrill persuading voice and a gruff resisting voice – confusedly reached his ears. After a while, the voices left off speaking – a chain was undone, a bolt drawn back – the door opened – and Trottle stood face to face with two persons, a woman in advance, and a man behind her, leaning back flat against the wall.

'Wish you good evening, sir,' says the woman, in such a sudden way, and in such a cracked voice, that it was quite startling to hear her. 'Chilly weather, ain't it, sir? Please to walk in. You come from good Mr Forley, don't you, sir?'

'Don't you, sir?' chimes in the man hoarsely, making a sort of gruff echo of himself, and chuckling after it, as if he thought he had made a joke.

If Trottle had said, 'No,' the door would have been probably closed in his face. Therefore, he took circumstances as he found them, and boldly ran all the risk, whatever it might be, of saying, 'Yes.'

'Quite right sir,' says the woman. 'Good Mr Forley's letter told us his particular friend would be here to represent him, at dusk, on Monday the thirteenth – or, if not on Monday the thirteenth, then on Monday the twentieth, at the same time, without fail. And here you are on Monday the thirteenth, ain't you, sir? Mr Forley's particular friend, and dressed all in black – quite right, sir! Please to step into the dining-room – it's always kep scoured and clean against Mr Forley comes here – and I'll fetch a candle in half a minute. It gets so dark in the evenings, now, you hardly know where you are, do you, sir? And how is good Mr Forley in his health? We trust he is better, Benjamin, don't we? We are so sorry not to see him as usual, Benjamin, ain't we? In half a minute, sir, if you don't mind waiting, I'll be back with the candle. Come along, Benjamin.'

'Come along, Benjamin,' chimes in the echo, and chuckles again as if he thought he had made another joke.

Left alone in the empty front-parlour, Trottle wondered what was coming next, as he heard the shuffling, scraping footsteps go slowly down the kitchen-stairs. The front-door had been carefully chained up and bolted behind him on his entrance; and there was not the least chance of his being able to open it to effect his escape, without betraying himself by making a noise.

Not being of the Jarber sort, luckily for himself, he took his situation quietly, as he found it, and turned his time, while alone, to account, by summing up in his own mind the few particulars which he had discovered thus far. He had found out, first, that Mr Forley was in the habit of visiting the house regularly. Second, that Mr Forley being prevented by illness from seeing the people put in charge as usual, had appointed a friend to represent him; and had written to say so. Third, that the friend had a choice of two Mondays, at a particular time in the evening, for doing his errand; and that Trottle had accidentally hit on this time, and on the first of the Mondays, for beginning his own investigations. Fourth, that the similarity between Trottle's black dress, as servant out of livery, and the dress of the messenger (whoever he might be), had helped the error by which Trottle was profiting. So far, so good. But what was the messenger's errand? and what chance was there that he might not come up and knock at the door himself, from minute to minute, on that very evening?

While Trottle was turning over this last consideration in his mind, he heard the shuffling footsteps come up the stairs again, with a flash of candlelight going before them. He waited for the woman's coming in with some little anxiety; for the twilight had been too dim on his getting into the house to allow him to see either her face or the man's face at all clearly.

The woman came in first, with the man she called Benjamin at her heels, and set the candle on the mantelpiece. Trottle takes leave to describe her as an offensively cheerful old woman, awfully lean and wiry, and sharp all over, at eyes, nose, and chin – devilishly brisk, smiling, and restless, with a dirty false front and a dirty black cap, and short fidgety arms, and long hooked fingernails – an unnaturally lusty old woman, who walked with a spring in her wicked old feet, and spoke with a smirk on her wicked old face – the sort of old woman (as Trottle thinks) who ought to have lived in the dark ages, and been ducked in a horse-pond, instead of flourishing in the nineteenth century, and taking charge of a Christian house.

'You'll please to excuse my son, Benjamin, won't you, sir?' says this witch without a broomstick, pointing to the man behind her, propped against the bare wall of the dining-room, exactly as he had been propped against the bare wall of the passage. 'He's got his inside dreadful bad again, has my son Benjamin. And he won't go to bed, and he will follow me about the house, upstairs and downstairs, and in my lady's chamber, as the song says, you know. It's his indisgestion, poor dear, that sours his temper and makes him so aggravating – and indisgestion is a wearing thing to the best of us, ain't it, sir?'

'Ain't it, sir?' chimes in aggravating Benjamin, winking at the candlelight like an owl at the sunshine.

Trottle examined the man curiously, while his horrid old mother was speaking of him. He found 'My son Benjamin' to be little and lean, and buttoned-up slovenly in a frowsy old greatcoat that fell down to his ragged carpet-slippers. His eyes were very watery, his cheeks very pale, and his lips very red. His breathing was so uncommonly loud, that it sounded almost like a snore. His head rolled helplessly in the monstrous big collar of his greatcoat; and his limp, lazy hands pottered about the wall on either side of him, as if they were groping for a imaginary bottle. In plain English, the complaint of 'My son Benjamin' was drunkenness, of the stupid, pig-headed, sottish kind. Drawing this conclusion easily enough, after a moment's observation of the man, Trottle found himself, nevertheless, keeping his eyes fixed much longer than was necessary on the ugly drunken face rolling about in the monstrous big coat collar, and looking at it with a curiosity that he could hardly account for at first. Was there something familiar to him in the man's features? He turned away from them for an instant, and then turned back to him again. After that second look, the notion forced itself into his mind, that he had certainly seen a face somewhere, of which that sot's face appeared like a kind of slovenly copy. 'Where?' thinks he to himself, 'where did I last see the man whom this aggravating Benjamin, here, so very strongly reminds me of?'

It was no time, just then – with the cheerful old woman's eye searching him all over, and the cheerful old woman's tongue talking at him, nineteen to the dozen – for Trottle to be ransacking his memory for small matters that had got into wrong corners of it. He put by in his mind that very curious circumstance respecting Benjamin's face, to be taken up again when a fit opportunity offered itself; and kept his wits about him in prime order for present necessities.

'You wouldn't like to go down into the kitchen, would you?' says the witch without the broomstick, as familiar as if she had been Trottle's mother, instead of Benjamin's. 'There's a bit of fire in the grate, and the sink in the back kitchen don't smell to matter much today, and it's uncommon chilly up here when a person's flesh don't hardly cover a person's bones. But you don't look cold, sir, do you? And then, why, Lord bless my soul, our little bit of business is so very, very little, it's hardly worth while to go downstairs about it, after all. Quite a game at business, ain't it, sir? Give-and-take, that's what I call it – give-and-take!'

With that, her wicked old eyes settled hungrily on the region round about Trottle's waistcoat-pocket, and she began to chuckle like her son, holding out one of her skinny hands, and tapping cheerfully in the palm with the knuckles of the other. Aggravating Benjamin, seeing what she was about, roused up a little, chuckled and tapped in imitation of her, got an idea of his own into his muddled head all of a sudden, and bolted it out charitably for the benefit of Trottle.

'I say!' says Benjamin, settling himself against the wall and nodding his head viciously at his cheerful old mother. 'I say! Look out. She'll skin you!'

Assisted by these signs and warnings, Trottle found no difficulty in understanding that the business referred to was the giving and taking of money, and that he was expected to be the giver. It was at this stage of the proceedings that he first felt decidedly uncomfortable, and more than half inclined to wish he was on the street-side of the house-door again.

He was still cudgelling his brains for an excuse to save his pocket, when the silence was suddenly interrupted by a sound in the upper part of the house.

It was not at all loud – it was a quiet, still, scraping sound – so faint that it could hardly have reached the quickest ears, except in an empty house.

'Do you hear that, Benjamin?' says the old woman. 'He's at it again, even in the dark, ain't he? P'raps you'd like to see him, sir!' says she, turning on Trottle, and poking her grinning face close to him. 'Only name it; only say if you'd like to see him before we do our little bit of business – and I'll show good Forley's friend upstairs, just as if he was good Mr Forley himself. *My* legs are all right, whatever Benjamin's may be. I get younger and younger, and stronger and stronger, and jollier and jollier, every day – that's what I do! Don't mind the stairs on my account, sir, if you'd like to see him.'

'Him?' Trottle wondered whether 'him' meant a man, or a boy, or a domestic animal of the male species. Whatever it meant, here was a chance of putting off that uncomfortable give-and-take-business, and, better still, a chance perhaps of finding out one of the secrets of the mysterious house. Trottle's spirits began to rise again and he said 'Yes,' directly, with the confidence of a man who knew all about it.

Benjamin's mother took the candle at once, and lighted Trottle briskly to the stairs; and Benjamin himself tried to follow as usual. But getting up several flights of stairs, even helped by the banisters, was more, with his particular complaint, than he seemed to feel himself inclined to venture on. He sat down obstinately on the lowest step, with his head against the wall, and the tails of his big greatcoat spreading out magnificently on the stairs behind him and above him, like a dirty imitation of a court lady's train.

'Don't sit there, dear,' says his affectionate mother, stopping to snuff the candle on the first landing.

'I shall sit here,' says Benjamin, aggravating to the last, 'till the milk comes in the morning.'

The cheerful old woman went on nimbly up the stairs to the first floor, and Trottle followed, with his eyes and ears wide open. He had seen nothing out of the common in the front-parlour, or up the staircase, so far. The house was dirty and dreary and close-smelling – but there was nothing about it to excite the least curiosity, except the faint scraping sound, which was now beginning to get a little clearer – though still not at all loud – as Trottle followed his leader up the stairs to the second floor.

Nothing on the second-floor landing, but cobwebs above and bits of broken plaster below, cracked off from the ceiling. Benjamin's mother was not a bit out of breath, and looked all ready to go to the top of the monument if necessary. The faint scraping sound had got a little clearer still; but Trottle was no nearer to guessing what it might be, than when he first heard it in the parlour downstairs.

On the third, and last, floor, there were two doors; one, which was shut, leading into the front garret; and one, which was ajar, leading into the back garret. There was a loft in the ceiling above the landing; but the cobwebs all over it vouched sufficiently for its not having been opened for some little time. The scraping noise, plainer than ever here, sounded on the other side of the back garret door; and, to Trottle's great relief, that was precisely the door which the cheerful old woman now pushed open.

Trottle followed her in; and, for once in his life, at any rate, was struck dumb with amazement, at the sight which the inside of the room revealed to him.

The garret was absolutely empty of everything in the shape of furniture. It must have been used at one time or other, by somebody engaged in a profession or a trade which required for the practice of it a great deal of light; for the one window in the room, which looked out on a wide open space at the back of the house, was three or four times as large, every way, as a garret-window usually is. Close under this window, kneeling on the bare boards with his face to the door, there appeared, of all the creatures in the world to see alone at such a place and at such a time, a mere mite of a child – a little, lonely, wizen, strangely clad boy, who could not, at the most, have been more than five years old. He had a greasy old blue shawl crossed over his breast, and rolled up, to keep the ends from the ground, into a great big lump on his back. A strip of something which looked like the remains of a woman's flannel petticoat, showed itself under the shawl, and, below that again, a pair of rusty black stockings, worlds too large for him, covered his legs and his shoeless feet. A pair of old clumsy muffetees, which had worked themselves up on his little frail red arms to the elbows, and a big cotton nightcap that had dropped down to his very eyebrows, finished off the strange dress which the poor little man seemed not half big enough to fill out, and not near strong enough to walk about in.

But there was something to see even more extraordinary than the clothes the child was swaddled up in, and that was the game which he was playing at, all by himself; and which, moreover, explained in the most unexpected manner the faint scraping noise that had found its way downstairs, through the half-opened door, in the silence of the empty house.

It has been mentioned that the child was on his knees in the garret, when Trottle first saw him. He was not saying his prayers, and not crouching down in terror at being alone in the dark. He was, odd and unaccountable as it may appear, doing nothing more or less than playing at a charwoman's or housemaid's business of scouring the floor. Both his little hands had tight hold of a mangy old blacking-brush, with hardly any bristles left in it, which he was rubbing backwards and forwards on the boards, as gravely and steadily as if he had been at scouring-work for years, and had got a large family to keep by it. The coming-in of Trottle and the old woman did not startle or disturb him in the least. He just looked up for a minute at the candle, with a pair of very bright, sharp eyes, and then went on with his work again, as if nothing had happened. On one side of him was a battered pint saucepan without a handle, which was his make-believe pail; and on the other a morsel of slate-coloured cotton rag, which stood for his flannel to wipe up with. After scrubbing bravely for a minute or two, he took the bit of rag, and mopped up, and then squeezed make-believe water out into his make-believe pail, as grave as any judge that ever sat on a Bench. By the time he thought he had got the floor pretty dry, he raised himself upright on his knees, and blew out a good long breath, and set his little red arms akimbo, and nodded at Trottle.

'There!' says the child, knitting his little downy eyebrows into a frown. 'Drat the dirt! I've cleaned up. Where's my beer?'

Benjamin's mother chuckled till Trottle thought she would have choked herself.

'Lord ha' mercy on us!' says she, 'just hear the imp. You would never think he was only five years old, would you, sir? Please to tell good Mr Forley you saw him going on as nicely as ever, playing at being me scouring the parlour floor, and calling for my beer afterwards. That's his regular game, morning, noon, and night – he's never tired of it. Only look how snug we've been and dressed him. That's my shawl a keepin his precious little body warm, and Benjamin's nightcap a keepin his precious little head warm, and Benjamin's stockings, drawed over his trousers, a keepin his precious little legs warm. He's snug and happy if ever a imp was yet. "Where's my beer!" – say it again, little dear, say it again!'

If Trottle had seen the boy, with a light and a fire in the room, clothed like other children, and playing naturally with a top, or a box of soldiers, or a bouncing big India-rubber ball, he might have been as cheerful under the circumstances as Benjamin's mother herself. But seeing the child reduced (as he could not help suspecting) for want of proper toys and proper child's company, to take up with the mocking of an old woman at her scouring-work, for something to stand in the place of a game, Trottle, though not a family man, nevertheless felt the sight before him to be, in its way, one of the saddest and the most pitiable that he had ever witnessed.

'Why, my man,' says he, 'you're the boldest little chap in all England. You don't seem a bit afraid of being up here all by yourself in the dark.'

'The big winder,' says the child, pointing up to it, 'sees in the dark; and I see with the big winder.' He stops a bit, and gets up on his legs, and looks hard at Benjamin's mother. 'I'm a good 'un,' says he, 'ain't I? I save candle.'

Trottle wondered what else the forlorn little creature had been brought up to do without, besides candlelight; and risked putting a question as to whether he ever got a run in the open air to cheer him up a bit. O, yes, he had a run now and then, out of doors (to say nothing of his runs about the house), the lively little cricket – a run according to good Mr Forley's instructions, which were followed out carefully, as good Mr Forley's friend would be glad to hear, to the very letter.

As Trottle could only have made one reply to this, namely, that good Mr Forley's instructions were, in his opinion, the instructions of an infernal scamp; and as he felt that such an answer would naturally prove the deathblow to all further discoveries on his part, he gulped down his feelings before they got too many for him, and held his tongue, and looked round towards the window again to see what the forlorn little boy was going to amuse himself with next.

The child had gathered up his blacking-brush and bit of rag, and had put them into the old tin saucepan; and was now working his way, as well as his clothes would let him, with his make-believe pail hugged up in his arms, towards a door of communication which led from the back to the front garret.

'I say,' says he, looking round sharply over his shoulder, 'what are you two stopping here for? I'm going to bed now – and so I tell you!'

With that, he opened the door, and walked into the front room. Seeing Trottle take a step or two to follow him, Benjamin's mother opened her wicked old eyes in a state of great astonishment.

'Mercy on us!' says she, 'haven't you seen enough of him yet?'

'No,' says Trottle. 'I should like to see him go to bed.'

Benjamin's mother burst into such a fit of chuckling that the loose extinguisher in the candlestick clattered again with the shaking of her hand. To think of good Mr Forley's friend taking ten times more trouble about the imp than good Mr Forley himself! Such a joke as that, Benjamin's mother had not often met with in the course of her life, and she begged to be excused if she took the liberty of having a laugh at it.

Leaving her to laugh as much as she pleased, and coming to a pretty positive conclusion, after what he had just heard, that Mr Forley's interest in the child was not of the fondest possible kind, Trottle walked into the front room, and Benjamin's mother, enjoying herself immensely, followed with the candle.

There were two pieces of furniture in the front garret. One, an old stool of the sort that is used to stand a cask of beer on; and the other a great big rickety straddling old truckle bedstead. In the middle of this bedstead, surrounded by a dim brown waste of sacking, was a kind of little island of poor bedding – an old bolster, with nearly all the feathers out of it, doubled in three for a pillow; a mere shred of patchwork counterpane, and a blanket; and under that, and peeping out a little on either side beyond the loose clothes, two faded chair cushions of horsehair, laid along together for a sort of makeshift mattress. When Trottle got into the room, the lonely little boy had scrambled up on the bedstead with the help of the beer-stool, and was kneeling on the outer rim of sacking with the shred of counterpane in his hands, just making ready to tuck it in for himself under the chair cushions.

'I'll tuck you up, my man,' says Trottle. 'Jump into bed, and let me try.'

'I mean to tuck myself up,' says the poor forlorn child, 'and I don't mean to jump. I mean to crawl, I do – and so I tell you!'

With that, he set to work, tucking in the clothes tight all down the sides of the cushions, but leaving them open at the foot. Then, getting up on his knees, and looking hard at Trottle as much as to say, 'What do you mean by offering to help such a handy little chap as me?' he began to untie the big shawl for himself, and did it, too, in less than half a minute. Then, doubling the shawl up loose over the foot of the bed, he says, 'I say, look here,' and ducks under the clothes, head first, worming his way up and up softly, under the blanket and counterpane, till Trottle saw the top of the large nightcap slowly peep out on the bolster. This oversized headgear of the child's had so shoved itself down in the course of his journey to the pillow, under the clothes, that when he got his face fairly out on the bolster, he was all nightcap down to his mouth. He soon freed himself, however, from this slight encumbrance by turning the ends of the cap up gravely to their old place over his eyebrows – looked at Trottle – said, 'Snug, ain't it? Goodbye!' – popped his face under the clothes again – and left nothing to be seen of him but the empty peak of the big nightcap standing up sturdily on end in the middle of the bolster.

'What a young limb it is, ain't it?' says Benjamin's mother, giving Trottle a cheerful dig with her elbow. 'Come on! you won't see no more of him tonight!'

'And so I tell you!' sings out a shrill, little voice under the bedclothes, chiming in with a playful finish to the old woman's last words.

If Trottle had not been, by this time, positively resolved to follow the wicked secret which accident had mixed him up with, through all its turnings and windings, right on to the end, he would have probably snatched the boy up then and there, and carried him off from his garret prison, bedclothes and all. As it was, he put a strong check on himself, kept his eye on future possibilities, and allowed Benjamin's mother to lead him downstairs again.

'Mind them top banisters,' says she, as Trottle laid his hand on them. 'They are as rotten as medlars every one of 'em.'

'When people come to see the premises,' says Trottle, trying to feel his way a little farther into the mystery of the house, 'you don't bring many of them up here, do you?'

'Bless your heart alive!' says she, 'nobody ever comes now. The outside of the house is quite enough to warn them off. Mores the pity, as I say. It used to keep me in spirits, staggering 'em all, one after another, with the frightful high rent – specially the women, drat 'em. "What's the rent of this house?" – "Hundred and twenty pound a-year!" – "Hundred and twenty? why, there ain't a house in the street as lets for more than eighty!" – "Likely enough, ma'am; other landlords may lower their rents if they please; but this here landlord sticks to his rights, and means to have as much for his house as his father had before him!" – "But the neighbourhood's gone off since then!" – "Hundred and twenty pound, ma'am." – "The landlord must be mad!" – "Hundred and twenty pound, ma'am." – "Open the door you impertinent woman!" Lord! what a happiness it was to see 'em bounce out, with that awful rent a-ringing in their ears all down the street!'

She stopped on the second-floor landing to treat herself to another chuckle, while Trottle privately posted up in his memory what he had just heard. 'Two points made out,' he thought to himself: 'the house is kept empty on purpose, and the way it's done is to ask a rent that nobody will pay.'

'Ah, deary me!' says Benjamin's mother, changing the subject on a sudden, and twisting back with a horrid, greedy quickness to those awkward money-matters which she had broached down in the parlour. 'What we've done, one way and another for Mr Forley, it isn't in words to tell! That nice little bit of business of ours ought to be a bigger bit of business, considering the trouble we take, Benjamin and me, to make the imp upstairs as happy as the day is long. If good Mr Forley would only please to think a little more of what a deal he owes to Benjamin and me – '

'That's just it,' says Trottle, catching her up short in desperation, and seeing his way, by the help of those last words of hers, to slipping cleverly through her fingers. 'What should you say, if I told you that Mr Forley was nothing like so far from thinking about that little matter as you fancy? You would be disappointed, now, if I told you that I had come today without the money?' – (her lank old jaw fell, and her villainous old eyes glared, in a perfect state of panic, at that!) – 'But what should you say, if I told you that Mr Forley was only waiting for my report, to send me here next Monday, at dusk, with a bigger bit of business for us two to do together than ever you think for? What should you say to that?'

The old wretch came so near to Trottle, before she answered, and jammed him up confidentially so close into the corner of the landing, that his throat, in a manner, rose at her.

'Can you count it off, do you think, on more than that?' says she, holding up her four skinny fingers and her long crooked thumb, all of a tremble, right before his face.

'What do you say to two hands, instead of one?' says he, pushing past her, and getting downstairs as fast as he could.

What she said Trottle thinks it best not to report, seeing that the old hypocrite, getting next door to light-headed at the golden prospect before her, took such liberties with unearthly names and persons which ought never to have approached her lips, and rained down such an awful shower of blessings on Trottle's head, that his hair almost stood on end to hear her. He went on downstairs as fast as his feet would carry him, till he was brought up all standing, as the sailors say, on the last flight, by aggravating Benjamin, lying right across the stair, and fallen off, as might have been expected, into a heavy drunken sleep.

The sight of him instantly reminded Trottle of the curious half likeness which he had already detected between the face of Benjamin and the face of another man, whom he had seen at a past time in very different circumstances. He determined, before leaving the house, to have one more look at the wretched muddled creature; and accordingly shook him up smartly, and propped him against the staircase wall, before his mother could interfere.

'Leave him to me; I'll freshen him up,' says Trottle to the old woman, looking hard in Benjamin's face, while he spoke.

The fright and surprise of being suddenly woke up, seemed, for about a quarter of a minute, to sober the creature. When he first opened his eyes, there was a new look in them for a moment, which struck home to Trottle's memory as quick and as clear as a flash of light. The old maudlin sleepy expression came back again in another instant, and blurred out all further signs and tokens of the past. But Trottle had seen enough in the moment before it came; and he troubled Benjamin's face with no more enquiries.

'Next Monday, at dusk,' says he, cutting short some more of the old woman's palaver about Benjamin's indisgestion. 'I've got no more time to spare, ma'am, tonight: please to let me out.'

With a few last blessings, a few last dutiful messages to good Mr Forley, and a few last friendly hints not to forget next Monday at dusk, Trottle contrived to struggle through the sickening business of leave-taking; to get the door opened; and to find himself, to his own indescribable relief, once more on the outer side of the house to let.

Let at Last

'There, ma'am!' said Trottle, folding up the manuscript from which he had been reading, and setting it down with a smart tap of triumph on the table. 'May I venture to ask what you think of that plain statement, as a guess on my part (and not on Mr Jarber's) at the riddle of the empty house?'

For a minute or two I was unable to say a word. When I recovered a little, my first question referred to the poor forlorn little boy.

'Today is Monday the twentieth,' I said. 'Surely you have not let a whole week go by without trying to find out something more?'

'Except at bedtime, and meals, ma'am,' answered Trottle, 'I have not let an hour go by. Please to understand that I have only come to an end of what I have written, and not to an end of what I have done. I wrote down those first particulars, ma'am, because they are of great importance, and also because I was determined to come forward with my written documents, seeing that Mr Jarber chose to come forward, in the first instance, with his. I am now ready to go on with the second part of my story as shortly and plainly as possible, by word of mouth. The first thing I must clear up, if you please, is the matter of Mr Forley's family affairs. I have heard you speak of them, ma'am, at various times; and I have understood that Mr Forley had two children only by his deceased wife, both daughters. The eldest daughter married, to her father's entire satisfaction, one Mr Bayne, a rich man, holding a high government situation in Canada. She is now living there with her husband, and her only child, a little girl of eight or nine years old. Right so far, I think, ma'am?'

'Quite right,' I said.

'The second daughter,' Trottle went on, 'and Mr Forley's favourite, set her father's wishes and the opinions of the world at flat defiance, by running away with a man of low origin – a mate of a merchant-vessel, named Kirkland. Mr Forley not only never forgave that marriage, but vowed that he would visit the scandal of it heavily in the future on husband and wife. Both escaped his vengeance, whatever he meant it to be. The husband was drowned on his first voyage after his marriage, and the wife died in child-bed. Right again, I believe, ma'am?'

'Again quite right.'

'Having got the family matter all right, we will now go back, ma'am, to me and my doings. Last Monday, I asked you for leave of absence for two days; I employed the time in clearing up the matter of Benjamin's face. Last Saturday I was out of the way when you wanted me. I played truant, ma'am, on that occasion, in company with a friend of mine, who is managing clerk in a lawyer's office; and we both spent the morning at Doctors' Commons, over the last will and testament of Mr Forley's father. Leaving the will-business for a moment, please to follow me first, if you have no objection, into the ugly subject of Benjamin's face. About six or seven years ago (thanks to your kindness) I had a week's holiday with some friends of mine who live in the town of Pendlebury. One of those friends (the only one now left in the place) kept a chemist's shop, and in that shop I was made acquainted with one of the two doctors in the town, named Barsham. This Barsham was a first-rate surgeon, and might have got to the top of his profession, if he had not been a first-rate blackguard. As it was, he both drank and gambled; nobody would have anything to do with him in Pendlebury; and, at the time when I was made known to him in the chemist's shop, the other doctor, Mr Dix, who was not to be compared with him for surgical skill, but who was a respectable man, had got all the practice; and Barsham and his old mother were living together in such a condition of utter poverty, that it was a marvel to everybody how they kept out of the parish workhouse.'

'Benjamin and Benjamin's mother!'

'Exactly, ma'am. Last Thursday morning (thanks to your kindness, again) I went to Pendlebury to my friend the chemist, to ask a few questions about Barsham and his mother. I was told that they had both left the town about five years since. When I enquired into the circumstances, some strange particulars came out in the course of the chemist's answer. You know I have no doubt, ma'am, that poor Mrs Kirkland was confined while her husband was at sea, in lodgings at a village called Flatfield, and that she died and was buried there. But what you may not know is, that Flatfield is only three miles from Pendlebury; that the doctor who attended on Mrs Kirkland was Barsham; that the nurse who took care of her was Barsham's mother; and that the person who called them both in, was Mr Forley. Whether his daughter wrote to him, or whether he heard of it in some other way, I don't know; but he was with her (though he had sworn never to see her again when she married) a month or more before her confinement, and was backwards and forwards a good deal between Flatfield and Pendlebury. How he managed matters with the Barshams cannot at present be discovered; but it is a fact that he contrived to keep the drunken doctor sober, to everybody's amazement. It is a fact that Barsham went to the poor woman with all his wits about him. It is a fact that he and his mother came back from Flatfield after Mrs Kirkland's death, packed up what few things they had, and left the town mysteriously by night. And, lastly, it is also a fact that the other doctor, Mr Dix, was not called in to help, till a week after the birth *and burial* of the child, when the mother was sinking from exhaustion – exhaustion (to give the vagabond, Barsham, his due) not produced, in Mr Dix's opinion, by improper medical treatment, but by the bodily weakness of the poor woman herself – '

'Burial of the child?' I interrupted, trembling all over. 'Trottle! you spoke that word "burial" in a very strange way – you are fixing your eyes on me now with a very strange look – '

Trottle leaned over close to me, and pointed through the window to the empty house.

'The child's death is registered, at Pendlebury,' he said, 'on Barsham's certificate, under the head of Male Infant, Still-Born. The child's coffin lies in the mother's grave, in Flatfield churchyard. The child himself – as surely as I live and breathe, is living and breathing now – a castaway and a prisoner in that villainous house!'

I sank back in my chair.

'It's guesswork, so far, but it is borne in on my mind, for all that, as truth. Rouse yourself, ma'am, and think a little. The last I hear of Barsham, he is attending Mr Forley's disobedient daughter. The next I see of Barsham, he is in Mr Forley's house, trusted with a secret. He and his mother leave Pendlebury suddenly and suspiciously five years back; and he and his mother have got a child of five years old, hidden away in the house. Wait! please to wait – I have not done yet. The will left by Mr Forley's father, strengthens the suspicion. The friend I took with me to Doctors' Commons, made himself master of the contents of that will; and when he had done so, I put these two questions to him. "Can Mr Forley leave his money at his own discretion to anybody he pleases?" "No," my friend says, "his father has left him with only a life interest in it." "Suppose one of Mr Forley's married daughters has a girl, and the other a boy, how would the money go?" "It would all go," my friend says, "to the boy, and it would be charged with the payment of a certain annual income to his female cousin. After her death, it would go back to the male descendant, and to his heirs." Consider that, ma'am! The child of the daughter whom Mr Forley hates, whose husband has been snatched away from his vengeance by death, takes his whole property in defiance of him; and the child of the daughter whom he loves, is left a pensioner on her low-born boy-cousin for life! There was good – too good reason – why that child of Mrs Kirkland's should be registered still-born. And if, as I believe, the register is founded on a false certificate, there is better, still better reason, why the existence of the child should be hidden, and all trace of his parentage blotted out, in the garret of that empty house.'

He stopped, and pointed for the second time to the dim, dust-covered garret-windows opposite. As he did so, I was startled – a very slight matter sufficed to frighten me now – by a knock at the door of the room in which we were sitting.

My maid came in, with a letter in her hand. I took it from her. The mourning card, which was all the envelope enclosed, dropped from my hands.

George Forley was no more. He had departed this life three days since, on the evening of Friday.

'Did our last chance of discovering the truth,' I asked, 'rest with *him*? Has it died with *his* death?'

'Courage, ma'am! I think not. Our chance rests on our power to make Barsham and his mother confess; and Mr Forley's death, by leaving them helpless, seems to put that power into our hands. With your permission, I will not wait till dusk today, as I at first intended, but will make sure of those two people at once. With a policeman in plain clothes to watch the house, in case they try to leave it; with this card to vouch for the fact of Mr Forley's death; and with a bold acknowledgement on my part of having got possession of their secret, and of being ready to use it against them in case of need, I think there is little doubt of bringing Barsham and his mother to terms. In case I find it impossible to get back here before dusk, please to sit near the window, ma'am, and watch the house, a little before they light the street-lamps. If you see the front-door open and close again, will you be good enough to put on your bonnet, and come across to me immediately? Mr Forley's death may, or may not, prevent his messenger from coming as arranged. But, if the person does come, it is of importance that you, as a relative of Mr Forley's, should be present to see him, and to have that proper influence over him which I cannot pretend to exercise.'

The only words I could say to Trottle as he opened the door and left me, were words charging him to take care that no harm happened to the poor forlorn little boy.

Left alone, I drew my chair to the window; and looked out with a beating heart at the guilty house. I waited and waited through what appeared to me to be an endless time, until I heard the wheels of a cab stop at the end of the street. I looked in that direction, and saw Trottle get out of the cab alone, walk up to the house, and knock at the door. He was let in by Barsham's mother. A minute or two later, a decently dressed man sauntered past the house, looked up at it for a moment, and sauntered on to the corner of the street close by. Here he leant against the post, and lighted a cigar, and stopped there smoking in an idle way, but keeping his face always turned in the direction of the house-door.

I waited and waited still. I waited and waited, with my eyes riveted to the door of the house. At last I thought I saw it open in the dusk, and then felt sure I heard it shut again softly. Though I tried hard to compose myself, I trembled so that I was obliged to call for Peggy to help me on with my bonnet and cloak, and was forced to take her arm to lean on, in crossing the street.

Trottle opened the door to us, before we could knock. Peggy went back, and I went in. He had a lighted candle in his hand.

'It has happened, ma'am, as I thought it would,' he whispered, leading me into the bare, comfortless, empty parlour. 'Barsham and his mother have consulted their own interests, and have come to terms. My guess-work is guesswork no longer. It is now what I felt it was – Truth!'

Something strange to me – something which women who are mothers must often know – trembled suddenly in my heart, and brought the warm tears of my youthful days thronging back into my eyes. I took my faithful old servant by the hand, and asked him to let me see Mrs Kirkland's child, for his mother's sake.

'If you desire it, ma'am,' said Trottle, with a gentleness of manner that I had never noticed in him before. 'But pray don't think me wanting in duty and right feeling, if I beg you to try and wait a little. You are agitated already, and a first meeting with the child will not help to make you so calm, as you would wish to be, if Mr Forley's messenger comes. The little boy is safe upstairs. Pray think first of trying to compose yourself for a meeting with a stranger; and believe me you shall not leave the house afterwards without the child.'

I felt that Trottle was right, and sat down as patiently as I could in a chair he had thoughtfully placed ready for me. I was so horrified at the discovery of my own relation's wickedness that when Trottle proposed to make me acquainted with the confession wrung from Barsham and his mother, I begged him to spare me all details, and only to tell me what was necessary about George Forley.

'All that can be said for Mr Forley, ma'am, is, that he was just scrupulous enough to hide the child's existence and blot out its parentage here, instead of consenting, at the first, to its death, or afterwards, when the boy grew up, to turning him adrift, absolutely helpless in the world. The fraud has been managed, ma'am, with the cunning of Satan himself. Mr Forley had the hold over the Barshams, that they had helped him in his villainy, and that they were dependent on him for the bread they eat. He brought them up to London to keep them securely under his own eye. He put them into this empty house (taking it out of the agent's hands previously, on pretence that he meant to manage the letting of it himself); and by keeping the house empty, made it the surest of all hiding places for the child. Here, Mr Forley could come, whenever he pleased, to see that the poor lonely child was not absolutely starved; sure that his visits would only appear like looking after his own property. Here the child was to have been trained to believe himself Barsham's child, till he should be old enough to be provided for in some situation, as low and as poor as Mr Forley's uneasy conscience would let him pick out. He may have thought of atonement on his deathbed; but not before – I am only too certain of it – not before!'

A low, double knock startled us.

'The messenger!' said Trottle, under his breath. He went out instantly to answer the knock; and returned, leading in a respectable-looking elderly man, dressed like Trottle, all in black, with a white cravat, but otherwise not at all resembling him.

'I am afraid I have made some mistake,' said the stranger.

Trottle, considerately taking the office of explanation into his own hands, assured the gentleman that there was no mistake; mentioned to him who I was; and asked him if he had not come on business connected with the late Mr Forley. Looking greatly astonished, the gentleman answered, 'Yes.' There was an awkward moment of silence, after that. The stranger seemed to be not only startled and amazed, but rather distrustful and fearful of committing himself as well. Noticing this, I thought it best to request Trottle to put an end to further embarrassment, by stating all particulars truthfully, as he had stated them to me; and I begged the gentleman to listen patiently for the late Mr Forley's sake. He bowed to me very respectfully, and said he was prepared to listen with the greatest interest.

It was evident to me – and, I could see, to Trottle also – that we were not dealing, to say the least, with a dishonest man.

'Before I offer any opinion on what I have heard,' he said, earnestly and anxiously, after Trottle had done, 'I must be allowed, in justice to myself, to explain my own apparent connection with this very strange and very shocking business. I was the confidential legal adviser of the late Mr Forley, and I am left his executor. Rather more than a fortnight back, when Mr Forley was confined to his room by illness, he sent for me, and charged me to call and pay a certain sum of money here, to a man and woman whom I should find taking charge of the house. He said he had reasons for wishing the affair to be kept a secret. He begged me so to arrange my engagements that I could call at this place either on Monday last, or today, at dusk; and he mentioned that he would write to warn the people of my coming, without mentioning my name (Dalcott is my name), as he did not wish to expose me to any future importunities on the part of the man and woman. I need hardly tell you that this commission struck me as being a strange one; but, in my position with Mr Forley, I had no resource but to accept it without asking questions, or to break off my long and friendly connection with my client. I chose the first alternative. Business prevented me from doing my errand on Monday last – and if I am here today, notwithstanding Mr Forley's unexpected death, it is emphatically because I understood nothing of the matter, on knocking at this door; and therefore felt myself bound, as executor, to clear it up. That, on my word of honour, is the whole truth, so far as I am personally concerned.'

'I feel quite sure of it, sir,' I answered. 'You mentioned Mr Forley's death, just now, as unexpected. May I enquire if you were present, and if he has left any last instructions?'

'Three hours before Mr Forley's death,' said Mr Dalcott, 'his medical attendant left him apparently in a fair way of recovery. The change for the worse took place so suddenly, and was accompanied by such severe suffering, to prevent him from communicating his last wishes to anyone. When I reached his house, he was insensible. I have since examined his papers. Not one of them refers to the present time or to the serious matter which now occupies us. In the absence of instructions I must act cautiously on what you have told me; but I will be rigidly fair and just at the same time. The first thing to be done,' he continued, addressing himself to Trottle, 'is to hear what the man and woman, downstairs, have to say. If you can supply me with writing-materials, I will take their declarations separately on the spot, in your presence, and in the presence of the policeman who is watching the house. Tomorrow I will send copies of those declarations, accompanied by a full statement of the case, to Mr and Mrs Bayne in Canada (both of whom know me well as the late Mr Forley's legal adviser); and I will suspend all proceedings, on my part, until I hear from them, or from their solicitor in London. In the present posture of affairs this is all I can safely do.'

We could do no less than agree with him, and thank him for his frank and honest manner of meeting us. It was arranged that I should send over the writing-materials from my lodgings; and, to my unutterable joy and relief, it was also readily acknowledged that the poor little orphan boy could find no fitter refuge than my old arms were longing to offer him, and no safer protection for the night than my roof could give. Trottle hastened away upstairs, as actively as if he had been a young man, to fetch the child down.

And he brought him down to me without another moment of delay, and I went on my knees before the poor little mite, and embraced him, and asked him if he would go with me to where I lived? He held me away for a moment, and his wan, shrewd little eyes looked sharp at me. Then he clung close to me all at once, and said: 'I'm a-going along with you, I am – and so I tell you!'

For inspiring the poor neglected child with this trust in my old self, I thanked Heaven, then, with all my heart and soul, and I thank it now!

I bundled the poor darling up in my own cloak, and I carried him in my own arms across the road. Peggy was lost in speechless amazement to behold me trudging out of breath upstairs, with a strange pair of poor little legs under my arm; but, she began to cry over the child the moment she saw him, like a sensible woman as she always was, and she still cried her eyes out over him in a comfortable manner, when he at last lay fast asleep, tucked up by my hands in Trottle's bed.

'And Trottle, bless you, my dear man,' said I, kissing his hand, as he looked on: 'the forlorn baby came to this refuge through you, and he will help you on your way to Heaven.'

Trottle answered that I was his dear mistress, and immediately went and put his head out at an open window on the landing, and looked into the back street for a quarter of an hour.

That very night, as I sat thinking of the poor child, and of another poor child who is never to be thought about enough at Christmastime, the idea came into my mind which I have lived to execute, and in the realisation of which I am the happiest of women this day.

'The executor will sell that house, Trottle?' said I.

'Not a doubt of it, ma'am, if he can find a purchaser.'

'I'll buy it.'

I have often seen Trottle pleased; but, I never saw him so perfectly enchanted as he was when I confided to him, which I did, then and there, the purpose that I had in view.

To make short of a long story – and what story would not be long, coming from the lips of an old woman like me, unless it was made short by main force! – I bought the house. Mrs Bayne had her father's blood in her; she evaded the opportunity of forgiving and generous reparation that was offered her, and disowned the child; but, I was prepared for that, and loved him all the more for having no one in the world to look to, but me.

I am getting into a flurry by being over-pleased, and I dare say I am as incoherent as need be. I bought the house, and I altered it from the basement to the roof, and I turned it into a Hospital for Sick Children.

Never mind by what degrees my little adopted boy came to the knowledge of all the sights and sounds in the streets, so familiar to other children and so strange to him; never mind by what degrees he came to be pretty, and childish, and winning, and companionable, and to have pictures and toys about him, and suitable playmates. As I write, I look across the road to my Hospital, and there is the darling (who has gone over to play) nodding at me out of one of the once lonely windows, with his dear chubby face backed up by Trottle's waistcoat as he lifts my pet for 'Grandma' to see.

Many an eye I see in that house now, but it is never in solitude, never in neglect. Many an eye I see in that house now, that is more and more radiant every day with the light of returning health. As my precious darling has changed beyond description for the brighter and the better, so do the not less precious darlings of poor women change in that house every day in the year. For which I humbly thank that Gracious Being whom the restorer of the Widow's son and of the Ruler's daughter, instructed all mankind to call their Father.

HUNTED DOWN

Most of us see some romances in life. In my capacity as chief manager of a Life Assurance office, I think I have within the last thirty years seen more romances than the generality of men, however unpromising the opportunity may, at first sight, seem.

As I have retired and live at my ease, I possess the means, that I used to want, of considering what I have seen at leisure. My experiences have a more remarkable aspect, so reviewed, than they had when they were in progress. I have come home from the play now, and can recall the scenes of the drama upon which the curtain has fallen, free from the glare, bewilderment and bustle of the theatre.

Let me recall one of these romances of the real world.

There is nothing truer than physiognomy, taken in connection with manner. The art of reading that book of which eternal wisdom obliges every human creature to present his or her own page, with the individual character written on it, is a difficult one, perhaps, and is little studied. It may require some natural aptitude, and it must require (for everything does) some patience and some pains. That these are not usually given to it – that numbers of people accept a few stock commonplace expressions of the face as the whole list of characteristics, and neither seek nor know the refinements that are truest – that you, for instance, give a great deal of time and attention to the reading of music, Greek, Latin, French, Italian, Hebrew, if you please, and do not qualify yourself to read the face of the master or mistress looking over your shoulder teaching it to you – I assume to be five hundred times more probable than improbable. Perhaps a little self-sufficiency may be at the bottom of this; facial expression requires no study from you, you think; it comes by nature to you to know enough about it, and you are not to be taken in.

I confess, for my part, that I *have* been taken in, over and over again. I have been taken in by acquaintances, and I have been taken in (of course) by friends; far oftener by friends than by any other class of persons. How came I to be so deceived? Had I quite misread their faces?

No. Believe me, my first impression of those people, founded on face and manner alone, was invariably true. My mistake was in suffering them to come nearer to me and explain themselves away.

2

The partition which separated my own office from our general outer office in the City was of thick plate-glass. I could see through it what passed in the outer office, without hearing a word. I had it put up in place of a wall that had been there for years – ever since the house was built. It is no matter whether I did or did not make the change in order that I might derive my first impression of strangers, who came to us on business, from their faces alone, without being influenced by anything they said. Enough to mention that I turned my glass partition to that account, and that a Life Assurance office is at all times exposed to be practised upon by the most crafty and cruel of the human race.

It was through my glass partition that I first saw the gentleman whose story I am going to tell.

He had come in without my observing it, and had put his hat and umbrella on the broad counter, and was bending over it to take some papers from one of the clerks. He was about forty or so, dark, exceedingly well dressed in black – being in mourning – and the hand he extended with a polite air, had a particularly well-fitting black-kid glove upon it. His hair, which was elaborately brushed and oiled, was parted straight up the middle; and he presented this parting to the clerk, exactly (to my thinking) as if he had said, in so many words: 'You must take me, if you please, my friend, just as I show myself. Come straight up here, follow the gravel path, keep off the grass, I allow no trespassing.'

I conceived a very great aversion to that man the moment I thus saw him.

He had asked for some of our printed forms, and the clerk was giving them to him and explaining them. An obliged and agreeable smile was on his face, and his eyes met those of the clerk with a sprightly look. (I have known a vast quantity of nonsense talked about bad men not looking you in the face. Don't trust that conventional idea. Dishonesty will stare honesty out of countenance any day in the week if there is anything to be got by it.)

I saw, in the corner of his eyelash, that he became aware of my looking at him. Immediately he turned the parting in his hair toward the glass partition, as if he said to me with a sweet smile, 'Straight up here, if you please. Off the grass!'

In a few moments he had put on his hat and taken up his umbrella, and was gone.

I beckoned the clerk into my room, and asked, 'Who was that?'

He had the gentleman's card in his hand. 'Mr Julius Slinkton, Middle Temple.'

'A barrister, Mr Adams?'

'I think not, sir.'

'I should have thought him a clergyman, but for his having no Reverend here,' said I.

'Probably, from his appearance,' Mr Adams replied, 'he is reading for orders.'

I should mention that he wore a dainty white cravat, and dainty linen altogether.

'What did he want, Mr Adams?'

'Merely a form of proposal, sir, and form of reference.'

'Recommended here? Did he say?'

'Yes, he said he was recommended here by a friend of yours. He noticed you, but said that as he had not the pleasure of your personal acquaintance he would not trouble you.'

'Did he know my name?'

'Oh yes, sir! He said, "There *is* Mr Sampson, I see!" '

'A well-spoken gentleman, apparently?'

'Remarkably so, sir.'

'Insinuating manners, apparently?'

'Very much so, indeed, sir.'

'Hah!' said I. 'I want nothing at present, Mr Adams.'

Within a fortnight of that day I went to dine with a friend of mine, a merchant, a man of taste, who buys pictures and books, and the first man I saw among the company was Mr Julius Slinkton. There he was, standing before the fire, with good large eyes and an open expression of face; but still (I thought) requiring everybody to come at him by the prepared way he offered, and by no other.

I noticed him ask my friend to introduce him to Mr Sampson, and my friend did so. Mr Slinkton was very happy to see me. Not too happy;

there was no overdoing of the matter; happy in a thoroughly well-bred, perfectly unmeaning way.

'I thought you had met,' our host observed.

'No,' said Mr Slinkton. 'I did look in at Mr Sampson's office, on your recommendation; but I really did not feel justified in troubling Mr Sampson himself, on a point in the everyday routine of an ordinary clerk.'

I said I should have been glad to show him any attention on our friend's introduction.

'I am sure of that,' said he, 'and am much obliged. At another time, perhaps, I may be less delicate. Only, however, if I have real business; for I know, Mr Sampson, how precious business time is, and what a vast number of impertinent people there are in the world.'

I acknowledged his consideration with a slight bow. 'You were thinking,' said I, 'of effecting a policy on your life.'

'Oh dear no! I am afraid I am not so prudent as you pay me the compliment of supposing me to be, Mr Sampson. I merely enquired for a friend. But you know what friends are in such matters. Nothing may ever come of it. I have the greatest reluctance to trouble men of business with enquiries for friends, knowing the probabilities to be a thousand to one that the friends will never follow them up. People are so fickle, so selfish, so inconsiderate. Don't you, in your business, find them so every day, Mr Sampson?'

I was going to give a qualified answer; but he turned his smooth, white parting on me with its 'Straight up here, if you please!' and I answered, 'Yes.'

'I hear, Mr Sampson,' he resumed presently, for our friend had a new cook, and dinner was not so punctual as usual, 'that your profession has recently suffered a great loss.'

'In money?' said I.

He laughed at my ready association of loss with money, and replied, 'No, in talent and vigour.'

Not at once following out his allusion, I considered for a moment. '*Has* it sustained a loss of that kind?' said I. 'I was not aware of it.'

'Understand me, Mr Sampson. I don't imagine that you have retired. It is not so bad as that. But Mr Meltham – '

'Oh, to be sure!' said I. 'Yes! Mr Meltham, the young actuary of the "Inestimable". '

'Just so,' he returned in a consoling way.

'He is a great loss. He was at once the most profound, the most original, and the most energetic man I have ever known connected with Life Assurance.'

I spoke strongly; for I had a high esteem and admiration for Meltham; and my gentleman had indefinitely conveyed to me some suspicion that he wanted to sneer at him. He recalled me to my guard by presenting that trim pathway up his head, with its infernal 'Not on the grass, if you please – the gravel.'

'You knew him, Mr Slinkton?'

'Only by reputation. To have known him as an acquaintance, or as a friend, is an honour I should have sought if he had remained in society, though I might never have had the good fortune to attain it, being a man of far inferior mark. He was scarcely above thirty, I suppose?'

'About thirty.'

'Ah!' he sighed in his former consoling way. 'What creatures we are! To break up, Mr Sampson, and become incapable of business at that time of life! – Any reason assigned for the melancholy fact?'

('Humph!' thought I, as I looked at him. 'But I *won't* go up the track, and I *will* go on the grass.')

'What reason have you heard assigned, Mr Slinkton?' I asked, point-blank.

'Most likely a false one. You know what rumour is, Mr Sampson. I never repeat what I hear; it is the only way of paring the nails and shaving the head of rumour. But when *you* ask me what reason I have heard assigned for Mr Meltham's passing away from among men, it is another thing. I am not gratifying idle gossip then. I was told, Mr Sampson, that Mr Meltham had relinquished all his avocations and all his prospects, because he was, in fact, brokenhearted. A disappointed attachment I heard – though it hardly seems probable, in the case of a man so distinguished and so attractive.'

'Attractions and distinctions are no armour against death,' said I.

'Oh, she died? Pray pardon me. I did not hear that. That, indeed, makes it very, very sad. Poor Mr Meltham! She died? Ah, dear me! Lamentable, lamentable!'

I still thought his pity was not quite genuine, and I still suspected an unaccountable sneer under all this, until he said, as we were parted, like the other knots of talkers, by the announcement of dinner: 'Mr

Sampson, you are surprised to see me so moved on behalf of a man whom I have never known. I am not so disinterested as you may suppose. I have suffered, and recently too, from death myself. I have lost one of two charming nieces, who were my constant companions. She died young – barely three-and-twenty; and even her remaining sister is far from strong. The world is a grave!'

He said this with deep feeling, and I felt reproached for the coldness of my manner. Coldness and distrust had been engendered in me, I knew, by my bad experiences; they were not natural to me; and I often thought how much I had lost in life, losing trustfulness, and how little I had gained, gaining hard caution. This state of mind being habitual to me, I troubled myself more about this conversation than I might have troubled myself about a greater matter. I listened to his talk at dinner, and observed how readily other men responded to it, and with what a graceful instinct he adapted his subjects to the knowledge and habits of those he talked with. As, in talking with me, he had easily started the subject I might be supposed to understand best, and to be the most interested in, so, in talking with others, he guided himself by the same rule. The company was of a varied character; but he was not at fault, that I could discover, with any member of it. He knew just as much of each man's pursuit as made him agreeable to that man in reference to it, and just as little as made it natural in him to seek modestly for information when the theme was broached.

As he talked and talked – but really not too much, for the rest of us seemed to force it upon him – I became quite angry with myself. I took his face to pieces in my mind, like a watch, and examined it in detail. I could not say much against any of his features separately; I could say even less against them when they were put together. 'Then is it not monstrous,' I asked myself, 'that because a man happens to part his hair straight up the middle of his head, I should permit myself to suspect, and even to detest, him?'

(I may stop to remark that this was no proof of my sense. An observer of men who finds himself steadily repelled by some apparently trifling thing in a stranger is right to give it great weight. It may be the clue to the whole mystery. A hair or two will show where a lion is hidden. A very little key will open a very heavy door.)

I took my part in the conversation with him after a time, and we got on remarkably well. In the drawing-room, I asked the host how long he had known Mr Slinkton. He answered, not many months; he had met him at the house of a celebrated painter then present, who had known him well when he was travelling with his nieces in Italy for their health. His plans in life being broken by the death of one of them, he was reading with the intention of going back to college as a matter of form, taking his degree, and going into orders. I could not but argue with myself that here was the true explanation of his interest in poor Meltham, and that I had been almost brutal in my distrust on that simple head.

3

On the very next day but one I was sitting behind my glass partition, as before, when he came into the outer office, as before. The moment I saw him again without hearing him, I hated him worse than ever.

It was only for a moment that I had this opportunity; for he waved his tight-fitting black glove the instant I looked at him, and came straight in.

'Mr Sampson, good-day! I presume, you see, upon your kind permission to intrude upon you. I don't keep my word in being justified by business, for my business here – if I may so abuse the word – is of the slightest nature.'

I asked, was it anything I could assist him in?

'I thank you, no. I merely called to enquire outside whether my dilatory friend had been so false to himself as to be practical and sensible. But, of course, he has done nothing. I gave him your papers with my own hand, and he was hot upon the intention, but of course he has done nothing. Apart from the general human disinclination to do anything that ought to be done, I dare say there is a specialty about assuring one's life. You find it like will-making. People are so superstitious, and take it for granted they will die soon afterwards.'

'Up here, if you please; straight up here, Mr Sampson. Neither to the right nor to the left.' I almost fancied I could hear him breathe the words as he sat smiling at me, with that intolerable parting exactly opposite the bridge of my nose.

'There is such a feeling sometimes, no doubt,' I replied; 'but I don't think it obtains to any great extent.'

'Well,' said he, with a shrug and a smile, 'I wish some good angel would influence my friend in the right direction. I rashly promised his mother and sister in Norfolk to see it done, and he promised them that he would do it. But I suppose he never will.'

He spoke for a minute or two on indifferent topics, and went away.

I had scarcely unlocked the drawers of my writing-table next morning, when he reappeared. I noticed that he came straight to the door in the glass partition, and did not pause a single moment outside.

'Can you spare me two minutes, my dear Mr Sampson?'

'By all means.'

'Much obliged,' laying his hat and umbrella on the table; 'I came early, not to interrupt you. The fact is, I am taken by surprise in reference to this proposal my friend has made.'

'Has he made one?' said I.

'Ye–es,' he answered, deliberately looking at me; and then a bright idea seemed to strike him – 'or he only tells me he has. Perhaps that may be a new way of evading the matter. By Jupiter, I never thought of that!'

Mr Adams was opening the morning's letters in the outer office. 'What is the name, Mr Slinkton?' I asked.

'Beckwith.'

I looked out at the door and requested Mr Adams, if there were a proposal in that name, to bring it in. He had already laid it out of his hand on the counter. It was easily selected from the rest, and he gave it me. Alfred Beckwith. Proposal to effect a policy with us for two thousand pounds. Dated yesterday.

'From the Middle Temple, I see, Mr Slinkton.'

'Yes. He lives on the same staircase with me; his door is opposite. I never thought he would make me his reference though.'

'It seems natural enough that he should.'

'Quite so, Mr Sampson; but I never thought of it. Let me see.' He took the printed paper from his pocket. 'How am I to answer all these questions?'

'According to the truth, of course,' said I.

'Oh, of course!' he answered, looking up from the paper with a smile; 'I meant they were so many. But you do right to be particular. It stands to reason that you must be particular. Will you allow me to use your pen and ink?'

'Certainly.'

'And your desk?'

'Certainly.'

He had been hovering about between his hat and his umbrella for a place to write on. He now sat down in my chair, at my blotting-paper and inkstand, with the long walk up his head in accurate perspective before me, as I stood with my back to the fire.

Before answering each question he ran over it aloud, and discussed it. How long had he known Mr Alfred Beckwith? That he had to calculate by years upon his fingers. What were his habits? No difficulty about them; temperate in the last degree, and took a little too much exercise, if anything. All the answers were satisfactory. When he had written them all, he looked them over, and finally signed them in a very pretty hand. He supposed he had now done with the business. I told him he was not likely to be troubled any further. Should he leave the papers there? If he pleased. Much obliged. Good-morning.

I had had one other visitor before him; not at the office, but at my own house. That visitor had come to my bedside when it was not yet daylight, and had been seen by no one else but by my faithful confidential servant.

A second reference paper (for we required always two) was sent down into Norfolk, and was duly received back by post. This, likewise, was satisfactorily answered in every respect. Our forms were all complied with; we accepted the proposal, and the premium for one year was paid.

4

For six or seven months I saw no more of Mr Slinkton. He called once at my house, but I was not at home; and he once asked me to dine with him in the Temple, but I was engaged. His friend's assurance was effected in March. Late in September or early in October I was down at Scarborough for a breath of sea-air, where I met him on the beach. It was a hot evening; he came toward me with his hat in his hand; and there was the walk I had felt so strongly disinclined to take in perfect order again, exactly in front of the bridge of my nose.

He was not alone, but had a young lady on his arm.

She was dressed in mourning, and I looked at her with great interest. She had the appearance of being extremely delicate, and her face was remarkably pale and melancholy; but she was very pretty. He introduced her as his niece, Miss Niner.

'Are you strolling, Mr Sampson? Is it possible you can be idle?'

It *was* possible, and I *was* strolling.

'Shall we stroll together?'

'With pleasure.'

The young lady walked between us, and we walked on the cool sea sand, in the direction of Filey.

'There have been wheels here,' said Mr Slinkton. 'And now I look again, the wheels of a hand-carriage! Margaret, my love, your shadow without doubt!'

'Miss Niner's shadow?' I repeated, looking down at it on the sand.

'Not that one,' Mr Slinkton returned, laughing. 'Margaret, my dear, tell Mr Sampson.'

'Indeed,' said the young lady, turning to me, 'there is nothing to tell – except that I constantly see the same invalid old gentleman at all times, wherever I go. I have mentioned it to my uncle, and he calls the gentleman my shadow.'

'Does he live in Scarborough?' I asked.

'He is staying here.'

'Do you live in Scarborough?'

'No, I am staying here. My uncle has placed me with a family here, for my health.'

'And your shadow?' said I, smiling.

'My shadow,' she answered, smiling too, 'is – like myself – not very robust, I fear; for I lose my shadow sometimes, as my shadow loses me at other times. We both seem liable to confinement to the house. I have not seen my shadow for days and days; but it does oddly happen, occasionally, that wherever I go, for many days together, this gentleman goes. We have come together in the most unfrequented nooks on this shore.'

'Is this he?' said I, pointing before us.

The wheels had swept down to the water's edge, and described a great loop on the sand in turning. Bringing the loop back towards us, and spinning it out as it came, was a hand-carriage, drawn by a man.

'Yes,' said Miss Niner, 'this really is my shadow, uncle.'

As the carriage approached us and we approached the carriage, I saw within it an old man, whose head was sunk on his breast, and who was enveloped in a variety of wrappers. He was drawn by a very quiet but very keen-looking man, with iron-grey hair, who was slightly lame. They had passed us, when the carriage stopped, and the old gentleman within, putting out his arm, called to me by my name. I went back, and was absent from Mr Slinkton and his niece for about five minutes.

When I rejoined them, Mr Slinkton was the first to speak. Indeed, he said to me in a raised voice before I came up with him: 'It is well you have not been longer, or my niece might have died of curiosity to know who her shadow is, Mr Sampson.'

'An old East India director,' said I. 'An intimate friend of our friend's, at whose house I first had the pleasure of meeting you. A certain Major Banks. You have heard of him?'

'Never.'

'Very rich, Miss Niner; but very old, and very crippled. An amiable man, sensible – much interested in you. He has just been expatiating on the affection that he has observed to exist between you and your uncle.'

Mr Slinkton was holding his hat again, and he passed his hand up the straight walk, as if he himself went up it serenely, after me.

'Mr Sampson,' he said, tenderly pressing his niece's arm in his, 'our affection was always a strong one, for we have had but few near ties. We have still fewer now. We have associations to bring us together that are not of this world, Margaret.'

'Dear uncle!' murmured the young lady, and turned her face aside to hide her tears.

'My niece and I have such remembrances and regrets in common, Mr Sampson,' he feelingly pursued, 'that it would be strange indeed if the relations between us were cold or indifferent. If I remember a conversation we once had together, you will understand the reference I make. Cheer up, dear Margaret. Don't droop, don't droop. My Margaret! I cannot bear to see you droop!'

The poor young lady was very much affected, but controlled herself. His feelings, too, were very acute. In a word, he found himself under such great need of a restorative that he presently went away to take a bath of sea-water, leaving the young lady and me sitting by a point of rock, and probably presuming – but that, you will say, was a pardonable indulgence in a luxury – that she would praise him with all her heart.

She did, poor thing! With all her confiding heart, she praised him to me, for his care of her dead sister and for his untiring devotion in her last illness. The sister had wasted away very slowly, and wild and terrible fantasies had come over her toward the end, but he had never been impatient with her, or at a loss; had always been gentle, watchful and self-possessed. The sister had known him, as she had known him, to be the best of men, the kindest of men, and yet a man of such admirable strength of character as to be a very tower for the support of their weak natures while their poor lives endured.

'I shall leave him, Mr Sampson, very soon,' said the young lady; 'I know my life is drawing to an end; and when I am gone, I hope he will marry and be happy. I am sure he has lived single so long only for my sake, and for my poor, poor sister's.'

The little hand-carriage had made another great loop on the damp sand, and was coming back again, gradually spinning out a slim figure of eight, half a mile long.

'Young lady,' said I, looking around, laying my hand upon her arm and speaking in a low voice, 'time presses. You hear the gentle murmur of that sea?'

She looked at me with the utmost wonder and alarm, saying, 'Yes!'

'And you know what a voice is in it when the storm comes?'

'Yes!'

'You see how quiet and peaceful it lies before us, and you know what an awful sight of power without pity it might be, this very night!'

'Yes!'

'But if you had never heard or seen it, or heard of it in its cruelty, could you believe that it beats every inanimate thing in its way to pieces, without mercy, and destroys life without remorse?'

'You terrify me, sir, by these questions!'

'To save you, young lady, to save you! For God's sake, collect your strength and collect your firmness! If you were here alone, and hemmed in by the rising tide on the flow to fifty feet above your head, you could not be in greater danger than the danger you are now to be saved from.'

The figure on the sand was spun out, and straggled off into a crooked little jerk that ended at the cliff very near us.

'As I am, before heaven and the judge of all mankind, your friend, and your dead sister's friend, I solemnly entreat you, Miss Niner, without one moment's loss of time, to come to this gentleman with me!'

If the little carriage had been less near to us, I doubt if I could have got her away; but it was so near that we were there before she had recovered the hurry of being urged from the rock. I did not remain there with her two minutes. Certainly within five, I had the inexpressible satisfaction of seeing her – from the point we had sat on, and to which I had returned –

half supported and half carried up some rude steps notched in the cliff by the figure of an active man. With that figure beside her, I knew she was safe anywhere.

I sat alone on the rock, awaiting Mr Slinkton's return. The twilight was deepening and the shadows were heavy, when he came round the point, with his hat hanging at his buttonhole, smoothing his wet hair with one of his hands, and picking out the old path with the other and a pocket-comb.

'My niece not here, Mr Sampson?' he said, looking about.

'Miss Niner seemed to feel a chill in the air after the sun was down, and has gone home.'

He looked surprised, as though she were not accustomed to do anything without him; even to originate so slight a proceeding.

'I persuaded Miss Niner,' I explained.

'Ah!' said he. 'She is easily persuaded – for her good. Thank you, Mr Sampson; she is better within doors. The bathing-place was farther than I thought, to say the truth.'

'Miss Niner is very delicate,' I observed.

He shook his head and drew a deep sigh. 'Very, very, very. You may recollect my saying so. The time that has since intervened has not strengthened her. The gloomy shadow that fell upon her sister so early in life seems, in my anxious eyes, to gather over her, ever darker, ever darker. Dear Margaret, dear Margaret! But we must hope.'

The hand-carriage was spinning away before us at a most indecorous pace for an invalid vehicle, and was making most irregular curves upon the sand. Mr Slinkton, noticing it after he had put his handkerchief to his eyes, said: 'If I may judge from appearances, your friend will be upset, Mr Sampson.'

'It looks probable, certainly,' said I.

'The servant must be drunk.'

'The servants of old gentlemen will get drunk sometimes,' said I.

'The major draws very light, Mr Sampson.'

'The major does draw light,' said I.

By this time the carriage, much to my relief, was lost in the darkness. We walked on for a little, side by side over the sand, in silence. After a short while he said, in a voice still affected by the emotion that his niece's state of health had awakened in him, 'Do you stay here long, Mr Sampson?'

'Why, no. I am going away tonight.'

'So soon? But business always holds you in request. Men like Mr Sampson are too important to others to be spared to their own need of relaxation and enjoyment.'

'I don't know about that,' said I. 'However, I am going back.'

'To London?'

'To London.'

'I shall be there, too, soon after you.'

I knew that as well as he did. But I did not tell him so. Any more than I told him what defensive weapon my right hand rested on in my pocket, as I walked by his side. Any more than I told him why I did not walk on the sea side of him with the night closing in.

We left the beach, and our ways diverged. We exchanged good-night, and had parted indeed, when he said, returning, 'Mr Sampson, *may* I ask? Poor Meltham, whom we spoke of – dead yet?'

'Not when I last heard of him; but too broken a man to live long, and hopelessly lost to his old calling.'

'Dear, dear, dear!' said he, with great feeling. 'Sad, sad, sad! The world is a grave!' And so went his way.

It was not his fault if the world were not a grave; but I did not call that observation after him, any more than I had mentioned those other things just now enumerated. He went his way, and I went mine with all expedition. This happened, as I have said, either at the end of September or beginning of October. The next time I saw him, and the last time, was late in November.

5

I had a very particular engagement to breakfast in the Temple. It was a bitter north-easterly morning, and the sleet and slush lay inches deep in the streets. I could get no conveyance, and was soon wet to the knees; but I should have been true to that appointment though I had to wade to it up to my neck in the same impediments.

The appointment took me to some chambers in the Temple. They were at the top of a lonely corner house overlooking the river. The name Mr Alfred Beckwith was painted on the outer door. On the door opposite, on the same landing, the name Mr Julius Slinkton. The doors of both sets of chambers stood open, so that anything said aloud in one set could be heard in the other.

I had never been in those chambers before. They were dismal, close, unwholesome and oppressive; the furniture, originally good, and not yet old, was faded and dirty – the rooms were in great disorder; there was a strong prevailing smell of opium, brandy and tobacco; the grate and fire-irons were splashed all over with unsightly blotches of rust; and on a sofa by the fire, in the room where breakfast had been prepared, lay the host, Mr Beckwith, a man with all the appearances of the worst kind of drunkard, very far advanced upon his shameful way to death.

'Slinkton is not come yet,' said this creature, staggering up when I went in; 'I'll call him – Halloa! Julius Caesar! Come and drink!' As he hoarsely roared this out, he beat the poker and tongs together in a mad way, as if that were his usual manner of summoning his associate.

The voice of Mr Slinkton was heard through the clatter from the opposite side of the staircase, and he came in. He had not expected the pleasure of meeting me. I have seen several artful men brought to a stand, but I never saw a man so aghast as he was when his eyes rested on mine.

'Julius Caesar,' cried Beckwith, staggering between us, 'Mist' Sampson! Mist' Sampson, Julius Caesar! Julius, Mist' Sampson, is the friend of my soul. Julius keeps me plied with liquor, morning, noon and night. Julius is a real benefactor. Julius threw the tea and coffee out of the window when I used to have any. Julius empties all the water-jugs of their contents, and fills 'em with spirits. Julius winds me up and keeps me going. Boil the brandy, Julius!'

There was a rusty and furred saucepan in the ashes – the ashes looked like the accumulation of weeks – and Beckwith, rolling and staggering between us as if he were going to plunge headlong into the fire, got the saucepan out, and tried to force it into Slinkton's hand.

'Boil the brandy, Julius Caesar! Come! Do your usual office. Boil the brandy!'

He became so fierce in his gesticulations with the saucepan that I expected to see him lay open Slinkton's head with it. I therefore put out my hand to check him. He reeled back to the sofa, and sat there panting, shaking and red-eyed, in his rags of dressing-gown, looking at us both. I noticed then that there was nothing to drink on the table but brandy, and nothing to eat but salted herrings, and a hot, sickly, highly peppered stew.

'At all events, Mr Sampson,' said Slinkton, offering me the smooth gravel path for the last time, 'I thank you for interfering between me and this unfortunate man's violence. However you came here, Mr Sampson, or with whatever motive you came here, at least I thank you for that.'

'Boil the brandy,' muttered Beckwith.

Without gratifying his desire to know how I came there, I said, quietly, 'How is your niece, Mr Slinkton?'

He looked hard at me, and I looked hard at him.

'I am sorry to say, Mr Sampson, that my niece has proved treacherous and ungrateful to her best friend. She left me without a word of notice or explanation. She was misled, no doubt, by some designing rascal. Perhaps you may have heard of it.'

'I did hear that she was misled by a designing rascal. In fact, I have proof of it.'

'Are you sure of that?' said he.

'Quite.'

'Boil the brandy,' muttered Beckwith. 'Company to breakfast, Julius Caesar. Do your usual office – provide the usual breakfast, dinner, tea and supper. Boil the brandy!'

The eyes of Slinkton looked from him to me, and he said, after a moment's consideration, 'Mr Sampson, you are a man of the world, and so am I. I will be plain with you.'

'Oh no, you won't,' said I, shaking my head.

'I tell you, sir, I will be plain with you.'

'And I tell you you will not,' said I. 'I know all about you. *You* plain with anyone? Nonsense, nonsense!'

'I plainly tell you, Mr Sampson,' he went on, with a manner almost composed, 'that I understand your object. You want to save your funds, and escape from your liabilities; these are old tricks of trade with you office-gentlemen. But you will not do it, sir; you will not succeed. You have not an easy adversary to play against, when you play against me. We shall have to enquire, in due time, when and how Mr Beckwith fell into his present habits. With that remark, sir, I put this poor creature, and his incoherent wanderings of speech, aside, and wish you a good-morning and a better case next time.'

While he was saying this, Beckwith had filled a half-pint glass with brandy. At this moment, he threw the brandy at his face, and threw the glass after it. Slinkton put his hands up, half blinded with the spirit, and cut with the glass across the forehead. At the sound of the breakage, a fourth person came into the room, closed the door, and stood at it; he was a very quiet but very keen-looking man, with iron-grey hair, and slightly lame.

Slinkton pulled out his handkerchief, assuaged the pain in his smarting eyes, and dabbled the blood on his forehead. He was a long time about it, and I saw that in the doing of it, a tremendous change came over him, occasioned by the change in Beckwith – who ceased to pant and tremble, sat upright, and never took his eyes off him. I never in my life saw a face in which abhorrence and determination were so forcibly painted as in Beckwith's then.

'Look at me, you villain,' said Beckwith, 'and see me as I really am. I took these rooms, to make them a trap for you. I came into them as a drunkard, to bait the trap for you. You fell into the trap, and you will never leave it alive. On the morning when you last went to Mr Sampson's office, I had seen him first. Your plot has been known to both of us, all along, and you have been counterplotted all along. What? Having been cajoled into putting that prize of two thousand pounds in your power, I was to be done to death with brandy, and, brandy not proving quick enough, with something quicker? Have I never seen you, when you thought my senses gone, pouring from your little bottle into my glass? Why, you murderer and forger, alone here with you in the dead of night, as I have so often been, I have had my hand upon the trigger of a pistol, twenty times, to blow your brains out!'

This sudden starting up of the thing that he had supposed to be his imbecile victim into a determined man, with a settled resolution to hunt him down and be the death of him, mercilessly expressed from head to foot, was, in the first shock, too much for him. Without any figure of speech, he staggered under it. But there is no greater mistake than to suppose that a man who is a calculating criminal is, in any phase of his guilt, otherwise than true to himself, and perfectly consistent with his whole character. Such a man commits murder, and murder is the natural culmination of his course; such a man has to outface murder, and will do it with hardihood and effrontery. It is a sort of fashion to express surprise that any notorious criminal, having such crime upon his conscience, can so brave it out. Do you think that if he had it on his conscience at all, or had a conscience to have it upon, he would ever have committed the crime?

Perfectly consistent with himself, as I believe all such monsters to be, this Slinkton recovered himself, and showed a defiance that was sufficiently cold and quiet. He was white, he was haggard, he was changed; but only as a sharper who had played for a great stake and had been outwitted and had lost the game.

'Listen to me, you villain,' said Beckwith, 'and let every word you hear me say be a stab in your wicked heart. When I took these rooms, to throw myself in your way and lead you on to the scheme that I knew my appearance and supposed character and habits would suggest to such a devil, how did I know that? Because you were no stranger to me. I knew you well. And I knew you to be the cruel wretch who, for so much money, had killed one innocent girl while she trusted him implicitly, and who was by inches killing another.'

Slinkton took out a snuffbox, took a pinch of snuff, and laughed.

'But see here,' said Beckwith, never looking away, never raising his voice, never relaxing his face, never unclenching his hand. 'See what a dull wolf you have been, after all! The infatuated drunkard who never drank a fiftieth part of the liquor you plied him with, but poured it away, here, there, everywhere – almost before your eyes; who bought over the fellow you set to watch him and to ply him, by outbidding you in his bribe, before he had been at his work three days; with whom you have observed no caution, yet who was so bent on ridding the earth of you as a wild beast, that he would have defeated you if you had been ever so prudent; that drunkard whom you have, many a time, left on the floor of this room, and who has even let you go out of it, alive and undeceived, when you have turned him over with your foot – has, almost as often, on the same night, within an hour, within a few minutes, watched you awake, had his hand at your pillow when you were asleep, turned over your papers, taken samples from your bottles and packets of powder, changed their contents, rifled every secret of your life!'

He had had another pinch of snuff in his hand, but had gradually let it drop from between his fingers to the floor; where he now smoothed it out with his foot, looking down at it the while.

'That drunkard,' said Beckwith, 'who had free access to your rooms at all times, that he might drink the strong drinks that you left in his way and be the sooner ended, holding no more terms with you than he would hold with a tiger, has had his master-key for all your locks, his test for all your poisons, his clue to your cipher-writing. He can tell you, as well as you can tell him, how long it took to complete that deed, what doses there were, what intervals, what signs of gradual decay upon mind and body; what distempered fancies were produced, what observable changes, what physical pain. He can tell you, as well as you can tell him, that all this was recorded day by day, as a lesson of experience for future service. He can tell you, better than you can tell him, where that journal is at this moment.'

Slinkton stopped the action of his foot, and looked at Beckwith.

'No,' said the latter, as if answering a question from him. 'Not in the drawer of the writing-desk that opens with a spring; it is not there, and it never will be there again.'

'Then you are a thief!' said Slinkton.

Without any change whatever in the inflexible purpose, which it was quite terrific even to me to contemplate, and from the power of which I had always felt convinced it was impossible for this wretch to escape, Beckwith returned, 'And I am your niece's shadow, too.'

With an imprecation Slinkton put his hand to his head, tore out some hair, and flung it to the ground. It was the end of the smooth walk; he destroyed it in the action, and it will soon be seen that his use for it was past.

Beckwith went on: 'Whenever you left here, I left here. Although I understood that you found it necessary to pause in the completion of that purpose, to avert suspicion, still I watched you close, with the poor confiding girl. When I had the diary, and could read it word by word – it was only about the night before your last visit to Scarborough – you remember the night? you slept with a small flat vial tied to your wrist – I sent to Mr Sampson, who was kept out of view. This is Mr Sampson's trusty servant standing by the door. We three saved your niece among us.'

Slinkton looked at us all, took an uncertain step or two from the place where he had stood, returned to it, and glanced about him in a very curious way – as one of the meaner reptiles might, looking for a hole to hide in. I noticed at the same time, that a singular change took place in the figure of the man – as if it collapsed within his clothes, and they consequently became ill-shapen and ill-fitting.

'You shall know,' said Beckwith, 'for I hope the knowledge will be bitter and terrible to you, why you have been pursued by one man, and why, when the whole interest that Mr Sampson represents would have expended any money in hunting you down, you have been tracked to death at a single individual's charge. I hear you have had the name of Meltham on your lips sometimes?'

I saw, in addition to those other changes, a sudden stoppage come upon his breathing.

'When you sent the sweet girl whom you murdered (you know with what artfully made-out surroundings and probabilities you sent her) to Meltham's office, before taking her abroad to originate the transaction that doomed her to the grave, it fell to Meltham's lot to see her and to speak with her. It did not fall to his lot to save her, though I know he would freely give his own life to have done it. He admired her – I would say he loved her deeply, if I thought it possible that you could understand the word. When she was sacrificed, he was thoroughly assured of your guilt. Having lost her, he had but one object left in life, and that was to avenge her and destroy you.'

I saw the villain's nostrils rise and fall convulsively; but I saw no moving at his mouth.

'That man Meltham,' Beckwith steadily pursued, 'was as absolutely certain that you could never elude him in this world, if he devoted himself to your destruction with his utmost fidelity and earnestness, and if he divided the sacred duty with no other duty in life, as he was certain that in achieving it he would be a poor instrument in the hands of Providence, and would do well before heaven in striking you out from among living men. I am that man, and I thank God that I have done my work!'

If Slinkton had been running for his life from swift-footed savages, a dozen miles, he could not have shown more emphatic signs of being oppressed at heart and labouring for breath than he showed now, when he looked at the pursuer who had so relentlessly hunted him down.

'You never saw me under my right name before; you see me under my right name now. You shall see me once again in the body, when you are tried for your life. You shall see me once again in the spirit, when the cord is round your neck, and the crowd are crying against you!'

When Meltham had spoken these last words, the miscreant suddenly turned away his face, and seemed to strike his mouth with his open hand. At the same instant, the room was filled with a new and powerful odour and, almost at the same instant, he broke into a crooked run, leap, start – I have no name for the spasm – and fell, with a dull weight that shook the heavy old doors and windows in their frames.

That was the fitting end of him.

When we saw that he was dead, we drew away from the room, and Meltham, giving me his hand, said, with a weary air, 'I have no more work on earth, my friend. But I shall see her again elsewhere.'

It was in vain that I tried to rally him. He might have saved her, he said; he had not saved her, and he reproached himself; he had lost her, and he was broken-hearted.

'The purpose that sustained me is over, Sampson, and there is nothing now to hold me to life. I am not fit for life; I am weak and spiritless; I have no hope and no object; my day is done.'

In truth, I could hardly have believed that the broken man who then spoke to me was the man who had so strongly and so differently impressed me when his purpose was before him. I used such entreaties with him, as I could; but he still said, and always said, in a patient, undemonstrative way – nothing could avail him – he was broken-hearted.

He died early in the next spring. He was buried by the side of the poor young lady for whom he had cherished those tender and unhappy regrets; and he left all he had to her sister. She lived to be a happy wife and mother; she married my sister's son, who succeeded poor Meltham; she is living now, and her children ride about the garden on my walking-stick when I go to see her.

A CHRISTMAS TREE

I have been looking on, this evening, at a merry company of children assembled round that pretty German toy, a Christmas tree. The tree was planted in the middle of a great round table, and towered high above their heads. It was brilliantly lighted by a multitude of little tapers; and everywhere sparkled and glittered with bright objects. There were rosy-cheeked dolls, hiding behind the green leaves; and there were real watches (with movable hands, at least, and an endless capacity of being wound up) dangling from innumerable twigs; there were French-polished tables, chairs, bedsteads, wardrobes, eight-day clocks, and various other articles of domestic furniture (wonderfully made, in tin, at Wolverhampton), perched among the boughs, as if in preparation for some fairy house-keeping; there were jolly, broad-faced little men, much more agreeable in appearance than many real men – and no wonder, for their heads took off, and showed them to be full of sugar-plums; there were fiddles and drums; there were tambourines, books, work-boxes, paint boxes, sweet-meat-boxes, peep-show boxes, and all kinds of boxes; there were trinkets for the elder girls, far brighter than any grown-up gold and jewels; there were baskets and pincushions in all devices; there were guns, swords, and banners; there were witches standing in enchanted rings of pasteboard, to tell fortunes; there were teetotums, humming-tops, needle-cases, pen-wipers, smelling-bottles, conversation-cards, bouquet-holders; real fruit, made artificially dazzling with gold leaf; imitation apples, pears, and walnuts, crammed with surprises; in short, as a pretty child, before me, delightedly whispered to another pretty child, her bosom friend, 'There was everything, and more.' This motley collection of odd objects, clustering on the tree like magic fruit, and flashing back the bright looks directed towards it from every side – some of the diamond-eyes admiring it were hardly on a level with the table, and a few were languishing in timid wonder on the bosoms of pretty mothers, aunts, and nurses – made a lively realisation of the fancies of childhood; and set me thinking how all the trees that grow and all the things that come into existence on the earth, have their wild adornments at that well-remembered time.

Being now at home again, and alone, the only person in the house awake, my thoughts are drawn back, by a fascination which I do not care to resist, to my own childhood. I begin to consider, what do we all remember best upon the branches of the Christmas tree of our own young Christmas days, by which we climbed to real life.

Straight, in the middle of the room, cramped in the freedom of its growth by no encircling walls or soon-reached ceiling, a shadowy tree arises; and, looking up into the dreamy brightness of its top – for I observe in this tree the singular property that it appears to grow downward towards the earth – I look into my youngest Christmas recollections!

All toys at first, I find. Up yonder, among the green holly and red berries, is the tumbler with his hands in his pockets, who wouldn't lie down, but whenever he was put upon the floor, persisted in rolling his fat body about, until he rolled himself still, and brought those lobster eyes of his to bear upon me – when I affected to laugh very much, but in my heart of hearts was extremely doubtful of him. Close beside him is that infernal snuffbox, out of which there sprang a demoniacal counsellor in a black gown, with an obnoxious head of hair, and a red cloth mouth, wide open, who was not to be endured on any terms, but could not be put away either; for he used suddenly, in a highly magnified state, to fly out of mammoth snuffboxes in dreams, when least expected. Nor is the frog with cobbler's wax on his tail, far off; for there was no knowing where he wouldn't jump; and when he flew over the candle, and came upon one's hand with that spotted back – red on a green ground – he was horrible. The cardboard lady in a blue-silk skirt, who was stood up against the candlestick to dance, and whom I see on the same branch, was milder, and was beautiful; but I can't say as much for the larger cardboard man, who used to be hung against the wall and pulled by a string; there was a sinister expression in that nose of his; and when he got his legs round his neck (which he very often did), he was ghastly, and not a creature to be alone with.

When did that dreadful mask first look at me? Who put it on, and why was I so frightened that the sight of it is an era in my life? It is not a hideous visage in itself; it is even meant to be droll, why then were its stolid features so intolerable? Surely not because it hid the wearer's face. An apron would have done as much; and though I should have preferred even the apron away, it would not have been absolutely insupportable, like the mask. Was it the immovability of the mask? The doll's face was immovable, but I was not afraid of *her*. Perhaps that fixed and set change coming over a real face, infused into my quickened heart some remote suggestion and dread of the universal change that is to come on every face, and make it still? Nothing reconciled me to it. No drummers, from whom proceeded a melancholy chirping on the turning of a handle; no regiment of soldiers, with a mute band, taken out of a box, and fitted, one by one, upon a stiff and lazy little set of lazy-tongs; no old woman, made of wires and a brown-paper composition, cutting up a pie for two small children; could give me a permanent comfort, for a long time. Nor was it any satisfaction to be shown the mask, and see that it was made of paper, or to have it locked up and be assured that no one wore it. The mere recollection of that fixed face, the mere knowledge of its existence any-where, was sufficient to awake me in the night all perspiration and horror, with, 'O I know it's coming! O the mask!'

I never wondered what the dear old donkey with the panniers – there he is! was made of, then! His hide was real to the touch, I recollect. And the great black horse with the round red spots all over him – the horse that I could even get upon – I never wondered what had brought him to that strange condition, or thought that such a horse was not commonly seen at Newmarket. The four horses of no colour, next to him, that went into the waggon of cheeses, and could be taken out and stabled under the piano, appear to have bits of fur-tippet for their tails, and other bits for their manes, and to stand on pegs instead of legs, but it was not so when they were brought home for a Christmas present. They were all right, then; neither was their harness unceremoniously nailed into their chests, as appears to be the case now. The tinkling works of the music-cart, I *did* find out, to be made of quill toothpicks and wire; and I always thought that little tumbler in his shirt sleeves, perpetually swarming up one side of a wooden frame, and coming down, head foremost, on the other, rather a weak-minded person – though good-natured; but the Jacob's ladder, next him, made of little squares of red wood, that went flapping and clattering over one another, each developing a different picture, and the whole enlivened by small bells, was a mighty marvel and a great delight.

Ah! The doll's house! – of which I was not proprietor, but where I visited. I don't admire the Houses of Parliament half so much as that stone-fronted mansion with real glass windows, and doorsteps, and a real balcony – greener than I ever see now, except at watering places; and even they afford but a poor imitation. And though it *did* open all at once, the entire house-front (which was a blow, I admit, as cancelling the fiction of a staircase), it was but to shut it up again, and I could believe. Even open, there were three distinct rooms in it: a sitting-room and bedroom, elegantly furnished, and best of all, a kitchen, with uncommonly soft fire-irons, a plentiful assortment of diminutive utensils – oh, the warming-pan! – and a tin man-cook in profile, who was always going to fry two fish. What Barmecide justice have I done to the noble feasts wherein the set of wooden platters figured, each with its own peculiar delicacy, as a ham or turkey, glued tight on to it, and garnished with something green, which I recollect as moss! Could all the temperance societies of these later days, united, give me such a tea-drinking as I have had through the means of yonder little set of blue crockery, which really would hold liquid (it ran out of the small wooden cask, I recollect, and tasted of matches), and which made tea, nectar. And if the two legs of the ineffectual little sugar-tongs did tumble over one another, and want purpose, like Punch's hands, what does it matter? And if I did once shriek out, as a poisoned child, and strike the fashionable company with consternation, by reason of having drunk a little teaspoon, inadvertently dissolved in too hot tea, I was never the worse for it, except by a powder!

Upon the next branches of the tree, lower down, hard by the green roller and miniature gardening-tools, how thick the books begin to hang. Thin books, in themselves, at first, but many of them, and with deliciously smooth covers of bright red or green. What fat black letters to begin with! 'A was an archer, and shot at a frog.' Of course he was. He was an apple-pie also, and there he is! He was a good many things in his time, was A, and so were most of his friends, except X, who had so little versatility, that I never knew him to get beyond Xerxes or Xantippe – like Y, who was always confined to a yacht or a yew tree; and Z condemned for ever to be a zebra or a zany. But, now, the very tree itself changes, and becomes a bean-stalk – the marvellous bean-stalk up which Jack climbed to the giant's house! And now, those dreadfully interesting, double-headed giants, with their clubs over their shoulders, begin to stride along the boughs in a perfect throng, dragging knights and ladies home for dinner by the hair of their heads. And Jack – how noble, with his sword of sharpness, and his shoes of swiftness! Again those old meditations come upon me as I gaze up at him; and I debate within myself whether there was more than one Jack (which I am loth to believe possible), or only one genuine original admirable Jack, who achieved all the recorded exploits.

Good for Christmastime is the ruddy colour of the cloak, in which – the tree making a forest of itself for her to trip through, with her basket –

Little Red Riding-Hood comes to me one Christmas Eve to give me information of the cruelty and treachery of that dissembling wolf who ate her grandmother, without making any impression on his appetite, and then ate her, after making that ferocious joke about his teeth. She was my first love. I felt that if I could have married Little Red Riding-Hood, I should have known perfect bliss. But, it was not to be; and there was nothing for it but to look out the wolf in the Noah's Ark there, and put him late in the procession on the table, as a monster who was to be degraded. O the wonderful Noah's Ark! It was not found seaworthy when put in a washing-tub, and the animals were crammed in at the roof, and needed to have their legs well shaken down before they could be got in, even there – and then, ten to one but they began to tumble out at the door, which was but imperfectly fastened with a wire latch – but what was *that* against it! Consider the noble fly, a size or two smaller than the elephant: the ladybird, the butterfly – all triumphs of art! Consider the goose, whose feet were so small, and whose balance was so indifferent, that he usually tumbled forward, and knocked down all the animal creation. Consider Noah and his family, like idiotic tobacco-stoppers; and how the leopard stuck to warm little fingers; and how the tails of the larger animals used gradually to resolve themselves into frayed bits of string!

Hush! Again a forest, and somebody up in a tree – not Robin Hood, not Valentine, not the Yellow Dwarf (I have passed him and all Mother Bunch's wonders, without mention), but an eastern King with a glittering scimitar and turban. By Allah! two eastern Kings, for I see another, looking over his shoulder! Down upon the grass, at the tree's foot, lies the full length of a coal-black giant, stretched asleep, with his head in a lady's lap; and near them is a glass box, fastened with four locks of shining steel, in which he keeps the lady prisoner when he is awake. I see the four keys at his girdle now. The lady makes signs to the two Kings in the tree, who softly descend. It is the setting-in of the bright Arabian nights.

Oh, now all common things become uncommon and enchanted to me. All lamps are wonderful; all rings are talismans. Common flowerpots are full of treasure, with a little earth scattered on the top; trees are for Ali Baba to hide in; beef steaks are to throw down into the valley of diamonds, that the precious stones may stick to them, and be carried by the eagles to their nests, whence the traders, with loud cries, will scare them. Tarts are made, according to the recipe of the vizier's son of

Bussorah, who turned pastrycook after he was set down in his drawers at the gate of Damascus; cobblers are all Mustaphas, and in the habit of sewing up people cut into four pieces, to whom they are taken blindfold.

Any iron ring let into stone is the entrance to a cave which only waits for the magician, and the little fire, and the necromancy, that will make the earth shake. All the dates imported come from the same tree as that unlucky date, with whose shell the merchant knocked out the eye of the genie's invisible son. All olives are of the stock of that fresh fruit, concerning which the commander of the faithful overheard the boy conduct the fictitious trial of the fraudulent olive merchant; all apples are akin to the apple purchased (with two others) from the Sultan's gardener for three sequins, and which the tall black slave stole from the child. All dogs are associated with the dog, really a transformed man, who jumped upon the baker's counter, and put his paw on the piece of bad money. All rice recalls the rice which the awful lady, who was a ghoul, could only peck by grains, because of her nightly feasts in the burial-place. My very rocking-horse – there he is, with his nostrils turned completely inside-out, indicative of blood! – should have a peg in his neck, by virtue thereof to fly away with me, as the wooden horse did with the Prince of Persia, in the sight of all his father's court.

Yes, on every object that I recognise among those upper branches of my Christmas tree, I see this fairy light! When I wake in bed, at daybreak, on the cold, dark, winter mornings, the white snow dimly beheld, outside, through the frost on the window-pane, I hear Dinarzade. 'Sister, sister, if you are yet awake, I pray you finish the history of the young king of the black islands.' Scheherazade replies, 'If my lord the Sultan will suffer me to live another day, sister, I will not only finish that, but tell you a more wonderful story yet.' Then, the gracious Sultan goes out, giving no orders for the execution, and we all three breathe again.

At this height of my tree I begin to see, cowering among the leaves – it may be born of turkey, or of pudding, or mince pie, or of these many fancies, jumbled with Robinson Crusoe on his desert island, Philip Quarll among the monkeys, Sandford and Merton with Mr Barlow, Mother Bunch, and the mask – or it may be the result of indigestion, assisted by imagination and over-doctoring – a prodigious nightmare. It is so exceedingly indistinct, that I don't know why it's frightful – but I know it is. I can only make out that it is an immense array of shapeless things, which appear to be planted on a vast exaggeration of the lazy-tongs that used to bear the toy soldiers, and to be slowly coming close to my eyes, and receding to an immeasurable distance. When it comes closest, it is worse. In connection with it I descry remembrances of winter nights incredibly long; of being sent early to bed, as a punishment for some small offence, and waking in two hours, with a sensation of having been asleep two nights; of the laden hopelessness of morning ever dawning; and the oppression of a weight of remorse.

And now, I see a wonderful row of little lights rise smoothly out of the ground, before a vast green curtain. Now, a bell rings – a magic bell, which still sounds in my ears unlike all other bells – and music plays, amidst a buzz of voices, and a fragrant smell of orange-peel and oil. Anon, the magic bell commands the music to cease, and the great green curtain rolls itself up majestically, and the play begins! The devoted dog of Montargis avenges the death of his master, foully murdered in the Forest of Bondy; and a humorous peasant with a red nose and a very little hat, whom I take from this hour forth to my bosom as a friend (I think he was a waiter or an hostler at a village inn, but many years have passed since he and I have met), remarks that the sassigassity of that dog is indeed surprising; and evermore this jocular conceit will live in my remembrance fresh and unfading, overtopping all possible jokes, unto the end of time. Or now, I learn with bitter tears how poor Jane Shore, dressed all in white, and with her brown hair hanging down, went starving through the streets; or how George Barnwell killed the worthiest uncle that ever man had, and was afterwards so sorry for it that he ought to have been let off. Comes swift to comfort me, the pantomime – stupendous phenomenon! – when clowns are shot from loaded mortars into the great chandelier, bright constellation that it is; when harlequins, covered all over with scales of pure gold, twist and sparkle, like amazing fish; when Pantaloon (whom I deem it no irreverence to compare in my own mind to my grandfather) puts red-hot pokers in his pocket, and cries 'Here's somebody coming!' or taxes the clown with petty larceny, by saying, 'Now, I sawed you do it!' when Everything is capable, with the greatest ease, of being changed into Anything; and 'Nothing is, but thinking makes it so.' Now, too, I perceive my first experience of the dreary sensation – often to return in afterlife – of being unable, next day, to get back to the dull, settled world; of wanting to live for ever in the bright atmosphere I have quitted; of doting on the little fairy, with the wand like a celestial barber's pole, and pining for a fairy immortality along with her.

Ah, she comes back, in many shapes, as my eye wanders down the branches of my Christmas tree, and goes as often, and has never yet stayed by me!

Out of this delight springs the toy-theatre – there it is, with its familiar proscenium, and ladies in feathers, in the boxes! – and all its attendant occupation with paste and glue, and gum, and water colours, in the getting-up of 'The Miller and his Men', and 'Elizabeth, or the Exile of Siberia'. In spite of a few besetting accidents and failures (particularly an unreasonable disposition in the respectable Kelmar, and some others, to become faint in the legs, and double up, at exciting points of the drama), a teeming world of fancies so suggestive and all-embracing, that, far below it on my Christmas tree, I see dark, dirty, real theatres in the daytime, adorned with these associations as with the freshest garlands of the rarest flowers, and charming me yet.

But hark! The waits are playing, and they break my childish sleep! What images do I associate with the Christmas music as I see them set forth on the Christmas tree? Known before all the others, keeping far apart from all the others, they gather round my little bed. An angel, speaking to a group of shepherds in a field; some travellers, with eyes uplifted, following a star; a baby in a manger; a child in a spacious temple, talking with grave men; a solemn figure, with a mild and beautiful face, raising a dead girl by the hand; again, near a city gate, calling back the son of a widow, on his bier, to life; a crowd of people looking through the opened roof of a chamber where he sits, and letting down a sick person on a bed, with ropes; the same, in a tempest, walking on the water to a ship; again, on a seashore, teaching a great multitude; again, with a child upon his knee, and other children round; again, restoring sight to the blind, speech to the dumb, hearing to the deaf, health to the sick, strength to the lame, knowledge to the ignorant; again, dying upon a cross, watched by armed soldiers, a thick darkness coming on, the earth beginning to shake, and only one voice heard, 'Forgive them, for they know not what they do.'

Still, on the lower and maturer branches of the tree, Christmas associations cluster thick. Schoolbooks shut up; Ovid and Virgil silenced; the rule of three, with its cool impertinent enquiries, long disposed of; Terence and Plautus acted no more, in an arena of huddled desks and forms, all chipped, and notched, and inked; cricket-bats, stumps, and balls, left higher up, with the smell of trodden grass and the softened noise of shouts in the evening air; the tree is still fresh, still gay. If I no more come home at Christmastime, there will be boys and girls (thank heaven!) while the world lasts; and they do! Yonder they dance and play upon the branches of my tree, God bless them, merrily, and my heart dances and plays too!

And I do come home at Christmas. We all do, or we all should. We all come home, or ought to come home, for a short holiday – the longer, the better – from the great boarding-school, where we are for ever working at our arithmetical slates, to take, and give a rest. As to going a visiting, where can we not go, if we will; where have we not been, when we would; starting our fancy from our Christmas tree!

Away into the winter prospect. There are many such upon the tree! On, by low-lying, misty grounds, through fens and fogs, up long hills, winding dark as caverns between thick plantations, almost shutting out the sparkling stars; so, out on broad heights, until we stop at last, with sudden silence, at an avenue. The gate-bell has a deep, half-awful sound in the frosty air; the gate swings open on its hinges; and, as we drive up to a great house, the glancing lights grow larger in the windows, and the opposing rows of trees seem to fall solemnly back on either side, to give us place. At intervals, all day, a frightened hare has shot across this whitened turf; or the distant clatter of a herd of deer trampling the hard frost, has, for the minute, crushed the silence too. Their watchful eyes beneath the fern may be shining now, if we could see them, like the icy dewdrops on the leaves; but they are still, and all is still. And so, the lights growing larger, and the trees falling back before us, and closing up again behind us, as if to forbid retreat, we come to the house.

There is probably a smell of roasted chestnuts and other good comfortable things all the time, for we are telling winter stories – ghost stories, or more shame for us – round the Christmas fire; and we have never stirred, except to draw a little nearer to it. But, no matter for that. We came to the house, and it is an old house, full of great chimneys where wood is burnt on ancient dogs upon the hearth, and grim portraits (some of them with grim legends, too) lower distrustfully from the oaken panels of the walls. We are a middle-aged nobleman, and we make a generous supper with our host and hostess and their guests – it being Christmastime, and the old house full of company – and then we go to bed. Our room is a very old room. It is hung with tapestry. We don't like the portrait of a cavalier in green, over the fireplace. There are great black beams in the ceiling, and there is a great black bedstead, supported at the foot by two great black figures, who seem to have come off a couple of tombs in the old baronial church in the park, for our particular accommodation. But, we are not a superstitious nobleman, and we don't mind. Well! we dismiss our servant, lock the door, and sit before the fire in our dressing-gown, musing about a great many things. At length we go to bed. Well! we can't sleep. We toss and tumble, and can't sleep. The embers on the hearth burn fitfully and make the room look ghostly. We can't help peeping out over the counterpane, at the two black figures and the cavalier – that wicked-looking cavalier – in green. In the flickering light they seem to advance and retire: which, though we are not by any means a superstitious nobleman, is not agreeable. Well! we get nervous – more and more nervous. We say 'This is very foolish, but we can't stand this; we'll pretend to be ill, and knock up somebody.' Well! we are just going to do it, when the locked door opens, and there comes in a young woman, deadly pale, and with long fair hair, who glides to the fire, and sits down in the chair we have left there, wringing her hands. Then, we notice that her clothes are wet. Our tongue cleaves to the roof of our mouth, and we can't speak; but, we observe her accurately. Her clothes are wet; her long hair is dabbled with moist mud; she is dressed in the fashion of two hundred years ago; and she has at her girdle a bunch of rusty keys. Well! there she sits, and we can't even faint, we are in such a state about it. Presently she gets up, and tries all the locks in the room with the rusty keys, which won't fit one of them; then, she fixes her eyes on the portrait of the cavalier in green, and says, in a low, terrible voice, 'The stags know it!' After that, she wrings her hands again, passes the bedside, and goes out at the door. We hurry on our dressing-gown, seize our pistols (we always travel with pistols), and are following, when we find the door locked. We turn the key, look out into the dark gallery; no one there. We wander away, and try to find our servant. Can't be done. We pace the gallery till daybreak; then return to our deserted room, fall asleep, and are awakened by our servant (nothing ever haunts him) and the shining sun. Well! we make a wretched breakfast, and all the company say we look queer. After breakfast, we go over the house with our host, and then we take him to the portrait of the cavalier in green, and then it all comes out. He was false to a young housekeeper once attached to that family, and famous for her beauty, who drowned herself in a pond, and whose body was discovered, after a long time, because the stags refused to drink of the water. Since which, it has been whispered that she traverses the house at midnight (but goes especially to that room where the cavalier in green was wont to sleep), trying the old locks with the rusty keys. Well! we tell our host of what we have seen, and a shade comes over his features, and he begs it may be hushed up; and so it is. But, it's all true; and we said so, before we died (we are dead now) to many responsible people.

There is no end to the old houses, with resounding galleries, and dismal state-bedchambers, and haunted wings shut up for many years, through which we may ramble, with an agreeable creeping up our back, and encounter any number of ghosts, but (it is worthy of remark perhaps) reducible to a very few general types and classes; for, ghosts have little originality, and 'walk' in a beaten track. Thus, it comes to pass, that a certain room in a certain old hall, where a certain bad lord, baronet, knight, or gentleman, shot himself, has certain planks in the floor from which the blood *will not* be taken out. You may scrape and scrape, as the present owner has done, or plane and plane, as his father did, or scrub and scrub, as his grandfather did, or burn and burn with strong acids, as his great-grandfather did, but, there the blood will still be – no redder and no paler – no more and no less – always just the same. Thus, in such another house there is a haunted door, that never will keep open; or another door that never will keep shut, or a haunted sound of a spinning-wheel, or a hammer, or a footstep, or a cry, or a sigh, or a horse's tramp, or the rattling of a chain. Or else, there is a turret-clock, which, at the midnight hour, strikes thirteen when the head of the family is going to die; or a shadowy, immovable black carriage which at such a time is always seen by somebody, waiting near the great gates in the stable-yard. Or thus, it came to pass how Lady Mary went to pay a visit at a large wild house in the Scottish Highlands, and, being fatigued with her long journey, retired to bed early, and innocently said, next morning, at the breakfast-table, 'How odd, to have so late a party last night, in this remote place, and not to tell me of it, before I went to bed!' Then, every one asked Lady Mary what she meant? Then, Lady Mary replied, 'Why, all night long, the carriages were driving round and round the terrace, underneath my window!' Then, the owner of the house turned pale, and so did his lady, and Charles Macdoodle of Macdoodle signed to Lady Mary to say no more, and every one was silent. After breakfast, Charles Macdoodle told Lady Mary that it was a tradition in the family that those rumbling carriages on the terrace betokened death. And so it proved, for, two months afterwards, the lady of the mansion died. And Lady Mary, who was a maid of honour at court, often told this story to the old Queen Charlotte; by this token that the old King always said, 'Eh, eh? What, what? Ghosts, ghosts? No such thing, no such thing!' And never left off saying so, until he went to bed.

Or, a friend of somebody's whom most of us know, when he was a young man at college, had a particular friend, with whom he made the compact that, if it were possible for the spirit to return to this earth after its separation from the body, he of the twain who first died, should reappear to the other. In course of time, this compact was forgotten by our friend; the two young men having progressed in life, and taken diverging paths that were wide asunder. But, one night, many years afterwards, our friend being in the North of England, and staying for the night in an inn, on the Yorkshire Moors, happened to look out of bed; and there, in the moonlight, leaning on a bureau near the window, steadfastly regarding him, saw his old college friend! The appearance being solemnly addressed, replied, in a kind of whisper, but very audibly, 'Do not come near me. I am dead. I am here to redeem my promise. I come from another world, but may not disclose its secrets!' Then, the whole form becoming paler, melted, as it were, into the moonlight, and faded away.

Or, there was the daughter of the first occupier of the picturesque Elizabethan house, so famous in our neighbourhood. You have heard about her? No! Why, *she* went out one summer evening at twilight, when she was a beautiful girl, just seventeen years of age, to gather flowers in the garden; and presently came running, terrified, into the hall to her father, saying, 'Oh, dear father, I have met myself!' He took her in his arms, and told her it was fancy, but she said, 'Oh no! I met myself in the broad walk, and I was pale and gathering withered flowers, and I turned my head, and held them up!' And, that night, she died; and a picture of her story was begun, though never finished, and they say it is somewhere in the house to this day, with its face to the wall.

Or, the uncle of my brother's wife was riding home on horseback, one mellow evening at sunset, when, in a green lane close to his own house, he saw a man standing before him, in the very centre of a narrow way. 'Why does that man in the cloak stand there!' he thought. 'Does he want me to ride over him?' But the figure never moved. He felt a strange sensation at seeing it so still, but slackened his trot and rode forward. When he was so close to it, as almost to touch it with his stirrup, his horse shied, and the figure glided up the bank, in a curious, unearthly manner – backward, and without seeming to use its feet – and was gone. The uncle of my brother's wife, exclaiming, 'Good heaven! It's my cousin Harry, from Bombay!' put spurs to his horse, which was suddenly in a profuse sweat, and, wondering at such strange behaviour, dashed round to the front of his house. There, he saw the same figure, just passing in at the long French window of the drawing-room, opening on the ground. He threw his bridle to a servant, and hastened in after it. His sister was sitting there, alone. 'Alice, where's my cousin Harry?' 'Your cousin Harry, John?' 'Yes. From Bombay. I met him in the lane just now, and saw him enter here, this instant.' Not a creature had been seen by anyone; and in that hour and minute, as it afterwards appeared, this cousin died in India.

Or, it was a certain sensible old maiden lady, who died at ninety-nine, and retained her faculties to the last, who really did see the orphan boy; a story which has often been incorrectly told, but, of which the real truth is this – because it is, in fact, a story belonging to our family – and she was a connection of our family. When she was about forty years of age, and still an uncommonly fine woman (her lover died young, which was the reason why she never married, though she had many offers), she went to stay at a place in Kent, which her brother, an Indian merchant, had newly bought. There was a story that this place had once been held in trust by the guardian of a young boy; who was himself the next heir, and who killed the young boy by harsh and cruel treatment. She knew nothing of that. It has been said that there was a cage in her bedroom in which the guardian used to put the boy. There was no such thing. There was only a closet. She went to bed, made no alarm whatever in the night, and in the morning said composedly to her maid when she came in, 'Who is the pretty forlorn-looking child who has been peeping out of that closet all night?' The maid replied by giving a loud scream, and instantly decamping. She was surprised; but she was a woman of remarkable strength of mind, and she dressed herself and went downstairs, and closeted herself with her brother. 'Now, Walter,' she said, 'I have been disturbed all night by a pretty, forlorn-looking boy, who has been con- stantly peeping out of that closet in my room, which I can't open. This is some trick.' 'I am afraid not, Charlotte,' said he, 'for it is the legend of the house. It is the orphan boy. What did he do?' 'He opened the door softly,' said she, 'and peeped out. Sometimes, he came a step or two into the room. Then, I called to him, to encourage him, and he shrunk, and shuddered, and crept in again, and shut the door.' 'The closet has no communication, Charlotte,' said her brother, 'with any other part of the house, and it's nailed up.' This was undeniably true, and it took two carpenters a whole forenoon to get it open, for examination. Then, she was satisfied that she had seen the orphan boy. But, the wild and terrible part of the story is, that he was also seen by three of her brother's sons, in succession, who all died young. On the occasion of each child being taken ill, he came home in a heat, twelve hours before, and said, Oh, Mamma, he had been playing under a particular oak tree, in a certain meadow, with a strange boy – a pretty, forlorn-looking boy, who was very timid, and made signs! From fatal experience, the parents came to know that this was the orphan boy, and that the course of that child whom he chose for his little playmate was surely run.

Legion is the name of the German castles, where we sit up alone to wait for the spectre – where we are shown into a room, made comparatively cheerful for our reception – where we glance round at the shadows, thrown on the blank walls by the crackling fire – where we feel very lonely when the village innkeeper and his pretty daughter have retired, after laying down a fresh store of wood upon the hearth, and setting forth on the small table such supper-cheer as a cold roast capon, bread, grapes, and a flask of old Rhine wine – where the reverberating doors close on their retreat, one after another, like so many peals of sullen thunder – and where, about the small hours of the night, we come into the knowledge of divers supernatural mysteries. Legion is the name of the haunted German students, in whose society we draw yet nearer to the fire, while the schoolboy in the corner opens his eyes wide and round, and flies off the footstool he has chosen for his seat, when the door accidentally blows open. Vast is the crop of such fruit, shining on our Christmas tree; in blossom, almost at the very top; ripening all down the boughs!

Among the later toys and fancies hanging there – as idle often and less pure – be the images once associated with the sweet old waits, the softened music in the night, ever unalterable! Encircled by the social thoughts of Christmastime, still let the benignant figure of my childhood stand unchanged! In every cheerful image and suggestion that the season brings, may the bright star that rested above the poor roof, be the star of all the

Christian world! A moment's pause, O vanishing tree, of which the lower boughs are dark to me as yet, and let me look once more! I know there are blank spaces on thy branches, where eyes that I have loved have shone and smiled; from which they are departed. But, far above, I see the raiser of the dead girl, and the widow's son; and God is good! If age be hiding for me in the unseen portion of thy downward growth, O may I, with a grey head, turn a child's heart to that figure yet, and a child's trustfulness and confidence!

Now, the tree is decorated with bright merriment, and song, and dance, and cheerfulness. And they are welcome. Innocent and welcome be they ever held, beneath the branches of the Christmas tree, which cast no gloomy shadow! But, as it sinks into the ground, I hear a whisper going through the leaves. 'This, in commemoration of the law of love and kindness, mercy and compassion. This, in remembrance of me!'

WHAT CHRISTMAS IS AS
WE GROW OLDER

Time was, with most of us, when Christmas Day encircling all our limited world like a magic ring, left nothing out for us to miss or seek; bound together all our home enjoyments, affections, and hopes; grouped everything and every one around the Christmas fire; and made the little picture shining in our bright young eyes, complete.

Time came, perhaps, all so soon, when our thoughts over-leaped that narrow boundary; when there was someone (very dear, we thought then, very beautiful, and absolutely perfect) wanting to the fullness of our happiness; when we were wanting too (or we thought so, which did just as well) at the Christmas hearth by which that someone sat; and when we intertwined with every wreath and garland of our life that someone's name.

That was the time for the bright visionary Christmases which have long arisen from us to show faintly, after summer rain, in the palest edges of the rainbow! That was the time for the beatified enjoyment of the things that were to be, and never were, and yet the things that were so real in our resolute hope that it would be hard to say, now, what realities achieved since, have been stronger!

What! Did that Christmas never really come when we and the priceless pearl who was our young choice were received, after the happiest of totally impossible marriages, by the two united families previously at daggers-drawn on our account? When brothers and sisters-in-law who had always been rather cool to us before our relationship was effected, perfectly doted on us, and when fathers and mothers overwhelmed us with unlimited incomes? Was that Christmas dinner never really eaten, after which we arose, and generously and eloquently rendered honour to our late rival, present in the company, then and there exchanging friendship and forgiveness, and founding an attachment, not to be surpassed in Greek or Roman story, which subsisted until death? Has that same rival long ceased to care for that same priceless pearl, and married for money, and become usurious? Above all, do we really know, now, that we should probably have been miserable if we had won and worn the pearl, and that we are better without her?

That Christmas when we had recently achieved so much fame; when we had been carried in triumph somewhere, for doing something great and good; when we had won an honoured and ennobled name, and arrived and were received at home in a shower of tears of joy; is it possible that *that* Christmas has not come yet?

And is our life here, at the best, so constituted that, pausing as we advance at such a noticeable milestone in the track as this great birthday, we look back on the things that never were, as naturally and full as gravely as on the things that have been and are gone, or have been and still are? If it be so, and so it seems to be, must we come to the conclusion that life is little better than a dream, and little worth the loves and strivings that we crowd into it?

No! Far be such miscalled philosophy from us, dear reader, on Christmas Day! Nearer and closer to our hearts be the Christmas spirit, which is the spirit of active usefulness, perseverance, cheerful discharge of duty, kindness and forbearance! It is in the last virtues especially, that we are, or should be, strengthened by the unaccomplished visions of our youth; for, who shall say that they are not our teachers to deal gently even with the impalpable nothings of the earth!

Therefore, as we grow older, let us be more thankful that the circle of our Christmas associations and of the lessons that they bring, expands! Let us welcome every one of them, and summon them to take their places by the Christmas hearth.

Welcome, old aspirations, glittering creatures of an ardent fancy, to your shelter underneath the holly! We know you, and have not outlived you yet. Welcome, old projects and old loves, however fleeting, to your nooks among the steadier lights that burn around us. Welcome, all that was ever real to our hearts; and for the earnestness that made you real, thanks to heaven! Do we build no Christmas castles in the clouds now? Let our thoughts, fluttering like butterflies among these flowers of children, bear witness! Before this boy, there stretches out a future, brighter than we ever looked on in our old romantic time, but bright with honour and with truth. Around this little head on which the sunny curls lie heaped, the graces sport, as prettily, as airily, as when there was no scythe within the reach of time to shear away the curls of our first-love. Upon another girl's face near it – placider but smiling bright – a quiet and contented little face, we see Home fairly written. Shining from the word, as rays shine from a star, we see how, when our graves are old, other hopes than ours are young, other hearts than ours are moved; how other ways are smoothed; how other happiness blooms, ripens, and decays – no, not decays, for other homes and other bands of children, not yet in being nor for ages yet to be, arise, and bloom and ripen to the end of all!

Welcome, everything! Welcome, alike what has been, and what never was, and what we hope may be, to your shelter underneath the holly, to your places round the Christmas fire, where what is sits open-hearted! In yonder shadow, do we see obtruding furtively upon the blaze, an enemy's face? By Christmas Day we do forgive him! If the injury he has done us may admit of such companionship, let him come here and take his place. If otherwise, unhappily, let him go hence, assured that we will never injure nor accuse him.

On this day we shut out Nothing!

'Pause,' says a low voice. 'Nothing? Think!'

'On Christmas Day, we will shut out from our fireside, Nothing.'

'Not the shadow of a vast city where the withered leaves are lying deep?' the voice replies. 'Not the shadow that darkens the whole globe? Not the shadow of the city of the dead?'

Not even that. Of all days in the year, we will turn our faces towards that city upon Christmas Day, and from its silent hosts bring those we loved, among us. City of the dead, in the blessed name wherein we are gathered together at this time, and in the Presence that is here among us according to the promise, we will receive, and not dismiss, thy people who are dear to us!

Yes. We can look upon these children angels that alight, so solemnly, so beautifully among the living children by the fire, and can bear to think how they departed from us. Entertaining angels unawares, as the patriarchs did, the playful children are unconscious of their guests; but we can see them – can see a radiant arm around one favourite neck, as if there were a tempting of that child away. Among the celestial figures there is one, a poor misshapen boy on earth, of a glorious beauty now, of whom his dying mother said it grieved her much to leave him here, alone, for so many years as it was likely would elapse before he came to her – being such a little child. But he went quickly, and was laid upon her breast, and in her hand she leads him.

There was a gallant boy, who fell, far away, upon a burning sand beneath a burning sun, and said, 'Tell them at home, with my last love, how much I could have wished to kiss them once, but that I died contented and had done my duty!' Or there was another, over whom they read the words, 'Therefore we commit his body to the deep,' and so consigned him to the lonely ocean and sailed on. Or there was another, who lay down to his rest in the dark shadow of great forests, and, on earth, awoke no more. O shall they not, from sand and sea and forest, be brought home at such a time!

There was a dear girl – almost a woman – never to be one – who made a mourning Christmas in a house of joy, and went her trackless way to the silent city. Do we recollect her, worn out, faintly whispering what could not be heard, and falling into that last sleep for weariness? O look upon her now! O look upon her beauty, her serenity, her changeless youth, her happiness! The daughter of Jairus was recalled to life, to die; but she, more blest, has heard the same voice, saying unto her, 'Arise for ever!'

We had a friend who was our friend from early days, with whom we often pictured the changes that were to come upon our lives, and merrily imagined how we would speak, and walk, and think, and talk, when we came to be old. His destined habitation in the city of the dead received him in his prime. Shall he be shut out from our Christmas remembrance? Would his love have so excluded us? Lost friend, lost child, lost parent, sister, brother, husband, wife, we will not so discard you! You shall hold your cherished places in our Christmas hearts, and by our Christmas fires; and in the season of immortal hope, and on the birthday of immortal mercy, we will shut out nothing!

The winter sun goes down over town and village; on the sea it makes a rosy path, as if the sacred tread were fresh upon the water. A few more moments, and it sinks, and night comes on, and lights begin to sparkle in the prospect. On the hillside beyond the shapelessly diffused town, and in the quiet keeping of the trees that gird the village-steeple, remembrances are cut in stone, planted in common flowers, growing in grass, entwined with lowly brambles around many a mound of earth. In town and village, there are doors and windows closed against the weather, there are flaming logs heaped high, there are joyful faces, there is healthy music of voices. Be all ungentleness and harm excluded from the temples of the household gods, but be those remembrances admitted with tender encouragement! They are of the time and all its comforting and peaceful reassurances; and of the history that reunited even upon earth the living and the dead; and of the broad beneficence and goodness that too many men have tried to tear to narrow shreds.

THE POOR RELATION'S STORY

He was very reluctant to take precedence of so many respected members of the family, by beginning the round of stories they were to relate as they sat in a goodly circle by the Christmas fire; and he modestly suggested that it would be more correct if 'John our esteemed host' (whose health he begged to drink) would have the kindness to begin. For as to himself, he said, he was so little used to lead the way that really – But as they all cried out here, that he must begin, and agreed with one voice that he might, could, would, and should begin, he left off rubbing his hands, and took his legs out from under his armchair, and did begin.

I have no doubt (said the poor relation) that I shall surprise the assembled members of our family, and particularly John our esteemed host to whom we are so much indebted for the great hospitality with which he has this day entertained us, by the confession I am going to make. But, if you do me the honour to be surprised at anything that falls from a person so unimportant in the family as I am, I can only say that I shall be scrupulously accurate in all I relate.

I am not what I am supposed to be. I am quite another thing. Perhaps before I go further, I had better glance at what I *am* supposed to be.

It is supposed, unless I mistake – the assembled members of our family will correct me if I do, which is very likely (here the poor relation looked mildly about him for contradiction); that I am nobody's enemy but my own. That I never met with any particular success in anything. That I failed in business because I was unbusiness-like and credulous – in not being prepared for the interested designs of my partner. That I failed in love, because I was ridiculously trustful – in thinking it impossible that Christiana could deceive me. That I failed in my expectations from my uncle Chill, on account of not being as sharp as he could have wished in worldly matters. That, through life, I have been rather put upon and disappointed in a general way. That I am at present a bachelor of between fifty-nine and sixty years of age, living on a limited income in the form of a quarterly allowance, to which I see that John our esteemed host wishes me to make no further allusion.

The supposition as to my present pursuits and habits is to the following effect.

I live in a lodging in the Clapham Road – a very clean back room, in a very respectable house – where I am expected not to be at home in the daytime, unless poorly; and which I usually leave in the morning at nine o'clock, on pretence of going to business. I take my breakfast – my roll and butter, and my half-pint of coffee – at the old-established coffee-shop near Westminster Bridge; and then I go into the City – I don't know why – and sit in Garraway's Coffee House, and on 'Change, and walk about, and look into a few offices and counting-houses where some of my relations or acquaintance are so good as to tolerate me, and where I stand by the fire if the weather happens to be cold. I get through the day in this way until five o'clock, and then I dine: at a cost, on the average, of one and threepence. Having still a little money to spend on my evening's entertainment, I look into the old-established coffee-shop as I go home, and take my cup of tea, and perhaps my bit of toast. So, as the large hand of the clock makes its way round to the morning hour again, I make my way round to the Clapham Road again, and go to bed when I get to my lodging – fire being expensive, and being objected to by the family on account of its giving trouble and making a dirt.

Sometimes, one of my relations or acquaintances is so obliging as to ask me to dinner. Those are holiday occasions, and then I generally walk in the Park. I am a solitary man, and seldom walk with anybody. Not that I am avoided because I am shabby; for I am not at all shabby, having always a very good suit of black on (or rather Oxford mixture, which has the appearance of black and wears much better); but I have got into a habit of speaking low, and being rather silent, and my spirits are not high, and I am sensible that I am not an attractive companion.

The only exception to this general rule is the child of my first cousin, Little Frank. I have a particular affection for that child, and he takes very kindly to me. He is a diffident boy by nature; and in a crowd he is soon run over, as I may say, and forgotten. He and I, however, get on exceedingly well. I have a fancy that the poor child will in time succeed to my peculiar position in the family. We talk but little; still, we under-stand each other. We walk about, hand in hand; and without much speaking he knows what I mean, and I know what he means. When he was very little indeed, I used to take him to the windows of the toy-shops, and show him the toys inside. It is surprising how soon he found out that I would have made him a great many presents if I had been in circumstances to do it.

Little Frank and I go and look at the outside of the Monument – he is very fond of the Monument – and at the bridges, and at all the sights that are free. On two of my birthdays, we have dined on à-la-mode beef, and gone at half-price to the play, and been deeply interested. I was once walking with him in Lombard Street, which we often visit on account of my having mentioned to him that there are great riches there – he is very fond of Lombard Street – when a gentleman said to me as he passed by, 'Sir, your little son has dropped his glove.' I assure you, if you will excuse my remarking on so trivial a circumstance, this accidental mention of the child as mine, quite touched my heart and brought the foolish tears into my eyes.

When Little Frank is sent to school in the country, I shall be very much at a loss what to do with myself, but I have the intention of walking down there once a month and seeing him on a half holiday. I am told he will then be at play upon the Heath; and if my visits should be objected to, as unsettling the child, I can see him from a distance without his seeing me, and walk back again. His mother comes of a highly genteel family, and rather disapproves, I am aware, of our being too much together. I know that I am not calculated to improve his retiring disposition; but I think he would miss me beyond the feeling of the moment if we were wholly separated.

When I die in the Clapham Road, I shall not leave much more in this world than I shall take out of it; but, I happen to have a miniature of a bright-faced boy, with a curling head, and an open shirt-frill waving down his bosom (my mother had it taken for me, but I can't believe that it was ever like), which will be worth nothing to sell, and which I shall beg may be given to Frank. I have written my dear boy a little letter with it, in which I have told him that I felt very sorry to part from him, though bound to confess that I knew no reason why I should remain here. I have given him some short advice, the best in my power, to take warning of the consequences of being nobody's enemy but his own; and I have endeavoured to comfort him for what I fear he will consider a bereavement, by pointing out to him, that I was only a superfluous something to every one but him; and that having by some means failed to find a place in this great assembly, I am better out of it.

Such (said the poor relation, clearing his throat and beginning to speak a little louder) is the general impression about me. Now, it is a remarkable circumstance which forms the aim and purpose of my story, that this is all wrong. This is not my life, and these are not my habits. I do not even live in the Clapham Road. Comparatively speaking, I am very seldom there. I reside, mostly, in a – I am almost ashamed to say the word, it sounds so full of pretension – in a castle. I do not mean that it is an old baronial habitation, but still it is a building always known to every one by the name of a castle. In it, I preserve the particulars of my history; they run thus: It was when I first took John Spatter (who had been my clerk) into partnership, and when I was still a young man of not more than five-and-twenty, residing in the house of my uncle Chill, from whom I had considerable expectations, that I ventured to propose to Christiana. I had loved Christiana a long time. She was very beautiful, and very winning in all respects. I rather mistrusted her widowed mother, who I feared was of a plotting and mercenary turn of mind; but, I thought as well of her as I could, for Christiana's sake. I never had loved anyone but Christiana, and she had been all the world, and O far more than all the world, to me, from our childhood!

Christiana accepted me with her mother's consent, and I was rendered very happy indeed. My life at my uncle Chill's was of a spare dull kind, and my garret chamber was as dull, and bare, and cold, as an upper prison room in some stern northern fortress. But, having Christiana's love, I wanted nothing upon earth. I would not have changed my lot with any human being.

Avarice was, unhappily, my uncle Chill's master-vice. Though he was rich, he pinched, and scraped, and clutched, and lived miserably. As Christiana had no fortune, I was for some time a little fearful of confessing our engagement to him; but, at length I wrote him a letter, saying how it all truly was. I put it into his hand one night, on going to bed.

As I came downstairs next morning, shivering in the cold December air; colder in my uncle's unwarmed house than in the street, where the winter sun did sometimes shine, and which was at all events enlivened by cheerful faces and voices passing along; I carried a heavy heart towards the long, low breakfast-room in which my uncle sat. It was a large room with a small fire, and there was a great bay window in it which the rain had marked in the night as if with the tears of houseless people. It stared upon a raw yard, with a cracked stone pavement, and some rusted iron railings half uprooted, whence an ugly outbuilding that had once been a dissecting-room (in the time of the great surgeon who had mortgaged the house to my uncle), stared at it.

We rose so early always, that at that time of the year we breakfasted by candlelight. When I went into the room, my uncle was so contracted by the cold, and so huddled together in his chair behind the one dim candle, that I did not see him until I was close to the table.

As I held out my hand to him, he caught up his stick (being infirm, he always walked about the house with a stick), and made a blow at me, and said, 'You fool!'

'Uncle,' I returned, 'I didn't expect you to be so angry as this.' Nor had I expected it, though he was a hard and angry old man.

'You didn't expect!' said he; 'when did you ever expect? When did you ever calculate, or look forward, you contemptible dog?'

'These are hard words, uncle!'

'Hard words? Feathers, to pelt such an idiot as you with,' said he. 'Here! Betsy Snap! Look at him!'

Betsy Snap was a withered, hard-favoured, yellow old woman – our only domestic – always employed, at this time of the morning, in rubbing my uncle's legs. As my uncle adjured her to look at me, he put his lean grip on the crown of her head, she kneeling beside him, and turned her face towards me. An involuntary thought connecting them both with the Dissecting Room, as it must often have been in the surgeon's time, passed across my mind in the midst of my anxiety.

'Look at the snivelling milksop!' said my uncle. 'Look at the baby! This is the gentleman who, people say, is nobody's enemy but his own. This is the gentleman who can't say no. This is the gentleman who was making such large profits in his business that he must needs take a partner, t'other day. This is the gentleman who is going to marry a wife without a penny, and who falls into the hands of Jezebels who are speculating on my death!'

I knew, now, how great my uncle's rage was; for nothing short of his being almost beside himself would have induced him to utter that concluding word, which he held in such repugnance that it was never spoken or hinted at before him on any account.

'On my death,' he repeated, as if he were defying me by defying his own abhorrence of the word. 'On my death – death – death! But I'll spoil the speculation. Eat your last under this roof, you feeble wretch, and may it choke you!'

You may suppose that I had not much appetite for the breakfast to which I was bidden in these terms; but, I took my accustomed seat. I saw that I was repudiated henceforth by my uncle; still I could bear that very well, possessing Christiana's heart.

He emptied his basin of bread and milk as usual, only that he took it on his knees with his chair turned away from the table where I sat. When he had done, he carefully snuffed out the candle; and the cold, slate-coloured, miserable day looked in upon us.

'Now, Mr Michael,' said he, 'before we part, I should like to have a word with these ladies in your presence.'

'As you will, sir,' I returned; 'but you deceive yourself, and wrong us, cruelly, if you suppose that there is any feeling at stake in this contract but pure, disinterested, faithful love.'

To this, he only replied, 'You lie!' and not one other word.

We went, through half-thawed snow and half-frozen rain, to the house where Christiana and her mother lived. My uncle knew them very well. They were sitting at their breakfast, and were surprised to see us at that hour.

'Your servant, ma'am,' said my uncle to the mother. 'You divine the purpose of my visit, I dare say, ma'am. I understand there is a world of pure, disinterested, faithful love cooped up here. I am happy to bring it all it wants, to make it complete. I bring you your son-in-law, ma'am – and you, your husband, miss. The gentleman is a perfect stranger to me, but I wish him joy of his wise bargain.'

He snarled at me as he went out, and I never saw him again.

*   *   *

It is altogether a mistake (continued the poor relation) to suppose that my dear Christiana, over-persuaded and influenced by her mother, married a rich man, the dirt from whose carriage wheels is often, in these changed times, thrown upon me as she rides by. No, no. She married me.

The way we came to be married rather sooner than we intended, was this. I took a frugal lodging and was saving and planning for her sake, when, one day, she spoke to me with great earnestness, and said: 'My dear Michael, I have given you my heart. I have said that I loved you, and I have pledged myself to be your wife. I am as much yours through all changes of good and evil as if we had been married on the day when such words passed between us. I know you well, and know that if we should be separated and our union broken off, your whole life would be shadowed, and all that might, even now, be stronger in your character for the conflict with the world would then be weakened to the shadow of what it is!'

'God help me, Christiana!' said I. 'You speak the truth.'

'Michael!' said she, putting her hand in mine, in all maidenly devotion, 'let us keep apart no longer. It is but for me to say that I can live contented upon such means as you have, and I well know you are happy. I say so from my heart. Strive no more alone; let us strive together. My dear Michael, it is not right that I should keep secret from you what you do not suspect, but what distresses my whole life. My mother: without considering that what you have lost, you have lost for me, and on the assurance of my faith: sets her heart on riches, and urges another suit upon me, to my misery. I cannot bear this, for to bear it is to be untrue to you. I would rather share your struggles than look on. I want no better home than you can give me. I know that you will aspire and labour with a higher courage if I am wholly yours, and let it be so when you will!'

I was blest indeed, that day, and a new world opened to me. We were married in a very little while, and I took my wife to our happy home. That was the beginning of the residence I have spoken of; the castle we have ever since inhabited together, dates from that time. All our children have been born in it. Our first child – now married – was a little girl, whom we called Christiana. Her son is so like Little Frank, that I hardly know which is which.

* * *

The current impression as to my partner's dealings with me is also quite erroneous. He did not begin to treat me coldly, as a poor simpleton, when my uncle and I so fatally quarrelled; nor did he afterwards gradually possess himself of our business and edge me out. On the contrary, he behaved to me with the utmost good faith and honour.

Matters between us took this turn. On the day of my separation from my uncle, and even before the arrival at our counting-house of my trunks (which he sent after me, *not* carriage paid), I went down to our room of business, on our little wharf, overlooking the river; and there I told John Spatter what had happened. John did not say, in reply, that rich old relatives were palpable facts, and that love and sentiment were moonshine and fiction. He addressed me thus: 'Michael,' said John, 'we were at school together, and I generally had the knack of getting on better than you, and making a higher reputation.'

'You had, John,' I returned.

'Although,' said John, 'I borrowed your books and lost them; borrowed your pocket-money, and never repaid it; got you to buy my damaged knives at a higher price than I had given for them new; and to own to the windows that I had broken.'

'All not worth mentioning, John Spatter,' said I, 'but certainly true.'

'When you were first established in this infant business, which promises to thrive so well,' pursued John, 'I came to you, in my search for almost any employment, and you made me your clerk.'

'Still not worth mentioning, my dear John Spatter,' said I; 'still, equally true.'

'And finding that I had a good head for business, and that I was really useful *to* the business, you did not like to retain me in that capacity, and thought it an act of justice soon to make me your partner.'

'Still less worth mentioning than any of those other little circumstances you have recalled, John Spatter,' said I; 'for I was, and am, sensible of your merits and my deficiencies.'

'Now, my good friend,' said John, drawing my arm through his, as he had had a habit of doing at school; while two vessels outside the windows of our counting-house – which were shaped like the stern windows of a ship – went lightly down the river with the tide, as John and I might then be sailing away in company, and in trust and confidence, on our voyage of life; 'let there, under these friendly circumstances, be a right understanding between us. You are too easy, Michael. You are nobody's enemy but your own. If I were to give you that damaging character among our connection, with a shrug, and a shake of the head, and a sigh; and if I were further to abuse the trust you place in me – '

'But you never will abuse it at all, John,' I observed.

'Never!' said he; 'but I am putting a case – I say, and if I were further to abuse that trust by keeping this piece of our common affairs in the dark, and this other piece in the light, and again this other piece in the twilight, and so on, I should strengthen my strength, and weaken your weakness, day by day, until at last I found myself on the high road to fortune, and you left behind on some bare common, a hopeless number of miles out of the way.'

'Exactly so,' said I.

'To prevent this, Michael,' said John Spatter, 'or the remotest chance of this, there must be perfect openness between us. Nothing must be concealed, and we must have but one interest.'

'My dear John Spatter,' I assured him, 'that is precisely what I mean.'

'And when you are too easy,' pursued John, his face glowing with friendship, 'you must allow me to prevent that imperfection in your nature from being taken advantage of, by anyone; you must not expect me to humour it – '

'My dear John Spatter,' I interrupted, '*I don't* expect you to humour it. I want to correct it.'

'And I, too,' said John.

'Exactly so!' cried I. 'We both have the same end in view; and, honourably seeking it, and fully trusting one another, and having but one interest, ours will be a prosperous and happy partnership.'

'I am sure of it!' returned John Spatter. And we shook hands most affectionately.

I took John home to my castle, and we had a very happy day. Our partnership throve well. My friend and partner supplied what I wanted, as I had foreseen that he would, and by improving both the business and myself, amply acknowledged any little rise in life to which I had helped him.

*   *   *

I am not (said the poor relation, looking at the fire as he slowly rubbed his hands) very rich, for I never cared to be that; but I have enough, and am above all moderate wants and anxieties. My castle is not a splendid place, but it is very comfortable, and it has a warm and cheerful air, and is quite a picture of Home.

Our eldest girl, who is very like her mother, married John Spatter's eldest son. Our two families are closely united in other ties of attachment. It is very pleasant of an evening, when we are all assembled together – which frequently happens – and when John and I talk over old times, and the one interest there has always been between us.

I really do not know, in my castle, what loneliness is. Some of our children or grandchildren are always about it, and the young voices of my descendants are delightful – O, how delightful! – to me to hear. My dearest and most devoted wife, ever faithful, ever loving, ever helpful and sustaining and consoling, is the priceless blessing of my house; from whom all its other blessings spring. We are rather a musical family, and when Christiana sees me, at any time, a little weary or depressed, she steals to the piano and sings a gentle air she used to sing when we were first betrothed. So weak a man am I, that I cannot bear to hear it from any other source. They played it once, at the theatre, when I was there with Little Frank; and the child said wondering, 'Cousin Michael, whose hot tears are these that have fallen on my hand!'

Such is my castle, and such are the real particulars of my life therein preserved. I often take Little Frank home there. He is very welcome to my grandchildren, and they play together. At this time of the year – the Christmas and New Year time – I am seldom out of my castle. For, the associations of the season seem to hold me there, and the precepts of the season seem to teach me that it is well to be there.

'And the castle is – ' observed a grave, kind voice among the company.

'Yes. My castle,' said the poor relation, shaking his head as he still looked at the fire, 'is in the air. John our esteemed host suggests its situation accurately. My castle is in the air! I have done. Will you be so good as to pass the story?'

THE CHILD'S STORY

Once upon a time, a good many years ago, there was a traveller, and he set out upon a journey. It was a magic journey, and was to seem very long when he began it, and very short when he got halfway through.

He travelled along a rather dark path for some little time, without meeting anything, until at last he came to a beautiful child. So he said to the child, 'What do you do here?' And the child said, 'I am always at play. Come and play with me!'

So, he played with that child, the whole day long, and they were very merry. The sky was so blue, the sun was so bright, the water was so sparkling, the leaves were so green, the flowers were so lovely, and they heard such singing-birds and saw so many butterflies, that everything was beautiful. This was in fine weather. When it rained, they loved to watch the falling drops, and to smell the fresh scents. When it blew, it was delightful to listen to the wind, and fancy what it said, as it came rushing from its home – where was that, they wondered! – whistling and howling, driving the clouds before it, bending the trees, rumbling in the chimneys, shaking the house, and making the sea roar in fury. But, when it snowed, that was best of all; for, they liked nothing so well as to look up at the white flakes falling fast and thick, like down from the breasts of millions of white birds; and to see how smooth and deep the drift was; and to listen to the hush upon the paths and roads.

They had plenty of the finest toys in the world, and the most astonishing picture-books: all about scimitars and slippers and turbans, and dwarfs and giants and genii and fairies, and blue-beards and bean-stalks and riches and caverns and forests and Valentines and Orsons: and all new and all true.

But, one day, of a sudden, the traveller lost the child. He called to him over and over again, but got no answer. So, he went upon his road, and went on for a little while without meeting anything, until at last he came to a handsome boy. So, he said to the boy, 'What do you do here?' And the boy said, 'I am always learning. Come and learn with me.'

So he learned with that boy about Jupiter and Juno, and the Greeks and the Romans, and I don't know what, and learned more than I could tell – or he either, for he soon forgot a great deal of it. But, they were not always learning; they had the merriest games that ever were played. They rowed upon the river in summer, and skated on the ice in winter; they were active afoot, and active on horseback; at cricket, and all games at ball; at prisoner's base, hare and hounds, follow my leader, and more sports than I can think of; nobody could beat them. They had holidays too, and Twelfth cakes, and parties where they danced till midnight, and real theatres where they saw palaces of real gold and silver rise out of the real earth, and saw all the wonders of the world at once. As to friends, they had such dear friends and so many of them, that I want the time to reckon them up. They were all young, like the handsome boy, and were never to be strange to one another all their lives through.

Still, one day, in the midst of all these pleasures, the traveller lost the boy as he had lost the child, and, after calling to him in vain, went on upon his journey. So he went on for a little while without seeing anything, until at last he came to a young man. So, he said to the young man, 'What do you do here?' And the young man said, 'I am always in love. Come and love with me.'

So, he went away with that young man, and presently they came to one of the prettiest girls that ever was seen – just like Fanny in the corner there – and she had eyes like Fanny, and hair like Fanny, and dimples like Fanny's, and she laughed and coloured just as Fanny does while I am talking about her. So, the young man fell in love directly – just as Somebody I won't mention, the first time he came here, did with Fanny. Well! he was teased sometimes – just as Somebody used to be by Fanny; and they quarrelled sometimes – just as Somebody and Fanny used to quarrel; and they made it up, and sat in the dark, and wrote letters every day, and never were happy asunder, and were always looking out for one another and pretending not to, and were engaged at Christmastime, and sat close to one another by the fire, and were going to be married very soon – all exactly like Somebody I won't mention, and Fanny!

But, the traveller lost them one day, as he had lost the rest of his friends, and, after calling to them to come back, which they never did, went on upon his journey. So, he went on for a little while without seeing anything, until at last he came to a middle-aged gentleman. So, he said to the gentleman, 'What are you doing here?' And his answer was, 'I am always busy. Come and be busy with me!'

So, he began to be very busy with that gentleman, and they went on through the wood together. The whole journey was through a wood, only it had been open and green at first, like a wood in spring; and now began to be thick and dark, like a wood in summer; some of the little trees that had come out earliest, were even turning brown. The gentleman was not alone, but had a lady of about the same age with him, who was his wife; and they had children, who were with them too. So, they all went on together through the wood, cutting down the trees, and making a path through the branches and the fallen leaves, and carrying burdens, and working hard.

Sometimes, they came to a long green avenue that opened into deeper woods. Then they would hear a very little, distant voice crying, 'Father, father, I am another child! Stop for me!' And presently they would see a very little figure, growing larger as it came along, running to join them. When it came up, they all crowded round it, and kissed and welcomed it; and then they all went on together.

Sometimes, they came to several avenues at once, and then they all stood still, and one of the children said, 'Father, I am going to sea,' and another said, 'Father, I am going to India,' and another, 'Father, I am going to seek my fortune where I can,' and another, 'Father, I am going to Heaven!' So, with many tears at parting, they went, solitary, down those avenues, each child upon its way; and the child who went to Heaven, rose into the golden air and vanished.

Whenever these partings happened, the traveller looked at the gentleman, and saw him glance up at the sky above the trees, where the day was beginning to decline, and the sunset to come on. He saw, too, that his hair was turning grey. But, they never could rest long, for they had their journey to perform, and it was necessary for them to be always busy.

At last, there had been so many partings that there were no children left, and only the traveller, the gentleman, and the lady, went upon their way in company. And now the wood was yellow; and now brown; and the leaves, even of the forest trees, began to fall.

So, they came to an avenue that was darker than the rest, and were pressing forward on their journey without looking down it when the lady stopped.

'My husband,' said the lady. 'I am called.'

They listened, and they heard a voice a long way down the avenue, say, 'Mother, mother!'

It was the voice of the first child who had said, 'I am going to Heaven!' and the father said, 'I pray not yet. The sunset is very near. I pray not yet!'

But, the voice cried, 'Mother, mother!' without minding him, though his hair was now quite white, and tears were on his face.

Then, the mother, who was already drawn into the shade of the dark avenue and moving away with her arms still round his neck, kissed him, and said, 'My dearest, I am summoned, and I go!' And she was gone. And the traveller and he were left alone together.

And they went on and on together, until they came to very near the end of the wood: so near, that they could see the sunset shining red before them through the trees.

Yet, once more, while he broke his way among the branches, the traveller lost his friend. He called and called, but there was no reply, and when he passed out of the wood, and saw the peaceful sun going down upon a wide purple prospect, he came to an old man sitting on a fallen tree. So, he said to the old man, 'What do you do here?' And the old man said with a calm smile, 'I am always remembering. Come and remember with me!'

So the traveller sat down by the side of that old man, face to face with the serene sunset; and all his friends came softly back and stood around him. The beautiful child, the handsome boy, the young man in love, the father, mother, and children: every one of them was there, and he had lost nothing. So, he loved them all, and was kind and forbearing with them all, and was always pleased to watch them all, and they all honoured and loved him. And I think the traveller must be yourself, dear grandfather, because this is what you do to us, and what we do to you.

THE SCHOOLBOY'S STORY

Being rather young at present – I am getting on in years, but still I am rather young – I have no particular adventures of my own to fall back upon. It wouldn't much interest anybody here, I suppose, to know what a screw the Reverend is, or what a griffin *she* is, or how they do stick it into parents – particularly hair-cutting, and medical attendance. One of our fellows was charged in his half's account twelve and sixpence for two pills – tolerably profitable at six and threepence apiece, I should think – and he never took them either, but put them up the sleeve of his jacket.

As to the beef, it's shameful. It's *not* beef. Regular beef isn't veins. You can chew regular beef. Besides which, there's gravy to regular beef, and you never see a drop to ours. Another of our fellows went home ill, and heard the family doctor tell his father that he couldn't account for his complaint unless it was the beer. Of course it was the beer, and well it might be!

However, beef and Old Cheeseman are two different things. So is beer. It was Old Cheeseman I meant to tell about; not the manner in which our fellows get their constitutions destroyed for the sake of profit.

Why, look at the pie-crust alone. There's no flakiness in it. It's solid – like damp lead. Then our fellows get nightmares, and are bolstered for calling out and waking other fellows. Who can wonder!

Old Cheeseman one night walked in his sleep, put his hat on over his nightcap, got hold of a fishing-rod and a cricket-bat, and went down into the parlour, where they naturally thought from his appearance he was a ghost. Why, he never would have done that if his meals had been wholesome. When we all begin to walk in our sleep, I suppose they'll be sorry for it.

Old Cheeseman wasn't second Latin master then; he was a fellow himself. He was first brought there, very small, in a post-chaise, by a woman who was always taking snuff and shaking him – and that was the most he remembered about it. He never went home for the holidays. His accounts (he never learnt any extras) were sent to a Bank, and the Bank paid them; and he had a brown suit twice a-year, and went into boots at twelve. They were always too big for him, too.

In the midsummer holidays, some of our fellows who lived within walking distance, used to come back and climb the trees outside the playground wall, on purpose to look at Old Cheeseman reading there by himself. He was always as mild as the tea – and *that's* pretty mild, I should hope! – so when they whistled to him, he looked up and nodded; and when they said, 'Halloa, Old Cheeseman, what have you had for dinner?' he said, 'Boiled mutton'; and when they said, 'An't it solitary, Old Cheeseman?' he said, 'It is a little dull sometimes': and then they said, 'Well goodbye, Old Cheeseman!' and climbed down again. Of course it was imposing on Old Cheeseman to give him nothing but boiled mutton through a whole vacation, but that was just like the system. When they didn't give him boiled mutton, they gave him rice pudding, pretending it was a treat. And saved the butcher.

So Old Cheeseman went on. The holidays brought him into other trouble besides the loneliness; because when the fellows began to come back, not wanting to, he was always glad to see them; which was aggravating when they were not at all glad to see him, and so he got his head knocked against walls, and that was the way his nose bled. But he was a favourite in general. Once a subscription was raised for him; and, to keep up his spirits, he was presented before the holidays with two white mice, a rabbit, a pigeon, and a beautiful puppy. Old Cheeseman cried about it – especially soon afterwards, when they all ate one another.

Of course Old Cheeseman used to be called by the names of all sorts of cheeses – Double Glo'sterman, Family Cheshireman, Dutchman, North Wiltshireman, and all that. But he never minded it. And I don't mean to say he was old in point of years – because he wasn't – only he was called from the first, Old Cheeseman.

At last, Old Cheeseman was made second Latin Master. He was brought in one morning at the beginning of a new half, and presented to the school in that capacity as 'Mr Cheeseman'. Then our fellows all agreed that Old Cheeseman was a spy, and a deserter, who had gone over to the enemy's camp, and sold himself for gold. It was no excuse for him that he had sold himself for very little gold – two pound ten a quarter and his washing, as was reported. It was decided by a Parliament which sat about it, that Old Cheeseman's mercenary motives could alone be taken into account, and that he had 'coined our blood for drachmas'. The Parliament took the expression out of the quarrel scene between Brutus and Cassius.

When it was settled in this strong way that Old Cheeseman was a tremendous traitor, who had wormed himself into our fellows' secrets on purpose to get himself into favour by giving up everything he knew, all courageous fellows were invited to come forward and enrol themselves in a society for making a set against him. The president of the society was first boy, named Bob Tarter. His father was in the West Indies, and he owned, himself, that his father was worth millions. He had great power among our fellows, and he wrote a parody, beginning: 'Who made believe to be so meek That we could hardly hear him speak, Yet turned out an Informing Sneak? Old Cheeseman.' – and on in that way through more than a dozen verses, which he used to go and sing, every morning, close by the new master's desk. He trained one of the low boys, too, a rosy-cheeked little brass who didn't care what he did, to go up to him with his Latin grammar one morning, and say it so: *Nominativus Pronominum* – Old Cheeseman, *raro exprimitur* – was never suspected, *nisi distinctionis* – of being an informer, *aut emphasis gratia* – until he proved one. *Ut* – for instance, *vos damnastis* – when he sold the boys. *Quasi* – as though, *dicat* – he should say, *Pretaerea nemo* – I'm a Judas! All this produced a great effect on Old Cheeseman. He had never had much hair; but what he had, began to get thinner and thinner every day. He grew paler and more worn; and sometimes of an evening he was seen sitting at his desk with a precious long snuff to his candle, and his hands before his face, crying. But no member of the society could pity him, even if he felt inclined, because the president said it was Old Cheeseman's conscience.

So Old Cheeseman went on, and didn't he lead a miserable life! Of course the Reverend turned up his nose at him, and of course *she* did – because both of them always do that at all the masters – but he suffered from the fellows most, and he suffered from them constantly. He never told about it, that the society could find out; but he got no credit for that, because the president said it was Old Cheeseman's cowardice.

He had only one friend in the world, and that one was almost as powerless as he was, for it was only Jane. Jane was a sort of wardrobe woman to our fellows, and took care of the boxes. She had come at first, I believe, as a kind of apprentice – some of our fellows say from a charity, but I don't know – and after her time was out, had stopped at so much a year. So little a year, perhaps I ought to say, for it is far more likely. However, she had put some pounds in the Savings' Bank, and she was a very nice young woman. She was not quite pretty; but she had a very frank, honest, bright face, and all our fellows were fond of her. She was uncommonly neat and cheerful, and uncommonly comfortable and kind. And if anything was the matter with a fellow's mother, he always went and showed the letter to Jane.

Jane was Old Cheeseman's friend. The more the society went against him, the more Jane stood by him. She used to give him a good-humoured look out of her still-room window, sometimes, that seemed to set him up for the day. She used to pass out of the orchard and the kitchen garden (always kept locked, I believe you!) through the playground, when she might have gone the other way, only to give a turn of her head, as much as to say 'Keep up your spirits!' to Old Cheeseman. His slip of a room was so fresh and orderly that it was well known who looked after it while he was at his desk; and when our fellows saw a smoking hot dumpling on his plate at dinner, they knew with indignation who had sent it up.

Under these circumstances, the society resolved, after a quantity of meeting and debating, that Jane should be requested to cut Old Cheese-man dead; and that if she refused, she must be sent to Coventry herself. So a deputation, headed by the president, was appointed to wait on Jane, and inform her of the vote the society had been under the painful necessity of passing. She was very much respected for all her good qualities, and there was a story about her having once waylaid the Reverend in his own study, and got a fellow off from severe punishment, of her own kind comfortable heart. So the deputation didn't much like the job. However, they went up, and the president told Jane all about it. Upon which Jane turned very red, burst into tears, informed the president and the deputation, in a way not at all like her usual way, that they were a parcel of malicious young savages, and turned the whole respected body out of the room. Consequently it was entered in the society's book (kept in astronomical cypher for fear of detection), that all communication with Jane was interdicted: and the president addressed the members on this convincing instance of Old Cheeseman's undermining.

But Jane was as true to Old Cheeseman as Old Cheeseman was false to our fellows – in their opinion, at all events – and steadily continued to be his only friend. It was a great exasperation to the society, because Jane was as much a loss to them as she was a gain to him; and being more inveterate against him than ever, they treated him worse than ever. At last, one morning, his desk stood empty, his room was peeped into, and found to be vacant, and a whisper went about among the pale faces of our fellows that Old Cheeseman, unable to bear it any longer, had got up early and drowned himself.

The mysterious looks of the other masters after breakfast, and the evident fact that old Cheeseman was not expected, confirmed the society in this opinion. Some began to discuss whether the president was liable to hanging or only transportation for life, and the president's face showed a great anxiety to know which. However, he said that a jury of his country should find him game; and that in his address he should put it to them to lay their hands upon their hearts and say whether they as Britons approved of informers, and how they thought they would like it themselves. Some of the society considered that he had better run away until he found a forest where he might change clothes with a woodcutter, and stain his face with blackberries; but the majority believed that if he stood his ground, his father – belonging as he did to the West Indies, and being worth millions – could buy him off.

All our fellows' hearts beat fast when the Reverend came in, and made a sort of a Roman, or a field marshal, of himself with the ruler; as he always did before delivering an address. But their fears were nothing to their astonishment when he came out with the story that Old Cheeseman, 'so long our respected friend and fellow-pilgrim in the pleasant plains of knowledge', he called him – O yes! I dare say! Much of that! – was the orphan child of a disinherited young lady who had married against her father's wish, and whose young husband had died, and who had died of sorrow herself, and whose unfortunate baby (Old Cheeseman) had been brought up at the cost of a grandfather who would never consent to see it, baby, boy, or man: which grandfather was now dead, and serve him right – that's my putting in – and which grandfather's large property, there being no will, was now, and all of a sudden and for ever, Old Cheeseman's! Our so long respected friend and fellow-pilgrim in the pleasant plains of knowledge, the Reverend wound up a lot of bothering quotations by saying, would 'come among us once more' that day fort-night, when he desired to take leave of us himself, in a more particular manner. With these words, he stared severely round at our fellows, and went solemnly out.

There was precious consternation among the members of the society, now. Lots of them wanted to resign, and lots more began to try to make out that they had never belonged to it. However, the president stuck up, and said that they must stand or fall together, and that if a breach was made it should be over his body – which was meant to encourage the society: but it didn't. The president further said, he would consider the position in which they stood, and would give them his best opinion and advice in a few days. This was eagerly looked for, as he knew a good deal of the world on account of his father's being in the West Indies.

After days and days of hard thinking, and drawing armies all over his slate, the president called our fellows together, and made the matter clear. He said it was plain that when Old Cheeseman came on the appointed day, his first revenge would be to impeach the society, and have it flogged all round. After witnessing with joy the torture of his enemies, and gloating over the cries which agony would extort from them, the probability was that he would invite the Reverend, on pretence of conversation, into a private room – say the parlour into which parents were shown, where the two great globes were which were never used – and would there reproach him with the various frauds and oppressions he had endured at his hands. At the close of his observations he would make a signal to a prizefighter concealed in the passage, who would then appear and pitch into the Reverend, till he was left insensible. Old Cheeseman would then make Jane a present of from five to ten pounds, and would leave the establishment in fiendish triumph.

The president explained that against the parlour part, or the Jane part, of these arrangements he had nothing to say; but, on the part of the society, he counselled deadly resistance. With this view he recommended that all available desks should be filled with stones, and that the first word of the complaint should be the signal to every fellow to let fly at Old Cheeseman. The bold advice put the society in better spirits, and was unanimously taken. A post about Old Cheeseman's size was put up in the playground, and all our fellows practised at it till it was dinted all over.

When the day came, and places were called, every fellow sat down in a tremble. There had been much discussing and disputing as to how Old Cheeseman would come; but it was the general opinion that he would appear in a sort of triumphal car drawn by four horses, with two livery servants in front, and the prizefighter in disguise up behind. So, all our fellows sat listening for the sound of wheels. But no wheels were heard, for Old Cheeseman walked after all, and came into the school without any preparation. Pretty much as he used to be, only dressed in black.

'Gentlemen,' said the Reverend, presenting him, 'our so long respected friend and fellow-pilgrim in the pleasant plains of knowledge, is desirous to offer a word or two. Attention, gentlemen, one and all!'

Every fellow stole his hand into his desk and looked at the president. The president was all ready, and taking aim at old Cheeseman with his eyes.

What did Old Cheeseman then, but walk up to his old desk, look round him with a queer smile as if there was a tear in his eye, and begin in a quavering, mild voice, 'My dear companions and old friends!'

Every fellow's hand came out of his desk, and the president suddenly began to cry.

'My dear companions and old friends,' said Old Cheeseman, 'you have heard of my good fortune. I have passed so many years under this roof – my entire life so far, I may say – that I hope you have been glad to hear of it for my sake. I could never enjoy it without exchanging congratulations with you. If we have ever misunderstood one another at all, pray, my dear boys, let us forgive and forget. I have a great tenderness for you, and I am sure you return it. I want in the fullness of a grateful heart to shake hands with you every one. I have come back to do it, if you please, my dear boys.'

Since the president had begun to cry, several other fellows had broken out here and there: but now, when Old Cheeseman began with him as first boy, laid his left hand affectionately on his shoulder and gave him his right; and when the president said 'Indeed, I don't deserve it, sir; upon my honour I don't'; there was sobbing and crying all over the school. Every other fellow said he didn't deserve it, much in the same way; but Old Cheeseman, not minding that a bit, went cheerfully round to every boy, and wound up with every master – finishing off the Reverend last.

Then a snivelling little chap in a corner, who was always under some punishment or other, set up a shrill cry of 'Success to Old Cheeseman! Hooray!' The Reverend glared upon him, and said, 'Mr Cheeseman, sir.' But, Old Cheeseman protesting that he liked his old name a great deal better than his new one, all our fellows took up the cry; and, for I don't know how many minutes, there was such a thundering of feet and hands, and such a roaring of Old Cheeseman, as never was heard.

After that, there was a spread in the dining-room of the most magnificent kind. Fowls, tongues, preserves, fruits, confectionaries, jellies, neguses, barley-sugar temples, trifles, crackers – eat all you can and pocket what you like – all at Old Cheeseman's expense. After that, speeches, whole holiday, double and treble sets of all manners of things for all manners of games, donkeys, pony-chaises and drive yourself, dinner for all the masters at the Seven Bells (twenty pounds a head our fellows estimated it at), an annual holiday and feast fixed for that day every year, and another on Old Cheeseman's birthday – Reverend bound down before the fellows to allow it, so that he could never back out – all at Old Cheeseman's expense.

And didn't our fellows go down in a body and cheer outside the Seven Bells? O no!

But there's something else besides. Don't look at the next storyteller, for there's more yet. Next day, it was resolved that the society should make it up with Jane, and then be dissolved. What do you think of Jane being gone, though! 'What? Gone for ever?' said our fellows, with long faces. 'Yes, to be sure,' was all the answer they could get. None of the people about the house would say anything more. At length, the first boy took upon himself to ask the Reverend whether our old friend Jane was really gone? The Reverend (he has got a daughter at home – turn-up nose, and red) replied severely, 'Yes, sir, Miss Pitt is gone.' The idea of calling Jane, Miss Pitt! Some said she had been sent away in disgrace for taking money from Old Cheeseman; others said she had gone into Old Cheeseman's service at a rise of ten pounds a year. All that our fellows knew, was, she was gone.

It was two or three months afterwards, when, one afternoon, an open carriage stopped at the cricket field, just outside bounds, with a lady and gentleman in it, who looked at the game a long time and stood up to see it played. Nobody thought much about them, until the same little snivelling chap came in, against all rules, from the post where he was scout, and said, 'It's Jane!' Both Elevens forgot the game directly, and ran crowding round the carriage. It *was* Jane! In such a bonnet! And if you'll believe me, Jane was married to Old Cheeseman.

It soon became quite a regular thing when our fellows were hard at it in the playground, to see a carriage at the low part of the wall where it joins the high part, and a lady and gentleman standing up in it, looking over. The gentleman was always Old Cheeseman, and the lady was always Jane.

The first time I ever saw them, I saw them in that way. There had been a good many changes among our fellows then, and it had turned out that Bob Tarter's father wasn't worth millions! He wasn't worth anything.

Bob had gone for a soldier, and Old Cheeseman had purchased his discharge. But that's not the carriage. The carriage stopped, and all our fellows stopped as soon as it was seen.

'So you have never sent me to Coventry after all!' said the lady, laughing, as our fellows swarmed up the wall to shake hands with her. 'Are you never going to do it?'

'Never! never! never!' on all sides.

I didn't understand what she meant then, but of course I do now. I was very much pleased with her face though, and with her good way, and I couldn't help looking at her – and at him too – with all our fellows clustering so joyfully about them.

They soon took notice of me as a new boy, so I thought I might as well swarm up the wall myself, and shake hands with them as the rest did. I was quite as glad to see them as the rest were, and was quite as familiar with them in a moment.

'Only a fortnight now,' said Old Cheeseman, 'to the holidays. Who stops? Anybody?'

A good many fingers pointed at me, and a good many voices cried 'He does!' For it was the year when you were all away; and rather low I was about it, I can tell you.

'Oh!' said Old Cheeseman. 'But it's solitary here in the holiday time. He had better come to us.'

So I went to their delightful house, and was as happy as I could possibly be. They understand how to conduct themselves towards boys, *they* do. When they take a boy to the play, for instance, they *do* take him. They don't go in after it's begun, or come out before it's over. They know how to bring a boy up, too. Look at their own! Though he is very little as yet, what a capital boy he is! Why, my next favourite to Mrs Cheeseman and Old Cheeseman, is young Cheeseman.

So, now I have told you all I know about Old Cheeseman. And it's not much after all, I am afraid. Is it?

NOBODY'S STORY

He lived on the bank of a mighty river, broad and deep, which was always silently rolling on to a vast undiscovered ocean. It had rolled on, ever since the world began. It had changed its course sometimes, and turned into new channels, leaving its old ways dry and barren; but it had ever been upon the flow, and ever was to flow until time should be no more. Against its strong, unfathomable stream, nothing made head. No living creature, no flower, no leaf, no particle of animate or inanimate existence, ever strayed back from the undiscovered ocean. The tide of the river set resistlessly towards it; and the tide never stopped, any more than the earth stops in its circling round the sun.

He lived in a busy place, and he worked very hard to live. He had no hope of ever being rich enough to live a month without hard work, but he was quite content, *God* knows, to labour with a cheerful will. He was one of an immense family, all of whose sons and daughters gained their daily bread by daily work, prolonged from their rising up betimes until their lying down at night. Beyond this destiny he had no prospect, and he sought none.

There was overmuch drumming, trumpeting, and speech-making, in the neighbourhood where he dwelt; but he had nothing to do with that. Such clash and uproar came from the Bigwig family, at the unaccountable proceedings of which race, he marvelled much. They set up the strangest statues, in iron, marble, bronze, and brass, before his door; and darkened his house with the legs and tails of uncouth images of horses. He wondered what it all meant, smiled in a rough good-humoured way he had, and kept at his hard work.

The Bigwig family (composed of all the stateliest people thereabouts, and all the noisiest) had undertaken to save him the trouble of thinking for himself, and to manage him and his affairs. 'Why truly,' said he, 'I have little time upon my hands; and if you will be so good as to take care of me, in return for the money I pay over' – for the Bigwig family were not above his money – 'I shall be relieved and much obliged, considering that you know best.' Hence the drumming, trumpeting, and speech-making, and the ugly images of horses which he was expected to fall down and worship.

'I don't understand all this,' said he, rubbing his furrowed brow confusedly. 'But it *has* a meaning, maybe, if I could find it out.'

'It means,' returned the Bigwig family, suspecting something of what he said, 'honour and glory in the highest, to the highest merit.'

'Oh!' said he. And he was glad to hear that.

But, when he looked among the images in iron, marble, bronze, and brass, he failed to find a rather meritorious countryman of his, once the son of a Warwickshire wool-dealer, or any single countryman whomsoever of that kind. He could find none of the men whose knowledge had rescued him and his children from terrific and disfiguring disease, whose boldness had raised his forefathers from the condition of serfs, whose wise fancy had opened a new and high existence to the humblest, whose skill had filled the working man's world with accumulated wonders. Whereas, he did find others whom he knew no good of, and even others whom he knew much ill of.

'Humph!' said he. 'I don't quite understand it.'

So, he went home, and sat down by his fireside to get it out of his mind.

Now, his fireside was a bare one, all hemmed in by blackened streets; but it was a precious place to him. The hands of his wife were hardened with toil, and she was old before her time; but she was dear to him. His children, stunted in their growth, bore traces of unwholesome nurture; but they had beauty in his sight. Above all other things, it was an earnest desire of this man's soul that his children should be taught. 'If I am sometimes misled,' said he, 'for want of knowledge, at least let them know better, and avoid my mistakes. If it is hard to me to reap the harvest of pleasure and instruction that is stored in books, let it be easier to them.'

But, the Bigwig family broke out into violent family quarrels concerning what it was lawful to teach to this man's children. Some of the family insisted on such a thing being primary and indispensable above all other things; and others of the family insisted on such another thing being primary and indispensable above all other things; and the Bigwig family, rent into factions, wrote pamphlets, held convocations, delivered charges, orations, and all varieties of discourses; impounded one another in courts lay and courts ecclesiastical; threw dirt, exchanged pummellings, and fell together by the ears in unintelligible animosity. Meanwhile, this man, in his short evening snatches at his fireside, saw the demon ignorance arise there, and take his children to itself. He saw his daughter perverted into a heavy, slatternly drudge; he saw his son go moping down the ways of low sensuality, to brutality and crime; he saw the dawning light of intelligence in the eyes of his babies so changing into cunning and suspicion, that he could have rather wished them idiots.

'I don't understand this any the better,' said he; 'but I think it cannot be right. Nay, by the clouded Heaven above me, I protest against this as my wrong!'

Becoming peaceable again (for his passion was usually short-lived, and his nature kind), he looked about him on his Sundays and holidays, and he saw how much monotony and weariness there was, and thence how drunkenness arose with all its train of ruin. Then he appealed to the Bigwig family, and said, 'We are a labouring people, and I have a glimmering suspicion in me that labouring people of whatever condition were made – by a higher intelligence than yours, as I poorly understand it – to be in need of mental refreshment and recreation. See what we fall into, when we rest without it. Come! Amuse me harmlessly, show me something, give me an escape!'

But, here the Bigwig family fell into a state of uproar absolutely deafening. When some few voices were faintly heard, proposing to show him the wonders of the world, the greatness of creation, the mighty changes of time, the workings of nature and the beauties of art – to show him these things, that is to say, at any period of his life when he could look upon them – there arose among the Bigwigs such roaring and raving, such pulpiting and petitioning, such maundering and memorialising, such name-calling and dirt-throwing, such a shrill wind of parliamentary questioning and feeble replying – where 'I dare not' waited on 'I would' – that the poor fellow stood aghast, staring wildly around.

'Have I provoked all this,' said he, with his hands to his affrighted ears, 'by what was meant to be an innocent request, plainly arising out of my familiar experience, and the common knowledge of all men who choose to open their eyes? I don't understand, and I am not understood. What is to come of such a state of things!'

He was bending over his work, often asking himself the question, when the news began to spread that a pestilence had appeared among the labourers, and was slaying them by thousands. Going forth to look about him, he soon found this to be true. The dying and the dead were mingled in the close and tainted houses among which his life was passed. New poison was distilled into the always murky, always sickening air. The robust and the weak, old age and infancy, the father and the mother, all were stricken down alike.

What means of flight had he? He remained there, where he was, and saw those who were dearest to him die. A kind preacher came to him, and would have said some prayers to soften his heart in his gloom, but he replied: 'O what avails it, missionary, to come to me, a man condemned to residence in this foetid place, where every sense bestowed upon me for my delight becomes a torment, and where every minute of my numbered days is new mire added to the heap under which I lie oppressed! But, give me my first glimpse of Heaven, through a little of its light and air; give me pure water; help me to be clean; lighten this heavy atmosphere and heavy life, in which our spirits sink, and we become the indifferent and callous creatures you too often see us; gently and kindly take the bodies of those who die among us, out of the small room where we grow to be so familiar with the awful change that even its sanctity is lost to us; and, Teacher, then I will hear – none know better than you, how willingly – of Him whose thoughts were so much with the poor, and who had compassion for all human sorrow!'

He was at work again, solitary and sad, when his master came and stood near to him dressed in black. He, also, had suffered heavily. His young wife, his beautiful and good young wife, was dead; so, too, his only child.

'Master, 'tis hard to bear – I know it – but be comforted. I would give you comfort, if I could.'

The master thanked him from his heart, but, said he, 'O you labouring men! The calamity began among you. If you had but lived more healthily and decently, I should not be the widowed and bereft mourner that I am this day.'

'Master,' returned the other, shaking his head, 'I have begun to understand a little that most calamities will come from us, as this one did, and that none will stop at our poor doors, until we are united with that great squabbling family yonder, to do the things that are right. We cannot live healthily and decently, unless they who undertook to manage us provide the means. We cannot be instructed unless they will teach us; we cannot be rationally amused, unless they will amuse us; we cannot but have some false gods of our own, while they set up so many of theirs in all the public places. The evil consequences of imperfect instruction, the evil consequences of pernicious neglect, the evil consequences of unnatural restraint and the denial of humanising enjoyments, will all come from us, and none of them will stop with us. They will spread far and wide. They always do; they always have done – just like the pestilence. I understand so much, I think, at last.'

But the master said again, 'O you labouring men! How seldom do we ever hear of you, except in connection with some trouble!'

'Master,' he replied, 'I am Nobody, and little likely to be heard of (nor yet much wanted to be heard of, perhaps), except when there is some trouble. But it never begins with me, and it never can end with me. As sure as death, it comes down to me, and it goes up from me.'

There was so much reason in what he said, that the Bigwig family, getting wind of it, and being horribly frightened by the late desolation, resolved to unite with him to do the things that were right – at all events, so far as the said things were associated with the direct prevention, humanly speaking, of another pestilence. But, as their fear wore off, which it soon began to do, they resumed their falling out among themselves, and did nothing. Consequently the scourge appeared again – low down as before – and spread avengingly upward as before, and carried off vast numbers of the brawlers. But not a man among them ever admitted, if in the least degree he ever perceived, that he had anything to do with it.

So Nobody lived and died in the old, old, old way; and this, in the main, is the whole of Nobody's story.

Had he no name, you ask? Perhaps it was Legion. It matters little what his name was. Let us call him Legion.

If you were ever in the Belgian villages near the field of Waterloo, you will have seen, in some quiet little church, a monument erected by faithful companions in arms to the memory of Colonel A, Major B, Captains C, D and E, Lieutenants F and G, Ensigns H, I and J, seven noncommissioned officers, and one hundred and thirty rank and file, who fell in the discharge of their duty on the memorable day. The story of Nobody is the story of the rank and file of the earth. They bear their share of the battle; they have their part in the victory; they fall; they leave no name but in the mass. The march of the proudest of us, leads to the dusty way by which they go. O! Let us think of them this year at the Christmas fire, and not forget them when it is burnt out.

THE BOARDING-HOUSE

Mrs Tibbs was, beyond all dispute, the most tidy, fidgety, thrifty little personage that ever inhaled the smoke of London; and the house of Mrs Tibbs was, decidedly, the neatest in all Great Coram Street. The area and the area-steps, and the street-door and the street-door steps, and the brass handle, and the door-plate, and the knocker, and the fanlight, were all as clean and bright as indefatigable whitewashing, and hearth-stoning, and scrubbing and rubbing, could make them. The wonder was that the brass doorplate, with the interesting inscription 'Mrs Tibbs', had never caught fire from constant friction, so perseveringly was it polished. There were meat-safe-looking blinds in the parlour windows, blue and gold curtains in the drawing-room and spring roller blinds, as Mrs Tibbs was wont in the pride of her heart to boast, 'all the way up'. The bell-lamp in the passage looked as clear as a soap-bubble; you could see yourself in all the tables and French-polish yourself on any one of the chairs. The banisters were beeswaxed; and the very stair-wires made your eyes wink, they were so glittering.

Mrs Tibbs was somewhat short of stature and Mr Tibbs was by no means a large man. He had, moreover, very short legs, but, by way of indemnification, his face was peculiarly long. He was to his wife what the o is in 90 – he was of some importance *with* her – he was nothing without her. Mrs Tibbs was always talking. Mr Tibbs rarely spoke; but, if it were at any time possible to put in a word, when he should have said nothing at all, he had that talent. Mrs Tibbs detested long stories, and Mr Tibbs had one, the conclusion of which had never been heard by his most intimate friends. It always began, 'I recollect when I was in the volunteer corps, in eighteen hundred and six' – but, as he spoke very slowly and softly, and his better half very quickly and loudly, he rarely got beyond the introductory sentence. He was a melancholy specimen of the storyteller. He was the Wandering Jew of Joe Millerism.

Mr Tibbs enjoyed a small independence from the pension-list – about £43 15s. 10d. a year. His father, mother, and five interesting scions from the same stock, drew a like sum from the revenue of a grateful country, though for what particular service was never known. But, as this said independence was not quite sufficient to furnish two people with *all* the luxuries of this life, it had occurred to the busy little spouse of Tibbs that the best thing she could do with a legacy of £700 would be to take and furnish a tolerable house – somewhere in that partially explored tract of country which lies between the British Museum and a remote village called Somers Town – for the reception of boarders. Great Coram Street was the spot pitched upon. The house had been furnished accordingly; two female servants and a boy engaged; and an advertisement inserted in the morning papers informing the public that 'Six individuals would meet with all the comforts of a cheerful musical home in a select private family, residing within ten minutes' walk of' – everywhere. Answers out of number were received, with all sorts of initials; all the letters of the alphabet seemed to be seized with a sudden wish to go out boarding and lodging; voluminous was the correspondence between Mrs Tibbs and the applicants and most profound was the secrecy observed. 'E.' didn't like this; 'I.' couldn't think of putting up with that; 'I. O. U.' didn't think the terms would suit him; and 'G. R.' had never slept in a French bed. The result, however, was that three gentlemen became inmates of Mrs Tibbs's house, on terms which were 'agreeable to all parties'. In went the advertisement again, and a lady with her two daughters, proposed to increase – not their families, but Mrs Tibbs's.

'Charming woman, that Mrs Maplesone!' said Mrs Tibbs, as she and her spouse were sitting by the fire after breakfast; the gentlemen having gone out on their several avocations. 'Charming woman, indeed!' repeated little Mrs Tibbs, more by way of soliloquy than anything else, for she never thought of consulting her husband. 'And the two daughters are delightful. We must have some fish today; they'll join us at dinner for the first time.'

Mr Tibbs placed the poker at right angles with the fire shovel and essayed to speak, but recollected he had nothing to say.

'The young ladies,' continued Mrs T., 'have kindly volunteered to bring their own piano.'

Tibbs thought of the volunteer story, but did not venture it.

A bright thought struck him

'It's very likely – ' said he.

'Pray don't lean your head against the paper,' interrupted Mrs Tibbs; 'and don't put your feet on the steel fender; that's worse.'

Tibbs took his head from the paper, and his feet from the fender, and proceeded. 'It's very likely one of the young ladies may set her cap at young Mr Simpson, and you know a marriage – '

'A what!' shrieked Mrs Tibbs. Tibbs modestly repeated his former suggestion.

'I beg you won't mention such a thing,' said Mrs T. 'A marriage, indeed! – to rob me of my boarders – no, not for the world.'

Tibbs thought in his own mind that the event was by no means unlikely, but, as he never argued with his wife, he put a stop to the dialogue by observing it was 'time to go to business'. He always went out at ten o'clock in the morning and returned at five in the afternoon with an exceedingly dirty face and smelling mouldy. Nobody knew what he was or where he went; but Mrs Tibbs used to say with an air of great importance that he was engaged in the City.

The Miss Maplesones and their accomplished parent arrived in the course of the afternoon in a hackney-coach, and accompanied by a most astonishing number of packages. Trunks, bonnet-boxes, muff-boxes and parasols, guitar-cases and parcels of all imaginable shapes, done up in brown paper and fastened with pins, filled the passage. Then, there was such a running up and down with the luggage, such scampering for warm water for the ladies to wash in and such a bustle and confusion and heating of servants and curling-irons as had never been known in Great Coram Street before. Little Mrs Tibbs was quite in her element, bustling about, talking incessantly and distributing towels and soap like a head nurse in a hospital. The house was not restored to its usual state of quiet repose until the ladies were safely shut up in their respective bedrooms, engaged in the important occupation of dressing for dinner.

'Are these gals 'andsome?' enquired Mr Simpson of Mr Septimus Hicks, another of the boarders, as they were amusing themselves in the drawing-room, before dinner, by lolling on sofas and contemplating their pumps.

'Don't know,' replied Mr Septimus Hicks, who was a tallish, white-faced young man, with spectacles, and a black ribbon round his neck instead of a neckerchief – a most interesting person; a poetical walker of the hospitals and a 'very talented young man'. He was fond of 'lugging' into conversation all sorts of quotations from *Don Juan*, without fettering himself by the propriety of their application; in which particular he was remarkably independent. The other, Mr Simpson, was one of those young men who are in society what walking gentlemen are on the stage, only infinitely worse skilled in his vocation than the most indifferent artist. He was as empty-headed as the great bell of St Paul's, always dressed according to the caricatures published in the monthly fashion and spelt character with a k.

'I saw a devilish number of parcels in the passage when I came home,' simpered Mr Simpson.

'Materials for the toilet, no doubt,' rejoined the *Don Juan* reader.

> 'Much linen, lace, and several pair
> Of stockings, slippers, brushes, combs, complete;
> With other articles of ladies fair,
> To keep them beautiful, or leave them neat.'

'Is that from Milton?' enquired Mr Simpson.

'No – from Byron,' returned Mr Hicks, with a look of contempt. He was quite sure of his author, because he had never read any other. 'Hush! Here come the gals,' and they both commenced talking in a very loud key.

'Mrs Maplesone and the Miss Maplesones, Mr Hicks. Mr Hicks Mrs Maplesone and the Miss Maplesones,' said Mrs Tibbs, with a very red face, for she had been superintending the cooking operations below stairs and looked like a wax doll on a sunny day. 'Mr Simpson, I beg your pardon – Mr Simpson – Mrs Maplesone and the Miss Maplesones' – and *vice versa*. The gentlemen immediately began to slide about with much politeness and to look as if they wished their arms had been legs, so little did they know what to do with them. The ladies smiled, curtseyed and glided into chairs and dived for dropped pocket-handkerchiefs; the gentlemen leant against two of the curtain-pegs; Mrs Tibbs went through an admirable bit of serious pantomime with a servant who had come up to ask some question about the fish-sauce; and then the two young ladies looked at each other; and everybody else appeared to discover something very attractive in the pattern of the fender.

'Julia, my love,' said Mrs Maplesone to her younger daughter, in a tone loud enough for the remainder of the company to hear – 'Julia.'

'Yes, ma.'

'Don't stoop.' This was said for the purpose of directing general attention to Miss Julia's figure, which was undeniable. Everybody looked at her, accordingly, and there was another pause.

'We had the most uncivil hackney-coachman today you can imagine,' said Mrs Maplesone to Mrs Tibbs, in a confidential tone.

Mr Septimus Hicks

'Dear me!' replied the hostess, with an air of great commiseration. She couldn't say more, for the servant again appeared at the door and commenced telegraphing most earnestly to her 'missis'.

'I think hackney-coachmen generally *are* uncivil,' said Mr Hicks in his most insinuating tone.

'Positively I think they are,' replied Mrs Maplesone, as if the idea had never struck her before.

'And cabmen, too,' said Mr Simpson. This remark was a failure, for no one intimated, by word or sign, the slightest knowledge of the manners and customs of cabmen.

'Robinson, what *do* you want?' said Mrs Tibbs to the servant, who, by way of making her presence known to her mistress, had been giving sundry hems and sniffs outside the door during the preceding five minutes.

'Please, ma'am, master wants his clean things,' replied the servant, taken off her guard. The two young men turned their faces to the window, and 'went off' like a couple of bottles of ginger-beer; the ladies put their handkerchiefs to their mouths; and little Mrs Tibbs bustled out of the room to give Tibbs his clean linen – and the servant warning.

Mr Calton, the remaining boarder, shortly afterwards made his appearance and proved a surprising promoter of the conversation. Mr Calton was a superannuated beau – an old boy. He used to say of himself that although his features were not regularly handsome, they were striking. They certainly were. It was impossible to look at his face without being reminded of a chubby street-door knocker, half-lion half-monkey; and the comparison might be extended to his whole character and conversation. He had stood still, while everything else had been moving. He never originated a conversation, or started an idea; but if any commonplace topic were broached, or, to pursue the comparison, if anybody *lifted him up*, he would hammer away with surprising rapidity. He had the *tic douloureux* occasionally, and then he might be said to be muffled, because he did not make quite as much noise as at other times, when he would go on prosing, rat-tat-tat, the same thing over and over again. He had never been married; but he was still on the lookout for a wife with money. He had a life interest worth about £300 a year – he was exceedingly vain and inordinately selfish. He had acquired the reputation of being the very pink of politeness, and he walked round the park, and up Regent Street, every day.

This respectable personage had made up his mind to render himself exceedingly agreeable to Mrs Maplesone – indeed, the desire of being as amiable as possible extended itself to the whole party; Mrs Tibbs having considered it an admirable little bit of management to represent to the gentlemen that she had *some* reason to believe the ladies were fortunes, and to hint to the ladies that all the gentlemen were 'eligible'. A little flirtation, she thought, might keep her house full, without leading to any other result.

Mrs Maplesone was an enterprising widow of about fifty: shrewd, scheming and good-looking. She was amiably anxious on behalf of her daughters; in proof whereof she used to remark that she would have no objection to marry again, if it would benefit her dear girls – she could have no other motive. The 'dear girls' themselves were not at all insensible to the merits of 'a good establishment'. One of them was twenty-five; the other, three years younger. They had been at different watering-places, for four seasons; they had gambled at libraries, read books in balconies, sold at fancy fairs, danced at assemblies, talked sentiment – in short, they had done all that industrious girls could do – but, as yet, to no purpose.

'What a magnificent dresser Mr Simpson is!' whispered Matilda Maplesone to her sister Julia.

'Splendid!' returned the youngest. The magnificent individual alluded to wore a maroon-coloured dress-coat, with a velvet collar and cuffs of the same tint – very like that which usually invests the form of the distinguished unknown who condescends to play the 'swell' in the pantomime at 'Richardson's Show'.

'What whiskers!' said Miss Julia.

'Charming!' responded her sister; 'and what hair!' His hair was like a wig, and distinguished by that insinuating wave which graces the shining locks of those *chefs-d'oeuvre* of art surmounting the waxen images in Bartellot's window in Regent Street; his whiskers meeting beneath his chin, seemed strings wherewith to tie it on, ere science had rendered them unnecessary by her patent invisible springs.

'Dinner's on the table, ma'am, if you please,' said the boy, who now appeared for the first time, in a revived black coat of his master's.

'Oh! Mr Calton, will you lead Mrs Maplesone? – Thank you.' Mr Simpson offered his arm to Miss Julia; Mr Septimus Hicks escorted the lovely Matilda; and the procession proceeded to the dining room. Mr Tibbs was introduced, and Mr Tibbs bobbed up and down to the three ladies like a figure in a Dutch clock, with a powerful spring in the middle of his body, and then dived rapidly into his seat at the bottom of the table, delighted to screen himself behind a soup-tureen, which he could just see over and that was all. The boarders were seated, a lady and gentleman alternately, like the layers of bread and meat in a plate of sandwiches; and then Mrs Tibbs directed James to take off the covers. Salmon, lobster sauce, giblet-soup and the usual accompaniments were discovered: potatoes like petrifactions and bits of toasted bread the shape and size of blank dice.

'Soup for Mrs Maplesone, my dear,' said the bustling Mrs Tibbs. She always called her husband 'my dear' before company. Tibbs, who had been eating his bread and calculating how long it would be before he should get any fish, helped the soup in a hurry, made a small island on the tablecloth and put his glass upon it to hide it from his wife.

'Miss Julia, shall I assist you to some fish?'

'If you please – very little – oh! plenty, thank you' (a bit about the size of a walnut put upon the plate).

'Julia is a *very* little eater,' said Mrs Maplesone to Mr Calton.

The knocker gave a single rap. He was busy eating the fish with his eyes: so he only ejaculated, 'Ah!'

'My dear,' said Mrs Tibbs to her spouse after everyone else had been helped, 'what do *you* take?' The enquiry was accompanied with a look intimating that he mustn't say fish, because there was not much left. Tibbs thought the frown referred to the island on the tablecloth; he therefore coolly replied, 'Why – I'll take a little – fish, I think.'

'Did you say fish, my dear?' (another frown).

'Yes, dear,' replied the villain, with an expression of acute hunger depicted in his countenance. The tears almost started to Mrs Tibbs's eyes as she helped her 'wretch of a husband', as she inwardly called him, to the last eatable bit of salmon on the dish.

'James, take this to your master, and take away your master's knife.' This was deliberate revenge, as Tibbs never could eat fish without one. He was, however, constrained to chase small particles of salmon round and round his plate with a piece of bread and a fork, the number of successful attempts being about one in seventeen.

'Take away, James,' said Mrs Tibbs, as Tibbs swallowed the fourth mouthful – and away went the plates like lightning.

'I'll take a bit of bread, James,' said the poor 'master of the house', more hungry than ever.

'Never mind your master now, James,' said Mrs Tibbs, 'see about the meat.' This was conveyed in the tone in which ladies usually give admonitions to servants in company, that is to say, a low one; but which, like a stage whisper, from its peculiar emphasis, is most distinctly heard by everybody present.

A pause ensued, before the table was replenished – a sort of parenthesis in which Mr Simpson, Mr Calton and Mr Hicks produced respectively a bottle of sauterne, bucellas and sherry, and took wine with everybody – except Tibbs. No one ever thought of him.

Between the fish and an intimated sirloin, there was a prolonged interval.

Here was an opportunity for Mr Hicks. He could not resist the singularly appropriate quotation –

> 'But beef is rare within these oxless isles;
> Goats' flesh there is, no doubt, and kid, and mutton,
> And, when a holiday upon them smiles,
> A joint upon their barbarous spits they put on.'

'Very ungentlemanly behaviour,' thought little Mrs Tibbs, 'to talk in that way.'

'Ah,' said Mr Calton, filling his glass. 'Tom Moore is my poet.'

'And mine,' said Mrs Maplesone.

'And mine,' said Miss Julia.

'And mine,' added Mr Simpson.

'Look at his compositions,' resumed the knocker.

'To be sure,' said Simpson, with confidence.

'Look at *Don Juan*,' replied Mr Septimus Hicks.

'Julia's letter,' suggested Miss Matilda.

'Can anything be grander than the *Fire Worshippers*?' enquired Miss Julia.

'To be sure,' said Simpson.

'Or *Paradise and the Peri*,' said the old beau.

'Yes; or *Paradise and the Peer*,' repeated Simpson, who thought he was getting through it capitally.

'It's all very well,' replied Mr Septimus Hicks, who, as we have before hinted, never had read anything but *Don Juan*. 'Where will you find anything finer than the description of the siege at the commencement of the seventh canto?'

'Talking of a siege,' said Tibbs, with a mouthful of bread – 'when I was in the volunteer corps, in eighteen hundred and six, our commanding officer was Sir Charles Rampart; and one day, when we were exercising on the ground on which the London University now stands, he says, says he, "Tibbs" (calling me from the ranks), "Tibbs – " '

'Tell your master, James,' interrupted Mrs Tibbs, in an awfully distinct tone, 'tell your master if he *won't* carve those fowls, to send them to me.' The discomfited volunteer instantly set to work, and carved the fowls almost as expeditiously as his wife operated on the haunch of mutton. Whether he ever finished the story is not known, but, if he did, nobody heard it.

As the ice was now broken, and the new inmates more at home, every member of the company felt more at ease. Tibbs himself most certainly did, because he went to sleep immediately after dinner. Mr Hicks and the ladies discoursed most eloquently about poetry and the theatres and Lord Chesterfield's *Letters*; and Mr Calton followed up what everybody said with continuous double knocks. Mrs Tibbs highly approved of every observation that fell from Mrs Maplesone; and as Mr Simpson sat with a smile upon his face and said 'Yes' or 'Certainly' at intervals of about four minutes each, he received full credit for understanding what was going forward. The gentlemen rejoined the ladies in the drawing-room very shortly after they had left the dining-parlour. Mrs Maplesone and Mr Calton played cribbage, and the 'young people' amused themselves with music and conversation. The Miss Maplesones sang the most fascinating duets, and accompanied themselves on guitars, ornamented with bits of ethereal blue ribbon. Mr Simpson put on a pink waistcoat and said he was in raptures; and Mr Hicks felt in the seventh heaven of poetry or the seventh canto of *Don Juan* – it was the same thing to him. Mrs Tibbs was quite charmed with the newcomers; and Mr Tibbs spent the evening in his usual way – he went to sleep, and woke up, and went to sleep again, and woke at supper-time.

*   *   *

We are not about to adopt the licence of novel-writers, and to let 'years roll on'; but we will take the liberty of requesting the reader to suppose that six months have elapsed, since the dinner we have described, and that Mrs Tibbs's boarders have, during that period, sang and danced and gone to theatres and exhibitions together, as ladies and gentlemen, wherever they board, often do. And we will beg them, the period we have mentioned having elapsed, to imagine further, that Mr Septimus

Hicks received, in his own bedroom (a front attic), at an early hour one morning, a note from Mr Calton, requesting the favour of seeing him, as soon as convenient to himself, in his (Calton's) dressing-room on the second-floor back.

'Tell Mr Calton I'll come down directly,' said Mr Septimus to the boy. 'Stop – is Mr Calton unwell?' enquired this excited walker of hospitals, as he put on a bed-furniture-looking dressing-gown.

'Not as I knows on, sir,' replied the boy. ' Please, sir, he looked rather rum, as it might be.'

'Ah, that's no proof of his being ill,' returned Hicks, unconsciously. 'Very well: I'll be down directly.' Downstairs ran the boy with the message, and down went the excited Hicks himself, almost as soon as the message was delivered. 'Tap, tap.' 'Come in.' – Door opens, and discovers Mr Calton sitting in an easy-chair. Mutual shakes of the hand exchanged and Mr Septimus Hicks motioned to a seat. A short pause. Mr Hicks coughed and Mr Calton took a pinch of snuff. It was one of those interviews where neither party knows what to say. Mr Septimus Hicks broke silence.

'I received a note – ' he said, very tremulously, in a voice like a Punch with a cold.

'Yes,' returned the other, 'you did.'

'Exactly.'

'Yes.'

Now, although this dialogue must have been satisfactory, both gentlemen felt there was something more important to be said; therefore they did as most men in such a situation would have done – they looked at the table with a determined aspect. The conversation had been opened, however, and Mr Calton had made up his mind to continue it with a regular double knock. He always spoke very pompously.

'Hicks,' said he, 'I have sent for you, in consequence of certain arrangements which are pending in this house, connected with a marriage.'

'With a marriage!' gasped Hicks, compared with whose expression of countenance, Hamlet's, when he sees his father's ghost, is pleasing and composed.

'With a marriage,' returned the knocker. 'I have sent for you to prove the great confidence I can repose in you.'

'And will you betray me?' eagerly enquired Hicks, who in his alarm had even forgotten to quote.

'I betray *you*! Won't *you* betray *me*?'

'Never: no one shall know, to my dying day, that you had a hand in the business,' responded the agitated Hicks, with an inflamed countenance and his hair standing on end as if he were on the stool of an electrifying machine in full operation.

'People must know that, some time or other – within a year, I imagine,' said Mr Calton, with an air of great self-complacency. 'We *may* have a family.'

'*We!* – That won't affect you, surely?'

'The devil it won't!'

'No! how can it?' said the bewildered Hicks. Calton was too much enwrapped in the contemplation of his happiness to see the equivoque between Hicks and himself; and threw himself back in his chair. 'Oh, Matilda!' sighed the antique beau, in a lackadaisical voice, and applying his right hand a little to the left of the fourth button of his waistcoat, counting from the bottom. 'Oh, Matilda!'

'What Matilda?' enquired Hicks, starting up.

'Matilda Maplesone,' responded the other, doing the same.

'I marry her tomorrow morning,' said Hicks.

'It's false,' rejoined his companion: 'I marry her!'

'You marry her?'

'I marry her!'

'You marry Matilda Maplesone?'

'Matilda Maplesone.'

'*Miss* Maplesone marry *you*?'

'Miss Maplesone! No; Mrs Maplesone.'

'Good heaven!' said Hicks, falling into his chair: 'You marry the mother, and I the daughter!'

'Most extraordinary circumstance!' replied Mr Calton, 'and rather inconvenient too; for the fact is, that owing to Matilda's wishing to keep her intention secret from her daughters until the ceremony had taken place, she doesn't like applying to any of her friends to give her away. I entertain an objection to making the affair known to my acquaintance just now; and the consequence is, that I sent to you to know whether you'd oblige me by acting as father.'

'I should have been most happy, I assure you,' said Hicks, in a tone of condolence; 'but, you see, I shall be acting as bridegroom. One character is frequently a consequence of the other; but it is not usual to act in both at the same time. There's Simpson – I have no doubt he'll do it for you.'

'I don't like to ask him,' replied Calton, 'he's such a donkey.'

Mr Septimus Hicks looked up at the ceiling, and down at the floor; at last an idea struck him. 'Let the man of the house, Tibbs, be the father,' he suggested; and then he quoted, as peculiarly applicable to Tibbs and the pair –

'O Powers of Heaven! what dark eyes meets she there?
'Tis – 'tis her father's – fixed upon the pair.'

'The idea has struck me already,' said Mr Calton: 'but, you see, Matilda, for what reason I know not, is very anxious that Mrs Tibbs should know nothing about it till it's all over. It's a natural delicacy, after all, you know.'

'He's the best-natured little man in existence, if you manage him properly,' said Mr Septimus Hicks. 'Tell him not to mention it to his wife, and assure him she won't mind it, and he'll do it directly. My marriage is to be a secret one, on account of the mother and *my* father; therefore he must be enjoined to secrecy.'

A small double knock, like a presumptuous single one, was that instant heard at the street-door. It was Tibbs; it could be no one else; for no one else occupied five minutes in rubbing his shoes. He had been out to pay the baker's bill.

'Mr Tibbs,' called Mr Calton in a very bland tone, looking over the banisters.

'Sir!' replied he of the dirty face.

'Will you have the kindness to step upstairs for a moment?'

'Certainly, sir,' said Tibbs, delighted to be taken notice of. The bedroom-door was carefully closed, and Tibbs, having put his hat on the floor (as most timid men do), and been accommodated with a seat, looked as astounded as if he were suddenly summoned before the familiars of the Inquisition.

'A rather unpleasant occurrence, Mr Tibbs,' said Calton, in a very portentous manner, 'obliges me to consult you, and to beg you will not communicate what I am about to say to your wife.'

Tibbs acquiesced, wondering in his own mind what the deuce the other could have done, and imagining that at least he must have broken the best decanters.

Mr Calton resumed: 'I am placed, Mr Tibbs, in rather an unpleasant situation.'

Tibbs looked at Mr Septimus Hicks, as if he thought Mr H.'s being in the immediate vicinity of his fellow-boarder might constitute the unpleasantness of his situation; but as he did not exactly know what to say, he merely ejaculated the monosyllable, 'Lor!'

'Now,' continued the knocker, 'let me beg you will exhibit no manifestations of surprise, which may be overheard by the domestics, when I tell you – command your feelings of astonishment – that two inmates of this house intend to be married tomorrow morning.' And he drew back his chair, several feet, to perceive the effect of the unlooked-for announcement.

If Tibbs had rushed from the room, staggered downstairs and fainted in the passage – if he had instantaneously jumped out of the window into the mews behind the house in an agony of surprise – his behaviour would have been much less inexplicable to Mr Calton than it was when he put his hands into his inexpressible pockets and said, with a half-chuckle, 'Just so.'

'You are not surprised, Mr Tibbs?' enquired Mr Calton.

'Bless you, no, sir,' returned Tibbs; 'after all, its very natural. When two young people get together, you know – '

'Certainly, certainly,' said Calton, with an indescribable air of self-satisfaction.

'You don't think it's at all an out-of-the-way affair then?' asked Mr Septimus Hicks, who had watched the countenance of Tibbs in mute astonishment.

'No, sir,' replied Tibbs; 'I was just the same at his age.' He actually smiled when he said this.

'How devilish well I must carry my years!' thought the delighted old beau, knowing he was at least ten years older than Tibbs at that moment.

'Well, then, to come to the point at once,' he continued, 'I have to ask you whether you will object to act as father on the occasion?'

'Certainly not,' replied Tibbs; still without evincing an atom of surprise.

'You will not?'

'Decidedly not,' reiterated Tibbs, still as calm as a pot of porter with the head off.

Mr Calton seized the hand of the petticoat-governed little man and vowed eternal friendship from that hour. Hicks, who was all admiration and surprise, did the same.

'Now, confess,' asked Mr Calton of Tibbs, as he picked up his hat, 'were you not a little surprised?'

'I b'lieve you!' replied that illustrious person, holding up one hand; 'I b'lieve you! When I first heard of it.'

'So sudden,' said Septimus Hicks.

'So strange to ask *me*, you know,' said Tibbs.

'So odd altogether!' said the superannuated love-maker; and then all three laughed.

'I say,' said Tibbs, shutting the door which he had previously opened, and giving full vent to a hitherto corked-up giggle, 'what bothers me is, what *will* his father say?'

Mr Septimus Hicks looked at Mr Calton.

'Yes; but the best of it is,' said the latter, giggling in his turn, 'I haven't got a father – he! he! he!'

'You haven't got a father. No; but *he* has,' said Tibbs.

'*Who* has?' enquired Septimus Hicks.

'Why, *him*.'

'Him, who? Do you know my secret? Do you mean me?'

'You! No; you know who I mean,' returned Tibbs with a knowing wink.

'For heaven's sake, whom do you mean?' enquired Mr Calton, who, like Septimus Hicks, was all but out of his senses at the strange confusion.

'Why Mr Simpson, of course,' replied Tibbs; 'who else could I mean?'

'I see it all,' said the Byron-quoter; 'Simpson marries Julia Maplesone tomorrow morning!'

'Undoubtedly,' replied Tibbs, thoroughly satisfied, 'of course he does.'

It would require the pencil of Hogarth to illustrate – our feeble pen is inadequate to describe – the expression which the countenances of Mr Calton and Mr Septimus Hicks respectively assumed at this unexpected announcement. Equally impossible is it to describe, although perhaps it is easier for our lady readers to imagine, what arts the three ladies could have used so completely to entangle their separate partners. Whatever they were, however, they were successful. The mother was perfectly aware of the intended marriage of both daughters; and the young ladies were equally acquainted with the intention of their estimable parent. They agreed, however, that it would have a much better appearance if each feigned ignorance of the other's engagement; and it was equally desirable that all the marriages should take place on the same day, to prevent the discovery of one clandestine alliance operating prejudicially on the others. Hence, the mystification of Mr Calton and Mr Septimus Hicks, and the pre-engagement of the unwary Tibbs.

On the following morning, Mr Septimus Hicks was united to Miss Matilda Maplesone. Mr Simpson also entered into a 'holy alliance' with Miss Julia – Tibbs acting as father, 'his first appearance in that character'. Mr Calton, not being quite so eager as the two young men, was rather struck by the double discovery; and as he had found some difficulty in getting anyone to give the lady away, it occurred to him that the best mode of obviating the inconvenience would be not to take her at all. The lady, however, 'appealed', as her counsel said on the trial of the cause, *Maplesone v. Calton*, for a breach of promise, 'with a broken heart, to the outraged laws of her country'. She recovered damages to the amount of £1,000 which the unfortunate knocker was compelled to pay. Mr Septimus Hicks having walked the hospitals, took it into his head to walk off altogether. His injured wife is at present residing with her mother at Boulogne. Mr Simpson, having the misfortune to lose his wife six weeks after marriage (by her eloping with an officer during his temporary sojourn in the Fleet Prison, in consequence of his inability to discharge her little mantua-maker's bill), and being disinherited by his father, who died soon afterwards, was fortunate enough to obtain a permanent engagement at a fashionable haircutter's; hairdressing being a science to which he had frequently directed his attention. In this situation he had necessarily many opportunities of making himself acquainted with the habits and style of thinking of the exclusive portion of the nobility of this kingdom. To this fortunate circumstance are we indebted for the production of those brilliant efforts of genius, his fashionable novels, which so long as good taste, unsullied by exaggeration, cant and quackery, continues to exist, cannot fail to instruct and amuse the thinking portion of the community.

It only remains to add that this complication of disorders completely deprived poor Mrs Tibbs of all her inmates, except the one whom she could have best spared – her husband. That wretched little man returned home, on the day of the wedding, in a state of partial intoxication; and, under the influence of wine, excitement and despair, actually dared to brave the anger of his wife. Since that ill-fated hour he has constantly taken his meals in the kitchen, to which apartment, it is understood, his witticisms will be in future confined, a turn-up bedstead having been conveyed there by Mrs Tibbs's order for his exclusive accommodation. It is possible that he will be enabled to finish, in that seclusion, his story of the volunteers.

The advertisement has again appeared in the morning papers. Results must be reserved for another chapter.

* * *

'Well!' said little Mrs Tibbs to herself, as she sat in the front parlour of the Coram Street mansion one morning, mending a piece of stair-carpet off the first landing – 'Things have not turned out so badly, either, and if I only get a favourable answer to the advertisement, we shall be full again.'

Mrs Tibbs resumed her occupation of making worsted latticework in the carpet, anxiously listening to the twopenny postman, who was hammering his way down the street at the rate of a penny a knock. The house was as quiet as possible. There was only one low sound to be heard – it was the unhappy Tibbs cleaning the gentlemen's boots in the back kitchen, and accompanying himself with a buzzing noise, in wretched mockery of humming a tune.

The postman drew near the house. He paused – so did Mrs Tibbs. A knock – a bustle – a letter – post paid.

Wednesday evening

T. I. presents compt. to I. T. and T. I. begs To say that i see the advertisement And she will Do Herself the pleasure of calling On you at 12 o'clock tomorrow morning.

T. I. as To apologise to I. T. for the shortness Of the notice But i hope it will not unconvenience you.

I remain yours Truly

Little Mrs Tibbs perused the document, over and over again; and the more she read it, the more was she confused by the mixture of the first and third person; the substitution of the 'i' for the 'T. I.'; and the transition from the 'I. T.' to the 'you'. The writing looked like a skein of thread in a tangle, and the note was ingeniously folded into a perfect square, with the direction squeezed up into the right-hand corner, as if it were ashamed of itself. The back of the epistle was pleasingly ornamented with a large red wafer, which, with the addition of divers ink-stains, bore a marvellous resemblance to a black beetle trodden upon. One thing, however, was perfectly clear to the perplexed Mrs Tibbs. Somebody was to call at twelve. The drawing-room was forthwith dusted for the third time that morning; three or four chairs were pulled out of their places and a corresponding number of books carefully upset in order that there might be a due absence of formality. Down went the piece of stair-carpet before noticed, and up ran Mrs Tibbs 'to make herself tidy'.

The clock of New St Pancras Church struck twelve, and the Foundling, with laudable politeness, did the same ten minutes afterwards, St something else struck the quarter, and then there arrived a single lady with a double knock, in a pelisse the colour of the interior of a damson pie; a bonnet of the same, with a regular conservatory of artificial flowers; a white veil and a green parasol with a cobweb border.

The visitor (who was very fat and red-faced) was shown into the drawing-room, Mrs Tibbs presented herself and the negotiation commenced.

'I called in consequence of an advertisement,' said the stranger, in a voice as if she had been playing a set of Pan's pipes for a fortnight without leaving off.

'Yes!' said Mrs Tibbs, rubbing her hands very slowly and looking the applicant full in the face – two things she always did on such occasions.

'Money isn't no object whatever to me,' said the lady, 'so much as living in a state of retirement and obtrusion.'

Mrs Tibbs, as a matter of course, acquiesced in such an exceedingly natural desire.

'I am constantly attended by a medical man,' resumed the pelisse wearer; 'I have been a shocking unitarian for some time – I, indeed, have had very little peace since the death of Mr Bloss.'

Mrs Tibbs looked at the relict of the departed Bloss and thought he must have had very little peace in his time. Of course she could not say so; so she looked very sympathising.

'I shall be a good deal of trouble to you,' said Mrs Bloss; 'but for that trouble I am willing to pay. I am going through a course of treatment which renders attention necessary. I have one mutton chop in bed at half-past eight, and another at ten, every morning.'

Mrs Tibbs, as in duty bound, expressed the pity she felt for anybody placed in such a distressing situation; and the carnivorous Mrs Bloss proceeded to arrange the various preliminaries with wonderful despatch. 'Now mind,' said that lady, after terms were arranged; 'I am to have the second-floor front, for my bedroom?'

'Yes, ma'am.'

'And you'll find room for my little servant Agnes?'

'Oh! certainly.'

'And I can have one of the cellars in the area for my bottled porter.'

'With the greatest pleasure – James shall get it ready for you by Saturday.'

'And I'll join the company at the breakfast-table on Sunday morning,' said Mrs Bloss. 'I shall get up on purpose.'

'Very well,' returned Mrs Tibbs, in her most amiable tone; for satisfactory references had 'been given and required', and it was quite certain that the newcomer had plenty of money. 'It's rather singular,' continued Mrs Tibbs, with what was meant for a most bewitching smile, 'that we have a gentleman now with us, who is in a very delicate state of health – a Mr Gobler. His apartment is the back drawing-room.'

'The next room?' enquired Mrs Bloss.

'The next room,' repeated the hostess.

'How very promiscuous!' ejaculated the widow.

'He hardly ever gets up,' said Mrs Tibbs in a whisper.

'Lor!' cried Mrs Bloss, in an equally low tone.

'And when he is up,' said Mrs Tibbs, 'we never can persuade him to go to bed again.'

'Dear me!' said the astonished Mrs Bloss, drawing her chair nearer Mrs Tibbs. 'What is his complaint?'

'Why, the fact is,' replied Mrs Tibbs, with a most communicative air, 'he has no stomach whatever.'

'No what?' enquired Mrs Bloss, with a look of the most indescribable alarm.

'No stomach,' repeated Mrs Tibbs, with a shake of the head.

'Lord bless us! what an extraordinary case!' gasped Mrs Bloss, as if she understood the communication in its literal sense, and was astonished at a gentleman without a stomach finding it necessary to board anywhere.

'When I say he has no stomach,' explained the chatty little Mrs Tibbs, 'I mean that his digestion is so much impaired, and his interior so deranged, that his stomach is not of the least use to him – in fact, it's an inconvenience.'

'Never heard such a case in my life!' exclaimed Mrs Bloss. 'Why, he's worse than I am.'

'Oh, yes!' replied Mrs Tibbs – 'certainly.' She said this with great confidence, for the damson pelisse suggested that Mrs Bloss, at all events, was not suffering under Mr Gobler's complaint.

'You have quite incited my curiosity,' said Mrs Bloss, as she rose to depart. 'How I long to see him!'

'He generally comes down, once a week,' replied Mrs Tibbs; 'I dare say you'll see him on Sunday.' With this consolatory promise Mrs Bloss was obliged to be contented. She accordingly walked slowly down the stairs, detailing her complaints all the way; and Mrs Tibbs followed her, uttering an exclamation of compassion at every step. James (who looked very gritty, for he was cleaning the knives) fell up the kitchen-stairs and opened the street-door; and, after mutual farewells, Mrs Bloss slowly departed, down the shady side of the street.

It is almost superfluous to say that the lady whom we have just shown out at the street-door (and whom the two female servants are now inspecting from the second-floor windows) was exceedingly vulgar, ignorant and selfish. Her deceased better-half had been an eminent cork-cutter, in which capacity he had amassed a decent fortune. He had no relative but his nephew, and no friend but his cook. The former had the insolence one morning to ask for the loan of fifteen pounds; and, by way of retaliation, he married the latter next day; he made a will immediately afterwards, containing a burst of honest indignation against his nephew (who supported himself and two sisters on £100 a year), and a bequest of his whole property to his wife. He felt ill after breakfast, and died after dinner. There is a mantelpiece-looking tablet in a civic parish church, setting forth his virtues and deploring his loss. He never dishonoured a bill or gave away a halfpenny.

The relict and sole executrix of this noble-minded man was an odd mixture of shrewdness and simplicity, liberality and meanness. Bred up as she had been, she knew no mode of living so agreeable as a boarding-house: and having nothing to do, and nothing to wish for, she naturally imagined she must be ill – an impression which was most assiduously promoted by her medical attendant Dr Wosky and her handmaid Agnes: both of whom, doubtless for good reasons, encouraged all her extravagant notions.

Since the catastrophe recorded in the last chapter, Mrs Tibbs had been very shy of young-lady boarders. Her present inmates were all lords of the creation, and she availed herself of the opportunity of their assemblage at the dinner-table to announce the expected arrival of

Mrs Bloss. The gentlemen received the communication with stoical indifference and Mrs Tibbs devoted all her energies to prepare for the reception of the valetudinarian. The second-floor front was scrubbed, and washed, and flannelled, till the wet went through to the drawing-room ceiling. Clean white counterpanes, and curtains, and napkins, water-bottles as clear as crystal, blue jugs and mahogany furniture, added to the splendour and increased the comfort of the apartment. The warming-pan was in constant requisition, and a fire lighted in the room every day. The chattels of Mrs Bloss were forwarded by instalments. First, there came a large hamper of Guinness's stout and an umbrella; then, a train of trunks; then, a pair of clogs and a bandbox; then, an easy-chair with an air-cushion; then, a variety of suspicious looking packages; and – 'though last not least' – Mrs Bloss and Agnes: the latter in a cherry-coloured merino dress, openwork stockings and shoes with sandals: like a disguised Columbine.

The installation of the Duke of Wellington as Chancellor of the University of Oxford was nothing, in point of bustle and turmoil, to the installation of Mrs Bloss in her new quarters. True, there was no bright doctor of civil law to deliver a classical address on the occasion; but there were several other old women present, who spoke quite as much to the purpose, and understood themselves equally well. The chop-eater was so fatigued with the process of removal that she declined leaving her room until the following morning; so a mutton-chop, pickle, a pill, a pint bottle of stout and other medicines were carried upstairs for her consumption.

'Why, what *do* you think, ma'am?' enquired the inquisitive Agnes of her mistress, after they had been in the house some three hours; 'what *do* you think, ma'am? the lady of the house is married.'

'Married!' said Mrs Bloss, taking the pill and a draught of Guinness – 'married! Unpossible!'

'She is indeed, ma'am,' returned the Columbine; 'and her husband, ma'am, lives – he – he – he – lives in the kitchen, ma'am.'

'In the kitchen!'

'Yes, ma'am: and he – he – he – the housemaid says, he never goes into the parlour except on Sundays; and that Mrs Tibbs makes him clean the gentlemen's boots; and that he cleans the windows, too, sometimes; and that one morning early, when he was in the front balcony cleaning the drawing-room windows, he called out to a gentleman on the opposite side of the way, who used to live here, "Ah! Mr Calton, sir, how are you?" '

Here the attendant laughed till Mrs Bloss was in serious apprehension of her chuckling herself into a fit.

'Well, I never!' said Mrs Bloss.

'Yes. And please, ma'am, the servants gives him gin and water sometimes; and then he cries and says he hates his wife and the boarders and wants to tickle them.'

'Tickle the boarders!' exclaimed Mrs Bloss, seriously alarmed.

'No, ma'am, not the boarders, the servants.'

'Oh, is that all!' said Mrs Bloss, quite satisfied.

'He wanted to kiss me as I came up the kitchen-stairs, just now,' said Agnes, indignantly; 'but I gave it him – a little wretch!'

This intelligence was but too true. A long course of snubbing and neglect; his days spent in the kitchen, and his nights in the turn-up bedstead, had completely broken the little spirit that the unfortunate volunteer had ever possessed. He had no one to whom he could detail his injuries but the servants, and they were almost of necessity his chosen confidants. It is no less strange than true, however, that the little weaknesses which he had incurred, most probably during his military career, seemed to increase as his comforts diminished. He was actually a sort of journeyman Giovanni of the basement storey.

The next morning being Sunday, breakfast was laid in the front parlour at ten o'clock. Nine was the usual time, but the family always breakfasted an hour later on Sabbath. Tibbs enrobed himself in his Sunday costume – a black coat, and exceedingly short, thin trousers; with a very large white waistcoat, white stockings and cravat, and Blucher boots – and mounted to the parlour aforesaid. Nobody had come down and he amused himself by drinking the contents of the milkpot with a teaspoon.

A pair of slippers were heard descending the stairs. Tibbs flew to a chair; and a stern-looking man, of about fifty, with very little hair on his head, and a Sunday paper in his hand, entered the room.

'Good-morning, Mr Evenson,' said Tibbs, very humbly, with something between a nod and a bow.

'How do you do, Mr Tibbs?' replied he of the slippers, as he sat himself down, and began to read his paper without saying another word.

'Is Mr Wisbottle in town today, do you know, sir?' enquired Tibbs, just for the sake of saying something.

'I should think he was,' replied the stern gentleman. 'He was whistling "The Light Guitar", in the next room to mine, at five o'clock this morning.'

'He's very fond of whistling,' said Tibbs, with a slight smirk.

'Yes – I ain't,' was the laconic reply.

Mr John Evenson was in the receipt of an independent income, arising chiefly from various houses he owned in the different suburbs. He was very morose and discontented. He was a thorough radical, and used to attend a great variety of public meetings for the express purpose of finding fault with everything that was proposed. Mr Wisbottle, on the other hand, was a high Tory. He was a clerk in the Woods and Forests Office, which he considered rather an aristocratic employment; he knew the peerage by heart, and could tell you, offhand, where any illustrious personage lived. He had a good set of teeth and a capital tailor. Mr Evenson looked on all these qualifications with profound contempt; and the consequence was that the two were always disputing, much to the edification of the rest of the house. It should be added that, in addition to his partiality for whistling, Mr Wisbottle had a great idea of his singing powers. There were two other boarders, besides the gentleman in the back drawing-room – Mr Alfred Tomkins and Mr Frederick O'Bleary. Mr Tomkins was a clerk in a wine-house; he was a connoisseur in paintings and had a wonderful eye for the picturesque. Mr O'Bleary was an Irishman, recently imported; he was in a perfectly wild state and had come over to England to be an apothecary, a clerk in a government office, an actor, a reporter or anything else that turned up – he was not particular. He was on familiar terms with two small Irish members, and got franks for everybody in the house. He felt convinced that his intrinsic merits must procure him a high destiny. He wore shepherd's-plaid inexpressibles, and used to look under all the ladies' bonnets as he walked along the streets. His manners and appearance reminded one of Orson.

'Here comes Mr Wisbottle,' said Tibbs; and Mr Wisbottle forthwith appeared, in blue slippers and a shawl dressing-gown, whistling *'Di piacer'*.

'Good-morning, sir,' said Tibbs again. It was almost the only thing he ever said to anybody

'How are you, Tibbs?' condescendingly replied the amateur; and he walked to the window, and whistled louder than ever.

'Pretty air, that!' said Evenson, with a snarl and without taking his eyes off the paper.

'Glad you like it,' replied Wisbottle, highly gratified.

'Don't you think it would sound better if you whistled it a little louder?' enquired the mastiff.

'No; I don't think it would,' rejoined the unconscious Wisbottle.

'I'll tell you what, Wisbottle,' said Evenson, who had been bottling up his anger for some hours – 'the next time you feel disposed to whistle "The Light Guitar" at five o'clock in the morning, I'll trouble you to whistle it with your head out the window. If you don't, I'll learn the triangle – I will, by – '

The entrance of Mrs Tibbs (with the keys in a little basket) interrupted the threat, and prevented its conclusion.

Mrs Tibbs apologised for being down rather late; the bell was rung; James brought up the urn and received an unlimited order for dry toast and bacon. Tibbs sat down at the bottom of the table, and began eating watercresses like a Nebuchadnezzar. Mr O'Bleary appeared and Mr Alfred Tomkins. The compliments of the morning were exchanged and the tea was made.

'God bless me!' exclaimed Tomkins, who had been looking out of the window. 'Here – Wisbottle – pray come here – make haste.'

Mr Wisbottle started from the table, and everyone looked up.

'Do you see,' said the connoisseur, placing Wisbottle in the right position – 'a little more this way: there – do you see how splendidly the light falls upon the left side of that broken chimney-pot at No. 48?'

'Dear me! I see,' replied Wisbottle, in a tone of admiration.

'I never saw an object stand out so beautifully against the clear sky in my life,' ejaculated Alfred. Everybody (except John Evenson) echoed the sentiment; for Mr Tomkins had a great character for finding out beauties which no one else could discover – he certainly deserved it.

'I have frequently observed a chimney-pot in College Green, Dublin, which has a much better effect,' said the patriotic O'Bleary, who never allowed Ireland to be outdone on any point.

The assertion was received with obvious incredulity, for Mr Tomkins declared that no other chimney-pot in the United Kingdom, broken or unbroken, could be so beautiful as the one at No. 48.

The room-door was suddenly thrown open and Agnes appeared, leading in Mrs Bloss, who was dressed in a geranium-coloured muslin gown, and displayed a gold watch of huge dimensions; a chain to match; and a splendid assortment of rings, with enormous stones. A general rush was made for a chair and a regular introduction took place. Mr John Evenson made a slight inclination of the head; Mr Frederick O'Bleary, Mr Alfred Tomkins and Mr Wisbottle bowed like the mandarins in a grocer's shop; Tibbs rubbed hands, and went round in circles. He was observed to close one eye, and to assume a clockwork sort of expression with the other; this has been considered as a wink, and it has been reported that Agnes was its object. We repel the calumny and challenge contradiction.

Mrs Tibbs enquired after Mrs Bloss's health in a low tone. Mrs Bloss, with a supreme contempt for the memory of Lindley Murray, answered the various questions in a most satisfactory manner; and a pause ensued, during which the eatables disappeared with awful rapidity.

'You must have been very much pleased with the appearance of the ladies going to the drawing-room the other day, Mr O'Bleary?' said Mrs Tibbs, hoping to start a topic.

'Yes,' replied Orson, with a mouthful of toast.

'Never saw anything like it before, I suppose?' suggested Wisbottle.

'No – except the Lord Lieutenant's levees,' replied O'Bleary.

'Are they at all equal to our drawing-rooms?'

'Oh, infinitely superior!'

'Gad! I don't know,' said the aristocratic Wisbottle, 'the Dowager Marchioness of Publiccash was most magnificently dressed, and so was the Baron Slappenbachenhausen.'

'What was he presented on?' enquired Evenson.

'On his arrival in England.'

'I thought so,' growled the radical; 'you never hear of these fellows being presented on their going away again. They know better than that.'

'Unless somebody pervades them with an apintment,' said Mrs Bloss, joining in the conversation in a faint voice.

'Well,' said Wisbottle, evading the point, 'it's a splendid sight.'

'And did it never occur to you,' enquired the radical, who never would be quiet; 'did it never occur to you, that you pay for these precious ornaments of society?'

'It certainly *has* occurred to me,' said Wisbottle, who thought this answer was a poser; 'it *has* occurred to me, and I am willing to pay for them.'

'Well, and it has occurred to me too,' replied John Evenson, 'and I ain't willing to pay for 'em. Then why should I? – I say, why should I?' continued the politician, laying down the paper, and knocking his knuckles on the table. 'There are two great principles – demand – '

'A cup of tea if you please, dear,' interrupted Tibbs.

'And supply – '

'May I trouble you to hand this tea to Mr Tibbs?' said Mrs Tibbs, interrupting the argument, and unconsciously illustrating it.

The thread of the orator's discourse was broken. He drank his tea and resumed the paper.

'If it's very fine,' said Mr Alfred Tomkins, addressing the company in general, 'I shall ride down to Richmond today, and come back by the steamer. There are some splendid effects of light and shade on the Thames; the contrast between the blueness of the sky and the yellow water is frequently exceedingly beautiful.' Mr Wisbottle hummed, 'Flow on, thou shining river.'

'We have some splendid steam-vessels in Ireland,' said O'Bleary.

'Certainly,' said Mrs Bloss, delighted to find a subject broached in which she could take part.

'The accommodations are extraordinary,' said O'Bleary.

'Extraordinary indeed,' returned Mrs Bloss. 'When Mr Bloss was alive, he was promiscuously obligated to go to Ireland on business. I went with him, and truly the manner in which the ladies and gentlemen were accommodated with berths is not creditable.'

Tibbs, who had been listening to the dialogue, looked aghast, and evinced a strong inclination to ask a question, but was checked by a look from his wife. Mr Wisbottle laughed, and said Tomkins had made a pun; and Tomkins laughed too, and said he had not.

The remainder of the meal passed off as breakfasts usually do. Conversation flagged and people played with their teaspoons. The gentlemen looked out at the window; walked about the room; and, when they got near the door, dropped off one by one. Tibbs retired to the back parlour, by his wife's orders, to check the greengrocer's weekly account; and ultimately Mrs Tibbs and Mrs Bloss were left alone together.

'Oh dear!' said the latter, 'I feel alarmingly faint; it's very singular.' (It certainly was, for she had eaten four pounds of solids that morning.) 'By the by,' said Mrs Bloss, 'I have not seen Mr What's-his-name yet.'

'Mr Gobler?' suggested Mrs Tibbs.

'Yes.'

'Oh!' said Mrs Tibbs, 'he is a most mysterious person. He has his meals regularly sent upstairs, and sometimes don't leave his room for weeks together.'

'I haven't seen or heard nothing of him,' repeated Mrs Bloss.

'I dare say you'll hear him tonight,' replied Mrs Tibbs; 'he generally groans a good deal on Sunday evenings.'

'I never felt such an interest in anyone in my life,' ejaculated Mrs Bloss. A little double-knock interrupted the conversation; Dr Wosky was announced, and duly shown in. He was a little man with a red face – dressed of course in black, with a stiff white neckerchief. He had a very good practice, and plenty of money, which he had amassed by invariably humouring the worst fancies of all the females of all the families he had ever been introduced into. Mrs Tibbs offered to retire but was entreated to stay.

'Well, my dear ma'am, and how are we?' enquired Wosky, in a soothing tone.

'Very ill, doctor – very ill,' said Mrs Bloss, in a whisper

'Ah! we must take care of ourselves – we must, indeed,' said the obsequious Wosky, as he felt the pulse of his interesting patient.

'How is our appetite?'

Mrs Bloss shook her head.

'Our friend requires great care,' said Wosky, appealing to Mrs Tibbs, who of course assented. 'I hope, however, with the blessing of providence, that we shall be enabled to make her quite stout again.' Mrs Tibbs wondered in her own mind what the patient would be when she was made quite stout.

'We must take stimulants,' said the cunning Wosky – 'plenty of nourishment, and, above all, we must keep our nerves quiet; we positively must not give way to our sensibilities. We must take all we can get,' concluded the doctor, as he pocketed his fee, 'and we must keep quiet.'

'Dear man!' exclaimed Mrs Bloss, as the doctor stepped into the carriage.

'Charming creature indeed – quite a lady's man!' said Mrs Tibbs, and Dr Wosky rattled away to make fresh gulls of delicate females, and pocket fresh fees.

As we had occasion, in a former paper, to describe a dinner at Mrs Tibbs's, and as one meal went off very like another on all ordinary occasions, we will not fatigue our readers by entering into any other detailed account of the domestic economy of the establishment. We will therefore proceed to events, merely premising that the mysterious tenant of the back drawing-room was a lazy, selfish hypochondriac; always complaining and never ill. As his character in many respects closely assimilated to that of Mrs Bloss, a very warm friendship soon sprang up between them. He was tall, thin and pale; he always fancied he had a severe pain somewhere or other, and his face invariably wore a pinched, screwed-up expression; he looked, indeed, like a man who had got his feet in a tub of exceedingly hot water against his will.

For two or three months after Mrs Bloss's first appearance in Coram Street, John Evenson was observed to become, every day, more sarcastic and more ill-natured; and there was a degree of additional importance in his manner, which clearly showed that he fancied he had discovered something which he only wanted a proper opportunity of divulging. He found it at last.

One evening, the different inmates of the house were assembled in the drawing-room engaged in their ordinary occupations. Mr Gobler and Mrs Bloss were sitting at a small card-table near the centre window, playing cribbage; Mr Wisbottle was describing semicircles on the music-stool, turning over the leaves of a book on the piano and humming most melodiously; Alfred Tomkins was sitting at the round table, with his elbows duly squared, making a pencil sketch of a head considerably larger than his own; O'Bleary was reading Horace, and trying to look as if he understood it; and John Evenson had drawn his chair close to Mrs Tibbs's work-table and was talking to her very earnestly in a low tone.

'I can assure you, Mrs Tibbs,' said the radical, laying his forefinger on the muslin she was at work on; 'I can assure you, Mrs Tibbs, that nothing but the interest I take in your welfare would induce me to make this communication. I repeat, I fear Wisbottle is endeavouring to gain the affections of that young woman, Agnes, and that he is in the habit of meeting her in the storeroom on the first floor, over the leads. From my bedroom I distinctly heard voices there, last night. I opened my door immediately, and crept very softly on to the landing; there I saw Mr Tibbs, who, it seems, had been disturbed also. – Bless me, Mrs Tibbs, you change colour!'

'No, no – it's nothing,' returned Mrs T. in a hurried manner; 'it's only the heat of the room.'

'A flush!' ejaculated Mrs Bloss from the card-table; 'that's good for four.'

'If I thought it was Mr Wisbottle,' said Mrs Tibbs, after a pause, 'he should leave this house instantly.'

'Go!' said Mrs Bloss again.

'And if I thought,' continued the hostess with a most threatening air, 'if I thought he was assisted by Mr Tibbs – '

'One for his nob!' said Gobler.

'Oh,' said Evenson, in a most soothing tone – he liked to make mischief – 'I should hope Mr Tibbs was not in any way implicated. He has always appeared to me very harmless.'

'I have generally found him so,' sobbed poor little Mrs Tibbs, crying like a watering-pot.

'Hush! hush! pray – Mrs Tibbs – consider – we shall be observed – pray, don't!' said John Evenson, fearing his whole plan would be interrupted. 'We will set the matter at rest with the utmost care, and I shall be most happy to assist you in doing so.' Mrs Tibbs murmured her thanks.

'When you think everyone has retired to rest tonight,' said Evenson very pompously, 'if you'll meet me without a light, just outside my bedroom door, by the staircase window, I think we can ascertain who the parties really are, and you will afterwards be enabled to proceed as you think proper.'

Mrs Tibbs was easily persuaded; her curiosity was excited, her jealousy was roused, and the arrangement was forthwith made. She resumed her work and John Evenson walked up and down the room with his hands in his pockets, looking as if nothing had happened. The game of cribbage was over and conversation began again.

'Well, Mr O'Bleary,' said the humming-top, turning round on his pivot, and facing the company, 'what did you think of Vauxhall the other night?'

'Oh, it's very fair,' replied Orson, who had been enthusiastically delighted with the whole exhibition.

'Never saw anything like that Captain Ross's set-out – eh?'

'No,' returned the patriot, with his usual reservation – 'except in Dublin.'

'I saw the Count de Canky and Captain Fitzthompson in the Gardens,' said Wisbottle; 'they appeared much delighted.'

'Then it *must* be beautiful,' snarled Evenson.

'I think the white bears is partickerlerly well done,' suggested Mrs Bloss. 'In their shaggy white coats, they look just like Polar bears – don't you think they do, Mr Evenson?'

'I think they look a great deal more like omnibus cads on all fours,' replied the discontented one.

'Upon the whole, I should have liked our evening very well,' gasped Gobler; 'only I caught a desperate cold which increased my pain dreadfully! I was obliged to have several shower-baths, before I could leave my room.'

'Capital things those shower-baths!' ejaculated Wisbottle.

'Excellent!' said Tomkins.

'Delightful!' chimed in O'Bleary. (He had once seen one, outside a tinman's.)

'Disgusting machines!' rejoined Evenson, who extended his dislike to almost every created object, masculine, feminine or neuter.

'Disgusting, Mr Evenson!' said Gobler, in a tone of strong indignation. – 'Disgusting! Look at their utility – consider how many lives they have saved by promoting perspiration.'

'Promoting perspiration, indeed,' growled John Evenson, stopping short in his walk across the large squares in the pattern of the carpet – 'I was ass enough to be persuaded some time ago to have one in my bedroom. 'Gad, I was in it once, and it effectually cured *me*, for the mere sight of it threw me into a profuse perspiration for six months afterwards.'

A titter followed this announcement, and before it had subsided James brought up 'the tray', containing the remains of a leg of lamb which had made its début at dinner; bread; cheese; an atom of butter in a forest of parsley; one pickled walnut and the third of another; and so forth. The boy disappeared and returned again with another tray, containing glasses and jugs of hot and cold water. The gentlemen brought in their spirit-bottles; the housemaid placed divers plated bedroom candlesticks under the card table; and the servants retired for the night.

Chairs were drawn round the table, and the conversation proceeded in the customary manner. John Evenson, who never ate supper, lolled on the sofa and amused himself by contradicting everybody. O'Bleary ate as much as he could conveniently carry and Mrs Tibbs felt a due degree of indignation thereat; Mr Gobler and Mrs Bloss conversed most affectionately on the subject of pill-taking and other innocent amusements; and Tomkins and Wisbottle 'got into an argument'; that is to say, they both talked very loudly and vehemently, each flattering himself that he had got some advantage about something and neither of them having more than a very indistinct idea of what they were talking about. An hour or two passed away; and the boarders and the plated candlesticks retired in pairs to their respective bedrooms. John Evenson pulled off his boots, locked his door, and determined to sit up until Mr Gobler had retired. He always sat in the drawing-room an hour after everybody else had left it, taking medicine and groaning.

Great Coram Street was hushed into a state of profound repose: it was nearly two o'clock. A hackney-coach now and then rumbled slowly by; and occasionally some stray lawyer's clerk, on his way home to Somers Town, struck his iron heel on the top of the coal cellar with a noise resembling the click of a smoke-jack. A low, monotonous, gushing sound was heard, which added considerably to the romantic dreariness of the scene. It was the water 'coming in' at number eleven.

'He must be asleep by this time,' said John Evenson to himself, after waiting with exemplary patience for nearly an hour after Mr Gobler had left the drawing-room. He listened for a few moments; the house was perfectly quiet; he extinguished his rush light, and opened his bedroom door. The staircase was so dark that it was impossible to see anything.

'S–s–s!' whispered the mischief-maker, making a noise like the first indication a catherine-wheel gives of the probability of its going off.

'Hush!' whispered somebody else.

'Is that you, Mrs Tibbs?'

'Yes, sir.'

'Where?'

'Here;' and the misty outline of Mrs Tibbs appeared at the staircase window, like the ghost of Queen Anne in the tent scene in *Richard*.

'This way, Mrs Tibbs,' whispered the delighted busybody: 'give me your hand – there! Whoever these people are, they are in the storeroom now, for I have been looking down from my window, and I could see that they accidentally upset their candlestick, and are now in darkness. You have no shoes on, have you?'

'No,' said little Mrs Tibbs, who could hardly speak for trembling.

'Well; I have taken my boots off, so we can go down, close to the storeroom door, and listen over the banisters;' and downstairs they both crept accordingly, every board creaking like a patent mangle on a Saturday afternoon.

'It's Wisbottle and somebody, I'll swear,' exclaimed the radical in an energetic whisper, when they had listened for a few moments.

'Hush – pray let's hear what they say!' exclaimed Mrs Tibbs, the gratification of whose curiosity was now paramount to every other consideration.

'Ah! if I could but believe you,' said a female voice coquettishly, 'I'd be bound to settle my missis for life.'

'What does she say?' enquired Mr Evenson, who was not quite so well situated as his companion.

'She says she'll settle her missis's life,' replied Mrs Tibbs. 'The wretch! they're plotting murder.'

'I know you want money,' continued the voice, which belonged to Agnes; 'and if you'd secure me the five hundred pound, I warrant she should take fire soon enough.'

'What's that?' enquired Evenson again. He could just hear enough to want to hear more.

'I think she says she'll set the house on fire,' replied the affrighted Mrs Tibbs. 'But thank God I'm insured in the Phoenix!'

'The moment I have secured your mistress, my dear,' said a man's voice in a strong Irish brogue, 'you may depend on having the money.'

'Bless my soul, it's Mr O'Bleary!' exclaimed Mrs Tibbs, in a parenthesis.

'The villain!' said the indignant Mr Evenson.

'The first thing to be done,' continued the Hibernian, 'is to poison Mr Gobler's mind.'

'Oh, certainly,' returned Agnes.

'What's that?' enquired Evenson again, in an agony of curiosity and a whisper.

'He says she's to mind and poison Mr Gobler,' replied Mrs Tibbs, aghast at this sacrifice of human life.

'And in regard of Mrs Tibbs – ' continued O'Bleary. Mrs Tibbs shuddered.

'Hush!' exclaimed Agnes, in a tone of the greatest alarm, just as Mrs Tibbs was on the extreme verge of a fainting fit. 'Hush!'

'Hush!' exclaimed Evenson, at the same moment to Mrs Tibbs.

'There's somebody coming *up*stairs,' said Agnes to O'Bleary.

'There's somebody coming *down*stairs,' whispered Evenson to Mrs Tibbs.

'Go into the parlour, sir,' said Agnes to her companion. 'You will get there before whoever it is gets to the top of the kitchen stairs.'

'The drawing-room, Mrs Tibbs!' whispered the astonished Evenson to his equally astonished companion; and for the drawing-room they both made, plainly hearing the rustling of two persons, one coming downstairs and one coming up.

'What can it be?' exclaimed Mrs Tibbs. 'It's like a dream. I wouldn't be found in this situation for the world!'

'Nor I,' returned Evenson, who could never bear a joke at his own expense. 'Hush! here they are at the door.'

'What fun!' whispered one of the newcomers. – It was Wisbottle.

'Glorious!' replied his companion, in an equally low tone. – This was Alfred Tomkins. 'Who would have thought it?'

'I told you so,' said Wisbottle, in a most knowing whisper. 'Lord bless you, he has paid her most extraordinary attention for the last two months. I saw 'em when I was sitting at the piano tonight.'

'Well, do you know I didn't notice it?' interrupted Tomkins.

'Not notice it!' continued Wisbottle. 'Bless you; I saw him whispering to her, and she crying; and then I'll swear I heard him say something about tonight when we were all in bed.'

'They're talking of *us*!' exclaimed the agonised Mrs Tibbs, as the painful suspicion, and a sense of their situation, flashed upon her mind.

'I know it – I know it,' replied Evenson, with a melancholy consciousness that there was no mode of escape.

'What's to be done? we cannot both stop here!' ejaculated Mrs Tibbs, in a state of partial derangement.

'I'll get up the chimney,' replied Evenson, who really meant what he said.

'You can't,' said Mrs Tibbs, in despair. 'You can't – it's a register stove.'

'Hush!' repeated John Evenson.

'Hush – hush!' cried somebody downstairs.

'What a deuced hushing!' said Alfred Tomkins, who began to get rather bewildered.

'There they are!' exclaimed the sapient Wisbottle, as a rustling noise was heard in the storeroom.

'Hark!' whispered both the young men.

'Hark!' repeated Mrs Tibbs and Evenson.

'Let me alone, sir,' said a female voice in the storeroom.

'Oh, Hagnes!' cried another voice, which clearly belonged to Tibbs, for nobody else ever owned one like it, 'Oh, Hagnes – lovely creature!'

'Be quiet, sir!' (A bounce.)

'Hag –'

'Be quiet, sir – I am ashamed of you. Think of your wife, Mr Tibbs. Be quiet, sir!'

'My wife!' exclaimed the valorous Tibbs, who was clearly under the influence of gin and water, and a misplaced attachment; 'I 'ate her! Oh, Hagnes! when I was in the volunteer corps, in eighteen hundred and – '

'I declare I'll scream. Be quiet, sir, will you?' (Another bounce and a scuffle.)

'What's that?' exclaimed Tibbs, with a start.

'What's what?' said Agnes, stopping short.

'Why that!'

'Ah! you have done it nicely now, sir,' sobbed the frightened Agnes, as a tapping was heard at Mrs Tibbs's bedroom door, which would have beaten any dozen woodpeckers hollow.

'Mrs Tibbs! Mrs Tibbs!' called out Mrs Bloss. 'Mrs Tibbs, pray get up.' (Here the imitation of a woodpecker was resumed with tenfold violence.)

'Oh, dear – dear!' exclaimed the wretched partner of the depraved Tibbs. 'She's knocking at my door. We must be discovered! What will they think?'

'Mrs Tibbs! Mrs Tibbs!' screamed the woodpecker again.

'What's the matter!' shouted Gobler, bursting out of the back drawing-room, like the dragon at Astley's.

'Oh, Mr Gobler!' cried Mrs Bloss, with a proper approximation to hysterics; 'I think the house is on fire, or else there's thieves in it. I have heard the most dreadful noises!'

'The devil you have!' shouted Gobler again, bouncing back into his den, in happy imitation of the aforesaid dragon, and returning immediately with a lighted candle. 'Why, what's this? Wisbottle! Tomkins! O'Bleary! Agnes! What the deuce! all up and dressed?'

'Astonishing!' said Mrs Bloss, who had run downstairs and taken Mr Gobler's arm.

'Call Mrs Tibbs directly, somebody,' said Gobler, turning into the front drawing-room. – 'What! Mrs Tibbs and Mr Evenson!!'

'Mrs Tibbs and Mr Evenson!' repeated everybody, as that unhappy pair were discovered: Mrs Tibbs seated in an armchair by the fireplace and Mr Evenson standing by her side.

We must leave the scene that ensued to the reader's imagination. We could tell how Mrs Tibbs forthwith fainted away and how it required the united strength of Mr Wisbottle and Mr Alfred Tomkins to hold her in her chair; how Mr Evenson explained, and how his explanation was

*Mrs Tibbs seated in an armchair by the fireplace and
Mr Evenson standing by her side*

evidently disbelieved; how Agnes repelled the accusations of Mrs Tibbs by proving that she was negotiating with Mr O'Bleary to influence her mistress's affections in his behalf; and how Mr Gobler threw a damp counterpane on the hopes of Mr O'Bleary by avowing that he (Gobler) had already proposed to, and been accepted by, Mrs Bloss; how Agnes was discharged from that lady's service; how Mr O'Bleary discharged himself from Mrs Tibbs's house, without going through the form of previously discharging his bill; and how that disappointed young gentleman rails against England and the English, and vows there is no virtue or fine feeling extant, 'except in Ireland'. We repeat that we *could* tell all this, but we love to exercise our self-denial and we therefore prefer leaving it to be imagined.

The lady whom we have hitherto described as Mrs Bloss, is no more. Mrs Gobler exists; Mrs Bloss has left us for ever. In a secluded retreat in Newington Butts, far, far removed from the noisy strife of that great boarding-house, the world, the enviable Gobler and his pleasing wife revel in retirement: happy in their complaints, their table and their medicine, wafted through life by the grateful prayers of all the purveyors of animal food within three miles round.

We would willingly stop here, but we have a painful duty imposed upon us which we must discharge. Mr and Mrs Tibbs have separated by mutual consent, Mrs Tibbs receiving one moiety of £43 15s. 10d., which we before stated to be the amount of her husband's annual income, and Mr Tibbs the other. He is spending the evening of his days in retirement; and he is spending also, annually, that small but honourable independence. He resides among the original settlers at Walworth; and it has been stated, on unquestionable authority, that the conclusion of the volunteer story has been heard in a small tavern in that respectable neighbourhood.

The unfortunate Mrs Tibbs has determined to dispose of the whole of her furniture by public auction, and to retire from a residence in which she has suffered so much. Mr Robins has been applied to to conduct the sale, and the transcendent abilities of the literary gentlemen connected with his establishment are now devoted to the task of drawing up the preliminary advertisement. It is to contain, among a variety of brilliant matter, seventy-eight words in large capitals and six original quotations in inverted commas.

MR MINNS AND HIS COUSIN

Mr Augustus Minns was a bachelor, of about forty as he said – of about eight-and-forty as his friends said. He was always exceedingly clean, precise and tidy, perhaps somewhat priggish, and the most retiring man in the world. He usually wore a brown frock-coat without a wrinkle, light inexplicables without a spot, a neat neckerchief with a remarkably neat tie and boots without a fault; moreover, he always carried a brown silk umbrella with an ivory handle. He was a clerk in Somerset House, or, as he said himself, he held 'a responsible situation under government'. He had a good and increasing salary, in addition to some £10,000 of his own (invested in the funds), and he occupied a first floor in Tavistock Street, Covent Garden, where he had resided for twenty years, having been in the habit of quarrelling with his landlord the whole time: regularly giving notice of his intention to quit on the first day of every quarter, and as regularly countermanding it on the second. There were two classes of created objects which he held in the deepest and most unmingled horror: these were dogs and children. He was not unamiable, but he could, at any time, have viewed the execution of a dog or the assassination of an infant with the liveliest satisfaction. Their habits were at variance with his love of order; and his love of order was as powerful as his love of life. Mr Augustus Minns had no relations, in or near London, with the exception of his cousin, Mr Octavius Budden, to whose son, whom he had never seen (for he disliked the father), he had consented to become godfather by proxy. Mr Budden having realised a moderate fortune by exercising the trade or calling of a corn-chandler, and having a great predilection for the country, had purchased a cottage in the vicinity of Stamford Hill, whither he retired with the wife of his bosom, and his only son, Master Alexander Augustus Budden. One evening, as Mr and Mrs B. were admiring their son, discussing his various merits, talking over his education and disputing whether the classics should be made an essential part thereof, the lady pressed so strongly upon her husband the propriety of cultivating the friendship of Mr Minns in behalf of their son that Mr Budden at last made up his mind that it should not be his fault if he and his cousin were not in future more intimate.

'I'll break the ice, my love,' said Mr Budden, stirring up the sugar at the bottom of his glass of brandy and water, and casting a sidelong look at his spouse to see the effect of the announcement of his determination, 'by asking Minns down to dine with us, on Sunday.'

'Then pray, Budden, write to your cousin at once,' replied Mrs Budden. 'Who knows, if we could only get him down here, but he might take a fancy to our Alexander and leave him his property? Alick, my dear, take your legs off the rail of the chair!'

'Very true,' said Mr Budden, musing, 'very true indeed, my love!'

On the following morning, as Mr Minns was sitting at his breakfast-table, alternately biting his dry toast and casting a look upon the columns of his morning paper, which he always read from the title to the printer's name, he heard a loud knock at the street-door; which was shortly afterwards followed by the entrance of his servant, who put into his hands a particularly small card, on which was engraven in immense letters, MR OCTAVIUS BUDDEN, AMELIA COTTAGE (Mrs B.'s name was Amelia), POPLAR WALK, STAMFORD HILL.'

'Budden!' ejaculated Minns, 'what can bring that vulgar man here! say I'm asleep – say I'm out, and shall never be home again – anything to keep him downstairs.'

'But please, sir, the gentleman's coming up,' replied the servant, and the fact was made evident by an appalling creaking of boots on the staircase accompanied by a pattering noise, the cause of which, Minns could not, for the life of him, divine.

'Hem! – show the gentleman in,' said the unfortunate bachelor. Exit servant and enter Octavius, preceded by a large white dog, dressed in a suit of fleecy hosiery, with pink eyes, large ears and no perceptible tail.

The cause of the pattering on the stairs was but too plain. Mr Augustus Minns staggered beneath the shock of the dog's appearance.

'My dear fellow, how are you?' said Budden, as he entered. He always spoke at the top of his voice, and always said the same thing half a dozen times. 'How are you, my hearty?'

'How do you do, Mr Budden? – pray take a chair!' politely stammered the discomfited Minns.

'Thank you – thank you – well – how are you, eh?'

'Uncommonly well, thank you,' said Minns, casting a diabolical look at the dog, who, with his hind legs on the floor and his fore paws resting on the table, was dragging a bit of bread and butter out of a plate, preparatory to devouring it, with the buttered side next the carpet.

Mr Minns and Mr Budden his cousin

'Ah, you rogue!' said Budden to his dog; 'you see, Minns, he's like me, always at home, eh, my boy! – Egad, I'm precious hot and hungry! I've walked all the way from Stamford Hill this morning.'

'Have you breakfasted?' enquired Minns.

'Oh, no! – came to breakfast with you; so ring the bell, my dear fellow, will you? and let's have another cup and saucer, and the cold ham. – Make myself at home, you see!' continued Budden, dusting his boots with a table-napkin. 'Ha! – ha! – ha! – 'pon my life, I'm hungry.'

Minns rang the bell, and tried to smile.

'I decidedly never was so hot in my life,' continued Octavius, wiping his forehead; 'well, but how are you, Minns? 'Pon my soul, you wear capitally!'

'D'ye think so?' said Minns; and he tried another smile.

' 'Pon my life, I do!'

'Mrs B. and – what's his name – quite well?'

'Alick – my son, you mean; never better – never better. But at such a place as we've got at Poplar Walk, you know, he couldn't be ill if he tried. When I first saw it, by Jove! it looked so knowing, with the front garden, and the green railings, and the brass knocker, and all that – I really thought it was a cut above me.'

'Don't you think you'd like the ham better,' interrupted Minns, 'if you cut it the other way?' He saw, with feelings which it is impossible to describe, that his visitor was cutting or rather maiming the ham, in utter violation of all established rules.

'No, thank ye,' returned Budden, with the most barbarous indifference to crime, 'I prefer it this way, it eats short. But I say, Minns, when will you come down and see us? You will be delighted with the place; I know you will. Amelia and I were talking about you the other night, and Amelia said – another lump of sugar, please; thank ye – she said, don't you think you could contrive, my dear, to say to Mr Minns, in a friendly way – come down, sir – damn the dog! he's spoiling your curtains, Minns – ha! – ha! – ha!' Minns leaped from his seat as though he had received the discharge from a galvanic battery.

'Come out, sir! – go out, hoo!' cried poor Augustus, keeping, never-theless, at a very respectful distance from the dog, having read of a case of hydrophobia in the paper of that morning. By dint of great exertion, much shouting and a marvellous deal of poking under the tables with a stick and umbrella, the dog was at last dislodged and placed on the landing outside the door, where he immediately commenced a most appalling howling, at the same time vehemently scratching the paint off the two nicely varnished bottom panels until they resembled the interior of a backgammon-board.

'A good dog for the country that!' coolly observed Budden to the distracted Minns, 'but he's not much used to confinement. But now, Minns, when will you come down? I'll take no denial, positively. Let's see, today's Thursday. Will you come on Sunday? We dine at five, don't say no – do.'

After a great deal of pressing, Mr Augustus Minns, driven to despair, accepted the invitation and promised to be at Poplar Walk on the ensuing Sunday at a quarter before five to the minute.

'Now mind the direction,' said Budden: 'the coach goes from the Flowerpot, in Bishopsgate Street, every half-hour. When the coach stops at the Swan, you'll see, immediately opposite you, a white house.'

'Which is your house – I understand,' said Minns, wishing to cut short the visit, and the story, at the same time.

'No, no, that's not mine; that's Grogus's, the great ironmonger's. I was going to say – you turn down by the side of the white house till you can't go another step further – mind that! – and then you turn to your right, by some stables – well; close to you, you'll see a wall with "Beware of the Dog" written on it in large letters – ' (Minns shuddered) – 'go along by the side of that wall for about a quarter of a mile – and anybody will show you which is my place.'

'Very well – thank ye – goodbye.'

'Be punctual.'

'Certainly – good-morning.'

'I say, Minns, you've got a card.'

'Yes, I have; thank ye.' And Mr Octavius Budden departed, leaving his cousin looking forward to his visit on the following Sunday with the feelings of a penniless poet to the weekly visit of his Scotch landlady.

Sunday arrived; the sky was bright and clear; crowds of people were hurrying along the streets, intent on their different schemes of pleasure for the day; everything and everybody looked cheerful and happy except Mr Augustus Minns.

The day was fine, but the heat was considerable; when Mr Minns had fagged up the shady side of Fleet Street, Cheapside and Threadneedle Street, he had become pretty warm, tolerably dusty and it was getting late into the bargain. By the most extraordinary good fortune, however, a coach was waiting at the Flowerpot, into which Mr Augustus Minns got, on the solemn assurance of the cad that the vehicle would start in three minutes – that being the very utmost extremity of time it was allowed to wait by Act of Parliament. A quarter of an hour elapsed, and there were no signs of moving. Minns looked at his watch for the sixth time.

'Coachman, are you going or not?' bawled Mr Minns, with his head and half his body out of the coach window.

'Di–rectly, sir,' said the coachman, with his hands in his pockets, looking as much unlike a man in a hurry as possible. 'Bill, take them cloths off.' Five minutes more elapsed: at the end of which time the coachman mounted the box, from whence he looked down the street, and up the street, and hailed all the pedestrians for another five minutes.

'Coachman! if you don't go this moment, I shall get out,' said Mr Minns, rendered desperate by the lateness of the hour, and the impossibility of being in Poplar Walk at the appointed time.

'Going this minute, sir,' was the reply – and, accordingly, the machine trundled on for a couple of hundred yards, and then stopped again. Minns doubled himself up in a corner of the coach and abandoned himself to his fate as a child, a mother, a bandbox and a parasol became his fellow-passengers.

The child was an affectionate and an amiable infant; the little dear mistook Minns for his other parent, and screamed to embrace him.

'Be quiet, dear,' said the mamma, restraining the impetuosity of the darling, whose little fat legs were kicking and stamping and twining themselves into the most complicated forms in an ecstasy of impatience. 'Be quiet, dear, that's not your papa.'

'Thank heaven I am not!' thought Minns, as the first gleam of pleasure he had experienced that morning shone like a meteor through his wretchedness.

Playfulness was agreeably mingled with affection in the disposition of the boy. When satisfied that Mr Minns was not his parent, he endeavoured to attract his notice by scraping his drab trousers with his dirty shoes, poking his chest with his mamma's parasol, and other nameless endearments peculiar to infancy, with which he beguiled the tediousness of the ride, apparently very much to his own satisfaction.

When the unfortunate gentleman arrived at the Swan, he found to his great dismay that it was a quarter past five. The white house, the stables, the 'Beware of the Dog' – every landmark was passed, with a rapidity not unusual to a gentleman of a certain age when too late for dinner. After the lapse of a few minutes, Mr Minns found himself opposite a yellow brick house with a green door, brass knocker and door plate, green window-frames and ditto railings, with 'a garden' in front, that is to say, a small loose bit of gravelled ground, with one round and two scalene triangular beds, containing a fir tree, twenty or thirty bulbs and an unlimited number of marigolds. The taste of Mr and Mrs Budden was further displayed by the appearance of a cupid on each side of the door, perched upon a heap of large chalk flints, variegated with pink conch-shells. His knock at the door was answered by a stumpy boy, in drab livery, cotton stockings and high-lows, who, after hanging his hat on one of the dozen brass pegs which ornamented the passage, denominated by courtesy 'The Hall', ushered him into a front drawing-room commanding a very extensive view of the backs of the neighbouring houses. The usual ceremony of introduction, and so forth, over, Mr Minns took his seat: not a little agitated at finding that he was the last comer, and, somehow or other, the Lion of about a dozen people, sitting together in a small drawing-room, getting rid of that most tedious of all time, the time preceding dinner.

'Well, Brogson,' said Budden, addressing an elderly gentleman in a black coat, drab knee-breeches and long gaiters, who, under pretence of inspecting the prints in an *Annual*, had been engaged in satisfying himself on the subject of Mr Minns's general appearance by looking at him over the tops of the leaves – 'Well, Brogson, what do ministers mean to do? Will they go out, or what?'

'Oh – why – really, you know, I'm the last person in the world to ask for news. Your cousin, from his situation, is the most likely person to answer the question.'

Mr Minns assured the last speaker that although he was in Somerset House, he possessed no official communication relative to the projects of his majesty's ministers. But his remark was evidently received incredulously; and no further conjectures being hazarded on the subject, a long pause ensued, during which the company occupied themselves in coughing and blowing their noses, until the entrance of Mrs Budden caused a general rise.

The ceremony of introduction being over, dinner was announced, and downstairs the party proceeded accordingly – Mr Minns escorting Mrs

Budden as far as the drawing-room door, but being prevented, by the narrowness of the staircase, from extending his gallantry any farther. The dinner passed off as such dinners usually do. Ever and anon, amidst the clatter of knives and forks, and the hum of conversation, Mr B.'s voice might be heard, asking a friend to take wine, and assuring him he was glad to see him; and a great deal of by-play took place between Mrs B. and the servants, respecting the removal of the dishes, during which her countenance assumed all the variations of a weatherglass, from 'stormy' to 'set fair'.

Upon the dessert and wine being placed on the table, the servant, in compliance with a significant look from Mrs B., brought down 'Master Alexander', habited in a sky-blue suit with silver buttons; and possessing hair of nearly the same colour as the metal. After sundry praises from his mother, and various admonitions as to his behaviour from his father, he was introduced to his godfather.

'Well, my little fellow – you are a fine boy, ain't you?' said Mr Minns, as happy as a tomtit on birdlime.

'Yes.'

'How old are you?'

'Eight, next We'nsday. How old are *you*?'

'Alexander,' interrupted his mother, 'how dare you ask Mr Minns how old he is!'

'He asked me how old *I* was,' said the precocious child, to whom Minns had from that moment internally resolved that he never would bequeath one shilling. As soon as the titter occasioned by the observation had subsided, a little smirking man with red whiskers, sitting at the bottom of the table, who during the whole of dinner had been endeavouring to obtain a listener to some stories about Sheridan, called, out, with a very patronising air, 'Alick, what part of speech is *be*.'

'A verb.'

'That's a good boy,' said Mrs Budden, with all a mother's pride.

'Now, you know what a verb is?'

'A verb is a word which signifies to be, to do or to suffer; as, I am – I rule – I am ruled. Give me an apple, ma.'

'I'll give you an apple,' replied the man with the red whiskers, who was an established friend of the family, or in other words was always invited by Mrs Budden, whether Mr Budden liked it or not, 'if you'll tell me what is the meaning of *be*.'

'Be?' said the prodigy, after a little hesitation – 'an insect that gathers honey.'

'No, dear,' frowned Mrs Budden; 'b double e is the substantive.'

'I don't think he knows much yet about *common* substantives,' said the smirking gentleman, who thought this an admirable opportunity for letting off a joke. 'It's clear he's not very well acquainted with *proper names*. He! he! he!'

'Gentlemen,' called out Mr Budden, from the end of the table, in a stentorian voice and with a very important air, 'will you have the goodness to charge your glasses? I have a toast to propose.'

'Hear! hear!' cried the gentlemen, passing the decanters.

After they had made the round of the table, Mr Budden proceeded, 'Gentlemen; there is an individual present – '

'Hear! hear!' said the little man with red whiskers.

'*Pray* be quiet, Jones,' remonstrated Budden.

'I say, gentlemen, there is an individual present,' resumed the host, 'in whose society, I am sure we must take great delight – and – and – the conversation of that individual must have afforded to everyone present the utmost pleasure.' ('Thank heaven, he does not mean me!' thought Minns, conscious that his diffidence and exclusiveness had prevented his saying above a dozen words since he entered the house.) 'Gentlemen, I am but a humble individual myself, and I perhaps ought to apologise for allowing any individual feeling of friendship and affection for the person I allude to, to induce me to venture to rise, to propose the health of that person – a person that, I am sure – that is to say, a person whose virtues must endear him to those who know him – and those who have not the pleasure of knowing him, cannot dislike him.'

'Hear! hear!' said the company, in a tone of encouragement and approval.

'Gentlemen,' continued Budden, 'my cousin is a man who – who is a relation of my own.' (Hear! hear!) Minns groaned audibly. 'Who I am most happy to see here, and who, if he were not here, would certainly have deprived us of the great pleasure we all feel in seeing him.' (Loud cries of hear!) 'Gentlemen, I feel that I have already trespassed on your attention for too long a time. With every feeling – of – with every sentiment of – of – '

'Gratification' – suggested the friend of the family.

' – Of gratification, I beg to propose the health of Mr Minns.'

'Standing, gentlemen!' shouted the indefatigable little man with the whiskers – 'and with the honours. Take your time from me, if you please. Hip! hip! hip! – Za! – Hip! hip! hip! – Za! – Hip hip! – Za–a–a!'

All eyes were now fixed on the subject of the toast, who by gulping down port wine at the imminent hazard of suffocation, endeavoured to conceal his confusion. After as long a pause as decency would admit, he rose, but, as the newspapers sometimes say in their reports, 'we regret that we are quite unable to give even the substance of the honourable gentleman's observations'. The words 'present company – honour – present occasion', and 'great happiness' – heard occasionally, and repeated at intervals, with a countenance expressive of the utmost confusion and misery, convinced the company that he was making an excellent speech; and, accordingly, on his resuming his seat, they cried 'Bravo!' and manifested tumultuous applause. Jones, who had been long watching his opportunity, then darted up.

'Budden,' said he, 'will you allow *me* to propose a toast?'

'Certainly,' replied Budden, adding in an undertone to Minns right across the table, 'Devilish sharp fellow that: you'll be very much pleased with his speech. He talks equally well on any subject.' Minns bowed, and Mr Jones proceeded: 'It has on several occasions, in various instances, under many circumstances, and in different companies, fallen to my lot to propose a toast to those by whom, at the time, I have had the honour to be surrounded. I have sometimes, I will cheerfully own – for why should I deny it? – felt the overwhelming nature of the task I have undertaken, and my own utter incapability to do justice to the subject. If such have been my feelings, however, on former occasions, what must they be now – now – under the extraordinary circumstances in which I am placed.' (Hear! hear!) 'To describe my feelings accurately, would be impossible; but I cannot give you a better idea of them, gentlemen, than by referring to a circumstance which happens, oddly enough, to occur to my mind at the moment. On one occasion, when that truly great and illustrious man, Sheridan, was – '

Now, there is no knowing what new villainy in the form of a joke would have been heaped on the grave of that very ill-used man, Mr Sheridan, if the boy in drab had not at that moment entered the room in a breathless state, to report that, as it was a very wet night, the nine o'clock stage had come round to know whether there was anybody going to town, as, in that case, he (the nine o'clock) had room for one inside.

Mr Minns started up; and, despite countless exclamations of surprise and entreaties to stay, persisted in his determination to accept the vacant place. But the brown silk umbrella was nowhere to be found; and as the coachman couldn't wait, he drove back to the Swan, leaving word for Mr Minns to 'run round' and catch him. However, as it did not occur to Mr Minns for some ten minutes or so, that he had left the brown silk umbrella with the ivory handle in the other coach coming down; and, moreover, as he was by no means remarkable for speed, it is no matter of surprise that when he accomplished the feat of 'running round' to the Swan, the coach – the last coach – had gone without him.

It was somewhere about three o'clock in the morning when Mr Augustus Minns knocked feebly at the street-door of his lodgings in Tavistock Street, cold, wet, cross and miserable. He made his will next morning, and his professional man informs us, in that strict confidence in which we inform the public, that neither the name of Mr Octavius Budden, nor of Mrs Amelia Budden, nor of Master Alexander Augustus Budden, appears therein.

SENTIMENT

The Miss Crumptons, or to quote the authority of the inscription on the garden-gate of Minerva House, Hammersmith, 'The Misses Crumpton', were two unusually tall, particularly thin and exceedingly skinny personages: very upright and very yellow. Miss Amelia Crumpton owned to thirty-eight and Miss Maria Crumpton admitted she was forty; an admission which was rendered perfectly unnecessary by the self-evident fact of her being at least fifty. They dressed in the most interesting manner – like twins – and looked as happy and comfortable as a couple of marigolds run to seed. They were very precise, had the strictest possible ideas of propriety, wore false hair and always smelt very strongly of lavender.

Minerva House, conducted under the auspices of the two sisters, was a 'finishing establishment for young ladies', where some twenty girls of the ages of from thirteen to nineteen, inclusive, acquired a smattering of everything and a knowledge of nothing; instruction in French and Italian; dancing lessons twice a week; and other necessaries of life. The house was a white one, a little removed from the roadside, with close palings in front. The bedroom windows were always left partly open, to afford a bird's-eye view of numerous little bedsteads with very white dimity furniture, and thereby impress the passer-by with a due sense of the luxuries of the establishment; and there was a front parlour hung round with highly varnished maps which nobody ever looked at, and filled with books which no one ever read, appropriated exclusively to the reception of parents, who, whenever they called, could not fail to be struck with the very deep appearance of the place.

'Amelia, my dear,' said Miss Maria Crumpton, entering the school-room one morning with her false hair in papers, as she occasionally did in order to impress the young ladies with a conviction of its reality. 'Amelia, my dear, here is a most gratifying note I have just received. You needn't mind reading it aloud.'

Miss Amelia, thus advised, proceeded to read the following note with an air of great triumph: ' "Cornelius Brook Dingwall Esq. MP presents his compliments to Miss Crumpton, and will feel much obliged by Miss Crumpton's calling on him, if she conveniently can, tomorrow morning at one o'clock, as Cornelius Brook Dingwall Esq. MP is anxious to see Miss Crumpton on the subject of placing Miss Brook Dingwall under her charge. Adelphi. Monday morning." A Member of Parliament's daughter!' ejaculated Amelia, in an ecstatic tone.

'A Member of Parliament's daughter!' repeated Miss Maria, with a smile of delight, which, of course, elicited a concurrent titter of pleasure from all the young ladies.

'It's exceedingly delightful!' said Miss Amelia; whereupon all the young ladies murmured their admiration again. Courtiers are but schoolboys and court-ladies schoolgirls.

So important an announcement at once superseded the business of the day. A holiday was declared in commemoration of the great event; the Miss Crumptons retired to their private apartment to talk it over; the smaller girls discussed the probable manners and customs of the daughter of a Member of Parliament; and the young ladies verging on eighteen wondered whether she was engaged, whether she was pretty, whether she wore much bustle and many other *whethers* of equal importance.

The two Miss Crumptons proceeded to the Adelphi at the appointed time next day, dressed, of course, in their best style, and looking as amiable as they possibly could – which, by the by, is not saying much for them. Having sent in their cards, through the medium of a red-hot looking footman in bright livery, they were ushered into the august presence of the profound Dingwall.

Cornelius Brook Dingwall Esq. MP was very haughty, solemn and portentous. He had, naturally, a somewhat spasmodic expression of countenance, which was not rendered the less remarkable by his wearing an extremely stiff cravat. He was wonderfully proud of the MP attached to his name, and never lost an opportunity of reminding people of his dignity. He had a great idea of his own abilities, which must have been a great comfort to him, as no one else had; and in diplomacy, on a small scale, in his own family arrangements, he considered himself unrivalled. He was a county magistrate and discharged the duties of his station with all due justice and impartiality; frequently committing poachers, and occasionally committing himself. Miss Brook Dingwall was one of that numerous class of young ladies, who, like adverbs, may be known by their answering to a commonplace question, and doing nothing else.

On the present occasion, this talented individual was seated in a small library at a table covered with papers doing nothing, but trying to look busy, playing at shop. Acts of Parliament and letters directed to 'Cornelius Brook Dingwall Esq. MP' were ostentatiously scattered over the table, at a little distance from which Mrs Brook Dingwall was seated at work. One of those public nuisances, a spoiled child, was playing about the room, dressed after the most approved fashion – in a blue tunic with a black belt a quarter of a yard wide, fastened with an immense buckle – looking like a robber in a melodrama, seen through a diminishing glass.

After a little pleasantry from the sweet child, who amused himself by running away with Miss Maria Crumpton's chair as fast as it was placed for her, the visitors were seated, and Cornelius Brook Dingwall Esq. opened the conversation.

He had sent for Miss Crumpton, he said, in consequence of the high character he had received of her establishment from his friend, Sir Alfred Muggs.

Miss Crumpton murmured her acknowledgments to him (Muggs), and Cornelius proceeded.

'One of my principal reasons, Miss Crumpton, for parting with my daughter, is that she has lately acquired some sentimental ideas, which it is most desirable to eradicate from her young mind.' (Here the little innocent before noticed, fell out of an armchair with an awful crash.)

'Naughty boy!' said his mamma, who appeared more surprised at his taking the liberty of falling down than at anything else; 'I'll ring the bell for James to take him away.'

'Pray don't check him, my love,' said the diplomatist, as soon as he could make himself heard amidst the unearthly howling consequent upon the threat and the tumble. 'It all arises from his great flow of spirits.' This last explanation was addressed to Miss Crumpton.

'Certainly, sir,' replied the antique Maria: not exactly seeing, however, the connection between a flow of animal spirits and a fall from an armchair.

Silence was restored, and the MP resumed: 'Now, I know nothing so likely to effect this object, Miss Crumpton, as her mixing constantly in the society of girls of her own age; and, as I know that in your establishment she will meet such as are not likely to contaminate her young mind, I propose to send her to you.'

The youngest Miss Crumpton expressed the acknowledgments of the establishment generally. Maria was rendered speechless by bodily pain. The dear little fellow, having recovered his animal spirits, was standing upon her most tender foot, by way of getting his face (which looked like a capital O in a red-lettered playbill) on a level with the writing-table.

'Of course, Lavinia will be a parlour boarder,' continued the enviable father; 'and on one point I wish my directions to be strictly observed. The fact is that some ridiculous love affair, with a person much her inferior in life, has been the cause of her present state of mind. Knowing that of course, under your care, she can have no opportunity of meeting this person, I do not object to – indeed, I should rather prefer – her mixing with such society as you see yourself.'

This important statement was again interrupted by the high-spirited little creature, in the excess of his joyousness, breaking a pane of glass and nearly precipitating himself into an adjacent area. James was rung for; considerable confusion and screaming succeeded; two little blue legs were seen to kick violently in the air as the man left the room, and the child was gone.

'Mr Brook Dingwall would like Miss Brook Dingwall to learn everything,' said Mrs Brook Dingwall, who hardly ever said anything at all.

'Certainly,' said both the Miss Crumptons together.

'And as I trust the plan I have devised will be effectual in weaning my daughter from this absurd idea, Miss Crumpton,' continued the legislator, 'I hope you will have the goodness to comply, in all respects, with any request I may forward to you.'

The promise was of course made; and after a lengthened discussion, conducted on behalf of the Dingwalls with the most becoming diplomatic gravity, and on that of the Crumptons with profound respect, it was finally arranged that Miss Lavinia should be forwarded to Hammersmith on the next day but one, on which occasion the half-yearly ball given at the establishment was to take place. It might divert the dear girl's mind. This, by the way, was another bit of diplomacy.

Miss Lavinia was introduced to her future governess, and both the Miss Crumptons pronounced her 'a most charming girl'; an opinion which, by a singular coincidence, they always entertained of any new pupil.

Courtesies were exchanged, acknowledgments expressed, condescension exhibited and the interview terminated.

Preparations, to make use of theatrical phraseology, 'on a scale of magnitude never before attempted', were incessantly made at Minerva House to give every effect to the forthcoming ball. The largest room in the house was pleasingly ornamented with blue calico roses, plaid tulips, and other equally natural-looking artificial flowers, the work of the young ladies themselves. The carpet was taken up, the folding-doors were taken down, the furniture was taken out and rout-seats were taken in. The linen-drapers of Hammersmith were astounded at the sudden demand for blue sarsenet ribbon and long white gloves. Dozens of geraniums were purchased for bouquets, and a harp and two violins were bespoke from town, in addition to the grand piano already on the premises. The young ladies who were selected to show off on the occasion, and do credit to the establishment, practised incessantly, much to their own satisfaction, and greatly to the annoyance of the lame old gentleman over the way; and a constant correspondence was kept up between the Misses Crumpton and the Hammersmith pastrycook.

The evening came; and then there was such a lacing of stays and tying of sandals and dressing of hair as never can take place with a proper degree of bustle out of a boarding-school. The smaller girls managed to be in everybody's way, and were pushed about accordingly; and the elder ones dressed, and tied, and flattered, and envied one another, as earnestly and sincerely as if they had actually *come out*.

'How do I look, dear?' enquired Miss Emily Smithers, the belle of the house, of Miss Caroline Wilson, who was her bosom friend, because she was the ugliest girl in Hammersmith, or out of it.

'Oh! charming, dear. How do I?'

'Delightful! you never looked so handsome,' returned the belle, adjusting her own dress, and not bestowing a glance on her poor companion.

'I hope young Hilton will come early,' said another young lady to Miss somebody else, in a fever of expectation.

'I'm sure he'd be highly flattered if he knew it,' returned the other, who was practising *l'été*.

'Oh! he's so handsome,' said the first.

'Such a charming person!' added a second.

'Such a *distingué* air!' said a third.

'Oh, what *do* you think?' said another girl, running into the room; 'Miss Crumpton says her cousin's coming.'

'What! Theodosius Butler?' said everybody in raptures.

'Is *he* handsome?' enquired a novice.

'No, not particularly handsome,' was the general reply; 'but, oh, so clever!'

Mr Theodosius Butler was one of those immortal geniuses who are to be met with in almost every circle. They have, usually, very deep, monotonous voices. They always persuade themselves that they are wonderful persons, and that they ought to be very miserable, though they don't precisely know why. They are very conceited, and usually possess half an idea; but, with enthusiastic young ladies, and silly young gentlemen, they are very wonderful persons. The individual in question, Mr Theodosius, had written a pamphlet containing some very weighty considerations on the expediency of doing something or other; and as every sentence contained a good many words of four syllables, his admirers took it for granted that he meant a good deal.

'Perhaps that's he,' exclaimed several young ladies, as the first pull of the evening threatened destruction to the bell of the gate.

An awful pause ensued. Some boxes arrived and a young lady – Miss Brook Dingwall, in full ball costume, with an immense gold chain round her neck, her dress looped up with a single rose, an ivory fan in her hand and a most interesting expression of despair in her face.

The Miss Crumptons enquired after the family, with the most excruciating anxiety, and Miss Brook Dingwall was formally introduced to her future companions. The Miss Crumptons conversed with the young ladies in the most mellifluous tones, in order that Miss Brook Dingwall might be properly impressed with their amiable treatment.

Another pull at the bell. Mr Dadson, the writing-master, and his wife. The wife in green silk, with shoes and cap-trimmings to correspond; the writing-master in a white waistcoat, black kneeshorts and ditto silk stockings, displaying a leg large enough for two writing-masters. The young ladies whispered to one another, and the writing-master and his wife flattered the Miss Crumptons, who were dressed in amber, with long sashes, like dolls.

Repeated pulls at the bell, and arrivals too numerous to particularise: papas and mammas, and aunts and uncles, the owners and guardians of the different pupils; the singing-master, Signor Lobskini, in a black wig; the pianoforte player and the violins; the harp, in a state of intoxication; and some twenty young men, who stood near the door, and talked to one another, occasionally bursting into a giggle. A general hum of conversation. Coffee handed round, and plentifully partaken of by fat mammas, who looked like the stout people who come on in pantomimes for the sole purpose of being knocked down.

The popular Mr Hilton was the next arrival; and he having, at the request of the Miss Crumptons, undertaken the office of master of the ceremonies, the quadrilles commenced with considerable spirit. The young men by the door gradually advanced into the middle of the room, and in time became sufficiently at ease to consent to be introduced to partners. The writing-master danced every set, springing about with the most fearful agility, and his wife played a rubber in the back parlour – a little room with five bookshelves, dignified by the name of the study. Setting her down to whist was a half-yearly piece of generalship on the part of the Miss Crumptons; it was necessary to hide her somewhere, on account of her being a fright.

The interesting Lavinia Brook Dingwall was the only girl present who appeared to take no interest in the proceedings of the evening. In vain was she solicited to dance; in vain was the universal homage paid to her as the daughter of a Member of Parliament. She was equally unmoved by the splendid tenor of the inimitable Lobskini, and the brilliant execution of Miss Laetitia Parsons, whose performance of 'The Recollections of Ireland' was universally declared to be almost equal to that of Moscheles himself. Not even the announcement of the arrival of Mr Theodosius Butler could induce her to leave the corner of the back drawing-room in which she was seated.

'Now, Theodosius,' said Miss Maria Crumpton, after that enlightened pamphleteer had nearly run the gauntlet of the whole company, 'I must introduce you to our new pupil.'

Theodosius looked as if he cared for nothing earthly.

'She's the daughter of a Member of Parliament,' said Maria. Theodosius started.

'And her name is – ?' he enquired.

'Miss Brook Dingwall.'

'Great heaven!' poetically exclaimed Theodosius, in a low tone.

Miss Crumpton commenced the introduction in due form. Miss Brook Dingwall languidly raised her head.

'Edward!' she exclaimed, with a half-shriek, on seeing the well-known nankeen legs.

Fortunately, as Miss Maria Crumpton possessed no remarkable share of penetration, and as it was one of the diplomatic arrangements that no attention was to be paid to Miss Lavinia's incoherent exclamations, she was perfectly unconscious of the mutual agitation of the parties; and therefore, seeing that the offer of his hand for the next quadrille was accepted, she left him by the side of Miss Brook Dingwall.

'Oh, Edward!' exclaimed that most romantic of all romantic young ladies, as the light of science seated himself beside her, 'Oh, Edward, is it you?'

Mr Theodosius assured the dear creature, in the most impassioned manner, that he was not conscious of being anybody but himself.

'Then why – why – this disguise? Oh! Edward McNeville Walter, what have I not suffered on your account?'

'Lavinia, hear me,' replied the hero, in his most poetic strain. 'Do not condemn me unheard. If anything that emanates from the soul of such a wretch as I can occupy a place in your recollection – if any being, so vile, deserve your notice – you may remember that I once published a pamphlet (and paid for its publication) entitled "Considerations on the Policy of Removing the Duty on Beeswax".'

'I do – I do!' sobbed Lavinia.

'That,' continued the lover, 'was a subject to which your father was devoted heart and soul.'

'He was – he was!' reiterated the sentimentalist.

'I knew it,' continued Theodosius, tragically; 'I knew it – I forwarded him a copy. He wished to know me. Could I disclose my real name? Never! No, I assumed that name which you have so often pronounced in tones of endearment. As McNeville Walter, I devoted myself to the stirring cause; as McNeville Walter I gained your heart; in the same character I was ejected from your house by your father's domestics; and in no character at all have I since been enabled to see you. We now meet again, and I proudly own that I am – Theodosius Butler.'

The young lady appeared perfectly satisfied with this argumentative address and bestowed a look of the most ardent affection on the immortal advocate of beeswax.

'May I hope,' said he, 'that the promise your father's violent behaviour interrupted, may be renewed?'

'Let us join this set,' replied Lavinia, coquettishly – for girls of nineteen *can* coquette.

'No,' ejaculated he of the nankeens. 'I stir not from this spot, writhing under this torture of suspense. May I – may I – hope?'

'You may.'

'The promise is renewed?'

'Now, Theodosius, I must introduce you to our new pupil.'

'It is.'

'I have your permission?'

'You have.'

'To the fullest extent?'

'You know it,' returned the blushing Lavinia. The contortions of the interesting Butler's visage expressed his raptures.

We could dilate upon the occurrences that ensued. How Mr Theodosius and Miss Lavinia danced, and talked, and sighed for the remainder of the evening – how the Miss Crumptons were delighted thereat. How the writing-master continued to frisk about with one-horse power, and how his wife, from some unaccountable freak, left the whist-table in the little back parlour and persisted in displaying her green headdress in the most conspicuous part of the drawing-room. How the supper consisted of small triangular sandwiches in trays and a tart here and there by way of variety; and how the visitors consumed warm water disguised with lemon and dotted with nutmeg, under the denomination of negus. These, and other matters of as much interest, however, we pass over, for the purpose of describing a scene of even more importance.

A fortnight after the date of the ball, Cornelius Brook Dingwall Esq. MP was seated at the same library-table and in the same room as we have before described. He was alone, and his face bore an expression of deep thought and solemn gravity – he was drawing up 'A Bill for the Better Observance of Easter Monday'.

The footman tapped at the door – the legislator started from his reverie and 'Miss Crumpton' was announced. Permission was given for Miss Crumpton to enter the *sanctum*; Maria came sliding in, and when she had taken her seat with a due portion of affectation, the footman retired and the governess was left alone with the MP. Oh! how she longed for the presence of a third party! Even the facetious young gentleman would have been a relief.

Miss Crumpton began the duet. She hoped Mrs Brook Dingwall and the handsome little boy were in good health.

They were. Mrs Brook Dingwall and little Frederick were at Brighton. 'Much obliged to you, Miss Crumpton,' said Cornelius, in his most dignified manner, 'for your attention in calling this morning. I should have driven down to Hammersmith, to see Lavinia, but your account was so very satisfactory, and my duties in the House occupy me so much, that I determined to postpone it for a week. How has she gone on?'

'Very well indeed, sir,' returned Maria, dreading to inform the father that she had gone off.

'Ah, I thought the plan on which I proceeded would be a match for her.'

Here was a favourable opportunity to say that somebody else had been a match for her. But the unfortunate governess was unequal to the task.

'You have persevered strictly in the line of conduct I prescribed, Miss Crumpton?'

'Strictly, sir.'

'You tell me in your note that her spirits gradually improved.'

'Very much indeed, sir.'

'To be sure. I was convinced they would.'

'But I fear, sir,' said Miss Crumpton, with visible emotion, 'I fear the plan has not succeeded quite so well as we could have wished.'

No!' exclaimed the prophet. 'Bless me! Miss Crumpton, you look alarmed. What has happened?'

'Miss Brook Dingwall, sir – '

'Yes, ma'am?'

'Has gone, sir' – said Maria, exhibiting a strong inclination to faint.

'Gone!'

'Eloped, sir.'

'Eloped! – Who with – when – where – how?' almost shrieked the agitated diplomatist.

The natural yellow of the unfortunate Maria's face changed to all the hues of the rainbow as she laid a small packet on the member's table.

He hurriedly opened it. A letter from his daughter, and another from Theodosius. He glanced over their contents – 'Ere this reaches you, far distant – appeal to feelings – love to distraction – beeswax – slavery,' &c., &c. He dashed his hand to his forehead, and paced the room with fearfully long strides, to the great alarm of the precise Maria.

'Now mind; from this time forward,' said Mr Brook Dingwall, suddenly stopping at the table, and beating time upon it with his hand; 'from this time forward, I never will, under any circumstances whatever, permit a man who writes pamphlets to enter any other room of this house but the kitchen. I'll allow my daughter and her husband one hundred and fifty pounds a year, and never see their faces again; and, dam'me! ma'am, I'll bring in a bill for the abolition of finishing-schools.'

Some time has elapsed since this passionate declaration. Mr and Mrs

Butler are at present rusticating in a small cottage at Ball's Pond, pleasantly situated in the immediate vicinity of a brickfield. They have no family. Mr Theodosius looks very important, and writes incessantly; but, in consequence of a gross combination on the part of publishers, none of his productions appear in print. His young wife begins to think that ideal misery is preferable to real unhappiness; and that a marriage contracted in haste and repented at leisure is the cause of more substantial wretchedness than she ever anticipated.

On cool reflection, Cornelius Brook Dingwall Esq. MP was reluctantly compelled to admit that the untoward result of his admirable arrangements was attributable, not to the Miss Crumptons, but to his own diplomacy. He, however, consoles himself, like some other small diplomatists, by satisfactorily proving that if his plans did not succeed, they ought to have done so. Minerva House is *in statu quo*, and 'The Misses Crumpton' remain in the peaceable and undisturbed enjoyment of all the advantages resulting from their finishing-school.

THE TUGGSES AT RAMSGATE

Once upon a time there dwelt, in a narrow street on the Surrey side of the water, within three minutes' walk of old London Bridge, Mr Joseph Tuggs – a little dark-faced man with shiny hair, twinkling eyes, short legs and a body of very considerable thickness, measuring from the centre button of his waistcoat in front to the ornamental buttons of his coat behind. The figure of the amiable Mrs Tuggs, if not perfectly symmetrical, was decidedly comfortable; and the form of her only daughter, the accomplished Miss Charlotte Tuggs, was fast ripening into that state of luxuriant plumpness which had enchanted the eyes, and captivated the heart, of Mr Joseph Tuggs in his earlier days. Mr Simon Tuggs, his only son and Miss Charlotte Tuggs's only brother, was as differently formed in body as he was differently constituted in mind from the remainder of his family. There was that elongation in his thoughtful face, and that tendency to weakness in his interesting legs, which tell so forcibly of a great mind and romantic disposition. The slightest traits of character in such a being possess no mean interest to speculative minds. He usually appeared in public in capacious shoes with black cotton stockings; and was observed to be particularly attached to a black glazed stock, without tie or ornament of any description.

There is perhaps no profession, however useful; no pursuit, however meritorious; which can escape the petty attacks of vulgar minds. Mr Joseph Tuggs was a grocer. It might be supposed that a grocer was beyond the breath of calumny; but no – the neighbours stigmatised him as a chandler; and the poisonous voice of envy distinctly asserted that he dispensed tea and coffee by the quartern, retailed sugar by the ounce, cheese by the slice, tobacco by the screw and butter by the pat. These taunts, however, were lost upon the Tuggses. Mr Tuggs attended to the grocery department; Mrs Tuggs to the cheesemongery; and Miss Tuggs to her education. Mr Simon Tuggs kept his father's books, and his own counsel.

One fine spring afternoon, the latter gentleman was seated on a tub of weekly Dorset, behind the little red desk with a wooden rail, which ornamented a corner of the counter, when a stranger dismounted from a cab and hastily entered the shop. He was habited in black cloth, and bore with him a green umbrella and a blue bag.

'Mr Tuggs?' said the stranger, enquiringly.

'*My* name is Tuggs,' replied Mr Simon.

'It's the other Mr Tuggs,' said the stranger, looking towards the glass door which led into the parlour behind the shop, and on the inside of which the round face of Mr Tuggs senior was distinctly visible, peeping over the curtain.

Mr Simon gracefully waved his pen, as if in intimation of his wish that his father would advance. Mr Joseph Tuggs, with considerable celerity, removed his face from the curtain and placed it before the stranger.

'I come from the Temple,' said the man with the bag.

'From the Temple!' said Mrs Tuggs, flinging open the door of the little parlour and disclosing Miss Tuggs in perspective.

'From the Temple!' said Miss Tuggs and Mr Simon Tuggs at the same moment.

'From the Temple!' said Mr Joseph Tuggs, turning as pale as a Dutch cheese.

'From the Temple,' repeated the man with the bag; 'from Mr Cower's, the solicitor's. Mr Tuggs, I congratulate you, sir. Ladies, I wish you joy of your prosperity! We have been successful.' And the man with the bag leisurely divested himself of his umbrella and glove, as a preliminary to shaking hands with Mr Joseph Tuggs.

Now the words 'we have been successful' had no sooner issued from the mouth of the man with the bag, than Mr Simon Tuggs rose from the tub of weekly Dorset, opened his eyes very wide, gasped for breath, made figures of eight in the air with his pen and finally fell into the arms of his anxious mother and fainted away without the slightest ostensible cause or pretence.

'Water!' screamed Mrs Tuggs.

'Look up, my son,' exclaimed Mr Tuggs.

'Simon! dear Simon!' shrieked Miss Tuggs.

'I'm better now,' said Mr Simon Tuggs. 'What! successful!' And then, as corroborative evidence of his being better, he fainted away again, and was borne into the little parlour by the united efforts of the remainder of the family and the man with the bag.

To a casual spectator, or to anyone unacquainted with the position of the family, this fainting would have been unaccountable. To those who understood the mission of the man with the bag, and were moreover acquainted with the excitability of the nerves of Mr Simon Tuggs, it was quite comprehensible. A long-pending lawsuit respecting the validity of a will had been unexpectedly decided; and Mr Joseph Tuggs was the possessor of twenty thousand pounds.

A prolonged consultation took place that night in the little parlour – a consultation that was to settle the future destinies of the Tuggses. The shop was shut up at an unusually early hour; and many were the unavailing kicks bestowed upon the closed door by applicants for quarterns of sugar or half-quarterns of bread or penn'orths of pepper, which were to have been 'left till Saturday', but which fortune had decreed were to be left alone altogether.

'We must certainly give up business,' said Miss Tuggs.

'Oh, decidedly,' said Mrs Tuggs.

'Simon shall go to the bar,' said Mr Joseph Tuggs.

'And I shall always sign myself "Cymon" in future,' said his son.

'And I shall call myself Charlotta,' said Miss Tuggs.

'And you must always call *me* "ma", and father "pa",' said Mrs Tuggs.

'Yes, and pa must leave off all his vulgar habits,' interposed Miss Tuggs.

'I'll take care of all that,' responded Mr Joseph Tuggs, complacently. He was, at that very moment, eating pickled salmon with a pocketknife.

'We must leave town immediately,' said Mr Cymon Tuggs.

Everybody concurred that this was an indispensable preliminary to being genteel. The question then arose, Where should they go?

'Gravesend?' mildly suggested Mr Joseph Tuggs. The idea was unanimously scouted. Gravesend was *low*.

'Margate?' insinuated Mrs Tuggs. Worse and worse – nobody there but tradespeople.

'Brighton?' Mr Cymon Tuggs opposed an insurmountable objection. All the coaches had been upset, in turn, within the last three weeks; each coach had averaged two passengers killed and six wounded; and, in every case, the newspapers had distinctly understood that 'no blame whatever was attributable to the coachman'.

'Ramsgate?' ejaculated Mr Cymon, thoughtfully. To be sure; how stupid they must have been not to have thought of that before! Ramsgate was just the place of all others.

Two months after this conversation, the City of London to Ramsgate steamer was running gaily down the river. Her flag was flying, her band was playing, her passengers were conversing; everything about her seemed gay and lively. No wonder – the Tuggses were on board.

'Charming, ain't it?' said Mr Joseph Tuggs, in a bottle-green greatcoat, with a velvet collar of the same, and a blue travelling-cap with a gold band.

'Soul-inspiring,' replied Mr Cymon Tuggs – he was entered at the bar. 'Soul-inspiring!'

'Delightful morning, sir!' said a stoutish, military-looking gentleman in a blue surtout buttoned up to his chin and white trousers chained down to the soles of his boots.

Mr Cymon Tuggs took upon himself the responsibility of answering the observation. 'Heavenly!' he replied.

'You are an enthusiastic admirer of the beauties of nature, sir?' said the military gentleman.

'I am, sir,' replied Mr Cymon Tuggs.

'Travelled much, sir?' enquired the military gentleman.

'Not much,' replied Mr Cymon Tuggs.

'You've been on the continent, of course?' enquired the military gentleman.

'Not exactly,' replied Mr Cymon Tuggs – in a qualified tone, as if he wished it to be implied that he had gone halfway and come back again.

'You of course intend your son to make the grand tour, sir?' said the military gentleman, addressing Mr Joseph Tuggs.

As Mr Joseph Tuggs did not precisely understand what the grand tour was, or how such an article was manufactured, he replied, 'Of course.' Just as he said the word, there came tripping up, from her seat at the stern of the vessel, a young lady in a puce-coloured silk cloak and boots of the same; with long black ringlets, large black eyes, brief petticoats and unexceptionable ankles.

'Walter, my dear,' said the young lady to the military gentleman.

'Yes, Belinda, my love,' responded the military gentleman to the black-eyed young lady.

'What have you left me alone so long for?' said the young lady. 'I have been stared out of countenance by those rude young men.'

'What! stared at?' exclaimed the military gentleman, with an emphasis which made Mr Cymon Tuggs withdraw his eyes from the young lady's face with inconceivable rapidity. 'Which young men where?' and the military gentleman clenched his fist, and glared fearfully on the cigar-smokers around.

'Be calm, Walter, I entreat,' said the young lady.

'I won't,' said the military gentleman.

'Do, sir,' interposed Mr Cymon Tuggs. 'They ain't worth your notice.'

'No – no – they are not, indeed,' urged the young lady.

'I *will* be calm,' said the military gentleman. 'You speak truly, sir. I thank you for a timely remonstrance which may have spared me the guilt of manslaughter.' Calming his wrath, the military gentleman wrung Mr Cymon Tuggs by the hand.

'My sister, sir!' said Mr Cymon Tuggs; seeing that the military gentleman was casting an admiring look towards Miss Charlotta.

'My wife, ma'am – Mrs Captain Waters,' said the military gentleman, presenting the black-eyed young lady.

'My mother, ma'am – Mrs Tuggs,' said Mr Cymon. The military gentleman and his wife murmured enchanting courtesies; and the Tuggses looked as unembarrassed as they could.

'Walter, my dear,' said the black-eyed young lady, after they had sat chatting with the Tuggses some half-hour.

'Yes, my love,' said the military gentleman.

'Don't you think this gentleman (with an inclination of the head towards Mr Cymon Tuggs) is very much like the Marquis Carriwini?'

'Lord bless me, very!' said the military gentleman.

'It struck me the moment I saw him,' said the young lady, gazing intently, and with a melancholy air, on the scarlet countenance of Mr Cymon Tuggs. Mr Cymon Tuggs looked at everybody; and finding that everybody was looking at him, appeared to feel some temporary difficulty in disposing of his eyesight.

'So exactly the air of the marquis,' said the military gentleman.

'Quite extraordinary!' sighed the military gentleman's lady.

'You don't know the marquis, sir?' enquired the military gentleman.

Mr Cymon Tuggs stammered a negative.

'If you did,' continued Captain Walter Waters, 'you would feel how much reason you have to be proud of the resemblance – a most elegant man, with a most prepossessing appearance.'

'He is – he is indeed!' exclaimed Belinda Waters energetically. As her eye caught that of Mr Cymon Tuggs, she withdrew it from his features in bashful confusion.

All this was highly gratifying to the feelings of the Tuggses; and when, in the course of further conversation, it was discovered that Miss Charlotta Tuggs was the *facsimile* of a titled relative of Mrs Belinda Waters, and that

Mrs Tuggs herself was the very picture of the Dowager Duchess of Dobbleton, their delight in the acquisition of so genteel and friendly an acquaintance knew no bounds. Even the dignity of Captain Walter Waters relaxed, to that degree that he suffered himself to be prevailed upon by Mr Joseph Tuggs to partake of cold pigeon-pie and sherry on deck; and a most delightful conversation, aided by these agreeable stimulants, was prolonged, until they ran alongside Ramsgate Pier.

'Goodbye, dear!' said Mrs Captain Waters to Miss Charlotta Tuggs, just before the bustle of landing commenced; 'we shall see you on the sands in the morning; and, as we are sure to have found lodgings before then, I hope we shall be inseparables for many weeks to come.'

'Oh! I hope so,' said Miss Charlotta Tuggs, emphatically.

'Tickets, ladies and gen'lm'n,' said the man on the paddle-box.

'Want a porter, sir?' enquired a dozen men in smock-frocks.

'Now, my dear!' said Captain Waters.

'Goodbye!' said Mrs Captain Waters – 'goodbye, Mr Cymon!' and with a pressure of the hand which threw the amiable young man's nerves into a state of considerable derangement, Mrs Captain Waters disappeared among the crowd. A pair of puce-coloured boots were seen ascending the steps, a white handkerchief fluttered, a black eye gleamed. The Waterses were gone, and Mr Cymon Tuggs was alone in a heartless world.

Silently and abstractedly did that too sensitive youth follow his revered parents and a train of smock-frocks and wheelbarrows along the pier, until the bustle of the scene around recalled him to himself. The sun was shining brightly; the sea, dancing to its own music, rolled merrily in; crowds of people promenaded to and fro; young ladies tittered; old ladies talked; nursemaids displayed their charms to the greatest possible advantage; and their little charges ran up and down and to and fro and in and out, under the feet and between the legs of the assembled concourse, in the most playful and exhilarating manner. There were old gentlemen, trying to make out objects through long telescopes; and young ones, making objects of themselves in open shirt-collars; ladies, carrying about portable chairs and portable chairs carrying about invalids; parties, waiting on the pier for parties who had come by the steamboat; and nothing was to be heard but talking, laughing, welcoming and merriment.

'Fly, sir?' exclaimed a chorus of fourteen men and six boys, the moment Mr Joseph Tuggs, at the head of his little party, set foot in the street.

'Here's the gen'lm'n at last!' said one, touching his hat with mock politeness. 'Werry glad to see you, sir – been a-waitin' for you these six weeks. Jump in, if you please, sir!'

'Nice light fly and a fast trotter, sir,' said another: 'fourteen mile a hour, and surroundin' objects rendered inwisible by ex–treme welocity!'

'Large fly for your luggage, sir,' cried a third. 'Werry large fly here, sir – reg'lar bluebottle!'

'Here's *your* fly, sir!' shouted another aspiring charioteer, mounting the box and inducing an old grey horse to indulge in some imperfect reminiscences of a canter. 'Look at him, sir! – temper of a lamb and haction of a steam-ingein!'

Resisting even the temptation of securing the services of so valuable a quadruped as the last named, Mr Joseph Tuggs beckoned to the proprietor of a dingy conveyance of a greenish hue, lined with faded striped calico; and, the luggage and the family having been deposited therein, the animal in the shafts, after describing circles in the road for a quarter of an hour, at last consented to depart in quest of lodgings.

'How many beds have you got?' screamed Mrs Tuggs out of the fly to the woman who opened the door of the first house which displayed a bill intimating that apartments were to be let within.

'How many did you want, ma'am?' was, of course, the reply.

'Three.'

'Will you step in, ma'am?' Down got Mrs Tuggs. The family were delighted. Splendid view of the sea from the front windows charming! A short pause. Back came Mrs Tuggs again. – One parlour and a mattress.

'Why the devil didn't they say so at first?' enquired Mr Joseph Tuggs, rather pettishly.

'Don't know,' said Mrs Tuggs.

'Wretches!' exclaimed the nervous Cymon. Another bill – another stoppage. Same question – same answer – similar result.

'What do they mean by this?' enquired Mr Joseph Tuggs, thoroughly out of temper.

'Don't know,' said the placid Mrs Tuggs.

'Orvis the vay here, sir,' said the driver, by way of accounting for the circumstance in a satisfactory manner; and off they went again, to make fresh enquiries and encounter fresh disappointments.

It had grown dusk when the 'fly' – the rate of whose progress greatly belied its name – after climbing up four or five perpendicular hills, stopped before the door of a dusty house with a bay window from which you could obtain a beautiful glimpse of the sea – if you thrust half of your body out of it, at the imminent peril of falling into the area. Mrs Tuggs alighted. One ground-floor sitting-room, and three cells with beds in them upstairs. A double-house. Family on the opposite side. Five children milk-and-watering in the parlour and one little boy, expelled for bad behaviour, screaming on his back in the passage.

'What's the terms?' said Mrs Tuggs. The mistress of the house was considering the expediency of putting on an extra guinea; so she coughed slightly and affected not to hear the question.

'What's the terms?' said Mrs Tuggs, in a louder key.

'Five guineas a week, ma'am, *with* attendance,' replied the lodging-house keeper. (Attendance means the privilege of ringing the bell as often as you like, for your own amusement.)

'Rather dear,' said Mrs Tuggs.

'Oh dear, no, ma'am!' replied the mistress of the house, with a benign smile of pity at the ignorance of manners and customs which the observation betrayed. 'Very cheap!'

Such an authority was indisputable. Mrs Tuggs paid a week's rent in advance, and took the lodgings for a month. In an hour's time, the family were seated at tea in their new abode.

'Capital srimps!' said Mr Joseph Tuggs.

Mr Cymon eyed his father with a rebellious scowl as he emphatically said, '*Shrimps.*'

'Well, then, shrimps,' said Mr Joseph Tuggs. 'Srimps or shrimps, don't much matter.'

There was pity, blended with malignity, in Mr Cymon's eye as he replied, 'Don't matter, father! What would Captain Waters say if he heard such vulgarity?'

'Or what would dear Mrs Captain Waters say,' added Charlotta, 'if she saw mother – ma, I mean – eating them whole, heads and all!'

'It don't bear thinking of!' ejaculated Mr Cymon, with a shudder. 'How different,' he thought, 'from the Dowager Duchess of Dobbleton!'

'Very pretty woman, Mrs Captain Waters, is she not, Cymon?' enquired Miss Charlotta.

A glow of nervous excitement passed over the countenance of Mr Cymon Tuggs as he replied, 'An angel of beauty!'

'Hallo!' said Mr Joseph Tuggs. 'Hallo, Cymon, my boy, take care.

Married lady, you know;' and he winked one of his twinkling eyes knowingly.

'Why,' exclaimed Cymon, starting up with an ebullition of fury, as unexpected as alarming, 'why am I to be reminded of that blight of my happiness and ruin of my hopes? Why am I to be taunted with the miseries which are heaped upon my head? Is it not enough to – to – to – ' and the orator paused; but whether for want of words, or lack of breath, was never distinctly ascertained.

There was an impressive solemnity in the tone of this address, and in the air with which the romantic Cymon, at its conclusion, rang the bell and demanded a flat candlestick, which effectually forbade a reply. He stalked dramatically to bed, and the Tuggses went to bed too, half an hour afterwards, in a state of considerable mystification and perplexity.

If the pier had presented a scene of life and bustle to the Tuggses on their first landing at Ramsgate, it was far surpassed by the appearance of the sands on the morning after their arrival. It was a fine, bright, clear day, with a light breeze from the sea. There were the same ladies and gentlemen, the same children, the same nursemaids, the same telescopes, the same portable chairs. The ladies were employed in needlework, or watch-guard making, or knitting, or reading novels; the gentlemen were reading newspapers and magazines; the children were digging holes in the sand with wooden spades and collecting water therein; the nursemaids, with their youngest charges in their arms, were running in after the waves and then running back with the waves after them; and, now and then, a little sailing-boat either departed with a gay and talkative cargo of passengers or returned with a very silent and particularly uncomfortable-looking one.

'Well, I never!' exclaimed Mrs Tuggs, as she and Mr Joseph Tuggs and Miss Charlotta Tuggs and Mr Cymon Tuggs, with their eight feet in a corresponding number of yellow shoes, seated themselves on four rush-bottomed chairs, which, being placed in a soft part of the sand, forthwith sank down some two feet and a half – 'Well, I never!'

Mr Cymon, by an exertion of great personal strength, uprooted the chairs and removed them farther back.

'Why, I'm blessed if there ain't some ladies a-going in!' exclaimed Mr Joseph Tuggs, with intense astonishment.

'Lor, pa!' exclaimed Miss Charlotta.

'There *is*, my dear,' said Mr Joseph Tuggs. And, sure enough, four young ladies, each furnished with a towel, tripped up the steps of a bathing-machine. In went the horse, floundering about in the water; round turned the machine; down sat the driver; and presently out burst the young ladies aforesaid, with four distinct splashes.

'Well, that's sing'ler, too!' ejaculated Mr Joseph Tuggs, after an awkward pause. Mr Cymon coughed slightly.

'Why, here's some gentlemen a-going in on this side!' exclaimed Mrs Tuggs, in a tone of horror.

Three machines – three horses – three flounderings – three turnings round – three splashes – three gentlemen, disporting themselves in the water like so many dolphins.

'Well, *that's* sing'ler!' said Mr Joseph Tuggs again. Miss Charlotta coughed this time, and another pause ensued. It was agreeably broken.

'How d'ye do, dear? We have been looking for you all the morning,' said a voice to Miss Charlotta Tuggs. Mrs Captain Waters was the owner of it.

'How d'ye do?' said Captain Walter Waters, all suavity; and a most cordial interchange of greetings ensued.

'Belinda, my love,' said Captain Walter Waters, applying his glass to his eye and looking in the direction of the sea.

'Yes, my dear,' replied Mrs Captain Waters.

'There's Harry Thompson!'

'Where?' said Belinda, applying her glass to her eye.

'Bathing.'

'Lor, so it is! He don't see us, does he?'

'No, I don't think he does,' replied the captain. 'Bless my soul, how very singular!'

'What?' enquired Belinda.

'There's Mary Golding, too.'

'Lor! – where?' (Up went the glass again.)

'There!' said the captain, pointing to one of the young ladies before noticed, who, in her bathing costume, looked as if she was enveloped in a patent Mackintosh of scanty dimensions.

'So it is, I declare!' exclaimed Mrs Captain Waters. 'How very curious we should see them both!'

'Very,' said the captain, with perfect coolness.

'It's the reg'lar thing here, you see,' whispered Mr Cymon Tuggs to his father.

'I see it is,' whispered Mr Joseph Tuggs in reply. 'Queer, though – ain't it?' Mr Cymon Tuggs nodded assent.

'What do you think of doing with yourself this morning?' enquired the captain. 'Shall we lunch at Pegwell?'

'I should like that very much indeed,' interposed Mrs Tuggs. She had never heard of Pegwell; but the word 'lunch' had reached her ears, and it sounded very agreeably.

'How shall we go?' enquired the captain; 'it's too warm to walk.'

'A shay?' suggested Mr Joseph Tuggs.

'Chaise,' whispered Mr Cymon.

'I should think one would be enough,' said Mr Joseph Tuggs aloud, quite unconscious of the meaning of the correction. 'However, two shays if you like.'

'I should like a donkey *so* much,' said Belinda.

'Oh, so should I!' echoed Charlotta Tuggs.

'Well, we can have a fly,' suggested the captain, 'and you can have a couple of donkeys.'

A fresh difficulty arose. Mrs Captain Waters declared it would be decidedly improper for two ladies to ride alone. The remedy was obvious. Perhaps young Mr Tuggs would be gallant enough to accompany them.

Mr Cymon Tuggs blushed, smiled, looked vacant and faintly protested that he was no horseman. The objection was at once overruled. A fly was speedily found; and three donkeys – which the proprietor declared on his solemn asseveration to be 'three parts blood, and the other corn' – were engaged in the service.

'Kim up!' shouted one of the two boys who followed behind to propel the donkeys, when Belinda Waters and Charlotta Tuggs had been hoisted and pushed and pulled into their respective saddles.

'Hi – hi – hi!' groaned the other boy behind Mr Cymon Tuggs. Away went the donkey, with the stirrups jingling against the heels of Cymon's boots and Cymon's boots nearly scraping the ground.

'Way – way! Wo–o–o–!' cried Mr Cymon Tuggs as well as he could, in the midst of the jolting.

'Don't make it gallop!' screamed Mrs Captain Waters, behind.

'My donkey *will* go into the public-house!' shrieked Miss Tuggs in the rear.

'Hi–hi–hi!' groaned both the boys together; and on went the donkeys as if nothing would ever stop them.

Everything has an end, however; even the galloping of donkeys will cease in time. The animal which Mr Cymon Tuggs bestrode, feeling sundry uncomfortable tugs at the bit the intent of which he could by no means divine, abruptly sidled against a brick wall and expressed his uneasiness by grinding Mr Cymon Tuggs's leg on the rough surface. Mrs Captain Waters's donkey, apparently under the influence of some playfulness of spirit, rushed suddenly, head first, into a hedge and declined to come out again; and the quadruped on which Miss Tuggs was mounted expressed his delight at this humorous proceeding by firmly planting his forefeet against the ground and kicking up his hindlegs in a very agile, but somewhat alarming, manner.

This abrupt termination to the rapidity of the ride naturally occasioned some confusion. Both the ladies indulged in vehement screaming for several minutes; and Mr Cymon Tuggs, besides sustaining intense bodily pain, had the additional mental anguish of witnessing their distressing situation without having the power to rescue them, by reason of his leg being firmly screwed in between the animal and the wall. The efforts of the boys, however, assisted by the ingenious expedient of twisting the tail of the most rebellious donkey, restored order in a much shorter time than could have reasonably been expected, and the little party jogged slowly on together.

'Now let 'em walk,' said Mr Cymon Tuggs. 'It's cruel to overdrive 'em.'

'Werry well, sir,' replied the boy, with a grin at his companion, as if he understood Mr Cymon to mean that the cruelty applied less to the animals than to their riders.

'What a lovely day, dear!' said Charlotta.

'Charming; enchanting, dear!' responded Mrs Captain Waters.

'What a beautiful prospect, Mr Tuggs!'

Cymon looked full in Belinda's face, as he responded – 'Beautiful, indeed!' The lady cast down her eyes, and suffered the animal she was riding to fall a little back. Cymon Tuggs instinctively did the same.

There was a brief silence, broken only by a sigh from Mr Cymon Tuggs.

'Mr Cymon,' said the lady suddenly, in a low tone, 'Mr Cymon – I am another's.'

Mr Cymon expressed his perfect concurrence in a statement which it was impossible to controvert.

'If I had not been – ' resumed Belinda; and there she stopped.

'What – what?' said Mr Cymon earnestly. 'Do not torture me. What would you say?'

'If I had not been' – continued Mrs Captain Waters – 'if, in earlier life, it had been my fate to have known, and been beloved by, a noble youth – a kindred soul – a congenial spirit – one capable of feeling and appreciating the sentiments which – '

'Heavens! what do I hear?' exclaimed Mr Cymon Tuggs. 'Is it possible! can I believe my – Come up!' (This last unsentimental parenthesis was addressed to the donkey, who, with his head between his forelegs, appeared to be examining the state of his shoes with great anxiety.)

'Hi–hi–hi,' said the boys behind. 'Come up,' expostulated Cymon Tuggs again. 'Hi–hi–hi,' repeated the boys. And whether it was that the animal felt indignant at the tone of Mr Tuggs's command or felt alarmed by the noise of the deputy proprietor's boots running behind him; or whether he burned with a noble emulation to outstrip the other donkeys; certain it is that he no sooner heard the second series of 'hi–hi's' than he started away, with a celerity of pace which jerked Mr Cymon's hat off instantaneously and carried him to the Pegwell Bay Hotel in no time, where he deposited his rider, without giving him the trouble of dismounting, by sagaciously pitching him over his head into the very doorway of the tavern.

Great was the confusion of Mr Cymon Tuggs when he was put right end uppermost by two waiters; considerable was the alarm of Mrs Tuggs in behalf of her son; agonising were the apprehensions of Mrs Captain Waters on his account. It was speedily discovered, however, that he had not sustained much more injury than the donkey – he was grazed and the animal was grazing – and then it *was* a delightful party to be sure! Mr and Mrs Tuggs and the captain had ordered lunch in the little garden behind – small saucers of large shrimps, dabs of butter, crusty loaves and bottled ale. The sky was without a cloud; there were flowerpots and turf before them; the sea, from the foot of the cliff, stretching away as far as the eye could discern anything at all; vessels in the distance with sails as white, and as small, as nicely-got-up cambric handkerchiefs. The shrimps were delightful, the ale better, and the captain even more pleasant than either. Mrs Captain Waters was in *such* spirits after lunch! – chasing first the captain across the turf and among the flowerpots; and then Mr Cymon Tuggs; and then Miss Tuggs; and laughing, too, quite boisterously. But as the captain said, it didn't matter; who knew what they were, there? For all the people of the house knew, they might be common people. To which Mr Joseph Tuggs responded, 'To be sure.' And then they went down the steep wooden steps, a little farther on, which led to the bottom of the cliff; and looked at the crabs, and the seaweed, and the eels, till it was more than fully time to go back to Ramsgate again. Finally, Mr Cymon Tuggs ascended the steps last and Mrs Captain Waters last but one; and Mr Cymon Tuggs discovered that the foot and ankle of Mrs Captain Waters were even more unexceptionable than he had at first supposed.

Taking a donkey towards his ordinary place of residence is a very different thing and a feat much more easily to be accomplished than taking him from it. It requires a great deal of foresight and presence of mind in the one case to anticipate the numerous flights of his discursive imagination; whereas, in the other, all you have to do is to hold on and place a blind confidence in the animal. Mr Cymon Tuggs adopted the latter expedient on his return; and his nerves were so little discomposed by the journey that he distinctly understood they were all to meet again at the library in the evening.

The library was crowded. There were the same ladies and the same gentlemen who had been on the sands in the morning and on the pier the day before. There were young ladies, in maroon-coloured gowns and black velvet bracelets, dispensing fancy articles in the shop and presiding over games of chance in the concert-room. There were marriageable daughters, and marriage-making mammas, gaming and promenading and turning over music and flirting. There were some male beaux doing the sentimental in whispers and others doing the ferocious in moustache. There were Mrs Tuggs in amber, Miss Tuggs in sky-blue, Mrs Captain Waters in pink. There was Captain Waters in a braided surtout; there was Mr Cymon Tuggs in pumps and a gilt waistcoat; there was Mr Joseph Tuggs in a blue coat and a shirt-frill.

'Numbers three, eight and eleven!' cried one of the young ladies in the maroon-coloured gowns.

'Numbers three, eight and eleven!' echoed another young lady in the same uniform.

'Number three's gone,' said the first young lady. 'Numbers eight and eleven!'

'Numbers eight and eleven!' echoed the second young lady.

'Number eight's gone, Mary Ann,' said the first young lady.

'Number eleven!' screamed the second.

'The numbers are all taken now, ladies, if you please,' said the first. The representatives of numbers three, eight and eleven, and the rest of the numbers, crowded round the table.

'Will you throw, ma'am?' said the presiding goddess, handing the dice-box to the eldest daughter of a stout lady with four girls.

There was a profound silence among the lookers-on.

'Throw, Jane, my dear,' said the stout lady. An interesting display of bashfulness – a little blushing in a cambric handkerchief – a whispering to a younger sister.

'Amelia, my dear, throw for your sister,' said the stout lady; and then she turned to a walking advertisement of Rowland's Macassar Oil, who stood next her, and said, 'Jane is so *very* modest and retiring; but I can't be angry with her for it. An artless and unsophisticated girl is *so* truly amiable that I often wish Amelia was more like her sister!'

The gentleman with the whiskers whispered his admiring approval.

'Now, my dear!' said the stout lady. Miss Amelia threw – eight for her sister, ten for herself.

'Nice figure, Amelia,' whispered the stout lady to a thin youth beside her.

'Beautiful!'

'And *such* a spirit! I am like you in that respect. I can*not* help admiring that life and vivacity. Ah!' (a sigh) 'I wish I could make poor Jane a little more like my dear Amelia!'

The young gentleman cordially acquiesced in the sentiment; both he, and the individual first addressed, were perfectly contented.

'Who's this?' enquired Mr Cymon Tuggs of Mrs Captain Waters, as a short female, in a blue velvet hat and feathers, was led into the orchestra by a fat man in black tights and cloudy Berlins.

'Mrs Tippin, of the London theatres,' replied Belinda, referring to the programme of the concert.

The talented Tippin, having condescendingly acknowledged the clapping of hands and shouts of 'bravo!' which greeted her appearance, proceeded to sing the popular cavatina of 'Bid Me Discourse', accompanied on the piano by Mr Tippin; after which, Mr Tippin sang a comic song, accompanied on the piano by Mrs Tippin; the applause consequent upon which was only to be exceeded by the enthusiastic approbation bestowed upon an air with variations on the guitar, by Miss Tippin, accompanied on the chin by Master Tippin.

Thus passed the evening; thus passed the days and evenings of the Tuggses and the Waterses for six weeks. Sands in the morning – donkeys at noon – pier in the afternoon – library at night – and the same people everywhere.

On that very night six weeks, the moon was shining brightly over the calm sea, which dashed against the feet of the tall gaunt cliffs with just enough noise to lull the old fish to sleep without disturbing the young ones, when two figures were discernible – or would have been, if anybody had looked for them – seated on one of the wooden benches which are stationed near the verge of the western cliff. The moon had climbed higher into the heavens by two hours' journeying since those figures first sat down – and yet they had moved not. The crowd of loungers had thinned and dispersed; the noise of itinerant musicians had died away; light after light had appeared in the windows of the different houses in the distance; blockade-man after blockade-man had passed the spot, wending his way towards his solitary post; and yet those figures had remained stationary. Some portions of the two forms were in deep shadow, but the light of the moon fell strongly on a puce-coloured boot and a glazed stock. Mr Cymon Tuggs and Mrs Captain Waters were seated on that bench. They spoke not, but were silently gazing on the sea.

'Walter will return tomorrow,' said Mrs Captain Waters, mournfully breaking silence.

Mr Cymon Tuggs sighed like a gust of wind through a forest of gooseberry bushes as he replied, 'Alas! he will.'

'Oh, Cymon!' resumed Belinda, 'the chaste delight, the calm happiness, of this one week of Platonic love, is too much for me!' Cymon was about to suggest that it was too little for him, but he stopped himself and murmured unintelligibly.

'And to think that even this gleam of happiness, innocent as it is,' exclaimed Belinda, 'is now to be lost for ever!'

'Oh, do not say for ever, Belinda,' exclaimed the excitable Cymon, as two strongly defined tears chased each other down his pale face – it was so long that there was plenty of room for a chase. 'Do not say for ever!'

'I must,' replied Belinda.

'Why?' urged Cymon, 'oh why? Such Platonic acquaintance as ours is so harmless that even your husband can never object to it.'

'My husband!' exclaimed Belinda. 'You little know him. Jealous and revengeful; ferocious in his revenge – a maniac in his jealousy! Would you be assassinated before my eyes?' Mr Cymon Tuggs, in a voice broken by emotion, expressed his disinclination to undergo the process of assassination before the eyes of anybody.

'Then leave me,' said Mrs Captain Waters. 'Leave me, this night, for ever. It is late: let us return.'

Mr Cymon Tuggs sadly offered the lady his arm and escorted her to her lodgings. He paused at the door – he felt a Platonic pressure of his hand. 'Good-night,' he said, hesitating.

'Good-night,' sobbed the lady. Mr Cymon Tuggs paused again.

'Won't you walk in, sir?' said the servant. Mr Tuggs hesitated. Oh, that hesitation! He *did* walk in.

'Good-night!' said Mr Cymon Tuggs again, when he reached the drawing-room.

'Good-night!' replied Belinda; 'and if, at any period of my life, I – Hush!' The lady paused and stared with a steady gaze of horror on the ashy countenance of Mr Cymon Tuggs. There was a double knock at the street-door.

'It is my husband!' said Belinda, as the captain's voice was heard below.

'And my family!' added Cymon Tuggs, as the voices of his relatives floated up the staircase.

'The curtain! The curtain!' gasped Mrs Captain Waters, pointing to the window before which some chintz hangings were closely drawn.

'But I have done nothing wrong,' said the hesitating Cymon.

'The curtain!' reiterated the frantic lady: 'you will be murdered.' This last appeal to his feelings was irresistible. The dismayed Cymon concealed himself behind the curtain with pantomimic suddenness.

Enter the captain, Joseph Tuggs, Mrs Tuggs and Charlotta.

'My dear,' said the captain, 'Lieutenant Slaughter.' Two ironshod boots and one gruff voice were heard by Mr Cymon to advance and acknowledge the honour of the introduction. The sabre of the lieutenant rattled heavily upon the floor as he seated himself at the table. Mr Cymon's fears almost overcame his reason.

'The brandy, my dear!' said the captain. Here was a situation! They were going to make a night of it! And Mr Cymon Tuggs was pent up behind the curtain and afraid to breathe!

'Slaughter,' said the captain, 'a cigar?'

Now, Mr Cymon Tuggs never could smoke without feeling it

indispensably necessary to retire, immediately, and never could smell smoke without a strong disposition to cough. The cigars were introduced; the captain was a professed smoker; so was the lieutenant; so was Joseph Tuggs. The apartment was small, the door was closed, the smoke powerful: it hung in heavy wreaths over the room, and at length found its way behind the curtain. Cymon Tuggs held his nose, his mouth, his breath. It was all of no use – out came the cough.

'Bless my soul!' said the captain, 'I beg your pardon, Miss Tuggs. You dislike smoking?'

'Oh, no; I don't indeed,' said Charlotta.

'It makes you cough.'

'Oh dear no.'

'You coughed just now.'

'Me, Captain Waters! Lor! how can you say so?'

'Somebody coughed,' said the captain.

'I certainly thought so,' said Slaughter. No; everybody denied it.

'Fancy,' said the captain.

'Must be,' echoed Slaughter.

Cigars resumed – more smoke – another cough – smothered, but violent.

'Damned odd!' said the captain, staring about him.

'Sing'ler!' ejaculated the unconscious Mr Joseph Tuggs.

Lieutenant Slaughter looked first at one person mysteriously, then at another; then, laid down his cigar, then approached the window on tiptoe and pointed with his right thumb over his shoulder in the direction of the curtain.

'Slaughter!' ejaculated the captain, rising from table, 'what do you mean?'

The lieutenant, in reply, drew back the curtain and discovered Mr Cymon Tuggs behind it, pallid with apprehension and blue with wanting to cough.

'Aha!' exclaimed the captain, furiously. 'What do I see? Slaughter, your sabre!'

'Cymon!' screamed the Tuggses.

'Mercy!' said Belinda.

'Platonic!' gasped Cymon.

'Your sabre!' roared the captain: 'Slaughter – unhand me – the villain's life!'

'The curtain! You will be murdered.' This last appeal to his feelings was irresistible. The dismayed Cymon concealed himself behind the curtain with pantomimic suddenness.

'Murder!' screamed the Tuggses.

'Hold him fast, sir!' faintly articulated Cymon.

'Water!' exclaimed Joseph Tuggs – and Mr Cymon Tuggs and all the ladies forthwith fainted away, and formed a tableau.

Most willingly would we conceal the disastrous termination of the six weeks' acquaintance. A troublesome form and an arbitrary custom, however, prescribe that a story should have a conclusion in addition to a commencement; we have therefore no alternative. Lieutenant Slaughter brought a message – the captain brought an action. Mr Joseph Tuggs interposed – the lieutenant negotiated. When Mr Cymon Tuggs recovered from the nervous disorder into which misplaced affection and exciting circumstances had plunged him, he found that his family had lost their pleasant acquaintance; that his father was minus fifteen hundred pounds and the captain plus the precise sum. The money was paid to hush the matter up but it got abroad notwithstanding; and there are not wanting some who affirm that three designing impostors never found more easy dupes than did Captain Waters, Mrs Waters and Lieutenant Slaughter in the Tuggses at Ramsgate.

HORATIO SPARKINS

'Indeed, my love, he paid Teresa very great attention on the last assembly night,' said Mrs Malderton, addressing her spouse, who, after the fatigues of the day in the City, was sitting with a silk handkerchief over his head and his feet on the fender, drinking his port; – 'very great attention; and I say again, every possible encouragement ought to be given him. He positively must be asked down here to dine.'

'Who must?' enquired Mr Malderton.

'Why, you know whom I mean, my dear – the young man with the black whiskers and the white cravat, who has just come out at our assembly and whom all the girls are talking about. Young – dear me! what's his name? – Marianne, what *is* his name?' continued Mrs Malderton, addressing her younger daughter, who was engaged in netting a purse and looking sentimental.

'Mr Horatio Sparkins, ma,' replied Miss Marianne, with a sigh.

'Oh! yes, to be sure – Horatio Sparkins,' said Mrs Malderton. 'Decidedly the most gentlemanlike young man I ever saw. I am sure, in the beautifully made coat he wore the other night, he looked like – like – '

'Like Prince Leopold, ma – so noble, so full of sentiment!' suggested Marianne, in a tone of enthusiastic admiration.

'You should recollect, my dear,' resumed Mrs Malderton, 'that Teresa is now eight-and-twenty; and that it really is very important that something should be done.'

Miss Teresa Malderton was a very little girl, rather fat, with vermilion cheeks, but good-humoured, and still disengaged, although, to do her justice, the misfortune arose from no lack of perseverance on her part. In vain had she flirted for ten years; in vain had Mr and Mrs Malderton assiduously kept up an extensive acquaintance among the young eligible bachelors of Camberwell, and even of Wandsworth and Brixton; to say nothing of those who 'dropped in' from town. Miss Malderton was as well known as the lion on the top of Northumberland House, and had an equal chance of 'going off'.

'I am quite sure you'd like him,' continued Mrs Malderton, 'he is so gentlemanly!'

'So clever!' said Miss Marianne.

'And has such a flow of language!' added Miss Teresa.

'He has a great respect for you, my dear,' said Mrs Malderton to her husband. Mr Malderton coughed, and looked at the fire.

'Yes I'm sure he's very much attached to pa's society,' said Miss Marianne.

'No doubt of it,' echoed Miss Teresa.

'Indeed, he said as much to me in confidence,' observed Mrs Malderton.

'Well, well,' returned Mr Malderton, somewhat flattered; 'if I see him at the assembly tomorrow, perhaps I'll ask him down. I hope he knows we live at Oak Lodge, Camberwell, my dear?'

'Of course – and that you keep a one-horse carriage.'

'I'll see about it,' said Mr Malderton, composing himself for a nap; 'I'll see about it.'

Mr Malderton was a man whose whole scope of ideas was limited to Lloyd's, the Exchange, the India House and the Bank. A few successful speculations had raised him from a situation of obscurity and comparative poverty to a state of affluence. As frequently happens in such cases, the ideas of himself and his family became elevated to an extraordinary pitch as their means increased; they affected fashion, taste and many other fooleries, in imitation of their betters, and had a very decided and becoming horror of anything which could, by possibility, be considered low. He was hospitable from ostentation, illiberal from ignorance and prejudiced from conceit. Egotism and the love of display induced him to keep an excellent table; convenience and a love of the good things of this life ensured him plenty of guests. He liked to have clever men, or what he considered such, at his table, because it was a great thing to talk about; but he never could endure what he called 'sharp fellows'. Probably he cherished this feeling out of compliment to his two sons, who gave their respected parent no uneasiness in that particular. The family were ambitious of forming acquaintances and connections in some sphere of society superior to that in which they themselves moved; and one of the necessary consequences of this desire, added to their utter ignorance of the world beyond their own small circle, was that anyone who could lay claim to an acquaintance with people of rank and title had a sure passport to the table at Oak Lodge, Camberwell.

The appearance of Mr Horatio Sparkins at the assembly had excited no small degree of surprise and curiosity among its regular frequenters. Who could he be? He was evidently reserved, and apparently melancholy.

Was he a clergyman? – He danced too well. A barrister? – He said he was not called. He used very fine words and talked a great deal. Could he be a distinguished foreigner, come to England for the purpose of describing the country, its manners and customs, and frequenting public balls and public dinners with the view of becoming acquainted with high life, polished etiquette and English refinement? – No, he had not a foreign accent. Was he a surgeon, a contributor to the magazines, a writer of fashionable novels or an artist? – No; to each and all of these surmises there existed some valid objection. – 'Then,' said everybody, 'he must be *somebody*.' – 'I should think he must be,' reasoned Mr Malderton, within himself, 'because he perceives our superiority, and pays us so much attention.'

The night succeeding the conversation we have just recorded, was 'assembly night'. The double-fly was ordered to be at the door of Oak Lodge at nine o'clock precisely. The Miss Maldertons were dressed in sky-blue satin trimmed with artificial flowers; and Mrs M. (who was a little fat woman), in ditto ditto, looked like her elder daughter multiplied by two. Mr Frederick Malderton, the elder son, in full-dress costume, was the very *beau idéal* of a smart waiter; and Mr Thomas Malderton, the younger, with his white dress-stock, blue coat, bright buttons and red watch-ribbon, strongly resembled the portrait of that interesting but rash young gentleman, George Barnwell. Every member of the party had made up his or her mind to cultivate the acquaintance of Mr Horatio Sparkins. Miss Teresa, of course, was to be as amiable and interesting as ladies of eight-and-twenty on the lookout for a husband usually are. Mrs Malderton would be all smiles and graces. Miss Marianne would request the favour of some verses for her album. Mr Malderton would patronise the great unknown by asking him to dinner. Tom intended to ascertain the extent of his information on the interesting topics of snuff and cigars. Even Mr Frederick Malderton himself, the family authority on all points of taste, dress and fashionable arrangement; who had lodgings of his own in town; who had a free admission to Covent Garden theatre; who always dressed according to the fashions of the months; who went up the water twice a week in the season; and who actually had an intimate friend who once knew a gentleman who formerly lived in Albany – even he had determined that Mr Horatio Sparkins must be a devilish good fellow and that he would do him the honour of challenging him to a game at billiards.

The first object that met the anxious eyes of the expectant family on their entrance into the ballroom was the interesting Horatio, with his hair brushed off his forehead and his eyes fixed on the ceiling, reclining in a contemplative attitude on one of the seats.

'There he is, my dear,' whispered Mrs Malderton to Mr Malderton.

'How like Lord Byron!' murmured Miss Teresa.

'Or Montgomery!' whispered Miss Marianne.

'Or the portraits of Captain Cook!' suggested Tom.

'Tom – don't be an ass!' said his father, who checked him on all occasions, probably with a view to prevent his becoming 'sharp' which was very unnecessary.

The elegant Sparkins attitudinised with admirable effect until the family had crossed the room. He then started up with the most natural appearance of surprise and delight; accosted Mrs Malderton with the utmost cordiality; saluted the young ladies in the most enchanting manner; bowed to, and shook hands with Mr Malderton, with a degree of respect amounting almost to veneration; and returned the greetings of the two young men in a half-gratified, half-patronising manner, which fully convinced them that he must be an important, and, at the same time, condescending personage.

'Miss Malderton,' said Horatio, after the ordinary salutations, and bowing very low, 'may I be permitted to presume to hope that you will allow me to have the pleasure – '

'I don't *think* I am engaged,' said Miss Teresa, with a dreadful affectation of indifference – 'but, really – so many – '

Horatio looked handsomely miserable.

'I shall be most happy,' simpered the interesting Teresa, at last. Horatio's countenance brightened up, like an old hat in a shower of rain.

'A very genteel young man, certainly!' said the gratified Mr Malderton, as the obsequious Sparkins and his partner joined the quadrille which was just forming.

'He has a remarkably good address,' said Mr Frederick.

'Yes, he is a prime fellow,' interposed Tom, who always managed to put his foot in it – 'he talks just like an auctioneer.'

'Tom!' said his father solemnly, 'I think I desired you, before, not to be a fool.' Tom looked as happy as a cock on a drizzly morning.

'How delightful!' said the interesting Horatio to his partner, as they promenaded the room at the conclusion of the set – 'how delightful, how refreshing it is, to retire from the cloudy storms, the vicissitudes and the troubles of life, even if it be but for a few short fleeting moments: and to spend those moments, fading and evanescent though they be, in the delightful, the blessed society of one individual – whose frowns would be death, whose coldness would be madness, whose falsehood would be ruin, whose constancy would be bliss; the possession of whose affection would be the brightest and best reward that heaven could bestow on man?'

'What feeling! what sentiment!' thought Miss Teresa, as she leaned more heavily on her companion's arm.

'But enough – enough!' resumed the elegant Sparkins, with a theatrical air. 'What have I said? what have I – I – to do with sentiments like these! Miss Malderton' – here he stopped short – 'may I hope to be permitted to offer the humble tribute of – '

'Really, Mr Sparkins,' returned the enraptured Teresa, blushing in the sweetest confusion, 'I must refer you to papa. I never can, without his consent, venture to – '

'Surely he cannot object – '

'Oh, yes. Indeed, indeed, you know him not!' interrupted Miss Teresa, well knowing there was nothing to fear, but wishing to make the interview resemble a scene in some romantic novel.

'He cannot object to my offering you a glass of negus,' returned the adorable Sparkins, with some surprise.

'Is that all?' thought the disappointed Teresa. 'What a fuss about nothing!'

'It will give me the greatest pleasure, sir, to see you to dinner at Oak Lodge, Camberwell, on Sunday next at five o'clock, if you have no better engagement,' said Mr Malderton, at the conclusion of the evening, as he and his sons were standing in conversation with Mr Horatio Sparkins.

Horatio bowed his acknowledgments, and accepted the flattering invitation.

'I must confess,' continued the father, offering his snuffbox to his new acquaintance, 'that I don't enjoy these assemblies half so much as the comfort – I had almost said the luxury – of Oak Lodge. They have no great charms for an elderly man.'

'And after all, sir, what is man?' said the metaphysical Sparkins. 'I say, what is man?'

'Ah! very true,' said Mr Malderton; 'very true.'

'We know that we live and breathe,' continued Horatio; 'that we have wants and wishes, desires and appetites – '

'Certainly,' said Mr Frederick Malderton, looking profound.

'I say, we know that we exist,' repeated Horatio, raising his voice, 'but there we stop; there, is an end to our knowledge; there, is the summit of our attainments; there, is the termination of our ends. What more do we know?'

'Nothing,' replied Mr Frederick – than whom no one was more capable of answering for himself in that particular. Tom was about to hazard something, but, fortunately for his reputation, he caught his father's angry eye and slunk off like a puppy convicted of petty larceny.

'Upon my word,' said Mr Malderton the elder, as they were returning home in the fly, 'that Mr Sparkins is a wonderful young man. Such surprising knowledge! such extraordinary information! and such a splendid mode of expressing himself!'

'I think he must be somebody in disguise,' said Miss Marianne. 'How charmingly romantic!'

'He talks very loud and nicely,' timidly observed Tom, 'but I don't exactly understand what he means.'

'I almost begin to despair of your understanding anything, Tom,' said his father, who, of course, had been much enlightened by Mr Horatio Sparkins's conversation.

'It strikes me, Tom,' said Miss Teresa, 'that you have made yourself very ridiculous this evening.'

'No doubt of it,' cried everybody – and the unfortunate Tom reduced himself into the least possible space. That night, Mr and Mrs Malderton had a long conversation respecting their daughter's prospects and future arrangements. Miss Teresa went to bed considering whether, in the event of her marrying a title, she could conscientiously encourage the visits of her present associates – and dreamed, all night, of disguised noblemen, large routs, ostrich plumes, bridal favours and Horatio Sparkins.

Various surmises were hazarded on the Sunday morning as to the mode of conveyance which the anxiously expected Horatio would adopt. Did he keep a gig? – was it possible he could come on horseback? – or would he patronise the stage? These, and other various conjectures of equal importance, engrossed the attention of Mrs Malderton and her daughters during the whole morning after church.

'Upon my word, my dear, it's a most annoying thing that that vulgar brother of yours should have invited himself to dine here today,' said Mr Malderton to his wife. 'On account of Mr Sparkins's coming down, I purposely abstained from asking anyone but Flamwell. And then to think of your brother – a tradesman – it's insufferable! I declare I wouldn't have him mention his shop before our new guest – no, not for a thousand pounds! I wouldn't care if he had the good sense to conceal the disgrace he is to the family; but he's so fond of his horrible business that he *will* let people know what he is.'

Mr Jacob Barton, the individual alluded to, was a large grocer; so vulgar, and so lost to all sense of feeling, that he actually never scrupled to avow that he wasn't above his business: 'he'd made his money by it, and he didn't care who know'd it'.

'Ah! Flamwell, my dear fellow, how d'ye do?' said Mr Malderton, as a little spoffish man, with green spectacles, entered the room. 'You got my note?'

'Yes, I did; and here I am in consequence.'

'You don't happen to know this Mr Sparkins by name? You know everybody.'

Mr Flamwell was one of those gentlemen of remarkably extensive information whom one occasionally meets in society, who pretend to know everybody, but in reality know nobody. At Malderton's, where any stories about great people were received with a greedy ear, he was an especial favourite; and, knowing the kind of people he had to deal with, he carried his passion of claiming acquaintance with everybody to the most immoderate length. He had rather a singular way of telling his greatest lies in a parenthesis, and with an air of self-denial, as if he feared being thought egotistical.

'Why, no, I don't know him by that name,' returned Flamwell, in a low tone, and with an air of immense importance. 'I have no doubt I know him, though. Is he tall?'

'Middle-sized,' said Miss Teresa.

'With black hair?' enquired Flamwell, hazarding a bold guess.

'Yes,' returned Miss Teresa, eagerly.

'Rather a snub nose?'

'No,' said the disappointed Teresa, 'he has a Roman nose.'

'I said a Roman nose, didn't I?' enquired Flamwell. 'He's an elegant young man?'

'Oh, certainly.'

'With remarkably prepossessing manners?'

'Oh, yes!' said all the family together. 'You must know him.'

'Yes, I thought you knew him, if he was anybody,' triumphantly exclaimed Mr Malderton. 'Who d'ye think he is?'

'Why, from your description,' said Flamwell, ruminating, and sinking his voice, almost to a whisper, 'he bears a strong resemblance to the Honourable Augustus Fitz-Edward Fitz-John Fitz-Osborne. He's a very talented young man, and rather eccentric. It's extremely probable he may have changed his name for some temporary purpose.'

Teresa's heart beat high. Could he be the Honourable Augustus Fitz-Edward Fitz-John Fitz-Osborne! What a name to be elegantly engraved upon two glazed cards, tied together with a piece of white satin ribbon! 'The Honourable Mrs Augustus Fitz-Edward Fitz-John Fitz-Osborne!' The thought was transport.

'It's five minutes to five,' said Mr Malderton, looking at his watch: 'I hope he's not going to disappoint us.'

'There he is!' exclaimed Miss Teresa, as a loud double-knock was heard at the door. Everybody endeavoured to look – as people when they particularly expect a visitor always do – as if they were perfectly unsuspicious of the approach of anybody.

The room-door opened – 'Mr Barton!' said the servant.

'Confound the man!' murmured Malderton. 'Ah! my dear sir, how d'ye do! Any news?'

'Why no,' returned the grocer, in his usual bluff manner. 'No, none partickler. None that I am much aware of. How d'ye do, gals and boys? Mr Flamwell, sir – glad to see you.'

'Here's Mr Sparkins!' said Tom, who had been looking out at the window, 'on *such* a black horse!' There was Horatio, sure enough, on a large black horse, curvetting and prancing along, like an Astley's super-numerary. After a great deal of reining in and pulling up, with the accompaniments of snorting, rearing and kicking, the animal consented to stop at about a hundred yards from the gate, where Mr Sparkins dismounted and confided him to the care of Mr Malderton's groom. The ceremony of introduction was gone through, in all due form. Mr Flamwell looked from behind his green spectacles at Horatio with an air of mysterious importance; and the gallant Horatio looked unutterable things at Teresa.

'Is he the Honourable Mr Augustus What's-his-name?' whispered Mrs Malderton to Flamwell, as he was escorting her to the dining-room.

'Why, no – at least not exactly,' returned that great authority – 'not exactly.'

'Who *is* he then?'

'Hush!' said Flamwell, nodding his head with a grave air, importing that he knew very well, but was prevented, by some grave reasons of state, from disclosing the important secret. It might be one of the ministers making himself acquainted with the views of the people.

'Mr Sparkins,' said the delighted Mrs Malderton, 'pray divide the ladies. John, put a chair for the gentleman between Miss Teresa and Miss Marianne.' This was addressed to a man who, on ordinary occasions, acted as half-groom, half-gardener; but who, as it was important to make an impression on Mr Sparkins, had been forced into a white neckerchief and shoes, and touched up and brushed to look like a second footman.

The dinner was excellent; Horatio was most attentive to Miss Teresa, and everyone felt in high spirits, except Mr Malderton, who, knowing the propensity of his brother-in-law, Mr Barton, endured that sort of agony which the newspapers inform us is experienced by the surrounding neighbourhood when a potboy hangs himself in a hayloft, and which is 'much easier to be imagined than described'.

'Have you seen your friend Sir Thomas Noland lately, Flamwell?' enquired Mr Malderton, casting a sidelong look at Horatio to see what effect the mention of so great a man had upon him.

'Why, no – not very lately. I saw Lord Gubbleton the day before yesterday.'

'Ah! I hope his lordship is very well?' said Malderton, in a tone of the greatest interest. It is scarcely necessary to say that until that moment he had been quite innocent of the existence of such a person.

'Why, yes; he was very well – very well indeed. He's a devilish good fellow. I met him in the City and had a long chat with him. Indeed, I'm rather intimate with him. I couldn't stop to talk to him as long as I could wish, though, because I was on my way to a banker's, a very rich man and a Member of Parliament, with whom I am also rather, indeed I may say very, intimate.'

'I know whom you mean,' returned the host, consequentially – in reality knowing as much about the matter as Flamwell himself. 'He has a capital business.'

This was touching on a dangerous topic.

'Talking of business,' interposed Mr Barton, from the centre of the table. 'A gentleman whom you knew very well, Malderton, before you made that first lucky spec of yours, called at our shop the other day, and – '

'Barton, may I trouble you for a potato?' interrupted the wretched master of the house, hoping to nip the story in the bud.

'Certainly,' returned the grocer, quite insensible of his brother-in-law's object – 'and he said in a very plain manner – '

'*Floury*, if you please,' interrupted Malderton again; dreading the termination of the anecdote and fearing a repetition of the word 'shop'.

'He said, says he,' continued the culprit, after despatching the potato; 'says he, how goes on your business? So I said, jokingly you know my way – says I, I'm never above my business, and I hope my business will never be above me. Ha, ha!'

'Mr Sparkins,' said the host, vainly endeavouring to conceal his dismay, 'a glass of wine?'

'With the utmost pleasure, sir.'

'Happy to see you.'

'Thank you.'

'We were talking the other evening,' resumed the host, addressing Horatio partly with the view of displaying the conversational powers of his new acquaintance and partly in the hope of drowning the grocer's stories – 'we were talking the other night about the nature of man. Your argument struck me very forcibly.'

'And me,' said Mr Frederick. Horatio made a graceful inclination of the head.

'Pray, what is your opinion of woman, Mr Sparkins?' enquired Mrs Malderton. The young ladies simpered.

'Man,' replied Horatio, 'man, whether he ranged the bright, gay, flowery plains of a second Eden or the more sterile, barren, and I may say, commonplace regions to which we are compelled to accustom ourselves in times such as these; man, under any circumstances or in any place – whether he were bending beneath the withering blasts of the frigid zone or scorching under the rays of a vertical sun – man, without woman, would be – alone.'

'I am very happy to find you entertain such honourable opinions, Mr Sparkins,' said Mrs Malderton.

'And I,' added Miss Teresa. Horatio looked his delight and the young lady blushed.

'Now, it's my opinion – ' said Mr Barton.

'I know what you're going to say,' interposed Malderton, determined not to give his relation another opportunity, 'and I don't agree with you.'

'What!' enquired the astonished grocer.

'I am sorry to differ from you, Barton,' said the host, in as positive a manner as if he really were contradicting a position which the other had laid down, 'but I cannot give my assent to what I consider a very monstrous proposition.'

'But I meant to say – '

'You never can convince me,' said Malderton, with an air of obstinate determination. 'Never.'

'And I,' said Mr Frederick, following up his father's attack, 'cannot entirely agree in Mr Sparkins's argument.'

'What!' said Horatio, who became more metaphysical, and more argumentative, as he saw the female part of the family listening in wondering delight – 'what! Is effect the consequence of cause? Is cause the precursor of effect?'

'That's the point,' said Flamwell.

'To be sure,' said Mr Malderton.

'Because, if effect is the consequence of cause, and if cause does precede effect, I apprehend you are wrong,' added Horatio.

'Decidedly,' said the toad-eating Flamwell.

'At least, I apprehend that to be the just and logical deduction?' said Sparkins, in a tone of interrogation.

'No doubt of it,' chimed in Flamwell again. 'It settles the point.'

'Well, perhaps it does,' said Mr Frederick; 'I didn't see it before.'

'I don't exactly see it now,' thought the grocer; 'but I suppose it's all right.'

'How wonderfully clever he is!' whispered Mrs Malderton to her daughters, as they retired to the drawing-room.

'Oh, he's quite a love!' said both the young ladies together; 'he talks like an oracle. He must have seen a great deal of life.'

The gentlemen being left to themselves, a pause ensued, during which everybody looked very grave, as if they were quite overcome by the profound nature of the previous discussion. Flamwell, who had made up his mind to find out who and what Mr Horatio Sparkins really was, first broke silence.

'Excuse me, sir,' said that distinguished personage, 'I presume you have studied for the bar? I thought of entering once, myself – indeed, I'm rather intimate with some of the highest ornaments of that distinguished profession.'

'N–no!' said Horatio, with a little hesitation; 'not exactly.'

'But you have been much among the silk gowns, or I mistake?' enquired Flamwell, deferentially.

'Nearly all my life,' returned Sparkins.

The question was thus pretty well settled in the mind of Mr Flamwell. He was a young gentleman 'about to be called'.

'I shouldn't like to be a barrister,' said Tom, speaking for the first time, and looking round the table to find somebody who would notice the remark.

No one made any reply.

'I shouldn't like to wear a wig,' said Tom, hazarding another observation.

'Tom, I beg you will not make yourself ridiculous,' said his father. 'Pray listen, and improve yourself by the conversation you hear, and don't be constantly making these absurd remarks.'

'Very well, father,' replied the unfortunate Tom, who had not spoken a word since he had asked for another slice of beef at a quarter-past five, and it was then eight.

'Well, Tom,' observed his good-natured uncle, 'never mind! *I* think with you. *I* shouldn't like to wear a wig. I'd rather wear an apron.'

Mr Malderton coughed violently. Mr Barton resumed – 'For if a man's above his business – '

The cough returned with tenfold violence, and did not cease until the unfortunate cause of it, in his alarm, had quite forgotten what he intended to say.

'Mr Sparkins,' said Flamwell, returning to the charge, 'do you happen to know Mr Delafontaine of Bedford Square?'

'I have exchanged cards with him; since which, indeed, I have had an opportunity of serving him considerably,' replied Horatio, slightly colouring; no doubt at having been betrayed into making the acknowledgment.

'You are very lucky, if you have had an opportunity of obliging that great man,' observed Flamwell, with an air of profound respect.

'I don't know who he is,' he whispered to Mr Malderton, confidentially, as they followed Horatio up to the drawing-room. 'It's quite clear, however, that he belongs to the law, and that he is somebody of great importance and very highly connected.'

'No doubt, no doubt,' returned his companion.

The remainder of the evening passed away most delightfully. Mr Malderton, relieved from his apprehensions by the circumstance of Mr Barton's falling into a profound sleep, was as affable and gracious as possible. Miss Teresa played the 'Fall of Paris', as Mr Sparkins declared, in a most masterly manner, and both of them, assisted by Mr Frederick, tried over glees and trios without number, they having made the pleasing discovery that their voices harmonised beautifully. To be sure, they all sang the first part; and Horatio, in addition to the slight drawback of having no ear, was perfectly innocent of knowing a note of music; still, they passed the time very agreeably and it was past twelve o'clock before Mr Sparkins ordered the mourning-coach-looking steed to be brought out – an order which was only complied with on the distinct under-standing that he was to repeat his visit on the following Sunday.

'But perhaps Mr Sparkins will form one of our party tomorrow evening?' suggested Mrs M. 'Mr Malderton intends taking the girls to see the pantomime.' Mr Sparkins bowed, and promised to join the party in box 48 in the course of the evening.

'We will not tax you for the morning,' said Miss Teresa, bewitchingly; 'for ma is going to take us to all sorts of places, shopping. I know that gentlemen have a great horror of that employment.' Mr Sparkins bowed again, and declared that he should be delighted, but business of importance occupied him in the morning. Flamwell looked at Malderton significantly. 'It's term time!' he whispered.

At twelve o'clock on the following morning, the 'fly' was at the door of Oak Lodge to convey Mrs Malderton and her daughters on their expedition for the day. They were to dine and dress for the play at a friend's house. First driving thither with their bandboxes, they departed on their first errand to make some purchases at Messrs Jones, Spruggins and Smith's of Tottenham Court Road; after which, they were to go to Redmayne's in Bond Street; thence, to innumerable places that no one had ever heard of. The young ladies beguiled the tediousness of the ride by eulogising Mr Horatio Sparkins, scolding their mamma for taking them so far to save a shilling, and wondering whether they should ever reach their destination. At length, the vehicle stopped before a dirty-looking ticketted linen-draper's shop, with goods of all kinds and labels of all sorts and sizes in the window. There were dropsical figures of seven with a little three-farthings in the corner, 'perfectly invisible to the naked eye'; three hundred and fifty thousand ladies' boas, *from* one shilling and a penny-halfpenny; real French kid shoes, at two and ninepence per pair; green parasols, at an equally cheap rate; and 'every description of goods', as the proprietors said – and they must know best – 'fifty per cent under cost price'.

'Lor! ma, what a place you have brought us to!' said Miss Teresa; 'what *would* Mr Sparkins say if he could see us!'

'Ah! what, indeed!' said Miss Marianne, horrified at the idea.

'Pray be seated, ladies. What is the first article?' enquired the obsequious master of the ceremonies of the establishment, who, in his large white neckcloth and formal tie, looked like a bad 'portrait of a gentleman' in the Somerset House exhibition.

'I want to see some silks,' answered Mrs Malderton.

'Directly, ma'am. – Mr Smith! Where *is* Mr Smith?'

'Here, sir,' cried a voice at the back of the shop.

'Pray make haste, Mr Smith,' said the MC. 'You never are to be found when you're wanted, sir.'

Mr Smith, thus enjoined to use all possible dispatch, leaped over the counter with great agility and placed himself before the newly arrived customers. Mrs Malderton uttered a faint scream; Miss Teresa, who had been stooping down to talk to her sister, raised her head, and beheld – Horatio Sparkins!

'We will draw a veil', as novel-writers say, over the scene that ensued. The mysterious, philosophical, romantic, metaphysical Sparkins – he who, to the interesting Teresa, seemed like the embodied idea of the young dukes and poetical exquisites in blue silk dressing-gowns and ditto ditto slippers of whom she had read and dreamed, but had never expected to behold, was suddenly converted into Mr Samuel Smith, the assistant at a 'cheap shop'; the junior partner in a slippery firm of some three weeks' existence. The dignified evanishment of the hero of Oak Lodge, on this unexpected recognition, could only be equalled by that of a furtive dog with a considerable kettle at his tail. All the hopes of the Maldertons were destined at once to melt away, like the lemon ices at a company's dinner; Almack's was still to them as distant as the North Pole; and Miss Teresa had as much chance of a husband as Captain Ross had of the north-west passage.

Mrs Malderton uttered a faint scream; Miss Teresa, who had been stooping down to talk to her sister, raised her head, and beheld – Horatio Sparkins!

Years have elapsed since the occurrence of this dreadful morning. The daisies have thrice bloomed on Camberwell Green; the sparrows have thrice repeated their vernal chirps in Camberwell Grove; but the Miss Maldertons are still unmated. Miss Teresa's case is more desperate than ever; but Flamwell is yet in the zenith of his reputation; and the family have the same predilection for aristocratic personages, with an increased aversion to anything *low*.

THE BLACK VEIL

One winter's evening, towards the close of the year 1800, or within a year or two of that time, a young medical practitioner, recently established in business, was seated by a cheerful fire in his little parlour, listening to the wind which was beating the rain in pattering drops against the window or rumbling dismally in the chimney. The night was wet and cold; he had been walking through mud and water the whole day, and was now comfortably reposing in his dressing-gown and slippers, more than half asleep and less than half awake, revolving a thousand matters in his wandering imagination. First, he thought how hard the wind was blowing and how the cold, sharp rain would be at that moment beating in his face if he were not comfortably housed at home. Then, his mind reverted to his annual Christmas visit to his native place and dearest friends; he thought how glad they would all be to see him, and how happy it would make Rose if he could only tell her that he had found a patient at last and hoped to have more and to come down again, in a few months' time, and marry her, and take her home to gladden his lonely fireside and stimulate him to fresh exertions. Then he began to wonder when his first patient would appear or whether he was destined, by a special dispensation of providence, never to have any patients at all; and then he thought about Rose again, and dropped to sleep and dreamed about her, till the tones of her sweet merry voice sounded in his ears and her soft tiny hand rested on his shoulder.

There *was* a hand upon his shoulder, but it was neither soft nor tiny, its owner being a corpulent round-headed boy who, in consideration of the sum of one shilling per week and his food, was let out by the parish to carry medicine and messages. As there was no demand for the medicine, however, and no necessity for the messages, he usually occupied his unemployed hours – averaging fourteen a day – in abstracting peppermint drops, taking animal nourishment and going to sleep.

'A lady, sir – a lady!' whispered the boy, rousing his master with a shake.

'What lady?' cried our friend, starting up, not quite certain that his dream was an illusion and half expecting that it might be Rose herself – 'What lady? Where?'

'*There*, sir!' replied the boy, pointing to the glass door leading into the surgery, with an expression of alarm which the very unusual apparition of a customer might have tended to excite.

The surgeon looked towards the door and started himself, for an instant, on beholding the appearance of his unlooked-for visitor.

It was a singularly tall woman, dressed in deep mourning and standing so close to the door that her face almost touched the glass. The upper part of her figure was carefully muffled in a black shawl, as if for the purpose of concealment; and her face was shrouded by a thick black veil. She stood perfectly erect; her figure was drawn up to its full height, and though the surgeon felt that the eyes beneath the veil were fixed on him, she stood perfectly motionless, and evinced, by no gesture whatever, the slightest consciousness of his having turned towards her.

'Do you wish to consult me?' he enquired, with some hesitation, holding open the door. It opened inwards, and therefore the action did not alter the position of the figure, which still remained motionless on the same spot.

She slightly inclined her head, in token of acquiescence.

'Pray walk in,' said the surgeon.

The figure moved a step forward; and then, turning its head in the direction of the boy – to his infinite horror – appeared to hesitate.

'Leave the room, Tom,' said the young man, addressing the boy, whose large round eyes had been extended to their utmost width during this brief interview. 'Draw the curtain, and shut the door.'

The boy drew a green curtain across the glass part of the door, retired into the surgery, closed the door after him, and immediately applied one of his large eyes to the keyhole on the other side.

The surgeon drew a chair to the fire and motioned the visitor to a seat. The mysterious figure slowly moved towards it. As the blaze shone upon the black dress, the surgeon observed that the bottom of it was saturated with mud and rain.

'You are very wet,' he said.

'I am,' said the stranger, in a low deep voice.

'And you are ill?' added the surgeon, compassionately, for the tone was that of a person in pain.

'I am,' was the reply – 'very ill; not bodily, but mentally. It is not for myself, or on my own behalf,' continued the stranger, 'that I come to you. If I laboured under bodily disease, I should not be out, alone, at such an hour or on such a night as this; and if I were afflicted with it, twenty-four hours hence, God knows how gladly I would lie down and pray to die. It is for another that I beseech your aid, sir. I may be mad to ask it for him – I think I am; but, night after night, through the long dreary hours of watching and weeping, the thought has been ever present to my mind; and though even I see the hopelessness of human assistance availing him, the bare thought of laying him in his grave without it makes my blood run cold!' And a shudder, such as the surgeon well knew art could not produce, trembled through the speaker's frame.

There was a desperate earnestness in this woman's manner that went to the young man's heart. He was young in his profession and had not yet witnessed enough of the miseries which are daily presented before the eyes of its members to have grown comparatively callous to human suffering.

'If,' he said, rising hastily, 'the person of whom you speak be in so hopeless a condition as you describe, not a moment is to be lost. I will go with you instantly. Why did you not obtain medical advice before?'

'Because it would have been useless before – because it is useless even now,' replied the woman, clasping her hands passionately.

The surgeon gazed, for a moment, on the black veil, as if to ascertain the expression of the features beneath it: its thickness, however, rendered such a result impossible.

'You *are* ill,' he said, gently, 'although you do not know it. The fever which has enabled you to bear, without feeling it, the fatigue you have evidently undergone, is burning within you now. Put that to your lips,' he continued, pouring out a glass of water – 'compose yourself for a few moments, and then tell me, as calmly as you can, what the disease of the patient is and how long he has been ill. When I know what it is necessary I should know to render my visit serviceable to him, I am ready to accompany you.'

The stranger lifted the glass of water to her mouth, without raising the veil; put it down again untasted; and burst into tears.

'I know,' she said, sobbing aloud, 'that what I say to you now seems like the ravings of fever. I have been told so before, less kindly than by you. I am not a young woman; and they do say that as life steals on towards its final close, the last short remnant, worthless as it may seem to all beside, is dearer to its possessor than all the years that have gone before, connected though they be with the recollection of old friends long since dead and young ones – children perhaps – who have fallen off from and forgotten one as completely as if they had died too. My natural term of life cannot be many years longer and should be dear on that account; but I would lay it down without a sigh – with cheerfulness – with joy – if what I tell you now were only false or imaginary. Tomorrow morning he of whom I speak will be I *know*, though I would fain think otherwise, beyond the reach of human aid; and yet, tonight, though he is in deadly peril, you must not see and could not serve him.'

'I am unwilling to increase your distress,' said the surgeon, after a short pause, 'by making any comment on what you have just said, or appearing desirous to investigate a subject you are so anxious to conceal; but there is an inconsistency in your statement which I cannot reconcile with probability. This person is dying tonight, and I cannot see him when my assistance might possibly avail; you apprehend it will be useless tomorrow, and yet you would have me see him then! If he be, indeed, as dear to you as your words and manner would imply, why not try to save his life before delay and the progress of his disease render it impracticable?'

'God help me!' exclaimed the woman, weeping bitterly, 'how can I hope strangers will believe what appears incredible, even to myself? You will *not* see him then, sir?' she added, rising suddenly.

'I did not say that I declined to see him,' replied the surgeon; 'but I warn you, that if you persist in this extraordinary procrastination, and the individual dies, a fearful responsibility rests with you.'

'The responsibility will rest heavily somewhere,' replied the stranger bitterly. 'Whatever responsibility rests with me, I am content to bear and ready to answer.'

'As I incur none,' continued the surgeon, 'by acceding to your request, I will see him in the morning, if you leave me the address. At what hour can he be seen?'

'*Nine*,' replied the stranger.

'You must excuse my pressing these enquiries,' said the surgeon, 'but is he in your charge now?'

'He is not,' was the rejoinder.

'Then if I gave you instructions for his treatment through the night, you could not assist him?'

The woman wept bitterly, as she replied, 'I could not.'

Finding that there was but little prospect of obtaining more information by prolonging the interview; and anxious to spare the woman's feelings, which, subdued at first by a violent effort, were now irrepressible and most painful to witness; the surgeon repeated his promise of calling in the morning at the appointed hour. His visitor, after giving him a direction to an obscure part of Walworth, left the house in the same mysterious manner in which she had entered it.

It will be readily believed that so extraordinary a visit produced a considerable impression on the mind of the young surgeon; and that he speculated a great deal and to very little purpose on the possible circumstances of the case. In common with the generality of people, he had often heard and read of singular instances in which a presentiment of death, at a particular day or even minute, had been entertained and realised. At one moment he was inclined to think that the present might be such a case; but, then, it occurred to him that all the anecdotes of the kind he had ever heard were of persons who had been troubled with a foreboding of their own death. This woman, however, spoke of another person – a man; and it was impossible to suppose that a mere dream or delusion of fancy would induce her to speak of his approaching dissolution with such terrible certainty as she had spoken. It could not be that the man was to be murdered in the morning, and that the woman, originally a consenting party, and bound to secrecy by an oath, had relented, and, though unable to prevent the commission of some outrage on the victim, had determined to prevent his death if possible by the timely interposition of medical aid? The idea of such things happening within two miles of the metropolis appeared too wild and preposterous to be entertained beyond the instant. Then his original impression that the woman's intellects were disordered recurred; and, as it was the only mode of solving the difficulty with any degree of satisfaction, he obstinately made up his mind to believe that she was mad. Certain misgivings upon this point, however, stole upon his thoughts at the time, and presented themselves again and again through the long dull course of a sleepless night; during which, in spite of all his efforts to the contrary, he was unable to banish the black veil from his disturbed imagination.

The back part of Walworth, at its greatest distance from town, is a straggling miserable place enough, even in these days; but, five-and-thirty years ago, the greater portion of it was little better than a dreary waste, inhabited by a few scattered people of questionable character, whose poverty prevented their living in any better neighbourhood or whose pursuits and mode of life rendered its solitude desirable. Very many of the houses which have since sprung up on all sides were not built until some years afterwards; and the great majority even of those which were sprinkled about, at irregular intervals, were of the rudest and most miserable description.

The appearance of the place through which he walked in the morning was not calculated to raise the spirits of the young surgeon, or to dispel any feeling of anxiety or depression which the singular kind of visit he was about to make had awakened. Striking off from the high road, his way lay across a marshy common, through irregular lanes, with here and there a ruinous and dismantled cottage fast falling to pieces with decay and neglect. A stunted tree or pool of stagnant water, roused into a sluggish action by the heavy rain of the preceding night, skirted the path occasionally; and, now and then, a miserable patch of garden-ground, with a few old boards knocked together for a summerhouse and old palings imperfectly mended with stakes pilfered from the neighbouring hedges, bore testimony at once to the poverty of the inhabitants and the little scruple they entertained in appropriating the property of other people to their own use. Occasionally, a filthy-looking woman would make her appearance from the door of a dirty house, to empty the contents of some cooking utensil into the gutter in front or to scream after a little slipshod girl who had contrived to stagger a few yards from the door under the weight of a sallow infant almost as big as herself; but scarcely anything was stirring around; and so much of the prospect as could be faintly traced through the cold damp mist which hung heavily over it presented a lonely and dreary appearance perfectly in keeping with the objects we have described.

After plodding wearily through the mud and mire; making many enquiries for the place to which he had been directed; and receiving as many contradictory and unsatisfactory replies in return; the young man at length arrived before the house which had been pointed out to him as the object of his destination. It was a small low building, one storey above the ground, with even a more desolate and unpromising exterior than any he had yet passed. An old yellow curtain was closely drawn across the window upstairs, and the parlour shutters were closed, but not fastened. The house was detached from any other, and, as it stood at an angle of a narrow lane, there was no other habitation in sight.

When we say that the surgeon hesitated and walked a few paces beyond the house before he could prevail upon himself to lift the knocker, we say nothing that need raise a smile upon the face of the boldest reader. The police of London were a very different body in that day; the isolated position of the suburbs, when the rage for building and the progress of improvement had not yet begun to connect them with the main body of the city and its environs, rendered many of them (and this in particular) a place of resort for the worst and most depraved characters. Even the streets in the gayest parts of London were imperfectly lighted at that time; and such places as these were left entirely to the mercy of the moon and stars. The chances of detecting desperate characters, or of tracing them to their haunts, were thus rendered very few, and their offences naturally increased in boldness as the consciousness of comparative security became the more impressed upon them by daily experience. Added to these considerations, it must be remembered that the young man had spent some time in the public hospitals of the metropolis; and, although neither Burke nor Bishop had then gained a horrible notoriety, his own observation might have suggested to him how easily the atrocities to which the former has since given his name might be committed. Be this as it may, whatever reflection made him hesitate, he *did* hesitate: but, being a young man of strong mind and great personal courage, it was only for an instant – he stepped briskly back and knocked gently at the door.

A low whispering was audible, immediately afterwards, as if some person at the end of the passage were conversing stealthily with another on the landing above. It was succeeded by the noise of a pair of heavy boots upon the bare floor. The door-chain was softly unfastened; the door opened; and a tall, ill-favoured man, with black hair and a face, as the surgeon often declared afterwards, as pale and haggard as the countenance of any dead man he ever saw, presented himself.

'Walk in, sir,' he said in a low tone.

The surgeon did so, and the man having secured the door again, by the chain, led the way to a small back parlour at the extremity of the passage.

'Am I in time?'

'Too soon!' replied the man. The surgeon turned hastily round, with a gesture of astonishment not unmixed with alarm, which he found it impossible to repress.

'If you'll step in here, sir,' said the man, who had evidently noticed the action – 'if you'll step in here, sir, you won't be detained five minutes, I assure you.'

The surgeon at once walked into the room. The man closed the door and left him alone.

It was a little cold room, with no other furniture than two deal chairs and a table of the same material. A handful of fire, unguarded by any fender, was burning in the grate, which brought out the damp if it served no more comfortable purpose, for the unwholesome moisture was stealing down the walls in long slug-like tracks. The window, which was broken and patched in many places, looked into a small enclosed piece of ground almost covered with water. Not a sound was to be heard, either within the house or without. The young surgeon sat down by the fireplace to await the result of his first professional visit.

He had not remained in this position many minutes, when the noise of some approaching vehicle struck his ear. It stopped; the street-door was opened; a low talking succeeded, accompanied with a shuffling noise of footsteps, along the passage and on the stairs, as if two or three men were engaged in carrying some heavy body to the room above. The creaking of the stairs, a few seconds afterwards, announced that the newcomers having completed their task, whatever it was, were leaving the house. The door was again closed, and the former silence was restored.

Another five minutes had elapsed, and the surgeon had resolved to explore the house in search of someone to whom he might make his errand known, when the room-door opened and his last night's visitor, dressed in exactly the same manner, with the veil lowered as before, motioned him to advance. The singular height of her form, coupled with the circumstance of her not speaking, caused the idea to pass across his brain for an instant that it might be a man disguised in woman's attire. The hysteric sobs which issued from beneath the veil, and the convulsive attitude of grief of the whole figure, however, at once exposed the absurdity of the suspicion; and he hastily followed.

The woman led the way upstairs to the front room and paused at the door to let him enter first. It was scantily furnished with an old deal box, a few chairs, and a tent bedstead, without hangings or cross-rails, which was covered with a patchwork counterpane. The dim light admitted through the curtain which he had noticed from the outside rendered the objects in the room so indistinct, and communicated to all of them so uniform a hue, that he did not, at first, perceive the object on which his eye at once rested when the woman rushed frantically past him and flung herself on her knees by the bedside.

Stretched upon the bed, closely enveloped in a linen wrapper and covered with blankets, lay a human form, stiff and motionless. The head and face, which were those of a man, were uncovered, save by a bandage which passed over the head and under the chin. The eyes were closed. The left arm lay heavily across the bed and the woman held the passive hand.

The surgeon gently pushed the woman aside and took the hand in his.

'My God!' he exclaimed, letting it fall involuntarily – 'the man is dead!'

The woman started to her feet and beat her hands together.

'Oh! don't say so, sir,' she exclaimed, with a burst of passion amounting almost to frenzy. 'Oh! don't say so, sir! I can't bear it! Men have been brought to life before, when unskilful people have given them up for lost; and men have died who might have been restored if proper means had been resorted to. Don't let him lie here, sir, without one effort to save him! This very moment life may be passing away. Do try, sir – do, for heaven's sake!' – And while speaking, she hurriedly chafed, first the forehead and then the breast, of the senseless form before her; and then wildly beat the cold hands, which, when she ceased to hold them, fell listlessly and heavily back on the coverlet.

'It is of no use, my good woman,' said the surgeon, soothingly, as he withdrew his hand from the man's breast. 'Stay – undraw that curtain!'

'Why?' said the woman, starting up.

'Undraw that curtain!' repeated the surgeon in an agitated tone.

'I darkened the room on purpose,' said the woman, throwing herself before him as he rose to undraw it. – 'Oh! sir, have pity on me! If it can be of no use, and he is really dead, do not expose that form to other eyes than mine!'

'This man died no natural or easy death,' said the surgeon. 'I *must* see the body!' With a motion so sudden that the woman hardly knew that he had slipped from beside her, he tore open the curtain, admitted the full light of day and returned to the bedside.

'There has been violence here,' he said, pointing towards the body and gazing intently on the face from which the black veil was now, for the first time, removed. In the excitement of a minute before, the female had thrown off the bonnet and veil, and now stood with her eyes fixed upon him. Her features were those of a woman about fifty, who had once been handsome. Sorrow and weeping had left traces upon them which not time itself would ever have produced without their aid; her face was deadly pale; and there was a nervous contortion of the lip and an unnatural fire in her eye which showed too plainly that her bodily and mental powers had nearly sunk beneath an accumulation of misery.

'There has been violence here,' said the surgeon, preserving his searching glance.

'There has!' replied the woman.

'This man has been murdered.'

'That I call God to witness he has,' said the woman, passionately; 'pitilessly, inhumanly murdered!'

'By whom?' said the surgeon, seizing the woman by the arm.

'Look at the butchers' marks, and then ask me!' she replied.

The surgeon turned his face towards the bed and bent over the body which now lay full in the light of the window. The throat was swollen and a livid mark encircled it. The truth flashed suddenly upon him.

'This is one of the men who were hanged this morning!' he exclaimed, turning away with a shudder.

'It is,' replied the woman, with a cold, unmeaning stare.

'Who was he?' enquired the surgeon.

'*My son,*' rejoined the woman; and fell senseless at his feet.

It was true. A companion, equally guilty with himself, had been acquitted for want of evidence; and this man had been left for death, and executed. To recount the circumstances of the case, at this distant period, must be unnecessary, and might give pain to some persons still alive. The history was an everyday one. The mother was a widow without friends or money, and had denied herself necessaries to bestow them on her orphan boy. That boy, unmindful of her prayers and forgetful of the sufferings she had endured for him – incessant anxiety of mind and voluntary starvation of body – had plunged into a career of dissipation and crime. And this was the result; his own death by the hangman's hands, and his mother's shame and incurable insanity.

For many years after this occurrence, and when profitable and arduous avocations would have led many men to forget that such a miserable being existed, the young surgeon was a daily visitor at the side of the harmless mad woman; not only soothing her by his presence and kindness, but alleviating the rigour of her condition by pecuniary donations for her comfort and support, bestowed with no sparing hand. In the transient gleam of recollection and consciousness which preceded her death, a prayer for his welfare and protection, as fervent as mortal ever breathed, rose from the lips of this poor friendless creature. That prayer flew to heaven and was heard. The blessings he was instrumental in conferring have been repaid to him a thousandfold; but, amid all the honours of rank and station which have since been heaped upon him, and which he has so well earned, he can have no reminiscence more gratifying to his heart than that connected with the black veil.

THE STEAM EXCURSION

Mr Percy Noakes was a law student, inhabiting a set of chambers on the fourth floor in one of those houses in Gray's Inn Square which command an extensive view of the gardens and their usual adjuncts – flaunting nurserymaids and town-made children with parenthetical legs. Mr Percy Noakes was what is generally termed – 'a devilish good fellow'. He had a large circle of acquaintance and seldom dined at his own expense. He used to talk politics to papas, flatter the vanity of mammas, do the amiable to their daughters, make pleasure engagements with their sons and romp with the younger branches. Like those paragons of perfection, advertising footmen out of place, he was always 'willing to make himself generally useful'. If any old lady, whose son was in India, gave a ball, Mr Percy Noakes was master of the ceremonies; if any young lady made a stolen match, Mr Percy Noakes gave her away; if a juvenile wife presented her husband with a blooming cherub, Mr Percy Noakes was either godfather or deputy-godfather; and if any member of a friend's family died, Mr Percy Noakes was invariably to be seen in the second mourning coach, with a white handkerchief to his eyes, sobbing – to use his own appropriate and expressive description – 'like winkin'!'

It may readily be imagined that these numerous avocations were rather calculated to interfere with Mr Percy Noakes's professional studies. Mr Percy Noakes was perfectly aware of the fact, and had, therefore, after mature reflection, made up his mind not to study at all – a laudable determination, to which he adhered in the most praiseworthy manner. His sitting-room presented a strange chaos of dress-gloves, boxing-gloves, caricatures, albums, invitation-cards, foils, cricket-bats, cardboard drawings, paste, gum and fifty other miscellaneous articles, heaped together in the strangest confusion. He was always making something for somebody or planning some party of pleasure, which was his great *forte*. He invariably spoke with astonishing rapidity; was smart, spoffish and eight-and-twenty.

'Splendid idea, 'pon my life!' soliloquised Mr Percy Noakes, over his morning coffee, as his mind reverted to a suggestion which had been thrown out on the previous night by a lady at whose house he had spent the evening. 'Glorious idea! – Mrs Stubbs.'

'Yes, sir,' replied a dirty old woman with an inflamed countenance, emerging from the bedroom with a barrel of dirt and cinders. This was the laundress. 'Did you call, sir?'

'Oh! Mrs Stubbs, I'm going out. If that tailor should call again, you'd better say – you'd better say I'm out of town, and shan't be back for a fortnight; and if that bootmaker should come, tell him I've lost his address or I'd have sent him that little amount. Mind he writes it down; and if Mr Hardy should call – you know Mr Hardy?'

'The funny gentleman, sir?'

'Ah! the funny gentleman. If Mr Hardy should call, say I've gone to Mrs Taunton's about that water-party.'

'Yes, sir.'

'And if any fellow calls and says he's come about a steamer, tell him to be here at five o'clock this afternoon, Mrs Stubbs.'

'Very well, sir.'

Mr Percy Noakes brushed his hat, whisked the crumbs off his inexpressibles with a silk handkerchief, gave the ends of his hair a persuasive roll round his forefinger, and sallied forth for Mrs Taunton's domicile in Great Marlborough Street, where she and her daughters occupied the upper part of a house. She was a good-looking widow of fifty, with the form of a giantess and the mind of a child. The pursuit of pleasure, and some means of killing time, were the sole end of her existence. She doted on her daughters, who were as frivolous as herself.

A general exclamation of satisfaction hailed the arrival of Mr Percy Noakes, who went through the ordinary salutations and threw himself into an easy-chair near the ladies' work-table with the ease of a regularly established friend of the family. Mrs Taunton was busily engaged in planting immense bright bows on every part of a smart cap on which it was possible to stick one; Miss Emily Taunton was making a watch-guard; Miss Sophia was at the piano, practising a new song – poetry by the young officer, or the police-officer, or the custom-house officer, or some other interesting amateur.

'You good creature!' said Mrs Taunton, addressing the gallant Percy. 'You really are a good soul! You've come about the water-party, I know.'

'I should rather suspect I had,' replied Mr Noakes, triumphantly. 'Now, come here, girls, and I'll tell you all about it.' Miss Emily and Miss Sophia advanced to the table.

'Now,' continued Mr Percy Noakes, 'it seems to me that the best way will be to have a committee of ten, to make all the arrangements and manage the whole set-out. Then, I propose that the expenses shall be paid by these ten fellows jointly.'

'Excellent, indeed!' said Mrs Taunton, who highly approved of this part of the arrangements.

'Then, my plan is that each of these ten fellows shall have the power of asking five people. There must be a meeting of the committee, at my chambers, to make all the arrangements, and these people shall be then named; every member of the committee shall have the power of black-balling anyone who is proposed; and one black ball shall exclude that person. This will ensure our having a pleasant party, you know.'

'What a manager you are!' interrupted Mrs Taunton again.

'Charming!' said the lovely Emily.

'I never did!' ejaculated Sophia.

'Yes, I think it'll do,' replied Mr Percy Noakes, who was now quite in his element. 'I think it'll do. Then, you know, we shall go down to the Nore and back; and have a regular capital cold dinner laid out in the cabin before we start, so that everything may be ready without any confusion; and we shall have the lunch laid out, on deck, in those little tea-garden-looking concerns by the paddle-boxes – I don't know what you call 'em. Then, we shall hire a steamer expressly for our party, and a band, and have the deck chalked, and we shall be able to dance quadrilles all day; and then, whoever we know that's musical, you know, why they'll make themselves useful and agreeable; and – and – upon the whole, I really hope we shall have a glorious day, you know!'

The announcement of these arrangements was received with the utmost enthusiasm. Mrs Taunton, Emily and Sophia were loud in their praises.

'Well, but tell me, Percy,' said Mrs Taunton, 'who are the ten gentle-men to be?'

'Oh! I know plenty of fellows who'll be delighted with the scheme,' replied Mr Percy Noakes; 'of course we shall have – '

'Mr Hardy!' interrupted the servant, announcing a visitor. Miss Sophia and Miss Emily hastily assumed the most interesting attitudes that could be adopted on so short a notice.

'How are you?' said a stout gentleman of about forty, pausing at the door in the attitude of an awkward harlequin. This was Mr Hardy, whom we have before described, on the authority of Mrs Stubbs, as 'the funny gentleman'. He was an Astley-Cooperish Joe Miller – a practical joker, immensely popular with married ladies and a general favourite with young men. He was always engaged in some pleasure excursion or other, and delighted in getting somebody into a scrape on such occasions. He could sing comic songs, imitate hackney-coachmen and fowls, play airs on his chin and execute concertos on the Jews'-harp. He always ate and drank most immoderately and was the bosom friend of Mr Percy Noakes. He had a red face, a somewhat husky voice and a tremendous laugh.

'How *are* you?' said this worthy, laughing, as if it were the finest joke in the world to make a morning call, and shaking hands with the ladies with as much vehemence as if their arms had been so many pump-handles.

'You're just the very man I wanted,' said Mr Percy Noakes, who proceeded to explain the cause of his being in requisition.

'Ha! ha! ha!' shouted Hardy, after hearing the statement, and receiving a detailed account of the proposed excursion. 'Oh, capital! glorious! What a day it will be! what fun! – But, I say, when are you going to begin making the arrangements?'

'No time like the present – at once, if you please.'

'Oh, charming!' cried the ladies. 'Pray, do!'

Writing materials were laid before Mr Percy Noakes and the names of the different members of the committee were agreed on, after as much discussion between him and Mr Hardy as if the fate of nations had depended on their appointment. It was then agreed that a meeting should take place at Mr Percy Noakes's chambers on the ensuing Wednesday evening at eight o'clock, and the visitors departed.

Wednesday evening arrived; eight o'clock came and eight members of the committee were punctual in their attendance. Mr Loggins, the solicitor, of Boswell Court, sent an excuse, and Mr Samuel Briggs, the ditto of Furnival's Inn, sent his brother: much to his (the brother's) satisfaction and greatly to the discomfiture of Mr Percy Noakes. Between the Briggses and the Tauntons there existed a degree of implacable hatred, quite unprecedented. The animosity between the Montagues and Capulets was nothing to that which prevailed between these two illustrious houses. Mrs Briggs was a widow, with three daughters and two sons; Mr Samuel, the elder, was an attorney, and Mr Alexander, the younger, was under articles to his brother. They resided in Portland Street, Oxford Street, and moved in the same orbit as the Tauntons –

hence their mutual dislike. If the Miss Briggses appeared in smart bonnets, the Miss Tauntons eclipsed them with smarter. If Mrs Taunton appeared in a cap of all the hues of the rainbow, Mrs Briggs forthwith mounted a toque with all the patterns of the kaleidoscope. If Miss Sophia Taunton learnt a new song, two of the Miss Briggses came out with a new duet. The Tauntons had once gained a temporary triumph with the assistance of a harp, but the Briggses brought three guitars into the field and effectually routed the enemy. There was no end to the rivalry between them.

Now, as Mr Samuel Briggs was a mere machine, a sort of self-acting legal walking-stick; and as the party was known to have originated, however remotely, with Mrs Taunton, the female branches of the Briggs family had arranged that Mr Alexander should attend instead of his brother; and as the said Mr Alexander was deservedly celebrated for possessing all the pertinacity of a bankruptcy-court attorney, combined with the obstinacy of that useful animal which browses on the thistle, he required but little tuition. He was especially enjoined to make himself as disagreeable as possible; and, above all, to black-ball the Tauntons at every hazard.

The proceedings of the evening were opened by Mr Percy Noakes. After successfully urging on the gentlemen present the propriety of their mixing some brandy and water, he briefly stated the object of the meeting, and concluded by observing that the first step must be the selection of a chairman, necessarily possessing some arbitrary – he trusted not unconstitutional – powers, to whom the personal direction of the whole of the arrangements (subject to the approval of the committee) should be confided. A pale young gentleman, in a green stock and spectacles of the same, a member of the honourable society of the Inner Temple, immediately rose for the purpose of proposing Mr Percy Noakes. He had known him long and this he would say, that a more honourable, a more excellent or a better-hearted fellow never existed. – (Hear, hear!) The young gentleman, who was a member of a debating society, took this opportunity of entering into an examination of the state of the English law from the days of William the Conqueror down to the present period; he briefly adverted to the code established by the ancient Druids; slightly glanced at the principles laid down by the Athenian lawgivers; and concluded with a most glowing eulogium on picnics and constitutional rights.

Mr Alexander Briggs opposed the motion. He had the highest esteem for Mr Percy Noakes as an individual, but he did consider that he ought not to be entrusted with these immense powers – (oh, oh!) He believed that in the proposed capacity Mr Percy Noakes would not act fairly, impartially or honourably; but he begged it to be distinctly understood that he said this without the slightest personal disrespect. Mr Hardy defended his honourable friend, in a voice rendered partially unintelligible by emotion and brandy and water. The proposition was put to the vote, and there appearing to be only one dissentient voice, Mr Percy Noakes was declared duly elected and took the chair accordingly.

The business of the meeting now proceeded with rapidity. The chairman delivered in his estimate of the probable expense of the excursion, and everyone present subscribed his portion thereof. The question was put that the *Endeavour* be hired for the occasion; Mr Alexander Briggs moved as an amendment that the word *Fly* be substituted for the word *Endeavour*, but after some debate consented to withdraw his opposition. The important ceremony of balloting then commenced. A tea-caddy was placed on a table in a dark corner of the apartment and everyone was provided with two backgammon men, one black and one white.

The chairman with great solemnity then read the following list of the guests whom he proposed to introduce – Mrs Taunton and two daughters, Mr Wizzle, Mr Simson. The names were respectively balloted for, and Mrs Taunton and her daughters were declared to be black-balled. Mr Percy Noakes and Mr Hardy exchanged glances.

'Is your list prepared, Mr Briggs?' enquired the chairman.

'It is,' replied Alexander, delivering in the following – 'Mrs Briggs and three daughters, Mr Samuel Briggs.' The previous ceremony was repeated, and Mrs Briggs and three daughters were declared to be black-balled. Mr Alexander Briggs looked rather foolish and the remainder of the company appeared somewhat overawed by the mysterious nature of the proceedings.

The balloting proceeded; but, one little circumstance which Mr Percy Noakes had not originally foreseen, prevented the system from working quite as well as he had anticipated. Everybody was black-balled. Mr Alexander Briggs, by way of retaliation, exercised his power of exclusion in every instance, and the result was that after three hours had been consumed in hard balloting, the names of only three gentlemen were found to have been agreed to. In this dilemma what was to be done?

either the whole plan must fall to the ground, or a compromise must be effected. The latter alternative was preferable; and Mr Percy Noakes therefore proposed that the form of balloting should be dispensed with and that every gentleman should merely be required to state whom he intended to bring. The proposal was acceded to; the Tauntons and the Briggses were reinstated; and the party was formed.

The next Wednesday was fixed for the eventful day, and it was unanimously resolved that every member of the committee should wear a piece of blue sarsenet ribbon round his left arm. It appeared from the statement of Mr Percy Noakes that the boat belonged to the General Steam Navigation Company, and was then lying off the Custom House; and, as he proposed that the dinner and wines should be provided by an eminent city purveyor, it was arranged that Mr Percy Noakes should be on board by seven o'clock to superintend the arrangements, and that the remaining members of the committee, together with the company generally, should be expected to join her by nine o'clock. More brandy and water was despatched; several speeches were made by the different law students present; thanks were voted to the chairman; and the meeting separated.

The weather had been beautiful up to this period, and beautiful it continued to be. Sunday passed over and Mr Percy Noakes became unusually fidgety – rushing, constantly, to and from the Steam Packet Wharf, to the astonishment of the clerks and the great emolument of the Holborn cabmen. Tuesday arrived and the anxiety of Mr Percy Noakes knew no bounds. He was every instant running to the window to look out for clouds; and Mr Hardy astonished the whole square by practising a new comic song for the occasion in the chairman's chambers.

Uneasy were the slumbers of Mr Percy Noakes that night; he tossed and tumbled about, and had confused dreams of steamers starting off, and gigantic clocks with the hands pointing to a quarter-past nine, and the ugly face of Mr Alexander Briggs looking over the boat's side and grinning, as if in derision of his fruitless attempts to move. He made a violent effort to get on board, and awoke. The bright sun was shining cheerfully into the bedroom and Mr Percy Noakes started up for his watch in the dreadful expectation of finding his worst dreams realised.

It was just five o'clock. He calculated the time – he should be a good half-hour dressing himself; and as it was a lovely morning, and the tide would be then running down, he would walk leisurely to Strand Lane and have a boat to the Custom House.

He dressed himself, took a hasty apology for a breakfast and sallied forth. The streets looked as lonely and deserted as if they had been crowded, overnight, for the last time. Here and there, an early apprentice, with quenched-looking sleepy eyes, was taking down the shutters of a shop; and a policeman or milkwoman might occasionally be seen pacing slowly along; but the servants had not yet begun to clean the doors or light the kitchen fires and London looked the picture of desolation. At the corner of a by-street, near Temple Bar, was stationed a 'street-breakfast'. The coffee was boiling over a charcoal fire and large slices of bread and butter were piled one upon the other, like deals in a timberyard. The company were seated on a form, which, with a view both to security and comfort, was placed against a neighbouring wall. Two young men, whose uproarious mirth and disordered dress bespoke the conviviality of the preceding evening, were treating three 'ladies' and an Irish labourer. A little sweep was standing at a short distance, casting a longing eye at the tempting delicacies; and a policeman was watching the group from the opposite side of the street. The wan looks and gaudy finery of the thinly-clad women contrasted as strangely with the gay sunlight as did their forced merriment with the boisterous hilarity of the two young men, who, now and then, varied their amusements by 'bonneting' the proprietor of this itinerant coffee-house.

Mr Percy Noakes walked briskly by, and when he turned down Strand Lane, and caught a glimpse of the glistening water, he thought he had never felt so important or so happy in his life.

'Boat, sir?' cried one of the three watermen who were mopping out their boats, and all whistling. 'Boat, sir?'

'No,' replied Mr Percy Noakes, rather sharply; for the enquiry was not made in a manner at all suitable to his dignity.

'Would you prefer a wessel, sir?' enquired another, to the infinite delight of the 'Jack-in-the-water'.

Mr Percy Noakes replied with a look of supreme contempt.

'Did you want to be put on board a steamer, sir?' enquired an old fireman-waterman, very confidentially. He was dressed in a faded red suit, just the colour of the cover of a very old *Court Guide*.

'Yes, make haste – the *Endeavour* – off the Custom House.'

'*Endeavour*!' cried the man who had convulsed the 'Jack' before. 'Vy, I see the *Endeavour* go up half an hour ago.'

'So did I,' said another; 'and I should think she'd gone down by this time, for she's a precious sight too full of ladies and gen'lemen.'

Mr Percy Noakes affected to disregard these representations, and stepped into the boat, which the old man, by dint of scrambling and shoving and grating, had brought up to the causeway. 'Shove her off!' cried Mr Percy Noakes, and away the boat glided down the river, Mr Percy Noakes seated on the recently mopped seat and the watermen at the stairs offering to bet him any reasonable sum that he'd never reach the 'Custum-us'.

'Here she is, by Jove!' said the delighted Percy, as they ran alongside the *Endeavour*.

'Hold hard!' cried the steward over the side, and Mr Percy Noakes jumped on board.

'Hope you will find everything as you wished, sir. She looks uncommon well this morning.'

'She does, indeed,' replied the manager, in a state of ecstasy which it is impossible to describe. The deck was scrubbed, and the seats were scrubbed, and there was a bench for the band, and a place for dancing, and a pile of camp-stools, and an awning; and then Mr Percy Noakes bustled down below, and there were the pastrycook's men, and the steward's wife, laying out the dinner on two tables the whole length of the cabin; and then Mr Percy Noakes took off his coat and rushed backwards and forwards, doing nothing but quite convinced he was assisting everybody; and the steward's wife laughed till she cried, and Mr Percy Noakes panted with the violence of his exertions. And then the bell at London Bridge wharf rang; and a Margate boat was just starting; and a Gravesend boat was just starting, and people shouted, and porters ran down the steps with luggage that would crush any men but porters; and sloping boards, with bits of wood nailed on them, were placed between the outside boat and the inside boat; and the passengers ran along them, and looked like so many fowls coming out of an area; and then the bell ceased, and the boards were taken away, and the boats started, and the whole scene was one of the most delightful bustle and confusion.

The time wore on; half-past eight o'clock arrived; the pastrycook's men went ashore; the dinner was completely laid out; and Mr Percy Noakes locked the principal cabin, and put the key in his pocket, in order that it might be suddenly disclosed, in all its magnificence, to the eyes of the astonished company. The band came on board and so did the wine.

Ten minutes to nine, and the committee embarked in a body. There was Mr Hardy, in a blue jacket and waistcoat, white trousers, silk stockings and pumps – in full aquatic costume, with a straw hat on his head and an immense telescope under his arm; and there was the young gentleman with the green spectacles, in nankeen inexplicables, with a ditto waistcoat and bright buttons, like the pictures of Paul – not the saint but he of Virginia notoriety. The remainder of the committee, dressed in white hats, light jackets, waistcoats and trousers, looked something between waiters and West India planters.

Nine o'clock struck, and the company arrived in shoals. Mr Samuel Briggs, Mrs Briggs and the Misses Briggs made their appearance in a smart private wherry. The three guitars, in their respective dark green cases, were carefully stowed away in the bottom of the boat, accompanied by two immense portfolios of music, which it would take at least a week's incessant playing to get through. The Tauntons arrived at the same moment with more music, and a lion – a gentleman with a bass voice and an incipient red moustache. The colours of the Taunton party were pink; those of the Briggses a light blue. The Tauntons had artificial flowers in their bonnets; here the Briggses gained a decided advantage – they wore feathers.

'How d'ye do, dear?' said the Misses Briggs to the Misses Taunton. (The word 'dear' among girls is frequently synonymous with 'wretch'.)

'Quite well, thank you, dear,' replied the Misses Taunton to the Misses Briggs; and then, there was such a kissing, and congratulating, and shaking of hands, as might have induced one to suppose that the two families were the best friends in the world, instead of each wishing the other overboard, as they most sincerely did.

Mr Percy Noakes received the visitors, and bowed to the strange gentleman, as if he should like to know who he was. This was just what Mrs Taunton wanted. Here was an opportunity to astonish the Briggses.

'Oh! I beg your pardon,' said the general of the Taunton party, with a careless air. – 'Captain Helves – Mr Percy Noakes – Mrs Briggs – Captain Helves.'

Mr Percy Noakes bowed very low, the gallant captain did the same with all due ferocity and the Briggses were clearly overcome.

'Our friend, Mr Wizzle, being unfortunately prevented from coming,' resumed Mrs Taunton, 'I did myself the pleasure of bringing the captain, whose musical talents I knew would be a great acquisition.'

'In the name of the committee I have to thank you for doing so and to offer you welcome, sir,' replied Percy. (Here the scraping was renewed.) 'But pray be seated – won't you walk aft? Captain, will you conduct Miss Taunton? – Miss Briggs, will you allow me?'

'Where could they have picked up that military man?' enquired Mrs Briggs of Miss Kate Briggs, as they followed the little party.

'I can't imagine,' replied Miss Kate, bursting with vexation; for the very fierce air with which the gallant captain regarded the company had impressed her with a high sense of his importance.

Boat after boat came alongside and guest after guest arrived. The invites had been excellently arranged: Mr Percy Noakes having considered it as important that the number of young men should exactly tally with that of the young ladies as that the quantity of knives on board should be in precise proportion to the forks.

'Now, is everyone on board?' enquired Mr Percy Noakes. The committee (who, with their bits of blue ribbon, looked as if they were all going to be bled) bustled about to ascertain the fact, and reported that they might safely start.

'Go on!' cried the master of the boat from the top of one of the paddle-boxes.

'Go on!' echoed the boy, who was stationed over the hatchway to pass the directions down to the engineer; and away went the vessel with that agreeable noise which is peculiar to steamers and which is composed of a mixture of creaking, gushing, clanging and snorting.

'Hoi–oi–oi–oi–oi–oi–o–i–i–i!' shouted half a dozen voices from a boat a quarter of a mile astern.

'Ease her!' cried the captain; 'do these people belong to us, sir?'

'Noakes,' exclaimed Hardy, who had been looking at every object far and near through the large telescope, 'it's the Fleetwoods and the Wakefields – and two children with them, by Jove!'

'What a shame to bring children!' said everybody; 'how very inconsiderate!'

'I say, it would be a good joke to pretend not to see 'em, wouldn't it?' suggested Hardy, to the immense delight of the company generally. A council of war was hastily held, and it was resolved that the newcomers should be taken on board, on Mr Hardy solemnly pledging himself to tease the children during the whole of the day.

'Stop her!' cried the captain.

'Stop her!' repeated the boy; whizz went the steam, and all the young ladies, as in duty bound, screamed in concert. They were only appeased by the assurance of the martial Helves that the escape of steam consequent on stopping a vessel was seldom attended with any great loss of human life.

Two men ran to the side; and after some shouting and swearing and angling for the wherry with a boat-hook, Mr Fleetwood and Mrs Fleetwood and Master Fleetwood and Mr Wakefield and Mrs Wakefield and Miss Wakefield were safely deposited on the deck. The girl was about six years old, the boy about four; the former was dressed in a white frock with a pink sash and dog's-eared-looking little spencer, a straw bonnet and a green veil, six inches by three and a half; the latter, was attired for the occasion in a nankeen frock, between the bottom of which and the top of his plaid socks a considerable portion of two small mottled legs was discernible. He had a light blue cap with a gold band and tassel on his head, and a damp piece of gingerbread in his hand, with which he had slightly embossed his countenance.

The boat once more started off; the band played 'Off She Goes': the major part of the company conversed cheerfully in groups; and the old gentlemen walked up and down the deck in pairs, as perseveringly and gravely as if they were doing a march against time for an immense stake. They ran briskly down the Pool; the gentlemen pointed out the Docks, the Thames Police-Office and other elegant public edifices; and the young ladies exhibited a proper display of horror at the appearance of the coal-whippers and ballast-heavers. Mr Hardy told stories to the married ladies, at which they laughed very much in their pocket-handkerchiefs, and hit him on the knuckles with their fans, declaring him to be 'a naughty man – a shocking creature' – and so forth; and Captain Helves gave slight descriptions of battles and duels, with a most bloodthirsty air, which made him the admiration of the women and the envy of the men. Quadrilling commenced; Captain Helves danced one set with Miss Emily Taunton, and another set with Miss Sophia Taunton. Mrs Taunton was in ecstasies. The victory appeared to be complete; but alas! the inconstancy of man! Having performed this necessary duty, he attached himself solely to Miss Julia Briggs, with whom he danced no less than three sets consecutively, and from whose side he evinced no intention of stirring for the remainder of the day.

Mr Hardy having played one or two very brilliant fantasias on the

Jews'-harp, and having frequently repeated the exquisitely amusing joke of slily chalking a large cross on the back of some member of the committee, Mr Percy Noakes expressed his hope that some of their musical friends would oblige the company by a display of their abilities.

'Perhaps,' he said in a very insinuating manner, 'Captain Helves will oblige us?' Mrs Taunton's countenance lighted up, for the captain only sang duets, and couldn't sing them with anybody but one of her daughters.

'Really,' said that warlike individual, 'I should be very happy, but – '

'Oh! pray do,' cried all the young ladies.

'Miss Emily, have you any objection to join in a duet?'

'Oh! not the slightest,' returned the young lady, in a tone which clearly showed she had the greatest possible objection.

'Shall I accompany you, dear?' enquired one of the Miss Briggses, with the bland intention of spoiling the effect.

'Very much obliged to you, Miss Briggs,' sharply retorted Mrs Taunton, who saw through the manoeuvre; 'my daughters always sing without accompaniments.'

'And without voices,' tittered Mrs Briggs, in a low tone.

'Perhaps – ' said Mrs Taunton, reddening, for she guessed the tenor of the observation though she had not heard it clearly – 'Perhaps it would be as well for some people, if their voices were not quite so audible as they are to other people.'

'And, perhaps, if gentlemen who are kidnapped to pay attention to some persons' daughters, had not sufficient discernment to pay attention to other persons' daughters,' returned Mrs Briggs, 'some persons would not be so ready to display that ill-temper which, thank God, distinguishes them from other persons.'

'Persons!' ejaculated Mrs Taunton.

'Persons,' replied Mrs Briggs.

'Insolence!'

'Creature!'

'Hush! hush!' interrupted Mr Percy Noakes, who was one of the very few by whom this dialogue had been overheard. 'Hush! – pray, silence for the duet.'

After a great deal of preparatory crowing and humming, the captain began the following duet from the opera of *Paul and Virginia*, in that grunting tone in which a man gets down, heaven knows where, without the remotest chance of ever getting up again. This, in private circles, is frequently designated 'a bass voice'.

> 'See [sang the captain] from o–ce–an ri–sing
> Bright flames the or–b of d–ay.
> From yon gro–ove, the varied so–ongs – '

Here the singer was interrupted by varied cries of the most dreadful description, proceeding from some grove in the immediate vicinity of the starboard paddle-box.

'My child!' screamed Mrs Fleetwood. 'My child! it is his voice I know it.'

Mr Fleetwood, accompanied by several gentlemen, here rushed to the quarter from whence the noise proceeded, and an exclamation of horror burst from the company; the general impression being that the little innocent had either got his head in the water or his legs in the machinery.

'What is the matter?' shouted the agonised father, as he returned with the child in his arms.

'Oh! oh! oh!' screamed the small sufferer again.

'What is the matter, dear?' enquired the father once more – hastily stripping off the nankeen frock for the purpose of ascertaining whether the child had one bone which was not smashed to pieces.

'Oh! oh! – I'm so frightened!'

'What at, dear? – what at?' said the mother, soothing the sweet infant.

'Oh! he's been making such dreadful faces at me,' cried the boy, relapsing into convulsions at the bare recollection.

'He! – who?' cried everybody, crowding round him.

'Oh! – him!' replied the child, pointing at Hardy, who affected to be the most concerned of the whole group.

The real state of the case at once flashed upon the minds of all present, with the exception of the Fleetwoods and the Wakefields. The facetious Hardy, in fulfilment of his promise, had watched the child to a remote part of the vessel, and, suddenly appearing before him with the most awful contortions of visage, had produced his paroxysm of terror. Of course, he now observed that it was hardly necessary for him to deny the accusation; and the unfortunate little victim was accordingly led below, after receiving sundry thumps on the head from both his parents for having the wickedness to tell a story.

This little interruption having been adjusted, the captain resumed and Miss Emily chimed in, in due course. The duet was loudly applauded, and, certainly, the perfect independence of the parties deserved great commendation. Miss Emily sang her part, without the slightest reference to the captain; and the captain sang so loud, that he had not the slightest idea what was being done by his partner. After having gone through the last few eighteen or nineteen bars by himself, therefore, he acknowledged the plaudits of the circle with that air of self-denial which men usually assume when they think they have done something to astonish the company.

'Now,' said Mr Percy Noakes, who had just ascended from the fore-cabin where he had been busily engaged in decanting the wine, 'if the Misses Briggs will oblige us with something before dinner, I am sure we shall be very much delighted.'

One of those hums of admiration followed the suggestion which one frequently hears in society when nobody has the most distant notion what he is expressing his approval of. The three Misses Briggs looked modestly at their mamma, and the mamma looked approvingly at her daughters, and Mrs Taunton looked scornfully at all of them. The Misses Briggs asked for their guitars, and several gentlemen seriously damaged the cases in their anxiety to present them. Then there was a very interesting production of three little keys for the aforesaid cases, and a melodramatic expression of horror at finding a string broken, and a vast deal of screwing and tightening and winding and tuning during which Mrs Briggs expatiated to those near her on the immense difficulty of playing a guitar and hinted at the wondrous proficiency of her daughters in that mystic art. Mrs Taunton whispered to a neighbour that it was 'quite sickening!' and the Misses Taunton looked as if they knew how to play but disdained to do it.

At length, the Misses Briggs began in real earnest. It was a new Spanish composition, for three voices and three guitars. The effect was electrical. All eyes were turned upon the captain, who was reported to have once passed through Spain with his regiment, and who must be well acquainted with the national music. He was in raptures. This was sufficient; the trio was encored; the applause was universal; and never had the Tauntons suffered such a complete defeat.

'Bravo! bravo!' ejaculated the captain; – 'bravo!'

'Pretty! isn't it, sir?' enquired Mr Samuel Briggs, with the air of a self-satisfied showman. By the by, these were the first words he had been heard to utter since he left Boswell Court the evening before.

'De–lightful!' returned the captain, with a flourish and a military cough; – 'de–lightful!'

'Sweet instrument!' said an old gentleman with a bald head, who had been trying all the morning to look through a telescope inside the glass of which Mr Hardy had fixed a large black wafer.

'Did you ever hear a Portuguese tambourine?' enquired that jocular individual.

'Did *you* ever hear a tom-tom, sir?' sternly enquired the captain, who lost no opportunity of showing off his travels, real or pretended.

'A what?' asked Hardy, rather taken aback.

'A tom-tom.'

'Never!'

'Nor a gum-gum?'

'Never!'

'What *is* a gum-gum?' eagerly enquired several young ladies.

'When I was in the East Indies,' replied the captain – (here was a discovery – he had been in the East Indies!) – 'when I was in the East Indies, I was once stopping a few thousand miles up the country, on a visit at the house of a very particular friend of mine, Ram Chowdar Doss Azuph al Bowlar – a devilish pleasant fellow. As we were enjoying our hookahs, one evening, in the cool veranda in front of his villa, we were rather surprised by the sudden appearance of thirty-four of his Kit-ma-gars (for he had rather a large establishment there), accompanied by an equal number of Con-su-mars, approaching the house with a threatening aspect and beating a tom-tom. The Ram started up – '

'Who?' enquired the bald gentleman, intensely interested.

'The Ram – Ram Chowdar – '

'Oh!' said the old gentleman, 'beg your pardon; pray go on.'

' – Started up and drew a pistol. "Helves," said he, "my boy," he always called me, my boy – "Helves," said he, "do you hear that tom-tom?" "I do," said I. His countenance, which before was pale, assumed a most frightful appearance; his whole visage was distorted and his frame shaken by violent emotions. "Do you see that gum-gum?" said he. "No," said I, staring about me. "You don't?" said he. "No, I'll be damned if I do," said I; "and what's more, I don't know what a gum-gum is," said I. I really thought the Ram would have dropped. He drew me aside, and with an expression of agony I shall never forget, said in a low whisper – '

'Dinner's on the table, ladies,' interrupted the steward's wife.

At length, the Misses Briggs began in real earnest. The effect was electrical.

'Will you allow me?' said the captain, immediately suiting the action to the word, and escorting Miss Julia Briggs to the cabin, with as much ease as if he had finished the story.

'What an extraordinary circumstance!' ejaculated the same old gentleman, preserving his listening attitude.

'What a traveller!' said the young ladies.

'What a singular name!' exclaimed the gentlemen, rather confused by the coolness of the whole affair.

'I wish he had finished the story,' said an old lady. 'I wonder what a gum-gum really is?'

'By Jove!' exclaimed Hardy, who until now had been lost in utter amazement. 'I don't know what it may be in India, but in England I think a gum-gum has very much the same meaning as a humbug.'

'How illiberal! how envious!' cried everybody, as they made for the cabin, fully impressed with a belief in the captain's amazing adventures. Helves was the sole lion for the remainder of the day – impudence and the marvellous are pretty sure passports to any society.

The party had by this time reached their destination and put about on their return home. The wind, which had been with them the whole day, was now directly in their teeth; the weather had become gradually more and more overcast and the sky, water and shore were all of that dull, heavy, uniform lead-colour which housepainters daub in the first instance over a street-door which is gradually approaching a state of convalescence. It had been 'spitting' with rain for the last half-hour and now began to pour in good earnest. The wind was freshening very fast, and the waterman at the wheel had unequivocally expressed his opinion that there would shortly be a squall. A slight emotion on the part of the vessel, now and then, seemed to suggest the possibility of its pitching to a very uncomfortable extent in the event of its blowing harder; and every timber began to creak, as if the boat were an overladen clothes-basket. Seasickness, however, is like a belief in ghosts – everyone entertains some misgivings on the subject, but few will acknowledge any. The majority of the company, therefore, endeavoured to look peculiarly happy, feeling all the while especially miserable.

'Don't it rain?' enquired the old gentleman before noticed, when, by dint of squeezing and jamming, they were all seated at table.

'I think it does – a little,' replied Mr Percy Noakes, who could hardly hear himself speak in consequence of the pattering on the deck.

'Don't it blow?' enquired someone else.

'No, I don't think it does,' responded Hardy, sincerely wishing that he could persuade himself that it did not; for he sat near the door and was almost blown off his seat.

'It'll soon clear up,' said Mr Percy Noakes, in a cheerful tone.

'Oh, certainly!' ejaculated the committee generally.

'No doubt of it!' said the remainder of the company, whose attention was now pretty well engrossed by the serious business of eating, carving, taking wine and so forth.

The throbbing motion of the engine was but too perceptible. There was a large, substantial, cold boiled leg of mutton at the bottom of the table, shaking like blancmange; a previously hearty sirloin of beef looked as if it had been suddenly seized with the palsy; and some tongues, which were placed on dishes rather too large for them, went through the most surprising evolutions, darting from side to side and from end to end like a fly in an inverted wineglass. Then the sweets shook and trembled, till it was quite impossible to help them and people gave up the attempt in despair; and the pigeon-pies looked as if the birds, whose legs were stuck outside, were trying to get them in. The table vibrated and started like a feverish pulse, and the very legs were convulsed – everything was shaking and jarring. The beams in the roof of the cabin seemed as if they were put there for the sole purpose of giving people headaches, and several elderly gentlemen became ill-tempered in consequence. As fast as the steward put the fire-irons up, they *would* fall down again; and the more the ladies and gentlemen tried to sit comfortably on their seats, the more the seats seemed to slide away from the ladies and gentlemen. Several ominous demands were made for small glasses of brandy; the countenances of the company gradually underwent most extraordinary changes; one gentle-man was observed suddenly to rush from table without the slightest ostensible reason, and dart up the steps with incredible swiftness: thereby greatly damaging both himself and the steward, who happened to be coming down at the same moment.

The cloth was removed; the dessert was laid on the table; and the glasses were filled. The motion of the boat increased; several members of the party began to feel rather vague and misty, and looked as if they had only just got up. The young gentleman with the spectacles, who had been in a fluctuating state for some time – at one moment bright and at another dismal, like a revolving light on the sea-coast – rashly announced his wish to propose a toast. After several ineffectual attempts to preserve his perpendicular, the young gentleman, having managed to hook himself to the centre leg of the table with his left hand, proceeded as follows –

'Ladies and gentlemen. A gentleman is among us – I may say a stranger – ' (here some painful thought seemed to strike the orator; he paused, and looked extremely odd) – 'whose talents, whose travels, whose cheerfulness – '

'I beg your pardon, Edkins,' hastily interrupted Mr Percy Noakes; 'Hardy, what's the matter?'

'Nothing,' replied the 'funny gentleman', who had just life enough left to utter two consecutive syllables.

'Will you have some brandy?'

'No!' replied Hardy in a tone of great indignation, and looking as comfortable as Temple Bar in a Scotch mist; 'what should I want brandy for?'

'Will you go on deck?'

'No, I will *not*.' This was said with a most determined air, and in a voice which might have been taken for an imitation of anything; it was quite as much like a guinea-pig as a bassoon.

'I beg your pardon, Edkins,' said the courteous Percy; 'I thought our friend was ill. Pray go on.'

A pause.

'Pray go on.'

'Mr Edkins *is* gone,' cried somebody.

'I beg your pardon, sir,' said the steward, running up to Mr Percy Noakes, 'I beg your pardon, sir, but the gentleman as just went on deck – him with the green spectacles – is uncommon bad, to be sure; and the young man as played the wiolin says that unless he has some brandy he can't answer for the consequences. He says he has a wife and two children, whose wery subsistence depends on his breaking a wessel, and he expects to do so every moment. The flageolet's been wery ill, but he's better, only he's in a dreadful prusperation.'

All disguise was now useless; the company staggered on deck; the gentlemen tried to see nothing but the clouds; and the ladies, muffled up in such shawls and cloaks as they had brought with them, lay about on the seats and under the seats in the most wretched condition. Never was such a blowing, and raining, and pitching, and tossing, endured by any pleasure party before. Several remonstrances were sent down below on

The countenances of the company gradually underwent most extraordinary changes; one gentleman was observed suddenly to rush from table without the slightest ostensible reason

the subject of Master Fleetwood, but they were totally unheeded in consequence of the indisposition of his natural protectors. That interesting child screamed at the top of his voice until he had no voice left to scream with; and then Miss Wakefield began and screamed for the remainder of the passage.

Mr Hardy was observed, some hours afterwards, in an attitude which induced his friends to suppose that he was busily engaged in contemplating the beauties of the deep; they only regretted that his taste for the picturesque should lead him to remain so long in a position very injurious at all times, but especially so to an individual labouring under a tendency of blood to the head.

The party arrived off the Custom House at about two o'clock on the Thursday morning, dispirited and worn out. The Tauntons were too ill to quarrel with the Briggses, and the Briggses were too wretched to annoy the Tauntons. One of the guitar-cases was lost on its passage to a hackney-coach, and Mrs Briggs has not scrupled to state that the Tauntons bribed a porter to throw it down an area. Mr Alexander Briggs opposes vote by ballot – he says from personal experience of its inefficacy; and Mr Samuel Briggs, whenever he is asked to express his sentiments on the point, says he has no opinion on that or any other subject.

Mr Edkins – the young gentleman in the green spectacles – makes a speech on every occasion on which a speech can possibly be made: the eloquence of which can only be equalled by its length. In the event of his not being previously appointed to a judgeship, it is probable that he will practise as a barrister in the New Central Criminal Court.

Captain Helves continued his attention to Miss Julia Briggs, whom he might possibly have espoused if it had not unfortunately happened that Mr Samuel arrested him, in the way of business, pursuant to instructions received from Messrs Scroggins and Payne, whose town-debts the gallant captain had condescended to collect, but whose accounts, with the indiscretion sometimes peculiar to military minds, he had omitted to keep with that dull accuracy which custom has rendered necessary. Mrs Taunton complains that she has been much deceived in him. He introduced himself to the family on board a Gravesend steam-packet, and certainly, therefore, ought to have proved respectable.

Mr Percy Noakes is as light-hearted and careless as ever.

THE GREAT WINGLEBURY DUEL

The little town of Great Winglebury is exactly forty-two miles and three-quarters from Hyde Park corner. It has a long, straggling, quiet high-street, with a great black and white clock at a small red townhall, halfway up – a marketplace – a cage – an assembly room – a church – a bridge – a chapel – a theatre – a library – an inn – a pump – and a post-office. Tradition tells of a 'Little Winglebury', down some cross-road about two miles off; and, as a square mass of dirty paper, supposed to have been originally intended for a letter, with certain tremulous characters inscribed thereon, in which a lively imagination might trace a remote resemblance to the word 'Little', was once stuck up to be owned in the sunny window of the Great Winglebury post-office, from which it only disappeared when it fell to pieces with dust and extreme old age, there would appear to be some foundation for the legend. Common belief is inclined to bestow the name upon a little hole at the end of a muddy lane about a couple of miles long, colonised by one wheelwright, four paupers and a beer-shop; but, even this authority, slight as it is, must be regarded with extreme suspicion, inasmuch as the inhabitants of the hole aforesaid concur in opining that it never had any name at all, from the earliest ages down to the present day.

The Winglebury Arms, in the centre of the high-street, opposite the small building with the big clock, is the principal inn of Great Winglebury – the commercial inn, posting-house and excise-office, the 'Blue' house at every election and the judge's house at every assizes. It is the headquarters of the Gentlemen's Whist Club of Winglebury Blues (so called in opposition to the Gentlemen's Whist Club of Winglebury Buffs, held at the other house, a little farther down); and whenever a juggler, or waxwork man, or concert-giver, takes Great Winglebury in his circuit, it is immediately placarded all over the town that Mr So-and-so, 'trusting to that liberal support which the inhabitants of Great Winglebury have long been so liberal in bestowing, has at a great expense engaged the elegant and commodious assembly-rooms attached to the Winglebury Arms'. The house is a large one, with a red brick and stone front; a pretty spacious hall, ornamented with evergreen plants, terminates in a perspective view of the bar, and a glass case, in which are displayed a choice variety of delicacies ready for dressing, to catch the eye of a newcomer the moment he enters, and excite his appetite to the highest possible pitch. Opposite doors lead to the 'coffee' and 'commercial' rooms; and a great wide, rambling staircase – three stairs and a landing – four stairs and another landing – one step and another landing – half a dozen stairs and another landing – and so on – conducts to galleries of bedrooms, and labyrinths of sitting-rooms, denominated 'private', where you may enjoy yourself, as privately as you can in any place where some bewildered being walks into your room every five minutes by mistake, and then walks out again to open all the doors along the gallery until he finds his own.

Such is the Winglebury Arms, at this day, and such was the Winglebury Arms some time since – no matter when – two or three minutes before the arrival of the London stage. Four horses with cloths on – change for a coach – were standing quietly at the corner of the yard surrounded by a listless group of post-boys in shiny hats and smock-frocks, engaged in discussing the merits of the cattle; half a dozen ragged boys were standing a little apart, listening with evident interest to the conversation of these worthies; and a few loungers were collected round the horse-trough awaiting the arrival of the coach.

The day was hot and sunny, the town in the zenith of its dullness, and with the exception of these few idlers, not a living creature was to be seen. Suddenly, the loud notes of a key-bugle broke the monotonous stillness of the street; in came the coach, rattling over the uneven paving with a noise startling enough to stop even the large-faced clock itself. Down got the outsides, up went the windows in all directions, out came the waiters, up started the ostlers and the loungers and the post-boys and the ragged boys, as if they were electrified – unstrapping and unchaining and unbuckling and dragging willing horses out, and forcing reluctant horses in, and making a most exhilarating bustle. 'Lady inside, here!' said the guard. 'Please to alight, ma'am,' said the waiter. 'Private sitting-room?' interrogated the lady. 'Certainly, ma'am,' responded the chambermaid. 'Nothing but these 'ere trunks, ma'am?' enquired the guard. 'Nothing more,' replied the lady. Up got the outsides again and the guard and the coachman; off came the cloths, with a jerk. 'All right,' was the cry; and away they went. The loungers lingered a minute or two in the road, watching the coach until it turned the corner, and then loitered away one by one. The street was clear again, and the town, by contrast, quieter than ever.

'Lady in number twenty-five,' screamed the landlady. 'Thomas!'

'Yes, ma'am.'

'Letter just been left for the gentleman in number nineteen. Boots at the Lion left it. No answer.'

'Letter for you, sir,' said Thomas, depositing the letter on number nineteen's table.

'For me?' said number nineteen, turning from the window, out of which he had been surveying the scene just described.

'Yes, sir' – (waiters always speak in hints, and never utter complete sentences) – 'yes, sir – Boots at the Lion, sir – Bar, sir – Missis said number nineteen, sir – Alexander Trott Esq., sir? – Your card at the bar, sir, I think, sir?'

'My name *is* Trott,' replied number nineteen, breaking the seal. 'You may go, waiter.' The waiter pulled down the window-blind, and then pulled it up again – for a regular waiter must do something before he leaves the room – adjusted the glasses on the sideboard, brushed a place that was *not* dusty, rubbed his hands very hard, walked stealthily to the door and evaporated.

There was, evidently, something in the contents of the letter of a nature, if not wholly unexpected, certainly extremely disagreeable. Mr Alexander Trott laid it down, and took it up again, and walked about the room on particular squares of the carpet, and even attempted, though unsuccessfully, to whistle an air. It wouldn't do. He threw himself into a chair, and read the following epistle aloud –

'*Blue Lion and Stomach-Warmer*
'*Great Winglebury*
'*Wednesday morning*

'Sɪʀ – Immediately on discovering your intentions, I left our counting-house and followed you. I know the purport of your journey; that journey shall never be completed.

'I have no friend here, just now, on whose secrecy I can rely. This shall be no obstacle to my revenge. Neither shall Emily Brown be exposed to the mercenary solicitations of a scoundrel, odious in her eyes and contemptible in everybody else's; nor will I tamely submit to the clandestine attacks of a base umbrella-maker.

'Sir. From Great Winglebury church a footpath leads through four meadows to a retired spot known to the townspeople as Stiffun's Acre.

[Mr Trott shuddered.] I shall be waiting there alone, at twenty minutes before six o'clock tomorrow morning. Should I be disappointed in seeing you there, I will do myself the pleasure of calling with a horsewhip.

'HORACE HUNTER

'PS There is a gunsmith's in the high-street; and they won't sell gunpowder after dark – you understand me.

'PPS You had better not order your breakfast in the morning until you have met me. It may be an unnecessary expense.'

'Desperate-minded villain! I knew how it would be!' ejaculated the terrified Trott. 'I always told father that once start me on this expedition, and Hunter would pursue me like the Wandering Jew. It's bad enough as it is, to marry with the old people's commands and without the girl's consent; but what will Emily think of me if I go down there breathless with running away from this infernal salamander? What *shall* I do? What *can* I do? If I go back to the City, I'm disgraced for ever – lose the girl – and, what's more, lose the money too. Even if I did go on to the Browns' by the coach, Hunter would be after me in a post-chaise; and if I go to this place, this Stiffun's Acre' (another shudder), 'I'm as good as dead. I've seen him hit the man at the Pall Mall shooting-gallery in the second buttonhole of the waistcoat, five times out of every six, and when he didn't hit him there, he hit him in the head.' With this consolatory reminiscence Mr Alexander Trott again ejaculated, 'What shall I do?'

Long and weary were his reflections, as, burying his face in his hands, he sat ruminating on the best course to be pursued. His mental direction-post pointed to London. He thought of the 'governor's' anger, and the loss of the fortune which the paternal Brown had promised the paternal Trott his daughter should contribute to the coffers of his son. Then the words 'To Brown's' were legibly inscribed on the said direction-post, but Horace Hunter's denunciation rang in his ears; last of all it bore, in red letters, the words, 'To Stiffun's Acre'; and then Mr Alexander Trott decided on adopting a plan which he presently matured.

First and foremost, he despatched the under-boots to the Blue Lion and Stomach-Warmer, with a gentlemanly note to Mr Horace Hunter intimating that he thirsted for his destruction and would do himself the pleasure of slaughtering him next morning, without fail. He then wrote another letter, and requested the attendance of the other boots – for they kept a pair. A modest knock at the room door was heard. 'Come in,' said Mr Trott. A man thrust in a red head with one eye in it, and being again desired to 'come in', brought in the body and the legs to which the head belonged and a fur cap which belonged to the head.

'You are the upper-boots, I think?' enquired Mr Trott.

'Yes, I am the upper-boots,' replied a voice from inside a velveteen case with mother-of-pearl buttons – 'that is, I'm the boots as b'longs to the house; the other man's my man, as goes errands and does odd jobs. Top-boots and half-boots, I calls us.'

'You're from London?' enquired Mr Trott.

'Driv a cab once,' was the laconic reply.

'Why don't you drive it now?' asked Mr Trott.

'Over-driv the cab, and driv over a 'ooman,' replied the top-boots, with brevity.

'Do you know the mayor's house?' enquired Mr Trott.

'Rather,' replied the boots, significantly, as if he had some good reason to remember it.

'Do you think you could manage to leave a letter there?' interrogated Trott.

'Shouldn't wonder,' responded boots.

'But this letter,' said Trott, holding a deformed note with a paralytic direction in one hand, and five shillings in the other – 'this letter is anonymous.'

'A – what?' interrupted the boots.

'Anonymous – he's not to know who it comes from.'

'Oh! I see,' responded the reg'lar, with a knowing wink, but without evincing the slightest disinclination to undertake the charge – 'I see – bit o' Sving, eh?' and his one eye wandered round the room, as if in quest of a dark lantern and phosphorus-box. 'But, I say!' he continued, recalling the eye from its search, and bringing it to bear on Mr Trott. 'I say, he's a lawyer, our mayor, and ensured in the County. If you've a spite agen him, you'd better not burn his house down – blessed if I don't think it would be the greatest favour you could do him.' And he chuckled inwardly.

If Mr Alexander Trott had been in any other situation, his first act would have been to kick the man downstairs by deputy; or, in other words, to ring the bell and desire the landlord to take his boots off. He contented himself, however, with doubling the fee and explaining that the letter merely related to a breach of the peace. The top-boots retired, solemnly pledged to secrecy; and Mr Alexander Trott sat down to a fried sole, Maintenon cutlet, Madeira and sundries, with greater composure than he had experienced since the receipt of Horace Hunter's letter of defiance.

The lady who alighted from the London coach had no sooner been installed in number twenty-five, and made some alteration in her travelling-dress, than she indited a note to Joseph Overton Esquire, solicitor and mayor of Great Winglebury, requesting his immediate attendance on private business of paramount importance a summons which that worthy functionary lost no time in obeying; for after sundry openings of his eyes, divers ejaculations of 'Bless me!' and other manifestations of surprise, he took his broad-brimmed hat from its accustomed peg in his little front office and walked briskly down the high-street to the Winglebury Arms; through the hall and up the staircase of which establishment he was ushered by the landlady, and a crowd of officious waiters, to the door of number twenty-five.

'Show the gentleman in,' said the stranger lady, in reply to the foremost waiter's announcement. The gentleman was shown in accordingly.

The lady rose from the sofa; the mayor advanced a step from the door; and there they both paused for a minute or two, looking at one another as if by mutual consent. The mayor saw before him a buxom, richly dressed female of about forty; the lady looked upon a sleek man, about ten years older, in drab shorts and continuations, black coat, neckcloth and gloves.

'Miss Julia Manners!' exclaimed the mayor at length, 'you astonish me.'

'That's very unfair of you, Overton,' replied Miss Julia, 'for I have known you long enough not to be surprised at anything you do, and you might extend equal courtesy to me.'

'But to run away – actually run away – with a young man!' remonstrated the mayor.

'You wouldn't have me actually run away with an old one, I presume?' was the cool rejoinder.

'And then to ask me – me – of all people in the world – a man of my age and appearance – mayor of the town – to promote such a scheme!' pettishly ejaculated Joseph Overton; throwing himself into an armchair, and producing Miss Julia's letter from his pocket, as if to corroborate the assertion that he *had* been asked.

'Now, Overton,' replied the lady, 'I want your assistance in this matter, and I must have it. In the lifetime of that poor old dear, Mr Cornberry, who – who – '

'Who was to have married you, and didn't, because he died first; and who left you his property unencumbered with the addition of himself,' suggested the mayor.

'Well,' replied Miss Julia, reddening slightly, 'in the lifetime of the poor old dear, the property had the incumbrance of your management; and all I will say of that is that I only wonder it didn't die of consumption instead of its master. You helped yourself then – help me now.'

Mr Joseph Overton was a man of the world, and an attorney; and as certain indistinct recollections of an odd thousand pounds or two, appropriated by mistake, passed across his mind, he hemmed deprecatingly, smiled blandly, remained silent for a few seconds and finally enquired, 'What do you wish me to do?'

'I'll tell you,' replied Miss Julia – 'I'll tell you in three words. Dear Lord Peter – '

'That's the young man, I suppose – ' interrupted the mayor.

'That's the young *nobleman*,' replied the lady, with a great stress on the last word. 'Dear Lord Peter is considerably afraid of the resentment of his family; and we have therefore thought it better to make the match a stolen one. He left town, to avoid suspicion, on a visit to his friend, the Honourable Augustus Flair, whose seat, as you know, is about thirty miles from this, accompanied only by his favourite tiger. We arranged that I should come here alone in the London coach; and that he, leaving his tiger and cab behind him, should come on, and arrive here as soon as possible this afternoon.'

'Very well,' observed Joseph Overton, 'and then he can order the chaise, and you can go on to Gretna Green together, without requiring the presence or interference of a third party, can't you?'

'No,' replied Miss Julia. 'We have every reason to believe – dear Lord Peter not being considered very prudent or sagacious by his friends, and they having discovered his attachment to me – that, immediately on his absence being observed, pursuit will be made in this direction – to elude which, and to prevent our being traced, I wish it to be understood in this house that dear Lord Peter is slightly deranged, though perfectly harmless; and that I am, unknown to him, awaiting his arrival to convey him in a post-chaise to a private asylum – at Berwick, say. If I don't show myself much, I dare say I can manage to pass for his mother.'

The thought occurred to the mayor's mind that the lady might show herself a good deal without fear of detection; seeing that she was about double the age of her intended husband. He said nothing, however, and the lady proceeded.

'With the whole of this arrangement dear Lord Peter is acquainted; and all I want you to do is to make the delusion more complete by giving it the sanction of your influence in this place, and assigning this as a reason to the people of the house for my taking the young gentleman away. As it would not be consistent with the story that I should see him until after he has entered the chaise, I also wish you to communicate with him and inform him that it is all going on well.'

'Has he arrived?' enquired Overton.

'I don't know,' replied the lady.

'Then how am I to know!' enquired the mayor. 'Of course he will not give his own name at the bar.'

'I begged him, immediately on his arrival, to write you a note,' replied Miss Manners; 'and to prevent the possibility of our project being discovered through its means, I desired him to write anonymously, and in mysterious terms, to acquaint you with the number of his room.'

'Bless me!' exclaimed the mayor, rising from his seat, and searching his pockets – 'most extraordinary circumstance – he has arrived – mysterious note left at my house in a most mysterious manner, just before yours – didn't know what to make of it before, and certainly shouldn't have attended to it. – Oh! here it is.' And Joseph Overton pulled out of an inner coat-pocket the identical letter penned by Alexander Trott. 'Is this his lordship's hand?'

'Oh yes,' replied Julia; 'good, punctual creature! I have not seen it more than once or twice, but I know he writes very badly and very large. These dear, wild young noblemen, you know, Overton – '

'Ay, ay, I see,' replied the mayor. – 'Horses and dogs, play and wine – grooms, actresses and cigars – the stable, the green-room, the saloon and the tavern; and the legislative assembly at last . . . Here's what he says,' he pursued; ' "Sir – A young gentleman in number nineteen at the Winglebury Arms is bent on committing a rash act tomorrow morning at an early hour." (That's good – he means marrying.) "If you have any regard for the peace of this town, or the preservation of one – it may be two – human lives" – What the deuce does he mean by that?'

'That he's so anxious for the ceremony, he will expire if it's put off, and that I may possibly do the same,' replied the lady with great complacency.

'Oh! I see – not much fear of that; – well – "two human lives, you will cause him to be removed tonight." (He wants to start at once.) "Fear not to do this on your responsibility, for tomorrow the absolute necessity of the proceeding will be but too apparent. Remember: number nineteen. The name is Trott. No delay; for life and death depend upon your promptitude." Passionate language, certainly. Shall I see him?'

'Do,' replied Miss Julia; 'and entreat him to act his part well. I am half afraid of him. Tell him to be cautious.'

'I will,' said the mayor.

'Settle all the arrangements.'

'I will,' said the mayor again.

'And say I think the chaise had better be ordered for one o'clock.'

'Very well,' said the mayor once more; and, ruminating on the absurdity of the situation in which fate and old acquaintance had placed him, he desired a waiter to herald his approach to the temporary representative of number nineteen.

The announcement, 'Gentleman to speak with you, sir,' induced Mr Trott to pause halfway in the glass of port, the contents of which he was in the act of imbibing at the moment; to rise from his chair; and to retreat a few paces towards the window, as if to secure a retreat, in the event of the visitor assuming the form and appearance of Horace Hunter. One glance at Joseph Overton, however, quieted his apprehensions. He courteously motioned the stranger to a seat. The waiter, after a little jingling with the decanter and glasses, consented to leave the room; and Joseph Overton, placing the broad-brimmed hat on the chair next him, and bending his body gently forward, opened the business by saying in a very low and cautious tone, 'My lord – '

'Eh?' said Mr Alexander Trott, in a loud key, with the vacant and mystified stare of a chilly somnambulist.

'Hush – hush!' said the cautious attorney: 'to be sure – quite right – no titles here – my name is Overton, sir.'

'Overton?'

'Yes: the mayor of this place – you sent me a letter with anonymous information, this afternoon.'

'I, sir?' exclaimed Trott with ill-dissembled surprise; for, coward as he was, he would willingly have repudiated the authorship of the letter in question. 'I, sir?'

'Yes, you, sir; did you not?' responded Overton, annoyed with what he supposed to be an extreme degree of unnecessary suspicion. 'Either this letter is yours, or it is not. If it be, we can converse securely upon the subject at once. If it be not, of course I have no more to say.'

'Stay, stay,' said Trott, 'it *is* mine; I *did* write it. What could I do, sir? I had no friend here.'

'To be sure, to be sure,' said the mayor, encouragingly, 'you could not have managed it better. Well, sir; it will be necessary for you to leave here tonight in a post-chaise and four. And the harder the boys drive, the better. You are not safe from pursuit.'

'Bless me!' exclaimed Trott, in an agony of apprehension, 'can such things happen in a country like this? Such unrelenting and cold-blooded hostility!' He wiped off the concentrated essence of cowardice that was oozing fast down his forehead, and looked aghast at Joseph Overton.

'It certainly is a very hard case,' replied the mayor with a smile, 'that, in a free country, people can't marry whom they like, without being hunted down as if they were criminals. However, in the present instance the lady is willing, you know, and that's the main point, after all.'

'Lady willing,' repeated Trott, mechanically. 'How do you know the lady's willing?'

'Come, that's a good one,' said the mayor, benevolently tapping Mr Trott on the arm with his broad-brimmed hat; 'I have known her, well, for a long time; and if anybody could entertain the remotest doubt on the subject, I assure you I have none, nor need you have.'

'Dear me!' said Mr Trott, ruminating. 'This is *very* extraordinary!'

'Well, Lord Peter,' said the mayor, rising.

'Lord Peter?' repeated Mr Trott.

'Oh – ah, I forgot. Mr Trott, then – Trott – very good, ha! ha! Well, sir, the chaise shall be ready at half-past twelve.'

'And what is to become of me until then?' enquired Mr Trott, anxiously. 'Wouldn't it save appearances, if I were placed under some restraint?'

'Ah!' replied Overton, 'very good thought – capital idea indeed. I'll send somebody up directly. And if you make a little resistance when we put you in the chaise it wouldn't be amiss – look as if you didn't want to be taken away, you know.'

'To be sure,' said Trott – 'to be sure.'

'Well, my lord,' said Overton, in a low tone, 'until then, I wish your lordship a good-evening.'

'Lord – lordship?' ejaculated Trott again, falling back a step or two and gazing, in unutterable wonder, on the countenance of the mayor.

'Ha–ha! I see, my lord – practising the madman? – very good indeed – very vacant look – capital, my lord, capital – good-evening, Mr – Trott – ha! ha! ha!'

'That mayor's decidedly drunk,' soliloquised Mr Trott, throwing himself back in his chair, in an attitude of reflection.

'He is a much cleverer fellow than I thought him, that young noble-man – he carries it off uncommonly well,' thought Overton, as he went his way to the bar, there to complete his arrangements. This was soon done. Every word of the story was implicitly believed, and the one-eyed boots was immediately instructed to repair to number nineteen to act as custodian of the person of the supposed lunatic until half-past twelve o'clock. In pursuance of this direction, that somewhat eccentric gentle-man armed himself with a walking-stick of gigantic dimensions and repaired, with his usual equanimity of manner, to Mr Trott's apartment, which he entered without any ceremony and mounted guard in by quietly depositing himself on a chair near the door, where he proceeded to beguile the time by whistling a popular air with great apparent satisfaction.

'What do you want here, you scoundrel?' exclaimed Mr Alexander Trott, with a proper appearance of indignation at his detention.

The boots beat time with his head, as he looked gently round at Mr Trott with a smile of pity, and whistled an *adagio* movement.

'Do you attend in this room by Mr Overton's desire?' enquired Trott, rather astonished at the man's demeanour.

'Keep yourself to yourself, young feller,' calmly responded the boots, 'and don't say nothing to nobody.' And he whistled again.

'Now mind!' ejaculated Mr Trott, anxious to keep up the farce of wishing with great earnestness to fight a duel if they'd let him. 'I protest against being kept here. I deny that I have any intention of fighting with anybody. But as it's useless contending with superior numbers, I shall sit quietly down.'

'You'd better,' observed the placid boots, shaking the large stick expressively.

'Under protest, however,' added Alexander Trott, seating himself with indignation in his face, but great content in his heart. 'Under protest.'

'Oh, certainly!' responded the boots; 'anything you please. If you're happy, I'm transported; only don't talk too much – it'll make you worse.'

'Make me worse?' exclaimed Trott, in unfeigned astonishment: 'the man's drunk!'

'You'd better be quiet, young feller,' remarked the boots, going through a threatening piece of pantomime with the stick.

'Or mad!' said Mr Trott, rather alarmed. 'Leave the room, sir, and tell them to send somebody else.'

'Won't do!' replied the boots.

'Leave the room!' shouted Trott, ringing the bell violently: for he began to be alarmed on a new score.

'Leave that 'ere bell alone, you wretched loo–nattic!' said the boots, suddenly forcing the unfortunate Trott back into his chair and brandishing the stick aloft. 'Be quiet, you miserable object, and don't let everybody know there's a madman in the house.'

'He *is* a madman! He *is* a madman!' exclaimed the terrified Mr Trott, gazing on the one eye of the red-headed boots with a look of abject horror.

'Madman!' replied the boots, 'dam'me, I think he *is* a madman with a vengeance! Listen to me, you unfort'nate. Ah! would you?' (a slight tap on the head with the large stick, as Mr Trott made another move towards the bell-handle) – 'I caught you there! did I?'

'Spare my life!' exclaimed Trott, raising his hands imploringly.

'I don't want your life,' replied the boots, disdainfully, 'though I think it 'ud be a charity if somebody took it.'

'No, no, it wouldn't,' interrupted poor Mr Trott, hurriedly, 'no, no, it wouldn't! I – I'd rather keep it!'

'Oh, wery well,' said the boots: 'that's a mere matter of taste ev'ry one to his liking. Hows'ever, all I've got to say is this here: You sit quietly down in that chair, and I'll sit hoppersite you here, and if you keep quiet and don't stir, I won't damage you; but, if you move hand or foot till half-past twelve o'clock, I shall alter the expression of your countenance so completely that the next time you look in the glass you'll ask vether you're gone out of town, and ven you're likely to come back again. So sit down.'

'I will – I will,' responded the victim of mistakes; and down sat Mr Trott and down sat the boots too, exactly opposite him, with the stick ready for immediate action in case of emergency.

Long and dreary were the hours that followed. The bell of Great Winglebury church had just struck ten, and two hours and a half would probably elapse before succour arrived. For half an hour, the noise occasioned by shutting up the shops in the street beneath betokened

*I won't damage you; but, if you move hand or foot till half-past
twelve o'clock, I shall alter the expression of your countenance*

something like life in the town and rendered Mr Trott's situation a little less insupportable; but, when even these ceased, and nothing was heard beyond the occasional rattling of a post-chaise as it drove up the yard to change horses and then drove away again, or the clattering of-horses' hoofs in the stables behind, it became almost unbearable. The boots occasionally moved an inch or two to knock superfluous bits of wax off the candles, which were burning low, but instantaneously resumed his former position; and as he remembered to have heard, somewhere or other, that the human eye had an unfailing effect in controlling mad people, he kept his solitary organ of vision constantly fixed on Mr Alexander Trott. That unfortunate individual stared at his companion in his turn until his features grew more and more indistinct – his hair gradually less red – and the room more misty and obscure. Mr Alexander Trott fell into a sound sleep, from which he was awakened by a rumbling in the street, and a cry of 'Chaise-and-four for number twenty-five!' A bustle on the stairs succeeded; the room door was hastily thrown open and Mr Joseph Overton entered, followed by four stout waiters and Mrs Williamson, the stout landlady of the Winglebury Arms.

'Mr Overton!' exclaimed Mr Alexander Trott, jumping up in a frenzy. 'Look at this man, sir; consider the situation in which I have been placed for three hours past – the person you sent to guard me, sir, was a madman – a madman – a raging, ravaging, furious madman.'

'Bravo!' whispered Mr Overton.

'Poor dear!' said the compassionate Mrs Williamson, 'mad people always thinks other people's mad.'

'Poor dear!' ejaculated Mr Alexander Trott. 'What the devil do you mean by poor dear! Are you the landlady of this house?'

'Yes, yes,' replied the stout old lady, 'don't exert yourself, there's a dear! Consider your health, now; do.'

'Exert myself!' shouted Mr Alexander Trott; 'it's a mercy, ma'am, that I have any breath to exert myself with! I might have been assassinated three hours ago by that one-eyed monster with the oakum head. How dare you have a madman, ma'am – how dare you have a madman, to assault and terrify the visitors to your house?'

'I'll never have another,' said Mrs Williamson, casting a look of reproach at the mayor.

'Capital, capital,' whispered Overton again, as he enveloped Mr Alexander Trott in a thick travelling-cloak.

'Capital, sir!' exclaimed Trott, aloud; 'it's horrible. The very recollection makes me shudder. I'd rather fight four duels in three hours, if I survived the first three, than I'd sit for that time face to face with a madman.'

'Keep it up, my lord, as you go downstairs,' whispered Overton, 'your bill is paid, and your portmanteau in the chaise.' And then he added aloud, 'Now, waiters, the gentleman's ready.'

At this signal, the waiters crowded round Mr Alexander Trott. One took one arm; another, the other; a third, walked before with a candle; the fourth, behind with another candle; the boots and Mrs Williamson brought up the rear; and downstairs they went: Mr Alexander Trott expressing alternately at the very top of his voice either his feigned reluctance to go or his unfeigned indignation at being shut up with a madman.

Mr Overton was waiting at the chaise-door, the boys were ready mounted, and a few ostlers and stable nondescripts were standing round to witness the departure of 'the mad gentleman'. Mr Alexander Trott's foot was on the step when he observed (which the dim light had prevented his doing before) a figure seated in the chaise, closely muffled up in a cloak like his own.

'Who's that?' he enquired of Overton, in a whisper.

'Hush, hush,' replied the mayor: 'the other party of course.'

'The other party!' exclaimed Trott, with an effort to retreat.

'Yes, yes; you'll soon find that out, before you go far, I should think – but make a noise, you'll excite suspicion if you whisper to me so much.'

'I won't go in this chaise!' shouted Mr Alexander Trott, all his original fears recurring with tenfold violence. 'I shall be assassinated – I shall be – '

'Bravo, bravo,' whispered Overton. 'I'll push you in.'

'But I won't go,' exclaimed Mr Trott. 'Help here, help! They're carrying me away against my will. This is a plot to murder me.'

'Poor dear!' said Mrs Williamson again.

'Now, boys, put 'em along,' cried the mayor, pushing Trott in and slamming the door. 'Off with you, as quick as you can, and stop for nothing till you come to the next stage – all right!'

'Horses are paid, Tom,' screamed Mrs Williamson; and away went the chaise, at the rate of fourteen miles an hour, with Mr Alexander Trott and Miss Julia Manners carefully shut up in the inside.

Mr Alexander Trott remained coiled up in one corner of the chaise and his mysterious companion in the other for the first two or three miles, Mr Trott edging more and more into his corner, as he felt his companion gradually edging more and more from hers, and vainly endeavouring in the darkness to catch a glimpse of the furious face of the supposed Horace Hunter.

'We may speak now,' said his fellow-traveller, at length; 'the post-boys can neither see nor hear us.'

'That's not Hunter's voice!' – thought Alexander, astonished.

'Dear Lord Peter!' said Miss Julia, most winningly: putting her arm on Mr Trott's shoulder. 'Dear Lord Peter. Not a word?'

'Why, it's a woman!' exclaimed Mr Trott, in a low tone of excessive wonder.

'Ah! Whose voice is that?' said Julia; ' 'tis not Lord Peter's.'

'No – it's mine,' replied Mr Trott.

'Yours!' ejaculated Miss Julia Manners; 'a strange man! Gracious heaven! How came you here!'

'Whoever you are, you might have known that I came against my will, ma'am,' replied Alexander, 'for I made noise enough when I got in.'

'Do you come from Lord Peter?' enquired Miss Manners.

'Confound Lord Peter,' replied Trott pettishly. 'I don't know any Lord Peter. I never heard of him before tonight, when I've been Lord Peter'd by one and Lord Peter'd by another, till I verily believe I'm mad, or dreaming – '

'Whither are we going?' enquired the lady tragically.

'How should *I* know, ma'am?' replied Trott with singular coolness; for the events of the evening had completely hardened him.

'Stop stop!' cried the lady, letting down the front glasses of the chaise.

'Stay, my dear ma'am!' said Mr Trott, pulling the glasses up again with one hand, and gently squeezing Miss Julia's waist with the other. 'There is some mistake here; give me till the end of this stage to explain my share of it. We must go so far; you cannot be set down here alone, at this hour of the night.'

The lady consented; the mistake was mutually explained. Mr Trott was a young man, had highly promising whiskers, an undeniable tailor and an insinuating address – he wanted nothing but valour, and who wants that with three thousand a year? The lady had this, and more; she wanted a young husband, and the only course open to Mr Trott to retrieve his disgrace was a rich wife. So they came to the conclusion that it would be a pity to have all this trouble and expense for nothing; and that as they were so far on the road already, they had better go to Gretna Green and marry each other; and they did so. And the very next preceding entry in the Blacksmith's book was an entry of the marriage of Emily Brown with Horace Hunter. Mr Hunter took his wife home, and begged pardon, and *was* pardoned; and Mr Trott took *his* wife home, begged pardon too, and was pardoned also. And Lord Peter, who had been detained beyond his time by drinking champagne and riding a steeplechase, went back to the Honourable Augustus Flair's, and drank more champagne and rode another steeplechase and was thrown and killed. And Horace Hunter took great credit to himself for practising on the cowardice of Alexander Trott; and all these circumstances were discovered in time and carefully noted down; and if you ever stop a week at the Winglebury Arms, they will give you just this account of The Great Winglebury Duel.

MRS JOSEPH PORTER

Most extensive were the preparations at Rose Villa, Clapham Rise, in the occupation of Mr Gattleton (a stockbroker in especially comfortable circumstances), and great was the anxiety of Mr Gattleton's interesting family as the day fixed for the representation of the Private Play, which had been 'many months in preparation', approached. The whole family was infected with the mania for Private Theatricals; the house, usually so clean and tidy, was, to use Mr Gattleton's expressive description, 'regularly turned out o' windows'; the large dining-room, dismantled of its furniture, and ornaments, presented a strange jumble of flats, flies, wings, lamps, bridges, clouds, thunder and lightning, festoons and flowers, daggers and foils, and various other messes in theatrical slang included under the comprehensive name of 'properties'. The bedrooms were crowded with scenery, the kitchen was occupied by carpenters. Rehearsals took place every other night in the drawing-room, and every sofa in the house was more or less damaged by the perseverance and spirit with which Mr Sempronius Gattleton, and Miss Lucina, rehearsed the smothering scene in *Othello* – it having been determined that that tragedy should form the first portion of the evening's entertainments.

'When we're a *leetle* more perfect, I think it will go admirably,' said Mr Sempronius, addressing his *corps dramatique* at the conclusion of the hundred and fiftieth rehearsal. In consideration of his sustaining the trifling inconvenience of bearing all the expenses of the play, Mr Sempronius had been, in the most handsome manner, unanimously elected stage-manager. 'Evans,' continued Mr Gattleton the younger, addressing a tall, thin, pale young gentleman with extensive whiskers – 'Evans, you play Roderigo beautifully.'

'Beautifully,' echoed the three Miss Gattletons; for Mr Evans was pronounced by all his lady friends to be 'quite a dear'. He looked so interesting, and had such lovely whiskers: to say nothing of his talent for writing verses in albums and playing the flute! Roderigo simpered and bowed.

'But I think,' added the manager, 'you are hardly perfect in the – fall – in the fencing-scene, where you are – you understand?'

'It's very difficult,' said Mr Evans, thoughtfully; 'I've fallen about a good deal in our counting-house lately, for practice, only I find it hurts one so. Being obliged to fall backward you see, it bruises one's head a good deal.'

'But you must take care you don't knock a wing down,' said Mr Gattleton the elder, who had been appointed prompter, and who took as much interest in the play as the youngest of the company. 'The stage is very narrow, you know.'

'Oh! don't be afraid,' said Mr Evans, with a very self-satisfied air; 'I shall fall with my head "off", and then I can't do any harm.'

'But, egad,' said the manager, rubbing his hands, 'we shall make a decided hit in *Masaniello*. Harleigh sings that music admirably.'

Everybody echoed the sentiment. Mr Harleigh smiled, and looked foolish – not an unusual thing with him – hummed 'Behold how brightly breaks the morning', and blushed as red as the fisherman's nightcap he was trying on.

'Let's see,' resumed the manager, telling the number on his fingers, 'we shall have three dancing female peasants, besides Fenella, and four fishermen. Then, there's our man Tom; he can have a pair of ducks of mine and a check shirt of Bob's and a red nightcap and he'll do for another – that's five. In the choruses, of course, we can sing at the sides; and in the market-scene we can walk about in cloaks and things. When the revolt takes place, Tom must keep rushing in on one side and out on the other with a pickaxe, as fast as he can. The effect will be electrical; it will look exactly as if there were an immense number of 'em. And in the eruption-scene we must burn the red fire and upset the tea-trays and make all sorts of noises – and it's sure to do.'

'Sure! sure!' cried all the performers *una voce* – and away hurried Mr Sempronius Gattleton to wash the burnt cork off his face and superintend the 'setting up' of some of the amateur-painted, but never-sufficiently-to-be-admired, scenery.

Mrs Gattleton was a kind, good-tempered, vulgar soul, exceedingly fond of her husband and children, and entertaining only three dislikes. In the first place, she had a natural antipathy to anybody else's unmarried daughters; in the second, she was in bodily fear of anything in the shape of ridicule; lastly – almost a necessary consequence of this feeling – she regarded, with feelings of the utmost horror, one Mrs Joseph Porter over the way. However, the good folks of Clapham and its vicinity stood very much in awe of scandal and sarcasm; and thus Mrs Joseph Porter was courted, and flattered, and caressed, and invited, for much the same reason that induces a poor author, without a farthing in his pocket, to behave with extraordinary civility to a twopenny postman.

'Never mind, ma,' said Miss Emma Porter, in colloquy with her respected relative, and trying to look unconcerned; 'if they had invited me, you know that neither you nor pa would have allowed me to take part in such an exhibition.'

'Just what I should have thought from your high sense of propriety,' returned the mother. 'I am glad to see, Emma, you know how to designate the proceeding.' Miss P., by the by, had only the week before made 'an exhibition' of herself for four days, behind a counter at a fancy fair, to all and every of her majesty's liege subjects who were disposed to pay a shilling each for the privilege of seeing some four dozen girls flirting with strangers and playing at shop.

'There!' said Mrs Porter, looking out of window; 'there are two rounds of beef and a ham going in – clearly for sandwiches; and Thomas, the pastrycook, says there have been twelve dozen tarts ordered, besides blancmange and jellies. Upon my word! think of the Miss Gattletons in fancy dresses, too!'

'Oh, it's too ridiculous!' said Miss Porter, hysterically.

'I'll manage to put them a little out of conceit with the business, however,' said Mrs Porter; and out she went on her charitable errand.

'Well, my dear Mrs Gattleton,' said Mrs Joseph Porter, after they had been closeted for some time, and when, by dint of indefatigable pumping, she had managed to extract all the news about the play, 'well, my dear, people may say what they please; indeed we know they will, for some folks are *so* ill-natured. Ah, my dear Miss Lucina, how d'ye do? I was just telling your mamma that I have heard it said, that – '

'What?'

'Mrs Porter is alluding to the play, my dear,' said Mrs Gattleton; 'she was, I am sorry to say, just informing me that – '

'Oh, now pray don't mention it,' interrupted Mrs Porter; 'it's most absurd – quite as absurd as young What's-his-name saying he wondered how Miss Caroline, with such a foot and ankle, could have the vanity to play Fenella.'

'Highly impertinent, whoever said it,' said Mrs Gattleton, bridling up.

'Certainly, my dear,' chimed in the delighted Mrs Porter; 'most undoubtedly! Because, as I said, if Miss Caroline *does* play Fenella, it doesn't follow, as a matter of course, that she should think she has a pretty foot; – and then – such puppies as these young men are – he had the impudence to say that – '

How far the amiable Mrs Porter might have succeeded in her pleasant purpose it is impossible to say, had not the entrance of Mr Thomas Balderstone, Mrs Gattleton's brother, familiarly called in the family 'Uncle Tom', changed the course of conversation, and suggested to her mind an excellent plan of operation on the evening of the play.

Uncle Tom was very rich and exceedingly fond of his nephews and nieces; as a matter of course, therefore, he was an object of great importance in his own family. He was one of the best-hearted men in existence: always in a good temper, and always talking. It was his boast that he wore top-boots on all occasions and had never worn a black silk neckerchief; and it was his pride that he remembered all the principal plays of Shakespeare from beginning to end – and so he did. The result of this parrot-like accomplishment was that he was not only perpetually quoting himself, but that he could never sit by and hear a misquotation from the 'Swan of Avon' without setting the unfortunate delinquent right. He was also something of a wag; never missed an opportunity of saying what he considered a good thing and invariably laughed until he cried at anything that appeared to him mirth-moving or ridiculous.

'Well, girls!' said Uncle Tom, after the preparatory ceremony of kissing and how-d'ye-do-ing had been gone through – 'how d'ye get on? Know your parts, eh? – Lucina, my dear, Act ii, Scene i – place, left – cue – "Unknown fate . . . " – What's next, eh? – Go on – "The heavens – " '

'Oh, yes,' said Miss Lucina, 'I recollect –

The heavens forbid
But that our loves and comforts should increase
Even as our days do grow!'

'Make a pause here and there,' said the old gentleman, who was a great critic. ' "But that our loves and comforts should increase" – emphasis on the last syllable, "*crease*" – loud, "even" – one, two, three, four; then loud again, "as our days do grow", emphasis on *days*. That's the way, my dear; trust to your uncle for emphasis. Ah! Sem, my boy, how are you?'

'Very well, thankee, uncle,' returned Mr Sempronius, who had just appeared, looking something like a ringdove with a small circle round each eye: the result of his constant corking. 'Of course we see you on Thursday.'

'Of course, of course, my dear boy.'

'What a pity it is your nephew didn't think of making you prompter, Mr Balderstone!' whispered Mrs Joseph Porter; 'you would have been invaluable.'

'Well, I flatter myself, I *should* have been tolerably up to the thing,' responded Uncle Tom.

'I must bespeak sitting next you on the night,' resumed Mrs Porter; 'and then, if our dear young friends here should be at all wrong, you will be able to enlighten me. I shall be so interested.'

'I am sure I shall be most happy to give you any assistance in my power.'

'Mind, it's a bargain.'

'Certainly.'

'I don't know how it is,' said Mrs Gattleton to her daughters, as they were sitting round the fire in the evening, looking over their parts, 'but I really very much wish Mrs Joseph Porter wasn't coming on Thursday. I am sure she's scheming something.'

'She can't make us ridiculous, however,' observed Mr Sempronius Gattleton, haughtily.

The long-looked-for Thursday arrived in due course, and brought with it, as Mr Gattleton senior philosophically observed, 'no disappointments, to speak of'. True, it was yet a matter of doubt whether Cassio would be enabled to get into the dress which had been sent for him from the masquerade warehouse. It was equally uncertain whether the principal female singer would be sufficiently recovered from the influenza to make her appearance; Mr Harleigh, the Masaniello of the night, was hoarse and rather unwell, in consequence of the great quantity of lemon and sugar-candy he had eaten to improve his voice; and two flutes and a violoncello had pleaded severe colds. What of that? the audience were all coming. Everybody knew his part; the dresses were covered with tinsel and spangles; the white plumes looked beautiful; Mr Evans had practised falling until he was bruised from head to foot and quite perfect; Iago was sure that, in the stabbing-scene, he should make 'a decided hit'. A self-taught deaf gentleman, who had kindly offered to bring his flute, would be a most valuable addition to the orchestra; Miss Jenkins's talent for the piano was too well known to be doubted for an instant; Mr Cape had practised the violin accompaniment with her frequently; and Mr Brown, who had kindly undertaken, at a few hours' notice, to bring his violoncello, would, no doubt, manage extremely well.

Seven o'clock came, and so did the audience; all the rank and fashion of Clapham and its vicinity was fast filling the theatre. There were the Smiths, the Gubbinses, the Nixons, the Dixons, the Hicksons, people with all sorts of names, two aldermen, a sheriff in perspective, Sir Thomas Glumper (who had been knighted in the last reign for carrying up an address on somebody's escaping from nothing); and last, not least, there were Mrs Joseph Porter and Uncle Tom, seated in the centre of the third row from the stage – Mrs P. amusing Uncle Tom with all sorts of stories and Uncle Tom amusing everyone else by laughing most immoderately.

Ting, ting, ting! went the prompter's bell at eight o'clock precisely and dash went the orchestra into the overture to *The Men of Prometheus*. The pianoforte player hammered away with laudable perseverance; and the violoncello, which struck in at intervals, 'sounded very well, considering'. The unfortunate individual, however, who had undertaken to play the flute accompaniment 'at sight', found, from fatal experience, the perfect truth of the old adage 'ought of sight, out of mind'; for, being very near-sighted and being placed at a considerable distance from his music-book, all he had an opportunity of doing was to play a bar now and then in the wrong place and put the other performers out. It is, however, but justice to Mr Brown to say that he did this to admiration. The overture, in fact, was not unlike a race between the different instruments; the piano came in first by several bars, and the violoncello next, quite distancing the poor flute; for the deaf gentleman *too-too'd* away, quite unconscious that he was at all wrong, until apprised, by the applause of the audience, that the overture was concluded. A considerable bustle and shuffling of feet was then heard upon the stage, accompanied by whispers of 'Here's a pretty go! – what's to be done?' &c. The audience applauded again, by way of raising the spirits of the performers; and then Mr Sempronius desired the prompter, in a very audible voice, to 'clear the stage, and ring up'.

Ting, ting, ting! went the bell again. Everybody sat down; the curtain shook, rose sufficiently high to display several pair of yellow boots paddling about – and there remained.

Ting, ting, ting! went the bell again. The curtain was violently convulsed, but rose no higher; the audience tittered; Mrs Porter looked at Uncle Tom; Uncle Tom looked at everybody, rubbing his hands and

The curtain at length rose, and discovered Mr Sempronius Gattleton
'solus', and decked for Othello.

laughing with perfect rapture. After as much ringing with the little bell as a muffin-boy would make in going down a tolerably long street, and a vast deal of whispering, hammering and calling for nails and cord, the curtain at length rose, and discovered Mr Sempronius Gattleton *solus*, and decked for Othello. After three distinct rounds of applause, during which Mr Sempronius applied his right hand to his left breast, and bowed in the most approved manner, the manager advanced and said –

'Ladies and gentlemen – I assure you it is with sincere regret, that I regret to be compelled to inform you that Iago who was to have played Mr Wilson – I beg your pardon, ladies and gentlemen, but I am naturally somewhat agitated' (applause) – 'I mean, Mr Wilson, who was to have played Iago, is – that is has been – or, in other words, ladies and gentle-men, the fact is, that I have just received a note in which I am informed that Iago is unavoidably detained at the post-office this evening. Under these circumstances, I trust – a – a – amateur performance – a–another gentleman undertaken to read the part – request indulgence for a short time – courtesy and kindness of a British audience.' Overwhelming applause. Exit Mr Sempronius Gattleton and curtain falls.

The audience were, of course, exceedingly good-humoured; the whole business was a joke; and accordingly they waited for an hour with the utmost patience, being enlivened by an interlude of rout-cakes and lemonade. It appeared by Mr Sempronius's subsequent explanation that the delay would not have been so great had it not so happened that when the substitute Iago had finished dressing, and just as the play was on the point of commencing, the original Iago unexpectedly arrived. The former was therefore compelled to undress and the latter to dress for his part; which, as he found some difficulty in getting into his clothes, occupied no inconsiderable time. At last, the tragedy began in real earnest. It went off well enough, until the third scene of the first act, in which Othello addresses the Senate; the only remarkable circumstance being that as Iago could not get on any of the stage boots, in consequence of his feet being violently swelled with the heat and excitement, he was under the necessity of playing the part in a pair of Wellingtons, which contrasted rather oddly with his richly embroidered pantaloons. When Othello started with his address to the Senate (whose dignity was represented by the duke, a carpenter, two men engaged on the recommendation of the gardener, and a boy), Mrs Porter found the opportunity she so anxiously sought.

Mr Sempronius proceeded –

> ' "Most potent, grave, and reverend signiors,
> My very noble and approv'd good masters,
> That I have ta'en away this old man's daughter,
> It is most true; – rude am I in my speech – " '

'Is that right?' whispered Mrs Porter to Uncle Tom.

'No.'

'Tell him so, then.'

'I will. Sem!' called out Uncle Tom, 'that's wrong, my boy.'

'What's wrong, uncle?' demanded Othello, quite forgetting the dignity of his situation.

'You've left out something. "True I have married – " '

'Oh, ah!' said Mr Sempronius, endeavouring to hide his confusion as much and as ineffectually as the audience attempted to conceal their half-suppressed tittering by coughing with extraordinary violence –

> . . . ' "true I have married her;
> The very head and front of my offending
> Hath this extent; no more." '

(*Aside*) 'Why don't you prompt, father?'

'Because I've mislaid my spectacles,' said poor Mr Gattleton, almost dead with the heat and bustle.

'There, now it's "rude am I",' said Uncle Tom.

'Yes, I know it is,' returned the unfortunate manager, proceeding with his part.

It would be useless and tiresome to quote the number of instances in which Uncle Tom, now completely in his element and instigated by the mischievous Mrs Porter, corrected the mistakes of the performers; suffice it to say that having mounted his hobby, nothing could induce him to dismount; so, during the whole remainder of the play, he performed a kind of running accompaniment by muttering everybody's part as it was being delivered in an undertone. The audience were highly amused, Mrs Porter delighted, the performers embarrassed; Uncle Tom never was better pleased in all his life; and Uncle Tom's nephews and nieces had never, although the declared heirs to his large property, so heartily wished him gathered to his fathers as on that memorable occasion.

Several other minor causes, too, united to damp the ardour of the *dramatis personae*. None of the performers could walk in their tights or move their arms in their jackets; the pantaloons were too small, the boots too large and the swords of all shapes and sizes. Mr Evans, naturally too tall for the scenery, wore a black velvet hat with immense white plumes, the glory of which was lost in 'the flies'; and the only other inconvenience of which was that when it was off his head he could not put it on, and when it was on he could not take it off. Notwithstanding all his practice, too, he fell with his head and shoulders as neatly through one of the side scenes, as a harlequin would jump through a panel in a Christmas pantomime. The pianoforte player, overpowered by the extreme heat of the room, fainted away at the commencement of the entertainments, leaving the music of *Masaniello* to the flute and violoncello. The orchestra complained that Mr Harleigh put them out and Mr Harleigh declared that the orchestra prevented his singing a note. The fishermen who were hired for the occasion revolted to the very life, positively refusing to play without an increased allowance of spirits; and, their demand being complied with, getting drunk in the eruption-scene as naturally as possible. The red fire, which was burnt at the conclusion of the second act, not only nearly suffocated the audience but nearly set the house on fire into the bargain; and, as it was, the remainder of the piece was acted in a thick fog.

In short, the whole affair was, as Mrs Joseph Porter triumphantly told everybody, 'a complete failure'. The audience went home at four o'clock in the morning, exhausted with laughter, suffering from severe headaches and smelling terribly of brimstone and gunpowder. The Messrs Gattleton, senior and junior, retired to rest, with the vague idea of emigrating to Swan River early in the ensuing week.

Rose Villa has once again resumed its wonted appearance; the dining-room furniture has been replaced; the tables are as nicely polished as formerly; the horsehair chairs are ranged against the wall, as regularly as ever; Venetian blinds have been fitted to every window in the house to intercept the prying gaze of Mrs Joseph Porter. The subject of theatricals is never mentioned in the Gattleton family, unless, indeed, by Uncle Tom, who cannot refrain from sometimes expressing his surprise and regret at finding that his nephews and nieces appear to have lost the relish they once possessed for the beauties of Shakespeare and quotations from the works of that immortal bard.

A PASSAGE IN THE LIFE OF
MR WATKINS TOTTLE

Matrimony is proverbially a serious undertaking. Like an overweening predilection for brandy and water, it is a misfortune into which a man easily falls and from which he finds it remarkably difficult to extricate himself. It is of no use telling a man who is timorous on these points that it is but one plunge, and all is over. They say the same thing at the Old Bailey, and the unfortunate victims derive as much comfort from the assurance in the one case as in the other.

Mr Watkins Tottle was a rather uncommon compound of strong uxorious inclinations and an unparalleled degree of anti-connubial timidity. He was about fifty years of age; stood four feet six inches and three-quarters in his socks – for he never stood in stockings at all – plump, clean and rosy. He looked something like a vignette to one of Richardson's novels, and had a clean cravatish formality of manner and kitchen-pokerness of carriage which Sir Charles Grandison himself might have envied. He lived on an annuity, which was well adapted to the individual who received it in one respect – it was rather small. He received it in periodical payments on every alternate Monday; but he ran himself out, about a day after the expiration of the first week, as regularly as an eight-day clock, and then, to make the comparison complete, his landlady wound him up and he went on with a regular tick.

Mr Watkins Tottle had long lived in a state of single blessedness, as bachelors say, or single cursedness, as spinsters think; but the idea of matrimony had never ceased to haunt him. Wrapped in profound reveries on this never-failing theme, fancy transformed his small parlour in Cecil Street, Strand, into a neat house in the suburbs; the half-hundredweight of coals under the kitchen-stairs suddenly sprang up into three tons of the best Wallsend; his small French bedstead was converted into a regular matrimonial four-poster; and in the empty chair on the opposite side of the fireplace, imagination seated a beautiful young lady, with a very little independence or will of her own, and a very large independence under a will of her father's.

'Who's there?' enquired Mr Watkins Tottle, as a gentle tap at his room-door disturbed these meditations one evening.

'Tottle, my dear fellow, how *do* you do?' said a short elderly gentleman with a gruffish voice, bursting into the room, and replying to the question by asking another.

'Told you I should drop in some evening,' said the short gentleman, as he delivered his hat into Tottle's hand after a little struggling and dodging.

'Delighted to see you, I'm sure,' said Mr Watkins Tottle, wishing internally that his visitor had 'dropped in' to the Thames at the bottom of the street, instead of dropping into his parlour. The fortnight was nearly up, and Watkins was hard up.

'How is Mrs Gabriel Parsons?' enquired Tottle.

'Quite well, thank you,' replied Mr Gabriel Parsons, for that was the name the short gentleman revelled in. Here there was a pause; the short gentleman looked at the left hob of the fireplace; Mr Watkins Tottle stared vacancy out of countenance.

'Quite well,' repeated the short gentleman, when five minutes had expired. 'I may say remarkably well.' And he rubbed the palms of his hands as hard as if he were going to strike a light by friction.

'What will you take?' enquired Tottle, with the desperate suddenness of a man who knew that unless the visitor took his leave, he stood very little chance of taking anything else.

'Oh, I don't know – have you any whisky?'

'Why,' replied Tottle, very slowly, for all this was gaining time, 'I *had* some capital and remarkably strong whisky last week; but it's all gone – and therefore its strength – '

'Is much beyond proof; or, in other words, impossible to be proved,' said the short gentleman; and he laughed very heartily, and seemed quite glad the whisky had been drunk. Mr Tottle smiled – but it was the smile of despair. When Mr Gabriel Parsons had done laughing, he delicately insinuated that, in the absence of whisky, he would not be averse to brandy. And Mr Watkins Tottle, lighting a flat candle very ostentatiously; and displaying an immense key, which belonged to the street-door, but which, for the sake of appearances, occasionally did duty in an imaginary wine cellar; left the room to entreat his landlady to charge their glasses and charge them in the bill. The application was successful; the spirits were speedily called – not from the vasty deep, but the adjacent wine-vaults. The two short gentlemen mixed their grog; and then sat cosily down before the fire – a pair of shorts, airing themselves.

'Tottle,' said Mr Gabriel Parsons, 'you know my way – offhand, open, say what I mean, mean what I say, hate reserve and can't bear affectation. One is a bad domino which only hides what good people have about 'em, without making the bad look better; and the other is much about the same thing as pinking a white cotton stocking to make it look like a silk one. Now listen to what I'm going to say.'

Here the little gentleman paused and took a long pull at his brandy and water. Mr Watkins Tottle took a sip of his, stirred the fire, and assumed an air of profound attention.

'It's of no use humming and ha'ing about the matter,' resumed the short gentleman – 'you want to get married.'

'Why,' replied Mr Watkins Tottle evasively; for he trembled violently, and felt a sudden tingling throughout his whole frame; 'why – I should certainly – at least, I *think* I should like – '

'Won't do,' said the short gentleman. 'Plain and free – or there's an end of the matter. Do you want money?'

'You know I do.'

'You admire the sex?'

'I do.'

'And you'd like to be married?'

'Certainly.'

'Then you shall be. There's an end of that.' Thus saying, Mr Gabriel Parsons took a pinch of snuff and mixed another glass.

'Let me entreat you to be more explanatory,' said Tottle. 'Really, as the party principally interested, I cannot consent to be disposed of in this way.'

'I'll tell you,' replied Mr Gabriel Parsons, warming with the subject, and the brandy and water – 'I know a lady – she's stopping with my wife now – who is just the thing for you. Well educated; talks French; plays the piano; knows a good deal about flowers, and shells, and all that sort of thing; and has five hundred a year, with an uncontrolled power of disposing of it, by her last will and testament.'

'I'll pay my addresses to her,' said Mr Watkins Tottle. 'She isn't *very* young – is she?'

'Not very; just the thing for you. I've said that already.'

'What coloured hair has the lady?' enquired Mr Watkins Tottle.

'Egad, I hardly recollect,' replied Gabriel, with coolness. 'Perhaps I ought to have observed, at first, that she wears a front.'

'A what?' ejaculated Tottle.

'One of those things with curls, along here,' said Parsons, drawing a straight line across his forehead, just over his eyes, in illustration of his meaning. 'I know the front's black; I can't speak quite positively about her own hair, because, unless one walks behind her and catches a glimpse of it under her bonnet, one seldom sees it; but I should say that it was *rather* lighter than the front – a shade of a greyish tinge, perhaps.'

Mr Watkins Tottle looked as if he had certain misgivings of mind. Mr Gabriel Parsons perceived it and thought it would be safe to begin the next attack without delay.

'Now, were you ever in love, Tottle?' he enquired.

Mr Watkins Tottle blushed up to the eyes and down to the chin and exhibited a most extensive combination of colours as he confessed the soft impeachment.

'I suppose you popped the question more than once, when you were a young – I beg your pardon – a younger – man,' said Parsons.

'Never in my life!' replied his friend, apparently indignant at being suspected of such an act. 'Never! The fact is that I entertain, as you know, peculiar opinions on these subjects. I am not afraid of ladies, young or old – far from it; but, I think, that in compliance with the custom of the present day, they allow too much freedom of speech and manner to marriageable men. Now, the fact is that anything like this easy freedom I never could acquire; and as I am always afraid of going too far, I am generally, I dare say, considered formal and cold.'

'I shouldn't wonder if you were,' replied Parsons, gravely; 'I shouldn't wonder. However, you'll be all right in this case; for the strictness and delicacy of this lady's ideas greatly exceed your own. Lord bless you, why, when she came to our house, there was an old portrait of some man or other, with two large, black, staring eyes, hanging up in her bedroom; she positively refused to go to bed there till it was taken down, considering it decidedly wrong.'

'I think so, too,' said Mr Watkins Tottle; 'certainly.'

'And then, the other night – I never laughed so much in my life,' resumed Mr Gabriel Parsons; 'I had driven home in an easterly wind, and caught a devil of a face-ache. Well; as Fanny – that's Mrs Parsons, you know – and this friend of hers, and I and Frank Ross were playing a rubber, I said, jokingly, that when I went to bed I should wrap my head in Fanny's flannel petticoat. She instantly threw up her cards, and left the room.'

'Quite right!' said Mr Watkins Tottle; 'she could not possibly have behaved in a more dignified manner. What did you do?'

'Do? – Frank took dummy; and I won sixpence.'

'But didn't you apologise for hurting her feelings?'

'Devil a bit. Next morning at breakfast, we talked it over. She contended that any reference to a flannel petticoat was improper; men ought not to be supposed to know that such things were. I pleaded my coverture; being a married man.'

'And what did the lady say to that?' enquired Tottle, deeply interested.

'Changed her ground, and said that Frank being a single man, its impropriety was obvious.'

'Noble-minded creature!' exclaimed the enraptured Tottle.

'Oh! both Fanny and I said, at once, that she was regularly cut out for you.'

A gleam of placid satisfaction shone on the circular face of Mr Watkins Tottle, as he heard the prophecy.

'There's one thing I can't understand,' said Mr Gabriel Parsons, as he rose to depart; 'I cannot, for the life and soul of me, imagine how the deuce you'll ever contrive to come together. The lady would certainly go into convulsions if the subject were mentioned.' Mr Gabriel Parsons sat down again and laughed until he was weak. Tottle owed him money, so he had a perfect right to laugh at Tottle's expense.

Mr Watkins Tottle feared, in his own mind, that this was another characteristic which he had in common with this modern Lucretia. He, however, accepted the invitation to dine with the Parsonses on the next day but one, with great firmness – and looked forward to the introduction, when again left alone, with tolerable composure.

The sun that rose on the next day but one had never beheld a sprucer personage on the outside of the Norwood stage than Mr Watkins Tottle; and when the coach drew up before a cardboard-looking house with disguised chimneys and a lawn like a large sheet of green letter-paper, there certainly had never lighted to his place of destination a gentleman who felt more uncomfortable.

The coach stopped, and Mr Watkins Tottle jumped – we beg his pardon – alighted, with great dignity. 'All right!' said he, and away went the coach up the hill with that beautiful equanimity of pace for which 'short' stages are generally remarkable.

Mr Watkins Tottle gave a faltering jerk to the handle of the garden-gate bell. He essayed a more energetic tug, and his previous nervousness was not at all diminished by hearing the bell ringing like a fire alarm.

'Is Mr Parsons at home?' enquired Tottle of the man who opened the gate. He could hardly hear himself speak, for the bell had not yet done tolling.

'Here I am,' shouted a voice on the lawn – and there was Mr Gabriel Parsons in a flannel jacket, running backwards and forwards from a wicket to two hats piled on each other, and from the two hats to the wicket, in the most violent manner, while another gentleman with his coat off was getting down the area of the house, after a ball. When the gentleman without the coat had found it – which he did in less than ten minutes – he ran back to the hats, and Gabriel Parsons pulled up. Then the gentleman without the coat called out 'play' very loudly, and bowled. Then Mr Gabriel Parsons knocked the ball several yards and took another run. Then the other gentleman aimed at the wicket, and didn't hit it; and Mr Gabriel Parsons, having finished running on his own account, laid down the bat and ran after the ball, which went into a neighbouring field. They called this cricket.

'Tottle, will you "go in"?' enquired Mr Gabriel Parsons, as he approached him, wiping the perspiration off his face.

Mr Watkins Tottle declined the offer, the bare idea of accepting which made him even warmer than his friend.

'Then we'll go into the house, as it's past four, and I shall have to wash my hands before dinner,' said Mr Gabriel Parsons. 'Here, I hate ceremony, you know! Timson, that's Tottle – Tottle, that's Timson; bred for the church, which I fear will never be bread for him'; and he chuckled at the old joke. Mr Timson bowed carelessly. Mr Watkins Tottle bowed stiffly. Mr Gabriel Parsons led the way to the house. He was a rich sugar-baker, who mistook rudeness for honesty and abrupt bluntness for an open and candid manner; many besides Gabriel mistake bluntness for sincerity.

Mrs Gabriel Parsons received the visitors most graciously on the steps, and preceded them to the drawing-room. On the sofa was seated a lady of very prim appearance and remarkably inanimate. She was one of those persons at whose age it is impossible to make any reasonable guess; her features might have been remarkably pretty when she was younger, and they might always have presented the same appearance. Her complexion – with a slight trace of powder here and there – was as clear as that of a well-made wax doll, and her face as expressive. She was handsomely dressed, and was winding up a gold watch.

'Miss Lillerton, my dear, this is our friend Mr Watkins Tottle; a very old acquaintance I assure you,' said Mrs Parsons, presenting the Strephon of Cecil Street, Strand. The lady rose, and made a deep courtesy; Mr Watkins Tottle made a bow.

'Splendid, majestic creature!' thought Tottle.

Mr Timson advanced, and Mr Watkins Tottle began to hate him. Men generally discover a rival, instinctively, and Mr Watkins Tottle felt that his hate was deserved.

'May I beg,' said the reverend gentleman – 'May I beg to call upon you, Miss Lillerton, for some trifling donation to my soup, coals and blanket distribution society?'

'Put my name down for two sovereigns, if you please,' responded Miss Lillerton.

'You are truly charitable, madam,' said the Reverend Mr Timson, 'and we know that charity will cover a multitude of sins. Let me beg you to understand that I do not say this from the supposition that you have many sins which require palliation; believe me when I say that I never yet met anyone who had fewer to atone for than Miss Lillerton.'

Something like a bad imitation of animation lighted up the lady's face, as she acknowledged the compliment. Watkins Tottle incurred the sin of wishing that the ashes of the Reverend Charles Timson were quietly deposited in the churchyard of his curacy, wherever it might be.

'I'll tell you what,' interrupted Parsons, who had just appeared with clean hands and a black coat, 'it's my private opinion, Timson, that your "distribution society" is rather a humbug.'

'You are so severe,' replied Timson, with a Christian smile; he disliked Parsons, but liked his dinners.

'So positively unjust!' said Miss Lillerton.

'Certainly,' observed Tottle. The lady looked up; her eyes met those of Mr Watkins Tottle. She withdrew them in a sweet confusion and Watkins Tottle did the same – the confusion was mutual.

'Why,' urged Mr Parsons, pursuing his objections, 'what on earth is the use of giving a man coals who has nothing to cook, or giving him blankets when he hasn't a bed, or giving him soup when he requires substantial food? – "like sending them ruffles when wanting a shirt". Why not give 'em a trifle of money, as I do, when I think they deserve it, and let them purchase what they think best? Why? – because your subscribers wouldn't see their names flourishing in print on the church-door – that's the reason.'

'Really, Mr Parsons, I hope you don't mean to insinuate that I wish to see *my* name in print on the church-door,' interrupted Miss Lillerton.

'I hope not,' said Mr Watkins Tottle, putting in another word, and getting another glance.

'Certainly not,' replied Parsons. 'I dare say you wouldn't mind seeing it in writing, though, in the church register – eh?'

'Register! What register?' enquired the lady gravely.

'Why, the register of marriages, to be sure,' replied Parsons, chuckling at the sally, and glancing at Tottle. Mr Watkins Tottle thought he should have fainted for shame, and it is quite impossible to imagine what effect the joke would have had upon the lady if dinner had not been, at that moment, announced. Mr Watkins Tottle, with an unprecedented effort of gallantry, offered the tip of his little finger; Miss Lillerton accepted it gracefully, with maiden modesty; and they proceeded in due state to the dinner-table, where they were soon deposited side by side. The room was very snug, the dinner very good and the little party in spirits. The conversation became pretty general, and when Mr Watkins Tottle had extracted one or two cold observations from his neighbour, and had taken wine with her, he began to acquire confidence rapidly. The cloth was removed; Mrs Gabriel Parsons drank four glasses of port on the plea of being a nurse just then; and Miss Lillerton took about the same number of sips, on the plea of not wanting any at all. At length, the ladies retired, to the great gratification of Mr Gabriel Parsons, who had been coughing and frowning at his wife for half an hour previously – signals which Mrs Parsons never happened to observe, until she had been pressed to take her ordinary quantum, which, to avoid giving trouble, she generally did at once.

'What do you think of her?' enquired Mr Gabriel Parsons of Mr Watkins Tottle, in an undertone.

'I dote on her with enthusiasm already!' replied Mr Watkins Tottle.

'Gentlemen, pray let us drink "the ladies",' said the Reverend Mr Timson.

'The ladies!' said Mr Watkins Tottle, emptying his glass. In the fullness of his confidence, he felt as if he could make love to a dozen ladies, offhand.

'Ah!' said Mr Gabriel Parsons, 'I remember when I was a young man – fill your glass, Timson.'

'I have this moment emptied it.'

'Then fill again.'

'I will,' said Timson, suiting the action to the word.

'I remember,' resumed Mr Gabriel Parsons, 'when I was a younger man, with what a strange compound of feelings I used to drink that toast, and how I used to think every woman was an angel.'

'Was that before you were married?' mildly enquired Mr Watkins Tottle.

'Oh! certainly,' replied Mr Gabriel Parsons. 'I have never thought so since; and a precious milksop I must have been, ever to have thought so at all. But, you know, I married Fanny under the oddest and most ridiculous circumstances possible.'

'What were they, if one may enquire?' asked Timson, who had heard the story, on an average, twice a week for the last six months. Mr Watkins Tottle listened attentively, in the hope of picking up some suggestion that might be useful to him in his new undertaking.

'I spent my wedding-night in a back-kitchen chimney,' said Parsons, by way of a beginning.

'In a back-kitchen chimney!' ejaculated Watkins Tottle. 'How dreadful!'

'Yes, it wasn't very pleasant,' replied the small host. 'The fact is, Fanny's father and mother liked me well enough as an individual, but had a decided objection to my becoming a husband. You see, I hadn't any money in those days, and they had; and so they wanted Fanny to pick up somebody else. However, we managed to discover the state of each other's affections somehow. I used to meet her, at some mutual friends' parties; at first we danced together, and talked, and flirted, and all that sort of thing; then, I used to like nothing so well as sitting by her side – we didn't talk so much then, but I remember I used to have a great notion of looking at her out of the extreme corner of my left eye and then I got very miserable and sentimental, and began to write verses and use Macassar oil. At last I couldn't bear it any longer, and after I had walked up and down the sunny side of Oxford Street in tight boots for a week – and a devilish hot summer it was too –. in the hope of meeting her, I sat down and wrote a letter, and begged her to manage to see me clandestinely, for I wanted to hear her decision from her own mouth. I said I had discovered, to my perfect satisfaction, that I couldn't live without her, and that if she didn't have me, I had made up my mind to take prussic acid, or take to drinking, or emigrate, so as to take myself off in some way or other. Well, I borrowed a pound, and bribed the housemaid to give her the note, which she did.'

'And what was the reply?' enquired Timson, who had found, before, that to encourage the repetition of old stories is to get a general invitation.

'Oh, the usual one! Fanny expressed herself very miserable; hinted at the possibility of an early grave; said that nothing should induce her to swerve from the duty she owed her parents; implored me to forget her, and find out somebody more deserving, and all that sort of thing. She said she could, on no account, think of meeting me unknown to her pa and ma; and entreated me, as she should be in a particular part of Kensington Gardens at eleven o'clock next morning, not to attempt to meet her there.'

'You didn't go, of course?' said Watkins Tottle.

'Didn't I? – Of course I did. There she was, with the identical house–maid in perspective, in order that there might be no interruption. We walked about, for a couple of hours; made ourselves delightfully miserable; and were regularly engaged. Then, we began to "correspond" that is to say, we used to exchange about four letters a day; what we used to say in 'em I can't imagine. And I used to have an interview, in the kitchen, or the cellar, or some such place, every evening. Well, things went on in this way for some time; and we got fonder of each other every day. At last, as our love was raised to such a pitch, and as my salary had been raised too, shortly before, we determined on a secret marriage. Fanny arranged to sleep at a friend's, on the previous night; we were to be married early in the morning; and then we were to return to her home and be pathetic. She was to fall at the old gentleman's feet, and bathe his boots with her tears; and I was to hug the old lady and call her "mother", and use my pocket-handkerchief as much as possible. Married we were, the next morning; two girls – friends of Fanny's – acting as bridesmaids, and a man who was hired for five shillings and a pint of porter officiating as father. Now, the old lady unfortunately put off her return from Ramsgate, where she had been paying a visit, until the next morning; and as we placed great reliance on her, we agreed to postpone our confession for four-and-twenty hours. My newly-made wife returned home, and I spent my wedding-day in strolling about Hampstead Heath, and execrating my father-in-law. Of course, I went to comfort my dear little wife at night, as

A back kitchen, with a stone floor and a dresser – upon which, in the absence of chairs, we used to sit and make love.'

much as I could, with the assurance that our troubles would soon be over. I opened the garden-gate, of which I had a key, and was shown by the servant to our old place of meeting – a back kitchen, with a stone floor and a dresser – upon which, in the absence of chairs, we used to sit and make love.'

'Make love upon a kitchen-dresser!' interrupted Mr Watkins Tottle, whose ideas of decorum were greatly outraged.

'Ah! On a kitchen-dresser!' replied Parsons. 'And let me tell you, old fellow, that if you were really over head and ears in love and had no other place to make love in, you'd be devilish glad to avail yourself of such an opportunity. However, let me see – where was I?'

'On the dresser,' suggested Timson.

'Oh – ah! Well, here I found poor Fanny, quite disconsolate and uncomfortable. The old boy had been very cross all day, which made her feel still more lonely; and she was quite out of spirits. So, I put a good face on the matter, and laughed it off, and said we should enjoy the pleasures of a matrimonial life more by contrast; and, at length, poor Fanny brightened up a little. I stopped there till about eleven o'clock, and just as I was taking my leave for the fourteenth time, the girl came running down the stairs, without her shoes, in a great fright, to tell us that the old villain – heaven forgive me for calling him so, for he is dead and gone now! – prompted I suppose by the prince of darkness, was coming down, to draw his own beer for supper – a thing he had not done before, for six months, to my certain knowledge; for the cask stood in that very back kitchen. If he discovered me there, explanation would have been out of the question; for he was so outrageously violent, when at all excited, that he never would have listened to me. There was only one thing to be done. The chimney was a very wide one; it had been originally built for an oven; went up perpendicularly for a few feet, and then shot backward and formed a sort of small cavern. My hopes and fortune – the means of our joint existence almost – were at stake. I scrambled in like a squirrel; coiled myself up in this recess; and, as Fanny and the girl replaced the deal chimney-board, I could see the light of the candle which my un-conscious father-in-law carried in his hand. I heard him draw the beer; and I never heard beer run so slowly. He was just leaving the kitchen and I was preparing to descend when down came the infernal chimney-board with a tremendous crash. He stopped and put down the candle and the jug of beer on the dresser; he was a nervous old fellow and any unexpected noise annoyed him. He coolly observed that the fireplace was never used and, sending the frightened servant into the next kitchen for a hammer and nails, actually nailed up the board and locked the door on the outside. So, there was I, on my wedding-night, in the light kersey-mere trousers, fancy waistcoat and blue coat that I had been married in in the morning, in a back-kitchen chimney, the bottom of which was nailed up and the top of which had been formerly raised some fifteen feet, to prevent the smoke from annoying the neighbours. And there,' added Mr Gabriel Parsons, as he passed the bottle, 'there I remained till half-past seven the next morning, when the housemaid's sweetheart, who was a carpenter, unshelled me. The old dog had nailed me up so securely that, to this very hour, I firmly believe that no one but a carpenter could ever have got me out.'

'And what did Mrs Parsons's father say when he found you were married?' enquired Watkins Tottle, who, although he never saw a joke, was not satisfied until he heard a story to the very end.

'Why, the affair of the chimney so tickled his fancy, that he pardoned us offhand, and allowed us something to live on till he went the way of all flesh. I spent the next night in his second-floor front, much more comfortably than I had spent the preceding one; for, as you will probably guess – '

'Please, sir, missis has made tea,' said a middle-aged female servant, bobbing into the room.

'That's the very housemaid that figures in my story,' said Mr Gabriel Parsons. 'She went into Fanny's service when we were first married, and has been with us ever since; but I don't think she has felt one atom of respect for me since the morning she saw me released, when she went into violent hysterics, to which she has been subject ever since. Now, shall we join the ladies?'

'If you please,' said Mr Watkins Tottle.

'By all means,' added the obsequious Mr Timson; and the trio made for the drawing-room accordingly.

Tea being concluded, and the toast and cups having been duly handed, and occasionally upset, by Mr Watkins Tottle, a rubber was proposed. They cut for partners – Mr and Mrs Parsons and Mr Watkins Tottle and Miss Lillerton. Mr Timson, having conscientious scruples on the subject of card-playing, drank brandy and water and kept up a running spar with Mr Watkins Tottle. The evening went off well; Mr Watkins Tottle was in high spirits, having some reason to be gratified with his reception by Miss Lillerton; and before he left, a small party was made up to visit the Beulah Spa on the following Saturday.

'It's all right, I think,' said Mr Gabriel Parsons to Mr Watkins Tottle as he opened the garden gate for him.

'I hope so,' he replied, squeezing his friend's hand.

'You'll be down by the first coach on Saturday,' said Mr Gabriel Parsons.

'Certainly,' replied Mr Watkins Tottle. 'Undoubtedly.'

But fortune had decreed that Mr Watkins Tottle should not be down by the first coach on Saturday. His adventures on that day, however, and the success of his wooing, are subjects for another chapter.

*   *   *

Gabriel Parsons, as he very complacently paced up and down the fourteen feet of gravel which bordered the 'lawn', on the Saturday morning which had been fixed upon for the Beulah Spa jaunt.

'No, sir; I haven't seen it,' replied a gardener in a blue apron, who let himself out to do the ornamental for half a crown a day and his 'keep'.

'Time Tottle was down,' said Mr Gabriel Parsons, ruminating – 'Oh, here he is, no doubt,' added Gabriel, as a cab drove rapidly up the hill; and he buttoned his dressing-gown and opened the gate to receive the expected visitor. The cab stopped and out jumped a man in a coarse Petersham greatcoat, whity-brown neckerchief, faded black suit, gamboge-coloured top-boots and one of those large-crowned hats, formerly seldom met with, but now very generally patronised by gentlemen and costermongers.

'Mr Parsons?' said the man, looking at the superscription of a note he held in his hand and addressing Gabriel with an enquiring air.

'My name *is* Parsons,' responded the sugar-baker.

'I've brought this here note,' replied the individual in the painted tops, in a hoarse whisper: 'I've brought this here note from a gen'lm'n as come to our house this mornin'.'

'I expected the gentleman at my house,' said Parsons, as he broke the seal, which bore the impression of her majesty's profile as it is seen on a sixpence.

'I've no doubt the gen'lm'n would ha' been here,' replied the stranger, 'if he hadn't happened to call at our house first; but we never trusts no gen'lm'n furder nor we can see him – no mistake about that there' –

added the unknown, with a facetious grin; 'beg your pardon, sir, no offence meant, only – once in, and I wish you may – catch the idea, sir?'

Mr Gabriel Parsons was not remarkable for catching anything suddenly but a cold. He therefore only bestowed a glance of profound astonishment on his mysterious companion and proceeded to unfold the note of which he had been the bearer. Once opened and the idea was caught with very little difficulty. Mr Watkins Tottle had been suddenly arrested for £33 10s. 4d., and dated his communication from a lockup house in the vicinity of Chancery Lane.

The lockup house in the vicinity of Chancery Lane

'Unfortunate affair this!' said Parsons, refolding the note.

'Oh! nothin' ven you're used to it,' coolly observed the man in the Petersham.

'Tom!' exclaimed Parsons, after a few minutes' consideration, 'just put the horse in, will you? – Tell the gentleman that I shall be there almost as soon as you are,' he continued, addressing the sheriff-officer's Mercury.

'Wery well,' replied that important functionary; adding, in a confidential manner, 'I'd adwise the gen'lm'n's friends to settle. You see it's a mere trifle; and, unless the gen'lm'n means to go up afore the court, it's hardly worth while waiting for detainers, you know. Our governor's wide awake, he is. I'll never say nothin' agin him, nor no man; but he knows what's o'clock, he does, uncommon.' Having delivered this eloquent, and, to Parsons, particularly intelligible harangue, the meaning of which was eked out by divers nods and winks, the gentleman in the boots reseated himself in the cab, which went rapidly off and was soon out of sight. Mr Gabriel Parsons continued to pace up and down the pathway for some minutes, apparently absorbed in deep meditation. The result of his cogitations seemed to be perfectly satisfactory to himself, for he ran briskly into the house; said that business had suddenly summoned him to town; that he had desired the messenger to inform Mr Watkins Tottle of the fact; and that they would return together to dinner. He then hastily equipped himself for a drive, and mounting his gig, was soon on his way to the establishment of Mr Solomon Jacobs, situate (as Mr Watkins Tottle had informed him) in Cursitor Street, Chancery Lane.

When a man is in a violent hurry to get on, and has a specific object in view, the attainment of which depends on the completion of his journey, the difficulties which interpose themselves in his way appear not only to be innumerable, but to have been called into existence especially for the occasion. The remark is by no means a new one, and Mr Gabriel Parsons had practical and painful experience of its justice in the course of his drive. There are three classes of animated objects which prevent your driving with any degree of comfort or celerity through streets which are but little frequented – they are pigs, children and old women. On the occasion we are describing, the pigs were luxuriating on cabbage stalks; and the shuttle-cocks fluttered from the little deal battledores, and the children played in the road; and women, with a basket in one hand, and the street-door key in the other, *would* cross just before the horse's head, until Mr Gabriel Parsons was perfectly savage with vexation and quite hoarse with hoi-ing and imprecating. Then, when he got into Fleet Street, there was 'a stoppage', in which people in vehicles have the satisfaction of remaining stationary for half an hour and envying the slowest pedestrians, and where policemen rush about and seize hold of horses' bridles and back them into shop-windows, by way of clearing the road and preventing confusion. At length Mr Gabriel Parsons turned into Chancery Lane, and having enquired for, and been directed to Cursitor Street (for it was a locality of which he was quite ignorant), he soon found himself opposite the house of Mr Solomon Jacobs. Confiding his horse and gig to the care of one of the fourteen boys who had followed him from the other side of Blackfriars Bridge on the chance of his requiring their services, Mr Gabriel Parsons crossed the road and knocked at an inner door, the upper part of which was of glass, grated like the windows of this inviting mansion with iron bars – painted white to look comfortable.

The knock was answered by a sallow-faced, red-haired, sulky boy, who, after surveying Mr Gabriel Parsons through the glass, applied a large key to an immense wooden excrescence, which was in reality a lock, but which, taken in conjunction with the iron nails with which the panels were studded, gave the door the appearance of being subject to warts.

'I want to see Mr Watkins Tottle,' said Parsons.

'It's the gentleman that come in this morning, Jem,' screamed a voice from the top of the kitchen-stairs, which belonged to a dirty woman who had just brought her chin to a level with the passage floor. 'The gentleman's in the coffee-room.'

'Upstairs, sir,' said the boy, just opening the door wide enough to let Parsons in without squeezing him, and double-locking it the moment he had made his way through the aperture. 'First floor – door on the left.'

Mr Gabriel Parsons thus instructed, ascended the uncarpeted and ill-lighted staircase, and after giving several subdued taps at the before-mentioned 'door on the left', which were rendered inaudible by the hum of voices within the room and the hissing noise attendant on some frying operations which were carrying on below stairs, turned the handle and entered the apartment. Being informed that the unfortunate object of his visit had just gone upstairs to write a letter, he had leisure to sit down and observe the scene before him.

The room – which was a small, confined den – was partitioned off into boxes, like the commonroom of some inferior eating-house. The dirty floor had evidently been as long a stranger to the scrubbing-brush as to carpet or floor-cloth: and the ceiling was completely blackened by the flare of the oil-lamp by which the room was lighted at night. The grey ashes on the edges of the tables, and the cigar ends which were plentifully scattered about the dusty grate, fully accounted for the intolerable smell of tobacco which pervaded the place; and the empty glasses and half-saturated slices of lemon on the tables, together with the porter pots beneath them, bore testimony to the frequent libations in which the individuals who honoured Mr Solomon Jacobs by a temporary residence in his house indulged. Over the mantel-shelf was a paltry looking-glass, extending about half the width of the chimney-piece; but by way of counterpoise, the ashes were confined by a rusty fender about twice as long as the hearth.

From this cheerful room itself, the attention of Mr Gabriel Parsons was naturally directed to its inmates. In one of the boxes two men were playing at cribbage with a very dirty pack of cards, some with blue, some with green and some with red backs – selections from decayed packs. The cribbage board had been long ago formed on the table by some ingenious visitor with the assistance of a pocketknife and a two-pronged fork, with which the necessary number of holes had been made in the table at proper distances for the reception of the wooden pegs. In another box a stout, hearty-looking man, of about forty, was eating some dinner which his wife – an equally comfortable-looking personage – had brought him in a basket; and in a third, a genteel-looking young man was talking earnestly, and in a low tone, to a young female, whose face was concealed by a thick veil but whom Mr Gabriel Parsons immediately set down in his own mind as the debtor's wife. A young fellow of vulgar manners, dressed in the very extreme of the prevailing fashion, was pacing up and down the room, with a lighted cigar in his mouth and his hands in his pockets, ever and anon puffing forth volumes of smoke and occasionally applying, with much apparent relish, to a pint pot, the contents of which were 'chilling' on the hob.

'Four pence more, by gum!' exclaimed one of the cribbage-players, lighting a pipe, and addressing his adversary at the close of the game; 'one 'ud think you'd got luck in a pepper-cruet, and shook it out when you wanted it.'

'Well, that a'n't a bad un,' replied the other, who was a horse dealer from Islington.

'No; I'm blessed if it is,' interposed the jolly-looking fellow, who, having finished his dinner, was drinking out of the same glass as his wife, in truly conjugal harmony, some hot gin and water. The faithful partner of his cares had brought a plentiful supply of the anti-temperance fluid in a large flat stone bottle, which looked like a half-gallon jar that had been successfully tapped for the dropsy. 'You're a rum chap, you are, Mr Walker – will you dip your beak into this, sir?'

'Thank'ee, sir,' replied Mr Walker, leaving his box and advancing to the other to accept the proffered glass. 'Here's your health, sir, and your good 'ooman's here. Gentlemen all – yours, and better luck still. Well, Mr Willis,' continued the facetious prisoner, addressing the young man with the cigar, 'you seem rather down today – floored, as one may say. What's the matter, sir? Never say die, you know.'

'Oh! I'm all right,' replied the smoker. 'I shall be bailed out tomorrow.'

'Shall you, though?' enquired the other. 'Dam'me, I wish I could say the same. I am as regularly over head and ears as the *Royal George*, and stand about as much chance of being *bailed out*. Ha! ha! ha!'

'Why,' said the young man, stopping short, and speaking in a very loud key, 'look at me. What d'ye think I've stopped here two days for?'

' 'Cause you couldn't get out, I suppose,' interrupted Mr Walker, winking to the company. 'Not that you're exactly obliged to stop here, only you can't help it. No compulsion, you know, only you must – eh?'

'A'n't he a rum un?' enquired the delighted individual, who had offered the gin and water, of his wife.

'Oh, he just is!' replied the lady, who was quite overcome by these flashes of imagination.

'Why, my case,' frowned the victim, throwing the end of his cigar into the fire, and illustrating his argument by knocking the bottom of the pot on the table at intervals – 'my case is a very singular one. My father's a man of large property, and I am his son.'

'That's a very strange circumstance!' interrupted the jocose Mr Walker, *en passant*.

' – I am his son, and have received a liberal education. I don't owe no man nothing – not the value of a farthing, but I was induced, you see, to put my name to some bills for a friend – bills to a large amount, I may say a very large amount, for which I didn't receive no consideration. What's the consequence?'

'Why, I suppose the bills went out, and you came in. The acceptances weren't taken up, and you were, eh?' enquired Walker.

'To be sure,' replied the liberally educated young gentleman. 'To be sure; and so here I am, locked up for a matter of twelve hundred pound.'

'Why don't you ask your old governor to stump up?' enquired Walker, with a somewhat sceptical air.

'Oh! bless you, he'd never do it,' replied the other, in a tone of expostulation – 'Never!'

'Well, it is very odd to – be – sure,' interposed the owner of the flat bottle, mixing another glass, 'but I've been in difficulties, as one may say, now for thirty year. I went to pieces when I was in a milk-walk, thirty year ago; arterwards, when I was a fruiterer, and kept a spring wan; and arter that again in the coal and 'tatur line – but all that time I never see a youngish chap come into a place of this kind who wasn't going out again directly, and who hadn't been arrested on bills which he'd given a friend and for which he'd received nothing whatsomever – not a fraction.'

'Oh! it's always the cry,' said Walker. 'I can't see the use on it; that's what makes me so wild. Why, I should have a much better opinion of an individual if he'd say at once in an honourable and gentlemanly manner as he'd done everybody he possibly could.'

'Ay, to be sure,' interposed the horse-dealer, with whose notions of bargain and sale the axiom perfectly coincided, 'so should I.' The young gentleman, who had given rise to these observations, was on the point of offering a rather angry reply to these sneers, but the rising of the young man before noticed, and of the female who had been sitting by him, to leave the room, interrupted the conversation. She had been weeping bitterly, and the noxious atmosphere of the room acting upon her excited feelings and delicate frame rendered the support of her companion necessary as they quitted it together.

There was an air of superiority about them both, and something in their appearance so unusual in such a place, that a respectful silence was observed until the *whirr–r–bang* of the spring door announced that they were out of hearing. It was broken by the wife of the ex-fruiterer.

'Poor creetur!' said she, quenching a sigh in a rivulet of gin and water. 'She's very young.'

'She's a nice-looking 'ooman too,' added the horse-dealer.

'What's he in for, Ikey?' enquired Walker of an individual who was spreading a cloth, with numerous blotches of mustard upon it, on one of the tables, and whom Mr Gabriel Parsons had no difficulty in recognising as the man who had called upon him in the morning.

'Vy,' responded the factotum, 'it's one of the rummiest rigs you ever heard on. He come in here last Vensday, which by the by he's a-going over the water tonight – hows'ever that's neither here nor there. You see I've been a-going back'ards and for'ards about his business, and ha' managed to pick up some of his story from the servants and them; and so far as I can make it out, it seems to be summat to this here effect – '

'Cut it short, old fellow,' interrupted Walker, who knew from former experience that he of the top-boots was neither very concise nor intelligible in his narratives.

'Let me alone,' replied Ikey, 'and I'll ha' vound up and made my lucky in five seconds. This here young gen'lm'n's father – so I'm told, mind ye – and the father o' the young voman, have always been on very bad, out-and-out, rig'lar knock-me-down sort o' terms; but somehow or another, when he was a wisitin' at some gentlefolk's house, as he knowed at college, he came into contract with the young lady. He seed her several times, and then he up and said he'd keep company with her, if so be as she vos agreeable. Vell, she vos as sweet upon him as he vos upon her, and so I s'pose they made it all right; for they got married 'bout six months arterwards, unbeknown, mind ye, to the two fathers – leastways so I'm told. When they heard on it – my eyes, there was such a combustion! Starvation vos the very least that vos to be done to 'em. The young gen'lm'n's father cut him off vith a bob, 'cos he'd cut himself off vith a wife; and the young lady's father he behaved even worser and more unnat'ral, for he not only blow'd her up dreadful, and swore he'd never see her again, but he employed a chap as I knows – and as you knows, Mr Valker, a precious sight too well – to go about and buy up the bills and them things on which the young husband, thinking his governor 'ud come round agin, had raised the vind just to blow himself on vith for a time; besides vich, he made all the interest he could to set other people agin him. Consequence vos, that he paid as long as he could; but things he never expected to have to meet till he'd had time to turn himself round, come fast upon him, and he vos nabbed. He vos brought here, as I said afore, last Vensday, and I think there's about – ah, half a dozen detainers agin him downstairs now. I have been,' added Ikey, 'in the purfession these fifteen year, and I never met vith such windictiveness afore!'

'Poor creeturs!' exclaimed the coal-dealer's wife once more: again resorting to the same excellent prescription for nipping a sigh in the bud.

'Ah! when they've seen as much trouble as I and my old man here have, they'll be as comfortable under it as we are.'

'The young lady's a pretty creature,' said Walker, 'only she's a little too delicate for my taste – there ain't enough of her. As to the young cove, he may be very respectable and what not, but he's too down in the mouth for me – he ain't game.'

'Game!' exclaimed Ikey, who had been altering the position of a green-handled knife and fork at least a dozen times, in order that he might remain in the room under the pretext of having something to do. 'He's game enough ven there's anything to be fierce about; but who could be game, as you call it, Mr Walker, with a pale young creetur like that hanging about him? – It's enough to drive any man's heart into his boots to see 'em together – and no mistake at all about it. I never shall forget her first comin' here; he wrote to her on the Thursday to come – I know he did, 'cos I took the letter. Uncommon fidgety he was all day to be sure, and in the evening he goes down into the office, and he says to Jacobs, says he, "Sir, can I have the loan of a private room for a few minutes this evening, without incurring any additional expense – just to see my wife in?" says he. Jacobs looked as much as to say, "Strike me bountiful if you ain't one of the modest sort!" but as the gen'lm'n who had been in the back parlour had just gone out, and had paid for it for that day, he says – wery grave – "Sir," says he, "it's agin our rules to let private rooms to our lodgers on gratis terms, but," says he, "for a gentleman, I don't mind breaking through them for once." So then he turns round to me, and says, "Ikey, put two mould candles in the back parlour, and charge 'em to this gen'lm'n's account," vich I did. Vell, by and by a hackney-coach comes up to the door, and there, sure enough, was the young lady, wrapped up in a hopera-cloak, as it might be, and all alone. I opened the gate that night, so I went up when the coach come, and he vos a waitin' at the parlour door – and wasn't he a trembling, neither? The poor creetur see him, and could hardly walk to meet him. "Oh, Harry!" she says, "that it should have come to this; and all for my sake," says she, putting her hand upon his shoulder. So he puts his arm round her pretty little waist, and leading her gently a little way into the room, so that he might be able to shut the door, he says, so kind and soft-like – "Why, Kate," says he –

'Here's the gentleman you want,' said Ikey, abruptly breaking off in his story, and introducing Mr Gabriel Parsons to the crestfallen Watkins

Tottle, who at that moment entered the room. Watkins advanced with a wooden expression of passive endurance and accepted the hand which Mr Gabriel Parsons held out.

'I want to speak to you,' said Gabriel, with a look strongly expressive of his dislike of the company.

'This way,' replied the imprisoned one, leading the way to the front drawing-room, where rich debtors did the luxurious at the rate of a couple of guineas a day.

'Well, here I am,' said Mr Watkins, as he sat down on the sofa; and placing the palms of his hands on his knees, anxiously glanced at his friend's countenance.

'Yes; and here you're likely to be,' said Gabriel, coolly, as he rattled the money in his unmentionable pockets, and looked out of the window.

'What's the amount with the costs?' enquired Parsons, after an awkward pause.

'£37 3s. 10d.'

'Have you any money?'

'Nine and sixpence halfpenny.'

Mr Gabriel Parsons walked up and down the room for a few seconds before he could make up his mind to disclose the plan he had formed; he was accustomed to drive hard bargains, but was always most anxious to conceal his avarice. At length he stopped short, and said, 'Tottle, you owe me fifty pounds.'

'I do.'

'And from all I see, I infer that you are likely to owe it to me.'

'I fear I am.'

'Though you have every disposition to pay me if you could?'

'Certainly.'

'Then,' said Mr Gabriel Parsons, 'listen: here's my proposition. You know my way of old. Accept it – yes or no – I will or I won't. I'll pay the debt and costs, and I'll lend you £10 more (which, added to your annuity, will enable you to carry on the war well) if you'll give me your note of hand to pay me one hundred and fifty pounds within six months after you are married to Miss Lillerton.'

'My dear – '

'Stop a minute – on one condition; and that is, that you propose to Miss Lillerton at once.'

'At once! My dear Parsons, consider.'

'It's for you to consider, not me. She knows you well from reputation, though she did not know you personally until lately. Notwithstanding all her maiden modesty, I think she'd be devilish glad to get married out of hand with as little delay as possible. My wife has sounded her on the subject, and she has confessed.'

'What – what?' eagerly interrupted the enamoured Watkins.

'Why,' replied Parsons, 'to say exactly what she has confessed, would be rather difficult, because they only spoke in hints, and so forth; but my wife, who is no bad judge in these cases, declared to me that what she had confessed was as good as to say that she was not insensible of your merits – in fact, that no other man should have her.'

Mr Watkins Tottle rose hastily from his seat, and rang the bell.

'What's that for?' enquired Parsons.

'I want to send the man for the bill stamp,' replied Mr Watkins Tottle.

'Then you've made up your mind?'

'I have' – and they shook hands most cordially. The note of hand was given – the debt and costs were paid – Ikey was satisfied for his trouble, and the two friends soon found themselves on that side of Mr Solomon Jacobs's establishment on which most of his visitors were very happy when they found themselves once again – to wit, the *out*side.

'Now,' said Mr Gabriel Parsons, as they drove to Norwood together – 'you shall have an opportunity to make the disclosure tonight, and mind you speak out, Tottle.'

'I will – I will!' replied Watkins, valorously.

'How I should like to see you together,' ejaculated Mr Gabriel Parsons. – 'What fun!' and he laughed so long and so loudly that he disconcerted Mr Watkins Tottle and frightened the horse.

'There's Fanny and your intended walking about on the lawn,' said Gabriel, as they approached the house. 'Mind your eye, Tottle.'

'Never fear,' replied Watkins, resolutely, as he made his way to the spot where the ladies were walking.

'Here's Mr Tottle, my dear,' said Mrs Parsons, addressing Miss Lillerton. The lady turned quickly round, and acknowledged his courteous salute with the same sort of confusion that Watkins had noticed on their first interview, but with something like a slight expression of disappointment or carelessness.

'Did you see how glad she was to see you?' whispered Parsons to his friend.

'Why, I really thought she looked as if she would rather have seen somebody else,' replied Tottle.

'Pooh, nonsense!' whispered Parsons again – 'it's always the way with women, young or old. They never show how delighted they are to see those whose presence makes their hearts beat. It's the way with the whole sex, and no man should have lived to your time of life without knowing it. Fanny confessed it to me, when we were first married, over and over again – see what it is to have a wife.'

'Certainly,' whispered Tottle, whose courage was vanishing fast.

'Well, now, you'd better begin to pave the way,' said Parsons, who, having invested some money in the speculation, assumed the office of director.

'Yes, yes, I will – presently,' replied Tottle, greatly flurried.

'Say something to her, man,' urged Parsons again. 'Confound it! pay her a compliment, can't you?'

'No! not till after dinner,' replied the bashful Tottle, anxious to postpone the evil moment.

'Well, gentlemen,' said Mrs Parsons, 'you are really very polite; you stay away the whole morning, after promising to take us out, and when you do come home, you stand whispering together and take no notice of us.'

'We were talking of the *business*, my dear, which detained us this morning,' replied Parsons, looking significantly at Tottle.

'Dear me! how very quickly the morning has gone,' said Miss Lillerton, referring to the gold watch, which was wound up on state occasions whether it required it or not.

'I think it has passed very slowly,' mildly suggested Tottle.

('That's right – bravo!') whispered Parsons.

'Indeed!' said Miss Lillerton, with an air of majestic surprise.

'I can only impute it to my unavoidable absence from your society, madam,' said Watkins, 'and that of Mrs Parsons.'

During this short dialogue, the ladies had been leading the way to the house.

'What the deuce did you stick Fanny into that last compliment for?' enquired Parsons, as they followed together; 'it quite spoilt the effect.'

'Oh! it really would have been too broad without,' replied Watkins Tottle, 'much too broad!'

'He's mad!' Parsons whispered to his wife, as they entered the drawing-room, 'mad from modesty.'

'Dear me!' ejaculated the lady, 'I never heard of such a thing.'

'You'll find we have quite a family dinner, Mr Tottle,' said Mrs Parsons, when they sat down to table: 'Miss Lillerton is one of us, and, of course, we make no stranger of you.'

Mr Watkins Tottle expressed a hope that the Parsons family never would make a stranger of him; and wished internally that his bashfulness would allow him to feel a little less like a stranger himself.

'Take off the covers, Martha,' said Mrs Parsons, directing the shifting of the scenery with great anxiety. The order was obeyed, and a pair of boiled fowls, with tongue and etceteras, were displayed at the top, and a fillet of veal at the bottom. On one side of the table two green sauce-tureens, with ladles of the same, were setting to each other in a green dish; and on the other was a curried rabbit, in a brown suit, turned up with lemon.

'Miss Lillerton, my dear,' said Mrs Parsons, 'shall I assist you?'

'Thank you, no; I think I'll trouble Mr Tottle.'

Watkins started – trembled – helped the rabbit – and broke a tumbler. The countenance of the lady of the house, which had been all smiles previously, underwent an awful change.

'Extremely sorry,' stammered Watkins, assisting himself to curry and parsley and butter in the extremity of his confusion.

'Not the least consequence,' replied Mrs Parsons, in a tone which implied that it was of the greatest consequence possible, directing aside the researches of the boy, who was groping under the table for the bits of broken glass.

'I presume,' said Miss Lillerton, 'that Mr Tottle is aware of the interest which bachelors usually pay in such cases; a dozen glasses for one is the lowest penalty.'

Mr Gabriel Parsons gave his friend an admonitory tread on the toe. Here was a clear hint that the sooner he ceased to be a bachelor and emancipated himself from such penalties, the better. Mr Watkins Tottle viewed the observation in the same light, and challenged Mrs Parsons to take wine, with a degree of presence of mind, which, under all the circumstances, was really extraordinary.

'Miss Lillerton,' said Gabriel, 'may I have the pleasure?'

'I shall be most happy.'

'Tottle, will you assist Miss Lillerton, and pass the decanter. Thank you.' The usual pantomimic ceremony of nodding and sipping gone through, 'Tottle, were you ever in Suffolk?' enquired the master of the house, who was burning to tell one of his seven stock stories.

'No,' responded Watkins, adding, by way of a saving clause, 'but I've been in Devonshire.'

'Ah!' replied Gabriel, 'it was in Suffolk that a rather singular circumstance happened to me many years ago. Did you ever happen to hear me mention it?'

Mr Watkins Tottle *had* happened to hear his friend mention it some four hundred times. Of course he expressed great curiosity, and evinced the utmost impatience to hear the story again. Mr Gabriel Parsons forthwith attempted to proceed, in spite of the interruptions to which, as our readers must frequently have observed, the master of the house is often exposed in such cases. We will attempt to give them an idea of our meaning.

'When I was in Suffolk – ' said Mr Gabriel Parsons.

'Take off the fowls first, Martha,' said Mrs Parsons. 'I beg your pardon, my dear.'

'When I was in Suffolk,' resumed Mr Parsons, with an impatient glance at his wife, who pretended not to observe it, 'which is now years ago, business led me to the town of Bury St Edmund's. I had to stop at the principal places in my way, and therefore, for the sake of convenience, I travelled in a gig. I left Sudbury one dark night – it was wintertime – about nine o'clock; the rain poured in torrents, the wind howled among the trees that skirted the roadside, and I was obliged to proceed at a foot-pace, for I could hardly see my hand before me, it was so dark – '

'John,' interrupted Mrs Parsons, in a low, hollow voice, 'don't spill that gravy.'

'Fanny,' said Parsons impatiently, 'I wish you'd defer these domestic reproofs to some more suitable time. Really, my dear, these constant interruptions are very annoying.'

'My dear, I didn't interrupt you,' said Mrs Parsons.

'But, my dear, you did interrupt me,' remonstrated Mr Parsons.

'How very absurd you are, my love! I must give directions to the servants; I am quite sure that if I sat here and allowed John to spill the gravy over the new carpet, you'd be the first to find fault when you saw the stain tomorrow morning.'

'Well,' continued Gabriel with a resigned air, as if he knew there was no getting over the point about the carpet, 'I was just saying, it was so dark that I could hardly see my hand before me. The road was very lonely, and I assure you, Tottle (this was a device to arrest the wandering attention of that individual, which was distracted by a confidential communication between Mrs Parsons and Martha, accompanied by the delivery of a large bunch of keys), I assure you, Tottle, I became somehow impressed with a sense of the loneliness of my situation – '

'Pie to your master,' interrupted Mrs Parsons, again directing the servant.

'Now, pray, my dear,' remonstrated Parsons once more, very pettishly. Mrs P. turned up her hands and eyebrows, and appealed in dumb show to Miss Lillerton. 'As I turned a corner of the road,' resumed Gabriel, 'the horse stopped short, and reared tremendously. I pulled up, jumped out, ran to his head, and found a man lying on his back in the middle of the road, with his eyes fixed on the sky. I thought he was dead; but no, he was alive, and there appeared to be nothing the matter with him. He jumped up, and putting his hand to his chest and fixing upon me the most earnest gaze you can imagine, exclaimed – 'Pudding here,' said Mrs Parsons.

'Oh! it's no use,' exclaimed the host, now rendered desperate. 'Here, Tottle; a glass of wine. It's useless to attempt relating anything when Mrs Parsons is present.'

This attack was received in the usual way. Mrs Parsons talked *to* Miss Lillerton and *at* her better half; expatiated on the impatience of men generally; hinted that her husband was peculiarly vicious in this respect, and wound up by insinuating that she must be one of the best tempers that ever existed, or she never could put up with it. Really what she had to endure sometimes was more than anyone who saw her in everyday life could by possibility suppose. The story was now a painful subject, and therefore Mr Parsons declined to enter into any details and contented himself by stating that the man was a maniac, who had escaped from a neighbouring madhouse.

The cloth was removed; the ladies soon afterwards retired, and Miss Lillerton played the piano in the drawing-room overhead, very loudly, for the edification of the visitor. Mr Watkins Tottle and Mr Gabriel Parsons sat chatting comfortably enough, until the conclusion of the second bottle, when the latter, in proposing an adjournment to the drawing-room, informed Watkins that he had concerted a plan with his wife for leaving him and Miss Lillerton alone soon after tea.

'I say,' said Tottle, as they went upstairs, 'don't you think it would be better if we put it off till – till – tomorrow?'

'Don't *you* think it would have been much better if I had left you in that wretched hole I found you in this morning?' retorted Parsons bluntly.

'Well – well – I only made a suggestion,' said poor Watkins Tottle, with a deep sigh.

Tea was soon concluded, and Miss Lillerton, drawing a small work-table on one side of the fire and placing a little wooden frame upon it, something like a miniature clay-mill without the horse, was soon busily engaged in making a watch-guard with brown silk.

'God bless me!' exclaimed Parsons, starting up with well-feigned surprise, 'I've forgotten those confounded letters. Tottle, I know you'll excuse me.'

If Tottle had been a free agent, he would have allowed no one to leave the room on any pretence, except himself. As it was, however, he was obliged to look cheerful when Parsons quitted the apartment.

He had scarcely left, when Martha put her head into the room, with – 'Please, ma'am, you're wanted.'

Mrs Parsons left the room, shut the door carefully after her, and Mr Watkins Tottle was left alone with Miss Lillerton.

For the first five minutes there was a dead silence – Mr Watkins Tottle was thinking how he should begin, and Miss Lillerton appeared to be thinking of nothing. The fire was burning low; Mr Watkins Tottle stirred it and put some coals on.

'Hem!' coughed Miss Lillerton; Mr Watkins Tottle thought the fair creature had spoken. 'I beg your pardon,' said he.

'Eh?'

'I thought you spoke.'

'No.'

'Oh!'

'There are some books on the sofa, Mr Tottle, if you would like to look at them,' said Miss Lillerton, after the lapse of another five minutes.

'No, thank you,' returned Watkins; and then he added, with a courage which was perfectly astonishing, even to himself, 'Madam, that is Miss Lillerton, I wish to speak to you.'

'To me!' said Miss Lillerton, letting the silk drop from her hands, and sliding her chair back a few paces. 'Speak – to me!'

'To you, madam – and on the subject of the state of your affections.'

The lady hastily rose and would have left the room; but Mr Watkins Tottle gently detained her by the hand, and holding it as far from him as the joint length of their arms would permit, he thus proceeded: 'Pray do not misunderstand me, or suppose that I am led to address you, after so short an acquaintance, by any feeling of my own merits – for merits I have none which could give me a claim to your hand. I hope you will acquit me of any presumption when I explain that I have been acquainted through Mrs Parsons, with the state – that is, that Mrs Parsons has told me – at least, not Mrs Parsons, but – ' here Watkins began to wander, but Miss Lillerton relieved him.

'Am I to understand, Mr Tottle, that Mrs Parsons has acquainted you with my feeling – my affection – I mean my respect, for an individual of the opposite sex?'

'She has.'

'Then, what?' enquired Miss Lillerton, averting her face with a girlish air, 'what could induce *you* to seek such an interview as this? What can your object be? How can I promote your happiness, Mr Tottle?'

Here was the time for a flourish. 'By allowing me,' replied Watkins, falling bump on his knees and breaking two brace-buttons and a waist-coat-string in the act – 'By allowing me to be your slave, your servant – in short, by unreservedly making me the confidant of your heart's feelings – may I say for the promotion of your own happiness – may I say, in order that you may become the wife of a kind and affectionate husband?'

'Disinterested creature!' exclaimed Miss Lillerton, hiding her face in a white pocket-handkerchief with an eyelet-hole border.

Mr Watkins Tottle thought that if the lady knew all, she might possibly alter her opinion on this last point. He raised the tip of her middle finger ceremoniously to his lips, and got off his knees, as gracefully as he could. 'My information was correct?' he tremulously enquired, when he was once more on his feet.

'It was.' Watkins elevated his hands and looked up to the ornament in the centre of the ceiling, which had been made for a lamp, by way of expressing his rapture.

'Our situation, Mr Tottle,' resumed the lady, glancing at him through one of the eyelet-holes, 'is a most peculiar and delicate one.'

'It is,' said Mr Tottle.

'Our acquaintance has been of *so* short duration,' said Miss Lillerton.

*Falling bump on his knees and breaking two brace-buttons and a waistcoat-
string in the act – 'By allowing me to be your slave, your servant*

'Only a week,' assented Watkins Tottle.

'Oh! more than that,' exclaimed the lady, in a tone of surprise.

'Indeed!' said Tottle.

'More than a month – more than two months!' said Miss Lillerton.

'Rather odd, this,' thought Watkins. 'Oh!' he said, recollecting Parsons's assurance that she had known him from report, 'I understand. But, my dear madam, pray, consider. The longer this acquaintance has existed, the less reason is there for delay now. Why not at once fix a period for gratifying the hopes of your devoted admirer?'

'It has been represented to me again and again that this is the course I ought to pursue,' replied Miss Lillerton, 'but pardon my feelings of delicacy, Mr Tottle – pray excuse this embarrassment – I have peculiar ideas on such subjects, and I am quite sure that I never could summon up fortitude enough to name the day to my future husband.'

'Then allow *me* to name it,' said Tottle eagerly.

'I should like to fix it myself,' replied Miss Lillerton, bashfully, but I cannot do so without at once resorting to a third party.'

'A third party!' thought Watkins Tottle; 'who the deuce is that to be, I wonder!'

'Mr Tottle,' continued Miss Lillerton, 'you have made me a most disinterested and kind offer – that offer I accept. Will you at once be the bearer of a note from me to – to Mr Timson?'

'Mr Timson!' said Watkins.

'After what has passed between us,' responded Miss Lillerton, still averting her head, 'you must understand whom I mean; Mr Timson, the – the – clergyman.'

'Mr Timson, the clergyman!' ejaculated Watkins Tottle, in a state of inexpressible beatitude and positive wonder at his own success. 'Angel! Certainly – this moment!'

'I'll prepare it immediately,' said Miss Lillerton, making for the door; 'the events of this day have flurried me so much, Mr Tottle, that I shall not leave my room again this evening; I will send you the note by the servant.'

'Stay – stay,' cried Watkins Tottle, still keeping a most respectful distance from the lady; 'when shall we meet again?'

'Oh! Mr Tottle,' replied Miss Lillerton, coquettishly, 'when we are married, I can never see you too often, nor thank you too much;' and she left the room.

Mr Watkins Tottle flung himself into an armchair and indulged in the most delicious reveries of future bliss, in which the idea of 'five hundred pounds per annum, with an uncontrolled power of disposing of it by her last will and testament', was somehow or other the foremost. He had gone through the interview so well, and it had terminated so admirably, that he almost began to wish he had expressly stipulated for the settlement of the annual five hundred on himself.

'May I come in?' said Mr Gabriel Parsons, peeping in at the door.

'You may,' replied Watkins.

'Well, have you done it?' anxiously enquired Gabriel.

'Have I done it!' said Watkins Tottle. 'Hush – I'm going to the clergyman.'

'No!' said Parsons. 'How well you have managed it!'

'Where does Timson live?' enquired Watkins.

'At his uncle's,' replied Gabriel, 'just round the lane. He's waiting for a living and has been assisting his uncle here for the last two or three months. But how well you have done it – I didn't think you could have carried it off so!'

Mr Watkins Tottle was proceeding to demonstrate that the Richardsonian principle was the best on which love could possibly be made, when he was interrupted by the entrance of Martha, with a little pink note folded like a fancy cocked-hat.

'Miss Lillerton's compliments,' said Martha, as she delivered it into Tottle's hands, and vanished.

'Do you observe the delicacy?' said Tottle, appealing to Mr Gabriel Parsons. '*Compliments*, not *love*, by the servant, eh?'

Mr Gabriel Parsons didn't exactly know what reply to make, so he poked the forefinger of his right hand between the third and fourth ribs of Mr Watkins Tottle.

'Come,' said Watkins, when the explosion of mirth, consequent on this practical jest, had subsided, 'we'll be off at once – let's lose no time.'

'Capital!' echoed Gabriel Parsons; and in five minutes they were at the garden-gate of the villa tenanted by the uncle of Mr Timson.

'Is Mr Charles Timson at home?' enquired Mr Watkins Tottle of Mr Charles Timson's uncle's man.

'Mr Charles *is* at home,' replied the man, stammering; 'but he desired me to say he couldn't be interrupted, sir, by any of the parishioners.'

'I am not a parishioner,' replied Watkins.

'Is Mr Charles writing a sermon, Tom?' enquired Parsons, thrusting himself forward.

'No, Mr Parsons, sir; he's not exactly writing a sermon, but he is practising the violoncello in his own bedroom, and gave strict orders not to be disturbed.'

'Say I'm here,' replied Gabriel, leading the way across the garden; 'Mr Parsons and Mr Tottle, on private and particular business.'

They were shown into the parlour, and the servant departed to deliver his message. The distant groaning of the violoncello ceased; footsteps were heard on the stairs; and Mr Timson presented himself, and shook hands with Parsons with the utmost cordiality.

'How do you do, sir?' said Watkins Tottle, with great solemnity.

'How do *you* do, sir?' replied Timson, with as much coldness as if it were a matter of perfect indifference to him how he did, as it very likely was.

'I beg to deliver this note to you,' said Watkins Tottle, producing the cocked-hat.

'From Miss Lillerton!' said Timson, suddenly changing colour. 'Pray sit down.'

Mr Watkins Tottle sat down, and while Timson perused the note, fixed his eyes on an oyster-sauce-coloured portrait of the Archbishop of Canterbury which hung over the fireplace.

Mr Timson rose from his seat when he had concluded the note, and looked dubiously at Parsons. 'May I ask,' he enquired, appealing to Watkins Tottle, 'whether our friend here is acquainted with the object of your visit?'

'Our friend is in *my* confidence,' replied Watkins, with considerable importance.

'Then, sir,' said Timson, seizing both Tottle's hands, 'allow me in his presence to thank you most unfeignedly and cordially for the noble part you have acted in this affair.'

'He thinks I recommended him,' thought Tottle. 'Confound these fellows! they never think of anything but their fees.'

'I deeply regret having misunderstood your intentions, my dear sir,' continued Timson. 'Disinterested and manly, indeed! There are very few men who would have acted as you have done.'

Mr Watkins Tottle could not help thinking that this last remark was anything but complimentary. He therefore enquired, rather hastily, 'When is it to be?'

'On Thursday,' replied Timson – 'on Thursday morning at half-past eight.'

'Uncommonly early,' observed Watkins Tottle, with an air of triumphant self-denial. 'I shall hardly be able to get down here by that hour.' (This was intended for a joke.)

'Never mind, my dear fellow,' replied Timson, all suavity, shaking hands with Tottle again most heartily, 'so long as we see you to breakfast, you know – '

'Eh!' said Parsons, with one of the most extraordinary expressions of countenance that ever appeared in a human face.

'What!' ejaculated Watkins Tottle, at the same moment.

'I say that so long as we see you to breakfast,' replied Timson, 'we will excuse your being absent from the ceremony, though of course your presence at it would give us the utmost pleasure.'

Mr Watkins Tottle staggered against the wall and fixed his eyes on Timson with appalling perseverance.

'Timson,' said Parsons, hurriedly brushing his hat with his left arm, 'when you say "us", whom do you mean?'

Mr Timson looked foolish in his turn, when he replied, 'Why – Mrs Timson that will be this day week: Miss Lillerton that is – '

'Now don't stare at that idiot in the corner,' angrily exclaimed Parsons, as the extraordinary convulsions of Watkins Tottle's countenance excited the wondering gaze of Timson – 'but have the goodness to tell me in three words the contents of that note?'

'This note,' replied Timson, 'is from Miss Lillerton, to whom I have been for the last five weeks regularly engaged. Her singular scruples and strange feeling on some points have hitherto prevented my bringing the engagement to that termination which I so anxiously desire. She informs me here that she sounded Mrs Parsons with the view of making her her confidante and go-between, that Mrs Parsons informed this elderly gentleman, Mr Tottle, of the circumstance, and that he, in the most kind and delicate terms, offered to assist us in any way, and even undertook to convey this note, which contains the promise I have long sought in vain – an act of kindness for which I can never be sufficiently grateful.'

'Good night, Timson,' said Parsons, hurrying off and carrying the bewildered Tottle with him.

'Won't you stay – and have something?' said Timson.

'No, thank ye,' replied Parsons; 'I've had quite enough;' and away he went, followed by Watkins Tottle in a state of stupefaction.

Mr Gabriel Parsons whistled until they had walked some quarter of a mile past his own gate, when he suddenly stopped, and said, 'You are a clever fellow, Tottle, ain't you?'

'I don't know,' said the unfortunate Watkins.

'I suppose you'll say this is Fanny's fault, won't you?' enquired Gabriel.

'I don't know anything about it,' replied the bewildered Tottle.

'Well,' said Parsons, turning on his heel to go home, 'the next time you make an offer, you had better speak plainly and not throw a chance away. And the next time you're locked up in a sponging-house, just wait there till I come and take you out, there's a good fellow.'

How, or at what hour, Mr Watkins Tottle returned to Cecil Street is unknown. His boots were seen outside his bedroom-door next morning; but we have the authority of his landlady for stating that he neither emerged therefrom nor accepted sustenance for four-and-twenty hours. At the expiration of that period, and when a council of war was being held in the kitchen on the propriety of summoning the parochial beadle to break his door open, he rang his bell and demanded a cup of milk and water. The next morning he went through the formalities of eating and drinking as usual, but a week afterwards he was seized with a relapse, while perusing the list of marriages in a morning paper, from which he never perfectly recovered.

A few weeks after the last-named occurrence, the body of a gentleman unknown was found in the Regent's Canal. In the trousers-pockets were four shillings and threepence halfpenny; a matrimonial advertisement from a lady, which appeared to have been cut out of a Sunday paper; a toothpick – and a card case, which it is confidently believed would have led to the identification of the unfortunate gentleman but for the circumstance of there being none but blank cards in it. Mr Watkins Tottle had absented himself from his lodgings shortly before. A bill, which has not been taken up, was presented next morning; and a bill, which has not been taken down, was soon afterwards affixed in his parlour window.

THE BLOOMSBURY CHRISTENING

Mr Nicodemus Dumps, or, as his acquaintance called him, 'Long Dumps', was a bachelor, six feet high and fifty years old; cross, cadaverous, odd and ill-natured. He was never happy but when he was miserable; and always miserable when he had the best reason to be happy. The only real comfort of his existence was to make everybody about him wretched – then he might be truly said to enjoy life. He was afflicted with a situation in the bank worth five hundred a year, and he rented a 'first-floor furnished', at Pentonville, which he originally took because it commanded a dismal prospect of an adjacent churchyard. He was familiar with the face of every tombstone, and the burial service seemed to excite his strongest sympathy. His friends said he was surly – he insisted he was nervous; they thought him a lucky dog, but he protested that he was 'the most unfortunate man in the world'. Cold as he was, and wretched as he declared himself to be, he was not wholly unsusceptible of attachments. He revered the memory of Hoyle, as he was himself an admirable and imperturbable whist-player, and he chuckled with delight at a fretful and impatient adversary. He adored King Herod for his massacre of the innocents; and if he hated one thing more than another, it was a child. However, he could hardly be said to hate anything in particular, because he disliked everything in general; but perhaps his greatest antipathies were cabs, old women, doors that would not shut, musical amateurs and omnibus cads. He subscribed to the Society for the Suppression of Vice, for the pleasure of putting a stop to any harmless amusements; and he contributed largely towards the support of two itinerant Methodist parsons, in the amiable hope that if circumstances rendered any people happy in this world, they might perchance be rendered miserable by fears for the next.

Mr Dumps had a nephew who had been married about a year, and who was somewhat of a favourite with his uncle because he was an admirable subject to exercise his misery-creating powers upon. Mr Charles Kitterbell was a small, sharp, spare man, with a very large head and a broad, good-humoured countenance. He looked like a faded giant, with the head and face partially restored; and he had a cast in his eye which rendered it quite impossible for anyone with whom he conversed to know where he was looking. His eyes appeared fixed on the wall, and he was staring you out of countenance; in short, there was no catching his eye, and perhaps it is a merciful dispensation of providence that such eyes are not catching. In addition to these characteristics, it may be added that Mr Charles Kitterbell was one of the most credulous and matter-of-fact little personages that ever took *to* himself a wife, and *for* himself a house in Great Russell Street, Bedford Square. (Uncle Dumps always dropped the 'Bedford Square' and inserted in lieu thereof the dreadful words 'Tottenham Court Road'.)

'No, but, uncle, 'pon my life you must – you must promise to be godfather,' said Mr Kitterbell, as he sat in conversation with his respected relative one morning.

'I cannot, indeed I cannot,' returned Dumps.

'Well, but why not? Jemima will think it very unkind. It's very little trouble.'

'As to the trouble,' rejoined the most unhappy man in existence, 'I don't mind that; but my nerves are in that state – I cannot go through the ceremony. You know I don't like going out. For God's sake, Charles, don't fidget with that stool so; you'll drive me mad.' Mr Kitterbell, quite regardless of his uncle's nerves, had occupied himself for some ten minutes in describing a circle on the floor with one leg of the office-stool on which he was seated, keeping the other three up in the air and holding fast on by the desk.

'I beg your pardon, uncle,' said Kitterbell, quite abashed, suddenly releasing his hold of the desk and bringing the three wandering legs back to the floor with a force sufficient to drive them through it.

'But come, don't refuse. If it's a boy, you know, we must have two godfathers.'

'*If* it's a boy!' said Dumps; 'why can't you say at once whether it *is* a boy or not?'

'I should be very happy to tell you, but it's impossible I can undertake to say whether it's a girl or a boy if the child isn't born yet.'

'Not born yet!' echoed Dumps, with a gleam of hope lighting up his lugubrious visage. 'Oh, well, it *may* be a girl and then you won't want me; or if it is a boy, it *may* die before it is christened.'

'I hope not,' said the father that expected to be, looking very grave.

'I hope not,' acquiesced Dumps, evidently pleased with the subject. He was beginning to get happy. 'I hope not, but distressing cases frequently occur during the first two or three days of a child's life; fits, I am told, are exceedingly common, and alarming convulsions are almost matters of course.'

'Lord, uncle!' ejaculated little Kitterbell, gasping for breath.

'Yes; my landlady was confined – let me see – last Tuesday: an uncommonly fine boy. On the Thursday night the nurse was sitting with him upon her knee before the fire, and he was as well as possible. Suddenly he became black in the face, and alarmingly spasmodic. The medical man was instantly sent for, and every remedy was tried, but – '

'How frightful!' interrupted the horror-stricken Kitterbell.

'The child died, of course. However, your child *may* not die; and if it should be a boy, and should *live* to be christened, why I suppose I must be one of the sponsors.' Dumps was evidently good natured on the faith of his anticipations.

'Thank you, uncle,' said his agitated nephew, grasping his hand as warmly as if he had done him some essential service. 'Perhaps I had better not tell Mrs K. what you have mentioned.'

'Why, if she's low-spirited, perhaps you had better not mention the melancholy case to her,' returned Dumps, who of course had invented the whole story; 'though perhaps it would be but doing your duty as a husband to prepare her for the *worst*.'

A day or two afterwards, as Dumps was perusing a morning paper at the chop-house which he regularly frequented, the following paragraph met his eyes –

Births – On Saturday, the 18th inst., in Great Russell Street, the lady of Charles Kitterbell Esq. of a son.

'It *is* a boy!' he exclaimed, dashing down the paper, to the astonishment of the waiters. 'It *is* a boy!' But he speedily regained his composure as his eye rested on a paragraph quoting the number of infant deaths from the bills of mortality.

Six weeks passed away, and as no communication had been received from the Kitterbells, Dumps was beginning to flatter himself that the child was dead, when the following note painfully resolved his doubts –

Great Russell Street
Monday morning

DEAR UNCLE – You will be delighted to hear that my dear Jemima has left her room, and that your future godson is getting on capitally. He was very thin at first, but he is getting much larger, and nurse says he is filling out every day. He cries a good deal, and is a very singular colour, which made Jemima and me rather uncomfortable; but as nurse says it's natural, and as of course we know nothing about these things yet, we are quite satisfied with what nurse says. We think he will be a sharp child; and nurse says she's sure he will, because he never goes to sleep. You will readily believe that we are all very happy, only we're a little worn out for want of rest, as he keeps us awake all night; but this we must expect, nurse says, for the first six or eight months. He has been vaccinated, but in consequence of the operation being rather awkwardly performed, some small particles of glass were introduced into the arm with the matter. Perhaps this may in some degree account for his being rather fractious; at least, so nurse says. We propose to have him christened at twelve o'clock on Friday, at Saint George's Church in Hart Street, by the name of Frederick Charles William. Pray don't be later than a quarter before twelve. We shall have a very few friends in the evening, when of course we shall see you. I am sorry to say that the dear boy appears rather restless and uneasy today: the cause, I fear, is fever.

Believe me, dear uncle,

Yours affectionately,

CHARLES KITTERBELL

PS – I open this note to say that we have just discovered the cause of little Frederick's restlessness. It is not fever, as I apprehended, but a small pin, which nurse accidentally stuck in his leg yesterday evening. We have taken it out, and he appears more composed, though he still sobs a good deal.

It is almost unnecessary to say that the perusal of the above interesting statement was no great relief to the mind of the hypochondriacal Dumps. It was impossible to recede, however, and so he put the best face – that is to say, an uncommonly miserable one – upon the matter; and purchased a handsome silver mug for the infant Kitterbell, upon which he ordered the initials F. C. W. K., with the customary untrained grape-vine-looking flourishes and a large full stop, to be engraved forthwith.

Monday was a fine day, Tuesday was delightful, Wednesday was equal to either and Thursday was finer than ever; four successive fine days in London! Hackney-coachmen became revolutionary and crossing-sweepers began to doubt the existence of a First Cause. The *Morning Herald* informed its readers that an old woman in Camden Town had been heard to say that the fineness of the season was 'unprecedented in the memory of the oldest inhabitant'; and Islington clerks, with large families and small salaries, left off their black gaiters, disdained to carry their once green cotton umbrellas and walked to town in the conscious pride of white stockings and cleanly brushed Bluchers. Dumps beheld all this with an eye of supreme contempt – his triumph was at hand. He knew that if it had been fine for four weeks instead of four days, it would rain when he went out; he was lugubriously happy in the conviction that Friday would be a wretched day – and so it was. 'I knew how it would be,' said Dumps, as he turned round opposite the Mansion House at eleven o'clock on the Friday morning. 'I knew how it would be. I am concerned, and that's enough;' – and certainly the appearance of the day was sufficient to depress the spirits of a much more buoyant-hearted individual than himself. It had rained, without a moment's cessation, since eight o'clock; everybody that passed up Cheapside, and down Cheapside, looked wet, cold and dirty. All sorts of forgotten and long-concealed umbrellas had been put into requisition. Cabs whisked about, with the 'fare' as carefully boxed up behind two glazed calico curtains as any mysterious picture in any one of Mrs Radcliffe's castles; omnibus horses smoked like steam-engines; nobody thought of 'standing up' under doorways or arches – they were painfully convinced it was a hopeless case; and so everybody went hastily along, jumbling and jostling, and swearing and perspiring, and slipping about like amateur skaters behind wooden chairs on the Serpentine on a frosty Sunday.

Dumps paused; he could not think of walking, being rather smart for the christening. If he took a cab he was sure to be spilt, and a hackney-coach was too expensive for his economical ideas. An omnibus was waiting at the opposite corner – it was a desperate case – he had never heard of an omnibus upsetting or running away, and if the cad did knock him down, he could 'pull him up' in return.

'Now, sir!' cried the young gentleman who officiated as 'cad' to the

'Lads of the Village', which was the name of the machine just noticed. Dumps crossed.

'This vay, sir!' shouted the driver of the 'Harkaway', pulling up his vehicle immediately across the door of the opposition – 'This vay, sir – he's full.' Dumps hesitated, whereupon the 'Lads of the Village' commenced pouring out a torrent of abuse against the 'Harkaway'; but the conductor of the 'Admiral Napier' settled the contest in a most satisfactory manner, for all parties, by seizing Dumps round the waist and thrusting him into the middle of his vehicle, which had just come up and only wanted the sixteenth inside.

'All right,' said the 'Admiral', and off the thing thundered, like a fire-engine at full gallop, with the kidnapped customer inside, standing in the position of a half doubled-up bootjack and falling about with every jerk of the machine, first on the one side and then on the other, like a 'Jack-in-the-green' on May Day, setting to the lady with a brass ladle.

'For heaven's sake, where am I to sit?' enquired the miserable man of an old gentleman, into whose stomach he had just fallen for the fourth time.

'Anywhere but on my *chest*, sir,' replied the old gentleman in a surly tone.

'Perhaps the *box* would suit the gentleman better,' suggested a very damp lawyer's clerk, in a pink shirt and a smirking countenance.

After a great deal of struggling and falling about, Dumps at last managed to squeeze himself into a seat, which, in addition to the slight disadvantage of being between a window that would not shut, and a door that must be open, placed him in close contact with a passenger who had been walking about all the morning without an umbrella, and who looked as if he had spent the day in a full water-butt – only wetter.

'Don't bang the door so,' said Dumps to the conductor, as he shut it after letting out four of the passengers; 'I am very nervous – it destroys me.'

'Did any gen'lm'n say anythink?' replied the cad, thrusting in his head, and trying to look as if he didn't understand the request.

'I told you not to bang the door so!' repeated Dumps, with an expression of countenance like the knave of clubs, in convulsions.

'Oh! vy, it's rather a sing'ler circumstance about this here door, sir, that it von't shut without banging,' replied the conductor; and he opened the door very wide, and shut it again with a terrific bang, in proof of the assertion.

'I beg your pardon, sir,' said a little prim, wheezing old gentleman, sitting opposite Dumps, 'I beg your pardon; but have you ever observed, when you have been in an omnibus on a wet day, that four people out of five always come in with large cotton umbrellas without a handle at the top or the brass spike at the bottom?'

'Why, sir,' returned Dumps, as he heard the clock strike the half hour, 'it never struck me before; but now you mention it, I – Hallo! hallo!' shouted the persecuted individual, as the omnibus dashed past Drury Lane, where he had directed to be set down. 'Where is the cad?'

'I think he's on the box, sir,' said the young gentleman before noticed in the pink shirt, which looked like a white one ruled with red ink.

'I want to be set down!' said Dumps in a faint voice, overcome by his previous efforts.

'I think these cads want to be *set down*,' returned the attorney's clerk, chuckling at his sally.

'Hallo!' cried Dumps again.

'Hallo!' echoed the passengers. The omnibus passed St Giles's church.

'Hold hard!' said the conductor; 'I'm blowed if we ha'n't forgot the gen'lm'n as vas to be set down at Doory Lane. – Now, sir, make haste, if you please,' he added, opening the door, and assisting Dumps out with as much coolness as if it was 'all right'. Dumps's indignation was for once getting the better of his cynical equanimity. 'Drury Lane!' he gasped, with the voice of a boy in a cold bath for the first time.

'Doory Lane, sir? – yes, sir – third turning on the right-hand side, sir.'

Dumps's passion was paramount: he clutched his umbrella, and was striding off with the firm determination of not paying the fare. The cad, by a remarkable coincidence, happened to entertain a directly contrary opinion, and heaven knows how far the altercation would have proceeded, if it had not been most ably and satisfactorily brought to a close by the driver.

'Hallo!' said that respectable person, standing up on the box, and leaning with one hand on the roof of the omnibus. 'Hallo, Tom! tell the gentleman if so be as he feels aggrieved, we will take him up to the Edge– er [Edgeware] Road for nothing, and set him down at Doory Lane when we comes back. He can't reject that, anyhow.'

The argument was irresistible: Dumps paid the disputed sixpence and in a quarter of an hour was on the staircase of 14 Great Russell Street.

Everything indicated that preparations were making for the reception of 'a few friends' in the evening. Two dozen extra tumblers and four ditto wineglasses – looking anything but transparent, with little bits of straw in them – were on the slab in the passage, just arrived. There was a great smell of nutmeg, port wine and almonds on the staircase; the covers were taken off the stair-carpet, and the figure of Venus on the first landing looked as if she were ashamed of the composition-candle in her right hand, which contrasted beautifully with the lamp-blacked drapery of the goddess of love. The female servant (who looked very warm and bustling) ushered Dumps into a front drawing-room, very prettily furnished with a plentiful sprinkling of little baskets, paper table-mats, china watchmen, pink and gold albums and rainbow-bound little books on the different tables.

'Ah, uncle!' said Mr Kitterbell, 'how d'ye do? Allow me – Jemima, my dear – my uncle. I think you've seen Jemima before, sir?'

'Have had the *pleasure*,' returned big Dumps, his tone and look making it doubtful whether in his life he had ever experienced the sensation.

'I'm sure,' said Mrs Kitterbell, with a languid smile, and a slight cough. 'I'm sure – hem – any friend – of Charles's – hem much less a relation, is – '

'I knew you'd say so, my love,' said little Kitterbell, who, while he appeared to be gazing on the opposite houses, was looking at his wife with a most affectionate air: 'Bless you!' The last two words were accompanied with a simper, and a squeeze of the hand, which stirred up all Uncle Dumps's bile.

'Jane, tell nurse to bring down baby,' said Mrs Kitterbell, addressing the servant. Mrs Kitterbell was a tall, thin young lady, with very light hair and a particularly white face – one of those young women who almost invariably, though one hardly knows why, recall to one's mind the idea of a cold fillet of veal. Out went the servant, and in came the nurse, with a remarkably small parcel in her arms, packed up in a blue mantle trimmed with white fur. This was the baby.

'Now, uncle,' said Mr Kitterbell, lifting up that part of the mantle which covered the infant's face, with an air of great triumph, '*who* do you think he's like?'

'He! he! Yes, who?' said Mrs K., putting her arm through her husband's and looking up into Dumps's face with an expression of as much interest as she was capable of displaying.

'Good God, how small he is!' cried the amiable uncle, starting back with well-feigned surprise; '*remarkably* small indeed.'

*In came the nurse, with a remarkably small parcel in her arms, packed
up in a blue mantle trimmed with white fur. This was the baby.*

'Do you think so?' enquired poor little Kitterbell, rather alarmed. 'He's a monster to what he was – ain't he, nurse?'

'He's a dear,' said the nurse, squeezing the child and evading the question – not because she scrupled to disguise the fact, but because she couldn't afford to throw away the chance of Dumps's half-crown.

'Well, but who is he like?' enquired little Kitterbell.

Dumps looked at the little pink heap before him, and only thought at the moment of the best mode of mortifying the youthful parents.

'I really don't know *who* he's like,' he answered, very well knowing the reply expected of him.

'Don't you think he's like *me*?' enquired his nephew with a knowing air.

'Oh, *decidedly* not!' returned Dumps, with an emphasis not to be misunderstood. 'Decidedly not like you. – Oh, certainly not.'

'Like Jemima?' asked Kitterbell, faintly.

'Oh, dear no; not in the least. I'm no judge, of course, in such cases; but I really think he's more like one of those little carved representations that one sometimes sees blowing a trumpet on a tombstone!' The nurse stooped down over the child and with great difficulty prevented an explosion of mirth. Pa and ma looked almost as miserable as their amiable uncle.

'Well!' said the disappointed little father, 'you'll be better able to tell what he's like by and by. You shall see him this evening with his mantle off.'

'Thank you,' said Dumps, feeling particularly grateful.

'Now, my love,' said Kitterbell to his wife, 'it's time we were off. We're to meet the other godfather and the godmother at the church, uncle – Mr and Mrs Wilson from over the way – uncommonly nice people. My love, are you well wrapped up?'

'Yes, dear.'

'Are you sure you won't have another shawl?' enquired the anxious husband.

'No, sweet,' returned the charming mother, accepting Dumps's proffered arm; and the little party entered the hackney-coach that was to take them to the church, Dumps amusing Mrs Kitterbell by expatiating largely on the danger of measles, thrush, teethcutting and other interesting diseases to which children are subject.

The ceremony (which occupied about five minutes) passed off without anything particular occurring. The clergyman had to dine some distance from town, and had two churchings, three christenings and a funeral to perform in something less than an hour. The godfathers and godmother, therefore, promised to renounce the devil and all his works – 'and all that sort of thing' – as little Kitterbell said – 'in less than no time'; and with the exception of Dumps nearly letting the child fall into the font when he handed it to the clergyman, the whole affair went off in the usual business-like and matter-of-course manner, and Dumps re-entered the bank gates at two o'clock with a heavy heart, and the painful conviction that he was regularly booked for an evening party.

Evening came – and so did Dumps's pumps, black silk stockings and white cravat, which he had ordered to be forwarded, per boy, from Pentonville. The depressed godfather dressed himself at a friend's counting-house, from whence, with his spirits fifty degrees below proof, he sallied forth – as the weather had cleared up, and the evening was tolerably fine – to walk to Great Russell Street. Slowly he paced up Cheapside, Newgate Street, down Snow Hill and up Holborn ditto, looking as grim as the figurehead of a man-of-war, and finding out fresh causes of misery at every step. As he was crossing the corner of Hatton Garden, a man, apparently intoxicated, rushed against him, and would have knocked him down had he not been providentially caught by a very genteel young man who happened to be close to him at the time. The shock so disarranged Dumps's nerves, as well as his dress, that he could hardly stand. The gentleman took his arm, and in the kindest manner walked with him as far as Furnival's Inn. Dumps, for about the first time in his life, felt grateful and polite; and he and the gentlemanly-looking young man parted with mutual expressions of goodwill.

'There are at least some well-disposed men in the world,' ruminated the misanthropical Dumps, as he proceeded towards his destination.

Rat–tat–ta–ra–ra–ra–ra–rat – knocked a hackney-coachman at Kitterbell's door, in imitation of a gentleman's servant, just as Dumps reached it; and out came an old lady in a large toque and an old gentleman in a blue coat and three female copies of the old lady in pink dresses and shoes to match.

'It's a large party,' sighed the unhappy godfather, wiping the perspiration from his forehead and leaning against the area railings. It was some time before the miserable man could muster up courage to knock at the door, and when he did, the smart appearance of a neighbouring greengrocer (who had been hired to wait for seven and sixpence, and whose calves alone were worth double the money), the lamp in the passage and the Venus on the landing, added to the hum of many voices and the sound of a harp and two violins, painfully convinced him that his surmises were but too well founded.

'How are you?' said little Kitterbell, in a greater bustle than ever, bolting out of the little back parlour with a corkscrew in his hand, and various particles of sawdust, looking like so many inverted commas, on his inexpressibles.

'Good God!' said Dumps, turning into the aforesaid parlour to put his shoes on, which he had brought in his coat-pocket, and still more appalled by the sight of seven fresh-drawn corks and a corresponding number of decanters. 'How many people are there upstairs?'

'Oh, not above thirty-five. We've had the carpet taken up in the back drawing-room, and the piano and the card-tables are in the front. Jemima thought we'd better have a regular sit-down supper in the front parlour, because of the speechifying, and all that. But, Lord! uncle, what's the matter?' continued the excited little man, as Dumps stood with one shoe on, rummaging his pockets with the most frightful distortion of visage. 'What have you lost? Your pocketbook?'

'No,' returned Dumps, diving first into one pocket and then into the other, and speaking in a voice like Desdemona with the pillow over her mouth.

'Your card-case? snuffbox? the key of your lodgings?' continued Kitterbell, pouring question on question with the rapidity of lightning.

'No! no!' ejaculated Dumps, still diving eagerly into his empty pockets.

'Not – not – the *mug* you spoke of this morning?'

'Yes, the *mug*!' replied Dumps, sinking into a chair.

'How *could* you have done it?' enquired Kitterbell. 'Are you sure you brought it out?'

'Yes! yes! I see it all!' said Dumps, starting up as the idea flashed across his mind; 'miserable dog that I am – I was born to suffer. I see it all: it was the gentlemanly-looking young man!'

'Mr Dumps!' shouted the greengrocer in a stentorian voice, as he ushered the somewhat recovered godfather into the drawing-room half an hour after the above declaration. 'Mr Dumps!' – everybody looked at the door, and in came Dumps, feeling about as much out of place as a salmon might be supposed to be on a gravel-walk.

'Happy to see you again,' said Mrs Kitterbell, quite unconscious of the unfortunate man's confusion and misery; 'you must allow me to introduce you to a few of our friends – my mamma, Mr Dumps – my papa and sisters.' Dumps seized the hand of the mother as warmly as if she was his own parent, bowed *to* the young ladies and *against* a gentleman behind him and took no notice whatever of the father, who had been bowing incessantly for three minutes and a quarter.

'Uncle,' said little Kitterbell, after Dumps had been introduced to a select dozen or two, 'you must let me lead you to the other end of the room, to introduce you to my friend Danton. Such a splendid fellow! – I'm sure you'll like him – this way' – Dumps followed as tractably as a tame bear.

Mr Danton was a young man of about five-and-twenty, with a considerable stock of impudence and a very small share of ideas; he was a great favourite, especially with young ladies of from sixteen to twenty-six years of age, both inclusive. He could imitate the French-horn to admiration, sang comic songs most inimitably and had the most insinuating way of saying impertinent nothings to his doting female admirers. He had acquired, somehow or other, the reputation of being a great wit, and, accordingly, whenever he opened his mouth, everybody who knew him laughed very heartily.

The introduction took place in due form. Mr Danton bowed, and twirled a lady's handkerchief, which he held in his hand, in a most comic way. Everybody smiled.

'Very warm,' said Dumps, feeling it necessary to say something.

'Yes. It was warmer yesterday,' returned the brilliant Mr Danton. – A general laugh.

'I have great pleasure in congratulating you on your first appearance in the character of a father, sir,' he continued, addressing Dumps – 'godfather, I mean.' The young ladies were convulsed, and the gentlemen in ecstasies.

A general hum of admiration interrupted the conversation and announced the entrance of nurse with the baby. An universal rush of the young ladies immediately took place. (Girls are always *so* fond of babies in company.)

'Oh, you dear!' said one.

'How sweet!' cried another, in a low tone of the most enthusiastic admiration.

'Heavenly!' added a third.

'Oh! what dear little arms!' said a fourth, holding up an arm and fist about the size and shape of the leg of a fowl cleanly picked.

'Did you ever!' – said a little coquette with a large bustle, who looked like a French lithograph, appealing to a gentleman in three waistcoats – 'Did you ever!'

'Never, in my life,' returned her admirer, pulling up his collar.

'Oh! *do* let me take it, nurse,' cried another young lady. 'The love!'

'Can it open its eyes, nurse?' enquired another, affecting the utmost innocence. – Suffice it to say, that the single ladies unanimously voted him an angel, and that the married ones, *nem. con.*, agreed that he was decidedly the finest baby they had ever beheld – except their own.

The quadrilles were resumed with great spirit. Mr Danton was universally admitted to be beyond himself; several young ladies enchanted the company and gained admirers by singing 'We Met', 'I Saw Her at the Fancy Fair' and other equally sentimental and interesting ballads. 'The young men,' as Mrs Kitterbell said, 'made themselves very agreeable'; the girls did not lose their opportunity; and the evening promised to go off excellently. Dumps didn't mind it: he had devised a plan for himself – a little bit of fun in his own way – and he was almost happy! He played a rubber and lost every point. Mr Danton said he could not have lost every point, because he made a point of losing; everybody laughed tremendously. Dumps retorted with a better joke and nobody smiled, with the exception of the host, who seemed to consider it his duty to laugh till he was black in the face at everything. There was only one drawback – the musicians did not play with quite as much spirit as could have been wished. The cause, however, was satisfactorily explained; for it appeared, on the testimony of a gentleman who had come up from Gravesend in the afternoon, that they had been engaged on board a steamer all day, and had played almost without cessation all the way to Gravesend and all the way back again.

The 'sit-down supper' was excellent; there were four barley-sugar temples on the table, which would have looked beautiful if they had not melted away when the supper began; and a water-mill, whose only fault was that instead of going round, it ran over the tablecloth. Then there were fowls, and tongue, and trifle, and sweets, and lobster salad, and potted beef – and everything. And little Kitterbell kept calling out for clean plates and the clean plates did not come: and then the gentlemen who wanted the plates said they didn't mind, they'd take a lady's; and then Mrs Kitterbell applauded their gallantry, and the greengrocer ran about till he thought his seven and sixpence was very hardly earned; and the young ladies didn't eat much for fear it shouldn't look romantic, and the married ladies ate as much as possible for fear they shouldn't have enough; and a great deal of wine was drunk and everybody talked and laughed considerably.

'Hush! hush!' said Mr Kitterbell, rising and looking very important. 'My love (this was addressed to his wife at the other end of the table), take care of Mrs Maxwell, and your mamma, and the rest of the married ladies; the gentlemen will persuade the young ladies to fill their glasses, I am sure.'

'Ladies and gentlemen,' said Long Dumps, in a very sepulchral voice and rueful accent, rising from his chair like the ghost in *Don Juan*, 'will you have the kindness to charge your glasses? I am desirous of proposing a toast.'

A dead silence ensued, and the glasses were filled – everybody looked serious.

'Ladies and gentlemen,' slowly continued the ominous Dumps, 'I – ' (here Mr Danton imitated two notes from the French-horn, in a very loud key, which electrified the nervous toast-proposer and convulsed his audience).

'Order! order!' said little Kitterbell, endeavouring to suppress his laughter.

'Order!' said the gentlemen.

'Danton, be quiet,' said a particular friend on the opposite side of the table.

'Ladies and gentlemen,' resumed Dumps, somewhat recovered, and not much disconcerted, for he was always a pretty good hand at a speech – 'In accordance with what is, I believe, the established usage on these occasions, I, as one of the godfathers of Master Frederick Charles William Kitterbell – ' (here the speaker's voice faltered, for he remembered the mug) – 'venture to rise to propose a toast. I need hardly say that it is the health and prosperity of that young gentleman, the particular event of whose early life we are here met to celebrate – ' (applause). Ladies and gentlemen, it is impossible to suppose that our friends here, whose sincere well-wishers we all are, can pass through life without some trials, considerable suffering, severe affliction and heavy losses!' – Here the arch traitor paused, and slowly drew forth a long, white pocket handkerchief –

his example was followed by several ladies. 'That these trials may be long spared them is my most earnest prayer, my most fervent wish' (a distinct sob from the grandmother). 'I hope and trust, ladies and gentlemen, that the infant whose christening we have this evening met to celebrate may not be removed from the arms of his parents by premature decay' (several cambrics were in requisition): ' – that his young and now *apparently* healthy form, may not be wasted by lingering disease.' (Here Dumps cast a sardonic glance around, for a great sensation was manifest among the married ladies.) 'You, I am sure, will concur with me in wishing that he may live to be a comfort and a blessing to his parents.' ('Hear, hear!' and an audible sob from Mr Kitterbell.) 'But should he not be what we could wish – should he forget in aftertimes the duty which he owes to them – should they unhappily experience that distracting truth, "how sharper than a serpent's tooth it is to have a thankless child" – ' Here Mrs Kitterbell, with her handkerchief to her eyes, and accompanied by several ladies, rushed from the room and went into violent hysterics in the passage, leaving her better half in almost as bad a condition, and a general impression in Dumps's favour; for people like sentiment, after all.

It need hardly be added that this occurrence quite put a stop to the harmony of the evening. Vinegar, hartshorn and cold water were now as much in request as negus, rout-cakes and *bon-bons* had been a short time before. Mrs Kitterbell was immediately conveyed to her apartment, the musicians were silenced, flirting ceased and the company slowly departed. Dumps left the house at the commencement of the bustle and walked home with a light step and (for him) a cheerful heart. His landlady, who slept in the next room, has offered to make oath that she heard him laugh, in his peculiar manner, after he had locked his door. The assertion, however, is so improbable, and bears on the face of it such strong evidence of untruth, that it has never obtained credence to this hour.

The family of Mr Kitterbell has considerably increased since the period to which we have referred; he has now two sons and a daughter; and as he expects, at no distant period, to have another addition to his blooming progeny, he is anxious to secure an eligible godfather for the occasion. He is determined, however, to impose upon him two conditions. He must bind himself, by a solemn obligation, not to make any speech after supper; and it is indispensable that he should be in no way connected with 'the most miserable man in the world'.

THE DRUNKARD'S DEATH

We will be bold to say that there is scarcely a man in the constant habit of walking, day after day, through any of the crowded thoroughfares of London, who cannot recollect among the people whom he 'knows by sight', to use a familiar phrase, some being of abject and wretched appearance whom he remembers to have seen in a very different condition, whom he has observed sinking lower and lower, by almost imperceptible degrees, and the shabbiness and utter destitution of whose appearance, at last, strike forcibly and painfully upon him as he passes by. Is there any man who has mixed much with society, or whose avocations have caused him to mingle, at one time or other, with a great number of people, who cannot call to mind the time when some shabby, miserable wretch, in rags and filth, who shuffles past him now in all the squalor of disease and poverty, was a respectable tradesman, or clerk, or a man following some thriving pursuit with good prospects and decent means? – or cannot any of our readers call to mind from among the list of their quondam acquaintance, some fallen and degraded man, who lingers about the pavement in hungry misery – from whom everyone turns coldly away, and who preserves himself from sheer starvation, nobody knows how? Alas! such cases are of too frequent occurrence to be rare items in any man's experience; and but too often arise from one cause – drunkenness – that fierce rage for the slow, sure poison that oversteps every other consideration; that casts aside wife, children, friends, happiness and station; and hurries its victims madly on to degradation and death.

Some of these men have been impelled, by misfortune and misery, to the vice that has degraded them. The ruin of worldly expectations, the death of those they loved, the sorrow that slowly consumes, but will not break the heart, has driven them wild; and they present the hideous spectacle of madmen, slowly dying by their own hands. But by far the greater part have wilfully, and with open eyes, plunged into the gulf from which the man who once enters it never rises more, but into which he sinks deeper and deeper down until recovery is hopeless.

Such a man as this once stood by the bedside of his dying wife, while his children knelt around and mingled loud bursts of grief with their innocent prayers. The room was scantily and meanly furnished; and it needed but a glance at the pale form from which the light of life was fast passing away to know that grief and want and anxious care had been busy at her heart for many a weary year. An elderly woman, with her face bathed in tears, was supporting the head of the dying woman – her daughter – on her arm. But it was not towards her that the wan face turned; it was not her hand that the cold and trembling fingers clasped; they pressed the husband's arm; the eyes so soon to be closed in death rested on his face, and the man shook beneath their gaze. His dress was slovenly and disordered, his face inflamed, his eyes bloodshot and heavy. He had been summoned from some wild debauch to the bed of sorrow and death.

A shaded lamp by the bedside cast a dim light on the figures around and left the remainder of the room in thick, deep shadow. The silence of night prevailed without the house and the stillness of death was in the chamber. A watch hung over the mantel-shelf; its low ticking was the only sound that broke the profound quiet, but it was a solemn one, for well they knew, who heard it, that before it had recorded the passing of another hour, it would beat the knell of a departed spirit.

It is a dreadful thing to wait and watch for the approach of death; to know that hope is gone and recovery impossible; and to sit and count the dreary hours through long, long nights – such nights as only watchers by the bed of sickness know. It chills the blood to hear the dearest secrets of the heart – the pent-up, hidden secrets of many years – poured forth by the unconscious, helpless being before you; and to think how little the reserve and cunning of a whole life will avail, when fever and delirium tear off the mask at last. Strange tales have been told in the wanderings of dying men; tales so full of guilt and crime that those who stood by the sick person's couch have fled in horror and affright, lest they should be scared to madness by what they heard and saw; and many a wretch has died alone, raving of deeds the very name of which has driven the boldest man away.

But no such ravings were to be heard at the bedside by which the children knelt. Their half-stifled sobs and moaning alone broke the silence of the lonely chamber. And when at last the mother's grasp relaxed, and, turning one look from the children to the father, she vainly strove to speak and fell backward on the pillow, all was so calm and tranquil that she seemed to sink to sleep. They leant over her; they called upon her name, softly at first, and then in the loud and piercing tones of desperation. But there was no reply. They listened for her breath, but no sound came. They felt for the palpitation of the heart, but no faint throb responded to the touch. That heart was broken and she was dead!

The husband sank into a chair by the bedside and clasped his hands upon his burning forehead. He gazed from child to child, but when a weeping eye met his, he quailed beneath its look. No word of comfort was whispered in his ear, no look of kindness lighted on his face. All shrank from and avoided him; and when at last he staggered from the room, no one sought to follow or console the widower.

The time had been when many a friend would have crowded round him in his affliction and many a heartfelt condolence would have met him in his grief. Where were they now? One by one, friends, relations, the commonest acquaintance even, had fallen off from and deserted the drunkard. His wife alone had clung to him in good and evil, in sickness and poverty, and how had he rewarded her? He had reeled from the tavern to her bedside in time to see her die.

He rushed from the house and walked swiftly through the streets. Remorse, fear, shame, all crowded on his mind. Stupefied with drink, and bewildered with the scene he had just witnessed, he re-entered the tavern he had quitted shortly before. Glass succeeded glass. His blood mounted and his brain whirled round. Death! Everyone must die, and why not *she*? She was too good for him; her relations had often told him so. Curses on them! Had they not deserted her and left her to whine away the time at home? Well she was dead, and happy perhaps. It was better as it was. Another glass – one more! Hurrah! It was a merry life while it lasted; and he would make the most of it.

Time went on; the four children who were left to him grew up and were children no longer. The father remained the same – poorer, shabbier and more dissolute-looking, but the same confirmed and irreclaimable drunkard. The boys had, long ago, run wild in the streets and left him; the girl alone remained, but she worked hard, and words or blows could always procure him something for the tavern. So he went on in the old course and a merry life he led.

One night, as early as ten o'clock – for the girl had been sick for many days, and there was, consequently, little to spend at the public-house – he bent his steps homeward, bethinking himself that if he would have her able to earn money, it would be as well to apply to the parish surgeon, or, at all events, to take the trouble of enquiring what ailed her, which he had not yet thought it worth while to do. It was a wet December night; the wind blew piercing cold and the rain poured heavily down. He begged a few halfpence from a passer-by, and having bought a small loaf (for it was his interest to keep the girl alive, if he could), he shuffled onwards as fast as the wind and rain would let him.

At the back of Fleet Street, and lying between it and the waterside, are several mean and narrow courts, which form a portion of Whitefriars; it was to one of these that he directed his steps.

The alley into which he turned might, for filth and misery, have competed with the darkest corner of this ancient sanctuary in its dirtiest and most lawless time. The houses, varying from two storeys in height to four, were stained with every indescribable hue that long exposure to the weather, damp and rottenness can impart to tenements composed originally of the roughest and coarsest materials. The windows were patched with paper and stuffed with the foulest rags; the doors were falling from their hinges; poles with lines on which to dry clothes projected from every casement, and sounds of quarrelling or drunkenness issued from every room.

The solitary oil lamp in the centre of the court had been blown out, either by the violence of the wind or the act of some inhabitant who had excellent reasons for objecting to his residence being rendered too conspicuous; and the only light which fell upon the broken and uneven pavement was derived from the miserable candles that here and there twinkled in the rooms of such of the more fortunate residents as could afford to indulge in so expensive a luxury. A gutter ran down the centre of the alley – all the sluggish odours of which had been called forth by the rain; and as the wind whistled through the old houses, the doors and shutters creaked upon their hinges and the windows shook in their frames, with a violence which every moment seemed to threaten the destruction of the whole place.

The man whom we have followed into this den walked on in the darkness, sometimes stumbling into the main gutter and at others into some branch repositories of garbage which had been formed by the rain, until he reached the last house in the court. The door, or rather what was left of it, stood ajar, for the convenience of the numerous lodgers; and he proceeded to grope his way up the old and broken stair to the attic storey.

He was within a step or two of his room door, when it opened, and a girl, whose miserable and emaciated appearance was only to be equalled by that of the candle which she shaded with her hand, peeped anxiously out.

'Is that you, father?' said the girl.

'Who else should it be?' replied the man gruffly. 'What are you trembling at? It's little enough that I've had to drink today, for there's no drink without money and no money without work. What the devil's the matter with the girl?'

'I am not well, father – not at all well,' said the girl, bursting into tears.

'Ah!' replied the man, in the tone of a person who is compelled to admit a very unpleasant fact, to which he would rather remain blind, if he could. 'You must get better somehow, for we must have money. You must go to the parish doctor, and make him give you some medicine. They're paid for it, damn 'em. What are you standing before the door for? Let me come in, can't you?'

'Father,' whispered the girl, shutting the door behind her, and placing herself before it, 'William has come back.'

'Who!' said the man with a start.

'Hush,' replied the girl, 'William; brother William.'

'And what does he want?' said the man, with an effort at composure – 'money? meat? drink? He's come to the wrong shop for that, if he does. Give me the candle – give me the candle, fool – I ain't going to hurt him.' He snatched the candle from her hand, and walked into the room.

Sitting on an old box, with his head resting on his hand and his eyes fixed on a wretched cinder fire that was smouldering on the hearth, was a young man of about two-and-twenty, miserably clad in an old coarse jacket and trousers. He started up when his father entered.

'Fasten the door, Mary,' said the young man hastily – 'Fasten the door. You look as if you didn't know me, father. It's long enough, since you drove me from home; you may well forget me.'

'And what do you want here, now?' said the father, seating himself on a stool on the other side of the fireplace. 'What do you want here, now?'

'Shelter,' replied the son. 'I'm in trouble: that's enough. If I'm caught I shall swing; that's certain. Caught I shall be, unless I stop here; that's *as* certain. And there's an end of it.'

'You mean to say you've been robbing or murdering, then?' said the father.

'Yes, I do,' replied the son. 'Does it surprise you, father?' He looked steadily in the man's face, but he withdrew his eyes and bent them on the ground.

'Where's your brothers?' he said, after a long pause.

'Where they'll never trouble you,' replied his son: 'John's gone to America and Henry's dead.'

'Dead!' said the father, with a shudder which even he could not repress.

'Dead,' replied the young man. 'He died in my arms – shot like a dog, by a gamekeeper. He staggered back, I caught him, and his blood trickled down my hands. It poured out from his side like water. He was weak, and it blinded him, but he threw himself down on his knees, on the grass, and prayed to God that if his mother was in heaven, He would hear her prayers for pardon for her youngest son. "I was her favourite boy, Will," he said, "and I am glad to think, now, that when she was dying, though I was a very young child then, and my little heart was almost bursting, I knelt down at the foot of the bed, and thanked God for having made me so fond of her as to have never once done anything to bring the tears into her eyes. Oh, Will, why was she taken away and father left?" There's his dying words, father,' said the young man; 'make the best you can of 'em. You struck him across the face, in a drunken fit, the morning we ran away; and here's the end of it.'

The girl wept aloud; and the father, sinking his head upon his knees, rocked himself to and fro.

'If I am taken,' said the young man, 'I shall be carried back into the country, and hung for that man's murder. They cannot trace me here, without your assistance, father. For aught I know, you may give me up to justice; but unless you do, here I stop until I can venture to escape abroad.'

For two whole days, all three remained in the wretched room, without stirring out. On the third evening, however, the girl was worse than she had been yet, and the few scraps of food they had were gone. It was indispensably necessary that somebody should go out; and as the girl was too weak and ill, the father went, just at nightfall.

He got some medicine for the girl, and a trifle in the way of pecuniary assistance. On his way back, he earned sixpence by holding a horse; and he turned homewards with enough money to supply their most pressing wants for two or three days to come. He had to pass the public-house. He lingered for an instant, walked past it, turned back again, lingered once more and finally slunk in. Two men whom he had not observed were on the watch. They were on the point of giving up their search in despair when his loitering attracted their attention; and when he entered the public-house, they followed him.

'You'll drink with me, master,' said one of them, proffering him a glass of liquor.

'And me too,' said the other, replenishing the glass as soon as it was drained of its contents.

The man thought of his hungry children and his son's danger. But they were nothing to the drunkard. He *did* drink; and his reason left him.

'A wet night, Warden,' whispered one of the men in his ear, as he at length turned to go away after spending in liquor one half of the money on which, perhaps, his daughter's life depended.

'The right sort of night for our friends in hiding, Master Warden,' whispered the other.

'Sit down here,' said the one who had spoken first, drawing him into a corner. 'We have been looking arter the young un. We came to tell him it's all right now, but we couldn't find him 'cause we hadn't got the precise direction. But that ain't strange, for I don't think he know'd it himself, when he come to London, did he?'

'No, he didn't,' replied the father.

The two men exchanged glances.

'There's a vessel down at the docks, to sail at midnight, when it's high water,' resumed the first speaker, 'and we'll put him on board. His passage is taken in another name, and what's better than that, it's paid for. It's lucky we met you.'

'Very,' said the second.

'Capital luck,' said the first, with a wink to his companion.

'Great,' replied the second, with a slight nod of intelligence.

'Another glass here; quick' – said the first speaker. And in five minutes more, the father had unconsciously yielded up his own son into the hangman's hands.

Slowly and heavily the time dragged along, as the brother and sister, in their miserable hiding-place, listened in anxious suspense to the slightest sound. At length, a heavy footstep was heard upon the stair; it approached nearer; it reached the landing; and the father staggered into the room.

The girl saw that he was intoxicated, and advanced with the candle in her hand to meet him; she stopped short, gave a loud scream, and fell senseless on the ground. She had caught sight of the shadow of a man reflected on the floor. They both rushed in, and in another instant the young man was a prisoner and handcuffed.

'Very quietly done,' said one of the men to his companion, 'thanks to the old man. Lift up the girl, Tom – come, come, it's no use crying, young woman. It's all over now and can't be helped.'

The young man stooped for an instant over the girl and then turned fiercely round upon his father, who had reeled against the wall and was gazing on the group with drunken stupidity.

'Listen to me, father,' he said, in a tone that made the drunkard's flesh creep. 'My brother's blood, and mine, is on your head: I never had kind look, or word, or care, from you, and alive or dead, I never will forgive you. Die when you will, or how, I will be with you. I speak as a dead man now, and I warn you, father, that as surely as you must one day stand before your Maker, so surely shall your children be there, hand in hand, to cry for judgement against you.' He raised his manacled hands in a threatening attitude, fixed his eyes on his shrinking parent and slowly left the room; and neither father nor sister ever beheld him more, on this side of the grave.

When the dim and misty light of a winter's morning penetrated into the narrow court and struggled through the begrimed window of the wretched room, Warden awoke from his heavy sleep and found himself alone. He rose and looked round him; the old flock mattress on the floor was undisturbed; everything was just as he remembered to have seen it last; and there were no signs of anyone, save himself, having occupied the room during the night. He enquired of the other lodgers and of the neighbours but his daughter had not been seen or heard of. He rambled through the streets and scrutinised each wretched face among the crowds that thronged them with anxious eyes. But his search was fruitless and he returned to his garret when night came on, desolate and weary.

For many days he occupied himself in the same manner, but no trace of his daughter did he meet with and no word of her reached his ears. At length he gave up the pursuit as hopeless. He had long thought of the probability of her leaving him and endeavouring to gain her bread in quiet, elsewhere. She had left him at last to starve alone. He ground his teeth and cursed her!

He begged his bread from door to door. Every halfpenny he could wring from the pity or credulity of those to whom he addressed himself, was spent in the old way. A year passed over his head; the roof of a jail was the only one that had sheltered him for many months. He slept under archways and in brickfields – anywhere where there was some warmth or shelter from the cold and rain. But in the last stage of poverty, disease and houseless want, he was a drunkard still.

At last, one bitter night, he sank down on a doorstep faint and ill. The premature decay of vice and profligacy had worn him to the bone. His cheeks were hollow and livid; his eyes were sunken and their sight was dim. His legs trembled beneath his weight and a cold shiver ran through every limb.

And now the long-forgotten scenes of a mis-spent life crowded thick and fast upon him. He thought of the time when he had a home – a happy, cheerful home – and of those who peopled it, and flocked about him then, until the forms of his elder children seemed to rise from the grave and stand about him – so plain, so clear and so distinct they were that he could touch and feel them. Looks that he had long forgotten were fixed upon him once more; voices long since hushed in death sounded in his ears like the music of village bells. But it was only for an instant. The rain beat heavily upon him; and cold and hunger were gnawing at his heart again.

He rose, and dragged his feeble limbs a few paces further. The street was silent and empty; the few pedestrians who passed by, at that late hour, hurried quickly on, and his tremulous voice was lost in the violence of the storm. Again that heavy chill struck through his frame and his blood seemed to stagnate beneath it. He coiled himself up in a projecting doorway and tried to sleep.

But sleep had fled from his dull and glazed eyes. His mind wandered strangely, but he was awake, and conscious. The well-known shout of drunken mirth sounded in his ear, the glass was at his lips, the board was covered with choice rich food – they were before him: he could see them all, he had but to reach out his hand and take them – and, though the illusion was reality itself, he knew that he was sitting alone in the deserted street, watching the raindrops as they pattered on the stones; that death was coming upon him by inches – and that there were none to care for or help him.

Suddenly he started up, in the extremity of terror. He had heard his own voice shouting in the night air, he knew not what or why. Hark! A groan! – another! His senses were leaving him: half-formed and incoherent words burst from his lips; and his hands sought to tear and lacerate his flesh. He was going mad, and he shrieked for help till his voice failed him.

He raised his head and looked up the long dismal street. He recollected that outcasts like himself, condemned to wander day and night in those dreadful streets, had sometimes gone distracted with their own lone-liness. He remembered to have heard many years before that a homeless wretch had once been found in a solitary corner, sharpening a rusty knife to plunge into his own heart, preferring death to that endless, weary wandering to and fro. In an instant his resolve was taken, his limbs received new life; he ran quickly from the spot and paused not for breath until he reached the riverside.

He crept softly down the steep stone stairs that lead from the com-mencement of Waterloo Bridge down to the water's level. He crouched into a corner and held his breath as the patrol passed. Never did prisoner's heart throb with the hope of liberty and life half so eagerly as did that of the wretched man at the prospect of death. The watch passed close to him but he remained unobserved; and after waiting till the sound of footsteps had died away in the distance, he cautiously descended and stood beneath the gloomy arch that forms the landing-place from the river.

The tide was in and the water flowed at his feet. The rain had ceased, the wind was lulled and all was, for the moment, still and quiet – so quiet, that the slightest sound on the opposite bank, even the rippling of the water against the barges that were moored there, was distinctly audible to his ear. The stream stole languidly and sluggishly on. Strange and fantastic forms rose to the surface and beckoned him to approach; dark gleaming eyes peered from the water and seemed to mock his hesitation, while hollow murmurs from behind urged him onwards. He retreated a few paces, took a short run, desperate leap, and plunged into the river.

Not five seconds had passed when he rose to the water's surface – but what a change had taken place in that short time, in all his thoughts and feelings! Life – life in any form, poverty, misery, starvation – anything but death. He fought and struggled with the water that closed over his head and screamed in agonies of terror. The curse of his own son rang in his ears. The shore – but one foot of dry ground – he could almost touch the step. One hand's breadth nearer, and he was saved – but the tide bore him onward, under the dark arches of the bridge, and he sank to the bottom.

Again he rose and struggled for life. For one instant – for one brief instant – the buildings on the river's banks, the lights on the bridge through which the current had borne him, the black water and the fast-flying clouds were distinctly visible – once more he sank and once again he rose. Bright flames of fire shot up from earth to heaven and reeled before his eyes, while the water thundered in his ears and stunned him with its furious roar.

A week afterwards the body was washed ashore, some miles down the river, a swollen and disfigured mass. Unrecognised and unpitied, it was borne to the grave; and there it has long since mouldered away!

THOUGHTS ABOUT PEOPLE

It is strange with how little notice, good, bad or indifferent, a man may live and die in London. He awakens no sympathy in the breast of any single person; his existence is a matter of interest to no one save himself; he cannot be said to be forgotten when he dies, for no one remembered him when he was alive. There is a numerous class of people in this great metropolis who seem not to possess a single friend, and whom nobody appears to care for. Urged by imperative necessity in the first instance, they have resorted to London in search of employment and the means of subsistence. It is hard, we know, to break the ties which bind us to our homes and friends, and harder still to efface the thousand recollections of happy days and old times which have been slumbering in our bosoms for years, and only rush upon the mind to bring before it associations connected with the friends we have left, the scenes we have beheld too probably for the last time and the hopes we once cherished, but may entertain no more. These men, however, happily for themselves, have long forgotten such thoughts. Old country friends have died or emigrated; former correspondents have become lost, like themselves, in the crowd and turmoil of some busy city; and they have gradually settled down into mere passive creatures of habit and endurance.

We were seated in the enclosure of St James's Park the other day, when our attention was attracted by a man whom we immediately put down in our own mind as one of this class. He was a tall, thin, pale person, in a black coat, scanty grey trousers, little pinched-up gaiters and brown beaver gloves. He had an umbrella in his hand – not for use, for the day was fine – but, evidently, because he always carried one to the office in the morning. He walked up and down before the little patch of grass on which the chairs are placed for hire, not as if he were doing it for pleasure or recreation, but as if it were a matter of compulsion, just as he would walk to the office every morning from the back settlements of Islington. It was Monday; he had escaped for four-and-twenty hours from the thraldom of the desk and was walking here for exercise and amusement – perhaps for the first time in his life. We were inclined to think he had never had a holiday before, and that he did not know what to do with himself. Children were playing on the grass; groups of people were loitering about, chatting and laughing; but the man walked steadily up and down, unheeding and unheeded, his spare, pale face looking as if it were incapable of bearing the expression of curiosity or interest.

There was something in the man's manner and appearance which told us, we fancied, his whole life, or rather his whole day, for a man of this sort has no variety of days. We thought we almost saw the dingy little back office into which he walks every morning, hanging his hat on the same peg and placing his legs beneath the same desk, first taking off that black coat which lasts the year through and putting on the one which did duty last year and which he keeps in his desk to save the other. There he sits till five o'clock, working on, all day, as regularly as the dial over the mantelpiece, whose loud ticking is as monotonous as his whole existence; only raising his head when someone enters the counting-house, or when, in the midst of some difficult calculation, he looks up to the ceiling as if there were inspiration in the dusty skylight with a green knot in the centre of every pane of glass. About five, or half-past, he slowly dismounts from his accustomed stool, and again changing his coat, proceeds to his usual dining-place, somewhere near Bucklersbury. The waiter recites the bill of fare in a rather confidential manner – for he is a regular customer – and after enquiring, 'What's in the best cut?' and 'What was up last?' he orders a small plate of roast beef with greens and half a pint of porter. He has a small plate today, because greens are a penny more than potatoes, and he had 'two breads' yesterday, with the additional enormity of 'a cheese' the day before. This important point settled, he hangs up his hat – he took it off the moment he sat down – and bespeaks the paper after the next gentleman. If he can get it while he is at dinner, he eats with much greater zest; balancing it against the waterbottle, and eating a bit of beef, and reading a line or two, alternately. Exactly at five minutes before the hour is up, he produces a shilling, pays the reckoning, carefully deposits the change in his waistcoat-pocket (first deducting a penny for the waiter), and returns to the office, from which, if it is not foreign post night, he again sallies forth in about half an hour. He then walks home, at his usual pace, to his little back room at Islington, where he has his tea; perhaps solacing himself during the meal with the conversation of his landlady's little boy, whom he occasionally rewards with a penny for solving problems in simple addition. Sometimes there is a letter or two to take up to his employer's in Russell Square; and then, the wealthy man of business, hearing his voice, calls out from the dining-parlour, 'Come in,

*He eats with much greater zest; balancing the paper against the waterbottle,
and eating a bit of beef, and reading a line or two, alternately*

Mr Smith:' and Mr Smith, putting his hat at the feet of one of the hall chairs, walks timidly in, and being condescendingly desired to sit down, carefully tucks his legs under his chair, and sits at a considerable distance from the table while he drinks the glass of sherry which is poured out for him by the eldest boy, and after drinking which, he backs and slides out of the room, in a state of nervous agitation from which he does not perfectly recover until he finds himself once more in the Islington Road. Poor, harmless creatures such men are; contented but not happy; broken-spirited and humbled, they may feel no pain, but they never know pleasure.

Compare these men with another class of beings who, like them, have neither friend nor companion, but whose position in society is the result of their own choice. These are generally old fellows with white heads and red faces, addicted to port wine and Hessian boots, who from some cause, real or imaginary – generally the former, the excellent reason being that they are rich, and their relations poor – grow suspicious of everybody, and do the misanthropical in chambers, taking great delight in thinking themselves unhappy and making everybody they come near miserable. You may see such men as these anywhere; you will know them at coffee-houses by their discontented exclamations and the luxury of their dinners; at theatres, by their always sitting in the same place and looking with a jaundiced eye on all the young people near them; at church, by the pomposity with which they enter, and the loud tone in which they repeat the responses; at parties, by their getting cross at whist and hating music. An old fellow of this kind will have his chambers splendidly furnished, and collect books, plate and pictures about him in profusion; not so much for his own gratification, as to be superior to those who have the desire, but not the means, to compete with him. He belongs to two or three clubs, and is envied, and flattered, and hated by the members of them all. Sometimes he will be appealed to by a poor relation – a married nephew perhaps – for some little assistance: and then he will declaim with honest indignation on the improvidence of young married people, the worthlessness of a wife, the insolence of having a family, the atrocity of getting into debt with a hundred and twenty-five pounds a year, and other unpardonable crimes, winding up his exhortations with a complacent review of his own conduct and a delicate allusion to parochial relief. He dies, some day after dinner, of apoplexy, having bequeathed his property to a public society, and the institution erects a tablet to his memory, expressive of their admiration of his Christian conduct in this world and their comfortable conviction of his happiness in the next.

But, next to our very particular friends, hackney-coachmen, cabmen and cads, whom we admire in proportion to the extent of their cool impudence and perfect self-possession, there is no class of people who amuse us more than London apprentices. They are no longer an organised body, bound down by solemn compact to terrify his majesty's subjects whenever it pleases them to take offence in their heads and staves in their hands. They are only bound, now, by indentures, and, as to their valour, it is easily restrained by the wholesome dread of the New Police, and a perspective view of a damp station-house, terminating in a police-office and a reprimand. They are still, however, a peculiar class, and not the less pleasant for being inoffensive. Can any one fail to have noticed them in the streets on Sunday? And were there ever such harmless efforts at the grand and magnificent as the young fellows display! We walked down the Strand, a Sunday or two ago, behind a little group; and they furnished food for our amusement the whole way. They had come out of some part of the City; it was between three and four o'clock in the afternoon, and they were on their way to the park. There were four of them, all arm in arm, with white kid gloves like so many bridegrooms, light trousers of unprecedented patterns and coats for which the English language has yet no name – a kind of cross between a greatcoat and a surtout, with the collar of the one, the skirts of the other and pockets peculiar to themselves.

Each of the gentlemen carried a thick stick, with a large tassel at the top, which he occasionally twirled gracefully round; and the whole four, by way of looking easy and unconcerned, were walking with a paralytic swagger irresistibly ludicrous. One of the party had a watch, about the size and shape of a reasonable Ribstone pippin, jammed into his waistcoat-pocket, which he carefully compared with the clocks at St Clement's and the New Church, the illuminated clock at Exeter 'Change, the clock of St Martin's Church and the clock of the Horse Guards. When they at last arrived in St James's Park, the member of the party who had the best-made boots on, hired a second chair expressly for his feet, and flung himself on this two-pennyworth of sylvan luxury with an air which levelled all distinctions between Brookes's and Snooks's, Crockford's and Bagnigge Wells.

We may smile at such people, but they can never excite our anger. They are usually on the best terms with themselves, and it follows almost as a matter of course, in good humour with everyone about them. Besides, they are always the faint reflection of higher lights; and, if they do display a little occasional foolery in their own proper persons, it is surely more tolerable than precocious puppyism in the Quadrant, whiskered dandyism in Regent Street and Pall Mall, or gallantry in its dotage anywhere.

MISS EVANS AND THE EAGLE

Mr Samuel Wilkins was a carpenter, a journeyman carpenter of small dimensions, decidedly below the middle size – bordering, perhaps, upon the dwarfish. His face was round and shining, and his hair carefully twisted into the outer corner of each eye till it formed a variety of that description of semi-curls usually known as 'aggerawators'. His earnings were all-sufficient for his wants, varying from eighteen shillings to one pound five, weekly – his manner undeniable – his Sabbath waistcoats dazzling. No wonder that, with these qualifications, Samuel Wilkins found favour in the eyes of the other sex: many women have been captivated by far less substantial qualifications. But Samuel was proof against their blandishments until at length his eyes rested on those of a being for whom, from that time forth, he felt fate had destined him. He came, and conquered – proposed, and was accepted – loved, and was beloved. Mr Wilkins 'kept company' with Jemima Evans.

Miss Evans (or Ivins, to adopt the pronunciation most in vogue with her circle of acquaintance) had adopted in early life the useful pursuit of shoe-binding, to which she had afterwards superadded the occupation of a straw-bonnet maker. Herself, her maternal parent and two sisters formed an harmonious quartet in the most secluded portion of Camden Town; and here it was that Mr Wilkins presented himself, one Monday afternoon, in his best attire, with his face more shining and his waistcoat more bright than either had ever appeared before. The family were just going to tea, and were *so* glad to see him. It was quite a little feast; two ounces of seven-and-sixpenny green and a quarter of a pound of the best fresh; and Mr Wilkins had brought a pint of shrimps, neatly folded up in a clean belcher, to give a zest to the meal, and propitiate Mrs Ivins. Jemima was 'cleaning herself' upstairs; so Mr Samuel Wilkins sat down and talked domestic economy with Mrs Ivins, whilst the two youngest Miss Ivinses poked bits of lighted brown paper between the bars under the kettle, to make the water boil for tea.

'I wos a thinking,' said Mr Samuel Wilkins, during a pause in the conversation – 'I wos a thinking of taking J'mima to the Eagle tonight.' – 'O my!' exclaimed Mrs Ivins. 'Lor! how nice!' said the youngest Miss Ivins. 'Well, I declare!' added the youngest Miss Ivins but one. 'Tell

J'mima to put on her white muslin, Tilly,' screamed Mrs Ivins, with motherly anxiety; and down came J'mima herself soon afterwards in a white muslin gown carefully hooked and eyed, a little red shawl, plentifully pinned, a white straw bonnet trimmed with red ribbons, a small necklace, a large pair of bracelets, Denmark satin shoes and open-work stockings, white cotton gloves on her fingers and a cambric pocket-handkerchief, carefully folded up, in her hand – all quite genteel and ladylike. And away went Miss J'mima Ivins and Mr Samuel Wilkins and a dress-cane with a gilt knob at the top, to the admiration and envy of the street in general and to the high gratification of Mrs Ivins and the two youngest Miss Ivinses in particular. They had no sooner turned into the Pancras Road than who should Miss J'mima Ivins stumble upon, by the most fortunate accident in the world, but a young lady as she knew, with *her* young man! – And it is so strange how things do turn out sometimes – they were actually going to the Eagle too. So Mr Samuel Wilkins was introduced to Miss J'mima Ivins's friend's young man, and they all walked on together, talking, and laughing, and joking away like anything; and when they got as far as Pentonville, Miss Ivins's friend's young man *would* have the ladies go into the Crown, to taste some shrub, which, after a great blushing and giggling, and hiding of faces in elaborate pocket-handkerchiefs, they consented to do. Having tasted it once, they were easily prevailed upon to taste it again; and they sat out in the garden tasting shrub, and looking at the buses alternately, till it was just the proper time to go to the Eagle; and then they resumed their journey, and walked very fast for fear they should lose the beginning of the concert in the Rotunda.

'How 'ev'nly!' said Miss J'mima Ivins, and Miss J'mima Ivins's friend, both at once, when they had passed the gate and were fairly inside the gardens. There were the walks, beautifully gravelled and planted – and the refreshment-boxes, painted and ornamented like so many snuffboxes – and the variegated lamps shedding their rich light upon the company's heads – and the place for dancing ready chalked for the company's feet – and a Moorish band playing at one end of the gardens – and an opposition military band playing away at the other. Then, the waiters were rushing to and fro with glasses of negus, and glasses of brandy and water, and bottles of ale, and bottles of stout; and ginger-beer was going off in one place, and practical jokes were going on in another; and people were crowding to the door of the Rotunda; and in short the whole scene was, as Miss J'mima

Mr Wilkins 'kept company' with Jemima Evans

Ivins, inspired by the novelty, or the shrub, or both, observed – 'one of dazzling excitement'. As to the concert-room, never was anything half so splendid. There was an orchestra for the singers, all paint, gilding and plate-glass; and such an organ! Miss J'mima Ivins's friend's young man whispered it had cost 'four hundred pound', which Mr Samuel Wilkins said was 'not dear neither'; an opinion in which the ladies perfectly coincided. The audience were seated on elevated benches round the room, and crowded into every part of it; and everybody was eating and drinking as comfortably as possible. Just before the concert commenced, Mr Samuel Wilkins ordered two glasses of rum and water 'warm with – ' and two slices of lemon, for himself and the other young man, together with 'a pint o' sherry wine for the ladies, and some sweet carraway-seed biscuits'; and they would have been quite comfortable and happy, only a strange gentleman with large whiskers *would* stare at Miss J'mima Ivins, and another gentleman in a plaid waistcoat *would* wink at Miss J'mima Ivins's friend; on which Miss Jemima Ivins's friend's young man exhibited symptoms of boiling over, and began to mutter about 'people's imperence', and 'swells out o' luck'; and to intimate, in oblique terms, a vague intention of knocking somebody's head off; which he was only prevented from announcing more emphatically by both Miss J'mima Ivins and her friend threatening to faint away on the spot if he said another word.

The concert commenced – overture on the organ. 'How solemn!' exclaimed Miss J'mima Ivins, glancing, perhaps unconsciously, at the gentleman with the whiskers. Mr Samuel Wilkins, who had been muttering apart for some time past, as if he were holding a confidential conversation with the gilt knob of the dress-cane, breathed hard – breathing vengeance, perhaps – but said nothing. 'The soldier tired,' Miss Somebody in white satin. 'Ancore!' cried Miss J'mima Ivins's friend. 'Ancore!' shouted the gentleman in the plaid waistcoat immediately, hammering the table with a stout bottle. Miss J'mima Ivins's friend's young man eyed the man behind the waistcoat from head to foot, and cast a look of interrogative contempt towards Mr Samuel Wilkins. Comic song, accompanied on the organ. Miss J'mima Ivins was convulsed with laughter – so was the man with the whiskers. Everything the ladies did, the plaid waistcoat and whiskers did, by way of expressing unity of sentiment and congeniality of soul; and Miss J'mima Ivins and Miss J'mima Ivins's friend grew lively and talkative, as Mr Samuel Wilkins and Miss J'mima Ivins's friend's young man grew morose and surly in inverse proportion.

Now, if the matter had ended here, the little party might soon have recovered their former equanimity; but Mr Samuel Wilkins and his friend began to throw looks of defiance upon the waistcoat and whiskers. And the waistcoat and whiskers, by way of intimating the slight degree in which they were affected by the looks aforesaid, bestowed glances of increased admiration upon Miss J'mima Ivins and friend. The concert and vaudeville concluded, they promenaded the gardens. The waistcoat and whiskers did the same; and made divers remarks complimentary to the ankles of Miss J'mima Ivins and friend, in an audible tone. At length, not satisfied with these numerous atrocities, they actually came up and asked Miss J'mima Ivins and Miss J'mima Ivins's friend to dance, without taking no more notice of Mr Samuel Wilkins and Miss J'mima Ivins's friend's young man than if they was nobody!

'What do you mean by that, scoundrel!' exclaimed Mr Samuel Wilkins, grasping the gilt-knobbed dress-cane firmly in his right hand. 'What's the matter with *you*, you little humbug?' replied the whiskers. 'How dare you insult me and my friend?' enquired the friend's young man. 'You and your friend be hanged!' responded the waistcoat. 'Take that,' exclaimed Mr Samuel Wilkins. The ferrule of the gilt-knobbed dress-cane was visible for an instant, and then the light of the variegated lamps shone brightly upon it as it whirled into the air, cane and all. 'Give it him,' said the waistcoat. 'Horficer!' screamed the ladies. Miss J'mima Ivins's beau and the friend's young man lay gasping on the gravel, and the waistcoat and whiskers were seen no more.

Miss J'mima Ivins and friend, being conscious that the affray was in no slight degree attributable to themselves, of course went into hysterics forthwith; declared themselves the most injured of women; exclaimed, in incoherent ravings, that they had been suspected – wrongfully suspected – oh! that they should ever have lived to see the day – and so forth; suffered a relapse every time they opened their eyes and saw their unfortunate little admirers; and were carried to their respective abodes in a hackney-coach and a state of insensibility, compounded of shrub, sherry and excitement.

THE MISPLACED ATTACHMENT
OF MR JOHN DOUNCE

If we had to make a classification of society, there is a particular kind of men whom we should immediately set down under the head of 'Old Boys'; and a column of most extensive dimensions the old boys would require. To what precise causes the rapid advance of old-boy population is to be traced, we are unable to determine. It would be an interesting and curious speculation, but, as we have not sufficient space to devote to it here, we simply state the fact that the numbers of the old boys have been gradually augmenting within the last few years, and that they are at this moment alarmingly on the increase.

Upon a general review of the subject, and without considering it minutely in detail, we should be disposed to subdivide the old boys into two distinct classes – the gay old boys and the steady old boys. The gay old boys are paunchy old men in the disguise of young ones, who frequent the Quadrant and Regent Street in the daytime, the theatres (especially theatres under lady management) at night and who assume all the foppishness and levity of boys, without the excuse of youth or in-experience. The steady old boys are certain stout old gentlemen of clean appearance, who are always to be seen in the same taverns, at the same hours every evening, smoking and drinking in the same company.

There was once a fine collection of old boys to be seen round the circular table at Offley's every night, between the hours of half-past eight and half-past eleven. We have lost sight of them for some time. There were, and may be still, for aught we know, two splendid specimens in full blossom at the Rainbow Tavern in Fleet Street, who always used to sit in the box nearest the fireplace, and smoked long cherry-stick pipes which went under the table, with the bowls resting on the floor. Grand old boys they were – fat, red-faced, white-headed old fellows – always there – one on one side the table and the other opposite – puffing and drinking away in great state. Everybody knew them, and it was supposed by some people that they were both immortal.

Mr John Dounce was an old boy of the latter class (we don't mean immortal, but steady), a retired glove and braces maker, a widower, resident with three daughters – all grown up, and all unmarried – in Cursitor Street, Chancery Lane. He was a short, round, large-faced, tubbish sort of man, with a broad-brimmed hat and a square coat; and had that grave, but confident, kind of roll, peculiar to old boys in general. Regular as clockwork – breakfast at nine – dress and tittivate a little – down to the Sir Somebody's Head – a glass of ale and the paper – come back again, and take daughters out for a walk – dinner at three – glass of grog and pipe – nap – tea – little walk – Sir Somebody's Head again – capital house – delightful evenings. There were Mr Harris, the law-stationer, and Mr Jennings, the robe-maker (two jolly young fellows like himself), and Jones, the barrister's clerk – rum fellow that Jones – capital company – full of anecdote! – and there they sat every night till just ten minutes before twelve, drinking their brandy and water, and smoking their pipes, and telling stories, and enjoying themselves with a kind of solemn joviality particularly edifying.

Sometimes Jones would propose a half-price visit to Drury Lane or Covent Garden, to see two acts of a five-act play, or a new farce, perhaps, or a ballet, on which occasions the whole four of them went together; none of your hurrying and nonsense, but having their brandy and water first, comfortably, and ordering a steak and some oysters for their supper against they came back, and then walking coolly into the pit, when the 'rush' had gone in, as all sensible people do, and did when Mr Dounce was a young man, except when the celebrated Master Betty was at the height of his popularity, and then, sir – then – Mr Dounce perfectly well remembered getting a holiday from business, and going to the pit doors at eleven o'clock in the forenoon, and waiting there, till six in the afternoon, with some sandwiches in a pocket-handkerchief and some wine in a phial; and fainting after all, with the heat and fatigue, before the play began; in which situation he was lifted out of the pit into one of the dress boxes, sir, by five of the finest women of that day, sir, who compassionated his situation and administered restoratives and sent a black servant, six foot high, in blue and silver livery, next morning with their compliments, and to know how he found himself, sir – by Gad! Between the acts Mr Dounce and Mr Harris and Mr Jennings used to stand up and look round the house, and Jones – knowing fellow that Jones – knew everybody – pointed out the fashionable and celebrated Lady So-and-So in the boxes, at the mention of whose name Mr Dounce, after brushing up his hair and adjusting his neckerchief, would inspect the aforesaid Lady So-and-So through an immense glass, and remark either that she was a 'fine woman – very fine woman, indeed', or that 'there might be a little more of her, eh, Jones?' Just as the case might happen to be. When the dancing began, John Dounce and the other old boys were particularly anxious to see what was going forward on the stage, and Jones – wicked dog that Jones – whispered little critical remarks into the ears of John Dounce, which John Dounce retailed to Mr Harris and Mr Harris to Mr Jennings; and then they all four laughed, until the tears ran down out of their eyes.

When the curtain fell, they walked back together, two and two, to the steaks and oysters; and when they came to the second glass of brandy and water, Jones – hoaxing scamp, that Jones – used to recount how he had observed a lady in white feathers, in one of the pit boxes, gazing intently on Mr Dounce all the evening, and how he had caught Mr Dounce, whenever he thought no one was looking at him, bestowing ardent looks of intense devotion on the lady in return; on which Mr Harris and Mr Jennings used to laugh very heartily, and John Dounce more heartily than either of them, acknowledging, however, that the time *had* been when he *might* have done such things; upon which Mr Jones used to poke him in the ribs, and tell him he had been a sad dog in his time, which John Dounce with chuckles confessed. And after Mr Harris and Mr Jennings had preferred their claims to the character of having been sad dogs too, they separated harmoniously and trotted home.

The decrees of Fate, and the means by which they are brought about, are mysterious and inscrutable. John Dounce had led this life for twenty years and upwards, without wish for change or care for variety, when his whole social system was suddenly upset and turned completely topsy-turvy – not by an earthquake, or some other dreadful convulsion of nature, as the reader would be inclined to suppose, but by the simple agency of an oyster; and thus it happened.

Mr John Dounce was returning one night from the Sir Somebody's Head, to his residence in Cursitor Street – not tipsy, but rather excited, for it was Mr Jennings's birthday and they had had a brace of partridges for supper and a brace of extra glasses afterwards and Jones had been more than ordinarily amusing – when his eyes rested on a newly-opened oyster-shop, on a magnificent scale, with natives laid, one deep, in circular marble basins in the windows, together with little round barrels of oysters directed to lords and baronets and colonels and captains in every part of the habitable globe.

Behind the natives were the barrels, and behind the barrels was a young lady of about five-and-twenty, all in blue, and all alone – splendid creature, charming face and lovely figure! It is difficult to say whether Mr John Dounce's red countenance, illuminated as it was by the flickering gaslight in the window before which he paused, excited the lady's risibility, or whether a natural exuberance of animal spirits proved too much for that staidness of demeanour which the forms of society rather dictatorially prescribe. But certain it is that the lady smiled; then put her finger upon her lip, with a striking recollection of what was due to herself; and finally retired, in oyster-like bashfulness, to the very back of the counter. The sad-dog sort of feeling came strongly upon John Dounce: he lingered – the lady in blue made no sign. He coughed – still she came not. He entered the shop.

'Can you open me an oyster, my dear?' said Mr John Dounce.

'Dare say I can, sir,' replied the lady in blue, with playfulness. And Mr John Dounce ate one oyster, and then looked at the young lady, and then ate another, and then squeezed the young lady's hand as she was opening the third, and so forth, until he had devoured a dozen of those at eight-pence in less than no time.

'Can you open me half a dozen more, my dear?' enquired Mr John Dounce.

'I'll see what I can do for you, sir,' replied the young lady in blue, even more bewitchingly than before; and Mr John Dounce ate half a dozen more of those at eightpence.

'You couldn't manage to get me a glass of brandy and water, my dear, I suppose?' said Mr John Dounce, when he had finished the oysters, in a tone which clearly implied his supposition that she could.

'I'll see, sir,' said the young lady: and away she ran out of the shop, and down the street, her long auburn ringlets shaking in the wind in the most enchanting manner; and back she came again, tripping over the coal-cellar lids like a whipping-top, with a tumbler of brandy and water, which Mr John Dounce insisted on her taking a share of, as it was regular ladies' grog – hot, strong, sweet, and plenty of it.

So the young lady sat down with Mr John Dounce, in a little red box with a green curtain, and took a small sip of the brandy and water, and a small look at Mr John Dounce, and then turned her head away, and went through various other serio-pantomimic fascinations, which forcibly reminded Mr John Dounce of the first time he courted his first wife, and which made him feel more affectionate than ever; in pursuance of which

'Can you open me an oyster, my dear?' said Mr John Dounce.

affection, and actuated by which feeling, Mr John Dounce sounded the young lady on her matrimonial engagements, on which the young lady denied having formed any such engagements at all – she couldn't abear the men, they were such deceivers; thereupon Mr John Dounce enquired whether this sweeping condemnation was meant to include other than very young men; on which the young lady blushed deeply – at least she turned away her head, and said Mr John Dounce had made her blush, so of course she *did* blush – and Mr John Dounce was a long time drinking the brandy and water; and, at last, John Dounce went home to bed, and dreamed of his first wife, and his second wife, and the young lady, and partridges, and oysters, and brandy and water, and disinterested attachments.

The next morning, John Dounce was rather feverish with the extra brandy and water of the previous night; and, partly in the hope of cooling himself with an oyster, and partly with the view of ascertaining whether he owed the young lady anything, or not, went back to the oyster-shop. If the young lady had appeared beautiful by night, she was perfectly irresistible by day; and, from this time forward, a change came over the spirit of John Dounce's dream. He bought shirt-pins; wore a ring on his third finger; read poetry; bribed a cheap miniature-painter to perpetrate a faint resemblance to a youthful face, with a curtain over his head, six large books in the background, and an open country in the distance (this he called his portrait); 'went on' altogether in such an uproarious manner that the three Miss Dounces went off on small pensions, he having made the tenement in Cursitor Street too warm to contain them; and, in short, comported and demeaned himself in every respect like an unmitigated old Saracen, as he was.

As to his ancient friends, the other old boys, at the Sir Somebody's Head, he dropped off from them by gradual degrees; for, even when he did go there, Jones – vulgar fellow that Jones – persisted in asking 'when it was to be?' and 'whether he was to have any gloves?' together with other enquiries of an equally offensive nature, at which not only Harris laughed, but Jennings also; so, he cut the two, altogether, and attached himself solely to the blue young lady at the smart oyster-shop.

Now comes the moral of the story – for it has a moral after all. The last-mentioned young lady, having derived sufficient profit and emolument from John Dounce's attachment, not only refused, when matters came to a crisis, to take him for better for worse, but expressly declared, to use her own forcible words, that she 'wouldn't have him at no price'; and John Dounce, having lost his old friends, alienated his relations and rendered himself ridiculous to everybody, made offers successively to a schoolmistress, a landlady, a feminine tobacconist and a housekeeper; and, being directly rejected by each and every one of them, was accepted by his cook, with whom he now lives, a henpecked husband, a melancholy monument of antiquated misery and a living warning to all uxorious old boys.

THE DANCING ACADEMY

Of all the dancing academies that ever were established, there never was one more popular in its immediate vicinity than Signor Billsmethi's of the 'King's Theatre'. It was not in Spring Gardens or Newman Street or Berners Street or Gower Street or Charlotte Street or Percy Street or any other of the numerous streets which have been devoted time out of mind to professional people, dispensaries and boarding-houses; it was not in the West End at all – it rather approximated to the eastern portion of London, being situated in the populous and improving neighbourhood of Gray's Inn Lane. It was not a dear dancing academy – four and sixpence a quarter is decidedly cheap upon the whole. It was *very* select, the number of pupils being strictly limited to seventy-five, and a quarter's payment in advance being rigidly exacted. There was public tuition and private tuition – an assembly-room and a parlour. Signor Billsmethi's family were always thrown in with the parlour, and included in parlour price; that is to say, a private pupil had Signor Billsmethi's parlour to dance *in*, and Signor Billsmethi's family to dance *with*; and when he had been sufficiently broken in in the parlour, he began to run in couples in the assembly-room.

Such was the dancing academy of Signor Billsmethi when Mr Augustus Cooper, of Fetter Lane, first saw an unstamped advertisement walking leisurely down Holborn Hill, announcing to the world that Signor Bill-smethi, of the King's Theatre, intended opening for the season with a Grand Ball.

Now, Mr Augustus Cooper was in the oil and colour line – just of age, with a little money, a little business and a little mother, who, having managed her husband and *his* business in his lifetime, took to managing her son and *his* business after his decease; and so, somehow or other, he had been cooped up in the little back parlour behind the shop on week-days, and in a little deal box without a lid (called by courtesy a pew) at Bethel Chapel on Sundays, and had seen no more of the world than if he had been an infant all his days; whereas Young White, at the gas-fitter's over the way, three years younger than him, had been flaring away like winkin' – going to the theatre – supping at harmonic meetings – eating oysters by the barrel – drinking stout by the gallon – even out all night, and coming home as cool in the morning as if nothing had happened. So Mr Augustus Cooper made up his mind that he would not stand it any longer, and had that very morning expressed to his mother a firm determination to be 'blowed', in the event of his not being instantly provided with a street-door key. And he was walking down Holborn Hill, thinking about all these things, and wondering how he could manage to get introduced into genteel society for the first time, when his eyes rested on Signor Billsmethi's announcement, which it immediately struck him was just the very thing he wanted; for he should not only be able to select a genteel circle of acquaintance at once, out of the five-and-seventy pupils at four and sixpence a quarter, but should qualify himself at the same time to go through a hornpipe in private society, with perfect ease to himself and great delight to his friends. So, he stopped the unstamped advertisement – an animated sandwich, composed of a boy between two boards – and having procured a very small card with the Signor's address indented thereon, walked straight at once to the Signor's house – and very fast he walked too, for fear the list should be filled up, and the five-and-seventy completed, before he got there. The Signor was at home, and, what was still more gratifying, he was an Englishman! Such a nice man – and so polite! The list was not full, but it was a most extraordinary circumstance that there was only just one vacancy, and even that one would have been filled up, that very morning, only Signor Billsmethi was dissatisfied with the reference, and, being very much afraid that the lady wasn't select, wouldn't take her.

'And very much delighted I am, Mr Cooper,' said Signor Billsmethi, 'that I did *not* take her. I assure you, Mr Cooper – I don't say it to flatter you, for I know you're above it – that I consider myself extremely fortunate in having a gentleman of your manners and appearance, sir.'

'I am very glad of it too, sir,' said Augustus Cooper.

'And I hope we shall be better acquainted, sir,' said Signor Billsmethi.

'And I'm sure I hope we shall too, sir,' responded Augustus Cooper.

Just then, the door opened, and in came a young lady, with her hair curled in a crop all over her head, and her shoes tied in sandals all over her ankles.

'Don't run away, my dear,' said Signor Billsmethi; for the young lady didn't know Mr Cooper was there when she ran in, and was going to run out again in her modesty, all in confusion-like. 'Don't run away, my dear,' said Signor Billsmethi, 'this is Mr Cooper – Mr Cooper, of Fetter

*Signor Billsmethi, of the King's Theatre, intended opening
for the season with a Grand Ball*

Lane. Mr Cooper, my daughter, sir – Miss Billsmethi, sir, who I hope will have the pleasure of dancing many a quadrille, minuet, gavotte, country-dance, fandango, double-hornpipe, and farinagholkajingo with you, sir. She dances them all, sir; and so shall you, sir, before you're a quarter older, sir.'

And Signor Bellsmethi slapped Mr Augustus Cooper on the back, as if he had known him a dozen years – so friendly – and Mr Cooper bowed to the young lady, and the young lady curtseyed to him, and Signor Billsmethi said they were as handsome a pair as ever he'd wish to see; upon which the young lady exclaimed, 'Lor, pa!' and blushed as red as Mr Cooper himself – you might have thought they were both standing under a red lamp at a chemist's shop; and before Mr Cooper went away it was settled that he should join the family circle that very night – taking them just as they were – no ceremony nor nonsense of that kind – and learn his positions in order that he might lose no time, and be able to come out at the forthcoming ball.

Well; Mr Augustus Cooper went away to one of the cheap shoe-makers' shops in Holborn, where gentlemen's dress-pumps are seven and sixpence and men's strong walking just nothing at all, and bought a pair of the regular seven-and-sixpenny, long-quartered town-mades, in which he astonished himself quite as much as his mother, and sallied forth to Signor Billsmethi's. There were four other private pupils in the parlour: two ladies and two gentlemen. Such nice people! Not a bit of pride about them. One of the ladies in particular, who was in training for a Columbine, was remarkably affable; and she and Miss Billsmethi took such an interest in Mr Augustus Cooper and joked and smiled and looked so bewitching that he got quite at home and learnt his steps in no time. After the practising was over, Signor Billsmethi and Miss Billsmethi and Master Billsmethi and a young lady and the two ladies and the two gentlemen danced a quadrille – none of your slipping and sliding about, but regular warm work, flying into corners and diving among chairs and shooting out at the door – something like dancing! Signor Billsmethi in particular, notwithstanding his having a little fiddle to play all the time, was out on the landing every figure, and Master Billsmethi, when everybody else was breathless, danced a hornpipe, with a cane in his hand and a cheese-plate on his head, to the unqualified admiration of the whole company. Then, Signor Billsmethi insisted, as they were so happy, that they should all stay to supper, and proposed sending Master

Billsmethi for the beer and spirits, whereupon the two gentlemen swore, 'strike 'em wulgar if they'd stand that', and were just going to quarrel who should pay for it, when Mr Augustus Cooper said he would, if they'd have the kindness to allow him – and they *had* the kindness to allow him; and Master Billsmethi brought the beer in a can and the rum in a quart pot. They had a regular night of it; and Miss Billsmethi squeezed Mr Augustus Cooper's hand under the table; and Mr Augustus Cooper returned the squeeze, and returned home too, at something to six o'clock in the morning, when he was put to bed by main force by the apprentice, after repeatedly expressing an uncontrollable desire to pitch his revered parent out of the second-floor window and to throttle the apprentice with his own neck-handkerchief.

Weeks had worn on, and the seven-and-sixpenny town-mades had nearly worn out, when the night arrived for the grand dress-ball at which the whole of the five-and-seventy pupils were to meet together for the first time that season, and to take out some portion of their respective four-and-sixpences in lamp-oil and fiddlers. Mr Augustus Cooper had ordered a new coat for the occasion – a two-pound-tenner from Turnstile. It was his first appearance in public; and, after a grand Sicilian shawl-dance by fourteen young ladies in character, he was to open the quadrille department with Miss Billsmethi herself, with whom he had become quite intimate since his first introduction. It *was* a night! Everything was admirably arranged. The sandwich-boy took the hats and bonnets at the street-door; there was a turn-up bedstead in the back parlour, on which Miss Billsmethi made tea and coffee for such of the gentlemen as chose to pay for it, and such of the ladies as the gentlemen treated; red port-wine negus and lemonade were handed round at eighteen-pence a head; and in pursuance of a previous engagement with the public-house at the corner of the street, an extra potboy was laid on for the occasion. In short, nothing could exceed the arrangements, except the company. Such ladies! Such pink silk stockings! Such artificial flowers! Such a number of cabs! No sooner had one cab set down a couple of ladies, than another cab drove up and set down another couple of ladies, and they all knew not only one another, but the majority of the gentlemen into the bargain, which made it all as pleasant and lively as could be. Signor Billsmethi, in black tights, with a large blue bow in his buttonhole, introduced the ladies to such of the gentlemen as were strangers: and the ladies talked away – and laughed they did – it was delightful to see them.

As to the shawl-dance, it was the most exciting thing that ever was beheld; there was such a whisking and rustling and fanning and getting ladies into a tangle with artificial flowers and then disentangling them again! And as to Mr Augustus Cooper's share in the quadrille, he got through it admirably. He was missing from his partner, now and then, certainly, and discovered on such occasions to be either dancing with laudable perseverance in another set, or sliding about in perspective, without any definite object; but, generally speaking, they managed to shove him through the figure, until he turned up in the right place. Be this as it may, when he had finished, a great many ladies and gentlemen came up and complimented him very much, and said they had never seen a beginner do anything like it before; and Mr Augustus Cooper was perfectly satisfied with himself, and everybody else into the bargain; and 'stood' considerable quantities of spirits and water, negus and compounds for the use and behoof of two or three dozen very particular friends, selected from the select circle of five-and-seventy pupils.

Now, whether it was the strength of the compounds, or the beauty of the ladies, or what not, it did so happen that Mr Augustus Cooper encouraged, rather than repelled, the very flattering attentions of a young lady in brown gauze over white calico who had appeared particularly struck with him from the first; and when the encouragements had been prolonged for some time, Miss Billsmethi betrayed her spite and jealousy thereat by calling the young lady in brown gauze a 'creeter', which induced the young lady in brown gauze to retort in certain sentences containing a taunt founded on the payment of four-and-sixpence a quarter, which reference Mr Augustus Cooper, being then and there in a state of considerable bewilderment, expressed his entire concurrence in. Miss Billsmethi, thus renounced, forthwith began screaming in the loudest key of her voice, at the rate of fourteen screams a minute; and being unsuccessful, in an onslaught on the eyes and face, first of the lady in gauze and then of Mr Augustus Cooper, called distractedly on the other three-and-seventy pupils to furnish her with oxalic acid for her own private drinking; and, the call not being honoured, made another rush at Mr Cooper, and then had her stay-lace cut and was carried off to bed. Mr Augustus Cooper, not being remarkable for quickness of apprehension, was at a loss to understand what all this meant, until Signor Billsmethi explained it in a most satisfactory manner by stating to the pupils that Mr Augustus Cooper had made and confirmed divers promises of marriage to his daughter on divers occasions and had now basely deserted her; on which, the indignation of the pupils became universal; and as several chivalrous gentlemen enquired rather pressingly of Mr Augustus Cooper whether he required anything for his own use, or, in other words, whether he 'wanted anything for himself', he deemed it prudent to make a precipitate retreat. And the upshot of the matter was that a lawyer's letter came next day, and an action was commenced next week; and that Mr Augustus Cooper, after walking twice to the Serpentine for the purpose of drowning himself, and coming twice back without doing it, made a confidante of his mother, who compromised the matter with twenty pounds from the till: which made twenty pounds four shillings and sixpence paid to Signor Billsmethi, exclusive of treats and pumps. And Mr Augustus Cooper went back and lived with his mother, and there he lives to this day; and as he has lost his ambition for society, and never goes into the world, he will never see this account of himself, and will never be any the wiser.

MAKING A NIGHT OF IT

Damon and Pythias were undoubtedly very good fellows in their way: the former for his extreme readiness to put in special bail for a friend; and the latter for a certain trump-like punctuality in turning up just in the very nick of time, scarcely less remarkable. Many points in their character have, however, grown obsolete. Damons are rather hard to find in these days of imprisonment for debt (except the sham ones, and they cost half a crown); and, as to the Pythiases, the few that have existed in these degenerate times have had an unfortunate knack of making themselves scarce at the very moment when their appearance would have been strictly classical. If the actions of these heroes, however, can find no parallel in modern times, their friendship can. We have Damon and Pythias on the one hand. We have Potter and Smithers on the other; and, lest the two last-mentioned names should never have reached the ears of our unenlightened readers, we can do no better than make them acquainted with the owners thereof.

Mr Thomas Potter, then, was a clerk in the city, and Mr Robert Smithers was a ditto in the same; their incomes were limited, but their friendship was unbounded. They lived in the same street, walked into town every morning at the same hour, dined at the same slap-bang every day, and revelled in each other's company every night. They were knit together by the closest ties of intimacy and friendship, or, as Mr Thomas Potter touchingly observed, they were 'thick-and-thin pals, and nothing but it'. There was a spice of romance in Mr Smithers's disposition, a ray of poetry, a gleam of misery, a sort of consciousness of he didn't exactly know what, coming across him he didn't precisely know why – which stood out in fine relief against the offhand, dashing, amateur-pickpocket sort of manner which distinguished Mr Potter in an eminent degree.

The peculiarity of their respective dispositions extended itself to their individual costume. Mr Smithers generally appeared in public in a surtout and shoes, with a narrow black neckerchief and a brown hat, very much turned up at the sides – peculiarities which Mr Potter wholly eschewed, for it was his ambition to do something in the celebrated 'kiddy' or stagecoach way, and he had even gone so far as to invest capital in the purchase of a rough blue coat with wooden buttons, made upon the fireman's principle, in which, with the addition of a low-crowned, flower-pot-saucer-shaped hat, he had created no inconsiderable sensation at the Albion in Little Russell Street and divers other places of public and fashionable resort.

Mr Potter and Mr Smithers had mutually agreed that, on the receipt of their quarter's salary, they would jointly and in company 'spend the evening' – an evident misnomer – the spending applying, as everybody knows, not to the evening itself but to all the money the individual may chance to be possessed of, on the occasion to which reference is made; and they had likewise agreed that, on the evening aforesaid, they would 'make a night of it' – an expressive term, implying the borrowing of several hours from tomorrow morning, adding them to the night before, and manufacturing a compound night of the whole.

The quarter-day arrived at last – we say at last, because quarter days are as eccentric as comets: moving wonderfully quick when you have a good deal to pay, and marvellously slow when you have a little to receive. Mr Thomas Potter and Mr Robert Smithers met by appointment to begin the evening with a dinner; and a nice, snug, comfortable dinner they had, consisting of a little procession of four chops and four kidneys, following each other, supported on either side by a pot of the real draught stout, and attended by divers cushions of bread and wedges of cheese.

When the cloth was removed, Mr Thomas Potter ordered the waiter to bring in two goes of his best Scotch whisky, with warm water and sugar, and a couple of his 'very mildest' Havannahs, which the waiter did. Mr Thomas Potter mixed his grog and lighted his cigar; Mr Robert Smithers did the same; and then Mr Thomas Potter jocularly proposed as the first toast 'the abolition of all offices whatever' (not sinecures, but counting-houses), which was immediately drunk by Mr Robert Smithers, with enthusiastic applause. So they went on, talking politics, puffing cigars and sipping whisky and water, until the 'goes' – most appropriately so called – were both gone, which Mr Robert Smithers perceiving, immediately ordered in two more goes of the best Scotch whisky, and two more of the very mildest Havannahs; and the goes kept coming in, and the mild Havannahs kept going out, until, what with the drinking, and lighting, and puffing, and the stale ashes on the table, and the tallow-grease on the cigars, Mr Robert Smithers began to doubt the mildness of the Havannahs, and to feel very much as if he had been sitting in a hackney-coach with his back to the horses.

As to Mr Thomas Potter, he *would* keep laughing out loud, and volunteering inarticulate declarations that he was 'all right'; in proof of which, he feebly bespoke the evening paper after the next gentleman, but finding it a matter of some difficulty to discover any news in its columns, or to ascertain distinctly whether it had any columns at all, walked slowly out to look for the moon, and, after coming back quite pale with looking up at the sky so long, and attempting to express mirth at Mr Robert Smithers' having fallen asleep, by various galvanic chuckles, laid his head on his arm, and went to sleep also. When he awoke again, Mr Robert Smithers awoke too, and they both very gravely agreed that it had been extremely unwise to eat so many pickled walnuts with the chops, as it was a notorious fact that they always made people queer and sleepy; indeed, if it had not been for the whisky and cigars, there was no knowing what harm they mightn't have done 'em. So they took some coffee, and after paying the bill – twelve and twopence the dinner, and the odd ten pence for the waiter – thirteen shillings in all – started out on their expedition to manufacture a night.

It was just half-past eight, so they thought they couldn't do better than go at half-price to the slips at the City Theatre, which they did accordingly. Mr Robert Smithers, who had become extremely poetical after the settlement of the bill, enlivening the walk by informing Mr Thomas Potter in confidence that he felt an inward presentiment of approaching dissolution, and subsequently embellishing the theatre by falling asleep with his head and both arms gracefully drooping over the front of the boxes.

Such was the quiet demeanour of the unassuming Smithers, and such were the happy effects of Scotch whisky and Havannahs on that interesting person! But Mr Thomas Potter, whose great aim it was to be considered as a 'knowing card', a 'fast-goer', and so forth, conducted himself in a very different manner, and commenced going very fast indeed – rather too fast, at last, for the patience of the audience to keep pace with him. On his first entry, he contented himself by earnestly calling upon the gentlemen in the gallery to 'flare up', accompanying the demand with another request, expressive of his wish that they would instantaneously 'form a union', both which requisitions were responded to in the manner most in vogue on such occasions.

'Give that dog a bone!' cried one gentleman in his shirt-sleeves. 'Where have you been a-having half a pint of intermediate beer?' cried a second.

'Tailor!' screamed a third. 'Barber's clerk!' shouted a fourth. 'Throw him o–VER!' roared a fifth; while numerous voices concurred in desiring Mr Thomas Potter to 'go home to his mother!' All these taunts Mr Thomas Potter received with supreme contempt, cocking the low-crowned hat a little more on one side whenever any reference was made to his personal appearance and, standing up with his arms akimbo, expressing defiance melodramatically.

The overture – to which these various sounds had been an *ad libitum* accompaniment – concluded, the second piece began, and Mr Thomas Potter, emboldened by impunity, proceeded to behave in a most unprecedented and outrageous manner. First of all, he imitated the shake of the principal female singer; then, groaned at the blue fire; then, affected to be frightened into convulsions of terror at the appearance of the ghost; and, lastly, not only made a running commentary, in an audible voice, upon the dialogue on the stage, but actually awoke Mr Robert Smithers, who, hearing his companion making a noise and having a very indistinct notion where he was or what was required of him, immediately, by way of imitating a good example, set up the most unearthly, unremitting and appalling howling that ever audience heard. It was too much. 'Turn them out!' was the general cry. A noise, as of shuffling of feet and men being knocked up with violence against wainscoting, was heard; a hurried dialogue of 'Come out!' – 'I won't!' – 'You shall!' – 'I shan't!' – 'Give me your card, sir!' – 'You're a scoundrel, sir!' and so forth, succeeded. A round of applause betokened the approbation of the audience, and Mr Robert Smithers and Mr Thomas Potter found themselves shot with astonishing swiftness into the road, without having had the trouble of once putting foot to ground during the whole progress of their rapid descent.

Mr Robert Smithers, being constitutionally one of the slow-goers, and having had quite enough of fast-going in the course of his recent expulsion to last until the quarter-day then next ensuing at the very least, had no sooner emerged with his companion from the precincts of Milton Street than he proceeded to indulge in circuitous references to the beauties of sleep, mingled with distant allusions to the propriety of returning to Islington and testing the influence of their patent Bramahs over the street-door locks to which they respectively belonged. Mr Thomas Potter, however, was valorous and peremptory. They had come out to make a night of it: and a night must be made. So Mr Robert

All these taunts Mr Thomas Potter received with supreme contempt

Smithers, who was three parts dull, and the other dismal, despairingly assented; and they went into a wine-vaults, to get materials for assisting them in making a night; where they found a good many young ladies, and various old gentlemen, and a plentiful sprinkling of hackney-coachmen and cab-drivers, all drinking and talking together; and Mr Thomas Potter and Mr Robert Smithers drank small glasses of brandy, and large glasses of soda, until they began to have a very confused idea, either of things in general or of anything in particular; and, when they had done treating themselves they began to treat everybody else; and the rest of the entertainment was a confused mixture of heads and heels, black eyes and blue uniforms, mud and gaslights, thick doors and stone paving.

Then, as standard novelists expressively inform us – 'all was a blank!' and in the morning the blank was filled up with the words 'STATION-HOUSE', and the station-house was filled up with Mr Thomas Potter, Mr Robert Smithers and the major part of their wine-vault companions of the preceding night, with a comparatively small portion of clothing of any kind. And it was disclosed at the police-office, to the indignation of the bench and the astonishment of the spectators, how one Robert Smithers, aided and abetted by one Thomas Potter, had knocked down and beaten, in divers streets, at different times, five men, four boys and three women; how the said Thomas Potter had feloniously obtained possession of five door-knockers, two bell-handles and a bonnet; how Robert Smithers, his friend, had sworn at least forty pounds' worth of oaths, at the rate of five shillings apiece; terrified whole streets full of her majesty's subjects with awful shrieks and alarms of fire; destroyed the uniforms of five policemen; and committed various other atrocities, too numerous to recapitulate. And the magistrate, after an appropriate reprimand, fined Mr Thomas Potter and Mr Thomas Smithers five shillings each, for being, what the law vulgarly terms, drunk; and thirty-four pounds for seventeen assaults at forty shillings ahead, with liberty to speak to the prosecutors.

The prosecutors *were* spoken to, and Messrs Potter and Smithers lived on credit for a quarter as best they might; and, although the prosecutors expressed their readiness to be assaulted twice a week, on the same terms, they have never since been detected in 'making a night of it'.

MEDITATIONS IN MONMOUTH STREET

We have always entertained a particular attachment towards Monmouth Street, as the only true and real emporium for second-hand wearing apparel. Monmouth Street is venerable from its antiquity, and respectable from its usefulness. Holywell Street we despise; the red-headed and red-whiskered Jews who forcibly haul you into their squalid houses, and thrust you into a suit of clothes, whether you will or not, we detest.

The inhabitants of Monmouth Street are a distinct class; a peaceable and retiring race, who immure themselves for the most part in deep cellars, or small back parlours, and who seldom come forth into the world, except in the dusk and coolness of the evening, when they may be seen seated in chairs on the pavement, smoking their pipes, or watching the gambols of their engaging children as they revel in the gutter, a happy troop of infantine scavengers. Their countenances bear a thoughtful and a dirty cast, certain indications of their love of traffic; and their habitations are distinguished by that disregard of outward appearance and neglect of personal comfort, so common among people who are constantly immersed in profound speculations, and deeply engaged in sedentary pursuits.

We have hinted at the antiquity of our favourite spot. 'A Monmouth Street laced coat' was a byword a century ago; and still we find Monmouth Street the same. Pilot greatcoats with wooden buttons have usurped the place of the ponderous laced coats with full skirts; embroidered waistcoats with large flaps have yielded to double-breasted checks with roll-collars; and three-cornered hats of quaint appearance have given place to the low crowns and broad brims of the coachman school; but it is the times that have changed, not Monmouth Street. Through every alteration and every change, Monmouth Street has still remained the burial-place of the fashions; and such, to judge from all present appearances, it will remain until there are no more fashions to bury.

We love to walk among these extensive groves of the illustrious dead, and to indulge in the speculations to which they give rise; now fitting a deceased coat, then a dead pair of trousers, and anon the mortal remains of a gaudy waistcoat, upon some being of our own conjuring up, and endeavouring, from the shape and fashion of the garment itself, to bring its former owner before our mind's eye. We have gone on speculating in this way, until whole rows of coats have started from their pegs, and buttoned up, of their own accord, round the waists of imaginary wearers; lines of trousers have jumped down to meet them; waistcoats have almost burst with anxiety to put themselves on; and half an acre of shoes have suddenly found feet to fit them and gone stumping down the street with a noise which has fairly awakened us from our pleasant reverie and driven us slowly away, with a bewildered stare, an object of astonishment to the good people of Monmouth Street, and of no slight suspicion to the policemen at the opposite street corner.

We were occupied in this manner the other day, endeavouring to fit a pair of lace-up half-boots on an ideal personage, for whom, to say the truth, they were full a couple of sizes too small, when our eyes happened to alight on a few suits of clothes ranged outside a shop-window, which, it immediately struck us, must at different periods have all belonged to, and been worn by, the same individual, and had now, by one of those strange conjunctions of circumstances which will occur sometimes, come to be exposed together for sale in the same shop. The idea seemed a fantastic one, and we looked at the clothes again with a firm determination not to be easily led away. No, we were right; the more we looked, the more we were convinced of the accuracy of our previous impression. There was the man's whole life written as legibly on those clothes as if we had his autobiography engrossed on parchment before us.

The first was a patched and much-soiled skeleton suit; one of those straight blue cloth cases in which small boys used to be confined, before belts and tunics had come in and old notions had gone out: an ingenious contrivance for displaying the full symmetry of a boy's figure, by fastening him into a very tight jacket, with an ornamental row of buttons over each shoulder, and then buttoning his trousers over it, so as to give his legs the appearance of being hooked on, just under the armpits. This was the boy's dress. It had belonged to a town boy, we could see: there was a shortness about the legs and arms of the suit and a bagging at the knees peculiar to the rising youth of London streets. A small day-school he had been at, evidently. If it had been a regular boys' school they wouldn't have let him play on the floor so much, and rub his knees so white. He had an indulgent mother too, and plenty of halfpence, as the numerous smears of some sticky substance about the pockets, and just below the chin, which even the salesman's skill could not succeed in disguising,

The inhabitants of Monmouth Street seated in chairs on the pavement, smoking their pipes, or watching the gambols of their engaging children as they revel in the gutter

sufficiently betokened. They were decent people, but not overburdened with riches, or he would not have so far outgrown the suit when he passed into those corduroys with the round jacket; in this he went to a boys' school, however, and learnt to write – and in ink of pretty tolerable blackness, too, if the place where he used to wipe his pen might be taken as evidence.

A black suit and the jacket changed into a diminutive coat. His father had died, and the mother had got the boy a message-lad's place in some office. A long-worn suit that one; rusty and threadbare before it was laid aside, but clean and free from soil to the last. Poor woman! We could imagine her assumed cheerfulness over the scanty meal, and the refusal of her own small portion, that her hungry boy might have enough. Her constant anxiety for his welfare, her pride in his growth mingled some-times with the thought, almost too acute to bear, that as he grew to be a man his old affection might cool, old kindnesses fade from his mind, and old promises be forgotten – the sharp pain that even then a careless word or a cold look would give her – all crowded on our thoughts as vividly as if the very scene were passing before us.

These things happen every hour, and we all know it; and yet we felt as much sorrow when we saw, or fancied we saw – it makes no difference which – the change that began to take place now, as if we had just conceived the bare possibility of such a thing for the first time. The next suit, smart but slovenly; meant to be gay, and yet not half so decent as the threadbare apparel; redolent of the idle lounge, and the blackguard companions, told us, we thought, that the widow's comfort had rapidly faded away. We could imagine that coat – imagine! we could see it; we *had* seen it a hundred times – sauntering in company with three or four other coats of the same cut, about some place of profligate resort at night.

We dressed, from the same shop-window in an instant, half a dozen boys of from fifteen to twenty; and putting cigars into their mouths, and their hands into their pockets, watched them as they sauntered down the street, and lingered at the corner, with the obscene jest and the oft-repeated oath. We never lost sight of them, till they had cocked their hats a little more on one side, and swaggered into the public-house; and then we entered the desolate home, where the mother sat late in the night, alone; we watched her as she paced the room in feverish anxiety, and every now and then opened the door, looked wistfully into the dark and empty street, and again returned, to be again and again disappointed. We beheld the look of patience with which she bore the brutish threat, nay, even the drunken blow; and we heard the agony of tears that gushed from her very heart as she sank upon her knees in her solitary and wretched apartment.

A long period had elapsed, and a greater change had taken place, by the time of casting off the suit that hung above. It was that of a stout, broad-shouldered, sturdy-chested man; and we knew at once, as anybody would who glanced at that broad-skirted green coat with the large metal buttons, that its wearer seldom walked forth without a dog at his heels and some idle ruffian, the very counterpart of himself, at his side. The vices of the boy had grown with the man, and we fancied his home then – if such a place deserve the name.

We saw the bare and miserable room, destitute of furniture, crowded with his wife and children, pale, hungry and emaciated; the man cursing their lamentations, staggering to the tap-room, from whence he had just returned, followed by his wife and a sickly infant, clamouring for bread; and heard the street-wrangle and noisy recrimination that his striking her occasioned. And then imagination led us to some metropolitan work-house, situated in the midst of crowded streets and alleys, filled with noxious vapours, and ringing with boisterous cries, where an old and feeble woman, imploring pardon for her son, lay dying in a close dark room, with no child to clasp her hand, and no pure air from heaven to fan her brow. A stranger closed the eyes that settled into a cold unmeaning glare, and strange ears received the words that murmured from the white and half-closed lips.

A coarse round frock, with a worn cotton neckerchief, and other articles of clothing of the commonest description, completed the history. A prison, and the sentence – banishment or the gallows. What would the man have given then, to be once again the contented humble drudge of his boyish years; to have been restored to life, but for a week, a day, an hour, a minute, only for so long a time as would enable him to say one word of passionate regret to, and hear one sound of heartfelt forgiveness from, the cold and ghastly form that lay rotting in the pauper's grave! The children wild in the streets, the mother a destitute widow: both deeply tainted with the deep disgrace of the husband and father's name, and impelled by sheer necessity down the precipice that had led him to a lingering death, possibly of many years' duration, thousands of miles away. We had no clue to the end of the tale; but it was easy to guess its termination.

We took a step or two further on, and by way of restoring the naturally cheerful tone of our thoughts, began fitting visionary feet and legs into a cellar-board full of boots and shoes, with a speed and accuracy that would have astonished the most expert artist in leather living. There was one pair of boots in particular – a jolly, good-tempered, hearty-looking pair of tops, that excited our warmest regard; and we had got a fine, red-faced, jovial fellow of a market-gardener into them, before we had made their acquaintance half a minute. They were just the very thing for him. There were his huge fat legs bulging over the tops, and fitting them too tight to admit of his tucking in the loops he had pulled them on by; and his knee-cords with an interval of stocking; and his blue apron tucked up round his waist; and his red neckerchief and blue coat, and a white hat stuck on one side of his head; and there he stood with a broad grin on his great red face, whistling away, as if any other idea but that of being happy and comfortable had never entered his brain.

This was the very man after our own heart; we knew all about him; we had seen him coming up to Covent Garden in his green chaise-cart, with the fat, tubby little horse, half a thousand times; and even while we cast an affectionate look upon his boots, at that instant the form of a coquettish servant-maid suddenly sprang into a pair of Denmark satin shoes that stood beside them, and we at once recognised the very girl who accepted his offer of a ride, just on this side the Hammersmith suspension-bridge, the very last Tuesday morning we rode into town from Richmond.

A very smart female, in a showy bonnet, stepped into a pair of grey cloth boots, with black fringe and binding, that were studiously pointing out their toes on the other side of the top-boots, and seemed very anxious to engage his attention, but we didn't observe that our friend the market-gardener appeared at all captivated with these blandishments; for beyond giving a knowing wink when they first began, as if to imply that he quite understood their end and object, he took no further notice of them. His indifference, however, was amply recompensed by the excessive gallantry of a very old gentleman with a silver-headed stick, who tottered into a pair of large list shoes that were standing in one corner of the board, and indulged in a variety of gestures expressive of his admiration of the lady in the cloth boots, to the immeasurable amusement of a young fellow we put into a pair of long-quartered pumps, who we thought would have split the coat, that slid down to meet him, with laughing.

We had been looking on at this little pantomime with great satisfaction for some time, when, to our unspeakable astonishment, we perceived that the whole of the characters, including a numerous *corps de ballet* of boots and shoes in the background, into which we had been hastily thrusting as many feet as we could press into the service, were arranging themselves in order for dancing; and some music striking up at the moment, to it they went without delay. It was perfectly delightful to witness the agility of the market-gardener. Out went the boots, first on one side, then on the other, then cutting, then shuffling, then setting to the Denmark satins, then advancing, then retreating, then going round, and then repeating the whole of the evolutions again, without appearing to suffer in the least from the violence of the exercise.

Nor were the Denmark satins a bit behindhand, for they jumped and bounded about, in all directions; and though they were neither so regular, nor so true to the time as the cloth boots, still, as they seemed to do it from the heart, and to enjoy it more, we candidly confess that we preferred their style of dancing to the other. But the old gentleman in the list shoes was the most amusing object in the whole party; for, besides his grotesque attempts to appear youthful, and amorous, which were sufficiently entertaining in themselves, the young fellow in the pumps managed so artfully that every time the old gentleman advanced to salute the lady in the cloth boots, he trod with his whole weight on the old fellow's toes, which made him roar with anguish, and rendered all the others like to die of laughing.

We were in the full enjoyment of these festivities when we heard a shrill and by no means musical voice exclaim, 'Hope you'll know me agin, imperence!' and on looking intently forward to see from whence the sound came, we found that it proceeded, not from the young lady in the cloth boots, as we had at first been inclined to suppose, but from a bulky lady of elderly appearance who was seated in a chair at the head of the cellar-steps, apparently for the purpose of superintending the sale of the articles arranged there.

A barrel-organ, which had been in full force close behind us, ceased playing; the people we had been fitting into the shoes and boots took to flight at the interruption; and as we were conscious that in the depth of our meditations we might have been rudely staring at the old lady for half an hour without knowing it, we took to flight too, and were soon immersed in the deepest obscurity of the adjacent 'Dials.'

LONDON RECREATIONS

The wish of persons in the humbler classes of life to ape the manners and customs of those whom fortune has placed above them is often the subject of remark, and not unfrequently of complaint. The inclination may, and no doubt does, exist to a great extent among the small gentility – the would-be aristocrats – of the middle classes. Tradesmen and clerks, with fashionable novel-reading fam-ilies, and circulating-library-subscribing daughters, get up small assemblies in humble imitation of Almack's, and promenade the dingy 'large room' of some second-rate hotel with as much complacency as the enviable few who are privileged to exhibit their magnificence in that exclusive haunt of fashion and foolery. Aspiring young ladies, who read flaming accounts of some 'fancy fair in high life', suddenly grow desperately charitable; visions of admiration and matrimony float before their eyes; some wonderfully meritorious in-stitution, which, by the strangest accident in the world, has never been heard of before, is discovered to be in a languishing condition: Thomson's great room, or Johnson's nursery-ground, is forthwith engaged, and the aforesaid young ladies, from mere charity, exhibit themselves for three days, from twelve to four, for the small charge of one shilling per head! With the exception of these classes of society, however, and a few weak and insignificant persons, we do not think the attempt at imitation to which we have alluded prevails in any great degree. The different character of the recreations of different classes has often afforded us amusement; and we have chosen it for the subject of our present sketch, in the hope that it may possess some amusement for our readers.

If the regular City man, who leaves Lloyd's at five o'clock, and drives home to Hackney, Clapton, Stamford Hill or elsewhere, can be said to have any daily recreation beyond his dinner, it is his garden. He never does anything to it with his own hands; but he takes great pride in it notwithstanding; and if you are desirous of paying your addresses to the youngest daughter, be sure to be in raptures with every flower and shrub it contains. If your poverty of expression compel you to make any distinction between the two, we would certainly recommend your bestowing more admiration on his garden than his wine. He always takes a walk round it before he starts for town in the morning, and is particularly anxious that the fishpond should be kept specially neat. If you call on him on Sunday in summertime, about an hour before dinner, you will find him sitting in an armchair on the lawn behind the house, with a straw hat on, reading a Sunday paper. A short distance from him you will most likely observe a handsome parakeet in a large brass-wire cage; ten to one but the two eldest girls are loitering in one of the side walks accompanied by a couple of young gentlemen, who are holding parasols over them – of course only to keep the sun off – while the younger children, with the under nurserymaid, are strolling listlessly about, in the shade. Beyond these occasions, his delight in his garden appears to arise more from the consciousness of possession than actual enjoyment of it. When he drives you down to dinner on a weekday, he is rather fatigued with the occupations of the morning and tolerably cross into the bargain; but when the cloth is removed, and he has drunk three or four glasses of his favourite port, he orders the French windows of his dining-room (which of course look into the garden) to be opened, and throwing a silk handkerchief over his head, and leaning back in his armchair, descants at considerable length upon its beauty, and the cost of maintaining it. This is to impress you – who are a young friend of the family – with a due sense of the excellence of the garden and the wealth of its owner; and when he has exhausted the subject, he goes to sleep.

There is another and a very different class of men whose rec-reation is their garden. An individual of this class resides some short distance from town – say in the Hampstead Road, or the Kilburn Road, or any other road where the houses are small and neat and have little slips of back garden. He and his wife – who is as clean and compact a little body as himself – have occupied the same house ever since he retired from business twenty years ago. They have no family. They once had a son, who died at about five years old. The child's portrait hangs over the mantelpiece in the best sitting-room, and a little cart he used to draw about is carefully preserved as a relic.

In fine weather the old gentleman is almost constantly in the garden; and when it is too wet to go into it, he will look out of the window at it, by the hour together. He has always something to do there, and you will see him digging, and sweeping, and cutting, and planting, with manifest delight. In springtime, there is no end to the sowing of seeds, and sticking little bits of wood over them, with labels, which look like epitaphs to their memory; and in the evening, when the sun has gone down, the perseverance with which he lugs a great watering-pot about is perfectly astonishing. The only other recreation he has is the newspaper, which he peruses every day, from beginning to end, generally reading the most interesting pieces of intelligence to his wife during breakfast. The old lady is very fond of flowers, as the hyacinth-glasses in the parlour-window and geranium-pots in the little front court testify. She takes great pride in the garden too: and when one of the four fruit-trees produces rather a larger gooseberry than usual, it is carefully preserved under a wine-glass on the sideboard, for the edification of visitors, who are duly informed that Mr So-and-so planted the tree which produced it, with his own hands. On a summer's evening, when the large watering-pot has been filled and emptied some fourteen times, and the old couple have quite exhausted themselves by trotting about, you will see them sitting happily together in the little summerhouse, enjoying the calm and peace of the twilight, and watching the shadows as they fall upon the garden and, gradually growing thicker and more sombre, obscure the tints of their gayest flowers – no bad emblem of the years that have silently rolled over their heads, deadening in their course the brightest hues of early hopes and feelings which have long since faded away. These are their only recreations, and they require no more. They have within themselves the materials of comfort and content; and the only anxiety of each is to die before the other.

This is no ideal sketch. There *used* to be many old people of this description; their numbers may have diminished, and may decrease still more. Whether the course female education has taken of late days – whether the pursuit of giddy frivolities and empty nothings has tended to unfit women for that quiet domestic life, in which they show far more beautifully than in the most crowded assembly, is a question we should feel little gratification in discussing: we hope not.

Let us turn now to another portion of the London population, whose recreations present about as strong a contrast as can well be conceived – we mean the Sunday pleasurers; and let us beg our readers to imagine themselves stationed by our side in some well-known rural 'tea-gardens'.

The heat is intense this afternoon, and the people, of whom there are additional parties arriving every moment, look as warm as the tables which have been recently painted, and have the appearance of being red-hot. What a dust and noise! Men and women – boys and girls – sweethearts and married people – babies in arms and children in chaises –

pipes and shrimps – cigars and periwinkles – tea and tobacco. Gentlemen, in alarming waistcoats and steel watch-guards, promenading about, three abreast, with surprising dignity (or as the gentleman in the next box facetiously observes, 'cutting it uncommon fat!') – ladies, with great, long, white pocket-handkerchiefs like small tablecloths in their hands, chasing one another on the grass in the most playful and interesting manner, with the view of attracting the attention of the aforesaid gentlemen – husbands in perspective ordering bottles of ginger-beer for the objects of their affections, with a lavish disregard of expense; and the said objects washing down huge quantities of 'shrimps' and 'winkles,' with an equal disregard of their own bodily health and subsequent comfort – boys, with great silk hats just balanced on the top of their heads, smoking cigars, and trying to look as if they liked them – gentlemen in pink shirts and blue waistcoats, occasionally upsetting either themselves or somebody else with their own canes.

Some of the finery of these people provokes a smile, but they are all clean, and happy, and disposed to be good-natured and sociable. Those two motherly-looking women in the smart pelisses, who are chatting so confidentially, inserting a 'ma'am' at every fourth word, scraped an acquaintance about a quarter of an hour ago: it originated in admiration of the little boy who belongs to one of them – that diminutive specimen of mortality in the three-cornered pink satin hat with black feathers. The two men in the blue coats and drab trousers, who are walking up and down, smoking their pipes, are their husbands. The party in the opposite box are a pretty fair specimen of the generality of the visitors. These are the father and mother and old grandmother; a young man and woman, and an individual addressed by the euphonious title of 'Uncle Bill', who is evidently the wit of the party. They have some half-dozen children with them, but it is scarcely necessary to notice the fact, for that is a matter of course here. Every woman in 'the gardens' who has been married for any length of time must have had twins on two or three occasions; it is impossible to account for the extent of juvenile population in any other way.

Observe the inexpressible delight of the old grandmother at Uncle Bill's splendid joke of 'tea for four: bread and butter for forty'; and the loud explosion of mirth which follows his wafering a paper 'pigtail' on the waiter's collar. The young man is evidently 'keeping company' with Uncle Bill's niece: and Uncle Bill's hints – such as, 'Don't forget me at

Gentlemen, in alarming waistcoats and steel watch-guards,
promenading about, three abreast, with surprising dignity

the dinner, you know,' 'I shall look out for the cake, Sally,' 'I'll be godfather to your first – wager it's a boy,' and so forth, are equally embarrassing to the young people and delightful to the elder ones. As to the old grandmother, she is in perfect ecstasies, and does nothing but laugh herself into fits of coughing, until they have finished the 'gin and water warm with,' of which Uncle Bill ordered 'glasses round' after tea, 'just to keep the night air out, and do it up comfortable and riglar arter sitch an astonishing hot day!'

It is getting dark, and the people begin to move. The field leading to town is quite full of them; the little hand-chaises are dragged wearily along, the children are tired and amuse themselves and the company generally by crying, or resort to the much more pleasant expedient of going to sleep – the mothers begin to wish they were at home again – sweethearts grow more sentimental than ever, as the time for parting arrives – the gardens look mournful enough by the light of the two lanterns which hang against the trees for the convenience of smokers – and the waiters, who have been running about incessantly for the last six hours, think they feel a little tired as they count their glasses and their gains.

GREENWICH FAIR

If the parks be 'the lungs of London', we wonder what Greenwich Fair is – a periodical breaking out, we suppose, a sort of spring-rash: a three days' fever, which cools the blood for six months afterwards, and at the expiration of which London is restored to its old habits of plodding industry as suddenly and completely as if nothing had ever happened to disturb them.

In our earlier days, we were a constant frequenter of Greenwich Fair, for years. We have proceeded to, and returned from, it in almost every description of vehicle. We cannot conscientiously deny the charge of having once made the passage in a spring-van, accompanied by thirteen gentlemen, fourteen ladies, an unlimited number of children and a barrel of beer; and we have a vague recollection of having, in later days, found ourself the eighth outside, on the top of a hackney-coach, at something past four o'clock in the morning, with a rather confused idea of our own name or place of residence. We have grown older since then, and quiet, and steady: liking nothing better than to spend our Easter, and all our other holidays, in some quiet nook, with people of whom we shall never tire; but we think we still remember something of Greenwich Fair and of those who resort to it. At all events we will try.

The road to Greenwich during the whole of Easter Monday is in a state of perpetual bustle and noise. Cabs, hackney-coaches, 'shay' carts, coal-waggons, stages, omnibuses, sociables, gigs, donkey-chaises – all crammed with people (for the question never is what the horse can draw, but what the vehicle will hold) – roll along at their utmost speed; the dust flies in clouds, ginger-beer corks go off in volleys, the balcony of every public-house is crowded with people, smoking and drinking, half the private houses are turned into tea-shops, fiddles are in great request, every little fruit-shop displays its stall of gilt gingerbread and penny toys; turnpike men are in despair; horses won't go on, and wheels will come off; ladies in 'carawans' scream with fright at every fresh concussion, and their admirers find it necessary to sit remarkably close to them, by way of encouragement; servants-of-all-work, who are not allowed to have followers, and have got a holiday for the day, make the most of their time with the faithful admirer who waits for a stolen interview at the corner of the street every night when they go to fetch the beer – apprentices grow sentimental and straw-bonnet makers kind. Everybody is anxious to get on, and actuated by the common wish to be at the fair, or in the park, as soon as possible.

Pedestrians linger in groups at the roadside, unable to resist the allurements of the stout proprietress of the 'Jack-in-the-box, three shies a penny', or the more splendid offers of the man with three thimbles and a pea on a little round board, who astonishes the bewildered crowd with some such address as, 'Here's the sort o' game to make you laugh seven years arter you're dead, and turn ev'ry air on your ed grey vith delight! Three thimbles and vun little pea – with a vun, two, three and a two, three, vun; catch him who can, look on, keep your eyes open, and niver say die! niver mind the change, and the expense; all fair and above board; them as don't play can't vin, and luck attend the ryal sportsman! Bet any gen'lm'n any sum of money, from harf-a-crown up to a suverin, as he doesn't name the thimble as kivers the pea!' Here some greenhorn whispers his friend that he distinctly saw the pea roll under the middle thimble – an impression which is immediately confirmed by a gentleman in top-boots, who is standing by, and who, in a low tone, regrets his own inability to bet, in consequence of having unfortunately left his purse at home, but strongly urges the stranger not to neglect such a golden opportunity. The 'plant' is successful, the bet is made, the stranger of course loses and the gentleman with the thimbles consoles him, as he pockets the money, with an assurance that it's 'all the fortin of war! this time I vin, next time you vin; niver mind the loss of two bob and a bender! Do it up in a small parcel, and break out in a fresh place. Here's the sort o' game,' &c. – and the eloquent harangue, with such variations as the speaker's exuberant fancy suggests, is again repeated to the gaping crowd, reinforced by the accession of several newcomers.

The chief place of resort in the daytime, after the public-houses, is the park, in which the principal amusement is to drag young ladies up the steep hill which leads to the Observatory, and then drag them down again, at the very top of their speed, greatly to the derangement of their curls and bonnet-caps and much to the edification of lookers-on from below. 'Kiss in the Ring', and 'Threading my Grandmother's Needle', too, are sports which receive their full share of patronage. Lovesick swains, under the influence of gin and water and the tender passion, become violently affectionate: and the fair objects of their regard enhance the value of stolen kisses, by a vast deal of struggling, and holding down of heads, and cries of 'Oh! Ha' done, then, George – Oh, do tickle him for me, Mary – Well, I never!' and similar Lucretian ejaculations. Little old men and women, with a small basket under one arm and a wine-glass without a foot in the other hand, tender 'a drop o' the right sort' to the different groups; and young ladies, who are persuaded to indulge in a drop of the aforesaid right sort, display a pleasing degree of reluctance to taste it, and cough afterwards with great propriety.

The old pensioners, who, for the moderate charge of a penny, exhibit the mast-house, the Thames and shipping, the place where the men used to hang in chains and other interesting sights through a telescope, are asked questions about objects within the range of the glass which it would puzzle a Solomon to answer; and requested to find out particular houses in particular streets which it would have been a task of some difficulty for Mr Horner (not the young gentleman who ate mince-pies with his thumb, but the man of Colosseum notoriety) to discover. Here and there, where some three or four couples are sitting on the grass together, you will see a sunburnt woman in a red cloak 'telling fortunes' and prophesying husbands, which it requires no extraordinary obser-vation to describe for the originals are before her. Thereupon, the lady concerned laughs and blushes, and ultimately buries her face in an imitation cambric handkerchief, and the gentleman described looks extremely foolish, and squeezes her hand, and fees the gypsy liberally; and the gypsy goes away, perfectly satisfied herself, and leaving those behind her perfectly satisfied also; and the prophecy, like many other prophecies of greater importance, fulfils itself in time.

But it grows dark: the crowd has gradually dispersed, and only a few stragglers are left behind. The light in the direction of the church shows that the fair is illuminated; and the distant noise proves it to be filling fast. The spot, which half an hour ago was ringing with the shouts of boisterous mirth, is as calm and quiet as if nothing could ever disturb its serenity: the fine old trees, the majestic building at their feet, with the noble river beyond, glistening in the moonlight, appear in all their beauty and under their most favourable aspect; the voices of the boys, singing their evening hymn, are borne gently on the air; and the humblest mechanic who has been lingering on the grass so pleasant to the feet that beat the same dull round from week to week on the paved streets of London, feels proud to think, as he surveys the scene before him, that he belongs to the country which has selected such a spot as a retreat for its oldest and best defenders in the decline of their lives.

Five minutes' walking brings you to the fair; a scene calculated to awaken very different feelings. The entrance is occupied on either side by the vendors of gingerbread and toys: the stalls are gaily lighted up, the most attractive goods profusely disposed, and unbonneted young ladies, in their zeal for the interest of their employers, seize you by the coat, and use all the blandishments of 'Do, dear' – 'There's a love' – 'Don't be cross, now' &c. to induce you to purchase half a pound of the real spice nuts, of which the majority of the regular fair-goers carry a pound or two as a present supply, tied up in a cotton pocket-handkerchief. Occasionally you pass a deal table on which are exposed pen'orths of pickled salmon (fennel included), in little white saucers, oysters, with shells as large as cheese-plates, and divers specimens of a species of snail (*wilks*, we think they are called), floating in a somewhat bilious-looking green liquid. Cigars, too, are in great demand; gentlemen must smoke, of course, and here they are, two a penny, in a regular authentic cigar-box, with a lighted tallow candle in the centre.

Imagine yourself in an extremely dense crowd, which swings you to and fro, and in and out, and every way but the right one; add to this the screams of women, the shouts of boys, the clanging of gongs, the firing of pistols, the ringing of bells, the bellowings of speaking-trumpets, the squeaking of penny dittos, the noise of a dozen bands, with three drums in each, all playing different tunes at the same time, the hallooing of showmen and an occasional roar from the wild-beast shows; and you are in the very centre and heart of the fair.

This immense booth, with the large stage in front, so brightly illuminated with variegated lamps and pots of burning fat, is 'Richardson's', where you have a melodrama (with three murders and a ghost), a pantomime, a comic song, an overture and some incidental music all done in five-and-twenty minutes.

The company are now promenading outside in all the dignity of wigs, spangles, red-ochre and whitening. See with what a ferocious air the gentleman who personates the Mexican chief paces up and down, and with what an eye of calm dignity the principal tragedian gazes on the crowd below, or converses confidentially with the harlequin! The four clowns, who are engaged in a mock broadsword combat, may be all very well for the low-minded holidaymakers; but these are the people for the reflective portion of the community. They look so noble in those Roman dresses, with their yellow legs and arms, long black curly heads, bushy eyebrows and scowl expressive of assassination and vengeance, and everything else that is grand and solemn. Then, the ladies – were there ever such innocent and awful-looking beings as they walk up and down the platform in twos and threes, with their arms round each other's waists or leaning for support on one of those majestic men! Their spangled muslin dresses and blue satin shoes and sandals (a *leetle* the worse for wear) are the admiration of all beholders; and the playful manner in which they check the advances of the clown is perfectly enchanting.

'Just a-going to begin! Pray come for'erd, come for'erd,' exclaims the man in the countryman's dress, for the seventieth time: and people force their way up the steps in crowds. The band suddenly strikes up, the harlequin and columbine set the example, reels are formed in less than no time, the Roman heroes place their arms akimbo, and dance with considerable agility; and the leading tragic actress and the gentleman who enacts the 'swell' in the pantomime foot it to perfection. 'All in to begin,' shouts the manager, when no more people can be induced to 'come for'erd', and away rush the leading members of the company to do the dreadful in the first piece.

A change of performance takes place every day during the fair, but the story of the tragedy is always pretty much the same. There is a rightful heir, who loves a young lady, and is beloved by her; and a wrongful heir, who loves her too, and isn't beloved by her; and the wrongful heir gets hold of the rightful heir, and throws him into a dungeon, just to kill him off when convenient, for which purpose he hires a couple of assassins – a good one and a bad one who, the moment they are left alone, get up a little murder on their own account, the good one killing the bad one, and the bad one wounding the good one. Then the rightful heir is discovered in prison, carefully holding a long chain in his hands and seated despondingly in a large armchair; and the young lady comes in to two bars of soft music and embraces the rightful heir; and then the wrongful heir comes in to two bars of quick music (technically called 'a hurry'), and goes on in the most shocking manner, throwing the young lady about as if she was nobody, and calling the rightful heir 'Ar-recreant – ar-wretch!' in a very loud voice, which answers the double purpose of displaying his passion and preventing the sound being deadened by the sawdust. The interest becomes intense; the wrongful heir draws his sword, and rushes on the rightful heir; a blue smoke is seen, a gong is heard, and a tall white figure (who has been all this time behind the armchair, covered over with a tablecloth) slowly rises to the tune of 'Oft in the stilly night'. This is no other than the ghost of the rightful heir's father, who was killed by the wrongful heir's father, at sight of which the wrongful heir becomes apoplectic, and is literally 'struck all of a heap', the stage not being large enough to admit of his falling down at full length. Then the good assassin staggers in, and says he was hired in conjunction with the bad assassin, by the wrongful heir, to kill the rightful heir; and he's killed a good many people in his time, but he's very sorry for it, and won't do so any more – a promise which he immediately redeems by dying offhand without any nonsense about it. Then the rightful heir throws down his chain; and then two men, a sailor and a young woman (the tenantry of the rightful heir) come in, and the ghost makes dumb motions to them, which they, by supernatural interference, understand – for no one else can; and the ghost (who can't do anything without blue fire) blesses the rightful heir and the young lady by half suffocating them with smoke; and then a muffin-bell rings and the curtain drops.

The exhibitions next in popularity to these itinerant theatres are the travelling menageries, or, to speak more intelligibly, the 'wild-beast shows', where a military band in beefeaters' costume, with leopard-skin caps, play incessantly; and where large highly coloured representations of tigers tearing men's heads open and a lion being burnt with red-hot irons to induce him to drop his victim are hung up outside, by way of attracting visitors.

The principal officer at these places is generally a very tall, hoarse man, in a scarlet coat, with a cane in his hand, with which he occasionally raps the pictures we have just noticed by way of illustrating his description – something in this way. 'Here, here, here: the lion, the lion' (tap), 'exactly as he is represented on the canvas outside' (three taps); 'no waiting, remember; no deception. The fe–ro–cious lion' (tap, tap) 'who bit off the gentleman's head last Cambervel vos a twelvemonth, and has killed on the awerage three keepers a year ever since he arrived at matoority. No extra charge on this account recollect; the price of admission is only sixpence.' This address never fails to produce a considerable sensation, and sixpences flow into the treasury with wonderful rapidity.

The dwarfs are also objects of great curiosity, and as a dwarf, a giantess, a living skeleton, a wild Indian, 'a young lady of singular beauty, with perfectly white hair and pink eyes', and two or three other natural curiosities, are usually exhibited together for the small charge of a penny, they attract very numerous audiences. The best thing about a dwarf is that he has always a little box, about two feet six inches high, into which, by long practice, he can just manage to get, by doubling himself up like a boot-jack; this box is painted outside like a six-roomed house, and as the crowd see him ring a bell, or fire a pistol out of the first-floor window, they verily believe that it is his ordinary town residence, divided like other mansions into drawing-rooms, dining-parlour and bedchambers. Shut up in this case, the unfortunate little object is brought out to delight the throng by holding a facetious dialogue with the proprietor, in the course of which, the dwarf (who is always particularly drunk) pledges himself to sing a comic song inside, and pays various compliments to the ladies, which induce them to 'come for'erd' with great alacrity. As a giant is not so easily moved, a pair of indescribables of most capacious dimensions and a huge shoe are usually brought out, into which two or three stout men get all at once, to the enthusiastic delight of the crowd, who are quite satisfied with the solemn assurance that these habiliments form part of the giant's everyday costume.

The grandest and most numerously frequented booth in the whole fair, however, is 'The Crown and Anchor' – a temporary ballroom we forget how many hundred feet long, the price of admission to which is one shilling. Immediately on your right hand as you enter, after paying your money, is a refreshment place, at which cold beef, roast and boiled, French rolls, stout, wine, tongue, ham, even fowls, if we recollect right, are displayed in tempting array. There is a raised orchestra, and the place is boarded all the way down, in patches, just wide enough for a country dance.

There is no master of the ceremonies in this artificial Eden – all is primitive, unreserved and unstudied. The dust is blinding, the heat insupportable, the company somewhat noisy and in the highest spirits possible: the ladies, in the height of their innocent animation, dancing in the gentlemen's hats, and the gentlemen promenading 'the gay and festive scene' in the ladies' bonnets, or with the more expensive ornaments of false noses and low-crowned, tinder-box-looking hats: playing children's drums, and accompanied by ladies on the penny trumpet.

The noise of these various instruments, the orchestra, the shouting,

There is no master of the ceremonies in this artificial Eden –
all is primitive, unreserved and unstudied

the 'scratchers' and the dancing is perfectly bewildering. The dancing itself beggars description – every figure lasts about an hour, and the ladies bounce up and down the middle with a degree of spirit which is quite indescribable. As to the gentlemen, they stamp their feet against the ground every time 'hands four round' begins, go down the middle and up again, with cigars in their mouths and silk handkerchiefs in their hands, and whirl their partners round, nothing loth, scrambling and falling and embracing and knocking up against the other couples until they are fairly tired out and can move no longer. The same scene is repeated again and again (slightly varied by an occasional 'row') until a late hour at night; and a great many clerks and 'prentices find themselves next morning with aching heads, empty pockets, damaged hats and a very imperfect recollection of how it was they did *not* get home.

EARLY COACHES

We have often wondered how many months' incessant travelling in a post-chaise it would take to kill a man; and wondering by analogy, we should very much like to know how many months of constant travelling in a succession of early coaches an unfortunate mortal could endure. Breaking a man alive upon the wheel, would be nothing to breaking his rest, his peace, his heart – everything but his fast – upon four; and the punishment of Ixion (the only practical person, by the by, who has discovered the secret of perpetual motion) would sink into utter insignificance before the one we have suggested. If we had been a powerful churchman in those good times when blood was shed as freely as water, and men were mowed down like grass in the sacred cause of religion, we would have lain by very quietly till we got hold of some especially obstinate miscreant, who positively refused to be converted to our faith, and then we would have booked him for an inside place in a small coach, which travelled day and night; and, securing the remainder of the places for stout men with a slight tendency to coughing and spitting, we would have started him forth on his last travels, leaving him mercilessly to all the tortures which the waiters, landlords, coachmen, guards, boots, chambermaids and other familiars on his line of road might think proper to inflict.

Who has not experienced the miseries inevitably consequent upon a summons to undertake a hasty journey? You receive an intimation from your place of business – wherever that may be, or whatever you may be – that it will be necessary to leave town without delay. You and your family are forthwith thrown into a state of tremendous excitement; an express is immediately dispatched to the washerwoman's; everybody is in a bustle; and you, yourself, with a feeling of dignity which you cannot altogether conceal, sally forth to the booking-office to secure your place. Here a painful consciousness of your own unimportance first rushes on your mind – the people are as cool and collected as if nobody were going out of town, or as if a journey of a hundred odd miles were a mere nothing. You enter a mouldy-looking room, ornamented with large posting-bills, the greater part of the place enclosed behind a huge, lumbering, rough counter, and fitted up with recesses that look like the dens of the smaller animals in a travelling menagerie, without the bars. Some half-dozen people are 'booking' brown-paper parcels, which one of the clerks flings into the aforesaid recesses with an air of recklessness which you, remembering the new carpetbag you bought in the morning, feel considerably annoyed at; porters, looking like so many Atlases, keep rushing in and out, with large packages on their shoulders; and while you are waiting to make the necessary enquiries, you wonder what on earth the booking-office clerks can have been before they were booking-office clerks; one of them, with his pen behind his ear and his hands behind him, is standing in front of the fire like a full-length portrait of Napoleon; the other, with his hat half off his head, enters the passengers' names in the books with a coolness which is inexpressibly provoking; and the villain whistles – actually whistles – while a man asks him what the fare is outside all the way to Holyhead! – in frosty weather, too! They are clearly an isolated race, evidently possessing no sympathies or feelings in common with the rest of mankind. Your turn comes at last, and having paid the fare, you tremblingly enquire – 'What time will it be necessary for me to be here in the morning?' – 'Six o'clock,' replies the whistler, carelessly pitching the sovereign you have just parted with, into a wooden bowl on the desk. 'Rather before than arter,' adds the man with the semi-roasted unmentionables, with just as much ease and com-placency as if the whole world got out of bed at five. You turn into the street, ruminating as you bend your steps homewards on the extent to which men become hardened in cruelty by custom.

If there be one thing in existence more miserable than another, it most unquestionably is the being compelled to rise by candlelight. If you have ever doubted the fact, you are painfully convinced of your error on the morning of your departure. You left strict orders, overnight, to be called at half-past four, and you have done nothing all night but doze for five minutes at a time and start up suddenly from a terrific dream of a large church-clock with the small hand running round, with astonishing rapidity, to every figure on the dial-plate. At last, completely exhausted, you fall gradually into a refreshing sleep – your thoughts grow confused – the stage-coaches, which have been 'going off' before your eyes all night, become less and less distinct, until they go off altogether; one moment you are driving with all the skill and smartness of an experienced whip – the next you are exhibiting, *á la* Ducrow, on the off-leader; anon you are closely muffled up, inside, and have just recognised in the person of the

You enter a mouldy-looking room, ornamented with large posting-bills, the greater part of the place enclosed behind a huge, lumbering, rough counter

guard an old schoolfellow, whose funeral, even in your dream, you remember to have attended eighteen years ago. At last you fall into a state of complete oblivion, from which you are aroused, as if into a new state of existence, by a singular illusion. You are apprenticed to a trunk-maker; how, or why, or when, or wherefore, you don't take the trouble to enquire; but there you are, pasting the lining in the lid of a portmanteau. Confound that other apprentice in the back shop, how he is hammering! – rap, rap, rap – what an industrious fellow he must be! you have heard him at work for half an hour past, and he has been hammering incessantly the whole time. Rap, rap, rap, again – he's talking now – what's that he said? Five o'clock! You make a violent exertion, and start up in bed. The vision is at once dispelled; the trunk-maker's shop is your own bedroom, and the other apprentice your shivering servant, who has been vainly endeavouring to wake you for the last quarter of an hour at the imminent risk of breaking either his own knuckles or the panels of the door.

You proceed to dress yourself, with all possible dispatch. The flaring flat candle with the long snuff gives light enough to show that the things you want are not where they ought to be, and you undergo a trifling delay in consequence of having carefully packed up one of your boots in your over-anxiety of the preceding night. You soon complete your toilet, however, for you are not particular on such an occasion, and you shaved yesterday evening; so, mounting your Petersham greatcoat and green travelling shawl, and grasping your carpetbag in your right hand, you walk lightly downstairs, lest you should awaken any of the family, and after pausing in the common sitting-room for one moment, just to have a cup of coffee (the said common sitting-room looking remarkably comfortable, with everything out of its place, and strewed with the crumbs of last night's supper), you undo the chain and bolts of the street-door and find yourself fairly in the street.

A thaw, by all that is miserable! The frost is completely broken up. You look down the long perspective of Oxford Street, the gaslights mournfully reflected on the wet pavement, and can discern no speck in the road to encourage the belief that there is a cab or a coach to be had – the very coachmen have gone home in despair. The cold sleet is drizzling down with that gentle regularity which betokens a duration of four-and-twenty hours at least; the damp hangs upon the housetops and lamp-posts and clings to you like an invisible cloak. The water is 'coming in' in every area, the pipes have burst, the water-butts are running over; the rage in accelerating her progress and in knocking the little scanty blue bonnet of the unfortunate child over its still more scanty and faded-looking face.

In the last box, which is situated in the darkest and most obscure corner of the shop, considerably removed from either of the gaslights, are a young delicate girl of about twenty, and an elderly female, evidently her mother from the resemblance between them, who stand at some distance back, as if to avoid the observation even of the shopman. It is not their first visit to a pawnbroker's shop, for they answer without a moment's hesitation the usual questions, put in a rather respectful manner and in a much lower tone than usual, of 'What name shall I say? – Your own property, of course? Where do you live? – Housekeeper or lodger?' They bargain, too, for a higher loan than the shopman is at first inclined to offer, which a perfect stranger would be little disposed to do; and the elder female urges her daughter on, in scarcely audible whispers, to exert her utmost powers of persuasion to obtain an advance of the sum, and expatiate on the value of the articles they have brought to raise a present supply upon. They are a small gold chain and a 'Forget me not' ring: the girl's property, for they are both too small for the mother; given her in better times; prized, perhaps, once, for the giver's sake, but parted with now without a struggle; for want has hardened the mother, and her example has hardened the girl, and the prospect of receiving money, coupled with a recollection of the misery they have both endured from the want of it – the coldness of old friends – the stern refusal of some, and the still more galling compassion of others – appears to have obliterated the consciousness of self-humiliation, which the idea of their present situation would once have aroused.

In the next box is a young female whose attire, miserably poor but extremely gaudy, wretchedly cold but extravagantly fine, too plainly bespeaks her station. The rich satin gown with its faded trimmings, the worn-out thin shoes and pink silk stockings, the summer bonnet in winter, and the sunken face, where a daub of rouge only serves as an index to the ravages of squandered health never to be regained and lost happiness never to be restored, and where the practised smile is a wretched mockery of the misery of the heart, cannot be mistaken. There is something in the glimpse she has just caught of her young neighbour, and in the sight of the little trinkets she has offered in pawn, that seems to have awakened in this woman's mind some slumbering recollection, and to have changed, for an instant, her whole demeanour. Her first hasty impulse was to bend forward as if to scan more minutely the appearance of her half-concealed companions; her next, on seeing them involuntarily shrink from her, to retreat to the back of the box, cover her face with her hands and burst into tears.

There are strange chords in the human heart which will lie dormant through years of depravity and wickedness, but which will vibrate at last to some slight circumstance apparently trivial in itself but connected by some undefined and indistinct association with past days that can never be recalled and with bitter recollections from which the most degraded creature in existence cannot escape.

There has been another spectator, in the person of a woman in the common shop; the lowest of the low; dirty, unbonneted, flaunting and slovenly. Her curiosity was at first attracted by the little she could see of the group; then her attention. The half-intoxicated leer changed to an expression of something like interest, and a feeling similar to that we have described, appeared for a moment, and only a moment, to extend itself even to her bosom.

Who shall say how soon these women may change places? The last has but two more stages – the hospital and the grave. How many females situated as her two companions are, and as she may have been once, have terminated the same wretched course in the same wretched manner! One is already tracing her footsteps with frightful rapidity. How soon may the other follow her example! How many have done the same!